The
Burning
White

By Brent Weeks

Perfect Shadow: A Night Angel Novella

THE NIGHT ANGEL TRILOGY

The Way of Shadows
Shadow's Edge
Beyond the Shadows

Night Angel: The Complete Trilogy
The Night Angel Trilogy: 10th Anniversary Edition

THE LIGHTBRINGER SERIES

The Black Prism
The Blinding Knife
The Broken Eye
The Blood Mirror
The Burning White

The
Burning
White

Lightbringer: Book 5

BRENT WEEKS

www.orbitbooks.net

Copyright © 2019 by Brent Weeks

Cover design by Lauren Panepinto
Cover illustration by Gene Mollica
Cover copyright © 2019 by Hachette Book Group, Inc.
Maps by Chad Roberts Design

Orbit
Hachette Book Group
1290 Avenue of the Americas
New York, NY 10104
orbitbooks.net

First Edition: October 2019
Simultaneously published in Great Britain by Orbit

Orbit is an imprint of Hachette Book Group.
The Orbit name and logo are trademarks of Little, Brown Book Group Limited.

The publisher is not responsible for websites (or their content) that are not owned by the publisher.

The Hachette Speakers Bureau provides a wide range of authors for speaking events. To find out more, go to www.hachettespeakersbureau.com or call (866) 376-6591.

Library of Congress Cataloging-in-Publication Data
Names: Weeks, Brent, author.
Title: The burning white / Brent Weeks.
Description: First edition. | New York : Orbit, 2019. | Series: Lightbringer ; book 5
Identifiers: LCCN 2019027655 | ISBN 9780316251303 (hardcover) |
    ISBN 9780316402873 (library ebook)
Subjects: GSAFD: Fantasy fiction.
Classification: LCC PS3623.E4223 B87 2019 | DDC 813/.6—dc23
LC record available at https://lccn.loc.gov/2019027655

ISBNs: 978-0-316-25130-3 (hardcover), 978-0-316-53474-1 (signed edition),
    978-0-316-53472-7 (Barnes and Noble signed edition),
    978-0-316-25128-0 (ebook)

Printed in the United States of America

LSC-C

10 9 8 7 6 5 4 3 2 1

To my wife, Kristi, who is far too practical to have suggested
I quit my job to write and far too wise to keep repeating
for five years, "Let's not have a backup plan."
Yet she did.
&
To my stubborn readers, who deserve to be rewarded.*

*I said "deserve to be." Not "will be."

Contents

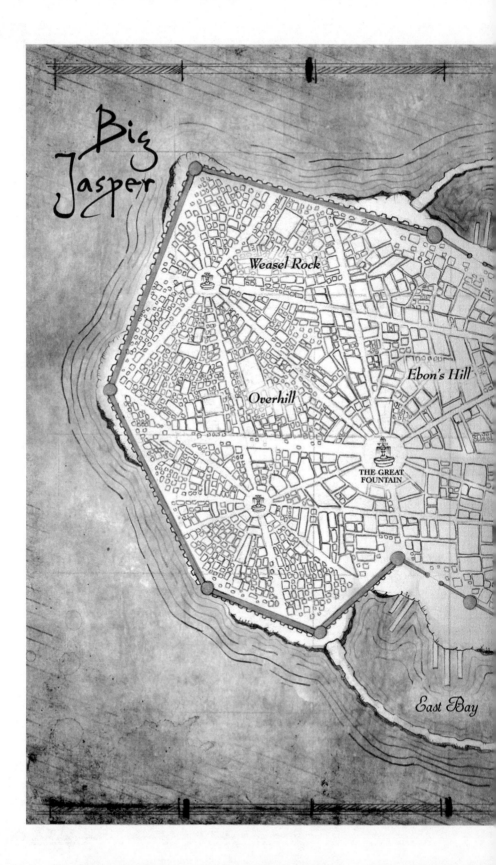

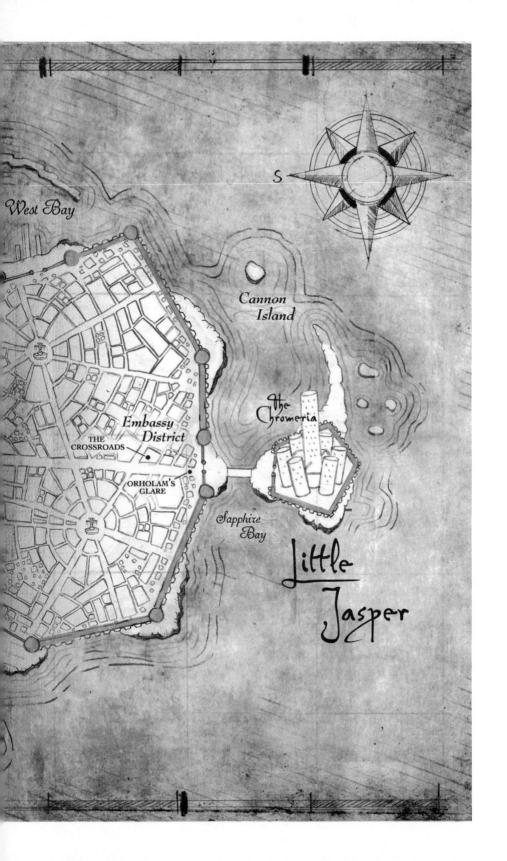

The Lightbringer Series Recap

In the empire of the Seven Satrapies, some people are born with the ability to transform light into luxin: a physical, tangible substance that exists in one of nine colors. The process is known as drafting, and each drafted color has unique physical and metaphysical properties and innumerable uses, from construction to warfare. Trained at the empire's capital, the Chromeria, drafters lead lives of privilege, with politicians and powerful families vying for their services. In exchange, they agree that once they exhaust their ability to safely use magic—signaled when the halos of their irises are broken by the colors they draft—they will be killed by the emperor, the Prism, in a ceremony on the most holy day of the year: Sun Day. Drafters who have broken the halo are called wights, and they descend into madness if they are not Freed; those who run from the ritual Freeing are hunted to their deaths. Only the Prism can draft with limitless power, and he or she alone can balance all the colors in the satrapies to prevent luxin from overwhelming the lands and creating chaos. Every seven years, or on a multiple of seven years, the Prism also gives up his or her life, and the ruling council installs a new Prism. If the Prism refuses death, he or she is likewise hunted down by the elite squadron assigned to protecting the empire: the Blackguard.

Book One: *The Black Prism*

Kip Delauria is scrounging for shards of luxin on a battlefield of the False Prism's War outside Rekton. He comes upon a green wight, Gaspar Elos, bound and trying to escape. Satrap Garadul has declared himself king and is planning to lay waste to Rekton; there is an army camped not far away. Kip races to the home of red dyer Master

Danavis, who urges Kip to find his friends and run. During his escape attempt, Kip inadvertently drafts. Later he finds his mother, Lina, gravely injured, hidden in a cave with one of his friends. She gives him a rosewood box containing a mysterious jewel-encrusted dagger before dying.

At the Chromeria, Prism Gavin Guile receives a message from Lina, telling him that he has a son in Rekton named Kip. Gavin soon sets off with Blackguard Karris White Oak. They make their way to Tyrea on a luxin skimmer/glider of his own creation, which allows them to cross the entire Cerulean Sea in a day. Upon their arrival they discover that Rekton has been destroyed, and they find Kip trying to defend himself from Garadul's Mirrormen. Gavin quickly dispatches the soldiers, realizing that Garadul is trying to set up his own Chromeria and has declared himself king. Gavin recognizes Kip as his bastard and claims him; Garadul takes the dagger before they leave.

Gavin and Kip make their way back to the Chromeria, where Kip is immediately tested to see what he can draft. He is discovered to be a superchromat and is revealed to be a blue/green bichrome. He also reunites with Aliviana (Liv) Danavis—a friend from his hometown and daughter of Corvan.

Meanwhile in Tyrea, Karris has set out on her own. She finds Corvan Danavis—Dazen's greatest general in the False Prism's War—in a basement, the lone survivor of the brutal massacre in Rekton. Karris is captured by the king's forces, and she discovers that King Garadul's right hand, a polychrome wight who calls himself the Color Prince, is the one inciting rebellion. He is Karris's brother, whom she'd thought long dead. Corvan begins to make his way to Garriston to warn the governor.

Back at the Chromeria, it is revealed that Gavin is in fact Dazen, masquerading as his older brother. The real Gavin Guile ('the prisoner') is still alive, held in a blue luxin prison far beneath the Prism's Tower. Prism Guile meets with the Spectrum, the governing body of the Seven Satrapies, and tells them what Garadul is planning. Gavin decides to make his way to Garriston with Kip, Blackguard Commander Ironfist, and Liv—who is to be Kip's tutor. Once they arrive in Garriston, Gavin deposes Governor Crassos and takes command. He reunites with and reinstates General Danavis, giving his old friend command of Garriston's defenses.

Gavin plans to build a magnificent yellow luxin wall around Garriston in an attempt to save the otherwise vulnerable city. Brightwater Wall is nearly complete when a cannonball destroys the gate as Gavin is finishing it. Meanwhile, Kip sneaks away to infiltrate Garadul's camp as a spy to find Karris, and Liv goes with him; Kip is captured, and Liv is invited to join the Color Prince. Liv saves both Kip and Karris by agreeing to join the Color Prince if he'll spare Kip's and Gavin's lives.

During the Battle of Garriston, Gavin goes down after drafting white luxin, Kip kills King Garadul, and the rest of the forces retreat to the docks. Kip helps rescue Ironfist, and they run across the ocean to one of the barges, where Kip races to meet another threat: a young polychrome, Zymun, who has been assigned to assassinate Gavin. Zymun's attempt fails when Kip intercedes. Kip takes the dagger Zymun used and realizes it is the same blade his mother gave him; he recovers the knife, which now has a blue gem in the hilt.

Gavin realizes he has lost the ability to see or draft blue. The prisoner has broken out of the blue prison to find himself inside a green one.

Book Two: *The Blinding Knife*

Gavin and the refugees from Garriston are aboard the barges, and he tries to reconcile with the fact that he has lost blue. He saves the refugees from a sea demon, then departs with Karris for Seers Island, where he negotiates with the Third Eye, a powerful Seer, to get permission for the refugees to build a home on her island. The Third Eye knows who he really is and that he has already lost blue. She gives Gavin some useful advice about the *bane*, and Gavin later kills the blue bane by himself.

After they make their way back to the Chromeria, Kip goes through Blackguard training against the wishes of Commander Ironfist. Kip makes some friends and meets Teia, a color-blind *paryl* drafter and a slave. The war isn't going well for the Chromeria, and Ironfist announces that the Blackguard will graduate the top fourteen candidates instead of the usual seven. As hard as training is, the new interest Kip's grandfather, Andross Guile, has taken in him is worse. Andross demands Kip play Nine Kings for extremely high stakes.

Gavin and Karris return to the Chromeria after getting the refugees settled in their new home. He meets with the Spectrum, and Seers Island is renamed New Tyrea, giving it power as a satrapy and Danavis as satrap. Karris is ambushed and beaten by men hired by Andross Guile.

A librarian, Rea Siluz, introduces Kip to Janus Borig, an eccentric old artist who creates priceless original Nine Kings cards infused with magic. Janus warns Kip that her life is in danger, and soon Kip discovers Borig's house burned and Janus mortally wounded by two mysterious assassins. Kip recovers a deck of completely new cards, kills the assassins, steals their shimmercloaks, and gives the items to Ironfist and Gavin. Kip eventually ranks fourteenth in his Blackguard testing and is revealed to be not a bichrome, but a full-spectrum polychrome.

Meanwhile, Liv has sworn fealty to the Color Prince and his cause. His army begins to make their way from Garriston toward Ru, a large city in Atash. Gavin travels to Ru with Kip and a team of Blackguards. They go on scouting missions. Gavin reveals his skimmer to the Blackguards, and together they sink the *Gargantua*, an enormous ship owned by pirate king Pash Vecchio.

Gavin and Karris reconcile and marry just before they go to war against the Color Prince. With the new Blackguard inductees and the Chromeria's forces, they must destroy a green bane that is birthing a new god, Atirat. Ironfist and Teia lead a team in an assault on a watchtower. The green bane emerges from the sea; Gavin, Kip, and Karris fight their way to it, killing wights in their wake. Amid the chaos, Gavin realizes he has lost the ability to see or draft green. Liv directs a huge beam of light to the bane spire, awakening the new green god Atirat.

Back at the watchtower, Teia, Ironfist, and company aim cannon fire at the bane, causing the spire to explode. Using the explosion as a distraction, Kip drives his dagger—the powerful Blinding Knife— into the green god Atirat, killing it. They have killed a god and sunk a bane, but ultimately lose Ru to the Color Prince.

After the battle, while still on a Chromeria ship, Kip and Gavin meet with Andross Guile. Kip realizes that Andross is a color wight and moves to confront his grandfather. Kip draws the Blinding Knife and stabs Andross in the shoulder. Gavin tries to intervene but can only redirect the knife into his own body. Gavin falls overboard, and Kip jumps after him.

They are quickly picked up by the *Bitter Cob*, led by pirate captain Gunner, a crazed cannoneer who was on a ship Gavin had earlier destroyed; the Blinding Knife has grown into a huge gun-sword. Gunner decides to keep Gavin and the gun-sword, throwing Kip back into the ocean as a tribute to Ceres.

Andross discovers he is no longer a wight.

Kip is picked up in a small boat by Zymun, Gavin and Karris's long-lost illegitimate son.

Gavin wakes to find he can't draft, is completely color-blind...and a slave rower.

Book Three: *The Broken Eye*

Kip and Zymun are adrift at sea until Kip escapes and swims his way to shore. He struggles to survive, withstanding dehydration, injury, and hallucinations for several weeks as he attempts to return home to the Jaspers.

Ironfist and the other Blackguards have returned to the Chromeria, where Kip is presumed dead. The Spectrum meet to decide what to do about the war and Gavin's absence; Andross is made promachos, commander in chief of the Chromeria's military. Teia is recruited by Murder Sharp, a skilled paryl assassin for the Order of the Broken Eye. Karris, who is now married to the Prism, is removed from the Blackguard to become spymistress for the White.

Upon his homecoming, Kip tells the Spectrum and Karris that Gavin is still alive and forges a tenuous alliance with Andross. He trains and studies under Karris and reunites with his old Blackguard squad: Cruxer, Ben-hadad, Big Leo, Teia, Ferkudi, Winsen, Goss, and Daelos. Andross grants the group access to restricted libraries so they can research heretical Nine Kings cards and the Lightbringer, a long-prophesied savior of the satrapies, hoping they'll gain information to win the war. The group meets and befriends Quentin Naheed, a humble and brilliant young luxiat and scholar.

Back across the ocean, Gavin—color-blind and unable to draft—is a galley slave on Gunner's pirate ship. His oarmate is an old prophet nicknamed Orholam. After months of sailing on the open sea, Gavin is freed by Antonius Malargos, a naïve young Ruthgari noble. They sail for Rath, a large port city in Ruthgar, where Gavin is handed over to Antonius's cousin Eirene. She imprisons Gavin and plots with the Nuqaba of Paria (who possesses the orange seed crystal). They decide to spare Gavin's life but plan to burn out his eyes.

Teia confesses to Ironfist and the White that she had been stealing for her owner, Aglaia Crassos, and that she has been ensnared by the Order of the Broken Eye. Under the White's orders, Teia becomes a double agent for the Chromeria, infiltrating the Order; she immediately undertakes various missions to prove her loyalty to the Order. Teia soon gets a message from Karris that someone is planning to kill Kip, and she hurries with Cruxer and Winsen to try to help their friend. They save Kip and kill the Blackguards who were trying to assassinate him.

While meeting with Andross, Kip learns that his grandfather knows about Zymun, who is on his way to the Jaspers, and that when he arrives, he will be named Prism-elect—unless Kip can find Andross's missing Nine Kings deck, as well as the originals Kip saved from Janus Borig's house.

Kip, after confessing his feelings to Teia and telling her about Tisis's proposal that they marry, goes down to the Prism's training room and finds the lost Nine Kings cards in a punching bag. When Kip accidentally absorbs all the cards, he falls dead and enters the Great Library, where he meets an immortal: Abaddon.

Meanwhile, Karris and Ironfist learn where Gavin is and plan to go rescue him. They leave with a team of Blackguards and rescue Gavin from the giant hippodrome, but not before one of Gavin's eyes is burned out with a red-hot metal rod. When they return, they take Gavin to a chirurgeon they trust to hide him while Karris goes to look for Kip.

Back in the training room, Teia finds Kip's body. She revives him, but Kip is distraught to find the images have disappeared from the cards. He has stolen Abaddon's shimmercloak, which he gives to Teia. Kip has trouble sorting out reality from the visions he saw on the cards.

Teia follows Andross to his estate on Big Jasper, where she overhears him meeting with Zymun about Zymun's future with the Guile family, and then with Murder Sharp plotting to assassinate the White. She reports this to Kip, and the two of them rush to the White's rooms to find her dying. The day after Orea's passing, Karris finds herself at the ceremony for selecting a new White—and that she is a nominee.

During the ceremony, Andross removes Ironfist from the Blackguard and publicly banishes Kip and his friends from the Chromeria. They all make their way back to the tower, where Kip and his squad are given uniform blacks, supplies, and a new name: the Mighty. They decide to board a ship to flee the Chromeria, but before they can leave, Zymun orders the newly formed Lightguard to kill Kip and his friends; Goss is killed and Daelos is gravely wounded before they can meet Tisis Malargos at the docks. Kip and Tisis marry, then set sail for Blood Forest with the Mighty, who have pledged fealty to Kip.

Karris discovers that the ceremony for selecting a new White has been rigged using orange luxin hexes, even though the sacred ritual is supposed to be guided by Orholam. When two of the other candidates attack her, Karris kills them and becomes Karris White.

Ironfist finds his brother, Tremblefist, dying. He confesses that he knows Ironfist has been working for the Order of the Broken Eye since he came to the Chromeria. Ironfist then meets with the leader of the Order, the Old Man of the Desert—who is revealed to be Andross's secretary and slave, Grinwoody.

Meanwhile, Liv Danavis has been hunting the superviolet seed crystal at the command of the Color Prince. But though the Color Prince tries to make her wear a black luxin choker to keep her under his control, she captures the seed crystal on her own.

Gavin wakes up to find himself inside the blue prison cell he built beneath the Prism's Tower.

Book Four: *The Blood Mirror*

Teia and Murder Sharp kidnap Marissia, stealing documents from her that were vital to Karris's rule as the new White. Gavin wakes up to find that Marissia is with him in the blue cell to tend to his injuries. She confesses that she was not only Orea Pullawr's spymistress, but also her granddaughter. As soon as Gavin is on the mend, Andross arrives and takes Marissia away, presumably to her death.

Karris survives her first meeting with Andross as the White, where he agrees to handle the issue of her killing two men during the selection process. Karris then meets her estranged son, Zymun, who tells her of his traumatic childhood; she swears that she'll never abandon him again.

Teia has her first meeting with the Old Man of the Desert, who tasks her with getting close to Karris. He tells her to tag someone for him to have assassinated, as a 'gift' for her loyalty thus far. This meeting is followed by one with newly promoted Commander Fisk, whom she feels uneasy around after the Mighty find out he was compromised. Fisk tells her that he believes she stayed behind for Kip and that he and the Blackguard will be there for the Mighty when they need him. He also informs her that she will be taking her final vows as a full Blackguard the following day; she is to stand vigil that night. Teia then goes down to the cells to see the prisoners who will be executed on Sun Day to find Quentin, who has been arrested for murdering Lucia during the Blackguard training. She tags him with paryl to mark him for assassination but removes the tag before the execution ceremony.

During Sun Day, Karris condemns High Luxiat Tawleb to Orholam's Glare for ordering Quentin to assassinate Kip. His execution is followed by Pheronike's, a spy for the Color Prince; while he burns, Pheronike releases Nabiros, a three-headed djinn that had possessed him. Karris spares Quentin, choosing to make him a slave as an example of the Magisterium's greed and corruption.

Meanwhile, Kip and Tisis have been trying, unsuccessfully, to consummate their marriage—an issue that becomes urgent as their wedding will be annulled if they don't. Tisis wants to accompany the Mighty when they go to fight in Blood Forest. On the way, their ship finds itself in the middle of an enormous luxin storm, and Kip saves them by pushing apart twisted streams of *chi* and paryl until the ship is able to pass. The effort leaves him blind for three days, but Rea Siluz heals his eyes. After Kip wakes up, the Mighty head out on Benhadad's newly designed skimmer, and Tisis begins to demonstrate her worth to the squad.

Gavin has been talking to the dead man in the blue cell, who admits that Gavin will-cast the dead men into the prisons to torture his brother. The dead man also reveals that Gavin is the Black Prism—a black drafter who absorbed the power to draft all colors by killing other drafters. Gavin attempts to escape from the cells and makes it through green and into a small cove to find none other than his father, Andross, there, waiting for him. Andross tries to strike a deal with Gavin, but instead Gavin ends up in the yellow cell, where he left his brother's body after shooting him.

The Mighty meet the Ghosts of Shady Grove, a group of will-casters led by Conn Ruadhán Arthur; they convince him to join Kip's army. They successfully start raiding the Blood Robes and come upon the Cwn y Wawr ('Dogs of Dawn'), a band of skilled warrior-drafters with highly trained dogs. The Ghosts have a fraught history with the Cwn y Wawr, but the two groups are able to set aside their differences to fight together.

Elsewhere, Liv has become the superviolet god Ferrilux, and meets Samila Sayeh/Mot in Rekton. Samila tells Liv that the White King has her bane, but that Liv can only claim it if she agrees to become bound to him and wear the black luxin. She refuses.

Eirene has sent Antonius, cousin to her and Tisis, to bring Tisis back, but Tisis is able to convince him to join Kip's army and swear fealty to him instead. With his army growing, Kip sets his sights on saving a besieged city.

Gavin sees that his brother is not in the yellow luxin cell, and after talking to the dead man there, realizes that he never imprisoned his brother; he killed the real Gavin at Sundered Rock, and drafting black erased his memory of the event. Andross, Felia, and Orea had all known the truth about Gavin and waited to see how and whether he would recover from his madness/memory loss. Gavin eventually passes out from eating drugged bread and wakes up in the black luxin prison.

Teia is sent on a mission to Paria by both the Order and Karris, charged with killing the Nuqaba by the Order and Satrapah Tilleli Azmith (the Nuqaba's spymistress) by Karris. During her mission, she discovers that the Nuqaba is Haruru, Ironfist's sister, and that Ironfist is alive and imprisoned by her. Teia completes her mission, but Ironfist discovers her, and Teia then returns to report to Karris that Ironfist is alive.

Corvan and his newlywed wife, the Third Eye, spend their last night together before her assassination by Murder Sharp. She reveals that Kip marches to Dúnbheo to free it, not having seen the White King's trap.

Gavin spends months in the black cell, and eventually discovers the dead man there is not a will-casting, but something else entirely. Grinwoody appears sometime later, revealing that he is the Old Man of the Desert and that he will free Gavin if he agrees to sail to White Mist Reef, climb the Tower of Heaven, and kill Orholam—what the Old Man believes is the nexus of magic in the satrapies—using the Blinding Knife. Gavin agrees, places a piece of black luxin that will ensure his obedience over his eye socket, and walks to the ship. It is the *Golden Mean*, captained by none other than Gunner.

Teia is given a final mission by the Order to test her. She is told to murder someone (Gavin) once he has completed a quest for the Order. If she fails, they will murder her father.

Karris meets with Andross, who tells her that Ironfist has declared himself king of Paria. She then has to kill Blackguard Gavin Greyling, who broke his halos while out searching for her husband. After his Freeing, Karris orders that the Blackguard is to search for Gavin no more, accepting that he is dead.

Liv decides to join the White King and realize her full powers as a goddess, seeing that he is preparing to sail the bane to invade the Chromeria.

Kip and his army successfully free the besieged city of Dúnbheo, at great personal cost to Conn Arthur, who deserts following the battle. Kip deposes the nobles and claims the city for himself and his army. He and Tisis profess their love for each other and are finally able to consummate their marriage. Kip uses every color of luxin to repair an ancient mural in their room, known as *Túsaíonn Domhan*, 'A World Begins.'

Author's Note

Astute readers—or those who accidentally read Author's Notes—will notice that Teia's first scenes happen at the same time several characters' last scenes occurred in *The Blood Mirror*.

Am I cheating? Retroactively patching up continuity errors?

Nah. I'd already written these overlapping scenes, and they don't change what the other characters do, but I decided to pull them from *The Blood Mirror* and put them here instead.

Why? One of the challenges of writing an epic story over multiple volumes is balancing dramatic unities against one another. The Lightbringer series tells one huge, unified story, but my goal has been for each book to comprise its own story so that both journey and destination satisfy. Sometimes the desires of an individual novel yield to the demands of the whole series—say, when big plot questions are raised in one volume but not answered until several books later. Other times I think an individual novel has the better claim.

This series certainly doesn't need more complexity, and thus the vast majority of the scenes *are* presented in chronological order. But what's a writer to do when a character jumps the gun and gets into her book five problems while the other characters are still wrapping up their book four problems? (In this case, Teia.)

A strict chronological presentation would interrupt the other characters' book four finales, and then, when book five came out, what Teia had done mere hours before would have to be reintroduced. Worse, that ordering would undercut our end-of-book satisfaction— that precious, fragile feeling that though this epic journey will continue, we've reached a logical base camp.

Characters warming themselves around a fire and looking up at the mountain peak they'll attempt tomorrow? That's a good tease.

Characters never stopping hiking and the book simply ending? That's bad structure.

In another case here, a character off in the hinterlands has his most interesting scenes occur back-to-back in a single day, while everyone else's are spread over weeks.

Chronological order may be the simplest, but where one character's actions won't (yet) affect other characters, I've chosen to present a small number of scenes in the order I think gives the best reading experience instead.

Trust me, when the characters come back together, it all works out.

The chronology, that is. Not necessarily the events.

—Brent Weeks
in a hole in the ground, outside Portland, Oregon

The
Burning
White

Beware of shedding blood unnecessarily ... for blood never sleeps.
    —AN-NASIR SALAH AD-DIN YUSUF IBN AYYUB (SALADIN)

Chapter 1

The White King's plan to destroy Kip Guile only began with an assassination. The assassination began with the scent of cloves.

"I love being in the Mighty, don't get me wrong," Big Leo was telling Ferkudi, "but sometimes the bodyguard duty is too much for only five of us, don't you think? The Blackguard always has at least a hundred warriors. That's like ten times as many. Fifteen? Dammit, twenty. You see? That's how tired I am. And sure, they gotta guard more people than we—"

Ferkudi sniffed.

Big Leo stopped. He took his eyes off the chattering nobles for the first time all night and glanced at him. Like most things he did, Ferkudi sniffed *different*, huffing in his air in little triads, short, short, long.

The two of them had pulled door-guard duty for the big dinner party hailing Kip (Breaker to the Mighty) as the Liberator of Dúnbheo. After his initial chilly reception by the Council of Divines—and a couple of hangings—the nobles of Blood Forest's cultural capital were trying to make nice.

When Ferkudi said nothing, Big Leo took the sniff as agreement. He continued, "I mean, no one's going to make a move on the city's big savior tonight, right? It ever bother you no one seems to notice *Lord Kip Guile* didn't save the city all by himself?"

Everything was fine, Leo thought. No one was acting strangely. Sure, there were some nerves as everyone was trying to figure out how to turn Breaker into an ally, but the noise of the crowd was right. People even seemed to be enjoying themselves.

Ferkudi sniffed.

"Don't tell me you're coming down with a cold," Leo said, not looking over this time.

Ferkudi inhaled deeply, like a war-bound soldier carefully filling his mnemonic storehouses with the scent of his wife's hair.

"What?" Ferkudi said blankly. "Cold? Huh?"

"Yeah, all right. What was I—oh, yeah, I mean Breaker saves the city, distributes all our food to the starving? And fixes that ceiling-art-whatever-thing? That *meant* something to these people. He's like a god here now. If the Council of Divines or any of the Blood Forest nobles makes a move against him, the people would riot. They'd burn the nobles' heart trees, string up every last one of—"

Ferkudi interrupted. "Anyone get added to the guest list late?"

Ferkudi loved lists, all lists. When the palace chatelaine had shown him her immaculately organized ledgers, the look on his face had been a baggage train of astonishment, then disbelief, then rapture, and finally utter infatuation for the bespectacled sexagenarian and her perfect figures. Kip—Breaker—had been turning Ferkudi's odd brain to good use in his now daily wranglings with traders and bankers and nobles. The Mighty mostly used it for humor: setting Ferkudi to ranking units of the army by sewage produced had been a recent favorite. (By weight? No, by volume. How long after excretion?)

But when you pulled door duty, there was nothing humorous about reconciling the guest list. "Absolutely not!" Big Leo said, stone serious. Something in his growl or his changing stance sent a few nearby nobles back a step.

It was a discipline they'd learned from the Blackguard—there were *never* to be late additions or surprise guests when they provided security, ever. If a Blackguard saw someone at an event who wasn't on the master list, he or she had free rein to consider them a threat.

But that only worked when the Blackguards could identify every guest by sight. Maybe Ferkudi could do that on the Mighty's second night in Dúnbheo, but Big Leo certainly couldn't. A flare of white-knuckled rage shot through him. The five of them, being asked to protect the Lightbringer himself? Impossible!

Damn you, Cruxer, it's been a year. You should have recruited fifty of us by now.

But everything still looked fine.

"Ferk?" he said.

"I talked with the cooks," the big round-shouldered young man said, sniffing again. "There were no dishes with cloves."

Cloves. Superviolet luxin smelled something like cloves. Big Leo felt a frisson down his spine.

"Breaker's the only declared superviolet in the room," Big Leo said.

Kip sat at the head table, where he was chatting amicably with an older woman who was some kind of authority on cultural antiquities.

He was much too far away for the scent to be coming from him.

"A secret message?" Big Leo said. Superviolet was often used for diplomatic messages. This was precisely the kind of crowd that would carry those, and even a noble could get jostled, breaking some fragile superviolet luxin scrawled on a parchment.

Or the cooks could have added cloves to one of the dishes at the last moment. Right?

Hell, for all Big Leo knew, maybe some lady walking past had clove-scented perfume.

'Falsely declaring an assassination attempt is the worst thing you can do...' Blackguard Commander Ironfist had once lectured them, '...except stand over the body of your ward. Announcing an assassination attempt means throwing a burning torch into the powder magazine of history. *You* are the people trusted with guns and spears and drafting while the most powerful and paranoid people in the world sleep and sup and talk and f...fornicate.' They'd laughed, but the point was serious: several Prisms had been murdered by cuckolded spouses and scorned lovers. 'When powerful paranoid people see you burst into a room shouting, armed and drafting, you *will* see pistols somehow appear on people who you know have been searched and cleared. You will see munds somehow turn out to be able to draft. You will see people innocent of everything except stupidity give you reasons to believe they need killing.

'In a false alarm, you may see people die for no reason other than that you yelled. You may kill them yourself.

'Given all that, some say calling a false alarm is shameful,' Commander Ironfist had said. 'But I say a Blackguard who doesn't shout a Nine Kill once in their life isn't working on edge. We protect the most important people in the world. Work on edge.'

The code was shorthand for the number of attackers, the suspected intent, and capabilities. A normal shout might be One Kill Five (a solo attacker, attempting assassination, likely a red drafter) or Two Grab Ten (two attackers attempting kidnapping, armed with muskets). Nine was 'unspecified' and the most likely to be wrong.

Big Leo looked over at Ferkudi, praying he'd say he'd been mistaken.

Ferkudi was glowering at the room, his brain grinding forward as slowly as a millstone and just as implacably.

Behind their smiles, not a few of the Blood Forest conns might *want* Kip dead, but none would dare to move against him openly, certainly not with his army deployed inside their city. But someone else had good reason to want Kip dead. Someone who would stop at nothing. The White King.

He shouldn't have anyone serving him, not in this city. But he might.

Big Leo's eyes met Ferkudi's. There was no hesitation there.

"Nine Kill Seven!" Big Leo bellowed—

Just as Ferkudi yelled, "Nine Kill Naught!"

What?! 'Naught' wasn't superviolet. 'Naught' meant a *paryl*-using assassin.

But their voices had already flown like torches from their hands to land amid friends and foes and fools, the nervous and naïve, all of them paranoid and powerful.

And the black powder of history roared in reply.

Chapter 2

Kip Guile had become a thousand hands holding two thousand cords, each one twisting in his fists, tearing away in every direction, each believing their own petty happiness was more important than the survival of them all. He smiled at mousy Lady Proud Hart, finding a measure of real joy in her excited jabbering about his repairs of the ceiling art *Túsaíonn Domhan*, 'A World Begins.' He wondered if what he was doing now was easier or harder than that repair, weaving the myriad magics together into one yoke and then pulling the whole from extinction into new life.

Except here the two thousand cords were conns and banconns, merchant princes, gentleman pirates, emissaries, slavers, spies, confidence women, and deserters, and exiles and refugees in their tens of thousands—and even one shy and fabulously wealthy art collector. Some cords turned to shape without complaint, adding weight but also more usefulness. Many resisted his pull, rightly distrustful of another war, another Guile. Many tried to twist him to their selfish ends. But behind others, even tonight, Kip could feel an undue tension, pulling against him.

He wasn't looking to weave an emperor's robe for himself, for

Orholam's sake, he was making a simple yoke, that he might heave the Seven Satrapies away from the edge of an abyss.

It was the White King. Koios was at work here in this very room tonight. Kip could feel it.

"With your discovery that the old masters used truly full-spectrum magic, Great Lord Guile," Lady Proud Hart was saying, "nine colors! not seven! who'd have dared believe it?—with that insight, we can bring art back to life that has not graced this earth with its true beauty in centuries. Yes, yes, the Chromeria will be peeved, but surely art is a demi-creation that brings great glory to the Creator Himself, no? The creation of beauty *is* worship! Who can deny it?" She was a tiny woman, the foremost expert on Forester antiquities in the world, or so Tisis had told him. She was also very connected and universally loved here. "With you leading the efforts, Conn Guile—oh dear, did I let that slip? Did you know yet that the Divines are planning to confer the title on you tonight? A little present. Unofficially, of course, until the formal—"

Across the room, Ferkudi and Big Leo suddenly shouted, "Nine Kill Naught!" and "Nine Kill Seven!" simultaneously.

For an embarrassingly long moment, Kip didn't understand why they'd be so rude as to scream during a civilized dinner party.

In one instant, Kip's greatest dread was that Lady Proud Hart was warming to asking him to repair dozens of fragile, priceless works of art himself. There was no way he wouldn't destroy half of them if he tried. He *was* the f'ing Turtle-Bear.

In the next instant, dual cracking noises woke him from a social fear to a physical one, like a man wakened from a fitful sleep by a thief in his room. Lux torches snapped open, Ben-hadad threw one blue and one green torch onto the banquet table, each flaring and burning and spitting magnesium heat, scorching the priceless walnut.

Kip suddenly lurched backward as Cruxer heaved on his shoulders, yanking him and his chair to get him out of any possible line of fire as quickly as possible.

Cruxer suddenly stopped the chair's skidding feet with his own, pulling the chair hard toward the ground and catapulting Kip into the air.

Kip flipped over backward, only belatedly tucking his knees.

When they'd practiced this, he'd landed on his feet. One time.

Not this time. He crashed onto his hands and knees behind Cruxer.

By the time Kip stood, Cruxer had slammed an oblivious serving girl out of the way and off her feet with a hard shove and planted himself in front of Kip, whose back was now against the wall. Cruxer, with one side of his blue spectacles knocked askew, was staring at the blue burning lux torch on the table and drafting.

The tall bodyguard whirled each hand in circles, building a blue luxin shield, swiping left and right, painting the air itself with crystalline protection.

To not make a stationary target of himself, Kip dodged left and right within the space behind Cruxer, drafting as much off the lux torches as he could while trying to identify a threat.

Ferkudi and Big Leo were barreling through the wide common hall to get to his side. The music of lyre and timbrel and psantria fell silent.

Kip had asked for a small party—which meant (not counting those laboring in the kitchens and stockyards) a hundred lords and ladies and lackeys and lickspittles, thirty-some servants and slaves, fifty men-at-arms (who, on Cruxer's insistence, were allowed no more armament than a table knife), and a dozen performers.

All of them were shrinking back from the center of the room and the high table. Some of the men-at-arms were covering their charges with their own bodies or hauling them toward the doors. Other men-at-arms were still stupefied like blinking heifers, too dull to do the only work for which they'd been hired.

A hundred people in the room, and not one whom Kip could see as a threat.

In a far corner of the room, the petite Winsen had jumped up on a servant's sideboard to get a view of the whole room, his bow already strung, arrow nocked but not drawn, its point sweeping left and right with Winsen's gaze.

Then Kip's view was obscured as Cruxer finished the shield-bubble of blue luxin.

It wasn't elegant work. Despite being made of translucent blue luxin, it was nearly opaque, but Kip knew it was strong. Cruxer did nothing halfway.

"More men," Cruxer muttered. "We need more men."

It was only then that Kip finally processed the last bits: 'Nine Kill Seven' meant a possible assassination attempt by an unknown number of drafters, possibly involving a superviolet. With no one charging forward now, that sounded like a false alarm. Nine Kills were often false alarms.

But 'Nine Kill Naught' meant a paryl drafter.

An assassin from the Order of the Broken Eye. A Shadow.

Which meant the assassin might be *invisible*, the kind of monster who could reach through clothes and flesh and luxin unseen and stop your very heart.

With a pop like an impudent kid clicking his tongue, Cruxer's solid shield-bubble of blue luxin burst and simply fell to dust.

Aghast, Cruxer hesitated, baffled at how something he'd built to be impervious could simply *fail*, but Kip was suddenly loosed. Paryl was fragile. It could slide through luxin or flesh, into joints or hearts. But it couldn't stretch, couldn't cut, couldn't survive violent motion.

As some nerve was invisibly tweaked, Cruxer's knee buckled under him even as Kip dove away.

Kip rolled to his feet and ran straight for the high table. Last thing he wanted with a paryl assassin nearby was to trap himself against a wall. Shouting, "Paryl!" he leapfrogged over the head table between the great clay jugs of wine.

In typically flamboyant Forester fashion, there was a tradition at big parties for the conn to line up all the wine he intended to serve his guests in great jugs on the head table as a sign of his largesse and wealth. The guests, for their part, were expected to drink all of it. Naturally, the jugs got bigger as the egos did.

Here, for the man who had saved the city, some of the most brilliant examples of the big jugs ever crafted were lined up along the entire length of the high table like a rank of alcoholic soldiers.

In all the majesty of his gracefulness, the Turtle-Bear clipped one of them as he cleared the table. He rolled into the open space in the center of the big U of all the tables.

The priceless glazed clay jug painted with gold zoomorphic swirls and studded with precious stones tottered, teetered with the countervailing motion of the sloshing wine inside, tilted, toppled—and smashed.

A fortune of wine and pottery sprayed in every direction.

Beyond the spreading of wine, Kip was already looking for the assassin in sub-red, maybe near Cruxer.

Everyone else had retreated toward the walls or bolted for the doors, creating a shrieking knot of humanity.

Nothing.

Even with a shimmercloak, it took a gifted Shadow to hide himself or herself from sub-red vision.

Like the fearsome twin tusks of a charging iron bull, Ferkudi and Big Leo rushed to flank Kip.

Cruxer was still down, kicking his leg to restore feeling to it, breaking up the paryl. He was physically out of the fight for a while, but his eyes were up and he was already barking orders, no fear at all in his voice, despite his helplessness. "Ferk, Leo, wide! Keep moving! Paryl!"

Big Leo had already unlimbered the heavy chain he usually draped around his neck and tucked into his belt. He began whirring it in the air around him, sweeping it into a shifting shell of shimmering steel. No fragile fingers of paryl would make it through that. Because of Teia, the Mighty had an idea of what paryl could do.

Ferkudi, the grappler, had knots of luxin in and around each hand—a coruscating chunk of crystalline blue luxin in his right, and a spreading shillelagh of woody green in his left. He would count on deflecting any attacks with luxin just long enough to close the distance so he could seize an attacker.

Kip thought, if sub-red doesn't work...

Still moving erratically, still scanning, Kip began narrowing his eyes to *chi*. It occurred to him a little late that the last time he'd messed with chi, he'd been blind for three days.

Too late.

The thunderclap of a pistol fired at close range rocked Kip. He saw fire gush from a barrel sweeping right past his face, heard the snap of a lead ball, and felt the concussive force flattening his cheek like a boxer's punch.

In the barren, total focus that answers the sound of Death's footfall, the world faded. No sound. No people. There was only the pistol, floating in midair held in a disembodied, gloved hand by the invisible killer. As the pistol jumped, the Shadow's shimmercloak rippled with the shock wave, momentarily giving shape to the assassin.

A black burning powder cloud raced hard on the musket ball's heels.

The burning cloud stung Kip's face as he fell. He'd not noticed his feet tangled, but he definitely saw a second pistol sliding into visibility as it emerged from the cover of the shimmercloak.

Another boom and then a clatter.

Kip hit the ground on his side and saw Ferkudi leaping through the air over him, trying to snatch the assassin, blue luxin and green forming great jagged claws to make his arm span twice as wide.

Ferkudi caught nothing, though, his sweeping arms and luxin claws snapping shut on empty air. He landed on his chest with a thump and lost the luxin, both claws breaking apart and beginning to disintegrate on the floor.

Big Leo followed hard on Ferkudi's attack, flinging his chain out to its full reach in a wide circle at waist height.

The last link caught the edge of the retreating Shadow's cloak and threw it wide. The sudden glimpse of boots and trousers and belt where the rest of the man was invisible gave the impression they were staring through a tear in reality. Disrupted by the blow, the magics in a section of the cloak sizzled out of sync with any colors in the room before settling again as the assassin spun out of reach.

Then the cloak draped down again, covering him with its invisibility.

As Kip pulled himself together, deafened but unhurt, Big Leo pressed his advantage against the assassin, charging after the Shadow like a hound on the scent. His chain whipped out again, hitting nothing—

But there was a glimpse of boots as the assassin dove toward one wall.

This time, the whirling heavy chain came down with all the force in the warrior's mountainous body. It cracked the floor tiles and shot sparks, but hit no flesh—the Shadow was fast.

People shrieked, cowering back in fear as Big Leo charged toward them. The Shadow must be nearly among them. If Big Leo struck again, he was going to kill or maim more than one of the bystanders.

But Big Leo pulled up short, flicking out the end of the chain just short of the crowd, who were panicked now, pushing one another through the nearest door as if pushing a cork down into a wine bottle.

With the easy grace of a squad that's worked together so long they act like one body, Big Leo diverted the tornado of heavy chain for one instant as Ferkudi barreled past him.

Big Leo couldn't attack too close to the crowd. Ferkudi had no such compunctions. Again, with arms and luxin spread and all of his considerable bulk at a full sprint, Ferkudi made a flying leap at the portion of the bunched crowd where he guessed the Shadow was.

Ferkudi's tackle sent at least a dozen people flying—none of them the Shadow, and he went down in a tangle with all of them.

Which only left one way the Shadow could have gone—right back in front of the high table.

Kip saw Ben-hadad, wearing his knee brace but still hobbled by his injury from when they'd fled the Chromeria, standing at the far end of the high table. He had his heavy crossbow loaded and aimed—right at the crowd. But to shoot at the Shadow was to shoot at the crowd beyond it. The frustration was writ all over his bespectacled face.

Ben, Kip knew, felt useless. That all his brilliance was for naught. Couldn't fight. Couldn't help his friends who were in mortal peril. Couldn't shoot unless he got the perfect opportunity—which he couldn't, with these panicked strangers everywhere.

Then, faster than Kip could think, Ben-hadad swiveled on his good leg so that he was aiming parallel with the table's front edge. He fired his bolt at nothing Kip could see—

—and blew out the front of every one of the priceless wine jugs lined up on the high table. They jetted rivers of wine onto the floor in front of the high table as if someone had opened spigots on all of them.

Then, in orderly succession, they tumbled and exploded on the floor.

The wide wave of wine washed every which way. Then the wave parted around two barriers, momentarily indistinct, then surrounded and revealed. Wine covered the floor everywhere, except in two, foot-shaped depressions.

Kip nearly unleashed the bolt of magical death he'd gathered in his right hand, until he saw the stunned face of Lady Proud Hart directly in the line of fire behind where the invisible Shadow was standing. The noblewoman was still seated. Hadn't moved from her place, frozen by shock.

Then there was splashing as the Shadow realized he'd been discovered, and bolted.

Wine-wet footprints marked his passage, but Kip had it now. If this Shadow was too good at his work to be seen in sub-red, then...

Kip's eyes spasmed to an inhuman narrowness as he peered at the world through chi. Faint skeletons grinned at him everywhere through their flesh suits. Metal in cold black and bones like pink shadows; all else was merely colored fog.

In chi, though, the shimmercloak flared with weird energies, magic boiling off it in clouds like a sweaty horse steaming on a cold morning.

The Shadow stopped running, his shoes finally dry enough not to leave footprints. He turned back into the middle of the room, checking that he was unseen, skeletal hands pulling the folds of the cloak in place.

Kip kept moving his head, as if he, too, were blind.

The Shadow drew a short sword, but kept it tucked down, covered by his cloak. He walked toward Kip, secure in his invincibility.

Orholam, he wasn't giving up, even though they were all on alert now. Kip couldn't decide if it was overweening pride or terrifying professionalism that the man thought he could still pull this job off against these odds.

Waiting until the Shadow was close, Kip suddenly looked directly at him. "You've a message for me," Kip said. "What is it?"

The Shadow stopped as suddenly as if he'd been slapped. Kip could see the man's skull dip as he checked himself. *No, no, I'm still invisible. It's a bluff.*

"You've got a message," Kip said.

The skeleton-man paused, as if he thought Kip was trying to fool him into speaking and giving his position away. After a moment, he shook his head slightly.

"Ah," Kip said, gazing straight where the man's veiled eyes must be. The air began humming with Kip's gathering power. "Then you *are* the message."

The Shadow twitched as he finally accepted that Kip really could see him. He lunged forward, stabbing—

And Kip's pent-up fury of tentacled-green and razored-blue death blasted into the assassin and threw him across the room.

The danger past, Kip released chi, and was immediately reminded why he hated chi. Drafting chi was like riding a horse that kicked you every time you got on, and every time you got off. In the face.

Kip fell to his knees, his eyes burning, lightning stabbing back into his head, tears blinding him. He squeezed his eyes tight shut, but when he opened them, they were still locked in chi vision, people around the room showing up only as dim shadows and skeletons and metal-bearers.

Chi was the worst.

Kip willed his eyes to open to their normal apertures, and mercifully, they did. This time, thank Orholam, chi hadn't stricken him blind.

Big Leo materialized, standing over Kip, as Ferkudi went over to make sure the Shadow was dead. Ben-hadad and Cruxer limped over, leaning on each other, Cruxer looking better by the step.

Only Winsen hadn't moved. He still perched on his table in the corner of the room, an arrow still nocked, never having shot. He wasn't usually shy about shooting in questionable circumstances.

Ferkudi stood back up. The Shadow was, indeed, dead. Very dead. Gory, don't-look-at-that-mess-if-you-want-to-sleep-tonight dead.

It was a mistake.

Not killing the man, but that he'd obliterated him: Kip had destroyed a shimmercloak.

No one reproved him. No one said he should have done better, as Andross Guile or Gavin Guile would have. Maybe they didn't even think it.

But he did. He'd been out of control.

It was a reminder that he'd been drafting a lot. In its unfettered strength, green had taken him further than he wanted to go. If nothing else killed him first, it would be green that got him in the end. Indeed, he hadn't looked at his own eyes in a mirror in a while, fearing what the bloody glass would tell him.

"What the hell, Win?!" Big Leo demanded. "Where were you?"

But the lefty still stood silent, a bundle of arrows held with the bow in his right hand for quick drawing, as if he didn't even hear them.

Big Leo blew out an exasperated breath, dismissing him. "And what the hell's with you, Ferk? You say you smell *cloves*—and then shout Nine Kill Naught?"

"My goof," Ferkudi said as if he'd said he wanted wine with dinner but then decided he'd really wanted beer. "Saffron. Not cloves. I meant I smelled saffron. Paryl smells like saffron. Superviolet is cloves. Always get those two mixed up."

"You confused saffron and *cloves*? They don't smell anything alike!"

"They're both yummy."

Big Leo rubbed his face with a big hand. "Ferk, you are the dumbest smart guy I know."

"No I'm not!" Ferkudi said, a big grin spreading over his face. "I'm the smartest dumb guy you know."

"Yeah," Ben-hadad said, "*I'm* the dumbest smart guy you know. I smelled saffron half an hour ago, out by the palace's front doors. Didn't even think about it. Breaker, my apologies." He knuckled his forehead. "I think it's customary to offer my resignation?"

"None of that," Cruxer said. "This is none of your faults. It's mine. You've all been right. The Mighty's too small. We're spread too thin. And that's on me." Kip had kept it secret that Teia was infiltrating the Order of the Broken Eye, but he had mentioned that Karris was afraid the Order had people even in the Blackguard itself, which had made Cruxer stop any talk of adding to the Mighty, fearing that whoever they welcomed in might be a traitor.

'How can you be certain one of us isn't with the Order already?' Winsen had asked. 'I say we add people. Might as well get a few shifts' rest while we wait to get stabbed in the back.'

As if they weren't already sometimes nervous about Winsen, what with his alien gaze, total disregard for danger, and overeagerness to shoot.

"You all did your part," Cruxer continued. "And you all did your parts brilliantly. I mean, except Winsen, who I think might be angling for a Blackguard name. What do you think of Dead Weight?"

The Mighty were all just starting to laugh, delighted, turning toward Winsen, when Kip saw something go cruel and hungry in the little man's eyes. Win had never taken mockery well.

Win's obsidian arrow point swept left as the archer drew the nocked arrow fully, pointing straight at Cruxer, who was standing tall, flat-footed.

There was no time for him to evade. Win's move was as fast as a man stepping in a hole while expecting solid ground. The bowstring came back to his lips in the swift kiss of a departing parent and then leapt away.

He couldn't miss—

—but he did.

He loosed another arrow and was drawing a third before the Mighty dove left and right. Kip was throwing a green shield in front of himself—I always knew it would be Win. That saurian calm. That unnatural detachment.

Big Leo crushed Kip to the ground, disrupting his drafting and blotting out all vision as he offered his own body as a shield.

"Whoa! Whoa! Whoa!" Winsen shouted. "Easy, Ferk! Ben! Easy, Ben!"

Kip unearthed himself from the living mountain that was Big Leo and saw Winsen with bow lifted high in surrender.

Ben-hadad had his crossbow leveled at the archer, his fingers heavy on the trigger plate. Ferkudi was slowing down, already having charged over most of the distance, closing off Winsen's view of Kip— and therefore angle of fire—with his own bulk. Cruxer had his arm drawn back, blue luxin boiling, hardening into a lance.

"I know one thing about the Shadows," Winsen said loudly. He dropped the arrows from his right hand to show he was no threat. "They often work in pairs."

There was a clatter behind the Mighty. Metal hitting stone—not three paces behind them.

War-blinded by the threat in front of them, not one of them had looked back. But they did now.

A cloaked figure was shimmering back into visibility, Winsen's two arrows protruding from his chest. A Shadow. He pitched facedown.

None of them said a word as the Shadow twitched in death.

The Mighty fanned out, securing Kip, checking that the dead assassin was really dead.

Then Commander Cruxer cleared his throat. "Did I say Dead Weight? I meant, uh, Dead Eye."

They chuckled. It was an apology.

Except Ferkudi. "You can't call him Dead Eye. There's already an Archer from a year behind us called that. Beat Win's score at the three hundred paces by four p—"

"Ferk!" Cruxer said, not looking at him, his smile cracking. "Dead Shot it is."

"Oh, definitely not, Commander," Ferkudi said. "That's been used like seven times. Most recent one's retired now, but still alive. Very disrespectful to take a living Blackguard's n—"

"*Ferk*," Cruxer said, his smile tightening.

"I'd settle for you calling me 'Your Holiness,'" Win offered.

"No," Cruxer said.

"'*Commander* Winsen'?" Winsen suggested.

Cruxer sighed.

Chapter 3

Maybe it isn't treason.

Teia ghosted through the barracks after her meeting with the Old Man of the Desert and Murder Sharp, wondering if it would be the last time she ever set foot here. As she packed in early-morning darkness, her brothers and sisters of the Blackguard slept.

Brothers and sisters, she thought. Huh. What would that make Commander Ironfist? Their father? It sure had felt like it.

What kind of person would kill her own father?

No. No! This is to *save* my father. My real father.

She hoisted her pack to her shoulders and looked around the barracks as if hoping someone would see her, stop her.

What am I doing? Saying goodbye?

Pathetic. This is all gone. This is all already gone.

Besides, her closest remaining friends weren't even here: Gav and Gill Greyling and Essel and Tlatig were all out on one of the semi-clandestine Gavin Guile search expeditions that so many of the Blackguards had been doing for the last year. The trips weren't exactly allowed—responsibility for seeking the lost Prism had passed to other hands—but they weren't exactly forbidden, either.

Even if Gavin Guile had only been the Blackguards' professional patron, not their Promachos who had fought for them on the fields of battle and bled for them in the halls of power, earning himself a Black-guard name and all the Blackguards' devotion; even then, even if it had only been an affront to their pride and not an assault on their love, los-ing a Prism was an unbearable blot on the Blackguards' honor.

Their chief purpose was to protect him, and he'd been kidnapped right under their noses.

They would do anything to get him back. It's what a family does.

The day they'd lost him had been the day everything went north for Teia. Karris had become the White. Zymun became Prism-elect. Commander Ironfist had been fired. Kip and the Mighty had nearly been killed escaping, and Tremblefist had died silencing the cannons to save them.

Teia had stupidly decided to stay behind. She'd told herself she could do more good here.

Do good?! Mostly she'd learned to use her magic to murder slaves.

She wasn't even *good* at her bad work.

She'd botched the assassination of Ironfist's sister so badly that he'd immediately figured out who'd sent her and who she was—Teia was the reason Ironfist had declared himself a king rather than a satrap.

And now, in his revenge, the Chromeria had lost Paria.

Out of the original seven satrapies, that left them with only two and a half: Abornea, Ruthgar, and half of Blood Forest.

The empire had been a seven-legged feast table; now it was a top-heavy end table teetering on two golden legs. The only question was which way it would fall.

Best for Teia to side with the Order, then. Kingdoms rise and empires fall, but the cockroaches survive.

And that's what this next kill for the Old Man meant, when Teia stripped away all her pretenses. It meant siding once and for all with the Order. Not pretending anymore. No longer a double agent, an agent.

She arrived at Little Jasper's back docks in the last minutes before dawn, feeling as sere and barren inside as the wind-scoured Red Cliffs.

Her father wouldn't want her to buy his life at such a price, but Teia had worried for far too long what other people wanted.

Though the Old Man hadn't come right out and said it, Teia's next kill was Ironfist.

To guarantee her obedience, the Order held her father hostage. He would leave their company a rich man or not at all.

'This is the pain that will transform you into Teia Sharp,' the Old Man had said.

May Orholam—absent or blind or uncaring as He was—send that vile man and all the Order with him to the ninth hell.

Teia didn't know how or why, but Ironfist was either on that odd bone-white ship she spied coming into the dock now, or he waited wherever it was sailing next.

It wasn't 'betrayal,' technically. He'd declared himself a king. That made *him* the traitor.

And killing a traitor wasn't wrong...Right?

Ironfist had been like a father to her, but in infiltrating the Blackguard for the Order, he'd betrayed the man who was like a father to them all: savant and savior, paterfamilias and Promachos, godlike Gavin Guile.

Ironfist had sworn loyalty to Gavin! He'd administered those very oaths to half the rest of the Blackguard! Before the blades come out, you have to decide where you stand. King Ironfist had decided to stand for himself. He'd thrown off his loyalty to Gavin, and now he must be trying to do the same with the Order.

Why else would they be sending Teia to assassinate him? He was one of their own.

Had been, anyway.

Now Teia would be the shield that came down on his neck. Hers would be the hand that brought his head to her masters.

It would hurt to kill Ironfist. But it wouldn't break her. She was beyond that now.

Invisible in the master cloak, Teia made her way out onto the lonely dock. Cheerless dawn was threatening the horizon as sailors prepared the ship in hushed tones. There was no harbormaster present, nor any of the usual dockhands or slaves or attendants Teia would have expected. It was a ghost ship—fitting for the departing condemned.

Three figures stood on the quay. One was hunched and swaddled as if ill, or perhaps to hide his height. The second was a broadly gesticulating man with a wild, woolly beard with match cords woven into it and a gold-brocaded jacket worn open over his bare chest, despite the chill of the morning. The third figure had his back to Teia. There was something in his carriage that spoke of being human freight, a slave about to be passed from one man to another. Teia had seen that broken shuffle before; in truth, she'd walked like that herself.

So she dismissed that one, flaring her eyes to paryl to look at the others just as the heavily cloaked man presented a sword.

Its appearance hit her like a rapid blow to the nose, leaving her blinking: that blade should have shone white in her paryl vision. Metal always did, with minute variations of tone for different metals. This thing was *invisible*.

No, the shimmercloaks made things invisible—when you looked at an active shimmercloak, you saw whatever lay beyond it. This was a bar of black, heavy nothingness. Usually, darkness is a hole, an absence, as death is the absence of life.

This was a piece of hungry night, of darkness breathing.

This was more than Death, hammered and folded into killing shape. This was not made by the hand of man. Perhaps in the youth of Old Man Time, some dead demigod, after his descent to the all-devouring depths of the ninth hell, had rallied instead of despaired at his imprisonment there. He'd charged hell's gates from the inside. Then, confronting the three-headed hound who guarded that way, terrifying all lesser souls, he smashed its faces on the gates, using its snarling snouts as battering rams, snapping lupine teeth and bones, one, two, and three, throwing the mighty gates from their hinges.

Then the demigod had gone his way, triumphant to the heavens, heedless of the hellhound he left behind.

If such might be true, then this blade was one of hell's jagged, broken fangs.

The cloaked man laid it across his gloved palms and offered it up.

But not to the flamboyant captain.

And there was another blow. A paryl marker, visible only to her, the sign that this man was her target, hung in the air above the wretch she'd dismissed as a slave.

He couldn't be—he *wasn't* Ironfist.

He wasn't Ironfist.

Even from the back it was clear this man was too small. Broad across his hunched shoulders, square-jawed, but light-skinned and not tall enough. Hair covered with a grubby hat. He was just some broken old warrior.

All the cold courage she'd been knotting tight loosed its tension from her limbs and she could suddenly breathe.

She didn't have to kill Ironfist.

Something like a prayer of thanks made its way to her teeth. But there it stopped.

Why would the Old Man think I'd have a hard time killing some stranger?

The man a sailor had referred to as Captain Gunner whistled a melodious little trill. "C'mon!" he said, waggling his bushy eyebrows at the slave. He had a winsome, goofy grin, but he struck Teia as not very stable, and very, very dangerous. "What'll it be? Death or glory?"

Apparently, the poor bastard was being offered some kind of choice. Not much of one, though, since no matter what he did Teia was going to be killing him afterward.

"Let's sail," the slave said, straightening his stooped shoulders and taking up the blade. Some spirit came back into him, and recognition clobbered Teia like a left hook to the neck. "Death *and* glory, Cap'n Gunner," said none other than Gavin Guile.

The Prism himself, Gavin Guile. The price for saving Teia's father was that she assassinate Emperor Gavin Fucking Guile.

Chapter 4

The young goddess strode barefoot through the hidden shipyards in a dress mostly faded to blue from the original bright murex purple it had been when the White King had given it to her. That had been before he tried to kill her. Invisible to most, tornadoes of the airy spidersilk luxin billowed from her, spiraling out in orderly whorls, the patterns repeating themselves on every scale. Tendrils stuck to those in her path and wormed their way into them. And tradesmen and shipbuilders and the unpaid laborers whom no one here called slaves found reasons to move aside, most without even noticing her.

The dirty warehouse she approached made a tawdry throne room for a man who would be a king of the gods, but it had kept its secrets safe.

As she passed through the crowds that magically parted for her, she heard the cadences of their speeches warble, disparate words from a hundred conversations suddenly aligning, the pitches rising and falling in perfect uniformity with every other—and then falling simultaneously to silence, as everyone noticed.

Most were baffled, some alarmed. The words had been their own; the speakers hadn't intended such conformity. Surely here, among the new pagans, odd magic was the norm. Wights of every color walked the streets. Six of the *bane* had been gathered in closer proximity than perhaps ever before in history. But this magic was different.

Aliviana, born Aliviana Danavis, now the goddess Ferrilux, passed the wights guarding the doors. The superviolet wights were the easiest of all: they could belong to her in an instant, if she willed it. The dull, animalistic sub-reds were the most challenging for her; they goggled bestial eyes at all those around them, as if everyone else had heard a tone to which they were deaf. One of the burned freaks even stared at her, but couldn't comprehend why Aliviana might be important.

The cadences and then the silence rippled through the petitioners in two slow waves before her, only to burst at the circle of the White King's nine bodyguards, all formerly elite drafter-warriors who had made the leap halfway to godhood and were now polychrome wights with black-luxin-edged vechevorals and ataghans and scorpions and flyssas and man catchers, even in their weapons preferring the old and provincial to the modern and universal.

Liv's superviolet luxin died where she touched those spears, as all magic died when it touched living black luxin.

That these wights had such weapons told her that the White King had been experimenting with his black seed crystal. She wondered if he understood that he was playing with the most dangerous magic in all the world, and something tightened uneasily in her stomach.

An emotion, perhaps.

She could dredge up a name for it from her memory, if she tried, but she simply didn't care to.

"That's far enough!" the White King boomed.

And then everyone could see her, her will-crafting broken as if it were a spell. The people fell away from her, some literally so, tumbling over their neighbors in their astonishment and fear.

Weapons came to wights' hands, but not even the reds or sub-reds moved to attack without the White King's command.

A superviolet will-crafting compels only one's reason, as an orange hex-crafting compels only one's emotions, so anyone at all could have broken her webs with a shouted word.

But instead of noticing the artistry of her drafting that had allowed her to shift the vision of six hundred twenty-seven people and seventy-three wights, the people seemed impressed with their king instead. As if he had commanded her to be visible and she had no choice but to comply. As if it were proof that his magic was greater.

Her rage needed no help finding its name. It was quite well fixed to the condescending, pompous polychrome wight who now stood before an ivory throne.

Born Koios White Oak before a fire at his family's mansion on Big Jasper had robbed him of his good looks and humanity and illusions, the White King was an imposing figure, she could admit. To his burn-scarred flesh, he added luxin and hexes. He'd refined his control of both in the time she'd been gone. He wore gold-edged white silk trousers of some flowing design that reminded her of something from an ancient woodcut, a fashion from the time of the nine kingdoms. He wore a matching tunic laced tight over his thin body with gold cords, with knots at ritual intervals. Rather than looking ruddy or pallid or freckled from his Forester heritage, his skin was now white as the noonday sun. His many and grotesque lumpy burn scars were somehow invisible, whether by the arts of cosmetics or will-crafting. She doubted he'd actually been healed; the White King was all about appearances, not changing underlying realities. His eyelids were kohled black so as to accentuate their many colors, and his ivory skin was studded with glued-on jewels and protruding luxin.

"You look well, Koios," Aliviana said. "It seems I'm not the only one who's changed since you sent me away with an assassin whom you ordered to either murder me or chain me up like your other pet djinn."

"Daughter! Our new Ferrilux!" the White King said. "You speak like one who has become the goddess of pride indeed! You have blossomed into all I had hoped you might be, with a little additional cheek thrown in for good measure."

He chuckled, and his people seemed to take that as a sign that it was safe to laugh, and they did.

It was an odd sound, laughter; one she had neither made nor heard for a year, twelve days and twenty hours, seven seconds. Only after it was gone did Aliviana think that she should have been listening to the messages that laughter carried. Was it the laughter of a people afraid of their king, or of people in awe of and in love with him?

Too late.

The unfamiliar emotional freight had gone unweighed, and her memory could no more call it back to take its measure than one could call back an insult carelessly offered.

"May I have a word? In private?" she asked.

Her jaw strained suddenly against her effort to open it. *Don't grovel*, Beliol hissed.

No one else could hear him. Careful not to let her irritation show on her face, she slammed the thought down and even triggered her zygomatic major muscle. From this distance, the White King might take it for a pleasant smile. "Please," she added.

Chapter 5

"Another nightmare?" Tisis asked. "You think the assassination attempt...?"

"No. The other thing again." Kip scooted to the edge of their bed. He'd left his side sweat-damp.

"I'd kind of hoped..." Tisis's sigh echoed his own. He could tell she'd been up for a while, meeting with her spies or something. She'd even selected clothes for him. She thought he slept too little, and tried to protect him.

"How'd I ever find you?" he asked her.

"The first time, I was sabotaging your initiation. I think the second was when I was jerking off your grandfather."

"Honey, I didn't mean—"

"Just so you know, in case you ever thought I might make comparisons, you are—"

"No, let's not!" Kip said.

Tisis was not a disinterested party when it came to discussing these particular dreams. Dreams of Andross Guile.

"Should I summon the attendants?" Tisis already had the small bell in hand, a sign that he was already late.

He held out a staying hand. "Can I tell you something? Something bizarre?"

Of course he could, but she didn't put down the bell.

"I dreamed of him as a young man. He's going to woo a bride and trying to save the Guile family as he does so, and he doesn't even realize—for all his smarts—that he's broken, utterly broken by his own brother's recent death." He paused.

"So far...not that bizarre," Tisis said. Her own lack of sleep was making her shorter with him than usual.

Kip looked down at the Turtle-Bear tattoo on the inside of his wrist. The inks or luxins that made the colors were all still vibrant from the Battle of Greenwall a few days before; it would fade, in time. He'd been using every color of luxin recently. The wick of his life was burning fast. Maybe that had something to do with the dreams.

"They're not dreams, exactly," Kip said. "I think they're dreams of a card."

"But you forget most of what you see when you wake. Exactly like a dream."

"Well, yes. I didn't say it wasn't a dream at all. Just that it's a dream of a card."

"You said you'd never touched the full Andross Guile card. That he was too clever to allow all of his experiences to be captured."

He had said that. Janus Borig had convinced Kip's grandfather to let her do two very partial cards, stubs, that showed only particular scenes, similar to what an untalented Mirror could make, or what a good Mirror would make of an item. The card needn't show the maker of that item's entire life story; the card's focus would be limited to the item itself. Kip had only touched a stub card. So he thought. "And I believed it fully to be true," Kip said. "But these dreams…"

"Nightmares," she said. "And, as they're of that creature, it's fitting that your dreams are twisted. This is the man who hired an assassin to murder you—his own grandson—before you'd even met, who forced you to play literal games for Teia's life and freedom, who has killed Orholam only knows how many innocents in his life, and not incidentally arranged for my future husband to walk in on the most humiliating moment of my life, after he'd convinced me to whore myself. Thinking you're living that disgusting *thing's* life? That's a nightmare. And you never touched his card, so it's also a delusion. And considering everything you need to do—yesterday—it's a distraction, too." Tisis rang the bell to summon the servants more loudly than necessary. "You're going to be late," she said.

And then she was gone.

She wasn't really mad at him, he knew. She'd apologize for this tonight. They were all of them adjusting to the burdens of their new, magnified positions and the quagmire they'd stepped into. Tisis was trying to take care of Kip as well as everything else—first, even—and it must seem to her that he wasn't even trying to help her help him. He was spending precious minutes talking about dreams while he was late to a council of war?

But he hadn't even told her the worst part, the thing out of all the landscape of impossibilities that had actually struck him as bizarre before he even woke. The young Andross Guile that Kip had seen from the inside during his dream? Kip had sort of *liked* him.

"No need to cry, Your High and Mighty, I'm here," Winsen said.

Kip looked up, surprised. He hadn't even heard the door open.

Winsen. Why did it have to be Winsen?

Kip wasn't crying, anyway. Just feeling morose. Not that he expected Winsen to understand fine gradations of emotions.

"Where are the servants?" Kip asked.

"I asked them to step out so I could assassinate you," Winsen said.

"You're not gonna let that go, are you?" Kip thought he only thought it, but it slipped out. Damn, just when he thought he was getting better at governing his tongue, Kip the Lip showed up again.

"Let it go?" Winsen said. "You all looked at me like I was really gonna kill you. Except Ferk. But that's only because he's too dumb. I think he was just running over to give me a lecture on weapon safety."

"You know," Kip said, rubbing his eyes, "I kind of hate you sometimes."

"Yeah, but you hate me less than anyone else does."

For a moment, Kip was stunned to silence by the near compliment.

"And the feeling's mutual!" Win said, as if to save them from having a moment. "You all done with your beauty rest, princess? Can we go now—you know, to that meeting you ordered us all to be at a half hour ago? Cruxer's been shittin' cobbles."

"Thank you for that," Kip said.

Winsen grunted, as if straining to pass a cobblestone.

Kip was a stone.

Kip didn't give him the pleasure of a reproof or any sign of amusement. Winsen didn't stop grunting.

Kip cracked a grin. "Dammit, Winsen!"

Winsen waggled his eyebrows.

Kip wanted nothing more than to grab yesterday's tunic and head out. "I'd love to just charge down there, but I do actually need to get dressed properly. Tisis and I had a long conversation on why I do actually need to dress like…you know, the rich and careful way I've been dressing—so as to encourage people not to see me as overly young or sloppy or a barbarian."

Too late, Kip realized that Winsen was not the person Kip wanted to recount any more of that conversation with.

"Hey, don't look at me," Winsen said. "I totally understand why you spend a Blackguard's yearly wages on a single set of clothes. I'd do it myself if I'd been paid in the last six months. Or, you know, ever."

Kip rang the summons bell again, louder.

"I understand your need to project yourself at a certain standard," Winsen said, as if offended. He lowered his voice momentarily. "And how much work it takes to try to make you look good. And I know Cruxer's irritated at waiting, so I sent your servants on ahead of us."

"Oh gods," Kip said. "You're not gonna have the servants *primp* me in front of the Mighty!" Being naked in front of the Mighty was nothing. But being bathed (by strangers!), and tweezed, and picked at, and salved, and massaged, and having strangers chatter things like,

'Should we emphasize or de-emphasize the surprising and obvious power of his buttocks?'

Torture.

Winsen said, "Me? And embarrass you like that? Your Grace, I am shocked!"

Chapter 6

Hope leaped in Teia like a gazelle from a lion's grip.

Gavin Guile is alive! And he's *here*!

That had to mean that the man with the Hellfang blade was the Old Man of the Desert himself—for who else would the Old Man trust with such a weapon or such a prisoner?

And if that was the Old Man, Teia could follow him from here *now* and find his lair and his real identity and report to Karris and maybe even find word of where her father was—

But lose Gavin. The former Prism had already boarded the *Golden Mean* with Captain Gunner. Sailors were preparing the ship to leave immediately.

Teia had made it halfway up the quay, following the Old Man back to the Chromeria, when she saw the Blackguards standing at their posts out back. They either hadn't been there when she came down or they'd been hidden. Friends! Comrades! She could tell them and—

They saluted the Old Man as he approached.

Not a Blackguard salute. A Braxian salute.

Teia skidded to a stop. They were his.

And the Old Man had known she was coming down here. He'd ordered her to board the ship, after all. That meant those Blackguards were here not for him but for her.

They were here in case she decided to disobey and not board the ship.

Which meant they must be sub-reds. The Old Man trusted no one, especially not his well-nigh-invisible assassins. He was not a man—or woman perhaps, Teia still couldn't assume—who would hone a blade to razor sharpness and then let it cut his own throat.

Teia's heart sank like a panting gazelle into the lion's patient paws.

The Order didn't know it, but she could defeat sub-red with a sufficiently dense cloud of paryl now. But it was a blustery morning, and a gust of wind would be the death of her.

It would be a huge gamble to try to make it past the traitor Blackguards without being seen.

And Gavin would be lost to the wide sea and whatever desperate mission the Old Man was sending him on. If Teia *did* make it past these Blackguards, how long would it take her to reach Karris? How long to get her alone so Teia could report the truth?

How could Karris mobilize skimmers without breaking Teia's cover? There were other Blackguard traitors than these two, Teia knew.

What contingency plans did the Old Man have ready, just in case Gavin were rescued?

He wouldn't let him be taken alive, would he? No. Gavin had seen him, heard his voice.

There had to be a course here where Teia did everything right and somehow averted disaster, but she was paralyzed. If Gavin left on that ship without her, her father was dead.

I'm seriously considering obeying them again. Her belly filled with sick horror.

She walked back to the ship as in a trance and climbed the gangplank with lead in her shoes.

There was no way out. Her thoughts of defiance had lasted less than two minutes.

Gavin Guile was amidships. The captain was removing his chains.

Teia shuddered with a slave's visceral revulsion at the fetters. She eyed his wrists, looking for sores as instinctively as another woman might check a man's fingers for a wedding band. There were none.

Wherever Gavin Guile had been held, he hadn't been chained. The other possibility—that he might not have fought his chains—was unthinkable. Everyone fights the chains. Most, like Teia, gave up after a few cuts. When your own mother puts you in chains, you think maybe you deserve them.

To her shame, Teia didn't even have scars on her wrists.

But thinking of that called to mind Ironfist in that terrible room, over the pooled blood of his sister, whom Teia'd just killed. Ironfist, tearing his chains out of the wall in his rage and agony. But even he hadn't broken his chains, had he?

No one breaks the chains, T. You can only ask to be let out nicely. After you do what they demand.

She didn't know what she was doing. She should go belowdecks. Hide like she was supposed to do until they were far out to sea. Obey. It was a strain to stay invisible for so long, to be so open and sensitive to the light, which was only swelling by the minute as the sun fingered the horizon. But she couldn't pull herself away.

The Prism had always been the height of majesty, of virility, potency. She'd heard other Blackguards say in hushed tones, 'Whatever else we do, whatever happens, we were Blackguards in the time of Gavin Guile.' Here was a man who was emperor who actually deserved it.

Seeing Zymun get ready to step into his place had made Teia sharply aware of how rare that was. Gavin made you believe in the Great Chain of Being; that some humans really were one step below Orholam, that they were surely made of fundamentally different stuff than you were.

The man before her threatened to give the lie to all that. Haggard, pathetic, ill, in sloppy clothes over a body with dirt so caked on that it seemed a washing would foul the water without cleansing the man. He must have lost as much weight as Kip had in Kip's time at the Chromeria, but Gavin hadn't had the weight to lose.

But she saw a glimpse of the old Gavin Guile charisma like a glint of sunlight off a distant lighthouse as he shook his head at some comment Captain Gunner had just made and gave a lopsided grin. " 'Good furred muffins'? Orholam's saggy nipples, man, never change," Gavin said to Gunner.

The grin—that quintessential Guile grin that Teia knew so well from his son—exposed a missing dogtooth. That hadn't been gone before his imprisonment. It made Teia touch her own, still sore even after Karris's own chirurgeon's ministrations.

Nor had his eye been missing before. Gavin now wore a patch on his left eye with an unsettling black jewel in it. Gunner was just relieving him of the black sword, carefully wrapping it in cloths and handing it off to a nervous sailor to take below.

"Speaking of change, you need to," Gunner said. "No, no, you know I hain't religious. I mean, I give my 'spects to the Nine Ladies and the sea witches and keep my friendly spat with Ceres"—he spat into the water—"ya shriveled, sandy old cunt—and naturally, I tip a bowl for Borealis and Arcturus and the Bitch o' Storms, but that's just salt sense for a man of my avocation. I weren't talkin' meta—meta... metanoumenistically. I meant your bestments. Vestments? See? I trya talk to you god-botherers and it gets me kerfaffled. Change your clothes, man. You stink to low heaven. Soap and a rag and a bucket o' clean until you shine like you're polished as frequent as your mama's nethers. Only thing worse 'n a stanky sailor's a stanky prince."

"Technically, I'm an emperor," Gavin said.

"So two things worse. Anyhoo, as our mutual fiend there in the wrappings wants this pale little gold beauty back on the waves two bells past. But there's a way to do things when gettin' a ship ship-shape, things to check. Crew to kick in the pucker. So get yourself clean afore you come belowdecks. My new girl deserves the best. I'll have a man bring you fresh clothes."

"These are actually new. Generous guy. Gave me new clothes in addition to the starvation and imprisonment and the black eye. I—"

Captain Gunner gave him a flat, dangerous look. "They've got a miasma about 'em. Bad luck. You fold 'em nice and leave them on the dock. Five minutes."

Gavin nodded agreeably, but Teia could see gears turning in his head, quick as Kip: So I'm being put in my place. Fair enough . . . Captain. He mumbled, "Was a joke. Little joke. Black eye. Never mind."

"Tolerable sailors, this lot. All Order folk, though," Captain Gunner said, looking at the men and women scurrying about at their tasks.

"Oh, good. Now I feel better about consigning them to certain death," Gavin said. "I'll clean up before I come below."

"End don't try en' run."

"Running's not in my cards, I'm afraid," Gavin said with some forced good humor.

Indeed, the man looked like he could barely stand. But as Captain Gunner departed, Gavin Guile climbed up the stairs of the sterncastle and accepted a bucket and sponge.

Teia watched him invisibly. She should go belowdecks, out of the way of rushing sailors. She was invisible, not incorporeal, and her presence was supposed to be a secret at least until they were on their way. But she couldn't bear to be shut in with her self-loathing just yet.

No wonder the Old Man hadn't told her who her target was. If he'd had even a sliver of a doubt about her loyalty, he *couldn't* tell her. And no wonder he'd thought it would be a painful kill for her: it wasn't that he thought she had any special personal connection with Gavin Guile; it was that she was a Blackguard. Her whole life, her entire calling, was dedicated to protecting the Prism. She had only ever wanted to be a Blackguard, and this murder asked her to betray the very essence of that.

That was the pain that would make her a Sharp. Teia Sharp.

But Gavin Guile wasn't merely a Prism, was he? Not merely a fig-urehead emperor, or even a good man. He was Kip's father. Karris's husband. To the Blackguards who still searched the seas and the Seven Satrapies for him, he had earned the Name 'Promachos,' 'The One Who Goes Before Us to Fight.' The image it evoked was the point of the spear, the man who runs ahead into battle, who leads it from the front, who never shies from the danger he asks others to risk.

My father, for Kip's.

My father is a nobody. Gavin Guile is a man who shakes history. But my *father*...

Sailors were scurrying around, double-checking knots before Cap'n Gunner arrived to see that they'd done everything right. She dodged through the rushing men and made it up the sterncastle ladder.

Gavin was wasting no time. He'd stripped naked and was scrubbing vigorously at his arms and chest, rubbing his skin ruddy and flinging water about.

Teia realized she wasn't embarrassed by his nudity. Perhaps it was because he looked sick, faded so far from his former sun-hot glory that she felt only pity. Perhaps it was because she, not yet eighteen years old and still never having lain with a man, had seen so many people naked now in using paryl constantly that nudity simply didn't mean anything to her. Perhaps it was because she had to kill him, and you couldn't let a target be fully human. A target was meat and blood and breath to be stilled, not a father, not a lover, not a leader you'd adored.

A year ago, she would have been embarrassed, regardless.

She'd been different then. Better.

"Grab me that razor?" Gavin said. "This beard."

Teia looked around the sterncastle to see who he was talking to. There was no one here. The nearby sailors had all disappeared.

Gavin said, "I'm ragged and beaten and half-blind and melancholy and exhausted, but I'm not deaf."

Teia had been *damn near* silent.

"And you stepped in a water drop," Gavin admitted. He smirked, as if he knew his life was in danger but he just didn't care. "Which shimmercloak is that?"

"The fox," Teia said, defeated. "How would—"

"The fox? That's the one burnt all to hell. That means you're new. And short. Woman, by your voice. Who are you working for?"

"I've been sent to kill you," Teia said. "I mean, after you do whatever you've agreed to do."

"The Order itself, then?" Gavin asked, still scrubbing his face and neck. He barely moved his mouth, didn't look toward her, and spoke in a near mumble to keep his voice from carrying. Not a dumb man, Gavin Guile. "There is, after all, more than one group that would like me dead. Though several of them might hire the Order, I suppose..."

"I work for the Order itself. Everyone else thinks you're already dead, so far as I know."

Teia wasn't sure why she said that. She worked for the Order? No, she still hadn't decided, right? Why didn't she say she worked for the Chromeria first, a lie to give him hope? He looked like he could use some.

"It's enough to make you wonder, isn't it?" Gavin said, picking up the razor and starting to shave. He didn't seem to even consider using the little blade against her—with how weak he was, maybe he'd already rejected the notion. "I mean, bad guys double-crossing you after they blackmail you into helping them? What's next?"

"It is kinda shitty," Teia admitted.

"So. Deep cover or doubting convert?" Gavin asked.

"What? Why would you ask that?"

"Because we're talking." He tested the smoothness of his cheeks with a hand, then set down the razor, farther out of reach than necessary. "If you were fully theirs, there'd be no need for you to approach me in the few minutes before we sail when you can still change your mind. Less than a few minutes, now. You have a decision to make. It's hard to go against the Order, after you've seen what they do." He scrubbed an armpit and smelled the sponge afterward. Wrinkled his nose, coughed.

"Deep cover," she said. Why was it so hard to let him know that?

"Very deep, if you'd kill the Prism to maintain it."

"You think I've already decided," she said, piqued.

"Adrasteia!" he whispered, triumphantly. "Kip's Blackguard partner. Knew I'd heard that voice before."

She didn't think that before now she'd spoken two sentences in front of Gavin Guile, and he remembered her *voice*? Dammit. The man was a legend for a reason.

"They have my dad," she said. Wasn't sure why she said that, either.

It had been so long since she'd had anyone to talk to at all. Karris was the nearest thing, and Karris was her commander. A friendly commander was still not quite a friend. Not in these times.

Or maybe there was a reason so many had given their confessions to this man.

"Ah," Gavin said, getting it. He scrubbed his other armpit. "So those goons guarding the passage back into the Chromeria are subreds, then. To make sure you go."

"I can drop them," Teia said. "Probably."

"All four?" he asked, amused.

Four? She'd only seen two. "Two before the others attack...?" It came out with a silent 'maybe' on the end, which she hated.

And I'm in deep cover. You'd think I'd be a better liar.

"And then everyone on this ship joins the fight," Gavin said. "Not on our side, in case you were getting your hopes up."

"What if we jump off at the last moment? Takes a while to turn a ship around...even if a few jump off and swim to pursue, we'd have a good head start." It was desperation talking, though.

Gavin didn't answer. He looked toward the rising sun. He was trembling merely from the effort of scrubbing his legs. A running leap from the ship, past how many people?

He couldn't even run. Certainly couldn't fight.

"What if—what if I had another cloak? Could you...?" Gavin Guile had once been able to do everything anyone else could do with drafting. Maybe he, too, had discovered paryl dispersal clouds thick enough to fool sub-reds.

But he just shook his head. "It was just an idle game. I can't go with you regardless."

Teia couldn't take four men by herself while trying to protect Gavin. Were all four Blackguards, or just the two?

What was Teia going to do? Try to carry him and keep him invisible, then fight four men by herself? Four men with muskets?

"It's beautiful, isn't it?" Gavin Guile said, looking at the sunrise. "I can't see the colors. The Blinding Knife took that from me, and I—fool that I was—for a long time I cursed every new dawn for the beauty I recalled but could no longer see. Instead, I should've blessed every dawn for the beauty it granted everyone else, regardless of my handicap. I should've blessed Orholam for the memory He gave that let me call to mind so perfectly the thousand hues and tones of a summer dawn. I was an ingrate."

"We need you," Teia said. "I need you. I can't stop them."

"You can get past them?" he asked. "You can escape if you're alone?"

"Paryl cloud. Works for sub-red, even paryl itself, if you're good enough and there's no wind."

"Funny. I never really bothered with paryl. They all said it was useless, and it always hurt my eyes when I tried to play with it. Of course, I didn't know it had any real use. Now...Shimmercloaks. Magic swords. It's like I've lived long enough to see all my childhood stories come to life. Just need a dragon now." He paused. "On second thought, no dragons. I think we're fine without dragons."

He pulled on his new trousers. Threw on the loose tunic. "Tell Karris I live. Tell her...tell her to give me twelve months before she marries some other lucky bastard. I'll either be back by then or I won't be back ever. And you, go save your dad."

"I can't," Teia said. "He's hidden. I've got no way to find him. All the Order's cells are kept separ—"

They were interrupted by Captain Gunner coming up to the waist of the ship from belowdecks.

"It's just a matter of will, Adrasteia," Gavin said. "You grab the one thread your fingers can reach, and you pull until the whole cloth unravels."

"It's not that simple. They're—"

"And if you can't save your father, then you poison the well. You rip them out by the root. And every time your heart inclines to mercy, if you love your father, you remember whatever tiny shred of devotion you hold toward that poor man, and you make sure they don't steal and murder any other little girl's father ever again."

She trembled with sudden rage that he would question her love. Cold, hot, fierce, impotent, and utterly misplaced rage. "The extra cloak. You want it?" she asked flatly.

"Do I look like the hooded-man type to you? No. What waits for me is not a subterfuge kind of job."

"Anything else you want me to tell her? I mean, if I do."

"It was my father who kidnapped and imprisoned me," he said. "Karris will ask. But he thought I was insane when he did so. He thought he was saving the satrapies. I have no rage left for him. She shouldn't fight him. He'll kill her, too, if he thinks he has to."

"All right, boys!" Gunner shouted, climbing halfway up the stern-castle toward his wheel and turning to address the sailors. "We're about to sail to legend—or infamy!"

"Not antonyms," Gavin said under his breath.

"Wait," Teia said as she was plotting her course through the milling bodies to still get to the dock. "Why is your father working with the Order?"

"Oh, he's not. Not on *this* anyway," Gavin mumbled to the deck as he folded his old clothing. "This is all on—" He stopped himself, it seemed, from saying a name. "On your old man, not mine. Andross needs the Blinding Knife to make a new Prism. Which is another excellent reason I can't get off this ship. I'm useless now, but the Knife isn't. I need to try to save it."

"My old man?" Teia asked. "You say that like you know who the Old Man is...or who *she* is?"

"I'd love to tell you, but if I do, or even hint, this stone"—he tapped the black jewel on his eye patch, and winced as if it hurt more than he'd expected—"goes through my brain. Nasty little bit of magic, or nice little bit of bluffing, but I'm not desperate enough to call those cards to the table yet. Besides, telling you would only help if you went back now. I thought you were going to kill me. Your father for me. Good trade, if he's a halfway decent man. Of course, if you come with us, you'll most likely die with all the rest of us on this fools' errand. But maybe the Order will honor their promise? I mean, they lied to me and plan to double-cross me, but…one can hope."

"Or one can fight," Teia said. She didn't know if she was arguing with him or agreeing now.

Damned Guiles, getting you twisted up inside.

But she didn't move.

"You do strike me as one not inclined to run away. Which way is running away now, though?" he asked, chuckling to himself. It was a dangerous mood, like he was this close to doing something incredibly rash.

With obvious difficulty, Gavin stood and stared up at the Prism's Tower soaring high above them, like a man who would never see it again.

"I'm finished," Gavin said loudly to the sailors.

He meant bathing.

"Draw the mooring lines!" Gunner shouted as he approached the sterncastle. "Lift the gangplank! Rowers ready!" Then Gunner wheeled suddenly and pointed sharply at Gavin. "Guile! I see what you're doing!"

Teia's blood froze.

Gunner wagged his finger. "Black eye. Gave you a black eye. That's funny. Took me a moment. Forgot how you be. Always liked that white of yourn."

Gavin forced a smile and lifted his chin in acknowledgment. Under his breath, he said, "Time makes a coward's decisions for her."

" 'White of yourn,' thet ain't right," Gunner grumbled. "Whiting bit. Bidding white. Biding…shit!"

Waiting, waiting just a few more seconds, meant trusting the Order. Casting in her lot with them completely. It meant helping them. It meant doing evil, hoping that an evil man would do her some good.

How stupid do they think I am?

Stupid enough to get on this boat.

True. But I'm not stupid enough to stay.

"Biting wit!" Gunner crowed. "Ha!"

Drawing her paryl cloud around her, Teia jumped up on the hand-

rail, running down it to the ship's waist, stepping over Gunner's hand

and onto a finial as his bearded, bushy head swung under her as he began to climb.

She dropped to the deck and dodged between sailors, past the two men lifting the plank. With a heave, she leapt—

—and she wasn't going to make it. Her feet were going to strike the dock's side just short of the front edge.

She lifted her feet, tucking her knees as if in a deep squat, and barely cleared the gap, but the position left her nothing to absorb the shock of landing. She tumbled head over heels, barely having the wherewithal to swirl the cloak and cloud back over her body as she stopped.

One of the Order sailors lifting the plank paused, staring right at where she was. He lifted a hand to shade his eyes, and Teia saw that she had jumped right between him and the rising sun—which was either brilliant or the worst possible thing she could have done. Any part of her that had been exposed would have thrown a shadow over his face. On the other hand, he was now looking directly into the rising sun.

The sailor on the other side of the heavy plank looked over at the man, peeved he'd stopped. "You fookin' gonna help me stow this fookin' thing, ya beaver shite eater?"

The man cast his eye around the dock again, puzzled, but then he said, "Man can't appreciate a sunrise for two fookin' heartbeats? You and your dysent'ry gams, foulin' a liminal moment."

"It'll be a *sub*liminal moment if you don't start helping, because I'mma knock you the fook out."

"Take one deep breath through that poo pincher disfiguring your gob for a moment, won'tcha? It's a sunrise."

"It's Orholam's Eye coming up. Curse it like ya ought."

"What kinda lead-souled, hieroproctical—"

"Lead-soled? You're the one with heavy feet, you laggard son of a slattern mum—"

"Don't you talk about our mum that way. If she'd been faithful to dad, you'd not be here. And I weren't talking about that kind of soul, not that you'd be familiar..."

Teia lost the rest as another man came to the rail with a long pole to push the ship away from the dock far enough for the slaves belowdecks to get their oars out.

She watched as the gap between her and obedience grew until it was unbridgeable.

She was committed.

The Old Man's command had been the kind of ultimatum on

which a whole world turns: murder Gavin and become fully one of us and be given all you could want or hope for, or else.

I choose 'or else.'

For no reason that Teia could understand, for no reason that made any sense at all, her heart suddenly soared.

She'd failed in her every single attempt against the Order so far. But she would not fail again.

She straightened her back and drew her powers about her. As far as the Old Man knew, she was gone for at least a month and a half, if not twice that.

The Order didn't have their own skimmers yet, so that meant six weeks at least before anyone could return with word of her absence—and therefore, her disobedience.

She couldn't tell the commander or even her friends that she lived, lest someone betray her, or let it slip to someone who would. So she must become a ghost, moving invisibly through the world of men, leaving nothing but terror and death.

In commissioning Teia to infiltrate the Order of the Broken Eye, Karris had wanted her to destroy the Order utterly, so they wouldn't be able to enslave and blackmail and murder ever again. Teia had always understood her mission was necessary, but now it was personal.

She had six weeks.

Six weeks to find someone in the Order of the Broken Eye, to follow that thread to the leadership, and that would lead her to what she needed: their papers. Even if one leader could memorize a list of all the secret members of the Order, his underlings couldn't be expected to. Codes had to change and adjustments be made. On top of that, there would be deeds and titles, lists of properties owned and the places they met. The membership lists would go to Karris so she could round up people for hanging or to go on Orholam's Glare. But the papers would also give Teia places to search and Braxian cultists to interview—or torture, if necessary—to tell her where her father was being held.

Six weeks to find her father and free him. Six weeks to find those who would do him harm, and to end the threat forever.

Teia had never fantasized about being frightening, had only wanted to be a shield—a big, obvious guardian against the violence of others. But against these people? She felt something gloriously strong and ugly and beautiful rising in her heart, easing the worry on her brow, and turning her mouth to a smile.

The Order had made her. They were about to learn how well.

One of those masked Blackguards who'd saluted the Old Man of the Desert had moved with a bit of a limp. That was her thread to pull.

Let the haunting begin.

Chapter 7

"On the one hand, I couldn't be more horrified," Tisis Guile said, looking out the window in a flowing red summer dress accented with a vibrant green that perfectly matched the emerald luxin in her eyes.

The moment she'd stepped through the living white-oak doorway of the Palace of the Divines two days ago, Tisis had assumed the wardrobe of young royalty and a mien of measured grace and slow eloquence like a favorite pair of old boots. Strangely, the guise had endured without wrinkle or rumple, her cadences and tones and even accent seamless over the long, full days of affectation since they'd arrived.

It had taken Kip several days to realize the persona wasn't a pretense. Though Tisis absolutely *was* trying to impress both the nobility and the servants, this was no false face. She had grown up in the corridors of power in Rath and Green Haven and the Chromeria, and only at the last had she had her retinue forcibly limited by Andross Guile.

Far from being a façade, for the first time, Kip was seeing his wife in the full flower of her natural environment.

Thank Orholam he'd first seen her at her weakest. She'd intimidated the hell out of him *then*, when she'd been vulnerable, isolated, uncertain.

"On the other hand," she said, letting the curtain fall, "I couldn't be prouder."

For this one thing, thank you, Grandpa Guile. You did me a good turn when—well, when you pretty much forced this stunning woman to marry me and made her think it was her own idea.

Kip was really going to have to tell her about that someday.

She noticed his smile slip, but before she could ask anything, Kip said, "Huh? What?"

He'd been staring at decrees and reports and budgets for so long he was drifting. She was horrified about something? Proud?

"What's going on?" Big Leo asked Tisis, gesturing outside. "Something wrong out there with the queue?"

After word had gotten out about Kip's magical restorations to *Túsaíonn Domhan*, everyone wanted to see the masterpiece ceiling functioning as it had been intended, so Kip had simply said whoever wanted to see it could.

That was how he and Tisis ended up sleeping in nondescript guest chambers: his permission had been taken as an order, and now there was a constant line out the door, out the Palace of the Divines, down the steps, and into the square below. People who had far better things to do in this wracked and wretched city were instead waiting hour upon hour to see Kip's handiwork, even sleeping in line, watched by attentive guards. He and Tisis decided to move to another room rather than expel those who'd waited so long at the end of every day.

"Come see," Tisis said, not to Kip, though.

The Mighty crowded around the windows, peeking carefully. Except for Winsen, who, with his typical subtlety, pulled the curtain fully back to stare down into the courtyard.

All of them were bored. Kip couldn't blame them. While they all waited for their only paryl drafter to finish her quiet scans of the room, with her eyes midnight orbs against her true black skin, Kip had things to do. The rest of them didn't.

Though Kip had never thought of him as the devious sort, Cruxer had been the one to initiate room searches. As it turned out, several other chambers in a row that had been provided for the Mighty's meetings had been riddled with spy holes.

It wasn't the only way Kip and his Nightbringers, outwardly hailed as liberators, had been passively resisted, and carefully made to feel unwelcome. The Divines were either not half as clever as they thought, or they believed themselves to be untouchable. Kip hoped they weren't stupid, but they were treating him like he was, and it was a burr under his saddle.

Regardless, until the woman finished her paryl scans, the Mighty couldn't talk strategy.

Kip hadn't appreciated how good Teia was at drafting paryl until Súil had given him a basis for comparison. She was nice, but she needed breaks every few minutes, and even when she was working, she was *slow*.

He considered taking over the scanning himself, but that would shame her. It would also reveal more of the full extent of his abilities to any spies who might be watching.

The Mighty missed Teia for a dozen reasons, but her speed was one they'd mentioned repeatedly. Kip had agreed with them but offered no more, telling them only that Karris had needed Teia. Paryl's ability to see through clothing for hidden weapons was so useful for a Black-guard that Kip hadn't needed to lie to them about Teia's real work hunting the Order—that had felt like a secret that wasn't his to give away and one too dangerous to share.

But the Mighty had brought up Teia's absence more as they realized how important it was to trust your paryl drafter absolutely. In fraught times, how do you trust a stranger who can kill you without leaving any evidence, whose powers can't be detected or countered except by someone who shares them?

No wonder paryl drafters had so often been hunted down through-out history, their arts no longer taught, but instead buried and for the most part happily forgotten.

But the biggest problem with having Súil around was that it made him miss Teia. And all that didn't bear thinking about.

Kip had been lucky last night. The Mighty stopping two Shadows? How did that happen, really? The Mighty were good, but ... the Shad-ows must have been inexperienced or lazy, underprepared, undisci-plined. Would the Old Man of the Desert really spend two Shadows to send a message? Kip had said that, but it had been bravado.

You can't admit that all of your best people together barely stopped two of the enemy, and only because they'd been incredibly lucky. So was it luck, or was the Old Man telling Kip he could kill him that eas-ily, or ... what was the alternative? Divine intervention?

Kip only wished he could believe that.

If it were a message, though, what was the message?

This whole city was starting to infuriate him. Not just the attempted eavesdropping. The passive resistance. The bureaucracy. 'That's not the way we do ...' 'Ancient tradition dictates ...' 'The peo-ple will be mortally offended, but if my lord wills it ...' 'The priests are being summoned for a grand council to vote to allow just that, my lord, but so many of them are old, it's taken longer than expected. Doubtless they'll meet today. But I'm afraid if you preempt their authority ...'

But there were things only he could do, and that he could only do if he stayed. Things only Kip cared enough to do. Things only he could get away with. That wasn't even counting the things he should do that he could do better than anyone else. Worse, he didn't know who he could trust enough to leave in charge.

The longer he stayed, the more fighters flocked to his banners and the better the intelligence he received. More time also meant more resources he could gather for his army.

But the longer he stayed, the more time he gave the White King to learn what Kip had accomplished and move to counter what he would do next.

He was going to go full Andross Guile on those old bastards.

He looked at the papers stacked on his desk. A year's worth of commitments and decisions.

Two more days. I can give it two days. What can I accomplish in two more days? Enough?

"Breaker," Cruxer said beside Tisis at the window, "*there's a crowd*."

"So? There was a crowd yesterday." Kip started sorting the stacks into what he could possibly hope to do in two days.

"I went out there this morning again," Cruxer said. "I recognized some of them. Same people. They're not leaving after they see the ceiling."

"They want to wait in the queue to see it again, that's their business," Kip said.

"They aren't in the queue," Cruxer said, troubled. "Yesterday they came curious. They left exultant. Today they're...expectant?"

"I think they're hoping to make you king," Tisis said quietly.

"Uh-huh," Kip said, not looking up. "Too much to do today, sorry," he said.

He would meet with the merchant in the next two days. Definitely. His question was, how much of a fight did he put up over these shortages? Of course the discrepancies were never 'surpluses,' but he couldn't be certain *whose* fingers had lightened the shipments. Men on his side, or on the merchant's, or the merchant himself, swindling Kip? Contracts with 'neutral' traders were the worst, especially this asshole Marco Vellera.

Kip was pretty sure Marco Vellera was actually Benetto-Bastien Bonbiolo, one of the four Ilytian pirate kings. Or three kings and a queen at the moment, technically—there was a rumor that a king had been on the *Gargantua* when Gavin and Kip sank it. They still called them kings, though; apparently 'the Ilytian pirate monarchs' didn't have the same ring to it. Kip's problem was that Vellera was undoubtedly not selling supplies only to him but also to Koios, and to Satrap Briun Willow Bough as well.

He hated that, but there was no recourse for it. If you started seizing merchants' caravans, you bankrupted the merchants. Bankrupt more than one, and the reasonable ones stop coming, leaving you to deal with the greedy who'll gouge you, or the desperate who might steal from you outright; you end up paying with one kind of coin or another.

So far, Kip thought his own performance as a leader was decidedly lacking. He couldn't win every game like Andross Guile, and he couldn't break every game like Gavin Guile, so he was forced to do his best to rebound a loss from one game (the financial war) into a win in another (the shooting war).

Blubber bounces back, boys.

Kip was first on Marco Vellera's trade route, so he was surreptitiously buying up the supplies he guessed the White King needed most.

Finding the coin to do all these things was what half the stacks of papers on the tables were all about. It involved a lot of bending the truth to a lot of very concerned bankers.

"Breaker, she's *serious*," Cruxer said.

Kip didn't even look up. "Uh-huh. Happens to everyone who dabbles in the art-restoration business. Hazard of the trade, getting offered a crown."

"Art?" Ferkudi asked.

"Fixing the ceiling?" Ben-hadad prompted.

"Oh, right! Right." Ferkudi looked up. "What's wrong with the ceiling?"

"Crowd's not that big. Oh, they've seen us," Winsen said, now beside Cruxer. "Crux? How does a High Magister wave? Like so?" He waved a devil-may-care wave, and Kip could hear the crowd go mad with excitement.

" 'Not that big'?" Kip said, suddenly rooted to the desk, papers forgotten.

"Nor that small," Tisis said.

"How not small is 'not small'?" Kip asked.

"I dunno," Winsen said. "Maybe twenty thousand?"

"What?!" Kip shot to his feet.

"He's joking," Tisis said. "Maybe a thousand?"

"Nine hundred fifty-seven," Ferkudi said.

They all stopped. They looked at him.

"You didn't just count them all . . ." Winsen said.

"Huh? Of course not," Ferkudi said, as if Win was crazy. "I was guessing. Why does everyone else always guess round numbers? They're not any more likely." He suddenly looked troubled. "They *aren't* more likely, are they?"

But Kip suddenly remembered. They were worried about spies listening in. Tisis was only bluffing, trying to give the Divines something to worry about—to soften them up for what Kip planned next. She wasn't serious.

"Breaker," Cruxer said as Kip stepped up to the window himself, curious. There must be a small crowd at least, for Tisis's play to have any teeth.

But Cruxer put a hand on his chest, stopping him. "*Kip!* Don't you step into view unless you plan to become a king. With all that that entails. For all of us."

"You're serious," Kip said. Since when did Cruxer call him Kip?

"Never more." The look in Cruxer's eyes was inscrutable, and Kip suddenly wasn't sure what his friend would do if he tried to take that last step.

Ever righteous, would Cruxer see Kip taking a crown as treason?

But as if he'd just wondered the same thing, Cruxer dropped his hand as if Kip were burning white-hot.

"Where can I stand where they won't see me?" Kip asked.

"Let 'em see you," Winsen said. " 'King's Guard' has a nice ring to it. Lot better than 'Winsen, Kip Guile's Mighty Right Hand, You Know, the Suave and Dashing One.' "

" 'Right hand'?" Cruxer asked, eyebrows climbing.

Winsen shrugged, helpless. "I can't stop people from talking, Commander."

" 'Suave'?" Ferkudi asked.

Ben-hadad said, " 'Dashing'? 'Dashing Away from the Fight,' maybe."

"Least I *can* dash, Hop-Along," Winsen sneered. "Funny, I don't remember the cripple complaining about my speed when I saved his gimpy ass last night. And I am suave, Ferkudi. Certainly compared with the village idiot of the Mighty."

"Oh, I'm sure you are," Ferkudi said. "I mean, if you say so. It was a real question. I don't know what 'suave' means." He cut off suddenly. "Hold the door! Who's the village idiot of the Mighty?"

"Was that a real question, too?" Ben-hadad muttered.

Kip peered past the edge of a curtain—and then he understood what Cruxer had meant. Hundreds of people were gathered, yelling and waving crude little green flags and banners he couldn't read from here.

"They might not look like much…" Tisis said.

"The banners or the people?" Ben-hadad asked.

Tisis went on quietly without answering. "But you encourage these ones, and they get excited. They spread the word that becoming king is what you really want but maybe you just can't say it. Tomorrow the crowd's bigger. If no one stops them, that day or the next, some disaffected nobles join in, hoping their early allegiance will curry favor. The next day, others are joining fast, no one wanting to be the last."

"They can't be serious," Kip said. King?

"They *believe*," Ferkudi said, like it was simple.

Winsen said, "I know we're not supposed to say the magic words…"

"But you're going to say them anyway?" Cruxer said.

Winsen said, "How are you surprised by this? Being a king? There've been hundreds of kings—"

"Not since the Seven Satrapies were founded," Kip said.

"Being a king's like barely the second rung on the ladder to the heavens, and you're heading pretty near the top of it."

Ben-hadad said, "Don't say it."

"You're the *Lightbringer*, the *Luíseach* here or whatever," Winsen said.

"He said it," Ben-hadad said.

"He just had to say it," Big Leo said.

"Win, the rest of you, too?! Are you *serious* with this?!" Kip said. "Setting that up—even talking about it with the kitchen staff or, or anyone!—it's totally destructive for everything we're trying to do here. If you encourage that kind of talk, we might do a hundred amazing things, but if we don't do *one* thing from some stupid prophecy, maybe even one we don't know about—or even if some idiot wrote it down wrong or translated it wrong three hundred years ago or whatever—then all of a sudden, everyone on our side loses heart, because I look like a fraud. Rather than being a leader who's helping save a satrapy, I look like some delusional megalomaniac who thinks he's Lucidonius come again! Do you really not see how that's a problem?!"

"Right, we've heard it before," Winsen said. "It's too late. You're asking us to pretend because you don't like the pressure? Tough shit. People already *are* joining us because they believe in you. Sure, deny it publicly, play it however you want, but the cards are on the table, you—"

"Enough!" Tisis said. "Win, you're a moron. Do you not remember why we're here?"

"We invaded?" Winsen asked. "Liberated, I mean."

"*Here*, here," she said.

Kip saw it dawn on the slight archer: Oh, right, spies might be listening to every word. Shit.

"Kip," Tisis said, "ignore him."

Of course, all of them were trying to think whether Winsen—or Kip—had said anything that would be disastrous if it had been overheard.

Tisis went on: "The real reason the people here might dream of you   41 as their king is simple. In their hour of need, Satrap Willow Bough did nothing for them. The Chromeria did practically nothing. You? You saved these people from the Blood Robes. And then you saved them from their own nobles, literally saved their lives when you fed them. And then you gave them reason to be proud of their city and their history when you fixed *Túsaíonn Domhan*. You gave them a new heart. You breathed new life into them; how can they forget that big empty throne in the audience chamber? Why would they *not* want you to be king?"

"Pfft. They're desperate," Kip said. "But they're not desperate for *me* to be king. Me, so obviously a foreigner? I mean, who cares what my grandfather's titles say? Look at me. Come on. They're just desperate *to be saved*. I'm just a vessel to pour their hopes into."

"Could do worse," Ben-hadad said.

"That's a rousing endorsement! I've got one cheek on the throne already!" Kip said.

"Room's clear," Cruxer announced suddenly. "One minute while our people put the luxin seals in place, then we can speak freely."

"Finally," Ben-hadad said. "I'm so glad Winsen will no longer have to hold back how he really feels."

"We're not so good at this being-devious thing, are we?" Big Leo asked.

He hadn't meant it as a shot at Kip, but Kip couldn't help but think it reflected most on him. He should have discovered if there were spies, and whose. He should've figured out exactly what lies to funnel to that person to make them do what he wanted.

Andross Guile would have.

Cruxer said, "Súil, thank you. Excellent work. You're getting faster, aren't you?"

She beamed through a sheen of sweat.

Cruxer was good at that, looking out for people. It was one of the reasons Kip loved him.

They all broke to get their packs and papers. Everyone in the room had responsibilities and reports to deliver.

As Tisis quickly donned nondescript clothing, then ducked out, Kip looked at his own papers for the strategy session, but he had no heart to go over them again. "You called me 'Kip'?" he asked Cruxer quietly.

"Mmm."

"That wasn't an accident or a pretense for the spies, was it?"

Cruxer looked for a moment like he wanted to deny it, but a lie wouldn't escape the cage of his teeth. "Our Breaker was a Blackguard scrub. Sure, he'd break some rules, break expectations, a bully's arm, a chair"—he flashed a grin at that memory—"but I don't think that boy would break the empire. I guess it slipped out. I guess I've been wondering if maybe you're more their Lord Guile than our Breaker. Maybe it was an ill omen, that name."

"You gave it to me," Kip said.

"I hadn't forgotten," Cruxer said. "Lot of things about that year that I regret."

"Ah, come on! 'King Breaker,'" Winsen said. They hadn't realized he was still close. "How can you not love that? Say...Bennie?"

"'Bennie'?" Ben-hadad asked.

Winsen said, "Yeah. You think a man destined to kill kings might be called a king-breaker, Bennie?"

Ben-hadad looked at him flatly. He tested the heft of the cane he still used half the time.

"You know...Breaker would be King Breaker, the...king-breaker?" Winsen asked. "Because the White King is, you know, a king..."

"You're only coming to this now?" Ben-hadad asked. "Ferkudi asked about that a year ago."

Coming up to stand beside Ben-hadad, Big Leo rumbled, "Looks like maybe your earlier question's a little more complicated than you thought."

"Question?" Winsen asked. "Which question?"

"'Who's the village idiot of the Mighty?'" Ben-hadad and Big Leo said at the same time. They raised their eyebrows in unison at Winsen.

Big Leo put out a massive paw for a fist salute. Ben-hadad met it without having to look.

Winsen answered with a finger salute for each of them.

"Enough grab-ass," Cruxer said, the phrase and even the intonation borrowed from old Commander Ironfist. "Everyone to the table."

Somehow, Tisis had set up and activated the war map with all the most current updates already. She briefly kissed Kip's cheek—they were trying to be less irritating with their affections around the Mighty—and left. Moments later, Kip's drafters sealed the doors.

Everyone began examining the big map. Kip had been doing a little trick Súil had taught him, using a small amount of paryl, which was highly sensitive to other colors, to make a form of a small portion of the three-dimensional map, then quickly filling in the colors with other luxins to make a fragile copy of Green Haven and its surroundings. He turned it around and tilted it to get a sense of how the changes in elevation might affect sight lines, and the flow of horses and men in a battle.

But he was really just stalling.

Cruxer turned to him. "Over to you, milord. How bad is our situation?"

Kip squeezed his outspread fingers, and the luxin city in his hands snapped and fell into multicolored dust. "Asking it that way really implies that things are bad. And they're not."

"Oh, thank Orholam," Ben-hadad said, "because with what we heard last night, and then when Tisis first came in this morning, her expression—"

"They're *appalling*," Kip said. "Awful, bleak, dire . . ."

"But surely not—" Ferkudi said.

"Hopeless?" Kip asked.

They all fell silent.

Then Ben-hadad asked, "Was that a question, or an answer?"

"Yes," Kip said. "Green Haven is under siege, and they're led by incompetents and fools. If the capital falls, the satrapy falls. We're the only ones who can possibly save them. But the Council of the Divines isn't willing to give us the support they promised they would if we saved this city. Worse, they may not even have it. They also won't give us access to the palace's Great Mirror array, which probably won't even help us much even *if* I win another pointless fight over it. Our most popular and capable general, Conn Arthur, has snapped and deserted. Sibéal Siofra has disappeared, too. Maybe she went after him, but she's not only his best friend, she also held my one long-shot hope of getting the pygmies to join us in the war. Let's see, what's next? The big one? Sure! In trying to gain the initiative, I've blundered horribly instead. Immediately after the battle, when I sent nearly all the Nightbringers' will-casters and their animal partners on ahead of us to attack the White King's supply lines to disrupt their siege? Tisis has just discovered that the White King did the same to us first, weeks if not months ago. He's blocked the Great River behind us. We don't know where. We can't get any intel or reinforcements from the rest of the Seven Satrapies. And now, after I've sent away our most powerful forces, it appears one of the bandit kings—a lovely fellow named Daragh the Coward—has gained sudden wealth and a huge number of recruits and may lay siege to us here within days. I suspect he's been bought by the White King. So you tell me: is 'hopeless' a question, or the answer?"

Some of this was news even since last night, and they all took a
44   moment to absorb it.

What would you do here, father?

Kip suddenly stood, because the first step at least was obvious.

Maybe it was time to see if he was the son of Gavin Guile after all. He looked over at Cruxer, and his commander's throat bobbed as he saw what Kip intended.

Kip flashed him a grin.

And maybe it was the grin that did it, the intimation of confidence, for instead of raising an objection, Cruxer nodded. He was in with Kip, categorically.

Kip strode to the windows, head high, threw back the drapes, and waved to the damned crowd, smiling broadly.

They cheered. Of course they did.

Chapter 8

Teia thought there were two kinds of women most aware of how many people at a party are staring at them: a pretty one who opts for much more daring clothing than usual, and a hideous one who's dressed the same way and only becomes aware of her mistake as her carriage pulls away, leaving her stranded. She'd never really been the former, but right now she felt a hell of a lot like the latter.

Please don't look my way. Please don't look my way.

She moved through the Chromeria with her heart in her throat. If the wrong eyes spotted her, she wouldn't face scorn. She'd face death, and consign her father to it as well.

A couple hours ago, she'd felt like some kind of avenging nocturnal angel: I'll be a ghost, haunting their dreams!

That would make them nightmares, she supposed.

I'll haunt their nightmares!... But do you *haunt* nightmares? Why not a nice empty house? Maybe in the countryside. With cheese, maybe. And wine.

I am *not* good at this being-scary business.

As she ascended the Prism's Tower invisibly, she felt less like a phantom and more like a mouse in the stables. No one noticed her, but if they did, it was far more likely to be disastrous for her than for them. And that was just on the slaves' stairs.

An invisible assassin breaking into the White's quarters was, after all, exactly the kind of thing that the Blackguard had been formed to stop. She'd done it before, but she'd also rushed across a busy street without looking and lived—that didn't make it a good idea to do it repeatedly.

In the first hours after leaving Gavin Guile alive, Teia had retrieved a few of her things from the barracks—again dodging invisibly around her compatriots and friends. Because any of them might be working for the Order of the Broken Eye, she had to appear to have simply vanished. The Old Man of the Desert would check, after all.

Whoever he or she was, they had certainly not survived this long—like a tapeworm in the guts of the Chromeria itself—without being fanatically careful.

She'd had to take a few hours to plot, and to rest.

The truth was, even after training for the last year with the master cloak, the longest Teia could comfortably stay invisible was still only a couple hours.

Now, with night full upon the Jaspers and the shift change about to begin, it was time to sneak into Karris's room and tell her that her husband, Gavin, was alive. Further, he'd been *here* in the Chromeria itself, mere hours ago.

And Teia hadn't saved him. Oh, and she hadn't reported earlier, when there might have been a good chance at rescue.

It was not a report Teia relished giving.

She made it into the room on the heels of Watch Captain Blunt and Kerea—neither of whom was a sub-red, thank Orholam. They checked the room's balcony, the slaves' closet, and the windows, even though, as Teia saw immediately, Karris wasn't asleep, nor alone.

The young White was in her bed, lying on her back, resting. Blackguard Trainer Samite stood at the foot of her bed, at ease. Her face was stone, and she didn't move, even when Watch Captain Blunt hesitated at the door, his scheduled sweep of the room completed. He motioned to his younger partner to leave.

After she stepped out, wordlessly, he snapped a salute to Samite, and left.

Samite didn't return the salute; she barely dipped her chin.

She wasn't usually rude. If anything, oddly, losing her hand had made her less of a hard-ass than before.

Teia had taken advantage of the Blackguards' noise in moving about the room to position herself in a dark corner behind Samite's back—the woman was facing the window and the door, where threats were likely to appear. They'd also dull her night vision.

Pretty quickly, Teia realized that Samite intended to stand guard all night. Not good.

Why? What the hell was going on?

Long minutes passed, and none of them moved. Teia was going to have to think of something to get rid of Samite, or she was going to be here all night.

And it's harder to be totally silent for an entire night than one might guess. Teia relaxed her hold on paryl. She didn't have the strength to stay fully invisible all night, but with the darkness and Samite staring the other way, she shouldn't have to.

"You can go," Karris said from the bed. Finally.

Please obey, Trainer Samite. Please?

But Samite merely squared her shoulders. Though not tall, she was built like a draft horse.

After a long minute, Samite said, "Being this kind of hard? Not good. This kind of hard is brittle. You should weep for him."

For him? Huh? For Gavin? That had to be it. But why was this happening now? So far as Karris knew, Gavin had been absent for nearly a year.

"*You're* not weeping," Karris said. There was nothing of tears in her voice, either.

Ah, so not Gavin, then? Who would they both weep for?

"I'm on duty," Samite said. "This is your *break* from duty. These hours are when you need to regroup so you can put on your face tomorrow."

Karris scoffed.

"The dumbest scrub learns that if you don't take off your blacks and give 'em a wash, you're gonna stink, and you'll wear through 'em in no time. That applies to your clothes, too, O Iron White."

Teia had never heard someone speak so scornfully to Karris, not even when she'd just been Karris White Oak.

"Do I need to order you to go?" Karris asked coldly.

"Not the kind of order I'm required to obey," Samite said. She turned her back and folded her arms.

"What, you think I'm a danger to myself? I'm not going to *kill* myself." The condescension was thick in Karris's voice. Teia had never heard her talk that way to anyone, either.

Then she remembered these two had been in the same cohort. They'd known each other for nearly twenty years, and been through everything together.

You can be a bitch to a heart-friend, when you really have to.

But Samite merely applied the servant's veto—she pretended not to hear: what I have just heard is a fool's order; my mistress is no fool; ergo my mistress obviously didn't give it.

Karris sank back into her covers. Speaking to the ceiling, she asked, "Have you ever done it?"

"It's not such a horrible thing," Samite said. "Dying for something you believe in. For someone you believe in. And he did. More than anything."

"Have you ever done it? Personally?"

"You know I haven't," Samite said a few moments later, back still turned.

What the hell? They were talking about a Freeing. Someone must have broken the halo recently. One of the Blackguards?

Teia's chest went tight. No.

A scroll of the names of every Blackguard Teia knew started unfurling before her mind's eye. Who was close to bursting their halo? She felt a sting of guilt at the realization that losing some of her comrades wouldn't bother her at all.

"You want to know a secret?" Karris asked. Her voice was bitter as the black kopi she loved. She sat up. "A secret I barely even dare whisper even here? Here, in my own rooms, to you, my oldest fri…" She trailed off.

"What?" Samite asked. Teia drafted the paryl she'd been holding loosely and disappeared before Samite turned around.

The one-handed warrior's face was forgiving toward this woman who'd been such a bitch moments ago.

But Karris didn't give the answer. Instead, she looked suddenly ill.

"Oh my God," Karris said. "This is why Prisms go mad. This is why Gavin was always so wretched at Freeings."

"What are you talking about?" Samite asked, tense.

"I knew it was hard, Sami. I thought I knew. But…it's not hard."

Samite's face was writ with the same confusion Teia felt. Killing their own wasn't hard? Karris had killed before; surely she knew that the physical act wasn't so difficult most of the time, so she meant something else.

"Oh *God*," the White blasphemed, though perhaps such a desperate tone made uttering the holy title a prayer rather than a curse. "Oh God." Her pale skin went death-white. Her fingers grabbed wads of the covers and she gulped convulsively to keep from vomiting.

"What…?" Samite asked.

"It's not *hard*, Sami," Karris said. "I killed that boy, and the veil lifted. This. What we're doing. It's not hard. Koios is right. What we're doing is *wrong*. And if it's wrong when Gav Greyling offers me his life willingly, how much worse is it when we drag women to the

Prism's knife as they scream and wail and beg us to think of their children?"

Teia felt as if a horse had kicked her. Seeing the White herself lose faith?

Oh, that was pretty bad.

And admit that the Blood Robes were right?

That was also bad.

But that wasn't the part that Teia's mind couldn't hold—like cupped, imploring hands as someone emptied a full pitcher of blood into them. She couldn't hold the name.

Gav Greyling. The young, roguish, cute idiot. The lout. He'd only just stopped his obnoxious fake flirting with her.

That asshole. He was just now becoming the friend she needed so, so badly.

He was...

Karris had Freed him?

Obviously he'd broken the halo. Probably out on one of the expeditions to find Gavin. And they'd brought him back, knowing what had to be done.

Karris had knifed his heart. Personally.

But after all the people Karris had had Teia kill...all the murders of innocent slaves and the kidnapping and murder of Marissia, all the shit she'd ordered Teia to do and to be party to, she, the White herself, was losing faith merely because she'd had to hold the knife? Once?

Now she flinches?! How dare she.

Sure, you're only human. You're allowed to have your doubts.

But you can't doubt *this*. You're the White. Any doubts you had should have been dealt with years ago.

If *you* doubt, why should anyone believe?

Among the Blackguard, Gav's was an honorable death. A combat death. It was counted as succumbing to your wounds from battle. A hero's death. It was giving your all, and more. It was being willing to give not just your life but even more, your sanity. Most Blackguards, if they felt the halo break, tried to die on the field. Easier that way for everyone. Safer.

But if you didn't, what you asked in return for your sacrifice was that your friends would end you before you dishonored yourself by hurting those you loved. If possible, if you lived so long, you were accorded the honor of being Freed by your highest commanders, those you trusted with your body and your soul, the head of the Blackguard, or a High Luxiat, or the Prism himself. Nothing short of the dawn Sun Day ritual itself was too important to be interrupted for a Blackguard's Freeing.

The people who'd put you in the place where you needed to die in order to serve them would hold the knife.

And all you asked for all your suffering and sacrifice was a steady hand on the knife and a steady look in the eye. You asked them to affirm the meaning not just of your death but of your whole life, of the oath of service you'd given and that you were upholding even after breaking the halo, when everything in you screamed to break troth. You asked them to have the basic decency to honor your sacrifice.

How could you become the White, and look into the eyes of a good man who was dying for you, and *blink*?

The Iron White, they called her.

It was a bitter taste in Teia's mouth. A mock.

Teia felt the darkness all around her like dead, cold fingers touching her cheek; cold, wormy breath blowing down on her hood, wheezing. But as she drafted paryl now, she couldn't say any more that the darkness was merely a cloak around her than you could say the air was merely around you once you breathed it in.

She opened herself to darkness and it took her. It gave her power, but it changed her, too.

Darkness tore the hem of its robe, and that flapping hem became a fluttering raven that took a perch on her pallid heart.

The winsome, goofy smile of Gav Greyling was no more. And nevermore would be.

Teia would give Karris her report. Not today. But eventually. Teia would do her duty. She always did. The monsters she fought were still monsters. Her friends still her friends. Her commanders still, unfortunately, her commanders. Doubts are for old warriors, not young ones.

But on a personal level? Fuck you, Karris.

You're making everything you put me through, everything you made me do, be for nothing. Now you've given me a dead friend. Why would I give you a live husband?

You took my Gavin. Why should I give you yours?

Teia waited until morning. As the Iron White slept in her soft bed, Adrasteia's mind never wavered, her determination never faltered, her focus never flagged, her will never failed. Witness to weakness, she was implacable.

When the morning shift came in, she slipped out the door and got to work.

Chapter 9

Kip was following Tisis through the verdant vibrancy of the forest. The air was thick as hot soup, the ground spongy underfoot with mosses and fanning ferns, but there was no trail. The clouds broke overhead with the kind of downpour that could last a few minutes or all morning. Kip was drenched in warm sky spit within seconds.

It was kind of miserable being out here, actually. And a total relief.

His Nightbringers only nominally controlled this land, not even a league from Greenwall. It should be safe—aside from the snakes. They had scouts farther out, after all, and this was in the direction least likely for them to be attacked by Daragh the Coward's bandits, or any unlikely sneak attack from Koios. Cruxer was still nervous, of course. But this had to be secret, so only Kip, Cruxer, Ferkudi, and Tisis had slipped away.

"What's your read on this?" Tisis asked.

"This?" Kip asked. They'd already agreed he couldn't make a decision until he learned more. That was the whole point of actually hiking out here rather than just sending orders. "You mean..."

"Daragh," she said, gesturing to the scroll case at her belt as if doing so again.

Oh, that. He'd missed it in the rain and with staring at his footing. Daragh the Coward wanted to meet with Kip.

Kip first suspected he was trying to gain time to spread his forces out to shut down supply or reinforcement, but Daragh had asked to meet in person, in neutral territory.

As if there were any such thing.

They'd sent a message back saying that if Daragh didn't trust Kip would honor a flag of truce, then he obviously wouldn't trust any deal he might make with Kip, so a meeting was pointless. Thus Daragh could meet him in the city or not at all.

"There's a reason his bandits haven't attacked us directly all this time," Kip said.

"Depends how you define 'us,'" Tisis said.

The bandits literally lived by enslaving and pillaging, with raping thrown in for good measure and murder as their primary tool. That Daragh the Coward hadn't attacked Kip's *forces* per se was incidental to her: their victims were Foresters, and that by itself made them Tisis's people.

"I'm trying to see it—for the moment—as he does," Kip said. He'd explained this already. In Daragh's mind, he had avoided attacking Kip's people, even as Kip had passed through territory he considered his own. That didn't happen by accident, not with men like this. So to him, that should mean he and Kip could still work something out.

Tisis would rather fight. Regardless. To her Koios was an invader, but Daragh the Coward was a traitor, which was worse. She might not forgive Kip if he fought the invader but forgave the traitor.

Which made her right morally but wrong strategically.

That was tomorrow's problem.

They came to the small encampment suddenly, set in a hollow hidden by a hill. General Antonius Malargos greeted them outside the longhouse.

The year of being in authority had transformed Antonius. He'd been the gawky young red drafter, terminally the little-brother figure to his cousin Tisis—whom he still adored. He was still lean, but there was a focus to him now, a strength that knew itself and hadn't given up its striving to grow more. His people loved him because he loved them, and because he was bold. That he had the Malargos good looks didn't hurt, either. He had an intuitive grasp of tactics, and would throw himself headlong wherever he sensed weakness.

This was, after all, the young man who'd leaped from his own ship as it was being captured by pirates to steal the pirates' own ship—and in so doing saved Kip's father.

Oddest of all for a man so bold, Antonius accepted instruction from those he respected.

He himself had no sense at all of strategy; his eyes glazed during those discussions, but he was young yet. Logistics were beyond him completely, but he could have others attached to him to help with those—though it would always have to be someone with a steel spine, because Antonius had little patience for those who said things couldn't be done.

Kip liked him a lot.

"My people here will keep quiet," Antonius said.

He had only ten men here. Even at that, Kip wasn't certain he was right. Antonius's total faith in his people inspired deep loyalty in return. But Kip knew that the same person might show different kinds of loyalty in different kinds of fights.

And this was not a fight Kip or anyone wanted.

"They know what has to be done with deserters," Antonius said. Either because he was just that obvious, or to put some backbone in them. So maybe he wasn't that certain of how quiet they would keep, after all.

Ferkudi took up a position outside the door. Cruxer stepped inside first. Kip followed, bracing himself for what he might have to do.

In the shadows of this longhouse with no fire burning at its center, stood a pygmy woman, dirty, her eyes exhausted red: Sibéal Siofra. Next to her, chained to great stakes driven into the ground, smeared with ash and grease such as hunters employ to melt into the forest, but also dirty and disheveled from hard days and nights, knelt an enormous bear of a man, his every jutting muscle covered with red hair, the bereaved deserter and Kip's former second-in-command, Conn Ruadhán Arthur.

"My lord," Sibéal said, "there's no need for the chains. The conn here got into some booze while foraging. Just lost track of time. Got lost on his way back. But we're back now and reporting for duty. With all apologies for our absence."

She was floating the possibility for the lash, not the noose.

But Conn Arthur snorted, shaking his head. "You spent days dragging my ass back here, and that's the best you could come up with, Sibéal?"

Kip ignored him, turning to Antonius. "It's my understanding they came in of their own will. That they were returning, not captured. That right?"

"*She* was certainly returning of her own will..." He hesitated. Antonius could tell that Kip was trying to point him in some direction, but he couldn't see what it was.

"And he was with her—when she returned voluntarily," Kip said. "So that'd be dereliction of duty, not desertion."

"That's, uh, that's right," Lord Antonius said, relieved.

The law was the law, but Kip didn't want to hang his friend.

"So that's what happened?" Kip asked. "I'm very disappointed in you two."

"That's not what happened," Conn Arthur growled at the floor.

"Stop!" Sibéal shouted at him. "Think about what you're doing!"

"I'll not let you be whipped for what I've done," he said. He lifted his shaggy head to look at Kip with heavy eyes. "My lord, I told you I was going to desert. I did. It's not on her. She came and dragged me back."

"Damn you," Sibéal whispered.

She deflated, and Kip's heart fell too. She'd risked her life trying to save her friend, but some men don't want to be saved.

It wasn't her fault. It was Kip's. Conn Arthur had tried to resign, but Kip had thought without their work and the company of people who loved him that Ruadhán would die, so he'd forbidden it.

Ruadhán had left anyway.

"You tried," General Antonius told Kip. "We all did. There's no win here. He doesn't want to live."

He was right. This was bigger than one bereaved man who couldn't bear to fight anymore. If Kip let his friend off now, it'd destroy morale. People would say there was one rule for Kip's friends and one for everyone else. To save a man sunken in self-pity and ungrateful for his second—no, his *third*—chance would make that even worse. It would cast doubt on Kip's judgment.

But hanging him? Did Kip want to be known as the man who hanged his own friends?

Andross Guile would do it. Hell, Gavin would probably do it, too.

Antonius said, "Sibéal doubtless noticed things wherever it is they went. She reports on it, and we say she was out scouting. I don't think any punishment's necessary for her."

Kip looked at the others for any ideas and saw only grief.

Cruxer said, "Not all the soldiers killed by war die on the field. It's no one's fault." He cocked his head at a thought. "Well, it's the White King's fault. May he burn in hell. But it's not yours."

No one else had anything to say. No plans. No ways out.

"You go," young General Antonius said. "I'll handle it."

Kip looked to Conn Arthur, but the big man didn't even meet his gaze.

"Everyone out," Kip said.

They looked at him, and saw the resolve in his face. Tisis went out first, then the Blackguards, except Cruxer, who stood guard impassively. He wasn't going to leave no matter what Kip said, not with a man as dangerous as Conn Arthur might become if he'd gone truly mad.

Kip stopped Antonius, though. "General," he said. "I'll need your dagger."

The general nodded grimly and passed Kip a big, ornate dagger he'd gotten from his aunt Eirene Malargos. It was a showy piece, but very fine, too. The woman had an eye for quality.

Then they were alone in the damp and the dark and the smoky close air of the longhouse. It felt close to the earth in here. Real, solid, and dirty. Here, with clan and family tight around them, people made love on just a few blankets and rushes on the floor, and they gave birth on the same floor, and played with their children, and bickered, and ate, and died, all here, packed close. It was still sometimes shocking to Kip's Tyrean sensibilities, but such a life felt connected, too. Unashamed.

He breathed in the heavy air and let it flow through him.

"You remember that time we did the survey after that raid went sideways?" Kip said. "You know, at Three Bridges, to see how many of us were hurt? What was the number?"

Conn Arthur squinted up at him for a moment. "All of us."

"All of us," Kip said. "But the main force of the Blood Robes was moving on to Yellow Top, where all the women and kids had been sent. We knew they were looking for vengeance. We were already overextended, but no one else could get there. You remember what we did?"

Conn Arthur stared belligerently at the ground, but the thews in his neck were tight. "With all due respect, my lord, I need a noose, not a pep talk."

Sibéal Siofra made to speak, but Kip flashed her the scout signal they used in the woods that she should be silent.

"We busted our asses to get there first," Kip said. "The healthiest of us scouting ahead to make sure we didn't fall into an ambush— and we got there in time to save those people. And that story spread, Ruadhán. It's a huge part of why people joined up, because they saw what we would do at our own cost to save strangers. Because to us, those women and kids and old people weren't strangers. They were our people. And we'd be damned if we let them die without a fight."

"Some fights you can't win," Ruadhán growled, and Kip felt Cruxer go tight despite the big man's chains.

"We're all wounded," Kip said. "And we've got work to do. I need hands. I need *your* hands. *We* need your hands. The men who lie down and die do no good for anyone. Don't get me wrong; I want you to live because I love you, but I also want you to live so you can fight for us. This is bigger than you, bigger than your griefs, your failures, your brother. It's bigger than him. He helped us. He saved hundreds or thousands of lives. He was heroic at the end, and that makes a huge difference. It matters.

"But he's dead, man. He died saving lives, and now you won't *live* to do the same. I don't feel sorry for you, Ruadhán, I'm pissed off you won't help when we've got work to do."

"I've got nothing left," Conn Arthur said, as if Kip was refusing to see the obvious.

"When it serves life, there's a time to choose death," Kip said. "Absolutely. And your brother made that choice, but he took too damn long to make it. He was selfish, and he got other people killed."

"Don't talk about my brother."

"There's a time to choose life, Conn, and you're taking too damn long to make it," Kip said. "You're in a pit, so I'm throwing you a rope, but I ain't gonna fuckin' climb for you. You dyin' today? It hurts me more than you. But if you choose to live, I want you to live for one reason—because you're going to make yourself useful. You're worried it hurts our traditions for me to let you live? Yes. It does. People will think you got preferential treatment? Yes, they will. Because you are. Not because I love you, but because I think you can do what others can't for this people, this satrapy. I think you'll be more help than harm. A lot more. If you climb out of this pit, you're on the hook to prove me right. You're on the hook to work every day to show you're worth the third chance I'm giving you, and someday, when it's your turn, when it's wise, you're on the hook to give that chance to someone else." Kip blew out a breath in exasperation. "Look at your fucking shoulders, man. You were made to bear burdens. You are strong as fuck, and you're not acting like it. So, if you want to stay and curl up and die? Then fuck you. You've already wasted too much of my time." Kip turned away, but then paused.

He pulled a knife from his belt and stared at Ruadhán, eye to eye.

"It'd tear up the men to hang you," Kip said. "So you want to die? Have the goddam decency to think of someone else a bit, would you?"

Kip dropped the knife and the key, outside the cell. Ruadhán would have to strain against his chains to get either of them.

Kip gave Sibéal the signal to get out of the longhouse. Stony-faced, silent, she went, not daring to look at Conn Arthur, who was still staring at the ground anyway.

Then Kip strode out as if it weren't tearing out his heart not to offer soft words to his suffering friend.

But Kip knew all about the slimy, steep-sided pit of self-pity. Sometimes, a hard kick in the ass can do what a soft word in the ear can't.

Or so he hoped.

Outside, the men searched his face for any clue of what they must do, but none dared ask him anything. Kip found Sibéal. "You'd already said your goodbyes?"

"Yeah, I didn't know how soon you'd hang us. It was like he was already d—"

"You know it's better for you if he takes the knife."

A guilty look flashed over her face, then was hidden by anger. She knew. "Why the hell would you say that? He's my best friend."

"You could finally move on."

56

She moved to angrily deny it, but words fell dead with no spirit to give them life.

"Is it so obvious?" she asked.

Kip suddenly remembered glances he'd seen others exchange about the two. He'd never spoken of it to anyone. He'd only realized Sibéal loved that big idiot minutes ago. Others had, he saw now, known it for much longer. He said, "Obvious enough to a few who love you."

Her people's uncanny smile on her lips twisted bitterly. "I've made myself a laughingstock."

"No one's laughing."

Sibéal got quiet. They breathed the forest air together. "I'm pretty sure he loves me, too, and just hates himself too much to see it."

Kip said nothing. It was a poison that had to be drained, that she'd held in for too long, and that had spurred her to actions that could well have cost her her life.

"It wouldn't all be so bad if I didn't want kids," she said. "I mean, we have ways to know when not to take a man to bed, to avoid his seed taking root. But...all that effort to fix the problem doesn't fix the problem when you want the problem, does it? I want a child. Hell, I want lots of them, if this war ever ends. I want loud, shrieking, giggling, climbing-over-me-and-clinging-to-my-legs life everywhere. A house bursting at the seams with life after all this..." Her voice fell off. "But I want *him*."

Kip hesitated, but then said, "Do you think it's a coincidence that you've chosen to fall in love with a man in an impossible situation that he himself created?"

"What do you mean? What do you mean I've *chosen* to—"

"You've done exactly the same thing he has. You're in a pit, too, Sibéal. And if you want to, even if he dies, you can stay in yours. You can curl up in grief around your sweet, doomed love. You can take that tragedy and wrap yourself up in it like a blanket to keep you feeling warm and self-righteous, because *this world done you wrong.* You could've gotten out earlier, and if so, sure, what happens in there today would be a terrible blow—losing a dear friend is always tragic, but people lose friends in war, and still go home and have those babies and that full house. You could've gotten out earlier and easier, but you didn't.

"You're here now. So you can stay in this shit, or you can climb out, too. And I'm sorry to say it, but I don't have a rope to throw you or a key to offer. Climbing out will be tougher than it would be to tell yourself what a noble martyr you are and live half a life, cuddled up with your misery. But you're making a choice, like it or not. This isn't happening *to* you. You can choose to love him and have his babies—and, yeah, probably die in childbirth. Or you can choose to love him and not have babies, or adopt—plenty of war orphans already, and there'll be more before we're done. Or choose to move on. Or choose to sink into self-pity and self-loathing. I even respect a couple of those. But whatever you choose, I expect you to make yourself useful in the meantime. If he kills himself in there in the next few minutes, you get to clean up the blood and the shit, and you get to bury him. You brought this mess on us when you brought him back. If he can't find the guts to use the knife or to live, then you get to be the hangman. None of these other men and women deserve to have that on them. Last, as we both hope, if he comes out, choosing to live, you get to clean him up. Maybe it'll be a good chance to tell him what *you* are choosing for your life.

"Regardless," Kip said, "report for duty first thing tomorrow morning; I want you to brief me on the lands you've scouted. Oh, and Captain Siofra? Never fucking leave your post without permission again."

Chapter 10

"To work," Kip said to the Mighty gathered around the table with him once more. "Strategy first. The banking meeting will come next. Big Leo, Ferk, you're in on that one. Tactics we'll save for when General Antonius and the trainers can be here. Ferkudi, I'll need you to lead a logistics meeting later. Bring your ledgers. I know you don't need 'em, but everyone else does. Ben-hadad, you're in that one, too. I know you are each doing the work of two or three people, so let's be quick. Now the big question: what do we have to do to win?"

"Define 'win,' " Winsen said.

"Winsen, shut up," Cruxer said.

"No, I'm serious. I'm not being a jackass." He shrugged. "This time."

Big Leo said, "We win once we kill the White King and all his leadership. That's winning. Nothing short of that."

Ben-hadad took off his flip-down spectacles. "What if, by that definition, we can't win?"

"You think we can't win?" Ferkudi asked.

"Worse," Ben-hadad said. "Breaker doesn't."

They all looked at Kip. "I never said that," he said.

But they all knew him.

"Focus on the problem," Cruxer said. "We have to lift the siege on Green Haven or we'll lose the satrapy. If we lose the capital, we lose Blood Forest. We do that and the other satrapies fall eventually. Maybe we can't beat him alone, but we're not alone. Winning is stopping him here, showing he can be defeated and trusting the rest of the empire to do their part, too, albeit later than we'd like."

"No, we have to do more than that," Ben-hadad said. "The White King has multiple paths to victory. Big Leo was right. We have to kill him. Even if he loses here, he can go on and win elsewhere, drawing strength from everything he's already conquered, and then come back. With the land he holds and the revenues he commands, the longer this war goes on, the more certain our defeat."

Cruxer said, "To lift the siege, we either have to leave right away or we'll get besieged ourselves here. Even if the bandits can't keep us under siege for more than a few weeks, that'll be long enough for Green Haven to fall. But if we leave, we leave Dúnbheo defenseless."

"I kind of like the idea of those old bastards on the Council of Divines being led away in chains. They deserve it for all their lies," Winsen said.

"But everyone else here doesn't," Cruxer said.

"Dúnbheo was under siege," Ben-hadad said. "Of course they lied to us. What were they gonna do? Tell us they're not worth saving? Admit they didn't have any food or supplies to share? They're corrupt idiots, but not stupid idiots."

Cruxer said, "Dúnbheo has ceremonial and symbolic power. History. The whole satrapy is taking heart as they get news of our victory over the next days and weeks. The Divines might have convinced themselves the city still has strategic value as well."

"Aw, Cruxer, always trying to see the best in everyone except yourself," Winsen said. "It's cute."

"Shut up, Win," Big Leo rumbled.

"The thing is," Kip said, feeling like he was groping around the foot of a really big idea, "Koios knew it didn't. If he'd already seized Loch Lána and had a plan in motion to strangle the Great River, why try to take Dúnbheo?"

"The symbolic value," Ben-hadad said. "This city is still Blood Forest's pagan heart—and there's still that huge throne in that audience chamber. A throne unpolished by a king's waxing moons in four centuries. If the White King sits there, he becomes a king in truth—the first king since Lucidonius."

"But if that was it," Kip said, "why wouldn't he have come here himself, to make sure the city fell?"

"A general has to delegate," Ben-hadad said. "If you see a general fighting on the front lines, you're seeing a damned foo—" He cut off as he realized something. He looked at Kip and cringed. "Uh, I mean, usually, you're seeing a man choosing glory over victory."

"Breaker fights on the front lines," Ferkudi said.

"Thanks, guys," Kip said.

"I did say 'usually,' " Ben-hadad grumbled.

Kip had moved fast, trying to cut the White King's lines of supply and reinforcement while getting supplies and reinforcements of his own—the word of Kip's victory saving Dúnbheo should have given the Spectrum a good reason to bet fully on him. Instead, the White King had beaten him to the exact same strategy.

Kip had been doing everything right to make allies. At great cost, he'd done all he could to make friends, and here he was, alone and unsupported.

Again.

No, no, that wasn't true. He *and his people* were alone and unsupported. He wasn't poor Kip Delauria of Rekton anymore. He was Kip Guile of Blood Forest. And if the fights felt the same—the isolation, the self-doubt—maybe all those earlier fights had been readying him for this one.

"Maybe there are other forces Koios is worried about threatening his siege," Ben-hadad said. "The pygmies, maybe? Or maybe the Chromeria's finally decided to stop sitting on its thumbs and is attacking from Atash? Or maybe he's so certain of victory, he's in no rush."

"He's attacked aggressively everywhere else, from Garriston to Idoss to Ru to Ox Ford," Kip said. "Now he changes?"

"If we leave Dúnbheo, he can paint us as abandoning them to die. If we don't leave, he can paint us as cowards abandoning Green Haven to die. That's worth a few weeks for him, isn't it?" Ben-hadad said.

Big Leo said, "Does it give us enough time to call back the Night Mares?"

I should've kept the Night Mares with me, scouting. If I had, this never would have happened.

Moving fast doesn't help if you move exactly the wrong direction.

Dim people ride a mule to their conclusions; bright ones ride a race-horse. But not always in the right direction.

"No," Kip said. "They're our fastest troops. That's why I sent them. Before any messengers could catch up with them, they'd have split in a hundred directions anyway, trying to rally the villages."

"So have we already lost?" Ben-hadad asked. He was skipping ahead of the rest of them to the final judgment. That was just how fast his mind worked. Ben might well become a great general in time, but his true genius lay with the *machinae* he could imagine, and then actually make, and then perfect. Few people could do even one of those things.

Of them all, Ben-hadad was the one who should change history—and would, if Kip didn't get him killed first.

Kip pulled back his sleeve where the Turtle-Bear tattoo was vibrant with all the colors he'd recently drafted. "Turtle-bears can do many things, but one thing they're shit at: they don't know how to give up."

"Are you telling me you have a plan?" Cruxer asked.

"Does this have something to do with why you went to the window yesterday?" Ben-hadad asked.

The crowd today, as Tisis had predicted, was easily twice as large.

The seals on the door cracked open, but there was the appropriate knock, so no one was alarmed. Tisis came in. Kip was glad to see her. "News?" he asked.

She nodded. "I have an update on our...cicatriferous friend."

Private nicknames were useful when you were worried about being overheard, so they'd privately coined that for Daragh the Coward, who was famous for his many scars.

"Good news, I hope?" Kip asked.

"No," she said. She looked ill. "But there's something else first."

She blew out a breath as she looked around at the Mighty. She tossed her petasos onto the table. "I'm in charge of the scouts. This map is mine. Kip invented it, but all the intel on it is work I cleared. It's all from interviews I conducted, reports I checked. I'm responsible for what's on it and for what's not. I denote reports I don't trust or have questions about. Anything that's wrong on here is my fault. And I loused up, badly. I still have no idea how Koios took the river without me hearing about it. There are rumors now about river monsters, which I assume and really hope are river wights—I don't know, and I still can't confirm them. Regardless, it's an enormous failure. I've got people checking *everything*, but it may be weeks before we know what went wrong. There should have been some refugee, some report. Maybe there was. Maybe I filtered it out. I must have. I've got ideas about what happened, but I'm not even going to offer guesses right now. Not after this."

Tucking an errant strand of blonde hair behind an ear, she looked at everyone in turn around the table, except Kip. "I failed you, and I'm sorry. It won't happen again."

There was only silence. No one protested that she hadn't bungled things badly.

She looked over at Winsen. "If you give me shit, Win—"

"I won't," he said.

"…I'll deserve it," she said, finishing over his words.

He looked at her one moment more. Then he shrugged. "I won't."

Dammit, Winsen, don't you go surprising me with a glimmer of humanity.

Finally she looked at Kip, "My lord. I failed you most of all. I'd like to offer my—"

"Denied. Give us your report," he said.

She didn't want anything soft from him, not after such a failure, not in front of these men, whose acceptance she craved so much.

They accepted her as one of the Mighty, but she was different. It wasn't or wasn't only that she was a woman; Teia had obviously belonged with them, different as her own abilities were from theirs. But Tisis feared they only tolerated *her* for Kip's sake. She feared they thought her weak because she was no warrior.

The worst thing Kip could do in this moment was coddle her. It would alienate her from them forever.

She took a deep breath. "With the Blood Robe deserters and the refugees and escaped slaves from the war, I've been tracking upward of fifty bandit groups, but I concentrated on Iphitos the Archer, Bardan the Grave Digger, Colm the Cannibal, with Daragh the Coward having a smaller band, but claiming territory we've traversed. I tried to get agents in with these various bandits, but each band requires anyone who joins to do one terrible thing or another as initiation to weed out such infiltrators. Do you know how many *good guys* are willing to murder innocent people in order to infiltrate a gang of bad guys?"

"None, I'm sure," Cruxer said.

Kip could think of one: Teia.

He didn't say it, of course. Not to his wife.

"Anyway, so I couldn't get good sources, but now that Daragh the Coward's army is within two days' march, I'm working on getting figures of the composition of his forces now."

They all chewed on that.

"He's a bandit, not a soldier. You think we can buy him off?" Ben-hadad said.

"With what money?" Ferkudi asked.

"You were saying, earlier? About a plan?" Cruxer prompted Kip.

There were few options, and none of them good. No use bemoaning it. Kip said, "Pull the last remaining Night Mares we have from messenger duty. Send them to surround Daragh the Coward's camp tonight and tomorrow. Tell them to let themselves be seen, though. Then move stealthily to another side of their camp and be seen again. They're to do all they can to appear to be a much larger force." Kip looked around the room, seeing sudden hope in some of their faces. He trusted these men with his life. He trusted them even with his fallibilities. "Truth is, calling it a plan would be generous. And it relies way too much on an open question."

"What's that?" Ferkudi asked.

"What's an 'open question'?" Winsen asked him. "'Well, you see, son, when a mommy question and a daddy question love each other very much—'"

In unison, Big Leo, Ben-hadad, and Cruxer said, "Shut up, Win."

"What's the question?" Cruxer asked, trying to get them back on track, as ever.

Kip said, "How much am I really Gavin Guile's son?"

Chapter 11

Aliviana had stood in place for two thousand seven hundred seconds, hands folded in front of her, chin high. In their hundreds, the petitioners had vacated the hall. Gods don't inconvenience themselves for mortals.

But apparently, they do inconvenience one another. Her patience had worn thin after the first six hundred and twenty seconds. It was such a transparent power play to make her wait while he took his time that her estimation of the White King fell by the minute.

Then she realized he wasn't merely waiting to see if he could goad her into some outburst; he was taking counsel. He sat silent on his throne with the air of one listening to attendants. Very interesting. She would have to speak with Beliol about that later.

"Your old love is in Dúnbheo," the White King said finally.

"He humiliated the forces you sent to take the city, you mean." Of course she'd told Koios about Kip, a long time ago. Including that the love had been one way, and the other way. None of which mattered now. What mattered was letting Koios know she had her own means of knowing things.

But he didn't look surprised she knew. "I'd have preferred to crush young Guile, but entangling him will serve almost as well. If my generals fail in the task I leave them, I can return when my reign is secure with ten times the forces and all the gods. His time is almost finished."

He was studying her as if this were a test. "Do you think I *care*?" she asked.

"Don't you?" he asked.

She thought about it, really thought about it. "I...liked Kip," she said finally. "Really liked him, actually. Not in the puppy-panting-after-my-heels way that he liked me, naturally. But he was a good kid. Too damaged, though. Too self-loathing for one to ever really take him seriously. Who needs all that? But I...admired that he was loyal. He tried to do what was right, no matter the cost. I see now that that was a weakness. He took loyalty to illogical extremes. You can't help others when you're dead yourself. It's a miracle he's not dead already, come to think of it. Kip...Kip has always been doomed, hasn't he? I shall miss him, but mortals die. It is our burden to watch their lights bloom in the darkness and then fade back into it after a few short years, isn't it? I shall mourn his passing—no, no, that's not exactly true, and will be less true as time goes on. I shall note his death when I learn of it, perhaps even regretfully, so whether I do that now or in some years, what's the difference?"

"Here I thought you came to threaten me," the White King said.

"Threaten?" she asked, surprised.

"You've refused to bend the knee to me. Your message spoke of a partnership instead, so surely you have some 'or else,'" Koios said. He sat down now on his ivory throne as if she were merely another petitioner come to beg some favor of him. It was a power display, to sit when the other must stand. He even pretended nonchalance, but his muscles, though bent into a slouch, were taut for action.

She noticed such things. She had quite the eye for detail now.

"Oh, I see," she said. "That helps immensely. You're taking me being enslaved to you as the default, so my defiance of that order irks you, and you assume I must have some force backing me up, some power that allows me to insult you to your face by not groveling. That is quite illuminating. Instead, the true default is that we each reign over separate realms, and we can either join together—if such is mutually profitable—or we can go to war, which most certainly would not be. Comprehending easily this truth, which seems to have eluded you, I spoke of partnership."

"That is not the way of things."

"Aha," she said. "So. You're not quite the ideologue you pretend to be, bringing a new order of justice and freedom to the realms; you're simply a maniac. Well, then, I can deal with that, too."

His eyes flashed and he sat up. His bodyguards rippled as if they were directly connected to his will—which, she thought, perhaps they were. She would have to study that. His lungs filled. At his neck, his pulse throbbed faster.

"In that case," she said before he could go on, "you want threats of me. Yes, I will join with Kip. If it's necessary."

He scoffed. "Are you naïve, or are you stupid, coming here with talk like that?"

She didn't like false dichotomies. They itched like a spot on her back she couldn't reach. They made her eyelid twitch. "Perhaps you require a display of power? Really? The king of the djinn needs that?"

Suddenly, he grinned despite himself. Then he laughed. "I think I missed you, Liv."

She didn't like being called Liv anymore. But she held her tongue.

"No one speaks to me that way. Not anymore. Not that I like it, mind you," he said. "But it seems that when one bans certain kinds of talk, it doesn't just stop that one thing; it radiates out and silences so much. I hold a humorless court, I'm afraid, and I'm probably some-what to blame for that."

Probably? Somewhat?

But again, she held her tongue.

"We can skip the displays of power," he said, "but...it's the 'God of Gods,' if you will."

"'Gods' plural? You got *two* of them to worship you? Which ones?" she asked.

His bodyguards went wide-eyed. That was helpful to her new study. It told her they still had some will of their own.

"All of them," the White King said flatly.

"Surely not dry old Samila Sayeh."

"They *all* worship me," the White King said.

"If you define 'worship' as bowing at the right times, lighting incense, and mumbling prayers, I'm sure that's true."

"I am their *god*," the White King said.

"That, however, I'm certain is not true. What's the point in being a god if you have to worship another god? No. They don't really worship you; they fear you. Which is excellent, as far as it goes. Fear is a powerful motivator, though one that may fade in time. They remember what you were, and they do or will hope to transform themselves as you have transformed yourself. You are not categorically *other* to them. One can revere what one wishes to emulate. One can't revere what one wishes to replace. I'm sure each one will serve you for a time, and then you can kill them and replace them. The replacements will serve much longer, never having known you as merely a man. The new gods, if not corrupted by the old ones, may then revere you indeed, and then your reign will be secure. Or more secure. But it will take a few purges."

The pique faded, and she watched his mouth quirk backward momentarily as his lower eyelids tensed.

"You're asking yourself," she said, " 'Is she the first to guess my plan, or only the first to do so to my face?' "

"*You* don't fear me," he said. "That makes you more dangerous than any of them."

"Not true on the first part, and for the second, it really depends what you mean by dangerous," she said. "I do fear you, still. My mortal nature hasn't faded so much yet. But fear has lost much of its motivating power. I don't wear your chain, and I tell the truth. That may make me dangerous. It also can make me helpful, especially when one is surrounded by those who constantly lie."

"Then tell me about Kip...truthfully," he said.

"Kip?"

"Your threat."

"Oh, that. Well. I could work with him. Very easily. He's never tried to kill me or make me his slave. I can trust him. All things I can't say of you."

"And yet here you are," Koios said. "Ready to make a deal to kill him and all his friends. How terribly ungrateful of you."

She blinked. She'd not thought of gratitude in a long while. No matter. "I know I could trust Kip forever. But 'forever' is such a short span for mortals. Kip will die soon. He's burning too hot, rising too fast, and loved by too many. He has something of greatness in him, and that makes small, powerful men feel small and powerless, and there's nothing they hate more."

"Says the girl goddess," Koios said wryly.

"Says the small, powerful man," she said.

He was actually so shocked that he didn't move at all for a long moment. It must have indeed been long and long since he had felt genuinely offended.

"The point is that you're exactly right," she said. "Kip and I have certain similarities in rising fast and high by our wits. What I—"

"Did you know that an earthquake made the Red Cliffs? It thrust the seabed into the very sky. Those who climb still see the imprints of fishes a thousand paces above the sea. You see, in a great upheaval like that, or like the coming of the God of Gods, mountains are plunged into the sea, and low places are flung up to the heavens," the White King said. "So when we find fish on a mountaintop, let us not praise them too quickly for making the climb."

Liv saw several of the bodyguards grinning, as if he'd really put her back in her place.

"The point is," Liv said, "Kip will die. I don't intend to, ever, and I can't trust whomever comes after him to keep whatever deal we make, no matter what oaths we swear. If I align myself with the Chromeria, they'll come after me eventually. They'll have to. By my very nature I'm an abomination to them. I'd forever be a compromise they made, and their...What was your word again? Their 'gratitude' toward me would eventually die. Worse, so would their fear. You, however, won't."

"Won't...what? Betray you?"

"Die. Or forget. I understand you. You and I have reached the same conclusion. Everything you've done has been predicated on your understanding coupled with intelligence and patience."

"Compliments?" the White King said. "That must have been painful for you."

She had no idea what he was talking about. "Statements of fact are almost never painful to me." That was true, of course. And they were becoming less so as she grew into her full nature.

She had also nearly forgotten how painfully inefficient most conversations were. "May I continue?"

"Please," he said, and the symmetry of him saying 'please' to her in return for her earlier 'please' and thus closing the loop made her feel inordinately better.

"You and I understand that the nine kingdoms were doomed to fall, not because of who won the Deimachia, but by the very fact of it. Once the War of the Gods began, all of them were doomed, and their kingdoms, too. The very physics of this world are set against any one color dominating for long. Any can reign for a time, but with every additional year of the colors being out of balance, it takes more and more effort even to draft the dominant color, and less and less for one's enemies to draft theirs. It's a fool's game, and you're not that kind of fool. This is why you haven't become a god yourself. Inside the system, you would be entrapped by the system. You wouldn't be able to help attempting to dominate the colors. It is in the nature of the inner-spectrum colors to do so."

"But not of your color?" he said.

She scowled. Did he not know? "Do you not know?" she asked.

"Enlighten me," he said.

She scowled harder. If she lectured him on superviolet, she would want to tell him about chi, and whatever else he clearly didn't understand. It was very hard for her not to finish a thing once begun. It was one of the weaknesses of her color that she had noticed, and she wished to keep those from him for as long as possible. Still, if she wished to live through today, she had to portray herself as just enough of a threat, and not too much, and a wellspring of useful information—enough so as to get him to swear the oath with her.

"Superviolet stands far apart, is rational, and strictly abides oaths," she said, introducing the idea. "Only chi is safer to you, but it's so far from human concerns as to be useless. Plus they get cancers and die within a few years. Blue is safe so long as the hierarchies above and below it are stable. Green can be corralled if given enough freedom. Yellow believes itself to be perfectly positioned to stand atop that hierarchy, and is most dangerous. Orange is wily, but hates direct conflict. Red and sub-red must be manipulated but are too chaotic to be threatening and are easily read and therefore misled. Paryl is profoundly influenced by any color at all, and therefore any magic. It can easily be made a puppet. But a paryl god could be as dangerous as a yellow, given a century or two. If her mind and will weren't destroyed by a long tutelage of being controlled by every magic, one such might invert her weakness and attempt to control every magic instead.

"A less intelligent full-spectrum polychrome would have made himself the yellow god, hoping to balance all the others. Instead, you seek something harder, to take power over all the gods at once, because once held, that's a power you could actually keep. You will become a king of djinn. Or, apologies, a god of gods."

"Thank you," the White King said.

She nodded.

"And you, you hardly fear me at all?"

"You'll have better than my fear: you'll know you can trust me."

"Really? You bear me no ill feeling for when that rash fool Phyros Seaborn tried to chain you with the black luxin?"

She shook her head, baffled. If Phyros Seaborn had put the living black-luxin necklace on her neck, it would have plunged through her very spine if she'd tried to remove it or if she'd disobeyed the White

King. She'd killed Phyros for trying to make her a slave. "Yours was a logical effort. Exactly what you should've attempted at the time. In truth, I resent you implying Phyros did it without your orders more than I resent the attempt."

"A mistake," the White King said. "I was curious to see how far you'd embraced your godhood. A mortal would be furious with me."

It struck her oddly. "I remember a peculiar joy in being carried along at times by fury. It made me feel powerful." She shrugged. "That's no longer necessary. Nor is you chaining me."

"Oh?"

"The power of order for one of my metaphysical nature is proportional to my power absolutely."

It took him a moment to understand. "Ah. Ferrilux doesn't lie."

"I suppose that's close enough," she said. If one disdains nuance.

But apparently she'd not kept her face blank.

His lip curled.

She remembered again that though she had left most emotion behind, he had most certainly not. Her statements of fact could be taken as insufferable arrogance. How tiresome. She sighed. "What it means is that if I take an oath, I could break it, in my current state. But doing so would set me back two to three centuries. During all that time I would be vulnerable."

"And in two or three centuries?" he asked with a smile that showed no contraction of the orbicularis oculi. It was not the part of his face that had been burned; thus the tell was true.

"In two or three centuries I hope I shall never be in such a vulnerable position that I shall need to take an oath."

He gave a thin smile, as if she were a particularly dense child. "What I'm asking is, will you be able to break an oath you make, then?"

"An oath bonds one's will and one's nature in a temporalized and external rubric," she said.

He was nodding, but he had a blank look.

"That's the *whole point* of an oath," she said. How could a man of intelligence not see this immediately? "All liars weaken themselves, but breaking an oath would break *me*. Besides," she said, "we'll give each other plenty of space."

He raised his eyebrows.

"When you win, King Koios, because of the way"—'the stupid way,' she didn't say; she had to speak truth, but she didn't have to speak all the truth all the time—"you've chosen to wipe out most of your warriors and all the Chromeria's, you'll be very, very weak for a decade or two. Stronger than everyone else, however, so your weakness won't matter. Unless..."

"Unless?" His eyebrows knit.

"You've heard the Everdark Gates are open? It's true. And I can tell you that the Angari wave-tamers have been truly fascinated this past year by what's happening in their seas, and by what's happening here. They're hungry for new lands to conquer, and they believe that the Gates' failure is a sign of favor from their gods."

"I'll happily fight their gods with my own."

"Then you'll die happily. The first wave they're amassing is three times the size of all your armies together, I should say. And I mean your armies now, before all the losses you'll take with this island siege you have planned. Nor are they lacking for magic of their own. I'm no Gaspar Estratega, but I believe they would defeat you even if your forces and the Chromeria's fought united against them. However, you needn't fight at all. I can close the Everdark Gates again. And the Angari are seafaring people, whose gods are sea gods. They have tamed creatures that are much like our own sea demons. But because they love only the sea, if the Gates are shut, they will not attempt an attack through the mountains and the deserts that have kept them from our lands for so long."

"You'll save me from a threat that isn't even real?" The condescending smile crept back onto his face.

"Send your people, then," she said. "Confirm it for yourself. Time draws short, but perhaps you have time if you've duplicated the skimmers by now? No? Sad. But I assure you, if we don't have an agreement before you invade the Jaspers, I'll fight for Kip. I'll have to. Because afterward you won't need me, and I won't be able to challenge you."

"How rational of you," he said.

"Was that supposed to be an insult?"

"I hope you've also come up with some good reasons why I shouldn't kill you now, bringing a threat like that here. Or have you forgotten so much about fury?"

She was bored of this conversation. He treated *her* like a moron while acting like one himself half the time.

"Do you need a list of my threats?" she asked. "Backup plans? Dead man's switches? I have such things. But if I do list them, you'll be fretting on them for the next hundred years. Me putting such things into words gives them substance, turns them into worries—worms that will chew into the bulwarks of our peace, weakening them with every passing year. It's a poor option. Instead, I would like today to be the last time we think of each other as adversaries. Let us instead become distant allies, brought together for a short period to sort out our mutual concerns and then happily parting to do what we will with our own distant lands."

"So let's run this hypothetical," he said. "We make an alliance. A partnership, as you said. I need you now not to join Kip, and perhaps even to shut the Everdark Gates. And let's say I accept that because of your nature, I can trust you forever. But I will grow in power far more than you will, and I will close my vulnerabilities in time. Why would you trust me to keep my oaths?"

"Because I bring you a gift. Will-crafting. We've both done it in this room this very day. Do you know why the Chromeria forbids will-crafting in all but the most rudimentary forms?"

"They have an especial delight in forbidding things. I've given up caring why."

"You shouldn't have. An oath binds one's will to a word, but a drafter *can* bind her will to something more permanent."

She saw his eyes light up. He was a smart man. If an oath could be magically binding, and anchored to something permanent, any drafter he could force to take an oath of fealty to him would be unable to break that oath—ever.

"This works with gods?" he asked.

"You won't be as good at doing it as I am," she said honestly. "And your gods will have a very long time to work against it. You'll still have to kill them, after a time. Yes, of course I know you plan to do that. Mortals, however? I wouldn't say it's permanent, but if it takes them a hundred years to unwind a spell and most of them don't live half so long, that's a distinction without a difference, isn't it? That is why the Chromeria abandoned an entire branch of magical study. It was one of the first pieces of lore the Chromeria erased. True slavery to the gods, for life."

"That is a handsome gift," he said. "And now that you've given me the lead, perhaps that's all I require of you."

A threat. Again. "It will likely take you a hundred years to find a superviolet who can do what I've already done, though maybe you'll get very lucky and it will only take you ten. But these next ten years are when you'll be most vulnerable. If you can live ten years, you'll likely live forever. So I know you might kill me out of pique today, but I'm gambling that you'll take the deal where we both win, both in the short term and in the long."

"What do you want?" he asked.

"You can have all the lands of the Seven Satrapies. The nine kingdoms, whatever you wish to call them. You may also have all of the Cerulean Sea. The Everdark Gates, however, will belong to neither of us. A no-man's-land. Everything within them is yours; everything outside them is mine. No people, no magic, not so much as a rowboat or letter or child is to be sent from one realm to the other. We'll have mirrors set up on either side to message each other in case of emergencies. Otherwise, nothing. If you wish, have your wars among your humans. Let there be peace between the gods."

Chapter 12

Kip had just done the most brilliant and cynical thing of his entire political career: he'd listened to his wife.

Yesterday, in the privy council chamber, they'd met with the six remaining Divines. With many, many words, the Divines communicated their chagrin at the assassination attempt and commitment to find those responsible. They wished—they said—to help Kip and his marvelous companions in any way possible; therefore, he must understand that this particular refusal wasn't personal and this particular request was in fact impossible and this small change Kip requested was one they were quite willing to accommodate but would mortally offend some other important group (and that group's support was necessary for the following list of reasons).

Yesterday, for many long minutes, Kip had actually listened to them. They knew what they were talking about, after all. They had run this city for generations. He'd adjourned the meeting with the thought that it was, frankly, just damned hard to govern a city.

"...which sadly has, from time immemorial, been the prerogative of the Keeper herself."

'Prerogative.' The word had stuck to Kip for some reason. Not because it was that odd of a word but because of the landscape of other words used by these old men (never an old woman on the Council of Divines, at least not that survived into the records). 'Prerogative' joined 'tradition' and 'customs' and even 'demesne,' the violation of any of which would either 'needlessly cause terrible offense' or 'deeply alienate' or 'create antipathy' or 'endanger all you've accomplished.'

The circumlocutions suddenly sounded familiar, strumming an old and much-hated chord from his past: Kip was being handled.

Mother used to do this, with her drugs, listing all the reasons it was impossible to quit just now.

Power was the Divines' drug, and Kip was threatening their supply.

What would you do here, father? he'd asked himself.

How had Gavin done it? All Gavin's life, he'd broken through all the horseshit like this, upending other people's games and yet emerging not only unscathed but beloved.

Well, let's see: He was basically all-powerful, and he cajoled, charmed, and used wit and humor to take the edge off of whatever he was going to do anyway. Plus he was incredibly handsome, which never hurt. Oh, and when people defied him, sometimes he'd kill all of them.

So no one went into a meeting with Gavin Guile entirely fearlessly, which meant that when he was charming instead, and told them how it was going to be, most people found themselves nodding along, or even laughing along, admitting it was all for the best.

Kip wasn't all those things, but maybe, between emulating his father and his grandfather, he might be enough.

That was why Kip had gone to the window and waved to the crowd. But that hadn't been a full plan, only an intuition of one.

While the old men were conferring with one another again yesterday, Kip had said to the Mighty, 'I want to turtle-bear their porcelain shop and give the old Divines a heart attack or three. Ideas?'

'Oh, I have ideas!' Big Leo said.

'Ripping people's arms off is not an idea,' Kip said. 'It's a daydream.'

'You didn't even let me tell you what I'd do with them,' Big Leo complained.

'I didn't say I didn't share it,' Kip said. Morning had expired, and with his realization that he was being handled, so had his patience. 'Also Lord Golden Briar has the worst breath I've ever smelled.'

'You're telling me that's his *breath*?' Ben-hadad asked. 'I thought—'

'*Gentlemen*,' Cruxer said as the men came back.

'Yeah, we don't know if they're *all* deaf,' Ferkudi said, too loudly. 'I've been watching, and Lord Appleton is faking that old-man shuffle.'

Lord Appleton looked over.

'They're none of them dumb, either,' Kip said, carefully screening his mouth against lipreading with a lifted cup.

Winsen hissed, 'Unlike our pal whose name rhymes with Jerkudi.'

After the meeting adjourned on more empty promises and stalling, Kip had listened to his wife's idea.

So today, they met the Divines in one of the side gardens, where Tisis made much of the flowers. Then Kip suggested she see some of the exotics the people had been bringing. In no hurry, they made their way to the front of the palace. Kip split his time between pleasantries to the old Divines and greeting people waiting in the long queue to see *Túsaíonn Domhan* that wrapped around the building, more and more spending his time on the people, much to the Divines' consternation.

Finally, on the way to the front of the palace, they picked up the hundreds of admirers to whom Kip had waved yesterday. Cruxer had not been a fan of this part of the plan, but the people kept a respectful distance once the Mighty demonstrated what that was. They themselves weren't quite certain what they wanted of Kip.

The Divines looked more and more uncomfortable, but when Lord Aodán Appleton suggested reconvening inside, Kip pretended not to hear. And finally, they made it to the mound of flowers that had been piled out in front of the palace, partly in thanks to Kip's Nightbringers for liberating the city and partly to cover the smell of the putrefying and still hanging Divine and conn.

By tradition, the men's bodies were to stay in place for several days more yet. The stench was nearly intolerable. Kip stopped at the top of the steps as Tisis pretended to admire the flowers here. The Divines were painfully aware of their dead compatriots nearby, though none dared look at them.

Kip said, "You've told me we need a full council to have a quorum to vote on certain matters, matters that must be decided immediately. So let's agree—"

"New councillors! Yes!" Lord Rathcore said. "Just what a conn is for!"

"A conn?" Kip asked as if this were a surprise. It was supposed to be a great honor, and they'd been trying to extract all sorts of concessions from him in return while only hinting it might be possible. In reality, he was being asked to pay for the privilege of eating two slices of warm bread hiding a turd.

Being named conn *was* an honor, and it would give him legitimacy that wasn't derived from his father or grandfather. It would be something he'd earned himself. He wanted that, and they obviously sensed that.

But by law and tradition, a conn had significant limits to his power here. By assenting to a defined role and swearing to its oaths, Kip would be assenting to its limits, too. The Divines weren't offering a gift; they were offering Kip chains decorated with gold filigree.

"No," Kip said. "I don't have time for the frippery and delay. I'll give you my suggestions. You can approve them if you do so unanimously, yes? I suggest Lady Proud Hart and Lady Greenwood."

Their heads did not literally explode, but several of them turned shades redder.

"My lord," Lord Appleton said, "we could make you conn within the hour. It would honor our ways, and then perhaps we might even"—he looked like he was trying to swallow a mouthful of salt—"come to an agreement on *one* of those noble matriarchs."

"You're not hearing me," Kip said. "I don't want the position." He was feeling red, and he almost insulted the pointless position itself—which would have been an insult to the whole city.

"Milord," Lord Spreading Oak said patiently as if trying to counsel reason, "becoming conn is the only way for you to accomplish all you think you need to do."

"Funny," Kip said, "the last conn believed that was true, too." He looked up at the hanged, rotting Conn Hill. "Tell me, Lord Spreading Oak, if a man has as much power as a king but not the name, is he more or less than a king?"

By long tradition and by an explicit oath as he took office, a conn couldn't become a king. It was one of the stupider things they were trying to keep from Kip's grasp. King? He didn't even want to be a mayor!

A thrill went through the crowd at the very word 'king,' and the Divines alternately blanched and went purple. It was one nice thing about these northerners' pallid skin: it made them so easy to read sometimes.

Lord Spreading Oak could find no words.

Kip said, "My esteemed Lords Divine, when the bandit king Daragh the Coward arrives tomorrow with his thousands of raiders and runaway drafters and slave-takers and desperate men, I should like to be here to protect you. But later today, I'm meeting with Satrap Willow Bough's ambassador. He's going to ask to me to abandon Dúnbheo and bring my forces to lift the siege on Green Haven—also a worthy and necessary fight. Now, if I'm to stay, if I'm to help this city I so love, I need your help. Can you find it in your hearts to help me, please?"

The crowd heard only that Kip wanted to save them, again, and that the Divines were somehow driving him out of the city instead. Ugly suggestions rippled through them, and the air took on a palpable menace.

The Divines looked at the mob uneasily, and then at each other.

Chapter 13

"My mama suicided just like that," Gunner announced, heedless of all cues.

Gavin lay stretched out sunning himself on the hard, unforgiving deck of the ship's forecastle, his eyes closed, still adjusting to the harsh, bleached sunlight of freedom after his long stint in darkness.

Gunner's voice was like a child pounding on the door when you're in the middle of a bad lay: Gavin wasn't enjoying himself as much as he'd expected, but what he was doing was a lot more enjoyable than what he was being called to do.

"I'm sorry to hear that, Captain," he said, shading his eyes and cracking them open briefly—only because Gunner was the kind of man who might stomp on Gavin's head if he thought he wasn't being shown the proper respect.

Gavin had told himself he needed to get sun, needed to get his eyes reaccustomed to the light, needed to feel the light on his skin in case just maybe his disability was healing itself. Or something.

He was better at lying to others, though, than to himself. No, Gavin was lying about, seeking an idyll and finding himself merely idle.

Closing his eyes as if to fend off the captain through his obvious exhaustion, Gavin reached out his fingertips, wishing they might dip into the sapphire waters as they had that morning he touched the sea demon.

Eyes? Eye. Funny how he still thought of them in the plural, while at other times he couldn't ignore the jagged black monstrosity strapped to him in that eye patch, feeling like it was trying to burrow into his head.

"Y'ain't gonna ask, is ya?" Gunner said.

He moved into Gavin's sun, swaying with the waves, so that Orholam's one eye blinded Gavin's one eye only half the time.

76   Instead of conjuring that morning of peace, arms spread touching

the waters, and that numinous creature, the memory that came swimming serpentine to the surface was of the day he'd been shackled spread-eagled in the hippodrome, as Orholam stared down, pitiless or powerless, and Gavin's eye was burnt out by a very apologetic chirurgeon. When she wasn't burning out people's eyeballs with a white-hot poker, she was probably quite nice.

Ha. People had thought the same of him, on Sun Days, as he slaughtered so many.

"That evil eye of yourn," Gunner said with a shudder. That was his charming name for the black jewel that would kill Gavin if he tried to remove it. "It still shivs me the givers."

Go away, Gunner.

Come to think of it, perhaps many *had* denounced Gavin for the fraud he was, but his circle of privilege had kept those cries from his ears.

"Kin I touch it?" Gunner asked.

"Probably kill us both if you do. Go ahead."

What if Grinwoody—traitorous monster that he was—while certainly an asshole, was fundamentally correct? Gavin—nice and charismatic man that he was—had certainly served a monstrous function. All of the empire's power was predicated on its control of drafters: identifying, training, distributing, and then eliminating them.

Eliminating them? No. Executing them for crimes they *might* commit.

The Chromeria did this by defining morality and medicine for their own ends. They said that like dementia striking an elderly person, breaking the halo has no moral dimension. It's a sad, natural process that leads to a person acting contrary to their own character, and in ways that are terribly destructive. Gavin had fought wights; he'd seen the destruction they could wreak. *Could.*

But the Chromeria coupled this with a moral injunction. It's not wrong to break the halo, but it's wrong to run if you do. It's good, they said, to die right before you do. They said it's not suicide to volunteer to be killed. It's serving your community.

They defined Life as one of Orholam's Great Gifts, but carved out a remarkable exception. To most of the world, a drafter who'd served their community for one or two decades went on a last pilgrimage—Sun Day at the Chromeria—and simply never came back.

Drafters simply only lived to forty or forty-five. That was the way it was.

But Gavin had been the instrument of that brutal reality, ramming the knife through ribs, vomiting empty prayers at black heavens painted white. His conscience revolted at what he did, and he did it anyway.

He was the monstrous fist inside the velvet glove. If an institution requires the monstrous in order to operate—requires, not commits incidentally, *requires* in an essential way—is it not therefore itself fundamentally monstrous?

Can one commit murder and walk away clean?

Gunner huffed some sound between a grunt and a bark, still standing there. He hadn't touched Gavin's eye, but he'd been watching him all the while.

"What kinda shit horse is this? I get me a broken Guile?"

If an institution presents itself as uniquely moral but is secretly monstrous, isn't that proof that its very ideas are corrupt and corrupting, rather than that only some few of its practitioners are corrupt?

The implications were horrifying.

If the Chromeria was fundamentally corrupt, then they were all of them—the Chromeria, the Broken Eye, and the Blood Robes—equally horrific. All committed evil, and all excused their own evil as necessary.

Maybe it was worse than that. It wasn't that each defined the good differently and thus excused different evils; it was that right and wrong were meaningless concepts: there was only what flavor of power you preferred.

Can good fruit come from a bad tree?

"Blackberries," Gunner said, moving out of the sun once more, allowing Orholam's cursed eye to dazzle Gavin.

"What?" Gavin asked, grimacing against the light. "She killed herself with blackberries? How? The brambles?"

"No, that just sorter popped in me eggshelf. Egg bone? Shell. Eggshell." He rapped on his forehead with his knuckles. "Words, sentences, you know, not my own? Popped in there? Happens to ever'one, right?"

"Yeah, sure, right—no, no. I don't follow at all. How'd your mom die?" It was the most delicate way Gavin could think of to ask about a suicide. Seemed like Gunner wanted to talk about it, and Gavin probably needed to humor the man. He propped himself up on an elbow, squinting at the man standing over him.

"Wrong question," Gunner said. "You got it sorter back swords, don'tcha?"

Orholam help him, either Gunner was starting to make more sense, or his madness was contagious, because Gavin understood him perfectly.

He blew a long-suffering sigh. Very well. He sat up. He knew what Gunner meant about the wrong question. He was to ask not, 'How did she die, Gunner?' but, 'How'd she live?'

Oddly, with Gunner, this would actually be the quicker way to get to how she died (and thus, get him to go the hell away) than trying to get a straight answer. Gunner seemed a bit bored being a captain when there was neither ship nor storm to fight. He'd already trained his new crew to some acceptable degree of proficiency on the many cannons that worked in concert, and now even that diversion was denied him, as he'd decided to conserve the rest of their powder for the dangers to come.

"Smart man, y'are, Yer Guileship." Gunner grinned the big, happy gap-toothed grin of a man who was rarely understood and who prized it when he was.

Gunner took a deep breath, spat in the waves, muttered a curse to Ceres, and made the sign of the seven. "She uz pregnant most 'er time. Not with my pa's brats, and that was clear as the Atashian shallows, him bein' a sailor, en' gone most the time.

"He'd leave with her pregnant with one, and come back an' she was already bellyful with the next. Not that he were the subject of any hagioglyphics his ownself. Probably had 'least four other wives in other ports. He was the marrying sort. Gave my mama nothing but baby-batter and beatings, though. Finally died, or got took slave, I guess.

"I got my luck from her, though, cuz she mat a good man after that. Didn't beat her once, not even when she ast for it. Treated us li'l brats like 'is own, though we were a right handful a hell and hot coals. Arranged apprenticery for me, and afore he put me on a ship he taught me to fight so I wouldn't be made a buttboy.

"But kin you believe? All that good he done us, and Mama cheated on him, too. Some folk—my mama, me, you—we got the devil in us, Guile. Canna go straight, no gatter how many second chances we met."

Gatter? Met?

Matter. Get. No matter how many second chances we get.

Ah, Gavin thought. It had been a while since he'd heard the pirate speak at length. It took some getting used to.

Again Gunner spat over the gunwale with a muttered curse at Ceres.

"Papa didn't learn it out, but I did. I punched her in the face and gave her the raspy side a' my tongue. But I didn't hell tim neither. I had little brothers and sisters. What would they do without 'im, if he left 'er? Mama was so keen on makin' the beast with two backs with any dangerous man what winked at her that she never even noticed she uz setting her own house on fire by doin' it—with all us kids inside, burnin'. She was pregnant, that's what for I hit her in the face. She told 'im the black eye was from falling down. Uz a better lie than you'd think. Only thing she was ever good at was gettin' on her back in a hurry."

Please don't tell me you murdered her.

"S'pose the harpies took vengeance on her, since no one else would. Somethin' broke in 'er after she shat out that last babe. One night after we were all asleep, she cut her arms up good, almost bled dry. Papa patched her up. Never seen a man what done nothin' wrong look so hunted.

"Mama went on crying and carrying on most every day. Elgin, she named him. Algae, we all said. The baby, right?"

"Right," Gavin said. He felt sick to his stomach already, and he was worried this was only going to get worse.

"Pa was a smith. One day, when he wouldn't stop cryin', Mama quick snatched up Pa's hammer, and laid li'l Algae down on the work-bench, lined him up good—she uz gonna smash his head, we thought. Then she stopped herself, and she smashed her hand instead, smashed it jelly, kept smashing. Wouldn't stop. That wet, sloppy sound and her screamin' won't never come out me ears. Hear the echoes to this day, rattlin' from cliff to cliff inside my skull. Said she had ta be punished for wantin' a do such a thing."

Fuck, Gunner! I am trying to enjoy some goddam sunshine!

"To save her life, Pa had to cut the hand off and burn the stump dry and sizzly, while she cursed him and screamed and asked to die. I hope you never have to hear yer mama beggin' ta die, Guile."

No, mine didn't beg. She asked politely, and I killed her politely. Thanks for the reminder of that, asshole.

"We thought she was gettin' better, after that. Healin'. I was jus' 'bout to ship out. Her 'little man,' she called me. Made her so proud, she said. Not that it should mean much coming from her, she said. Broken woman, Guile. It ain't how it s'pos'd ta be. Well, one day she puts on her finest and wanders out to the bog. Lays down and spreads her arms out lick thet. Lick what you done earlier.

"Someone saw her. Threw her a rope, but the whole area was too treach'rous to get close. She wouldnae take the rope, right at her hand. Help, that near. I s'pose she reckoned she'd take different kinder escape. Thatcher—that's who threw the rope—ran to get help. But when we all come, she was gone. Sunk."

Gavin had entertained the notion at first that maybe Gunner was making sport of him, that he was going to reveal this was all a tale simply to wind him up and pass a few minutes of boredom at sea. Now he didn't think so.

Not at all.

The bouncy, ceaselessly grinning and hollering and spitting pirate who, having been raised amid a cacophony of accents himself, veered wildly between all of them and none, who covered his habitual malapropisms and neologisms by purposely creating as many as possible so that he might become larger than life—that legend was suddenly simply a slender Ilytian man, hitting middle age earlier than he ought, his face drawn, eyes haunted by things forever lost.

Gunner said, "I held this mammary like a puzzle box."

Mammary? Oh no. Memory. Don't laugh, Gavin. For the sake of all that is holy, do *not* laugh right now when Gunner's feeling this vulnerable.

"Puzzle box?" Gavin said. He cleared his throat. He deliberately looked up at the burning white of a celestial eye as bleached of all color as his own eye was. The pain braced him.

"Aye. The mam'ry. I squeeze it, palpate it, grab it with both hands, twist it round, pinch at it, trya sink my teeth in t' it..."

Don't. Even. Grin.

Gunner had to be putting him on. But Gavin looked at the man, and he gave no indication of levity.

"And here's thing," Gunner said. "I kin understand it when a man throws back a few too many drinks on a lonesome night, gets sour inside, and sucks at the teat of a musket for jus' long enough so that big ole 'fuck you' we scream at the world bounces back as 'fuck me' and he pulls the trigger. I kin understand when a girl climbs a tree and tries on a noose necklace for size and once she got it on thinkin', 'I come this far, why not?' and takin' that hop. Prob'ly e'ryone who looks oft a cliff thinks a taking the sharp drop with a sudden stop. E'ry sailor has thought of takin' that swim what fattens sharks. We all got the black moment when the evil eye of the barrel dares a starin' contest. And we're all a hair trigger's pull from the musket's dare. It's the devil's gift, ain't it? It's the heritage o' man, aye?"

Gavin's moment of humor had dried to a desert.

Though surely some folk lived who'd never known what it was like to only just barely hold on to life by your bloody fingernails, Gavin certainly did.

"Aye," he said quietly.

"But lyin' in a bog? Lettin' yourself sink slow? That requires real dedication." He snorted suddenly. "Heh. What's a real commitment to dying, Guile?"

"Huh?"

"*Dead*ication. Eh? Eh?"

But the flare of amusement faded faster than a flintlock's flash. Gunner squatted down close to him and in a low and somber tone, he said, "Tell me, Guile, do you reckon, at the better end, as the bog muck closed slow o'er her face, as she sucked it in and coughed on that first lungful...you reckon she fought to live?"

It was a question as dangerously loaded as the pistols at the quicksilver pirate's hips.

"I hope so," Gavin said quietly.

But it seemed Gunner wasn't even listening. He stood and looked away.

"Thatcher said afore he run to get help, Mama was muttering about Ceres, calling her goddess of crops, fertility, or some such...He said my mama was begging Ceres for sumpin'. Odd, what? Everyone knows Ceres is the bitch of the sea." Gunner spat overboard.

He went on. "Hungry goddess, either way, I s'pose. She who gives so much takes all she wants, too. As if it's right. But I don't think ennyun should go out like thet, stretched out like an offering afore god or goddess or man. I reckon I'd ruther go to the roar of the cannon." He jumped up on the barrel of a huge cannon that dominated the forecastle. He obviously had feelings for it, as other men adore their horse or a sword. "Maybe double or triple load and let rip. If I can't have it, no one can, eh?"

"I...suppose," Gavin said, frowning. It sounded like a damnable waste to him.

"Just like magic for you, then, eh?" Gunner turned and watched Gavin's expression sharply, while he still stood on the cannon, nearly over the water, arms not even extended for balance.

"I...What?"

"You can't have it, no one can?" Gunner pressed.

"Uh..."

"That's what you're doing. Ain't it? Killin' magic. *All* of it. For everyone. I was there. I heard the old man. Be a different world without magic, sure as a sailor on shore leave is on the look for tipples and nipples."

By Orholam's unseeing eye. Gunner was a sly old dog, wasn't he?

It was all a setup. Not the cruel kind Gavin suspected to make fun of him, but a vulnerable kind that was far more clever. 'Look, I've opened up with you. Why don't you open up with me?'

But Gunner was no Andross Guile. Having committed to telling his story to get Gavin to open up in turn, Gunner had told his own tale fully and truly. Now, feeling overexposed, he'd barely remembered his initial purpose in telling Gavin at all.

Gunner now only wanted to distract Gavin from the wound he'd unwittingly revealed.

"Oh, I see," Gavin said.

"You hafta!"

"Uh. Right. And I do."

"*Half* ta. Cuz you only got the one eye," Gunner said. "Instead a two? Never mind. Not very bright sometimes, are ya, Guile? Go on."

There was something about being called stupid by an illiterate that rankled more than it ought to have, but Gavin held back. He said, "You want to know if I'm going to do...*his* bidding." Curse you forever, Grinwoody.

Gavin couldn't say the name without risking that black jewel shooting through his brain. He didn't even know if he could talk about his mission to kill Orholam—which Grinwoody thought was simply an impersonal nexus of magic. Grinwoody, at least, thought sticking the Blinding Knife into that nexus would kill all magic in the world.

"I do," Gunner said. "Seems ya change every time I lay my orisons on ya. Yer name, your face, number of eyeballs and fingers, sometimes your heart. But you were never a quitter, not even when I had you pull that oar. Never gave up. Till now."

Gunner's point was something else entirely, but Gavin couldn't get past how he'd put 'when I had you pull that oar.' Oh, yes, let's do pretend my enslavement was nothing personal, you piece of human—

Then again, maybe it hadn't been.

As Prism, Gavin's own murders had fallen like rain on the heads of the just and the unjust alike.

Shit. There goes my righteous fury. That was the trouble of a consistency in moral affairs: holding yourself up to the measure you judge others by is three clicks past irritating.

So Gavin answered Gunner's question, answered it without even thinking of what the pirate might want to hear: "I don't know yet what I'm gonna do, but I reckon before the sucking sand closes over my face, you'll find me fighting," Gavin said.

Still standing heedlessly on the cannon, Gunner crossed his arms and stroked his raggedy black beard, eyeing him.

"Funny thing, then," Gunner said. "Fightin' only makes you sink faster."

Chapter 14

Ambassador Bram Red Leaf looked like a barrel of fat with little arms poking out. Like so many of the nobles of the Seven Satrapies, he didn't much resemble the people he was supposed to represent. Here in fair Blood Forest, he was dark-skinned, with light eyes and curly hair, and a sheen of sweat on his forehead despite the coolness of the morning.

Kip couldn't help but hate him a little. The man was a vision of what Kip would've become if he'd never joined the Blackguard.

He waved the man over to stand beside him while he examined his maps again. From all the refugees who'd come here before the siege, Tisis had gathered a wealth of new intelligence for Kip's maps. In no small part, she was trying to see how she'd missed Koios's getting around them to take the river with her scouts never hearing of it. Messengers were coming and going constantly, adding new points to the map even now, chatting in quiet voices. Currently, Tisis was working with four drafters and Sibéal Siofra to add points to the map. The pygmy woman wore a fresh demeanor and new clothes to go with it. There was a new self-respect that joined beautifully with her previous professionalism.

"Hello, Ambassador," Kip said. "Welcome to my humble council." He didn't say 'court.' Not yet.

"A pleasure to be received so graciously. An excellent day to you, Luíseach."

The words stopped even Tisis, who met Kip's gaze quickly.

Maybe if they lived long enough to become an old married couple someday, they'd be able to have whole conversations with a glance. Right now, all they said was simply, 'What?!'

In a voice that sounded overly casual even to his own ears, Kip said, "I've not claimed that title. Why would you claim it for me?"

The man patted his forehead with a handkerchief, but when he spoke, there was no reticence in his voice. "You're busy saving this satrapy, so I'll be as direct as people say you are: you let others claim you to be the Luíseach when it serves your purposes, and back off when it seems dangerous. Oh, don't get me wrong, I don't blame you. Problem with claiming a prophecy is that you have to fulfill all the conditions of it, though, huh?"

"You've come to play games," Kip said. He wondered if this conversation would have been different if they'd held it in the palace's great hall. As it was, this parlor now held only a few hundred scrolls and tomes, gleaming wood in the natural-unnatural patterns the old joiners here had loved, and only those courtiers closest to him. The Mighty were all here, either on guard, or at the window, or sending or awaiting messages from their other duties—other than Big Leo, who was demonstrating his mastery of the soldier's art of sleeping anywhere. The big man was sitting at the end of the map table, head back, even as his hands draped protectively over a brace of lamb shanks on a plate in front of him so the servants wouldn't take them away while he dozed.

A few other servants and palace slaves were bringing and taking letters and assisting Tisis with the great map, but it was nowhere near the crowd that would have attended an official audience, had Kip given one.

Come to think of it, a year ago, Kip would have thought *this* was quite a crowd. He was growing accustomed to a life lived before others. It was changing him.

"No games," Ambassador Red Leaf said. "But we've work to do, and rapidly, you and me. I simply wanted to show you I'm not a fool."

"Many would consider showing your cards immediately to be foolish indeed," Kip said. My grandfather, for one, the best player of them all.

"Many would. But not you. You have shown yourself capable of wielding the truth like a scalpel, but you prefer to use it as a hammer. You like to shock people into silence by telling truths they can't believe you'd actually say."

Kip said nothing. This man thought he was clever. Perhaps he was.

Truth was, Kip was a little unnerved. He'd never been aware of being *studied* before.

"Then let us be direct," Kip said. "What do you want of me?"

It had been Andross who told him to use the truth like a hammer. Andross, whom Kip could never equal, would have twisted this fat little man before him into knots, and had him thanking him for the pleasure.

"Satrap Willow Bough wants your army."

"Oh, he does?" Kip asked, all doe-eyed innocence.

"Don't make me bare my throat for nothing, my lord. I'm trying to avoid wasting your time."

Kip nodded his head magnanimously, granting the point as a certain someone did when a stupid person made a surprisingly good point. He'd seen that damned nod enough. "What power do you have to negotiate?"

"Total."

Kip paused for the second time in this brief conversation. He knew to let his arched brows and silence do all the work, but he said, "Meaning...?"

"Total. Without you Green Haven will fall. We've sent a hundred messages begging the Chromeria's help, Ruthgar's help, the pirate kings' help, anyone's help—appealing to treaties, to honor, to greed. We've offered anything and everything. In return, we've gotten promises, but no one's coming." Ambassador Bram Red Leaf cleared his throat. "My good lord Briun Willow Bough is"—despite the few ears here to hear his words, he lowered his voice—"not the most... naturally gifted of leaders. But he is sincere. He doesn't want his people to die. To save his satrapy, he would trade his very life, or if he must, his city."

"Interesting," Kip said. "I hadn't heard he was stupid."

Ambassador Red Leaf didn't so much as blink. He didn't play along like a sycophant would, nor did he rush to his master's defense.

So he was either disloyal or simply a man capable of holding his tongue.

"Now," Kip said, "*now* I'm impressed. Forgive the slander. I didn't mean it."

"That...that was a test?" the man asked.

Kip gave the nod again.

"And like a cur, I didn't defend him..." The fat man's sweaty upper lip thinned. "Please, please don't tell him."

Ah, but just because I *say* the test is over, that doesn't mean it *is*.

For one wild, inappropriate moment, Kip missed Andross Guile. With that man, Kip was always sprinting to catch up, was always the pupil at the master's feet. Every victory against him was hard fought and only half a victory at best. What a man Andross Guile could have been. Where had he gone wrong?

"What's Green Haven's situation?" Kip asked. It had, oddly, been harder to get solid intel on their allies than on their enemies.

"We have a hundred and ten thousand soldiers, five thousand eight hundred twelve drafters. Of those, honestly, maybe two thousand will be of use in battle. Two hundred pygmies with tygre-wolf mounts from Conn Siofra."

"Conn Siofra?" Kip asked, shocked. He looked over at Sibéal. He probably shouldn't have asked that out loud. Too late now. "Is that your father?"

"Little brother," she said. Kip thought he saw real joy in her pygmy smile. Then she said, "Usurper."

Well, shit. And now Kip looked ignorant of his own people in front of the ambassador. But it was beside the point. "Other troops?" Kip asked, irritated with himself.

"Twelve hundred cavalry, and a militia led by the woodsmen of forty thousand."

"And how many of your nearly one hundred sixty thousand have been blooded?" Kip asked. "Ten thousand?"

Bram's brow wrinkled as if he were trying to figure out some way to pad the total, as Kip's disgust had made it clear that that was a low number. "If one counts the militias?" the ambassador offered.

Aha. So the commoners in the militias weren't *worth* counting, despite that Kip's army—the *only* army to have success against the Blood Robes—was composed of such folk.

These morons.

What would Andross do here? Andross would consolidate power into the only hands that knew what to do with it: his own.

"So rather than giving commissions and better arms to your best fighters, you've consigned your only veterans into militias under officers who've never lifted a weapon themselves except to impress a lady."

Kip scrubbed his face. It took a lot to change a culture. Here the poorer sort of nobles—men whose sole patrimony had been their fathers' swords and the right to carry them—didn't want to share ranks with lumberjacks and poachers, and wouldn't until they saw for themselves that those were exactly the men who would keep them alive.

Those lumberjacks and poachers were the kind of men their own fathers and grandfathers had been when they earned those swords.

By the time they learned that truth, though, it would be too late for Blood Forest.

Maybe the White King was on to something. Just burn it down.

It was an idle thought, but a monstrous one.

It was too late to change the Foresters now, with the Blood Robes laying siege to the capital itself.

"How many Blood Robes?" Kip asked.

"Forty thousand, give or take. Maybe four thousand of those are drafters. Maybe two or three hundred wights. At least that many will-casters. I know we outnumber them heartily, but..." He patted his forehead again with his handkerchief. It had to be soaked by now. "But you're the only one who's been able to stop him anywhere. Everywhere we fight, they roll over us. And all our men know it. You might be the only commander for whom our soldiers would stand."

"You've seen my crowds," Kip said, waving toward the window. He didn't need to approach it.

The ambassador nodded. "They are yours indeed."

Kip said, "What's to stop me from letting you and the White King smash each other and then marching in, wiping out the remnants of your armies, and declaring myself king?"

The man pursed his wide mouth. It made him look like a frog. The question had clearly already occurred to him. "Your conscience, this people's loyalty to their own, and our incompetence."

"Incompetence?" Kip asked. The others were clear.

"Coming in and wiping up the remnants only works if there are only remnants left. If, however, the Blood Robes take Green Haven easily, with few losses of their own, you'd be facing the White King with his experienced troops and competent leaders who would have the advantages of our defenses, our materiel, and our wealth. Right now? With us inside the walls and you outside them, and the Blood Robes exposed, our odds together are better than good. But what are *your* odds if you have to try to take Green Haven by yourself, from them?"

So the man was clever after all.

Most people didn't even see their own weaknesses so well. Most wouldn't have been so adept at framing the question in terms of what would be good for Kip, rather than that he simply must help them because, well, he *must*.

"Any deal you make with me is binding, and you have full authority to make treaties? How do I know none will gainsay it afterward?" Kip asked. "You said yourself that you've promised everything to everyone."

"But we've given no one this." Ambassador Red Leaf produced a scroll with a single sentence written on it. He read it aloud: " 'On our oaths and holy honor, any deal Bram Red Leaf signs with Kip Guile shall be fully binding on the satraps, lords, and peoples of Blood Forest now and forever.' " Below that sentence was a candle's worth of sealing wax: the Willow Bough seal prominent, surrounded by constellations of every leading clan's seal and all of the remaining unaffiliated smaller clans', too.

Kip handed it over to Tisis, who had stopped even pretending to work on her map. She looked at it carefully. "Named, signed, and sealed by the head of each family," she said. "Every signature that I recognize—and that's most of them—is correct. And the wording... this means exactly what it says."

The ambassador said nothing. The scroll said it for him. Satrap

Briun Willow Bough might be no military leader, but he was clear-eyed about his situation. It was desperate, but he was taking desperate actions without panicking.

It made Kip like the man. It took uncommon strength of character to present yourself to a foreigner, a younger man, and one of dubious birth no less, and say, 'I'm in desperate straits. Will you please, please help?'

"I'll be named satrap," Kip said. "And put in full charge of the armies. I'll expect the resignations of everyone on the board of electors of the satrap so it can't be stripped from me in a few months, and I'll have the power of appointing new ones."

The room went dead silent.

Kip went on, "Briun Willow Bough will be allowed to keep all of his own lands but will vacate the palace, leaving it furnished and adequately staffed. He can take his own gold, but if he raids the treasury, I'll have him hanged. The city needs that coin and more, if we're to keep fighting. All the nobles above the salt will give me one part in five of their lands and possessions immediately, like so: they will divide their possessions and wealth into five as they see fit, and I will choose which part I take. In cases of indivisible properties, trades will be allowed as assessed by an independent party and accepted within one year, or else the part I deem the larger reverts to me. Any hidden undeclared assets will become my property, and future possession of them by other parties considered theft.

"All officers will resign their commissions and reapply to the same posts pending my approval—though there will be no cost for the second commission. Failure to reenlist will be considered desertion. Families I find especially helpful in the transition or the defense of the Forest will find their tax reduced to one part in seven."

It was even more audacious than he and Tisis had discussed, and everyone in the room froze.

Bram looked suddenly ill. "That would make you a dictator. I would be responsible for giving away a fifth of all Blood Forest's wealth. My lord, on behalf of my entire family, I signed that scroll myself."

"Then perhaps as you're being particularly helpful, you should only give a seventh?" Kip asked.

"No!" the ambassador said, mortified. "No, I'm sorry. We would be shamed to the tenth generation if it looked like you bought this treaty by paying us off."

He didn't pat his forehead now, though. He looked up with those keen eyes hidden in his chubby face like raisins poked deep into bread dough. "But you'll save us?"

"I'll certainly try," Kip said. "Unfortunately, the White King does get a say in how that turns out."

"Not some halfhearted effort, though," Bram insisted. "You'll send everyone. Tomorrow? You'll bind your future to ours?"

"Tomorrow's not going to happen. But we're mobilizing already. The day after. But are you really worried we'll betray you, after all we've done for these lands?" Tisis asked the ambassador, disbelieving.

"Those people out there may want to make you king," Bram said. "But you'd have to fight if you wanted to be king in anything more than name, and a civil war burns a lot of treasure and more goodwill. So maybe this agreement is your way to take the same power without having to fight for it. With what you're asking, you'd be instantly wealthy, with complete legitimacy to your power. We couldn't dislodge you. From there, how hard would it be for a man of your talents to make yourself king in truth? Rather than even fight at all, you might negotiate a peace with the White King. Maybe you already have."

Kip said, "You're standing in a city I liberated from the Blood Robes. We killed thousands of them, *this week*."

"I know, I know. I'm just—I just need to know that you'll save us. I can't give you everything and get only words in return."

"Of course we'll march to save Green Haven," Kip said, and he could see the relief wash over the man's face. "So we're agreed?"

The ambassador took a deep breath, but he'd already decided, Kip could tell. He wasn't even patting his sweat. "We're agreed," he said.

Someone in the room whooped.

"We are going to go kick some Blood Robe ass, my friends," Benhadad said.

"Satrap's Guard," Winsen said, testing it out. "Meh, it's not quite as good as King's Guard, but I'll take it."

Several others in the room—locals—looked stricken. Kip was going to abandon the city to Daragh the Coward?

Kip had no hope that word of that wouldn't get out quickly. He only hoped it didn't get to Daragh before their meeting. The timing here could get dicey.

"Bring in the scribes," Kip said. "I'll want twelve copies made to distribute throughout the satrapies. Lady Guile, would you look over the language?"

There you go, grandfather. I don't know if you could have done better yourself.

Maybe Kip was learning something about this diplomacy business after all.

90   'Kip'? Make that 'Satrap Guile.'

Chapter 15

"You still don't trust me," Aliviana said.

The White King didn't even turn from the mortal he was conversing with, some engineer or something. "You can't lie, my dear. Why would I trust you?"

"What is that supposed to mean?" She let the 'my dear' go this time.

He shot her that deprecatory look again. "You're honest. You have to be, so I trust you not to lie to me. I also trust you to be lousy at lying to anyone else."

"I'm not a child," she said.

Still not turning toward her, he said, "What do you want, Liv?" exactly as one would address a child.

The engineer made to withdraw.

"Why have I been denied being in charge of communications? I'm Ferrilux, goddess of superviolet. It is what I do."

"It is what you will do," Koios said. "Integrating our forces will take time, and I can't risk you bungling anything at this juncture."

"So you don't trust me not to bungle things?"

"Yes, that's exactly it," he said.

"Fuck you," she said.

He made no move toward her, but the papers in his hands suddenly went up in flames. The engineer staggered backward and fell with a yelp.

"My apologies," Koios said to the man finally.

"No trouble at all, Your Majesty," he said, slowly getting up and retreating. "I'll redraw the schematics and bring them back immediately."

"No need. It looks excellent. You may go."

Koios turned toward her. "Not in front of the mortals, please?"

"Done," she said. "I want access to all your research as you promised, and my bane. It's been two days since we took our oath—"

"You were supposed to show me how to make my own oath stones!"

"I did."

"You know my superviolets couldn't follow what you did."

Of course she did.

"You will know how to make oath stones before I leave, this I promise. After the battle. I couldn't very well hand you chains you could so easily put on me, now, could I?"

He took a deep breath. "You won. I shan't underestimate you again."

"We both win, Your Majesty," she said. "Now, let me help us win the real war. My research and my bane. Please. And if you'd tell me the plan, I could actually help it succeed. Which is, after all, the whole point, isn't it?"

He weighed her with his color-knotted eyes, waves of different luxins rising and falling within them as he called on each in turn. "Apology accepted," he said. "You'll have the superviolet research and command, and the bane."

She didn't leave.

"Today," he said. "By my word."

He glanced at the oath stone; she carried it at her neck. Last year, he'd tried to chain her with a black luxin necklace. Now, it pleased her to remind him of it with a chain that bound them both instead.

"You're really going to throw it in the sea?" he asked.

"When I leave. As I promised."

"What would happen if I destroyed it instead?"

"That would be very difficult. But if you succeeded... You bound your will to it, utterly. Break one, break the other. I've told you all this. It should not be news."

"It isn't. I wanted you to repeat it in different words so I could tell if you meant what your words seemed to mean before."

He strode over to a map.

"Kip is here," he said, not bothering to wait for her to reach him before he started. "We're here. Dúnbheo has massive numbers of ships and excellent docks, so coming down the Great River and turning up the coast here could take Kip's Nightbringers possibly as little as two weeks. Less if they pack only essentials and don't expect a protracted fight. Coming overland would likely take four weeks, three at best."

"And you said we're about three weeks from launching the armada," she said. It was significantly later than she'd first assumed, and that meant she might have to hedge this bet of joining Koios. "So if he doesn't figure out what you're doing for another week or two, he can't possibly make it?"

"He's got less time than that, actually," Koios said. His grin was skeletal under the hard blue luxin.

She raised her hands palm up.

"We've seized the Great River," the White King said, "right behind his back."

"You what? How'd you manage that?"

He looked immensely pleased with himself. "In many ways, my

wights are inferior to the Chromeria's drafters. But they're also fearless. We've made great strides with magics long buried."

"What? Some kind of night magic?"

"No luck with that. The *caoránaigh.*"

"What is that? Sea monsters?"

"Wights who've transformed their bodies as much as possible for the water. They took the names of old monsters to make people fear them. Actually, though, I wonder if what they are is exactly what those old monsters were. They can go wherever the rivers go, unseen, and board boats before anyone knows they're there."

"How many do you have?" Aliviana asked.

"Enough. Mercenaries on the shores for fortifications and intel. Wights in the woods, wights in the waters. No one escapes. The silence won't hold forever, but it's already held longer than I'd dared hope. Long enough."

"And if he figures out your little plan? What if—"

"Hardly 'little.' No one's ever done it before."

"For good reason!" she said. "What if Kip moves faster than you imagine? He's done it before, I hear. Surprising you time and again, defeating your forces over and over?"

"And always pushing deeper and deeper into Blood Forest as he did so."

"And why do you care? The capital's there, and you'll never hold the satrapy without Green Haven. Not for long. These people—"

"The people of this satrapy believe Kip is the Lightbringer. Their Luíseach."

She put her hands to her cheeks in mock horror. "Oh no, the Lightbringer! Whatever shall we do?" She shook her head. "Are we really going to start listening to what desperate peasants say? Do you know what they say about *you*?"

"I believe it, too."

"Excuse me?"

He didn't seem to be joking.

"This is Kip Delauria we're talking about, right? Of Rekton? I've known him all his life. He's not some mystical being, Lucidonius reborn or something. He's a fat kid. A cringing whinger. There's nothing in him of—"

"It doesn't matter. I don't care how you cover for your old boyfriend—"

"I'm not covering and he's not—"

"You misunderstand. I don't care if he really is the Lightbringer."

She couldn't follow that at all. Either he'd gone mad, or... "You know something I don't," she said.

He looked at her as if surprised by her astuteness.

That rankled. Underestimating me? Still? I will burn you.

The White King said, "As long as the Lightbringer's not on the Jaspers when I arrive, the Jaspers will fall."

"How do you know that? Because some prophecy says so? I thought all this superstitious horseshit was just a put-on until you fully seized power, like your 'freeing' of the slaves."

"Silence!" he roared.

His guards shifted uncomfortably, looking at each other uncertainly. Oh, hadn't everyone seen through that foolishness by now?

She turned her attention to Koios. She couldn't tell if he'd yelled because she was right or because she was wrong. Even as she was getting better at divining the tells that showed this emotion or that, her own emotions were growing more distant, more mysterious, and her intuition getting worse. Reading anger and fear didn't tell her for which reasons he was angry and afraid.

"You don't understand how this works at all, do you?" he sneered. "Hell, it could be real."

"This *prophecy*?" she asked.

"Since Guile burned me, I've seen things that bent my mind in half. The Chromeria's too quick to dismiss what it doesn't control. I'm sorry to see that you do the same. Maybe you didn't escape their tutelage soon enough. Maybe their weakness infected you."

"How dare you!" she said, but he didn't even stop.

Him talking about things that had bent his mind in half didn't bode well. Even if the Chromeria oversold the dangers of going wight, this man was a wight seven times over, and was trying for nine.

"But the accuracy of the prophecy doesn't matter," he went on. "The *belief* in it is what matters. The prophecy I'm talking about is not well-known—but by the time my armada arrives, it will be. Everyone on Big and Little Jasper will know they need this young Guile—that their own prophecies, written by one of their most credible prophets, say they need him."

"You'll be making things even easier for Kip, then. If you position him as the only hope for the satrapies, you'll be helping unite the satrapies behind him. Do you not see that as more than a little dangerous? I'm no strategist, but maybe uniting our enemies isn't the best idea?"

Actually saying she was no strategist was a bit difficult. It was only partly true. Far more difficult still was accepting the look he gave her: like she was stupid.

"The loyalists will know that their sole and slim hope of victory rests on Kip being there when I arrive—and he won't be. So they'll know they're doomed. Do you know what happens when people know that if they fight you, they're doomed to certain death and gruesome tortures? I do. I've tested it out."

"So you have priests on the Jaspers to spread your messages."

"I've got more than that, but you don't need to know all my plans."

"And you're certain Kip can't get there?"

"I know how long it takes to move an army a lot better than he does. Even moving at the greatest possible speed, he can't arrive here in time to stop us unless he marches from Dúnbheo in the next two days. And I've arranged for that to be impossible."

She didn't know how he intended to do that, but at the least it meant the White King had people in Dúnbheo, and a way to communicate with them rapidly, exactly as she'd suspected.

"And how do you have any idea who he is at all? He's surprised you again and again. He's destroyed your forces at every turn. You've never even met him."

"You think I underestimate your friend?"

"He is a Guile," Liv said.

"A Guile made me this!" the king roared, and his skin flared hot and red.

But he calmed suddenly. The fierce heat died down. Liv saw one of the king's bodyguards gulp.

"Pardon," Koios said. "I misspoke. I made myself into this regal shape before you, carved of pure will. But a Guile made it necessary. Kip's uncle Dazen, when he was about Kip's age. Or had you forgotten?"

"I only knew there was a fire," Liv said, and her voice came out softer than she'd have liked.

"Dazen planned to elope with my sister Karris. The family needed her to marry Gavin, the elder brother. Love be damned. And we might remarry her after forcing a divorce, of course. But not to her ex-husband's brother. It would smack of old taboos, and our family honor couldn't take that. Nor could we give Andross Guile such power over us. So we set a trap for Dazen. Sealed the windows. Chained the doors and gates shut after he got in. He was only a blue/green bichrome, and it was after midnight. We got Karris's maid to take his lenses under some pretense, to pack with Karris's things or some such. He was disarmed." His eyes took on a distant look, red pain outlined with spiky black hatred, or black hatred impregnated with red pain, such that the two had mingled to a hue that stained the soul forever.

"We set upon him. Started beating him. It got out of hand. All the years of White Oaks being humiliated and outmaneuvered. Those smiling, beautiful, adored and entitled and *deified* fucking Guile brothers. There was this moment when Rodin tried to stop us, and my brothers and I looked at each other…and without a word, the rest of us decided to kill Dazen. And in that split second where we hesitated? That son of a bitch split light. He was a natural Prism, as the world hadn't seen since Vician's Sin. Four hundred years—and we stumble upon a true Prism. I remember the look in his eyes as it happened. I think he was as surprised as we were.

"Rodin threw up a shield—trying to help the *Guile*, against his own brothers. That's what Guiles do, Aliviana. They turn brother against brother. Rodin went down first in the crossfire."

You mean you killed him. Or one of your brothers did. Otherwise you'd blame Dazen for that murder, too.

"But it was still one bloodied man against all the rest of us, and we were drafters all. And he had no light! Around corners so he couldn't draft off them, we popped mag torches, and then we came at him. And you want to know what this lightsplitter does next?"

"What?"

"He *absorbs* everything we throw at him. Luxin missiles and streams of fire. Darts. Spears. Blades and waves. Projectiles and pure heat. Everything."

"What?! That's not how lightsplitting works—" Liv started.

"Black luxin. As if he didn't have enough tricks. He soaked up everything we threw at him, and he threw it all back at us. Killed us all. Only I made it to the courtyard fountain. Others of our household tried to take refuge with me there from the smoke and heat and flames, but I fought them off lest we all die. The water heated, unbearably. I burned, boiling like a crab in a kettle. And only that night's breeze kept the smoke from killing me as it did so many others. Some mercy. The pain is with me daily, still."

"I'm sorry," Liv said. It didn't seem at all adequate, but what could be?

"It's no matter. Dazen Guile destroyed the old Koios White Oak that I had been that night, but he showed me the key to what I could become. He showed me that black luxin is possible. And soon, I learned to draft it. I'm no lightsplitter, but with black luxin, I can do everything I need in order to destroy the Guiles. All of them."

"Even your sister?" Liv asked.

His eyes flashed. "She's a White Oak in my eyes, unless she chooses to be a Guile. I wouldn't choose Rodin's fate for her, but if she chooses to stand with the Guiles…?"

"She'll deserve it," Liv said. She guessed then, from the hardness in his eyes, that it had been Koios himself who'd killed his brother that day. Koios had seen the vulnerability Rodin opened. The rest of the White Oak brothers would be reluctant to attack for fear of harming Rodin, and Koios couldn't let that stand.

He'd killed his own brother, and blamed Dazen.

He was crazy, but only in the implacable I-don't-care-what-my-victory-costs-you sense. And he'd been that way before the fire.

He said, "So now, tell me, Aliviana Danavis, my new Ferrilux, do you think that I—of all people—will underestimate a Guile?"

"I see that you have very good reasons not to."

"But you have no faith in me? You really do have the arrogance of Ferrilux, don't you?"

That didn't merit a response.

"Kip is easily handled," he said. "Kip is like his father, not his grandfather. He reacts to the needs in front of him. He sees people, not numbers, not cards to play. To him, no one is disposable. He is brilliant, else I would have destroyed him already—and you're right, I've tried. But the way to beat Kip remains simple: I'll beat him with present needs and battles and victories far away from where they might matter. In terms of that game his grandfather likes so much, it doesn't matter what card Kip pulls. He's playing at the wrong table. And I'll keep him there until the real game is decided."

She hesitated, but again, she was getting worse about not speaking her mind. "That...eases my mind a great deal, but you've only established that if he stays in Dúnbheo a few more days, he can't get here with his full army."

"Do you want to know how delicious I find this?" the king said.

"What?" Was he even listening to her?

"We are the old gods reborn, Aliviana. We are the nightmare that has kept luxiats and magisters awake at night for a thousand years. Do you not see the irony? I tried to kill Dazen Guile—and I couldn't! Orholam sent the Chromeria the only man who could possibly save them from me. And I couldn't kill him, but *they* did."

"Your Highness," Liv said, "what if Kip comes at speed, with only his elite drafters?"

The White King's eyes lit with the cold blue of crackling luxin. "Oh, I hope he does. Come, my dear—" He stopped, seeming to note her fury at being called his 'dear.' "Pardon," the White King said. "I meant, come with me, my fierce young partner. Let me show you the real reason our temples were known as the 'bane.'"

Chapter 16

So that's where we're gonna die.

For the entire trip, a vast, swirling bank of clouds on the horizon had cloaked White Mist Reef like an anonymous assassin, but today Gavin's doom stood stripped of outer garments.

In ages past, it had been said that the heavens were held from falling down onto the earth by one pillar alone, as the Prism alone held up the Chromeria.

In times past, before the swirling storms, before the mist itself, it had been said that the tent of the sky itself was upheld by one tent pole. As they now came to the Chromeria, the faithful from all over the world had once made pilgrimage to climb it. The luxiats said that only after Vician's Sin had Orholam hidden the tower and the island, raising a reef to bar any entry to such holy ground, and raising the mist itself to hide His own connection to the earth. In grief at their disobedience and rejection of him, He'd covered His face from the world.

So the luxiats said.

Others said an isle of glass lay there, and the reef and the mist had risen after an earthquake had plunged the isle into the sea.

Even as a child, Gavin had wondered how much of either tale was true. He'd longed to come here one day to see for himself.

As a young Prism, he'd wanted to come here to confront Orholam, but he'd always wanted to live more.

He'd always assumed the descriptions he'd read of White Mist Tower must be either fanciful or poetic, describing the feelings evoked by seeing a tragically formerly holy place, rather than literal descriptions of the thing itself. The ancients were an emotional tribe, after all, as much given to hyperbole as were sailors.

White Mist Tower wasn't literally a tower, but it did look eerily like a tower carved from blocks of white mist. Gavin squinted against the distance. As if imprisoned inside a glass shell, the clouds of the 'tower' spiraled in a dense circle, swirling constantly but not in accord with the prevailing wind. The outlines of that ephemeral tower were unmoved by the nautical winds, and sprawled wider than the entire island they obscured. White Mist Tower wasn't like a tornado or waterspout. Those were diffuse, mutable, and mobile. This tower was of equal thickness from where its foot rested atop the reef itself to where its head was lost in the heavens.

Though it was still at least a day's travel away, even from here and even on a bright sunlit day like today, the mixture of the natural and unnatural about the form was stomach-twisting. Gavin could only imagine the effect on sailors on more foreboding days, seeing a natural mist suddenly yield to that monstrosity without warning.

"Big lux storm last night," Gunner said, coming up to Gavin at the railing. "And you, sleeping through all the rough action like my last port-girlie done, trustin' daddy Gunner to take you safe through the storm."

Yuck. "Lux storm?" Gavin asked instead.

"Common roun' here."

"They are?!" Gavin asked. "I've never read anything about that."

"You Chromeriacs. If it ain't writ down, it don't exist for ya," Gunner said, shaking his head. "Takes a big storm to get this good a view'a the mist tower. Purty, uh? Hope it stays this nice when we trya shoot the gap inna reef."

But Gavin had suddenly lost interest in the enormous tower of mist far before them, or their navigational choices. "A lux storm? Really?"

"Nornj 'un. Queerest thing ya ever seen. Sheets, orange sheets. You know how folks call lots a rain 'sheets a rain'?"

"Sure."

"Not like that. This uz like a ribbon unfurlin' from the skies to the depths. Gorgeous. Gorgeous, 'cept for the vijuns."

"Visions?" Gavin asked. Gunner hadn't woken him for *that*?

"Some says a man sees what's in his heart out there."

"That's not how orange works."

"Innit?" Gunner asked sharply. "Lots of experience with lorange ux storms, eh?"

Orange lux storms.

"No," Gavin admitted.

"Pro'lem of rewardin' men o' will, like your Chromeria do. You all impose whatcha think oughta be, ignoring what *is* when it ain't convenient." Gunner twisted a bit of his beard and poked it between his teeth. Then sucked on it. "One little plop as the sheet first dropped, like a hard turd hittin' a full chamber pot, then nothing except a rush. Solid connection from the seas to the heavens. Afterward, some the men swore they saw a whale." He shrugged. "Like I said. Vijuns."

"A whale?"

"Black whale. Immense. O' course, I'm not sure what other color a whale would look like at night, and no one ever says, 'Oh, take a looksie at that relatively small whale.'" Gunner twisted his lips. "Heard plenty of sailor stories, even when men weren't in a hallucino-jammy—halloosina—halluxination storm. But a whale? I near whipped a man this mornin' what wouldn't stop goin' on with his lies, swearin' a black whale nudged the port quarterdeck, like a little kiss."

What the hell? There hadn't been whales in the Cerulean Sea in centuries. Scholars said the closing of the Everdark Gates had choked off some essential migration route, either sealing them out while they were gone or keeping them in to die.

"That's where you sleep, innit?" Gunner asked. His cunning eyes glittered.

"Eh?" Gavin asked. He could tell the question held some kind of danger, but he had no idea why.

"Port quarterdeck's where you fold your hands, aye?"

"What's it matter? It didn't happen," Gavin said. "You said so yourself."

"*I* know it di'n't happen. *You* know it. But when men who oughta fookin' hate a Guile start believin' mythical beasties o' the deep are paying homage to 'im, I gotta ask who *they* think you are. I esk that, and then I gotta esk myself who *you* think you are. Mebbe you been plyin' some o' that Guile grease, pullin the world 'round the tackle o' yer desires, eh? Liftin' men with the halyard o' yer will, all tricksy like ya be. Mebbe I gotta clap ya back in chains to reminder everyone what you is?"

"I've said nothing to them," Gavin said. It was almost literally true. Going on a mission like this, they were all dead men already. No need to bond with his enemies.

"Who is ya, Guile? Yestiddy you'd said you'd fight, afore your end. Whaddaya see when you look in the mirror? A fighter?"

What kind of question was that? Of course Gavin was a fighter.

"You fightin' *me*, Guile? After all what I done for ya?"

Gunner gripped Gavin's face suddenly, his hands sharp and hard with callus and sinew. He wrenched Gavin's chin toward himself and bored his eyes into Gavin's.

Gavin accepted it. Maybe he only *had been* a fighter. Maybe his talk of fighting at the end yesterday wasn't a wry boast; maybe it was an empty boast.

"O Dazen Guile," Gunner mocked. His eyes were glittering mirrors as dark and sharp and dangerous as living black luxin. "O Master of Land Ways and Sea Ways, Man of Low Cunning and High Artifice, what are ye now?"

What. Not who.

Gunner released his chin, abruptly dismissive.

He who had flown, literally flown, in the peerless machina he'd dubbed his condor, tasting a freedom no one ever had before; he, a genius whose field of play had encompassed the sky itself—he himself was being dragged where he didn't want to go, blackmailed, afraid, passive. He couldn't even blame actual chains now, as he might have when he'd been a slave—

—Enslaved! It's different!

He was crippled. Half-blind. Enslaved, yes. But enslaved, not *a slave*. His bondage had been a temporary condition, not an identity. Emperor Gavin Guile had setbacks, not losses. He was Gavin Guile, victor. Never Gavin Guile, victim.

But really.

Seriously now.

How long has it been since that was true?

"You really t'ink you're gonna fight the suckin' sand? Then why'd you wander into this bog in the first place?" Gunner said.

Suddenly another piece of this dangerous little man snapped into focus for Gavin. Gunner was the soul of tenacity. That was what had made him the best cannoneer in the world. When a mystery or even a whim took Gunner in its teeth, he would follow it to the bitter end. If a shot wobbled, another man might fire another ten rounds from his cannons to figure out why before abandoning it as fruitless; Gunner would empty a treasury to fire a thousand rounds until he understood exactly why one shot deviated a hand's breadth from the last.

"That's a shit question," Gavin said, forgetting for a moment who he wasn't. "The whole world's a bog. Some stay on a safe path, some step off it unwittingly, some are led off it, and some are pushed. All that matters is that once caught in the bog, some fight, some ask for help, and some lie down."

Gunner picked his teeth. "You been lyin' down lots."

That stung. When he wasn't sunning himself, ostensibly to accustom his eyes to the brightness of the sun, but really hoping to reawaken his magic and his color vision, Gavin had been sleeping like the dead. He woke late and went to his rack early, not to plot but to sleep. He was actually starting to feel human again after his imprisonment, no longer so easily tired—but before this past year had demolished him so thoroughly, he'd been one of the most highly energetic men he'd ever known. Gunner's barb was a reminder that he was not now what once he had been.

"A metaphor's a gun. You gotta know its range," Gavin said, with less defiance than he'd intended.

"Aye. But even a man firin' at greatest random hits the mark sometimes," Gunner said. "Like what your man Commander Ironfist done at Ru. Snatched your bacon from the coals, eh? But I guess you were speakin' o' metty-force. Metal farcically...?"

"They trip up the best of us," Gavin said, smirking.

Sudden as a summer squall races over the horizon, Gunner's face went murder dark. "And how 'bout the worst of us? You got a bone to prick with me, Guile?"

Gavin blinked. "It's, uh, it's only an expression. I meant it could happen to any of us."

"You di'n't say that. And a Guile never misspeaks. And when a Guile says 'the best of us,' he means hisself. You meant yourself, didn't you?"

"In this, uh, particular instance, I—You know something, Gunner? Captain Gunner, I mean. Sir."

"Something?! Do I know something?!" The little man drew himself to his full height and grabbed his wild beard in a defiant fist. He slapped his chest. "Cap'n Gunner knows half the mysteries of the sea and sky, and all lissome lies and winsome ways of a woman's wink, and more of the conundra of the cannonade than other cunts kin count!" He frowned at a sudden thought. "Also not bad with a fiddle."

Gavin took a deep breath. "You know why we're doing this?" Gavin asked.

Gunner ignored him. "Also a fair hand with a fiddle. Also a fine... Aha! A fair fine fiddler, too!"

"Do you know why we're doing this?" Gavin repeated.

"I heard ya! It's only din a few bays. Days. I ain't forgot. We go to ensconce our legends in the firmament of the Celestine! They'll be naming constellations after us. Me mostly, 'tis truth, but there's stars enough to go 'round."

"That ain't the why for me," Gavin said.

Gunner made his voice small, whiny, mocking: "'We're already legends!' says you. I know. So why for you? You really think you'll save your lady's skin? From the master o' *them*?" Gunner threw his chin toward his Order crew, meaning Grinwoody.

"You ever wonder if you're a good man, Gunner?"

"Eh?" Gunner scrunched his face like he was trying to pick some jerked meat out between his teeth with his tongue. "I'm tops at most things what I put my hand to. But being a man? Ain't really something you gotta try at if you're in our perfessions, aye? Not sure what kinda pirate worries 'bout how manly he is." Gunner stopped, looked at his first mate. "Pansy!"

The woman, with her hair glued in hard, spiky points, resembled a
flower in zero respects; she was at the ship's wheel on the sterncastle,

twenty paces away. Her body was as hard as a terebinth tree clinging to a wind-torn cliff, and her face was harder still. "Aye, Cap'n?" she shouted, even her voice harsh.

"Pansy, you ever worry 'bout how manly you are?"

She answered immediately. "Daily, Cap'n!"

"Didn't think so!" Gunner said. He scowled at Gavin.

Gavin couldn't tell if the pirate was taking the piss.

He tried another tack. "Captain, I got a head full o' books, enough to know a few things. For good and ill, history's written with a blood-dipped quill. Good men died, fighting against me, under the banners of bad men, held there perhaps by old loyalties or law. But that never bothered me. We who gamble in taking up arms with the intent to kill know that our own lives are our ante," Gavin said. "But I get this dream. Not every night, but often enough to dread sleep. In it, I'm manacled to a kneeler, and buckets of blameless blood march into a darkened room and pour themselves over my hands while I fight to get away, and all the time, they *shriek* at me. You ken?"

Gunner nodded.

Ridiculous. Gavin had never told anyone about that. Maybe he would've told Karris, if they'd had longer together.

"From the Freein'?" Gunner asked.

"Aye." 'Ayes' and 'ain'ts' now seasoned Gavin's speech like salt in jerked meat. "There was this girl…" He trailed off. And at the end, he'd given her death. He gave them all death.

It made him want to vomit all over again. How could I have done that?

"Ya killed her, I s'pose? So what? It's the voyage they sign on for, innit?" Gunner asked. "Yer drafters."

"It is," Gavin allowed, narrowly avoiding using another 'aye.'

"Then what's the pro'lem? They know the deal: Light duty mos' times, respect e'erwhere, good pay, and when they take the last lonely boat, their family gets a sack o' gold. They get all that, and in return they gotta obey and they get a short life. Sailors get nothing 'ceptin' the obedience and short life."

Putting it like that, it didn't sound like such a bad deal. Better than working a farm until the arthritis made every move hell, and then working it another ten years, prayin' you could hold on to life until your sons and daughters could fend for themselves.

Didn't sound like a bad deal, when you were fifteen years old and forty sounded ancient and they asked you to scrawl your damn idiot signature on the vow.

But it didn't seem like such a good deal when you were a father who still felt young and you held an infant in your arms who'd already never know her drafter mother, and the Prism who'd killed her first now asked you to hand over the child to some uncaring luxiat so he could slice your heart out, too.

It didn't seem like such a good deal when you were the man who held the knife and murdered artist kids like Aheyyad Brightwater.

"In all my time as the head of the faith," Gavin said, "I could never come up with more than two questions that were worth a damn. As it were."

It sailed over Gunner's head. In his world, 'damn' was for punctuation, not punning. And it wasn't the full truth anyway. Gavin had a third question, but he didn't let himself even think it too loudly.

Gavin looked at the great tower of cloud on the horizon, growing ever closer.

"Two questions?" Gunner prompted. "Or did you mean that metty-forcibly?"

"No. I mean, yes? First: is Orholam real? And second: if He is real, is He like we think He is?"

Gunner was looking at him like he wasn't making sense. "Uh... what?"

Gavin tried again. "You and I, Captain, we've seen the shit. The real problem with Orholam comes if He is who He says He is."

"And who else would he be?" Gunner asked. "Hand me that hoo-dad, wouldja?"

Gavin handed him a brush, then other tools, one by one, as Gunner proceeded to happily clean the great cannon on the front quarterdeck.

All his life, he'd kicked against the goads: Tell me I have to do this? I'll find my own way, and you can go to hell. When the dichotomy was 'Do I obey Grinwoody or do I defy him?' given Gavin's nature, that wasn't even a choice.

But defying Grinwoody meant either a fast death (say, by blurting out his name while wearing this stabby hellstone eye patch) or a slow one (by accepting failure and death), so Gavin, despairing and defiant but not suicidal, had chosen 'slow.'

'Slow' meant becoming passive. And his whole soul hated that. Sinking into sarcasm is the heart's last rebellion against a mind choosing helplessness.

Logical step to inexorable step, his answers had marched him into waters that now closed over his head. When your answers lead you logically to despair, you don't have the wrong answers; you have the right answers—to the wrong questions.

Gavin didn't want to give Grinwoody what he wanted, but there was

no way out. In his current state and situation, Gavin couldn't outsmart him or outfight him or out-magic him. He couldn't deny Grinwoody what he wanted.

But that was framing the problem exactly wrong. In truth, it didn't matter what Grinwoody wanted—it mattered what Gavin wanted.

Gavin didn't want Grinwoody to win...? Gavin didn't want to die...?

Divergent as those seemed, both of them were importantly distinct from wanting victory or wanting life.

What *do* I want?

Odd thing to wonder, here, when he had no power to get it. Before, he'd never asked it in any profound way. His 'great' goals for every seven years he served as Prism hadn't been great in any way. They'd been field dressings on a gaping wound of purposelessness. His house-broken dream had been merely to stay alive, to not be unmasked as a fraud.

Sure, that made sense for a month or two after the war while he healed.

But he'd never become more. Never dreamed more than declawed dreams.

He'd put his brother in the grave, but Dazen had also died at Sundered Rock.

What did Gavin want?

Which Gavin?

Time stretched, as if something were supposed to happen right now—but nothing did. Gavin looked around. Nothing. Odd. He sank back into his thoughts.

Maybe Gavin only wanted to win.

In Gavin's place, a *hero* would strive for some positive good. Say, to save the empire. That kind of goal would ready him to fight a diverse host of battles. He would be one man: integrated, of one purpose, strong whether he had to fight to save the empire from foreign enemies, or from traitors, or from those corrupting it, or if it needed renewing, he would be strong enough to undertake even its reformation. A hero might begin one kind of fight and then any of those others in turn and still be a whole man.

Such people had lived before: heroes and heroines with clear eyes and straight backs. And short lives, often. Sure, but villains got those, too, so maybe that was a wash.

It was all moot. Gavin wasn't a hero. He didn't believe in heroes anymore, and he didn't believe in a god who could let this world become what it was.

He'd been fighting Grinwoody because fighting was what Gavin did. So Gavin had been preparing, but passionlessly. He'd treated Grinwoody's demands as merely another prison that he had to figure out how to escape...and yet, even with his own life and all the world on the wager, Gavin hadn't found any heart for the effort.

He just didn't care to save the Chromeria. Not in the abstract.

He loved many people there. But the Chromeria itself was as corrupt as he was. The 'White King' was a murderer, a liar when it served him, and a wielder of oversimplifications, but Gavin couldn't object to the basic charge that the Chromeria was often shitty, and had been throughout history. Nor could he claim that the Magisterium, whose High Luxiats were entrenched beside those in power and empowered to speak against them, had, instead of standing against those abusing power, become indistinguishable from them. When was the last time a High Luxiat had called Gavin to account for something he'd done? Not since the first year, not even in private.

Gavin didn't believe Koios's reign would bring a society that was any better, certainly not so much better that it was worth the seas of blood he was spilling to establish it.

The universe had conspired to give Gavin one chance to go where he'd never dared go. Here, now, Gavin and only Gavin might actually confront Orholam—or prove He wasn't there at all.

What if, instead of turning all his genius to figuring out some third way out of Grinwoody's errand, treating the task as if it were merely another prison...

What if, instead, Gavin put his whole mind and heart and will into actually...succeeding?

He had to admit, the audacity of the quest was vastly appealing.

No, it was damn near irresistible.

Maybe the Old Man of the Desert was so clever he'd been counting on exactly this. It didn't matter. What *he* wanted was beside the point—if Gavin wanted it too.

Gavin hadn't had an audacious thought since he'd lost his powers. This? This wasn't audacious. This was legendary.

How do you prove once and for all that there's no God? How do you show that even if He *is* there, He's small and weak and unworthy of adoration? How do you prove that Orholam doesn't see, He doesn't hear, He doesn't care, He doesn't save?

You show up on His front door, uninvited. You go inside without knocking. You take a look around. And if you like the place...

A thrill shot through Gavin. It was his first great goal again, so carefully concealed for so long. There was nothing more impossible—

and that very thought was like a breath of clean air after months in the must and stench of himself in the black cell.

The Old Man of the Desert, Grinwoody, real name Amalu Anazâr, hoped to change the world's entire social and political order by killing magic itself. He believed that what lay at the center of White Mist Reef wasn't a personality, but simply the central node upon which the whole network of magic depended. He thought if Gavin destroyed that, all magic would fail.

Grinwoody thought that would change the world. He thought that was enough.

Grinwoody was wrong.

Throwing luxin around was merely a personal power. The genius of the Chromeria as an organization was that through education first and coercion later, they'd turned that power into communal power, then traditional power, first subservient to political power, then enmeshed with it, and finally indistinguishable from it. They had ensconced themselves in the world's politics and culture and religion and trade. But even if a sconce is originally placed high so that it may cast its light far, if the fire it held dies, the sconce remains, and it remains in its high place. So, too, the Chromeria's social and political and commercial and ceremonial power would falter if magic were lost, but it wouldn't necessarily be broken.

Destroying magic wasn't enough.

Fearing the lash, even freed of his chains, the slave will still pull at his oar, but men of unfettered soul, who though chained are still whole, will smash it like trash on the floor.

Magic was one major tool by which Orholam and Orholam's Chosen worked His will in the world, but they had others. People didn't send their daughters to be living and dying sacrifices to the Chromeria because of magic, but because they believed it was what Orholam demanded.

Gavin—High Lord Gavin Guile, Emperor, Promachos, and mighty Prism, Orholam's Chosen, the Highest Luxiat, the Defender of the Faith—Gavin the Liar Prince, the High Deceiver, was the only one who might be able to kill the religion itself. Down to its rotten root.

If that fell, everything built on it would, too.

He who'd been 'blessed' with the gift of black luxin could kill the Lord of Light and watch tumble all the horrors built on men's fear of Him. Half-blind and chained and toothless as he was, Gavin might stagger to the pillars that upheld the roof of the empire. He might find strength had come once more to his old muscular will—strength enough to lever apart the pillars upholding the very heavens and bring it all down. Gavin the Liar, who'd murdered innocents to uphold others' lies, could destroy the greatest lie of all.

Gavin would bring down the rebels, not in order to save the empire but in order to make it fall correctly.

Fuck the old way. Fuck the new way. As he had always been, he himself would be the third way. He would be himself, and he would be terrible. He would come back from death, come back from this journey to heaven and hell, and Gavin would invert all they had hoped. Gavin, the Son of the Morning, the Bright Hope of the World, had been cast down into a ninefold hell. But he hadn't stayed down. He'd broken through and escaped from one color of hell to another and another—until his own father had shut him into the inner darkness. The blackest heart of Chromeria, its very foundation.

From those depths, a nameless wretch had been sent to scale the heavens and kill God Himself. Who could return from such an impossible journey?

Only one man. Only one man might have been born for such a thing. Only one who could make and remake himself, who refused to die, who defied the schemes of those who held every advantage over him—and won.

Triumphant, with a cloak of fire and a crown of blood, Dazen the Black would return. He would bring down heaven and he would raze hell.

But.

Gavin could only triumph if he did what no one had ever done: he must make it through White Mist Reef, scale the Tower of Heaven, kill Orholam, and then make it back home to escape, outwit, and destroy the Order—he'd need to do all that by Sun Day if he were to save Karris.

Then he could live happily ever after.

Easy.

Of course, he could say nothing of all this. Not among these doomed servants of the Order.

But he wasn't one of the doomed anymore. Not in his own mind.

Looking over at Gunner, Gavin felt the old, reckless, confident Guile grin spread over his face for the first time in eons. "Gunner? Captain? Let's go find God. I'll bring the sword, just in case He's a dick."

Gunner's mercurial mood abruptly stilled. All the guns of his attention drew broadside. His eyes weighed Gavin, judging velocity, pitch, charge, spin. Eyes tightening, he calculated windage, current, the target's distance, speed, and parallax.

Gavin welcomed the judgment, fatal as it might be. The end began here. This was Gunner's destiny. He *would* join Gavin; he simply didn't know it yet.

Frankly, but fearlessly, his demeanor void of forced jollity or feigned madness, Gunner said, "You must know that's impossible."

"Impossible is what I do."

Chapter 17

By his own count, Daragh the Coward had four hundred seventeen scars—none of them on his back. It might not have been an exaggeration. The bandit lord had bragged that there was one scar for each kill. It was said that if the killed man hadn't possessed the skill to cut Daragh as they fought, Daragh cut himself. He bore one scar for each man. Deeper or longer for the men he respected.

He didn't kill women or children. Or, if one believed the darker rumors, he simply didn't think they counted enough to deserve their own scars when he did kill them.

Kip was the son of an emperor. He didn't want to be impressed at the sight of the man who'd strolled into the audience chamber this morning as if he owned it, but there was no denying that Daragh was impressive. Daragh the Coward didn't just have four hundred seventeen scars covering his arms and cheeks and forehead and fists: every one of his scars was hypertrophic. Hypertrophic scars didn't spread beyond the original wound like keloid scars did, but they did puff up, thick and red against Daragh's olive skin, cartilaginous and angry.

Apparently such scars often itched terribly.

Which made the bandit lord's skin a striped shrine not only to human mortality past, but to one man's misery past and present.

Kip regarded the bandit with lidded eyes. This wasn't going to be easy. He knew what he had to do.

Daragh the Coward wore his dark, curly hair in long dreadlocks piled into a tail on top of his head. He tucked his tight breeches into rich knee-high boots. Doubtless in order to better display his mutilated pelt, he wore no tunic, only a leather weapons harness, currently with many empty sheaths and pistol hooks, as the Mighty had resolutely refused his demands to come into Kip's presence armed.

Kip had been tired of being the center of attention all the time, so he'd expected to feel relieved as the smiling bandit king drew every eye.

Instead, Kip was surprised by how it irked him.

"Your *Highness*," Daragh said, making an elegant bow. He was flanked by two muscular men and followed by three more. Kip presumed they were all warrior-drafters.

" 'My lord' will do," Kip said.

"Ah, but you're not that, are you?" Daragh said pleasantly.

Really? You're going to play the shame-me-with-my-past card? Instead of saying anything, though, Kip merely stared at the man, as if monumentally bored by the stupid games this bandit was trying to play.

The moment stretched uncomfortably, and Kip the Lip somehow managed to hold his words like a disciplined line of infantry holding its fire while enemy cavalry charged into range.

Daragh broke first. He was, after all, the one who had requested this meeting. "Not *my* lord, that is. Not yet, anyway." He gave a gap-toothed grin, backing off from the other possible implication of his words: that Kip was a bastard.

"You fled from your owner seventeen years ago now," Kip said. "That's long enough to learn correct terms of address, even if one were possessed merely of low cunning and not much intelligence."

With some tightness around his eyes, Daragh the Coward smiled again, and Kip could well imagine him holding that same smile while he slid a dagger into your ribs. "We learn different things in the forests and firths than do the soft-handed boys that weaker men call lords."

Kip let the jab hit only air. "I should hope you've learned quite a lot, or we're both wasting our time. You see, Daragh...or, I'm sorry, my own education was geared more toward drafting and war than rhetoric and finer points of alionymics: do you prefer Master the Coward, or is it always Daragh the Coward...? Seems too long for ordinary daily usage. Just Daragh, perhaps? Dar-Dar?"

It had taken Tisis no small amount of prying to find that old nickname, and that Daragh hated it.

The bandit let it roll past, but wet his lips. "Daragh is fine for my friends."

Don't say, 'You can call me Daragh the Coward.'

"You can call me Daragh the Coward. Or Lord Daragh, if you prefer."

Kip sighed.

Grandfather, is this how you feel all the time? Playing against stupid people? "Lord? Baron of the Bayou, I suppose? The Earl of the Estuary? The Count Who Can't?" Kip didn't give him the time to reply. "Enough pleasantries. I would rather be serving this people, and for your part, *Lord* Daragh, you would doubtless rather be raping and murdering them, as you do, but we've things to discuss, don't we? The growth of my power has come at the expense of yours, yet you've been careful to avoid attacking me directly.

"That avoidance doubtless cost you both in money and in the respect of your people, but you're cunning: you wanted to keep an option open, just in case there was a time to jump onto my side. But now things have changed."

Surprisingly, Daragh kept quiet. He wanted to see how accurate Kip's read of him and his situation was.

That suited Kip. He would set the ground rules of this game, and skip past some of the introductory positioning. Except that he had to be careful not to go too far too fast: one of the things he needed not to do was to reach the crisis of this meeting too quickly.

"You've been at this a long time. You know exactly what it costs to keep your men fed. Everyone you'd ordinarily prey upon has fled, *and* you've still not attacked the easy pickings under my protection? Even as, in recent days, your forces have swelled far beyond what you can support through banditry in the best of times. That means you're making your big move. Perhaps you've realized there's not much security in retirement for a bandit. Or perhaps you're not thinking about the growing stiffness in your joints each morning or the pain in your aging back. You want to come back in from the cold, you want lands, you want to stop running, stop watching your back and become a lord—for him or for us. Maybe you don't even care. So you've taken the Wight King's coin and brought as many men here as you can afford to try to extract as much from us as you can.

"It's an obvious ploy," Kip said, though he'd thought himself pretty clever when he figured it out. "But regardless, you bring a not-inconsiderable number of men here, tested in killing if not actually in fighting against those who fight back. So come, let's make like horse traders. What do you want? I've much else to do today."

If Daragh the Coward was aghast at Kip's open assertion that he served the White King, he didn't show it. "My dear b—Lord Guile," he said as if catching himself. "I'm surprised. I come to a room full of people like you all, gracious lords and ladies that you are. But we're all Foresters, are we not? We're not so removed from the earth beneath our toes and the wind in our hair. I see the curiosity in every eye, and yet we've not even taken the time for proper introductions."

"How's that?" Kip said. The man was stalling, trying to reframe the discussion.

"You haven't asked me about my scars," Daragh said. "I—"

"No! No! Of course not!" Kip interrupted as if aghast at the idea.

"So you do know—"

"No, why would I? And I don't need to know. I was taught better than to draw attention to the disabilities of my guests. I'd never! It's uncouth to comment on things a man can't fix: say, a cleft lip, or a lame foot, or even a . . . a regrettable clumsiness at shaving."

The room erupted in shocked laughter.

The laughter hit Daragh the Coward so hard that Kip felt momentarily sorry for him. No one likes to be mocked, but mock a noble and he's still a noble. Mock a shopkeeper, she still owns her shop. But a bandit leader lives on his reputation. Turning this man's fearsome scars into an object of ridicule?

That could be fatal.

"But might I suggest"—Kip paused, as if he'd bumbled into rudeness and wanted to extricate himself—"perhaps . . . just let the beard grow out?"

Murder shot through Daragh the Coward's eyes. He shot a glance at stony Cruxer and then Big Leo, whose expressions said, 'Don't even think about it.' Clearly in the camps he'd lived in for nearly two decades, when one mocked another man, the possibility of personal violence was always on the table. He was unaccustomed to dealing with insults when that was gone.

"I bring five thousand men and you—" Daragh said, raising his voice.

"Five thousand?! Five?!" Kip interrupted. And here was where, if Tisis or Antonius was wrong, he was going to get his ass handed to him. "You have three thousand four hundred men; three hundred more who are casualties, well enough to walk but not to fight; and a thousand more camp followers. And that's counting the cavalry you were hoping to conceal twelve leagues from here in Little Wash. What kind of counting is this? The Count Who Can't Count indeed! Did you really never progress beyond using your fingers and toes?" Kip ticked off numbers on his fingers. " 'Three, four, five . . . oh fuck it, many!'? Or do you expect to negotiate with me while you lie?"

"I assure you our strength is felt far beyond our numbers," Daragh said. "Three hundred fifty drafters ride with us—three hundred forty-eight, for those of you who hold an abacus in one hand while you jerk your cock with the other."

The room went quiet again.

"Well, then, finally. Now we can begin," Kip said quietly, suddenly deathly calm. "Would you rather have a sign-up bonus of twenty denarii per soldier and fifty per cavalryman who brings his own horse and one hundred for every drafter, or would you like one-seventh of all our eventual loot, which will include anything we seize that was formerly the satrap's?"

Daragh the Coward blinked, blinked. Then the weasel came to the fore. "The sign-up, paid up front."

"Half up front," Kip countered. "Half after freeing Green Haven."

"Done." Daragh extended his hand to clasp on it.

Kip didn't move. "So, as it turns out, you're a bit of an abacus man yourself," he said, sneering. "Get out. You're small-time. Do you think a tattered peacock strutting in the mud impresses eagles?"

"So no deal?" Daragh asked, baffled.

Kip laughed derisively. "No, no deal."

Orholam damn it. Three *hundred*–some drafters? That was a real prize. And it was completely possible that Daragh had that many. A drafter was more likely than anyone to flee slavery or indenture, and the most likely to escape successfully.

But Daragh the Coward didn't leave.

He couldn't.

The reason for that was right there in his reputation. 'No scars on his back.' He'd surely put up with his men's complaining about his not raiding Kip's undefended lands. Daragh couldn't leave without at least an insulting offer on the table for him to reject.

Being sent away, like he hadn't been taken seriously by a boy half his age? A boy who'd mocked him?

That would be death to his reputation.

If the man weren't an inveterate murderer and rapist and many other things Kip knew but wished he didn't, Kip would have felt bad for treating him so unfairly.

Sold by Ilytian slavers to a rural Ruthgari lord far up the Great River, young Daragh had had the great misfortune of his master being murdered. The locals were intent on following an old custom: if a man was murdered, all of his slaves were killed for not stopping it.

The theory was that a man couldn't be murdered without his slaves being aware of the plot, or at least deciding not to step in to save him. Besides, who was more likely to murder you than your slaves themselves? One way to dissuade slaves from turning on their masters was to give all the slaves in a household the greatest possible incentive to protect their master, especially from each other.

The Chromeria had eventually succeeded in outlawing such

communal punishment, but outside the bubbles of direct influence they exerted in the cities and on the Jaspers, such slave massacres were rarely reported, rarely investigated, and rarely punished.

Daragh had escaped—some said it was the last time he'd ever run from a fight, thus his title. Then he'd crossed the Great River into Blood Forest and taken up banditry.

What else could an escaped slave do?

Having not grown up with slavery, Kip was still unsettled by the entire institution, and his discomfiture had only grown, the more familiar he'd become with it. His own first experiences with slavery, even with as uncomfortable as they'd been, hadn't been representative.

Speaking with Marissia, a slave to Gavin Guile? Marissia had more power and wealth than most nobles. Similarly, though technically slaves, in certain areas the Blackguards had authority above most lords', also often retired with wealth, and commanded far more respect than most drafters.

The Chromeria had slowly eroded the extent of slavery, believing it as intrinsically prone to abuse but also as ineradicable as lending at interest or prostitution. How else could debtors be forced to honor contracts when they might have no way to pay other than their own labor? What else could be done with enemies during war?

Would it please Orholam more if His people massacred all captured enemies? Were they supposed to build giant cages for the captured until hostilities ceased?

What if the hostilities lasted decades? Who would feed their foes for so long? Would they feed them still if war led to famine, as it so often did? Who would stand guard over these men? What kind of horrors must happen in such cages? Aside from being economically impossible, was it really humane to sequester men away from society and family? Man is a social animal. Even slaves were allowed human connections, the company of peers, perhaps the love of a woman or a man, and the hope of children—if often blighted hopes. What would long-term prisoners have?

So the Chromeria compromised. The biggest concession they'd won was that children of slaves were now born free.

With slaves' children born free, the only sources of new slaves were suddenly criminals, war, and piracy. Unsurprisingly, more things were made illegal, especially for poor young men and young women; piracy increased dramatically, and small wars were started on pretexts to allow raids for slave labor—which had, indeed, fed the fires of the unending Blood Wars.

When Gavin had violently ended the Blood Wars, he'd demanded that all the slaves taken by each side be allowed to return home.

In two war-torn and impoverished lands, it had sounded impossible. Ludicrous.

It had been the kind of administrative nightmare that Andross Guile adored. He and Felia Guile had woven diplomatic magic with the opportunity, giving Blood Forester lords lands in Ruthgar and Ruthgari lords lands in Blood Forest so as to stitch their interests back together. Certain exceptions were carved out (and bought) that enriched Andross. But he was more interested in using his clout to rebalance the powers in both satrapies so that troublesome elements were weakened but not too gravely insulted or reduced to where they had nothing to lose. Some great families found themselves vastly diminished—but their close allies stood too much to gain from Andross's reforms to join a revolt.

And no one wanted to fight Gavin Guile. So it worked.

All the slaves were returned unharmed, which made Gavin Guile greatly loved here. It also made slavery generally hated and also very expensive, as there was no supply of fresh slaves except at great expense from Ilytian 'traders' whose often-forged documents might invite more trouble than even a skilled slave could be worth.

It might have all meant that Kip was living during the last generation in Blood Forest to know slaves—if he weren't taking slaves himself.

Slavery was as evil as war, and both would continue to create broken men like Daragh until the end of time. In making war, Kip was surely responsible for making more such men.

O Lord of Lights, must my choices always be, by doing nothing, to allow evil to prevail, or to choose a lesser evil? Can I not do some good in my brief hour fretting upon this stage?

Daragh finished delivering the pitch Kip hadn't been listening to. Daragh stood with his legs wide, shoulders back, and his voice boomed with the intimation of shared victories, triumphs, and vengeance against their mutual foes.

"That's a good speech," Kip said. "Golly, what a deal!"

He said nothing more. He tilted his head, studying the angular scars on Daragh's cheeks and on his chest. Under them, it seemed, he could almost make out some older, looping scars. Script?

"So we have an agreement?" Daragh asked, eyes bright.

Kip said nothing. Come on, father, show the strength of your blood in me now. I don't think I can pull this off.

"You have some kind of counterproposal?" Daragh asked finally, flushing.

"This," Kip said, sighing, "is not about me. This is about what you choose, or really, what you and your men choose.

"You can choose to walk out and leave. When—well, let's be honest—*if* I reestablish order in this satrapy, you'll be outlaws, bandits again. Without, ever again, having any hope of pardon." He smiled amicably. "I assume that the reason you're all here is that you'd prefer not to do that. But, brief and harsh as it may be, your current life is still open to you. You're free to leave if you don't like the next choices. Because if you choose to join me, you also get to choose how.

"First option: You and your men become auxiliaries to my army. You'll keep your command structure and separate units. You'll be paid and fed and entitled to an equal share of the loot we capture, but you'll be responsible for your own arms and armature and infirmary care. For most of you, that means you'll go into battle lightly armored or not at all. I won't send you to willful slaughter, but you'll be used as auxiliaries have always been used: in the front, to break the enemy charges, where we can also make sure you don't run away. In the eyes of the Foresters and the rest of my army, you'll be more like…allies. Not compatriots or friends. Not countrymen.

"If you choose that option, after the war, all legal claims against you within Blood Forest will be pardoned. If you're guilty of other things in other satrapies, you're on your own for that, but we won't hand you over to anyone."

"That's a shit deal." Daragh sneered.

"You're rapists and murderers," Kip said. "Did you expect roses and a victory parade, or a hope at a new life and loot?"

"I expected—"

"The other option you can choose," Kip interrupted, "is that you be integrated into the army. Become Nightbringers. Your commanders will be given command of units of similar size to what they currently lead and become officers, without being required to pay for commissions. For ninety days, they will have an officer or noncommissioned officer assigned to them who will show them the ropes, interpret our signals, and translate unfamiliar orders and so forth. After ninety days, they sink or swim on their own.

"That gives your men time to learn, time to bond with their new units, and time for us all to get through this campaign. It'll give them time to decide if they want to live as honest men."

The bandit king's face creased with worry as he sensed the longing welling up in the men accompanying him. "And what about me? I'm the boss." Daragh grinned. "You going to put me in charge of your whole army?"

"I should love to have a man of your martial prowess command... half of my army," Kip said. "Your charisma's infectious and your audacity without measure. Your skills are unquestioned."

That caused a disapproving buzz through everyone gathered. Half the army?! Scandalous! Ridiculous. Offensive beyond words.

"Half the army isn't enough," Daragh said, seeing that he had to move fast before the pressure could mount against Kip, but bartering, audacious.

But Kip saw him fill with sudden hope, the acquisitive hunger of the raider he was.

"No, it's not," Kip said.

"But it's close," the man said, regaining his grin, judging the mood of the room easily, as he'd judged the moods of his free raiders so often before, seeing he had to provide a win for Kip. "I confess my mastery of cavalry lags behind my direction of foot soldiers. I should think we'll be most successful if I merely take over the infantry for now. For the good of the whole army."

Kip shook his head sadly. "I said, 'I should love to have a man of your martial prowess...' "

Give the bandit this, he had a keen sense of danger. The room went deathly calm, as if the air smelled of ozone, the earth straining up to reach the heavens for a lightning strike.

"We came under a flag of truce!" Daragh the Coward snarled. "You swore a troth!"

"And I keep my troth," Kip said quietly. He didn't need to speak loudly.

No one moved for their weapons. But you couldn't fully disarm drafters, although meeting in this room, with only white and black tones on all the walls, and all Kip's men wearing only the same, did everything possible to minimize that risk. As did dragging out the meeting so long—which Kip had done for this purpose: most drafters couldn't hold luxin packed inside their own bodies for very long, if they even knew how to pack it all. It slowly leaked away, so Kip had been disarming them, simply by going slowly.

"As you said," Kip went on, "you're the boss. You, Daragh the Coward, led these men into murder and theft and dishonor. Albeit with great difficulty, I can forgive their crimes and require others to do the same. But the blood of the innocent cries out for an answer. Your men's sins fall on *you*. You could have stopped the worst of it. You could have minimized the evil your men committed, even though you are bandits. Instead, you allowed, you incited, and you took part in all the worst that they did. You led your men to ever greater depravity.

"Nonetheless, you came under a flag of truce. I gave my troth. So. If you and your men leave now, as I promised, I will not kill any of you, nor—unless attacked—will I pursue you until after my army has defended Green Haven. No trickery. But if your men wish to have the new start I've offered—if they wish to live henceforth as honest, pardoned men, they will need to bring you, Daragh, either dead or in chains, to the foot of the stairs of the Palace of the Divines."

Kip looked at the hard-faced men around Daragh, ignoring him completely. "You have until tomorrow morning. It will take time to integrate you into the army."

"You can't do that!" Daragh shouted. "These are *my* men. They will do what I say! You can't buy them from me!"

"*I* am doing nothing," Kip said. "I'm pointing out three paths you each may choose: one, abandon the Forest in her hour of need and choose to be bandits until the day you die; two, serve as auxiliaries and remain on the edges of human society; or three, buy the chance to become honest men again. Daragh calls you *his* men?" Kip said to the others, pointedly ignoring Daragh. " 'His'? He speaks of 'buying'? As if you're slaves? I call you free men. Make your decision and pay the price for it. It's what free men do."

Tisis's intelligence was good, but she didn't have people everywhere. She hadn't been able to tell Kip anything about the men flanking Daragh the Coward. She and Kip had assumed that they were all drafters and formidable warriors—in case Kip broke the truce and tried to capture Daragh.

What Kip and Tisis didn't know was if these were also the most loyal men in Daragh's bandit army. Would Kip's words even be passed along at all?

Kip didn't like making promises that he wasn't sure he could keep, but he wouldn't be keeping any promises at all if he didn't get these bandits to join his army.

"This is horseshit," Daragh said. "You need me. You think you can offer us *scraps* while you feast?"

"Oh, 'free men.' That reminds me," Kip said as if he hadn't heard Daragh. Nor did he look at him now. "I know many of you escaped from other satrapies. If you do choose to integrate into my units, you'll earn not only your pardon for your crimes while a bandit but also papers of manumission upon your retirement or discharge— regardless of where in the Seven Satrapies you were enslaved. On the power of the Guiles and the wealth of the Malargoi, I swear this.

Further, if any of you earns a citation for valor in battle, he will also earn having his family redeemed." Kip raised his hand, as if he were taking an oath, but with his fingers spread. "Up to five family members manumitted, at my expense.

"But perhaps you will say, 'What if I fall heroically in battle but no one sees my heroism? Or what if my commander is stingy with recognition?' I'll be honest with you. I always will. I can't see everything, or root out every injustice, so let me add this: whether you earn a ribbon or not, if you die in battle or from wounds sustained in battle, five family members shall be redeemed, at my expense.

"If you pledge your hands to me," Kip vowed, looking at each of those stone-faced men, "I will repay you five times over. Honorable service, a pardon for wrongs, and freedom for you and those you love most. This I swear."

Freedom? Real freedom?

What Kip promised wasn't just an absence of the chains that all fugitive slaves found intolerable by definition—else they'd not have run in the first place. This was freedom from the stalking fear that hunted every fugitive, the fear that everything one had built up for many years might be taken away in an instant. And it was hope of being reunited with those one had thought forever lost.

Freedom? How could a fugitive slave think of anything else?

No matter how loyal and hardened the drafter-warriors flanking Daragh were, Kip's words *would* be passed along. It didn't matter what Daragh said as soon as he left this hall; he wouldn't be able to suppress them.

Of all the things that die, hope is the most easily resurrected.

Kip saw Daragh the Coward's hold on even the men flanking him crumbling. And Daragh saw it too.

"That is all," Kip said. "You may go."

He turned to Tisis and asked, still letting his voice project, "What's next? Is it time for breakfast, or do we have to deal with the embargo talks first?"

"The valor-award citations for the freeing of Dúnbheo, actually," Tisis said. "We need to decide how best to read those out. You'd wanted to make sure the men were recognized for what they did rather than just being handed a ribbon, but if we take even half a minute for each citation, the army will be standing there all morning."

Tisis, I could kiss you. The subtext was perfect: we give out plenty of valor citations.

Each of Daragh's men would later think, If they give out so many valor citations, how hard will it be to earn one myself?

"Very well," Kip said. "That first, then the embargo, and then breakfast, I suppose."

Daragh the Coward had finally gotten Kip's silent if unsubtle message—*I have many other things to do, most of them far more important than you*—and was striding, fuming, out of the audience chamber.

"Darling," Kip said out of the side of his mouth, but not turning toward her. "*Are* we giving out valor citations?"

"Of course we are," she said quietly. She cleared her throat. "Now."

"You just came up with that?" he asked.

"Yes?" she said.

"I love the hell out of you," he said.

"You better," she said.

He glanced over at her. She was still facing forward, regal, but she was beaming.

His next thought was less joyous: Citations. Great. Something else to add to the list.

As Daragh the Coward passed through the doors of the audience chamber, he stopped. He turned back, defiant.

Drawing up, his jaw jutting and his scarified chest puffed out, oiled muscles tensed, he roared from the vestibule, "Guile! You never asked about my name!"

Kip gave him a puzzled glance. Making a little motion to the soldiers to close the doors, he said, "Why would I give two shits what people call a dead man?"

Chapter 18

The rudeness of murder had always bothered him. That was how he knew he wasn't a monster, yet. It *still* bothered him.

Facing the predawn sun, praying alone, her husband having departed after a long night of lovemaking and tears, the Third Eye now sat up straight, her sunburnt arms saluting the rising light.

She had to be dead before the sun's disk broke the horizon. Those were his orders. Most likely, that was from the old, empty superstition that Orholam could see the Shadows once His Eye, the sun, rose. Regardless, there was no reason to take the chance of being interrupted by more mundane figures, either, so he moved forward.

It was always a mystical moment, ushering a soul unwillingly through the Great Gate into death. He already regretted how this job had to go: he wouldn't face her. He wouldn't feast on her fear or explore the fathomless mystery of watching a life cross over, hoping even after all these years to catch a glimpse of the soul in flight to…elsewhere.

He couldn't afford such consolations, not with a woman of this power. She was a Seer, the greatest Seer of them all, the Third Eye. She would die at her prayers, unafraid. He thought that, at least, was very decent of him.

But then suddenly she spoke—and not in prayer.

Clearly, but not loudly, not like someone calling for help, she said, "There is one thing that you cannot do, you who were once—but shall not henceforth be—Elijah ben-Kaleb. There is one thing you cannot do, despite all your awesome power."

It was as if he'd been sprinting and the earth dropped into an abyss beneath his feet. His true name. He froze. For the first time in years, he felt the squeeze of fear's heavy fist around his neck. She couldn't know his name. The shimmercloaks hid Shadows from mystical as well as mundane sight.

So was it a guess?

Ludicrous!

She knew Elijah Sharp was *here*, so she knew the Order hunted her and knew that they'd sent their best. That went beyond unnerving. What could a Seer in her position do with such knowledge?

But she knew more. She knew his father's name. She knew *everything*.

It was a trap, meant to make him flee!

Or delay! Or…

She was a *Seer. Anything* he did now could be playing straight into her schemes.

But he'd extended paryl webs across every entrance, and none had been tripped. He checked them again.

They were still alone.

What was that bit about him not being Elijah ben-Kaleb after today? What did she mean?

But the sun must surely be touching the horizon any moment. There was no time to sort out the muddle in his head.

"There is one thing you cannot do," she said. Her voice was quiet, her mien unthreatening, but there was no mistaking the strong steel in her. "You, son of Kaleb, son of a father whose very name means 'faithfulness,' you were trusted to live up to that name your father earned and gave to you as a free gift. Elijah ben-Kaleb, you were sent into the shadows as a candle unlit, sent to take the flame at the perfect moment to banish that darkness. But you decided the price was too high. You came to hate the cost of the flame. You didn't want your life consumed in giving light. But all our lives are wax, and time itself is heat unbearable, and every day we melt—but some of us take flame! I am such a soul, dying to bring light to a dark world.

"You? You felt your sacrifices were unseen and so your sins would be unseen, too. And so you were reborn to the shadows, and a name of light no longer fits you. No, nor that mockery they gave you. Sharp? Though molded into the shape of a blade and painted black, how sharp is melted wax? I, too, have a great gift, Elijah. And I, too, have been called to pay that selfsame price, to become a sacrifice seemingly unseen, to act with heroism unheralded."

He sometimes acted with a bit of delay, struggling to make sense of words spoken to him, and that was all that saved her now. Was she calling him dull?

He wasn't stupid!

But what 'price' was she going on about? And the thing she said he couldn't do? What was that?

There were only moments left, but he was already waiting, and she speaking. Both knew this was rapidly winding to a finish. His paryl webs were still undisturbed.

If this was a trap, it was a shitty one.

Gently, she said, "Elijah, even with the eye of a Seer, I cannot see you, but I see the darkness you cast into every life you touch. And though it slay me, I choose to spend my life bringing light instead. You think you came here of your own will? I think you were brought to me. You were not sent by malice but pulled by mercy. You will kill me, I've no doubt, but nothing can hide you from the All-Seeing one. I dub thee Elijah ben-Zoheth, and I tell you this: for all your power, Elijah ben-Zoheth, you cannot steal that which I freely give."

Then, in fear and rage, and in shame, exposed in the first light of the rising sun, he murdered her.

But afterward, for the entire long journey back to the Jaspers, he was troubled. He played that morning over and over in his mind. Had he blundered?

No. He couldn't have kidnapped her as he'd kidnapped that slave Marissia for the Andross Guile job. It was too dangerous, the area unfamiliar. More importantly, those weren't his orders—and the Old Man of the Desert was awfully particular about his orders being followed exactly, alpha to omega.

The roots of Sharp's broken teeth throbbed at the very idea of disobeying his master.

He'd done right. He'd done the only thing he could do. It didn't matter anyway. None of it meant anything.

But what had she freely given? He didn't understand. The Name? That didn't seem right. And what was that about anyway?

He knew its literal meaning, of course. He hadn't walked Abornea's shores for many years, but some things one doesn't forget. Why had the Third Eye used her last words to Name him? And what did she mean by dubbing him ben-Zoheth, the Son of Separation?

Chapter 19

After her long night, the dawn prayers in the company of the faithful lightened Karris's burdens; the pleasantly smiling Andross Guile waiting for her slammed them back in place. Then doubled them.

Andross *smiling*. Never a good sign.

It was a cloudless late-spring morning and the High Luxiats had opened the sanctuary's massive sliding doors that all the congregants could greet the beauty of Orholam's rising eye together. Karris's sole consolation for what was doubtless going to be a painful interaction was the vision of Andross squinting against the sun behind her.

"Orholam shine upon you, Promachos," Karris said. Orholam loves this man, too, she reminded herself, trying to squeeze some genuine feeling into her smile.

"May all your prayers be answered half as promptly," he said, "and twice as kindly." His smile was amused. He didn't miss much.

The only way to baffle Andross was with real kindness. She'd fallen short of that. Again. Dammit.

"Oh—" Karris stifled the curse. The White really wasn't supposed to curse. "Our meeting. The Parian situation. I forgot."

"Understandable. I should've reminded you."

Because Andross didn't forget. Andross never forgot. Anything. It was an infuriating reminder that his inhumanity didn't only make him less than human; all too often, it seemed to make him *more*.

"You really ought to get a secretary, someone who could be an overseer as well, ideally. As I have in Grinwoody, and Gavin had in, uh, what was her name?"

From a kinder man, the pretense that he'd forgotten might have been interpreted as him trying to bridge the gap between his own perfection and her own...not. She should really try interpreting Andross in the best possible light.

"Marissia," she said curtly. Dammit.

They began walking together toward her chambers. It had a better meeting space than his apartments, and going into his home alone felt like a fly volunteering to scout a spider's lair.

"Tragic she ran away," Andross said. "Slaves."

She hadn't run away. Andross had paid the Order—the Order!—to kidnap her. Not that Karris could admit she knew that, not without endangering Teia. But it did turn her stomach. Had Andross had a grudge against her husband's room slave, or had taking her been a way to keep Karris from learning all the things Andross feared Marissia might know? He would've interrogated her, and like many, he probably believed that slaves had to be interrogated under torture for their testimony to be trusted. And then he would've killed her. Just a bit of property destroyed: the price he had to pay to keep his kidnapping of her secret.

Marissia had been holding a bundle of Orea Pullawr's papers that the old White had intended for Karris. But Karris still hadn't figured out any way to learn if Andross had taken them or if the Order had kept them and never even told him about it.

He said, "You did check with your bankers, didn't you, to see that she didn't steal more from you? Terrifying that one might be betrayed by someone who slept in the Prism's very bedchamber, isn't it?"

He had to remind her of where Marissia had slept, didn't he? Not just in Gavin's suite, but so often in his bed.

I knew he'd use this to put me off balance. I'm the White now. Do it like I practiced.

"Gavin shared so much of his life with her," Karris said. "I'm sure she was simply afraid of what I might do to her without him here. She loved him very much."

She was actually surprised to find real compassion in her voice. And her heart.

Score one for the new White!

"Loved him? Slaves, always forgetting their place these days," Andross scoffed, shaking his head as he took a scroll case from his own man Grinwoody.

Yes, I'm sure everyone was well behaved back when you were young.

"It was my failure, not hers," Karris said instead. "It was no betrayal. I begrudge her nothing, though I admit it hurts that she left without a word. But she took nothing that wasn't hers."

"Other than her body."

"No. Gavin manumitted her," Karris said.

"Really? When? I wasn't aware of any papers filed on his behalf."

"In his will," Karris said. It was as good a time as any to admit she'd finally accepted the truth about his death that she'd denied for a year. "I'm filing them today."

Other than a quick upward flash of his eyebrows, though, he gave no indication he'd even heard, no vaunting, no I-told-you-so.

No, that wasn't true. He said nothing for several minutes. He didn't point out that the provisions of a will didn't apply until the deceased was pronounced legally dead, and that Marissia had 'run away' many months before that.

Indeed, Karris's first paranoia had involved suspecting Marissia herself in Gavin's abduction, but not one of them had panned out. And then Teia had told her what had really happened, and she'd been ashamed.

Karris and Andross stepped past the Blackguards, who'd finished checking the safety of the lift. One of Karris's attendants was reduced to the servile role of setting the counterweights, as the woman was considered junior to Grinwoody because Andross (as promachos) held the highest absolute rank. Naturally, one of the Blackguards stood at her elbow watching her—one of Karris's Blackguards, not Andross's, because while in the Chromeria the Blackguards considered the White the highest-ranking official, behind only the Prism, though the personnel assigned to guard the White and the promachos (and for that matter the Prism and the promachos, too) were all drawn from the same pool. Several of Andross's Lightguards also attended him, though they pretended not to be aware of their own place in the hierarchy (below the Blackguards in most matters at the Chromeria, though as free men and women, they were nominally socially above the technically servile Blackguards).

"I'm afraid your brother's nonsense really has riled them up," Andross said. "Freeing all slaves! Can you imagine?" Andross said. "Who would want a free woman to attend him when he's ill? Does anyone really want a person who works for *coin* to be the physicker who prods one's intimate places and knows one's ills and shameful diseases? Without the fear of the lash, would not one motivated by coin to sell one's secrets to whomever might bribe her? And what free woman would *choose* the work of laving lepers or massaging whores' prolapsed rectums or taking on the death sentence of palliating the 125 plagued? There is work not even the most penurious would choose. Your treasonous brother can't be ignorant of this, can he? Surely not. Who empties the chamber pots in his camps? Who collects the urine to tan the leather, who mucks the stables, who swives a dozen stinking ugly soldiers every night? Free men and women? Nonsense. There are just things that free people won't do."

He seemed utterly unaware that of the ten people sharing the lift, eight were slaves. Seemed unaware—and probably even was. He'd been so powerful and rich for so long that Karris could believe that. Andross remembered everything—but only everything he thought important. He was sly, but not omniscient, and he didn't think of others who didn't rise to the level of being players for his games.

Karris was the ninth person in the lift. Technically, as a Blackguard, she'd been a slave herself. She didn't believe Andross was unaware of *that* in the slightest. "I suppose it's a good thing, then," she said.

"Hmm?" he asked.

"That I was a slave myself," she said. "You expect me to believe you'd forgotten?" The second part slipped out of the corral before she could shut the gate. Sarcasm was not the appropriate mode for a White. Not a good one.

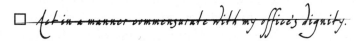

Dammit.

"Oh my," he said, putting a hand to his chest. "What a horrific gaffe." He made no effort to sound authentic.

"Do you know the thing about slights?" she asked. Thank Orholam she hadn't drafted red in a long time.

"What's that, dear?"

"They're *slight*."

"So is a bee sting," he said. Damn he was quick!

"What's a bee sting to an iron bull?" she said, just as quickly. She'd learned from long practice: never let a Guile keep talking. "Let it go. It's beneath you, father." If she let him talk, he'd make some crack about how she'd just compared herself to an iron bull. There was an Iron White joke in there somewhere, too, so she had to strike faster.

Thus, calling him 'father.'

He grimaced at the word. Then quirked his eyebrows as if accepting he'd deserved that for calling her 'dear.'

Karris had learned that she had to watch for the most fleeting expression on the promachos's face.

126   Those didn't lie. But everything else about him?

"Good thing—" she resumed. "I mean, if have your permission to finish my earlier thought?"

"Not so bad at slights yourself when you put your mind to it…or is withering scorn a bit different?" he asked, amused like a father whose toddler wishes to wrestle and actually thinks she'll win. "But please. Do finish."

She copied his eyebrow quirk, accepting the withering scorn in return for her own. But it pissed her off, deeply. It took her a moment to collect herself. "If there are certain things that free people won't do, then it's a good thing I was a slave."

"Why's that?"

"Because there's nothing I won't do to keep my people safe."

What was that twitch at the corners of his mouth with the rise of his eyebrows? A victory?

No. No? Maybe surprise melting into amusement.

"Funny. I said the same thing when I was a young man," Andross said. He smiled widely now. "I believe you mean it just as much as I did."

Which of course could be interpreted several ways.

But he was moving on. He said, "We'll see if that holds when the bill comes due, won't we? Because I'm sorry to say we may get to see what you're really willing to do for your people sooner than we'd like."

"What's that supposed to mean?" Needlessly confrontational, Karris. A more dignified White would've assumed an innocent air and said, 'Whatever do you mean? Are you going to bring me up to speed about the Parians now?'

Dealing with Andross Guile was *exhausting*. Karris was already mentally out of breath, and he didn't seem to be breaking a sweat.

"The sea chariots haven't verified it yet," Andross said. The lift had come to a stop, and the Blackguards opened the door, but he made no move to exit. "It's a large sea after all, but our spies in Azûlay agree: Your *King* Ironfist is sailing. Here. He'll likely arrive a week before or after Sun Day, depending on the weather. He's coming to negotiate."

The Blackguards in the lift and those outside it couldn't help but exchange looks, but Karris couldn't read their thoughts. She couldn't even untangle her own. Ironfist was coming back?

"If he wants to negotiate, why wouldn't he take a sea chariot?" she asked. "He knows how to build them."

"A secret it would have been nice for you not to put in the hands of a traitor," Andross muttered. "But you misunderstand." He glanced briefly at the slaves. All of them were cleared to serve at the highest levels, which meant they were trusted fully, but Andross trusted no one fully, except maybe Grinwoody. "They say he's furious. They say he's bringing an army. They say he wishes to negotiate *our surrender*."

It was a punch in the guts when you haven't had time to tense your belly. Fighting Ironfist? He was the kind of gentle warrior who got quiet and somber before he went into a battle. You *never* wanted to see him furious. In sparring, he'd bested his brother Tremblefist—the man whose battle rage had earned him a Name: the Butcher of Aghbalu.

Karris did not want to see Ironfist furious.

But forget fighting Ironfist himself. The people of the Chromeria, fighting against Parians? Their brothers? More than half of the Blackguards *were* Parians, and though she'd never question their loyalty, she also never wanted to put it to the test.

Especially not with a real enemy at the door. Even a victory over Ironfist would only guarantee losing to the White King, and the dissolution of the empire.

"Oh, but I left out the best part," Andross said, motioning that he was going to remain in the lift. "You'll pardon me. I've other urgent matters to attend to, given this news."

"What? What is it? Tell me the rest."

"King Ironfist trusts no one. Has no close advisers. Seems to think anyone at all could be a traitor." He opened his palm toward Grinwoody, but the wrinkled old slave didn't notice, seemed frozen. "*Grinwoody*," Andross said, exasperated.

The old man started and fumbled a scroll into Andross's outstretched hand.

Karris didn't like Grinwoody.

No, no, if a White is to be without stain—as a White must be—then she must be honest, with herself first of all.

Karris *hated* Grinwoody's guts. Not only because he was an extension of Andross's malevolent will, a spiked gauntlet on Andross's steel fist of command, but because he'd taken the Blackguard training—at far too advanced an age to usually get a chance. Then, when he'd passed all of it, on the eve of his final vows, he'd accepted a buyout of his contract to serve Andross. Karris, like every Blackguard, despised those who stole their expensive training and went elsewhere for the sake of more money. It spat on everything the Blackguard was. You bond with a fellow elite warrior-drafter, thinking they'll be your brother for life, and then he turns his back on you.

Regardless of his many years of faithful service to Andross, the Blackguards still thought of Grinwoody as a traitor. Which made it worse for everyone that as he was Andross's secretary and slave overseer, they had to deal with him constantly.

Him getting old and mentally missing a step sent an unkind (and unholy) thrill through her.

Andross was frowning, frustrated at having to take time from his real problems to manage a slave. That was a duty Grinwoody was supposed to handle for him.

"Five lashes, milord?" Grinwoody knew, even when he himself was the problem, to keep the interruption to his lord's day quick and quietly efficient.

"You're too damn old, you fool. Five would break you."

"Privilege suspension. One month," Grinwoody said.

Andross waved it off. "Where was I? No advisers. So there's no solid intelligence on his plans. Smart of him. He knows how we work. But. The suspicion among Paria's nobles is that this talk of our surrendering to him may be a feint."

"A 'feint'?" Karris asked.

"The Parian nobility believe there's something else Ironfist wants."

"Yes, thank you, I know what a feint *is*. I meant a feint to *what end*?" Karris snapped. Not the way the White should act at all.

"There were certain questions he's asked with 'uncommon intensity,' is how my spy put it."

Oh yes. Ironfist had stood at the elbow of the world's most powerful and devious personalities, seeing how they excelled and how they failed, and when, and often why. But it was one thing to study how the best people in the world do a thing; perhaps Ironfist was learning it was quite another to actually do it. Karris had been learning it herself for a year now.

It was like analyzing a fight versus taking the blows yourself.

Finding out exactly what you needed to know to act boldly and notifying all the people who needed to know, because they were the ones who would actually make it happen, while keeping spies in the dark about what you intended? That was not as easy as you'd think, even after years of watching it. A master worked art a mere spectator couldn't even see.

Karris herself still didn't know how the hell Andross did half the things *he* did.

"What kind of questions?" Karris asked, impatient. They were still holding up the lift.

Now she was getting paranoid, wondering if Andross was somehow using even that silence against her.

Important to remember: there isn't always a secret plan to make you look a fool. Andross was her ally, after all. At least against Ironfist.

"About the Prism-elect, naturally," Andross said. "But also about you, his old friend. People there can't believe he'll actually side with the White King. But for some odd reason he blames *me* for his sister's unfortunate accidental death. It comes out now that she had quite a penchant for riotous living. She used all manner of intoxicants, mixed together no less."

"That is odd," she said. "But at least the part about Ironfist not wanting to side against us is good...right?"

"In declaring himself king, he's committed treason. He believes I ordered his sister's murder—who, despite her flaws, was at least a legitimate Nuqaba. So him sending an army here is not good news in any fashion whatsoever."

"I didn't say it was good *news*. I said—"

Andross ran right over her words. "So what's his play? He paralyzes us from hostile action with an offer to ally with us, but then, once he's here with his army..."

Karris said, "He gives us some kind of ultimatum? He'll only join us if...what?"

What Andross didn't say aloud was that the Chromeria would lose the war if Paria sided against them. Without question, it would be the end of the empire. Full stop.

They would likely lose the war even if Paria simply decided on neutrality.

Andross said, "I don't know, and he's not telling anyone, but if he gives us such a choice, how outrageous would his demands have to be before we would say no?"

Short of asking them to abandon Orholam and worship the old gods instead? Short of that, Ironfist could likely ask anything at all. The Chromeria would have to agree.

Andross could obviously tell by the look on her face that she'd grasped the crux of it. She felt dread growing in the pit of her stomach. It was one thing to think, 'I am so dead.' It was quite another for a cowled man to escort you to the executioner's ax-bitten, bloodstained block.

"He seemed quite intent about...about you," Andross said, watching her carefully.

"You said that. But why?"

"He's declared himself king. Even if he wanted to, even if he's discovered that being a king isn't quite the prize everyone thinks, he *can't* submit to us now and hope to go back to the way things were before. Or so he must surely believe, with me as promachos. What guarantee could I give him that would make him trust me? He thinks I am a man of such low moral character that I have truck with assassins!"

Of course, Andross *had*—but he wasn't going to admit to it, not even only in front of slaves. Andross was no fool. (Though perhaps he believed Karris was.)

"Believing me so low," Andross said, "how could he trust any oath I gave him? If he believes I murdered his sister—who was guilty only of being slow to answer the Chromeria's call for help—he must doubtless believe I would murder him, an outright traitor."

Gee, old man, maybe if you didn't assassinate people, *maybe* people won't think you assassinate people.

But as soon as Karris had the thought, she realized how hypocritical it was. She was the one who'd made that job vastly more difficult by ordering Teia to assassinate the Parian satrapah as well. She was the one who'd knowingly sent a young woman—hardly more than a child—to do a job that even a master assassin might've botched. It was her fault in sending Teia at all that Teia had been unmasked by Ironfist. If the Nuqaba (and no one else) had simply died that night, Ironfist might never have known it was an assassination at all. He might have guessed it was some aggrieved local.

It was Karris, not just Andross, who'd turned Ironfist into an enemy.

"Thus," Andross said as if it were merely an interesting tidbit, "as far as I can presume, the only way Ironfist thinks he can keep himself safe from me—"

"You're really gifted at this, aren't you?" she said.

"What?" he asked, distracted.

"Putting yourself into other people's minds, figuring out how they think, figuring out what they know, and what they must be planning given what they know, and then using it to destroy them."

"*Gifted!* Gifted? I'm *skilled.* People call others 'gifted' when they don't want to believe they're worse at something because they're not willing to put in the work excellence requires. Regardless—I mean, if I have your permission to finish my thought?"

That. That was gratuitous. "By all means, please do," she said, nearly politely.

"Actually, let me qualify that. I spoke too soon. The rest stands, but the *destroying them* part? You're right. That's my gift." He flashed his eyebrows, as if it were all interesting, but tangential. "Now, where was I? Oh yes. If I guess correctly, given what he thinks he knows, Ironfist believes that the only way he can be safe from me…" Andross smiled, savoring the moment, "…is if he marries you."

"*What?!*" Surely Karris hadn't heard that right.

"How long has he been in love with you?"

"What, what? Never!"

"Well," Andross said with a shrug. "Perhaps it's solely political, then. We'll hope it doesn't come to it regardless. We'll hope he shows up with fewer soldiers and ships and drafters than rumored. These numbers often do get exaggerated. And he's a political novice, after all. We might yet outmaneuver him."

But Karris knew Ironfist, and Ironfist knew both her and Andross.

Ironfist wouldn't come here unless he was certain he could win. And implacable, righteous rage tends to make up for a lot of limitations.

"But if all goes poorly," Andross said, stepping off the lift. "I guess it's good news that you've accepted that Gavin's dead. You're a widow; your time of mourning is finished, and you're free to remarry."

Her mouth made an O, but no sound came out.

"After all," Andross said, "you just told me: you're willing to do whatever it takes to save your people, aren't you?"

He'd set her up. Somehow.

She'd never seen it coming.

It was like that time he'd hired those men to ambush and beat her. This time he was doing it with nothing more than his words, and this time, he got to watch her take the beating.

She couldn't muster any defense. She only looked at him, stricken as if she were down on the paving stones of that street again, taking kicks.

"You know, there's one good thing about my son dying," Andross said, timing his words perfectly with the closing of the lift's doors. "He didn't live to see you give up on him."

Chapter 20

"So, boss, remind me why we're going up here?" Winsen said as they ascended a bone-white spiral ramp to the roof of the Palace of the Divines.

"Two reasons," Kip said. "Ben really wanted to see the mechanism, and the Divines really, really didn't want him to."

"Good enough for me," Big Leo said. "Why so many of us? Are we expecting a hostile reception, or you just giving the nunks a chance to fail?"

Chagrined after the assassination attempt, Cruxer had been screening prospective new members for the Mighty. Fifteen of them followed the Mighty today. Kip shrugged and said quietly, "Every day's a new chance to fail."

Cruxer gave him a disapproving glance.

"What I meant is," Kip said more loudly, "if I had any idea what's so secret about their big secret, I might have an answer to that question."

"But you don't, because it's secret," Ferkudi said, nodding.

"It's just a big mirror, right?" Winsen asked.

"Like the *Blue Falcon* is just a boat," Ben-hadad said.

"Well...it is," Winsen said flatly.

Ben-hadad said, "You did not just say that my masterpiece, the finest skimmer ever created, is 'just a boat.'"

"No, actually *you* said that," Winsen said.

Ben-hadad paused in his limping up the stairs. He dropped his head in defeat.

"He's got you there," Ferkudi said loudly. "You did actually say that."

"Helluva view, huh?" Kip said, to forestall more sniping. The Palace of the Divines was topped by its heart tree, a massive white oak whose roots were artfully (and, he assumed, magically) woven through the walls of the palace below it. To the north and south of that great tree was a narrow band of old-growth forest with smaller white oaks descending down the sides of the palace as if it were simply a steep hill. That band of forest looped back into the palace's rear gardens.

The ramp was a white ribbon that circled the entirety of the palace, at two points of each revolution passing through that band of trees and moss and rocks, but suspended above the ground and never close enough to any of the trees to touch them.

There were interior stairs that would have taken them to the roof faster, but this looping, outside way was the more formal route, and he wanted to give the Foresters as much of his respect as possible. He didn't know why, but only the Divines, a conn, and the Keeper of the Flame and her people were supposed 'by ancient tradition' to approach the heart tree atop the Palace of the Divines.

Kip was breaking that tradition, so there was no need for him to stomp on their feelings any more than necessary.

"Why aren't you telling them the real reason?" Tisis asked him quietly.

"Those were real reasons," Kip said, but it came out as defensive.

His wife said nothing.

"Because I've got a feeling it won't work. It can't be as simple as I think, or they'd have done a better job with their defenses already. And..."

"And you don't want to fail in front of the nunks," Tisis said.

He pursed his lips and turned to admire the view. It was breathtaking. He'd never imagined a city so filled with trees and flowers and greenery of every shade, and here as they climbed, they were able to see over the great living wood-and-leaf curtain that was Greenwall. Beyond on one side lay many leagues of undulating forest canopy and crops, and on the other was the sparkling sapphire of Loch Lána.

"They're signing up for a job that might cost them their lives. To protect *me*," Kip said. "I don't want their first impression to be that they've made a huge mistake. That I'm not worth it."

He glanced over at her a few moments later. She had that perfectly serene look on her face that told him she was definitely mad at him.

Finally, after one last steep section, the white walkway deposited them before an ornate gatehouse on the roof that blocked their view of most of the giant white oak.

A woman stood before the building, blocking their way.

"Please, stay back," the brown-veiled woman said. She sounded kind, but Kip's heart was gripped by sudden fear. Something about the Keeper of the Flame struck him as wrong.

Her voice was more full of gravel than an old haze smoker's, but her erect carriage and lean figure spoke of a much younger woman. Her veils were bound tight against the contours of her face, with a choker high on her neck.

His own unbounded throat cut off his breath.

Luxurious braids of fire-copper hair woven and shaped with platinum thread and opals reached down her back like tongues of flame reaching down for hell instead of seeking its natural level with the æthereal fires.

Though no one used the title for her, everything about this woman shouted *priestess* to him. The pagan kind.

She raised black-gloved hands in amused surrender. "I'm happy to cooperate, but I'm not *safe*."

Not being able to see the woman's face bothered him. A condescending sneer would give those words different meaning than a patient smile.

She sighed, though he'd said nothing. She asked, "Do you trust these people to hold the fate of our satrapy and the entire war in their hands? Do you trust each of them not to loose secrets that might start a future war? If so, follow me."

Kip looked over at Cruxer. The man understood instantly.

"Nunks," the Commander said, "Gemel-six. Forget the hinge like last time, and you'll be doing froggers till sunset. Mighty, Aleph-eight. Everyone else, out."

Some high-level lord who'd somehow tagged along didn't move.

Cruxer turned a heavy gaze on the man.

"Surely you don't mean me," the man said innocently. "As the palace's—"

"I haven't killed a man in four days," Cruxer said without inflection.

The apple of the lord's throat bobbed. He seemed in sudden need of a chamber pot. He disappeared down the great ramp, nearly running.

The prospective new members Cruxer had selected for the Mighty followed, propping the door ajar at its foot and jamming a wedge into its hinges, lest it be closed and barred against them in an ambush. It left Kip and Tisis and the Mighty alone in what he now could only think of as less a gatehouse and more a temple. This wide building, whitewashed under thick branches of purple-blossoming wisteria, covered and controlled the entire approach to the enormous heart tree. The circuitous path up here now seemed less a gentle climb and more like a pilgrimage route.

The Mighty had already fanned out. Tisis stayed close to Kip, giving him room to take a wide stance himself, but near enough that Big Leo could interpose his considerable bulk between her and Kip and any threat. Ferkudi was the roamer, so no sudden assault might plan for exactly where he'd be. Ben-hadad was diagonally behind the Keeper of the Flame, where he could watch her and keep an eye on the two doors at the rear and side of the chamber. His crossbow was loaded, but pointed at the floor. Alone of the Mighty, Ben-hadad was able to maintain an amiable air despite total vigilance.

With hand signals, Cruxer put the Mighty on high alert.

This time, Kip wasn't sure why. Was Cruxer just that attuned to Kip's own tension, or had he noticed something explicitly that Kip was only feeling?

Winsen, who'd been scouting the back of the room, kicked a shim under one of the doors. The other swung out and had no easy way to bar it. Hand on his belt, Win opened that door and poked his head through.

"My appearance will be shocking, but I can see this will be necessary," the Keeper said.

As had been the tradition with other ancient titles, such as the Third Eye being known only by her title and never her name, the Keeper had also sacrificed her personal name in taking up her position. It was a tradition at least as old as the Tyrean Empire, and it still saw wan reflections in modern governance—Andross was sometimes referred to simply as the Red. The difference was that he was also known as Andross Guile.

"Forgive me if I move slowly," she said, "but I have no wish to provoke alarm."

Kip didn't know why his heart was gripped with fear. She'd banished all her attendants as soon as Kip arrived with his entourage, hot on the heels of Lord Appleton's message that the Keeper was to assist Kip in every way.

So only Kip could hear what Cruxer whispered: "She's wearing plate." Louder, he said, "Win, bookcase."

Plate? Under her clothes? Why?

Kip looked for it as she moved, though, and even then he could barely tell. Cruxer really was damn good at his work, and the plate was only partial. To make it less obvious that it was there, perhaps? Because surely anyone who knew you were wearing an armored tunic would simply stab you in the neck.

Assassinations weren't so common here. Or at least, not that outsiders heard.

Maybe trading in your name made it impossible for anyone to know who wore the veil?

For that matter, how sure was Kip that this woman was the real Keeper of the Flame?

Winsen climbed up a bookcase, as if it were something people did, and then stood atop it, strung bow and spare arrows in one hand, nocked arrow and string in the other, though pointed down.

The woman took a deep breath, bracing herself. She loosened the choker that held tight the layers of veils from her brow around her face and head. The outermost veil covered even her eyes, but the inner, tighter veils had small jeweled cutouts for her eyelashes—which told Kip that she wore the veils even while with her inner circle.

Slowly, she removed her veils one at a time, doffing and folding each with careful and identical motions. She'd done this many times. So if she was an impostor, she was one regularly.

At the last veil, she bowed her head and reached up to the base of her skull. Her fingers worked at the knot where the band around her forehead was tied.

The Mighty vibrated with tension like a bowstring drawn full to the lips, and held...*held*.

Slowly, she lifted not just the veil, not just the band around her forehead, but what seemed at first to be her entire scalp.

No, it was a cap, a wig into which the red hair was woven.

Revealed under the wig, her natural brown hair was patchy, her scalp mottled by open sores. She set aside the veil and wig and lifted her face.

And suddenly, even as he heard the sharp intake of breath through teeth beside him as Tisis saw and stifled a gasp, Kip's heart was moved not to disgust or fear but to pity.

Though she was not yet thirty years old, the Keeper's face was covered with weeping sores and distended by tumors. No wonder she kept herself wrapped like a corpse for the pyre—she would surely go to one soon. Everywhere, even where it was swollen by tumors, her skin gleamed. Little points of gritty golden light burned within her distressed skin everywhere, as if an exploding shell had pierced her with a hundred thousand fragments of ever-burning shrapnel.

It had a fatal beauty to it, pulsing brightly in time with her every heartbeat.

The Keeper held herself defiantly, though, apparently impervious to her wounds and to Kip's scrutiny as much as to her assured demise.

It was a resolve Kip knew well.

She wasn't horrified at her own ugliness nor dismayed by the warm death humming glee in her bones. She was stalwart despite what must be constant pain: she was like a runner who'd be damned if she would falter this close to the finish line.

And Kip knew with his heart: This wasn't a dying woman who happened to hold an important position. This was a woman dying *because* of her position. This was the warrior who'd volunteered for a fatal mission; this was a high priestess who'd offered herself for the sacrifice, approaching the altar and the knife. But she wasn't going to go quietly.

She unbuckled the fabric-covered plates from her forearms and then her broad, heavy skirts, and stood in her simple tunic and trousers, creased from her overgarments.

"Chi," Kip blurted. "You're a chi drafter, aren't you?"

Puzzlement flickered in her angry eyes. "Why would you say that? You haven't even touched chi since you got here. I've been watching your eyes and your soulbrand from the moment you arrived. I heard about the lightstorm out on the waters. They say you pulled apart paryl and chi twisted into waterspouts, drafting both at the same time. I don't know that anyone's done that before. Or is that a lie meant to pass to legend?"

Soulbrand?

"Do you know a lot about lies... Priestess?" Kip asked instead.

She blinked as if struck.

"I'm not here to give answers, but to hear them," Kip said.

"Not lies," she said, defensive, bitter. "Secrets. Secrets we must keep lest the Chromeria put us on Orholam's Glare."

Kip had no idea what a masterful drafter of chi could do, but it would be invisible to the Mighty, and to Kip—unless he acted immediately. The danger hadn't passed. Indeed, stripping a secret truth naked risked shame, and shame could spur violence.

What he did next was exactly the wrong thing to do. It was exactly the opposite of what Andross or Gavin would have done, but Kip waved the Mighty off.

Though the Mighty barely shifted their positions, the air changed immediately.

The Keeper noticed. The golden burning of her skin dimmed; her pulse slowed. But her shoulders slumped. "We only want to use the gift Orholam gave us," she said. "Drafting kills *every* drafter. But our color makes us ugly first, so ours is forbidden? Ours kills us faster, yes—in five or ten years rather than ten or twenty—but if we studied chi as every other color is studied, could we not learn what is safe? Why can we not bring our gifts in offering to the Lord of Lights, too? Why can we not serve mankind openly, as other drafters do? You, Lord Guile, have a wealth of colors. If you never draft chi again, you can serve with eight other colors. I have only the one. Are we chi drafters so monstrous that Orholam would have us destroyed? Or can God see beauty where the Magisterium sees only shame?"

"Tell me," Kip said. He looked down at his hands. He'd known, somehow. That ugly heat in his joints when he'd drafted chi—it had felt like he was cooking, like something was deeply wrong, deeply unsafe about the outer-spectrum color. With a sudden shot of hot fear like whiskey in his belly, he wondered if the same death taking this woman was growing in his own bones at this very moment.

Gently, he said again, "Please. Tell me."

The gathering storm of her righteous indignation frayed and scattered. Her lifted chin descended. The pulsing gold light slowed to a normal pace. A sigh released the last of her resistance.

"Our ancestors thought our cancers were a sign of a god's displeasure at some sin they'd committed. The priests said they bore the tumors as punishment on the people's behalf. They used their own suffering to control the people—even as they desperately searched for cures. Over many generations of careful notes, they figured out that chi kills everyone, even our families, if we have them. The more chi we use, the faster we die. Generally. Not always. This is my tenth year. It's quite long, as we reckon such things. I'm lucky, most say."

"You use chi for the Great Mirror?" Kip asked. "I thought the mirrors were controlled with superviolet."

She inclined her head, and Kip couldn't help but glance at features shaped as if by an angry child mashing clay. "May I put my raiments back on?" she asked. "For your protection... but for my vanity, too."

For my protection? What the hell does that mean?

"Of course," he said instead.

"I'll take you to the Great Mirror. It'll answer your questions better than I can."

Chapter 21

The warm, compassionate light of orange dawn had thawed Teia's iced fury. A little. Karris was unworthy of Teia's service, but Teia'd given too much to earn her position to serve poorly just because her commander was shit. She was better than that.

And to be fair, unlike Karris, Teia hadn't had to kill any of *her* friends to do her job. That had to take some getting used to, she guessed.

So before coming back to the Blackguard barracks, she'd dropped off a coded note for Karris in one of their dead drops. Teia couldn't bear actually speaking to the woman right now, but Karris deserved to know her husband was alive.

She was going to be furious that Teia hadn't told her right away. But Teia would deal with that later. Or never.

For now, she needed to find a safe place, if only to sleep. She would need to prepare, to hide whatever money and materials she stole— and she'd *need* to steal, which she hated. She'd need a place to eat, and sew disguises, and wash laundry. She'd scouted extra places before, but none of those that she'd already used would work. She had to start from zero.

Disappearing completely was the only way to be safe. To be a ghost. Anything less could get her father killed.

Sleep, though. Sleeping sounded better than, better than...she didn't know what. She was exhausted and it was coloring her every thought with a gray stupidity and every movement with black-and-blue clumsiness. She'd been up since before dawn yesterday, and not five minutes of that time had been the pink, pleasant kind of wakefulness, where you could drift in an unfocused haze.

The first and most hazardous step of her preparations was stopping at the Blackguard barracks and her old bunk. Yesterday morning, she hadn't grabbed the extra coin stick and pistol and tailor's kit she'd hidden under her bunk. She wouldn't have needed them if she'd gone on the ship as the Old Man ordered. Now the danger of going back to the barracks was outweighed by all the dangers she would be able to avoid later if she had the coins and pistol.

Simply by selling the pistol, she could get enough coin to rent a room for months in Overhill.

And hell, she was already *here.*

Despite the early-morning hour, Gill Greyling was seated on the side of his bunk. He blinked slowly, unseeing, staring at his dead brother's empty bunk. Stubble darkened his cheeks, and his uniform was wrinkled. He'd obviously been up all night.

Her breath froze inside her. So it was true.

Not that there had been much question, but it still seemed impossible. Gavin Greyling? Dead? *Gav?*

Teia's earlier black rage was washing out with the dawn, and she was afraid what weaknesses the new day's light would reveal.

Coming here was a terrible mistake.

She swallowed. Checked her paryl drafting, her invisibility, everything. It was all still in place.

All right. Breathe. Breathe.

There was nothing for her to do here. She couldn't give Gill any comfort. Even if anything she said could make a difference—and it wouldn't! it wouldn't!—she had to make everyone think she was just *gone.*

Everyone. No exceptions.

Though it felt like a betrayal of her Blackguard brothers and sisters to trust them so little, it wasn't distrust...exactly. It was just that anyone could slip up, and any slip-up meant failure of her mission, and her father's death.

T? That's pretty much the definition of distrust.

Fine. So I'm the asshole. But there are traitors loyal only to the Order of the Broken Eye who sleep in this very room.

Teia just didn't know who they were yet.

But she would. She swore it. That was coming. And it would start with whoever had that limp.

She crept invisibly into the women's section of the barracks, carefully inspected the underside of her bunk, and silently slid open the little box she'd nailed there.

Coin stick, pistol, tailor's kit.

Though there was no one in here, she stood quietly, carefully. It said something about how thin the Blackguard was stretched, even with all the rapid promotions of barely deserving scrubs into their ranks, that now, half an hour after dawn, the barracks were empty. All those who'd been on night shift should be coming in to sleep now. Instead, with Blackguards training all the Chromeria's other drafters to fight, double shifts were more common than ever. That work wasn't as strenuous as the constant vigilance required of a Blackguard when guarding a Color or the promachos, but it wasn't rest, either.

In the main barracks, she gazed once more upon Gill Greyling, looking haunted on his bunk. There was no one with him. No one at all in the barracks except the two of them.

He was too well liked for this. Maybe he'd demanded to be alone.

Teia didn't want to think that no one had thought to stay with him, or that Commander Fisk hadn't given anyone leave to do so.

War doesn't strip dignity only from the dead.

Red morning sun poured through windows, bloody light limning his solitary, hunched figure. She turned sharply, a sudden urge to weep strangling her. She stepped away.

The wood floor creaked under her shoe, and she froze in place. Heart pounding, she looked over her shoulder.

Gill had tightened.

He sat up straight, looked around the barracks, eyes searching. There was no one here.

Teia was suddenly acutely aware that Gill wasn't only a bereaved brother. He was a fully trained Blackguard, relentlessly molded to be attuned to hidden threats. And armed. And now alert. If he charged her—even in her general direction—what was she going to do?

Fight him?

Impossible! A single touch would be confirmation that she was *here*! A single glimpse of her would jeopardize everything she was trying to do against the Order. A single telling sound would reveal the existence of an *invisible* intruder. He would report it, or at least tell someone, and anyone who heard such a wild thing would tell others, and the Order would hear.

And the Order would know who it had to be.

Could she speak? Tell him? Trust him?

No. She trusted him. She did. She could trust Gill Greyling. But she had no idea how the man would behave in his grief. It might be one shock too many. Talk of shimmercloaks? The Order? Traitors in the Blackguard itself? That was at least three shocks too many.

Besides, she had no idea how long they'd be alone, even if she dared to try to brief him on secrets she'd been commanded to keep secret from everyone. She trusted him, she just couldn't . . . trust how he'd respond.

Ugh. That felt ugly and false.

She had to get out of here.

She began lifting her soft shoe slowly, heart pounding. She could feel the tension in the wood. There was no question: when she lifted that foot, the floor would creak again.

"Gav?" Gill whispered.

Teia's heart tumbled to the floor.

"Gavin? Is that you?" Gill asked plaintively.

Oh no. No, no, no.

"I can feel your presence. I know you're here. It's you, isn't it? Little brother . . ." His voice trailed off, and Teia saw him gulping convulsively against the threatening tears, joy and hope taking up arms against a tide of grief.

For a long moment, neither of them moved.

"Can you . . . can you give me another sign?" Gill asked.

She *had* to lift her foot. Gill was staring straight at her. She couldn't wait him out. Anyone might come in at any moment. Anyone who came in would surely go straight to Gill to offer some comfort—and Teia was blocking the aisle, rooted to the floor.

Teeth gritted, tears swimming in her eyes, she lifted her foot. The floor squeaked a protest. She retreated. From the barracks door, she looked back.

It was as if a great weight had been lifted from Gill's shoulders. He was standing, his face radiant. "I knew it!" he said. "I knew you wouldn't leave me . . ." His face twisted suddenly, a cavalry charge of tears of grief smashing against the shields of a smile, and his last word was a whisper. ". . . alone."

He wept then, and spoke to his dead little brother, and Teia couldn't stay, and she couldn't leave. Like a monster, she eavesdropped, and she knew it was a profound betrayal of those brothers she'd loved.

She was unforgiveable. Irredeemable.

She slowly sank into the sticky shadows of the hall. Her home. Human grief and human love and every species of human bonds and heart connections had floated at her fingertips, sometimes pushing in, sometimes waiting for her to reach out her hands and pull them to her once more. She'd been pushing it all away for the last year, and now as if by long practice her muscles of rejection had grown immensely strong, her humanity flown far from her.

No. No! This wasn't what she wanted, was it? From the darkness of her shadowy perch in the hall, she only watched as two figures rounded the corner of the tower's circular hallway into view. Essel and one-handed Trainer Samite fell silent as they approached the double doors of the barracks that they'd each gone through thousands of times.

With her hand hovering short of the door handle, Samite said, "Done this shit too many times this year."

"But not with a kid Gav's age," Essel said.

Through her teeth, Samite addressed only the floor. "I don't even know Gill that well. It shouldn't be me."

"It shouldn't be you giving him comfort," Essel agreed. "But right now it's nobody at all." Her tone was as soft and near as Teia felt cold and distant. Essel hesitated one moment more, giving Samite a chance, but then, as the trainer failed to marshal her courage as she had never failed in battle, Essel didn't reproach her. She only said quietly, "I'll go in now. You can come when you're ready."

But then Samite cursed quietly and opened the door. The two veterans disappeared inside together.

It was as if someone had held a long-lens up to each of Teia's eyes—backward. Every good thing Teia had ever wanted in life suddenly whooshed as far away as Orholam's Eye was to a woman pulled into the depths of the sea, drowning unseen.

Teia was exactly what she hated and condemned. She was Karris: offering those who deserved the truth a comforting lie instead, telling herself that her profound deception wasn't a betrayal.

In the hall, she passed a mirror and couldn't help but seek herself in its eyes.

Framed in a socket of rotting wood, with the tired, tarnished silver eyeshine of an aging nighttime carnivore, the dull, distorted glass revealed *nothing* where Teia stood—it showed a nullity more profound than darkness. All that was, still *was*, without her in the frame. Teia's absence was merely an empty bunk in the barracks, soon filled by another. She wasn't even a name on the lists of the war dead, a last sound heard a last time as it was read aloud to ears desperate not to hear some other name read out. She wasn't even one last scribble on a page to be posted publicly and skimmed over by some bereft family wondering if they would never hear any word at all of a lost son. The hole within her that had expanded with every murdered slave now reached beyond every bound of her body.

She was become absence itself.

She was more dead than Gav Greyling, who was still loved, who still had one who spoke to him.

Not so long ago, a fierce and fiery young Blackguard would have filled that mirror. Teia had been—she saw only now—beautifully *alive*. So, so young. But not less because of it. She'd been vibrant, strong, passionate. Playful.

An afterimage of her own old white-hot smile stole onto Teia's lips. Then it cooled, darkened.

Someone had murdered that spirited girl and turned her into a ghost. She could cast the guilt on others for that, but when she examined all the evidence honestly, she could still only see her own hand bloody on the knife.

*   *   *

With her thoughts hanging as heavy about her head as a burial shroud, as she left the Chromeria, Teia missed the low, slow scuff of rubber-soled shoes following her softly as a shadow.

Chapter 22

"Beautiful, ain't it?" a voice said behind Gavin. "And you and I'll make it through the mist wall. Just wish I wasn't going to drown before I reach shore."

Gavin froze. He knew that voice. The view of distant White Mist Tower that had so riveted him suddenly faded to insignificance.

"I'm a little too late, aren't I?" the old man continued. "You've already decided what you want, haven't you, oarmate? Then creation weeps at my failure."

"What's this?" Gunner demanded as Gavin turned.

"Stowaway, Cap'n," the first mate said. Pansy's hard face twisted like old oak gnarling. "Sorry for interruptin'."

"Well, I'll be!" Gunner shouted. He clapped his hands together, not once but in a weird quick rhythm.

"The men wanted to toss him overboard right off," she said. "I thought maybe a keelhaulin' instead? See if this luxin hull stays as clean as claimed, eh? Good for some entertainment, either way."

Bleeding from his mouth and nose, one eye swollen, and with both arms imprisoned by sailors with blood on their fists and grins on their faces, was none other than Gavin's old holier-than-thou oarmate, Orholam.

"No, no, no!" Gunner said, laughing. "This here's one of my old rowers! We go way back! You can't throw him to the sea! Ceres'd spit out such stringy meat!"

Orholam released a held breath, relieved. Apparently, he wasn't quite as certain of his prophecy as he'd claimed.

Gavin didn't particularly enjoy the rush of warm feelings that flowed over him at the sight of the old coot, but they had lived and worked and fought together during the worst part of Gavin's life.

Correction: the worst of my life up until that point. The cells under the Chromeria had been worse.

The prophet dared a small smile at his old owner.

Gunner repaid the smile with interest, but there was an edge to that smile that Gavin didn't like.

"Apologies for my tardiness, lord," Orholam said, head drooping once more. "I didn't think they'd take to the beating with such gusto."

"I ain't no lord," Gunner said. "I'm better. I'm a captain. A legend. I am—"

"I wasn't talking to you," Orholam said.

"Oh, then *I* forgive you," Gavin said quickly. The seed of an idea was sprouting in his mind. A prophet was a wild card to be snatched up as quickly as possible. Sailors were a superstitious lot. "But maybe—"

"Wasn't talking to you neither," Orholam said. "You're lord of shit-all now."

Gunner laughed at Gavin's expression.

"You're not makin' any friends, old man," Gavin shot back. "And it seems to me right now you need some."

Orholam said, " 'Need' is a strange word for this day. 'Friend' is even stranger."

"Stranger?" Captain Gunner said, stubbornly holding on to his glee. "What's *stranger* is that the fate of a god is given into my hand, *Orholam*."

"Nor for the last time," Orholam mumbled to the deck.

Captain Gunner roared, "Pansy!"

"I'm still right here...Captain," the woman said, at his elbow, non-plussed.

For the first time, Gavin's guile spied a little wedge into which he might force his will. So Pansy didn't particularly love serving Gunner, huh?

"Keelhaulin'. Psh," Gunner said. "Keel' this old boy? This old boy is *Orholam* hissown self. Orholam deserves spatial treatment." He smiled. It wasn't a kind smile.

Gavin saw Orholam swallow hard.

Oh, shit. Gavin's plan, half-formed as it was, required Orholam. Alive.

Offhand, Gunner said, "Strap him to the cannon."

His confidence vanishing, Orholam slumped, propped up only by the two sailors holding his arms, but he made no attempt at escape, resigned to his fate. Out here, at the center of the Cerulean Sea, where was there to run?

"Wh-why do this?" Gavin asked Gunner.

"Better question. Why not?" Gunner said.

The sailors draped Orholam over the cannon, hugging the barrel with both hands and feet. They stopped when they saw Gunner looking at them like they were complete morons.

"What're you thinkin' I wanna do? Warm his tenders with a few shots? *Scald* him to death through repeated firing?" Gunner demanded.

They looked back and forth at each other.

"Uh...over the *muzzle* then, Captain?" one asked. "Yessir! Right!"

Under Gunner's baleful eye, the sailors stripped Orholam to the waist. It only took them a short time to figure out how to tie the old rower over the mouth of the big cannon: his butt supported by ropes, arms and legs lashed down the barrel, facing toward the breech, torso strapped so as to cover the opening of the muzzle itself. The cannon's round shot was nearly as wide as the prophet's skinny chest.

The sailors began taking lighthearted bets on whether the shot would punch a hole cleanly through him, or if it would tear the prophet in half.

Gavin suddenly felt the old lens displacement he'd felt when in the space of a single hour he'd gone from a dignified discussion over tea in the palace at Ru during the Prisms' War to joining his men at their fires, with their jokes about hilarious murders they'd committed that

morning.

In the incongruities of war, sometimes you wonder, Am I even the same person?

But these men weren't soldiers. They'd not sacrificed their illusions and parts of their souls in order to pursue some noble ideal. He'd known that these sailors weren't good people; they were serving the Order of the Broken Eye. But hell, even Gavin himself was sort of serving the Order now. Seeing that they were assholes made him feel a lot better that they were on this suicide mission with him.

Let 'em die.

"Why kill Orholam, Gunner?" Gavin asked, louder.

Gunner looked at him sharply.

"Captain Gunner, I mean. Sir," Gavin said, suppressing a cringe.

But Gunner let it go, turning to Orholam instead. "My, my, my, I thrust out into the sea with all my charms, and what wonderous babes that old gruntin' labia-clapper slides easy into my harms. Arms."

He spat into the sea, then examined the swollen, bloodied face of his old slave: the sailors had been none too gentle when they found him hiding belowdecks.

Oddly, though, the prophet seemed to have already recovered his good spirits.

Minus the beating, the last year of not being chained to an oar had been good for Orholam. His cheeks weren't so hollow, and now he owned the modest tunic and trousers of a Parian tradesman. Any *burnous* or head covering he might have been wearing earlier had been taken, though, searched for weapons. The Order were big believers in paranoia.

But there was no mistaking Gavin's old oarmate, the man whose real name he'd never heard. In all Gavin's time as a galley slave, this man had spoken so rarely, and so infuriatingly full of religious platitudes, that he'd been dubbed 'Orholam.'

Orholam still had the reedy, strong arms of the oarsman he had been, and the bright eyes of the madman he doubtless still was.

"You got nothing to say, my own li'l *ora'lem Or'holam*?" Gunner said.

"You know Old Parian?" Gavin asked. Ora'lem Or'holam. Hidden Orholam?

"Hidden no more," Orholam said.

"Shut up, you," Gunner said. He addressed Gavin. "Good curses, Old Parian. My mama taught me. She loved to curse. Said it was the mark of a mature mind, cursin' fluently. Said every man should have fifty ways o' telling a man to bugger a viper's nest inside a cactus, and every woman double that many. I ever tell you about my mama?"

147

He couldn't have forgotten. Gavin surely never would.

Gunner regarded Orholam through bushy brows. "Orholam! You're a prophet. Prophet-size me what I'mma say next."

Orholam sighed. "Something about seeing as how I'm a stowaway, I can pay for my passage by giving you a prophecy for free."

"I'll be damned," one of the sailors holding Orholam's arms said.

"So wait," Gavin said. "Does that count?"

The sailors looked confused. The captain kept his face blank.

"You asked him for one prophecy, and he gave you one. A true one, too, by the look on your face. So . . . that pays his passage, right?"

Gunner's face looked like, while expecting brandy, he'd just quaffed bilge water.

"If you're getting one free glimpse into the future, it's too bad you wasted yours," Gavin said, "but he *did* give you what you demanded."

"That one didn't take prophecy to figure out," Orholam said, sighing. "I'm happy to oblige with another."

The crew, at least, seemed excited for the show to go on.

"How'd you do that?" Gunner demanded.

"After Guile here and young Lord Malargos freed us all from . . . well, from you, Captain, I took an oath never to lie again. It's been less pleasant to fulfill than even I'd guessed it would be. When men ask my vocation and I tell them I'm a prophet . . . let's just say, I get blindfolded and hit a lot. People ask me to say which one of them hit me. If I don't tell them, they think I can't, and thus I'm a fraud—which often gets me a beating. If I do tell them, though, they tend to try it again to see if I simply guessed correctly once, or twice, or three times. Not a fun game for me."

"Good news, then," Gunner said, seeming to have regained his footing. "There'll be no games."

"I wasn't implying—"

"When'd you take that oath?" Gunner asked.

"I said—"

"You shut up! You're a liar," Gunner said.

"I never lied to—"

"Not another word!" Gunner said. He thrust out his hand toward one of the sailors. "Linstock!"

"No, wait!" Orholam shouted. "Please—"

Gunner punched him in the face so fast the older man didn't even see it coming. His face snapped back so hard Gavin worried his neck was broken, and blood sprayed into the air, and then down his mouth and chin as his broken nose gushed blood.

"Prophets are hard to ken, but Gunner is not," Gunner said.

That actually was not at all true.

"Interplat me this, prophet," Gunner said. "What do you think I said when I meant not another word?"

Orholam opened his mouth to speak, then stopped, confused.

The sailors looked the same. One of them held out the linstock with a match cord affixed in it to the captain, but the captain didn't even seem aware of him now.

"What do you thean I mink!" Gunner bellowed, drawing back his fist again.

Gavin darted between them. "He's respecting you, Captain. Obeying you. If he answers, he'd be disobeying your order to be silent. See?"

"Ahhh! Stickin' up for your whoremate. But...that's true, ain't it?" Gunner said, stepping back. He twisted a bit of his beard and chewed on it. "My order to him did set the sails against the rowers, eh? 'Tain't fair, that. And I do believe in a fair taint."

"Then it's no wonder you enjoyed your time with Pansy's mother so much, Captain," Gavin said, deadpan.

Gunner guffawed as the sailors nearby chuckled or laughed aloud, though Pansy did not. Then Gunner stopped abruptly.

"You're a crafty little cunt, ain'tcha, Guile?"

Gavin said, "Once upon a time, I was actually reckoned a big cunt."

Gunner was not amused. "Don't get above your station, wee little man, or we'll make your lady parts more gapey than you'd wish, like Orh'lam's are about to be."

Orholam mumbled a protest but didn't speak. Gavin gulped. If every attempt at humor was a risk, attempts at humor with a happily homicidal madman were perhaps a risk not wisely taken.

"Gapey Guile, they'll call ya, eh, eh?" the captain asked.

The sailors chuckled dutifully, and then Gunner dismissed them to their work. They left the forecastle like it was an order. As they went, Gunner waggled his eyebrows at Gavin, grinning, suddenly convivial again.

Aha, Gavin had been speaking out of turn, so Gunner had merely been showing them who was in charge.

Gavin had gotten off lightly for such an offense. He wasn't even bloody.

My lucky day.

Now Gunner gazed at the horizon. "No one hates the sea like a sailor," he said.

He patted the big cannon that dominated the forecastle. The damned thing—now with bonus prophet adorning the muzzle—was *steel*. Steel, not brass. Gavin had never seen such a thing, always heard that steel couldn't be cast reliably this large. Either the Ilytians were making rapid advances in their metallurgy or every shot with this thing was risking a shrapnel-filled death for everyone on the forecastle.

Gunner hopped up on the cannon, his sentiment passing as quick as a whitecap. "Queer, eh? Boomer this big, out front? Should be too heavy so high up, made o' steel. Should make the ship squirrely as all hell, foulin' her center of weight."

"But it doesn't?" Gavin guessed. He had no delusions that Gunner had forgotten about Orholam, and whatever it was he had against the old man.

"Lighter than possible," Gunner said.

Well, obviously not, Gavin thought.

"Shoots true, too," Gunner said. "Accurate within your arm's stretch at a thousand paces. Greatest random is near thrice that."

"You name her?" Gavin asked, trying to anchor himself back on Gunner's good side.

Gunner had walked down the barrel until he was looming over Orholam. He stood on one foot, and with his opposite big toe lifted Orholam's chin to look at him. But Gavin's words distracted him. "Her? Her?! What the—how dumb are ya, Guile? Her! *Him.* C'mon. Cannons're always he's. Even you with your inky fingers gorta know that!" He did hip thrusts out over the empty air. "Boom! Boom!"

"Ah. Of course," Gavin said.

Gunner held on to nothing. He stared at the sky, he stared at the sea, he stared at his crew. He squatted now and patted the side of his cannon as a sane man might pat a horse's cheek. "Ol' Phin gave him the cognomenclature The Compelling Argument."

Gunner stood, and kicked a lever, then rode the cannon as it slid slowly back on a track. When it stopped, Orholam grunted, jarred against the muzzle pressed into his belly.

Gavin grinned. "He's, uh, he's beautiful. And it's a very fitting name."

"Captain, may I—" Orholam interjected timidly.

"You a slow learner, boy?" Gunner blazed, spittle flying.

Orholam swallowed.

"You'll get your chance to proffer a defiance." Gunner's eyes flicked upward. He tugged his beard. "Defense. 'Defiance' is good, though, eh, Gapin' Guile?"

Gavin nodded. "It works. It defiantly works."

Gunner missed it. That intense focus on one thing at a time that served him so well elsewhere meant the man often missed everything else.

"Shaped shells, you ever heard a such a thing?" Gunner asked. "Fer a cannon. And old Phin left forms so's I can make more. They gives me an extra two hunnerd paces, ackerate! BUT! I can use regular old round shot, too. And looksie this."

Gunner showed Gavin a set of levers that popped out near the muzzle. Gavin couldn't even pretend to understand.

"Puts *spin* on a ball, if you use a ball. Don't work for the shaped shells, unmoors the putty," Gunner said. More's the pity? "Costs yer some distance, but I can *curve* a cannonball. Up, down, or t'either side. Not much, mind you, and not sure what good it be—drop a ball tight o'er a wall, maybe? Phin was prollaby havin' fun. Showin' off like he do. You wanna see?"

"Love to!" Gavin said. There wasn't much entertainment out here, and Gunner treated him nearly like an equal, as long as Gavin played along with his whims. "But...um..."

Gavin motioned to the old man strapped over the muzzle.

"Oh, I hadn't forgot!" Gunner said. "You think I can curve it 'round him?"

Orholam's body was entirely blocking the muzzle.

"If it were possible, you'd be the one to do it," Gavin said. "But... I'm afraid he'd just foul the spin and mess it all up."

Gunner scowled. Orholam was nodding emphatically.

"Eh, still worth a shot!" Gunner said. He began checking the cannon with the unhurried efficiency of an old minstrel tuning her lute. Then he examined the harness that strapped the old prophet to the muzzle, arms and legs bound down the wide barrel, his belly and chest positioned to be turned into mist.

"It's going to make such a mess," Gavin said.

"Ol' Phin knew I love shit like this," Gunner said as if he hadn't spoken. "Curving cannonballs. That oughta be my new curse. Quite the gift. Almost makes me wish I hadn't played Hide the Musket in his old lady's skirts. Thet's on him, though. Man worked too much, he did. A woman's like a cannon herself. Keep her well lubricated, and she'll not just stand hard use but shine with it. But you cain't just empty your powder horn in her, then drop her back on the rack to rust! Phin shoulda knowed better. He's got three daughters."

Gunner blinked.

"I mean, not that he should've—been emptying anything...in his daughters. I mean, he shoulda knowed better than to marry a woman with appetites nearly as wide as her vengeful streak. By Ceres's swin-gin' saggies, I think she wanted us to get caught that last time. Had to be quick on the trigger with the old man stomping around downstairs, and her none too quiet. Then I had to climb on the roof and wait till nightfall to get away. Still. She shouldn'ta did that to Ol' Phin."

"It's all on her, huh?" Gavin asked.

Gunner looked at him like he was talking crazy. "Can't blame a sailor on shore leave for havin' an overcharged musket. I gone gam-bling, so I had no coin for whores. And I did try his daughters first! But...my luck was no better with them than it had been gambling."

You tried to woo his daughters first, and then their mother. Charming.

"But!" Gunner ejaculated. "I'll make it up to him by using this can-non as he intended."

"Eviscerating a man with his cannon will surely soothe any resent-ment he might have harbored for you swiving his wife."

"Agreed! Now, port or starbeard? I mean, I could go up or down, but it just look like I shot short or long to an ignorant layman like yerself."

"I don't know, Captain. Like you said, I'm ignorant, but if you plug the barrel, there's a risk of backfire, isn't there?"

"Backfire? We're talking iron and black powder 'gainst something as squishy as Orholam. Nah. Won't be a problem."

"I thought we were going to have some 'defiance' first."

"Huh?" Gunner asked.

"Orholam's defense?" Gavin prompted.

"The what?"

"The old man."

"Oh! Course, course." Gunner turned to the bound old man, who was sweating profusely now. Gunner said, "You coulda helped me, a lot. With what you kin do."

"I did help you. Every day," Orholam said. "Rowing?" He winced as he said the last, as if he couldn't help himself.

"Ahaha!" Gunner said, picking up the linstock and adjusting the match cord. "Funny, funny. I got me a sense of humor, too. Explosive one. Leaves 'em in pieces."

He opened the cage of a small lantern and lit the match cord from it. "I need the help o' yer magic peepers, not yer arms," Gunner said. "You done me a wrong, prophet. You gotta make right. Right now. What do you see? Say it plain or die."

"Please. You can't kill me."

"Now, *that* is a prophecy we can test real easy."

"I mean, if you kill me now, this whole world will be lost."

"Don't care," Gunner said. "I'll give you a count a four. And I ain't good at my number alls. One."

"We'll see White Mist Tower within the hour," the prophet said quickly.

"A bit late with that one," Gavin said, gesturing toward the distant tower.

"Ah shit," Orholam said, craning his neck and catching sight of the thing, apparently for the first time. "Did I say the tower? I meant the reef. We'll see and hear the reef itself within the hour."

"Really going out on a limb there, aren't you?" Gavin asked, though he wasn't sure why. He needed Orholam alive. What was he doing?

"Thanks, oarmate," Orholam said.

"My quibble's not with you; it's with your master," Gavin said.

Orholam said, "Love to have that discussion. Maybe we can do that sometime when I'm not strapped to a cannon by an angry madm—er, Master, uh, Master Gentleman?"

"About me," Gunner said, grabbing a handful of Orholam's salted beard. "Proffer-size about me. Or you will see an angry mad master gentleman. And no lies this time!"

"What's this about?" Gavin asked.

"Last time he told me I wouldn't lose the blade!"

Orholam said, "I said you'd live to give it willingly to Dazen Guile, not that you'd keep it at all times between when I told you that and when you finally gave it to him. And do you not wear it even now?"

"I gambled because a what you said! And I lost! Twice!" Gunner said. "You can't go making porphyries what don't mean what people think they do."

"Actually, I think that's the main business of prophets," Gavin said.

"Not with *me*. Understand?" Gunner said to Orholam, as if it had been he who talked back to him, not Gavin.

"You'll not die on the reef," Orholam said, fearful. "I swear it."

"So we make it! We shoot the gap! I told you I'd be in the books, Gilly!" Gunner expelled a big breath. "Do you see how many cannon I gotta use? Straight approach, or swinging 'round?"

But Gavin went to another tack. "Wait, wait. Not *on* the reef? So...does that mean the captain'll drown before he gets to the reef? He'll be battered to death by the ship breaking up?"

What was he doing? He needed the prophet *alive*.

"No! No. He'll live." But there was a sudden hesitation in the prophet's countenance.

"Orholam..." Gunner said, warning. "Tell me the whole truth." 153

The old man sank into himself. "You'll live, but the ship won't make it past the reef."

"No!" Gunner said, grabbing fistfuls of his hair. "Not my ship! Damn you, no! I gave everything for this ship!"

"What?" Gavin said. "No you didn't. You gambled for it. And you didn't even win. And it was *my* blade you gambled in the first place!"

"Mine!" Gunner said.

"So we'll never make it past the reef?" Gavin said.

"That's...not exactly what I said," Orholam said.

"Are we going to break up on the reef or no?" Gunner demanded.

"We're going to..." Orholam suddenly looked very, very reluctant. "It's ill luck to speak...of them."

Gunner's dark visage turned green. "Nay," he breathed. He spat in the sea. "Tell me."

"All eight," Orholam said. "Within the hour."

"All eight what?" Gavin asked. He was afraid that he already knew.

"Ceres's sons," Gunner whispered.

"Aye," Orholam said. "Soon now, I think."

The captain made the sign of the three and the four. "No. There's got to be a way."

Orholam said,

"Twenty-two there were, of the needed nine,
Who swam, immortal, 'gainst the scythe of time.
Now eight there are, of the needed nine,
Uluch Assan brings the end this time."

Uluch Assan. That was Gunner's birth name.

Gunner's face darkened. "This is *not* on me! What was I supposed to do? Let her kill us? I was a boy who begged onna the gun crew, not the captain o' that vessel. It wasn't my fault we sailed inta these waters!"

"*These* waters?" Gavin asked. "You mean you've been here before? You have! This was where you killed the—"

"Don't name 'em!" Gunner said. "It's bad luck."

"This was where you earned your name?" Gavin asked.

But neither of them answered him.

It suddenly made sense. How else would Gunner have known the sea demons were here, or the shape of the reef? Why else would Grinwoody have chosen Gunner to pilot his ship here, rather than one of his own people?

Orholam said, "The dark ones live on light—"

"What, like plants?" Gavin asked.

"No, the imbalances in it," he said.

154

"What are you talking about, 'the imbalances'?" Gavin said. "Prisms take care of any color imbalances."

"You're the first Prism to do that fully since Vician's Sin," Orholam said. "Since that time, the...the dark ones have been tolerated by the Chromeria for what they do. In subtle ways and explicit when necessary, drafters have been forbidden to harm them."

"But why? How's this fit with balancing?"

"It's really hard—" Orholam coughed unconvincingly. "It's hard to take a breath tied like this. I'm not sure if I can answer—"

Gunner lifted the burning match cord on the linstock close to the old man's face and then began moving it toward the fuse. "What if I say please?"

Orholam cleared his throat. "Most of the bane form here, and spin out through the sea. The dark ones devour the bane. Generally when the crystals are small and harmless. The bane only become truly dangerous when wights find them, because the bane can be used to amplify wights' powers. But when the bane are small, they're just food for the dark ones, forming constantly—just a consequence of magic in our world. Even a Prism balancing only minimizes how many appear. So in certain ways, this is your fault, too, Guile."

"Mine?!"

"See! I told you this wasn't on me!" Gunner said.

Orholam said, "With you balancing in truth, there were fewer bane, so the sea—err, so the dark ones had to go swim far from here to find other food. With them all feeding at the far corners of the seas, their net was spread too thin here to catch the sudden surge of bane that erupted once you so suddenly stopped balancing."

"So it's kind of *both* of our faults?" Gavin asked. "How do you know all this?"

"I'm a prophet. Knowing is what we do. It's not all about the future. In a world like ours, it's just as often about the past."

"Fine, then, no answer is fine," Gavin said. Maybe Orholam had been some kind of historian before he'd been captured and pressganged, chained to his oar. Maybe he'd once had access to books Gavin had never known. "What was that about 'the needed nine'?"

"Can you cut me loose yet?" Orholam asked. "It would be so much easier—"

"No!" Gunner growled.

"Nine of the dark ones survived into our era. Nine were enough to devour all the bane that formed. On the day Uluch Assan killed the ninth, Dazen Guile's gift awoke."

"My gift? Drafting black, you mean."

"I'm not going to be more specific."

"But you know."

"Oh yes. I kept misunderstanding what I needed to do and say here until Orholam revealed it all to me. But you don't deserve the same treatment. You haven't acted with the same obedience I have. You've distanced yourself from the truth, so the distance between you and the truth is your fault, not mine. Regardless, one might say, in a way, everything here—the war, the False Prism's War, all the death and misery and destruction—was one man's fault."

He called it the 'False Prism's War' rather than the Prisms' War. Fuck you, Orholam. "I'm tired of taking the blame for everything," Gavin said.

"He warn't talking 'bout you," Gunner said. There was a weariness in his voice.

"There was a tenuous, oh so tenuous, balance, but one that had stood for four centuries," Orholam said. "Others kicked out other legs of the stool, but you, Gunner, you kicked out the leg that made it all fall. That's why you get to be here now. You wanted the ultimate test for your gifts? It's coming. You want to be a legend? Maybe that, too. But your Name in history depends on what he does." He waggled a finger, but his arm was tied to the barrel, so it wasn't clear where he was pointing.

"Me?" Gavin asked. "Gunner's legend depends on me?"

"As does my own life."

"Your life?"

"Yes, but I've given up on that. Doesn't matter. You're not that man, Gavin Guile. What does matter is that if you don't succeed, Gunner will die out here."

"I thought you said I live!" Gunner protested.

"*Today*. But if Gavin—well, *this* Gavin, since one is supposed to be very careful with words when giving prophecy—if this man here fails, you'll eventually despair, drink seawater, and try to swim home. I think you drown while fighting sharks. Regardless, they eat you before or after you drown or a little of you before you drown—your left foot?—and then the rest of you after."

"Do I put up a good fight?" Gunner asked. He was standing delicately on his right foot as if the deck were covered in broken glass and he didn't want to put down his left foot. He made little fists with his toes.

Orholam twisted his mouth, a man trapped between his morality and his mortality. "For a man who's cooked in the sun for days without shelter and drunk seawater . . . you certainly, uh, give it your all."

"All of 'em are here?" Gunner asked.

"All eight," Orholam said.

"Do I kill any afore they get me?" Gunner asked.

"You don't kill any of the dark ones, and they don't get you," Orholam said.

Gavin expected Gunner to rage at that, but he got very quiet instead. He removed the match cord from the linstock. Stubbed it out on the great cannon, then buffed out the black smear with his coat sleeve.

"He's a beaut, ain't he?" Gunner said. "Makes me almost want to turn pirateer again, just to get the chance to try him in battle. Curved shots? Hell, he's got two dozen other tricks that are even better. I sailed out a few leagues from the Jaspers and popped off as many shots as I could for weeks, getting my mastery up. I can make a Compelling Argument myself, alone, on a mere count to fifty-seven. Four of that aim time. See that tank over there, Guile? Water. Pump that up afore battle, puts it under pressure. Every ten shots, Compie gets too hot. Spray that water inside and out, then that lever tilts the whole boy up to drain—whole thing! counterweighted so's I can do it myself— swab, tilt him back, and go on as afore. Adds only a fifteen count to the process. With the right crew and materiel, he can fire all day without getting overhot or cracking."

"He's really something," Gavin said, puzzled.

"Man'd be crazy to lie what you just told me," Gunner told Orholam. "So I think you're not just honest, you're brave. That deserves rewardin'."

He cut Orholam free.

Perhaps wisely, Orholam kept his mouth shut now, even as he rubbed feeling back into his legs and arms.

"White Mist Reef ain't like the Everdark Gates," Gunner said. "Men have shot the Gates afore. There are ways through. You need luck and a chart and a great crew, but it can be done. It's special, sure, but not legendary. But no one's made it through White Mist Reef. At least, none who've also made it back. No one. I thought if anyone could do it, it'd be you an' me, Guile."

"I suppose it would," Gavin said, uncertain where this was going.

"Magnificent critter, she was. We named her Ceres, said the whole sea must be hers. She followed us half a week while Captain scouted the reef, and seemed well-nigh content to hold back, until we tried to shoot the gap. Then she boiled the seas with her fury. We'd been expectin' it. Plan was to distract her with the shock and sounds of the rafts blowin' up in the waters 'round us. The gun captain was a fool, 157 though. Didn't set the fuses right. Got the timing wrong. Wouldn't listen when I told him. So when it all went to shit, I pushed him out a gunport and took charge. I walked our shots right in a line to the last raft, heavy-loaded with black powder. Six hundred paces out. My timin' never been so good. Ceres came up from beneath and just as she lifted that raft up inta the air in her jaws...My shot hit the barrels of black powder.

"For half a minute, I felt like a god. Everyone cheered. And then I felt ashamed. I watched that great beauty bubble and bleed and sink with her jaws all blown four directions, and the other dark ones stopped their circlin' and came fast to their dead sister. They tried to prop her up in the water. I swear, they grieved. And I knew then that what I done was wrong. I knew I was acurst. Been runnin' from Ceres's vengeance ever since."

"Why did you come back?" Gavin asked.

"A man gets tired a runnin', Guile."

Gunner disappeared then, and left Gavin and Orholam bewildered on the forecastle. "It's not a death sentence," Orholam said. "Well, not necessarily."

"Shut up," Gavin said.

Gunner reappeared. He tossed the Blinding Knife to Gavin. Orholam immediately began helping Gavin tie the long blade to his back with the very ropes he'd been bound with moments before. Gavin didn't even think to ask why.

"Well, look at that," Gunner said. Inexplicably, his bright mood had returned.

"Land ho!" a voice called from the crow's nest. The sailor hadn't even fully climbed the rigging to get in the nest, the clouds had parted so suddenly.

It was a bright spring day.

The sound of the surf rushing through the teeth of the coral came to them.

"Behold," Orholam said. "White Mist Reef."

"We go down fighting," Gunner announced.

" 'Old age hath yet his honor and his toil'?" Gavin quoted.

"Old farts always did like them lines," Gunner said. " 'Though much is taken, naught abides.' "

"I don't think that's how that—"

A shout rang out from the crow's nest: "Creature, hie!"

"Critter? What critter?!" Pansy called from the wheel.

Gunner and Gavin cursed in concert.

"Reef ho!" the lookout shouted. "And…a spout? A spout! It's a whale! A great black whale!"

"Aha!" Gunner said. He danced in a little circle, then waggled a finger in front of Orholam's face. "So much for that, eh? Sunk by a sea demon? Everyone knows whales and the dark ones won't tolerate each other—hair goat, a whale here means there can't be no—"

"More whales! A full pod, sir!" the lookout cried.

Gunner laughed aloud, delighted. It was an infectious sound. "A pod! That means they've driven away the—"

"No. Wait." The lookout's voice dropped so low Gavin could barely hear it. "No, that's not possible."

"Report!" Gunner shouted. "Damn your poxy orbs! Report!"

"Sea demons! Three—maybe four sea demons. Closing on the whale, fast."

The news settled on the crew like a burial shroud.

"Permission to go unchain the oar slaves, Captain?" Orholam asked, breaking the silence. He muttered. "They won't stop rowing, I can promise you that."

Gunner didn't answer him, still stunned by the news.

Orholam said quietly, "They all die regardless, but it'll give 'em hope. It's no small thing to give a man facing his doom."

"Permission denied," Gunner said, snapping back into action. "You!" he shouted at a man. "Get me a pack. Stuffed with rations and water and brandy. Much as you can carry. Get back soonest. Gun crews! Stations! Gunports open!"

The rattle of commands didn't stop. The reef was beyond the battle unfolding before them, and the wind was suddenly hard in their sails.

Gunner spared Gavin and Orholam a single look, if only to usher them off to one side as his gun crew came onto the foredeck. "Looks like you get to see a Compelling Argument for your own selfs, after all!" He patted the cannon and winked at them, his black mood unaccountably vanished.

"Some of us survive?" Gavin asked Orholam. Of course, it was superstitious nonsense, prophecy. Of course it was.

But when his fate flies from his own hands, a man takes comfort where he can.

"Oh, aye, some of us," Orholam said. "Gods have always been fond of prophets and madmen."

"And emperors?" Gavin suggested.

Orholam said, "I don't see any of those here."

Chapter 23

"You strike me as decent and fundamentally honest," Kip said, staring not at the Keeper but at the mechanism filling the great white oak tree towering above them.

"Thank you," the Keeper of the Flame said.

"Fundamentally honest, but you're not being honest now," Kip said, as if merely clarifying.

He pretended to ignore her, examining the Great Mirror. He'd never seen such an odd collision of materials. Nested metal frames on three axes were supported by limbs that had obviously been grown for the task, and the foliage itself had been husbanded so as to leave gaps for the light to come in and go out.

Kip had held suspicions that some things in the natural world were shaped by luxin as much as human drafters were. The extinct atasifusta trees were the most obvious candidates, but sea demons were said to be deeply entwined with magic, too, and his Night Mares said there was a special feel to giant elk, giant grizzlies, giant javelinas, and certain other animals. Certainly this tree was larger than any white oak he'd ever heard of.

She spoke up. "Perhaps you misread my discomfort. This entire area is virtually aglow with chi. Unless you and all your friends wish to get the same cancers that are killing me, we must keep this very brief."

The Keeper was once more ensconced in her golden armor and veils, so Kip was studying her more covertly: heeding her vocal inflections, her stance, where her feet pointed, her crossed arms, her chin tucked as if he'd go for her throat. For all that she'd said she would answer their questions, she had secrets here she was protecting.

"You've survived ten years of working with chi constantly. Are we to be fearful of dying after a quarter hour?" Kip asked.

"Chi is as unpredictable as a mad old bull, my lord. It's wisest to stay out of the corral."

Around him, the Mighty shuffled uneasily amid the verdant low underbrush of the old-growth forest here so oddly atop a palace, complete with mossy boulders and fallen tree limbs dissolving into the ground to feed mushrooms.

On a sudden hunch, Kip tightened his eyes all the way to chi. "That's why you wear the armor," he said. "That's what you meant when you said you're not safe."

The Keeper's body itself had become so infused with chi that it emanated chi. She had become a living lantern of lethal light. That was the reason for the heavy armor she wore—not to keep attacks *out* but to keep them *in.*

No wonder she didn't want anyone to stand close. No wonder others feared her so. No wonder the Chromeria feared chi and its drafters. Like paryl drafters, chi drafters could kill invisibly, but unlike their paryl counterparts, they did so unwittingly, unknowably, uncontrollably.

"That's correct," she said stiffly.

"You may have given us a cancer already," Kip said.

"Yes." Bitterness leaked through her clipped tones. It wasn't enough that she was dying, disfigured, and in pain, but she must be avoided by even caretakers, worse than a leper.

Kip didn't fight the sudden wave of fear that pushed through him, but neither did he step farther away. He looked for the seed of compassion he'd felt for her instead. He took a slow breath, choosing to see her as a brave and noble woman while ignoring himself. "You're a good person, strong and brave," Kip said, "so—"

"Are you mocking me, my lord?"

Oh, she was angry. Right on the edge. Or she was terrified.

"Actually," Kip said, "I was using this tricky rhetorical device we learn in the hinterlands of far Tyrea where I was born. We call it a 'compliment.'"

She didn't seem to know how to take that.

"So..." Kip said, "since you're that person. I can only figure that you've decided that deceiving me is the right thing for you to do. Can you help me understand why?"

"Excuse me?" she said.

"Answering a question with a question is a classic telltale of a lie."

"I haven't lied!" she said. "What do you want of us, Guile?"

"Your secret is no secret," Kip said. "You use the Great Mirror to pass messages to Green Haven. That's a stunning distance for a simple beam of light, so you can't be doing it directly. You've got to be using other smaller mirrors in between. Relay stations, like bonfires on hilltops. That's the only reason you'd need three axes for this mirror, so you could move the beam elsewhere in case one of those hilltop mirror stations is taken or needs repairs. But then it occurred to me that if you have mirror stations already, there's no reason you'd only communicate with Green Haven. With a few dozen stations, you could reach the entire satrapy. A message could be relayed from one end of the satrapy to the other in the course of a night. This is what I want from you—I want to use your network. I have people far afield. 161

If I can reach them, I can coordinate this satrapy's defenses in ways the Wight King couldn't hope to counter. He's blockaded the Great River. Do you know that? With your mirrors, I could find out where, and I could speak with our allies. Even if I could only get a message halfway across the satrapy but on the other side of the blockade, we could—"

"It's gone," she said.

"What?"

"There was such a network, long ago, before the Blood Wars. It was a huge defensive advantage—but the Ruthgari realized it, too. They murdered any chi drafters they could find and destroyed the mirror holds. Chi drafters have always been short-lived, and many of those few people who can learn to draft chi choose not to, given the costs. So we were always rare. The network fell centuries ago. A few mirrors still remain, some buried, hidden by their old keepers for the day when all could be restored, but they've no one tending them now. Where they're known at all, they're mere curiosities. Messages are only possible between here and Green Haven now, the old capital and the new."

"Why is it a secret, then?"

"We're not supposed to have it at all. The Chromeria wanted us to shut down all our defenses. They required it, but with the Ruthgari raiding, our ancestors broke that part of the treaty immediately. All this was centuries ago, mind you. The Chromeria didn't care, as long as we kept our defiance discreet. That need for discretion and their long revulsion for chi drafters has enforced us keeping a low profile. An overly zealous Magisterium or a hostile Prism could mean our deaths."

There was still something she wasn't telling him. "You use chi to adjust the mirror's positioning?" A yes-or-no question.

"We can use it for all sorts of things. Sending the beam of the signal, of course, being the most important," she said.

Not a direct answer. "You use chi to adjust the mirror's position?" he insisted.

She hesitated.

That was the problem with an unpracticed liar. She hoped to mislead Kip without lying outright. She hadn't considered exactly how far she was willing to go to hide her secrets, or what Kip was likely to already know.

"I thought it went without saying," she said.

"Odd thing to lie about," Kip mused.

"Are you quite dense?" she asked.

"Again a question in reply to a question," Kip said, as if commenting on the weather.

It was strange. What was it that allowed him to react so differently to her than to the Divines? She was lying to him. She'd just called him stupid. But he was able to see that this wasn't about him at all, so he didn't need to win here.

Stranger still, without him pushing back, she had nothing to push against, and she was falling over.

She said, "The Mirror has to be adjusted for weather conditions—some of which we understand and others we don't," she said. "For example, the light will travel differently after or during a rain or on a very humid day. Other times, it seems some quality of the sunlight itself changes how clearly the beams travel over these great distances. So minute movements are necessary even with our well-known target of Green Haven. Using even small amounts of chi repeatedly is, as you've seen, quite hazardous."

"Still hiding. Still deflecting," Kip said.

A perfect black globe broader across than Kip's shoulders rested in the trunk of the vast white oak itself, sunk into the wood—but leaving no rupture in the living wood, nor any oozing sap from a wound, nor any sign of the bark curling around it the way a natural tree might grow around a fence post. It looked as unnatural as if an image of a sphere had been superimposed on the tree trunk.

Inset around it were a number of similar black, featureless plates, only the oils of past fingers proving they weren't illusory.

But Kip wasn't drawn to those. Instead, he set his hands directly on the globe, and extended his will into it.

"What are you doing?" the Keeper of the Flame asked. "*Don't touch that!*"

He ignored her.

"You could die!" she said. She turned to Cruxer. "He could die! You have to stop him!"

None of the Mighty moved.

"We could *all* die if he does the wrong thing!" she said.

She reached a hand out to grab Kip, but suddenly found her arm held immobile.

"Then whatever he's doing," Cruxer said, his voice calmly professional but his grip on her arm unyielding, "I suggest you don't louse it up."

A touch of superviolet, and suddenly, above them, the vast shining disk that was the Great Mirror *wobbled*.

"Like I thought," Kip said. "You don't use chi to move the mirror. So what do you use it for?"

The mask hid all but a bit of her shaking her head. "Chi is more energetic than any other color. It can go farther, with less diffusion. The messages themselves are beams of chi."

Now, that was new. Kip had assumed they were reflecting the sun or a bonfire. "You reach Green Haven directly? All the way from here?!"

"Yes."

"Show me."

"I can't."

"You didn't get cancers doing nothing."

"There's...procedures."

"There's something in here, inside this globe. I can feel a hollow. Open it for me, would you?" Kip asked.

"I can't do that."

"Won't," Kip corrected. "No matter. Big Leo, you think you can smash this thing open with your chain?"

Big Leo grunted and slid the heavy fighting chain off his shoulders. His voice low and emotionless, he said, "Happy to try."

Winsen turned to Big Leo. "You know, if you do break it, they're gonna give him the credit, right? We should *never* have named him Breaker."

"Eh. I'm all right with that," Big Leo said. "Long as I get to use my chain."

O's beard, but he played the big dumb thug beautifully when he wanted to.

"You can't—no!" the Keeper said. She moved her body between Big Leo and the black globe.

Kip lifted a hand, and Big Leo stopped. "Keeper," Kip said, "I couldn't help but notice the band of trees all the way up and down the sides of the palace, all the way up to this one at the crown. Tell me about that. Seems like a lot of work. Why not just have the tree alone up here?"

He knew the answer. The locals said that beneath the surface, the roots of every tree in the city were connected with those of every other.

It might not be literally true, but it was a metaphor important enough to the old Foresters that they'd built an earthen ramp up and down their entire palace. The ancient kings and queens of this realm had wanted to proclaim that they were connected with all their people.

She seemed thrown off balance by his abrupt change in topic. "It's, it's...Trees are communal, Lord Guile," she said. "The roots inter-lace, passing along needed nutrients and even physical support to one

164

another, and especially to the tallest specimens. With the high winds up here, a white oak alone wouldn't stand for a year."

"Huh," Kip said. "Helping each other, passing along what's needed, even at some cost to themselves, so they all might thrive. United against the storm. It's almost as if there's a lesson we could learn from that."

"The trees support one another, Lord Guile. The largest don't only take, they also give."

"And you don't trust me to protect you. I don't blame you. You've given your life to be the Keeper of the Flame, and you'll do anything not to become the Loser of the Flame."

She folded her arms. "You already know, don't you?"

He said nothing.

"How?" she asked.

He drew in some superviolet and drew a line hanging in the air between the black orb set in the tree trunk just over a natural boulder and to the wall of the gatehouse. The color difference was barely perceptible to the naked eye. "Chi shadows," Kip said. "A lot more than you can draft unaided. And they're more intense off to the side, as if they hadn't been diffused by passing through the Keeper's body in the same way."

Her chin lifted, as if to offer another lie, but then descended. She suddenly had the air of one watching her life's work die, her legacy tainted, her order headed for genocide.

"They form all the time, you know," she said. "I don't think there's ever just one, despite what the Chromeria says. They're like lightning strikes, little discharge points for magic. And then they dissipate, usually. Unless someone with the right knowledge can get there first. Then she can stabilize it, build it if she wants. It calls to drafters, even over enormous distances if you grow it large enough. It's how the kings and queens of old summoned their drafter armies in the first place. They're dangerous, of course, especially these—"

"*These?* You have more than one?"

She sighed surrender. "There's another in Green Haven. But you have to understand...they're dangerous—very, very dangerous—but they're not *evil.* Some of us even believe the Chromeria secretly has seven of their own, if not nine. How else have they gathered drafters for so long? But my lord, the Chromeria will kill us all if they find out we have it. Call us blasphemers, heretics, apostates, pagans. Blindfold and burn us, or put out our eyes, or put us on the Glare. All we've wanted is to be accepted back into the fold."

"No. You wanted to keep power, too."

"We save lives with our training!" she protested.

And yet here she was dying, and dying young.

But she went on. "We'll be anathema. No one will be allowed to draft chi ever again, on pain of death. That's what it means, if you tell them."

She sighed again, but something about her seemed relieved. An honest woman indeed. But then, chi was ever so good at exposing secrets; Kip shouldn't have expected a chi drafter would love keeping them.

The Keeper walked to the globe. She touched it, and it opened like a flower. She reached a gloved hand inside and pulled out something smaller than her thumb. The air around her hand shimmered as if she held an invisible fire, but as she moved it, it spat out sparks of liquid-gold fire. The thing itself was hard to see at all from this distance, but it was much smaller than he'd expected. Kip had seen larger stones set in women's rings.

"Is that..." Cruxer started. "Is that solid chi? I didn't think such a thing existed! Chi luxin?!"

She shook her head. "Lord Guile," the Keeper said, her voice taking on a formal tone, "Luíseach, you have come to bring light, which means bringing shameful secrets to the light. Here is both our light and our shameful secret. Behold that which slays us, and that without which this city and my order is nothing. Behold the chi bane."

"Excellent," Kip said. "I'll take it."

Chapter 24

Gavin had charged toward a likely death several dozen times. This was different.

In the early part of the Prisms' War, the hours before every battle had been exhausting: the anxious mental rehearsals and the fears of cowardice and shaming himself publicly, the fears of death, and worse—in the mind of the young man he had been—the fear of living maimed or broken, which he'd thought were the same thing. There had been the righting of relationships: *Just, you know, in case*. There had been the writing of wills. There had been the selfish prayers; it was the closest he'd ever come to real piety.

For all the damnable emotional and mental sweat of it, it had served one purpose at least: the heightened state of fear and exhilaration had come effortlessly, giving incredible energy and even strength, allowing him to shrug off pain and fatigue, though at the cost of tunnel vision.

Over time, most of that had fallen away. It felt oddly like a loss.

Fear and excitement were gone, replaced with a butcher's efficiency. Today's fight was today's work. I know what to do. I know what I control and what I don't.

And while he always knew the possible costs, he'd had little time or energy to get worked up about it. There were things to do, things that would keep him alive.

Today was different. This was different.

He had nothing to do. He could only listen to the call of the overseer below his feet, keeping the slaves' rowing tempo. Eighteen months ago, that insistent beat would have meant terror and torn calluses and burning legs and lungs and new manacle cuts and blood. It now meant only the passage of time.

He had none of the old careful mental cataloging of his arsenal of luxin weapons to decide what best would match this much available light, this enemy, this battlefield, this likely enemy tactic. He had no generals to consult, no messengers to hear out or to send out, no scouts' reports, no orders to give, nor anyone who would listen to them if he tried.

As their galleon, the *Golden Mean*, shot across the waves, driven by both oar and wind, Gavin had no one to pick out of the enemy line and say, 'That one shall be mine first.'

All there was to do was wait, powerless.

Gavin's chest went tight as the rowers' drums, pounding, pounding.

There should have been some kind of towering storm. There wasn't. Today was the kind of day that makes landsmen romanticize the lives of sailors. The sun blazing overhead, the sea light and bright and clear and shallow. Blinding azure and turquoise and sapphire, Gavin guessed. And many other jewel colors denied him now.

He wished he could see them just one last time.

Under Captain Gunner's direction, the ship was circling in toward White Mist Reef, following the sea demons following the great black whale.

The sea demons hunting the whale hadn't noticed the little ship behind them yet, so it was a race against time to see if Gunner remembered correctly.

He was trying to remember the placement of a gap, Gavin never said aloud, from *two decades* ago. Gunner hadn't been the navigator back then, nor the navigator's boy. He'd been belowdecks, swabbing the cannons clean of burning embers that could ignite the next shot while it was being loaded.

Even if he remembered where the gap had been, there was no guarantee that in all those years the reef hadn't closed.

Gunner swore that White Mist Reef was a barrier reef with several gaps in its great circle. But if they didn't find one wide enough for the *Golden Mean* before one of the sea demons noticed them, they were dead. And the great tower of cloud hovering no more than a pace above the waves made it nearly impossible to see the gaps, if they were even there.

The great black whale breached fully again, avoiding another sea demon strike and coming down on its body instead, with a huge strike of its tail. There weren't three or four sea demons now. There were more like *six*. Hard to tell from five hundred paces.

"Is that the gap?" Gunner shouted up to the lookout in the crow's nest.

"No, sir!"

Gunner swore. He had good eyes, but White Mist Reef defied man's vision. The barrier reef itself rose from the sea floor to within a few hands'-breadths of the surface of the water. Stubborn coral had tried to grow higher, and their bleached skeletons were sometimes visible in the troughs between waves, white tips on the great claws that would tear a ship's soft belly open.

Driven by the cold currents blasting through the Everdark Gates into the warmer waters of the Cerulean Sea, the trade routes and currents and storm systems of the Seven Satrapies had always traveled clockwise around the coasts of the Seven Satrapies like a great wheel—or perhaps, having been created later than the currents, clocks moved storm-wise. So if the entire sea were an irregular wheel, here was the axle.

Gunner's teeth were bared. He shouted every command, even to those close by. A chase at sea is a slow chase, and their boat, fast as it was, was no match for the sea demons and the whale. They only kept them in sight because the massive creatures were fighting.

There wasn't much for Gunner to do. If he fired his guns now, he'd bring the sea demons' attention, but if he left the gun crews to steer the ship himself, the sea demons might be upon them before he could return. So he dodged from one station to the next, checking and rechecking wicks and ordering adjustments to the trim and the wheel through hand gestures to his first mate, and then flying up to the forecastle to check The Compelling Argument again and again.

Orholam had disappeared not long ago, but now he was suddenly at Gavin's shoulder, with a powder horn. "Nabbed it from the captain's quarters," he said. He pulled a musket ball pouch off the strap, though. "This, however, you won't be needing."

That's right. The baffling musket of the Blinding Knife didn't need to be loaded. It magically made its own shaped shells, turning light into luxin as if it were a drafter itself, only requiring a flint piece for the snap-cock jaws and black powder for every shot.

Gunner had blown an apple out of Gavin's mouth at forty paces with this rifled-barrel musket.

"What about you?" Gavin asked. "What are you doing?"

For some reason, Orholam was stripping off his tunic, but he had no rations or water. "Terrible swimmer," Orholam explained.

"Thought you said you were going to die. Are you trying to defy your own prophecy?"

"I told you the most likely thing. I'm just trying to do my part to make the less likely thing happen. But it ain't really on me."

"No, I imagine the sea demons have something to say about it."

"Them, neither," Orholam said. "My fate's up to you. And my own poor swimming. You'll have a chance to save me. But you won't. I don't blame you. You're just not that man. Still, I don't want to die, so you can't blame me for trying."

Gavin had no idea what to say to that.

"You know who they are, don't you?" Orholam asked, as if they hadn't been discussing his death.

"'They'?"

"The sea demons. They're you. Or what you would be if you only knew how."

"They're *me*? Well, fuck me, then." He began checking the action of the musket. Twist here and pull? "Can you tell me how to kill them, or not?"

"You know, I thought your problem was a lack of honesty. But your lack of compassion is worse."

"Compassion? For monsters?"

"They suffer, Dazen. For their broken oaths and cowardice, they have reaped unending centuries of isolation and madness and pain."

"Glad to see you're back to being cryptic. Kind of missed it," Gavin said with a little shake of his head. "But what the hell are you on about?"

Karris, I'm spending my last day with fools and madmen and traitors, and I'm afraid I fit right in.

Orholam said, "They're what happens when immensely talented and immoral drafters find an animal that's trusting and easy to soul-cast."

"They're what? What?"

"The sea giants were gentle creatures, so deeply attuned to luxin that their very bones react to it, intelligent, and nearly immortal. And they're now extinct, thanks to your predecessors. What's a Prism to do to escape his own Blackguards and his mortality itself?"

"Throw himself into a whale? Come on." Through curiosity or desperation or madness, drafters had will-cast almost every kind of animal—but soul-casting was another level entirely.

"No, no. Whales are far too willful, and too smart to trust men."

"Nobody's ever successfully soul-cast themselves," Gavin said dismissively.

"Depends what you mean by 'success.'"

Thinking you could do magic better than anyone else had ever done it before? That attitude wasn't exactly uncommon among drafters; it must be nearly ubiquitous among Prisms.

Good thing I'm not like that.

"This can't be true," Gavin said. "Of all people, I would know if it were."

"You? You don't even know how a Prism is made!"

"Made? You mean 'chosen.'"

"Time's up," Orholam said, his eyes perhaps sensing some change in the sea demons that Gavin's did not. "It was a pleasure to pull the same oar for a time, Man of Guile."

The old prophet stepped over and spoke to Gunner in hushed tones.

Gunner nodded. "Guile! You sees in lightsies and darksies, yes?"

Black and white? "Yes, Captain," Gavin said.

"Up ya go. To the next." He moistened his lips, peeved. "To the next. The *nest*. Fawk! Maybe you kin see what others cain't."

So Gavin slung the gun-sword over his back and began climbing the rigging. He'd regained enough strength for this, anyway.

But he wasn't even all the way up to the crow's nest when he saw something alarming.

"The whale!" he cried. "The whale's turned. It's headed straight this way!"

Gavin hauled himself into the crow's nest and flopped in awkwardly.

"Ten points a-port!" Gavin shouted. "Twelve hundred paces out!"

He was pretty good at distances, but it was a guess.

Almost as soon as he'd called it, Gunner cut to starboard. It was nice that a whale had been distracting the sea demons. But in the old tales, whales themselves had been the death of many a crew.

On the sea, no stranger is your friend.

And then Gavin saw it. "Gap!" he shouted. "Four hundred paces!"

But it was as if the sea demons themselves could hear his puny cry.

"They're turning!" Gavin shouted. "A thousand paces out now!"

Below him, Gunner was standing on the barrel of The Compelling Argument again, looking forward, though this time he had the fore skysail stay in his hand to keep his balance. He hopped down, and his hands became a blur on the whirling gears and pulleys. But Gavin could see that the great cannon was aimed wide of any of the sea demons.

"Captain—" he began.

But the roar of The Compelling Argument obliterated all else. The concussion made its own ring on the waves below it, and the sound and pressure knocked even Gavin backward, luckily into the crow's nest.

He pulled himself to a seated position in time to see a great explosive shell hit the water hundreds of paces to port from the sea demons. Water geysered around the impact.

Most impressive. Gavin would have applauded the sheer power of the thing if there weren't seven monstrous leviathans bearing down on them at this very—

Four. Four leviathans bearing down on them. What?

"Three of 'em peeled off, Captain!" Gavin shouted. "Headed for where the shell hit!"

That was it. Sea demons felt vibrations in the water. A distant cannon blast above the water was certainly felt, but an explosion *in* the water must have doubled or trebled its volume to those creatures.

"They're steaming hot!" Gavin shouted. "Four hundred paces. Our gap's in a hundred!"

"Whale ta port!" someone shouted below.

And so it was.

Like some kind of damned sheepdog loping easily alongside them, the whale was boxing them in, holding them tight to the reef. The open sea out beyond it was no option now.

"Cap'n!" the mate Pansy shouted. "We gotta swing wide!"

"No!" Gunner shouted, not even looking up as he cranked The Compelling Argument low to port.

"We'll not make that tight of a turn!" Pansy shouted.

"No!"

Orholam's balls. Gunner was gonna shoot the whale. Why was he going to shoot the whale?

As the big gun finished coming around, Gunner hopped up on its barrel.

"You're right!" he shouted to the whale as if they'd been conversing. "Fine! Damned if you ain't right!"

Swinging the boat wide was the only way they could make the right-angle turn to shoot the narrow gap in the reef. But the great black beast wasn't allowing that.

Gunner shouted, "Eight points port, on my mark, then full starboard on my mark. Got it, mate?!"

"Aye, Cap'n! Eight points port on mark, then full starboard on mark."

But Gunner had already disappeared below, bellowing orders to his gun crews.

Gavin threw a curse at the whale. This great, stupid fish might as well have been Andross Guile, hemming them in, denying them any real choice, making it look to any observer like they'd willfully rammed their own ship into the reef.

"Gap in seventy paces, Captain!" Gavin shouted. "Two sea demons at two hundred! Coming full speed in!"

The damned whale had disappeared.

Thanks, buddy. Stayed just long enough to get us killed, didn't ya?

But the water here wasn't deep enough for it to dive out of sight, and Gavin found it again quickly, veering out toward open sea.

Even as he threw one last mental curse to it, it veered back, straight toward the gap in the reef itself.

No, not at the gap, but on an intercepting course with the two remaining sea demons, who were flying like twin arrows at the *Golden Mean*—the interception point just happened to be right at the mouth of the gap.

The gap in the coral between the open sea and the protected lagoon inside was wide enough for the ship to pass through in ordinary circumstances: approached dead-on, with sails stowed, maneuvering by oar and with polemen on the decks. Normally, even in this light midafternoon chop, with care it would be perilous but possible.

But cutting a right-angle turn, under full sail and full speed? A single wave, a single untimely gust of wind could blow them into the teeth of the coral on either side.

There was nothing else for Gavin to say. Gunner could see it all for himself now. He was standing again on the barrel of his big cannon, dancing from one bare foot to the other because of the barrel's heat. But there was nothing comical in the utter concentration on his face, looking at that gap, and the oncoming sea demons, and the whale streaking in from the side. He'd readied the orders.

Now it was just a matter of timing, and Gunner was the best in the world at that.

"First mate . . . mark!"

"Mark!" she shouted, her hands spinning the wheel and then stopping it precisely.

The ship began to angle wide—but not wide enough!—and bleeding off speed—too much!

Gavin tried to calculate. The whale was maybe going to reach the sea demons just before they reached the ship, but where would the collision take them? Would the whale intercept both of the sea demons, or only one? What waves would crash into the boat?

Out only another hundred paces, the other sea demons had doubled back. Even if the whale took out both of the first two of them, if Gunner didn't get the ship through the gap in the first attempt, those others were going to demolish them.

Sailors on deck were praying, muttering, waiting with their hands on lines for their orders. Orholam had now stripped off all his clothes as if preparing for a swim. He saluted Gavin with a flagon of brandy and drank a deep draught. Crazy old bastard.

On the sterncastle, the first mate's forehead glistened with sweat, stance wide, knuckles tight on the wheel. She had all the look of a grizzled veteran who was terrified despite being a grizzled veteran.

Gavin looked up. The gap yawned before them, but there was no way they could make the turn.

"Reef the main now!" Gunner shouted. "First mate, now! Starboard oars, stop! Port oars, double-time, now, now! Second mate, on my—mark! Mark! Now!"

In quick succession, the first mate spun the wheel hard in toward the reef; the mainsail went half; and the starboard oars stopped, dragging water, creating a pivot point while the port oars kept pulling. A rattling chain drew Gavin's eyes to the rear.

The second mate had dropped the starboard anchor.

In the shallow water, it hit bottom and caught immediately. It was as if the ship had hit a wall, first jerking almost to a stop, timbers groaning, seams straining, men thrown from their feet, but then with too much forward momentum to stop, it slewed hard to starboard.

As the deck rolled, spraying a fan of water out, the crow's nest whipsawed back and forth. Gavin crashed into the railing, his feet actually rising off the wood for one terrifying moment before the motion ceased and then started the other way, with Gavin dropping into the nest and then crouching down as low as he could, bracing the railing against his shoulder to keep from being thrown overboard.

"Anchor free! Anchor free!" Gunner was shouting. "All oars full! First mate!"

"Yessir!" she shouted, already making corrections.

Some mechanism snapped loudly under the forces on the anchor—but the chain spun away and the deck surged up and forward.

"Sails full!" Gunner shouted, though they weren't ten paces from the reef—and they weren't aligned with the gap.

Unbelievably, they'd actually cut the corner too tightly.

They were going to hit the reef. But then Gavin saw that the boat was still drifting sideways, its momentum in the waves carrying it toward alignment with the gap.

They were barely going to clip the near edge of the reef.

But that'd be enough. It would tear off the prow easily. Even if it didn't, the crash would stop them dead in the waves as the sea demons arrived.

"Starboard guns..." Gunner shouted. "Now!"

The starboard guns all fired simultaneously, the hull shivering from the combined shock of the blasts, nudging the ship half a pace farther to port.

The sails filled with a snap as the ship rolled back on an even keel. Gunner was shouting to oarsmen, trying to get the starboard oars to lift from the water before they snapped off, trying to get them to push off of the reef as if they were polemen. He was demanding the port oars start pulling, but slowly so as not to drive them starboard. He had to repeat an order to the first mate, because he was already shouting his next at a gun crew and cranking The Compelling Argument himself.

Orholam's beard, they were going to make it!

Then Gavin's eyes rose to the sea to starboard—which had been behind them before they'd turned. Like a war-blind green recruit distracted by what was happening in front of and to each side of the ship, he'd not looked *behind* the ship in several minutes.

"Pull!" Gunner was shouting. "Damn your eyes, pull!"

Just behind the ship, the twin streaking lines of boiling waters of the sea demons and the black behemoth collided. Hot water sprayed over the decks as the huge beasts breached, and then as they crashed back into the sea, landing partially on the black whale, driving its great head into the coral, but then the sight of them was lost. A great trough from their bodies falling into the waters so near behind them slowed the ship as if it were suddenly going uphill—then sent a huge following wave into the stern, shoving the ship hard, straight toward the gap.

At first Gunner's orders couldn't be heard in the screams and the crash of water—but the ship rolled back on an even keel and the wind gusted and the sails snapped full, and the mast strained but held and it looked like they might pull through the gap safely.

"Pull!" Gunner shouted again.

Gavin's warning was lost in all the other shouts and sounds.

The oars port and starboard dropped simultaneously and pulled.

The ship nosed into the gap. Faces lit with hope. A few more moments—

Only Gavin had seen their doom. He shifted his feet to the very rail of the crow's nest as he cried out again, but nothing could save them.

Unseen until now, an eighth sea demon had appeared. Every sea demon was massive, but this one was twice the size of any of the others, so monstrously thick its body couldn't even fit beneath the waves here, a battering ram shearing through mud and coral and water alike, its body pumping like a bellows. But to Gavin's eyes it wasn't red, but burning white-hot, steam boiling from it.

The convulsing, gulping mouth of this greatest of the sea demons was the long-pursuing mouth of hell itself.

At the last moment it closed its great cruciform jaw to bring its head like a bony war hammer up and against the stern on the starboard side.

The collision lifted and crumpled the ship against the reef. Gavin saw the coral punch in the portside hull, tearing forecastle from deck as wanton boys fighting over an old book might tear off a cover.

The flexing mast, first bent from the shock of the collision with the sea demon and then loosed with the shock of the collision with the reef, catapulted Gavin skyward. His three-fingered hand hadn't a prayer of holding him. He twisted out into the air hopelessly, as sea and sky spun fast beneath him.

And then darkness opened its maw and swallowed him.

Chapter 25

Teia was being paranoid. She was sure of it.

Pretty sure.

The best thing about the near-total invisibility that the shimmercloak granted her wasn't the invisibility, not today. It was the 'near-total' part.

Total invisibility might allow her to relax. Instead, using the cloak here took everything Teia had: constant drafting to maintain the paryl cloud necessary to defeat any errant sub-red who would otherwise see a warm ghost passing by, will to activate the cloak, skill to follow how the cloak split the light hitting it at each moment, bending it around her form. Most Shadows—the Order's shimmercloak-using assassins—wouldn't do that. Couldn't, maybe.

Teia had to keep moving, and that meant she had to pay attention to any places where sources of paryl light weren't available. Those were rare, but given that being stuck with no paryl meant discovery, and discovery meant death, it was still important to look out for. Using the cloak while dodging all the churning humanity that shot through the Lily's Stem and into the turning flower that was the Chromeria itself took all her vigilance, all her dexterity, all her athleticism at moments that couldn't be predicted. That was the gift: not thinking.

In this past year, she'd adjusted to the quick glances necessary to keep her eyes unseen, to the dodging and darting while keeping the cloak tight about her form so her feet wouldn't show. She knew when to be visible and when to disappear, when to gather luxin and pack it so that she'd never be without if she had to dodge indoors or to some dark area where paryl was scarce.

But there was something in one's mind that refused to believe one was truly unseen. It was too unnatural. When eyes crossed one's face, something in the mind fiercely held that one had been ignored but wasn't actually *invisible*.

Thus, the paranoia that popped up at irregular intervals—a sticky, oily feeling, like a predator's eyes were on you in your bath.

And right now the feeling was strong.

The entrance to the luxin bridge called the Lily's Stem was a natural choke point. Here half a dozen of Andross Guile's Lightguards stood watch. They were thugs one and all, armed with muskets and blunderbusses smarter than most of them. Less conspicuously, four Blackguards would be somewhere farther back. Teia took her time finding them, hanging to the edges of the crowd so she wouldn't be bowled over while she searched. Being terrifically short was terrific when you wanted to disappear in a crowd, and horrific when you wanted to find anyone else.

She found them all, and knew them all. Not one was a sub-red or superviolet.

So she should relax a little.

But she couldn't. She kept flaring her eyes to paryl, kept circling, kept searching, searching, gnawing on that feeling like she was one of those tiny dogs trained to run in a wheel that turned a spit for cooking, and she'd been thrown an ox bone and couldn't crack it open with her weak little jaws.

She couldn't draft paryl or keep the cloak working forever, though.

Fine, I'm afraid. Since when has that stopped me?

She moved, slipping into the stream of humanity passing gushing into and then out of the Lily's Stem. The waves battered the covered luxin bridge as effectually as her fears. She moved fast, as fast as she could, riding right at the edge of foolhardiness. If her worst nightmare was true, and she was being pursued by some other Shadow, sent to murder her for her disobedience and to reclaim their Fox Cloak, they'd have a hard time matching this pace. Teia was damn good at this now.

Coming upon the exit of the bridge, she slipped into the back of a narrow wagon transporting empty tun and hogshead barrels from the Chromeria's larders. She wedged herself into a narrow spot where she could only see the sun, and thus not be seen herself, and let her invisibility go.

Without the paryl in her, it seemed the rational blue light from the luxin tunnel did much less to ease her. She felt shaken, jittery, a runner wobbly long before the last lap.

She had leagues to go yet before she was safe.

She pulled herself together, removed and rolled up the master cloak, and put on the Fox Cloak; loosed her belt, letting out the extra folds of her tunic to make a simple dress, colorful banding already stitched to it; pulled up her trouser legs and bound them at each knee; flipped her belt over to the opposite side, red for black; and rolled her sleeves up and her tall boots down. She donned a large necklace and bound her hair tight and pulled on a wig of wavy brunette.

Fear is a tortoise; its jaws will snap you clean in half if you let it—but it'll only catch you if you don't move, Teia'd learned.

Teia moved too fast for fear to follow.

Right now, she was just a lazy serving girl hitching a quick ride so she didn't have to walk. A little innocent mischief. She emerged from the barrels and slipped from the back of a wagon as it passed through a knot of people near an intersection.

In moments, she was better than invisible. She was anonymous. Unremarkable. Unseen.

The bright, rich districts—where the Chromeria's every be-serifed whim was captured by bespectacled scribes in official green ink and stamped with a reeve's seal and enforced by women armed with abacuses and bad attitudes and wearing ridiculous plumed hats—soon yielded to neighborhoods ruled by attitudes as foul and condescension as thick, but wielding tools sharper than a quill that writ decrees in a redder ink.

But Teia couldn't tell the difference between green and red anyway, and here her heart quieted some of its panicked thunder as of a summer squall passing into the distance.

She didn't let down her guard, of course. It was still a dangerous neighborhood, and the slight but perilous possibility of having picked up a tail was still present.

Her goal now was a series of blind alleys she'd discovered in a slightly nicer neighborhood nearby. The alleys led to...well, to nothing. Situated here on the dark side of Weasel Rock, the neighborhood wasn't the kind to attract passersby, but not quite a slum, either. The locals would avoid a dead end, but they also wouldn't allow any gangs to take up residence.

Teia could hide and wait for an hour or two for any pursuit. If none came, there was a spot where she could climb out of the alley to a rooftop in case her highly hypothetical pursuer followed this far, actually knew that this alley was a dead end, and tried to wait her out.

You poor bastards, she thought. You have no idea how good I've gotten.

No one's chasing you. They don't know there's anyone to chase. The Order doesn't even know you're here, T.

From little contextual clues, Teia'd guessed out that Murder Sharp was the best of the Order's Shadows. And further, that he was gone, which could mean he'd be gone for months yet. That meant any Shadow who might possibly come after her was second-rate. She was just being paranoid.

It was easy to impute legendary status to these people, but Teia had seen a little glimpse behind the façade. Anyone can kill if you give them invisibility. And the Order had to take those who were (1) murderous, (2) loyal, (3) able to split light, and (4) able to draft paryl.

That couldn't leave that many candidates.

Martial prowess, intelligence, flexibility? None of those could even make the list of requirements.

Being a bit scared made her careful, and that was good when the stakes were so high, but she couldn't make them out to be to gods or something.

She'd take up a position around the third sharp corner, she thought. Just in case she was a bit slow to take down her opponent and there was a fight. A brief fight. That she would win.

Stepping around the corner, she saw the briefest hint of distortion like a floater in her eye, so close she couldn't focus on it—and she ran nose-first into something that wasn't there. She reeled back, but instead of trying to keep her feet, she flopped to the side, her body reacting faster than her mind.

Someone! Not something! her mind shrilled. *Paryl! Move or die!*

Rolling, desperate, eyes streaming at the blow to her nose, Teia jumped to her feet, her hand stabbing down into the gun pouch at her hip, slipping over the smooth ball handle of the pistol.

And then someone unseen cuffed her upside the head, like she was a child, not an assassin. An arm circled around her chest and another around her neck, and as he tightened that arm on the sides of her neck—a dangerous move no Blackguard would use, because though it was meant not to, it *could* kill—she heard a voice, *his* voice.

"All my work, and you throw it away at the first tough job. You're such a disappointment, Adrasteia," Murder Sharp said.

The blackness was rising even faster than her terror, but Teia clawed at the pistol in its pouch. His foot was right next to her own, and there would be no time for aiming carefully before she lost consciousness.

Her straining fingertips brushed the polished-smooth pistol butt, and fingernails tore as she scrambled to lift the heavy, slick weapon up to her palm. But she did it. She did it faster than cowardice and a heartbeat before unconsciousness could claim the laurel crown. With a hot lead prayer, she pulled the trigger.

Nothing happened. Like a runner tripping within steps of the finish line, she wondered what might have betrayed her—a faulty flint? a broken cockjaw?

Blackness triumphing, her hands began pulling at his forearm like she was some moron who'd never trained against such things. Her knees sagged. It was too late to do all the right things. She was too weak for the chin turn, too...

Her last thought swam through the gathering wet darkness like some unseen loathsome sea creature sliding against her bare toes on a midnight swim: There'd been no mechanical failure. Teia had failed.

She hadn't cocked the pistol.

There was no way to try again. She was out of time and strength. There were no second chances here.

She slumped into the wages of that mortal sin: losing.

Chapter 26

Gavin knifed into the waves—tumbled, spun deeper. Black spots swam in his vision. He stabbed his hands forward and racked water back, back. It was several long strokes before he realized he was pulling himself deeper, like a disoriented eagle trying to swim, as if its pinions could beat the waves rather than the air.

He turned toward the greater light, and pulled for the sky.

His progress slowed. His chest convulsed. Vision darkened.

And then his hand pulled weakly on the air, and he bobbed to the surface. He gasped in a great breath, caught some wave with the air he inhaled, and coughed. He floundered, slapping at the water, gulping in air, trying to see.

The lagoon was calmer than the afternoon chop of the waves outside the reef. First he saw the remains of the ship, torn to pieces, part of the forecastle still perched on the reef it had been dropped on, the rest shearing away into a flotsam of broken wood and broken men and women.

Flung from the highest height, Gavin was the closest in toward land, but he saw others, their heads dotting the waves, yet alive. Some screamed with fear or injury, some clung to bits of crates or decking. Others danced to the sea's cruel, silent song, bobbing without a word, drowning: for the drowning haven't the breath to spare for screams.

Ceres hated anyone to interrupt her dancers, so in his terror, a drowning man would often force his rescuer under the waves himself, and Ceres would claim two victims rather than one. Fully half of the distance back to the ship from where he was now, Gavin saw Orholam, wet hair streaming over his face, hands plunging down and down, frenetic—dancing to that tune.

It took a strong and healthy swimmer to dare pull a man away from Ceres's fatal song. Gavin felt neither. He looked at the shore calling him.

Then he saw the fins cutting through the water.

Then he felt the stinging on his back. He was still wearing the gunsword, and in the fall, it had cut him. He was bleeding into the water; he had no idea how badly.

But he knew how blood called sharks.

Orholam bobbed up, up, up arrhythmically. He'd known he was going to die. Had accepted it as far as he could. Come to peace with it. *You're not that man, Gavin Guile.*

Gavin kicked off toward the old man.

He cursed himself with every stroke. What the hell am I doing? I don't even want to save him! I need to get my ass on that island so I can save Karris! I am more important than this old shit-brained—

A sailor clinging to a broken spar nearby screamed and kicked at the waves. Something slashed through the waters, and he screamed louder, lifting a bloody stump of a knee from the waves. He scrambled to climb fully onto his bit of spar, overbalanced, and fell into the water.

But Gavin was close now. He was committed. And—

Of course the old prophet went down before Gavin reached him.

Gavin dove and snatched at the disappearing form under the waves, caught something, and hauled him up by his beard.

The old man spit water into the air as they broke the surface. Alive. Damn!

But if it had been bad luck to reach the old man as he was on the verge of losing consciousness, now it was good—he didn't fight as Gavin pulled him into a weak grip with his left hand and kicked for shore.

By the time they made it to the shallows, all the screams had stopped, though in two places the sharks still churned the waves white in their frenzy.

Gavin stood, though his legs were wobbly and even the gentle sloshing of water that came up to his chest nearly knocked him down. "Stand. Come on," he told Orholam.

Behind them, still halfway out to the wreckage, Gavin saw a swimmer coming in, cutting strong and fast past dead bodies floating in the waves and heedless of the sharks.

Orholam stood, wheezing and spitting, and Gavin began hauling him toward the shore.

The figure resolved into the form of Pansy, the first mate, her hair still stuck in those iron-hard glued points. She was such a fast swimmer, Gavin could only wonder where must she have fallen to have not made it to shore before them.

They made it to water that only came up to their thighs, and Orholam said, "Please, please, let me rest." He leaned over, but Gavin pulled him on.

Coming up behind them, Pansy stood at last. She cleared the water from her eyes and heaved great, deep breaths. She leaned over, hands braced on her thighs, face barely clear of the waves.

In between breaths she said, "I don't...I don't think I want to be a sailor anymore."

"Let me *rest*!" Orholam said, slapping at Gavin's hand.

"I mean, not that I have any choice in the matter," she said, turning to gaze at the wreckage. "Seeing how a trip home is pretty much—"

She cut off abruptly, and Gavin heard a sharp intake of breath.

He saw the shadow streaking through the shallow water a moment after she did. Pansy spun and tried to leap forward through the waves, half jumping out of the waves and half swimming, clawing at the water, but the shark hit her hard and she crashed sideways through the water.

This time, Gavin didn't even think to save anyone else. He plunged toward the shore, wild with fear, lifting his feet free of the treacherous waters with strength he didn't even know he had.

And then he collapsed onto the dry sand.

From his hands and knees, he saw a dark stain spreading in the water, then a glimpse of torn flesh as another shark appeared and ripped at what had been Pansy only moments ago.

Moments later, Orholam trudged up next to him and dropped heavily onto the sand.

Turning from the sight of the sharks at their feast, Gavin crawled to shade, curled into a ball, and closed his eyes.

Chapter 27

"Karris Shadowblinder."

Nothing. Maybe it had been written the other way.

"Karris Atiriel," Kip whispered, watching the cookfires flicker in the darkness far below. "Anselm Malleus. Eva Ultafa."

With only Big Leo as bodyguard, Kip had climbed to the top of Greenwall. There, atop the massive living wall, on a magically grown walkway of well-nigh immortal branches and foliage that was ever-green, he surveyed those who had become his people, both inside the city of Dúnbheo and in a crescent on the shore of Loch Lána around it.

He was missing something, and his failure was going to get them all killed.

The city was eerily dark, not because of the privations of the Blood Robe siege Kip had so recently lifted but rather from the cultural For-ester deference to nature and the community: the awesome beauty of the stars was Orholam's gift to everyone, whereas a torch in the city was a selfish tool for one or two. One should weigh carefully whether the work you did by that light benefited the community more than the beauty you stole from them to do it.

With the urgent preparations to march, tonight there were more lights visible than usual, but with a cloudless sky, the scarce few lanterns of the city still barely dimmed the glory of the stars.

"Gaspar Estratega. Helane Troas. Viv Grayskin," Kip murmured. The stars, those æthereal fires above, called to the terrestrial fires below, like to like, and mirrored the thaumaturgical lights of Kip's war map. The vast beyond comprehension and the small beneath notice existed at once, in one city, one room, one mind.

"Zee Oakenshield. Telemachos the Bold."

All this, all the people below, would move at Kip's word. Though without mastery of all he should have mastered to deserve such obedience, he was their master. Where he said to go, they would go. They would live and fight and die by his will—and despite his desire, for there was no path Kip could see by which none would die, no matter what he did.

At most, he might make there be fewer deaths. At best, he might make the deaths purposeful. At the end, he *might* make their deaths buy victory and peace and some meager measure of justice, some semblance of stability, for a time.

Three years ago, Kip wouldn't have believed anyone would ever follow him. A year ago, he wouldn't have believed so many would. Now he only prayed that he would lead them well enough.

Hell, three years ago Kip never would have believed any woman would ever want him, much less one remotely like Tisis.

So why was he here, walking in the cold, trying to solve a gift as if it were a problem?

"Garibaldi Phlegethon. Euterpe Tamazight. The Chartopaíchtis."

Was that it? Had it seemed too easy to become satrap? Like a gift rather than an adroitly seized reward?

In hardly more than a day they'd have the big signing ceremony, and the army would march. People standing around while he signed a bit of paper? Kip hated that sort of thing. He'd insisted it be a small ceremony.

Tisis had suggested perhaps a large ceremony would be preferable, given that becoming a satrap was kind of a big deal, and many witnesses would be better than few.

But knowing that he had to assert his independence and indomitable will or lose the respect of his men, Kip had defiantly insisted on a large ceremony.

That showed *her* who wore the claws around here.

He called the war map to mind again, its lights overlaying the lights of the stars and the campfires, one reality atop another, like glassine immortals. Powerless here. Watchers, not helpers.

Kip felt like a mere observer himself now. He ran the lights forward and back as the White King's army invaded. In the night and the darkness, its moving colors became a universe entire. The whole map showed less than one-half of one satrapy, and he was a single splinter aflame among this constellation of torches against the darkness.

"Corvan Danavis." Ah, he'd said that name half a dozen times. "Darayaus Khurvash."

And that was the end of it. He couldn't think of anyone else. He'd named every single great tactician or strategist, every famous general or admiral, every warlord and great rogue, every scoundrel, every leader who came to mind who might, maybe, possibly, have some insight that would help him now and whose Nine Kings card he might have Viewed in that chaotic, compressed rush that had taken him to the Great Library.

Surely, surely in all the cards he'd Viewed of the most important people in history, surely he'd seen at least one person whose experiences could help him. Surely, somewhere in his fat skull was some bit of borrowed genius he could trigger that could set him at ease, that would have sharper insight than his own blunt wit.

But nothing happened.

Soon—maybe too soon—he'd take possession of more than he'd ever wanted, and instead of feeling elation, for some reason it irked him. It felt like failure, and he couldn't tell *why.*

Come on, Orholam, I'm fighting on Your side here. Gimme a break.

"The Master. Andross the Red," he said, unthinking.

His scalp tingled. He sucked in a breath.

Nothing happened. Or nothing more happened. That little tingling had been just him, right? That had been a shot of fear setting fire to his brain like straight brandy would set fire to his belly. That was just his dread of the old man, right?

Right.

He expelled a slow breath as nothing happened.

Oh, thank Orholam. Dodged a bullet there. He did *not* want to live that old dragon's life.

Not even if it saves you?

He turned that thought around in his hand as if it were a jagged hellstone that might lacerate him if his grip slipped even the slightest.

No, actually, not even then. To hell with him.

Andross had given Kip no help at all in the past year. He demanded reports, which Kip had sent. He'd sent none in return.

So I'm on my own, then. No magic will save me here. Nor a remembered life or borrowed experience. Nor man. Nor Orholam Himself, though we march in His cause.

He stood alone at one of the crenellations of Greenwall, next to some empty iron frame, perhaps for pots of hot oil or maybe for mounting a scorpion with which to shoot bolts as long as a spear into an enemy army.

No, it didn't look strong enough for either of those. Something else, then. Whatever.

Big Leo loomed behind Kip, so large and immobile that he didn't blend into the background, he became the background. The young warrior must have sensed Kip wanted to think and had barred the approach of any of the soldiers who otherwise constantly sidled close to the famous Kip Guile.

Famous. How strange.

The isolation was no favor. Kip looked out at all the lights above and below once more, and felt a crushing tightness in his chest as if it were all falling on him. Luíseach? Lightbringer? *Kip Almost* was supposed to be the axis around which all the satrapies turned? Kip, the louse-up from Rekton? Kip, who'd started this whole cataclysm by killing King Rask Garadul and allowing the White King to take power unopposed?

People believed in *Kip*.

But maybe they believed because they had to. He'd fooled them, and they clung desperately to him as the drowning do, 'cumbering his arms and legs, pulling him down.

What had his father Gavin said?

'Kip, you're not the Lightbringer, because there *is* no Lightbringer. That figure's a myth that's destroyed a thousand boys, and led a hundred thousand men to cynicism and disillusionment. It's a lie. A lie more tempting the more powerful you are. Like all lies, it destroys those who long entertain it.'

Kip should have listened. He was flotsam, trash washed down the Umber River, heading for the great cataract below Rekton. He was going to fall, and he was going to take all these people he loved with him.

"I believe," Big Leo said suddenly. His voice was a low rumble in the half-light.

"What?" Kip asked, turning to the big man, as if the words hadn't cut his darkness in twain.

But Big Leo didn't meet his eye, instead searching the darkness for nonexistent threats. His voice rumbled lower. "Nothin' else to say."

Kip studied the darkness, but saw nothing. *They believe, but I don't. Maybe I need a bit more of the Guile arrogance.*

Can a humble man do great things?

"That obvious, huh?" he asked, faking a grin.

Big Leo pursed his lips and finally met Kip's gaze. He shook his head slightly. *Not that obvious.*

"You always measure yourself by them," Big Leo said.

"Them?"

The warrior looked at him as if trying to determine whether he was being obtuse on purpose or simply by default. "Your father. Your grandfather."

"Oh. *Them*, them."

"Breaker?"

"Yeah?"

"Stop talking."

"Right."

Big Leo heaved a Big Leo–sized sigh, as if so many words were exhausting him. "Breaker, you got it all backward. I don't follow you because you're *almost them*. I follow you because you're *not* them."

So it was true: even the perfect man, Gavin Guile, had his detractors.

Find me the perfect man, and I will find you someone who dislikes him. Kip tried not to let the thought show on his face. It was a mental dodge, and it would infuriate his friend. He'd seen Big Leo angry—and it wasn't something he really wanted directed at himself.

"You know what I like about you?" Big Leo asked.

"Well, I hope more than one thing, but I'm always ready to hear anoth—"

"Words with you are never wasted."

A clear compliment? "Well, thank you!"

"You know what I hate about you?" Big Leo asked.

And here it had seemed like this was going so well. "Actually," Kip said, "I'm not that curious to—"

"It always seems like they are."

"Um. Well, thanks?" *You dick.* "Thanks for that, uh, deeply felt and oblique set of compliments."

"I wasn't done." Deep dissatisfaction had settled into resignation on Big Leo's face.

"Oh, I'd love to hear more compliments," Kip said.

It might have come out a little sarcastic.

"I am done with those."

I figured. "Go on."

"My favorite description of the Lightbringer? Says he'll be a man unmirrored."

"What's that even mean?" Kip asked.

"That's why I like it. It could be almost literal, although poetic. Don't know what the hell is wrong with prophets. Can't just say what they mean."

"I still don't get it." And why haven't I heard all of these things before?

"Unmirrored: like, a man who walks in front of a mirror, and it doesn't show him."

Kip had to think about it. Big Leo gave him time. "That person would just be invisible."

Big Leo sighed. "And who do we know—"

"Oh! Oh, so someone like Teia. Not invisible all the time, necessarily. Someone who can use a shimmercloak. Hmm."

It occurred to him then that he couldn't use a shimmercloak.

"Yeah, that would be too bad if that were true, huh?" Big Leo said. "Since you can't use a shimmercloak."

"You're doing wonders for my confidence, big guy."

"Don't worry about it."

Kip, of course, was suddenly very worried.

Big Leo said, "Lightsplitting is supposedly one of the gifts bestowed by Orholam during the installment of a Prism. So those who think you're the Lightbringer, and who also believe that interpretation, simply think you'll be installed as Prism sooner or later. Not really a big leap to think the Lightbringer would also be a Prism, eh? But usually—and maybe this is just because these scholars didn't know about shimmercloaks—usually the phrase is taken as a, uh, what do you call it, idiom. A man unmirrored could be a man unequaled. There's no one out there exactly like him, right?"

"Sure, that makes sense. It's pretty good—"

"No, it's not. It's a stupid descriptor. It's redundant. He's the Lightbringer. Of course he's unequaled. You don't need to say he's the most one-of-a-kind unique Lightbringer out there. In a set of one, he's the most *one* of the whole set? That makes no sense. There's just *one*."

"Prophecies can't have filler?" Kip asked.

"That's . . . actually a good question." Big Leo looked troubled. He started to turn away.

"No, wait. What were you going to say before?"

Big Leo stopped and seemed to chew his next words. "How I took it was that it could mean he's unequaled, or it could mean he's honest, 187 because every reflection imparts loss and distortion from the original, or it could mean he's different. He's *true*...in that he is his own self. Every mirror presents a flattened, pale copy, an image of a real thing. So maybe the Lightbringer is simply not like other people. In every set, he's the odd one, the exception. You know, like maybe he's the noble who's not a noble, the bastard who's not a bastard, the Tyrean who doesn't quite fit with the Tyreans, the Blackguard who doesn't quite fit the Blackguards, the unschooled kid who somehow got educated, the poor kid who got rich, the rich kid who doesn't act rich, the full-spectrum polychrome who's sort of Chromeria-trained and sort of not trained at all, the guy who's entitled to the highest horse but barely knows how to ride, yet always somehow gets where he needs to go, and fast."

I'd like to think 'barely knows how to ride' has been mostly remedied in this past year, Kip thought. But he didn't say it.

His tongue still escaped his control with some regularity, but not as often as it used to.

"And?" Kip asked. Big Leo obviously wanted to know that he had Kip's full attention.

"Brother, we need the Lightbringer. Desperately. This army, this satrapy, *all* the satrapies, the Chromeria, your friends. We all need *you* to be the Lightbringer, and those of us who stand with you here? We're betting our lives that you are. And that's why you're pissing me off."

"Huh?"

"You think you were powerful against Daragh the Coward or against Ambassador Red Leaf or with the Divines? You were stronger by far when you saw the Keeper and took pity on her, or when you saw Conn Arthur and showed him even greater pity by showing him none."

"Sure pissed off Cruxer," Kip said. The commander had said, 'You can forgive a man who breaks under a charge once out of weakness, but a man who lies to you day after day after day? He's not only a coward, he's *disloyal*. You're making a huge mistake.'

Big Leo waved it away. "Cruxer's still a mess over Lucia. He'll outgrow it. Now, shut up. I'm trying to lecture you."

"Please, proceed," Kip said, grinning.

Big Leo held his gaze until Kip's grin collapsed, then said, "Andross and Gavin couldn't have done what you did—because they're men invested in their own greatness. It makes them small next to you. Breaker, you didn't get this far by being like anyone else. So. If the Lightbringer's a man unmirrored, why the hell do you keep trying to be a mirror?"

Kip had immediate justifications, defenses, denials—dodges: I didn't know that stupid prophecy! Who else am I supposed to emulate if not the best and smartest people I know? And last and least true: I'm not trying to be them!

But instead of giving breath to any of it, he nodded, taking receipt of the words, a silent promise to think on them.

But Big Leo kept staring at him.

Big Leo *kept* staring at him.

It got awkward.

"Big Leo, do you want to know what I like about *you*?"

The big man pondered, eyes still locked on Kip.

Then, just as Kip was about to tell him, Big Leo said, "No."

He walked away.

Eventually, Kip turned back to his stars and his fire and his map, but none of them cast the light he needed.

He went to his room, but he didn't wake Tisis. He knew he should wake her, to talk, if not to make love. He should share the yoke that had settled heavy on his heart. But there weren't even two hours until he must wake. He let her lie and told himself it was love.

In the place of rest, instead he dreamed.

He dreamed of Andross Guile.

Chapter 28

~The Guile~
40 years ago. (Age 26.)

"I hope my art isn't boring you?"

Having only recently taken over as the head of my family and thereby made the lord of a house in crisis, my greatest expenditure in coming this deep into the Atashian highlands is in time. And this buffoon—whom I hope to make my father-in-law—is only making things worse. I've seen rocks worn down to nubs by the lapping of the sea's waves more quickly than this man moves us through his art collection.

"No indeed!" I say, and it's true. The *art* isn't boring me.

"Just a few more pieces before we return. We simply must get back   189 in time to see the fire dancers begin, young 'Andross. It's a treasured tradition on these brisk autumn nights!'"

Lord Dariush gives 'Andross' the old aspirative at the beginning, so it sounds almost like 'Handross.' When I first arrived, Lord Dariush told me he is a casual student of languages, and he loved that my name hearkens back to a rare dialect of Old Parian.

In the full week since then, I've deduced that by 'casual' he means he's fluent in six dead tongues, and has done his own translations of several ancient masterpieces. He derides his own efforts as derivative, an idle pastime not worth the parchment he scrawls them on: 'Still, it keeps me out of trouble. Some hunt fowls, I hunt vowels.' He'd laughed. I'd chuckled along dutifully.

An affable man, if inclined to laugh at his own jokes. By all reports, he is well loved here.

He is the first obscenely wealthy person I've met of whom that is true.

"You do love your traditions here, I've noticed. What is this?" The Dariush family has an art collection of wildly mixed quality, a common affliction among the newly rich: astonishing masterpieces cheek-by-jowl with quirky oddities and total garbage likely painted or drawn by family members.

This piece is a very nice facsimile of a Gollaïr. I've never liked his work myself. He discovered a technique of imbuing pigments with mildly unstable luxin, making them astonishingly bright—and then used the paints everywhere in his art with no sense of proportion and only moderate skill.

A second-rate natural scientist and a second-rate painter, Gollaïr's real genius had lain in getting others to believe he was a genius. He had amassed a large entourage, a vast fortune, and a golden reputation.

Then his pupil, Solarch, had shown what one could actually do with the tools Gollaïr had invented.

No Solarchs still survive. It emerged years after his death that Gollaïr had dedicated himself to destroying the young artist in every way. Even Solarch's eventual suicide had been suspicious, with some saying that perennial bogeyman the Order of the Broken Eye had been hired for the job. Before Solarch's early death, Gollaïr had secretly, through many different agents, bought up every last one of the young man's paintings. Then he'd burned them all before the young man's eyes.

Still, artists being assholes? What else was new?

190   Later painters had built on his discoveries, so Gollaïr was still

considered important, but mostly only to those who cared about the history of art, not the art itself.

Later counterfeiters succeeded in making the luxin pigments stable, and actually made better paints than Gollaïr ever had. So, oddly, the counterfeits lasted longer and now looked much better than any of the originals did. This painting still shone—thus, a counterfeit.

Even if it weren't a counterfeit, though, I certainly wouldn't hang his gaudy garbage on my walls.

"You've been staring at this one for quite some time," Lord Dariush said. "I'm so glad. It's one of the real prizes of my collection. What do you think?"

I really should have divided my time between more paintings if I was going to let my mind wander. He called it 'one of his real prizes'?

Ugh.

"Is this a Gollaïr?" I ask. Please say you know it's a counterfeit and you just like it. Bad taste I can deal with.

"Oh yes! An original! You know Gollaïr? Not many people do now."

Shit. I only wish I could say it aloud. I dream of the day when I have so much power that my sons may say aloud what they actually think.

I purse my lips. "I'm afraid I don't like his work at all, actually. My apologies. So much of art is subjective, though."

"Is it?" Lord Dariush asks.

Please don't try to convince me this trash is objectively good. I hurry on. "I certainly appreciate its importance, and I'm dazzled that someone could make luxins that still shine, what, two hundred and fifteen years later or something?" It's the closest I can hint at questioning if he's certain it's not a fake. I shouldn't have done it, but I can't help myself.

"Sounds about right," he says.

So he doesn't know it's a fake.

A counterfeit, as the prize of his collection. It makes him look a fool, and I've come so far and invested so much of my precious time that I don't want to believe it. I can't marry into a family of fools.

I won't do that to my sons or the rest of my line. A man has a duty.

But it just doesn't fit. Lord Dariush came from nothing and is now one of the three wealthiest people in the world. A bad judge of art I can believe, but a fool? Has he just been the largest fish in an inbred backwater up here?

"You really don't like it?" he presses.

I flash an awkward acknowledgment. "Maybe my judgment of the work itself is unfairly low because of what they say he did to that   191 young artist—what was his name?" Maybe. And maybe I'd rather not be trapped talking to you out of politeness, old man, and would like to see the woman I *had* intended to make my bride.

"You really don't remember the young artist's name?" he asks, teasing.

So he hasn't forgotten about the Guile memory. So many people do, no matter how they've heard it lauded.

I wince and offer a rueful grin. "Solarch," I say. "Gollaïr ruined him, right? Drove him to suicide?"

"Or had him murdered," Lord Dariush says. He waves dismissively. "Does that change your judgment of his work? Would you praise mediocre art crafted by someone because they are morally good? Or denigrate greatness because its creator was errant?"

'Errant' isn't the word for a man who sets out to destroy a pupil who rightly looks to him for protection and friendship. "These are really deep critical waters," I protest.

"Or these are real critically deep waters," he says.

Not dumb, to shoot that back so quickly.

Maybe a fool, but not dumb. Dim people ride a mule to their conclusions, bright ones a racehorse—but not always in the right direction.

He's still waiting. How did I get backed into having this conversation anyway?

"Growing up, I had a friend whose mother fancied herself a singer. A strangling cat would make more pleasing noises. She was... wretched. But I liked her very much. So. If I can like a person but hate their art, I can do the opposite as well. Those who can't do so reveal their own limitations, not Art's. So no, I don't think Gollaïr's villainy makes me judge him more harshly. I think his art deserves harsh judgment. But I understand he was a local here, and thus nets a bit more praise on that account. Just as every parent thinks their child is especially gifted, though at least half must be wrong."

Lord Dariush weighs me, curious. "Am I in that half?" he asks. It isn't clear whether he's speaking about the painting or about his daughter. A moment later, I see that the ambiguity was intentional.

Well, shit. Trying to avoid a ditch, I seem to have fallen into a pit instead.

But you know what? To the seventh hell with him. All these games. Seven days here, and I've only seen Felia from afar, while her widowed elder sister, Ninharissi, and her mother and even her little brother have vetted me. These cretins and their *traditions*.

"How much honesty do you want?" I ask.

"*More*," he says, his eyes fierce.

"More? Do you think me dishonest, or guarded?" I ask, dragging that accusation out like a worm to writhe in the hot glare of Orholam's Eye. Very well, then. I can use the tool that's fit for the job, even if it's honesty. But I go on before he has to answer. "Felia is clearly possessed of superior giftings when compared with all the people in the Seven Satrapies, else I'd not have trekked so far. But whether you think she is especially gifted among the circle of other eligible young women of our class, that I do not know, nor to what degree you believe so. Certainly, I should hope a father would see what is laudatory in his daughter."

And I expect it here, where there is a *traditional* bride price to be negotiated.

He doesn't blink, nor back down from his accusation of me giving him half truths. "One might do well to remember, then," he says, "that the feelings that affect our judgments that impact the value we place on what we're about to lose also affect the price we wish to exact for that loss, depending on our affection or disaffection for our counterpart."

"I'm not sure I follow." Actually, I do. I just don't like what I'm hearing.

"If I might inflate the bride price for my beloved daughter because of my love for her—perhaps even while believing my judgment is objective—how else might my other feelings factor into a negotiation?"

I'm not sure if he's heading for a subtler point here, because this seems like the obvious dressed up in a philosopher's garb. "If you don't like me, you're going to demand a higher price," I say.

Which is why I was *trying* not to call you stupid or blind or a fool with bad taste, old man.

"I suppose, then," he says, "if you are incapable of being a man unmirrored, then perhaps what you ought to have set as your first objective in this visit was figuring out exactly what I do like."

" 'A man unmirrored'?" I ask.

"An old colloquialism. A man who doesn't practice pulling faces in front of a mirror. A man who is himself. A forthright man," he says.

We have an absolute imbalance of power here, the two of us. He can say anything, unless my pride and I want to pack up and leave without even having spent even an hour with Felia.

And then it dawns on me.

This is *all* negotiation!

The old fox. No wonder he's rich.

I see it now. Frustrate me with delays and promises while he knows

I need to be elsewhere, and raise the stakes of my own time investment. The longer I've spent here, the harder and harder for me to walk away empty-handed. I'll be more willing to compromise—without him even having to broach the subject.

The manipulation of my emotions is lovely! Wonderful! Brilliant!

It's exactly what I've been hoping to add to the Guile line. I might even *learn* a thing or two from Lord Dariush.

Well. Unlikely.

But now I know the game. You want honesty from me, you wily old weasel? No, you want me to open the door to the henhouse so you don't have to go to all the work of wriggling under the floorboards is all.

"It really is sadly terrible, isn't it?" he asks, pensive, staring at the painting.

"Huh?" I ask.

"Poor brushwork, uneven tone, what should be complementary colors ever so slightly off."

I say nothing, disconcerted. It seems safest.

"But it's not a forgery," Lord Dariush says. "Gollaïr spent years figuring out his luxin pigments. He originally intended simply to sell his paints to artists, not use them himself. He knew he wasn't a good painter. But he worked up a few demonstration paintings with garish colors, intending them only to show what was possible—and they caused a sensation. People called him a genius, and he quite liked it. He started acting the artist, hoping only to buy time, but the worse he behaved, the more he was hailed. The more he demanded, the more he was given. He very quickly trapped himself. He was a barely competent drafter with poor color differentiation. But he couldn't get secret tutoring to become better at either drafting or at painting, because he was famous for both. It's common for successful artists to fear they're impostors, but some *are* impostors.

"And Gollaïr was their king. Finally, he was forced to take on a pupil by a patron whom he couldn't refuse, and he found that the boy wasn't just better than he; the boy was a master for the ages.

"For years Gollaïr had kept his fraud going, and he had almost begun to believe he was as good as he told everyone else said he was. Solarch threatened it all. After destroying the boy, Gollaïr publicly retired, but secretly he planned a triumphant return. He was studying the boy's technique from the one small painting that he hadn't destroyed. Not a figure study—Gollaïr knew he could never match Solarch on that—but a landscape using the boy's sense of color and much better luxin-work. And this painting is what Gollaïr made."

Lord Dariush smiles sadly, then goes on. "This shoddy thing is the last Gollaïr, and the only one whose pigments survive—that at least he learned from Solarch. But it still has all the same fundamental flaws of his other work. It was the best thing he ever did, but he never sold this last painting. He never even showed it. After he finished it, he retired to his estate and watched his reputation wither. He never picked up a brush again. It's said—but this part I don't know for certain—that every day he went to see this painting and his last Solarch. He kept them side by side, a reminder of what was and of what could have been."

"That's a . . . great story," I say blandly.

"You don't believe me?" he asks, offended.

"How much honesty did you say you wanted again?" I ask.

His eyes harden. "Don't insult me."

"A secret painting, made years later," I say in the same monotone. "Thus, it's no wonder that it is slightly different in style, and features clearly superior drafting than all the others, or that it's unknown to scholars. Thus it's not just a very odd Gollaïr; it's the best Gollaïr! It's unique, precious, and has such juicy history attached to it. In truth, Lord Dariush, I don't know whether you're telling me a tale, or if someone told you one and you believed them. But if someone told me a story that drove up the price and addressed all my concerns about a forgery so conveniently, I'd keep both hands on my coin purse. Especially if this painting was only available for a very limited time before the seller had to leave."

He stares hard at me, and I begin to wonder if I've gone terribly off course. Not with my guess, of course. With him.

Then he grins.

"Aha! Now we're getting somewhere," he says. "There's that carving-knife intellect Felia praises, finally out of the block, its edge glittering in the light. Feels good to let it cut some meat, doesn't it, boy? Feels good to speak your mind, doesn't it?"

I grin ruefully again, like we've just had a breakthrough together. "I wanted to make a good impression," I say.

Surprisingly, come to think of it, that's true.

"What if who you really are was enough to do that?" Lord Dariush asks.

Who I really am scares people. But I take it humbly, look down at the floor as if in thought.

"Well, my boy, it's almost time for us to conclude our tour," he says.

"So soon?" I tease.

"One more, before we head back," he says, "and I think you'll find its story even more incredible than the Gollaïr's."

"But shorter?" I ask.

"Easy, son. A little truth goes a long way."

"Aha," I say. "Now we're getting somewhere."

Despite himself, I see Lord Dariush grin.

Chapter 29

As soon as the lift departed with its smug burden, Karris sat down hard on the bench outside the checkpoint. She could hardly breathe. Ironfist. King Ironfist, asking if Gavin was really dead. Asking if Karris was still in mourning.

A marriage.

Andross was right. It was the only way Ironfist could be safe. It was the only move left open to him.

But... marriage? He didn't...

No, surely not.

Oh God. Karris hadn't exactly sent the assassin who'd killed his sister, but she had allowed it, and Teia wouldn't have been serving the Order at all if Karris hadn't allowed it. It was a fairly thin line between Karris and that particular blood guilt.

She took a deep breath. She should put her feelings aside now. She had to make plans. She had to take meetings. A full day awaited her.

At least, Karris hoped it did. She felt as if the earth had swallowed her, as if all her selfishness and shortsightedness was rearing up to strike her with poison condemnation.

She'd never done well alone, and now life had stripped away everyone from her. The burdens of her office meant that even amid those she loved, she was alone.

She took another breath, remembering a lovely day long ago when she'd gotten distracted and double-charged a musket in Blackguard drills. It had blown apart in another nunk's hands, though luckily it hadn't wounded him. Karris had gotten dressed down in front of everyone. Then she'd had a bruising quarrel with Samite, who hadn't stood up for her.

She'd been hiding in her bunk having a cry when none other than Orea Pullawr had pulled the covers back.

Karris had wanted to curl up and die already, but then being found like that, by the White herself?

Orea had said, 'Karris, isn't it? Child, do you know what tears and kisses and fine underthings have in common?'

The question had baffled her so much she'd stopped crying.

'They're best enjoyed in bed.'

'I was trying to—' Karris began mumbling. Kisses and fine underclothes? What? Oh! 'Well, the former, I mean!'

'And doing so with such vigor that I thought you and a friend were enjoying the latter. But—'

'What?!' Karris asked again.

'But,' Orea Pullawr repeated, 'I need a Blackguard, so put on your big-girl pants and save the tears for later. You're on duty.'

And so I am.

Remembering Orea's kindness helped a wan smile steal onto her face. It had been pure kindness, too. Karris had only realized much later that the 'duty' the White needed her for was some invented thing: the woman had obviously overheard Karris crying and came to distract her without shaming her.

And that had been how she'd begun her service to the older woman.

So. Duty now. Tears later.

She felt better.

But before she stood up, she leaned forward, feigning clearing a pebble from her shoe. She slid a hand along the underside of the bench. Not only was this bench a place she'd sat often when waiting for a Blackguard to get off duty (and these days to wait for the lift to arrive), but it was also outside the checkpoint on the White's level of the tower. Both she and Teia had easy access to this place. It made an excellent dead drop.

There was a note there.

Aha!

Karris hadn't seen the girl to get a report in person for a while. Any news had to mean good news in their secret war against the Order; if things went badly for her, Teia would simply *disappear*.

In her room a short while later, Karris opened the note and mentally decoded the brief message and the date it referred to.

Suddenly the air felt too thick to breathe.

Karris had only just—last night!—done what she'd sworn she would never do.

She'd finally accepted that Gavin was dead. She'd given up on him.

Worse, she'd admitted it to that old viper Andross, which committed her. She'd told him she would do anything to save her people. Many thousands of lives. The whole empire. She'd said she'd do anything, and she'd meant it.

If the terms for peace and an alliance against a mortal threat were so simple, how could she possibly refuse to marry Ironfist?

This was how.

The note read: "Gavin kidnapped by Order. In grave danger. But alive. I'm certain. —Teia"

Such short lines bringing such bright news shouldn't have the power to tear a woman's heart in two.

But they did.

No proof was offered. No evidence at all. Karris almost couldn't believe it. Maybe she shouldn't.

But she did.

And no one else would. She couldn't even offer Teia's word that Gavin was alive without betraying Teia's mission and jeopardizing her very life. Even if Karris made the girl come before Andross Guile and swear it all in person, Andross wouldn't believe her. Even if he believed her, he wouldn't care. Andross Guile didn't know anything about love; he loved only power. He didn't care about honor; he cared about survival. If the cost to buy Ironfist's army was Karris committing bigamy, Andross would say that that price—betraying her office and dishonoring her husband and her old friend—was cheap. If Karris tried to tell the truth, she would shame Ironfist, get Teia killed, and doom the empire.

The Blackguards sometimes repeated an old saying that sounded like bluster from those who didn't live and die by it. It was what they said when a brother or a sister had to take a battlefield Freeing: *Death before dishonor.* Now, to those who counted on her, one way or another, no matter what Karris did, she would bring death and dishonor both.

She sat on the bench and felt as if the world had slipped out of joint.

Ironfist had been a dear friend. A man she'd admired and appreciated for so long in so many ways that what began as a political marriage could become more in time...if it weren't based on deception. If it didn't shame and dishonor them both.

But how could she say no to him? Acceptance was so obviously the right thing to do on every conceivable level that her rejection would make him lose face. It would seem a profound personal rejection. It would shame him, and he wasn't only her former friend. He was a king. Rejecting him had consequences far beyond her.

But how could she *not* reject him? She was *married*. To a man she loved. To a man she'd waited for without any hope offered, waited and waited...until yesterday. And now she was going to give up on him, again?

Her own happiness was the last thing she could think of. She was the White.

Shortly before she'd died, Orea Pullawr had once asked Karris not to hate her. Karris still didn't know what for, but apparently there were hard truths in that mysterious bundle of papers the Order had stolen. But maybe the papers were irrelevant now. She understood what Orea had meant.

Not so long ago, Karris wouldn't have believed it was even possible to do the wrong things for the right reasons. Now she knew she would do things for entirely unselfish reasons, knowing she would regret them bitterly afterward.

She was the White now.

The White didn't wait for a man to come save her.

The White was the one who came to save.

She didn't seek her heart's desire instead of doing her duty; she made it her heart's desire to seek her duty.

So. 'Big-girl pants.' Thank you, Orea. The burden you left me is heavy, but a White Oak stands strong in the storm.

Karris had until Sun Day. She could search for Gavin until then. If she could produce him, she wouldn't have to remarry. Couldn't. If she found him, Gavin would forgive Ironfist's betrayal, and Ironfist would trust Gavin's word that his absolution would hold. Peace and alliance were still possible. The rift could be mended. Wounds healed.

She would have to destroy the Order before Sun Day, though. Utterly, if she hoped to live in peace. If they ever hoped to be safe again.

If she failed, when Sun Day came, she would do what she must. What the innocent lives she safeguarded demanded of her. She would keep her mouth shut and marry, thus dishonoring two men, herself, and the office that demanded purity.

But then, once her people were saved?

What moral authority had a White who had stained her robes dark with broken vows? How could that which was white hide a stain?

She wouldn't try. She wouldn't heap deceit upon deceit. Her people would live, but having proven herself unable to live with honor...

Her mind flashed suddenly to her father. In that horrible fire, the White Oak family had lost not only all her brothers and the estate itself, but also goods worth more than the indebted family could ever repay. Despite her attempt to elope with Dazen, Karris's engagement   199 to Gavin Guile must have looked like the only way to save the family. Gavin had known it, too, mocking him, talking in front of him in the most disgusting terms about what he was going to do with Karris—who drank herself into a stupor that night, hoping to make herself insensate. The eldest Guile son had done all he'd promised, too. Then he told Karris she wasn't good enough for him, not smart enough, not pretty enough, too boring, sexually dull. He told her he didn't care about her family's lost fortune—but that he could never marry a woman so far beneath himself in every other way. She hadn't fought him then, not even when he threw her out into the cold, clothes torn, hair disheveled, tear-streaked and drunk, only making it home when a street merchant steered her away from a wrong turn into a bad neighborhood and gave her something hot to drink.

She'd known she was pregnant immediately, because she had to be, because it was her worst fear, and she'd confronted her father, turning all her rage on the man who'd gambled her honor and his own and had lost.

He'd not defended himself. He'd quietly put his affairs in order and then he'd blown his head off.

She'd hated him for his weakness, but the young find it too easy to hate the weak.

How can a man live without honor? How can a woman?

Her father had wagered her in order to save his own fortunes; she would wager herself to save the very lives of her people. That made them different, even if she had to take the same exit.

But perhaps she would finally be able to forgive him, if it came to that. But it wouldn't come to that. She would make sure of it.

So. I have until Sun Day.

Karris felt oddly invigorated. She had a little more than a month to accomplish everything she could in her life, or nothing at all.

She was deep in the muck. It felt like quicksand sucking at her boots, but no matter. She was gonna fight like hell.

Chapter 30

As sensation returned to her dull carcass, Teia probably should've had some gratitude that she was waking up at all. The ropes strangled that in the crib.

She swallowed hard against hemp. She'd already visibly stirred. There could be no subterfuge now. That game was finished. And maybe every other one, too.

"Master? What the hell, Master?" she said. It was her last card. Not a good one.

"Master? Master." Behind her, his voice low, Murder Sharp seemed to be chewing on the word. "No, Adrasteia. You needed a master." He sounded suddenly mournful. "I couldn't be that for you. You needed me, and I was gone. The war called me away, and you went astray without me."

She hadn't been blindfolded. Why not?

It could be a mistake. Sharp was fearsome, but he wasn't very smart.

As if he could read her mind, Sharp suddenly grabbed her at the ropes at the nape of her neck and breathed into her ear—soft, trembly breaths smelling of mint leaves and darkness.

"What—what are you doing, Master Sharp?" It wasn't one rope around her neck, it was at least six, and they all bobbed with her fear.

She should be looking at the room, establishing exits, figuring what she might grab as a weapon—but her world had collapsed to a bubble of this man's breath and all the kinetic potential for violence in him, like a boulder tipping at the edge of a great cliff held back only by her attention on it.

"Anything. I. Want," he said.

She'd already forgotten her question.

His canine tooth closed gently on her earlobe, his stubble scratching her. Against her very will, gooseflesh raised across her arms. He wasn't the kind of man to— He was just tormenting her. Maybe if he was so amused, she had some hope.

He bit down hard and she yelled. She pursed her lips and cursed inwardly.

Sharp chuckled, pulling back. He didn't seem alarmed in the least, which told her that wherever they were, no shouting was going to bring her help.

"Oh, Adrasteia," he said. "Sweet, stupid child." He grabbed the ropes again and lifted her. She'd assumed her limbs must be bound to the chair. They weren't. Instead she was cocooned in ropes on top of the chair, so she stood with his motion, ready to lunge and drive her head into his face, but he kept her high and in front of him.

He stood her to her tiptoes and walked her straight to the wall, still lifting higher, so she had to strain higher simply to breathe. On reaching the wall, he lifted her off her feet and settled the rope over a hook.

Teia gagged. The many ropes around her neck weren't a noose

designed to choke the life out as quickly as possible, but they were holding her entire weight. Her elbows were bound behind her back, and her feet bound together, straining to reach the floor.

Sharp's frowning face came into view as her body turned. "Thought I estimated that right," he said. He examined the ropes behind her back in no apparent hurry to save her fucking life, thank you very much. With a finger, he thrummed the ropes here and there, checking the tension.

"What's this? You gettin' fat?" he asked.

She choked.

He blew out a breath and stepped behind her, his fingers tugging.

It was her chance. He wasn't looking at her eyes.

But he was already done. Her toes brushed the floor, and then touched. The first hiss of air slipped into her lungs, and then a slow but adequate breath. The ropes around her diaphragm didn't allow a full gasp, heightening the sensation of suffocation. But Teia'd learned something of torture, and she knew that sometimes the mere suggestion of suffocation was far better than the reality of it.

Teia breathed, and did nothing but breathe.

He was looking into her eyes again before it occurred to her to draft. She'd missed her chance. He was too strong for her. Too canny.

How do you move too fast for fear to follow when you can't move at all?

"I told you, Adrasteia. Disobedience isn't an option with the Order. I told you…" With eyes cold as the deep currents under her feet and brittle voice cracking like springtime ice under her, he said, "It's the *Order* of the Broken Eye, not the *Suggestion* of the Broken Eye."

She couldn't bear his disgust, or for him to see her fear.

Looking away in defeat, she saw this wasn't his lair. He had none of the accoutrements that would suggest it was even a safe house. It was just an empty dump. Except that he'd spread out his gear on the floor and there was a sheaf of parchments lying on his carefully folded shimmercloak.

Next to the parchments, which were bent from having been rolled, she saw a green or red ribbon.

"Recognize those?" he asked.

The White's papers. They were what had gotten Teia into all this.

She shook her head.

"You naughty, naughty girl," Murder Sharp said, like she was a dog who'd shat on the rug. "I got suspicious when you insisted on taking them. You were her cat's paw all along, weren't you?"

He'd seen her eyes stick to that package. She'd given herself away the day they'd kidnapped Marissia? Damn, damn, *damn*. "Why do you have them?" she asked carefully. Speaking wasn't fun with this much pressure on her throat. "I thought the Old Man owned you, heart and soul, blood and bone."

"I never disobey an order the Old Man gives. But sometimes it's weeks between when we can meet. Months. We can't be too careful. So I had to open the papers to make sure there were no traps, or plans we needed to know immediately. And then...I got curious."

"And?"

"And what I found...troubled me. But you have no idea, do you?"

"About what? I'd love to hear it." If only to stay alive a bit longer, thanks.

"They murder people. Just like we do—to keep power, you know? Your precious, righteous Spectrum, and I don't just mean Andross Guile. At first I felt such glee, reading Orea Pullawr's explanation in her own hand, the last confession of a woman who pretended to be so holy. Perhaps when I came to kill her, I was the hand of justice come to repay her many sins. She struck such a mournful tone. So apologetic. So desperate to explain. I *despised* her. But then I read more."

He scrubbed his hands through his short, fire-red hair and sat down on a footstool. It was the only furniture in the house, if a house it was.

Sharp lit a candle with a finger and thumb and a bit of sub-red. It hissed and spat oddly. He peered closely at her, and she knew that if she flared her eyes to paryl, he would kill her instantly.

"In the past two years," Sharp said, "I've seen the Chromeria try to do things the old way, balancing the colors by decree. Telling the reds to draft more, the blues to draft less, waiting a year. Seeing how many storms kill people where, and what happens to the crops or the animals or the forests here and there and everywhere. Everyone gets poor, people starve to death, and the storms rage anyway. Only... a bit less frequently. But if that's the only way to save things, even if everything else they say is lies, even if the Chromeria's being led by hypocrites and monsters...what if their way really is better? Better to kill a few here, where they feel it, than to let hundreds or thousands die throughout the satrapies, isn't it? We Braxians, we say our way's better: assassinate a few to save many, but how's that make sense? If the Chromeria is doing it all wrong, I suppose, turning Atash into desert so Tyrea can bloom, that's bad, right? But the records show we did the same. I mean the opposite. All we did was make sure that the thousands who died weren't *ours*. Who's the monster then? Maybe our way was best against the nine kings, but now?"

203

Sharp was not a good storyteller. Teia couldn't even tell when he was referring to which side.

"I have no idea what you're talking about," Teia said. "Can you start from the beginning?"

He shook his head, paused. Checked a denture as if it had felt loose.

"The Order ruined me," Sharp said. "Lied to me. Broke me in the worst way—they made me break myself." He reached into his mouth and took out his bottom set of teeth. He sat on the little stool and squinted at the teeth in order. With a tiny brush, he scraped away some tiny imperfection, wiggled a canine. He clucked his tongue between his jagged natural teeth, displeased, and tended to the rest of the dentures.

But he kept glancing up, noting her eyes at unpredictable intervals. She couldn't draft without getting caught. Dammit. She had to wait until he was more distracted.

He said, "It's a funny thing, you know, you and I."

"How's that?" Teia asked.

He hadn't looked up in perhaps a count of ten—as if he were daring her to try to draft. That she hadn't dared—that she might have missed her last chance through her lack of courage was infuriating, sickening, terrifying.

He dried the dentures and daubed paste from a jar along the length of the teeth channel with a tiny brush. Then he glanced over, quickly.

"It's funny that we both kind of want to be the other person—but only kind of," Sharp said. "You want to be a master of paryl. A killer. You're a brittle weakling, and you want to be strong. You want to be *scary*. But only kind of, because you don't want it badly enough to do what you need to become who you want to be. Me, I'm strong, but... I kind of want to be a traitor like you."

It was like a rope thrown toward a drowning woman.

"It's never betrayal to do what's right," Teia said.

He barked a laugh. "Think the Old Man would agree?"

"It's not too late for you," Teia said.

He tamped his gums and broken teeth dry by biting a towel. Then he fit the dentures back into his mouth. He pressed firmly on them and waited a moment. He sighed. "Oh, girl," he said. "Your naive-it, naïveté? naiveness? is a blindness worse than your shitty color-blind eyes. Do you know how many men I've killed?"

He was looking directly at her now. There was no chance to draft unless he turned away again.

"I—"

"Twenty-seven slaves, in my training. If you count those. They started me with worn-out old men. I knew those poor bastards'd soon be on the streets, dying, begging, miserable. Unwanted, uncared for. Not so hard to end a life that was gonna look like that. You're doing 'em a favor, aren't you? The Order worked me up from there, breaking me in until I was like an old, dependable pair of work boots."

It hit Teia like a punch in the stomach. She'd thought her training method was coincidental, that old slaves were the cheapest.

It was no coincidence. It was all by design.

They'd been chipping away at her conscience deliberately, by degrees.

And she'd helped them. Justifying it at every step. A victim, but a victim partaking in the evil done to her. Breaking herself. Sometimes she'd looked forward to trying out new paryl tricks on her victims, hadn't she? Experiments.

They're gonna die anyway. I might as well learn something from them.

Someone's going to kill them. Might as well be me. It's better that it's done by me, because...

Because why, exactly?

Someone's gonna do evil, might as well be me.

And if everyone in the world said that, what kind of world would it be?

Death had been certain for any one slave who'd stood before her. That man was going to die, regardless of what she did. But if she'd not killed that one, the Order wouldn't have purchased the next for her to kill.

Or the next. Or the next.

What if everyone in the world said, 'Someone's gonna do evil—but it won't be me'?

But Sharp was still talking. "They gave me reasons at first. You know, this one had done this terrible thing, this next had done something worse. From old slaves to young, young slaves to bad old free men, old free men to young free men to bad old luxiats to... to anyone, without question. Without remorse.

"Eighty-nine kills now in more years than I want to remember. Not all of them assassinations, either. Jobs go wrong, or sometimes you have to grab someone so you can try out a new technique for the next job. It takes a toll, you know? You'd think it's hardest at first, that after that you get over it. And you do, until sometimes you look back and think too much. Like I'm doing now, I guess.

"Last year, I killed Arys Sub-red in her very birthing chamber. We'd made love that morning." He smiled with real fondness, then shook himself. "Not that she loved me. I'd been very clear that I was willing to be good company and an attentive but temporary bedmate and no more. But she treated me...respectful. Honorably, I guess. You don't get that so much. We passed some of the sweetest hours of my life in each other's arms. I was...uh, fond of her, I guess, in a way I'd not thought I could be after...whatever. But that morning I threatened to strangle her newborn's first scream if she said the wrong thing. I would've done it, too." He shook his head. "What kind of man does that? Not a whole one. Not a man at all."

"You can still—"

"No!" he barked. "There is no redemption for men like me. And if there was, if some god would erase my crimes, I wouldn't want to serve a god so vile. Some things can't be forgiven. *Shouldn't* be. I've sworn the oaths. I've lived them. I've drunk of the communal bloodwine. So I've this much honor left to me, this much at least. At least I obey."

He slapped her face, shooting black stars over her vision, and then he pulled a blindfold over her face.

She heard him pull up the chair within a few feet and sit.

And as he sat with a great sigh, she could only hope he was dumber than she thought, because if the greatest evidence Murder Sharp held on to of his own goodness or honor was that he obeyed the Old Man, then every moment he let Teia live was an argument against all those things.

If he realized that her continuing existence undermined the very last thing he valued about himself? That moment would be her last.

Chapter 31

"May we have the room, please?" Tisis said. She'd just come in from one of her meetings with her spies, and was wearing attire for the forest, not the palace.

The windows of the privy council chamber were dark. Even the most ardent art aficionados had gone home. Kip had only three meetings left before he could call it a day. He'd been seated so long, his butt was going to come out of his chair square-shaped. Ferkudi's report on provisions was next: boring, but necessary information, doubtless with money requests attached.

What was after that, another banker to beg for a loan?

Kip sighed, then realized everyone was waiting on him. Not least his wife. "Please, please," he said.

He was not used to this 'lord' business.

"I could use a few more minutes with these numbers anyway," Ferkudi said as he and some subordinates and scribes and secretaries and the rest cleared out of the room.

Only Cruxer stayed in the chamber, with some of the Mighty's nunks outside. The man had to be even more tired than Kip, but he wasn't ready to leave Kip alone with anyone other than the original Mighty yet.

"They told me what you did," Tisis said.

"They did?" Kip asked stupidly. Which 'they'? What thing?

He really probably shouldn't be making decisions when he was this exhausted. He'd stacked the easy meetings up for the end of the day, but still.

"They did. Come with me," Tisis said.

As Kip stood laboriously, Cruxer paused in his checking the windows. They'd just cleared the room, and now they were leaving it? He made to go with them.

Tisis waved him off. "Sorry," she said. "Won't be long."

She took Kip's hand and pulled him toward the room's closet. She pulled out her ponytail. "I've been thinking about you all day," she said.

Kip's exhaustion was vanishing by the moment.

As she opened the closet door, she said, "Have you been thinking about me?"

With one meeting after another, all day long, each demanding total focus? He'd barely thought about her at all. But that didn't feel like the right thing to say at the moment, so he slid his hand up her cheek into her newly loosed blonde hair and pulled her head back to kiss her as he joined her in the little closet.

She snaked away from him after a moment to close the door behind them. It plunged them into darkness.

Kip's heart suddenly leapt with fear, all desire forgotten.

Locked in a closet. Helpless. Rats swarming.

A mag torch snapped, and they were bathed in green light. He saw the look of brazen desire on his wife's upturned face at the same time that she saw the terror on his.

Her hand paused from removing her belt, and she cringed. "Oh, shit! How'd I forget? Oh, honey, I'm so sorry. I've ruined it, haven't I?"

Kip took some deep breaths. He forced a grin. "Well, saying 'Oh, shit' that loudly is gonna make Cruxer wonder what I just did to you, but other than that? Nah."

She flashed a grin, but then sobered. "You're okay?"

"Not yet," he said honestly. His throat was tight. "Help me forget the where and remember the with-whom?"

Her smiled broadened, and there was nothing in all the world that could quicken his pulse like a devious, confident grin on his beautiful bride's face. "Draft a little green?" she asked.

"Green?!" he said, trying to keep his voice down. "The last time we tried some green in bed, do you remember what you did?"

"Just a little!" she whispered. The whites of her eyes were already swirling with green. More than a little, and she was shimmying her hips to remove her trousers.

But he didn't use green. Green was all wildness—which could be wonderful if one was looking to overcome shyness in the bedchamber—but that which is wild hates being caged, and Kip already felt near panic.

It actually took Kip several bifurcated minutes to forget the close confines of the closet. Then, as they made love in the tight space, her head bent back, her hair filling his nostrils with her scent, his hands on her hips, then on her still-covered breasts, her body pushing eagerly against him, slowly, slowly, that old grimy rat-infested closet's echo faded like bad music heading into the distance as blissful tones of a new song began close by.

And when they'd finished—as quietly as possible, for Cruxer's sake—he held her still against him and marveled. In the postcoital clarity, he was filled with such love for his wife that fear had been cast out.

The closet had been transformed: no more a trap, no more an echo of the darkest moments of his childhood—it was just a little room. Hemmed in on three sides, he'd wanted to bolt for the exit, but if he had, he'd have missed out on this.

He spun Tisis around and kissed her passionately.

She squeaked, surprised, but then leaned into him, her hand reaching down between them as she made a little moue that asked, 'Again?'

He pulled away from her lips. "I'd love to," he said.

She'd tilted her hips, but didn't press onto him now as she heard his hesitation.

Nor did he push forward. He'd meant to pull away from her hand as well, but didn't. "Do... *you* want to?" he asked.

"I'm more than *willing*," she said. "But I'm also certainly satisfied. I was trying to be quiet for Cruxer's sake." Her face went through several fast expressions. She said, "You're confusing me."

"You gave me a thought," he said. "A breakthrough, maybe. But part of me is screaming that I'd be a damned fool to—"

He cut off as she pushed deep onto him, pushing him off balance until his back hit the wall. Her eyelids fluttered for a moment, and then her eyes cleared and she looked up at him sweetly. "My lord," she said, "thank you for seeing to my needs. Now I believe you have others to attend to."

She pulled away and threw her clothes into place before he could stop her.

"You are merciless," he said. "And I adore you."

"What was your breakthrough?" she asked, pulling her belt on.

"Huh? Oh, oh, right," he said.

She sighed.

"What do you think is my greatest weakness?" Kip asked.

Tisis paused in pulling her hair back into its ponytail. "For real?"

"Yeah!"

"You're really going to ask that, right after we...had a moment?"

"Fine, fine, what's my greatest strength?"

"You have lots of great strengths—"

"No, I'm not hunting for compliments," Kip said. "It's what you've said before."

"You mean that you see with your heart? That you have compassion—could you put that away now?—that you have compassion that allows you to understand people, even in moments where another man would be sunk into his own needs and plans."

"Right! And thank you," Kip said, getting his own clothes back into place. "So the flip side is my great weakness. I see the small stuff, and I lose the big."

"The small stuff is the big stuff," Tisis said.

"With people, yeah. But not as a leader. Hey, you mind if I open the door now?"

"Do I look like I just had amazing sex?" Tisis asked.

Kip hesitated. "This isn't a trick question, is it?"

"Let me rephrase. Do I look like I just had sex in a closet?"

"Still not tracking."

"Do I look rumpled, Kip? Do I smell like—"

"No—oh, and yes. You and me both, actually."

She scowled, then gazed at the green mag torch. She drafted a little. "Okay, fine, now I don't care."

"You know, you really shouldn't—"

"Please lecture me about how much I'm drafting," she said sharply.

He shut his mouth. "Pot, meet kettle. Objection withdrawn."

"Go on, now," she said, opening the door.

Out in the fuller-spectrum light of the room, she definitely looked like she'd just had sex. Hair not all tucked into her ponytail, cheeks flushed, clothes a bit askew.

"Mirror's right there," Cruxer said, otherwise stony-faced. "And General Antonius is here to present tomorrow's training regimen and the daily report."

Tisis groaned. For all her earlier bluster, she was mortified when it came to her cousin learning anything about her sex life. They'd grown up together.

The call of a million duties delivered one after another, each somewhat different, and yet always stultifyingly the same, threatened to pull Kip back into their games.

"Ask him to wait," Kip said.

'Thank you,' Tisis mouthed, as Cruxer did so.

Kip sat silent, though.

He was being played. In the clamor of a million needs, he'd lost sight of his adversary. Koios had a plan. Nothing here—or at least very little—was by accident.

The thoughts swirled: an ambassador sweats when he shouldn't, and then doesn't when he should. Assassins fail at a job that should have been easy. A drafter wears armor, not to protect herself from her enemies but to protect her friends from herself. A map doesn't report what it should, and...maybe...

What if it also *did* show what it shouldn't?

Kip walked over to the map table.

He blacked out half a dozen of the blooming lights behind them—refugees' and scouts' reports that had come from the Great River behind them, reporting about various events, but that altogether told them the river was open when it actually hadn't been.

It had only taken *six* reports to lead them astray, because they didn't expect more: bandits were enslaving everyone in that area they could grab.

Now he ran the map backward and forward without those six reports, and saw a dark area in the map, right behind them, a shadow that they might otherwise have feared.

Koios had done that.

"These are the bad reports," Kip said. "These are the refugees who are spies."

Tisis was standing at the map table with him. "Yeah, these three for sure, and I'm checking into these ones now."

"They are," Kip said.

"How do you...?"

But he barely heard her. This darkness on the map had hid an enormous threat. What if there were another?

"Something's missing," Kip said. "Something...Cruxer, was there ever any emissary from the White King? Someone that the soldiers stopped? Any news of someone being waylaid by angry townspeople?"

"Uh-uh," Cruxer said.

"Why would there be?" Ben-hadad asked. Kip hadn't even noticed that Ben had come back into the room. "We just routed them. And then they tried to assassinate you."

Kip said, "There should be an emissary here to distract and confuse us. To sow discord if any could be sown. Not least, to try to see what condition the city's in."

"Koios surely expected you to execute anyone he sent," Cruxer said. "Lawless men expect lawless treatment."

Kip shook his head. "He doesn't mind sacrificing people. It's something else."

He looked at the map again. Advanced it. Rolled it all the way back to the battle of Ox Ford, nearly two years ago now. Advanced it again.

The reports lit up, beacons against a night of ignorance, cairns on a climb with precipices on every side. He squinted until the lights blurred, new lights appearing and old fading away as the reports aged and the map advanced time. It was like clouds passing over a night sky, blotting out the stars and revealing others. But some places stayed ever-black, little bits of the evernight, of eternal ignorance and blindness.

If you screened out a few reports, which could well be there to distract, then...the darkness had a shape.

There was an area of coastline almost entirely dark.

"What were those four reports? Here?" he asked Tisis.

She went back to the very beginning of one of her folders and told him some names. They had no meaning to him.

He pursed his lips.

She said, "But that was when I was just getting my networks set up. I didn't have many sources yet."

"Whose lands are those?" he asked.

She hadn't written that down, but she knew this satrapy well. She searched her memory for a few moments. "These ones are Red Leaf lands, a forest and farmland. This is Conal Briar Wood's estate, and this is old Aoife Bracken's grazing land, if she's still alive and it hasn't shifted to her stepson's family, uh, they're...Petrakoi? Alexandros Petrakis. Yeah."

"Shit," he said. He'd been hoping there was some connection with something, anything.

"Kip, they're both retainers to the Red Leafs."

"*Shiiit*," Kip said.

He darkened those four lights on the map, and now there was a blank area, east of Ox Ford. "What's this town near the coast?"

"Azuria, or maybe Apple Grove. Azuria Bay used to be a port until the harbor silted in. The moorage was a bit of a way up the river, can't remember the name. But it didn't generate enough revenue for the locals to be able to afford dredging it, and there are a lot of rocks farther out that made captains leery of it in the first place, so it slowly shriveled up and died. Apple Grove is the next village over, maybe a league away?"

Kip chortled.

"Oh ho. Master Danavis would be so disappointed in me. Cruxer, what do you do when your enemy is making a mistake?"

"Don't interrupt them," Cruxer said. "You taught us that a long time ago."

"Tisis, show me the language you've worked out with Ambassador Red Leaf."

He looked it over and clapped his hands. Good play, enemy mine! It almost worked.

"Well, you were wrong, Commander," Kip said.

"How so?"

"The White King did send his emissary. Ambassador Red Leaf is a traitor."

"What?!" Tisis asked. "But he gave us everything!"

"Everything to snare us," Kip said. "Commander, what message do you think those assassins were sending when they failed on purpose?"

Cruxer's brow furrowed. He still didn't buy that they had.

"Look," Kip said. "Let's say, for argument's sake, that they intended to fail...but didn't intend to die. What would you take from that?"

"Uh...'Don't mess with the Order, or we'll get you next time'?"

"Right. So where's the last place you'd go if you didn't want to run afoul of the Order?"

"Braxos?" Cruxer asked.

"Well, yes, yes...But you know, maybe a living city that someone might actually go to."

Cruxer shrugged. "I dunno. It's not like the Order publicly lets anyone know where their headquarters are."

"You're not really helping me here," Kip said. "How about if I said I wanted to go to the Chromeria? Would you be more or less afraid of the Order than if we stay here?"

"More, definitely."

"Thank you!" Kip looked at the treaty. "And this treaty commits me to take all our troops to lift the siege of Green Haven—and go with them personally."

"But that's where we want to go," Cruxer said.

"Right. Or we could stay here. There's a million reasons to stay here. A million problems to solve. A bandit army, for one. And what were they trying to do—before Daragh the Coward so kindly betrayed Koios and handed them over to us?"

Cruxer said, "Trying to trap us in the city so we couldn't go help lift the siege?"

"No," Kip said. "They don't care if we tried to lift the siege or if we fought here. They're armor, see?"

" 'Armor'?"

"But not just any armor! We thought they were blocking the Great River to keep out new threats from without—reinforcements and supplies and everything else. Now, it does do that, but that's not the main purpose. The White King hasn't thrown his whole might at Green Haven. Why not? He split his forces rather than overwhelm the city. Why? Because if he took the city, we would know that we had no chance of taking it back. So we wouldn't even try. See?

"He didn't block the river to keep things from coming *in*. His blockade is to keep something dangerous from going *out*. Do you see it now? We're trapped in a closet. Three walls, one door—and he knows what I'm going to do: either stay in here afraid, or rush out the door he shows us. He doesn't care which!"

"What do you mean?" Cruxer said. "Of course he cares!"

"I'm not saying he doesn't have preferences. He'd love for us to sit in this city and do nothing so his people can take Green Haven. But even if we save Green Haven—even if we push his forces out of Blood Forest entirely, how can we hold it if he holds the Great River and the rest of the Seven Satrapies?"

"Orholam's hoary head," Ben-hadad said. "That harbor. Cruxer, what do we know about the bane? I don't mean religiously. I mean practically, for war."

Cruxer scowled. "They lock down drafters of their color."

"And one other thing," Kip said.

Ben-hadad looked at him, horror dawning. "Oh no...They don't need a navy, just some supply ships and barges. That's why a little harbor could work."

"What? What do you mean?" Tisis asked. "What's the one other thing, Kip?"

"The bane *float*," Kip said. "At least, the one at Ru did. So what if the other can as well?"

"Plenty of lumber around Azuria to help support the heavier ones, if need be," Ben-hadad said.

"You're telling me..." Cruxer said.

"They're going to invade the Chromeria," Ben-hadad said. "Barges for ten or twenty thousand men and drafters and wights and food, and they just...cross. The Chromeria is surely using skimmers to scout now, but any skimmers that get close enough to spot the bane would simply die in the water because the drafters powering them couldn't draft. The Chromeria might only get a couple days' warning."

"And it wouldn't matter anyway," Kip said. "The Chromeria's defensive plans rely on drafters to do most of the fighting. If none of the drafters can do anything because the bane neutralize them... they'll panic. Everyone will. With drafters and wights and even five thousand warriors, the White King could take the Jaspers in a day."

"Well, that's fuckin' terrifying," Big Leo rumbled, coming in the door. "Doesn't do us much good, though, does it?"

"Sure it does," Kip said. "If we know what he's doing, we have a chance to stop him."

"How?" asked Big Leo.

"Gimme a break, man," Kip said, "I just figured out *his* plan. Give me a second or two to come up with ours, maybe?"

"Maybe we go scuttle the bane before they can leave?" Big Leo asked.

"Yes! A surprise attack. Move fast through the forest, descend on him like the raiders we are." Kip started to warm to the idea. He could stop the White King *and* not abandon Blood Forest. "We could send along the bulk of the army to relieve the siege at Green Haven, shoot down there by small rivers and streams, maybe reunite with the Night Mares and—"

"Breaker," Cruxer said. He looked over at Big Leo. "If they have the bane...then they have the bane. We're drafters. All of our elite warriors, all the Night Mares—we're all drafters. The bane can immobilize drafters of their color. If they have all the bane, we're the last people who could stop them."

214   It hit them all like a punch in the gut.

"We haven't lost. Not yet," Kip said. "I won't believe it."

Tisis came beside him and took his hand.

His heart plunged.

"*We* haven't," Big Leo said. "But maybe the Chromeria has."

"I guess that makes our decision for us," Cruxer said. He looked ill. "We can send messengers. Maybe see if they get around this navy to go warn the Chromeria."

"It won't make any difference," Big Leo said, "but we owe it to them to let them know what's coming. Maybe they can flee."

"You know damn well they won't," Tisis said. "Andross Guile won't believe someone's thought of something he hasn't."

At the Battle of Ru, everyone in the Seven Satrapies had seen what one bane could do—or could almost do. But they'd killed that one. Maybe that had lulled them all into a false complacency. No one could imagine that anyone could assemble seven bane together without anyone finding out about it. No one could imagine organizing large-scale warfare without drafters at the center of the strategy.

Kip said, "Fine, so let's say we give up the Chromeria for lost, which means we're giving up on the Seven Satrapies entirely. Then let's say we go free Green Haven, and have total success. Then we have...what? until next spring at best for the White King to regroup and attack us? We have until next spring to figure out how to win a war against drafters and wights and the bane—without using drafters, not even ourselves?"

He looked from face to face, but they all looked as gray and hopeless as he felt.

"And if the Chromeria falls," Cruxer said. "All the fleeing drafters are no help to us. *We* can't even help us."

"We'd have to retreat before every battle, leaving the munds to do all the fighting—against wights and drafters. They'll be slaughtered. We could fight a guerrilla war, but we'd have to be willing to give up every city, every decent-size town, and every person not able to travel fast and live off the land. There's no endgame there except hoping Koios simply decides it's not worth it to kill us. Anyone here think Koios will give up before we're all dead?"

Every face was grim.

Tisis said, "You've been awfully quiet, Ben. Any ideas?"

He fidgeted with his flip-up spectacles. He chewed on his lower lip. "Not for an attack, but maybe...maybe for a defense?"

Chapter 32

Karris White Oak had never felt so alone. She didn't know how long she could stand this.

She lifted her head from the prison of her folded arms at some sound from outside her rooms. She'd fallen asleep at her desk after another too-long night of studying and making plans and drinking too much kopi. Karris's room slave, Aspasia, wasn't confident enough in her position to make her go to bed. She had merely draped a blanket over her mistress's shoulders. It had fallen off.

Constantly surrounded by the Blackguards, who had been her family for nearly two decades, now Karris couldn't let herself trust any of them. She stood slowly, body aching, and wondered if it was only the night sleeping at her desk, or if she was getting old. She moved toward her bed, not bothering to undress as she glanced at a water clock. It was still two hours until dawn. She could get an hour of real sleep, anyway. Then the day's duties would accost her once more.

But she had barely slipped under the cold blankets when she heard a voice. The same voice that had wakened her, but now impossibly loud.

"Want to know your problem, Highness?" Samite said.

Let this just be a bad dream, Karris thought.

Highness wasn't one of her titles. "Not enough sleep," Karris said, not opening her eyes. "Please go away."

"You've got tits again. Never thought I'd see it."

"Excuse me?!" She opened her eyes. Samite was not alone. She closed them again. She was in no place to deal with people right now.

Gill Greyling's usually welcome voice intruded. "She's trying to be polite. She means you're getting fat."

"Ahem," said Commander Fisk. What the hell. When had he come in? "Excuse Gill. He meant soft."

"Chubby?" asked Essel.

"Chubby?!" Karris said. "My clothes still fit!" A little less comfortably, maybe, but still.

"Flabby?" asked Buskin.

"Tubby," suggested Vanzer.

What was this? Had *all* of them come? It was mortifying. Karris peeked from beneath her pillow. Orholam's granite belly, there were a dozen of them.

Karris stared daggers at some new kid she didn't even know. He swallowed. "I, uh, I hadn't noticed any change, High Lady."

"Hasn't been around long enough to know how tough you used to be," Vanzer said. "Sad."

"Long time ago," Essel said.

"Weren't they calling her the Iron White? More like the Hungry White," Gill said.

"You can't—you can't talk to me that way," Karris said plaintively.

"Bet she can't even do five pull-ups these days," Samite said.

"Excuse me!?" Karris sat bolt upright. She'd once matched the women's record for most pull-ups.

Half an hour later, she'd done those five pull-ups. Barely. And knew she was going to pay for it for days. And pay for everything else, too, training with the Blackguards. It was all coming back fast, though, and she realized how much she needed it. The clarity it brought.

In her time as White, she'd come to think of the hours spent training as hours lost—but now, again, she realized she accomplished more in the hours she still had than if she'd only worked.

Now, in the dawn's light, she sweated at the rear of a line of Blackguards, doing an advanced form. Standing on her left foot, she snapped out a side kick, sharp and crisp, holding her balance as she then spun and slapped her right elbow into her left hand, exactly at the moment fifty other Blackguards did. Kick, land on the opposite foot, kick again.

She wasn't a mind, housed in a body; she was body and mind united.

Dammit. How had she forgotten?

Her Blackguards loved her. They saw her. She didn't know exactly what she needed to do, but she knew she needed to fight for them. She needed to be worthy of these magnificent men and women.

The thought carried her through the rest of the morning's duties. She'd been elevated not to be honored but in order to serve. So this afternoon, she'd buried her reason for walking down this hallway amid a half dozen other tasks that took her to half of the towers of the Chromeria and even belowground, making numerous stops as if they were spur-of-the-moment decisions to check in on old friends, even to minister to an elderly luxiat who'd broken her wrist in a fall. All of it had been to bring her to this door, flanked by the new, short, and burly Blackguard who'd just been assigned to her detail, a kid named Amzîn.

Because she didn't know him, she didn't trust him. It had almost made her abandon her plan. To keep secrets, she had to trust no one, had to make today's stops seem casual. And she couldn't do that while checking the guard roster or requesting someone she knew.

Still, it put her alone, with a stranger. The young man who was supposed to be protecting her could well be a spy for the Order of the Broken Eye.

She could just go by this door. Pass it off as nothing. A whim.

In one of the stranger perquisites of her office, this little room was technically hers, albeit low in the bowels of the green tower, and thus much too far away from her apartments for her to use frequently as a second office or library. In her time as a Blackguard, she'd learned that previous Whites had sometimes used this second room as a discreet place for assignations. Karris was using it to tuck her own little secret away from sight.

"Do you want me to open the door, High Mistress?" Amzîn asked.

O sweet Orholam. He was just a kid! Built like a stump and as plain as the day was long, Amzîn had an incongruously high tenor voice. Seemed embarrassed about it, now that Karris had let her surprise at it show.

She owned everything in the room before her, including the person, so she had every right to go straight in.

"Knock, please," she said instead. It was a weird situation already; she didn't need to make it weirder.

Amzîn knocked too hard and rattled the door on its hinges. He actually flinched. Apparently didn't know his own strength.

Karris pretended not to notice.

"Please don't knock my door down!" a young man shouted from within. "It's unlocked!"

"Apologies, High Mistress," Amzîn mumbled.

Karris waved it away.

They stood for a moment longer, then Amzîn suddenly realized that by his training, he was supposed to open the door and go in first to assess the room for threats, and instead he was standing around. He blurted out, "Oh, shit!" and shoved the door open.

It slammed into the slight young man who'd come to open the door, and knocked him head over heels sprawling into the room.

Amzîn froze momentarily, but then checked the room like a professional.

Then he apologized profusely to the young luxiat in golden robes and many chains, who had only risen, wobbly, as far as his knees.

Quentin waved away Amzîn's proffered hand. "No, no, actually thank you. You've saved me all the effort of getting down gracefully in all this regalia." Facing Karris, Quentin lay himself prostrate, stretching out his hands toward her feet. "High Lady. Gracious One. Beloved Mistress. How may I serve you?"

"Please stand," Karris said. "I mean, if you can, under the weight of all that."

The wide Blackguard offered his hand again, but Quentin flinched. "Err, no...no, thank you."

"Amzîn?" Karris asked.

"High Lady?"

"First day solo?"

"Yes, High Lady," he said, pained. A Blackguard was supposed to be well-nigh invisible to his wards, and he was failing. Horribly.

"Why don't you take position out in the hallway? I think the threats to my health and well-being are much more likely to be out there...if you are."

He seemed at first relieved, and then at the whipcrack of the last words, stung. His face went from wounded to stoic quickly, though, give him that.

Karris wanted to be forgiving, but she'd been a Blackguard. Second-best wasn't good enough, and if this kid couldn't get better fast, she was going to be riding the watch captains for their bad judgment in promoting him.

Besides, she wasn't going to get close to another Blackguard kid. She'd probably just have to kill him in the end, like she had Gavin Greyling.

He slipped out quietly and professionally.

Orholam damn this war. With all the drafting she was requiring of everyone, Karris was going to be killing a lot of Gavin Greylings before the year was out.

"Seems like a lot more chains than when we last spoke," Karris said. She had much of the story already from others, which was good, because Quentin's modesty kept him from giving her the full truth.

"My spiritual director told me I can't sell them all," Quentin said. "If I'm to be your scourge of the luxiats, they should see both their wealth and the loss of it. At least until it seems like it's becoming a contest."

"How's that?" Karris asked.

He unfolded the tale succinctly. Ever since Karris had spared his life, recognizing his contrition at what he'd done was real, Quentin had taken on a unique position. She'd made him a slave—her slave—but required him to dress always in gold finery. It was both a personal penance for his own ambition and intended to be a corporate penance for all the luxiats who'd forgotten who they were supposed to be serving.

Quentin was hated and reviled by many of the luxiats, but no one 219 dared physically harm him—as far as Karris knew at least—because he was Karris's property, and they feared her. As well they should. But even if they hadn't used fists, Karris was certain many luxiats had used their words to hurt Quentin.

He'd taken every abuse and accepted it.

Soon, guilt-stricken by their own cruelty, some young luxiats had come to beg his forgiveness, and ended up confessing much more. With his intellectual gifts and deep study, the old Quentin had once been on track to becoming High Luxiat. Now he was a slave. As he listened, he condemned no one who came to him, and he seemed to be able to understand everyone, from high to low. He was a convicted murderer, but oddly also the most devout luxiat they knew.

Among the young luxiats at least, he'd become an important figure.

He thought he was merely an oddity, like a good-luck charm to them, but Karris knew he was becoming more than that. The young luxiats gave him alms.

And then, as Quentin's new reputation spread, so, too, did strangers.

It made him enemies among the older luxiats, who'd hated him already for rubbing their own shortcomings in their faces and now hated him more for being so apparently righteous, and admired (a convicted murderer, admired!) on top of it all.

Which now helped her understand what he meant about the donated jewelry he wore becoming a contest. As luxiats or lords gave to him, and saw their piece soon thereafter being worn, they might feel proud of it, but soon it would be gone—sold for another's bread. His wearing of it was to be a reminder that they didn't own it any longer, and if that stung, then good. If they gave without feeling a pinch, how did that help them learn to sacrifice? His no longer wearing it would be a further sign of how Orholam gives gifts, not that they may be hoarded but that they may be used. If that pained them, too, then that was good as well.

If, on the other hand, seeing him wear their jewelry started to give lords bragging rights, he would stop, and that could pain them, too.

He continued his studies—Karris had ordered him to do that, mainly so that he must always be among the luxiats—but he also volunteered in the worst precincts of Big Jasper, where he worked at charity hospitals and fed the poor, often helping in the sculleries himself. He'd been beaten and robbed several times—the gold clothing was the sign of an easy and lucrative mark. Once he'd been hit so hard he'd lost his hearing in one ear.

But he had no fear whatsoever, nor would he countenance stopping his work.

Of all people, white-bearded High Luxiat Amazzal had put a stop to the muggings. Karris's agents had reported that the old man had gone into Overhill himself, in plain clothing nearly as old as he was. He'd shown some toughs something (her agent couldn't see what) that made them very nervous. Then old High Luxiat Amazzal was taken to a building where some very powerful people with illegal interests were reputed to spend time gambling together. After half an hour, he left.

She got a note the next day from Amazzal: "Certain wayward sheep from my old flock have contacted me. They've noticed young Quentin's good works and wish them to continue. They tell me that henceforth, as well as they are able, he will be protected."

It was an odd construction—like it was their idea, not his. Like he hadn't paid for it with some kind of coin or another. But he hadn't been summoned by them, Karris was sure of that. She'd deployed a dozen spies on Amazzal, searching his offices, delving into his finances, following him everywhere he went, intercepting his correspondence and looking for codes, and noting every book he touched in case it was being used as a cipher key. Amazzal had been one of her prime candidates for being the Old Man of the Desert, the head of the Order of the Broken Eye.

Instead, his only secrets appeared to be secretly doing good works and depleting his own family fortunes at a rate that suggested he hoped to die without so much as a danar to his name. Though Amazzal looked the part perfectly, with his flowing beard and imposing voice, he wasn't a great High Luxiat.

But it looked more and more like he was a *good* one.

Nice as it was to find out that some men who appeared to be good actually were good, it also meant that in surveilling him, Karris had wasted time and resources.

She was running out of both.

"I've something very hard to ask of you," she said.

"I'm your slave, by law and by choice. You needn't *ask*," Quentin said.

Damn he was a weird kid.

"It'll be difficult and dangerous. It would put you in the company of a hardened murderer."

"I'm a murderer myself," he said.

Not a hardened one. "Any misstep could mean your death, and others'. It may be too hard for you."

"It won't be more than I can handle."

"You trust me too much," Karris said.

He laughed suddenly. "I don't trust you at all!"

She stepped back, offended. She was the White. And Quentin's owner.

"I've offended you. I'm sorry," he said. "But you misunderstand. I mean I don't place the locus of my trust in you or on your judgment, but in Orholam alone. You needn't take on His burden. Being the White would be too much for anyone to bear alone!"

She got it then, though he was so intelligent that he forgot that others weren't as quick as he was. He didn't need to trust *her*, because he trusted Orholam, who had put her in her position. Her choices mattered... but also *didn't* in some way that somehow made sense to luxiats, but never quite had to Karris.

Holy people can be so exhausting.

Well, she deserved whatever trouble Quentin gave her for what she was going to do to him. She said, "I'm sending you to someone who's killed a lot of innocent people—I don't know, twenty, twenty-five? All dead at my behest."

Quentin blanched. "You've ordered twenty murders?"

"I've ordered my agent to do what was necessary to accomplish what had to be done."

"To what end?" His voice, not low to start with, pitched squeaky.

To what end? It was the kind of archaic phrasing you'd hear from a kid who'd grown up with a wide variety of friends: friends writ on papyrus, friends writ on sheepskin, and friends writ on wood pulp—but not many of flesh and blood.

Karris said, "I want you to be her handler."

"Her—what? A handler? Me?"

"But I want you to do something harder than that. I want you to be her friend. Orholam's told me that you both need one, desperately." Almost as much as I do.

"Who are we talking—wait, you can't be serious."

*   *   *

Karris stepped out of the room a minute later. Her young Blackguard Amzîn was waiting, precisely where he was supposed to be, with perfect posture and alertness.

"Good kid," Karris said, closing the door behind her.

She saw the flicker of doubt in his eyes. She gave him leave to speak with a gesture.

"Isn't that the luxiat who murdered that girl?" he asked.

She nodded. "Sad story, huh? Promising young talent gets elevated too high too soon. Ends with a young woman with a bullet in her throat."

222   Amzîn got a pained look on his face, but it was the wrong kind

of pained look. He could tell she was doing more than repeating the facts, but he had no idea why.

She said, "You and me, Amzîn. You're the promising young talent. Let's do our best not to reprise the part where *someone* takes a bullet because of it, eh?"

Chapter 33

"*This*," Lord Dariush announces, spreading his arms grandly, "is the world's *last* surviving Solarch!"

He is so proud that I almost burst into inappropriate laughter.

"No," I say, but with not nearly the true degree of horror I feel. I infuse my disbelief more with 'No, really? How'd you manage that, you brilliant man?' than 'No, no, it's not.'

"Oh yes!" he says. He is *delighted*.

"This?" I allow myself, for anyone would have doubts, not just anyone with a brain.

And here, moments ago, I had hoped for this man's daughter to breed in some emotional brilliance to the Guile family line. Maybe his wife is very, very smart. I shall have to hope.

He chortles. "I told you you'd find it incredible."

I clear my throat. "I thought you meant the other definition of that word," I say.

"I know," he says. "I know. Study it. You'll see."

I'm never going to want to look at another painting in my life.

But, dutifully, I lean close and pretend to be enrapt.

I didn't come to Atash for art appreciation—unless one wishes to call enjoying the nude figure of this man's daughter 'art appreciation.'

Alas, there's not only been none of that, but I've barely even *seen* the woman I've come to woo and wed.

In a full week, I've seen more of her sister, Ninharissi, than I have of her, and when I *have* seen Felia, it's been at dinners—where I wasn't even seated next to her.

My pique is nearing the level of rage.

I've figured out why he's kept me from her now—it's all part of his maneuvering for these barbaric bride-price negotiations these savages practice—but it still rankles me.

"Speaking of definitions of words," he says, "how did your parents come to bestow such a name on you?"

"You've been wanting to ask that for days, haven't you?" I ask, as if amused.

I'm not. I think I'm coming to hate this man. I turn briefly away from the painting. Honestly, I've not caught even two details about it, I'm so focused on not letting my rage bleed through.

I shall need to take a break from drafting red, I think. I am not naturally a patient man, even without it.

He smiles. "Was it so obvious? I tried to wait until it wouldn't be rude."

"Uh-huh," I say, staring again back at the painting as if I care. "Well...I knew that a philologist such as yourself would be disappointed if I said my mother simply liked the sound of the words, so... I'll tell you that the name came to her in a dream."

He laughs. "Fair! Fair! I suppose not all men spend their lives trying to escape the shadow of their name."

"Did you try to escape yours, my lord? *Roshe Roshan Dârayava-hush* is no easy yoke for the shoulders of an infant. Nor even for a man to bear, one should think."

I don't quite suppress my pleasure at saying the name with precisely the correct diction and accent.

On the ship here, hoping to make a good impression on my father-in-law-to-be, I practiced for three dark days so I could say his name exactly as a local would. Three days I'll never have back, for one offhand sentence, to woo a woman I may no longer want.

But I continue nonchalantly. "Quite a lot to live up to."

Felia explained the name to me in one of her letters. It took her two full parchments, and she is not a woman to ramble. It means Judge Bright (or Light) Who Possesses Much Good (or Many Goods). 'Judge' placed first to hearken back to when petty kings (called 'judges' here) had ruled Atash. Judging—literally 'bringing justice'—was what Atashians understood as sole reason to *have* kings. It's something they're still quite proud of, centuries after the fact, believing it denoted some deep truth about their national character: here rulers were established in order to serve the people.

Funny how *that* didn't last. Denying reality only works as long as enough powerful people see a benefit in playing along.

So Lord Dariush—his name was usually shortened from Dârayavahush—had a name that meant the Rich, Smart, Good, and

Perceptive (or Able to See through the Surface of Things to the Truth) Bringer of Justice.

I'm sure the other children had no problems with a boy named *that*. Here I'd been angry at *my* mother that my name so easily devolved into the sarcastic 'Handy Andy' after a sudden growth spurt out of my youthful rotundity had left me clumsy—a good trade, I'll grant. Clumsiness can pass, fat is forever. 'Randy Andy' came after my first failed attempt at wooing a girl. (Quoting ancient Parian poetry, spoken of in my beloved books as being such a strong aphrodisiac that many kings had banned it, was not, as it turned out, appreciated by the puzzled thirteen-year-old target of my affections, neither in the original language nor in the best translation I could find.) 'Glossy Rossy' came during the same lovely oleofacurating pubertal years, and 'At-a-loss Andross' was from my first fight at age fourteen, when a lout called me Fart Eater and I'd asked what 'Fart Eater' even meant.

It would not be the last time the human race disappointed me. I'd learned then that reflecting the vacuity of the congenitally un-self-aware back to themselves will not inspire a philosophical awakening.

As it turns out, 'Do you see how stupid that is?' is a question you can only ask an intelligent person. Or more precisely, an intelligent person who is acting, saying, or believing something stupid. Thus, either one who is intelligent but not brilliant, or one who is young or uneducated or unequipped with formal logical apparatus.

I was indeed at a loss in that fight: lost in thought, thinking these things.

Then, coming to strategic grips with my intellectual discovery and realizing that the present situation called for a different type of solution altogether, I punched the lout across the nose.

Then I sat on his chest, grabbed a handful of his hair in my left hand, and said, 'That's Right-Cross Andross to you.'

Then I'd demonstrated my right cross again, careful to hold his head tight so it didn't rebound off the cobblestones. I wanted to teach him and his friends a lesson, not kill him.

I'd been so disappointed that 'Right-Cross Andross' hadn't caught on. 'Cross Ross' had.

Those stinky, sebaceous little semen secretors.

'Criss-cross Ross' came after one of my more maladroit early schemes had failed. That still stung—the failure, not the sophomoric onomatopoeia.

You know, on second thought, best not to remember the teen years.

The Guile memory is not always a gift.

Fortunately, though far-ranging, my mnemonic vacation has been brief. Nor is Lord Dariush one to hurry. And I had the good sense to drift while facing his little painting.

On actually studying it, I now wish I'd begun with my examination first and let my mind wander later.

Barely a foot square, the painting is prominently displayed where one must view it on the way to the solarium gallery's exit. The technique and colors and sensitivity are exquisite, and the style so idiosyncratic that one might see any painting by this master and know it to be his, regardless of the subject.

But the subject.

What in Orholam's lowest hell?

"What…is…this?" I can't help but ask.

"Some say that Solarch was a Mirror, and this is meant to be art for a Card, though I've seen no corroborating evidence of that."

I don't think that can be true. This is merely genius. As tragically misplaced and misapplied as it is undeniably, bafflingly superior.

This is a painting that would cause contemporary critics to scoff, his patron to grumble, and his competitors to throw down their brushes in agony and vexation.

Breathed by the greatest wordsmith ever to turn a phrase, this is a poem…about a bowel movement. This is the greatest composer of all time making fart jokes instead of penning concertos.

"It's…cute?" I say.

I can't take my eyes off it. The more I look, the more baffled I am.

"Cute, yes," Lord Dariush says. "Fat and rather adorable, isn't it?"

The abuse of talent is so outrageous, I can't help wondering if it's purposeful—perhaps Gollaïr, so certain that his own talents were being outstripped, had commissioned this piece simply to waste a few of Solarch's days on earth.

Some great painters can dash off a masterpiece in a day. Other styles require a year or more. This has the hallmarks of the latter. The paint so thick it gives a depth to the image, the colors balanced not only against each other, but also within the image so as to guide the eye from one pleasing line to the next.

It is a lovely travesty.

It is as if the fastest racer entered the great hippodrome of Aslal for the final laps of the mountains-to-sea race that caps the novennial Philocteian Games, and as every tribe in Paria cheered, he started skipping, backward, even as the other runners caught him up and passed him by to take the laurel crown.

One *might* skip quickly, even backward. Such speed might astound, in its own witless way, but…why?

What a shame.

"What, uh, what *is* it?" I ask finally.

After a long moment, Lord Dariush says, "It's a young dragon."

"This...doesn't look anything like..."

"In the highlands, our memories of dragons are rather different."

Memories? "You're...talking about a real animal?" I ask. "Something that gets translated 'dragon'?"

I suddenly have no read on this man at all: one moment sly, clever, even brilliant, the next superstitious, foolish, and queer. If he's actively delusional, I'll have to leave, regardless. We've enough madness already in the Guile family line without me breeding more into it by marrying his daughter.

Lord Dariush is engrossed in his viewing. "Dragons are vulnerable in their youth, but then they spring up seemingly all at once, terrifying in their might. Cuddly, though, huh? Little round belly and all!"

He chuckles, then tears his eyes away from what is clearly his favorite possession of everything he's shown me in the last week.

"What?" he asks suddenly, "Oh, a *real* animal? Oh, no. I mean, not to *my* knowledge. Maybe in the mists of time? But no, it's uh, it's uh, merely an important bit of our highland mythology. You see... hmmph. Do you know anything about scale-bearers? You know, serpents, lizards, geckos, the color-changers—some call them 'reptiles' now?"

"General knowledge," I say. "I've certainly seen snakes and salamanders, of course, but nothing specialized."

"Well, the sub-reds of Atash have studied them for centuries. Find them quite fascinating. They classify them as exotherms, whereas you and I and most animals are endotherms. We make heat internally; reptiles absorb it from their surroundings. If you believe heat to be a species of light, then animals who absorb it rather than give it off are rather suspect indeed. They are like little pits of darkness, light-devourers. Some say this is why men have always hated snakes." He waves it away. "But that's neither here nor there. My highland ancestors knew about exotherms and endotherms, and it's a factor in the tale."

"Go on," I say. Now I'm actually interested. A little.

"We humans, we're social. Sometimes we're scolding squirrels, or monkeys shrieking and flinging excrement. At better times, loyal dogs or wolves hunting together to take down prey that none of us could face alone. Like other endotherms, we care about our pack, in our cases the family, the tribe, the satrapy, even the empire. We care deeply about our position within those groups. We are *zoon politikon*, social animals. There's great strength in this, of course. A man alone in the wilderness will have trouble even surviving. We care for our sick, our elderly, and our children. But there's waste and danger to living in society, too. We obsess over trivialities.

"Consider Sulak and Ben-sulak, towns that, if not separated by a river, would have long grown together into one single city. Today, in one, a man is mocked for darkening his eyebrows with kohl. Across the river, his twin is considered brutish for *not* doing so. The former is considered barbaric for growing his beard, the latter childish because he lacks one. We go along with things that make no sense. This year our cloaks are worn so short they no longer keep us warm. Next year they'll be so long they'll make it impossible to run.

"Reptiles stand at the antipodes from this. They care nothing for what their sisters love or their fathers hate. They seek out company only when it's time to mate. There are some few men and women like this, of course, the broken ones, those born soulless, who possess neither empathy nor plans, nor can even be taught to feel much beyond their immediate fear, hunger, or lust. But most of us aren't like that at all."

Lord Dariush gestures to the painting. "See the fur? In our stories, the dragon is the wisest of all created beasts, for he has a dual nature: neither the blindnesses of the cold-blooded nor the weaknesses of the warm. Thus, we highlanders seek to emulate our 'dragon.' We discern when it is time to be a monkey of the tribe, and when it is time to be the cold lone serpent. Or whichsoever animals you will, given a particular circumstance."

"How do you know when to be which?" I ask. "Does the monkey in you get to decide, or the snake?"

Lord Dariush gives me a long appraisal. "You see the crux of the question. Quickly, too."

Was there, then, no answer? Or was it a stupid 'We muddle through as best we can, with our shitty metaphors and backward culture'?

Lord Dariush waits a moment longer, then he says, "Intriguing. You see the crux of the matter, but not the heart of it. You are so very, very fast to see the weakness in a system, but slow to go further to seek a charitable interpretation for it."

That stings. "Was this a test I've just failed?" Bugger your art, old man.

"Yes to the failure. No to the test. Tests are designed. This was inadvertent. Another slippage of your mask, I think."

"Putting one's best foot forward is hardly the same—"

Another slippage?

Dariush interrupts. "Hold that thought. I know you won't forget it. Back to the dragon, if you would, and my silly, backward tales."

228   "I never—!" I protest.

"No. You didn't. I withdraw that last." Dariush clears his throat. "The part that decides which nature to indulge or to express, the weak faculty that stands at the fulcrum between the dog and the serpent? That faculty is exactly what makes us human. Here in the highlands, we believe we are not *zoon politikon*. We are *zoon kritikon*, the animal that judges."

I... actually rather like that.

I wonder why. I'm not sure if it's because it's the most accurate way to think of this or merely the most charitable, but I do have 'cooler' blood in my own veins than most men do.

By this account, that doesn't condemn me as 'reptilian.' It makes me a bit of a dragon.

Much better. Much.

Lord Dariush goes on, though, musing now. "Sadly, the part of the myth that suggests that the whole of it is unreliable and infected by the old legends from the rest of the satrapies is that one day, they say, *naturally*, our Dragon, our very own Bringer of Fire will come."

"Bringer of Fire?" I ask. "Not the Bringer of Light?"

"It's a very clear distinction in our old tongue. But yes, clearly, that's the idea it parallels, to the point that it's become associated and confabulated and subsumed within the Lightbringer myths, like two lines of smoke from adjacent campfires, driven together by the winds of the Seven Satrapies' shared history." He sighs. "It's a very seductive idea, though, isn't it?"

"What's that?"

"A Lightbringer coming. Or a Bringer of Fire. A Luíseach. That your people's ideal man or woman, whether warrior or trickster or hero of whatever stripe you value most, will come and kick everyone else's asses?" He grinned as if to say, 'Humans, huh?'

"He comes just in time to save the highlands, I suppose," I ask, "like the Lightbringer and the Luíseach respectively? The mythoi really are catholic, aren't they?"

He shakes his head. "No to the 'saving.' This is where things get interesting to me, because that's different here. The Dragon won't come in time to save us. He'll be too late. He comes only to adjudge and avenge. So though our prophesied figure could actually be the same man as the Lightbringer, to us it won't matter. Thus when we highland Atashians toast each other in seasons of danger, we say, 'Here's to not living in the time of the Dragon.'"

Seeking to counter his earlier impression of my lack of charity, I try some light flattery: "I guess when you know your hero isn't going to come in time to save you, it does encourage self-reliance." The highlanders are well-known for their prickly, stupidly independent spirit.

'Self-reliance' is the kindest way I can think of to put it.

"That's how we like it," he says. Defensively.

I was *trying* to be nice.

"A people with calluses, indeed," I say, expecting him to finish the old truism.

Felia shares her father's love for translation and history, so from her letters I know it's 'a people *with* calluses.' There was a famous sloppy old translation (famous among that oh-so-wide circle of Atashian historical translators) that called the ancient Atashians 'a callused people, who all love what is dirty,' which was taken as an indictment of their crudeness and lack of civilized virtues.

That renowned scholar's apparent disdain for the Atashians colored several centuries of Chromeria scholarship. A more faithful translation—'a people with calluses, unified, rejoicing in the soil'— implies instead a people near to their work and to the land, who loved their labors and abhorred class distinctions. It's far more flattering.

But if I'd hoped to score any points with the reference, I'm disappointed. He misses it.

He says, "The gentlest people I know have callused hands. Would that I had more on my own. But I know no people more full of joy or love than mine are."

I try to clarify, but he offers no opening, saying, "I attribute that joy and love at least partly to this: When you know that when the end comes, it will go poorly for your people, it encourages you to suck the marrow from the bones of life. Where other nations pile coin and stare greedily at what others hold, we long for the treasure of time and spend it as others spend gold. We sing and dance and play. We embrace and make love each day. We wrestle and we sport and we ride. Our children learn to hunt and mend, and to fight so they may have hearts of courage at the end, and might."

The regular cadence of that tells me it likely comes from something else Atashian and probably renowned, but my studies haven't been so deep.

Perhaps it's another test I've failed.

If so, it's an excuse for rejecting all suitors, not a test. Surely no one else could do better than I. Maybe no father wants to make it easy on a suitor.

I see now I was arrogant, though, too soon to believe that this man who'd amassed one of the largest treasures in the Seven Satrapies would be a fool. A bumpkin perhaps, perhaps a man somewhat dulled from the keen sharpness of his prime, but not a fool. And if he wishes to reject my courtship in order to slake his pride, he is well on his way.

"You said we need to get back for the fire dancers?" I prompt, giving up on the painting, and so much more besides. Why is Felia even allowing this? Subjecting me to a week of this horseshit? Is she that weak, or is she simply not interested in my bid for her hand? It seems she isn't who she pretended to be in her letters at all. I expected more of her than this, else I'd not have wasted my time.

Grumpily, he says only, "Indeed. Ninharissi will be waiting for us." He sets off with long strides, not looking to see if I'm following.

Ninharissi, not Felia. Again.

I go after him, but I can't help but give one last look to the fat, round little dragonling hunched happily in a hairy, soft-scaled ball that is Oh So Important to these people.

Confounding. What a strange, primitive people.

If nothing changes my mind tonight, I'll leave tomorrow. I can't stand this family, their food, their idiot stories, their queer music, this rubbish they call art.

Lo, ye mortals! Behold the mighty Dragon!

Dragon, my ass. It's risible. It doesn't look anything like a dragon. It doesn't look like a monkey-lizard or scorpion-dog or anything else 'formidable.' The ridiculous little fatty looks like a turtle-bear.

Chapter 34

"It started up here," Ben-hadad said as all of the Mighty followed him out onto the rooftop garden dominated by the massive white oak heart tree. He gestured to the tree. "Tell me, what do trees need?"

"Can't you just tell us your big discovery?" Winsen asked.

"No, no, look, this is not me being brilliant—this time, I mean. Just play along. What do trees need?" Ben asked.

"Soil," Ferkudi said. "Hard to grow trees in the air."

Ben opened his mouth, closed it, then allowed, "Yes. Yes, I suppose that's true. But what else do they need?"

"Air?" Tisis asked.

"Well, sure, that too."

"Water?" Big Leo asked.

"Enough! Light! Trees need light. They need leaves. They need leaves to get the light, to grow, to survive, right?"

Everyone shrugged or nodded noncommittally.

Ben-hadad was clearly frustrated that they weren't the least intrigued. "Fine. Look at the tree. Look at where the branches are. More importantly, look at where they aren't."

Kip and Tisis were the only ones who appeared to be seriously trying to follow him.

The others seemed to be enjoying tormenting him a little. Ben's intellect was a wonderful addition to the team, but his arrogance about it—even if it was earned—sometimes piqued resentment.

"Not even you, commander?" Ben asked.

Cruxer was standing with arms folded, patiently waiting for the punchline. "You're the resident genius, Ben. I'm sure you're going to give us something worthwhile, but there's really no need for me to duplicate your work, is there? So speed it up, huh? I've got nunks who need training."

"The branches grow naturally," Kip said, "but the smaller branches and leaves are only allowed in certain quadrants. By design, surely. A trade-off between not blocking the mirror's signals and allowing the tree to get enough light to stay alive, right?"

"Almost!" Ben-hadad said. "I mean, yes, as far as it goes. See here?" He pointed to a plaque mounted on a rock near the trunk. "I can't read the words, but I was able to figure out that these symbols are numbers. They're coordinates, and once I realized that, I was able to take a known—the Great Mirror at Ru, actually, and—"

Cruxer cleared his throat.

"Right," Ben-hadad said. "Not important. But it was pretty ingenious how I—"

"I'm sure it was," Kip said quickly.

Ben-hadad got the point. Kip could see him mentally skipping ahead, with some reluctance.

"Anyway, these coordinates are ancient cities: and the leaves on this tree don't grow in the line of sight between them! These smaller numbers are towns and lookouts within Blood Forest. So by cross-referencing, we can find those places now. Maybe some have mirrors still. We can build our scouting web."

"That is great news," Kip said. But it doesn't really merit gathering all the Mighty, does it? "Great work."

"That's it?" Winsen asked, unimpressed.

"That's not enough?" Ben-hadad asked. He looked from face to face.

"I hate to side with Winsen on anything," Tisis said, throwing him a wink. He beamed. Oddly, he'd started becoming a big fan of Tisis recently, and she'd decided to cement that, if only because he was such an asshole if he didn't like you. She went on—"But I kind of expected more of a man of your towering intellect, Ben-hadad."

Kip looked at her. Siding with Winsen but then still giving a back-handed compliment to his perennial antagonist? Nicely done!

"And you'd be right to do so," Ben-hadad said triumphantly. "Because I calculated the angles the mirror would have to move to in order to send or receive signals from every one of these coordinates."

"When did you do this?" Cruxer asked.

"While Kip was chatting with the Keeper and we were all just standing around."

He'd done all this…in his head. Holy shit, Ben. If I get you killed, all of history is gonna hate me.

"Almost there," Ben-hadad said. "None of these coordinates require an angle of less than minus five degrees. Look at where the leaves *aren't*!"

"Huh?" Big Leo asked. "I'm still kind of reeling from all the trap stuff Breaker just told us. Can you pretend I'm dumber than you know I really am?"

Ferkudi said, "He means the mirror can point down. The tree has been grown specifically so the mirror can aim much lower than that."

Kip cracked his neck to one side, thinking. "But the tree's ancient. What if this is just an accident of its growth? Like, they had to prune it or whatever, and because of that some branches grew lower because they cut off all the higher branches?"

"I thought about that, and by—well, it doesn't matter how—I figured out it wasn't that. Any of you see the empty iron frames on Greenwall?" Ben-hadad asked.

"To hold burning pitch or whatever?" Kip asked.

"I sent servants looking in the old storerooms, and do you know what they found?"

"I know you're going to tell us," Cruxer said sternly. "And quickly."

"Mirrors," Ben-hadad said. "The Great Mirror can aim down, but in each sector there are branches growing that, if you pointed the mirror down, would get in the way. Those branches would cast big shadows."

"Okay…" Ferkudi said.

"The mirrors on the wall are mounted precisely so they can reflect the Great Mirror's light into those places that would otherwise be in shadow. Guys, every ancient city that could afford one built a Great Mirror. The scholars have always thought it was pure cultural dick-waving, you know, look how rich and important we are. Now we know they enabled communication—eventually—but not everyone would've had chi drafters. They've always been rare, and short-lived, and the ancient cities were hostile to drafters not of their kingdom's color. Yet they insisted on building the Greater and the Lesser Mirrors. Here, with the filters I found, you can point a beam of any color light you wish, anywhere, even right at the base of your own wall. Why?"

"To power your drafters in a battle?" Kip asked.

"Definitely... but for both religious and cultural reasons, the ancients in this city would have only had green drafters. They were at war with everyone else. So why have other color filters?"

No one answered.

Cruxer rubbed the bridge of his nose. "This *is* the short version, right?"

"Yes," Ben-hadad said.

"Then, what's the answer?"

"I don't know," Ben said.

They groaned.

"You're killin' us here, Ben," Big Leo said.

"No, no, no," Ben said. "Wait. I don't *know*... but I have some guesses. I know how engineers think and how they build—even over the centuries, we all have the same kind of minds. This Great Mirror can be moved quickly. You don't need to do that for messages—but you do in a battle. I'm certain that the Great Mirrors are defensive. They're artillery. I think the filters are for fighting wights. I don't know, but maybe if you shoot a huge beam of a complementary color at wights, it messes with their drafting or their minds? What does Orholam's Glare do? It overwhelms and then destroys a drafter or wight by giving them too much light. Now, if you had enough mirrors, all working together, say, under the direction of a full-spectrum polychrome, I bet you could negate the effect of even a bane."

"What are you..." Kip started.

"The ancients weren't stupid," Ben-hadad said. "But the Chromeria has been, in wiping out as much of the knowledge about the old gods as they could. The ancients would have known all about the bane. They would've known they were vulnerable to them—and they would've guarded against it. The Thousand Stars all over Big and Little Jasper? The Great Mirrors in the Chromeria's towers? They weren't meant just to give drafters a few extra minutes of light every day. The Chromeria is bristling with cannons built exactly for the kind of attack that's coming their way. But no one knows it. They don't even know an attack is coming, so there's no way any of them are going to figure it out once the bane are coming over the horizon. And even if they do, I think it'd take a full-spectrum polychrome of incredible power and concentration to use the mirrors all together."

Everyone had turned to look at Kip. He felt his face flushing.

"Breaker," Ben-hadad said, "Kip. They need the Lightbringer."

"I've never—I've never said I'm that," Kip said. It was like they were trying to foist an enormous burden onto his shoulders.

"It would explain the biggest conundrum of all," Cruxer said.

"What's that?" Ben asked.

"It'd explain why the White King has done so much to keep Breaker here."

"No," Kip said. He wasn't sure which part he was denying. "Anyway, the other reasons for him tying me up here are plenty."

"No, it makes sense," Big Leo said. "He's afraid of you."

"No, this is ridiculous. You guys, we've talked about this!" Kip said. "I'm not..." He lowered his voice, though they appeared to be completely alone up here.

"Wait, wait. What if—what if—forget all the extra stuff," Ben-hadad said. "All the religious garbage. All the myths and prophecies. Let 'em go. The core of what made Lucidonius Lucidonius was that he gave people light. He was the light-giver. Yeah, there was all the religious stuff he did and how he became a conqueror, but how did he give people light? He was a lens crafter. He discovered how to make colored lenses, and that technological leap changed drafters' lives forever. What if the Lightbringer is just as simple: you bring light. You *physically* bring light at the moment the Seven Satrapies need it most. What if that's it?"

"The Lightbringer's a lot more than that," Cruxer said.

"Shut up with that right now," Ben-hadad said. "Uh, with all due respect, commander." He turned. "Breaker, let other people call you whatever they want. You can figure out how to counteract the bane. You can send colored light to every corner of the Jaspers as quickly and precisely as a battle demands."

"What if it doesn't work that way? What if counteracting the bane isn't just a matter of directing the mirrors?"

"You'd figure it out," Ferkudi said, as if it were that simple.

They all nodded.

"And that's a monumental amount of drafting, even if I could figure it out."

"So we make you Prism first," Winsen said.

Kip threw his hands up. Oh, like that's no big deal. But a phrase rattled around inside of his head: 'You won't be the next Prism,' Janus Borig had said.

"Breaker, focus on the problem, not the title," Ben-hadad said. "It's our best chance—not just to save the Chromeria but to stop the White King once and for all, to save the empire, and Blood Forest, and hundreds of thousands of people, and even ourselves. If we stay, I don't know if this Great Mirror could stop a bane by itself. And I don't know why he'd bring all of them here, or even if he could. He wouldn't need to. This is our last chance. We've seen you tear apart a lux storm. You drafted a hundred different threads when you sank Pash Vecchio's great ship. No one else could do that. So, directing the Thousand Stars with speed and accuracy that no one else could equal? Figuring out a tough problem? You're the Turtle-Bear. Taking those on isn't arrogance; those are just things you can do."

Chapter 35

Teia heard the chair creak sharply as Murder Sharp popped to his feet.

He figured it out. Here's where it ends.

She couldn't see anything. She'd thought that might make it easier—if she didn't see his eyes go paryl-black to tell her that her death was coming.

It didn't.

"Ben-Kaleb," he said. "Ben-Zoheth! Dammit! Is that what she meant? Goddam soothsayers. The hell can't they talk straight? I should'a made it hurt."

What?

He cursed some more, and she could hear his footfalls as he paced.

"I want you to know this," he said, getting right in her face. "You ain't *good*, and us *bad*. Your Chromeria's as bad as we are. Near enough anyway."

"So I don't get to choose between good and bad?"

"Choose, yeah. I didn't get to choose, anyway." He started mumbling. "Separation, that's it. That's what separates me." He cursed the Chromeria then.

But Teia had a sudden revelation. She was an idiot. How had she not thought of this before?

Well, I've never been blindfolded since becoming proficient with
236 paryl.

Paryl could be cast through clothes. It could be sent out through flesh. If it could go out, surely it come *in*.

There was no reason she couldn't gather paryl through a blindfold and her closed eyelids.

Half to keep him talking, she said deadpan, "I'm stunned. All this time I've been so sure of our righteousness as I was murdering innocents. But...but maybe there's some subtlety to this that, uh, you could explain?"

"Maybe so," he growled. He was puzzled. He wasn't good at detecting sarcasm.

Which was probably much better for her continued health. But she couldn't stop herself.

Dammit, T! Are you trying to get yourself killed?

Her eyes relaxed to sub-red, and then those odd drafter's muscles pried them wider, wider. And there it was, sweet tenebrous paryl. A bare hint of it, though, between being indoors and the fact that whatever bounced around here wasn't focused.

The first wash of it slid into her, down her gullet like brandy going down hot.

She tilted her head, blackly amused, a hint of condescending amusement leaking through, "If I have to choose between 'sometimes not great' and 'always fucking evil,' is that supposed to be tough for me?"

The *skritch* of a foot pivoting on the gritty floor was her warning. He'd snatched something up from the table, and—*skritch*—something smashed into her face.

Her head felt like her skull had become a gambler's dice cup with a furious loser rattling her brain around, hoping by rage alone he might shake good luck out from bad.

She couldn't move, couldn't think. There was a thought, a plan that was trying to form. Blood filled her mouth. Her left dogtooth had smashed through her lip, and she felt a surge of terror. Is this what death tastes like?

Her head lolled on her chest. She'd lost the little paryl she'd already gathered.

She felt him grab a fistful of her hair at the forehead. He pushed back, banging her head against the wall, tearing hair from her scalp.

He shoved whatever he'd hit her with between her bloody teeth. It was leather and parchment? Oh, the pages he'd stolen from Marissia, bound in a folio.

"You take this," he said. "You take it and read it, and *you* decide if what they've done counts as 'not great.' You decide if all the blood on their hands demands vengeance." 237

Bound, helpless, bleeding, and having trouble focusing, with a butcher holding a fistful of her hair, Teia suddenly felt what she least expected:

Hope, is that you? Hey! Been a while! Don't make yourself such a stranger.

She made to speak, letting out a small grunt, but there was still the folio wedged between her teeth. She was careful not to resist Sharp in the slightest. She didn't even push at the folio with her tongue. His will was supreme.

"Take and read it?" Teia asked around the folio. So you're not going to kill me right now?

He grunted and then suddenly tore off her blindfold. Dammit!

Something about how her lips had flared to speak had caught his attention. He dropped the folio, unheeded, and held her chin with his left hand. He was fixated. She opened her mouth, docile, and he slid a finger around her teeth, one at a time, his thumb testing each one's edge.

The thought of biting him barely even flickered at the periphery of her mind, and then guttered out in the wind of fear.

He was transfixed. Lost, like a ratweed addict suffering withdrawals who catches a whiff of that poison he calls his love and salvation.

Murder Sharp never so much as glanced at her eyes. Teia should have drafted then and struck him down, but she didn't dare.

He leaned close, drawing out his own handkerchief and wiping away the blood carefully.

She should headbutt him in the face. Smash his nose and blind him. No one leaned forward after you broke their nose. He'd throw himself back, and she'd have a few moments to...

But she couldn't. Teia's nerve failed, and she was just a small girl, weak, utterly in the power of a larger man who was dripping with malice.

The expression on Sharp's face shifted, though, to the rapt concentration of a professional, intent yet dispassionately weighing the merits and demerits of her teeth against some Form of perfection he carried in his mind.

But his hunger wasn't gone. It merely stood patient, like a dog salivating at the door, tail wagging, knowing it would soon be fed.

Having somehow rejected her upper teeth as unworthy of further examination, he leaned over her to inspect the inner faces of her lower teeth.

He'd done this before, for Orholam's sake. Did he not remember?

She couldn't forget.

A stream of drool dribbled from the corner of his mouth. She flinched hard, blinking, near gagging.

Murder released her jaw. He stepped back, and dabbed at the slobber on his chin. He seemed suddenly embarrassed, like a man caught with an erection straining his trousers at an inopportune moment.

"What'd you say?" he asked. He was fully in control of himself now. Any opportunity she'd had, she'd squandered.

For a moment, to her shame, she couldn't even remember. Here was her chance to get some initiative back, and she couldn't—"You want me to read it?" she blurted.

"Read?"

"The folio," she said.

When he spoke again, his voice was old, as if regret had lifted a shovelful of the barren earth of his life, revealing a thick, gritty gray layer in the clay that betrayed an anger vast but long extinguished, as if its fires had consumed a forest of beliefs, trees roaring into red flight with sparks flung from their wingtips until every living thing traded green for red as Teia did, and lost all color as Teia's life had, and then embers fell from the sky like defiled gray snow, and even that cooled to ashes, and the ash had aged to soil.

"You're like me, Adrasteia, me in a shitty tin mirror anyway," he said, grim, lifeless. "Not as strong, not as fast, not as good a drafter. But we're both paryl drafters, sent as spies, as infiltrators to uproot the Broken Eye once and for all—that's what my Prism told me. Sayid Talim said my gift made me the only person who could do what had to be done. That I could end centuries of trouble. Surely saving untold numbers of lives was worth everything bad I had to do to get to where I could do what had to be done, right? Whenever I was troubled by the people I had to kill, he said I should think that I was saving a hundred in the long run for each one I killed now. He said it was war. Said we've been at war with them since the beginning. He said in war, if you can trade one life for a hundred, you have to take that choice every time.

"He was convincing himself more than me, I think.

"I didn't want to do it. I was too scared, too certain my nerve would fail me when it came time to kill some innocent. He said to let the blood be on his head, not mine. And then this man who pretended to be such a hard cold bastard, while he secretly fretted and drank himself to death, he told me he wasn't giving me a choice. He said it was war, and this was an order."

It was different, a little, but too much of it was eerily familiar.

Karris had given Teia that speech. And Karris had trembled in her chambers like a hypocrite—afterward—but before the crowds, she strutted with her back straight, as if she were Confidence made flesh. 239

"He told me that no one must know, because *anyone* could be a spy," Sharp said. His voice was tinged with bitter amusement. "He would tell no one and I couldn't, either. He said that if I were caught or even too close to getting caught, I should kill myself before the Order could find out too much, or trace my infiltration to him. He said in that event, he would personally beseech Orholam for forgiveness for my suicide, and for any...you know, lingering guilt I might *so wrongly* feel for all the murders." He sneered the last line, finally finding his anger's heat once more.

"What happened?" Teia asked softly.

"His nerves failed, or someone got to him, but the Blackguard imprisoned him quietly, saying he was ill. Everyone used to know what that meant. He was quietly wheeled from his chambers to the top of his tower to do the balancing every month. The Blackguard was a much larger force then, and it was impossible for me to get to him. I didn't have my own cloak yet, of course. So what happened? I guess *nothing* happened. He died. No one from the Chromeria ever said a word to me. I had no friends, because how can you have friends when you have a secret like that? How do you keep it secret if anyone's close enough to you to wonder where you spend so much of your time? Prism Talim had set me to sail in a sea of blood, and I'd lost sight of shore. He was my only anchor, and...with that cut loose...? What was I going to do?"

"Join the people you sold your soul to destroy," Teia said. *Obviously.*

Murder Sharp scanned her face.

T, you moron! Are you *trying* to die?

"But I guess," he said, "the real question is what are *you* going to do?"

"Huh?" she asked.

"They gave you the same assignment, same lies, didn't they? Gavin or Andross or Orea or Karris. One of them."

She gulped. If he asked her now who it was, what did she say?

He really didn't know?

"No, you don't need to tell me. I see the horror on your face."

She couldn't even understand what he meant for a moment. Oh, the horror that she'd heard the same lies, not horror at one of the names. She hadn't given Karris away.

Not yet.

"Who knows?" Sharp said. "Maybe you'll go left where I went right. It'd figure, huh? That's what mirror images do. Always confused me how that works."

240   Teia could say nothing.

"Never mind. The Old Man came to me after Talim died. Bastard didn't even leave last instructions for me in our dead drop. But no one signaled me, either, so I knew he'd kept my existence secret to the grave. Or forgotten me. What did it matter, then? No one was coming for me. No one saw me. No one had heard about me. No one cared. No one was going to save me. The Old Man didn't know about my mission, either. I was still safe. As safe as a spy gets when they're trying to do what we do, anyway, right? He said he wanted to trust me, but he didn't."

Teia had heard this story before, though somehow Murder Sharp had forgotten telling her—and she certainly hadn't heard about it from this perspective.

"He gave me the Biter—you know, that tooth-breaking tool? Oh, right, I showed it to you with the Old Man. Well, he gave me a job to do with it. I was supposed to find this noblewoman, orange drafter, break all her teeth, then kill her. Felia Dariush her name was. I'll never forget that night. The Old Man told me she'd infuriated some rival who wanted to marry the same man. The Old Man said it was hard to find people who were willing to kill drafters, hard to find people willing to kill women, and hardest to find people who'd take dangerous assignments on short notice. This job had to been done immediately. Course, he didn't tell me what he meant by 'immediately,' but I knew it was my chance—maybe my last chance—to work my way into his good graces."

"Shit," Teia said. She didn't want to, but she felt a kinship for him. The job assassinating the Nuqaba had been like that.

"Yeah. I botched the job. I wonder how different things would be if I hadn't. Not just for me, either.

"She was staying in a part of Big Jasper I didn't know well back then. I asked directions from some idiot kopi seller, and he told me the wrong street, gave me directions to Farhad Street instead of Farbod Street. Maybe I misunderstood his accent, or he mine. I broke into the house, and there was no young woman there, but there was a bed and a woman's clothing in the trunk, so I waited all night for her to come back, thinking I was at the right place. Some tavern girl comes back after dawn, and it's not her. Description is totally wrong. I ask someone else out in the street and figure out what I did wrong—and I run. I get to Felia's house and she's gone. I'm reckless as all hell—knowing this might mean my death if I fail, and I figure out she'd gone to the harbor. I got that feeling in my gut the whole time I'm running there—and I get there in time to see her ship disappear on the horizon. I ask where the boat's going. I ask for other boats going the same way, though I have no way to pay for passage. It turns out her rich daddy's boat is one of the fastest around, and no one knows where it's headed anyway. I ask if there's a boat heading for her home port, because I know I'm in it deep. I'm willing to gamble going to the wrong port on the bare chance I can fix it. But there isn't. Not for a week. And I know the Old Man won't let me live that long if I don't meet him when I'd said."

Holy hells, Teia thought.

"No matter how I practiced it in my head, it all sounded like a lame excuse, an unforgivable failure. The Old Man's not a fool. He doesn't expect perfection. He tolerates failure from those valuable to him. But this? A rich woman allowed to escape, when the Old Man was already suspicious? I'd look untrustworthy. And *that* he doesn't tolerate. So it was life-or-death. Do you know I didn't really have good teeth beforehand? Didn't even think about my smile. Didn't take care of myself. I'd probably not choose to keep a single one of those teeth now. Not like you. Very fortunate, you are."

She did not want to hear him rhapsodize about her teeth, not right now. Not ever. "That's...that's not the story you told in the Mirror Room," Teia said.

"Well, all that was a lie. I was trying to scare you into not getting distracted or greedy when you're on a job. The real problem with taking a bribe is that every delay gives your target more chances to get away or be saved. Don't do that."

Please stay utterly un-self-aware, Teia thought. "So, how am I supposed to know that this story is true this time?" she asked, trying to change the subject.

"Does it look like I'm trying to amuse anyone?"

"So that's why you broke all your own teeth? Because you were afraid the Old Man would think you'd taken a payoff to let that girl go?"

Too late, as he sucked air through his perfect dentures, she realized she shouldn't have said he was afraid. How could you call a man a coward who had shattered all his own teeth in order to live?

"I'm sorry—"

"Point is," Murder Sharp cut her off angrily, "*I* never had a choice. Not from the moment I was born with a paryl talent I didn't ask for. Elijah ben-Kaleb didn't have a choice who I would kill for the Chromeria, and Murder Sharp didn't have a choice who to kill for the Order. They're just the fuckin' same.

"Maybe that's what she meant," he mumbled. "Weird fuckin' lady. No coward, for sure, but she didn't even *fight*. Couldn't figure that out. 'Son of Separation.' Maybe this is how I separate myself from them."

He looked up at Teia with sudden resolve. "That's why I ain't killed you yet. Not fondness. Not weakness, for sure. You're gonna be my proof. I'm better than them. Better than your master, better than mine. Better than Orholam Himself, if He's up there, who didn't give me one choice since He cursed me with a talent for paryl. I, Elijah ben-Zoheth, am the god who holds you in his hand. I will give you the choice no one ever gave me. You read this folio, and you make your choice. Join us for real, or fight me, or run.

"You join the Order for real, and I'll never let 'em know you were a spy from the get-go. Or you can run. As long as you leave a trail so it's clear that you're running far away, the Order doesn't have anyone to spare right now to send after you. Or if they send me, now or later, I won't find you, on my honor. Or, if you're just that damned stubborn and stupid, and you want to fight..." He paused.

He sucked spit through his teeth a few times.

"Tell you what, I'll be as, uh, what-you-call-it? fair? sporting? generous? as I wish they would've been to me. You choose to fight, I won't tell them even then, unless you blow your own cover. You aren't supposed to be on the Jaspers at all. I haven't reported you—and I won't. But if you side with the Chromeria, I'll hunt you down myself, and I'll kill you. No mercy, no second chances. So I guess you'll have to try to kill me first. It can be a little hunt. That could be fun. We'll getta see who's best. Maybe I'll have a real challenge for once.

"So you choose. You want to join the Order for real, you show up at the Great Fountain tomorrow at noon. If you want to run, you best be on a boat off the Jaspers by then. If you want to fight me, uh... hmm... don't do either of those, I guess? Because if you're not at the Great Fountain at noon, the next time I see you, you die."

"I understand," Teia said.

He loosed her bonds, and she rubbed feeling back into her limbs. "Eyes," he said.

She made sure he could see her eyes weren't flared to paryl.

"Now, go," he said, handing her the folio. "You have some reading to do."

Teia took it carefully.

"No, wait," Sharp said suddenly. "Uh, if you run, I can't risk you using one of your old codes in the note, so just address it to your handler and, you know, 'I'm sorry' or something. Nothing else. No secret ink or codes or any of that. I'm ready to give you your life, but I don't need you endangering mine. So just leave that in your old bunk, under the pillow."

Where Sharp would look at it, of course.

243

"That would give you their name. I'd be betraying my handler." Unless I put someone else's name on it?

Dammit, I could have put that asshole Grinwoody's name on the note, and the Order would have killed him. Granted, shoving an innocent into the path of an arrow in flight like that wasn't exactly how a Blackguard was supposed to protect her ward, but between Karris and Grinwoody? Grinwoody could burn.

Shit. Teia'd thought too slow.

"Besides," Teia said. "If I leave anything *without* the right codes, my handler will know the Order got to me. Or some random innocent might take it."

Actually, that last wouldn't be a problem for Sharp. He didn't care that the message got through; he only cared to see the name on it.

Again, she wasn't thinking fast enough.

But he did look confused.

Sharp cursed. "True, true. Uh..."

Teia realized then that he really *was* at a loss. It wasn't a trap, or a devious plot by the Old Man to confirm her handler was Karris—whom he would surely have suspected.

"Just the words 'I'm sorry'?" Teia asked. "Then if someone does pass it on to my handler, they might be expected to recognize my handwriting, but no one's going to learn anything else from it, and if you see it, you'll know that I'm really—"

"No," he said. "You'd leave that note to try to trick me, even if you planned to fight me. Sorry, nope. That's the price. Do it my way if you want to run. Name probably won't be a surprise to the Old Man anyway. Probably will know who you're working for immediately as soon as that white boat gets back and you're not on it."

Shit! Sharp had gotten to the right solution through animal cunning instead of intelligence.

Or at least the wrong solution for Teia. If she put a name on that letter, she had to be willing for that person or anyone else who mistakenly touched the letter to die. If one of her Blackguard friends—Gill Greyling maybe? Essel?—tidied her bunk, they might find the note. Surely the Order would kill them, just in case they were a contact. Or it could be one of the slaves who tidied the floor. Even if she put that snake Andross's name on it, murdering him might be exactly the wrong thing for the Chromeria and the war.

And she sure as hell wasn't going to betray Karris. Karris was a betrayer. Teia wasn't.

Murder Sharp was shitty at this, but shitty in such a way that the choice he thought was giving her was actually no choice at all. He was a stupid man, but Teia wasn't much smarter, was she? She hadn't even thought fast enough to outsmart a moron.

Kip would've.

"Oh," Sharp said, like it was an afterthought, but there was a cruel edge to it, and Teia realized that what was coming was a trap. Sharp's cunning wasn't the kind that thought of every avenue for every plan; it was the kind that sought out chinks in the armor, like paryl slipping through the skin to your heart. "You've deceived us before. So if you choose to join the Order, you'll need to do something this time to convince me that you're serious. Because that's the first thing a spy would lie about, right? You already lied to join us, so you'd just do it again, right? So I'll need some proof. By your actions."

Oh God.

Sharp said, "You're my shitty tin mirror, so let's give you a test, don't you think? Just like I had."

She could tell he loved the dread he'd put on her face.

"It'd have to be something a spy would have a problem with doing, wouldn't it? Killin' some slave would be nothing to a tough, hardened little bitch like you, right?" he asked. "Nah, you're way past that. And we'll have to have a time pressure, so you don't get all sneaky smart or something and try to fool me. By tomorrow, then. By noon. Still meeting me at the Great Fountain."

"*Tomorrow*?!" Teia protested. "Are you forgetting that you tried your best at *your* task—and *failed*? And you're so much better than me. Always have been. You have to give me more time than—"

"You're right," he said, cutting her off. She shut up instantly. She wasn't out of this place yet; she couldn't afford to disrespect him. He seemed to actually be thinking about her objection. "It'd have to be something that's not *hard* to do, just difficult. Or do I mean difficult, but not hard? Hmm."

He was mocking her now, and she wasn't sure exactly how, which made her feel stupid.

I'm going to enjoy killing you, aren't I? You piece of shit.

A glowing crescent of his white teeth seemed to illuminate the shack with Sharp's cruel glee. He said, "If you want to join the Order for real, prove it by bringing me a sack. Waterproof. With a head in it."

"What?!"

"I don't trust you not to just go find some corpse, so I want to see a paryl blood clot in the brain, and dual hemorrhages so the eyes go all blackballed. It's a bad way to go. But on the other hand, it doesn't matter who you choose. Choose whoever you like. That makes it easy."

245

"I..." Always before, Teia had been assigned whom to murder. Someone else had chosen. This would mean choosing some innocent herself. Choosing some stranger and killing them in a horrific way.

How do you choose which innocent dies?

"Wait, wait. With your skills now, that's not difficult or hard, is it? You'd just kill another slave. You've already shown you're perfectly willing to do that."

"I don't—"

"No, no, I've got an idea," Sharp said. He nodded to himself. "Yeah, yeah, that'll do it, I think. A kid. Bring me a kid's head. You know, a little squirt. Say, eight to ten years old."

"A—a child?" Teia asked. One summer when she was growing up, there'd been someone in the city who snatched kids around her little sister's age. A few of the girls were found mutilated. More simply disappeared. The snatchings stopped after that horrible summer, but no one who lived through that time could ever hear about a missing child without remembering the horror and fear.

Now *Teia* was going to be the person who snatched and mutilated a child, like a bloodthirsty ghost in the night.

"Eight to ten years old," Sharp said. He pushed her out the door. "After you read the folio, you'll know why."

Chapter 36

"I suppose it should sound ungrateful to say that I was rather looking forward to being dead," Orholam said.

"You didn't look like you were looking forward to it out there," Gavin said, cracking one eye open. His shade had moved away from him, and it was miserably hot on the beach. He could only imagine he was already on his way to a fierce sunburn. And the damned sand fleas...

"Oh, I'm terrified of *dying*. Being dead, though? That's the thing." Orholam was sitting cross-legged on the sand, heedless of the bugs, dirt, and his own nudity.

Gavin stood up slowly, his body afire with aches. He still had the damned gun-sword strapped to him. Neither blade nor straps had made for easy rest. He began brushing off the worst of the dirt and bugs. "You're right," he said.

"I am?" Orholam asked.

"You do sound ungrateful."

"I meant to be the opposite," Orholam said. "Thank you. I was wrong about you."

"Well, I only did it for one reason," Gavin said. He gestured for them to move off the beach.

Orholam stood and then started walking. "And what's that?"

"Lots of men claim Orholam saved them from drowning," Gavin said.

"But what man can say he saved Orholam from drowning?" Orholam said. He chuckled.

Gavin grunted, irritated the man had taken his punchline.

"Guess we should both be grateful there's an island here at all, huh? If the story had been true about the isle sinking when the reef rose, we'd be shark supper."

"There's looking on the bright side!" the old man said.

Gavin grunted again. "How bad's my back? It cut me."

"Not terrible. Need to wash it, though, if you want to live."

Gavin examined the rest of himself for injuries. Arm had rope burn, but not bad. His head ached, tongue was dry, left leg hurt, but that was just a lightly pulled muscle. A few calluses torn off his hands. They'd gotten soft in his prison.

His left eye pit hurt like hell. The patch had stayed on, but saltwater had gotten into the hole, and sand was all around it. If he got sand into the empty orb of his eyeball, he'd be in such agony he wouldn't be able to accomplish anything.

Fantastic. Washing that was going to be just great.

Assuming, of course, they could find clean water at all.

"I already searched everything that washed up," Orholam said. "Only a little luck." He rapped on a little barrel small enough to fit under his arm.

"Black powder? That's enormous luck! With this musket, we can hunt!"

"Not powder. Salt fish," Orholam said apologetically. "Keep us for a few days if we can find some water. But nothing else. Maybe more'll wash in later, but I'd say we head inland and see if we can find the pilgrims' waystations. Whether they'll hold anything useful after a few centuries is another question, though."

"You couldn't find anything good?" Gavin asked, looking out to the lagoon. Fish was great, but water was more important, and tools to hunt with would've been the best.

He'd been so concerned about the beach and his own injuries that this was the first time he'd looked around. They were inside the great circular wall of mist that made the White Mist Tower; it was utterly clear here, with blue sky high above. The island was large enough that it would have streams if not a river, but that wall, maybe five hundred paces high, made Gavin claustrophobic. The outside world didn't exist here.

Halfway through alien cloud, part of their ship was visible perched on the reef crest. The stern, waist, and sails were completely gone, battered into flotsam, spread throughout the lagoon with the floating dead. Only the forecastle survived, with The Compelling Argument pointed at a jaunty angle into the sky. There appeared to be a figure moving there, but it might have been Gavin's imagination.

"Is that...?" he asked.

"Uluch Assan. Yes," Orholam said.

Gunner. "Hard man to kill," Gavin said.

"Not the only one," Orholam said.

"Don't suppose there's much we can do to help him," Gavin said. Though, come to think of it, he wasn't sure that he really wanted to help the crazy pirate.

"He's fishing," Orholam said, shielding his eyes against the sun.

Gavin couldn't see that well. But he chuckled. If only he could be like that madman, taking the day with equanimity, unperturbed by sea demons and reefs and shipwrecks and brushes with death.

"Huh!" Orholam said. "It was actually true!"

"What? What was?"

"I told him if he didn't want that cannon to fall into the sea, he'd have to keep his feet close. I thought I meant just nearby."

Gavin squinted and shaded his eyes. Gunner was moving, testing the deck, trying to step off it for some insane reason, perhaps thinking he could walk around the reef to some easier point to swim? But as soon as he lifted his foot, the entire deck began to shift, the end lifting, as the weight of The Compelling Argument threatened to tip it into the gap in the reef. The captain had to stay on the deck counterbalancing the big gun or it would tip into the sea.

Gunner sat back down on the deck railing and picked up his fishing pole again.

"Man doesn't know it's already lost," Gavin said.

"What you love isn't lost while you still have a mind to save it," Orholam said. "Sometimes."

He saw them looking at him, waved, and saluted with the skin of brandy. He seemed entirely unworried.

Gavin spread his arms helplessly like, 'We can't come save you.'

Gunner waved them off, happily. He stood on his right leg and pointed to his left foot, as if to show that the sharks hadn't gotten it. As if he didn't have a care in the world.

"Poor bastard," Gavin said. "Why do I have the feeling he'll outlive us all?"

"Not a risky bet if we don't find some water," Orholam said.

They moved inland. It was hard to tell how large the island was from the beach, with thick jungle obscuring their view. Judging from the gentle curve, maybe a couple leagues across? From the size of the outside of the reef as they'd sailed around it, though, it could have been ten leagues across.

They followed game trails until they came to a wide area where no trees were growing, though the ground was covered with low vegetation. The wide area continued in a broken line inland, uphill. It didn't look natural.

Gavin grabbed a shrub and pulled it up. The roots were only a hand's breadth deep, and below that were flat stones, interlocking.

An ancient road, not yet fully claimed by the jungle.

Gavin's heart leapt in his breast. Streets meant cities. Cities meant the possibility of shelter and access to clean water, which his thick tongue wanted more than anything.

They walked, slowly.

In less than an hour, they passed the first ruins. Nothing spectacular, just a few stone walls with no roof, all of it covered by moss and vines. But nearby, there was running water.

"Orholam!" Gavin said. "Can you go ahead and prophesy whether I'm going to get sick from this?"

"I have no idea. But I'm gonna drink."

And so they both did. They had nothing to use as a skin, so they drank until they nearly burst. Then Gavin carefully, slowly washed around his eye patch, careful not to let the black jewel lose contact with his eye—that would be his death, if Grinwoody's threat wasn't bluster. For one clumsy moment, he bobbled his grip, but luckily the eye patch held in place in his eye socket.

They headed on.

Within two hours of heading uphill, they rounded a turn and found more ruins. Lots more.

Amid the palm trees was an ancient, abandoned temple compound, all ancient stone arches and broad avenues with flagstones and great mosaics rent asunder with scrub grasses, and towering atasifusta trees, now extinct everywhere else in the Seven Satrapies. This was an entire ancient city, empty, if not old Tyrean itself then built in the style of the old Tyrean Empire, with horseshoe arches and stone carved like delicate lattices, once painted to look like climbing roses and ivy but now faded and chipped. The entire city was built around one central avenue, two blocks away from Gavin. He made his way to that street.

Stepping into the broad, open area—an ancient market?—Gavin had an unobstructed view toward the center of the island for the first time.

His heart stopped. All day, Gavin had expected to see the famed Tower of Heaven at any moment, but the jungle's canopy and the body of the rising mountain they'd been climbing had hidden it. Until now.

"This...this is not what I saw," Orholam said.

Overwhelming all the terrestrial wonders of this lost city was a great tower, surely as wide as all seven towers of the Chromeria put together, including all the grounds, and much, much taller.

Perfectly symmetrical, and bafflingly, blindingly black, the untapering cylinder was stabbed in the heart of the island. A crater ridge rose around it, as if some angry god had impaled the world here and only the black haft of his spear jutted from the wound.

Nothing relieved the unearthly emptiness of that black except a thin, pearlescent ribbon, a trail, spiraling around the outside of the great megalith.

And if its base would have covered half of the entire island of Little Jasper, its height was something else entirely. It had to be taller than Ruic Head or any of the Red Cliffs.

Gavin said, "Orholam's beard, pilgrims *climbed* that?"

Orholam had already recovered, and he just smiled at him like a fool.

"*I* have to climb that, don't I?" Gavin asked.

"We," Orholam said cheerily. "We *get* to climb that."

Chapter 37

Karris twitched in her sleep. She couldn't breathe.

She tried to snort. Nothing happened. No air entered her lungs.

Her eyes flew open. The room was pitch-black. There was nothing over her face, but as her tongue convulsed, no air flowed in.

She couldn't swallow.

Her body was paralyzed from the neck down.

"Shhh," a woman said. Soothing. "Shhh."

The woman stepped closer. Teia. Karris jerked at the recognition.

"I'm letting go," Teia whispered. "Be quiet now. You'll feel tingling, and then you'll be able to speak in a moment."

Speak?! She couldn't *breathe*!

Then her fingers tingled. Toes tingled. And rapidly, feeling returned to her body.

She gasped, then sat upright, her chest heaving.

"I brought you something," Teia said.

Karris's hair fell over her eyes, and she considered punching Teia in the throat. The goddam child, strangling her?! Who did she think she was? Was that paryl?

Teia pulled out a red leather-bound folio. She flipped the leather back for Karris to read the title page: 'Being the Secret History of the Chromeria: Written for and by the Whites.'

By the Whites?

And then Karris saw that there were dozens of signatures below the title. The last one was Orea Pullawr's, albeit a more florid hand than she'd had when she was young. The folio had been penned by Karris's predecessors in office. All of them.

A note on the next page said, "Entrusted to your care on the understanding that you will add no untrue or deceptive word, nor bring the black to excise any words written herein. We trust you here with the unvarnished history of our empire. For Orholam loves the truth, and will bring all things to light in time, but not all things should be known by all people."

A sheaf of loose papers was tucked in the back. Karris flipped to them.

They weren't histories, but instead names, contacts, accounts with bankers: all the things Orea Pullawr had wanted Karris to have, and to know.

"Where did you get this?" Karris asked. Her heart was pounding, and she wasn't sure now whether it was still from her fright or from excitement.

"From my master, who killed its previous owner and stole it." This was one of the ways Teia tried to minimize the dangers of eavesdroppers: no names to prick ears.

"How did you get this away from him? Did you kill him?"

"He gave it to me."

"Orholam Himself must have blinded him to its value."

Teia snorted and shook her head as if Karris were a hopelessly clueless mom and she her teenage daughter.

251

"What is your problem?" Karris asked. Even her excitement about the folio couldn't erase all her pique at the girl *paralyzing* her.

"Quiet!" Teia hissed. "My problem? First is that you're gonna get me killed if you can't even remember to whisper for five fucking minutes."

Karris gritted her teeth. She hadn't been *that* loud. Whispering now, she said, "You come and give me a gift like this, and then act like a spoiled child while you do it?"

Teia scoffed. "A child? A child?!" Now *she* wasn't remembering to whisper.

"I have questions," Karris said. Teia was a goddam child, but Karris wasn't. It was on her to forgive and compensate for the shortcomings of those she'd demanded serve in such hard positions. She wasn't being fair. "Please." She offered this last genuinely apologetically.

Teia calmed, but still said, "I don't have time for questions."

Firmly but with all the restraint she could muster, quashing the red rising in her at the fact the girl had used paryl on her spine—on her spine!—Karris said, "You have time."

"I am literally being hunted by *their* best assassin. He saw through me. He said he had a previous Prism pull the same trick with him as you did with me. Same big talk. Same assignment. But then he died, leaving him twisting in the breeze. No one knew who he was. What he'd done for him. He ended up joining *them* in truth. He captured me. And just let me go so he could have a little hunt. A contest. See who's really the best between us—as if I've got a chance."

"Orholam have mercy. How can I help?"

Teia shook her head like Karris was being a fool. "Help? You can't. You can only make things worse."

"Surely I can—"

"I need to go. You want to know everything I have on Gavin or not?" Teia said.

"Of course."

And then Teia reported about the ship and their conversation and the impossibility of reporting it all immediately.

Karris could tell Teia wanted to leave more with every passing minute, but she quizzed her on the Old Man of the Desert, whom she'd seen disguised. "Could it be Andross Guile?" she asked finally.

Teia shook her head. Andross had hired the Order before, and perhaps he was cunning enough to pretend to be someone else while hiring his own people, but no. "It was a good disguise, but there are things that are really, really hard to fake. This man or woman isn't as broad as Andross Guile is. You can add padding to affect a silhouette, but moving in the same way a larger person does, that's hard. So I think this person is probably thin, disguised with some padding, or maybe average with layers of jackets and the fine mail that breaks up paryl, but he or she isn't broad-chested and wearing all those layers, too. And the man had a presence about him, so I don't think it was a lieutenant standing in for the real Old Man. I think some secrets are so big, the Old Man attends to them himself. Or herself."

"And they threatened me?"

"To get... your husband to go along with them. A threat that I believe is credible. They do have people here, in the 'guard, I'm sure of it."

Karris breathed a heavy sigh. "I didn't think that... your masters were going to be a bigger threat than the White King."

"Not my masters. And not for long," Teia said. "I hope." She made to move to the door. "Oh, shit. One more thing. I realized we were so rushed before that I didn't tell you." She lowered her voice. "Ironfist. He was in the Order."

"What?!" Karris said.

"I don't know if he is anymore. Apparently, he joined them when he was a kid so they'd protect his sister from their family's enemies. And I guess they did. Then with me killing her, he thinks they betrayed him. Even though she was trying to murder him when I did kill her, he was... He was scary as hell. You ever see a man lose everything he's given his life for, all at once? I hadn't. And I've never known a man like him."

Me neither.

"It took me a while to put it all together, but... you know, he betrayed us in order to save his sister. Then his sister failed and betrayed him, and his brother died for us, and the people he betrayed us *to* then betrayed him." She got pensive, seemed to forget her urge to leave so quickly for a moment. "You know, not to do your job, but if he finds out you knew I was going to assassinate his sister, and you let me...? He won't be too happy."

Karris was reeling, but her first thought was horror. Oh, Ironfist, what have we done to you? In every part of your life, we've destroyed you.

What have you done to yourself? Joining the Order?

In ordering Teia to assassinate his sister, the Nuqaba, the Chromeria had betrayed him, but he'd betrayed them first.

Well, sort of. He hadn't known Karris or Gavin or any of the Blackguards when he'd taken his vow to the Order, had he? No wonder he'd held himself aloof, not just from Karris but from any woman. He'd known he was a hypocrite of the greatest degree, that he might be called on to do reprehensible things. He'd lived with that terrible, terrible secret and shame.

Then her gut sank as she realized what a new and horrible twist this put on them potentially marrying.

O God, protect us.

"Yeah," Teia said. "Sorry I didn't get you the news earlier."

"No, it wouldn't have changed anything." Except I would have felt rage first, rather than compassion. So maybe it was for the best.

"It's like your best friend dying, isn't it?" Teia said, her voice softer.

"I'm sorry for all this, Teia. But..."

"They're a blight. I know. It's gotta be done. And I'm the only one who can do this. Doesn't seem fair, but there it is. Now, sorry, but I really do have to go. Can you distract your door guards?"

"Hmm?"

"Invisible, not incorporeal," Teia said. "Can't float through things, and people tend to notice a door opening and closing by itself."

"Oh, right, right." Karris got up and threw on a robe. "You, uh, you haven't asked for your orders."

Teia looked at her quizzically, a shadow of derision returning to her sharp young face. The girl rubbed her cheek over her dogtooth as if it pained her. "Orders? An arrow in flight doesn't need orders. I'll return to you bloody or not at all."

She threw her hood over her head.

She was going to leave without another word. Karris grabbed her by the wrist, wishing she could shake some sense into the girl, wishing everything between them had been different.

"Nonetheless," she said gently. She rummaged through her desk and grabbed a paper. "Same code as usual."

Teia snagged it and tucked it away. Her cloak shimmered—and she was gone.

Karris went and opened her door to give Teia room to get out past the Blackguards. "Pardon me, Essel, could you check and see if any of my chamber servants are awake and would bring me some kopi? I hate to wake them at such an hour, so if none of them are up, it's not really necessary..."

Essel smiled. It had taken her a worryingly long time to recover from being knocked out the day Gavin had been kidnapped, but she was finally her old self again. "They *are* your chamber servants. That's what they do, High Lady."

"High Lady?" Karris said. "Essel, don't talk to me like we haven't danced the *gciorcal* on tables till past dawn together. One of us without a shift under her skirts."

"Yes, High Lady," Essel said. "I'll go check. You think you can keep it professional around here for one minute, Amzîn?"

"Yes, Watch Captain!" the young man said. "I will not stand here and wonder which of you was dancing without her shift, sir."

Essel stifled a laugh.

Karris raised her eyebrows, and young Amzîn blanched.

"I changed my mind," Karris said. "Amzîn, there's a kopi seller named Jalal on the back side of Ebon's Hill where the two main light-well streets intersect. Opens early. Go find a Blackguard in the barracks to cover the rest of your shift. Then I want you to run to the kopi seller and bring back as much hot kopi as you can carry. As quick as you can. I hate it lukewarm. Until your brain is faster than your tongue, your feet are going to have to be faster yet."

His mouth worked once or twice, but then he was off like a shot. Running so far was easy. Running so far carrying a hot drink? And being expected to bring it back before it cooled?

Essel came back to her post, "That...might have been my fault. I've been telling the boy stories of the old days of all the trouble we got into."

"Any of them true?"

"One or two," Essel said. "He's been terrified of you since his last gaffe. And the others have been none too gentle on him. They all feel like he's trying to take Gav Greyling's place. He's not, of course. But you know men at war. Not always fair."

"No, they're not."

"Nor women, neither."

Karris gave Essel a sharp look. "All right, all right. I hear you. I'll ease up."

"Just a little."

"Just a little," Karris said. "So, uh, which version of that story did you tell him?"

"The true one," Essel said, "where you were the one half-naked, and I was trying to convince you to go home."

"You wicked little liar!"

Essel just laughed.

Then she said, "Actually, after all this time, I can't remember which way is true. Or did it happen more than once?"

"More than once. For you," Karris said.

"Doing some work tonight?" Essel asked.

"Yeah."

"Want me stationed inside instead?"

Karris wanted the company, but said, "No. It's, um, no...not tonight, friend." She didn't know what was in the folio. No one should know it even existed.

Essel nodded, and Karris could tell her feelings were bruised. But   255

Essel was a professional. She asked immediately, "Want me to send to the kitchens for some kopi? It'll be at least an hour before the kid gets back. With lukewarm kopi, I'd guess, too."

"Sure," Karris said. "But don't let Amzîn know, would ya? Just in case. That old man's kopi really is the best."

Essel reached to close the door, then hesitated. "Gav was a great kid. I miss him, too."

Karris took a deep breath, letting the sorrow flow through her. "I miss a lot of us," she said.

Essel nodded, though there was a flash of sorrow there. Even between them there was a bit of death, a gap of secrets held, old trust between comrades abrogated—not by malice but by duty and war. She went.

*   *   *

In the next hours as Karris read, over perfectly hot kopi—it turned out Amzîn was a sub-red—the worries and tribulations of the night faded away as her attention was seized wholly by the advice and the stories the Whites before her had left to help her. Here were lessons from hundreds of years of women and men who'd led and protected drafters through the reigns of Prisms great and good and wretched and bitter and venial (not just one or two of those having reputations from other sources that differed widely from what the Whites past reported). But then they began referring to things that Karris couldn't understand. Sections were missing. There were blank lines, perfectly erased. Later Whites had clearly tried to piece together what was missing, obviously as perturbed as Karris was now.

And the revelations came in, like waves pounding wet sand in Karris's heart. And a new dedication, a new direction, and a new mission was born as the night yielded to the dawn in a single-breath prayer that broke from a chrysalis of horror and blasphemy at Karris's lips. "Oh my God," she repeated, as she flipped the pages one by one.

"Oh my God."

It wasn't a reverent salutation beginning some sacerdotal benediction; it was the curse of a warrior who'd just taken a mortal wound.

"Oh my God."

It wasn't the hushed intonation of a supplicant seeking divine favor; it was the shock of an officer coming upon the scene of a massacre, with his men standing, bloody, near the innocent slain.

But given time, horror fades, and repetition makes what was unthinkable now normal; the monstrous is made manageable. For mankind adapts to every horror.

This can't have happened.

This happened but not often.

This happened often, but this happens no longer.

This happens still but not often.

This happens often, but this is what must happen. This is what someone must do.

This is what *I* must do.

This is what I will do.

I am doing this.

I have done that, and it is what you must do in your turn.

"O my God," Karris said, "please, please, save us."

And the words were that commander's grief, as he held a dead child in his arms, at finding out the massacre hadn't been committed by some mortal foe but by his own men.

"O my God, save us from what we've done." Save us, Orholam, from *You*.

Chapter 38

~The Guile~
38 years ago. (Age 28.)

"This is like no prophecy I've ever seen, Andross," Felia says. She is nineteen years old and heavily pregnant with our first child. A son, she thinks. I've always wanted a girl first, to take care of me in my old age. It's a disappointment I can't hide from her, but she forgives me this, as she forgives so much else.

"I should hope not. This one might cost me drafting for thirty-eight years."

She ignores that. Through another scroll we discovered when it's likely the seal on the Everdark Gates will fail. That, plus this scroll, gives us either that the Lightbringer already came, years ago, and no one noticed; or that he is still to come thirty-eight years from now. So in order to see the prophecy fulfilled—if this prophecy is true—we'll have to *live* another thirty-eight years. That means giving up drafting. Not exactly how either of us wants to live.

She sighs. "For a prophecy, that which hasn't been redacted is so clear. Which makes me wonder if it's somehow deceptive. You understand.   257

You've seen the others: even the ones we know are from true prophets brim with phrases like 'when brother turns against brother, and men put power over religion' that obviously apply to every era. True, but useless. This...this is so different, it doesn't surprise me that other scholars have questioned its veracity, its provenance, even the prophet's sanity."

She's translated the scrolls for us. Felia has a knack for all learning, and with her charm and familial connections, she's had the opportunity to study every discipline that has captured her interest with its foremost scholars. She is like unto a desert, leaving men once fat with knowledge desiccated. She is a hooded lamp, never bragging of her brightness, but taking for fuel everything that comes to the hungry wick of her intellect. She is now doubtless one of the great linguists of our age, and few of the others even suspect it.

Holding the ancient scroll in my hand, I ask, "Is any other translation possible?"

She chews on a finger. We both wonder if she's missed something, so she goes through it phrase by phrase to see if I have any questions that might shine light on something she missed.

She says, " '*If upon that day*,' or 'at the time,' a constrained time, but usually it means 'on the same day' '*when the Everdark Gates open full*.' That's pretty clear: the Gates will have been open to some degree before then—and I do know that the translation of 'Everdark Gates' is certain; I've seen it elsewhere in even older scrolls. Unless you want to go really recursive, and say that '*the Everdark Gates*' means 'the gates of hell,' since we know that's how they got their name in the first place."

"Let's not get too deep here," I say. "The whole premise was that this prophecy is remarkably unambiguous."

"For a prophecy, yes," she said. "But you're right. Here we go: '*and the bane touch the Jaspers*' is when the bane—plural, no note of how many—literally touch the Jaspers. If on that day, '*there stands no Lightbringer*'—again, 'Lightbringer' is used elsewhere, no ambiguity—'*on the Jaspers' shore*'—not necessarily literally standing, it's often used colloquially the way we do: the Lightbringer is there, on the Jaspers, possibly literally on the shore of one island or the other. They didn't call them the Jaspers then, but they referred to the islands in a manner that was consistent. They thought of them as four islands, including Cannon Island and another low island that is believed to have been sunk when the Everdark Gates closed and the sea rose. I have translated that bit as 'the Jaspers' for simplicity. '*Then shall the Chromeria fall*.' In this context, 'fall' seems to mean both figuratively and literally. '*As a river of blood pours from the Prism's Tower*' is simply, 'As a river of blood pours from or around a tower the Prism in some special sense climbs'—thus, ownership: 'His or her tower.' The same word for tower is used again in the next sentence."

"Is '*a river of blood*' sacrifices, or a massacre?" I ask.

"The Freeings have been going on a long time without causing a fall of the satrapies, so I'm guessing that the fall of the satrapies begins with this massacre around the Prism or his seat of power."

"So maybe everyone on the Jaspers will be killed first," I say.

"And there's no clue who does it. Maybe the Angari who come in through the Everdark Gates? But I'm getting ahead of myself. '*Then will seven towers collapse, and with them, seven satrapies.*' Obviously the falls of the seven towers and satrapies are figurative—collapse, political dissolution. Sorry, I'm overexplaining, of course you know that."

"We're grasping at straws. *Too much* explanation might actually be the perfect amount to trigger some new understanding. Please go on."

She does: "'*Ye shall know the time is short when bane rise from the seas.*' I preserved the 'ye' instead of 'you' because he adopts a high tone here, an almost heraldic alarum. And apparently, this prophet believes the bane to be literal, physical things. He believes the *loci damnata* are real places, real temples of the false gods, the damned. '*Atirat will rise off Ruic Head.*' 'Off Ruic Head' is a little tricky. Ruic Head wasn't called Ruic Head at the time. It was the 'fist sinister of the Iron Mountains.' So the left hand of the Red Cliffs. Most agree that means Ruic Head, but it is a bit of an extrapolation. Further, 'off' could mean near or even on Ruic Head. It's more often 'inside Ruic Head,' so it might mean 'on Ruic Bay'? Or maybe 'buried in the ground beneath Ruic Head itself'? Alternately, if we wanted to take it a metaphorical direction, '*inside the left fist*' could merely mean 'in the power of' a political entity near Ruic Head, the city of Ru itself. But I don't think so."

"If a bane appears near Ruic Head, I imagine we'll notice," I say drily. "So it doesn't matter. The ambiguity will likely clear itself up in time."

She continues, "'*and she who births him will become Ferrilux.*' This could be an actual birth, but I've never heard of the gods literally giving birth to other gods, especially of such disparate colors as superviolet and green. And that Atirat rises from nearby doesn't suggest growing up from infancy; rather it suggests a god in full."

"So this woman will help Atirat…become Atirat?" I ask. We have so little idea how godhood is conferred or perhaps recognized. It is not something lost to the black, I don't think, though; I think it has always been secret.

Felia says, "And then this woman, this goddess, will at some indeterminate point later become Ferrilux, which is intriguing as Ferrilux is traditionally male. I've considered that this may be symbolic if the 'she' is a nation or a satrapy, but that would be a strange construction."

"Not that prophecies are noted for their plain language."

"Which makes this one all the more striking," Felia says. "It could be a poetic phrasing, because that seemed appropriate to the subject matter of goddesses?" She spreads her hands, as puzzled as I am.

"As you were," I say.

"Then *'She will open the Gates fully, which have been cracked.'* The 'have been cracked' isn't the same as our idiom 'opened a crack.' It means 'leaking' as in 'slightly broken,' like a cracked egg. Some believe—and I concur—that at some point during Lucidonius's or Vician's time, the Gates were fully closed and let no water at all through, which hasn't of course been the case for centuries. But this woman will open the gates all the way."

"Which would make us entirely vulnerable to the Angari."

"Maybe they aren't warlike anymore. It's been centuries," Felia says. "But then, this prophecy doesn't exactly strike such a hopeful note."

"On the other hand," I say, "if 'the Everdark Gates' actually does mean the gates of hell…there might be something worse than the Angari waiting to come through."

Felia purses her lips. "Not a hopeful note at all, huh? *'From Tyrea'* is the last fragment, and then the rest is redacted. She, the new Ferrilux, will come from Tyrea, or something or someone else? There's not enough context to guess."

I look at the words again:

If upon the day when the Everdark Gates open full and the bane touch the Jaspers, there stands no Lightbringer on the Jaspers' shore, then shall the Chromeria fall. As a river of blood pours from the Prism's Tower, then will seven towers collapse, and with them, seven satrapies. Ye shall know the time is short when bane rise from the seas. Atirat will rise off Ruic Head, and she who births him will become Ferrilux. She will open the Gates fully, which have been cracked. From Tyrea—

260

The words seem writ in fire to me. I have no doubt they are true. This prophecy alone doesn't give us the evidence we'd hoped for, but it gives us what's at stake, and the time frame.

"What do we do?" I ask.

Felia is the only one in the world of whom I would ask such a question.

She studies me with eyes aglow with orange luxin, with love, with intelligence, and with pride. A man cannot long endure a look of total love and acceptance without turning aside or being changed forever.

I hold her gaze.

She puts her hands on my forearms, looking up at me, and when she speaks, her voice is soft but unyielding. "How we direct all the resources of our wealth and our connections and our intelligences and our considerable powers hinges on your answer to one question. My husband, my lord..."

Suddenly, I can feel the waters of history streaming past us, the passions of men and the desires of nations, the Chromeria spinning like a great wheel of a water mill driven by the politics of satraps and satrapahs, ambitious Colors riding the wheel up and eventually down, but the mill's gears disengaged, its teeth whizzing purposelessly, all our power not even touching the great stationary millstone of history. But I stand at the lever. With one word, one decision, I may grind nations into wheat and chaff, I can be destroyer or savior. Both.

And I want to. If only to show that I *can*.

She studies me, and she knows. She translates my every blink and half-formed grin and twitched expression effortlessly, perfectly, my puzzling heart pellucid to her perspicacity. I am a text full open to her translation.

And yet she trusts me.

She speaks the question we have hinted at and dodged and joked about and hungered to know, but have never, never said aloud: she says, "After all we've seen and all we've learned...who are you, Andross Guile?"

"I am..." and the next words hang gleaming in the air like a glittering sword, a challenge, a taunt to those who had reached for it before me and been crushed by the unsupported weight of their presumption. "I am..." I say, and I leap into the teeth of history, and I break open its jaws with the lever of my audacity and power. "I, Andross Guile, am the Lightbringer."

Chapter 39

Kip and Tisis stood atop Greenwall where Ben-hadad had placed one of the mirrors he'd found in storage. It had fit perfectly in the frame, and with a little grease, it spun easily, just as Ben predicted. Kip had dismissed them all then. There were preparations to make, regardless of what he decided here tonight. Whatever he decided, he was going to get a lot of people killed.

He looked out over his city, his people, and what could be his satrapy.

Partly to avoid what he had to decide, but also partly because he was tired of everything being all about him all the time, he took his wife's hand and said, "What'd you do today, dear?"

"What do you think?" she asked.

"I sort of figured you were running half the satrapy," Kip said. He wasn't really joking. She was far more comfortable with governance than he was.

"Only half?" she asked.

They shared a smile.

Then she said, "Today I was placing and recruiting sources and acquiring a number of diaries from our new recruits' camp, including Daragh's, and securing the cooperation of several minstrels who were previously tasked with writing songs about the bandits' exploits. Then I was arranging interviews with camp girls, washerwomen, and servants from their old haunts. Within the week, we'll know exactly which of our new recruits is irredeemably villainous. I'll not only have a very good idea of which men are likely to commit future outrages, but I'll have sources nearby keeping an eye on them. Your part will be to keep some fluidity in the unit personnel assignments until then. I also took care of all my usual duties."

Kip cursed under his breath. "Dearest?"

"Yes, my love?"

"What happens when you realize you don't actually need me?"

"Oh, come now," she said, but she couldn't help but beam. "You tell us what we're going to do. I merely make sure it happens."

" 'Merely,' " Kip said, sarcastic, "because that's the easy part."

"And your own role is so simple that you're going to bed early?" she asked.

Which brought him crashing back to the present. And the future.

"You ever think you were destined for something greater?" Kip asked.

"Than what we're doing?" Tisis asked. "I thought my life would be way less *everything* than this." Then she asked, "You?"

"Think? No. I tried not to think, because I was sure I'd become like my mother, that I'd go from stuffing my face with food today to stuffing my nostrils with gutwrack tomorrow." Or haze, or ratweed, or *anything* to obliterate a day.

"Really?" she asked.

Her eyes filled with such empathy that he couldn't bear it.

"Sorry," he said, with a quick fake grin.

"But..." she said. "Why'd you ask?"

"Oh, a man asked me that question once. Green wight I ran into outside my hometown, just before...you know, the king's army came." It felt like a lifetime ago.

"Gaspar Elos?" she asked. Oh, right, he'd told her the story. He was probably boring her.

He nodded. "Funny," Kip said. "Back then, Koios's side imprisoned this wight and I freed him. How'd we switch sides?"

"You didn't. They're deceptive, Kip. Corrupted."

"Orholam's gift shouldn't be corruptible, should it? Shouldn't lead inevitably to death."

"Standing daily in the sun is a blessing; standing in the sun from dawn to dusk every day will burn even the darkest skin. Every gift must be received and released with the appropriate measure. Even the gift of life leads to death, Kip."

"It just feels wrong. Madness at the end of every road for us."

"What did he say?" Tisis asked.

Kip knew she meant Gaspar. How long had the wight's words festered under his skin like a jagged splinter? From the beginning, he supposed. Bury and ignore them as he would. Tell himself he couldn't be bothered by the words of a wight, a liar, an enemy, or simply a man who'd ruined himself and wanted to make sport of a vulnerable boy.

Yet still the splinter lay embedded in his psyche, inflamed.

" 'You ever wondered why you're stuck in such a small life?' he asked me. Of course I had! What young man doesn't? 'Do you know why you feel destined for something greater?' and for a moment I think I really believed he might be a messenger from Orholam Himself, come to give me meaning for my shitty life. Why had *I* found him? So randomly, out there alone, at that very hour? It was like it was appointed. Like maybe this was my great purpose calling." Kip trailed off. "What a child I was. So desperate and weak and full of hope that something great would simply happen to me."

"What did he say, Kip?"

"I don't know why I even care. I certainly shouldn't be deciding the fate of an empire on some throwaway insult. It doesn't matter."

"*Kip.*"

Kip licked his lips. "He said the reason I felt destined for something great was because I was an arrogant little shit." He shook his head and half chuckled. "Actually kind of funny."

"No. Cruel," Tisis said. "A sharp wit can puncture a wineskin overfull of ego. But any bully with a club-wit can shatter an empty crystal glass."

Kip shrugged. The man had said, 'There's a prophecy about you. Not Rekton you. You you.' But it had all been a setup for the taunt, hadn't it? He said, "Just a stranger. Dead one now."

She looked skeptical.

He shook it off. "I should get—"

She put a hand on his arm, stopping him. She was biting her bottom lip, intense. Then she took a deep breath. "I believe in you, but that's not enough, is it? You need to know. For you."

She didn't have to say about what.

"Don't you?" she asked.

"Know?" Kip asked.

"You're gonna play dumb? You? With me?"

They'd never talked about it directly, even as the Mighty assumed it. It was too precious, too big, too ridiculous for fat little Kip of Rekton to even dream.

He knew Tisis wouldn't ridicule him. Knew it absolutely. It wasn't in her.

But what if she did?

He cleared his throat. "I'm not that fat kid from Rekton anymore," Kip said. He shrugged. He braced himself on the ramparts, the masses of busy people below blending into one unvariegated carpet.

She stepped up beside him and put one hand atop his.

She looked out, and her face filled with pleasure at the people united, purposeful, hopeful—and it made him ache. Her satisfaction brought vigor to her beauty, a feminine strength, not fragile like a bloom that might be crushed underfoot, but adaptive, stubbornly growing toward the sun. Like a sapling in good soil, rushing into her strength, that she might bend before a storm, but grow; or be pressed down today and spring back up tomorrow, having grown taller yet

overnight.

Tisis was transforming before his eyes, and he knew he'd played a role in that beautiful mystery, that growing into what she was meant to be. It filled him with humility to be allowed to partake in something so sacred. And it filled him with impossible longing.

Kip looked out on all those thousands of people taking his direction, and though he knew it was there, he didn't see the glory of a community united, unselfish, moving toward a worthy goal. He saw thousands of people he could fail. Ten thousand ways he could fall short. And yet, how could he solve the paradoxical audacity in his breast?

He wanted to be even more.

How *dare* he?

"Kip, do you know what we do when we look at ourselves in a mirror?"

See ourselves? "Why do I have a feeling that whatever I say next is going to get me in trouble?"

"Shut up, Kip."

"See?!"

"*Kip.*" Level, stern, no-nonsense. If they lived so long, she had definite mother material in her.

Well, he'd certainly put enough father material in her for that to actually happen.

Which was kind of terrifying: Kip. A *father*.

No, he did *not* want to think about that right now.

"Sorry," he said. "Go ahead. You were saying?" He folded his hands and composed himself like an attentive student.

She studied him for a moment until she was certain he wasn't making light of things.

She spun the mounted mirror over and directed Kip's image at himself, which he didn't really appreciate. She said, "A mirror turns quiet voices blaring, and can blind you to the whole you by distracting you with details. It breaks you into imperfect pieces of a body rather than integrate you into a whole person. A mirror pushes its will into you, Kip. So if you think a mirror only reflects, if you think a mirror shows you the way you really are, you won't realize what it's doing, and you won't push back. You are that kid from Rekton, Kip."

"'Aren't,' you mean," he said. "Sorry, not important. You just misspoke. Go on."

She shook her head. "I didn't misspeak."

Yes, you did. He flashed a quick smile. It really didn't matter.

She rolled her eyes skyward. "Did you really have to give him a loud silent yes, too?!"

"You know," Kip said, "I usually feel smarter than this. And I don't usually feel all that smart."

She took his hands, and she was the comfort of a lantern in darkness. "You *are* that wounded, fearful child stuck in the closet with the rats." Her voice cracked momentarily, and lightning of her righteous wrath at what had been done to him flashed in the distance, but she went on. "And you are this man. And I have seen you..." Her eyes filled with tears, but she ignored them. "Kip, when you bring that little boy's heart and his compassion for brokenness into your rule, I have never seen anyone so powerful." She wet dry lips, mastering herself. "I think you owe that child abandoned in a locked closet with rats something, Kip. That boy? That boy you've poured scorn on, who you called a fat fuck? He survived because he *fought*. I think you owe him more than your *contempt*."

His cheeks were wet, but he whispered, "I stopped fighting."

The Guile memory was a curse. That memory was so clear when he thought about it that he tried to never think of it at all. Huddled in a ball on the floor, back slick with blood, exhausted, starving— Orholam, he hadn't even been fat yet then, had he?—the bodies of rats he'd smashed as he'd thrown his body this way and that, crushing some few of them. Those he'd crushed writhed while dying and were devoured first, as easier food. The pure disgust—rats!—had come first, and long since been scoured away. All that mattered in the end was that they not get his fingers, his toes, his groin, his face. All else he lacked the strength to protect.

He'd despised himself for his weakness. For flailing like a madman and having nothing left. For not being able to fight. For not having the courage to tear open one of the rats he'd killed to drink its blood to wet his parched lips.

At least not until it was too late, and the dead ones had already been devoured.

He was powerless, and it was his own fault. He'd known what he needed to do, and he hadn't done it.

And the rats would be back.

Tisis said, "Every slave stops fighting the chain. But some run every time the chains do come off. And you're *here*, Kip. And you have friends. And you trust people. And you love. Are those the hallmarks of the weak and contemptible?"

"Not...so much," he admitted.

"So what I'm looking forward to seeing is you pushing back at that old distorted mirror. I can't wait to see you repay that hurting boy for his gifts to you by finally bringing your piercing wisdom back to that child. Mirrors break us into pieces because that's how the eye focuses: one detail at a time, a prism splitting our whole experience, but the heart can be a second prism brought to the first, bringing that which is split back into a whole. So maybe it's no coincidence that the Seven Satrapies need healing and reintegration as much as you do. Maybe it's a sign that you're exactly the one to do it."

Kip swallowed. "Ah . . . so *that's* what you meant when you said you believed in me? Got it. That *is* a little different."

"Kip, I believe you're him."

She'd never said it aloud, and he'd never dared to ask.

He looked into her hopeful eyes, and now he saw reflected there a man made whole. He breathed her in, and she filled his lungs with confidence. She was countering lies, defying contempt—I'm the boy who felt destined for something greater, *because I was.* She wanted to know if all her efforts were actually making a difference: healing fissures, helping him accept boy and man both.

"I believe it with all my heart," she said. "And that's why I want you to stay."

"Excuse me?"

"The satrapies are finished. The empire's lost. But not everything is. These people need you. No one can lead them like you can. You can't abandon them in their hour of need. And if you stay—I mean, Lucidonius was able to sweep from Paria through all nine kings. You could do the same!"

"He faced nine kings who hated each other. We'd be facing them united."

"To all his people, the Chromeria is the big enemy. We don't know that Koios will be able to keep his people united after the Chromeria falls. To his people, they're the big enemy, his people aren't going to care about us way out here. We can rebuild. We'd still send messengers to the Chromeria, inviting anyone who wants to flee to join us."

"He can immobilize drafters. We have to figure out how to counter that, or the only way to fight would be to send wave after wave of fighters into his wights like grist into a mill until they're exhausted. It'd take a hundred thousand men to have a chance. Maybe twice that. Most would die, even in victory. I'd rather lose."

"You'll lose anyway," she said.

It felt like a stab in the back. "I thought you believed in me," he said.

"I don't mean to the White King. They'll kill you, Kip. The Chromeria. Even if you win. Even if you save them all and swear to leave the very next day. You won't live to see that day. My lord, my love. It doesn't matter what good you do them. This, too, is your inheritance: 267

no one trusts a Guile bearing gifts. You, coming with only a fraction of your army, but in all your power? They'll fear you, and hate you. Zymun? Your grandfather? The Order? Even the Magisterium. They've all killed for power—and you'll be the biggest threat yet. My love, they'll murder you. They'll believe they must."

She wasn't wrong.

"This is who I am," Kip said, and he raised his hands, fingers arched, stiff. "I used to think I was all thumbs. Turns out I was wrong. I'm all claws." Turtle-Bear.

She saw the look on his face, and he saw her world crumble. "Kip, my love, I didn't mean—"

"It's not your fault, it's not your doing. It's not about you."

But her face contorted in grief, and she sank to her knees. "Kip. Kip. This will be the death of you."

"O my love," Kip said gently. He pulled her to her feet and embraced her, just breathing in the scent of her, cherishing the comfort of her weight against him.

The next words had to be pushed up a hill before they could roll down the other side, unstoppable, but they had to be said. In the years to come, she would need to know that he had chosen this, clear-eyed, if not unafraid. He said, "My love. Haven't we always known? This was never going to end with me alive. After all, I am the Lightbringer."

Chapter 40

The door to Karris's rooms opened, and Samite strode in. "Hey, we missed you at training this morn..." She trailed off as she saw Karris's haggard face and puffy eyes, and then she swore. "Is there some new emergency the boys at the door don't know about? Because I swear to Orholam, if you're slipping back into some weak-ass limp-wristed bureaucrat's skin, I am going to kick your ass so far you need a long-lens to find it."

Samite was the trainer now, Karris thought, the ghost of a smile touching her lips. "Not a new emergency, no. An old one."

Late in the bundle of papers, where Karris had breezed past it at first, was a bit from Orea Pullawr. It had been a brief conversation

Orea and Karris had had years ago with each other, but here anonymized and left for the benefit of all the future Whites:

'I've left you a mess.'

'You are the White. It's your prerogative,' her strong right hand said.

'A prerogative I've invoked far too often. I hope your strong hands will succeed where mine have failed.'

And that was it. That was the entirety of her note. The occasion for those words originally had been when Orea's health had been failing and she'd had to take sometimes to her wheeled chair. It had been an actual mess, too trivial to summon the room slaves for, when Karris was simply standing there. She'd always liked making herself useful, so she'd cleaned it up.

That Orea had left that conversation in this missive without even noting her own name—Karris recognized it by the hand alone, but future Whites (if there were any) would have to guess who'd left this, so the exchange was generalized from one White to her successors: 'Clean up my messes. May you do better than I did. I'm sorry.'

She'd tried to say it to Karris before, saying something like, 'I hope you can find it in your heart to forgive me,' when Karris had no idea what forgiveness Orea could possibly want from her, or for what offense.

But now she knew, and it upended all her feelings for the old woman and spilled them on the floor in a tangle.

"Hey! Hey! Where'd you go?" Samite demanded. She snapped her fingers in front of Karris. "Uh-uh," she said. "You don't get to retreat. You don't pull back. Remember who you are, woman!"

Karris's eyes refocused, but she shook her head and scoffed. "Put your thumb right on it, didn't you?"

"No, no, no," Samite said. "You're not doing this."

"You don't know what I've just learned."

"I don't give two shits what you've learned," Samite said. "I'm worried about what you've forgotten."

"Sami, it's all worse than we thought. I thought it was bad when I killed Gav..." Karris started to open the letters to show her old friend, then stopped. "No, I can't," she said aloud, surprised that their rules still bound her inside, though she *should* respect them as little as Gavin did.

But no. She couldn't tell Samite. She couldn't tell anyone. This was her burden to carry. Her stomach twisted. She was alone, as she'd been alone since Gavin had been taken.

"Karris," Samite said softly, and in that word, not her title, not her full name, Karris saw the broad warrior lift off the mantle of Trainer Samite and become again her dear friend Sami.

"Thank you for standing for me the other night," Karris said. "I never said thank you for that, for standing watch. It was most ungracious of me."

Her friend waved it away with her one good hand. "Karris, do you remember Aghilas?"

Karris did. He'd been the fastest scrub in their cohort, and one of the strongest, too, but he hadn't made it into the Blackguard.

"Let me tell you a story."

"I don't have time for—come on, Sami."

"Before you and I met, I'd trained for years. *Years* to ready myself to attempt the Blackguard training. I'd spent hours every day making my body my slave. I still wasn't nearly the best, short reach, not naturally gifted, not fast, merely strong—and not even that strong, compared with most of the boys. I already felt resentful of the others, to tell you the truth.

"And then you showed up: this slip of a girl. Light-skinned, soft, pretty in all the wrong ways, good drafter with two colors but didn't have a clue how to use them in fighting yet. You were weak, slow, had no endurance. You had no business trying to be a Blackguard. We all knew you'd only been given the chance because you were noble-born.

"Truth is, Karris, I hated you. I was afraid they were gonna bend the rules to let you in."

"Well, you didn't need to worry about that. They kicked my ass—"

"And they did."

"What?" Karris asked, eyes tightening.

"They bent the rules. Maybe broke them, depending on whether you go by the rules as written, or as observed."

"They *what*?!" Karris asked. "They did not. I earned my—"

"You shocked the hell out of us, all of us," Samite went on, and Karris shut up, if only to hear the rest of this slander. "I remember the trainers looking at each other, while me and the other scrubs were waiting for you to finish one of our runs. You were a lap behind us all, and you puked—while running—and you broke stride as your stomach heaved, but you never stopped."

"I puked every day for a while there," Karris said, her mind casting back to what she'd always thought of as the best worst days of her life.

"You remember that day when the physickers came and yanked you out of training?"

As if Karris could forget it. Quietly, she said, "I thought I was done."

"You should've been," Samite said. "I know that now. Trainers tell each other things, not just the rules as written and what to let slide, but also how to keep kids from getting dead. You're lucky you didn't die. It's because of kids like you that they checked our piss every day. You remember that? We submitted to it thinking it was a test of whether we could stand awkwardness and humiliation, but it wasn't. A kid stops pissing regular, and then it comes out bloody—that kid's gonna kill himself from exertion."

"The physickers told me it was pretty bad," Karris admitted.

"When you were gone, Trainer Tzeddig stopped us and asked two questions."

"Oh? I never heard about that." The trainer had asked enough trick questions to make every scrub paranoid.

"She asked us, if we had to pair up that day and fight in teams, fighting to the death against the others, who we would like to have on our side: you or Aghilas. We all said Aghilas, of course—except Aghilas, who tried to be smart."

Aghilas had never been as funny as he thought. "She whack him upside the head?" Karris asked.

"She whacked him upside the head," Samite said with a smile. "Then she said we'd have to be fools not to choose Aghilas, that he was one of the most naturally gifted athletes she'd ever seen. He was fast, strong, and quick with a dozen weapons, or without any at all. Then she asked us if, in a few years, we had to go to war, who we'd want to have fight beside us: you or Aghilas."

Karris realized momentarily that she hadn't thought about her damned papers in several minutes, but she was enrapt.

"Some of us figured this had to be the trick part, so we said *you* instead of the obvious answer, but when she demanded why, none of us could say. You could see the traps opening up in front of your feet with that woman and still never avoid them. I hope I can be half the trainer she was."

"Well, what'd she say?" Karris demanded.

"Do you know why you piss blood when you're killing yourself from overexertion?"

"What?" she asked, not following.

"Your body panics. It starts devouring its own muscles."

"That sounds…unhelpful, when one's already overexerted."

"Trainer Tzeddig pointed after you, where the physickers were carrying you, and—" Samite's voice cracked with sudden emotion. She cleared her throat, but her eyes brimmed. "And she said, 'That girl Karris has all of two muscles to rub together, and she wants to be here with you so bad she's literally pissing them down her leg. She is working harder than anyone here. That *goddam* slip of a girl is working herself to death. Aghilas, do you know how good you could be if you worked half that hard? I don't, and I don't think you ever will, either. Last week we rigged the race so you couldn't do better than second—and you gave up and didn't finish in the top ten. You haven't stopped complaining since. You know who's never complained?'" Samite shook her head, tears spilling down her cheeks. "Orholam's stones, I remember it like it was yesterday. That woman was magnificent when she was chewing our asses."

Karris was barely holding back tears herself.

"Tzeddig said, 'That *little girl* will run through a brick wall for you. You give her a goal and death itself won't keep it from her. For years now I've trained the best fighters in the world, and I tell you that you haven't seen a person until you've seen how hard they'll push themselves and what they do *after* they reach their end and fail. So you tell me, when you go to war—and you will, may Orholam grant that it's merely a metaphorical one—but when you go to war, who do you want beside you?' And I tell you what, Karris, you weren't there, and Aghilas was. And a lot of us were afraid of him, and we knew we'd have to spar him that afternoon, and the next day, and the next, but almost everyone in the cohort chose you anyway."

They did? And now Karris couldn't stop the tears from spilling hot down her face.

"And then Trainer Tzeddig said, 'So now you've voted with your words. Let me tell you what you all already know: Karris isn't good enough to make it. Not yet. She'll get there: she's not just relentless, she's quick and she's a damn fast drafter too. But she's not good enough to get into the Blackguard. What you may not know is that she's got nothing else. The False Prism's War took it all from her: family, lands, wealth, and she's got enemies, too, who blame her for things, who see her vulnerability and are drooling to devour her. So I don't know where she'll be in a year, but it won't be here. She won't be able to try again. This is her only chance.' We all looked around at each other like we'd been punched in the gut. Then finally someone, maybe it was Fisk, asked, 'What do you mean we've voted *with our words*?' But Tzeddig didn't answer. Some of the older Blackguards were there, enjoying watching us get reamed, and Holdfast—remember him? Cruxer's father? Married Inana eventually?—he said, 'You know what Blackguards do? We stand for each other. When one of us can't make it, we carry him. You've all said you want to fight with Karris by your side, but the fact is, if she gets in, one of you standing here doesn't. So each of you make your choice. Vote with your cunning and your fists. You want Karris in? Make it happen.'"

Karris put a hand to her throat. "But—no one ever..."

"Who was gonna tell you? If you were a lock to make it in, maybe you'd stop working so hard. And some of the kids who were on the edge really *did* fight you. But those at the top eased your way a bit. It wasn't for you, Karris, you understand? It was for *us*. Because we knew an Aghilas would get us killed someday. You? You'd keep us alive. And that's what you're doing now, saving all of us, no matter what." Sami shrugged. "Anyway, that day changed my life. That was the day I stopped hating you. I realized that if you could get in on sheer grit, I could, too. So that day you kind of became my role model, and uh, you've never stopped. So when I lost my hand, I had this little moment where I thought my life was over and I'd have to retire. It'd kill me, you know? This work is everything for me. But then I thought, 'How can I quit now? I'm not pissing my muscles down my leg yet.'" Sami pursed her lips hard, but then went on as if her face weren't streaked with tears. "And that was it. That turned me around. Sure, I was still afraid. This isn't what I expected from my life. Death? Death I expected, someday. But living as a cripple? Seeing pity and fear in my brothers' and sisters' faces? This isn't what I expected from life, but this is what life expects from me. And you know what? I don't see myself as a cripple now. I just got a bad left hand to compensate for. And I don't see much pity anymore, and the nunks' fear of *being me* has become their fear *of* me. But the fact remains: I'm not what I was. A bit of my burden has to fall on someone else, but I've made my peace with that. Blackguards stand for each other. I can be humble enough to let 'em, even as I work to make myself useful—if not today, tomorrow. So if you need us to carry you for a day or two, we're here. We're *here*, Karris. But don't you dare give up, because that isn't who you are."

Samite studied her, then flashed a sudden smile. "You got that look on your face like my nunks get, you know? Like you're about to ask a stupid question. So let me answer it for you before you embarrass us both."

"What, I was—"

"'Who am I, then?'" Samite mocked. "That's what you were gonna say, wasn't it?"

"No," Karris lied, sounding way too much like a nunk who'd been caught out.

But Samite laughed. She'd known Karris too long.

"Karris, your answer for that's never been found in words. At least not any this simple Blackguard can put together. You've always made yourself known by your actions. Known and loved, too. So just keep doing what you do." Samite rolled her shoulders, as if trying to find some way to extricate herself from the messy emotions and pick up her gruff-trainer persona once more. "Now, uh, there's a stack of messengers and a line of papers outside your door—or maybe I got that backward. Regardless, uh, given the circumstances, I'll give you the rest of the morning off. See you at the training yards tomorrow?"

Slowly, despite the still-churning mess of thoughts and emotions roiling head and heart and stomach, and despite the headache she had—she always got headaches when she cried—slowly, Karris nodded, and she felt a little bit of herself coming back. "Bright and early," she promised.

Chapter 41

"I wanted to ask you something," Kip said, coming into the little room that Cruxer had made his office and bedroom. It was nauseatingly tidy. Even the stacks of schedules on the desk looked just so.

"Anything," Cruxer said. He'd just dribbled oil onto his blade, and now he picked up his whetstone, spinning a spear point into position.

"It's a sore spot."

Cruxer didn't waver. He began the soothing *wush-wush* of the whetstone.

Kip went on. "Big Leo said something I didn't understand. He said you were still grieving Lucia—"

"It hasn't been that long," Cruxer interrupted. It was uncharacteristic of him. He'd been in love with the young Blackguard scrub, and when she'd stepped into the line of fire, taking a bullet that had been meant for Kip, Cruxer's world had ended.

"No. It hasn't. And that wasn't at all what tripped me up. It was that he thought the reason you were angry about me giving Ruadhán another chance had something to do with her. He wouldn't say anything else when I asked him. So what's that about?"

"I'm fine with you giving Ruadhán another chance," Cruxer said. "Now."

"That actually confuses me more," Kip said.

Cruxer paused in his sharpening, then said, "You're the... you're the Breaker, not me. Different rules apply to you. I'm not a man who does new things. I'm a man who does the old things as well as they can be done. But here? I'm doing new things all the time. I'm making decisions over other people's lives, like I've got any right to do that. I'm worried all the time, Breaker. I keep looking around waiting to be punished," Cruxer said.

"Punished? For what?"

"Breaker, I'm eighteen years old. I'm styling myself a commander? I'm not even eligible to be a watch captain. I keep thinking Orholam's gonna give me what I deserve any moment."

"Is that who Orholam is to you?" Kip asked. "An Andross Guile waiting for you to transgress, so that He can expose you at the worst possible moment? Isn't He instead like Ironfist, who will correct your form, not because He enjoys showing you how you're messing up but because doing it wrong might get you hurt or killed someday?"

But Cruxer wasn't even hearing him. "I'm not the man anyone thinks I am. I'm a fraud. I had a hundred chances to come clean, and I never did. And do you know what punishment I got for that?"

"What are you talking about?"

"None. She paid for it."

"Lucia?" Kip said. "Her dying wasn't your fault!"

"She wasn't good enough to make it into the Blackguard—"

Kip accepted that. They'd all known it was true. "She absolutely had the spirit of the best of us, Crux. She saved my life. If this is on anyone, it's on—"

"She had the spirit, yes, but not the skills. She shouldn't have been there. Wouldn't have…" His face contorted.

"Wouldn't have?"

"I fell for her. Hard. Like, before we even talked. There was…" Cruxer's face brightened at the memory. "There was something radiant about her. Like you just want to watch her across the room and watch how spirits lighten as people talk to her. I started training her extra right away, not just to be near her, either. I knew, brother, I knew so early that she'd never make it in. I don't think she did. And I couldn't bear to be away from her."

He took a breath, steadying himself against his grief.

"She came from one of the slave-training houses, you know? If she failed out of Blackguard training, we both knew her owners would look for some other way to recoup their investment. Decent men who just want a domestic don't bid as much at the auction as men who want a domestic for whom they have…other uses as well. Good women who just want a domestic don't often bring a pretty one into their homes." He shook his head. "Have you ever seen the light in a girl's eyes die?" Cruxer met Kip's gaze for the first time in a while. "No, they didn't have slaves where you grew up, did they? That disgusting brutality isn't considered normal in oh-so-backward Tyrea, is it?" he said bitterly. "Well, I couldn't let it happen. Not to her."

"Oh, Cruxer." Kip covered his face.

"I thought, if I could just keep her in until the final testing, I could take my Blackguard price the next day and buy out her contract before her owners sold her. To free her, of course. I mean, I was nervous that maybe...even though she'd never acted like it, that maybe she'd attached herself to me hoping that would happen. You know, that she knew I was her only hope to get out. I wouldn't blame her for it. But as long as she was a slave, the worry's there, right? The infernal institution perverts everything it touches. So, I get my price, I free her. Maybe she loves me, too, and sticks around for a while. I mean, I was thinking marriage, but I wasn't going to put that on her. I wanted her to be free to go, if she wanted. But maybe someday..." He swallowed.

"So I cheated to keep her in. Our cohort was solid at the top places, but not at the bottom. A couple deep muscle bruises delivered during training the week before testing—hard kicks to a thigh or calf, not anything that would disable anyone, you know? Those kids were going to wash out anyway. What's the harm? I thought."

"Cruxer, everyone does that kind of thing, trying to keep their friends with them, and everyone knows it. It's part of—"

"It's *cheating*. It's wrong."

Except it wasn't. Not exactly.

The trainers and the watch captains and the Blackguards' commander all knew such scheming happened, and they didn't stop it. In fact, they didn't even mind, because allowing it rewarded cunning and alliance-making over pure technical fighting skill. Only fighters as incredibly skilled as Cruxer could be unaware of how the others schemed together; fighters as good as Cruxer always made it in regardless.

The rest of the scrubs stayed awake at night, wondering what they could possibly do to make it in. The commander and trainers accepted all the schemes and backstabbing because full Blackguards needed to know how cunning minds worked if they were to guard against such minds, addressing not only external threats but also internal political machinations.

But Kip wasn't going to convince Cruxer out of his guilt with justifications that others were cheating, too.

Cruxer said, "But of course, like every fraud, I got greedy. Keeping her in the Blackguard until the final testing wasn't good enough. I wanted to be around her all the time. There was no way she belonged in Aleph squad. I demanded it. Commander Ironfist took one look at me, and he *knew*. I never felt so naked and foolish in my life. He told me it was gonna lead to grief. He told me! He even offered to buy her contract himself if she failed out early—and I angrily denied everything. Breaker, he gave me a chance to have everything I wanted except that I wouldn't be the big hero in her eyes, and I lied to his face. I broke faith. I was a man under authority, and in my cowardice and weakness, I ripped myself out of my place in the Great Chain of Being. I stepped outside of Orholam's protection, and leader that I am, I brought Lucia with me. And she got killed for my sins. Orholam is good and merciful, so I've had many blessings since then. But the lesson remains. Those who break faith bring grief to those who love them most. And the sooner they're stopped, the better."

"So you didn't want mercy for Ruadhán, because you're afraid he'll hurt us."

"How many second chances does a man get? I would've said one, and that then he deserves everything he gets and worse. But you give Conn Arthur a third chance—and it feels *right*. You confuse me, and I can't tell if things work out for you because different rules apply to you, or if you're just the only person I know brave enough to try them."

So that was why Cruxer had almost stopped Kip from stepping in front of the window that day: anyone else, he would have stopped, but Kip?

The young commander scrubbed his fingers through his short curly hair. "It's different, right? Up near the top of the Great Chain, the lines get fuzzy. I know the Lightbringer is going to upend everything. *You* have to obey Orholam, and you have to figure out if following the Chromeria's will fits with that. Me? I hate that kind of thing. I'm not equipped for that stuff. Not made for it. You decide where Orholam calls us to go. Me? I follow you, unless you do something that outrages the light of conscience Orholam gave me."

"Or if I put myself in danger," Kip said.

"Well, I do get to save your dumb ass from yourself, yes," he said with a short-lived smile. "But that's not quite the same thing."

Kip nodded agreement, but his heart ached. How do you save a friend who's had a trauma burn the wrong lesson onto their heart in words of fire? "Cruxer... This rigidity in you, this fear? That's still the wound. Not the healing. You know that, right?"

"No. It's not. This is righteousness, and a man *must* fear he'll lose his integrity in a world like this or he'll never keep it."

"True... true," Kip said. And entirely beside the point. He tried 277 another tack. "There were two brothers. During a siege of an enemy city, they heroically broke through a burning sally port door. The city was taken, but they fell wounded and later shared a room as they convalesced from their burns," Kip said. "Day after day, they spoke as they were able.

" 'Fire's hot,' the first observed.

" 'Still hot, weeks later,' the second agreed.

" 'Burns are the worst,' the first said.

" 'The absolute worst,' the second agreed.

" 'Bravest thing I ever did,' the first said.

" 'Dumbest thing I ever did,' the second said.

"The first said, 'If we'd waited, a defender might've extinguished that fire, and many more of our friends would have gotten killed trying to take the city.'

"The second replied, 'If we'd waited, that burning door might've fallen down by itself, and we wouldn't be here, and no one would have gotten hurt saving us when we fell wounded.'

" 'There'll be another battle next month or next year, but we did what we had to, and we did it as well as we could,' the first said.

" 'There'll be another battle next month or next year, so we didn't really accomplish anything,' the second replied.

"Which one's right, Cruxer?" Kip asked.

Chapter 42

Dawn hadn't yet rolled over in her bed, much less brushed the horizon with groggy fingers to see if her lover still attended her. But despite the darkness, the armor-bearers and bakers and coal-carriers and dung-boys and the egglers and the fletchers were already up, their diurnal labors slowly displacing the stubborn nocturnal revelry of those soon leaving to greet death. The garrulous and the hateful and the inquisitive and the jocular would come later to see them off. Kin and lovers would trail behind, some mothers following for a league or more, unwilling to turn their faces from sons and daughters they might never see again.

Kip had come down from the wall and the mirror and his angry wife to walk from campfire to campfire, clapping shoulders and admiring weapons and offering a ready ear. Being seen, mostly, though it meant even more to those he touched and nodded to and questioned. A hundred times, he'd raised some offered skin, but had let neither beer nor brandy nor more exotic brews beyond his lips.

A hundred times, he saw a man he barely recognized in his people's eyes, and he didn't know if he could maintain the image of that hero and yet remain himself.

"There's a sadness about you," a logistics officer in her forties said. "You got respect, wealth, position, beautiful wife, friends—whole world in your purse. What's that about?"

She was one to know sorrow. When she'd refused to hand over the location of her daughter and several of her grandchildren, the Blood Robes had burned her brewery down—after locking two of her other grandchildren inside. The daughter who'd been saved couldn't forgive her for it, so she'd left it all and joined up.

Kip met her gaze. "I want to lead as well as you all deserve, and I'm afraid I won't."

Her eyes widened briefly at his honesty, and he could see her tuck that away to share it with others later.

They would love him more for it, he knew, but that hadn't been why he said it. Somewhere, oddly, he'd displaced some essential part of his fear. He wasn't, perhaps, fully the man they thought he was, but neither was he a fraud.

It also wasn't quite the whole truth. Tonight felt like a little death; tonight was goodbye—though he couldn't tell them that. Every hour of surprise that he gained on the White King and separately on his generals at Green Haven was an hour that might mean the difference between victory and defeat. So Kip had to endure this goodbye alone, even while in the company of those he'd come to love.

He joined the fire of some river sailors and longshoremen and asked a question about some intricate knot a man was using. When he didn't understand the answer about why a particular fiber was good for a task, he asked again, and then a follow-up; he dared to do so now because he wasn't afraid of looking stupid. Even if he would never understand the things these men understood easily, it was no essential threat to him. He did other things well. He didn't have to be good at everything.

Strangely, that lack of fear of failure made failures infrequent.

When he understood and asked if that meant you would use that particular knot with these cotton ropes in this kind of application, but only use it with a hemp rope in these other ones, they seemed to think he was a genius.

For a noble anyway, one offered, testing to see how prickly he was.

He laughed, though. "I see I'm not the only bastard here!"

They lit up. It was almost too easy, with men who wanted to like you.

Then he indulged his curiosity and threw a problem at them. "So let's say I've got a stallion. Fully barded. Sixteen hands. Weighs, what, probably nineteen and a half or twenty sevens? Got a wall fifteen paces high, but straight up, sheer. We can get right to the base. What ropes and knots do I use to lift him as quickly as possible to the top of the wall? And how long does it take? Let's say I've got access to hemp ropes and cotton, much as I need. Manpower's no problem, but time is."

They peppered him with a few other questions about what other supplies they had available. Pulleys? Nets? In a minute, they'd devised and refined a plan. Their pleasure in demonstrating their mastery told Kip he was on to something he should repeat at the other fires.

"No, no, no," a young sailor piped up suddenly after they'd all agreed on their answer. "You're doing it all wrong. I can get that horse to the top of the wall in half that time. We gotta think about this like our brothers the longshoremen here. We got these standard-size boxes, right?" He held his hands out to show how big they were.

"We already talked about that," one of the longshoreman interjected. "No matter how you lash 'em together, you can't make a platform or a sling with 'em. Ain't gonna be strong enough for—"

"So first thing you do is," the young man continued, his hands still held out to box size, "you cut the horse into pieces this big—"

Both the sailors and the longshoremen busted up laughing, though the longshoremen followed it with cursing at him for his cheek.

"Watch out, boys," Kip said, standing to go. "With that kind of approach to problem solving, you might have yourselves a future officer there."

They laughed again, and he moved on, but not before he took the boy's name. A quick wit's the flower of a keen mind. The boy might be an officer yet.

After some hours, he gave in to exhaustion. He couldn't see everyone, and dawn was coming.

But as he made his excuses and said his goodbyes, he was careful not to tell anyone that he'd see them later. With where they were going, he couldn't guarantee that he would; with where he was going, he could pretty much guarantee that he wouldn't.

Chapter 43

"Some of you have felt it," Karris said. "Your leaders in the Magisterium seem, curiously, to lack confidence." She was addressing a hundred young luxiats in a regular lecture hall. She'd told the magisters she wanted to offer them encouragement in a difficult time.

Instead, what she was telling them might get them all killed, and her with them.

'I've left you a mess. I hope your strong hands will succeed where mine have failed,' Orea had told her.

Well. This was where the rot began, so this is where Karris would begin, too. At some point, the shining, idealistic faces of the young luxiats before her would become old and powerful...and compromised, and even corrupt.

She didn't have a master plan yet, but she knew that what Orholam had for her to do began here.

"It's a puzzle, isn't it?" she said. "It's as if they almost think that the life-giving Lord in whom we believe is not, perhaps, so superior to the pagans' ancestor worship and ritual orgies, and their elevation of drafters as innately more valuable than other men and women. Why are our leaders so tentative? Is it merely because they are old? What is so wrong with us? Has one day passed since High Luxiat Tawleb's execution on Orholam's Glare that you haven't asked yourself, 'How could the High Magisterium itself shelter such a person?' A murderer in league with Nabiros himself? And then we saw Pheronike—not simply serving the immortal but somehow *hosting* him. How can such things be? Why is our faith spineless? Have we nothing to offer a dark world desperate for light?"

There was still time to bail out, to offer some anodyne exhortation to be faithful and do good.

Karris hadn't brought the red folio, but everything she did now was informed by it, and by the fact that Orholam had armed her with it. Why would Orea choose Karris to succeed her? Why, out of all those smarter, holier, and more impressive in a hundred ways, would Orholam choose her to be His White now?

It could only be because Karris was a warrior. So she sometimes needed direction? Orea's letter was that much: clean up the mess, whatever the cost. Fight. Die if necessary. Inspire others to join you in that, through your example. Karris could do that.

The red volume was, damnably, missing large chunks of its text. Apparently at least one of the later recipients of the work had ignored their pledge, or considered themselves not bound by an oath they hadn't consented to.

A later pen claimed that at one point, the folio had been sealed with some sort of a will-crafting magic so that it wouldn't even open until a new White had signed her name and assented with her will to the oath. Now oath-binding was another magic forbidden, and mercifully lost.

But despite what had been erased, what remained was enough. Karris wasn't the first of the Whites after the folio had been altered, and her predecessors had been brilliant and curious and indefatigable in restoring what they could. While some had written circumspectly, others were bruisingly blunt.

Careful to use the past tense, Karris said, "My own husband, the Lord Prism, the Highest Luxiat, himself did not believe in Orholam."

Gasps went up. They looked at her as if she were sullying the dead, and her own husband, no less. These young luxiats liked her a lot, she could tell, so they were doubly aghast.

"You're shocked," she said. "So it will grieve you to learn that none of the High Magisters were shocked at all by his disbelief. In fact, I'd be surprised if his atheism *wasn't* shared by some of them. They cared little. So long as Gavin kept up the pretense of faith, they were content. He did his duty faithfully, except that he had not the faith that undergirds those duties."

If they had dared to shout her down, they would have then. It was why she had excluded the High Luxiats and their staff, not by barring them from the meeting but by pretending it was yet another informal exhortation of the kind she'd done many times before.

Indeed, she'd met with three other classes recently and given them each an uninspiring lecture. Giving the same stultifying lecture, three times, had been enough to bore the important luxiats and magisters away.

All that in order to set this up.

The sole person of any standing in the room, a Magister Jens Galden, looked ill to the point of fainting. He stood at the back, and suddenly looked as if he were uncertain if he should bolt and go summon his superiors, or if he had better stay so he could keep a record of what outrage she spoke next.

She and Quentin had not chosen these young luxiats at random. Among their number was the order of the *auditarae*—a group dedicated to the preservation of contemporary and ancient history. The auditarae's discipline involved training their memories with various tricks and a great deal of practice to a point where they could listen to a speech of half an hour and replicate it point for point, if not word for word. Others of their order were trained in a traditional short-hand, and partnered with an auditarae, so that together they could compare their recollections and notes to form an accurate representation of the speech. This was not primarily for an accurate text of the speech—skilled shorthand was more than adequate for that—instead, the auditarae wrote annotated copy akin to a musical text, noting accents, rising or falling volume, pitch, speed, obvious sarcasm, physical movements, and other verbal flourishes or delivery idiosyncrasies. These, requiring judgment calls, were more art than science, and the auditarae worked first in isolation with their partner and then often compared their results with other auditarae.

Sometimes, the close examination revealed much more than the speaker had actually intended. Some auditarae became famous for their insight, and some of these (Karris had learned from Orea Pullawr) were recruited as spies.

"There are magics deeper than chromaturgy, and truths dangerous to tell. There are truths about the Chromeria and about the world that we have held from you. But hard truths buried in the soil of a lust for power become poisonous secrets. We've enforced ignorance, and allowed conjecture. We—your leaders, the Spectrum, and the High Magisterium—have nodded along, as incorrect suppositions hardened into tradition and tradition aged into doctrine. We told ourselves that the risk was too great. We asked: what was worse, a small body of lies, or letting dangerous powers free into the hands of any madman who might use them to harm the most vulnerable, or to harm us? If people learned the truth and rejected what we had done, we would surely lose power—and we thought that none could use power so well as we could. We told ourselves the lie that we were indispensable, that Orholam couldn't work without us, and thus we couldn't possibly let ourselves look bad.

"So we lied. Tell me, when has Orholam been a liar? Then how dare we lie for Him? How dare we say we do His work when we deceive our friends, and disciples, and flocks?" She laid a folio open flat on the podium. "This comes from the pen of the White Justinia Brook, two hundred and twelve years ago, in an address solely to the Whites who would follow her, like me: 'We have successfully, it seems, destroyed all knowledge of how to craft black luxin. This is a victory so profound that it cannot be overstated, nor likely ever understood, simply because of the nature of the victory. In the coming years it will be your duty, my fellow Whites, to relegate black luxin to myth. Of course, we've not stamped out the knowledge from the 283 oral storytelling cultures, but even those sources may be attacked and marginalized, even carefully corrupted. Let no books be written anew from their memories, and knowledge of the black may die out entirely. This, perforce, also means knowledge of white luxin will shrink. We have crafted as many of the Knives of Surrender as has been practical. I need not tell you how you must value each of these! If we lose them all, we will no longer be able to make Prisms, nor indeed, fight the *elohim* when they return.' "

The lecture hall had gone dead quiet. Everyone knew what they were hearing was dangerous. Everyone expected some adult to come along and stop it. But not a one of these young scholars wanted to leave. Prayerfully handpicked by Quentin, these were the intellectual cream of the luxiats. They lived to learn, and longed to teach.

She went on. "Then this comes from the White Orea Pullawr, my dear mentor, writing not quite two decades ago: 'Orholam save us. Black luxin has been rediscovered. Dazen Guile has drafted so much of it he nearly split the world at the Tyrean battlefield called Sundered Rock. I'd known black luxin could have some effect on memory. This drafting obliterated everything that happened in the entire battle from the memories of men within many leagues. All of them are, even now, reconstructing their own versions of the battle to explain the gaps in their memory, believing they've lost nothing. I've spread official accounts already, but with the loss of the Blinding Knife—the last of the old Knives of Surrender—I fear an apocalypse is upon us. I fear that the old gods are loosed upon us in judgment of our many sins. We know black luxin once more. We cannot survive unless we also rediscover white.' "

The hall was deathly silent. Some even of the young auditarae had forgotten to write down her words, mouths hanging open. Jens Galden was rooted to place. Even from this distance, the whites of his eyes showed round against his deep-olive skin.

"I am your White," Karris said. "And though you are not entitled to every truth from me, I will not lie to you. In white there is no room for darkness. White may become tainted—I shall fail—but when I do, I shall not hide the stain. I shall expose the truth, no matter how painful, and pay the penalty. This is what I pledge to do, because this is what the Chromeria should do. We are not called to perfection; we are called to correction. When we slip from the path, we will return to it. When we offend, we beg pardon and pay restitution. We do not call the crooked straight. Our courage is the courage to stand in the light, and to learn to love it.

"In this room, with this company, you may ask me any question you wish without fear of reprisal—and, auditarae, without attribution of the name of the questioner, thank you?"

The auditarae shared looks, and nodded, some vigorously, immediately, while others seemed more torn, but finally assented. She waited until they all agreed.

She said, "Now ask, and I will answer you."

No one spoke for a few moments. She saw some of them glancing at the older luxiat, who looked like he was halfway to wanting to know all the answers himself, but was more scandalized by Karris's betrayal of tradition.

"The gods!" someone yelled, not standing up, not asking to be recognized by her first, and not wanting to be recognized by Jens Galden. "Tell us about the elohim!"

Among the luxiats, there was a lot of debate about the gods. If they were purely fictitious or real; and if real, what was their nature, their connection to luxins, and to the old worship. Despite the pagans' rebellion, it was still a taboo subject, for the Magisterium feared even speaking of the gods might seduce the simpleminded to worship them once more.

Fertility cults? Orgies? Surely the simple would rush to their damnation at the mere rumor.

Of course, the appearance of Nabiros during Pheronike's execution on Orholam's Glare had made many luxiats ignore the old taboo. What were they to make of that? Had it been mass hysteria? An orange hex delusion? Could it have been *real*?

"The old gods are real," Karris said bluntly. "At least two hundred immortal powers are spread out amid the Thousand Worlds, though maybe that number refers only to the greatly powerful among them. Whatever their number, they are united in wishing nothing more than to kill and destroy and corrupt what Orholam has made, for He was their king, and they hate Him. In these last years of peace, our world has been either temporarily overlooked or barred from their direct influence. As we've seen, that peace has come to an end. I believe we may see more of these elohim, ere the end of this war."

"Stop!" Jens Galden shouted. "What are you doing? Why! You'll ruin us!"

And there you've done it, she thought. You probably didn't even know half of this yourself, and yet in the minds of these young luxiats, you've just confirmed it all.

Karris didn't raise her voice. She spoke as she would have spoken to the Blackguards at a mission briefing. "We are at war. We need unity if we're to fight. If the Magisterium cannot be united in light and in truth, how can the Seven Satrapies have any hope? The light of Orholam's Glare revealed the truth to us. Go now, and quickly," she told him. "I'm sure you have reports to make."

And so he rushed from the hall, nearly weeping.

But the door had barely clanged shut when a young woman asked, "Is there no hope, then? We stand against gods."

"Hope? Of course there is hope!" Karris said, "For know this—these gods can be banished from our world. The Whites of old believe that the nature of the old 'gods'—Anat, Dagnu, Molokh, Belphegor, Atirat, Mot, and Ferrilux—has confused us because it's always meant two different things. The ancients would have easily picked up what was meant by context. As powers of the air and sky, the elohim can make themselves physical only for short times. Perhaps only minutes or hours, but certainly not months or years. So when they hunger for the pleasures of the flesh—as we sons and daughters of the earth hunger to fly—they must partner with mortals to do it: usually a drafter of great ability, often a high priest or priestess of their religion. Thus, both the mortal and immortal would get the power and adoration they crave, and the limitations of embodiment wouldn't be so irksome for the immortal.

"Together, mortal and immortal could live for ages, though it was always the immortal who ruled. But in this union, they are made vulnerable—as Nabiros was. These fell immortals enter the body through the eyes, and so do they leave through them, if they may, as their host dies or is killed. This is why our ancestors blinded enemy priests and drafters, not through cruelty—or not through cruelty alone—but to trap the immortals in a form where they could then be banished from our world forever. We can even, the Whites of old believed, banish an immortal from *all* the Thousand Worlds, if we kill one with a Blinding Knife. This, I believe, is why we've had our long peace. Lucidonius gave us a gift of drafting colors more freely than ever, but he or his circle also gave us the ability to threaten the very elohim. The foul elohim who'd so long ruled here as gods decided to hunt less dangerous quarry on other worlds—until the time was ripe, until the Knives and the knowledge of their making could be lost. No doubt they had a hand in such losses, coming here and briefly risking embodiment in order to someday win their long war. But regardless of what they orchestrated beyond our knowing, we can know this: they believe that the time for their vengeance is now."

This was greeted with stunned quiet. It had taken her time and many readings to comprehend it all herself, and longer to distill it so,

286

knowing her words would be written down and must convey all she'd learned concisely and clearly.

These luxiats were not, she knew, ones whom anyone else would have chosen to use to pass on such earth-shattering news. But that they were young and idealistic and of humble estate, and holding forbidden and vital knowledge, was exactly what would make them unstoppable.

At least if they hurried and got out of here before the High Magisters arrived to stop them.

"What are we supposed to do?" they asked. "We're nobodies."

"That is a damned lie!" she shouted instantly, and the whole room flinched at the suddenness of her hard, hot anger. "*You* are Orholam's Thousand Stars. Stretch your hands high, reaching into the last light of the waning sun. Bring light where there is darkness. Those who love the light will flock to it, and those who hate the light will reveal themselves by their fear and hatred of you. Bring unity to these realms. Give new heart to the oppressed, and hope to the despairing. Starting with yourselves. Don't cower like Magister Galden. Stand tall. You scholars, search your books fearlessly and find if what I've said here is true. Or disprove it if you can, I pray you. Learn what I haven't learned. Find any lost knowledge that may help us. You auditarae, spread word of all this. If you believe what I've told you, then join me in the fight. If any can be found who will join this war, who will aid us, bring them here. We need people of courage. We need to reinspire drafters who've lost faith and run away. We need fighters. We need white luxin. We need at least one of those lost Knives.

"I will meet with you again," she said, "if I survive so long. There are those who will wish to silence me. I will, again, answer your questions truly if I can. But I don't wish you to be caught here with me, in case the worst comes to pass. There is, as yet, no record of your names. Magister Galden will remember some of you, no doubt, but I would rather only have endangered some than let all fall into shadow while I have yet life and light. So now go, by various doors and various ways, and take the light with you. Guard it well."

They scattered, and none of the High Magisters came, so Karris's plan had worked. So far.

She was being honest now and blameless, but earlier today each of the High Magisters had found themselves called upon to answer honest needs in far parts of Big Jasper. Being honest and blameless didn't mean she had to be without cunning.

After all, she was still Karris Guile.

Chapter 44

It's amazing, the things your mind will do when you have to stay awake for many hours with a slim but distinct possibility of suddenly needing to kill someone.

Certain boredom, with a chance of murder.

Blinking, crouching in this dark corner, shaking her limbs periodically to keep them from cramping, Teia was not, she finally had to admit, a ghost.

She could not pass through walls. For one thing, she had muscles that wanted to cramp—oh, and she had a bladder, albeit a tiny one (thanks for nothing, Orholam). She also wasn't dead. Yet. (Though it seemed she was trying to change that with alarming frequency.) Really, the only way she *was* like a ghost was that she was not something any rational adult would fear.

That's a great pep talk there, T. Your army of one has a shitty commander.

Oh yeah? Well, that's a *much* better pep talk.

Bollocks. Good point. Snottily made, but correct.

Good to see I can at least win an argument with myself.

Doesn't that also mean you just *lost* an argument with yourself?

Glass half-full. And shut up.

She stared at the slum building's door impatiently. Orholam's balls, would you finish up in there already?

Teia had never gotten close enough to identify the Blackguards at the back dock who'd attended the Old Man of the Desert, but she'd *thought* one of them had a hitch to his step, a slight limp on the left side. He'd also been tall, and most likely (having been brought to the back dock to make sure that Teia didn't simply head back inside) a sub-red drafter.

How many tall sub-reds had a bit of a limp in the Blackguard?

Unfortunately, the answer was *not* 'only one.' The constantly training warrior-drafters of the Blackguard accumulated injuries like misers hoard gold, and a slight limp didn't necessarily denote a permanent injury.

But there was a Blackguard who fit the bill so perfectly Teia hoped it was him. Old guy, nearly forty, had a hitch in his step that showed up only when he was tired. Sub-red/red bichrome named Halfcock. Teia didn't know how he'd gotten the name—an Archer had told her once not to ask, and Teia hadn't been curious enough to follow the obvious lead. He was infamous for being an asshole, though, especially to Archers.

It would all be so perfect if he were her traitor that Teia was pretty damn certain he wasn't. Still. She had to start somewhere, and his little trip tonight to see his...lover? handler? had seemed not only the most obvious place to start but also the only place to start.

Tomorrow, after this didn't pan out, she'd have to head to the Chromeria and sneak down to the training yard and start looking for anyone else with a limp.

She hadn't read the folio Murder Sharp gave her. He wanted her to read it, and that was reason enough not to. He thought it was going to change her mind? What, because it would tell her the Chromeria was terrible? She knew those people. She knew how good and how bad they were.

She was up to her neck in the tar pit of evil herself, but she hadn't sunk so far as to think everyone was just as bad as everyone else. The Chromeria tried to save lives—and sure, they failed a lot. Their leadership was often venal and weak and self-indulgent, so what? They weren't malevolent. They didn't take bright young girls and turn them into remorseless assassins.

Um...in your case they kind of did, T.

To infiltrate the Order! Not for fun.

Right, and I'm sure the Order has some really good reasons, too, about why they simply *have to*—

No. Uh-uh. I'm not the smartest girl in the world, but I'm smart enough to figure this out. The bad guys? They're the ones who smile as they send you to behead a kid.

Teia was a terrible human being, but she wasn't gonna behead a kid.

Maybe it was an odd place to plant her flag of moral compunctions: she'd killed innocents already. Did the age really matter? She could choose a slave kid who'd been pressed into service at one of the technically illegal brothels that catered to such things, and free him or her from an unbearably shitty life with the point of her blade. No one would raise a complaint. Such kids were disposable.

Just like me.

Maybe that was it. Once you stop telling yourself how much you're not like your neighbor, suddenly someone murdering your neighbor takes on a different hue.

Teia'd advanced in perfect time on the path to perfect conscience-lessness, hitting every beat, every step required, a compliant partner taking the devil's hand and following the devil's lead, and dancing to his tune, whirling round and round, skirts and morals flying as she spun, the dance floor itself a vortex to oblivion.

He had his hands up her skirts already.

All she had to do was to tell herself that one more step didn't matter, that she'd come this far, and this far was too far to give up now, that she'd be throwing away all her work—all her damnation—for nothing if she didn't kill this One Last Time. What, really, was the difference between twenty-seven kills and twenty-eight?

But dancing with the devil was damning enough. She wasn't gonna get in bed with him, take his seed, and watch herself grow into another Murder Sharp.

She flexed and massaged her legs to keep them from cramping.

This waiting thing wasn't good for her. Gave her too much time to think, and she went all sideways when she thought too much. Got maudlin. Full of regrets and hypothetical questions.

What would life be like if I'd gone with the Mighty?

Yeah, like *that* one.

Oh, poor Teia. Barf.

Besides, I'm not waiting. I'm stalking. I'm not sitting around hoping for a chance to murder someone. I'm *hunting*. I'm fierce. Even a little frightening.

Not a ghost; she was more like a fox, as her old shimmercloak showed. Not that she was particularly keen of hearing nor of smell. But if you dunked her in water, she did look about as small and frightening as a squirrel.

Ergo, practically indistinguishable from a fox.

No, no, that wasn't it.

No, she was nocturnal *like a fox*.

Mmm, well, not *entirely* nocturnal. Her prey didn't go about solely in the dark, so obviously she didn't either, but she was nocturnal-y. That's when the Order always met. At night, out of the sight of Orholam's Eye, the sun.

And like a fox she was very focused. Her eyes locked onto her target and she didn't let anything distract her as she glided toward her prey on silent paws. She let nothing interfere with her missions.

Which...makes me very concerned with my nocturnal-y missions.

I'm not a fox, I'm a teenage boy.

She nearly laughed out loud despite the danger and the dark. Hell, maybe because of it. Orholam's balls, she'd actually slapped her forehead. While on a mission!

But she paid that no heed. Instead, she tried to remember exactly how she'd come to the punch line so she could tell . . .

Kip.

It was a kick in the stones.

Gavin's wasn't the only ship that had sailed, was it? Kip was *gone*, and gone in more ways than one. Gone so that even if he came back to the Jaspers, he could never come back to Teia.

Enough! Come on, she wished she could tell any of the Mighty. Ben would laugh. Ferkudi would bray—when he got it in a week or so. Big Leo would grin despite himself, and Cruxer would sternly disapprove, but if she watched him, she'd see a lip twitch. But they were gone, too. Fighting, out there somewhere in the thick of it. Even if they came back, they'd come back different, suspicious, uncertain at first whether she could understand or whether she was one of *them* now—the gawkers, the people who asked you if you'd killed anyone, and how did it feel, or what the worst thing you'd seen was. But they'd warm, those boys of hers. They'd laugh, eventually, and they'd be her friends again, once they saw that she understood, once they saw that she'd waded in shit and hadn't come out clean, either.

But she had to brace herself that not all of them would come back. Worse, she had to brace herself that one or more of them wouldn't come back because she hadn't been there to guard their backs, seeing what they couldn't see.

Oh, did we reschedule the pity party? And I showed up without my hankie!

Teia huffed. She wondered if she should start chewing khat to help her keep focused.

You know what? Fuck the Mighty and all this crybaby shit, she just wanted a friend to be able to tell a dirty joke to.

She'd settle for having any friend at all.

T! Are you *serious* with this?

She cursed to herself until the long string of images of unlikely transpositions of body parts distracted her. She went through her lists again, checking the corners of the dead-end alley, the roofs, her own packed paryl, the time, the moisture on cobbles. She really wanted to take out her frustration with herself on this asshole. If he would show up, please.

This was the poorest end of a working neighborhood. The house he'd disappeared into was small and dingy. It had been created by slapping up two walls to connect the stronger walls of two large estates where they pinched together. The rich had long ago left this section of Overhill, and the estates on both sides had been diced up into dozens of homes, but they'd incorporated those walls, making this first a blind alley and then a section of street unclaimed by anyone.

It was illegal to block the rays of the Thousand Stars. Set at all the larger intersections, their light was supposed to be able to reach any part of the city, with radial streets like a spiderweb. Only the very rich and the very poor defied the law and got away with it.

The doubly blind alley meant that whoever lived in the house where Halfcock had disappeared had to enter from the opposite side of Northeast Circle Street, under the eyes of whatever guards might be atop the wall. Halfcock had instead used a ladder to climb onto the roofs of the bordering estate, and then down into the alley.

He really didn't want anyone to know he was here. Teia had no ladder, but since she'd assassinated the Nuqaba, she'd become a fearless climber.

No one else—except a Shadow like Teia—could follow Halfcock without being seen.

He might, of course, leave by the front door, in which case her waiting was for nothing. But if not, he'd isolated himself very, very effectively. There weren't even windows along the walls here.

He wasn't married, so he wasn't here meeting his wife. It was too late now for the woman Teia'd glimpsed through the briefly open door to be Halfcock's sister—unless he was simply staying the night, in which case Teia was wasting her time. He'd been there too long for it to be a prostitute, though Teia supposed some men might take half the night. All night even?

She wasn't really sure how all that worked, but somehow she'd assumed it was a business generally more concerned with pumping out a large volume of satisfied customers quickly than...

Hmm, there was a dirty joke in there somewhere.

Where was Ben-hadad when you needed him?

Anyway, so that left it being one of two things. Halfcock had a mistress. If so, it had to be someone forbidden. Blackguards were allowed fornication, but could be stripped of their rank for adultery, because that was a breach of faith. If a person couldn't keep their wedding vows, how could you trust them to keep the more difficult vows of Blackguard duty? Also, it opened them to blackmail. But sexual relationships weren't banned for single Blackguards—only sexual relations with other Blackguards, or married people, or foreign agents.

Aha, got it! Punchline!

Prostitution was a business generally more concerned with pumping out a large volume of satisfied customers rather than pumping a large volume out of one satisfied customer.

She filed that one away too, for no one. Prostitution wasn't terribly likely to come up in everyday conversation, unless you're in a squad for long periods of time with sexually frustrated young men.

Why was her mind going to all these things, anyway? She really needed a boyfriend, didn't she?

Yeah, T. What you really need is someone close enough to dig into your personal affairs.

I don't *have* personal affairs. That's why I need to get some.

We both know that 'getting some' isn't going to happen.

Oh, hells. *That's* what's going on. I'm at the new moon of my cycle. Just popped out an egg. That would explain why I've been damper than an Abornean pearl diver short of his quota on tax day.

Two regular moons in a row. She'd definitely not been training hard enough.

It also meant that finding a quick lay was out of the question. She would be super fertile right now. She had enough problems without adding any of *that*.

Right, because me and 'casual sex partner' usually go so well together.

The mission, T. Think about the mission.

Halfcock was one of the oldest Blackguards, a tall withered whip of a man who was an artist with dual short spears, but not well liked. Apparently, for a long time, he'd loved to regale everyone—regardless of their disinterest—with how he'd gotten that Blackguard name. He also loved to give definitive proof that it was not for the reason most would guess first—especially to women. The Archers were no strangers to seeing their brother Blackguards naked, nor were they moral paragons above gossiping about those whose physiques they found particularly praiseworthy or risible. Prohibitions on having sex with each other mostly held in the Blackguard, but no one could stop young athletic warriors in constant close proximity from *admiring* one another.

What Halfcock did was different. He looked for any excuse to pull it out, either to intimidate or to impress.

Once, Samite had shared a night guard posting with him alone. She said he'd done it again, and that when she made her total lack of admiration clear, he'd prodded her with it.

So Samite broke his jaw.

Unfortunately, then he'd thrashed her, despite the jaw.

He'd always been a hell of a fighter, and still was, despite his age.

No one else had witnessed the fight, and their stories of what had happened seemed to bear no relation to each other's, so he hadn't been drummed out of the Blackguard. Instead they'd both been punished for fighting each other while on duty.

That had been before Commander Ironfist's time, and since then, Halfcock hadn't given him enough reason to kick him out.

But everyone had believed Samite. Quietly, both the men and the women of the Blackguard made sure Halfcock never shared duty alone with an Archer ever again. The men took turns as his partner, like it was a burden no one should have to bear for too long. He was never promoted from the lowest ranks, and the watch captains gave him all the worst postings.

After Ironfist became the commander, he'd told Halfcock he would be allowed to retire early but with full benefits.

He refused to quit. Early retirement, normal retirement, late retirement—he refused each in turn. He was just a tough, stubborn son of a bitch all the way through.

There was nothing wrong with his skills, though. Sometimes at training, Teia would think he was mentally undressing her, so unrelenting and awkward was his gaze. Then he'd correct the position of her heel and tell her to turn her hips a fraction this way for a kick, and she'd feel the difference in the power instantly.

It had almost made her reappraise her own inherited hatred of him. But then, when she did it right the next time, he'd say, 'Better. But you're small and weak. You'll always be one of the worst Blackguards.'

With shooting muskets and drafting he was similarly skilled. He almost made a great trainer even as his own physical skills declined with age.

If he could have been trusted, he'd be exactly the type of person the Blackguard needed more of. Older warriors gave them continuity, which they desperately lacked. They'd seen it all, and done half of it, and knew how to fix what was wrong. People like that kept young Blackguards alive; they sharpened them and instilled tradition and pride in the whole corps.

Teia had fully absorbed the Archers' institutional disgust for Halfcock, but she wasn't *certain* that he deserved to die.

Him being an Order traitor would make sense of why he'd never retired, though. It had to be very difficult for the Order to get a man inside the Blackguard. Once they did, they wouldn't want him to retire. No, they would demand he draft as little as possible so that he could live and be in place as long as possible.

It made sense. It all pointed to Halfcock being in the Order. But a death sentence required a little more than suspicion.

It doesn't have to, T. You can kill anyone you want. You can kill anyone you want and get away with it. That's what makes you scary.

Call yourself a ghost or a fox or whatever you want. Your powers are the wet dream of anyone who hates.

Orholam's fear-shrunken stonesack, that—now, *that* was a pep talk.

The door opened. It was him.

Chapter 45

"We've new reasons to fear our enemies," Kip announced to his assembled thousands. His voice was carried with magic, but he still had to shout, and thus, keep it short. "But we've also new reasons to hope. I want you to know why we're doing what we're doing this morning."

The units had been arrayed so that they could be disentangled as quickly as possible without tipping Kip's hand that he was splitting his army. Word of any vast change would inevitably get out, and Kip wanted his men to have a chance to outrun the rumors of their coming.

Kip's goal this morning was simple: he had to tell his people that he was unexpectedly abandoning them, without them feeling like he was abandoning them. This army had come together largely because of him, and now he was leaving them, and he needed to do so without destroying their morale.

"We've had good news and bad," Kip said. "The bad news? The Wight Who Calls Himself King has collected bane from all over the world. Maybe all of them. The bane immobilize drafters. Whoever faces him will do so without their drafters. The good news? Neither the Wight King nor his best soldiers will be at Green Haven. You won't be facing them."

He could see relief wash over some faces. None of the drafters wanted to face a bane—something that could turn their own magic against them—that made their bowels turn to water. By the same token, none of the soldiers wanted to face wights and Blood Robe drafters without their own drafters.

"So you might ask, 'If they aren't going to be at Green Haven, where will they be?'" Kip said. "What could be more important to them?" Kip let that sink in. He glanced at Ambassador Red Leaf, who shared the stage with him, and was maintaining a pleasantly interested expression, betrayed only by a worried tightness around his eyes: why was Kip going on about this?

Kip continued, "They're taking their best troops and all the bane to the Chromeria. The Chromeria only has a few fighters, and many drafters to protect themselves. And they don't know what's coming. You have fought against some of the Wight King's best. Now imagine barely trained tower guards fighting wights and drafters, without any drafters of their own. Imagine what happens on the Jaspers when Koios wins over those he hates most."

Many of the men and women here had seen slaughters, had heard of neighboring villages completely wiped out. There were those here who cared little for the empire. It hadn't done much to defend them, after all. Others felt they'd been let down, but still had great affection for Gavin Guile, who'd ended the Blood Wars and brought two decades of peace. But no one in this passionate people could think of another Blood Robe massacre of innocents as some abstraction.

Cries went up, angry denials that they couldn't let this happen. Curses.

Few had gotten as far as thinking of what it might mean for them.

"There is hope," Kip said. "A slender one. I've learned that the Chromeria has a weapon that can defeat the bane. But the Chromeria doesn't know it. It doesn't know how to use it. And only one man can."

There were cries of 'Luíseach!' and 'Lightbringer!'

Kip bowed his head. They'd hadn't been slow on that one at all.

Then he lifted his head. "I don't know if I'm the Lightbringer, but I know this: if I'm not, many thousands of innocents will die on the Jaspers, and the empire will fall, and the Wight King will come here next. We have one best chance to stop him—and that's this chance, now. I don't know if I'm the Lightbringer, but I know Orholam won't abandon us now. I don't know that I'm the Lightbringer—but I believe!"

As they roared, and as the cries went up again, Kip's entire form was bathed in light. It pulsed, and their awe was redoubled.

Kip hadn't done that.

Dammit, wife, he thought. *That* was what that lotion she'd insisted on him using this morning was. A Prism-on-Sun-Day trick, Kip knew. He'd heard of it, though he'd never seen it himself. Still, old tricks endure because they work.

He wondered idly how much that balm had cost, and how many soldiers he could've fed or given better armor for that doubtless-princely sum.

Kip let them roar for a moment, then lowered his hands. He

glanced back at her; she was smiling innocently, but she gave a small signal to a superviolet drafter and his shine went down to a low burn.

"That leaves us with two problems," Kip said. It still took them a moment to quiet, so he repeated. "Two problems: First, we have little time. Too little. Most of you know how slowly a full army moves versus an elite corps. If we all go, we'll arrive only in time to pick over the bones of the dead. And the weapon will be destroyed. If we all go, we might as well not go at all. Second, if we all go, we abandon Green Haven. Even without the Wight King's best men, the city will fall before we could possibly return. That is, if we all go."

Kip let it sink in. These were a people of loud emotions. It made them easy to give a speech to.

"I'm not willing," Kip said, "to abandon anyone to the Blood Robes' *mercy*. But to save Green Haven and Big Jasper—to finally, once and for all stop the Blood Robes—we have to do something we don't want to do. We have to split our forces. Only I can wield the weapon at the Chromeria. To move fast enough to get there in time, I can only take a small force with me. You say you believe in me"— "We do!" a man shouted; Kip flashed a smile—"and the first thing I'm going to do is test your belief by leaving. You could think I'm abandoning you. I wouldn't blame you. But we each have a path laid out for us, and we have to serve as best we know. I'm charging you— most of you—with saving your brothers and sisters at Green Haven. It won't be easy, but I wouldn't leave you without giving you the best chance I know to be victorious.

"May I reintroduce you to your old general and your new satrap— Satrap Ruadhán Arthur!"

Ambassador Bram Red Leaf squeaked.

Kip hadn't exactly cleared that with him first.

The moment stretched, and Kip gestured broadly, almost bowing, directing their attention to the carpet in front of the platform as if they could expect their new leader to walk out onto it at any moment.

He heard a voice from below—Sibéal Siofra—saying, "You *will* wear it, damn you!"

Kip muttered, "Any time now, Arthur. Timing is kind of import—"

The carpet exploded upward in a mass of muscle and fur and sharp teeth as Conn Arthur's giant grizzly Tallach leapt out of the hole the carpet had been concealing. Thank Orholam that Tallach didn't also snarl. Kip had specifically instructed that none of the muskets be charged this morning and that none of the archers have their quivers or any arrows at hand. Some magically appeared anyway—but no one loosed an arrow in their shock.

Tallach stood on his hind legs, and from this special harness that allowed him to stand upright with the great bear, Conn Arthur suddenly appeared, standing at the bear's head. He was dressed as they were accustomed to seeing him—as a warrior, the chief of the will-casters, first of the Night Mares—with only a crown of laurels to denote his new position as Satrap of Blood Forest.

The acclaim was thunderous. Conn Arthur's—and Tallach's—absence had been felt keenly. This people loved him. If Kip was the Lightbringer, he belonged to all the satrapies—but Conn Arthur was theirs alone. He was Blood Forest, magnified, larger than life, from his red-hair-carpeted skin to his massively chiseled muscles to his giant grizzly to his huge emotions, both joy and grief and rage.

But Ambassador Red Leaf had almost recovered. Kip walked over to stand next to him, yielding the stage.

"This is not at all what we agreed," the ambassador began. Kip could tell he was working himself up to real rage. "You were to—"

"I know who you serve," Kip said.

"What are you—"

"My only question is why," Kip said quietly so they might not be overheard, "why did you turn traitor?"

"This is outrageous!" Bram hissed. He didn't shout it.

"Your lands are where Koios has been keeping his army, aren't they?" Kip said. "But it's not just land to you. It's people, isn't it? Your sister hasn't appeared in the capital in months. Nor your parents. Your son. All of them were last seen in lands that have gone dark. Hostages?"

"Nonsense. They fled long before there was any threat. They're in Varris Hollow and Glen Everry."

"So you admit there is a threat," Kip said. "Those lands are reputed to be empty."

Bram gawped.

Tallach had dropped to all fours and walked to the side of the stage, where Conn Arthur swung down easily. Still the applause continued.

"I think," Kip said, "that you aren't a traitor. Not exactly. I think you had to decide between loyalties, and you decided your loyalty to those you love came before your loyalty to a satrap you don't even respect and a cause you believed was doomed."

Bram looked at Kip, and something in him collapsed.

He nodded.

"I'm going to tell you what's going to happen," Kip said. "You're going to sign this paper. You're going to tell my wife everything you know"—Kip forestalled the man's stuttering objection—"which may be more than you think. You'll stay with Conn Arthur's—pardon

298

me—Satrap Arthur's forces for the next month. Enough time to prove it's your signature, and to make the terms binding. Then you'll be allowed to escape if you wish. In the meantime, I will send two elite units of Night Mares at speed to your family's holdings. They'll attempt to save everyone they can. I do that not because you're innocent but because they are. Your family will keep their holdings, but you will withdraw from public life and sign a full confession, which we will keep secret. If you cause more trouble, you'll be executed as the traitor you are. Deal?"

Conn Arthur came up front and center, as the ambassador's throat bobbed and his eyes blinked furiously.

"Deal," Bram said.

Before the word had faded from the air, Tisis had pushed an ink-wet quill in his hand and a parchment before him.

"What does it say?" he asked, his eyes imploring Kip.

"Does it matter?" Kip asked.

He signed it and affixed his seal.

Conn Arthur—no, High Lord Satrap Ruadhán Arthur, legitimately now—launched into a speech. He hated speeches, and hadn't known that Kip was about to make him a satrap, either, until the moment Sibéal had forced him to wear the laurel crown, so maybe it was no wonder he'd let the applause go on longer than he would have otherwise.

"Ten years ago," Satrap Arthur said, "there was a bump in the silver mines at Laurion—you know the term? It's a major collapse underground—and whenever it happens, everyone comes running to try to dig out those poor bastards who are trapped inside."

Kip's brow furrowed. He'd just used this little story this morning on Conn Arthur himself as he was convincing him to lead most of the army to Green Haven.

"To rescue their friends, the miners had to squeeze into areas that were so tight you couldn't swing a pick. So they cut half the handles off. You ever work with a tool with half the handle? Makes it exhausting, right? But it was all they could do. No choice. They had to take turns of just a few minutes. But each did what he or she could. They pulled together, and they did the job. They saved whoever could be saved. Now, on an ordinary day, you'd call a pickax with half a handle broken. You'd either throw it out or wait until it was repaired before you'd use it for work. But on that day, that broken tool was the only thing that could save lives.

"This job ain't what I want. But we got no time. So we don't get the choice of having the fight on the terms we'd like. We only get to choose if we're going to go help and save those who can be saved, or if we're going to give up. There's some days I feel broken, like I should be thrown out. Maybe you do, too. Guess what? I don't need you to be whole. I need you to be here. I need you to be willing to do what you can. Because in this fight, in this satrapy, you're exactly, exactly what I need. So will you serve?"

They shouted.

"Will you join me?"

Now they shouted again, louder. For a guy who said he didn't know how to give a speech, Satrap Arthur wasn't mucking it up too badly. He drew his sword.

"Will you fight?!" Arthur demanded, and he thrust the sword at the sky.

Weapons raised, they roared together, and Tallach roared with them, and it was a sound that shook the heavens.

A minute later, General Antonius took the platform, and began splitting the joyful army, the men bragging to one another about how they were going to plant their regimental flags in various unlikely or even anatomically impossible places of the Blood Robes' anatomy. Attending to all the logistics were Tisis and Ferkudi, feeding General Antonius all the necessary details. The Great River was utterly blocked, so Kip would be heading overland with less than two thousand of his most elite Nightbringer raiders, with two horses for everyone, the fastest of the wagons, and the best gear possible. But they wouldn't be taking any Night Mares, except for whatever of the Cwn y Wawr they could reach with messages to ask to join them.

Arthur made his way over to Kip. "So," he said, "how'd it go on your end with the ambassador?"

"You did exactly what we needed," Kip said.

"That mean I'm..."

"Legitimate?" Kip asked. The word had always been bladed for him, the bastard, but now it rolled out easily. "Yes, you are. They'll need to see the treaty, of course, and there is the matter of making sure there's a satrapy to be satrap of...but, yeah."

"This is, um"—Arthur adjusted the laurel crown on his head—"really weird. With where I was just a couple days ago."

"Uh-huh," Kip said.

"Say, you had me and Tallach jump up out of a pit on purpose, didn't you? Wait. You made me climb out of a pit—literally! You bastard."

"Maybe it was just good staging for the speech," Kip said. But he smiled.

"Maybe."

"Also, I don't know how you're calling *me* a bastard. You used my story."

Arthur grinned back. "Hell, like I know how to write a speech! Anyway, something something, imitation, flattery, something?"

"I should've been way harder on you," Kip said. "But there's no worse punishment I could think of than making you a satrap. Every boring meeting you have to sit through in the future, I want you to think if maybe you should've been nicer to me."

"Yeah, thanks!" Arthur said with a rueful grin.

Orholam but it was good to have him back, and have him back with some of his old spirit animating him.

The big man said, "You know, I just thought of something. The thing about using a pickax with half a handle: it's exhausting."

"Yeah?"

"So was that your subtle way of telling me it's exhausting to work with me?" Arthur asked.

"Dammit," Kip said, "I was planning to hit you with that some *other* day when you were being a pain in the ass."

Conn Arthur laughed.

Kip thought it was the first time he'd heard the man laugh, ever. It was a magical sound.

And for the first time in a long time, Kip thought that maybe, just maybe, they were gonna be all right.

Chapter 46

Before Teia could move, Halfcock doubled back suddenly at some sound she hadn't heard. Teia froze from old instinct, though she was invisible and hadn't made a sound.

A woman in her shift came to the door to say goodbye.

Probably not a prostitute, then.

Halfcock gave the woman a kiss, on the lips.

Probably not his sister, then.

And squeezed her butt.

Teia *really* hoped it wasn't his sister.

Playfully, the woman tried to pull him back inside.

Teia looked away. She didn't want to see anything approaching tenderness. She reminded herself that it was in this woman's economic interests to feign feelings for Halfcock. A mistress is more a mummer than a lover. This woman was interested in Halfcock's coin stick, not his meat stick.

Better?

Better, that derisive part of her that reminded her too much of Murder Sharp admitted.

Teia didn't know what she'd expected, but the woman was neither very pretty nor very young, both of which were things Teia associated with kept women. But then again, maybe if this woman were very pretty or very young, she wouldn't live in this neighborhood, nor be a mistress to a man like Halfcock, who had a terrible personality and—despite his skills—wasn't wealthy. The lowest level of Blackguards were expected to be young, and their elders didn't want them to have too much money on their hands lest they be corrupted by all those vices that the poor avoided.

Or so the old ones said, as they kept the money and the vices both for themselves.

After some words about how she'd hoped he would stay all night this time, and whispered promises Teia couldn't overhear, Halfcock pulled away.

Teia had made the right choice. This wasn't—thank Orholam—a meeting of Halfcock's cell of the Order, with this dingy house a front for a secret temple.

Well, unless that woman was in on it.

No, as far as Teia had been able to learn, members of the Order were not supposed to know one another's identities or fraternize in any special way. Far simpler that she was his mistress, and he was supporting her himself, and she was innocent of his Order ties. Or she might be cheating on a husband, if this was just somewhere they met to make love, but she was still innocent of Halfcock's Order ties.

Either way, not someone Teia could kill.

The conversation dragged on, and Teia sidled closer to eavesdrop.

"...understand...retire," she said. She was turned more away, so Teia couldn't hear her as well.

"We're not doing this again," Halfcock said.

Dammit. That would have been handy.

"Come inside," the woman said. "It's practically morning anyway, and I'm freezing. I'll make you breakfast."

"Does this place even have a stove?" he asked.

"Yeah, but I, uh, couldn't get the flue open."

"Oh, using me for my muscles, I see," he said.

Please don't go back inside.

"I thought we agreed you were going to leave right after I did," Halfcock continued.

"Eliazar is gonna be out all night with his friends regardless, and probably not come home until I can't smell the liquor on him."

"But you need to be home before he is," Halfcock insisted. "Just in case."

"I don't know that I *need*—"

"We agreed to certain rules," Halfcock said sharply. "That's all that keeps us safe."

Aha! So it was a love nest. And she was a married woman, it seemed.

Halfcock, you naughty, naughty boy.

Well, his punishment is coming.

"*Safe*," she scoffed. "You act like there are spies in every alley!"

He cursed. "Promise me," he said. "You wait two minutes after I leave, then you go."

"No," she said. "I'm tired. I'm sleeping here tonight." Then she lowered her voice and said something else Teia couldn't catch.

"No," he said, and then said something else Teia couldn't hear, but he was obviously getting mad.

The mistress tugged on Halfcock's nipple through his dark tunic. "Oh? How you gonna make me . . . big man?"

He looked at the sky like a man out of all patience. "You have got to be shitting me. I asked you twenty minutes ago if you wanted to go another—and you said no!"

"You were supposed to ask again."

"You do this to me every—" He trailed off, sighing at the sky again, but this time his gaze was like one gauging the time. "I am gonna bang you like an open storm door in a tempest, woman."

She wet her lower lip, a look of erotic triumph in her sudden smirk. "Oops, look at that. I left the storm door unlatched," she said, hiking her shift up.

He rushed up the steps, and she jumped up on his hips, embracing him, kissing him. He swept her inside, neither of them shutting the door in their haste.

Oh, for fuck's sake!

Yes, I think it's exactly for that, T.

She sat down, sighing. Everyone's got a love life but me. Is everyone getting that much action, or am I just unlucky enough to go out exactly when everyone else is getting lucky?

She stood. Not even a pity party was going to keep her awake if she kept resting.

Instead, she went to the door. Glanced inside.

Halfcock had his lover standing pinned against a wall, her legs around his waist, bouncing her against him as if she weren't nearly as big as he was. Impressive.

The look of rapture and the delighted gasps from the woman took Teia aback. For some reason she couldn't have articulated, she'd imagined that really amazing sex was reserved for the young and good-looking. Neither partner here was either.

Huh. Well, go to it, you two. Good for you.

I guess.

She looked beyond them. There wasn't much to the space. There was only a single room. A feather bed made neatly after the night's diversions (admirable Blackguard discipline there), towels, chamber pot, a stove with a bit of kindling and firewood stacked beside it. A thick lock and a bar on the front door, and presumably on the back as well, though Teia couldn't see that. The bed was the closest thing to a luxury; apparently Halfcock saved up for what he really valued.

Love nest indeed.

With loud primal grunts and a sudden alarming squeal, Halfcock finished.

His lover buried her face in his neck, clinging to his shoulders, urging him on. "Don't you dare, uh, stop. Don't you—"

Surprisingly, he didn't, and in half a minute, she cried out, spasming and pushing off the wall. With his trousers around his ankles, he staggered and stumbled, barely making it to the bed before they fell.

He dissolved laughing, and a few moments later, after she regained her breath, she joined him. She kissed his sweaty forehead over and over.

They're so goddam *happy*.

Great sex? That was one thing. Like, yeah, good for them. One last blast before dying. Let the man have his pleasures.

But joyous companionship?

Teia felt a purple bruise of bitterness that she hadn't even been aware of, like they'd just kicked it. It was ugly, ugly of her to hate them, but she did. Suddenly, intensely.

She wanted to hurt him.

This is no good, T. You need to expel this poison.

I chose this path. Dumbass that I am, I chose this.

Halfcock rolled off his lover, and Teia saw the reason the slattern had been gasping. The Blackguard's flag was only flying at half mast now, and Teia saw the full extent of the sarcasm behind his name.

Sure, a woman's body can stretch. We give birth, after all. But I can't imagine that even a woman who spoke with the fuzzy nostalgia of the 'ultimate feminine beauty' of pushing a baby into the light would want that kind of experience *every time she made love.*

And yet, hierovagus over there lay basking in juicy cetacean satiety.

She gazed at Halfcock with unabashed adoration.

"I don't want to keep hiding us," she said. "My son should know—"

He froze, trousers half-laced. Then he finished angrily. "Get the hell out. We're not talking about this again. I'm gonna be late for duty as is."

"Don't be angry with—"

"The hell I won't!" he said. "I can't *believe* you."

"Next week?" she asked, not moving from the bed.

"Up!" he said. "You're leaving first. You cannot sleep here. You gotta get back. Gimme your key. Eliazar can't—"

"You'll be here, though? Next week?" she asked.

He sighed. "Yes. Now, would you hurry?"

"And we'll talk?" she asked, getting up and pulling her dress over her head.

"Yes, yes!" he said.

She got dressed and pulled on a cloak as he dressed, too. He glanced toward the open back door, which they had never taken notice of all this time, and slammed it in Teia's face.

It scared her, though she knew she was invisible.

She heard no more raised voices, and two minutes later, the door opened again. She saw that the lanterns were extinguished in the room behind Halfcock, the front door barred, the folded blankets stacked, and the bedcovers pristine once more. He'd made his lover leave first, then cleaned up. The man might be in a hurry, but he simply *couldn't* leave a mess.

Too long living in a barracks does things to you.

The paryl was ready. Teia was ready. Through the velvet pistol bag at Halfcock's right hip, her paryl revealed the exact forward tilt of its grip. A scabbarded short sword was on his left hip.

She'd have to be quick.

Halfcock turned to close and lock the door, key in hand.

Before the door swung shut, she launched herself at the big Blackguard. With fingers of paryl, she enervated both of his knees just before she slammed a shoulder into the small of his back.

She drove his face and body into the door, her hands snatching at the pistol and the short sword.

Her timing was flawless.

305

Halfcock slammed through the door, smacking his face against the rough wood and careening to the ground inside.

His falling made the pistol bag and the scabbard both pull hard in her grasp, but Teia held on to both of them. She flicked them out behind her into the street. No time to examine the workings or check the load of an unfamiliar pistol, and her shoulder and face were throbbing from where she'd hit the big man. What was he, made of solid rock?

She kept her feet, though, which kept her clear of him. That and disarming him made it a victory, despite the fact that the collision had stunned her, too.

Halfcock's reflexes were better than she'd hoped, though. A lesser man would have been immobilized. Instead, he tried to launch himself up to his feet a moment before Teia could get a paryl grip on his spine.

His legs below the knee didn't obey him, and he fell again, farther into his house.

She flicked a kick at his neck.

It caught him mostly across his jaw instead. He rolled with the blow, his legs jamming against the doorframe, and the motion broke the paryl crystals paralyzing his knees.

Teia hesitated. On the long list of things she didn't want right now, getting stuck in an enclosed space with a bigger and stronger fighter was pretty high up. But she couldn't get the angle to get at his spine from here.

The advantages of being inside the little house—where they wouldn't be heard or interrupted—were only advantages if he was paralyzed. Her invisibility was far less helpful in a tight space, where she could be trapped.

But she had to attack or he'd escape and regroup.

She dodged in, kicking, just as he rolled head over heels farther into the house. She was aiming to stab the point of her boot into his kidney, but only half caught him.

He rolled, and rolled again—holy hells, he was fast!

In an instant, he was up on his feet, guarding his pained kidney, gasping, grunting.

He looked around, saw nothing. Maybe he didn't realize she was invisible yet. He circled quickly, hands up in a guard, trying to get a view out the door, where he assumed his attacker was.

The unexpected motions of his guard broke the reaching tendrils of Teia's solidifying paryl once again.

Chills shot down her back. She was good at fighting now. She was good at using paryl. She was getting good at using invisibility with the master cloak and even maintaining the fragile paryl cloud around it. But doing them all at the same time?

She was like a marksman also skilled at fencing and grappling, to whom someone had just handed two swords, a musket, and a brace of pistols and plopped her ten paces from a charging spearman. She had so many options to take down the threat, she was going to stand there with her hands full, choosing, until she got skewered.

Halfcock leapt, diving, rolling for the door.

She slashed with the knife she didn't even realize she'd drawn. It caught something as he went past, but he popped to his feet. He swept the door closed with a bang, flipped the bar down across it with one hand, and grabbed a blade mounted above it in quick succession.

With the closing of the door, it was suddenly pitch-black inside the single-room house.

It wasn't the boon it usually would be. Halfcock was a sub-red. Which meant—

Teia checked her paryl cloud, throwing back up the edges that had dissipated in the violence. She didn't make a shell anymore. She'd gotten better than that. A shell was easier, but fragile; anything could break it, and when it went, she lost all the paryl inside it too.

With one eye dilated to paryl and one merely to sub-red, she could see Halfcock's puzzlement. His eyes were dilated to sub-red, but he couldn't see her.

But Halfcock wasn't a thinker. He was already moving, circling, back against the wall, only out far enough to give his blade space. He spun his blade in an ascending flower.

Flowers looked impressive, but were terrible moves if you were actually fighting. Terrible, that is, unless you were fighting against someone you couldn't see and you hoped to hit their body by simply covering as much space as possible with your blade in the least time possible.

Intentional or not, that blurring steel, white in her paryl vision, was also a perfect shield against her paryl attacks.

She circled opposite him, keeping low and quiet. He was bleeding from her earlier slash, warmth throbbing bright in the sub-red spectrum down his back. It didn't look like enough to make him faint soon, though.

His jaw was tight. He was pretty sure that she was still in the room with him, but who could hide from sub-red?

Frustrated, he brought down a descending flower. Spinning a blade in a flower put his hands momentarily in predictable places, and Teia was ready. She grabbed hard for the nerves in his wrists.

The blade escaped from his enervated grip, but by terrible luck it flew right at Teia. It was twisting, sideways, impossible to judge exactly—she blocked with her own short blade, intercepting the blade, but the twisting hilt slapped around into her shoulder.

Harmless. Not even a cut. Flat of the blade.

It didn't hurt her at all—but it destroyed the paryl cloud, and cost her a full precious second—and her paryl grip on his wrists.

Halfcock lost the blade and as his eyes naturally followed it, he saw heat bloom, the whisper of a figure.

He charged, instantly.

One moment Teia was disengaging from a flying blade, stepping aside, up onto the stuffed feather mattress she'd been avoiding, trying to recover her stance, and the next her entire view was blotted out by a charging warrior three times her size.

Her foot slipped, but she didn't fall.

Luckier if she had.

She was crushed against the wall.

It drove the wind from her and smacked her neck against a wooden beam in the wall.

They dropped to the bed together. She had only mind to grope for her dagger. But it was gone.

Halfcock had driven his shoulder into her guts, but his face had met the wall with almost as much force.

She looked, hoping to see her dagger sticking out of him some-where, but it was nowhere to be seen. She tried to roll free, but his hip was on top of her shin, trapping her.

Levering her other foot against him, and arching her back to press against the wall, she tried to push his weight off her leg.

He rolled with it suddenly, surprising her and snatching her leg with a hand. It sent her flipping over him. She was obviously lighter than he'd expected.

He threw a punch at her leg, but missed. Catching a glimpse of his face, she saw the collision with the wall had made him tighten his eyes from sub-red back to the visible spectra. In the dark, he was momentarily blind.

But vision wasn't nearly as important when grappling.

She threw a knee into his face, and teeth and blood exploded every-where.

He roared, falling back on the bed, but the motherfucker did *not* let go of her leg.

Using her trapped foot to brace herself as if she were doing a great sit-up, Teia levered herself upright. She kicked at his kidney, once, twice. He blocked, blocked, trapped her right foot hard against his side, under his arm against his ribs again, and rolled to fling her over him.

But she'd been expecting it.

As he rolled, it freed her foot from the ground, allowing her to spin. She pulled herself down toward him with her trapped left leg, and jump-stomped on his head with her right.

He lost his grip, and she tumbled across the room away from him. This time she rolled to her feet first.

He shook his head like an enraged bull, snot and sweat and blood and bits of broken teeth streaming from him. He reached one hand out toward the wall, perhaps to steady himself, even as his eyes flared back to sub-red.

Where was all the paryl she'd packed? Had she lost it all?

Then Halfcock plucked Teia's dagger from where it had been buried in the wall, unseen by her, and his face filled with grim triumph as he saw the warm glow of her small figure against the dark cold.

He crouched to pounce—and dropped like a sack of slops before the pigs as Teia's last paryl pinched his spine.

She sealed the crystal—important to hold the paryl open while the target dropped, so they don't break the crystal with their fall. Then she turned her back and limped to the door. She opened it, trying to appear careless, but attuned to any sound in case she'd screwed up anything else.

Fresh, cold, alien paryl filled her lungs. It was power. It was life.

Life was good. Better than the alternative, today. She filled herself full of her monochrome power, then closed the door again. Barred it.

"So, Halfcock," she said, "let's talk about the Order."

Chapter 47

"We're missing something," Karris said as Andross approached her at her morning forms, and the sweat dripped from her trembling shoulders. But she kept her voice level. The exercise was making her mind sharp once more. "Something that may cost us the war."

"It's so nice to see you taking a break from our labors, daughter," Andross said, as if the Blackguard training yard were his home, not hers. "Grinwoody was just worrying for your health, wondering if you were pregnant. The weight gain, you understand."

That shot a bolt of fury through her. She almost lost her balance.

She could hear the smile in his voice. "Naturally, I punished him for such impudence. But I'm so glad to see you returning to the sweat and grime you rose from, like a flame eagle rising from the ashes of its old home—oh dear, pardon, that came out all muddled. I didn't mean to mention ashes to a White Oak."

She continued the form. Breath in, foot held above waist height, imagine a smug face for the next strike. She snapped it out, then held the position perfectly.

"I'm beginning to worry about *your* health, father," Karris said. Don't say it, Karris. "I know it's not age. You're very sharp for your advanced years. But you seem irritable, pissy... are you premenstrual perhaps? I know a good masseuse."

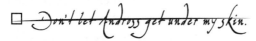

☐ Don't let Andross get under my skin.

"Oh, I know you do," Andross said. His voice was ice. "Rhoda works for me, you know. Has a lovely way of turning your neck just so, doesn't she? Just shy of where you worry it'll break. Hmm."

And now her fury stilled. The threat chilled her.

It was pure Andross Guile to try to drive a wedge between Karris and anyone who brought her joy. But as she thought about it, she had a hard time believing Andross would tolerate Rhoda's insouciant flamboyance, or Rhoda Andross's icy disapproval. No, Andross was simply aware that the woman worked for Karris, and was trying to make her paranoid.

Karris stopped the form and walked to a hook where her public-appropriate clothes hung, and patted herself with a towel. There were no servants here to fetch her things. Even Andross had come without a slave, leaving Grinwoody behind in an unusual display of respect: the promachos knew how the man's presence infuriated the Blackguards.

Karris pulled the loose tunic over her head, then called over to Samite, who was leading the exercise, "I'll make it up tonight. Twice as hard."

Samite nodded sharply amid her own forms. Her own face was beaded with sweat, not from the exertion but from the concentration. Oddly, the loss of most of her hand sometimes threw off her balance, and she wouldn't let herself falter.

Karris loved these people. They'd risked so much for her, in the past and now, too. They were helping her reconnect with herself, find her purpose.

And still Andross didn't ask about what she thought they were missing that would cost them the war. Didn't seem to care. Perhaps didn't respect her enough to even remember, much less to ask.

Fine. Be that as it may, regardless of who he is, I am called to be who *I* am.

☐ *No games. No fucking games.*

"I'm sorry, Promachos," Karris said. "I was out of line. What may I do to make it up to you?"

His eyebrows twitched up. He took off his lightly tinted spectacles that he wore in the darker hours, and squinted at her, pulling a darker pair from his pocket as the sunlight dawned over the wall and onto the topside yard—the lower areas having been yielded to the many hundreds of less experienced drafters needing training in the martial arts. But as Andross squinted at her, the light struck his face full, and Karris thought she glimpsed a cornucopia of colors in them. Red and the sparking of sub-red, of course, but also orange, and yellow, a hint of green? But Karris was certain that Andross's arc of colors only went from sub-red to yellow.

Odd, but maybe it was a reflection or natural coloration she'd never noticed. "It's your son," he said, putting on his dark spectacles. "You're ignoring him. He's come to me to complain about it."

"I'm too busy," Karris said. Zymun. Ugh.

"Yes, I see that." He said it as if her work here was worthless play.

"I've invited him to join me here. And at other occasions. Events. Duties."

"But never at dinners anymore," Andross said. "Or to your solar. Or your study. Or anywhere alone. So he says."

No games, Karris.

She took a deep breath. "He...touches me in ways he shouldn't."

"Ways he shouldn't?"

"You wish me to be explicit?" Karris asked.

"I wouldn't ask for clarification if I didn't want it."

"He touches me in ways that are sexual but that might be construed not to be. Kisses my lips, as a son might, maybe, but for too long, too softly. Wants to nuzzle my neck. Grazes my breasts. Wants to put his head in my lap. Trails his hands up and down my thigh, though I ask him to stop. *Sniffs* while he's there, as if he expects me to be aroused by it."

311

"That's enough." The disgust on Andross's face was stark. Apparently some things were out of bounds even for him. Marvel of marvels.

"Then he begs me not to reject him. Tells me how much it hurts that his own mother would push him away. This, as he strokes the small of my back."

"Enough. Enough!" He rubbed the bridge of his nose, then said quietly, "Shit."

"You knew he was like this," Karris said, heat rising in her.

"Lots of men bother the slave girls and pressure the servants. I'd hoped the endless stream of women happy to climb into his bed would sate his *appetites*."

"His is not an appetite for sex."

"Yes, thank you. I see that now."

"I won't allow him to be alone with me again," Karris said.

"You'll do what you damn well need to!" Andross said.

"I won't let him be alone with me again," Karris repeated calmly. "Nor any of my people. And if anyone is found willing to testify against him, he will be brought up on charges."

"This is why you put out that missive to the servants?"

"You know about that?" Karris asked.

"I thought you were trying to find the rumors so that you could silence them before they cause us embarrassment."

"Then you thought exactly the opposite of the truth," Karris said.

"No one's going to come forward," Andross said. "They never do. You're his mother. I'm his grandfather."

"Don't underestimate a thirst for justice. Or the fear of the Guiles. It may lead someone to strike first. And even an allegation from a sufficient source would be enough to stop our Prism-elect from becoming Prism in truth."

"No," Andross said.

"I'm just telling you, it's a card you ought to consider in your little games. There are other, better people who would make fine Prisms."

"I have plans for him, and you will not—you will not!—destroy him. I'll find out about anyone who comes to you."

"You won't harm them." She said it with a whipcrack in her voice, and he looked at her, surprised.

"No," he said. "I'll pay them off. But carefully, in such a way that it doesn't encourage more accusations."

"Father," Karris said, and there was no mockery in her voice at using the term, which made his brow knit. "Zymun cannot become Prism. He's stupidly impulsive and rapacious already. If you put more

power into his hands..."

"I'm not an idiot," Andross sneered. "Of course he'll never be Prism. But it doesn't mean he can't be useful in the interim."

What?! "You've brought a fire into our house, and locked all the doors and chained all the gates. I hope you know what you're doing better than my brothers did, or it'll all be ashes again. This time for House Guile."

Andross pursed his lips. "You don't have to meet with him. Ever. I'll take care of it."

Surprised, she said, "Thank you." And she meant it.

It was an odd thing, to know what she knew now, from the folio. Andross surely knew all the worst parts of what she'd read. He'd surely participated in some of them, and then had hidden that knowledge from even most (or all?) of the Colors now serving. He had participated in and ordered and committed murders.

But so had Orea Pullawr.

Karris found herself unwilling to forgive her old mentor, but also unwilling to condemn her. Why was it so different with Andross? Only because he seemed to truly enjoy being hated?

Then why did it trouble her so when he partially did the right thing?

Reluctantly, Andross said, "Now, what's this about something we're missing that's going to lose us the war? Zymun? You think he's going to wreck the effort?"

"No. I mean, I'm sure he'd tear apart the Seven Satrapies eventually—but no."

"What, then?" he asked irritably. He glanced to the edge of the yard, where Grinwoody had appeared, but waited respectfully. Andross had other business to attend to.

"It's my brother."

And then something fell into place, and her skin turned to gooseflesh that had little to do with the morning's cool air. She'd thought it a hundred times: Why me, Orholam? Why would You want me as Your White? And this was the answer: he was her brother, and she was a warrior. She was the only one who could stop him.

"Your brother the Wight King, I presume, not one of the ones who are ash?"

She took a breath and closed her eyes. Just when she wanted to see him as human. "Yes, the living brother."

"I'm waiting on tenterhooks," Andross said.

"He's going to attack us," Karris said. "Here. Soon."

"I looked into those rumors. Nothing to them."

"This is not from any rumor."

"You've had words from spies? Which ones? Where?"

Karris chewed on her lip.

"What is this...?" Andross asked.

"He's my brother. I know him. I can just...feel it."

Andross's face lit with incredulity. "No, dear. You *knew* him. You've seen him one time in almost twenty years. He is not who he was before two wars and the fire that took him."

"He's my brother. And he's going to strike first, just as he tried to strike first against Dazen."

"You think he hasn't learned his lesson from how that turned out for him?" Andross asked. "He was a child then. A boy amid the temperamental gang of his brothers, who thought their sister was being taken in by Guile deceit. He's had a lot of years since then, and *everything* he's done has been smart and forward thinking. He's got supplies pouring into his forces because he didn't let his men burn the fields as they marched through; they didn't destroy the mills and the orchards. They left lambs and calves behind. He means to rule, not just conquer." Andross lowered his voice. "He can win through sheer patience, Karris. If he attacks us now? He could lose everything."

"But you're counting on him waiting. Waiting gives you time to make something else happen that he can't foresee."

"Time is on his side."

"Only if he wants to rule," Karris said. And she thought of the look in his eyes when she'd met with him, a look of hatred implacable.

Andross tilted his head. "Of course he wants to rule. I just told you what he's done to prepare—"

"To prepare for an assault on us. Koios doesn't care how many of his own people die. What if he doesn't want to rule? What if he just wants vengeance on all of us for what we've done? Regardless, it's easier for him to build his new paradise on our graves."

Andross scowled, thinking it over, but then his scowl softened, and she already knew what he was going to say. "We've no reason to believe what you're saying."

"I just *gave* you a reason," Karris said.

"Your intuition? That's not reason. That's exactly the opposite of reason; that's a feeling. A worry. You want to base our war plan on your intuition now? Well! Let's recall our spies. What a waste of time, trying to actually find things out! We can just *feel* what our enemies are going to do from now on! It'll be so much more efficient!"

"Has anyone told you recently how much of an asshole you are?"

"No. But only because they're afraid of me."

"Well, I'm not." It was actually true at the moment she said it. And this, too, felt right. Her purpose was unfolding before her with every action that was in line with the Blackguard she was and every word she spoke that was true.

"Good for you. Are you going to say it now? Will it make you feel better?"

Karris didn't take the bait, didn't call him an asshole or any of the other words that so aptly applied. She said, "I'm taking over command of the drafters' training myself. Today. I've been helping for a long time, but they're all mine now. And I'm reclaiming a fair percentage of the incomes I'd allowed you to divert from Chromeria funding. I'll be using them here to shore up the islands' defenses."

"You will not. I'll not allow it. Also, we need to have a conversation about those pet luxiats of yours. Not now, but—"

"I'm fighting alongside you, father. You ask yourself, Is your time so worthless that you can throw it away in fighting against me instead? I require less money than you might lose if a single galley with supplies were plundered on its way here from Ruthgar."

He hesitated for a moment, then nodded. "Very well, but if I let you do this, then—"

"No! This is not a trade. It's not a game. You do what you must to save the satrapies. That's exactly what I'm doing, too."

"And when Ironfist arrives? You'll do what you have to then, too?" he asked.

"Yes," she said, and she felt it to the core of her being: this, too, was true.

Andross turned to go, but then stopped. "I've been intending to give you a gift, but I'm afraid it's fallen through."

"A gift?"

"Yes. Gavin's old room slave, Marissia. I know you have…missed having her help. It turns out she didn't run away after all. She was kidnapped. I traced her to an island off the Ruthgari coast where she was imprisoned. But it turns out she escaped with the help of mercenaries or pirates. One assumes she must have been desperate indeed to throw herself on the mercies of such people, but at least they didn't murder or enslave the servants on the island, so there is some reason to hope. Unfortunately, the lord those servants believed they were serving doesn't actually exist, so I've no more leads on who took her in the first place. Anyway, I thought you'd like to know you were right about her innocence, and that she is likely still alive. Who knows, maybe she'll come back to take up her chains once more." He smiled thinly.

No, Marissia would fear she was labeled a runaway. She'd surely believe that if she returned they would sell her to some lesser house—if not to a brothel or the mines. It was unlikely she'd heard Gavin had manumitted her in his will. Even if she had, she'd still have good reasons to fear coming back.

But all this was a smokescreen, Karris knew. Andross had been the one who'd ordered Marissia's kidnapping. Not that she could tell him she knew that.

So what did this mean? It was probably half true. He'd taken Marissia off the table himself, but had meant to keep her in reserve—thus, not murder but kidnapping and imprisonment, likely on one of his own islands. But then she'd escaped.

Good for her.

Oh, Marissia, how do I let you know that I mean you no ill? I would give you back your old position as spymaster in a second! But I couldn't keep you safe.

Go, Marissia, go and find yourself a good life.

If there are any left to be found in these war-racked lands.

"I'm afraid I'll have to muddle through as best I can without her," Karris said. "Thank you for...making the effort."

He stared at her closely, first as if waiting for her to say something cutting, as if her thanks was mere setup, but then seemingly surprised it wasn't. "Again," he said, then momentarily looked as if he were waffling whether to go on. "Again I see what Gavin liked so much about you."

He's gonna say 'weakness.' He's gonna punch me in the gut with *something* next.

But Karris forced her tense muscles to relax, and the insults to lie quiet on her tongue. Even if he hit her with something awful next, she was the White. She could do this.

For just a moment, Andross's eyes sparkled as if he knew exactly what she was feeling. A smile like none she'd ever seen on his face flashed, open and roguishly knowing, utterly beguiling. It dropped another twenty years from his aspect.

Then it was gone, and he was the old Andross once more—and he turned and left without another word.

And, remarkably, that was that. She took command of the drafters, and she took the money she needed, and his people did nothing to stop her.

Well, holy shit. It worked.

 *No games. No fucking games.*

Chapter 48

"I don't know what you're talking about. What order?" Halfcock said.

But terror had splashed over his face, and it drained away too slowly for Teia to miss it.

"Is that how we're going to do this?" Teia asked. "Really?"

"What are you doing, Teia? Where did you learn to do all this?" Halfcock asked as if he weren't paralyzed on the floor, utterly helpless.

"It was a good fight," Teia said. "You didn't blink when faced with an invisible opponent. You've got balls of steel. Balls that I let you empty first, so you're welcome for that."

Halfcock swallowed.

"Seems like a nice lady," Teia said.

"Just a whore."

"Huh. Too bad, then. Just another innocent killed in this war. But one has to be certain." Teia shrugged.

Orholam have mercy, is this who I've become? Casually threatening the murder of innocents?

"You're not with them," Halfcock said, stunned. "You're hunting them!" Obviously, the only Shadows he knew of were the Order's assassins. "That's—that's—that's wonderful! They were threatening me!"

"Uh-huh."

"You have to believe me," Halfcock said. "You have to believe me! I am not in the Order. I swear by Orholam! I swear to God!"

Now we're getting somewhere. "Who's Eliazar? Husband?" Teia asked.

"Son," Halfcock said, defeated. "From her first marriage."

"First marriage?"

"*Shit*," Halfcock said. "Look, can you let me—"

"Do I look like a fool to you?"

"Aliyah's my wife," Halfcock said.

"You're not forbidden to marry," Teia said. "Why the big secret?"

"Not a secret from *us*, a secret from *them*."

"*Us*, Halfcock? It's so hard to tell what a traitor means when he uses that word. Which 'us'?"

"*Us*, us! I'm not a traitor! I mean the Blackguard. Come on! I had to keep it secret from the Order."

"Now, why would you have to keep secrets from the Order?" Teia asked.

"I never really followed them. I was waiting for the perfect moment to betray them. I could run away if it were just me. I don't have family, but Aliyah does, and I knew the Order's vengeance would be terrible. You have to believe me. I was going to redeem myself."

"Redeem yourself, huh? Now, what'd you do that requires redemption?"

"Nothing. Nothing, I swear!"

"Uh-huh."

"Please. I know you all hate me. I know I did stupid shit when I was a kid. Yeah, I was an asshole. But I was a *kid*. I've been paying for that for longer than you've been alive. You're gonna kill me for that? You want to know why they gave me the name Halfcock?"

"Not really," Teia said.

"Our trainer said I was so fast that if I were anyone else, he'd be warning them about going off half-cocked. It was a compliment. But they hated me. So they called me Halfcocked around the trainers and Halfcock everywhere else. They told every new season of recruits I had the smallest cock in the Blackguard. They shit on everything good in my life. Samite was the worst of 'em, fucking man-hating tribadist. You tell me, you think she's fast enough to hit me in the jaw if she didn't throw that punch out of the blue?"

"I don't care about any of this," Teia said. "Are you stalling?" She double-checked her crystals.

"Don't kill me over an old lie," Halfcock said.

"I won't kill you over anyone's lies but yours," Teia said. "You say you were just infiltrating the Order? Fine. Give me the names you've learned."

He blanched. "You know it's not like that—"

"I know it's not *supposed* to be like that. Everyone's supposed to keep things carefully separate. But it just doesn't work, does it? Is Aliyah in the Order too? You're not supposed to be dipping your quill in the Order's ink. That'd be enough to get you both killed. Good reason to keep things secret. Hmm?"

"No, no, no. She's got nothing to do with them!"

Teia believed him. She'd overheard the woman pressuring Halfcock to make their relationship public. If she were in the Order, she'd never have done that.

"Names!" Teia hissed.

"I've been trying for years. You have to believe me. Because I'm a Blackguard my handler made me skip all but the high holy days, so I didn't have many chances. And then... Most people are so careful, even with me."

"Even with you?" Teia echoed.

"You ever been on a high holy day? The parties afterward tend to get sexual before dawn. We're supposed to keep our faces and any identifying characteristics covered—but, well, I got popular among a certain set of the women, on account of, you know, my endowments."

"I bet you stayed late for the orgy just on the hopes of being a better spy, right?"

"That's right!" he said.

Not keen on picking up sarcasm, old Halfcock.

"So you found someone," Teia said.

"Not a name, an address. A little love nest she keeps for her affairs. She's newer, and careless, but I'm certain she's from the nobility, and nobles tend to climb the Order's ranks quickly. She wanted me to come meet her—"

And here's where you lay your trap for me, Teia thought.

"—but I never dared," Halfcock finished.

"What?" Teia asked.

"I went by the place once. That's how I know it's a safe house. No one lives there, but it's well maintained. But there was no way I was going to go inside and openly disobey the Order. I wouldn't cheat on Aliyah that way, either."

But an orgy is fair game?

The hypocrisy of the statement actually made Teia believe him a little more, though.

"You have nothing else?" Teia asked.

"Nothing," he said.

She wasn't a skilled interrogator, but by the end of her talk with Halfcock, she learned one more thing: The Order had 'something big' planned for Sun Day. That was all he knew. Or maybe not on Sun Day. Maybe before. They would find out the specifics, he guessed, at their own ritual on Sun Day Eve, which the Braxians called the Feast of the Dying Light.

She probed for more a dozen times, a dozen ways, trying to see if he knew something else, maybe without realizing it. She asked about how his handler contacted him, how he knew where the meetings were on the high holy days, and a dozen other things—but he gave her nothing that helped. The Order had morons in its ranks, but only at the bottom. Whoever was directing Halfcock had been very careful and very skillful, and Halfcock had been too stupid or afraid to notice any patterns or slipups.

But still, he'd given Teia the next step up the Order's ladder. It was just what she needed: a noblewoman who didn't like to follow the rules that had kept the Order safe. Perfect.

"If you were really going to spy on them, you'd have waited outside that safe house," Teia said. "You'd have watched and seen who walked in."

"No, no, please. I thought of that, but only after I'd hurried away. I was afraid of them. Please!"

"Oh, I know. Your fear is real enough. Even Murder Sharp is afraid of them. I'm afraid of them, too. That's why you have to die, because every time it's come down to it, you've done what they wanted. And that's what you'd do again."

"Please, I'm a loyal Blackguard."

"You're not even loyal to your wife—if you're not lying about that, too. But just so you know, I'll let her live."

"I was gonna change! Everything was gonna be different!"

"I think you might even believe that," Teia said. "But I don't."

And then she killed him.

But something went wrong. Either there was some idiosyncrasy of his spine or Teia's control wasn't as fine as she thought. Instead of paralysis, she hit some bundle of nerves that sent his entire body into racking convulsions, bucking and flailing and screaming at a pitch and intensity she'd never have guessed he would reach, or even that he could. His screams shrieked like claws jagged across the slate of your mind and lodged in some animal part that begged you to run away or huddle in a corner, rocking back and forth, face to knees, ears plugged, whimpering.

It shook Teia's cold calm a bit, to be honest.

But there was worse to come. That old cliché she'd heard? The one she'd always figured men added to their war stories to make themselves sound tough, like they were better than weaker men or that the situation they'd been through was so, so hard? That thing about grown men crying for their mothers as they die? She'd always thought, Whatever, maybe that happens once in a while, maybe. Maybe with child soldiers or boys who can barely shave, but not with a grown man. Not with a warrior. Certainly, she thought, a man tougher than old saddle leather and more bitter than vinegared wine would never stop fighting. A hardened veteran weeping, tears and snot streaming unheeded down his face, gasping, "Mama help, mama help, mama, mama, mama..."?

She'd been so sure that never happened.

Huh.

Chapter 49

The dead savaged in the lagoon behind him didn't matter. The prophet and his logorrhea had no meaning. The world beyond the mist curtain had ceased to exist. Even the city, this nameless city below the black tower, held nothing to pique his curiosity.

This had been a waystation for pilgrims, once. The whole city had been organized around the physical and spiritual preparation of those who planned to attempt the climb. At its heyday, it must have hosted thousands every day.

But Gavin paid none of it any mind.

On the central boulevard, he found great mosaics of legends and saints ancient even to the ancient peoples who had made them. The boulevard had been lined with shops, once. By the remains of their painted pictographic signs, there had been cobblers and tailors and makers of packs and torches and walking sticks and bandages and dried meats and fruits. Doubtless a street or two back had housed the whorehouses and taverns, for all those pilgrims who wished, one last time, to sample the favorite sins they'd come to leave behind. Now empty buildings stared out at him like skulls stripped of flesh and eyes.

But as every secondary tone had darkened to the chromatic blindness in Gavin's sole remaining eye, so every secondary voice in curiosity's chorus had fallen quiet in his ears. The soloist rose before him. The answer to all things lay up there. And Karris's salvation, too—if Gavin were strong enough.

He came out from the shade of two mighty overarching atasifusta trees and saw a great gate, open, flanked by two large statues. All the work of human hands stopped at the gate. Not an outbuilding lay beyond, only the trail and jungle. The statues were warriors in identical scale armor and the spears common to the Tyrean era. But their faces were curious to Gavin: one a typical Tyrean with a prominent nose and brow, perhaps woolier hair than was common in Tyrea now, but the other one had flatter features, dark hair straight as wheat, and small eyes with a monolid like no one Gavin had ever seen.

"Is this some race of the immortals? A people from beyond even the Angari?" Gavin asked. "Or is it some quirk of Tyrean art?"

Orholam shrugged. "Look over here."

There were ceremonial baths by the road, fed by a lively stream.

They drank and washed and thought of little else for a time. A   321 mosaic wall behind the stone baths depicted men and women feasting and then washing in its waters. There were among them men with such eyes as the statue had, and other races and peoples Gavin had never seen in the Seven Satrapies. Men covered with tattoos and tall women and men half-sized, like Blood Forest's pygmies, though perhaps that was simply the ancient Tyrean art's way of depicting children.

All the figures were dressed in simple robes, and looked somber as they washed.

Apparently the old Tyrean Empire had been more cosmopolitan than the Seven Satrapies, or some races of men had simply passed from the earth.

Gavin washed his body. Nothing like having salt water and sand between your butt cheeks as you started a hike that might take weeks.

No, not weeks. They didn't have that long. Karris needed him to make it before Sun Day.

By the time Gavin was finished bathing, Orholam had washed himself, and had found water skins and clothing covered with odd pockets in airtight chests sealed with luxin. By their first good luck they'd had in a long time, the skins and clothing were actually functional. Four hundred years old and yet functional?

Then again, it was hardly the most astonishing magic here, so Gavin put it out of his mind.

That magic and their luck didn't extend to finding any edible food, though. Even the food they found likewise sealed away from the damp was, after all this time, little more than dust.

The water and the salt fish would be enough for a week, though. Gavin hoped it would be enough.

It would have to be. He wasn't going to take the time to fashion weapons, hunt animals, butcher and cure meat. He didn't know if Karris had that much time. Sun Day was coming.

They ate the fish, drank, filled the water skins, and then started. Old Parian text adorned the ground just under the gate, a line reference of some sort?

Ah, a prayer. For the pilgrimage.

Orholam spoke under his breath—saying the prayer, Gavin guessed, but he wasn't curious enough to find out if the old man recognized it, or knew Old Parian at all, for that matter. This whole trip had to be like a holy wet dream for the old kook.

The path was straight as an arrow's flight through the jungle. Some sections had been displaced by roots and new growth, others washed out by mudslides. Elsewhere, entire trees had fallen over the path and melted into soil, from which had bloomed flowers. But the path was impossible to lose.

Gavin kept an eye out for animals, but saw nothing larger than mice.

They climbed the crater's rim. The ridge here descended to a circular swamp before the queer black stone itself began. The straightness of the road had only aided its own erosion. Water from any rain cascaded fast down what had once been the road and had washed away all its stone.

There was nothing for it but to try to cross the swamp while the sun was still high.

It was muddy, mucky, brutal work, first sliding down the hill trying not to turn an ankle and then crossing the ooze, hoping not to plunge into some sinkhole or quicksand.

Orholam insisted on going first, in thanks for Gavin saving his life. Gavin followed in his footsteps. They didn't speak.

Nor did they make it across the swamp before evening fell.

Gavin said, "Mosquitoes are proof that God hates us and wants us to be miserable."

"I always thought of them as a strong hint to go inside and be with friends beside the fire, and be done with the day's labors."

"You're kind of a look-on-the-bright-side guy, aren't you?" Gavin asked. "I don't really remember that about you, back on the oar." He'd always been set apart, but then he'd been quietly pious, and though kind, he'd been morose.

"Life on the oar was its own life. Everything looks bright after that darkness."

The road was ruined on the other side by erosion, and the climb was misery. It was almost dark when they reached the first white gate, beyond which began the tower path itself.

This was the first of eight such gates, Gavin thought, if there weren't others on the other side of the tower. He'd been studying the black monstrosity all day. The tower was indeed a cylinder of equal thickness from foot to head, so the long path didn't curl around the outside of the tower but rather was cut into the tower so pilgrims would have the black stone not only below them and to one side but also overhanging above them as well.

And what black stone it was.

With only one good eye, and the other only good for monochrome, Gavin had held on to a great deal of skepticism about what his initial impression of the black stone was. Surely it couldn't be obsidian. Not an entire tower of it, glittering dangerously.

Obsidian was precious beyond words. If the whole tower was actually made of it, the pilgrims of old would have made off with all of it, and obsidian would no longer be as precious as it was.

But as they stood mere paces away from it now, it could be nothing else—unless there was some kind of hex here, fooling his eye.

Orholam appeared unfazed and was washing himself at a great stone basin off to one side before the gate, again fed with fresh running water off the tower side. Either the ancients had been quite a thirsty lot or they'd been obsessed with ritual cleanliness.

There was nothing ritual, though, about Gavin cleaning the muck from his legs and clothes. Again.

As the sun set, they finally confronted the gate itself, with its own statue of an immortal beyond it. The gate was fully as wide as the trail (though he thought he might be able to climb around the outside of it). The drop here was only thirty feet. The gate was starkly white against all the light-sucking black of the tower, its pearlescence shining in the sunset (probably pink, Gavin guessed). There were three mighty locks on it, side by side. Each labeled.

"My Old Parian vocabulary is limited," Gavin said. "Any idea?"

Orholam said, "The locks are Confession, Contrition, and Satisfaction."

"Not much good as locks, are they? The keys are still in them."

"Perhaps you should be grateful that the guardians who had to abandon this place decided that their own desire to save a relic of the place holiest to them should be suborned to the possible needs of strangers living long after them to make this climb."

"Fine," Gavin said, "I'm the asshole." He turned Confession, and the lock turned as smoothly as Andross Guile pivoting to stab you in the back.

"I'm sorry," Gavin said.

He turned Contrition.

"I won't do it again. Happy?"

He turned Satisfaction, and gave his best old Gavin Guile grin—marred somewhat, no doubt, by his missing dogtooth.

Orholam said, "There's a difference between charming and winsome. You're more the latter when you're less the former, Man of Guile. Shoes."

"Excuse me?"

"Leave your shoes. We walk now on holy ground."

"Are you serious? I haven't got time for this."

"You've got all the time you need as long as your feet are touching the holy mountain."

Gavin sighed. The obsidian of the path was polished, so it wasn't like he had that as an excuse, and the old man was going to keep harping on this.

He took off his shoes and moved forward onto the path. It was wide enough here for ten abreast, and the overhanging ceiling high enough not to invoke his claustrophobia.

The open gate revealed to the left an array of stones of varying sizes, and to the right, another statue, her paint worn thin by the elements. Her head was bowed, and at her bare feet, dropped from open hands, lay a scepter.

"Behold the spirit of Humility," Orholam said. "Here, you may expiate your Pride, the foundation of all sins. Here pilgrims select a stone to carry, symbolic of their own pride."

"Well, one would hate to offend local customs," Gavin said. He started to reach for the smallest of the stones.

"Hold," Orholam said. "A word about the pilgrimage, before you make a mistake you'll regret."

"There are booby traps?" Gavin asked.

"No!" Orholam said as if it were the stupidest thing he'd ever heard. "Why would luxiats try to kill people who are seeking Orholam? You want to know what your whole problem is, Guile?"

"Not really—"

"You've always feared men where you should have feared God."

"That...is at least half true."

"Shut up!" Orholam said. "Before you begin, do consider if you really wish to undertake this pilgrimage flippantly. Here's how it works. At each level, you'll pick a burden to carry representing your sin. At the next gate, you'll trade in your burden for a small stone, commonly called a boon stone, a mark of how far you made it."

"Ah, thus the pockets!" Gavin said, pulling at one of the seven funny-shaped pockets on his ancient tunic.

"When you arrive at the top—if you do—you may present them to Orholam, as a tribute that He makes holy. Some say that for each stone you present, Orholam grants a boon. Me, I don't think Orholam's favor can be bought."

Those are two different kinds of favors, Gavin thought. But he said aloud, "So everyone gets seven favors?"

"Few, I think, got the chance to test it."

This was starting to feel like an old magisters' examination. But fine, he'd passed plenty of those, often in ways that infuriated the magisters. He could do so again.

"If I pick the wrong rock, do I not get the boon stone?" Gavin asked.

"No, but it's written," Orholam said, "that you will find the correct stone to be the lightest burden."

"So the stones know somehow?" Gavin asked. "Clever, for stones."

"You've seen greater magic. Done greater yourself."

"No, I believe it. But, well, if you have stones here that weigh a man's sins, I should like to take some home. Come in right handy when adjudicating disputes."

"You could ask Orholam for that favor, if you wish."

Gavin moved toward one of the smaller stones. "So can I try a few..."

"The first stone you touch is the stone you take, for good or ill." He put his hands on his hips. "Are you really going to try to cheat a pilgrimage?"

"No!" Gavin said. He didn't sound convincing even to his own ears.

"Consider carefully, please."

"Consider what? The stones?" Gavin asked.

"Yes, those, in a moment, but no. Consider how you wish to start on this path. Start as you intend to go. You'll reap what you're planting."

"What's this thing?" Gavin asked, spotting an odd depression carved in the inner wall. He poked his head in. It looked like a chute, such as certain waterfalls carve. But—unfortunately—it was far too steep, slippery, and wide for him to climb directly. If he were hoping for a shortcut, he might as well simply scale the sheer walls of the tower instead.

"Lest you fear that hiking so burdened will slow you too much, know that this is where the celestial realms overlap the mundane. Time works differently here. Your first attempt will take less than two weeks, though here it will feel like only days have passed, so you'll finish by Sun Day, if you aren't too much of a sluggard. That's considered the most blessed day possible, naturally. You're highly favored to even have the chance."

"I feel real lucky," Gavin said.

"Your second attempt will feel like it takes the same amount of time, but during the attempt a year will pass. During the third, a decade."

"You get multiple chances?"

"Some people refuse to learn easy lessons, even repeated ones, yet still don't give up."

"Fools, you mean," Gavin said.

Orholam raised his eyebrows as if Gavin saying this was a bit rich.

But instead of the stern rebuke Gavin had expected, Orholam said, "Gentleness suits you better. I know you're not without it."

For some reason, it quieted Gavin. He wanted to mock all this, all this holiness that had spilled rivers of blood. He wanted to punish Orholam for all the bitterness in his own heart. But Gavin had to climb regardless.

What if he climbed and failed, then had to worry that it had been his failure, not anyone else's? Taking it seriously wouldn't cost him much of anything except his own sanctimonious attitude—and it might gain Karris her life.

Whether Orholam Himself or a nexus of magic awaited Gavin at the top of this climb, he had to get there in order to find out. Everything might depend on him taking this seriously.

Grinwoody had said Gavin had to kill the magical nexus called Orholam by Sun Day or Karris would die. How would the Old Man of the Desert even know?

But actually, if Gavin killed all magic in the world, then everyone everywhere would know it right away.

"Woo!" he said. "Let's expiate us some sins!" But though his tone was light, his heart was not.

Orholam didn't reprimand him.

Gavin moved to the biggest stone. He was pretty much filled to the brim with Pride.

The rock, though, was nearly as big as his own torso. There was no way he could carry that thing. He itched at his eye patch.

Well, I'm not the *most* arrogant person I know. Maybe I should grade myself against the people in my set. After all, my father is far more arrogant than I am. So…

He picked up the second largest stone. It was heavy as death. He grunted.

"You have to be kidding!" he said, straining.

"Let's go," Orholam said.

"One moment," Gavin said. He nudged the biggest stone to test its weight.

It rolled easily under his foot.

Shit.

Chapter 50

"Lord Luíseach," one of the new Mighty, Einin, said with a heavy accent as she entered Kip's dusty command tent. "The Cwn y Wawr captured a man on the road. Claims to be a messenger." Every one of the Mighty was extraordinary, but Einin stood out.

A huntress married to a farmer from some close-knit community far in the highlands, she was thirty years old (ancient compared to the rest of the Mighty), had borne ten children in her fourteen years of marriage, and had left her eight surviving children in her husband's care to come fight as soon as she heard about the White King's invasion. She'd found that her natural affinity for animals stemmed from a previously unknown ability to draft orange, red, and sub-red. Though she'd failed the requisite tests of strength four times, her speed, marksmanship, astonishingly keen intuition, and intellect had won her a place with the Mighty. Cruxer said the woman also had the pain tolerance of... well, a woman who'd borne ten children and claimed to enjoy the experience.

Kip had once idly asked her how she managed to go hunting when she'd had young children and her husband himself was out in the fields, before realizing that was how a close-knit community works. But she'd said instead, 'Some women thrive when they can be with their brats all day. Me? I'm a better mom when I can get out regularly and kill something.'

Then she'd laughed.

"High Lady Tisis Guile requests the honor of your presence for the interrogation," Einin said. Her mouth twisted. "Eh... milord."

"Yes?" Kip asked, thinking she had something else to say. And what was it with the formality?

"Nothing?" she said. "Oh, shi—sorry. Ahem. I'm still sortin' when I'm s'posed to add the 'milord's and all. Apologies. Er, my lord."

Standing beside Kip, Cruxer was rubbing his temples. "Smart woman, I swear she is," he mumbled.

"It's simple enough," Kip told Einin. He spoke quickly. "Every time you think you're supposed to add a 'milord,' don't. And every time you think you probably don't need to, do. And enunciate it fully 'my lord' every third time. Any more than that and people will think you're being sarcastic; any less and they'll think you're showing disrespect. Also make sure you pay attention to how often other people use name, surname, and full title—there's some nuances to it that are hard to explain, but really important, and most lords interpret mistakes as insults. Got it? Then, lead on!"

Cruxer could barely contain his laughter as Einin preceded them out of the tent, looking bewildered. He said, "You know she scares the hell out of the rest of the Mighty, right?"

"She kind of scares the hell out of me," Kip said.

"What do you think of Milard?" Cruxer said, pronouncing it just a bit off from how Einin's accent rendered 'milord.'

"As a Mighty name for her? Pretty much perfect. She's gonna hate it!" he said happily.

"It's a good kind of hate," Cruxer said with a smile.

Kip thought maybe he'd already gone crazy. He'd checked Cruxer's halos, but he couldn't blame it on luxin.

All he knew was that the weeks of torturous riding through hard country was the most joyful time of his life. He was riding toward his death; he'd never felt more alive: Connected with his bride, even when she wept on his chest in the cool privacy of their tent as he stroked her hair. Unified with the Mighty, granted the respect of men he respected profoundly. Filled with a sense of purpose that the course that lay before them was true and right and worthy, and all of them working at the very limit of their abilities.

Kip felt that all the disparate strands of his life were coming together. This was to be the final test. He was at the peak of his skills and strength and power, and either it would prove to be enough or he would fail utterly.

There was something to be said for moments of crisis that announce their coming beforehand, rather than leap at you from the shadows.

His use of the Great Mirror for signal-casting would help the army he was leaving behind enormously. Few of the old minor mirrors were still functional, and fewer still had acknowledged messages (meaning the locals were afraid to answer, had fled, or were ignorant of the mirrors' use), but two mirrors in the south and southeast parts of the Forest had answered, and were passing messages to the Night Mares in their areas. Those were the fastest of Kip's forces, and they'd be able to reach many other will-casters and rush to join the siege at Green Haven.

They would be no help to his own forces. No matter how he'd love to have them in any battle, he couldn't exactly bring will-cast bears and jaguars and tygre wolves and giant elk into a city. The Jaspers had cats but few dogs, and those required an exorbitant license fee. Kip had only recently realized that what he'd thought was a weird cultural idiosyncrasy was instead purposeful. There were few domestic animals on the Jaspers by design: the ancient Chromeria had feared being infiltrated and attacked by will-casters.

Still, two hundred of the Cwn y Wawr war dogs and their handlers had joined his sprint for the coast, and where the Chromeria would have barred wild animals from landing on their islands (or been forced to accept heretical will-casting), everyone on both sides could pretend the war dogs were simply highly trained dogs.

They found the grubby man bound and guarded. An equally grubby messenger bag lay before him, open and empty.

The rest of the Mighty—the old original crew—was already gathered.

"Where is it?" Kip asked.

"There isn't any scroll," Tisis said. "He claims he memorized it, and when he started, I stopped him so you could hear it first."

"Who's it from?" Kip asked.

The messenger spoke up. "My mistress says the name you would recognize as being hers is Aliviana Danavis, though it referred to one so utterly changed as to be unrecognizable."

Liv?!

"Where is she?" Kip asked.

"When I left her, she was in Azuria Bay. She directed me to give my message before answering any other questions, though, your pardon. With your permission, my lord?"

Kip waved the room clear of everyone but the Mighty, then nodded.

The messenger took a deep breath, then spoke, obviously recalling words verbatim: " 'Kip, Lord Guile. Who I used to be felt something for you. I am not she anymore. I'm not secretly on your side. I'm not going to save the day for you and stab Koios in the back. You're my hedged bet. Should you fight us where I think you will, I ask you fight me last. Should you win, I ask exile rather than death. Should we win, though, I'll be unable to give you the same.

" 'It's no fair trade. Therefore, without obligation that you give me anything back, I tender to you something first: The White King plans to attack the Jaspers directly. He's already constructed barges to carry all his men, and will float all the bane with them, paralyzing the Chromeria's drafters. You'll need to attack before he leaves Ruthgar to have a chance against him.' "

Big Leo bellowed a curse, picking up the man and shaking him. "That message would have been really fucking helpful three weeks ago!"

Tisis put a hand on Big Leo's arm, and he put the man down, but he continued to breathe heavily, as if on the very point of murderous rage.

It was an act—the warm, kindly Tisis and the murderous brute—but it was surprisingly effective.

"When were you sent?" Tisis asked gently.

"My lady sent me more than a month ago. I, uh, got caught behind enemy lines."

"Which *enemy*? Us?" Cruxer demanded.

"Yes?" the man said, pained. But then his eyes became haunted. "There were these huge dogs, but not dogs. Dogs that were more and less than dogs, more and less than men. Dogs like hounds straight from hell. They gave signals to each other like men, searched in grids like disciplined soldiers, and then—I saw them run a man down with speed and tear him apart with a fury and savagery that no snarling dog has ever matched. I saw it from afar, and I ran, and I couldn't—I couldn't..."

He could say no more.

He didn't have to.

It was sometimes easy to lose perspective on what Kip's army had become. His will-casters called themselves Night Mares. A joke, if a grim one.

But it was no joke to the men and women who fought an armored war dog the size of a horse.

"She messed up," Tisis said. "She tells us exactly what she means to do? But also without worrying we might take offense at it. Who does that? She doesn't try to mislead us into hoping she's still your friend, Kip? Why? Because she thinks the deal itself is clearly good enough. This is the hyperrationality of a superviolet wight lost deep in her color. She's still there, but she's not in control anymore. Because if you weighed them on a scale, the power of a dog is nothing compared to the power of a god; she sends a man without considering that phobias are irrational."

"I dunno that I'd call war-dog-o-phobia irrational," Ferkudi said. "I've seen what those dogs can do."

"I'd side with Ferk on this—pray to Orholam that never happens again," Ben-hadad said. "The dog was here, she's not. A man afraid of both is going to react to his fear of the one that's closest."

"Is a goddess ever really absent?" Tisis asked. "You remember that superviolet lux storm last year that was, like, *looking* for you? She sent that from Orholam alone knows how far away. What might she do now when she's so much closer?"

"Well," Ferk said, "so much for that."

"So much for what?" Kip asked. You never knew what brilliant insight Ferkudi might offer.

"Looks like I'm going to have to change underwear. Again. Third time today."

Or not offer.

"*Third* time?" Winsen asked.

"Eh, I've been timing exactly how fast I can empty my bladder when it's totally full. You know, to make marching more efficient—"

"Forget I asked," Winsen said.

But Ferkudi went on. "See, you scratch a trench parallel to the line of march and have the men relieve themselves in ranks as they reached it. Eliminate bathroom breaks or soiled clothing altogether. I had it down to a count of twelve this morning…I thought."

Tisis was rubbing her face.

"Yeah," he said to her, "more like a fourteen count."

"What do we do with this one?" Big Leo asked, rattling his thick fighting chain that was looped around the messenger's thin neck.

"Bad form to kill a messenger," Cruxer said.

"He didn't come as a messenger," Big Leo said. "We captured him. He didn't come under a flag of truce, nor openly, nor unarmed. Why should he get covered by those rules? I think he's more like a spy."

"I suppose it all depends on how we frame the problem, huh?" Cruxer asked, pensive.

"Liv is gone," Kip said, mostly to himself.

"In more than one way," Ben-hadad muttered.

"She's sailed," Kip said to the messenger, but mostly thinking aloud. "So we have no mistress to send you back to. And I can't let you go without risking it costing me lives. You're a Blood Robe, albeit one the White King would hang as a traitor with that message you've told us. Maybe you'd try to bring him back some intelligence valuable enough that you'd hope would make him spare you."

The man said, "No, I wouldn't. I swear—"

He stopped as soon as Kip started talking, though. Power means never having to shout to be heard. Kip said, "You're a man alone with no friends and many enemies, a soldier of a pagan rebel you betrayed, the servant of an absent goddess you failed. And now you're a problem for me."

"I'll take care of it," Winsen said emotionlessly.

Kip took a deep breath, thinking.

"Wait, wait, wait—" the man said, sinking to his knees, staring at Winsen with horror.

"You don't get a voice in this," Big Leo said, his voice a low rumble.

"One last part of the message!" the man said. "Look! This is valuable!"

"Get on with it," Big Leo said.

Desperate, the messenger talked, tripping over himself. "She said—she said if you could draw them into a fight at, at, at Paedrig's Field near Apple Grove that you could win. Demolish them. She said she'd activated the Great Mirror there for you. And she said if you made it by...hold on, I can remember this. She said you needed to provoke the battle by um, two hundred twelve days after the Festival of Ambrose Ultano."

Kip squinted. "What the hell, Liv?" It was a minor local festival in Rekton celebrated by little more than the cooking of fruit pies. Obviously, she'd picked the date in order to obscure it from anyone who might get the messenger to talk. Worse, it was a floating date based on the lunar calendar.

"Well, that doesn't sound like a trap at all," Winsen said.

"Shut up, Win," Cruxer said.

"Is that an order, sir?"

"Just shut up."

After doing the arithmetic in his head, twice, Kip called Ferkudi over and whispered to him for a bit.

"Yep, yep," Ferkudi said too loudly—the man was utterly guileless. "That's either tomorrow, or more likely yesterday, depending on how you calculate it. And if we push, and the river is passable all the way—unlikely, right?—but we could get to Apple Grove in...two days. More likely three or four."

"So there's no way we can get there by tomorrow?" Kip asked.

Ferkudi laughed. "No. Unless you can steal Orholam's own chariot like Phaethon or make a machina like a skimmer for the skies."

He'd meant them both as similar impossibilities, but it made Kip think of his father and the condor he'd made. Too bad he'd never told Kip how to construct one. Nor did Kip have his father's mind of how to invent things. Besides, the condor had needed a vast body of water to build up the requisite speed to glide. Kip didn't have that, either.

Low curses were muttered all around. No one trusted Aliviana Danavis, but if she was on their side, she'd just told them it was too late for them to win.

The messenger saw the black looks directed toward him. If the man had delivered his message when he was supposed to, they would have had a chance.

"You may have killed us all by dodging your duty," Cruxer snarled at the man. "Your cowardice. You knew what you had to do, and you couldn't simply do it, could you? *Could you!*" There was a depth of rage there that put the Mighty to glancing at each other.

"W-w-wait! She said, she said, she said for when you were done listening to her offer and were dismissing me, she said to tell you, 'This man is as much a treasure to me as Ramir's esteem was, back in Rekton. Please lavish commensurate honors upon him.'"

The man breathed again. He wet dry lips with his tongue. His eyes lit with hope as everyone turned to Kip.

"Oh, you have got to be joking," Big Leo said. "We have to let him go? Give him stuff? He's a spy!"

"That isn't what she said," Ben-hadad said, adjusting his spectacles. "Not necessarily. Breaker?"

It was an odd dislocation into memory. All his best friends were here, but they hadn't known the old Kip, when he'd lived in Rekton. They didn't share that life, those friends, those allegiances, fears, hatreds, and loathing.

The momentary reverie had apparently stretched beyond momentary, because Cruxer cleared his throat. "Since no one else is, I'll go ahead and ask the obvious: Lord Guile? How much did Aliviana Danavis value this Ramir's esteem?"

But Kip didn't answer. He had a vivid memory of being wildly infatuated with Liv and talking with her when she'd been back from the Chromeria once. As he was nervously trying to make conversation with the older, pretty girl, Kip had said Ram thinks this, Ram thinks that, maybe three or four times. Ramir had opinions about everything. And Liv had suddenly started berating Kip. 'Ramir's a small-town bully. He's trash. And you're licking his boots. What does that make you, Kip? You're *already* better than he'll ever be. Grow up!'

It had been highly confusing to him, being called a bootlicker and a baby but being praised at the same time.

Orholam's stones, it was embarrassing even to recall it.

She'd been right, too. Not that it mattered to the present situation, except that it verified the message was from her, and that it was going to be a bad day for her messenger.

"He's not having one of his trances again, is he?" Ferkudi asked.

"No," Tisis answered quietly. But she didn't prod him for an answer.

Resigned that they were going to have to give Kip some time to think it over, Ben-hadad looked over at Ferkudi. "What if a guy gets a shy bladder?"

"Huh? What's that?" Ferkudi asked.

Ben said, "You know, needs to pee, gets up to the trench, feels like people are watching, can't pee. Too much pressure."

"That's a thing?" Ferkudi asked, thunderstruck.

"It's a thing," Winsen said.

"That is *not* a thing," Ferkudi protested. "You gotta pee, you gotta pee."

"It's a thing," Big Leo rumbled. "I'm kind of a shy-bladder gentleman myself."

"Really?" Ben-hadad asked him. "Never noticed that about you."

"Huh," Ferkudi said. "I did not know that's a thing. That would explain some things that happened at the latrines when I was gathering data."

"And what were the women supposed to do, pee in the same trench? At the same speed?" Ben-hadad asked with a grin. "Were you going to run drills until they got up to snuff?"

"Of course. All those problems were next," Ferk said soberly. "But... well, I hung out by the privies and approached a lot of women to help me with my experiments, but I had real trouble finding volunteers. Not a single woman would help."

"You'll find those women in a different part of the camp," Winsen said dryly. "And they'll expect to be paid."

The rest of them laughed. Even Cruxer cracked a grin.

Orholam help him, even the poor messenger smiled.

"I don't get it," Ferkudi said. "You mean the tanners?"

But Kip turned toward the messenger. "Liv hated Ramir with a passion. She said his opinion was dung I should throw in a fire."

Everyone fell silent. The man froze, wide-eyed. Throw in a fire?

Kip continued, "So your goddess is letting me know I can kill you without offending her. She framed the words to deceive you, thinking your greed would drive you here."

"What a *bitch*," Tisis whispered.

"Not even loyal to her own," Winsen said.

"She didn't understand loyalty even before she went wight," Kip said. "So maybe it's just as well she's in the enemy's camp and not ours." He turned to the man. "I don't want to murder you. But you're a problem. So you solve it for me: Winsen's solution, or you choose to live a slave. We brand the date of next Sun Day on your arm. After that you go free. A year and a couple weeks of servitude, and your oath not to return to the fight."

"Only a year?" the man asked, suddenly hopeful again. Funny how fast our hopes can shrink.

"Anyone holding you past that date will face death." If our laws matter at all a year from now.

Kip pursed his lips as the man walked willingly to the blacksmith to be branded.

335

And *that* is how I justify becoming a slaver.

Tisis came to his side. "So we're headed to Apple Grove now? Even though it's either too late or a trap?"

Kip looked at her, pained.

Chapter 51

The door swung open silently, revealing the profile of a scrawny young scholar scratching a parchment with sure, fluid strokes while he studied a parchment whose fat, twin rolls dominated his desk.

"Are you here to kill me?" Quentin asked, not looking up to see who'd come into his recently locked room.

"No," Teia grunted, tucking away her picks.

"Then, one moment, please." He finished the long sentence he'd been writing. Then he used a boar's-hair brush and soapy water to clean the gold nib of his quill, shook a bit of fine sand on the damp ink, opened a case, and put away all his accoutrements. He grabbed a folded parchment from the box before closing it away.

There was some essential rightness to seeing Quentin with his scrolls and quills. His was a quieter excellence than Kip's drafting or Cruxer's flowing through the fighting forms, or Tlatig with her bow, but Teia knew that his mind was doing things that hers could never grasp.

When he looked up and saw Teia, his face showed no surprise.

"Of course it's you," he said. "Orholam wants us to be whole, does He not?"

Teia didn't really want a sermon from a traitor. She tossed her orders on the table. In Karris's hand they read, 'Quentin will be your handler, and will serve you in all ways. Trust him absolutely. Don't get him killed. I have plans for him.'

"What were your orders?" she asked.

"Karris told me the one who came would be my master and maybe even my friend. She said I needed to learn how to have both."

Teia was suddenly embarrassed for him. "I'm sorry," she said suddenly. "Maybe...maybe for a lot of things."

"I'm not," he said. "Just for the one thing. Nothing else."

" 'The one thing'? What do you mean?" she asked.

336   He looked at her, clear-eyed and steady. "Murdering Lucia, of

course. But I'm glad I got caught, glad I had to face up to what I'd done and what I'd become. I'm broken now, Teia, but I've never been so free. I know for the first time what it is to walk in the light. But never mind me. How may I serve you?"

"I—I have no idea."

"Then may I offer a suggestion?"

She nodded.

"When I saw my orders, I guessed it would be you, so I already got started."

" 'Started'? On what?"

He smiled, and scooted his papers toward her. She sat, and her blood went cold at the heading of his notes: 'Mist Walking: Myths/ Speculation, Ancient/Modern, & Educated Guesses.'

Her heart stopped. "Did she tell you I…?"

He shook his head. "Paryl. I think early on you must've believed it was useless, didn't you? Otherwise, you'd never have told anyone that you could use it. Hard to explain why you would qualify for Blackguard training if you were a mund, though, one supposes. Anyway, I found that a number of the books with the best information about Mist Walkers weren't even in the restricted libraries. You have to know which authors to trust, of course, but this hasn't been the hardest research I've done, by any means. Now, with you to tell me which information is true and which is exaggerated, I can winnow out which authors were fabulists or given to exaggeration among those I don't already know."

Only then did he seem to notice the stricken look on her face.

"Teia, what's wrong? I thought you would be excited."

"Quentin, do you have any idea what I'm involved in?"

"I thought that would be obvious," he said.

She gestured: 'Go on.'

"You're trying to discover how the most-likely-mythical Order of the Broken Eye was able to achieve whatever small measure of light diffraction they were, to the extent that latter storytellers would so grandiosely call it 'invisibility,' but which, according to the eminent leader of the Eighth Stoa, Ulgwar Pen, was more akin to good camoufla…What are you doing with that hood?"

Teia went invisible. Karris had said to trust him absolutely, right?

She held Quentin's gaze for a moment, knowing that her eyes would be visible while receiving light. Then she dipped her head to disappear completely.

His mouth dropped open, and Teia couldn't suppress a giggle.

That seemed to completely flip his apple cart.

Teia dropped the invisibility just as Quentin went wild-eyed.

"That—that...Ulgwar Pen had no idea what he was talking about!" Quentin said. "That *liar*! Everyone trusted—he made his reputation on that paper! There goes half my report!" He rubbed his temples. "That prompts the question: Was he deceived, or just wrong? Or, Orholam forbid, deliberately misleading? Surely a man of his standing wouldn't—well then, what does that say about his paper on the Two Hundred?" He stopped himself. "But I'm thinking like a scholastic. I'm on all the wrong questions, aren't I? Tell me."

Teia removed her hood. "The Order is real. They're assassinating people to this day. Not far away, either. They've been at work in the Chromeria itself. Karris assigned me to infiltrate their ranks and destroy them utterly, at any cost. You understand? I'm to do anything at all. Everything," Teia said. "I've had to kill innocents to prove myself, and even that hasn't been enough. Some of them trust me, but...one of their best assassins is hunting me. If I'm lucky, he alone suspects me. I can't run away, because I still have a chance to stop them—and if I run, they'll kill my father."

It was hilarious to see Quentin's brain explode twelve ways with bafflement. Under the strain of all she'd been through in the past year, Teia's sense of humor had gone so dark she couldn't see a dead-baby joke in front of her face. But the surprising part was how much of a relief it was simply to share—with *Quentin*! The last person in the world she would have thought would understand her new terrible life.

But the awful weight of her secret was halved instantly.

They talked, they planned, they shared what had happened in their lives—each holding back at least some parts, Teia could tell. She couldn't bring herself to tell Quentin about all the awful shit she'd done. But strangely, with how he reacted to the merely bad shit she did share, and the elliptical references to worse, she could imagine eventually telling him more. Maybe everything.

She'd expected him to radiate condemnation, but without pretending he knew exactly what she'd experienced, instead he radiated sorrow at what she'd been through, and acceptance of her, without accepting all she'd done.

She didn't know how he did that, but the tight knot in Teia's chest eased a little. She still felt like she was growing old too fast, like her youth was draining away like water through sand. But for an afternoon, she didn't feel like she was dying.

"I made up a joke," Teia said suddenly, as their time was winding down.

"Oh yeah? How's it go?" Quentin asked.

She suddenly realized her joke was not one to share with a holy man.

True, some of the Blood Forest luxiats were known to be a bit earthy from time to time, but on the whole, luxiats were not known for their ribald senses of humor. And Quentin, who didn't even like to hug, wasn't someone Teia could imagine ever being called 'earthy.'

She grimaced. "Nah, sorry. Forget I said anything. It's crude."

"I've never heard a crude joke before," Quentin said.

"You haven't?" she asked. She didn't think the luxiats were quite so far removed from—"Oh. You're kidding."

"Try me," he said.

"It's not...it's not even very funny." She sank into herself.

"I'm not expecting Aethelfric Yfargwvyn levels of wit here," Quentin said. "C'mon. It'll brighten a dark moment, even if it flops. Maybe especially then."

Aethel-who? "Now we've built it up," Teia protested, "it's about as funny as a fart joke. And less mature."

"I love flatus quips," Quentin protested.

"Yeah, see?!" she said. "Flatus? I mean, even that was dignified! Is that actually the proper name for—"

"It was actually a joke," he said.

She stopped. "Oh."

"Pretty bad, huh? Now you owe me a bad joke. C'mon, I even made it be a fart joke," he said. "Meet me halfway here."

"Okay. Fine." She tried to think of a different joke quickly. Something less gross. Some actual fart joke she'd heard. There had been off-color jokes in the barracks every day. But of course now she couldn't think of a single one.

She covered her face with her hands. I can't believe I'm doing this. "So I was out following a bad guy, and he'd gone inside this hovel with what I thought was his mistress and I had to wait for them to finish fu...meeting." She grimaced. "Anyway, when I first started doing this, I thought I was going to be like an avenging ghost, and all of a sudden I thought I was more like a fox, like my old shimmercloak—it had a fox on it?" This is awful. "Like I'm this fierce, keen, silent hunter who stalks unseen at night to kill, you know?"

"Uh-huh?" Quentin said.

"But then I thought, well, I don't only work at night, so I'm not entirely nocturnal. More like nocturnal-y." The worst joke ever. "But I am really focused on my missions. So, you know, I'm really worried about my nocturnal-y missions. So I thought, I'm not a fox. I'm a teenage boy!"

Quentin stared at her blankly.

"You know, a, a..."

Nothing. Total blank.

"What's a nocturnal emission?" Quentin asked.

The blood drained out of her face. No, no. Hell, no. She was not going to explain that!

"I think I've heard the term before," Quentin said, "but when I looked it up, it wasn't in any of the luxiats' dictionaries. Is it a specialized term? From what field? I'm so sorry, the whole joke hinges on that, and I've failed you. Maybe you could define it for me and then tell me the whole joke again?"

But then she noticed a tiny twitch of his lips.

"You asshole!" she said.

He burst out laughing. "Ah! the look on your face!"

"Goddammit, Quentin!"

"Easy, easy with the blasphemy!" he said, still laughing.

Oh, that was right. "Sorry, sorry," she said. Swearing and jokes about wet dreams were fair game, but saying 'God' was out of bounds. Or was it the 'damn' part? Her mouth twisted. "We are really different from each other, aren't we?"

"Oh, absolutely," he said. "But... also very much alike. I mean, you could say I'm like a fox and you're like a teenage—"

"Quentin!"

They both laughed, and Teia realized that for a precious hour, she hadn't felt alone.

And when she left to go do more terrible, necessary things, she banked that memory like a little glowing ember in her heart. She would take it out later, and breathe on it, and bask in that little warm glow.

That, that right there, is what it feels like to be human. That's what it feels like to have a friend.

She didn't know what her future held, but she knew she would need it.

Chapter 52

"Satrap Corvan Danavis is bringing his fleet here. To celebrate Sun Day with the Chromeria, he says," the diplomat Anjali Gates said.

Karris's breath caught. "'*Fleet*'? So our spies were right? But how'd he get a fleet? How could he afford that? The new Tyreans have nothing. Do you have any guesses on the number of drafters? Soldiers?"

The older woman fanned herself, though the morning was cool in Karris's rooms high in the Chromeria. The head of the diplomatic corps had come out of retirement to serve in the satrapies' time of need, and had proven herself a dozen times over.

"Not guesses. He told me the numbers himself, and from my experience, what he said seemed right. Four hundred drafters, four thousand fighters. He said he'd like to recruit among the pilgrims and drafters visiting the Chromeria while he's here, to pull together an expeditionary force against the White King. He would need to be in direct control, with a very specific writ of authority, and he gave details on exactly what funding, logistical support, and intelligence he'd need. It is quite impressive in both scope and completeness."

Taking up the pages and pages of requests, Karris was struck for a moment by the fact that she now knew exactly what all these numbers were. They all seemed in line, nothing excessive for the admittedly ambitious recruiting goals he had in mind. For whatever it was worth, her time training the drafters of the Chromeria was paying dividends.

"You look at these?" Karris asked.

"No indeed, High Lady," Anjali Gates said. There was a whiff of indignation around her, but she was sweating.

"They aren't sealed. I'd not be offended," Karris said.

"They were from his hand to yours. That's my trust, High Lady, and with it all my honor," Anjali said.

Karris flashed her eyebrows. Prickly sort. "Very well. You seemed, uh, discomfited. I'd supposed it was by what you'd read. Is it not?"

Anjali Gates flushed redder. "Oh. My apologies, High Lady. Hot flash. Damned things. Never at a convenient hour."

"Ah," Karris said awkwardly. Then she pretended not to feel awkward, which was also awkward, but hopefully only internally. Especially after the precedent Orea Pullawr had set, the White was often expected to be a mother figure. How can you be a mother figure to a woman old enough to be your own mother, especially when you miss such obvious signs?

Karris took a breath, while Anjali Gates pretended (more artfully) not to feel awkward at all. Diplomats got good at that sort of thing, Karris supposed. "I'm sorry. I didn't intend to embarrass you," Karris said. "I'm still learning."

"And if I may be so bold, learning very well, too, High Lady. You've engendered an enormous amount of trust in a difficult time. Most impressive."

Karris accepted the compliment with a nod of her head that didn't break eye contact. The White—as any diplomat would tell her—should not bow to anyone.

"Impressions of Danavis?" Karris asked.

Gates was ready for this sort of thing. "A man utterly in command of himself and his people, and deeply, deeply admired by them and promptly obeyed. As reported previously, he was recently widowered. There is a real air of grief about him, but not brokenness. He looked several times to a portrait he keeps of her. No signs of drunkenness or dissipation. It should not surprise me if he harbors great stores of rage; however, it seems he keeps them under lock and key. No truth whatever, I'd hazard, to the rumors of her killing herself. Now, there were some other numbers he mentioned..." Anjali Gates then lowered her voice so that no one might overhear, despite that they were in Karris's very rooms and no one other than Blackguards were in attendance. "He caught me when I caught him looking at her portrait, and he told me quite frankly that the Order of the Broken Eye had her assassinated so she might not help you with her visions. I asked if this suggested an alliance between the Order and the White King. He thought it likely, but said he had no proof."

Karris took a deep breath. The Order again. Aligned with the White King? Curse them to the deepest hell.

"Are those numbers also in these papers?" Karris asked for any eavesdropping ears. "Oh, of course, that's right, you didn't look. I may have to have you write them down for me, though, if they're not. I shan't remember all of that with everything else I have on my mind."

Karris thumbed through the pages. It looked like Satrap Corvan Danavis expected to recruit a lot of her drafters for the fight. It wasn't implausible from a practical standpoint: hot from the holy fervor of Sun Day, women and men might sign on for well nigh anything.

But putting her drafters under Corvan's command? Karris clucked her tongue. It certainly showed audacity—which was exactly what leading the fight against the White King would need.

But *where* would he attack? Had his Seer of a wife told him things that he didn't dare entrust to a diplomat messenger? Karris still believed her brother wanted to attack the Chromeria directly—but with what ships? From what port? When?

If she could attack him instead, either at sea or, even better, with his ships still in port, the Seven Satrapies might end this war without even more devastation.

Corvan might be the key to everything.

"He says these requests aren't meant as an opening to begin

negotiations," Anjali Gates said. "If you give him less than what he asks, he'll be able to tell you what successes you can hope for from his campaign, but he believes that striking hard and as quickly as possible will be the only hope for the Seven Satrapies to avoid collapse next spring. He plans to sail away from here to begin his attack only a day or two after Sun Day, and asks that as soon as his ships are seen on the horizon arriving, we allow no more ships to exit our ports."

"He still hopes to surprise the White King," Karris said. "It's worth a try." She knew her brother surely had many spies on both Big and Little Jasper, and one of them at least would *try* to sail to tell him about the arrival of unexpected forces.

But with her small fleet of skimmers, her people could overtake and stop any ship of spies. Surprising the White King was actually quite possible.

Apologizing again for her earlier gaffe, Karris dismissed the woman, and ushered in the next senior diplomat. This one to report the Ruthgari situation: Eirene Malargos was playing her cards close, stalling real action, but Karris's spies had learned that her allies—and allies they seemed, still—had discovered the secret of how to make their own skimmers, albeit of a seemingly more rudimentary design than the Chromeria's own.

Of course they had. It was easier for friends to spy on you than enemies, she supposed. Eirene had ships staffed and provisioned, ready to sail, but was still summoning troops. She could delay Karris's call to serve for as long as she wanted with that excuse. You can always wait for more troops, if you're as rich as a Malargos.

If Eirene were being honest with Karris, then she'd had no word from Kip's forces up the river since about the last time Karris herself had heard from them. Eirene suspected bandits were seizing supplies going up the river and had intercepted messengers, so she had long since dispatched messengers overland to Kip. But she'd had no word back yet. Dammit.

The scouts searching the seas for King Ironfist had found nothing. Dammit again.

On Karris's hunch, the Chromeria's small fleet was patrolling between the Jaspers and the Ruthgari coast, but the next messenger reported nothing new from their scouts—which could actually be good news.

The next reported a similar blank for those searching for the pirates who yearly preyed on the pilgrims who sailed for the Chromeria to celebrate Sun Day.

Karris had hoped to sink every last pirate with her skimmers, though it was early yet for the pirates to hunt so close to the Chromeria. Usually they started their piracy at the farther ports as pilgrims embarked. The Blackguards had gone to those coastal cities, sending their own personnel to hunt pirates as well as they were able to, because they didn't trust anyone else with the skimmers except Karris's and Andross's messengers.

Maybe Karris could send the Blackguards out en masse when the pirates came closer, and deal them a blow they'd never forget.

Maybe the pirate kings' and queen's fleets had tangled with Ironfist's, and they'd done one another such damage that none of them would come this year!

Right, Karris, and maybe the heavens will open up and shower down warriors to save the day! And chocolate. That'd be nice. Maybe a hot cup of kopi?

What Karris really needed was someone to serve her as she and Marissia had served the old White. She needed someone to recruit and manage her spies. She *should* choose Anjali Gates for the job: the woman was eminently capable, sharp, diligent, and exact, and willing to do excellent work without getting public recognition.

The last was a rarity on the Jaspers.

But Karris had delegated off so many duties already, only to add dozens more in taking over the drafters' war training and in quietly bolstering the islands' defenses, from refortifying walls that had had stones stolen from them for other construction over the years, to drilling the cannon crews of all the towers on overlapping fire and their supply chains for shot and powder if they ran out, to hiring the smiths to cast weapons and armor, to drilling free militias, even spurring on their training by offering prizes in archery competitions and melees.

None of it had been as cheap as she'd promised Andross, but he hadn't stopped her. Without ever saying a word of why, he acquiesced often now. It was almost as if he respected her a little, now. Almost.

He hadn't even demanded she stop meeting with her pet luxiats (as he called them). He seemed more amused that it had so infuriated some of the High Luxiats—and, she guessed, kept them busy being angry at her rather than at him.

She should summon Ambassador Gates and give her the job now. She knew she should.

But with all she'd passed off to other hands, the control of information was one thing she couldn't bear to give to anyone. Not now, not when the Order had people everywhere.

In peacetime, you might worry about a spy enriching a family unjustly or using their illicit knowledge to claim estates or negotiate or end trade agreements or even marriages. In wartime, though, a well-placed spy meant death for thousands. It could mean the death of the Seven Satrapies.

There was a knock at the door. Ugh, another meeting.

All this is what you were preparing me for, Orea, Karris thought, by putting me in charge of the spies. After my long tutelage everywhere else, you taught me to handle secrets and those who keep them. You taught me to judge whom to trust and how to trust someone halfway or three-quarters, rather than trusting fully or not at all, like I used to.

Thank you, Orea. Thank you.

Another knock.

"Send them in," Karris told her Blackguards.

One more meeting, she promised herself, then I'm getting the hell out of here to go to that little kopi shop myself.

Chapter 53

"YOU..."

The sound rose from a pitch so low Teia felt it first in her chest, but maybe that was only her anxious dreams. She rolled over. The closet was so small, no one could open it without the door pushing into her hip. This was as safe a place to sleep as anything got for her.

"HAVE." The voice had risen now, like a sea demon emerging from thalassic depths. Monstrous and raw, it was *basso profundo* deep, as if it had taken until now to find a cadence intelligible to her.

"MY CLOAK!"

The voice was a volcano rending the earth beneath her and vomiting fire past her face, the heat alone pummeling her into mute submission, agog, falling backward to tremble on uncertain ground.

"You cannot hide for long, thief. I will find you and take what is mine, and I will teach you what eternity means. I will snatch you from this time to a place where we can be uninterrupted for decades of torture, and then I'll bring you back, to your own family, your own home. You will betray your own father for one hour's cessation of pain, and then I will take you again, until you have broken yourself, and you beg to torture by your own hand them whom once you loved. I will flay you, I will tear off your fingernails, I will grind your bones to spike shards and make you dance as they pierce your skin. I will impale you from anus to broken teeth on the axle of my war chariot before I ride into battle. But no matter what pain you come to know, you will heal every time I allow you nightmarish sleep. You will not die. I, who am the Lord of Flies, will never let you more than glimpse that bourne."

This was not a nightmare. From any nightmare Teia had ever known when asleep, she would have woken by now, sheets drenched, cheeks wet with tears. But she could not wake.

This was not her psyche pawing through the jagged detritus of what had unsettled her in the day and sorting her fears. This wasn't a twisted confusion of things she knew. This was stark clarity. And he used terms she'd never heard.

This was not Teia speaking to herself.

At her sudden certainty, her throat clenched, at war with a stomach rebelling to empty itself.

Nor did he stop speaking.

"You shall be the asymptote of suffering incarnate, beyond whose limit is insanity, a land whose surcease of sorrow you shall never know. Eventually, you will choose me over freedom, me over love, *me* over every good. I, Abaddon, will be your god."

His voice had risen through the stones beneath her like grasping vines, and now they wrapped around her, imprisoning her, prodding into every gap, sliding sibilant across her skin.

"But whatever you say"—his voice had gone quieter, soothing, full of anticipation of pleasure—"however you praise me through your shattered nubs of teeth, no matter what you do or don't do, you will never know an end to suffering. Never. Not when you have served me for ten thousand faithful years. Not when your very sun expels its last exhausted breath of light and collapses into cold, dark dirt. You will suffer until you beg for your suffering not to end, for I will give you such uncertain respite from pain that each beat of rest is counted only in anticipation of the entire orchestra of pain reaching a new crescendo for which you are unprepared, and your nerves will have healed and regained old capacity for feeling. You will beg, for the pain renewed will be pain redoubled.

"Perhaps you hope I brag, perhaps you dare to disbelieve such suffering is possible, or you hope that you could not be so special to one such as I. And it's true. You're not special. For I have been offended before, and more grievously. But eternity is long, and the worlds are many, and time is vast when you may move about it at will. I am punishing a million such as you, even now. Would you like to see?"

346

For one moment, as her emotions skittered uncontrollably like a drop of water on a steaming-hot pan, Teia felt a flash of queer gratitude. For one heartbeat, Breaker broke her free of quicksand fear with memories of his quicksilver humor at all the wrong times. Though not in so many words, Kip the Lip had taught her this:

If you think you're helpless, if you think you're powerless; as long as you can speak, you're not helpless, and you're not powerless until you're too afraid to. If you're trapped in the darkness all alone, how do you know you're alone and not actually surrounded by an army of friends, also silent, also afraid in the dark, merely waiting for the sound of one voice to rouse them from fear, to fight for freedom?

Silence is isolation chosen. Silence is darkness, and every evil loves the dark.

Kip, Kip the Lip? You marvelous wrong-girl-marrying turd, you gave me this cloak that's gotten me out of and into every kind of mess, including this one. Kip, you tried to tell me about this guy, didn't you? I thought you were crazy. Maybe I was right, and crazy's contagious. But forget that. Kip, this one's for you, buddy.

"Eternity?" Teia interrupted, impressed. "That *is* a long time. And you're going to talk for all of it, aren't you? You're wrong about me not dying, though. I'll die of *boredom*."

It took Abaddon off guard. There was sudden quiet, and Teia felt those twisting tendrils of fear shrivel back.

"Mortal, you have no—"

"What, now you're mad so you're going to torture me worse? Longer? How's that work?" Teia asked as if he were unbelievably stupid. "You play music? Me neither, but even I know that you never start at a *fortissimo*. There's just no way you can go up. Raging along at a monotone as loud as possible? You're like an eight-year-old boy, screaming every word, from a total lack of either control or awareness. So get out of here, kid. You bother me."

But the presence wasn't gone. She hoped he was aghast at her audacity, that he would give up before her courage did.

"Oh please, do go on with the insults and the terribly convincing defiance," he said. "Because every word you speak helps me in my hunt for you. A young woman—that much is very helpful to know. Parian-born? Abornean perhaps? Lower-class, certainly, from the accent, with an urban muddle to it. Maybe raised in several cities? And uneducated, which usually goes with lower class, but not always. You claim not to play an instrument and then prove the truth of it by misusing terms. So, young—well, I won't say 'lady'—is there anything else you wish to say?"

Oh, shit.

"Yeah, one last thing," Teia said. "Thanks for the cloak, you little bitch."

If Teia had thought that Abaddon had been shouting at her in a fortissimo, the sudden draconic roar of a hatred that stretched to the very bounds of infinity quibbled that perhaps the immortal's former threats had been spoken *sotto voce*: her mortal ears simply weren't capable of hearing more than the minutest modulations in the volume of his mammoth voice.

The pressure of his scream clapped cupped hands on the ears of her mind, blowing blood from her every orifice at a pressure her psyche couldn't contain.

After she wandered a trackless season of dizzied pain, his voice descended to words that she could slowly begin to understand, now bated with acid malice. "You are an ant on the finger of a curious giant, daring to bite him. My amusement is at an end. You will soon know the—"

And then he was gone. Like a soap bubble popped on a blade of grass. Just. Gone. Leaving only a stretchy film of horror over her.

He knew her gender, her voice. Could guess she was on the Jaspers. And who else was close enough to Kip that he would entrust with such a treasure?

Abaddon was gone. For the moment. But he hunted, and where could she go that he would not find her?

But where had he gone?

A sense of peace came over her. A fathomless well of quiet, somehow qualitatively different from the silence that had come before. Peace.

And Teia slept once more.

But this she heard, first, before the soporific waves closed over her consciousness.

"Can we not save her?" a man asked mournfully, but his voice was layered as with his own echo. It was like no human voice.

"Too close. She might hear," a woman said, her quietly resounding voice soothing as a summer rain, warm as blankets by the fire.

"She'll think she dreams," he protested.

"Even dreams may move a mortal."

"I have time left there. I could protect her myself—" he started.

"Not while she has the cloak," the woman insisted. "If he knew we'd already found it, you know what that would mean for this world. He could rally many to his cause. Our only hope is in her stealth."

"And she has no hope at all? We demand that of her, without even asking?"

"She holds the most precious possession of—and willfully insulted—the former angel of death himself. We're not demanding anything of her she hasn't chosen already."

"This is our war. We owe it to—"

"And it *is* war! Or have you forgotten whose skins Abaddon used to make that abomination?!" The woman's voice had risen to thunder and lightning looking for a place to strike. "And now I've stirred her, and she will remember." She sighed. "Nor was that an accident, was it? Sometimes I wonder how *I* was assigned to the Guile and you to this woman."

"I think it was your love of spectacle, wasn't it?" the man answered, amused.

"You win this round, Nuri, but don't forget, we are on the same side."

There was a sudden rush as of something departing at great speed.

But Teia wasn't alone. The man spoke once more. "I am a watcher and a messenger, not a warrior, and the farthest thing from a rebel, no matter how that just sounded. I cannot fight for you except in words. Cannot stand for you except in prayer, Adrasteia, though that is stronger than you know. But this I promise you: If you fall and Abaddon seizes you, before he can take you away to his realms to do all he has promised, I will do everything in my power to kill you. That much I promise. But no more."

And then the immortal was gone.

"Wow. *Thanks*," Teia said. She meant it to come out as sarcasm. But she'd believed every threat Abaddon had uttered, and she found, to her horror, that her gratitude was sincere.

She woke fully into the darkness of her little closet, and slept no more.

Chapter 54

~Andross the Red~
25 years ago. (Age 41.)

"You know why it must be done," I say.

"No, we can't. We can't."

"Do you think I *want* to do this?" I ask. This is not what I need from my bride now. I need her to be the strong one. She won't even have to be there when it's done. She won't be the one who has to speak to Gavin and convince him to do the deed.

"What if we're wrong?" Felia breathes.

She is a fierce intellect, my Felia, though she hides it under soft smiles and a warm demeanor. Others see her as always just smart enough to understand their troubles, and they see not her perceptive questions. She is patient where I have never been, and when fools explain things to her that are not, she doesn't correct them. She plays a different game than I. Always has. It was part of my calculus when marrying her. Her strengths, plus mine, would make us unstoppable.

But only if our strengths are added, because our weaknesses subtract, too. We are both deep feelers.

Curse you, Ulbear Rathcore, for laying this trap at my feet. Curse you, Orea Pullawr, for all your pretenses at piety, while you go along with *this*. I will have my revenge. On both of you.

"Felia, how many languages do you know?"

"You know the answer to that."

"How many?"

"Nine, depending how one counts. Four of those more or less fluently, albeit with muddled accents. Three dexterously enough to pass as a native, given a bit of time to brush up."

"Did you get the translations wrong?"

She sighed. "I was certain of them at the time."

"Felia. In a scribe's serif stroke you see as if she laid bare all the secrets of her soul. You checked it a hundred times. We visited half the libraries of the world. You spoke with Janus Borig a dozen times. There was no mistake."

Her hands lay in her lap like dead birds. "My love," she says. "I was young and so, so full of myself. So proud. What if we're wrong?"

"If we're wrong, it will be terrible. Pointless sacrifices, meaningless deaths, talent wasted, and fortunes burned for nothing, as happens every day in these satrapies. But if we're right...If we're right but we blink—if we're right but we're not strong enough to do what must be done—all the world will pay. You will see *all* your sons die. You will bury me. You will see the Chromeria burn and the Jaspers awash in blood. You will live to see the beginning of the Blinder's thousand-year reign. Felia, it is because you are a great heart coupled with a great mind that Orholam has trusted you with this yoke beside me. A lesser soul would break."

350 "I *am* breaking!" she says. And tears explode.

A slave peeks in at the door, but I wave her away.

I can't go to Felia. I barely can stand myself. This was to be the burden we would carry together, but if she is fallen, I can't let her drag me down.

"For Orholam's sake, stand," I say. "My love, please."

For long moments, she is incapable of speech. She tries to weep quietly, but can't. "But...our sons!" she chokes out.

The words are barely discernible through her weeping, and part of me despises her for being weak. I need her now, and she thinks of the impossible.

I know better than to say, 'We can have more sons.' She will never share my bed again if I appear so callous. Nay, she will never so much as look at me again.

'Of red cunning, the youngest son cleaves father and father and father and son.'

How I loathe prophecy. It could mean anything or nothing. Which fathers, which son or sons? Which generation? It's worthless, meaningless. So why does it occur to me now?

I know why.

Sevastian. Curse you, Ulbear, curse you, Orea—and curse You, too, Orholam. How can I give You my son?

Chapter 55

Kip didn't know why it was that when you think someone is trying to kill you, it should be mildly disappointing to find out that they aren't.

They'd prepared for an enemy trap as they approached this little town. They'd arranged signals, scouted twice, set backup plans and rally points. Mostly they'd just thought they knew what was going to happen. And they'd been wrong. Which made Kip worry they'd fallen into another trap.

They'd wasted time, and they'd arrived at Apple Grove too late.

"Breaker, you need to come see this," Winsen said. His blue-and-yellow-stained eyes looked uneasy. Kip had never seen Winsen look uneasy.

"Just tell me it's not more of the dead," Kip said. He was in a black mood.

They'd arrived too late to stop the White King's armada before it launched from the next town over, and too late to stop a massacre here. They'd expected to be too late for the armada, but the massacre didn't make any sense.

"Not dead," Winsen said, "though I thought he was at first."

Kip mounted up and followed him, swinging Tisis into the saddle behind him. Cruxer, Ben-hadad, and Ferkudi fell in immediately.

The town hadn't been burned. It hadn't been disturbed in any way, merely left neglected, as if everyone had decided to leave while unaccountably abandoning their every worldly possession. The town was empty except for children between the ages of maybe one and three years old.

Everyone old enough to speak had been killed.

No massacre felt right, but this one felt very wrong. *Strange* wrong. Men inflamed with Atirat's lust for destruction don't leave buildings standing that they could burn. Those who massacre entire villages don't usually spare the young. Nor, afterward, do they pile up the bodies and burn them in an orderly manner until the ashes obscure what had happened, obviously staying to feed the bodies back into the hottest flames until every part is consumed.

It was careful, and massacres aren't careful work.

They'd done a decent job of hiding what they'd done, but Kip's war hounds could smell the tale.

Kip's first hope was that all the missing had been kidnapped by slavers, even as he wondered at what a world it was where one could *hope* such a thing. But the hounds smelled no departing tracks for those adults and older children. The people of Apple Grove had been rounded up, forced to give up valuables and jewelry, moved into a field, and slaughtered there. Maybe three hundred of them.

One of Kip's men found the stolen jewelry, all of it arrayed neatly on a table in one of the houses, as if asking to be taken by whoever came along.

The young children who had been allowed to live had been left with plenty of water and food.

But still. From everything they could tell—the war hounds had trouble with abstracts like units of time, but their handlers could make certain estimates that were confirmed by other trackers and evidence—the massacre had happened three or four weeks ago. These remaining children shouldn't have still been alive.

Not that all of them were. The war hounds led them to fresh graves. Small ones.

"Someone's been taking care of them," Tisis said. "They're too young to have survived this long by themselves."

Men and women from Kip's retinue were trying to comfort the children now, trying to engage them in play. It worked with a few. Others were still too traumatized to do anything more than mechanically chew the food offered them.

"What I'm taking you to see may be the answer to who's been taking care of the kids," Winsen said. "Or maybe he was part of the murdering. Hell, maybe both."

They rode up the main track away from the empty village for a few minutes, and then cut over into farmland, passing through apple orchards that had been tended until recently.

They rode up a hillside orchard to where the top flattened out.

Who massacres a village, doesn't take any loot, doesn't burn anything, and kills everyone except the kids too young to speak? Why would the White King hide what he'd done here? He'd massacred other cities and deliberately left people alive to spread the tale.

And why did the name of the town seem familiar? Kip was certain he'd heard it before, but he must not have thought it was important at the time, because he hadn't locked it in his memory.

"How'd you even think to come way out here?" Kip asked Winsen.

"Big Leo said something about this place from his parents' traveling days with their troupe. I wanted to get away from the brats' crying and thought I'd find some quiet out at these ruins. Didn't expect *this*."

They emerged from the orderly rows of trees into a wide clearing. It was almost a perfect circle. Even the great limbs of the old apple trees had been trimmed long, long ago to not intrude into the circle. Younger limbs did intrude, though, telling a tale of uneven husbandry or failing respect for old tradition.

In the center of the grassy circle stood a stone plinth, a few feet across and only as tall as a man. It was no great monument. Oddly, the earth around the base of the plinth was freshly cracked, as if something restless lay beneath it.

On top of the small plinth an adolescent sat cross-legged, hands draped over his knees. He was olive-skinned, with his raven hair in a short ponytail, naked to the waist, stringy rather than merely skinny, a leather band tied around one bicep, and wearing the deerskin trousers of a Blood Forest hunter. But in one relaxed hand he held a hellstone dagger that was surely worth more than two fistfuls of rubies.

It appeared he'd been using the dagger on himself, for his body was encrusted with blood old and new in shades of scarlet and crimson and brown. He'd striped himself, perhaps in ritual mourning, lines down his forearms, lines on his face. Cuts deep enough to scar but not to maim, with older wounds poulticed but the blood not washed from his skin nor from his cruor-encrusted trousers.

Fresh blood coursed down his forehead into his left eye. The boy didn't look up as Kip dismounted and came forward. Kip gestured for the others to stay back.

They ignored him; everything about this young hunter spoke death.

Some intuition held Kip back from speaking. He came before the young man and sat on the ground, legs akimbo in deliberate imitation, as if he were a disciple at the foot of his master.

I thought he was young. I was wrong.

The boy had eyes as old as a great oak that has seen the leaves brown and fall a thousand times, blossoming from green to grave, from bower to bier, leafy souls soaking the soil and feeding the tree again, like a cannibal hungry for the fruit of his own body.

Kip sat still, staring up at him. The old young man looked at him with the patience of the zephyrs chewing a mountain down, a quick form with a slow intent. The blood obscuring his left eye reminded Kip of the Parian tradition of the eye of mercy and the eye of justice, the good eye and the evil.

With the shedding of blood comes blindness.

And slowly, Kip's mimicry became imitation, and imitation became communion. Communion not with each other, but each settling into the cold embrace of time and their mortality, separate souls in the night, but the same night, different journeys to the same end.

And then, as the blood dried on the young man's obsidian blade and on his face, he became slowly familiar.

A swirl of the wind brought the young ancient's wild scent to Kip's nose, and suddenly Kip was gripped by blank, black fear. He was sitting before one of the most dangerous men in history.

Voice raw, Kip said, "Greetings, *Sealgaire na Scian*, Daimhin Web."

Daimhin's chest stopped in midbreath. Then, in a rocky voice like a man waking from a too-long slumber, "She said you would know me, Guile."

Like a rusty lock cracking open at the key that was Daimhin's name spoken aloud, Kip remembered the man's card, all of it: touching the white stag with his very hand, the village braggart who disbelieved him, the unrequited love, the hunt, then coming home to the village burned to the ground by the White King's outriders.

After that came the memories in blood: the hunting of men, dressing them like wild game, hung upside down, skinned and drained of blood to be found by their comrades outside their very tents. He remembered a dozen cruel games invented to terrorize the invading Blood Robes.

Who was the woman who'd told him of Kip coming?

"The Third Eye," Kip said.

"She sent her message with this. It's some leather I've never encountered." Daimhin gestured to the armband he wore above his bicep. "It intrigued me more than her words. Arrogant, I thought her. She claimed to see the future. But how dare she tell *me* what to do? I have become a god of vengeance, a spirit of the forest. She bade me come here. To stop this. Then she begged. Words as wind to twist my will."

"What is it?" Kip asked.

"Not snakeskin, nor any reptile known in these lands. I came here not to obey her but hoping she might tell me more. Perhaps this was some new animal to hunt, to test myself against. Perhaps I might lose my taste for hunting men. But it's not done that. I'm like a wolf that takes one lamb and then cannot help but raid for sheep, no matter the dangers." He fingered that leather band around his bicep, but Kip was too far away to see anything strange about it. "By the time I came, I was too late. Another village massacred while I was gone hunting."

"Like your home village was. But Apple Grove this time," Kip guessed.

Daimhin nodded bloody guilt.

"Why'd he do this?" Kip asked. Taking a village's livestock, burning a few huts to halt resistance, taking a few men or women, Kip could understand why an invader would do those...but this? Both recklessly insane and secretive.

An invader doesn't want its massacres to be secret. No one's intimidated by a massacre they never learn about.

"*He* didn't," Daimhin said. "If by him you mean the White King. I tracked those who did this. They didn't come from the White King's camp, and these men hid from the White King's patrols both coming and going. It was only twenty men, but some of them were drafters, and all were armed with good muskets. The villagers scattered at first, but then they recognized the leader. He'd been raised here among them. But after enough of them came back into town, he seized them, and he demanded those in hiding or at outlying farms come in. Started killing people until they did. Made promises of safe passage. Lies, naturally."

"You didn't learn all that from their tracks," Kip said.

"On their way back to their boats on the coast, these *arrachtaigh*,   355 these monsters, came across a Blood Robe patrol and had to hide. One of them got separated from the others. Got lost. I found him. We talked."

Kip didn't bother to ask if that man was still alive.

"Can you tell me anything else about them?" Kip asked.

"Height and weight for most of them, a few would just be guesses. They call themselves Lightguards, came on some type of boat they called a sea chariot. Second-in-command walks with a crutch."

"Aram," Ben-hadad said from behind Kip. "That sonuvabitch."

"Commander was a young man named Guile," Daimhin said. "I didn't ask many more questions. There were kids dying."

Kip's stomach sank. "Zymun."

No one protested that surely he wouldn't do such a thing.

"Why?" Cruxer asked.

"Zymun was raised here, right? Maybe it was a childhood grudge?" Tisis asked. "But why kill everyone else? He can't have hated *everyone*."

"I think once people saw him for what he was, they may well have all hated him," Cruxer said. "He's certainly capable of hating all of them."

"The massacre was to cover up whatever he came here to accomplish," Kip said.

"You think he met with the White King?" Tisis asked.

"Definitely possible. Maybe he was seen, and decided—" Kip started.

"No tracks that way," Daimhin said. "They might have taken their boats, I suppose, but there's a good road straight to the old city. He would have known about it if he grew up here. I don't think he came to meet with the wights."

"And they hid from the Blood Robe patrol," Ben-hadad said. "I don't think he was making an alliance with the White King, as convenient as that would be for us to expose."

Kip said, "Whatever he did here, he killed everyone in this village in such a way that we would think the White King ordered it, if we found out about it at all. By leaving the houses standing, refugees from elsewhere can move right in, and squatters don't often dig too deeply into why the houses they've moved into are empty."

"Nor do they appreciate when others ask where the original owners are," Big Leo said. "So they do the covering up for you."

"That's why he didn't let his men steal any jewelry," Kip said. "He didn't want them to keep any evidence of their crimes."

It was all...pretty clever, actually. Zymun was stupidly impulsive at times, but he was smart enough to realize he could disappear for three or four days and turn up saying he'd been in brothels, and everyone would believe it. A massacre, this far away? No one would even think to connect him to it. A year or two ago, it would have been impossible. It still would be, except that he had access to skimmers.

"But why not kill the children?" Winsen asked. "Why add the risk of letting them live?"

"Some of the men must've balked at it," Tisis said. "Many men will barter with evil, when they must. 'We'll kill the men, sure, but not the women. Fine, the women too, but not the kids. They can't even speak. They're no danger to us.' The Lightguard's rife with thugs and criminals, but they're not all... Zymun."

"That's the Lightguard for ya," Ben-hadad said, "willing to butcher helpless men, women, and children, but they draw the line at toddlers. Moral fucking paragons."

"We should kill all of them," Cruxer said. Fair as Cruxer was, there was nothing soft in him toward evil.

Kip had known Zymun was a snake, but his wanting to kill Kip so he could be assured of his own position had at least seemed understandable, if cruelly calculating and cold. Their grandfather was cruelly calculating and cold, too.

Murdering several hundred people... for what?... was a different thing entirely.

Kip couldn't imagine Andross Guile doing that.

"The babies died," Daimhin said with a voice like a swimmer in the great ocean seeing no land in sight, no ships, breath short, one last confession on his lips.

It brought Kip back to the present.

"Fourteen babies they didn't kill, but I couldn't save them. Not one. I couldn't find milk. No cow nor horse nor pig nor goat in the time I dared to be away. I went in to the camp followers who haven't yet left Azuria, tried to hire a wet nurse. They'd heard of me, though, from the Blood Robes. They feared me. They raised the hue and cry, said I was there to steal their women, tried to kill me.

"I came back. I could never go far again. I cut up food. The babies couldn't take it. I chewed up food, gave them little bits. They spat it up. They didn't even all die in my arms. There were too many dying for me to even give them that. I thought of giving them the black mercy, but I held out hope that someone would come at the last minute. The Third Eye had sent me to stop the massacre, but I'd failed. I hoped maybe she'd sent someone else to save the children." He took a deep breath. "But maybe I was the last hope. Or maybe the others failed, too."

His voice rolled across a vast distance, a messenger telling the facts, but tears rolled, blood and water mixing on his cheek.

"I was so happy when the crying stopped. Not relieved, mind you. *Happy*. I wept with joy. What kind of a horror could be 'happy'—"

"That's not joy," Kip interrupted. "That's a breakdown." The words kind of slipped out, but he also let them.

"Bugger off. You don't know me," Daimhin said, eyes coming to hard focus.

"Yes I do," Kip said. "The day you took your first stag, your hands were shaking so hard that when you cleaned it, your knife punctured its intestines. Your father never told anyone. He didn't want to shame you in front of the village. But you were ashamed, and your secret shame spurred you to become a better hunter. You expect perfection of yourself, and it's always been your shame that makes you redouble your efforts. It's brought you to heights unimaginable to other men... but it broke you here."

Kip could feel his Mighty getting tense even before he saw the white-knuckled grip Daimhin had on his obsidian knife.

Shame is a gorgon. Before you grab her serpentine hair to drag her into the light, remember what her hair *is*.

"Forgive me," Kip said. "I know you, but you don't know me. I shouldn't have spoken so." Except it had been on purpose, and the truth lay wriggling in the light like a rainbow trout thumping about the bottom of the boat, gasping in the air when it so wanted to breathe safe water. "The cutting. Tell me about it."

He knew it was an old pagan ritual way of mourning the dead, but Daragh the Coward had cut himself as bravado and as a mask. The same action might mean something very different in Daimhin Web.

The young man was on a jagged edge, looking as if he wasn't sure if he should attack Kip or throw himself at his feet or bolt into the forest. Instead, defeated, he sulked. "One for each one dead."

"But not too deep," Kip said. The hunter knew exactly how deeply to cut to cause a scar without impeding function.

"I have promises to keep," Daimhin said, as if it were simple.

"To the other children," Kip said, understanding him. "You've been taking care of them."

"Not well," Daimhin spat.

"You've made a vow that you'll take care of them forever." Kip had thought that the murderers had left the food. It had been Daimhin. "A penance?"

"I made them orphans," Daimhin said.

Came too late to stop them being made orphans by others. It was very different.

There had to be thirty children here. And this boy—maybe twenty years old? maybe years short of that—hunter and legend though he was, this *boy* was going to be their mother and father? It was insane.

And yet, war makes insanity a necessity.

"One might suggest..." Kip said. Then he wasn't sure if he should go on. But he bulled ahead. Drag it all into the light. Let the light sort it out, the evil and the good, and the good that had made its concessions to weakness and fallibility and human foibles. "If the Third Eye could see the future, wouldn't she have known you wouldn't make it in time to help, even if she asked? Maybe this wasn't your fault at all."

"She did ask," Daimhin Web said. As if it were simple.

"If she asked knowing you'd say no, is it really your fault?"

"She *did* ask," Daimhin said.

"Why would she ask if she knew he wouldn't get here in time?" Cruxer asked quietly, aggrieved. As if the Third Eye had piled guilt atop a boy too sensitive to hold its weight. Hard as he was, and as starkly as he liked to see the world separated into sheep and goats, at times Cruxer could show deep compassion. He could see that Daimhin the Hunter would never be only a hunter any longer. Cruxer, who'd been catapulted from an old life by his guilt over a death he couldn't stop, Cruxer understood.

If they made it through this damned war, Kip hoped to see that understanding, compassionate side of his dear friend flourish.

Tisis said quietly, "I think sometimes we can all see the future coming, and we can't help but act, even when we know it's too little or too late, too feeble. Sometimes we act even though we know it will mean our death," she said, locking her jade-green eyes with Kip's. "I don't think that makes us fools. I think it makes us great."

And you're staying with me, Kip thought. Does that make you a fool, or great, or both?

But Kip tore his eyes away from his remarkable bride, who was as undeserved as sunshine on a winter morning.

He saw perhaps the real reason for the Third Eye to send Daimhin: if she'd told him there were orphans for him to care for, he wouldn't have come. What were orphans to a hunter? But by lying, by telling him there was a massacre he could stop, she could save these orphans as Daimhin revealed a mettle he himself hadn't known he possessed.

After all, like everyone else, prophets can lie.

"Tell me about this, this clearing, that plinth," Kip said instead. "You came here for a reason. Or was it merely for the quiet?"

"Ha!" Daimhin said. But he breathed and looked at the sun for a time, and spun his hellstone knife and sheathed it, and jumped off the plinth with the grace of an artist whose body is his brush.

He turned and bowed to the plinth with a gravity that might have been mockery. He was a broken man indeed, teetering at the edge of madness.

"Seven groves, in seven lands," he said. "Apple, pear, fig, pomegranate, olive, orange, and atasifusta. Blood Forest, Ruthgar, Paria, Abornea, Ilyta, Tyrea, and Atash. Seven cities, seven mirrors, seven colored lenses. They were first meant to be a perfect circle, but compromises were made, so they became a circle as lopsided as our politics. This one had to be this close to the coast because treaties with the pygmies forbade the Tyrean Empire deeper access to the woods."

A prohibition that obviously hadn't stuck. Not that that was the point right now.

Daimhin said, "My forefathers were the keepers of this sacred grove, once upon a time. My father brought me here to visit once. Kind of a pilgrimage in our family, though we haven't lived here for generations. I came here hoping... for their understanding? Their forgiveness? Their wisdom? Ha. They failed, too, after all, and let us all be scattered into the deep forest. I hoped..." He snorted. "Maybe it was just for the quiet, after all."

"There was a city here, then?" Kip asked.

"Apple Grove was always small. I think most of the grove cities were. All were close or within a direct line of sight to great cities—Azuria, here, for one. They were intended to be isolated from the city's politics. As if such a thing is possible. But at least it is harder to capture two fortified positions than just one. It didn't work as intended, of course. The fort on Ruic Head was constructed solely to house Ru's Great Mirror, but Satrapah Naveen later moved the Great Mirror into Ru itself to show her power."

Kip hadn't been thinking in terms of the ancients when he'd been there, but it was true, the fort of Ruic Head was far too large for what the Chromeria thought it had been. The fort had thick timber walls, but it had been built on stone foundations. Before the relatively recent advent of cannons that could shoot great distances into the bay, there was no function for a fort there. A simple lookout tower would have sufficed. Maybe a lighthouse. There hadn't been need for an entire fort.

Which was interesting history and all, but if there were big mirrors in all these groves, where was the mirror that had been *here*?

But Tisis was already going in another direction. "Azuria?" she asked. "I've never even heard of a city called that."

"The pygmies didn't lose all their wars to the Tyrean Empire," Daimhin said. "They wiped out the city while it was still being built. Razed it. Crucified everyone in it or fed them to their tygre wolves.

My people fled without a fight after that. The ruins of Azuria are over beyond the new wall now, where the White King was. There's little there now except access to a good harbor."

"How do you know all this?" Kip asked.

"We deep Foresters keep our traditions alive in our songs, not on corruptible parchments or skins that can be changed." Daimhin's face clouded. "Or we did. I wasn't a singer of the songs and I don't know all the stories. They'll die now, I suppose. Already have, maybe, with my village."

And *that's* why you put the stories in books, Kip thought but didn't say. Books don't tend to get killed.

But that wasn't helpful. Nor kind. Nor the point.

Daimhin said, "I thought it was a coincidence that this Seer should contact me and want me to come here. It's been centuries since my people were here. I feel no connection to this land. I love my forests wild. I am no tender of domesticated trees."

"Arborist," Kip supplied. Also not helpful, but his mind was far away. "Did you say something about an orange grove? In Tyrea?"

"Yes."

"I don't suppose you know where that was?" Kip asked.

"I can't recall the name. Near the Great Dome."

" 'Great Dome'?" Tisis asked.

Kip felt like he'd plucked an invisible spiderweb, or perhaps a trip-wire. He remembered the old ruin in the orange grove where he'd gone so often. He said, "There were stories that Sundered Rock was once a great stone dome. Maybe it was, back when these groves were established." He turned back to Daimhin. "What happened here? What cracked the ground?"

"I assume something happened to make the Great Mirror move recently. But you're the drafter. You tell me," Daimhin said.

What mirror? Liv Danavis had directed them here saying she'd activated a mirror . . . but there was no mirror here, just a big empty field in the middle of an apple orchard.

But Daimhin was close enough now that the light caught on his leather armband. It shimmered a bit, like it was made of many tiny scales.

And that lute string of memory thrummed once more.

This moment was the kind of thing a Seer might see: Daimhin standing with his armband in the sun, talking to Kip, who was suddenly intensely interested in it, rather than the blood all over the young hunter or the blade in his hand or the cracked earth at his feet.

"Daimhin, do me a favor," Kip said. "Close your eyes, and think that you're in the blackest night, and that you want desperately to hide. Will yourself to disappear into the blackness."

After a moment of staring at him inscrutably, Daimhin closed his eyes. The armband shimmered and went a smoky, mottled black.

The others muttered imprecations, and when Daimhin opened his eyes and saw it, he seemed stunned.

"What does that mean?" Tisis asked.

"How did you know to do that?" Ben-hadad asked Kip.

"Because I've seen that kind of skin before," Kip said.

It was the same skin as what made the master cloak he'd given Teia. Kip had thought that cloak had been made of human skin—a light skin and a dark one stitched together—but he'd been wrong.

That shimmer reminded him of a being who changed his appearance at will, in far more complex ways than simple camouflage, who appeared beautiful when in reality he was ugly and burnt: Abaddon.

And then it reminded Kip of another immortal, whose glory had shimmered like the sun, but who had shifted herself effortlessly to walk among mortals: Rea Siluz.

"It's an immortal's skin," Kip said. "One of those from whose ranks came the old gods. Not men dressed in luxin and power to fool the gullible, the real gods. The Two Hundred. The Fallen. The djinn."

"I don't suppose they shed their skin?" Cruxer asked.

"I, I don't think so."

"So someone *skinned* one?" Cruxer asked.

"Who could do that?" Ben-hadad asked.

"Maybe we can," Winsen said flatly.

"Shut up, Win. Not funny," Cruxer said.

"No," Kip said. "I think Winsen's kind of right. We're fighting the *gods*. The Third Eye wants us to know... we can do it. They can be killed."

Chapter 56

Teia was running out of time. She leaned against the wall of a cooper's stall, half-shaded in the afternoon sun, nearly invisible not because of paryl magic but because she wore the hooded cloak low over her face and its stripes matched the tones of the wall and the shadows perfectly. She couldn't maintain her paryl cloud for hours, and hours it had been.

Sun Day was only ten days away. Whatever the Order was planning, it would spring then. Tens of thousands of pilgrims had swollen Big Jasper's streets. It seemed that for every person who sensibly kept away from making a pilgrimage because of the war, someone else came in their place, desperate because of the war.

She couldn't have let Halfcock live with what he knew of her, but by killing him, she'd given up her one certain lead to where the Braxians would meet the night before Sun Day. Halfcock hadn't known where their rituals would be held beforehand, and claimed he always would find a note in his pocket with directions when the time was close. So he couldn't tell her where it would be, but she could've followed him.

Now this safe house was her only lead.

A safe house no one had visited in three days.

It could be a trap, of course.

Worse, the longer she waited, the more likely it was that Murder Sharp would get wind of Halfcock's disappearance. Would that lead him here?

She gathered her paryl around her, going invisible, and moved through the street. She'd mastered it now, moving with her head down, shooting the quickest glances this way and that to see what she must, moving with the understanding that others didn't see her at all. It was a busy street, but the little house had a recessed doorway.

Teia slipped into it and started to work with the picks and anchors.

Through Quentin, Karris had made sure she had the best gear, but truth be told, Teia still wasn't much good with lockpicks.

The mechanism was neither new nor tight nor complicated, and it still took her almost ten sweating minutes and one ruined anchor to open the lock.

Opening the door a crack, Teia streamed a cloud of paryl vapor through the gap and into the room beyond. She felt nothing moving.

She looked back to the street and the bustle of carts, then opened the door—neither fast, which would draw the eye, nor too slow, which would make any who saw wonder why a door was swinging open by itself. Nope, this was just as if someone in the house had opened the door, changed their mind, and closed it again.

Her heart was in her throat as she stepped inside, hands baring daggers from sheaths, paryl readied for the attack. She pushed the door shut with one foot.

The trap would spring shut now, if there was one.

One breath passed with no attack.

Two.

She streamed out clouds of paryl again, moving from room to room quickly, not really noticing anything, merely feeling for life or empty places, trapdoors, hidden alcoves.

It was clear.

She breathed easy for the first time in half an hour.

Empty. Like she'd supposed it would be, after all her time watching the place.

Now to work.

There was a bed that was too rich for this neighborhood by half, a closet with various clothes rich and poor, and a woman's white Braxian robes.

That was good. At least it told Teia Halfcock had been honest with her about that much. This was someone in the Order's safe house.

Teia examined everything for some hint of who the woman was. The sheets were Ilytian cotton, but had no tailor's mark on them. The nicer clothing came from a variety of tailors around Big Jasper, but not a piece was monogrammed.

So whoever owned this place wasn't stupid, then.

Teia searched for two hours and found nothing.

She sat on the bed and sighed. What was she going to do? She could set Karris's people on it—the White did have many other eyes and ears—but Karris had asked that Teia reserve that for an emergency. Anything to do with the Order should be held closer than close, lest they all get killed.

What were her other options? If she set Karris's people on this, she could get back to hunting for her father, which almost certainly would be where Murder Sharp would have his best traps set. But some traps you have to risk.

It was hopeless. For months and months she'd been hunting the Order, and she had nothing. She was a total failure.

If she could just think. There had to be some way forward.

She closed her eyes.

When she opened them, she couldn't tell how long they'd been closed. Had she fallen asleep? No, surely not.

The rattle of a key in the lock sent a jolt through her. Shit! She hadn't even locked the door behind her.

But it bought her an extra couple of moments now, as whoever was on the other side had first locked the door, tried it, and now unlocked it.

She jumped to her feet, pulled the cloak shut, went invisible, and roughly smoothed the blankets from the depression her sitting on them had made.

The door cracked open, and a man poked his head in, a puzzled look on his face. When he saw no one was inside, he stepped in. He was fair-skinned, dressed in slaves' garb, dark hair oiled back, clean shaven.

He checked the rooms, and straightened out the wrinkles in the bedspread with a disapproving look. Just a slave checking the house for his mistress—of course she wouldn't clean a safe house herself.

Rich people. So helpless.

The slave busied himself, dusting the already clean surfaces, and Teia had to dodge him a few times, as silently as possible, regulating even her breath, and looking only at his feet. He was soon finished, but when he got to the door, he paused. "It's madness, Micael. Don't do it. It's the whipping post and salt packed in the wounds unto death if she catches you."

He reached his hand to the door, but instead of opening it, locked it.

He went to the sideboard, opened a drawer, and took out the silver. He laid the silver-polishing kit next to it, but he didn't polish the utensils, as if still momentarily at war with himself.

Then he held the front of his trousers away from his waist and scratched his pubic area with a fork.

He examined the tines carefully and then put it back away, glancing around guiltily.

Teia's mouth dropped open. She almost lost hold on her invisibility. But he worked systematically through the silver, until every piece had been down his pants.

"'Thank you, Mistress.' 'Your crop, Mistress?' 'With pleasure, Mistress.'" He repeated the phrases like they were a meditation prayer: he must have had to say them hundreds of times, but now he was reclaiming them. In the future, whenever he said those, he would think of this.

He was grinning like a maniac.

He moved to the bedroom, and he wiped his ass across every single one of the pillows, both sides. "'How did you sleep, Mistress? Oh, a scent? Odd. I'll have a stern word with the laundress. This old house *is* a little fusty, despite my best efforts. But I'll try harder, Mistress.'"

Teia had heard rumors of others doing this kind of thing when she'd been a slave, of course. She'd fantasized about it herself when her owner, that cunt Aglaia Crassos, had dreamed up some new humiliation for her or her friends. Watching someone deathly ill be forced to lick up their own vomit, or seeing a boy ten years old beaten to death because he'd peeked in on the mistress noisily having sex with someone.

Later she'd heard the same kinds of stories among slave owners, albeit repeated with more horror than glee: stories of slaves drying the dishes with their poxy undergarments, of men putting their cocks in the cups, or urinating and worse in the soup. They were the kinds of stories that played on the fears of those served and the fantasies of those enslaved, so of course they were popular.

But she hadn't thought anyone actually did it.

It was hatred to the point of suicide.

If she'd heard someone else tell this story, she'd laugh about it. But here, seeing this man do it, it was desperately unfunny. This Micael was risking torture and death merely to secretly dishonor a woman. He likely wouldn't even be here to see her use the forks or pillows. He was right: it was madness.

Enough, Micael. Just say her name. I don't need to see all this.

He finished doing everything he could think of, and went again to the door. "I should clean it all," he said. "Vengeance defiles the hand that enacts it. Orholam will bring justice in its appointed hour." He leaned his head on the doorframe, leaving a gap behind him.

He still blocked half the doorway, but Teia realized it was her best chance. She could easily leave after he left—but she had no way to relock the door, at least not in time to follow. Now or never!

She slipped out behind him, not even brushing his tunic.

She'd never been so happy to be petite in her life.

"No," Micael said. "Fuck her. *Fuck* her."

Say her name!

He left, and Teia followed him.

In several blocks he arrived at a small hovel, opened the door. It was apparently his own house. But there he stopped. Looking suddenly skyward, he said, "Orholam, You know she deserves it. If I stay my hand from vengeance, Orholam, You have to promise me..."

He stood there for a moment, then shook his head and sighed. Teia could tell he was walking back to his mistress's safe house to clean it up.

She didn't follow. She'd hoped that he would take her directly back to his mistress's estate, but it looked like she wasn't that lucky. Whoever the noblewoman was, she was too lazy to clean her own safe house, but she wasn't completely stupid. Her slave had his own hovel.

The Order really did do a good job enforcing all the disciplines of secrecy.

Quickly, Teia ransacked the slave's belongings. There were several tunics, with old bloodstains on the backs from whippings. Last, there was an overjacket with a family insignia on it.

Teia had been unlucky that it had taken her so long to find a time when she could get Halfcock alone and isolated. She'd been unlucky that the noblewoman hadn't been at her safe house, and that the slave had never said her name. She'd been unlucky that this slave was new and so Teia didn't recognize him and therefore his owner right away.

But finally. Finally luck turned its golden face full upon her.

For the first time in weeks, Teia smiled. Wonder of wonders, miracle of miracles, it seemed Orholam had as black a sense of humor as any soldier: according to this livery, the slave Micael belonged to Aglaia Crassos. Teia's very own former owner, that utter abomination, had joined the Order.

As Teia walked the streets home, she actually laughed aloud at a thought: Micael had prayed for vengeance on his owner. *Teia* was going to be an answer to prayer!

Aglaia was in the Order. Sooner or later, Teia was going to get to kill her.

Sooner, Teia thought. Definitely sooner. Just in case.

Chapter 57

Worried they were stepping into a trap—still—the Mighty didn't let Kip climb the luxin ladder until second to last, but at that point it didn't matter. He joined them atop the new wall.

The White King was no Gavin Guile. This wall was no Brightwater Wall; it wasn't luxin but simple wood, more a frontier fortification than a work of art. It wasn't high, either, less than three paces in most places. But it was vast, encompassing a half circle nearly a league across.

A nearly empty league, now.

"Huh! There's no one here," Ferkudi said.

The others looked at him. Big Leo cursed under his breath.

"Can I push him off the wall?" Winsen asked. "Please?"

"He'd probably survive," Ben-hadad said.

"You're right, that is a problem," Winsen said.

"Not the first time he's been dropped on his head, I'd wager," Big Leo said.

"Question is," Tisis said, "if he landed on his head, would that set him right, or make him *more* Ferkudi?"

Some scowled. Some shuddered.

"Yeah," Winsen said, "best not to risk it."

"Ah, come on, Ferk," Cruxer said, hugging the hurt dope around one boulder-sized shoulder. "You know we love ya."

It was a beautiful morning, sunny and clear. The forests were a green to make your eyes ache, rolling to the Cerulean Sea which was still and dark as wine from last night's glass at this early hour.

"But they're gone," Ferkudi said, re-restating the obvious. "There's no boats. Am I the only one surprised by this? Are you telling me we hurried for no reason?"

Ben-hadad was staring through a far-glass. "There are some people still here. Looks like they left most of the camp followers behind. At least, I hope that's most of them. If Daimhin Web's telling us the truth, though, that's only those who haven't already left."

"But no army," Winsen said.

"They're already gone," Kip said.

"What's that mean?" Ferkudi asked.

"It means we have to race them," Tisis said. "We didn't make it in time to stop them. We—or our messengers—have to warn the Chromeria." She glanced at Kip like, 'Are you sure you want to do this?'

"All of us," Kip said. "We'll join the fight."

Tisis sighed. "I know. Sorry."

"It'll be our last stand, won't it?" Ferkudi asked. He looked at the grim faces around him, then bobbed his big round head. "All right."

"Something occurred to me," Cruxer said. "Your half brother."

"Yeah?" Kip asked. He suspected where this was going.

"He's a straight-up murderer. No boundaries at all. And he's the Prism-elect. Prism fully in less than a week."

"On Sun Day, yep," Kip said.

"And he's got the Lightguard, which have already committed atrocities for him."

Kip nodded, as everyone looked harder at them both. He knew where this was going.

"We've got no evidence for what he did here," Cruxer said. "But he'll worry we do."

"Uh-huh," Kip said.

Tisis took his hand and squeezed. "I didn't say anything, I swear."

"I know," Kip said. "This was going to come up sooner or later."

"We're heading back to the Chromeria with purely good intentions," Cruxer said. "But men with impure eyes see dirt everywhere they look. We're headed for two kinds of fights, aren't we? And one of 'em isn't the kind where we can save you."

Kip looked from face to face: these boys he'd watched become men. He said, "I didn't know who he was then, but High General Corvan

Danavis half raised me, and he used to say politics are more dangerous than sharks or sea demons. We have to be ready to make sacrifices," Kip said. "That doesn't just mean you. It means me, too."

"If we go back, Zymun will kill you," Cruxer said.

"Nah," Kip said with a wink. "My grandfather will kill me first."

Chapter 58

"I will have my vengeance, Ravi."

"Shh, no names, no names!" the man whispered.

Though she was nearly dozing behind a curtain, Teia's ears pricked up immediately.

"In my own home?" Lady Aglaia Crassos scoffed.

Teia had been following Lady Crassos for days now. She'd learned all sorts of things about her, from her numerous lovers to her far more numerous business associates. The last few years had been disastrous for the Crassos family, starting with the death of Aglaia's brother at Gavin Guile's hands, so Aglaia had been cobbling together allies and coin in ways she'd never paid attention to earlier in her life. Teia couldn't even tell where the lines between lovers, business associates, and political allies might be drawn, either.

She'd made no secret of her hatred for the Guiles, though.

Which might have been why some of the men who met with Aglaia wanted to do so privately.

Teia had endangered herself unnecessarily at first, when she'd presumed a furtive little banker who was meeting with Aglaia must be in the Order. That had been merely an assignation: the man was married, and the only conspiracy he seemed to be part of was disguising the true extent of his fees from his clients.

So Teia tried not to get too excited as she drafted paryl once more—when was she going to go wight on this stuff? She'd been using so much!—and peeked out.

Aglaia was checking the jewels glued to her fingernails. "I only joined your little club to get vengeance on the Guiles, Ravi. And I want that magnificent asshole Murder Sharp to serve *me*. I want him to be the one who does it, and I want him to know he's serving *me*. Where is he? How do I hire him?"

Oh, so that was why Aglaia had been screwing a banker. She was angling for a future loan.

But Teia was only trying to feel matter-of-fact. This was her lead!

Ravi was a little beaver-faced man who fretted with his hat. "It doesn't work like that, and don't let them see you with that attitude. I'll...I'll speak with the priest on your behalf."

"The high priest, and I'll speak to him myself."

"I have no idea who that is!" Ravi said.

"Fine, then, the priest. Which one is he?" Horse-faced though she was, with her perfect braided blond hair and her tiny vest worked with coins, Aglaia could be attractive, Teia had to admit, and Ravi had certainly noticed her cleavage and the familiarity of her wearing house clothes in front of him.

He made a pained noise. "It doesn't work that way, *really*. Even I'm not supposed to know who he is, and I've been in the Order for three years. Each priest has several congregations and they're always very, very careful."

"If you figured it out, then I would have, too, within a few more weeks. I won't tattle on you, Ravi...sweetest."

"A little fear is appropriate. These people aren't *safe*."

She leaned forward, clasping her hands and making the most of her cleavage, and did she pout her lips just a little? Regardless, she waited until Ravi's eyes flicked down to her breasts, which only made it more withering when she said, "Get some stones, dear man. *We* are these people now."

His jaw twitched with momentary indignation, but then Teia saw that he was the small kind of man who, when insulted, tried to prove he didn't deserve the insult. "I suppose...maybe they'll forget that I was the one who brought you in. He's of medium height, thin..." He seemed to lose his nerve and stopped.

"We're masked and robed, Ravi. You've described half of them."

He gulped. "I just—I just have to think! The disguises rotate with where we meet. I can't remember!"

"Ravi," she said soothingly. "Haven't things gone well for you as long as you've been with me? Trust me, and things can go better yet."

He sighed, defeated. "It's Atevia Zelorn."

"Zelorn? The wine merchant?!"

"You can't approach him until after the Feast of the Dying Light. There's a huge party afterward. Stuff slips. He won't know it's me if you wait. Please, Lady Crassos, *please* be respectful. These people..."

"Of course, of course, my dear." Aglaia put a hand on Ravi's cheek, softly kissed his lips, then firmly pushed him away.

The man was reduced to a stammering flubberkin, which was frankly *bizarre*. It was painfully obvious that Aglaia despised him, wasn't it?

If Teia hadn't already reasons beyond counting to hate Aglaia, she would have added this easy manipulation to the list. Although it had been rather smoothly done, hadn't it? The woman wielded what she had like a chain whip.

Add another reason to the list of reasons to hate her: making Teia admire something about her. Sweet Orholam's garlicky breath, Teia was going to enjoy killing her.

She didn't think that the Order was going to kill any of the remaining Guiles just because Aglaia Crassos wished it, but she didn't know how much she should bet on that.

She couldn't let Aglaia get in touch with Murder Sharp. Right now, as far as Sharp was concerned, Aglaia was just one barely initiated member of the Order among many. But the woman's whole purpose in joining was vengeance on the Guiles, which Teia wasn't going to allow. But wouldn't the Order find it suspicious if Aglaia disappeared right after she insisted on killing a Guile?

Or would it be more suspicious if Ravi told the leadership how she'd disappeared before she even got to ask?

Well, there'd be no suspicion at all if Teia killed both of them now. After all, she had all she needed from them.

This is how life gets cheap. Someone teaches you how easy it is to kill. Someone gives you permission. The next moment it simply seems like the thing to do. You're stopping an unwanted flow of information, not sending immortal souls to their maker for judgment.

It was a hell of a thing, war. And yet part of her loved it.

Regardless of how she felt, though, this was still the thing to do. They had chosen treason. Teia was simply the satrapies' shield coming down on their necks.

There was nothing more to think about it.

The meeting ended soon after, and Teia followed Ravi Satish. Finding Aglaia again would be easy. Ravi was the more pressing.

Lord Ravi had come from one of the families dispossessed and bankrupted during the False Prism's War. He had little more than the clothes on his back, and no morals whatsoever. He supported his delusions about a return to power on illegal slave trading—mostly from drugging and enslaving sailors with the help of unscrupulous tavern owners.

He was the kind of man who would have lots of enemies—but not subtle ones.

Blunt force, Teia thought, as she followed him through the streets.

She didn't want any inexplicable (and therefore possibly caused by paryl) deaths to pique the Order's interest. A knife? A knife would work, too, but knifings were almost never clean. An assassin might kill with a single well-placed thrust, but usually a knife murder involved dozens of stabs and slashes, lots of mess and noise, and more danger. If she wanted a stabbing to look like the result of a drunken brawl or a sudden passion, she'd have to be willing to dice him up.

She'd done enough grappling recently, thanks. She'd rather not.

Blunt force it was. A single, furious smash over the head could result in death, and look almost accidental. Someone might hit a man he hated over the head, see what he'd done, and then flee. It could be almost soundless, too, where a knife fight would be more notable if it *weren't* heard than if it were.

At one point as she followed him, Lord Satish walked right along the edge of a quay he'd cut through as a shortcut. Teia had a sap, a leather casing covering a pouch of lead balls.

Hit him, grab his purse, and roll his body into the water! Quick!

But she hesitated, looking around to see if anyone might witness it, and when she was sure that there was no one looking, Lord Satish was already past the place where it would have been a good option.

She should've been more aware. She should always be thinking about what to do if an option presented itself. Dammit!

He led her to a boardinghouse. It didn't exactly have an inn on the first floor, more just a single hogshead barrel of wine, an old door propped on sawhorses to make a counter, and one currently occupied stool. Lord Ravi paid the wine pourer, was given a full tankard of wine, and told which room he could sleep in. Then the barman went back to chatting with the two women who were sharing the lone stool.

Teia noted which stairs creaked, then followed Ravi up, her lesser weight silent. She hadn't been close enough to hear which room he was in. She could only hope that the slaving business had been going well enough for him that he could afford to have the room to himself.

Which was kind of twisted, if she thought about it.

He opened the door, and Teia peeked over his shoulder. Empty. Perfect.

She didn't follow him in. Instead, she went downstairs and found the boardinghouse's utility closet. Boardinghouses always had things to fix, even if, like here, they didn't actually fix them all that often.

Nonetheless, she was able to find a hammer with an iron head. Good enough.

She ghosted back up the stairs. No sense in delaying things.

But she paused at the door.

One breath, T. You get one deep breath to panic. Then you move.

She took her long deep breath, and savored her paralysis like a warm bed on a cold morning. Then she exhaled slowly, shimmering into visibility and removing her hood.

She opened the door and stepped into the room like she owned the place. It was small, nondescript, not very clean, with fresh rushes thrown down on the bed on top of months of dirty ones. Ravi Satish was halfway into pulling his tunic over his head.

At the sound of the door opening and closing, he said, "What the hell? Arun told me I'd have this room to myself to—oh."

He finished shucking his tunic off and stopped speaking as he saw her.

"Dammit, that's what he told *me*," Teia said. "Did one of us get the wrong room?"

"Uh, second room on the right?" Ravi said.

"That's what he told me," Teia said, giving him a bold look.

"Arun's always been a joker. I'm going to have to thank him for this one, though."

"No," Teia said quietly. "No you're not." She took off the master cloak and hung it on a hook by the door.

Ravi picked up his tankard, still standing bare-chested. "I'm, uh, not sure I take your meaning."

"Would you be willing to share?"

"Share? The bed?" he asked.

"The wine. I'm parched." But she smirked as if the bed might be a possibility, later.

"Oh, the wine. Of course. Of course."

"Thank you," she said. She took the tankard and pretended to drink. She coughed. "Oooh," she said, "that is really bad."

"Does the trick, though," he said with a chuckle. He looked her up and down.

She set down the tankard on the lone table. Out of the way.

Then she turned back to him.

His eyes went round as he saw her hellstone stare. She pinched the nerves in his spine hard, and caught him as he fell.

She guided him to his knees, then released the nerves. "I know you're in the Order. If you believe in repentance," she whispered in his ear, "now's the time."

She would have a few seconds until he regained feeling. Should, anyway. She grabbed the hammer from the master cloak's pocket, stepped up to him, and swung with all her might.

Teia had never killed a man this way. She wasn't sure what she'd expected, but hadn't expected the hammer to *stick*. It crushed through his temple in a splatter of blood and bone and brain, and *stopped*.

Ravi crumpled to the ground, his skull clinging to the hammer harder than her fingers did.

He tumbled to the floor, but somehow, he wasn't dead.

"My teeth. You broke my teeth!" he moaned into the ground.

Teeth? What the hell?! But Teia was already moving, reaching out with paryl to squeeze his spine and grab his heart.

Make it stop. Dear Orholam, would you please just *die*?

He went limp as she found the right grip, but his heart kept stubbornly pumping on.

Then she saw them, glistening pearly beside his head. He'd broken his teeth against the floor as he fell.

But whinging about his teeth? When there was a hammer in his head?

Gradually, Teia found the nerves she needed, and Lord Ravi Satish died at her feet, sphincters relaxing, burbling, befouling his clothes and the air.

She rifled through his pockets to find his coin sticks and a knife, then stepped back quickly before the blood pool spreading from his head could reach her feet. The last thing she wanted to leave here was her small footprints.

She tore off his sleeve and looked at herself in the room's small polished bronze mirror. She blotted off the blood spatter on her face and neck and hand—there wasn't much, thank Orholam, and none at all she could see against her blacks.

She dipped his blade into the pool of blood, then flicked her wrist to distribute blood drops on the linens. Ravi's body had no cuts on it, so they'd guess that he'd cut his attacker before he himself was killed.

Then she tossed the knife across the room.

It clanged loudly, but no one was going to look into such a small sound in a place like this.

She left, invisible. Several blocks later, she stopped at the dock where she'd almost simply pushed him into the water, where she'd missed her chance at murder without drama, or blood, or pain. Without broken teeth and blood spatter.

She'd told herself this wasn't murder. It was sanctioned killing.

Granted: sanctioned without trial, commissioned in secret, committed in secret, and she would be prosecuted by the very state she served if she were caught, lest the Order find out how close the Chromeria had gotten to them. It had been murder in every sense except for a few words of permission spoken to the ephemeral air.

Teia hadn't done anything but work in months. She'd never gambled or drank or listened to the minstrels or watched the puppets or the light shows. She'd needed to train. She'd needed to hunt. She'd needed to train some more. There was always more to do that might later mean the difference between life and death.

She'd passed her name day, and even she hadn't noticed. She was becoming all warrior, all the bits of little girl and woman scraped away to leave only muscles and magic and blades.

If she were tough enough, and cold enough, and strong enough, she would go back to Aglaia Crassos's estate right now. Murder the woman, or kill her, if there was any difference anymore, and be done with this before anything else could go wrong.

You keep moving before your enemy can recover and counter. You don't stop until they can't recover, until they can never counter again.

But she wasn't tough, or strong, or cold in any way except physically right now.

It was time to find Quentin, and report, and then though she knew he didn't really like to be touched, he was going to hug her while she cried for five minutes, then she would go out again. And she was only going to cry about killing people, not about the whole damned world and her loneliness and her stupid sisters and Kip and, and, and.

Maybe ten good hard minutes. No more than ten. She'd have to make sure she ordered Quentin to be silent. He was good at that at least, orders. Not hugging. He'd probably be a terrible hugger, actually. Too little and bony and fragile and awkward to make you feel safe and warm and enveloped like Kip could...

Okay! None of that!

A woman makes do.

Ten minutes, scrawny Quentin, and I don't start crying until I'm where no one can see me.

Head high, she dropped her bloody cloth into the water, and the sea swallowed her sins, as it had swallowed so many before.

Chapter 59

"You want to know what's the worst?" Kip asked, staring at the plinth.

"Rhetorical questions?" Ben-hadad asked.

"Swamp ass," Big Leo said.

"A booger you can't reach," Ferkudi said. "Or mosquitoes. If you were trapped with mosquitoes *and* had a booger you couldn't reach, that'd be really bad."

"When you're two pumps shy of drawing the happy water up from your well and the woman's husband walks in?" Winsen asked.

"Insubordination?" Cruxer suggested. "Cluelessness? Obscenity?"

"No. Wiseasses," Kip said. "But after that? When someone tells you the solution to a problem is obvious, and then you can't figure it out."

"Huh," Ben-hadad said. "Never had that happen to me."

"I hate you guys," Kip said. "I know we've all got things to do, but what am I missing here?"

"The answer," Winsen said.

"Win, shut it," they all said.

Big Leo said, "Commander, were you lumping me with Ben's insubordination or Ferkudi's cluelessness?"

Cruxer ignored him, though, saying, "Liv Danavis—or whatever she is now—said she'd activated the Great Mirror here. But…there's no Great Mirror here. Right? I mean, is it hidden somewhere else in Apple Grove?"

They shook their heads. It was a small town, and their people had searched all of it. Even if the Mirror were half the size of the one housed in Ru or Dúnbheo, it would still be impossible to hide.

"And saying it's been 'activated' makes it sound like it's functional, so it's not lying in some barn or something; there has to be the whole frame system, right?" Kip asked. He looked at the plinth. Was it supposed to be the base of the frame, or where you'd set the frame?

"Well, then, it's obvious, especially given *that*," Ben-hadad said, pointing to the plinth. "The mirror's buried right under us."

"Well, yeah, *obviously*," Kip said. He looked over at the cracked earth at the base of the plinth. "The crack made that impossible to miss, right?"

He'd missed it. Apparently so had some of the others. They were looking down uneasily.

Kip said, "I meant, uh, since it's there, how do we raise it?"

"Sure you did, boss," Ben-hadad said. "Don't hate me 'cause I'm a genius."

"We don't. We hate you for all sorts of reasons," Winsen said easily.

Kip walked over to the plinth. There were no superviolet panels on it. It felt like it was just a marker. And maybe it had been, the ancient equivalent of 'Dig here.'

Ferkudi said, "Please don't tell me we have to dig it up."

"We?" Ben-hadad said. "I'm gonna be overseeing the drafters building our skimmers down at the coast. Actually, I should really be on my way."

But he didn't leave. Ben couldn't leave an unsolved puzzle.

Kip shielded his eyes against most of the light and looked into the chi, though it pained his eyes to compress them so far. He'd gone blind for three days the last time he'd used a lot of chi, and he couldn't afford that now.

He shot a pulse down into the earth, and it seemed to burn his skin in a line from his eyes, down his shoulders, along his entire arm. He tensed, but no one seemed to notice.

With its tremendous energy, the chi penetrated the earth easily, and he saw that Ben-hadad was right. Under a thin layer of grasses, the soil yielded from the native loam to a vast bowl of sand, and within that sand was a frame system, and lower still was a vast quantity of luxin. Green probably, considering the history of this satrapy. A temple? A shrine of some sort? It felt strange, though, as if being underground so long had changed it from solid luxin to a liquid. Or maybe it was just that he'd reached the limits of his tiny chi burst.

But that was all he could see in the tiny burst he'd shot out.

"It's a moot point," Cruxer said. "The Blood Robe army's gone. It'd be like building a siege engine when there's no siege...Unless..." Cruxer cleared his throat. "Our Lightbringer needs to tinker?"

They all looked at him.

"I've been thinking about it," Ben-hadad said, "and I keep coming up short. I mean, I get why the mirror towers would have been tremendously useful to the ancients. The kingdoms were broken into single colors, right? All the red drafters would go to Atash, greens here, and so on. They didn't have colored lenses, so simply fighting in bad light or at the wrong time of day or without decent sources would have been the death of many of them. So before lenses were developed, a king could gather thousands of precious or semiprecious stones—anything in their color—and use the Great Mirrors to beam their color out to their drafters. And when colored lenses were first invented, the Mirrors would still be useful—because they were so, so expensive and difficult to make. But, Breaker, I don't understand how the Mirrors are going to help us now: every drafter at the Chromeria has spectacles in their own color, and all the buildings are white by design. Sourcing isn't a problem for us. The real problem is how the bane paralyze us. Are you certain that the Great Mirrors even *do* anything about that? Like, you bombard a drafter—or even the bane—with a complementary color, or what?"

They all looked at Kip. It wasn't exactly a problem he hadn't thought about in the long days on the trail.

"Hand me your water skin, would you?" Kip asked Cruxer, who gave it to him immediately.

He shot a quick flash again, this time down the plinth.

It showed a dark panel on the structure, two paces below.

"Aha!" he said, gladly dropping the chi. He poured water over the blisters rising on his burning hand, handing the skin back absentmindedly. "I wonder."

He wasn't going to be able to worm superviolet all the way down into the soil by itself, but what if...

Connecting superviolet to chi, like foot soldiers following charging cavalry, Kip shot chi into the soil, clearing the way for the superviolet to reach the panel. It'd be way faster than digging.

He'd only have an instant. Unless he wanted to hold on to this hot coal that was chi for longer.

"Kip, do you think maybe it would be a good idea to take it slow with—" Tisis said.

And there, in the panel, he felt an obvious trigger, as if recently repaired, just waiting for his touch.

Thanks, Liv. It was only as the trigger clicked that he thought, *What if this is a trap?*

"Oops," he said.

With a muffled grinding of massive gears, the earth suddenly shifted under their feet.

"Run!" Kip shouted.

Only Tisis froze. She had no idea what was happening.

A two-paces-wide section of earth simply dropped into the ground beside them, tearing the grass free, exposing a chasm below and a glimpse of stone workings.

Kip stopped, grabbed Tisis, and threw her over his shoulder, sprinting for the trees. More ground gave way to the other side, the sand undergirding the grass sliding into oblivion, the sound of pouring sand and rumbling machinery filling his ears.

As always, he went to green first. The morning was bright, and the grass was emerald, the trees vibrant with dark-green leaves. The green rushed to him like a long-absent friend to an embrace.

But he wasn't going to make it to the safety of the trees. The Mighty had all seen that he was sprinting, and had bolted themselves. Only

Cruxer looked back now, horror and guilt etching his features: he'd run away without his wards.

The ground heaved upward for one moment and staggered him. Cruxer, looking over his shoulder, already slowing, was thrown headlong.

The bucking earth demolished Kip's chance to jump. He felt the ground go soft under his left foot and saw it disappear from where he was going to plant his right.

He blasted green luxin down as hard as he could, but carrying Tisis, it was too little to compensate; they were too heavy together.

Left hand under her ribs, he heaved her to safety, and plunged toward the depths.

He hit the wall of the abyss gracelessly and caught the edge, lost it, and grabbed some roots overhanging the blank wall. He slipped, slid down, and then caught a double handful.

He didn't even think to draft. The wind had been knocked from him when he hit the wall, and all he could do was clamp his eyes shut and hold on as tight as a kid fighting his big brother for a sweet.

The roots were tearing up his hands.

"Kip, let go!" Tisis shouted from above. She sounded in pain.

She must have said, 'Don't let go,' and he'd missed it. "I won't!" he shouted.

"No, Breaker. Let go," Cruxer said, suddenly there with her, looking over the edge of the abyss at him.

Kip looked down. His feet were almost touching the sunken ground. Oh.

He dropped onto the churned grass and sand.

Kip turned. The first thing he noticed was that there was a platform right where they'd all been standing moments before. It was untouched by the seismic chaos, its grass still undisturbed. Ah, because whoever had hidden the mirror hadn't meant it to be a death trap for whoever triggered it.

If he'd listened to his wife and looked a bit longer *before* messing with the control panel to a massive subterranean structure, he would have certainly seen it.

He glanced over at her. She was rubbing her ribs as if he'd bruised her when he'd thrown her to safety. *Safety.* What a hero.

But finally, his eye was drawn to the most obvious part of the gigantic machinery that had emerged from the soil. Perhaps working on the same principles as the mighty escape lines running from the Prism's Tower down into the city, massive counterweights must have dropped into hidden caverns in the earth in order to lever a great disk and a frame into the air, thirty paces high, with a huge pitted silver disk barely smaller than that held vertically in the frame.

But even as he watched, that silver casing cracked open, and a sheet of it slid off, first one side and then the other, revealing a giant lens and a giant mirror. Each cover spun out slowly, balancing on opposite arms.

There was no sign of the green temple below them, though. When this had all been buried, only the frame and mirror had been rigged to rise.

"Well, that was invigorating," Cruxer said, dusting himself off.

"Been too long since I nearly died," Big Leo said.

"Most bracing," Ben-hadad said, through obvious pain. "Speaking of braces..." He looked down at his leg, where his knee brace had snapped. "Looks like I have some repairs to do."

"I said 'Oops,'" Kip said, his heart still racing.

"You know, boss," Winsen said, not even being sarcastic about the 'boss' part, "I can protect you from all sorts of threats, but if you're gonna try to kill yourself, you just let me know that's what you're doing and I will get out of the way."

"Look at this thing," Tisis said, ignoring her own dishevelment from her fall, and not saying she'd told him so. "This is amazing. A gigantic weapon, hidden by the ancients. And we found it! It's actually here!"

"We don't know how to use it, so it's not really a weapon yet," Ben-hadad said. "Except maybe against impulsive Tyreans who can be hurt by very minor falls."

"But he *could've* figured it out," Tisis said. "Liv thought he could've, and so do I. And if he had, we could've used this to destroy the White King's army. I mean, if we'd gotten here before they left."

"Shit," Cruxer said.

"Shit," the others agreed.

"I said 'Oops,'" Kip said forlornly.

Chapter 60

Another day, another twenty meetings and two hundred letters, Karris thought as she ate her supper at her desk.

The latter was an exaggeration, but not by much. The trouble was that there was no telling which was hiding key information in plain sight: This rumor of sea monsters? This one of new lux storms in the Cracked Lands? This sighting of Gavin Guile smashing the Everdark Gates? This rumor about the pirate queen launching a laughably massive fleet to prey on Sun Day pilgrims? No, it was Pash Vecchio's fleet! And he was coming to invade Big Jasper!

Karris sighed, taking another spoonful of a delicious soup that she really wasn't appreciating as she should. There *were* fleets coming here—two of them at least, and decked out for war: one under Corvan Danavis and one under King Ironfist. And there were certainly thousands of pilgrims banded together, and there were certainly many pirates, too. But her spies themselves should winnow out the most ridiculous of the rumors—except she'd told them not to, fearing she'd miss something important.

Pash Vecchio had (possibly? likely?) worked with the White King before, and Gavin had sunk the pirate king's flagship, but such a blow was more likely to send the cur scurrying back to his islands than to try to take vengeance on a man he and everyone else believed to be dead.

Meanwhile, here, the Chromeria's fleet, gathered to conduct its own exercises in preparation for Corvan Danavis's arrival (and Karris's hoped-for invasion of Blood Forest—which she still needed to figure out how to pitch to Andross), had heard a rumor of some other pirate fleet and had sailed out immediately, without even telling Karris which direction they were headed.

It would be a good exercise for them, as long as they didn't sink any pilgrim vessels on their way. Karris had dispatched Blackguard skimmers to find out which direction they'd gone, and to check into another report she had that somehow that moron Caul Azmith had weaseled his way back into a small command with big sway. The nobleman had been the general who'd gotten tens of thousands of soldiers slaughtered at the Battle of Ox Ford. Those losses had nearly driven the Ruthgaris and the Parians to surrender and ally with the Blood Robes. Caul had resigned in disgrace before he could be fired. But the money to support the new fleet had to come from somewhere, and she'd known that the Azmiths were desperate for Caul to be given a chance to redeem himself. She'd allowed that he could serve with the fleet but had barred him from command.

She'd meant *all* command. The Azmiths had agreed. Now it seemed they'd gone around her. They'd apparently put him in a subcommand in control of a quarter of the fleet, under an admiral whom Azmith's familial connections allowed him to bully.

She had about a week to decide how to chasten them without losing their monetary support. If all else failed, she was going to have to bring Andross in on this one. He was good at bringing the recalcitrant to heel.

But still.

She knew she shouldn't set hopeless goals, but she couldn't help herself.

☐ *Avoid asking for Andross's help with the Armiths.*

Karris pushed her chair back. Her fingers were ink-stained. She rolled her neck.

☐ *Go for a massage.*

There, now *that* was a good goal.

"*Caleen,*" Karris said, to one of her secretary's slaves, "would you check on Rhoda's availability to give me a massage tomorrow morning after training?"

The girl hurried out.

Moments later, there was a knock at the door.

Karris looked for her Blackguard to open the door, then realized he'd been called away to do something or other quickly.

Huh, I have to open my own door. And it feels like an inconvenience! I really am getting soft.

Karris stood and stretched. Her soreness reminded her of the morning's training as much as of the day's sitting. She wasn't getting literally soft, at least. Not anymore.

She wasn't quite back to the body she'd had at twenty—but maybe that ship had sailed, too. Dammit.

She opened the door with a grin on her face. Her son Zymun stood there, smiling thinly. There were no Blackguards at their immediate posts outside the door.

Her blood went cold.

"Mother? May I come in?"

"I'm afraid I'm terribly busy—"

"Won't take but a moment." He glanced down the hall, where a Blackguard was striding back toward her post. Just someone taking an unscheduled break. Overstretched forces.

Was Karris going to throw him out? Make a scene? She'd avoided him until now, and knew he was furious about it, but throwing him out would shame him and make an enemy of him forever.

"Come in," she said reluctantly.

He looked around the room as he stepped inside, and his eyes lit with a quick, smug smile.

She turned and walked toward her desk to create space between them. She would not kiss him in greeting.

He cleared his throat, and she barely heard the scrape of wood under the sound.

Before she spun on her ankle, he'd barred the door.

"Open it," she commanded coldly. Her eyes went wide, but her spectacles were in her pocket, and drafting green from her curtains would take time.

"Mother?" he said plaintively. His shoulders slumped. "Are you *scared* of me?! What have I done to deserve this? Who's turned you against me? How have I offended you? One day we're talking and laughing over private dinners, and then my grandfather tells me you've taken a secret hatred for me into your heart. He forbade me to come see you. Forbade me even to apologize for anything I might have done... I'm so ashamed of myself. Can you just tell me what I did?"

"Your grandfather said *what*?!" Karris asked.

"Mother, I hurt you somehow, and now you're joining my enemies. I don't understand!" His eyes filled with tears.

Andross! That bastard! He'd pretended he was going to take Karris's side, and instead, this? Sowing *more* discord?

Zymun sank to a crouch, ashamed, and covered his eyes with his hands. "He said... he said he'd fought you for me, but you were pushing the Spectrum to get me disavowed as Prism-elect. He said he didn't know why you hated me, but that once you hated, you never turned away from your wrath, that you never forgave anyone. Not ever in all your life. He forbade me to come speak to you of it. Told me I'd only arouse you further. But he doesn't know you like I do. You're not like that... are you?"

She stepped forward, aghast. Furious. What the hell was Andross playing at?!

Her only warning was that Zymun didn't look up as he said the last words—'are you?'

He didn't search her face for any sign of forgiveness.

Her old Blackguard senses shrieked at her, but too late.

Zymun pounced, tackling her, and crushing her under his larger body. His eyes were full of color, but as devoid of feeling as a snake's. He'd hidden them with his hands to hide that he was drafting.

Now luxin snared her hands, her throat.

He punched her hard in the stomach, but she took the blow with practiced ease. She immediately began wending a foot up for a wrestling hold—

—and stopped as he pricked a dagger point under her eyelid.

The flat, dead look in his eyes gave her no read.

If he killed her, they'd put him on Orholam's Glare for sure. But he didn't even seem to be aware of that. Had no concern for consequences in the least. Not in this. Not in anything.

She stopped fighting.

In moments, he'd immobilized her with luxin bonds.

"You're scheming against me," he said. "I know it. No seat on the Spectrum? No place in the councils of war? No honors that are due me? You treat me like a *child*! And it ends now."

Quietly, calmly, despite the hand tight around her throat, Karris said, "May I speak, Zymun?"

"Son!" he said. "You call me *son*."

"They warned me," she said, her voice distant. "But I didn't see you. Not as you are. I let my guilt blind me. For a time, but no more."

"You'll give me what I want," Zymun said.

"Astonishing," she said as if amused, though her guts squirmed. "So close to being given all you want and you can't help but show your true colors. No. You're no son of mine, Zymun. I disown you. Disavow you. I admit, you certainly do bear a resemblance to the worst parts of me, and perhaps you have my own father's weak chin and venial disposition and shallow intellect, but you're not the small, lame, petty shadow of Gavin Guile that I thought you were; you bear no likeness to him at all. I shall have to ponder that harried month when I conceived you. It seems more and more undeniable that I must have gotten very drunk and fucked a village idiot."

"You…you *cunt*!"

"Get out," she said, ignoring her bonds, ignoring that he was on top of her and she was helpless. "And never speak to me again."

"I know how to break a woman," he hissed, spit flying in her face. "I've done it before. It's not so hard."

"You'll break nothing here," Karris said. "You'll walk out that door with your tail between your legs like the cur you are."

"Oh yeah?" he said. He lifted the hand with the dagger. "You stupid bitch, I'll—"

He cut off as two spear blades slid into view. One sharp blade slipped beneath his wrist, so the dagger couldn't descend without him slicing off his own hand. The other blade pressed along the side of Zymun's neck.

Gill Greyling stood behind Zymun, spears trembling in his grip, not with fear but with rage.

Karris had never been happier to see anyone in her life.

"Give me the excuse," Gill said. His voice was raspy. The man had been on edge perpetually since his brother died.

Zymun eased up, carefully dropping the dagger on the carpet, far out, raising his hands slowly and releasing the luxin to dust. "Could have sworn I barred that door," he said, good-naturedly, as if it had all been a joke. He rocked back on his heels and stood slowly.

Derisively, Karris laughed at him as if he were the stupidest man she'd ever met. "As if the Blackguard doesn't have ways to open the doors here?"

His face dropped, and the mask slipped to show the depth of the ugliness within him. He couldn't stand disrespect.

She only hoped he'd attack.

Gill would kill him—he wouldn't try to wound or incapacitate him, she knew. She knew her Blackguards.

She stood up and brushed the luxin dust off.

Now she was free, though, and this was all out in the open. She was honestly relieved. No more pretenses.

"Zymun," she said. "Until tonight, I didn't scheme against you. Not ever. But now I will. Thank you for bringing your true nature to light. History will judge me for giving birth to a monster. But at least I have the decency to hate him."

But his dead eyes betrayed nothing even of rage now. He walked out the door, then stopped and turned. "Oh, may I have my dagger, please? It was a gift from my grandfather."

"Try to take it," Gill said dangerously. "See what happens."

Zymun didn't move.

"What's your name again, Blackguard?" Zymun demanded.

"You don't remember?" Gill asked, looking at him contemptuously. "A true Guile would."

Chapter 61

"I have news about our hunt," Quentin said. He furrowed his thick brows. "Good news, barely good news, and definitely not good news."

Teia had managed to pull her shit together, somewhat, and hadn't asked Quentin for a hug the other day, despite having told him the outlines of how she'd killed Ravi and what she'd learned. She'd fled then to her solitude, only giving him the name 'Atevia Zelorn.'

She still wanted that hug, actually, but... Quentin was so damned *awkward*, and he didn't like to be touched. It would be selfish. And probably not satisfying. Right? "Go ahead," she said.

She'd asked to hear about his project first; it gave her time to gather her wits.

"Easy one first," he said. "Zelorn is indeed a wine merchant. Very successful one, too. Well-known among the nobility. Karris didn't have her people dig too deeply, though, lest it alarm anyone." He described where to find Zelorn's house, and his profile: physical description, style of clothing, three kids, six slaves, various servants between home and business, two long-term mistresses, and a pretty young wife who spent a lot of time crying about his many affairs, the pursuit of which seemed to be his main pastime.

Other than being a pagan priest, Teia thought.

"That was the *shallow* digging?" Teia asked.

"That's exactly how I reacted," Quentin said. "High Lady Guile said, 'Of course. Anyone in the upper nobility would dig that much into anyone they were considering doing even casual business with.'"

"Sometimes I think the nobles are just like the rest of us, and then other times..." Teia said.

"Also exactly my reaction," Quentin said.

"But that was the good news, though, wasn't it?" Teia asked. Though that was all helpful, she could've learned it herself—though any time she went out in public was a time she was risking Sharp finding her.

"Afraid so. Now, about the other project," he said. He opened a folio on his desk. "These are copies of all the final plans for each of the Chromeria's seven towers. Builders' notes, allotments of slaves, materials requests, stockpiles, and overages. Everything I could find. No budgets, irritatingly, which is what keyed me in—but I'm getting ahead of myself. If there's a hidden room in the Chromeria anywhere, it should show up here."

One of the jobs Teia had given Quentin was to search the Chromeria for the Old Man of the Desert's secret room. She knew he had one, if not more. She herself had lost caches of clothing and money and weapons simply to servants or strangers stumbling across them; there was no way the Old Man was going to risk the same happening to his code books; there was no way he'd risk someone interrupting him as he penned or decoded his secret messages. Secrecy required privacy, and the bigger the secret the more privacy required.

"That sounds pretty good...can you not read them? Are they in code or something?" Teia asked.

"No, I can read them. Now. I had to study up on construction techniques and terminology. Took me a while," the slender young man said.

"So...the bad news is...?"

"The plans show no space for any hidden rooms at all," Quentin said. "Everything is clear and public."

"Okay..."

"But I found an exterminator's report of a rat's nest...right here under the young discipuli's barracks."

Teia looked at the plans, but for her they might as well have been written in Old Tyrean. "Explain?"

"See, in the diagram here, there's no space at all. This is supposed to be hardwood planking directly over stone. But the rat catcher's report mentions finding a rat king...Do you know what that is?" He looked ill just speaking about it.

"No."

"You don't want to. Regardless, he said the rat king was two paces high. According to the plans, that's impossible. There's no space for it. So the plans are wrong. So I went outside, and using some trigonometry and an astrolabe, I was able to calculate the heights of the towers."

"And the Prism's Tower was taller than these plans say," Teia guessed.

"No. *All* of the towers are taller than these plans say. Four paces taller! And these are the most recent plans. So that means there isn't just one secret room, there's the equivalent of one secret *floor. In every tower.*"

"How do you hide an entire secret floor?"

"Cleverly, I guess. Maybe not all in one place? People look at the towers from the outside all the time, and point out their rooms and the rooms of their friends. I don't even know how you do it, honestly. I'm no master builder, but whoever did this certainly was. Of course, I am pretty sure that they must have the true plans *somewhere*. For the inevitable repairs, or to keep later workmen and servants away from them, if nothing else. So I'd guess the Black would have those, or the promachos."

"My money's on Andross Guile. The man's a maelstrom of secrets."

"I concur," Quentin said.

"Quen," Teia said. "No one says, 'I concur.'"

"I know, but it bothers you," he said with a quick grin.

She forced a smile, but then returned to the task. "It's not like we can ask Carver Black," she said. She sighed. Should she break into his rooms? His office? How long would it take her to find a book he'd hidden? Could she spare the time from hunting the Order itself to surveil him? What reason would Carver Black have to check the old tower plans? He might have those documents, not ever check them.

And who was to say Carver Black even knew? Would the Old Man of the Desert hide in a place Carver Black knew? Was Carver Black himself in the Order?

She sighed. It all made her head hurt. She would need years to untangle all this fully. And it wasn't like she could kill Carver Black without anyone noticing. No, her best bet wasn't to go after individuals to find if they were in the Order; it was to let the Order come to her. She rubbed her jaw gingerly.

She had to figure out some way to mark every person who attended their Feast of the Dying Light, the night before Sun Day. Maybe in the changing room? Could she mark their clothing?

Then Karris's soldiers could sweep down on the traitors on Sun Day morning and wipe them out in one fell swoop.

They could celebrate Sun Day by putting the Old Man of the Desert up on Orholam's Glare.

There was one man Teia would happily watch cook, screaming in agony as he died.

If she could survive so long. She rubbed her jaw again.

"Tooth still hurting?" Quentin asked. "I thought you were going to go see the White's barber about that before all this even started."

"I did. Not that I can tell, but he said it's better now than it would have been if I hadn't come to see him."

"A nonfalsifiable statement. Clever."

"I'm supposed to chew some herbs to help, but I always forget," she said. "I don't know what irritates me more: that he may be a charlatan or that this may be my fault because I don't follow instructions." She heard the whinging in her voice, and shut up.

Quentin looked at her, and didn't fill the sudden silence.

"It's killing me," she said.

"Your tooth? Not your tooth."

She sat on Quentin's bed. "Quentin, you're on a first-name basis with the guy: how can Orholam allow this?"

"This?" Quentin asked uncertainly.

"I'm a butcher, Quen. I've taken to scoring a notch on my knife for each kill."

He said nothing, but he wasn't fast enough to hide the brief flash of distaste on his lips.

"Not to brag about the number. To remind myself. Because I was forgetting. They all run together until I dream: Oh, the way that one slave gurgled on his blood because he bit his tongue so hard in his fear of me before I even touched him. How that other girl wept from the moment the door opened and never even got a word out because she was crying so hard. I remember how I despised her, how I wished she would die as bravely as some of the others had. Do you know, they gave me a break? The Order. Said that too many slaves had disappeared, and they needed to hold off until some more refugees came to the island so no one would get suspicious—and I felt *disappointed* because it would interrupt my studies. Disappointed. For only a moment, yes. But what the hell is that? I don't want to be this person I'm becoming, Quentin. Why would Orholam allow this?"

" 'If Orholam can do something, and if He cares about us, why doesn't He?' "

She nodded. "So what's the answer?"

"The answer's simple for the mind, but impossible for the heart. And the question, honestly asked, always comes from a wound." He said no more.

She waited, then understood. "So you're not going to tell me."

"Not when you're hurting and angry. You'll reject the answer, and then later you'll think of it as an answer you already found lacking and perhaps you'll neglect to consider it again. Having found a door's handle bristling with needles, you'll tell yourself it's probably locked anyway. When you come to the big questions, before you can get a true answer, you need to know whether you're approaching them rationally or emotionally."

A Blackguard guards his emotions, Teia thought. "So you're not going to tell me the rational answer until I can approach the question rationally," she said.

"It's not that it's a big Magisterium secret. You could go ask any luxiat and get the same answer today that I'll give you when you're ready—though some will phrase it more or less eloquently. But in my estimation, you'll profit more from it later. If you disagree, you're free to ask them."

"You're asking me to trust you when I don't understand something hard for me," she said. "That's supposed to parallel something, isn't it?"

"I didn't mean it to, but perhaps it does. Thanks for thinking I'm smarter than I am."

She pursed her lips to keep from smiling, though the hollow in her chest still ached.

"Now," he said, "you were abrupt last time. Seemed on edge. You killed this slaver, Ravi Satish. Easy kill?"

Sticking a hammer in his head? Easier than I thought. Fooling him? Pathetically easy. The rest? "Won't trouble my sleep," she said.

"And you're going out to hunt your old mistress presently. You're going to kill her?"

She nodded once, sharp as a falling guillotine.

"This is your first job that isn't purely professional."

"It's necessary," she said, quick and defensive. "If she contacts Murder Sharp, it brings him to her, and that puts him way too close to me. Plus she intends to contract a hit on a Guile. Not Andross, I'm sure. Sharp *probably* wouldn't take the job, but how could I explain that to Karris?"

"Those are all good reasons. Sufficient reasons," Quentin said. He let it hang there.

"Yeah," she said, trying to cover it over.

"Yeah?"

Teia felt stricken. He knew she wasn't being honest, and yet his eyes were filled with compassion. "She's low-level, Quen. I mean, she's a noble, so she'd rise quickly in their ranks...but she told Ravi she only joined them to try to get revenge on the Guiles for...something. Which, come to think of it, she ranted to me about a long time ago. Her brother was the governor of Garriston, and Gavin Guile killed him as a traitor or something? I don't know exactly. But it means she's not a true believer. And I know where the Order's meeting now. She doesn't *need* to die, not exactly. I mean, she's committed capital offenses, and she's covered under my writ, but if she were anyone else, and she got away? It wouldn't trouble me. She wouldn't be forming a new Order ten years from now. But I want to kill her almost as much as I want the Old Man."

"Then you know."

"I know what?"

Quentin looked at her, and his eyes were old and gentle. "Teia, this is the most dangerous job you've ever done. Not physically. This is where you can come to love what you do. The power of it. The righteous vengeance. This work wounds you, but this job is where you can get dirt in the wound."

"Like I haven't already?" she scoffed.

"To this point, you've been a shield, doing what you have to do, getting battered and torn protecting those you love. Now you decide what else you are. You can torture her, if you want. You can try to make her pay for all she did to your friends and to you. You can look into her eyes and wring whatever suffering from her you desire. No one can stop you."

"And no one should," Teia said coldly.

"Some luxiats say even the Two Hundred may yet repent, but from what you've told me of her, I daresay Aglaia's damnation is assured. What's in question is yours."

Chapter 62

With a grunt, Gavin set down the great, cumbersome Lust stone he'd borne for the entire circuit around the black tower on a pedestal. Above the pedestal was a statue, and beyond the statue another locked gate. This statue was of a kneeling man with face upturned, radiant, lambent in his white marble against all the sea of black stone here. All the statues had been the same white. The weight of the stone released a boon stone wider than his hand from the statue's grip.

"Chastity, I suppose?" Gavin asked, picking up the boon stone.

The prophet didn't have to answer.

"I'll be happy to give this one up to Orholam!" Gavin said.

The old man was as stone-faced as the statues, and a good deal less joyful.

"You know," Gavin said, "to hand over Chastity, because I don't want it?"

Orholam pursed his lips.

"Not like, give up my chastity *to* Orholam, like a sexual... You know what? Never mind. Just looking for a little levity, after the bludgeoning I just took with that round. You know what I mean?"

"No."

"So tell me, O, why aren't you pilgriming with me? Pilgriming.

Pilgrimaging? Huh. I'm the head of the faith and I don't know how people usually say it. I think I like pilgriming. Feels grim, and it's a bitter pill, right? No? Not working with me at all here, are you? Fine. Why aren't you pilgriming? No sins to purge? Too holy already?"

As Orholam sighed, Gavin took the Chastity boon stone and tucked it into a pocket in the pilgrim's tunic. It was heavy, but it fit perfectly.

When Grinwoody had commissioned Gavin for this task, he'd mentioned magical locks at every level that the fleeing guardians had left to keep out drafters of each associated color. That was why Gavin, unable now to draft, was supposedly the perfect candidate to assassinate Orholam—or the magical nexus called Orholam. So far, though, Gavin had only felt a whisper of resistance as he walked through each gate, and that may have been his imagination or his dread at what the next circle would hold.

They moved farther into the landing. There was one between each circle. Here, silently, they ate salt fish and drank water while Gavin recovered. The steep chute that Gavin had seen below had an opening here, and Gavin wondered how many pilgrims failed not on each level but on the spaces between them like this, where they pondered how terrible the next one would be.

How easy was it to give up and simply escape, too afraid to confront what lay next?

"I'm journeying for you," Orholam said finally, when Gavin had nearly forgotten his question. "If I did my own pilgrimage, I would take much less time on certain circles than you, leaving you alone. It's even possible I might take more time on certain circles. Dimly. Wrath, for one, would not be easy on me. But I'm here to walk with you, step for step, no matter how long you take. We're not meant to take the pilgrimage alone."

"So no pilgrimage for you at all?" Gavin asked.

"When my business with you is finished, I'll go back down and start my own climb."

"I'm really delighted that you are here for *me*, but I, uh, won't be joining you for yours. You know that, right?"

Orholam scoffed like yeah, he knew. Then he frowned.

"There's my old Wrath again, rearing up inside," Orholam said as if disappointed in himself.

"I piss you off that much, huh?" Gavin asked. And here he'd been being as respectful as he could manage. Wrath was going to be a tough circle for him, too.

"This is your chance to decide whether you want to be that old deceiver

Gavin Guile or if you want to be a Dazen Guile made new. I know you want that. You've made attempts before. This is an opportunity to change, Guile. And you've been offered more of those than most get. Take it."

The old prophet hunkered down with his own salt fish, turning his back on Gavin. The conversation, clearly, was finished.

Gavin sighed. Some company for his pilgrimage.

He'd mostly given up trying to understand the magic of whoever had created this tower. It had to be a highly advanced will-casting-focused magic, from the way it triggered Gavin's memories. He'd had multiple flashbacks during every circle: the makers of this thing had weaponized his own mind against him.

This wasn't a hike up a tower; it was a trek through everything he'd ever done wrong, everything he'd never done right. This was his every failure held up to the light and splintered into its component deadly sins through a black prism.

It was not a magic to be understood, merely one to be endured. He was gaining no new knowledge of magic, but only of himself.

How the tower's Tyrean makers (if this wasn't older than even their empire) had understood vice and virtue was different than what the Chromeria taught. He'd learned, and as the Highest Luxiat, even *taught* the seven virtues as being the four worldly virtues (prudence, courage, justice, temperance) and the three heavenly ones (charity, hope, and faith).

Believers were to meditate on these virtues, and how they might embody them better, as they made the sign of the four and the three touching hand, heart, and lips. If you counted hands as a collective singular, you would count them as number three, whereas if you counted each hand in turn separately, they would count as three and four—thus symbolizing a paradox, and the connection of all the virtues (or all the vices) to one another.

Here, though ultimately the lists basically covered the same territory as the Chromeria's, the tower's builders had divided up the pilgrimage into Seven Contrary Virtues: Patience against Wrath, Abstinence against Gluttony, Liberality against Greed, Diligence against Sloth, Chastity against Lust, Kindness against Envy, and Humility against Pride.

Gavin hadn't thought that Lust was going to be a difficult circle for him. After all, he'd been (unwillingly) chaste for quite a while now. Sure, he was as virile as the next two guys, but he hadn't been *promiscuous*—especially for a Prism with all the opportunities he'd had! But the memories he'd triggered at every step had focused not on numbers of women he'd taken to his bed but mostly on how he'd treated Marissia, not only in bed but out of it.

He'd prided himself on treating Marissia very, very well for a room slave. That she hadn't been a slave at all but was only masquerading as one was, if anything, a reason for *him* to be angry with *her*.

The tower hadn't let him off so easily. It hadn't cared whether she was slave or free. It triggered his own memories of how he'd treated her. They weren't flattering.

Marissia had been, in Gavin's careless estimation, supposed to feel only gratitude or desire toward him. That was pretty much the entire range of emotions he'd expected from her, and it was all he'd allowed her to express.

He'd seen undeniably over the years that the true range was far, far greater. He'd seen her despair, he'd seen her love for him, and her self-loathing at times, seemingly because she did love him—but he'd written them all off, as if they, and she, weren't worthy of his attention.

It must have been torture for her. Gavin would treat her well, showering her with compliments, thanking her for how well she was running his household and managing the servants and slaves. Some days he would ask her opinion on matters of all kinds, confide in her, give her gifts, and take her to his bed and make sure she reached her pleasure rather than merely take his own. Other days he would demand she serve him sexually at a moment's notice, pretending instant arousal and total desire—though her dryness betrayed the pretense, he'd ignored it or blamed her for it—then he'd banished her from the room as if she were no more than a rag to mop up his semen.

That's what room slaves are for, he'd told his protesting conscience. I treat her well!

And she had endured it, while knowing she could end her torture at any moment by revealing she wasn't a slave at all. But she had believed in her mission too much to do that. Or she'd loved him so much that she stayed, despite it all.

Or, his conscience asked, had the abuse so worn her down that she contented herself with taking the emotional scraps that fell from his table, and slowly come to believe it was all she deserved?

How long can everyone around you tell you that you're a slave, how long can every mirror show you to be a slave, and you not believe you really are one?

He had destroyed a great woman. He'd taken the best years of her life, and told himself he was doing right by her.

And he'd known better.

Fuck me. Fuck this climb.

He rubbed his face, inadvertently brushing the eye patch. It didn't hurt anymore. Now, if anything, that shock of sensation it sent through his whole body was pleasantly numbing.

After climbing the circles of Pride, and Envy, and Lust so far, the picture of himself that was emerging was as devastating as it was undeniable. But if this journey was supposed to be purgative, Gavin didn't see how. Purgatives are supposed to make you puke but then feel better.

Gavin didn't feel better, nor any more humble, kind, or chaste, only more aware of how much he wasn't those things.

Rubbing the eye patch deeper into his eye, oily pain canceling out sharp pain for a brief moment, he stood up and walked to the edge overlooking the sea.

"What the—? Gunner's gone!" Gavin said.

Slowly, troubled, Orholam said, "Yeah."

Gunner had been drinking out there.

He must have gotten drunk and fallen off. There was no way he would have abandoned his big gun to the waters, no way he would have tried to swim when there were still so, so many sharks gathered from leagues around to feed on all the bodies floating in the lagoon.

When sober, Gunner was a master of timing. If he'd decided he was going to have to abandon the gun and swim, he would have waited until everything calmed in the lagoon. A few days, at the least, while the sharks sated their hunger devouring all the bloating dead.

"You told him he was going to live," Gavin said, snarling.

"I know," Orholam said apologetically.

God damn. And Gavin had been starting to believe that Orholam wasn't a holy-talking charlatan, that—wherever it came from—he really did see the future sometimes, and the past.

Brushing past the old man, Gavin snarled, "What circle's next?"

"Wrath."

"*Perfect.*"

Chapter 63

"How many fights do we have left in us?" Kip asked Cruxer. It seemed like a good time to ask; Tisis was on the other side of their little fleet, checking on her reserve scouts, and she didn't like him dwelling on the death awaiting them.

The early-morning embarkation had been somber. Now they were crossing the Cerulean Sea at the maximally efficient skimmer speed: slow compared to what the craft were capable of, but preserving the lives of their drafters while still getting them to the Chromeria in two days.

Every one of the thousand drafters, two hundred Cwn y Wawr will-casters and war dogs, and one thousand elite soldiers knew they were heading for a fight for their own lives, for the future of the empire, and even for the future worship of Orholam Himself. Would the Seven Satrapies even exist, or would there be instead nine kingdoms with a high king? Would there be ten gods in this world, or One?

"Mentally we're tough," Cruxer said under the sound of the rushing wind. The sea was placid, the sun orange on the horizon, and the sky crystalline blue. It was one of those pristine summer mornings that made you feel that Orholam was full of joy when He created the world. "Emotionally, we all feel like we can fight forever."

That wasn't what Kip had meant, and they both knew it. He glanced back at the phalanxes of skimmers and sea chariots behind them. With drafters of various colors of luxin paired at the reeds of the different ships, their colors mixing as they jetted it into the water, the thousands of the Forest's best were painting Ceres's skin like artists each wielding a different tone, human colors rising in answer to the divine in the skies.

"Two or three hard skirmishes, maybe. One protracted battle. After that, we'll start losing significant numbers to luxin burnout. Too many of them have been making up for their lack of skill by drafting ever greater quantities. We might even lose a few on the passage."

"And the Mighty?" Kip asked, throat tightening. He already had his own guesses, of course. But he was trying to be dispassionate. A full year of raiding and the Battle at Dúnbheo had meant many fights to the death—and when your life is in peril today, why be careful with how much you draft so you can live another year fifteen years from now?

"The nunks are fine, of course," Cruxer said. "Ferkudi isn't too bad with blue, but his green is to the halos. Winsen will live forever. His yellow is barely halfway through his irises. Tisis is fine with her green. I've got four or five battles left in me. Ben-hadad is fine with yellow, but whenever he's near a fight, he tries too hard to compensate for his bad leg. His green and blue both are full. It's Big Leo who'll probably go first. He's straining his halos in both red and sub-red."

"We're insane for letting Ben-hadad even get close to a battle," Kip said. "He's great in a fight, but ultimately, he's just another drafter. But outside a fight, doing what he does? The man's a marvel. A once-in-a-generation genius. He's the one of us who could change the world the most."

Cruxer looked at him, shadows of Ironfist in his gaze. "You've pretty much summed up my thoughts exactly—"

"Glad we're agreed—"

"About you."

"Oh."

Cruxer shrugged. "Granted, you're a *bit* better in a fight. Maybe. Having two good legs and all." But the hint of a smile crept onto his face. He couldn't deadpan quite like Ironfist, not yet.

"Trouble is," Kip said, eyes staring at the morning's beauty but no longer seeing it, "a man isn't just the one thing he does best. Even if he's the best at that one thing that the world has ever seen."

Cruxer turned his palms up. "I haven't tried to keep you from fights, have I?"

"No," Kip admitted, coming back to focus.

"But lay off green. You go golem one more time, and you may break the halo yourself."

"Yeah. I've got other options."

"I know you do. Use them. It's always green with you."

"Yes, mother," Kip said. But they both knew Cruxer was right.

The Mighty didn't want to fight on the seas, but Ben had refused to let them go unarmed, in case a fight was necessary—maybe the White King had discovered how to make skimmers by now. Also, they'd heard wild rumors about will-cast sharks and other beasts. (Kip's Night Mares didn't think it could be done, though. Or not for long. Or not without them also attacking one's own people. Or...)

So the Nightbringers had muskets, a few swivel guns, and a pile of the sticky bombs they called hullwreckers now. The skimmers wouldn't be defenseless, but they wouldn't go looking for a slugfest with a galleon, either—a single cannonball strike anywhere would cause a catastrophic failure of the luxin. Ben-hadad said he already had plans to address that in the next generation of skimmers—if he lived so long.

He said it as if he'd started saying the sentence aloud intending to wink or grin, but changed his mind halfway through, like there was so much he would never discover in this life if he died, and that death felt more real now than it had in more than a year filled with fighting.

Cruxer had one of General Derwyn's drafters taking point a hundred paces out in front of them. A nautical equivalent of outriders protected him on either flank, but the main body traveled in cohorts of twenty craft each, with everything from two- to six-person craft.

Kip was trying to be patient, though he wanted to get to the Chromeria today—and could have, moving with only the Mighty. Moving even a small army at speed was an impressive feat of logistical acumen and leadership. Moving that army over water made it a feat wherein if you loused up, people drowned.

Kip supposed that he should be trying to enjoy the little remaining life he had. It was pretty much impossible to get any work done. Despite the wind blocker, he had to lean close to Cruxer to have a conversation, and it was just Cruxer, Kip, and two young drafters with fresh halos on reeds. Kip had tried talking to them, but that had put a panicked expression in their eyes. They couldn't concentrate on two things at once.

Funny he thought of them as kids. One of them had to be nearly his own age.

"Lord Commander!" one of them said, laboring to speak and still keep in time with her partner. "Scout returning!"

No sooner had she said the words than Kip saw the scout streaking toward them on a type of craft they'd come to call a flying pulpit. The scouts' special skimmers were made to be as light and fast as possible, so they'd dispensed with nearly everything: it consisted of a single chair mounted between two propulsion reeds with wings extending from the sides beneath the water. Each scout-drafter (all were small men with excellent upper-body strength) was strapped to his chair and carried a long-lens to see even farther. The craft were ludicrously fast, but they had to be launched at speed and couldn't stop moving or they'd sink.

The tenth scout was Izemrasen, who was approaching now. Forty years old, he was a ghotra-wearing Parian who'd been training to be a Blackguard when he fell during a wall climb and broke his back. His legs had turned useless and numb. A couple of unnoticed sores on them had gotten infected, and they'd had to be amputated. He'd lived through the operation, but his Chromeria sponsor had abandoned him (illegally), despite his strength as a green drafter.

Izemrasen hadn't had the coin or connections to bring the matter before a magistrate, and he ended up performing on the streets for food, doing acrobatics for coins. How he'd even made the trek through Blood Forest in the hopes that Kip's army would have some place for him, Kip didn't know, but the man was bursting with life and purpose now. Kip had never seen anyone more proud to don the uniform.

The scout turned in behind Kip's skimmer and docked in a slot made especially for it. Kip and Cruxer attached the hooks that bound the small skimmer to their larger one while he took a few deep breaths. Izemrasen's massive shoulders shone with sweat—he'd come back at the greatest possible speed.

"Two fleets, my lord," Izemrasen said. "Closing for battle, as far as I can tell. Definitely the Blood Robes on one side and the Chromeria on the other. Maybe a hundred fifty galleons on the Blood Robe side, but a lot of those seem to be trade ships with only a few cannons each. Chromeria's only got fifty-three galleons, but they're well-armed. They're flying banners of all seven satrapies."

"How far from here?" Cruxer asked.

"Three leagues? Four? I could be off."

Kip couldn't blame him. Distances were tricky at sea at the best of times, even with special tools. The scouts had trained to measure distances by their own speed over time, which they were supposed to keep constant—but Izemrasen had come back as quickly as possible.

"And how far from each other?"

"A bit more than a league? I'd guess the fight will start within half an hour, an hour? I don't really—I don't know anything about naval battles, my lords. My apologies. I'm still learning my work."

"As are we all," Kip said.

"There was something strange, though," Izemrasen said. "I mean, I don't know anything about naval warfare firsthand, but I have seen tapestries and paintings and such, and..." He tugged his ghotra forward from where the wind had pushed it back despite the hairpins. "The Chromeria's ships were out in big wings left and right, with multiple ranks and such—like the paintings. But the left wing was leading, a lot. Too much, it seemed to me. Unless there's some strategy...?"

"That's..." Kip said. "Who's on the left wing?"

Izemrasen said, "Uh...they were too far away for me to pick out their banners for sure, but given the style of ships and the colors, Ruthgar—and..." He scrunched his eyes closed, trying to remember. "A snake below it?"

"Coiled or striking?"

"Striking."

Kip turned. "Commander, please tell me that moron Caul Azmith isn't in charge of Ruthgar's fleet."

Cruxer shrugged. "Last we heard he'd been demoted because of his disastrous leadership at Ox Ford." Azmith had been commander of the armies—but his family was rich and powerful. Kip knew how those families worked now: he bet they'd bought his way onto a small command with the fleet, where they thought he couldn't do any harm.

"Orholam's balls. He broke ranks," Kip said. "He's charging, hoping to reclaim his lost glory."

"May Orholam save those men from their leader," Cruxer said, brow darkening, making the sign of the three and the four.

"But that wasn't all," Izemrasen said. "The White King's ships were all huddled together, real tight, almost in a ball. Not at all like any tapestry I've seen. I mean, I know artists exaggerate and try to make things look pretty, but isn't being encircled as bad in naval battles as it is in land ones?"

Messengers on small skimmers had pulled in beside Kip's craft, waiting for orders to relay.

"No bane visible?" Kip asked.

"No, sir. Didn't even feel anything, and I was paying attention like you said to."

"Ah, shit," Kip said. "They're doing the same damned thing they did at Ru!" Sinking a bane so the drafters don't feel it, raising it at the last moment—except this time it wasn't one color; it was all of them. "What kind of idiot falls into the same trap they've used on us before?!"

"Caul Azmith," Cruxer said with quiet fury.

"We have to warn them," Kip said.

"We're all *drafters*," Cruxer said.

"But we're the only ones who can get to them in time."

"We *can't* go."

Kip looked at him. "They'll all die if we don't."

"Breaker, when a man who can't swim jumps into the sea to save a drowning friend, you end up with two dead men, not zero."

Kip turned to the messengers. "I've new orders. Redistribute the supply ships. Take the empties to circle behind the White King's fleet after the battle and pick up survivors from the waves. Don't come in too fast or too close or they'll be sunk, too, but save as many as they can. I don't think the White King will double back. Izemrasen, you go get rest. You're gonna be lightsick as it is. You two on the reeds, go with the messengers. Commander Cruxer and I have it from here."

The young drafters stepped off the still-moving skimmer onto messengers' vessels. To another messenger, Kip said, "Tell our fleet to continue on. We'll catch up by nightfall."

Cruxer snorted.

"Or, you know, not at all," Kip said.

"Tisis is going to be pissed," Cruxer said. She was off checking on something on the other side of the fleet.

"Yep."

"Because this is a bad idea," Cruxer said.

"I know," Kip said.

Cruxer made the sign of the seven again and then took a reed. "You know, Blackguard training has very specific rules about keeping one's ward from putting himself in mortal peril unnecessarily." He looked at Kip's open, expectant face, and sighed. "So I guess it's a good thing we quit before we got to that part."

Chapter 64

Turning people into meat sacks was the easy part. The problem was disposing of the bodies. For all that Teia now knew dozens of ways to kill, she wasn't superhuman. Even in her blacks, holding a spear, and soaking wet, she weighed less than two sevs. She'd done tens of thousands of push-ups and curl ups. She'd run thousands of leagues. She'd swum until her shoulders were small blocks of granite. She'd lifted salt bags until veins bulged from her forearms even at rest, and she'd run relays with the Blackguard trainees until she could run down a gazelle on the open plains.

She could climb and jump and balance and fight and shoot a bow and fire a musket and draft—dear Orholam, at the insistence of her Archer sisters, she could even *dance* tolerably well now—but when it came to lifting a corpse that was more than double her weight, she was hopeless.

The good news was that she wouldn't need to drag Aglaia's body far.

In quick glances, Teia watched the noblewoman have her cosmetics applied by a severe old slave woman who was, despite her age and her own plain features, obviously an artist. It was evening, but Aglaia had come fresh-faced from a steam bath at an unmarked private club in the Embassies District. The old slave applied delicate layers of powders and creams with a sure and speedy hand. Teia used the time to scout the estate again.

It was a meeting night for the Order of the Broken Eye. That meant Aglaia had taken dinner in her room, as she apparently always did on the nights when she attended the Order's meetings, and she'd 'dismissed' the slaves except for this handmaid.

Of course, what a woman like Aglaia thought dismissing the slaves meant and what it really meant were very different. She would be angry if she came home and her dishes and food weren't cleared from her room and her bed wasn't turned down, a warming plate put between the sheets to prepare them for her.

As if these things happened by magic. As if she were giving her slaves a break rather than complicating their lives. For them, the dismissal meant, 'Get all the usual work done without me seeing you, and pretend not to see me leave, and never ask about where I'm going or where I've been, and there will be extra laundry in the morning.'

At long last, the slave finished her duties. As far as Teia could tell, the slave woman had done magic of a sort Gavin Guile himself would envy. Old Horse Face actually looked attractive, though Teia had no idea why Aglaia was putting on cosmetics. The woman would be donning a cloak and mask, which were required to stay on for the rest of the night.

Well, she thought so, anyway.

Aglaia looked at herself in her mirrors. She seemed dissatisfied with what she saw—for all the wrong reasons, Teia thought. But after a few exasperated sighs, Aglaia dismissed the slave woman.

Teia waited with the patience of a coiled serpent.

The door closed and Aglaia moved to a closet. She pulled a hat box off the highest shelf she could reach. She carried the box to a bed but didn't open it.

Teia crept forward invisibly on her rubber-sap-soled shoes, moving behind her prey.

Aglaia turned so abruptly, she almost collided with Teia.

Teia shrank bank, eyes downcast.

Aglaia moved forward quickly, but then stopped just as Teia was preparing to lash out with paryl.

Aglaia sat, grabbed a hair tie, and scowling at her reflection, rapidly bound up her long blonde hair into a sensible bun.

This was the moment Teia had been waiting for. She touched her chest where the vial of olive oil had once rested: it had been Aglaia's threat of sending her to be a brothel slave at the mines.

The blade came free of its leather sheath noiselessly.

"You are not afraid, Aglaia Indomita Crassos!" Aglaia told her reflection. "You think of Marcus. You think of what the Guiles did to him, and you make them pay."

It should have stirred something in Teia. Some human emotion. If not an emotion, a question at least. Paryl was supposed to make you more susceptible to feeling, but even handling paryl didn't do more than make Teia aware of the spot that was numb, like tapping frostbitten fingers against a stranger's flesh. There was pressure registering farther up your fingers, and you could see the touch. You remembered what feeling was like, but that spot had been pushed so far past pain it wasn't capable of anything at all.

But this was no time for thoughts or second thoughts.

This isn't payback. I am merely predator, you are merely prey. No torture. No final words.

Teia squeezed the nerves in each of Aglaia's shoulders and watched her arms fall unfeeling to her sides. As the woman looked down, wondering why her arms had dropped, Teia grabbed that sensible bun with one hand and rammed the dagger into the back of Aglaia's neck. With paryl illuminating the gap between skull and spine, Teia's blade slid in as easily as if Aglaia had lubed herself up for the unwanted penetration with olive oil, and penetrated to the hilt.

Aglaia's body went limp instantly, but Teia held her in place by her hair, that beautiful blonde hair that provided such a nice grip, and guided her back into her seat.

Teia wrenched the blade back and forth to ensure she'd fully severed the spine, then left it in Aglaia's neck as she grabbed a rag from a pocket.

She barely got the rag in place around the blade to blot up the blood before it leaked onto the fine chair's back.

Teia rolled Aglaia out of the chair and onto the bare floor, facedown, dagger up.

Then Teia left her prey and locked the door.

When she came back, she waited a few more heartbeats, and then used paryl to feel for life. You could punch a hole in a man's heart and he might yet move as you made a full count to ten. The body could be stubborn. It was faster with the spine, but it never hurt to be sure.

Aglaia Crassos was dead. Easy.

A bit of blood and spinal fluid seeped out around the dagger's blade and into the rag, but with the wound elevated and the heart stopped, there was no more bleeding than that. Teia had picked a short dagger deliberately so it wouldn't pierce all the way through the woman's neck. By design, but also by luck, she'd severed the spine without also slicing the big arteries in the neck.

The dead woman had pissed herself, but only a little, and her petticoats had held most of it. A few dribbles had escaped onto the wood floor and none onto the upholstered seat of the chair. Excellent.

Lest it get stained, Teia removed the master cloak and got to work. She untied the two bags she'd tied tight around her waist. The first held half a sev of rocks. The second was larger and made of waxed canvas.

Unhurried, Teia laid out that bag next to Aglaia's body and opened it. Then, carefully, she put the body onto the bag: lifting and moving feet, then knees, then hips, shoulders, and arms, keeping the dead woman's face down and wound up always. She slowly stuffed the body inside the bag, buttoning the buttons as she was able.

Then she left off buttoning the bag and cleaned the floor fastidiously. Last, she slid the dagger out of Aglaia's spine and cleaned the blade, and tucked the rag into the bag as well.

From here it got dicey.

She tested dragging the body, being carefully to keep the wound elevated.

Easy...on stone. Teia's disposal site was a latrine at the end of a long hallway—a long hallway with one of those runner carpets that's easier to kick out of the way than to keep in place. And Teia was going to be dragging a body down that. Dammit.

There was no way she could add the weight of all those rocks and do that.

That meant she was going to have to drag the body down the hall, then come back, get the rocks, take them down the hall, open the bag, put the rocks in, then lever the body somehow into the latrine.

If she were caught, would she kill the servant who saw her? How about a slave?

Yes, she thought. She'd already decided that. Why did she keep revisiting the choice? In this war, if innocents had to die, innocents had to die.

More innocents, she thought, seeing the faces again.

She pulled Aglaia's body out into the hall, rolling it until she got to the edge of the damned carpet runner. No blood seeped out, though on this patterned red carpet it wouldn't have been disastrous.

Hugging the corpse against herself to be able to pull it down the hall without leaking blood was somehow less repulsive to Teia than it would have been to hug Aglaia in life. This was simply meat. The vile part of it had departed, her spirit had been a putrescence worse than the merely physical odors of urine and decay.

Teia made it to the latrines. No problems. There was no blood. It was all clean. Professional.

Teia jogged back and grabbed her rocks. Made it back, put the rocks into the waxed bag with the body, and closed it again. The latrine opening wasn't overly wide, but mercifully Lady Crassos had been a big believer in girdles and the bag was cinched tight.

"One last thing, Lady," Teia said. She drew the short dagger again and stabbed it low in the corpse's stomach to pierce the intestines. She almost gagged at the gases it released as she withdrew the knife, but those were smells not out of place in a latrine.

She pierced the bag in several other places. The stones at Aglaia's feet would pull those lowest, so Teia made the holes near her head.

Then she began stuffing the body down the latrine. Bit by bit, each grunt and heave a labor pang, Teia squeezed Aglaia's body through the death canal and out of this life.

Shit you were, my lady, and to shit you return.

But the body only dropped a few feet. With a muffled clang, the rocks inside hit metal. Teia froze for a moment, then remembered. This mansion's indoor latrines had a metal plate below that swung open to drop waste and then swung closed again to keep the odors below from being blown constantly back up into the house.

Teia found the handle, and with effort because of the weight of the body on the plate, was able to slide it aside.

Lady Aglaia plopped like an especially large turd into the effluvia below. Teia slid the plate closed, went invisible, and waited in the hall.

With every corpse she left, Teia was inviting the Order to suspect her existence, so every kill had to account for the body somehow. Here, Teia had already scouted the mansion for disposal areas, going as far as directing paryl gas between the walls and eventually down the latrines. Here there was a holding area for the sewage—a septic pit?—Teia hadn't known anything about sewage.

But with what she'd learned from Quentin, she'd made her bag. Enough murdered bodies washed ashore every week on the Jaspers that Teia knew they bloated with gases and floated to the surface, white ghastly things. So she needed the rocks to keep Aglaia's body down. She'd pierced the stomach to allow the release of accumulating gases and pierced the bag to make sure it didn't inflate and buoy the body to the surface.

Their hope—they hadn't done this before—was that the body would decay naturally in the sewage but that the bag would slow the rate of decay. They didn't want the body to bob to the surface, where it had a chance of being seen. They also didn't want it to decay so quickly that anyone using the latrine would smell death.

Instead—they hoped—the air that blew through the sewage ducting would have a chance to take the smell of decay a little bit at a time.

Teia almost left before she remembered the hat box. As she slipped back into Lady Aglaia's chambers, she saw a slave on her way back up the steps to clean out the room.

Teia grabbed the hat box with its Order mask and robes and walked to the closet.

Damn. Me.

Aglaia had gotten the box down from the highest shelf she could reach. Unfortunately, Aglaia had been significantly taller than Teia was. The shelf was too high for Teia.

Teia hopped and tried to shove the box into its spot.

Not even close to high enough.

Oh, for Orholam's sake, a stupid hat box!

But any wrong detail could give her away—even stupid ones. She had to be a ghost, and ghosts don't leave evidence. She looked at the door. She had only one shot at this.

If she missed, it was going to be a disaster. This closet was a mess. Hat boxes were piled upon each other in huge piles. Even putting one on top of the pile with too much force might make the whole collection collapse.

Teia backed up and took a running leap and stabbed the costume box toward its spot with a little toss at the end.

She landed on her toes, in the closet, a hair's breadth away from colliding with the entire stack. She tipped forward. She couldn't see anything to balance herself against that wouldn't knock down everything.

But just as the door slid open, she regained her balance and threw the master cloak closed about her. But she stepped on the hem of the cloak as she stepped backward and fell—

Gracefully. She spun, taking the fall on her hip and tucking her knees so the cloak spun around her, covering them.

A servant walked in, yawning. She saw Aglaia's half-full tray of food.

She sat and ate with gusto. She didn't even look around. She hadn't noticed anything amiss.

Teia took a few deep breaths to steady herself and regain her grip of paryl. She'd come this close to losing it. And that would have meant another dead innocent, another body to dispose of.

While the girl was distracted, Teia stood. Then she got her first look at the hat box. She had left the closet door open, of course, and the hat box was perched at the top of its tower. Precariously.

The air billowing gently into the room from the open door was enough to set the whole stack swaying.

If Teia jumped and missed, it would all come down—and having just jumped, her cloak would be swirling around chaotically at the very moment the servant girl looked toward the sound.

There was nothing Teia could do but pray she didn't have to kill this pimply sixteen-year-old kitchen girl.

So she did nothing. The girl finished eating in no time and stood. She glanced toward the closet and walked over.

Oh, Orholam dammit, what had she seen?

But the girl just walked to the closet, stood on tiptoe and pushed the hat box back into place, and closed the closet. Then she grabbed the tray and left without a look back.

Teia breathed easily for the first time in many minutes.

She left quietly: out onto the balcony, a quick climb down to the street, and she was on her way to the Order's meeting to find the priest. It wasn't until she was halfway there that she realized that with this kill, she didn't feel damned, she didn't feel disgusted, she didn't feel satisfied. She hadn't felt anything at all.

Chapter 65

"Can someone explain to me again why we drafters are charging toward an enemy that can paralyze drafters?" Winsen deadpanned. "I'm so confused. We *are* all drafters, right?"

"We'll get there before they raise the bane," Kip said.

Of course he and Cruxer hadn't gone alone. The Mighty had all come. 'Oh, so if I'm going to be in egregious danger, we all are?' Kip had asked. 'We didn't make it that far in the training,' Cruxer had said.

Actually, not all of the Mighty had come. Though the new one, Einin, had joined them, Tisis hadn't. She'd been on a skimmer farther away, already formulating plans for Big Jasper with her own command. Kip hadn't waited to consult with her, much less asked her to come—but time was of the essence, and she was no good in this kind of fight.

Not that that was why she'd be furious.

Now the Mighty sped across the waves together. Their skimmers were able to interlock together, and with all of them working the reeds, they moved as fast as Izemrasen had.

"And you're so sure of that why?" Winsen asked.

"Because the White King is greedy," Kip said. "He likes a big spectacle. At Ru, he triggered the ambush when the bulk of our fleet was centered right over his trap. It destroyed the most ships possible with one stroke, but he'd have been better served if he'd waited until most of the ships were past the trap. He would have sunk fewer in the first strike, but he'd have trapped everyone else in the bay where he could kill them at his leisure."

"So what's that mean for us now?" Cruxer asked.

"It means he'll hold off until the last moment to spring his trap."

"Isn't the last moment sort of . . . now?" Winsen asked.

Kip turned on him. "What do you want, Winsen? You want to let all our friends die? I didn't get the scout's report until I got it. You want to live forever? Get out. I'm sick and tired of wondering if I can count on you."

"Bugger off," Winsen said. "You're the boss. Fine. Some accident of birth put you one notch above the rest of us. Fine. It's one notch, not twenty. You're the boss. I'll follow you. That's what we do. I'll follow you to my death today, or some other day if we get lucky, but don't expect me to enjoy it or kiss your ass on the way."

"Your bitching hurts morale," Kip said. "It weakens us."

The craft slowed perceptibly as Winsen stopped drafting, irate. "*I* weaken us?! Me?"

"You can be a whiny little shit sometimes," Ben-hadad said.

Winsen looked around to the others, and seemed baffled at their agreement.

Big Leo said, "This one time after I shit myself as we were escaping the Chromeria, I was cleaning my trousers and the stain . . . I was like, what! Winsen, what are you doing in my pants?"

Winsen's rage evaporated as they all laughed. "Dammit, Big Leo."

"Wait, you shit yourself in battle, too?" Ferkudi asked.

"Just the once," Big Leo said defensively. "It was my first fight!" Then he side-eyed Ferk. "Too?"

Everyone looked at Ferkudi.

"It was just a little pellet!" Ferkudi protested.

They laughed, and the blowing wind took their strife for the moment.

Kip looked over at Winsen, who met his gaze.

"I'm in," Winsen said. "I'll try, all right? I just don't want..." He wanted to say more, but he stopped himself.

It brought their present circumstances back into focus, though, even without him saying it. The Mighty looked at one another. That look was worse than scoffing. It was resignation.

"Good day for it," Ben-hadad said, looking at the beautiful blue sky.

"Good day for what?" Ferkudi asked.

Kip sighed. "He means it's a good day to die. Thank you very much, Ben."

"I never understood why people say that," Ferkudi said. "I don't really want to die any day, and most other people don't, either, I mean, except for suicides, right? So isn't *every* day a bad day to die? Ben-hadad, why *did* you say that?"

"Ferk," Cruxer said. "Ferk."

"It's one of the things for the Box, isn't it?" Ferkudi asked.

"Yes. Yes it is."

For Ferkudi, the Box of Things That Don't Make Sense But Make Sense to Other People Don't Worry About It It's Not Important was filled with many things: why people go back to lovers who treat them badly, why people like cats (pretty much the same thing), metaphors involving cutting cheese, why one would eat intestine, why women don't spend all their time looking at themselves naked, why the number system was based on ten but the time system wasn't, why it's normal for dogs to lick their balls in public but Blackguards aren't even allowed to clear their underwear from cleaving the moon, and why he got that question so often about being dropped on his head. As long as he had Cruxer's assurance that it wasn't important for him to figure out, he was perfectly content to put things in that box and put it away in a dark mental corner.

"Anyone feel it yet?" Kip asked.

Head shakes all around.

"How stupid is Caul Azmith?" Winsen said. "It's the same trap as last time. How can one man lose two fleets to the same trap?"

It was a good question. Not that the man wasn't dumb enough to do exactly that, but surely someone would have said something.

But it was finally obvious to Kip, unbelievable as the answer seemed. He said, "We killed a bane at Ru. They think that means it's gone forever. They don't believe us that the White King has any other bane at all. They must have gotten word that a lightly defended fleet was coming, and they rushed out to sink it. Not a bad strategy."

"If we were lying to them," Einin muttered.

"Why would they think we were lying to them?!" Ben-hadad demanded.

"They knew we were in a bad spot. We were asking for men and money. In the same kind of situation, Dúnbheo lied to us to get our help, why wouldn't we do the same?" Kip said.

They shared curses.

"What's the battle plan?" Big Leo asked.

"That depends on...Are those sails?" Kip said.

"There it is," Cruxer said.

It was exactly as Izemrasen had described, except now the two fleets had almost closed within cannon range. The White King's ships were bundled in a knot so tight it was impossible to see how many of them there were from Kip's vantage, but the Chromeria fleet was enveloping them with rank upon rank of ships.

The front ranks broke apart, every other ship slowly, slowly turning broadside. Then flashes of light blinked across the waves, followed by billows of black smoke floating up toward their sails—curiously silent from this far away. Those ships had turned forward again, as ahead of them those ships that had kept going now took their chance to turn broadside.

It was only then that the sound of the first cannons arrived, a distant thunder from that slow storm now covering most of the horizon.

No fire was returned from the White King's ships, and Kip couldn't see any result from the shelling, though scores must have died in the moments he'd been watching.

After the speed and chaos and dexterity required for ground combat, this naval positioning seemed graceless, ponderous. Give a man a sword and tell him to chase down another man, and the contest was decided within minutes; one ship chasing another could easily last all day.

And yet that apparent gracelessness was deceiving, Kip knew. There was a reason why famous admirals were famous. When you had to turn a ship weighing tens of thousands of sevens with only wind, and waves, and muscle, and had to judge exactly the rates at which your enemies could do the same, so that you could arrive at some future position where you could release a broadside at them before they could release one at you, it required a special brilliance to be successful. Add in needing to adjust any of your figures due to your slaves' exhaustion, injuries to crew, the weight of your ship and of your opponent's, timing to reload, then with possible damage to sails, rigging, oars, decks, or rudder, and you had to be brilliant to maneuver a single ship. Commanding a fleet must require another order of thinking altogether—especially when also having to deal with the egos of your subcommanders, like the idiot Caul Azmith, who'd broken ranks.

The single maneuver of interspersed fire, correctly executed, told Kip that whoever was admiral of the Chromeria's fleet now, he or she was probably a genius.

A genius who was about to suffer a crushing defeat.

"Too late to get the Chromeria to pull back," Kip said. "So we're looking for the White King's superviolet drafters, maybe in separate small boats. It seems the superviolets have to do something to trigger the bane to rise—so if we can kill them before they do that, we've got a chance."

"I don't see any boats out alone," Cruxer said.

"Winsen, you've got the best eyes," Kip said.

"Nothing. None alone," the young man said.

"If they're trying to get encircled," Cruxer said, "and they have more than one bane, then maybe they're planning to raise all the bane, all around them at once."

Kip caught where he was going. The bane would rise in a giant ring, matching the encircling Chromeria fleet—and destroying all of it simultaneously. "So the superviolets who are raising the bane have to be in the middle of the formation. The command skimmer's too big to penetrate between those ships. We'll have to split. Ben, I know you said you were working on making the *Blue Falcon IX* submersible, how's it going?"

"This is *Blue Falcon XIII*," Ben-hadad said quickly.

"I know how you work. I see the core ideas already here. This honeycomb structure here? You told me once in some other application that that's super strong."

Ben-hadad expelled a breath. "Last resort, understand? And no more than maybe half speed, at *most*. Slower for you and Big Leo. Even with the wind shield reinforced to be a wave shield, either the water will sweep you off or it'll disintegrate if you go too fast. But this generation was never meant—"

As he was speaking, an enormous cloud of ravens burst from the White King's fleet. But there was nothing random or independent about their flight.

"Razor wings," Einin said.

Winsen cursed aloud. The birds were will-cast to seek out rigging or crewmen and slice through them.

One of them exploded in midair.

"And they've figured out how to rig them to be bombs," Winsen said. "Bomb wings. Great."

"They can't carry much explosive," Kip said. "What are they doing? Ben?"

"They used pigeons before. But pigeons probably aren't smart enough to be taught to seek out the powder kegs," he said. "These are ravens. I'd guess they've will-cast them to seek out the gun decks."

Damn. A single crazed raven flapping and cawing and threatening to explode at any moment could delay an entire gun deck from firing, and that was if it *didn't* make it to the barrels of black powder.

"What else have they will-cast?" Ferkudi said. "Are those shark fins?"

Ben-hadad looked over at Cruxer. "Commander," he said. "You've got to stop us. This is suicide."

But Cruxer had his eyes closed. And when he opened them, a smile curled his lips and light lit his eyes. "Shh," he said, and his voice was a whisper under the storm. "Don't you feel it?"

"Feel what?"

"The wind behind us is greater than the wind against us."

Ben-hadad looked back and forth at the rest of them, their faces eager and fierce. The rattle of swivel guns and muskets and the taunting shouts of both sides rolled across the waves, and only seemed to inflame the Mighty further. "Why am I the only one bothered by that being *demonstrably fucking false*?!"

Kip gave a few more instructions: where they should meet afterward, what their sign would be that they had to retreat, and a quick check that they all had their flares and hullwreckers.

"Ready to separate on your mark," Big Leo said to Kip.

Kip knew he should be afraid. Or he should be worried that he was leading his friends to their deaths.

They might die. But he had a suspicion that they wouldn't.

They were only a few hundred paces out now.

"Remember," Kip said. "Nothing matters except stopping them from raising the bane. The Chromeria's fleet can lose even if the bane stay underwater, but it will *definitely* lose if the bane rise."

Big Leo said, "And we'll probably die, too."

They looked at him.

"You know, just in case anyone was lacking motivation," the big man said.

"Be Mighty and of courage," Kip told his friends. "Einin, stay with Cruxer. Winsen, you're with me this time; live or die. Together."

Winsen took his meaning, and his trust, and nodded. "Together... my lord."

Kip said, "And three, two, one, mark!"

Chapter 66

"There's a man here to see you, High Lord Promachos." The vice chamberlain cleared his throat as he stepped just inside Andross's door. "A Parian. He, uh, wouldn't give his name."

Grinwoody was off doing Orholam knew what again. As the slave aged, he was absent more and more often, and he always pretended it was on some business for Andross and not that he was lazy and due for replacement. But in his defense, Grinwoody would never let this happen.

Andross peered at his vice chamberlain. "Do I look like a village magistrate whom strangers may approach at will on the green?"

"No, High Excellency."

"Then *what do you mean* he wouldn't give his name?"

"He was very convincing, milord," one of the Blackguards at the door said, seeming intent to rescue the poor man. A new girl, Mina.

Andross sneered at her. "And this is why they used to only elevate Blackguards who could make it through the night without wetting the bed."

She withered.

But neither moved.

"He was very compelling, my lord, and he gave proofs enough to satisfy at each station," the other Blackguard, Presser, said.

Andross barked, "Not at this one. I'm busy. And you, Presser, you're old enough to shave by now, aren't you? You should know better. And keep your pup in line or I'll kick her down to a scrub."

"My lord, many pardons," the vice chamberlain said. "He said if you put him off, to remind you of what a young woman said of you, forty years ago now, 'A man of Parnassian storms and no wonder, for in you is joined a volcanic wit...'"

It was a crash of thunder heard when the sky is blue.

"What? He said no more?" Andross demanded.

"I asked. He knew no more of it, dangling as it is."

It took Andross so long he felt embarrassed. His memory— No! It had not failed him. Not yet. He was not so old. The scroll of years was merely so long, so densely packed with incident, and not filed in a library year by year. The man being a Parian had thrown him.

For she had been Atashian.

His first love. *Ninharissi.* He smiled despite himself.

No one had been on that balcony with them that day. No one else would dare send a messenger with such a 'proof,' either, that mixture of a challenge—could Andross remember so far back with such a small prompt?—but also respect, believing that of course Andross would remember back so far with such a small prompt.

The phrase had not even come at the climax of their relationship, though it had come on the night that had changed the entire course of both their lives, and of history itself.

"Shall I send him away?" Presser asked, shifting from foot to foot, rubbing circles awkwardly on one of his buttocks.

It was impossible that she should send him a message. No. Not exactly impossible. And it *was* impossible that it could have been sent by anyone else.

"Bring him in."

Andross had entertained a hope that he might recognize the old man. He didn't. Dark skin faded by the years, clothing fine and well maintained but showing wear. Thus, middling nobility or a rich merchant dressing a bit above his station. There were probably a dozen of the former sort that Andross could call to mind, and several hundred of the latter that he hadn't bothered to memorize.

"High Excellency," the man said after the longest possible pause and with the bare minimum tilt of his head.

A lordling, then. A merchant wouldn't dare so little respect.

"Do you know how the rest of that sentence goes?" Andross asked.

"No."

The old man added no honorific. Very odd. There was something familiar about those eyes, as blue as the morning sky, but Andross was certain he'd never met the man before. Perhaps he'd known a relation?

That didn't limit the circle much. Andross met thousands of people each year. One of the things that had most pained him about his long confinement had been not meeting people, not seeing others overawed at his presence, or having occasion to prove that their awe was justified.

It niggled more than a little that this old man seemed...what was it? Not exactly hostile. Disgusted, maybe.

Contemptuous?

Oho, now, that tempted Andross toward violence.

The old man shook his head. "Disappointing. Here I've forgiven you a thousand times for all the ruin you brought to my house. No, ten thousand. Every day three times with my prayers for every one of these long years, at least when I could bear it. And yet still my heart longs to hate you."

"Excuse me?" Andross asked. Blankly curious.

"I was told not to tell you my name, and that how long it took for you to guess it would tell us both something."

Oh please. "How tiresome," Andross said. "Do you have something for me, or not? *You* asked to see *me*, after all."

"No, I didn't ask for this at all. I was sent to see you. You are to finish the quote. She insisted you could." He clearly had his doubts.

Andross sighed. Better to get this over with, he supposed. "Ninharissi called me 'A man of Parnassian storms and no wonder, for in you are joined a volcanic wit and glacial emotions. When they mix, it is a cataclysm of fire and rain and lightning and molten rock, flames and floods, lava flows and mudslides, laying waste to everything and everyone in a thousand leagues.'"

His memory hadn't abandoned him after all. Who else could recall such, so perfectly?

"She adjudged you well," the old man said. "No wonder she wanted nothing to do with you."

It was a misstep. "Was Ninharissi your lady, then?" Andross asked.

"No. But I see why the Third Eye gave me those words to say. They were for both of us."

Of course. Now it made sense.

The message wasn't from Ninharissi herself, but merely from a Seer who had stolen them from the ether. A little magical eavesdropper, spying on a couple's intimate moments. Disgusting.

Andross had hoped the message was some word from beyond the grave, a treasure a dead woman had wished delivered to him while he was in these straits.

It was all very disappointing, but it made sense. Of course, only the Third Eye could see where she had never been, and into the past as well as into the future. She was an ally more dangerous than even Janus Borig, but couldn't be taken from the game, for she would be a foe far more dangerous still.

Thus, Andross had made no move against her, but he was glad she'd chosen to stay far away.

"How is Polyhymnia?" he asked. He wasn't supposed to know that name. No one was. But swive her for pretending to speak for one he loved. "Has she some guidance for the war?" He felt some hope. After all, Orholam's Seers might choose not to join sides in any normal war, but in a war against heretics and pagans? Surely this visit meant she was answering Andross's letters at last.

"I don't know who that is," the old man said, "but the Third Eye told me she'd be dead by the time I reached you. Murdered by the Order of the Broken Eye. She said anything she did to stop her assassination would only forestall it, wouldn't affect the course of the war, and would have other costs too great for her to countenance."

"Worthless to me, then. Figures. You know, I've met dozens of prophets and Seers through the years. Charlatans and half-wits, most of them. But at least those could be used against the kind of people who believe them. Yet the real ones were never any use at all."

The near-blasphemy spurred no anger from the old Parian. He only stared at Andross calmly.

"What are you here for, old man?" Andross asked.

The old man smiled, finally. "I overestimated you. I thought surely you would place me in an instant. The Third Eye said that for a man who'd had the light restored to his eyes, you were remarkably blind, for you hardly ever look at other people, except to see how you might use them."

Andross looked now. The age. The vocabulary. The diction. The red-gold buttons on his satchel, such as librarians use to carry their scrolls in Azûlay.

His heart suddenly clenched.

But the old man was already speaking: "You seduced my daughter. You convinced her to betray her oaths to her city and tribe and family. You turned her into a thief, and you left her banished, destitute, and pregnant."

Aha. He'd arrived at it only a moment too late. "Asafa ar Veyda de Lauria del Luccia verd'Avonte. A pleasure to meet a Keeper of the Word, Chief Librarian." This was Katalina Delauria's father; this was Kip's maternal grandfather.

Asafa's eyes were burning embers in a face like coal ready to take the flame. He said, "Before you took her from me, Lina and I were very close. She was my joy, my everything. For a time, she wrote me letters even after she fled in disgrace," Asafa said. "Long letters, unsparing of herself or others. She told me everything. And I've come, Andross Guile, to upend all you know and break your glacial heart."

Chapter 67

As the first cannons began firing at them, the command skimmer broke apart.

But the enemy had no Gunner directing their fire. The shots—twenty of them at least—all sailed wide, short, or long. Few of them were even close.

Still, there was the familiar jolt of excitement at being shot at with no effect. That bracing, 'Holy shit! I'm alive and I could have been dead and someone just wanted me dead and did all they could to make me dead, but I'm alive, hell yeah, you bastards!'

The Mighty were near enough the wall of galleys and galleons under the flying flags of broken chains on a black background that the roar of the guns was nearly simultaneous with the gushers of the smoke and the splash of the cannonballs, jetting water into the air.

Kip's eyes were dragged below the line of the cannons, though, in front of the ripples that spread around each as the shock waves left their imprint on the waters beside the ships.

In a unison not possible for wild animals, dozens—no, *hundreds*—of sharks rose, dorsal fins in ranks, heading straight for the Mighty.

A primal fear struck him then, thalassophobia, a dread that man was not made for the depths, that the water was not his home, that this vast sea was itself hostile to him, hateful. If the foils of his skimmer hit a shark, Kip might kill the shark, but the collision would certainly pitch him into the water.

He would be helpless. Torn apart by those alien, unforgiving teeth.

The skimmer shivering as a musket ball ricocheted off the deck broke Kip's brief paralysis. He aimed it down lower into the waves. The increased drag slowed him considerably.

Then, as he closed in on the sharks, he aimed skyward.

He shot into the air, and felt a jarring bump from beneath propelling him even higher.

It turned him off axis, but Ben-hadad—Orholam bless him for being such a damned genius—had built the skimmers well. The foils weren't edged but round, so when Kip hit the waves again, there was little danger of catching an edge and flipping over. Instead, Kip skipped over the waves a couple of times, then the foils dug into the waves and he was off again.

Directly toward dozens more sharks.

But before any of them could attack, on some unseen cue, the majority of them turned away and dove.

Kip had no time to figure out why they'd turned away, or what that dark immensity was far beneath the waves.

He also had lost track of what was happening with any of the rest of the Mighty. He could only keep himself alive now, and that took everything in him.

He was within forty paces of the first ships now, and though the teams were still reloading cannons and swivel guns, men on the galleons' decks were firing muskets toward him.

Splashes pocked the water as he juked one way and then the next.

At the last moment before he crashed into a galleon's hull, Kip veered his skimmer hard sideways and accelerated as quickly as he could.

The Mighty's lack of training as a squad on the skimmers nearly got him killed. He veered directly into Winsen's path, surprising the young man as much as the musketeers on the galley's deck.

Winsen popped his skimmer up into the air, and Kip ducked, taking a faceful of water even as he blasted luxin skyward. Winsen's skimmer was flung high into the air, and by the time Kip was able to clear his eyes, he heard a splash on the other side of the galleon.

Then he saw the stern of the next ship, looming directly before him, and he cut hard to port and inside the first circle of ships.

Kip glanced back just in time to see Big Leo follow his path, but this time a red wight was ready for him. The young woman with burn-scarred skin oozing pyrejelly set herself aflame and leapt through the air into Big Leo's path.

His immense chain swung in a quick arc and batted her aside as if she were an overexcited puppy jumping toward her master with muddy paws. She plunged into the waves, hissing and sizzling, and he swung that flaming chain once more above his head to regain his balance, slapped it into the waves to extinguish the last red luxin-fed flames, and came after Kip as they darted inside the outer circle of ships.

The second circle was entirely slave-rowed galleys without sails, their decks lower to the waves and packed with warriors, most of them only lightly armored.

Kip saw Cruxer speeding past an entire ship broadside, his skimmer shearing through slaves' oars while he himself needled the massed warriors on deck, shooting a storm of short blue luxin arrows from his hands, unguided and small but fiercely sharp. Whether hit themselves or just cowering before this terror, the warriors went down like sheaves of grain as a scythe passed across the deck. They folded in blood and screams.

Taking advantage of the chaos Cruxer was creating, Einin angled in to the ship and slapped a hullwrecker down near the waterline, then zipped away.

Winsen fought like a madman on a spring. He bounced his skimmer up to the height of a deck, loosed two arrows while he was in the air, put his hands back on the reeds, and bounced again as if the sea were made of boiled rubber. He killed the captain, the first mate at the wheel, he killed a bo's'n, he killed every officer and fighting man who looked important—and then he turned back around and kept killing until someone panicked and shouted the order to fire a broadside.

The young archer heard the order, though, and instead of popping back up from the waves, angled his skimmer downward and stayed underwater.

The broadside of twenty cannons boomed with a fury—raking death across the decks of its allied galleon in the outer circle.

Winsen popped up out of the waves, water sluicing off the skimmer as he barely held on, blinded and cursing, and no longer holding his favorite bow—but alive. Three sailors, muskets now reloaded, ran to the rail and aimed down at the temporarily immobilized young man.

Kip threw blue spikes as hard as he could from his awkward angle far beyond the ship himself. The first wasn't even close. The second shattered against the railing under the sailors' hands, barely a miss. The third flew low but passed underneath the railing and blasted the nearest sailor's legs out from under him.

Between the blue shrapnel exploding in their faces and their crewmate going down, the two unharmed sailors panicked. One froze. The other stepped backward, tripped, and accidentally discharged his musket into the air.

Seeing Winsen regain his balance and his velocity, Kip cut under the beakhead of the next ship and in.

The directed explosion of the hullwrecker snapped out behind them, and Kip saw a billow of smoke and showers of wood from the ship behind them.

At the Battle of Ru, the Blood Robes had used a single rowboat filled with superviolet drafters to raise the bane.

Kip had expected the same here, but perhaps with nine rowboats.

There were no rowboats.

This was a fucking dragon-ship.

A dozen galleys had been lashed together, the disparate parts melded into a whole with wood and burnt red luxin. Cut in the brutal style of early pagan art, this floating castle had the look of something crafted by a master artist equipped only with an ax. Brushed 419 white pine skin yielded to spikes carved from ivory tusks. The open maw, equipped with great spouts for shooting out burning red luxin, showed lips of burnt red luxin, like blackened, cracked skin. It had claws and eyes of atasifusta wood, ever-burning.

In a carven saddle, high on the dragon's back and raised high above the waves, was a black throne. Empty.

But that didn't mean the rest of the dragon-ship was empty. Like fire ants rushing up your trouser leg when you stepped full into their anthill, the Blood Robes on it were in a violent panic, frothing forth onto every surface Kip could see.

And all of them—red-robed though they were—were drafters or wights. There were hundreds.

But that wasn't what frightened Kip.

Behind the immense throne was a tower of chains and gears. Six great crank wheels were being turned by a dozen slaves each, and six taut chains with links as large as a man raised pulleys at their apex at the foot of the throne itself.

A great deal of chain had already accumulated around each of those crank wheels, and as Kip took a moment, he could feel a burgeoning tension in every color—like he'd felt in green before the Battle of Ru.

The bane were rising in a circle around the dragon-ship. All of them.

The Mighty were too late.

Kip's heart jumped, but then he felt something immense nearby. He blinked furiously and felt as if between blinks something happened to his eyes—had he been hit?

He glanced down, but in chi's spectrum, and his gaze saw something beyond his ken, a single slice of ocean down to the depths, being crossed by a monstrous shape.

A flutter of the eyes, as if clearing blood away. Blink. Nothing. Blink. Another slice, half a degree departed. A curve of pectoral fin. Blink. Gone. A fluke. Gone.

A whale?

She was turning, deep under the waves, even as dozens of sharks bit at her flanks and flukes.

It broke Kip out of his paralysis.

He hurled the retreat signal flares skyward for the Mighty and banked sharply away himself.

An explosion shook the distant waters out where the Mighty had penetrated the first ring of ships. Ah, Ben-hadad had put a hull-wrecker on another of the galleons.

420

But the inner ring that they had just penetrated had closed tight behind the Mighty.

Gunports were rattling open on this side of the ships as the cannon crews slowly reacted to the threat that was the Mighty. Had the Mighty proceeded to attack the center island dragon, the cannons wouldn't have been able to fire without endangering their own. But now the Mighty were turning back into range of safe and accurate fire.

A second explosion rocked the seas, this time on another of the ships in the inner circle, even as they sped toward it. Though the ship immediately sagged in the water, and all the cannon crews had been killed or stunned on that one ship, it did nothing to the others, who started opening up.

Nor was that ship going to sink in time. The bane was rising behind them, and if Kip and the Mighty didn't make it several leagues away within the next few minutes, they would all be paralyzed.

Throwing another signal flare, Kip sliced out a wide, fast circle, and each of the rest of the Mighty slotted in seamlessly, re-forming the command ship one at a time.

"Bane rising!" Kip gasped out as they finally locked in all together. He threw over the steering to Cruxer as he peered into the sea.

"Can't dive together!" Ben-hadad said. "Too much drag."

Cruxer steered their circle in close to the ship that they'd hit with the hullwrecker, hoping that the other ships would be reticent to fire up on their own comrades.

As they came out of that second circle, though, Winsen shouted a curse. He pointed back in toward the great dragon-ship. "Breaker!"

Kip ignored him.

"Breaker! Kip! For Orholam's sake, man—"

Kip glanced up, trying to narrow his eyes so that he wouldn't be blinded. He caught only a terror of skimmers streaming toward them—the White King had skimmers now?—no, they were sea chariots pulled by some kind of sea animals. Sharks? And sharks untethered and great swarms of razor wings clouding the sky.

But Kip said nothing. He jumped toward the rudder and cut so hard that all of them were nearly thrown off their feet and into the water.

Before they could even cry out in protest, the water exploded beside them in a flash of dark skin and immense presence as the black whale breached fully into the air, sharks snapping behind it, some of them launching into the air as well.

It was only the vast discipline ingrained in the Blackguard that kept them on their reeds, kept them moving. Razor wings hit the waves all around them, some exploding, some trying to slash their bodies.

The black whale came down on the stern of the ship Ben-hadad had bombed. Waves and flotsam exploded from the dying ship, a cacophony of screams and water and small explosions from the razor wings and dying men and animals.

Kip slewed the command skimmer back and forth as he nearly lost his feet, not so much in evasive moves as merely trying to regain his own balance, but when he came out of the tight arc, there seemed to be a gap—a trough of clear water.

He aimed the skimmer down into the trough and then up the other side.

The skimmer bottomed out in the trough, sliced into the following wave, then shot into the air, over crushed hull and lumber and dying men.

They didn't clear it completely, but the garbage they landed on yielded to the skimmer's foils and weight and speed.

Ahead of them, the black whale breached again, this time with only a single shark after it. Then it dove before it reached the second circle of ships.

It didn't matter. The outer circle was looser, and the first ship one of them had bombed was half sunk. Kip and the Mighty shot out into the open sea and safety.

He shot flares into the open sky—a retreat, in an old Chromeria code.

The Chromeria's fleet didn't heed it. Not that he could see.

There was nothing he could do.

They had tried. But that didn't make him feel like any less a coward as they fled.

"There were hundreds of drafters on that dragon-ship," Cruxer said. "We're good. Maybe we're each worth ten of them, but..."

"Not a hundred of them, each, not at once," Winsen said.

"I've shit myself before," Big Leo said. "But I've never run away."

"You didn't run away," Ferkudi said. "None of us did. I mean, except Breaker. He was steering. He gave the orders. So I guess he ran away, but the rest of us—"

"Ferk. Shut it," Cruxer said.

"They're gonna die back there, aren't they?" Ferkudi asked. "All those Chromeria drafters and sailors and soldiers. I mean, is there any possible way they might—"

"Ferk!" Cruxer said.

They skimmed in silence, and Kip wondered if at last he was the Breaker in truth. He had broken the Mighty's streak of victories; he had broken their foundational myth that they were invincible. In so doing had he broken the Mighty itself?

They were no longer heroes of lore, legends in the making, indomitable, unstoppable, unflappable, brave and just and right and true and forever.

Maybe they'd always just been boys who'd had some lucky fights.

Several minutes later, when the Mighty were so distant Kip didn't think they would know the outcome of this battle one way or the other, a sound like the earth shaking reached them, and mist exploded into the distant skies.

Big Leo said, "I feel like I just got in a fight with my big brother and he grabbed my fists and started hitting me in the face with them, chanting, 'Stop hitting yourself, stop hitting yourself.'"

Then a tugging sickness hit all of them, and even this far away they lost half their speed all at once. It was the call of a master to his slaves, certain of obedience.

The bane had surfaced.

Kip couldn't see it, couldn't feel it, couldn't witness it—and yet he knew that hundreds upon hundreds of their allies had just perished. Maybe their friends had been on those ships. He hadn't stopped the White King. He hadn't saved his friends.

He'd failed, and he couldn't think of any way that he could do anything but fail again when the bane reached the Jaspers.

Chapter 68

"I'm coming to the end of things, Quentin, I can feel it," Teia said.

"With the Order?" he asked, his voice low. He never forgot to be circumspect, even here in his own room. His room, it turned out, even had a secret exit into a seldom-used hallway. There were, Teia'd found, several old, dusty, and baggy cloaks of various colors and qualities hanging near the exit. Some White long ago had used this room probably not only for assignations but also as a staging area to go out incognito, probably to meet spies.

"No," she said. "I mean, sort of. With them, but not only with them. I feel like—I think maybe Orholam's letting me know that I'm going to die."

"It has been known to happen," he said, contemplative. "If so it's either a mercy, to tell one to repent, or it's a grace, to allow one to take   423 care of unfinished business. Do you feel you have unfinished business?"

She shrugged. Funny that he didn't think she needed to repent. "I mean, taking down the bad guys and finding my father, but not really like spiritually or whatnot."

She wasn't sure if that was true, but Quentin was a luxiat, and sometimes he went full-on luxiat on her. It was all right. She was glad he had something that worked for him, and he wasn't obnoxious about it.

He didn't say anything else. He was getting good at waiting silently. He'd joked once that the wisest luxiat is a silent luxiat. Finally, he said, "No one touches you, do they?"

It was heading toward night, and the sunset through the windows gave the wood in this chamber a ruddy glow. She'd always liked the light in Quentin's room. In this orangey, warm chamber, with his many books and the simple, well-burnished beauty of his hardwood shelves (and, perhaps, Quentin's company), there was no loneliness, only solitude.

"Hadn't thought about it," she said.

"I avoided touch for the longest time," he said. "I told myself I was just that way. Naturally averse to touch. It wasn't that. It was shame. It was worse after I murdered Lucia, of course, but I'd had it even before then. I'm trying to unlearn some things, Adrasteia, things that stand in the way of my mission. No one touches the destitute, the broken poor. It's been part of my work now to give them that connection, as valuable as the food and clothes I give them, I think. Of course, you minister to the body first, then the heart, and last, if you can, the soul. I think in this I've served you very poorly. Because you have enough to eat and are dressed well, and because you ask me smart questions, I've somehow missed your poverty."

" 'Poverty'? Ha. I've seen poverty. This ain't that." She motioned around herself vaguely: as if to say, 'Look at this room, these good clothes, all the privileges of my new station, the very nice meal a slave brought to Quentin's chamber only minutes ago.'

"You're a soldier with no brothers in arms, and you do heartbreaking work that no one can understand—not even those few you can tell about it. I don't understand; not even Karris can. You endure a poverty of heart. But poverty's lie to you is the same. Poverty tells you that you don't matter."

Teia felt suddenly naked. "Well, shit, Quentin."

"It wasn't a condemnation of you. The opposite, in fact."

"I do so think I matter," she said, but even she could hear the defensiveness in her voice. She wouldn't sound defensive if he were simply mistaken, would she?

"Adrasteia, you think that what you *do* matters. The mission matters. But outside of your mission, you believe you have no importance. That's a lie. A lie that's made you very good, very focused. Now the thing that you believed gave you your only significance is drawing to a close, so you're terrified. Of course you are. It's understandable, but it's not a premonition of death."

"I could die at any moment," she said. Sharp was hunting her, even now.

"That's true, but it's true of us all," he said.

"A little *more* true for me," she said.

"A point I'll concede," he said. "Though if Sharp catches you, they'll kill me, too."

"They what?" She'd never even thought of it.

"They'll kill anyone you spent much time with, trying to find your handler."

"How did I not think of that?" She felt a sudden nausea, but it was too late now. Even if she cut off all contact with Quentin today, they'd kill him regardless. She'd been seen with him and the Mighty before. It was how the Order worked. "I'm sorry," she said. "I swear I'll do my best not to let that happen."

"You'd do your best regardless, and I'll die when Orholam allows it, and no sooner. I'm glad to aid you, and honored to call you friend."

"Friend?" she asked.

"Is it such a high bar to clear?" he asked.

"No, it's not that. I suppose…I mean, you *have* been a friend to me, far better than I deserve."

"Oh, I disagree," he said.

"And I've been no friend to you," Teia said. "Our entire relationship is based on me taking."

He shrugged. "I don't see it that way."

"I didn't tell you what happened," she said. "With Aglaia."

Ah. Maybe she did have unfinished business.

"I took the lack of an answer as an answer."

So he thought she'd succumbed, that she'd tortured that evil bitch. "I didn't torture her. I didn't even speak to her."

"Did you kill her hard or easy?"

"Quick. I'm not sure there is *easy*. But it was instant. It was your words that inspired me, if you must know. Sort of."

Quentin took in a big breath. His eyes softened. "Well, then! I'm so proud of you, Adrasteia. Doing the right—"

425

"Don't be," she interrupted. "I didn't do the right thing. It was what you said about repentance. Or, actually, damnation."

"Hmm?"

"I was afraid if I tortured her, she might repent. Orholam is merciful, and I wanted to be sure I sent her straight to hell. I wanted her to suffer, but I could only spare a few minutes in that room, nervous of being interrupted. I wanted her to suffer forever, burn forever in whatever hell there is for her kind. I killed her fast so she wouldn't have any second chance to avoid that hell, if hell there is. So tell me, Quentin, tell me that I'm kind and good. Tell me that I *deserve* a friend."

A lump rose in her throat and she swallowed hard on it.

The compassion in his eyes didn't even waver. He shook his head. "I'm a *murderer*, Adrasteia. I killed an innocent! You expect me to reject you because you killed a bad woman too eagerly?"

Teia furrowed her brow. "Hadn't really thought of it that way."

"Even my hypocrisy knows *some* bounds," he said with a grin. "Besides," he said, "it doesn't work. Some people think they can force Orholam's hand. You know, like they can enjoy their sins for their whole life, then make a deathbed confession. That kind of thing. As if the Giver of Justice, the creator of the very concept, could be so easily fooled or manipulated. Do you think that you could, by plucking Aglaia out of time at this moment or that, really change her soul's destination? Do you think you're so powerful? Really? That matter is between her and Orholam. You have many powers, but that's not one of them! Granted, *trying* to send someone to hell is a serious matter. But you're not her judge. Being her executioner is quite enough weight for you to bear."

"You make it sound as if it all makes sense," Teia said. "As if it all works out."

"It does."

"All evidence to the contrary?"

"I never said we get to see it all work out."

"Then maybe it's time for us to finish that other discussion," Teia said. "Because I think I have an answer," Teia said. "You said when we approach the big questions, we need to know if we're approaching them rationally or emotionally. But the truth is we always approach them emotionally. There's always one answer we want. Though which answer that is varies from person to person."

"You're certain you're ready to talk about evil now?"

"Seems like *before* I do my best to kill people might be better for it than afterward."

He answered that with silence, and she actually took the time to think about it. Ready, really? She was and she wasn't. And her heart needed the words now, like a thirsty tongue needs water, even if it be a trickle licked off a stone and not a full glass.

"Ready enough to hear. Maybe not to accept," she admitted.

"Then you know your own heart better than most," Quentin said. "Very well, then. I'm a smart man, but often not a wise one, which can make for an impoverished theology or at least a poor application of it. But here's the best I've got. Why is there evil if Orholam loves us and has the power to stop it? My answer is that we are the apprentice painters, working under the master's watchful eye. He is a good master, and He has sworn not to make our work meaningless. Every smudge and every blot and every unsteady line we draw will remain. The master will soften a line or turn the darkest graffiti to chiaroscuro, but never will He take the palette knife to gouge out an imperfect piece of the work, for if He erased the imperfections made by our hands, where would He stop erasing? *Everything* we paint we paint imperfectly."

"Then the whole scheme is shit. He should paint it all Himself, were He not too lazy," Teia said. She wasn't doing a good job of listening, though, and she knew it.

Quentin flashed a quick, apologetic grin. "Sure, sure, if we are to call lazy the one who created the Ur, the Primes, and all the Thousand Worlds—not a heretical notion, by the by, despite what certain scholars...never mind. If we're to call lazy He who spread the stars with His cloak and blows the winds between them, who forms every beating heart and mountain and lake upon them, and is creating yet every life and love and every chick within each egg, bursting out into the light...if we're to do that, then I'm not sure the word 'lazy' has a stable definition. But certainly, we could conceive of Orholam as being so vast, so omnipotent, so intelligent that He could direct every moment of every man's and every woman's and every child's and every dog's day. He could do so, and the picture created thus would be flawless, and every head in the cosmos would nod as one that it was flawless, for they could not do otherwise than nod in unison. For in their perfection, they must recognize His perfection. They must bow and bob at His every command. They wouldn't need commands, for they would be but extensions of His fingers. Such creatures would be capable of everything except freedom, and therefore, everything except love. And for some reason, Orholam values love—not just of Him but our love toward others, toward even ourselves. The master takes joy when the apprentice grows in her mastery, when she sees the line for herself the first time, when her hand can finally paint what her heart conceives, and when she partakes of the beauty for the first time and the five hundredth."

"Murdered slaves and dead babies part of that beauty?" Teia asked bitterly.

Quentin folded his hands. "Part of the beauty? No. But part of the canvas. A wag asks from the secret bitterness of his heart, 'So then, is this the best of all possible worlds?' If Orholam is watching, and Orholam is acting, is this the best He can do? Because the best He can do appears to be shit."

Teia was still a bit surprised to hear Quentin use such language.

Quentin grinned, glad to have shocked her. "What? He made shit, too."

She grinned momentarily, but the ache didn't abate.

Quentin said, "There was a master who loved his slave, so he freed him immediately. Another master loved his slave, so he wrote into his will that the slave should be freed after he himself died. Which of these loved his slave?"

"The one who freed him."

"I agree!" Quentin said, "But the master who kept his slave would object that what he did was for the slave's own good: a free life is a dangerous one, the free man might end up destitute! The master would guarantee a good life for him, meaningful work, and protection—until he passed away and could guarantee it no longer."

"He's lying," Teia said. "Though maybe to himself first. It's none of the master's business what happens to that slave."

"But so long as the slave belongs to him, it literally *is* his business," Quentin said.

Teia blinked. "Well, sure, *financially*, but . . . but the master can't call it love, then. He's just making sure no one destroys his investment, the way a free man might destroy himself. The first master is assuming the financial loss in giving the slave his freedom. He's not investing in property; he's investing in a man. And not for his own enrichment but for the former slave's."

"What happens," Quentin asked, "if that freedman recognizes his master's love and continues working in his house, though now as a free man?"

"Everybody wins, I guess?" Teia said. "The master knows his former slave cares about him, and the former slave gets a fair wage and dignity and the ability to leave if things change."

"But the same work gets done?"

"I daresay that *more* work gets done in the good master's house. Slaves have ways of letting their will be felt."

"And yet you ask that Orholam be the kind of master who keeps His slaves as slaves forever and calls it love."

Quentin smiled, and she felt like she'd fallen into the kindliest trap ever. Despite Quentin's gentle demeanor, Teia felt like she'd been slapped.

"What? No." Teia shook her head. "Look, I hear you. But that doesn't close the gap for me. Sure, blame war on men. There's evil in my own heart. I fight it all the time. But...floods and cancer and famines? Why would there have to be those for us to have freedom? Why would that be the consequence of our evil choices? I don't get it. If Orholam made the whole system, He should have made it...I dunno. Better."

Quentin said, "There are those who claim that as men's rejection of Orholam's will for us has corrupted our very nature, so, too, those elohim who rebelled have corrupted the natural world. But I don't know. Personally, I think the proper response to those who've suffered a tragedy is not to teach them but to grieve with them. I've asked many times, and angrily, would it have upset some vast eternal plan if my father hadn't had a seizure and drowned while bathing me in the river when I was four years old? Why did our dog Red pull me out but not go back that time for my father, whom he'd saved from his fits before?"

And suddenly, Quentin was too overcome with emotion to speak.

It seemed to surprise him even more than it did her.

"I'm sorry," he said, clearing his throat. "I haven't told that story."

Teia got the idea that he meant ever, that he'd never told that story to anyone.

He dashed tears from his eyes and tried to smile to smooth it over. "I guess I can choose to be angry at that dog, or angry at Orholam for that day, or at Orholam for my father having the falling sickness in the first place. Or I can be grateful that He made dogs to love us and that Red saved my father from the fire and the waves four times before that day so that I might even be born, and I can be grateful that that beautiful animal saved me that day.

"In the face of life's black mysteries, answers feel barren. All I know is that I can only choose my attitude. The mysteries aren't thereby untangled, but when I choose gratitude, I see life flower. When I paint as if my art has meaning, not just for today but also for eternity, it doesn't make the aches go away, but I've come to trust that my master will use my pain for a purpose."

She saw the beauty in that way of seeing things. But it looked so far away from her vantage. She said, "You've got a lot of faith." But then, that's why you're a luxiat, she thought.

"No. I had a profoundly diseased set of beliefs—so diseased they led me to murdering a girl—and now I have a pretty finely attuned sense for what diseased beliefs look like. And the truth is, you don't need finely attuned senses to see them. You can judge a faith by the fruit it bears. When you see someone bitter with the world, ask yourself what they believe."

"And does that apply to me?" she asked. She was going for irony, but she was afraid her own words were pure bitterness.

He didn't answer. He didn't have to.

"Adrasteia, I believe you walk attended by the servants of the Most Holy. This is His work, His war, and He will not abandon you in your need. When you choose to do the task for which the maker made you, when you know yourself free, but you come back to the master's house to work anyway, you can excel in ways that others could never imagine. And you *are* excelling, even if you don't see it."

"I guess me excelling means nobody sees me, right? Especially the immortals. Well, at least the one."

She'd told Quentin about her dream about Abaddon. He'd blanched with fear but hadn't been very helpful in giving her anything solid about the creature. Too many contradictory claims in the texts, he said, many of them probably planted by the evil one himself.

"Be strong and of good courage, Adrasteia. We live in a world of earthquakes and landslides and floods, but we live in a world of eucatastrophes, too."

"I don't know what that even means."

"It means whether brought on by men or malevolent spirits, we live in a world where hell invades earth from time to time, with devastating consequences, far worse than anything we could imagine. But...but—almost always, so far as I can tell, at the hand of men and women of goodwill—*sometimes* heaven invades earth, too."

"You're a man of faith after all," she said.

"Maybe I am," he said, but sadly, for she saw his recognition that she was using the title to push him away.

"I feel so alone, Quentin."

"I wish I could be a better bridge for you," he said.

"These men I've been sent to k—"

"Those men are fools."

"What? They're the most capable spies I could even imagine. They've thrived in the shadow of the Chromeria itself."

"Fools."

"Have you not listened to my reports?" she asked.

"Cunning, perhaps, but fools. When we think the darkness hides our deeds from the Lord of Light, we are children who clap our hands over our eyes and shout that we're invisible. You are seen, Teia. Even in your cloak. You are known." He grinned, and it was scary to see the fierceness of judgment on his kind face as his voice lowered. "And, in the end, so are they."

She almost shivered, but she couldn't let it go. "Quentin, I need to tell you what I'm doing and where I'm going."

"No, you don't. Just in case I'm caught. I'm not terribly brave, and I'd soon fold under torture. You've said you're coming to the end. I believe you. I feel it, too. Adrasteia, you serve not just Karris, not just the Chromeria, but the Lord of Light Himself. You will know what must be done, and you will have the unique strength to do it."

She reached to her neck by old instinct. The vial was gone, long gone. "I hope you're right," she said. She grabbed one of Quentin's sheets of parchment and scribbled a quick note. "Take this to Karris."

"You know you shouldn't trust anything about them to writing."

"It's not about the Order," she said. "It's about you."

"What?"

"I don't know that we'll see each other again, Quentin. Ever. Karris promised me that if I did this, she'd give me anything."

He looked down at the note. "You've...you've asked that she free me?" His voice wavered, and he glanced up, profoundly humbled. "Why...why wouldn't you ask that they look for your father?"

Teia twisted her lips briefly. "If Karris is who I think she is, she'll do that anyway. Might as well get two requests for the price of one, eh?"

He snorted, but the sorrow didn't leave his eyes.

"Fare thee well, Quentin. You've been a most excellent friend to me."

He lifted a hand before she turned away.

"Adrasteia, before you go...may I hug you?"

She hesitated. His overture spooled out like a coil of rope over a chasm, thin as spidersilk, but also perhaps as strong. "I think...I think I would like that."

It wasn't magic. A hug didn't fix everything. Perhaps it didn't fix anything at all. But it did feel good.

Really, really good.

She might have cried then, finally. Maybe just a little.

Chapter 69

Kip had approached docking his armada at the Chromeria as if it were a military assault. His little army was his pry bar, and a pry bar is good for nothing if you can't wedge it into place.

So he hid most of his ships beyond the horizon, low and mastless as they were, and came in with Ben-hadad, Cruxer, and Tisis on skimmers, all of them dressed in blacks nearly identical to Blackguard garb.

The docks had been transformed in the time the Mighty had been gone: expanded to deal with the crush of refugees and the ships necessary to supply them from all over the satrapies, but also with additional fortifications. There were towers, more ballistae, and the walls themselves were taller and likely thicker, too.

They did all seem to be staffed by Andross Guile's Lightguard, though, making Kip almost hope some small violence was necessary.

He and the first wave broke up, seeking out the harbormaster and her apprentices and besieging them by any means necessary: Cruxer charming the woman with his good looks, Ben-hadad faking a medical emergency, Kip with a thousand questions, and Tisis distracting half a dozen journeymen herself with charm and cleavage, having changed into her finest silks and a giant hat that blocked the view of the men and women disembarking behind her. Meanwhile, other skimmers docked in a steady drip, drip, drip.

A few of the men who'd left Daragh the Coward to join Kip had been thieves (a really long time ago, before they'd totally, completely, utterly changed, sir!). Skilled ones, too, they bragged. He'd directed these to go deep into the crowds immediately, waiting on spotters who looked for any messengers sent toward the Chromeria. It was a slender hope, of course, with so many people jamming the docks.

Kip accepted an interruption by one of his new Mighty with the journeyman he was arguing with and headed for the Chromeria himself. Within two blocks, Ferkudi, Cruxer, and Winsen fell in with him.

Clearly, someone was awake, though, doubtless alarmed at the burgeoning number of unknown ships in their harbor, because Kip saw several messengers running from the Chromeria toward the docks. He even heard one waylaid by a barking dog. Apparently the Cwn y Wawr had landed successfully.

By now Tisis should be halfway to her safe house in a defensible mansion in a Ruthgari neighborhood. If Kip were arrested, she had to be safe. She would direct the army.

The streets of Big Jasper felt different than they had a year ago. Not only were they twice as crowded, dirtier, and more hostile, but they also felt smaller and more scared. What had seemed to Kip to be the center of the world, snug and smug in its towering superiority, was now a too-tall cairn, stone stacked on stone, wondering if the wind would blow it down.

They made it unimpeded all the way to the Lily's Stem and crossed that luxin bridge onto Little Jasper. An honor guard of Ruthgari soldiers in green fell in behind them—Eirene Malargos's ambassador's doing, no doubt. So Tisis's skimmer-sent letters had reached him.

Then they were joined by four of the Ruthgari Satrapah Ptolos's own guard. Actually, Kip wasn't even sure if Ruthgar was still led by Satrapah Ptolos these days. There had been rumblings that Eirene Malargos was considering taking over personally in this time of crisis instead of ruling from behind.

Someone had cleared out a path through the various petitioners and nobles in the great hall at ground level, and everyone turned to watch them walk through. Kip saw hostile faces from the white-clad Lightguards, but he and his entourage entered the lifts without being impeded.

No one asked where they were going. Their escorting soldiers set the plates and took them to the audience-hall level.

"Just, uh, in case I don't get another chance to say it," Ferkudi said. He cleared his throat. "Uh, it's been an honor to serve you, my lord."

Big Leo grunted an affirmation. Ben-hadad cleared his throat in agreement.

"More than that, for me," Cruxer said quietly, not turning his head, his shoulders back. "This work saved my life after, after Lucia passed. It's been purpose and a pursuit worthy of my whole heart."

The rest rumbled agreement, and Kip's heart swelled for these men who—

"Ah shit, you're all makin' me weepy," Winsen deadpanned. He dabbed at a dry eye.

Big Leo smacked the side of Winsen's head.

"Dammit, Leo!" Winsen said. "I keep telling you, don't—"

"You deserved that one," Big Leo said.

"Commander?" Winsen said.

"You deserved that one," Cruxer said.

"Fine," Winsen said. "Maybe a little. I just get cranky when I put my life in the hands of a man with a pucker like a paper press."

"What does that even mean?" Ferkudi asked. "And which man?"

Kip closed his eyes, a smile stealing over his face at their banter, at their inability to stay serious for more than a ten count. These men would face death for him—and they believed they were facing it for him now, in these serene halls. He'd brought them here, and they had no illusions that this place was safe.

"He's talking about the promachos," Cruxer told Ferkudi.

"Yeah, but still," Ferkudi said, "what does that mean?" He looked around. "Does this one go in the Box?"

"We killed Lightguards when we left," Cruxer said. "And those men's comrades surely gave their side of that story, and only their side of the story, while we were gone."

"I'm not stupid," Ferkudi said. "I know all that. What's that got to do with a promachos's pucker?"

Ben-hadad snorted. "I really hope that we live long enough for 'What's that got to do with a promachos's pucker?' to become a saying for us."

Big Leo said, "Our lives are...contiguous on the promachos's mood, Ferk, so Win's hoping that—that can't be right. 'Continuous'? No, not that, either."

"I really didn't think I was the subtle one," Winsen said.

" 'Contingent'?" Ben-hadad suggested.

"Ah, that's it," Big Leo said.

"I still don't—" Ferkudi said.

Kip felt a sudden surge of love for these big apes. They were nervous. Chatty. Nettlesome. And yet they were *here*. With him.

They could've had a secure kingdom in Blood Forest, for a while at least. Fame, for a while at least. And yet they were here, for him.

With the honor guard there with them, a mature man would never crack a joke. Kip was a fugitive, and honor guards could turn to actual guards all too easily.

Exactly how far being a Guile would benefit Kip depended completely on Andross Guile's whim.

"It means we hope the old man's been eating his prunes," Kip said as the lift doors opened.

"I still don't—"

"Orholam's scabby left nut, Ferk!" Ben-hadad said, turning, not noticing the doors were now fully open and dozens of nobles and retainers and men-at-arms lining the hallway were looking at them. "He means that if that batshit-crazy old man is cranky because he's constipated, we're fucked!"

Ben looked at the faces of his friends, and then followed those to the aghast faces in the hall behind him. "Oops."

Kip let him twist in the wind. Anything Kip did would merely make it seem like Ben-hadad was repeating an attitude Kip had modeled before. But give Ben-hadad this: his brain only stayed in panicked paralysis for a single heartbeat.

Ben-hadad limped out of the lift first, leaning heavily on his cane, exaggerating the limp. "War wound," he said, too loudly, rubbing his ear as if he were part deaf. "The wights knocked me a bit senseless."

Having seen that Andross Guile himself wasn't in the hallway, Kip let himself take a breath.

After all, if his grandfather decided to kill him, it wouldn't be over something like this. "Commander," Kip said. "See that your man is appropriately disciplined later. For the moment, we've things to do."

"Yes, my lord."

They strode forward past the whispers, and surrendered their weapons to the Blackguards standing at the audience-hall door.

Out of the side of his mouth, Ben-hadad muttered, "I said, 'Oops.'"

Kip recognized one—and only one—of the Blackguards at the door. Jin Holvar had recovered from her wounds, but looked older and grim as she extended her hands for their weapons.

"You know," Cruxer said to Kip, unbuckling his sword belt and handing it over, "it stings not to be able to go armed in front of the White and the promachos, especially given that you're family, and I'm a legacy, and all of us were so close to being Blackguards. I mean, I understand it. And it wouldn't be so bad if the Lightguards didn't get to go armed here while we don't. But they do."

Jin Holvar grimaced as if she agreed, but she maintained her Blackguard professionalism.

"No need to salt the wound," Kip said. "The Blackguards here already have to share duties with the men who murdered Goss—and he *was* a Blackguard nunk at the time, wasn't he?"

"Yeah, definitely, it's true. He was," Big Leo said, looking hard at Holvar but pretending to speak to Kip. "Even if a Blackguard wanted to forgive everything that happened to your old friends who had to flee afterward, that's still a huge offense, completely unprovoked as it was."

"Huge?" Ben-hadad said. "More than that. Unforgivable."

"It's all right," Cruxer said, leveling a hellstone stare right at the Lightguards flanking the Blackguards at the door. "Jin was in the infirmary that day with us. She knows the truth of what happened.

When men without honor attack you, there's little you can do to stop the first treacherous blow. All you can do is make them pay later. The Blackguard being the august, honorable company that it is, I'm sure they've made those cowards pay since then. *Sure* of it."

The faces of the Lightguards reddened and their knuckles went white, and the Blackguards nearby didn't look much better.

"We are much diminished," Jin Holvar said, stiff-spined. "A state not helped by our commander and then our best trainees abandoning us when we needed them most."

"Maybe you should have gone with us," Big Leo shot back.

"Maybe some would've if you'd given us the chance," Jin said. Before they could answer—or apologize, Kip suddenly felt like an ass—she pushed open the door.

Another gauntlet of expectant faces filled the audience chamber, but to Kip they were an undifferentiated blur. As war-blindness narrows your vision into a tiny cone, so was Kip's peripheral vision obliterated by his dread at what he was going to see on the dais at the front of the room.

He walked forward, hearing only his blood whooshing in his ears as he was announced. He should have been paying attention to which honorifics they added to glean clues about what kind of reception he was going to receive, but all he could see was Karris and Andross, standing together, one all in white, the other in red.

His half brother wasn't here. Thank Orholam for that.

The cares of war had had the opposite effects on Karris and Andross. Karris had lost weight, none of it muscle. She had never carried excess softness, but now she appeared to have buried her sorrows in relentless training. Her face was harsh and placid to gauntness. Her dress left her granite shoulders bare, and her hair was bleached to a platinum white. Everything she wore was either white leather, or shimmering white silk pulled taut, or steel. Even her cosmetics were cold, her cheekbones heightened to make her look angular and icy.

And then Kip saw her eyes. She was stunned at him.

And then he knew this was all her court dress. It was her war face. She was the Iron White. This wasn't a mask or a disguise: it wasn't *not* her, but it wasn't all of her, either.

He wasn't sure what she was seeing in him, but he turned his eyes to Promachos Andross Guile, from whom he would receive his doom.

Andross seemed to have thrived on war. He looked hale, vigorous. His skin was bronzed from the sun now, and he had an energy and assurance that made him a lodestone to the eyes. The misanthrope's bitterness had melted away into stern purpose. For the first time, Kip saw a bit of the Andross Guile his grandmother had fallen in love with.

"He looks like Gavin," Karris said beneath her breath. Kip didn't think he was supposed to hear it.

"No," Andross said. "He looks like Gavin's brother."

"Dazen? How so?" Karris asked, not looking away.

"Not Dazen," Andross said. "Sevastian."

Standing now before them, Kip made a low court bow. "High Lady White. High Lord Promachos."

As his eyes rose to their impassive faces, he felt a rage as sudden as the old earthquakes in Rekton. How dare they sit here doing nothing while his men fought and died? While slaves had fed them peeled grapes and dormouse pie, Conn Arthur had gutted his own brother, both brothers' lives burnt out defending satrapies that should have been far more united.

Other men's blood. Other men's sweat. Other men's tears and bile.

And they had denied him even the Blackguard. They played their games while satrapies burned. He had thought them giants, speaking from the heights. They weren't giants. They were dwarfs on a tower, shouting down with tinny voices at those who labored in the mud, hiding their puny legs under great fields of cloth as if large pretenses would make them larger than life.

Suddenly, Andross Guile broke the long silence, as if he had just seen something that pleased him.

"Grandson!" he said. "Welcome back!"

It was meant to shock Kip, to throw him off balance. But Kip was a child no longer. He wasn't about to lose the initiative.

"I come with dire news, and I come with help," Kip announced. "The Wight King is coming. He's destroyed your fleet. We tried to help, but it was a rout."

Gasps and little cries of denial from the audience.

"Koios is coming here?" Karris asked, a dry fury in the gaze she shot Andross. "Who could've guessed?"

The old man's face hardened. "And our fleet, which was supposed to be spread out in every direction protecting Sun Day pilgrims from pirates, just *happened* upon this fleet? And concentrated their forces?"

"They had sea chariots for scouting. If they saw an invasion fleet coming what do you expect they'd do?"

Andross Guile opened his mouth, but Kip cut him off, saying, "There's more."

"Out with it," Andross Guile said.

"Koios is floating the bane here. Six or seven of them. The bane paralyze drafters. It's why we couldn't help the fleet more than we did. He also has forty or fifty thousand soldiers. All this we've seen with our own eyes."

Throughout the hall, denial turned to horror. How was the Chromeria to fight fifty thousand soldiers and untold numbers of wights without its drafters?

"But there's good news," Kip said, raising his voice.

"Pray tell," Andross Guile said, eyes flashing.

Kip said, "I can stop them."

Chapter 70

"This is like one of those festival games, isn't it?" Gavin said, coming up to the gap. "The promise of an amazing prize if only you do something that looks simple... but is actually impossible." He looked into the abyss before his toes and tried to still the turning of his stomach.

"Many have made the jump with greater infirmities than your own."

"I'm *infirm* now, huh?"

They had climbed every circle, and Gavin had just tucked away the last boon stone into his constricting and now heavy pilgrim's garment. The crown of this great tower couldn't be more than a half circle away. But here, rather than sitting right in front of the next gate, the pilgrims' rest area sat right next to an enormous gap in the trail.

Orholam came up to stand beside Gavin at the precipice. "It's not so far."

"Not so far?" Gavin asked, incredulous. It had to be seven paces.

Gavin had endured a lifetime's worth of trials to get this far, and he'd kept his pilgrimage mind-set as well as he could. But this was impossible. Ludicrous. It was suicide.

He leaned forward over the abyss. Wind buffeted him, and he staggered back, heart seizing up in his chest.

He rubbed the black eye, but even that did nothing to soothe him.

"I can't make that kind of jump," Gavin said. "There's no way in hell *you* can make it."

"Nope. But like I said, this isn't my pilgrimage."

Gavin turned on the old man. "You're not going with me?"

"My task was to get you here," Orholam said. He smiled a toothy smile and patted himself on the back. " 'Good job, old boy. Well done!' 'Oh, Master, you're too kind. I was pretty good, though, wasn't I? Especially considering the load I had to carry up this tower!' " Plopping down his pack, Orholam sat and dangled his legs over the drop.

"Load?!" Gavin said. "I oughta kick you off this damned tower!"

"Meh. How do you think I plan to get down? Walk?"

"Huh?" Gavin asked.

"Below here, it's a...what do you call it? The entrance to the, uh, the thing you slide down."

"What? The chute?"

"*Chute*, that's it! Yeah, I mean, after the initial plunge, which is apparently quite bracing. You saw where it spits you out at the bottom of the tower. Safely, too, albeit likely with damp undergarments. This is a pilgrimage to the Father of Mercy. Failure doesn't mean death here. If you fall, you slide down the chute and start over. Or give up, I suppose."

"Start over?"

Gavin looked across the gap, despair welling up in him. How was he supposed to leap seven paces? Maybe at his strongest he might have leapt so far, but now?

"It's customary to take a meal as one contemplates this test. Hmm." Orholam was looking around. "There were benches and tables...once. Wood, I guess. No sign of them now after the centuries. Sad. Imagine the dedication of those who carried tables and chairs up through all that we've just seen, merely to ease the burdens of others who'd climbed! Come, sit."

Gavin was looking at the gap. In his prime, healthy, unencumbered, he could've cleared it. Probably.

Maybe.

"How strong are you, Guile? You look well—"

"Thank you."

"—considering your age and what you've been through."

"Let me take that back," Gavin said.

He had regained much of his strength, even through the climb, oddly. His body felt strong. Against the strop of successive circles, his mind had been honed to a keen edge.

But Orholam wasn't wrong in adding in that consideration of age: Gavin wasn't of that strength which in the old days shook the pillars of the earth.

"Are you going to throw the blade across?" Orholam asked, seeing Gavin contemplating its weight, turning it in his hands.

"And risk losing it in this wind? No way."

"Leave it here?" Orholam asked.

"And trust you with it?"

"You could do worse."

Jumping across while holding the Blinding Knife—Blinding Sword?—tempted serious injury. And that was if he could clear the gap at all with all the weight he was carrying. If the blade slowed his run up to the edge of the precipice even a little, Gavin wouldn't make it.

"How the hell would old people make it across this?" Gavin asked. "You said there were wood tables. Was there a plank or something, too? A little walk of faith, huge drop-off to either side, have to step exactly right or you fall?"

"That's how you see Him?"

"Accurately, you mean?"

Orholam shook his head sadly. "It's said that the gap adjusts to be a perfect test for each penitent."

"Adjusts?" Gavin asked. "So for some old lady, it'd be like a big step? You should've told me! I'd have brought an old lady with me. Oh wait, I sort of did. How about I make you go first?"

Orholam shrugged. "I'm not crossing. I'll jump if you try to make me."

"You're serious? You can't be serious. You got all the way here and *now* you're gonna quit? Half a turn from the top? You don't want to see if He really is there?"

"This isn't about me, Guile," the old rower said.

"It is now. I need you. If you're not going to help me, I deserve to know why." Right before I throw your geriatric ass off the no-chute side of the tower.

"That will of yours. No wonder it got you in trouble." Orholam sighed. "Very well. This is my penance. Many years ago, and for many years, I refused to go where Orholam told me to go. Now He told me to come here. And, as I understand, to go no farther. So here I am, standing at the door and knocking, but I won't go in uninvited."

" 'As you understand'? Change your understanding!"

"Here I stand. I can do no other."

"I guess I should've expected this much help from *Orholam* in my hour of need."

"I never claimed to be the Lord of Lights. I merely allowed myself to be used as a stand-in on our ship for enslaved men who couldn't understand how an invisible god could be present with them in their sufferings. I'm not Orholam Himself. "

440   "Oh, but you are. If He allows you to speak in His name, and you

lie, then He is weak or a liar or absent. You *are* Orholam here on earth, and in a way, so was I. But one of us is finished with the lies and dodging responsibility."

"How is it, my friend, that after all this climb, your heart is still hard against one who loves you most?"

"What you want's impossible. Fuck you, *friend*," Gavin said. "I'm sorry I ever saved you."

The old prophet seemed unperturbed. "I'll be here praying for you. That is, unless you do me some violence that prevents it. That edge over there will see me miss the chute and fall to my death."

The fires of rage burned only for a few moments more. Without further fuel, they dimmed. The old man wouldn't fight him.

Did Gavin really want to kill another person who didn't resist?

"No," Gavin said. "Killing deluded old men is exactly what I got tired of doing with my life. Plus I'm not going to let you die thinking you're a martyr."

He turned away. The gap remained. The gap was impossible.

Whatever happened to 'Impossible is what I do'?

The penitent's robes held Gavin's boon-stone burdens wonderfully, but they were burdens nonetheless. And heavy, no matter how well carried.

"Tell me again. What exactly happens if I fall?" Gavin asked.

"You slide down to the bottom, where you may either give up or climb again."

"All the way to the bottom? Are there shortcuts on the way back up? Ladders or something you didn't tell me about the first time? Is it easier the second time? I learned my lessons on my first trip, O wise and great master."

Orholam shook his head. "Oh! But there is an important bit I may not have told you? Didn't I tell you that where the celestial realm and ours overlap, time works somewhat differently?"

"Yes." And I *totally* believed you.

"It's nearly Sun Day now."

"What?" Gavin asked. It had certainly seemed a long climb, but long as in days, not weeks.

"If you fall? Your next climb will take a year. The next try takes ten. Some few have left behind all their lives and family to climb for a century, perhaps more."

"I know. You said that. I just didn't really believe you. We didn't see anyone else on our climb."

"And yet we passed many, and more passed us. You think the creator of the Thousand Worlds has made only one path of pilgrimage?" 441

Okay, lots of religious obfuscation there, but it was possible that there was some sort of anomaly here on this island that made time seem warped. If so, it made sense that primitive peoples would build a monument in such a place. How perception and reality overlapped with will-casting was something Gavin didn't understand well. No one did, he thought. He had to take the threat seriously.

Whether it was all lies or all the truth, though, he had to finish this climb.

He had no way of knowing if the chute was intact. A fall could well kill him, even if it wasn't meant to. Maybe it was true and earlier pilgrims had had multiple chances. That didn't matter. Gavin had to make it on the first try. Full stop.

He had to get to the top before Sun Day, or Karris would die. Magic had to die, or Karris would.

One try.

"Well, it's not like I haven't been here before," Gavin said, looking off the edge.

"On a real pilgrimage?" Orholam asked.

"How 'bout you pray silently, and not fall to your death?" Gavin suggested.

Orholam shut up. For once.

"*Here*, as in facing the impossible, with no help, certainly not from *you*," Gavin said.

Seven gates he'd cleared, claiming seven stones he was supposed to be able to redeem to get seven boons. Gavin had planned out what boons he'd asked of Orholam, too, with feebly growing hope in his heart:

1. That Karris will live

2. That I recover my powers

Perhaps this was a cheat, asking too many things, for it would require the restoration of his color vision, and to be able to draft all his colors again, and to split light again. He didn't know how legalistic Orholam would be with His boons, or how general Gavin could be, or how audacious the boons requested could be. But audacity had served him well in his life.

3. That I get vengeance on those who have wronged me

4. That I will reign again as Prism

5. That Kip will get the father he deserves

Whether that would be Gavin himself (only better than he was now), or if that was some other father figure, Gavin didn't know. Either, maybe.

6. That I will save the Seven Satrapies

Not just limp along through this war, but really, really make it. Thrive, even.

7. That Karris will forgive me

Maybe that was too much to ask. Maybe the boons couldn't force people to do what they didn't want to do. That would be the kind of stricture Orholam would abide, wouldn't it? Something easier, then:

7. That Marissia will find happiness

Yeah, she deserved that. That she would have an overflowing life somewhere, with someone better to her than he'd been.

That was the order, too. Funny, his priorities. The only one he thought was in an acceptable place was the first: Karris. Even a year ago, he'd not have put that there.

And really, the survival of the Seven Satrapies should be his highest priority.

Only one goal was fully un-self-interested. Nope, wait: No, not even saving the Seven Satrapies was really disinterested, was it? Hard to be the Prism over nothing, wasn't it?

"What do you call it when you realize you've been an asshole your whole life?" Gavin asked.

"A good start?" Orholam offered.

Gavin opened the pocket that held the boon stone for overcoming Lust. A beautiful green stone, Orholam had told him. Beautiful and weighty.

'That Marissia Will Find Happiness' lay heavy in his hand as he hefted it.

I didn't come this far to only come this far.

He tossed the boon stone off the side of the tower. Something shifted in the world, or in him, but he couldn't tell what it was.

No matter. He couldn't make the jump while he was still weighed down with so much.

He opened the pocket that held Greed's boon stone, but it caught in his fingers. He had to think for a long time what boon he would sacrifice here. In the end, he decided to give up 'That I Will Reign Again as Prism.' He tossed the orange stone aside and instantly felt lighter.

He shrugged his shoulders, tested how his body felt.

He stared heavenward, and dread filled him.

I feel lighter because I'm giving up my hopes.

"What are you doing?" Orholam asked.

"You know the thing about me?" Gavin asked.

"I know many things about you."

"The most important one."

"I think I'm not supposed to say aloud what I think that is," Orholam said. "I could pray for wisd—"

"I'll do whatever I must to win."

"A universal failing of the Guiles."

Next pocket, opened. Sloth's stone.

'That I Will Save the Seven Satrapies' dropped by the wayside.

It was a death.

"I should have known," Gavin said, "that any hope You'd give would be short-lived. Deceptive. You are astonishing in Your parsimony. You give and You take away, I suppose? Is that what we humble pilgrims are to learn?"

"It seems to me that He's taking nothing from you," Orholam said. "You're throwing them aside."

"The gap's too wide!" Gavin snarled.

But words changed nothing.

Red. Dagnu's stone. Gluttony. Kip. Was asking for happiness for Kip somehow Gavin being gluttonous?

It wasn't. Sure, Gavin wanted everything. Could never ask enough. But wasn't asking a boon for Kip *selfless*? How could Orholam oppose that?

I want to give him something so good, he'll never ask for the truth about his real father, whom I killed.

Gavin looked at the red boon stone. Sorry, Kip. You deserve better.

He tossed the stone aside, closing his eyes.

He bounced on his feet as if unaffected, testing his weight. Still too heavy, too encumbered. Three stones left. He knew what he *should* toss aside next. He opened sub-red. Anat's stone, goddess of Wrath. His vengeance. If Orholam made him focus his request, what would he choose? Vengeance on all wights for Sevastian's murder, as his Great Goal had once been? Vengeance on Koios White Oak for this damned war? Or was he pettier than that, his world even more constricted? Vengeance on his father?

He touched the raw wound that was the sub-red boon stone.

Tossing it away was like tearing away a scab that had an unhealed wound beneath it.

The warmth fled from the world, and it took some of the life from Gavin's limbs with it.

If I recover my powers, I can take vengeance myself. With my powers, I'm Prism Gavin Guile. With my powers, I can do anything. This time I won't waste it.

Now he had only two boons left he could ask: First, that Karris would live—that she would triumph! Yes, he would be audacious on her behalf. Second, that he recover all his powers, fully, with the full span of his years left in them, that he could last another twenty-one years as Prism, at least. With only two boons, he'd ask no half measures.

Gavin began limbering up his muscles. He checked the very edge of the precipice for grip, both as he would launch into his jump and where he would land. He would roll on the other side, he thought.

"When you fall, do you wish me to climb with you again, or do you want to come alone?" Orholam asked. "My instructions weren't clear about if I was supposed to accompany you for more than one attempt."

Gavin didn't deign to reply. He walked to the very edge. He examined it as if this were complicated.

It wasn't. He couldn't make it across. Certainly not so burdened.

He pulled the last two boon stones out: 'That Karris Will Live' and 'That I Recover My Powers.'

He weighed them in his hands.

If he fell, the next trip would take a year.

He didn't have a year. Nor did she. She'd be dead.

Fine, God. I can save her myself.

He hesitated before he could toss aside the blue that was her boon, though.

This *isn't* me putting my powers above her life. I can't trust Orholam. I can't trust anyone but myself.

This is... this is me committing myself to using my powers *for* her. I can't do anything for her if I'm dead. I gotta look out for myself first. For a little while. So I can serve everyone.

He threw away Karris's life.

His throat tightened. Without turning, he said, "You tell Orholam, next time you see Him, that this is bullshit. This whole thing. Everything He's done. All of it."

"Seems to me you'll do what you have to in order to be able to go tell Him yourself, Guile."

"Yeah, I will."

"It also seems to me that if you tossed the sword aside instead, you might be able to carry a couple of those stones. But what do I know?"

Somehow, Gavin hadn't even thought of the sword. He'd grown accustomed to the makeshift scabbard banging against him with every step.

"The sword's like my testicles, friend," Gavin said.

"Not the genitalia one usually hears a sword compared to."

"It can get in my way. It's a weak spot, but not one I'm willing to part with. Losing the sword is not an option."

445

So long as he had the sword, perhaps he could compel Orholam to give him a boon. Or kill Him, as Grinwoody demanded. But Gavin would do what it took. Whatever it took.

But he hadn't turned away from the gap as he spoke. He cracked open his left eye—the crystalline black eye—and he saw his trajectories. A hundred different attempts played out in front of him: he jumped too early; he stumbled on the last step; he tried to run along the wall for a few steps and then leap.

Again and again, he fell short, his body slamming into the wall on the other side, rebounding off the stones and into the abyss. There was no case even where he just barely grabbed the edge and then clambered up. Going from a full sprint to a full stop by colliding with a stone wall didn't leave a human grabbing much of anything.

Odd that the eye didn't account for the wind, he thought. Too irregular, perhaps. But it gusted fitfully up and across the gap, sometimes with startling force. It would certainly confound attempts at a wall run: a wrong gust would blast his feet from any step, and any lost step would mean a fall.

"Burn in hell, Orholam," Gavin said. He tossed the last boon stone aside.

"Why do you cling so tightly?" Orholam asked.

Now he looked again. The cold rationality of the black jewel showed him it was still too far. Just barely too far, but too far.

Tight, ill-fitting, pulling at his legs with every stride, the pilgrim's clothes had only been good for their pockets. Gavin stripped them off.

"Unique approach," Orholam said. "It may make for some real discomfort as you shoot down the, um, chute."

"I don't intend to fall," Gavin said.

"No one *intends* to fall," Orholam said. "Well. Except me. I intend to fall. So not really fall, I guess. Jump."

Still too far on all but the luckiest jump.

Gavin tore his pilgrim's clothes into strips, cutting them with the edge of the Blinding Knife where necessary. He bound the pieces together into a makeshift rope and then tied it around the hilt. He checked and double-checked his knots.

Then, before he went through with his stupid plan, he walked to the edge of the precipice again, set the sword at his feet, and looked at the jump through the cold eye of death.

Sure enough, he could still louse this up. But if he didn't carry the sword, more than half the time, he would clear the gap.

Those were the best odds he'd faced in years.

"Are you going to try what I think you're going to try?" Orholam asked.

"If you think it's a stupid idea, I agree with you," Gavin said. "So shut up."

He checked the rope yet again. No way was he going to come this far and then drop the Blinding Knife out into the abyss because he was careless.

The top of the tower was only a single level above him now: one gap and a single corkscrew turn of the stairs. With his hand protruding into empty air, he could spin the sword on the rope like a sling and toss *it* up onto the roof.

It took him half a dozen tries to get the sword to land above him, on the crown of the tower, and stick...up there somewhere. He had no idea what it looked like up there, so he had no idea if this could work.

His plan *had* been to throw the blade up there, jump the gap, and then run up to the roof to grab it again before Orholam Himself—or the magic nexus, or *whatever*—noticed.

But the sword stuck, and when he tugged on the rope and it stayed stuck, he couldn't help but hope that maybe *one* test in his life would turn out to be easier than he'd guessed. Maybe it was well and truly stuck. Maybe it could hold his weight. Maybe he could use the rope to swing across the gap. Maybe he could just climb the rope to the tower roof instead of risking his life on the jump.

He pulled harder.

The sword pulled free and flipped, speeding straight at his open-mouthed face.

He dodged out of the way at the last instant—and then nearly lost the rope and sword both from his nerveless fingers as the sword continued its fall.

"Throwing a sharp sword into the sky and then tugging it at your face?" Orholam said. "Not the smartest thing I've seen you do."

"Probably not the dumbest either," Gavin said. He started spinning the sword again.

"Hard to say. Lotta contenders."

Gavin shook his head. "I'm kind of going to miss you, old man."

"Only 'kind of'?"

"Only kind of."

It took Gavin another ten tries to get the blade to stay up there again. He pulled on it, and it slid easily off, almost striking him as it fell again.

Telling himself that it was better to take a few hours now than to take a year to make the climb again, he threw the sword back up onto the top of the tower dozens of times more. It never stuck fast enough for him to be able to put his own weight on it and simply climb. The roof must have no convenient ledges, and the sword was certainly no grapnel.

This was one test Gavin couldn't completely break by cheating: he wouldn't be climbing a rope to the top.

He'd have to jump the gap.

But at least he could do it without trying to hold a sword in his hand.

After one last good throw, where the sword seemed to land deeper and thus more safely than most of his tosses, Gavin said, "If I hand you this rope, will you promise just to hold on to it until I get up there and can take it back?"

"You're trying to pull a fast one on the Creator Himself," Orholam said. "You think I'm gonna help you with that?"

"I thought maybe you'd just hold a fucking rope," Gavin said. He spat at Orholam's feet.

Gavin spooled out the rope in his hand gingerly so as not to drop even the rope's own small weight onto the blade balanced above. He released the rope slowly, hand hovering in case it dropped suddenly.

But it stayed.

"What is that sword to you, Guile?" Orholam asked.

"It's my hope," Gavin said. "Be a pal and don't throw it into the abyss, would ya?"

"Guile." Orholam shook his head, reproving. "You know better. If it falls, it will be from your ineptitude, not my intervention. Orholam lets men choose; how could I do otherwise?"

Gavin took a deep breath. No point in delay. Delay would only give the winds time to nudge the blade toward the edge. Besides, he knew exactly where to place his feet to take the correct number of steps, and which type of jump was most likely to carry him across the chasm.

"Goodbye, old man," he said. "May we never see each other again."

"I think that unlikely," Orholam said. "But go now. Go find your answers, if you dare."

Gavin wiped the soles of his feet clean, rubbed his hands together, and breathed, breathed. He said, "A lack of daring has never been my problem."

Then he sprinted toward the gap.

And he leapt.

And he, Gavin Guile, who had fallen so far, only to climb so high; Gavin Guile the indomitable, the dauntless; Gavin Down but Never

Defeated; Gavin Guile soared through the air as the winds plucked at him and tried to turn him from his purpose—and he landed safely on the other side, rolling once and then coming to his feet.

He stood and whooped, recklessly baring his teeth at the gate so few had even seen.

It was simple gold, adorned in a spare Ptarsu style, latched but not locked. There were no boon stones here for having made the jump. Perhaps finishing the pilgrimage was supposed to be reward enough. Orholam lay beyond, supposedly.

Gavin pulled the gate open.

A membrane hovered in the air between him and the last stair: the lock to which Grinwoody had claimed only Gavin himself could be the key. The test only Gavin himself could pass.

Without hesitating, Gavin pushed into it. It bubbled and clung and gripped, seeming to catch on the fragments of his dead power like splinters catching on a wool tunic, but he pushed through, and soon stood gasping on the other side.

Then, grinning his fierce broken-toothed grin, victorious, he sprinted up the stairs two at a time to his destiny. Or his doom. Whichever.

Chapter 71

~Andross the Red~
18 years ago. (Age 48.)

Felia says, "The grammar here can be parsed half a dozen ways, as usual with the Scriptivist's prophecies, and that's without what was redacted. Worse, I've seen translations of it before. 'Breaking a great rock, the black fires of hell, on earth once more unleashed / did unleash / shall unleash / unleashes the...'"

"Does it help us?"

"I would have said no, if I'd known what it would cost us for you to get it from that girl..." And suddenly, she is blinking back tears. Her jaw is tight and she looks away. But then she is suddenly fierce. "Tell me. You never told me. Three weeks you were on a ship, coming home, and I can't stop smelling you, as if her scent would linger so long."

What is this? "You gave me permission. Explicitly."

"I didn't know it would feel like this!"

Felia is better than this. Next she'll be asking for information she doesn't want to know.

She hits my chest with an overhand blow that must hurt her more than it hurts me. "Don't you roll your eyes at me, Andy! Don't you dare!"

I go flat, a calm to her storm. I drop the paper on the table. I wave a hand to the slaves attending us in the open garden to begone, and a look to Grinwoody to let him know to tell them that if the others eavesdrop, they'll be beaten and sold to the galleys or the mines. Then I turn my attention back to my love.

"Ask what you will," I say. "But ask only what you want answered."

"Did you fuck her?"

"Yes," I answer immediately. I had thought that was implicit.

She swallows. "Damn you." She takes a few breaths, but I can't read whether she's regained herself. On her head be it. She will get only the truth of me, as I have sworn.

"Did you have to?"

"That was our deal," I say.

"I know what our deal was. I'm asking you to say it."

"I deemed it the best course."

"And how hard was it to convince you, Andy? I know you had many lovers before our marriage. Are you bored with me? I know that since Sevastian died I've not been the eager lover I once—"

"Stop! This had nothing to do with you, or that." I take a breath. There were deeper wells of suffering here than I was aware of. But her anger triggers something at my core, burning and furious.

I beat down the flames. As I so often do.

"Flirtation wasn't enough," I say. "I gently floated bribery, but her family is wealthy and she loved her position at the library. There was nothing I could give her. And she was so young and innocent, there was nothing to use as blackmail. I didn't have the time to hire agents to put pressures on those she loved, or the security that I could do so without her simply reporting it. So I seduced her."

"Did you enjoy it?" she practically spits.

I go cold. "It had been more than a month since I last shared your bed, and that had been a perfunctory goodbye, not the desperate love-making of a woman likely to be driven mad by jealousy, my dear. Yes, I enjoyed the release."

" '*Release*,' " she says. I used the word to imply that the sex had been a mere physical process, but somehow she turns it into an indictment of our whole marriage. As if I want to be released from her. From my vows.

But I've already said more than I would've, were I fully in control. "Anything else?" I growl.

"Did she enjoy it? How was it? For her. For you." Felia has retreated into cold bitch.

I take a deep breath, and then another, until the red recedes, until I can see her with compassion again. My Felia. She has been so alone, and everything she loves has been threatened. First Sevastian taken. Then Gavin's growing distance. Now this thing we must do with Dazen. And now me.

Felia is afraid she'll lose me, too.

"Did I give her the first orgasms of her life? Did I turn her into a wanton who craved my cock like the desert-parched crave water? Did she wake me in the morning with her mouth hot on me? Did she beg me for acts that you've avoided since soon after we wed? Did she pursue me as you have not in years? Is that what you want to ask? Why don't you ask this question, instead, and ask it of yourself: in the pursuit of my goals, was I ever a man to take half measures?"

"Never," she breathes, unblinking, but her hands have gone to her stomach, like a man with a gut wound in war, wanting to know how bad it is, needing to know, but not daring to find out.

"Why don't you ask what you really want to know? Did I hold her afterward? Did I let her sleep with her head on my shoulder in your place?" All the questions slip from my grasp like hounds eager for the hunt. I can't bear for her to be dishonest in this. Felia doesn't care about the mechanics of the thing, where we'd fornicated or how many times I'd brought the girl to the storms and the rain. She wants to know if she can be *replaced*.

The love of my life is fierce, and she is bleeding, and that's my fault as much as it is Orholam's and Orea's and Ulbear's.

"Fee," I say gently. "Let there be no darkness between us. Having decided the bed was the only battlefield by which I could seize our prize, you're damn right I didn't tiptoe over those marriage oaths you released me from. Doing that could have meant I did it all for nothing. Do you want to hear how I alternated between mumming the masterful, attentive lover such as she'll never know again in her life and the guilt-wrenched husband who needed to go back to his wife and children, just so that she was ever desperate for me and ever fearful to lose me? Do you want to know every step by which I isolated her from her family and friends so that when it came time to betray them and her duties, she was happy to do it, if only it meant

451

I would stay for another few weeks? And how when she gave me the scrolls, I left that very night, with no explanation at all, doubtless destroying her—because my heart ached for you? You think that one awkward, arrhythmic virgin could displace *you*? You think she could be your equal in the bedchamber or—"

"She's half my age, and hasn't borne three children, and as you said, I've not been—"

"Do you think I'm a man who could fall in love with a woman I don't respect?" I snap.

"A man will believe almost anything if one properly addresses what's below his waist."

"You think in four weeks—"

"The brief time makes it *worse*, Andross! I don't fear that I'm not the equal of that poor girl; I fear I'm not the equal of your imagination. A man can't fall in love at first sight with a woman; he falls in love with what he imagines she is. She is the canvas onto which he casts his hopes and dreams. And if the reports are right, this girl was a particularly lissome and nubile canvas indeed."

"What am I, seventeen?!"

"Why, because men old enough to know better have never traded their aging wives for younger, stupider ones?!"

"You know me too well for this. This is madness dressed up as fear. I've proven my troth a thousand times. You know about all the women who have tried to seduce me since we married. You know about the old lovers who've tried to ignite my interest again since I became the Red. I hold you in my eyes, Firuzeh Eszter Laleh Dariush. My Felia, my Felia Guile, how could I trade *you*? What kind of magic cunt would a woman have to have to even tempt me for an instant? From you? *You!* A woman who could be empress, should she will it? You think I would trade that girl's gullibility, her weakness, for your strength?"

But I still see fear in her eyes.

"If you believe that," I say, "you haven't lost me, you've lost yourself."

She searches my eyes, for any falseness, I suppose. If I could play so many others so skillfully, so cruelly, could I not play her, too? I try to open my gaze to her, as we did when we were young, but I can only see red.

After only a moment, I can see her gaze turn inward. "I don't feel strong. Not anymore."

"You're strong enough."

"I don't think so," she says.

I point and raise my voice. "Door's that way."

It's a slap in her face. She literally gasps. "Would you let me go? Easy as that? After all we've been through? All we've done?"

"Letting you leave me would be the hardest thing I've ever done. But this is war, no matter that only you and I see it now. If you're going to turn coward, I need to know before I trust you with my future and the world's."

"I'm not strong enough—"

"Strength is a choice. Courage is a habit. Unfortunately, cowardice is, too."

She looks me in the eye for the longest time. "We haven't made love since you got back."

I raise my hands, palms up. Whose choice was that?

But then I understand. Even this many years into our marriage, this new circumstance requires new responses: knowing her wounded, I've made overtures only. Hurting, reactive, she'd needed determined pursuit instead, while I had been certain that determined pursuit would get me an explosion of anger.

It would've. I see that now.

But perhaps we'd needed that to lance this boil. *I* hadn't needed the fight, hadn't wanted the mess and fallout of a huge argument, so I thought *we* didn't need it. An error.

She lets it go. Looks down. Turns back to the table.

She says, "The worst of it is that I've seen copies of this scroll before. So at first I thought it was all for...nothing."

As she finishes the sentence, I walk up behind her. I breathe in her hair, looming over her, hands bracing on the table to either side of her, but I don't touch her.

She puts her hand on my sleeve to push open the cage of my arms, but I hold, and she doesn't push hard.

"I need your everything, Fee," I tell her. "Without you, I am utterly alone in this world. A candle on a rampart with a storm coming. An ox dragged from the path by the weight of the empty yoke where his partner belongs. I can't do the work set before us without you, heart of my heart. I need your wisdom. I need your kindness. Your perspicacity. Your hand on the oar. I need that strength in you that you've always underestimated. Your hidden ferocity." I kiss her neck softly and am rewarded with a wave of gooseflesh. "You are my compass, my windlass, and my following wind. I need you like a singer needs a voice, like a tune needs a tempo, the chorus its pitch. I need you like a spearman needs his shield, the charger his harness, like the archer his bow. I need you like the crops need the sun, the dyer her colors, a drafter the light. I need you as the stars need the night. I need you as a poet needs words..."

Still she says nothing.

"And I want you. I want you like that night out in the vineyard at Stony Brook. I want you like that very unstealthy Sun Day Eve in our tent right next to your parents'. I want you like that morning atop the red tower with the luxiats banging on the door, wondering how it had been locked from outside." My voice lowers below a whisper of warm breath in her ear. "God, how I want you..."

The moment stretches, a privation and a punishment as I breathe the sweet scent of her. I long to grab her and take her, to make the decision for her that I can tell she doesn't want to make. But I don't.

Never has our union been of a weaker partner bowing ever to the whims of the greater. Nor can it be. In all the world, she is the one flower I will not crush beneath the wheels of the great siege engine that is my will.

She doesn't move.

The moment stretches beyond bearing.

I won't wait forever. I won't see my need turned to weakness, my hunger turned to starvation. I pull back.

But she snares my sleeve, and as a rider controls all the raging mass of a charging warhorse with a few narrow strips of leather, I am stopped.

Is this a partnership after all?

Sometimes I wonder if she is not far the greater of us.

She doesn't make me wait long enough to pursue the thought. She wants to know she has my full attention. She tilts her neck a little, to let her hair fall clear of the spot I kissed before.

I know she needs this. I know she wants to punish me a little. I know she needs to feel my pursuit, but it irks me, too, to be bidden like a dog. I am Andross Guile.

I shake my sleeve free of her grip and pull away, but before she can turn, before she can say a word, I grab her hair and kiss her roughly on the other side of her neck. Twisting her, I lift her onto the table and find her lips.

In the tales, every time true lovers come together, it is with such fervency and effortless skill that the heavens and the earth are shaken and nothing can ever be the same. Such is a lie, of course, but it's another expression of the central flaw of the glass that drama holds up to reality: everything depicted in that glass *matters*.

In reality, lovemaking rarely changes things. Most isn't even that memorable. In most lives, the heavens and the earth are shaken rarely by lovemaking, or perhaps never.

But sometimes they are.

Even with the ancestral gift of the Guile memory, the next minutes disappear in the turbulence of feelings unmoored from thought and pulled into the deep waters of passion.

"Sorry," I mutter, some time later.

I had absolutely intended to tear her Ilytian lace undergarments to show her my unbridled desire for her. The roughness following that had... not been the result of a rational internal dialectic.

"You can make it up to me—"

"I can, huh?"

"—but there's nothing to forgive."

"What?" And then it hits me. "You *hexed* me?"

"You can't hold it against me after I confess it, right?"

"Felia!" I don't know whether to be mad or a little proud of her. She used to be such a stickler for the Chromeria's rules.

"I wanted you to be rougher," she says matter-of-factly.

"You could've asked."

"I wanted you to apologize afterward. And to have to make it up to me. Speaking of which, you still need to."

"Make it up to you?"

"As in, right now. Carry me to our bed. I'm not sure I can walk."

*   *   *

"There were a couple of words that have changed meaning in our own language since those earlier translations, but it was all solid scholarship. And then I saw this." She points to a single point on the lambskin, right where the redaction begins.

"What's that?" I ask.

"A flaw in the leather? A stray quill mark? A stain of any kind from the intervening centuries." She shrugs. "A good translator or copyist wouldn't speculate, but only communicate what she knows. But when I look at the whole scroll, and see what's missing and how, it seems to me that whoever redacted this was in a hurry here. There are numerous places where he or she was sloppy. These three dots here at the end of the line, if I guess where the lines of text fell, could be all that remains of the three horns of a '*shin*.' This could be the foot of a '*khaf sofit*.' It could as easily be '*resh*' or '*nun sofit*' or '*tsadi sofit*' or '*zayin*' or '*dalet*,' but when I compare his earlier handwriting, his '*shin*'s were tall and elegant, and his '*khaf sofit*'s extended a little lower than the others."

455

She's getting into the minutiae. But she sees my impatience.

"If I'm right," she says, "then this dot"—she lays a piece of parchment over the area and draws a delicate curve—"is part of an aspirate, a breath mark, as in the way 'Or'holam' was once written. It's the right time period. Breath marks in punctuation only started falling out of scholarly usage some eighty years later, with Polyphrastes' *Dictions*."

"But this mark obviously isn't for 'Orholam.' You've discovered something else," I say.

" 'Discovered' is too strong. I've *'speculated.'* "

"Tell me."

"I'll show you instead." She lines up the parchment edge over the original scroll so that one edge just touches the breath mark and, farther down the absent line of text, the three dots of the missing 'khaf sofit' protrude. "You understand, what I'm doing here is by no means 'translation.' It's a guess, not scholarship."

I say nothing, and she picks up a quill, shaved precisely as the ancient Parians shaved theirs to give the proper calligraphic quality to edges and curves. Her lettering is not only beautiful, it is also such a match for the Scriptivist's handwriting that it would make a forger proud. The spacing and size of the letters is exact. She starts from the breath mark and moves left, unhurried. "There is nothing internally or in the other writings of the Scriptivist to support this," she says as she draws the 'khaf sofit,' its three horns coming above the edge of her parchment to touch the three dots on the scroll. She finishes the phrase and steps back.

" 'On a broken stone, the black fires of hell, on earth once more shall unleash the two hundred falling glories of heaven.' Literally, 'the falling stars.' But when it's 'two hundred,' it's never literal. The 'two hundred falling stars,' or 'fallen stars'—it's a euphemism sometimes shortened to 'the two hundred."

"The celestials," I say. "The elohim, the old gods."

"Those who rebelled against Orholam and were cast from His court."

"Or marched out in defiance of the tyrant, if the heretics have it true," I say.

"The Braxians?" Felia asks. "The Cracked Landers believe anything that justifies their thirst for power." She grows quiet. "Like all of us do, perhaps."

"You mean you and I?" I ask.

For a moment, her eyes are an open door to the soul bleeding within.

I forget, sometimes, that her greater sensitivity means that she suffers more than I even can.

"I don't want this," I say. "Do you? Are you perverting this translation so that we can do this to our boys? That's not the Felia I know you to be." Before tears can gather once more in her eyes, I say, "So don't lump us in with those desert assassins."

She is defeated. "My lord husband, look at Gavin's last letter to you." She hands me a parchment, not Gavin's letter, which was in code, but the decryption of it.

"How did you get this?" I ask.

"Read."

She's made a mark next to a paragraph: 'Father, I have him on the run now. Dazen doubtless hopes to retreat to the mountains around Kelfing, but we've a plan to entrap his army at a bend in the river near a town called Rekton.'

I look at the map Felia has spread on the table. She sweeps a hand over Tyrea, and the little dot that is Rekton on the Umber River. In orange luxin, names appear—old names, though. "At the height of the Tyrean Empire," she says, "there was a city here, its name lost to time. It was a holy city, consecrated to Anat Sub-red, before Karris Atiriel or her followers demolished it. There's a great dome of rock there. Anat's Dome, or Anat's Furnace, the Lady of the Desert's milk-swollen breast or her pregnant belly, they say. Upon it, the ancient Tyreans sacrificed their sons and fed their blood to the sands, begging the goddess to make their desert bloom." Her voice grows distant. "How blithely I condemned them as monsters, Andross. What mother worthy of the name could murder her sons and believe that, of such enormity, good would come? I couldn't imagine…How could we let this happen?"

"Felia," I say, "how can you even ask that? While you translate this? If there's no Lightbringer, we're doomed. Everything. Everyone. I—"

She brushes it off. "Karris Atiriel or her followers demolished the temple and city and put to the sword those who wouldn't flee. The wrecked town was settled by refugees from other places, who eventually called it Rekton.

"Andross, if Janus was right about Dazen, and if all these leaps of intuition are somehow correct…What if 'the black fires of hell' means 'burning hellstone'? 'Living hellstone'? 'A great rock' could be 'the Great Rock'…Andy, it could mean, 'Breaking the Great Rock, black luxin shall unleash the Two Hundred once more upon the earth.'" She takes a deep breath. "Gavin is trying to trap Dazen at Anat's Great Rock."

"And," I say, a dread birthed full grown from my heart in an instant, "Dazen can draft black luxin."

She looks out the ship's porthole. "What we've sacrificed—and what we've stolen from that poor librarian—has bought us all we needed to know to avert catastrophe, but too late. Gavin sent this letter a week ago. There's no way we can get to Rekton in time to stop them."

Chapter 72

There were only two ways Teia could uproot the entire Order of the Broken Eye, and tonight was her last chance to take the option that didn't involve dozens of loyal Chromeria soldiers dying. Tonight, it seemed, the priests of the various sects were meeting with the Old Man of the Desert himself to pull together the details for the Feast of the Dying Light.

Or, as not-evil fucks called it, Sun Day Eve.

The Braxians didn't celebrate the summer solstice as the longest day of the year; they celebrated it as the day after which the days would get shorter. That sort of made sense for the desert-dwelling Braxians, who'd suffered under the blistering, debilitating heat of their desert summers, but it still seemed kind of evil to Teia. Doubly so now, because these new Braxians weren't desert people at all; the new followers of the Order just hated Orholam.

She could be wrong, of course. She'd been shadowing Atevia—Shadowing? she thought.

No, T, stop thinking. Last time you thought too much, you nearly had to explain 'nocturnal emissions' to a luxiat.

She'd been, ahem, shadowing Atevia pretty much constantly, and she'd still missed the plant. The barrel-chested wine merchant/pagan priest had reached into a pocket and suddenly flinched in a way that made it obvious he'd found something there that hadn't been there before. Then he'd made his way hurriedly into a nearby alley, looked around furtively, and opened it. It must have been only a few words, because he closed it before Teia could lean around him to read it.

"Hate it when the old man does that," Atevia muttered. "What if I hadn't checked my pockets before tonight?"

Had he meant 'the old man,' or 'the Old Man'?

Teia followed him as he meandered around clearly looking for something, the note still in his hand.

She had to get that note! 'Before tonight'? That meant there was a meeting tonight, or 'before tonight,' didn't it?

Having failed, up till now, to find the Old Man's hidden office and a master list of the Order's members, Teia now only had two ways to destroy the Order of the Broken Eye. First, find out where they were holding their big joint ritual for the Feast of the Dying Light. Through some pretense, Karris could gather a bunch of soldiers at the last moment, not telling any of them or their commanders why, and then have them sprint to the place (so as to give no traitors time to send a messenger on ahead of them).

Then Karris's soldiers would attack the meeting directly.

There likely wouldn't be any arrests. The Order knew that if they were captured, Orholam's Glare awaited them. They would surely rather fight and die than face that. And the Order, fighting? That was a daunting prospect. How many Shadows would be gathered there with them?

Such a clash would likely be the end of the Order, but it would also likely be a bloodbath for both sides. And the Chromeria might still fail to get all its leaders. Teia would be there to help, but the leaders would have exit strategies, and everyone was disguised—how could Teia block every exit? She was only one person.

Maybe if she found the place early enough, she could scout it out and mark all the exits? But the Order would have Shadows and others double-checking that the site was secure beforehand.

That wasn't a situation she wanted to get into.

She might not have any choice.

The second option was much better: Teia would follow Atevia to this meeting with the Old Man and then track him to his lair, interrogate, and kill him. Somewhere, likely in that very room, he would have code books and a list of members, maybe even her father's location.

Even if things went wrong (and there were plenty that could), simply having the Old Man's identity in addition to Atevia's would be enough for Karris to triangulate the rest.

Once the Old Man and the priests were known to be dead, people like Aglaia who were on the outer circles of membership would start running for the exits—and when captured and facing the Glare, those folks would start giving up their contacts.

And Teia was close now; she could feel it. *Tonight.*

Teia had guessed that today or tonight there would have to be some sort of meeting of the priests to discuss the Feast. When your paranoia keeps you from trusting lower-level members of your cult with even the basic details (like, where a big party is going to be held), that meant the top-level people had to do all the grunt work. 'Where are we meeting?' 'Is it safe?' 'Is it clean?' 'Where do people change into their disguises?' 'Who's searching the guests for weapons this year?' 'Who's confirming that only people who belong are attending?'

Hell, if she was really lucky, she might get the Old Man's identity *and* the location of the Feast. Karris could attack the meeting in a safer way—trying to capture as many as possible but not worrying if some escaped—while Teia unraveled the organization from the top down.

Seeming dissatisfied, scowling at—at what? a missed contact?—Atevia sighed.

He threw up his palms, showing Teia that he was still holding that damned scrap of paper. Flash paper, it looked like, maybe? Then Atevia ducked into a tavern.

Orholam's burning piss but Teia had learned to hate doors.

Atevia seemed paranoid, so Teia didn't want to tread on his heels to follow him into the tavern. She didn't know if this door swung shut by itself, or if he'd have to pull it closed behind him—which would trap her between his bulk and a door that he was reaching to close.

If he so much as touched her, everything she'd done was for naught.

She stayed back, cursing to herself.

The door swung slowly shut by itself as Atevia strolled deep into the tavern. *Dammit*, she'd have been fine to follow him right in.

She waited for the next patron.

Who never came.

A minute passed. Had he left through a back door, a secret basement? Was he gone already? Had she missed her only chance?

Shit, shit, shit!

Just as she'd decided she really did have to open the door, invisible or not, the door opened from inside. Atevia stepped out, rubbing his fingers. Rubbing ash from his fingers.

Shit! He'd been looking for a fire for the message; that's what it was. And he hadn't found any lanterns outside, because it was so near to Sun Day it was both light outside and still quite warm. Thus, the tavern.

And now the note was gone. Argh! Teia'd failed *again*.

Desperate now not to lose him, she was falling in behind Atevia when she caught something out of the corner of her eye. It struck her as out of place, for some reason.

She stopped. Looked.

Just the tavern door opening. Swinging shut now, actually.

Nothing.

She turned back to Atevia, but then stopped. Nothing?

Who'd stepped out of the tavern?

She scanned the busy street, but there was no one close.

A chill shot down her back. Sinking backward, backward, she widened her eyes all the way to paryl.

And saw it: the whisper of the color-filtering edge of a paryl bubble. The Shadow inside was invisible, and if she hadn't looked in just the right place, she wouldn't have seen it.

The Shadow—was it Murder Sharp himself?—turned and moved the opposite way down the street.

Teia was frozen between them. It might not be Sharp. There were other Shadows. If she followed this person and it wasn't Sharp—

But then she saw the shape dip toward an alley and pause. A moment later, the paryl dropped and Murder Sharp appeared, settling his hood around his shoulders as if he were just another pedestrian emerging from the alley. He continued on his way, heading away from Teia and Atevia.

He must have been in charge of delivering the notes to summon the priests and then making sure they destroyed them afterward. Only Murder Sharp would be trusted with the priests' identities.

Teia's heart thudded. This was her chance!

But already Atevia was disappearing around a corner, fifty paces away. Sharp might be headed to the next priest, or he might be headed to the Old Man's secret office, or he might be headed home for a nap or even out to a tavern for all Teia knew. If she ran, she could kill him before he knew she was there and then...maybe Atevia would still be easy to find. Maybe he wasn't on his way to the meeting right now.

Or maybe this was a trap. How close must Teia have come to Murder Sharp when he'd been planting the note? They might have brushed shoulders, only saved by the fact that neither had been actively drawing in more paryl and that they both had to keep their gazes cast down most of the time, only stealing glimpses of the world lest their eyes be seen floating in the air.

If she'd gone into that tavern, she'd have surely bumped into him. Literally.

Holy shit.

But that didn't matter now. Focus, Teia!

Murder Sharp was the greatest danger to her by far...but Atevia was the key to her mission. He might not go to the meeting right this moment, but if he did, she would fail Karris, she'd fail every slave she'd murdered to get here, and she'd fail every person those pagan priests tonight would order killed in the future.

But letting Sharp go was like ignoring the loaded gun pointed at her head.

Am I a shield, or an assassin?

Teia clenched her fists so hard her knuckles popped—then ran after Atevia.

Chapter 73

"Clear the hall," Andross said loudly, before anyone else could react. "This isn't a matter for open court."

"Summon the Spectrum," Karris said to Trainer Fisk—except he wasn't a trainer any longer; the man who'd once helped cheaters try to keep Kip out of the Blackguard was now wearing a commander's band on his Blackguard blacks.

Commander Fisk? The Chromeria really is in trouble.

Already giving hand signs to the Blackguards at the door too fast for Kip to follow, Fisk then said, "Same orders as before, regarding..." He looked at Kip. "Ahem. The other young Lord Guile?"

"Yes!" Andross said, though Commander Fisk had been speaking to Karris. "For God's sake, don't let him in here, not for any reason."

Commander Fisk shot a glance at Karris, but obeyed. Clearly, he preferred to get his orders from her, though he was technically under both the promachos and the White.

Kip recognized two of the Blackguards as being from his own cohort, Tana and a light-skinned Abornean named Rivvyn Shmuel, who was as broad as his smile. They looked so, so young. The other two were so old they'd obviously been called out of retirement. Both had pretended not to recognize him, either from a misplaced sense that Blackguards shouldn't acknowledge anyone—sometimes the young were overzealous—or they'd believed that he and the Mighty had abandoned the Blackguard, and were shunning him.

Tana and one of the old Blackguards went outside the door. That still left Grinwoody here, which irked Kip. He'd never liked the wizened old legalist from the first moments they'd met. And if Andross seemed healthier than ever, Grinwoody had sunk further in on himself, curling up in his age like a dead spider.

"Tell me everything," Andross ordered.

" 'Us,' " Karris corrected.

Andross rolled his eyes. "Well, no one's thrown you out, daughter, so you're certainly permitted to listen in."

She smiled pleasantly while her knuckles went white on the arm of her chair. "How have you been, Kip?" she asked. "You do look so well. Married life appears to be agreeing with you."

"More than 'agreeing.' Tisis is an unalloyed blessing. The best thing in my life."

"Oh, I'm so happy to hear that!" Karris said. And if she started a new conversation to irk Andross, now she seemed truly involved in it. "It is so hard to find the right partner in this life, and seeing that you've done so brings me greater joy than you can know."

"Are you very much done?" Andross asked.

"Indeed!" Kip said as if answering Andross, but then said, "...High Lady White. And I've felt for some time now, grandfather, that I needed to thank you in person."

"What?" Andross asked.

"I'd not have married Tisis if not for you. You proved your wisdom and insight are beyond my comprehension. I was...quite dismissive of Tisis at first and would never have courted her. I wouldn't have guessed what an ideal partner and powerful ally she would be for me. You showed your superior insight and wisdom, and truly blessed me by arranging it."

Andross scowled, as if uncertain if Kip was mocking him or giving him a real compliment—which he actually was. If you wanted to compliment Andross Guile, Kip guessed, you should do it early in a conversation, before he did something to infuriate you—which he surely would. "Why are you talking about this now? Is she pregnant yet?"

"No," Kip said. And there it was. He was already mad.

"Then lay off the camp followers and get to plowing your own field, boy. You need lessons? A long, fatherly talk?"

Though he'd thought that his time in Blood Forest would have cured him of any shyness, Kip felt himself flushing hot.

Grinwoody spoke to Andross, none too quietly. "Perhaps the young lord suffers from a malady of the intimate sort? Spilling his seed before he reaches the fields? Softness rather than steel in the plow? I could suggest a physicker who might help."

"I'm sure you're quite expert in maladies of the intimate sort, *calun*," Kip said to Grinwoody. "But I've been quite satisfied in those matters, as has my wife, thank you."

"Faking, surely, but it's good she wishes you to feel competent," Andross said.

"It's your fault, you know," Karris said.

"Excuse me?" Andross asked.

"Gavin told me all about your books of genealogy, how the family looked at marriages like the horse breeders you all once were. He said it was the trade-off your family had made for its huge drafting potential and many other gifts—that your line had never had many children. And Felia had what, one sister? with very happily married and *active* parents, too, Gavin said."

Andross said, "Oh, I know the Guiles' lack of fecundity well enough, thank you. It was the reason I was willing to make such deep compromises in the areas of talent, intelligence, strength, and charisma when I decided to marry one of my sons to a White Oak. Along with their stubborn foolishness, your family had a history of breeding like rabbits. Unfortunately, it seems the last trait in you was trumped by all the former ones, as you wasted your childbearing years with your intransigence."

Karris was silenced, her mouth open.

Grinwoody smirked triumphantly, lickspittle that he was.

"But enough," Andross said. "A wise man provides himself a quiver full of arrows, but the warrior who finds himself down to two defectives doesn't simply give up fighting, does he?"

"'Two defectives'?" Kip said, accidentally speaking out loud. Andross seemed glad to have landed a blow. But Kip continued, "*Two*? So Zymun's finally been showing you his true colors, huh? Has he been raping the servants?"

He saw the sickened, guilty look on Karris's face and the flash of anger on Andross's.

"More than one, then?" Kip asked. As if Kip hadn't warned them Zymun was a serpent.

Shit! He shouldn't have asked about Zymun. It was enough for him to know that they knew something was deeply wrong with his half brother. He hadn't gathered any evidence yet that Zymun was gone on the dates of the massacre at Apple Grove. Once he did, he wanted to confront the man in front of them about it. But that time would come. Soon.

"To the matter at hand," Andross suggested.

For once, they were all quite willing to agree.

"What is this weapon you claim to have?" Andross asked.

"You haven't figured it out yet, grandfather?" Kip asked as if it were easy. "How to counter the bane?"

"I have many ideas. The question is what your single one is. And whether it's right."

"Our forebears knew about the bane, and they knew far more than we do," Kip started. "Yet another thing the Chromeria has hidden that endangers us all."

"They couldn't have imagined the nine kingdoms of old united," Karris said. "They surely couldn't have imagined fighting more than one bane at a time."

"Nonetheless," Kip said. "The ancients didn't leave us defenseless. The defenses are all around us."

"I'm not in the mood for games," Andross said.

"The Thousand Stars and the Tower Mirrors," Kip said. "They weren't intended to be expensive amusements or symbols of Orholam's kindness or even complicated instruments for executions— though they are all those things, too. They're weapons. They were made to fight the old gods."

Karris believed it instantly. Kip could see her faith on her face, as if everything was finally coming together, here at the end of things, perfectly in time. Andross looked like he was having to do far more work, fitting this potential revelation into an intricate rubric of what he already knew and all the terms and conditions this revelation would have to fulfill to be true. But his initial read seemed cautiously positive.

"How?" Andross asked. "How *exactly*?"

Kip swallowed. "I don't know exactly. That we have to fight six or seven bane rather than one like ancients would've prepared for? I think that's why we need someone who can juggle more things at the same time than anyone else. Someone with immense power, and someone with an implacable will, able to roll back the very stone of history careening down a hill to crush this empire."

"*Someone* really special, huh?" Andross said.

"You probably want to know about the threat, and how I'm sure of it," Kip said.

Andross looked like he wanted to nail Kip up on that 'someone' remark, but he let it go for the moment. So Kip gave them a summary of what had happened since they'd last had messages from each other.

It turned out that though both had sent numerous letters, few had gotten through, so repetition was necessary. Naturally, he skipped things that he didn't think they had any need to know. He was sure they were doing the same to him. And certain questions couldn't be asked, such as if Karris had heard anything from Teia. Kip had hoped she'd be on Blackguard duty when he came in. He'd have to wander by the barracks on his way out.

When he got to his account of the naval battle, Andross went purple with rage.

Not, it turned out, at Kip. Instead, it was with Caul Azmith. He looked, briefly, like he was going to blame Karris for it.

She said quietly, "I was able to bust him down to captain of a single ship. It was as big a step down as I could manage without your political backing. Which I didn't seem to have at the time. Maybe we should remember who made him a general in the first place?"

Kip could see the answer by the pinched look on Andross's face.

"If he manages to survive this battle," Andross said, "and his sort always do, somehow—a death will have to be arranged. Make a note of it, Grinwoody. And notify me the next time any of his relations are up for any type of office anywhere. That family needs to end."

"Not that I have any love for the Azmiths, but if we're gonna make a whole family pay when one of its members causes a few thousand deaths, the Guiles are in a whole lot of trouble," Kip said.

Andross's eyes flashed. "Didn't you come here to beg some favor of me? Reconsider your attitude, boy."

"Look, old man!" Cruxer burst out, from nowhere. "Kip left a throne to come here to save you. Wealth, position, security? He gave those up out of loyalty to the Chromeria—and even to *you*. You sent no help to us when we were dying for the Seven Satrapies, and yet here he is. Because he's a hundred times the man you are. So if anyone ought to check his attitude, it's you."

Everyone was stunned to silence.

Kip was reminded that Cruxer naturally deferred to authority, but this was also the young man who'd broken Aram's knee out of the blue when he saw authority endorsing injustice.

Andross waved to the Blackguards at the door. "Remove this failed Blackguard trainee. I can't abide mediocrity."

Cruxer didn't even look to Kip to countermand the order. He strode toward the door.

"Oh, Grinwoody," Andross said, projecting his voice so that Cruxer was sure to hear him, "check if Inana ux Holdfast is still getting a pension for her time in the Blackguard. And cancel it. Check to see if perhaps she's been overpaid for years and owes a ruinously large debt."

That was Cruxer's mother.

The young commander of the Mighty flinched as if struck, but he didn't turn.

He walked out.

Andross looked at Kip to see how he'd react.

"You're speaking," Kip said icily, "as if you'll be giving out pensions or collecting debts next week, much less next year."

"Make your demands," Andross said as if bored. Kip knew it was a put-on.

"I need to figure out the mirror array. So I need unfettered access to it, immediately."

"You haven't figured them out yet?"

Kip had already answered that. "I will," Kip said.

"You haven't figured out if they do what you claim, much less how," Andross said, darkly amused, "and yet you ask to be given a privilege that has been reserved to Prisms alone for centuries. I'll grant you this, you have grown into the Guile arrogance."

"It's not arrogance," Karris interjected. Her eyes were thoughtful. "Is it, Kip?"

"I don't claim to be free of it," Kip said. "But I don't think this is that."

"What is it, then? You think you can undercut your brother at the last moment?" Andross asked.

"Half brother," Kip said. "And no. It's not pride. It's purpose." Kip turned his hands up, as if offering himself.

His grandfather's eyes flicked to Kip's left wrist momentarily, and narrowed, and Kip saw him sink in thought. For a moment, Kip couldn't help but think, I just told you there's an invasion imminent. Shouldn't you be issuing some orders?

But Andross had shown himself quite willing to jump, once he decided which way. These few moments now, in his estimation, were worth the delay.

"Send a runner to Carver Black," Andross said to Grinwoody. "I want to meet him here before the Spectrum meeting."

Grinwoody bobbed and headed out.

Andross turned to Kip. "You would *bring light* against the bane. You would save the Jaspers and the empire. And it has to be you. Special, special you."

"Special in that I'm the only full-spectrum polychrome we've got who can do it."

"Nonsense. We've got plenty of full-spectrum polychromes."

"Plenty?" Karris asked. "Half a dozen? Ten, if some have come for Sun Day?"

"The time for the Chromeria to ignore things they don't like is over," Kip said. "High Lord Promachos, I've got a genius for drafting a lot of different colors not only serially but simultaneously. And I'm almost as Will-full as you are. I'm a Guile, and there's no one better equipped for this."

"Are you the Lightbringer?" Andross asked quietly.

It seemed as if history itself pulled sharply at the air through clenched teeth. No one moved.

Kip knew what he needed to say.

Voice firm, level: "I am."

And everyone breathed differently. The course was set. They were committed. Whether Andross was going to imprison or kill them for blasphemy, or if he'd fall in line behind them, was out of their hands now.

"The most important man in history," Andross said quietly. "Standing before me. My own...grandson." His tone was impossible to read. Mockery? Thoughtfulness?

But Kip thought he felt a current of grief in Andross's voice, as if he weren't mocking Kip but marveling at how the universe was mocking him.

"If it makes you feel better," Kip said, "the amount of luxin I'm talking about drafting will certainly kill me. Even if I look like the big hero for a moment, you'll be the most important man in the room again the very next day."

Kip could feel the Mighty looking at him. He hadn't talked about that part with them.

"You think that's what I care about?" Andross asked.

"Yes," Kip said instantly.

Winsen snorted.

Dammit, Win.

"We should make him Prism," Karris said. "It solves three problems for us at once."

"Three?" Andross asked. "What's the third?"

"Kip dying? Getting killed by all the luxin he drafts?" Karris asked.

"Funny, that sounded more like a solution to me," Andross said. He seemed to have sunk into a dark place where no one could follow.

Kip wasn't sure which problems Karris was talking about. That only a Prism was supposed to use the array atop the Prism's Tower was one.

Karris said, "Zymun will be furious if you let Kip impinge on what he believes to be his rights as Prism-elect, even if he isn't Prism yet. And we need to talk about *that* issue anyway. Our time is running out."

Ah, that was the second problem solved by naming Kip Prism first. Sort of. Zymun would still be furious, of course, just not in a position to do anything about it.

"It's impossible," Andross said.

"Displacing Zymun?" Karris asked.

"Making Kip Prism." As if those weren't the same thing for some reason.

"Why?" Karris asked.

"*Literally* impossible," Andross said.

"Oh, right. Shit," Karris said. Then she blanched and held her head in both hands and swore again.

"So...you figured it out," Andross said, not even turning to look at her. "Finally."

Figured what out? Kip thought.

"I wondered if you had," Andross said. "What with your little holy cadre of faithful young luxiats. Have you told *them* yet? Or was it they who told you?"

Kip wanted desperately to know what they were talking about, but he knew his best chance to find out was to keep his mouth shut.

Andross seemed amused that she didn't answer. "You're one of only two on the Spectrum who know now."

"You've been weeding out everyone else," Karris said. "Why?"

"Then you haven't figured it all out, after all. You might want to look into your beloved Orea Pullawr's legacy more closely. The old White wasn't quite so blameless as you've liked to believe. Her husband even less so."

"Really? Let's talk about blame," Karris said, suddenly fiery. "I think it's way past time you answered some questions of mine. And let's talk about my faithful luxiats. You know they say the Lightbringer's going to purify the faith. To me that sounds like I'm joining in his work. As the Red, much less as promachos, why wouldn't *you*?"

"We can talk about that later," Andross said, waving her to be quiet. "If I get around to it. So much to do." Dismissive asshole. Then he turned to Grinwoody, who had been holding one finger out, but inconspicuously, to draw his master's attention when he was ready. "Yes?"

Quietly Grinwoody said, "I've an errand. Your leave?"

Andross waved him to go, then stabbed a finger at Kip. "What's *that*?"

469

"What's what?" Kip asked.

"On your arm. Is that a *tattoo*?" Andross asked.

He meant the Turtle-Bear on Kip's left wrist with its freshly bright luxin lines in every color. Kip had been drafting a lot recently. He hadn't even thought to cover it up.

"We can talk about that later," Kip said. "If I get around to it. So much to do. There's a war coming? Maybe we should talk about that?"

"The adults will talk about that when Carver Black arrives," Andross said. "You know the Chromeria absolutely forbids tattoos."

"I know. I don't care." It was an old and remarkably stupid prohibition. During an early and contentious era before colored lenses were widely available, some lighter-skinned drafters had tattooed blocks of their drafting color on their arms to give themselves an ever-present color source. In a partisan power play, the dominant Parians, whose darker skin made color tattoos less helpful to them, had pushed through a prohibition on all tattoos to solidify their perennial hold on the Blackguard. What would happen to their dominance if lighter-skinned warriors could negate the advantages of dark skin *and* gain ever-present color sources simply by getting tattoos?

"You can't afford to thumb your nose at the Spectrum when you come begging favors. We'll talk more about that thing on your forearm, but for the moment, how about putting on something with sleeves?"

"Of course," Kip said. And in moments, he was pulling on Ferkudi's coat.

Andross studied him all the while. Then he pursed his lips. "Yes."

Yes? Oh, to the mirror array. He was granting permission. Thank Orholam.

A secretary produced a quill, parchment, and Andross's promachos seal. Andross wrote a brief note himself. As the secretary made copies, Andross drew up another writ granting Kip provisions and shelter for his forces.

"I've more defenders coming," Kip said, taking the parchments. "They'll need accommodation and supplies, too. We traveled at greatest possible speed."

"We'll take care of your people," Karris promised. She walked with him to the door as a sweating Carver Black came in. The man must have run.

"Is it true?" he asked. "They come?"

Kip nodded, and handed Black the scouting report he and the Mighty had written up before they'd made landfall. "I'm also leaving

Ferkudi with you to answer any questions. He's got a hell of an eye for detail."

Carver Black tore into the report, heading over to Andross, but Karris stayed behind.

"Kip, I have much to atone for, so I hope we get a chance to speak soon. One pressing question first, though. If you'll be on the Prism's array in some manner during the battle, then there's a question of the disposition of your forces. You won't be able to lead them personally. We'll need to integrate them with our forces."

"Yeah," Kip said. "It's not a problem I've got a great solution for yet." This was not a kind of fighting his people had trained for, nor was an effective defense a simple matter of putting warm bodies into the correct places.

"Then I wonder if you'd be willing to consider my solution," Karris said. "A general who I'd hoped would lead our invasion of Blood Forest is just arriving. If I get my way, he'll head up our defenses."

Yeah, hell no, I'm not handing my people over to anyone, Kip managed to not say aloud.

"Forgive me for speaking bluntly," he said instead, "but I'm afraid I've had my fill of the Chromeria's idea of effective military leadership."

She winced, accepting the justice of that, but then asked slyly, "Would it change anything if I told you the general I have in mind is Corvan Danavis?"

Chapter 74

With her heart in her throat, Teia shadowed the merchant through the pilgrim-clogged streets.

Unless she misjudged, the leaders of the Order of the Broken Eye would meet tonight, within hours. It would be Teia's last chance to fulfill her mission.

Through Quentin, Karris had left Teia a single question: 'If I give you anything and everything at my disposal, can we stamp out the Order of the Broken Eye within the next two days?' Teia was to leave a marker to get her yes or no to the White immediately.

All of Teia's hunting and killing had led her to this street, tracking

Atevia, and Atevia would lead her to the Old Man. The Old Man would either be carrying his papers or he would have to check them after this meeting, so he would surely head to his secret office.

Teia might be able to kill the Old Man of the Desert *today*, with the entire Order to follow as soon as Karris could mop them up.

When Atevia's steps took him to the Embassies District, Teia's chest tightened further. It didn't seem that a heretic would head *toward* the Chromeria and the attendant higher density of luxiats and spies of all kinds, not for an important meeting.

Then he turned in to the Crossroads, the former Tyrean embassy that had been converted into the city's finest restaurant and kopi house. Situated near the Lily's Stem and literally at a crossroads, it had long been a favorite haunt of diplomats, nobles, rich merchants, the idle rich who merely wanted to see and be seen, and everyone who wanted to do business with any of the above. Excellent food and drink, a fine and discreet brothel downstairs, superviolet bubbles for privacy upon request, private meeting rooms for hire, and dozens of egress routes all made it a haven for spies and those needing to meet with or even recruit them. There were so many legitimate reasons to enjoy the Crossroads, the illegitimate ones could hide in plain sight.

But all the things that made it a great place to meet clandestinely (as so many did) seemed to Teia to also make it the worst place to meet clandestinely: *because* so many did. Everyone was watching to see who everyone else was meeting with.

A certain kind of spy might enjoy hiding in plain sight, but Teia couldn't believe that the leadership of the Order of the Broken Eye would be so brazen. They weren't a brazen bunch.

She watched from a safe distance as he made the rounds, nodding to people who seemed engrossed in other meetings and dropping a quick word here and there with others, and had a longer, amenable conversation with someone who looked like a floor manager of the Crossroads, then took sips from a number of wineglasses a pretty young slave brought out on a tray, apparently discussing them with the manager.

Of course. Atevia was wine merchant to the nobility. The Crossroads would be a major account, or had the potential to be one, Teia supposed. Atevia was here for his actual business. Maintaining contacts with a huge number of important people was simply part of his job.

As Atevia seemed to be concluding his work with the manager, Teia slid closer.

The manager slipped out from their table and said, "Oh, there are some barrels in the cellar that I'm afraid have gone bad. Could you check on those for me?"

Atevia grinned and said, "Well...if you insist."

"Oh, I do," the manager said, winking. "There's a new, ahem, barrel I think you really need to sample."

Teia actually thought they were still talking about work until Atevia reached a hand down to adjust himself on the stairs.

Oh, gods, she really was naïve. Conspiratorial winks? The new *barrel* Atevia needed to sample...in the basement, which happened to be a brothel?

Dammit, T, how naïve can you be?

Teia had given up her chance to kill Murder Sharp—not to do anything productive, not to save anyone, but to wait around while Atevia emptied his coin purse before his big meeting tonight.

Suddenly, a bubbling cauldron of bile in her boiled and spilled over, hissing and spitting as it hit the flames of Teia's frustration and disappointment.

She wanted to wreck this man. She wanted to ruin him. She was going to follow him to his whore. She'd experiment on him: see if she could make him go limp, then back off, let him get aroused again, then make him go limp again. Hell, maybe she could figure out how to trigger his climax before he even touched the woman. That might be handy, too, not least for Teia to protect herself in the future— assuming she had one. And such practice wasn't exactly possible on terrified slaves, who don't tend to spend much time aroused.

As she followed Atevia into the Crossroad's basement, she knew she was acting out of all proportion.

She barely knew this man. Why did she hate him so particularly? Why did she want to punish this one so much?

Something about him grated her. So he was stupid, lustful, deceitful, small. Murder Sharp was worse—a hundred times worse—and she didn't hate *him*, not exactly. She feared Sharp. Hated how vulnerable he made her feel, tried to convince herself she could stop him from making her feel that way again, but she didn't despise him.

A beautiful hostess in a white silk chemise that barely hung past her pudenda greeted Atevia at the base of the stairs. She clearly recognized him.

The hostess's dark kinked hair was a perfect halo around her head, and when she walked, leading Atevia to a room, she stepped as if walking on a rope, her hips swaying with each deliberate step.

Atevia didn't look anywhere else.

The woman glanced back over her shoulder, saw his appreciation, and smiled beatifically. She was either a very good mummer or she actually enjoyed her work.

Amazing how we deceive ourselves, and tell ourselves we do good, Teia thought.

And then she was struck with the thought that maybe she wasn't exempt from that 'we.' This woman helped men cheat on their wives; Teia murdered people. She couldn't really look down on her. The woman was most likely a slave herself, making the best of a bad life she hadn't asked for.

Teia was the last person who should be judging her, but Teia's hatred was like a flame right now, lashing about, looking for fuel to feed on wherever it could.

She tried to hold off that fire, push it toward some barren, analytical place.

Why did she hate this man who seemed beguiled by the lowest of sins, lust? A mere sin of the body, of weakness. It was common, trivial.

Yet entangling. Teia's own mother had—

It hit Teia in the face.

Atevia Zelorn was the very image of Teia's mother. Blinded by lust, choosing to disregard the suffering of those who loved them, Atevia was selling out his family, while Teia's mother had literally sold her family. Teia's father had tried to give mother all the better things in life she said she needed, and had traveled farther and farther abroad to get them for her—which had only given her more opportunity to cheat on him.

Teia was going to destroy Atevia Zelorn for his treachery, but his treason to the Chromeria seemed paltry to her compared to how he'd betrayed his family. As her mother had.

And for what? For orgasms with strangers?

Teia hadn't had one yet, but to her it looked like the pleasure was something better than a good drunk but less intense than a poppy high. That couldn't be enough to destroy yourself over, could it?

But that wasn't all there was to cheating, was there? Her mother had seemed as eager for the sops to her vanity as she was for the love-making itself.

What did Atevia Zelorn gain for his treachery? Money? He had money. If he had more, what would he use it for? More visits to brothels? Chasing whores' feigned care when he had a woman who loved him back home?

Teia was going to wreck him, and when she killed him, she'd do it so the family wasn't humiliated, so they didn't have to pay for his sins. But he was going to pay—as her own mother had never had to.

The room had an antechamber, and the hostess held open the door but went no farther.

Teia slipped inside behind Atevia.

He closed the door behind him, locked it, and opened a side bureau. A curtain separated this antechamber from the rest of the room. As Atevia began undressing—no thanks—Teia streamed paryl at the curtain.

It was impenetrable to her gaze, filled with some metal. Huh?

She heard a door far on the other side of the curtain close and then a lock being slid home. What was this?

She turned and saw Atevia pulling on white robes. He draped a chain-mail veil over his face.

Teia's heart almost stopped. The veil. This wasn't a visit to a prostitute. This was the meeting.

Everything before this was pretense: the cellar barrel tasting was a pretense for a visit to a prostitute, which was the pretense for this.

Unfortunately, after he was dressed, Atevia stepped through the curtain without holding it open far enough for Teia to come in, too. He closed it carefully behind himself, shutting Teia out.

She could hear the men's voices clearly enough, but they exchanged greetings in some language Teia didn't understand, that she didn't even recognize.

Orholam have mercy, was the Order so good at keeping secrets that the leaders only spoke Braxian?

But apparently not all the men (three men? four?) were equally adept with the tongue. While a tenor gave his report fluently, he had to stop several times to clarify words for one of the others. "Yes, the bane," the tenor said. "All of them, if he is to be believed." Then he went back into Braxian. Then later, at a cough from the same man, who was confused again, the tenor said, "C'mon, *bawaba*, you have to know the word. We use it in our own ceremonies!"

"I just didn't hear you," the man complained. His voice seemed oddly familiar.

Teia wondered if Quentin knew Braxian. Or could learn it quickly. Well, of course he could learn it quickly. There were two books in Quentin's world: The Book of Everything Quentin Knows, and The Book of Everything Quentin Will Surely Know Soon.

But what was she going to do? Magic him into the room? Write down everything they said phonetically?

Good luck with that, T.

Then Atevia gave his own report. He was fluent, *damn* him.

When the slow one asked him to translate a word, Atevia did so   475 by using other Braxian vocabulary, which was apparently helpful enough for the other man—though not for Teia.

Yet another man spoke, and Teia heard the rumble of the voice distorter. Given how the others deferred to him, she guessed that could only be the Old Man of the Desert himself. He spoke the longest, with frequent questions for and from all of them, but Teia understood none of it except one instance of the word 'black powder' in a sentence otherwise unintelligible.

Apparently old Braxian had no word for that.

Wonderful.

Fragmentary as it was, she'd heard 'black powder,' 'bane,' and 'gates.' That, and the instructions that the faithful prepare themselves and bring their weapons.

When wasn't clear. To the Feast? After the Feast? Halfcock had said they had a plan, but what was it?

She'd been assuming the entire reason for the meeting was all last-second preparations for the Feast tomorrow night.

The least fluent one began his report. He had a nasal baritone, and he quickly gave up. "I'm sorry, I'm working on it, but by the Diakoptês, having to puzzle out how to actually speak Braxian from old scrolls? And it's not like I have any chances to practice with anyone. I can't—"

"Enough, proceed," the Old Man said.

Teia could hardly pay attention to him, though. From the lack of tension and the lapsing out of Braxian, it was clear that the more sensitive part of the meeting was finished. From here, she could tail one of the others, and from learning his identity, eventually reveal one additional congregation from that one additional priest. But if she were lucky, she could follow the Old Man of the Desert himself.

"There's a problem with the, the *abad el shams*. Shit, that's not right...the poppies. We have none." Oh, that was it! This priest had sounded familiar. He was the one with the haze smoker's harsh voice who'd ordered Teia to strip when they'd initiated her into the Order.

That bastard.

"*Ezay deh?*" the Old Man demanded.

"The Chromeria's been buying them up for medical supplies. One of our regular sources admitted that he'd guessed we wouldn't pay him as much as the Chromeria would, and he was too afraid to try to charge us more, so he sold all he had to them. He is willing to procure toad caps for us, though."

"Those taste positively foul. I can't bring a wine strong enough to cover the taste! Even with incense and spices," Atevia said, lapsing out of the Braxian as well.

"We could simply do without," the other man said. "As the old saying goes, '*Erdah be El sada lehad matofrago*,' right? Or with enough honey..."

The Old Man sighed. "I'll arrange for enough poppy to be accidentally released from the Chromeria's stores. Which of you will pick it up? Murder Sharp *maak yakhod balo menak*."

Murder Sharp what? What the hell was that?

"I can get it," Atevia said glumly. "Directions?"

Those, naturally, were all given in Braxian.

Teia wondered what would happen if she tried to kill these men here and now. Orholam, if she'd been thinking, she could have brought a grenado packed with shrapnel. With her skills and her cloak, though, what were her chances of killing them all if she went into that room now?

If she attacked though, even if she killed them all, she wouldn't get the list of all the members—and she needed that list. Without it, the Order could start right back up again. And she wouldn't find out where they had her father.

So she had to follow the Old Man. He was the center of everything. Follow him, identify him, wait until he went to his secret office. Then Teia could kill him and be certain the Order would implode.

She was close now, close to success for the first time. Close to saving her father.

They'd all entered the room from different directions, so it made sense they would leave different ways, too. And all cloaked and hooded, no doubt. She thought she'd gleaned as much as she could from eavesdropping—they were just talking about who was going to bring the drugs and alcohol to the party now, and not even in Braxian. Now she concentrated on getting the positioning of each of the priests within the room to try to give herself the best chance of following the correct one when they all left.

She was going to have to make a guess on which one to tail. The Old Man of the Desert had his paryl spectacles.

Teia would have to be masterful.

She guessed that the men would at least leave the room by the same ways they'd entered, in order to change back into their street clothes. That meant being in this room was useless to her. She already knew where Atevia lived.

It was time for Teia to gamble with her life yet again.

Invisible, she put an ear to the outer door. She couldn't hear anything. Pricey brothel, give it that—thick walls so you didn't hear what your neighbors were doing. More importantly, she supposed, they didn't hear you. She was going to have to risk it.

She eased the door open far enough to peek, saw the hostess leading a woman down the hall. Teia closed the door quietly. She extended paryl below the door and across the hall and waited. When she felt someone break the tendrils, she waited another couple of heartbeats and then eased the door open.

The hall was empty. The hostess was five paces farther down, showing the woman to a room.

The halls were a rabbit's warren—much larger than she would have guessed from above. Within a minute or so, though, Teia had scoped out several entrances to a larger chamber, where the Order's high priests were meeting, and a few nooks in which she might hide without using paryl.

None too soon, either. She was standing at an intersection when a door opened on each side. Identical cloaked figures stepped out simultaneously. She was on the opposite side from where Atevia had entered, so neither of these men were him. She had only two choices, and the Old Man of the Desert might not have been either of these men.

It was the flip of a coin.

This is on You, Orholam. If You want me—

The man to her left bobbed his head as he turned his back toward her and raised a finger toward his face as if pushing up a pair of spectacles.

Spectacles? Like the paryl spectacles the Old Man had?

Now the question was how far they worked. Teia could see paryl about thirty or forty paces out in sunlight, maybe twice that far in the dark. Were the spectacles that good? What if they were better?

She followed at a safe distance, thought she lost him when she was overly cautious coming out of the Crossroads, but identified him again by his gait—she hoped. The master cloak gave her a huge advantage, though, even when she didn't use it for invisibility. She started with it as a worn deep-blue cloak, folded it down on her shoulders and changed it to a green-and-black check pattern, and bound a scarf around her head quickly before she came up the stairs out of the basement, and then went with a muted brown to go with a wide-brimmed petasos she stole from a merchant's stall before she got to the Lily's Stem.

She had to hurry when he got to the Chromeria, but she lost him in the great hall. She caught a glimpse of a man who might be him, wearing a slave's garb and entering the servants' stairs.

Teia hesitated.

This was where things got even more dangerous. If he were aware of her at all, this would be where he sprang his trap. If she went invisibly, the Old Man might notice her paryl. If she went visibly, any Chromeria slave or servant might stop her coming up their stairs—she wasn't dressed as a slave, and sightseers and supplicants for the White often tried to jump the lines by doing that.

The last options were for Teia to go as a slave and possibly be recognized, or go as a Blackguard and definitely be recognized.

Would the staff know that a certain Blackguard was missing? What would Teia do if a Blackguard came down the stairs? The Blackguards often used the stairs for convenience or speed. After all, technically, they, too, were slaves.

Cursing inwardly at the stupidity of it all—Teia should be the one secure here, and the Old Man afraid, not the other way around!—Teia wrapped herself in a paryl cloud and darted into the door. She was exhausted from all her drafting, and from the tension, but she couldn't give up now.

Her boiled-rubber-soled shoes were nearly silent as she jogged up the steps.

Doors opened and doors closed, casting echoes down the great spiraling stairs where Kip and the Mighty had nearly died fighting last year. Too many openings and closings. The stairs were sometimes empty for several minutes, and at other times they were as busy as at the Lily's Stem. To her horror, now seemed like one of the latter times.

Teia poked her head out the first door she thought she might have heard, knowing it might be met with a sword.

But there was nothing.

She ran up another floor, threw the door open. A young slave woman setting down a clean bucket of water by her mop looked up, and seemed curious that she didn't see anyone there.

Next floor, nothing...nothing...nothing.

He was *here*. The Old Man was here in the Prism's Tower. He was close. But Teia hadn't found him in time. She'd hesitated too long, been too careful.

This had been her last chance to root out the Order of the Broken Eye without getting her friends killed. It had been her last chance to save her father.

Teia's last hope fizzled, sputtered, and went out.

She made her way woodenly to the dead drop and left her sign for Karris: Can we stamp out the Order? '*No.*'

Teia had failed.

Chapter 75

"In two or three days now," Karris said to her gathered luxiats, "all the work we've done will be tested. The King of Wights—the man who once was my brother—is coming. He will attack. And if he has his way, he will not stop until this island is nothing but blackened rubble and blood."

In the dangers and the heavy labor she'd demanded, her originally picked one hundred had first dwindled down to sixty-five luxiats, and then surged to nearly two hundred. Some were surely spies, but what did she care, so long as they helped her work?

She'd even said so, openly. She'd come to revel in the power of the truth.

"In our time together," she said, "you've served better than I could've asked. You've brought new purpose to the people of the Jaspers, and lent your muscles and your voices to our empire's defense and to Orholam's cause."

She could see in their faces that they felt uneasy at her praise, and at the timing. Midnight, for one of their meetings? They'd been careful about when they met, before, but not exactly clandestine.

This felt different. There was an urgency here.

"You think this sounds like a farewell," she said bluntly. "It may be. Too often, this empire has fought senseless wars over who would get to wear the purple. Too often it has fought for whomever or for whatever would put the most coins in its purse. This isn't one of those wars. This fight is for our survival and the survival of all we love. Looking back, we can have clear hearts about the work we've done: the defenses repaired, the stores refilled, the people inspired. Looking ahead, my charge to you is simple.

"Serve where there is need. Carry water to the thirsty. Carry the wounded to help. Comfort the dying. Carry gunpowder and shot. If you feel called, take up arms. But let me now be clear. I am not asking you to live for this people. I'm asking you to die for them. I'm not asking you to die as martyrs—have some humility and leave that for your betters." She grinned, and they laughed at her inversion: too humble for martyrdom? But then she grew serious. "I'm asking you to die as heroes. A martyr surrenders her life willingly; a hero fights to the end. Fight to the end."

She paused, and saw in the somber faces not fear but resolve.

"Know that I'm not asking you to go where I'm unwilling to lead. For some time I have had the growing sense that I shall die during this fight myself." A sense? Well, it had been only that—until she'd seen Teia's signal. Now it was a full-fledged premonition. The Order couldn't be stopped. All of Karris's grand purposes were being stymied.

A quiet chorus of denials went through the assembled young women and men, though, and their faces were writ with dismay.

"I'm not telling you that to elicit your pity or, Orholam forbid, your awe. I tell you because the knowledge of my own mortality has brought a question before me in a way I can't help but answer. It's a question I want to present humbly to you as well. Pray on it, and then act on your answer. Look to me to do the same." She took a moment to look at their faces. So young. So full of light and courage it broke her heart. "You and I have been called to serve. If the next days are our last, how dare we waste them in fear?"

She saw swallowing, and heads nodding. Many of those gathered were the bookish sort, not men or women who were quick to act. "Run the course Orholam lays before you. I know you'll make me proud."

There was no cheering at that. The weight of the moment had settled over all of them, her not least of all.

It was as honest as she could be without someone trying to stop her from doing what she knew she had to do. She'd made her peace with it.

When Ironfist demanded her hand as the price for his armies, there was no way to say no and still get those armies. She couldn't plead that Gavin was still alive without getting Teia killed—and nullifying all the young woman's sacrifices. The Order hadn't been stopped in time.

Karris's own words and actions hemmed her in now, and revealed the path she had to walk. I won't be without error, she'd promised, but when I do err, I'll pay the price for it.

In committing bigamy, she would save her people by dishonoring the two men who meant the most in the world to her. In deliberately breaking her oaths, she would dishonor her office and undermine every other oath she'd made. She would undermine everything she'd been trying to accomplish in the Magisterium.

There was no way out of her impending marriage that wouldn't cost lives and honor. So she would buy the armies with her own dishonor, and then her own life. She would go out and fight Koios, seeking death. And if death eluded her, she would suicide. Not out of despair, but to expiate dishonor. It wasn't death before dishonor. It would be death in order to make dishonor end.

It wasn't what she'd hoped for. It wasn't what she wanted. But she was willing.

No one seemed to want to leave, but finally, one awkward young man came forward. "High Lady," he said quietly. "This time I've spent serving with you has been the best thing in my life. This is why I wanted to be a luxiat. I have a premonition that I'm gonna die in this battle. Will you bless me?"

He knelt in front of her.

And so she blessed him. And then the next young luxiat. And then she blessed each and every one of them in turn, with an encouraging word here and there, but sometimes only a long, weighing look into their eyes, as she hoped she showed them Orholam's approval reflected in her own.

Last came Quentin in his silks and cumbersome gold chains. He didn't kneel as the others had; he merely waited, as any other slave would—at least until everyone else had left.

"You're planning to do something rash, aren't you?" he asked.

"Not rash, no. I've thought about it for quite some time."

"All this talk of dying..." Quentin shook his head. "Would you like to tell me more about that?"

"No," she said, and tried to soften the rebuff with a smile. But it came out sad.

Quentin cocked his head. "You told me once that you'd had a word from Orholam, through Orea White and the Third Eye? That He would repay you the years the locusts have eaten?"

"Yes," she said. Her lip twitched ruefully.

"You believed it once. Do you not anymore?"

"No. I believe it," she said. "But I don't know that I'll get to see it."

"How is that kind of belief different from not believing?" Quentin asked.

"We go to battle, Quentin. People better than me die every day," she said.

"People who don't have His promise."

"I'm a warrior. I don't shy away at the face of death. This is why I was entrusted with this office. To fight. To fight to the death if necessary."

"You're more than a warrior to Orholam, Karris—"

"I am well aware of my roles, thank you: the White, a trainer of drafters, a Blackguard, a warrior, a rather terrible mother—"

"You're also a daughter."

"I'm an *orphan*!" Karris retorted so fast she didn't know where it had come from. No, that wasn't true; it had come straight from red and green.

Quentin said, "How may one adopted by Orholam Himself be truly called an orphan?"

I found my father with half his brain dripping from the ceiling, that's how.

Sure. In some abstract, theological sense, Orholam was her father. But then, He was everyone's.

"And you've been drafting again," Quentin said. "Are *you* trying to be a hero, or a martyr?"

But she only said, "Maybe when you're older, you'll understand."

"That's a bit patronizing," Quentin said.

" '*Patronizing*' is having a child lecture me," she said.

"Not merely a child, a slave no less," Quentin said, lowering his gaze. "I stepped out of line, High Lady. I beg your pardon."

"Of course." But the red was still hot in her.

He knelt. "High Lady Guile, will you bless me?"

If she had only days left, how did she want to live? How much of a hypocrite was she to inspire the luxiats to live generously, obediently, selflessly—and then hold back now? She took a deep breath, willing down the green and the red.

And, thank Orholam, down they went.

"It would be my privilege," she said.

Chapter 76

"Well, this I don't believe," Tisis said. She stepped back from the door, where she'd just accepted a messenger's note.

They were staying in a fine house on the northern end of Big Jasper—as far from the Chromeria as possible. Kip wanted warning if Lightguards came to arrest him, and Cruxer didn't want to make it too easy for assassins from the Order to find him, either, so they were staying in a smaller bedroom in a house with many doors, with sub-red drafters stationed everywhere. Cruxer was also insisting they take different routes every time they traversed the Jaspers, and a dozen other precautions. Kip played along, though he thought if anyone wanted him dead badly enough, they could probably accomplish the deed.

"What's that?" he asked, bare-chested, arms in a fresh tunic he was donning for the evening. He thought he'd done pretty well speaking with two of the most powerful people in the world, but when Tisis presented him with freshly pressed clothes, the morning's nervous sweat had made her argument for her. These were for a different kind of battle, and if he had to go fight them somewhat alone, he was glad that Tisis was his shield bearer.

"A note from your grandfather."

"Did you check it for poison?" Kip asked.

"Kip."

"You're right; he'd rather deliver that in person."

"It's an invitation," Tisis said.

"For me to commit suicide?" Kip asked.

She read aloud, " 'High Lord Andross Guile, by the Light of Orholam Exalted Promachos of the United Seven Satrapies, High Lord Cardinal, Ascendant of Ruthgar, et cetera…' It actually says 'et cetera' like he's being brief. And the rest appears to be, um, in his own hand, I think?" She extended it to Kip, who quickly wrestled the tunic over his head.

Tisis set to the various laces while he read. Not that they didn't have servants for this sort of thing, but she liked taking care of him. He liked it, too. These small moments of closeness, of feeling normal, were treasures, he thought.

Something hit him as he saw that scrawl on the pages. "Whoa," Kip said.

"Right?" Tisis said.

"No, no, I haven't even read it yet. I just…I just felt like I had a flashback, but I have no idea to what. Like someone dropped a seed in my brain, but tamped hard the earth so it can't break the surface. Like I've seen that handwriting…" In a card. He shook his head as if to clear cobwebs. "They examined this for magic, right?"

"More than once. In every spectrum. Even chi."

That made Kip touch the pendant at his neck. He double-checked that there weren't any holes in the gallium. There weren't.

All right. No need for his chest to feel so tight. It was just a letter.

484   From the most controlling and malevolent man I personally know.

He read it: " 'Kip, would you please give me the honor and the great pleasure of joining me for a few games of Nine Kings?' "

Kip couldn't help but grin. What the hell?

" 'I fear this may be our last chance to play, and to speak frankly with each other. I have missed your company, though I understand if the feeling isn't mutual. I should be most gratified if you would join me immediately after dinner. Naturally, you may bring whatever protection you require, though we will play alone. I would love also to meet your bride anew. Perhaps tomorrow at breakfast?' "

"A bit to digest there, huh?" Tisis said. "I particularly like the bit about meeting me 'anew.' "

The last time Andross and Tisis had been in the same room together, Andross had arranged for Kip to walk in on her stroking the old man under the covers. "I actually kind of do like that part," Kip said. "Wouldn't mind forgetting about...that."

She twisted her face. "I'm halfway between mortified, still, and wanting to slap his evil face."

"I should like to see that very much," Kip said.

"But it would invite questions that I don't really want people asking," Tisis said. "You need to go, don't you?"

"It's too weird," Kip said. "Like, I'd say it's a forgery, because it's such a strange tone from him...but no forgery would opt for such a strange tone, would it?"

"I don't think so."

"With anyone else, I'd say it's an old man trying to mend fences before he dies or something. But..."

"But not Andross."

"No, not from the master himself." And there it was again: something thrumming in Kip's memory that he couldn't quite grab. The Master.

"The messenger apologized, said he came as soon as he could. But if you're supposed to meet after dinner, you need to go as soon as we can get you dressed. Do you think it's a trap?" she asked.

"They don't need a trap. We're in the web already," Kip said.

"I can't go with you, can I?" she said.

"If I get killed, you have to get our people off the island. Otherwise, they'll all stay and fight to avenge me. You know how these Foresters get."

"I'd fight to avenge you, too, you know," she said, smoothing his hair. "I'm a Forester myself."

"If it comes to that, you fight with a pen in one hand and a scepter in the other," Kip said. "You'll do far more damage."

"I know. But I don't have to like it." She swallowed, and he saw for one moment the depth of her fear for him. And he saw the bravery she showed in controlling it.

She straightened his light jacket—a fashion necessity, she assured him, despite the warmth of the evening—and tucked away his necklace. Finally, she laced his sleeves at the wrists to cover his Turtle-Bear tattoo and spritzed him with some scented water. "Remember how you walk. Shoulders back, string from the top of your head," she said, but all he heard was, 'I love you, I love you.'

"Like a marionette," Kip said, smiling at her in the mirror.

Her breath came out ragged.

She cleared her throat and, still looking at him in the mirror, said, "Lift your left arm."

"When I walk?" he asked.

She smacked him, but smiled.

He did it.

"Which arm did the man in the mirror raise?" she asked.

"Uh...his right?" Kip said. He hadn't meant it to come out as a question. He tried again, and immediately felt foolish. "Yep, definitely *his* right."

"You know why? No, don't give me that look."

He'd been giving her a look. He couldn't deny it. "Because our eyes—and how the light bounces—and stuff? I mean, the light travels correctly, but we reverse the image when we imagine that there's actually a person over on the other side of the mirror. Why are you frowning?"

"No, it's a hint." She shook her head. "I've been afraid of this meeting for you for a long time."

"You have?"

"I've been trying to arm you for it."

"Uh..."

"Kip, there are two kinds of mirrors a man should fear, because both push their will into him and can do so without him even realizing they're not objective or passive. The figure in the mirror raising the wrong arm is our hint that between reality and perception, things can get twisted."

"I remember. The first kind, anyway." She meant actual physical mirrors, where his own distorted perceptions could confirm lies about himself while he believed he was seeing objective truth.

"The second is others' regard. We judge ourselves by how others see us, and oftentimes that's exactly what we need to do in order to correct our errors of self-judgment. But you're going to see Andross Guile."

"Not a man who has much regard for anyone," Kip said.

"It's ten times worse, Kip. You meeting with your grandfather is more dangerous for you than facing ten thousand enemies."

"It's just a silly card game," Kip said. "I'll lose a few rounds, he'll feel superior, and we'll call it a day." But something in his guts twisted. Andross was going to make him put wagers on the games. Kip just knew it. Wagers he would certainly lose.

She sighed quietly. "Are you reassuring me or yourself?" But she didn't wait for him to answer. "Kip, he's dangerous to you because you admire him so much. You hate what he's done, sure. But you've compared yourself to him from the first time you met him. You've aspired to be what he is. And you're actually so much more than he is."

"He's smarter than I am."

"Sure. So? A man whose intelligence is leavened with humility is doubly wise."

"He's more cunning. More connected. More masterful. More knowledgeable. More—"

"He's a hundred things more! And not one of them matters. I worry what you'll see when you look in his eyes, Kip. Because he's warped. People come away from meeting him hating themselves and hating the world. People meet with you and they come away with hope. You're a thousand times the man he'll ever be—no matter what happens. No matter what."

Kip swallowed. "I love you."

"I know, you fat fuck," she said.

His eyebrows shot up, and she laughed at shocking him, and he remembered the phrase from their earlier talk about how he'd scorned himself.

But now her face went somber. Her hands rested on his shoulders, and he could tell she was appreciating how solid they were, how broad. "Remember to see yourself as you are in the eyes of those who love you. That's what it means when we say 'Orholam holds you in His eyes,' Kip. And I do, too. Swear to me you'll push back against everything else."

"Honey," Kip said, admonishing her, "I'm a Guile. I don't know how to *not* fight."

She grabbed him as he turned to go, her fingernails digging painfully into his arms. "Then you fight. Fight for all of us. I love you."

Chapter 77

Quentin wasn't in his room, but Teia was already in the damned tower, so she went looking for him in their old restricted library. She needed to report her failure.

The door was closed. Of course.

She sighed and eased it open, as if the wind had pushed it, peeked quickly, and let it close again.

No one was in sight.

She peeked again, then slipped inside.

The sound of laughter arrested her. Quentin, laughing? With someone else?

First, that was very strange, and then it oddly felt like he was cheating on her.

She ghosted closer, drawing paryl to her fingertips. She didn't recognize the man as she approached from behind, though. Tall, lanky, with long dark hair, a dark beard, the frame of spectacles over his ears. Baggy sailor's trousers, but a fine dark tunic, not a luxiat. She streamed paryl out toward him, the light cutting through his clothing to show her what weapons he carried.

It was veritable armory. Large pistols in queer sheaths at his hips, smaller ones on little frames up his sleeves loaded with springs, knives, and a sword-breaker, and two spare sets of spectacles.

This was no visiting scholar.

She felt a sudden sheen of sweat on her upper lip. Had Quentin ratted her out? Was he working with the Order?

"Perfectly safe," Quentin said. "No one comes here."

She reached across the room and slipped little blades of paryl into the man's neck. The paryl illuminated him further as she closed in on him. Some kind of odd, broken-and-repaired contraption encased one knee that had ugly scars around it; maybe an open luxin connection there?

Quentin was laughing along with a *wight*?

The little holy hypocrite. I thought I knew you, Quentin.

Teia readied a second strike for him.

"You can't expect the old boys to give up all their secrets without a fight," the stranger said, tucking a stray bit of hair behind his ears. Or securing his spectacles? There was something about that voice—

The man launched himself backward, staying in his chair as it tipped toward the floor. Before he slammed into the ground, he caught himself with both feet on the underside of the table, even as a mechanical *ka-chung* rang out. Teia found herself staring into two small pistol barrels that had sprung from the man's sleeves into his hands even as he hung upside down, tilting in his chair. Her paryl daggers into him had been shattered by his sharp movement. His spectacles glittered with sub-red. But behind everything unfamiliar, behind even the unfamiliar spectacles, were eyes she knew well.

"Oh, hello, Teia," Ben-hadad said.

He shoved hard against a spring-loaded pistol, resetting it. Then the other.

"I'll be damned," he said. "First time I've actually gotten both of them to work when I wanted. And neither accidentally fired. That would've been unfortunate. Oh, this one lost its flint. Of course it did. Again. Could you lift me back up? Little awkward here. Quentin, you gonna just stand there?"

Quentin looked over at Teia helplessly as she shimmered back into visibility. Ben-hadad was not a heavy man, but Quentin was the very antithesis of muscular. He couldn't lift him by himself.

Teia heaved Ben back to a sitting position.

He stood up and grinned. "Hey, look at me, huh?"

"...Yeah...I was..."

"And holy shit, little Teia, look at you," Ben-hadad said. "Bet no one calls you 'little Teia.' "

No one talks to me at all.

"No," she said. "You're back. You're back?"

"We're all back. Come to save the day."

Was he joking? It wasn't funny. "I'll put on my damsel hat. Whaddaya call it?"

"A wimple?" Quentin asked. "Sorry. Don't mind me. Not even here."

"No, not to save *you*, Teia. Shit. We needed you to save *us*. Can't think how many times we bitched about you being gone."

"Yeah?" she asked. There was suddenly something raw in her throat. They were standing close, but neither had moved to embrace. She suddenly thought she was going to cry. " 'All of us,' you said?"

"Yeah, Kip's back too."

"No, no, I meant, you're *all* back? Everyone? Everyone made it?"

"Oh, oh yeah. We're all right. Well, except Winsen, but then, he wasn't all right when we started. In fact, we've been trying to arrange for him to take a few good blows to the head to see if it might straighten him out a bit."

Teia smiled wanly.

"Nah," Ben said. "Actually, even Win is less of a dick than he used to be. A little bit less. Most of the time."

"Sometimes?"

"Yeah, only sometimes," Ben-hadad admitted.

"But you're okay? Really?"

"Yeah, I mean, I, I took the worst of it since we left." He gestured to his knee with the contraption, hidden under those baggy pants. "Actually, I guess you saw me get this injury. But I can walk now. Even run when I can't avoid it. Well, usually—just kind of broke my brace, but it'll be good in no time."

"Yeah?" she said.

"You been through the shit, huh?" Ben-hadad said, looking at her closely.

"Did Quentin tell...?"

"No, no," Ben-hadad said. And Teia saw that Ben wasn't only more self-assured and more grown-up-looking than when he'd left, his brash intelligence had also been tempered by suffering.

"You been through it, too," Teia said.

"A bit," he said with a quick, sad smile. "But I had the Mighty. Even if one of them is Winsen."

"Ha! I'd rather be alone," Teia said. But the word 'alone' bounced off the walls, ricocheting into her chest.

Ben-hadad's nose wrinkled. "No, you wouldn't. Would you?"

"No," Teia said, looking away. She couldn't break down. Ben didn't know what she'd done. Ben couldn't offer her absolution. "So how is everyone?"

"Kip's good," Ben-hadad said.

"That's not what I asked," she said. "But since you brought him up, sure, let's start there. How is he?" She thought her voice was admirably level. No hint that her heart was in her throat.

"Happily married."

"I, I didn't—! I wasn't asking— C'mon, Ben! Don't be like that."

"Teia, I know you. It's fine. It's what you wanted to know and I'm happy to tell you. You want to know about her?"

"No! No, not really, no." She cursed. "Maybe a bit?"

"She's one of the Mighty now. Has been for quite a while, I guess."

"Oh." She really did take my place in everything I loved, didn't she?

"She can't fight for shit. But she's saved our lives probably more than any of us. That's why we're Mighty, right? Different strengths, all pulling to the same purpose."

"Yeah, yeah, that's great." For you. Thanks for reminding me what I don't have, you clueless dick.

"We didn't know you were supposedly gone or whatever, so Tisis thought I might see you on duty. She gave me something for you."

"Why didn't she bring it herself?" Teia asked, suspicious.

"The Order sent a team to kill Kip back in Blood Forest, so with them and all our other enemies, we decided our leaders shouldn't all be in the same place. She's staying as far from the Chromeria as she can while still being on Big Jasper."

"They—what?!"

"Yeah, right, we've got a lot to catch up on. Can I just do this thing so Quentin can get back to telling you just how damned smart I am?"

"Language, please...?" Quentin said, wincing.

Ben-hadad looked at him quizzically.

"He's fine with any words except whatever dishonors Orholam or disrespects a listener," Teia explained. "Or something like that."

"It's a bit more nuanced than—" Quentin started.

"Let it go," Teia said. "Both of you. Ben? What are you talking about? What 'thing'?"

"Here," he said, digging into his pack. He pulled out a folded little cloth. "It was Tisis's idea, but..." He unfolded it. It was a patch of the Mighty. "We all wanted you to know. You didn't come with us, but no one stopped thinking of you as one of the Mighty, Teia. You're one of us. Cruxer says you've been absent without leave for way too long. He's said he's gonna make you run until you piss blood or something? I dunno, some saying he got from his father. And he said 'urinate,' of course, not 'piss.'"

She took the patch in trembling hands, and tears welled up in her eyes.

"Now, Quentin, tell her I'm brilliant!"

"None was gainsaying the claim," Quentin said. "Though none were yet queuing to support it, either."

Teia knew Quentin well enough now that she could tell he was teasing. But the flash of humor helped her push back the tears.

Maybe Quentin knew her a little bit, too.

"This is relevant, right?" she growled.

"A little," Quentin said.

"A little?!" Ben-hadad protested.

Quentin said, "Our old monopodal friend here, it turns out, is rather adept at reading schematics, and knows a fair bit more of engineering history than I do, as well. It's embarrassing really. I think I read straight past references to this very thing. It turns out that at the time of the Chromeria's construction, there were several different units of measure in use, with certain professions preferring one and others another. There were conversion tables, but always with a margin of error."

Teia had no idea what he was talking about, but sometimes it was faster to just listen, so she nodded along as Quentin continued. He was ridiculously excited about seeing someone else be smart in a realm he himself was ignorant of. Almost enough so that Teia found it contagious. Almost.

He went on. "It was a known problem, so there were corrections used on large-scale projects like this, but the head engineer made the teams work level by level and purposefully *didn't* correct for the conversion errors, and at each level, he brought in his own master carpenters and masons to 'fix things up' and conceal the errors."

"But," Ben-hadad said, finally breaking in on his own story, "there are certain things that really do have to be where the plans say they are: flues for the kitchen's fires, openings for the lightwells into classrooms and the signal crystals, and so forth, so by guessing which those might be, and knowing how much the total errors would be, then you see that the hidden rooms will be clustered high in the towers where the errors could accumulate, with maybe a few more in the depths of the bedrock of the basements."

"Not the basements," Teia said. Her heart was in her throat. "This'd be up high. Quickly accessible."

"That's what Quentin said you were looking for. So let's go."

"Go?" Teia asked.

"Yeah," Ben-hadad said, pointing to the pages of notes and equations he'd scribbled. "I've got ten or eleven possibilities for what I assume are four to nine spaces, depending on the size. I can either spend about four hours honing my equations to figure out which guesses are most likely...or we can just go look."

Teia felt like a huge weight she'd been carrying had suddenly been lifted from her shoulders. The Mighty were back. Her boys were home, and her total and abject failure to find the Old Man's office was about to be magically mended with a wave of Ben-hadad's brilliant equations.

For the first time in so long that it felt like the first time ever, she felt fluttering in her breast, a stretching out of the delicate wings of hope.

Chapter 78

Kip walked to Promachos Andross Guile's apartments clad for silken war. Under Tisis's direction, he'd been shaved and scrubbed and oiled, nails trimmed, hair cut, muscles pounded, joints stretched, measurements taken, complexion and eyes compared to various charts, clothing of various coloring and texture held up for her approval. Then she made him do push-ups and sit-ups and pull-ups. Washed him again, and made him do push-ups while she sat on his back before examining him critically one last time, nodding, and pulling on his tunic, strapping on his spectacles holster, checking his hair one last time, and pushing him out the door.

It felt ridiculous. He'd seen Andross just yesterday with none of this artifice. But he trusted Tisis, even if his entire upper body felt so swollen that he was going to have to twist sideways to get his shoulders through the door.

Cruxer knocked for him and was greeted by Grinwoody, who ushered them in with his typical greasy smile.

Andross's apartments were no longer the dingy dark they had been when Kip first came. Now they sparkled, window shades open wide to the light.

"Grandson, welcome! So good of you to accept my invitation," Andross said as if they were a normal family. He came over and took Kip by the shoulders, and there was a little flicker of surprise at how firm they were.

"I see you were right. I did choose well for you," Andross said.

"My lord?" Kip asked.

"Your bride. This is her doing, I can tell. When you left here...you were not, shall we say, who you are now?"

Kip wasn't sure if his grandfather somehow knew about his push-ups or meant something else entirely. "Sir?"

"Slimmed you down. Made you happy. Showed you how to dress appropriately. Before, you were a Guile in spirit, but only in spirit. You couldn't truly be a Guile until you looked like one. We're a handsome family, and it matters. I'd hoped that by giving you a beautiful wife I might inspire you to make something of yourself. I see it worked. And from what I hear, you'd not have fared nearly so well as you did if she were *only* a nice body. Can't tell you how pleased I am with that. It seemed terribly unjust that Eirene Malargos's sister had a reputation for being deeply stupid. I hoped and gambled that it wasn't true."

What am I really doing here? How had Kip forgotten what it was like to bear the full brunt of Andross Guile's abrasive personality? "As above, so below, huh?" Kip said.

"How's that?" Andross asked. He gestured. "Please, sit, sit."

"Like Orholam, you set the course before me. I merely ran it." Were they really going to pretend Andross had meant Kip well? That   **493** all the blessings Kip had enjoyed from his marriage were the point of what Andross had done? Taking a seat in a chair that probably cost more than a house in Rekton, Kip said, "I'm just so glad that the marriage also cemented the Malargos family to us, and kept Ruthgar from making a separate peace with Koios."

"Well, not everyone can start marriage with love, certainly not poor fat boys from the farthest reaches of the empire."

"Actually, poor fat boys from Tyrea have a pretty good chance of marrying for love. It's everything else they don't get."

Andross paused. "I'll yield to your greater experience on that. Regardless, good work making what I gave you your own."

And suddenly Kip wanted to bury his fist in his grandfather's pleasant, patronizing face.

"She's been a joy to me. Thank you," Kip said instead, smiling as if the old man were in his dotage and needed to be humored.

Andross caught it, and the jovial superiority drained from his face. But then he recovered. He wagged a finger and turned away. Grinwoody rolled a table over to them, covered with labeled decks and scores of cards spread faceup for modifying any of the decks.

"Have you had any chance to play?" Andross asked.

"None," Kip said. "But I feel I have a different perspective on some of the cards now. Not sure if that'll help me in the game, but it's been quite valuable in life."

"They're not so different," Andross said, "life and the game."

"Here I thought we were working to prevent that," Kip said.

"How so?" Andross asked. It was actually a bit of a relief that he wasn't tracking exactly with Kip's thoughts today. The old man was unnerving.

"We're trying to prevent there being nine kings again?" Kip said.

"Ha! Well. True," Andross said.

"Promachos Guile, we both know you're better at Nine Kings than I am. You're also the promachos. You can ask or order almost anything of me, and I'll simply have to give it to you. I'd love to play you sometime—without stakes other than perhaps my bruised ego. But not today. Maybe you've done everything you need to do to prepare for the coming battle, but I haven't. Every game I play against you is for stakes I can't afford, and with the decks stacked against me. I won't play."

Andross looked amused. "A good play itself."

"Thank you."

"Which is why I preemptively took it away from you."

"Excuse me?"

"Kip, do you think you're the first young man to see that the games of his elders are stacked against him? Do you think you're the first to rage against the game upon finding out that you're not much of a player?"

"Look, old man—"

"Yes, I am old, and how old are you now? Even out of your teens yet?"

That caught Kip up short. But he didn't bother to answer.

"Even in our world, where drafters, and the children of noble families, and most of all those who are both, must mature early, you are still very, very young."

"My uncle Dazen set the world on fire by the time he was my age," Kip countered. "And my—"

"You consider that an achievement?" Andross interrupted before Kip could start on his father's deeds.

"He moved the world by his will."

"No, he didn't. He didn't even set the world afire. He provided a spark to one powder keg among hundreds. He invited other fire throwers to his banners because he was so desperate for support, and they came because the old grievances were so strong."

"You backed him into a corner," Kip said. "And you did nothing to disperse all that powder, though you were in a position to do so. It was *your* failure."

"Perhaps you know less about that history than you think. You ascribe more power to me than I had at the time."

"Do I?" Kip said.

"I came from the outside myself, Kip. I was a nothing like you. I started from the bottom of the nobility to get where I am now. I had to make gambles, time and again, that would make your testicles quiver. And I didn't win every time. When the war broke out, I was still heavily in debt from all the bribes it cost me to get onto the Spectrum, and there were masterful players at that table who'd seen me coming and wanted me ruined, if not dead. You see me now and believe that I was ever thus."

"No, I hope that you weren't," Kip said. "You never got around to telling me how you closed off the chance for me to simply leave and not play your games."

Andross's eyes flashed, but then he suddenly smiled, and this time it hit his eyes. "This, this is why I've longed to play you again, Kip. You give me the uncomfortable pleasure of playing against an opponent who will bring out the best in me."

Kip couldn't help but suddenly remember those moments when

he'd actually missed sparring with the old man. But this was insanity; they didn't have time for this.

"But to answer your question: unattached young men are destabilizing," Andross said. "Like the lover of fire who burns down homes for pleasure and wouldn't altogether mind if the flames took him as well, a young man might tell you to go sodomize yourself, even if it's the worst possible thing he could do for his own interests. This is why young men go to war. It's why they gamble ruinous amounts. It's why they jump off heights to impress others and bear the pain of their injuries for the next fifty years. Anyone who might kill himself to hurt you is dangerous, hard to predict. You were one of those. You're not any longer. Why do you think I gave you a wife? Why do you think I gave you the Mighty? Why do you think I let you recruit your own army and have success with it? Because every bond is a fetter. Every extra thing you love makes you easier to predict."

"You didn't *give* those to me," Kip said.

"Didn't I?"

Fuuuuck.

Andross's eyes glittered at the doubt he saw in Kip's, and he went on. "I'd hoped you'd have a child on the way by now. I figured a young man who grew up without a father would be loath to abandon his own child. But you do have a wife to think of, and friends you wouldn't want anything bad to happen to."

Kip didn't want to believe that the very happiness he'd enjoyed had been afforded to him by Andross Guile, and he knew the man wasn't above taking credit for things he hadn't done, but he was the master.

The phrase pulsed in Kip's head: 'The Master.'

That card. But it triggered no further memories or visions.

"You know you're insufferable, right?" Kip asked.

"A common trait of the Guile men."

Kip shook his head, trying not to smile. Dammit. "How do you do this?" he asked.

Andross waited for him to clarify.

"How do I *like* you, after all you've done? I should..." I should abhor you, Kip thought, but it wasn't the time to say such things.

"Water seeks its own level," Andross said.

"What's that supposed to mean?" Kip said.

"It means we'll be playing three games."

"That doesn't answer my question in the slightest."

"The first two will have stakes high enough to keep your interest, and by the time we're finished with the third, you'll understand why

this is not only worth the time you'll be spending away from preparing for the battle, you'll understand that what we're doing will quite likely decide the battle."

"We're on the same side," Kip said, disbelieving. "If you want me to do something, just ask."

"I want you to play three games with me to decide the fate of the world," Andross said.

Kip had walked into that. He thought for a moment. What leverage did he have to refuse?

"Please," Andross said. He gave a serpent-cold smile.

"Since you asked so nicely," Kip said.

"Stakes for the first game are a secret for a secret. If I win, you tell me what happened to all of Janus Borig's cards. Everything you know. Including the ones you left out last time."

That sounded suspiciously non-terrible, though Kip knew there had to be some angle on it. "Understood. And if I win?"

Idly, Andross spun a ring on his finger. "I'll tell you your mother's story."

"You mean my real mother."

"Well, if you want Karris's real story, you'll have to ask her yourself. I think there are some things you might learn about the woman who called herself Katalina Delauria that might change how you feel about her."

"What do you mean by *that*? What do you know about my mother?" Kip demanded. He'd sworn he didn't care about her anymore, but his emotions went so hot so fast that he saw he'd only been fooling himself.

"Quite a lot more now than I did even a month ago. I had a visit with Lina's father. Most illuminating."

"I have another grandfather?!"

"Tragic story. Lina and Asafa were very close. They corresponded until she became convinced it was too dangerous for her to continue doing so. That, of course, was long after she'd run away. He'd love to meet you. Would you like to meet him?"

Run away?

Too dangerous?

Kip had a whole other *family*?

His grandfather's name was Asafa? Kip could meet him?

The questions piled on top of each other, throwing Kip's heart to the winds—until he saw Andross's coolly smug smirk.

This was Andross Guile's favorite thing in the world, wasn't it? Knocking people off balance, then lording his greater knowledge over them, then manipulating them with it: this was his real game.

"There's a battle coming. This is all moot," Kip said.

"I like to plan for the future, even if it looks like there is none. That's what makes us emerge from them stronger."

"Are you going to cheat?" Kip asked.

"Only if you let me," Andross said. "Are you familiar with Keffel's Variant?"

"I know what it *is*," Kip said. It was a set of custom rules that made for a faster game. He'd never played it.

"It's good for an analogy," Andross said. "And it'll give you a chance for luck to help you."

"Classic decks?" Kip asked. The variant started the game at noon rather than morning, when the most powerful cards could be played immediately, and had an initial mechanic where you drew seven cards but had to discard down to four. Using classic decks, you had some idea what your opponent would be going for. Typical games were a quick slugfest.

"No, my decks," Andross said.

Instantly, Grinwoody began sweeping cards from the surface of the table as if they'd been there for nothing.

Of course. Asshole. With the many cards out on the table, Andross had misled Kip into believing that Kip would be *constructing* his own deck. Instead, this was just another way of the old man putting him off balance.

"It's traditional that the guest be allowed to choose the deck pairing, isn't it?"

"I am...familiar with that tradition," Andross admitted.

"Hoped I wouldn't be, huh?" Kip asked with a quick grin.

Andross took a deep breath. "Beating you is going to be such fun. Do you know, I once stooped to playing Grinwoody? So capable in so many duties, and has surely seen me play a thousand times. Yet hopeless."

"Almost as bad as I am?" Kip asked.

Again Andross smiled.

Grinwoody said nothing, but now brought over a heavy tray, seeming to struggle with the weight with the infirmity of his age. He set it on the playing table and pulled back the top. It unfolded to reveal a score of decks, each nicely inset in a samite surface.

"You choose the pairing. I choose which deck."

"May I take a moment?" Kip asked as he started going through the decks.

"As you were so adamant to point out, we don't have all day,"

Andross said when Kip paused halfway through rifling through the second deck.

"Of course, grandfather," Kip said. "It's just been a while. Green Apple's Gambit?" he asked, gesturing to the deck in his hand.

"With four substitutions," Andross said. "As usually constructed, that deck's a little slow, I always thought it needed a tertiary path to victory, though in my games I've never used it."

"Never needed it?" Kip said.

"I've tended to be lucky," Andross said. It was, perhaps, the first modest thing Kip had ever heard come out of his mouth.

Dammit. Andross had here collected the legendary decks of history, but then made his own adjustments.

"Brier and Fire. Good one," Kip said, rifling. "But...lots of substitutions." He frowned.

He was at a greater disadvantage than he'd thought. It didn't matter how good his memory was, not with a time pressure like this. Studying each deck, recalling how close it was to the classic decks and rating its strengths, and then discarding most of the commentary he'd memorized to evaluate how strong it would be in this weird game variant?

Kip said, "I'd need days to prepare adequately for—oh, I see. This is an analogue for our defense against the White King. Not enough time to do what I'd like, so what do I do instead?"

Andross snapped his fingers, and Grinwoody disappeared to go fetch something. "Perhaps you read too much into a game."

It wasn't fair—but Kip had agreed to it. Any time he spent whinging was time wasted.

He had to look at the weird rules as part of the game, not as the terms of the game. He got to pick the decks, out of which Andross would choose which one he wanted. Most people would think it was obvious to choose decks that were as equal as possible. With equally good players, it would be.

But why had Andross chosen this variant? And why these decks?

Turn the question from a disinterested analytical query to a human question, and it suddenly made sense to Kip. "I see: I can't use my memory to simply pick the best decks and play it out as others have done before us. Neither the choice of decks nor the exact strategies involved in our game will have been covered by any book I might have read. So this is another test."

"Not a test. I simply don't want to play against your memories of what some card master from some earlier era did. I want to play against you," Andross said.

So Kip turned everything backward. At the disadvantage he was starting from, he needed a deck that counted on luck. Of course, the games' masters tended not to rely on luck, but many decks had secondary strategies—if you get unlucky and don't draw X, Y, or Z, you might still be able to win by using A and B together. Many of the classic decks, however, eschewed those secondary strategies in order to make the original strategy even stronger. They'd simply take the loss if they got particularly unlucky.

Over many iterations, skill prevailed over luck.

Which meant that skillful players naturally gravitated toward decks rewarding skillful play, and few players were more skillful than Andross. So Kip decided not to go with the classically paired decks at all. Instead, Kip looked for a two long-shot, luck-dependent decks that even Andross wouldn't have played against each other. In a minute, he had the two.

Andross frowned.

Each, in this variant, should be pretty weak—unless they drew one key card. The first deck was generally considered to be too complicated to be used regularly in standard play, Nine Mirrors. The second was Delayed Destruction, which hadn't been played in centuries because Sea Demon and another card in it whose name had been lost were now considered Black Cards—forbidden from legal play.

Kip wasn't sure what Andross would have used to shore up the deck, though, so he looked through the two decks for whatever changes the old man had made. "The hell?" Kip said. "What's this?"

Sea Demon was in the deck. Naturally. But so, too, was the nameless card, lost to the mists of time. It was not nameless here: "Sea *Giant?*"

"You've learned something about will-casting in this last year, I hear," Andross said.

"Indeed," Kip said. "And it's left me with many questions."

"Dolphins can be will-cast, but only by someone they like or by someone very strong. Whales can't be will-cast at all. There are accounts of men breaking their minds against them, like waves against the rocks of the Everdark Gates. But sea giants, enormous and peaceful as they were, sea giants were trivially easy to will-cast. It is how the pirate kings first established themselves. A few dozen will-cast sea giants and a pirate queen named Ceres established such a stranglehold on the sea that they named it Ceres's Sea. But then the other pirates attacked her, or she was murdered, and her followers couldn't control the sea giants, or she murdered the underlings she had in charge of the sea giants—or perhaps none of those stories are true, but however it was, somehow their reins slipped from human fingers. The sea giants went insane, and destroyed every ship they came upon, everywhere.

"Nautical trade came to a standstill. There's simply no defense against them. A few very strong will-casters had limited success against them, but it was rarely duplicated. Without nautical trade, every one of the nine kingdoms became utterly dependent upon its neighbors, and that only gave them all another reason for war. When the Chromeria gained control, the sea giants were hunted to extinction. The whales left thereafter. No one knows why."

"How do you know all this?" Kip asked.

Andross shrugged, as if to say, *Really?*

"These cards. They're *very* similar."

"They're the same, some say. Having no sea giants to compare our sea demons with, I have no way of telling. But some have said in bygone eras, before such talk was too dangerous, that our sea demons now are the last of those will-cast sea giants. They roam the seas, senescent, angry when roused from their near-immortal torpor."

"Reminds me of someone," Kip said.

"Damn, kid. I should beat you with my cane."

"You know interesting stuff," Kip said.

"Oh, high praise! You little shit. Have you decided yet?"

Kip shuffled through both decks one last time, trying to memorize them. Then he extended them.

Andross took Delayed Destruction, leaving Kip with Nine Mirrors. "Pick that for the name?" he asked.

"Not re...er, of course. I was hoping you'd ramble on about the Great Mirrors as a conversation piece," Kip said. "Have to confess, learning about them would probably be a lot more useful to my immediate future than learning about moldy old sea demons."

It actually would've been a clever plan, if Kip had been quick enough to think of it.

"Really?" Andross said.

"Not really. But I found a Great Mirror in Blood Forest. Triggered it. Huge thing, still pristine. Had been underground for centuries, it looked like. I don't suppose there's actually...nine of them?"

Andross gestured to Grinwoody to pour them some drinks while he shuffled his own cards, his liver-spotted hands moving as deftly as a cardsharp's. "The Nine Kings cards are a repository of ancient knowledge, some of it very unpopular with the censors of their eras, some of it unpopular with later ones." He flipped half his deck from one hand to another in a move that seemed to defy physical laws. "It's also just a game. How many Mirror cards in that deck?"

"Three?" Kip said. He hated that it came out as a question.

"But three doesn't sound scary. Three Mirrors? In a game called Nine Kings? Nine Mirrors, much better."

"Is that why you called us 'the Mighty'?" Kip asked. "For the name?"

"If I hadn't given you a Name, what would you have been? Six scared adolescents who'd dropped out of the Chromeria, who'd washed out of Blackguard training and been chased off the Jaspers by a half-trained band of thugs."

"Those thugs are your Lightguards. Who you also gave a pretty awesome name, much as we hate you for it. Hated." Kip cleared his throat.

" 'The Lightguard' is a name that either calls ironic attention to itself or, maybe one time in twenty, might have encouraged those thugs to make something of themselves. The latter is a gamble I lost, but I still win. They know everyone hates them, and they depend utterly on me, so they're fiercely loyal to me."

"Except for that incident where Zymun sent them to kill me and the Mighty."

"Well, yes, except for that. But they only obeyed him because he told them that they would actually be fulfilling my will by fulfilling his. He, too, is a Guile."

"I can't believe you're keeping him close," Kip said. "He's poison."

"He says the same about you. Shuffle?"

They shuffled for each other, and Kip kept his eyes tight on Andross's hands. One last cut of the decks, and they handed them back to each other.

Andross chose the setting as Big Jasper and set the sun-counter at noon. Kip went first.

He drew his cards: a tough polychrome named Katalina Galden, Red Spectacles, a musket, a good sword, Blue Spectacles, a green-drafting Blackguard with a musket proficiency, and a red-drafting Blackguard. It would have been a great hand for the normal game, good for offense and defense early. In a normal game, it would have put him in an early lead that Andross might never have recovered from.

But at full noon, and with two draws? Every card Kip kept in his hand was one less card he could draw, one less chance to get the powerful cards he needed. He flopped them all down.

"The discard pile is faceup in this variant," Andross said.

Kip hadn't recalled that. Great.

The old man studied Kip's overturned cards. "A tough call. But the right play."

"A compliment?" Kip asked.

"Doled out in heaping measure, when deserved," Andross said. He discarded three. They didn't help Kip at all. They were three cards you'd toss regardless of what you were pursuing.

"I knew her, you know."

"Katalina Galden?" Kip asked. "Any relation to that asshole Magister Jens Galden?"

Kip looked at the cards he'd drawn. Nothing. A big, heaping, steaming-on-a-cold-winter's-day pile-of-stinky nothing. He'd drawn most of the equipment in his deck, but no direct attacks and no one good enough to put the equipment on. If he'd kept Katalina Galden, he would have had a chance.

"Same family, though not likely by blood. I was actually speaking of Janus Borig," Andross said, drawing his own cards, imperturbable. "The woman who drew the new cards."

It was whiplash for Kip. He'd been walking down another mental path completely. And then he remembered. This was how Andross Guile operated: overload your opponent with too many things to think about, and then drop a bomb with a burning fuse in his lap and see what he did.

"How many people in history do you think were smarter than you are?" Kip asked.

But the counter didn't work.

"She was a dear friend of your grandmother's," Andross said. "For a long time. She, more than anyone, I think, is responsible for our family's troubles. She lied to me. She lied to us." She? Oh, she Janus Borig.

Kip got to go first, so he laid out nearly all of his cards. "How so?" Kip asked, suspicious.

"I was going to say, 'So beware of trusting anything she told you.' But instead you're surprised," Andross said. "So you think she's a truth teller? Because she's a Mirror? Because 'Mirror' implies a passivity?"

After his talk about mirrors with his wife not two hours ago, Kip felt like either history was bringing something together for him to understand or this was just one of those times where you learn a new word or concept and suddenly you're seeing it everywhere.

"I know this much," Kip said, trying not to show how troubled he was. "*She* didn't try to kill me before even meeting me."

503

"No, she was more interested in using you to kill someone else," Andross said. He played three coccas; they were smaller ships, but each capable of decent damage. If Kip got the direct attacks his deck depended on, he would have to waste valuable turns taking them out.

Kip was screwed. The game had barely started, and they both already knew he was going to lose. He looked at the card he'd drawn: Yellow Spectacles. Garbage.

Yeah, Luck, go bugger yourself.

"I'm sure anyone who has a message you can't control must be untrustworthy," Kip said, more furious at his cards than at his opponent. "From today forward I will get all my intelligence from you alone, grandfather."

A muscle in Andross's jaw twitched, but he took a slow breath. "Do you know, it's so frustrating. I'm making all the same mistakes with you I made with Dazen. I'm a better player than this. Fine." He seemed to be choosing his words with care, and Kip had to hide his astonishment that he'd thrown his grandfather off his own planned path for once.

"She told me," Andross said, "when I first ascended to the Red seat on the Spectrum, that she wanted to paint my portrait for her cards. It was meant to be hugely flattering, of course, a known Mirror telling me that I was worthy of a card. If one excludes the procedure and discovery and weapon and monster cards, that fact alone would acknowledge me as one of the four hundred fifty-seven most important people throughout history to that point. Slightly more, actually, but I didn't have an accurate count of the Black Cards then, and of course, there were many important people who never sat for their portrait, but they're the less famous for it. What the originals of these cards did, though, was known to very few."

Andross played Amir Bazak on one of the coccas, and Red Spectacles, and equipped them on him. Amir had turned himself into a human bomb, penetrating the enemy lines during a battle through subterfuge and then drafting so much red it killed him in an explosion that took out thousands and opened a gap in the line. It was a weak card, easily killed—if you had something to kill it with.

"But you knew," Kip said. It was hard to imagine Andross Guile not knowing any secret. "You knew what the cards did."

"I married well, into a family that knew…most of it," Andross said. "But Borig was clever. I think she'd already seen more than I guessed. She led me to believe that a card could only cover the time period up until its creation. Seems logical, right? And I believed that each person could only have one card. She lied. So tell me, my cleverer grandson, why would that be a problem?"

It wasn't the flattery of being told he was historically important, Kip realized. Though he imagined that flattery had meant quite a lot to Andross Guile, even if he didn't want to admit it.

But Andross would have pushed past the flattery.

Commemorating a mere Red? Andross had set his sights so much higher, and would soon achieve so much more. If Andross had believed that he was destined for much greater heights than merely being the youngest Red in history, then . . .

"Ah," Kip said. "You had plans. You knew that you were going to be promachos someday. Or maybe Prism? The White?"

"Something like that," Andross said. "Regardless, I should have known better. I was a young man, with a young man's weaknesses. I thought *potential* meant something. I thought I was so very devious in having her paint my card before I had done most of the things I'd planned. See, I was worried about what my enemies might do with such a card after it was completed. I knew I deserved a card. So if I could get her to do my card early, then even if my enemies got it, the information they learned about me, being solely retrospective, would be of limited use to them.

"But the truth was I hadn't done anything up to that point to deserve a card. Seizing control of my family, winning my bride from the pool of suitors and against a father who initially opposed me, becoming the Red? These are but the foundation stones of a legend, not a legend itself. But she was clever to come to me then, when I was overwhelmed with other concerns and susceptible to flattery. I couldn't take the time then to properly investigate the cards."

"They weren't only retrospective?" Kip asked. He played his garbage, and drew a Great Mirror. Too late.

Andross sipped his whiskey. He motioned that both ships and Amir Bazak would attack.

Kip couldn't stop the attack. The ships hurt him a little, and then Amir Bazak exploded and took out one of them, and badly damaged the other, but also took out almost all of Kip's life.

Andross said, "There are scholars' papers that say things like 'operating outside of time,' which sounds profound, until you think about it and realize it's nonsense. No, her lie was different. She told me—or I assumed—that it was only possible to have one card. After all, no one else has ever had more than one, and though I'm a proud man, I hadn't considered myself quite *that* special. Reflecting on it later, I realized that I didn't know that others *hadn't* had multiple cards made of them, with only one kept for later use. I only knew the cards that had entered the registers. It's possible the Mirrors have pulled this trick before. Lucidonius has no card, so far as we know, but there is an account of there being a Mirror during his era who met an early end. It was attributed to the Order, but they are a convenient scapegoat, aren't they?"

"You think Janus Borig made another card of you?"

"That's the question I think you will answer. Right. About. Now." Andross played Sea Demon.

Kip couldn't kill it in one turn, and the cocca alone could kill him next round, so it was now impossible for him to win.

He'd been focused during the game, focused on winning, on Andross's words, and that tight focus had allowed his mother to blur into insignificance in the background. But now she came back into his vision, only for him to see her retreating into the distance. Andross wouldn't give Kip her story; he never gave anyone anything, especially not something of great value to them.

Kip hadn't thought it would affect him, but suddenly it felt like losing his mother all over again—and even worse now. Andross wasn't going to let Kip find his grandfather, either, for his grandfather Asafa would likely tell Kip the story himself, and Andross wasn't about to give up a prize for nothing.

It was a moot point. Kip was going to die in this battle. It shouldn't hurt.

He didn't have time to prattle on with some old stranger anyway.

"Looks like a small man on a little ship wins it for you," Kip said. "An unlikely hero, what with sea demons and Great Mirrors about."

"But a hero nonetheless... because I was willing to lose him."

Kip folded his cards, conceding. "So Zymun and I are your little ships?" he asked.

Andross sipped his whiskey. "It's a game, not a metaphor, and you're the one who chose these decks. Not that I'm opposed to learning lessons from mere games or other unlikely places. Speaking of which, there's the matter of our first wager. I believe you have a story to tell me about what happened to Janus Borig's cards."

Chapter 79

Even as Gavin ran up the steps to the Tower of Heaven's roof, he noticed a change from the hewn conformity of all the stairs he'd climbed in the entire hike up until now.

The steps became irregular, a more natural shape, with uncut stone, albeit worn by the passage of many thousands of feet over untold years. Coming out on the top of White Mist Tower felt not like reaching the top of one of the Chromeria's seven towers but instead like summiting the stone crown of a mountain. The top wasn't carved flat, but gently curved.

It reminded him, quite suddenly, of the crest of Sundered Rock before he and his brother had shattered it.

So long lost in darkness, that memory surfaced as sharply as did the black stone beneath his feet. For the entire climb, the black stone of the tower had been an oddity. Was it meant to evoke the black humility of a luxiat's robes? The imagery had never gelled for Gavin. Luxiats showed they had no light of their own, but surely this pilgrimage should be toward light. Maybe a tower black at the base, but lighter as one climbed? That could make sense.

Instead, White Mist Tower was unrelieved black.

A part of Gavin knew he should move fast. He should grab the blade before anything else. He'd circled halfway around the tower with the last stair, which put the sword at the far side. But running before he knew what was here might be rushing heedless into danger—rather than running to safety. And a sight here struck him like Orholam's own raised fist.

Here, finally, at its topmost height, the Tower of Heaven poked its head above the wall of white mists that had obscured the rest of it for ages. Only here, at its crown, was Gavin high enough to see out beyond the mantle of cloud cloaking both tower and island.

The rising sun, dimmed for all the timeless days he'd been here, shone brilliant, awakening the horizon with fire. White fire, to Gavin's color-blind eyes, but the sun was beautiful yet, even stripped of its colors by a cruel god.

The thought brought him back to himself. Brought him back to threats and death and killing. He couldn't see the sword on the opposite side of the tower's top, hidden as it was by the rise of the stone hill that was the tower's center—but he didn't see anything else, either.

The summit was empty.

The pilgrimage ended in nothing.

I crossed half the world to come to God's own house, and He's not at home.

Probably never was.

But maybe this was an illusion, another will-casting, another test.

Gavin covered his color-blind eye and stared through the black jewel. It revealed only bleak nothingness rendered in starker tones than his natural orb saw. Brittle stone, a tower not of heaven but of lies. This temple was all façade. Men had labored for a thousand years to build this tower to the heavens, and when they reached it, they found themselves punished only with the death of their delusions and a loneliness plunging as deep as this tower was tall.

In piling up a tower to heaven, they only burrowed down exactly that deeply into hell. In the light of this open air, they'd found a darkness as great as the black cell under the Chromeria.

On the day they'd finished, there had surely been some festival, some celebration with serious prayers from serious luxiats. Together, those gathered had surely shouted to heaven, 'We built You a house! Come and live among us, Orholam! Fulfill the promise of the ages!'

What had they done when there had been no answer?

How long had it been before scandalized luxiats, seeing their own power dissolve with other men's beliefs, concocted some excuse for Orholam's absence?

They'd lied then as they did now, because all their power rested on it.

It was what Gavin had always suspected, but it was like suspecting your wife had cheated, dread growing in your heart as you became more certain, but the relationship not dying until you heard the admission from your becursed-beloved's own lips.

Gavin staggered. He fell to one knee. He clamped his eyes closed as his chest tightened and shut off his breath.

He covered the eye patch and opened only his natural eye, praying to no one, but *praying* that his wounded natural orb would see things differently. Perhaps the black stone told him bleaker news than it ought.

The darkness receded slowly from his vision like an oily film slowly sliding earthward, but even here in the beauty of a sunrise as he hadn't seen in what felt like ages untold, the fundamental truth remained: there was nothing here.

Nothing here meant everything Gavin had done—everything, for his whole life—was a breath exhaled into the storm. Worse, there being nothing here meant there was no nexus of magic. No nexus meant there was no nexus to kill.

That meant there was no way to save Karris.

What was Gavin to report to Grinwoody? 'I went but there was nothing there'? Who would believe that? Before the White Mist Reef had closed off the isle, disillusioned pilgrims must have said the same thing a hundred thousand times to those who'd not made the journey, and yet the people of the satrapies had chosen to believe instead the liars who'd returned swearing they'd encountered Orholam here.

Karris would die. Gavin would, too, even if he made it home. How could Grinwoody let him live?

He had no future.

But it was worse than a mission failed, and all Gavin's happiness stolen. It was worse than losing his life to that worm. Everything Gavin had ever done had been in the service of lies. His own, and others'.

His brother's death, and everyone he'd murdered for the Freeing, it had all been only men wrestling for power, cloaking themselves in respectability by invoking a god who had nothing to do with any of it, because He didn't exist.

But though broken and barely able to breathe, Gavin fought his way to his feet.

He'd knelt long enough.

So his suspicion was right, and his long-held intuition was wrong. So his first great goal would go unmet. The world was as it was. Only one thing was left for him to do.

He would pick up the sword, and he would hack at the very peak of the tower until he broke the Blinding Knife. He would carve the word 'Lies' into the very rock. And then, one last time, he would fly—as he hurled himself from the tower to a well-deserved death.

Chapter 80

Kip considered lying, of course. He was still a Guile.

"My father had hidden a box in a training bag. I was kicking it when I heard something break. I was drafting, maybe all the colors at once, and I opened the bag and the cards flew out onto my skin. I... somehow absorbed the cards. Not on purpose. I lost consciousness and nearly died, but Teia was able to revive me. When she pried the cards off my skin, they were blank."

"But you Viewed them," Andross said.

"Not in any way that I could make sense of," Kip said. "I saw them all at once. It killed me. Literally. My heart stopped. It, it felt like...It obliterated my mind. I couldn't tell who I was anymore."

"But they're not *lost*," Andross insisted. "You've the Guile memory."

"In any meaningful sense, yes, they're lost," Kip said.

" 'In any meaningful sense'? So in some other sense they're not. Tell me how they're not lost. Tell me what you experienced."

Of course it was like this. Kip had inadvertently destroyed the world's most valuable intelligence. Of course Andross was going to go after the scraps.

So Kip started talking. What did it matter, now, with their doom coming down on their heads? Kip ended up telling him about the Great Library and the immortal or djinn or whatever Abaddon was, with his broken ankles and pistol and that cracked mask of a visage. He skipped the master cloak. That was Teia's secret now, not Kip's.

Andross got a funny look as Kip told him about the immortal, but if it was disbelief, clearly he decided not to challenge Kip on it right now.

That was the great joy of speaking with Andross Guile, of course: you knew everything you said would be used against you sooner or later.

"Tell me every card name you remember."

Kip told him. It didn't take very long. He ended by saying, "And there was even a card that may have been you. I saw a man, maybe in a ship? The Master. He was writing a letter to the Color Prince, a treasonous letter about becoming Dagnu. He was cowled, though, as you used to be. And his hands were stained crimson like a red drafter who's gone wight."

"Ah, that's why you tried to assassinate me after the Battle of Ru," Andross said.

"That is...not what happened. And we both know it," Kip said.

"No, it's not," Andross admitted. "You remember no more of that card?"

"No. Not then or ever. One glimpse."

Andross believed him, he could tell.

"Now, I've fulfilled the terms of my wager," Kip said. "More than fulfilled them."

"Tell me about these flashbacks you 'sometimes' get."

"That wasn't part of the deal," Kip said.

510 "They're part of the cards you destroyed, and it may be the key to

saving us all, and who better to help you disentangle a puzzle than I?" Andross asked.

So Kip told him all about that, too.

Andross ended up shaking his head. "Off saving one satrapy when you could have been uncovering the mysteries of the Thousand Worlds that could save us all."

"Perhaps," Kip admitted, "but I'm not a man to sit idle while my people bleed."

It caught Andross up short. He marveled at it. "An honest statement of your limitations, but without apologies nor posturing that those limits somehow make you superior to other differently gifted men. Hmm. I know men twice your age who are less comfortable with themselves."

'Comfortable with myself'? Kip thought that was the first time anyone had ever said *that* about him. But he supposed he had made some progress on that front in the last few years.

"You didn't get all the new cards," Andross said.

"Excuse me?" Kip asked.

"Gavin left the bulk of them where he hoped you would find them, but some he considered too sensitive for you."

A shock passed through Kip, tightening his throat and turning his bowels to water. "How would you even know he did such a thing?"

"It's what I would do. There are some things I wouldn't want my own son to know."

"And?" Kip asked.

"Naturally, I found them."

"He left them for Karris, didn't he?" Kip guessed.

Andross Guile only hesitated a moment. "Curious," he said. "That's the kind of thing Felia would have done. That much of an intuitive leap, so quickly."

"Does Karris know about them?" Kip asked.

"Of course not. You don't show the other players your hole cards, especially not literal ones."

He flicked his gaze up to Grinwoody, who he suddenly realized was hanging on every word, as if he knew none of this. "More whiskey, calun," Kip said.

Of course Grinwoody's service was impeccable, silent, and swift, and emotionless. Maybe Kip should have called him by name to insult him.

"Where's this going?" Kip asked.

Andross weighed him while Grinwoody served them both. Though he'd chosen a fast-game variant, he now gave no indication of hurry in his manner and seemed not to worry at all about the calamity bearing down upon them.

"The truth?" Andross said.

A smart-ass comment leapt to mind, but Kip the Lip clamped his jaw tight shut. Hectoring Andross wasn't going to help anything.

Andross waved Grinwoody away. "Go, now, for a bit. Some few things are too secret even for you."

Grinwoody retreated to stand with his back turned toward them, close enough to hear and return instantly if Andross called. Andross produced a long key, opened a locked drawer in the table, and withdrew a card box. He handed it to Kip.

Nonchalantly, Kip flipped open the box. And his heart stopped.

It was the deck he'd absorbed. The new deck Janus Borig had painted—the deck Kip had destroyed, erased.

"Not originals," Andross said. "These cards can't be Viewed. They're paint and gold and parchment and lacquer only. There is no magic in them."

"How did you ...?"

"Janus had enemies. She kept this deck far from her home in a place she thought was safe. She hoped that if she were killed, some future Mirror would might be able to use these to re-create her work."

"How'd you get them?"

"Please," Andross Guile scoffed.

"You killed her? She was too dangerous to you."

"Don't be ridiculous. I don't destroy what I might better use. And I had many questions for her. Some other player did that, and not necessarily even a major one."

"Why have me describe them if you already have them all?" Kip asked.

"For one reason above all: it tells me you're honest, that you'll make good on a wager, even to me. I had to establish that first. Now, with that done, I believe it's time for our second game," Andross said. "If you win, I'll give you Gavin's card. The original."

Kip's heart seized. His father's card?! The original? That meant he could View it.

And if it truly wasn't retrospective, and if he used it properly, he could find where his father was now.

It was everything he'd hoped to do, simply offered by his grandfather.

But that was if he won.

If the reward for victory was so enormous, what would the cost of losing be?

512   "Wait," Kip said. "Why wouldn't you want me to View that card

regardless? Don't you want him back? What did you see when you Viewed it yourself?" Andross wasn't a full-spectrum polychrome, but surely he would have—

"I've not tried."

"You don't want to see yourself through his eyes," Kip said.

Andross's eyes flashed. "My reasons are my own. Perhaps if you win, you'll find out what they are. I don't know. That's what makes it such very, very good bait. I mean, such a very good wager."

"What's the price of defeat?" Kip asked.

A cat who'd stolen your dinner couldn't have grinned with the mixture of malevolence and self-satisfaction that Andross showed. "You lose, and I'll show you another card. You'll View it for me and tell me everything you see."

"That . . . doesn't sound that bad," Kip said.

"Well, then, you win, win or lose." Andross voice was so blithely pleasant, it could have been honey and melted butter.

Which was all the evidence Kip needed that it was covering the taste of arsenic.

Andross Guile would never offer uneven stakes that were tilted toward his opponent.

Kip wanted to think, How bad can it be?

But he remembered the card The Butcher of Aghbalu. He remembered the months of nightmares he'd had from watching the massacre unfold—no, not just watching but partaking in it, over and over. What if the card was one of *those* cards?

But it was his father against that.

Did it matter now? Kip wasn't going to be able to save him. But Karris deserved to know. The Blackguard deserved to know. Someone might help him, even if it wasn't Kip.

"Ah, one further stipulation," Andross said. "Whichever way the game goes, you have to View whichever card you get, and you have to answer my questions about it."

"So you win, win or lose, too," Kip said.

"Yes, isn't it nice that we can play a game so mutually beneficial?"

"Why do you want me to do this?" Kip asked.

"My son has a knack for showing up at the last moment and wrecking all sorts of plans. Usually the enemy's, but not always. Either card you View might tell us my son's location. Should he arrive quite suddenly in the next day or so, I should like very much to make sure that I enact the correct plan for this most important Sun Day."

Now, finally, Kip understood why Andross had said there was nothing more important for them to be doing than this. Preparations for battle? The people they each commanded could do most of those. Unfolding the past and the present itself? Only they could do this.

And it meant helping his father either way.

"Let's play," Kip said.

Andross chose conventional rules. Kip chose decks he was familiar with. He even added cards from the array Grinwoody brought in once more, based on what he guessed of how the Black Cards would affect the strategies.

It was close. Damn close.

He came to his last turn. His facedown deck held fourteen cards. He could only draw one, and any one of four cards left in that stack would give him the victory.

"Four," Andross said aloud. "Four winners. Out of fourteen."

"How do you know I don't have it in my hand already?"

"A man doesn't pray over his last draw when he has the winning card in hand."

Of course Andross knew exactly what Kip was looking for. Kip couldn't find it in himself to hate the old spider, not for this. Hating Andross Guile was like hating the weather. If the sun burns your head, you don't shake your fist at the sun; you blame yourself for not wearing a hat.

The game had been fair. Kip had watched for any cheats, eagle-eyed.

"You want to back out?" Andross asked, amused. "The odds are against you. Failure might break your spirit . . . *Breaker*." He said it with a light derision, as if Kip was trying on names like a child tries on his parents' fancy clothes and big hats.

"Not 'Breaker.' I prefer 'Diakoptês,'" Kip said. For some reason Grinwoody flinched at that. "My father told me once that the odds were against us, but that odds are for defying."

Kip drew.

He lost.

Chapter 81

"Grinwoody," Kip said. "Go fetch a bucket for me. I may vomit. Also, get a physicker. One with experience starting stopped hearts. Or better yet, the Blackguard Adrasteia."

"Teia's disappeared," Andross said. "Some time ago now. Absent without leave. I think they thought she might have gone to join you and your Mighty. No?"

Kip shook his head.

It was terrible, but the first thing Kip felt was relief. He wasn't going to have to face her yet. Not that that was really in the top ten things he ought to worry about right now.

Then his chest tightened as Andross went to a combination safe and opened it. He brought out a tiny vellum book, barely larger than a card itself. With careful fingers, he unwound the string from the button holding it shut and lay the covers open. Without touching any part of the card, he offered it.

Kip took the card by the edges, careful not to touch its face. He lay it on the table before him. The card depicted a golden ship, glowing in the sun, sails full-bellied, cutting through easy seas. It was exquisite art, as all of Janus Borig's had been, and obviously done by her hand.

"Some water, calun," Kip said. After all this time, he'd finally learned not to say please to a slave. Not that Grinwoody was any normal slave. "But open the window first. I need full-spectrum light." He turned to Andross. This card didn't look threatening in the least. "The *Golden Mean*? Is that the name of the ship?"

"Made by a pair of Abornean brothers, a shipwright and a yellow drafter, since sadly deceased in an apparent robbery. Possibly an assassination to keep them from talking. No, not done by my orders. Really, Kip, must you suspect me of everything?"

"What? No, I wasn't—"

"I saw the look on your face. Anyway, it was sold to an Ilytian cannon maker from Smussato named Phineas, and from there it's been seen in numerous ports, though of unknown ownership. Not least, it was here. On the Jaspers. Not five weeks ago."

"How do you know it has anything to do with Gavin?" Kip asked.

"Because I tried to View it myself."

"And?"

"Searching an item card for one person who's touched it isn't a matter of strength of will but of singularity of focus. I think you have that in a way I don't. When I look for Gavin, my attention is bifurcated, and my intentions are muddied. I was able to establish only that he has been on that ship in the recent past. You'll do better."

Grinwoody set down Kip's water, and there was an odd intensity about the man, a tension about him that touched those Blackguard senses that Kip had begun to develop, something that spoke of danger.

Kip looked at the older man then, but Grinwoody was all placid subservience. Surely he'd merely been echoing the tension in his master, who was meeting with a man Grinwoody surely thought might be a threat to Andross. After all, Grinwoody had had Blackguard training himself.

Kip dismissed it. Why was he focusing on a mere slave rather than on the fiercest intellect he'd ever known?

"Open the windows," Kip said.

But Grinwoody only looked to his master.

"The drapes are open," Andross said.

"That gives me seven colors," Kip said. "I have a feeling I'm going to need nine."

Andross gestured, and Grinwoody went and opened the large windows, bathing Kip in unfiltered light.

There wasn't need for much of any color, and Andross helpfully had blocks of every color large enough for Kip to draw source from, but as Kip finished with chi—his pupils squeezed down to nothing—he understood Andross's fear of the cards for the first time. Kip's gallium necklace felt heavy against his chest, concealing the chi bane within it, and Kip felt a twinge of fear as he thought for the first time, What if there's a card of this necklace? What if Andross knows everything?

But unhurried, Kip stared at the Golden Mean card on the table and set his fingers down on it, one by one, concentrating on his father alone.

Kip was the eager face of the prow cutting through azure waves, his decks gliding frictionless through the upbearing seas. He was the strain of the mast against the wind, two old friends leaning against each other as they walked home tipsy. His gunports opened like gills opening so he might breathe, and exhaling black smoke and shot, with the hurried walking of the crews and the shouted orders of a familiar voice. Gunner. And from the lack of distress in those somehow-distant voices of his crew, these were mere practice volleys with the many cannons.

Father, where are you?

"I feel him lying on the deck of the forecastle," Kip said, eyes closed. His senses were limited; it wasn't like standing on the ship himself, but more an awareness of things within a certain bubble of the ship. "He's skinny. Wearing an eye patch? Talking with someone, but I can't hear what they're saying. Now he's talking to Gunner. I recognize him, somehow. They've got a man strapped over the mouth of a cannon. A huge cannon mounted on the forecastle. Um...lost it." As Gavin stood up, his body no longer touching the deck, but only his feet doing so, he became harder to hold.

516   "There was some kind of luxin storm," Kip said. "But he slept

through it, maybe?" Kip had sharpened his focus to his father at the wrong time, it seemed. He would have liked to know what an orange-luxin storm looked like—but he wasn't going to try to go back now. "And now it's a new day. We're circling something for a while. An island and—whoa. There's a battle now. Maybe, maybe a battle. Lots of men running. Gavin's climbed up into the crow's nest. He's shouting." His mouth moved as he shouted, and Kip tried to read his lips. "I think he just shouted, 'Sea demon.' There's something terrible happening. They're firing my guns. They dropped my starboard anchor."

Kip grunted as the anchor tore free of his decks like someone tearing off a fingernail. Then the cannons boomed, his decks strained, the oars rattled out. "Something—" And then Kip felt the bony hammer of the sea demon's head crush him against the anvil of coral. Gavin was flung away. Decks tore like paper. Men were smashed, rigging tore, and bits of Kip's consciousness were flung into the seas: a shotgun blast of wood and rope and blood and metal.

He tore his fingers away from the card and found himself in the room once more. "He's gone."

"Gone? Dead?"

"I think so. He was flung from the crow's nest. The ship was crushed against a reef by a sea demon."

"Go back. Be certain!"

Kip didn't argue. He wasn't going to give up on his father, not while there was still a chance.

He found the time again and replayed it once more—though it felt like rubbing an open wound. He went beyond it, tried to search the seas.

He could feel the presence of sharks before his awareness faded from those scattered, dead bits of himself. "The bay is full of sharks," he heard himself saying. "With several sea demons outside it. But I can't feel him anywhere now. There's...there's a bit of the forecastle left, perched on the coral."

And that was it. Nothing for a time, and then the awareness of a single soul clambering up onto the forecastle.

But it wasn't Gavin Guile. It was Gunner.

Kip stayed with him for days, but Gavin never came, and Gunner only seemed to get more and more desperate.

He pulled his hand away once more and told what he'd seen. "Maybe...maybe he made it ashore?"

"Several sea demons, you said?" Andross asked.

Kip nodded. He wished suddenly that he could have seen Andross's face when he'd first given him the news that his last surviving son was now almost certainly dead. Maybe there would have been a flicker of humanity in it then, but now he spoke with the merciless focus of a captain steering his ship straight through a sandbar, scraping off the barnacles of wife and sons and grandsons and throwing into disarray everything in his life not bolted down, but always, always winning through the sand to victory and position and pride.

"He might have lived," Kip said. "A reef means there's an island close, right?" If he survived the initial collision. If he were flung into the bay rather than the open sea. If he weren't knocked unconscious by the fall. If he made it past the sharks.

If, if, if.

"Was there a wall of mist? At the reef?"

"Not...not that I was aware of?" Kip said. "But...awareness isn't so good in the cards. Why?"

Andross *hmph*ed. "There are stories that the sea demons circle White Mist Reef. If you saw several of them, he must have been there. I wonder why. But it doesn't matter. It's an island, you said. Even if he survived, even if he finds another ship, there are sea demons infesting the waters there. Very well. That tells me all I need to know. Gavin's dead, or at least dead to us. He's not coming back. Certainly not in time to help. Not in time to change anything. Which tells me that our last game is necessary."

His father was dead. There would be no Gavin Guile swooping in to save him at the last moment. It had been one thing to hear he was gone, and another to admit it might be true but hold on to hope, but now? "I'm done," Kip said, moving to stand. "I don't want to play anymore."

"You get out of that chair and I will pop your eyes out with my thumbs and fuck your skull until you bite off your swollen black tongue and drown in a bucket of your own blood."

For a moment Kip was a terrified little boy again, his mother hurling the cooking pot and the fire poker at him, shrieking at him like a wounded animal. He dropped back into his seat, baffled.

"The gold box," Andross said to Grinwoody, his voice abruptly cool once more, though he didn't take his eyes off Kip. "And the Ilytians. And put the decanter on the table."

Grinwoody brought a gold card box from the open safe. He put the crystal decanter of amber liquor on the playing table itself. Then he brought out the Ilytian bladed pistols Kip had last seen Gavin wearing. Andross checked them to confirm they were loaded and laid them across his lap, pointed toward Kip.

"Eighteen-year-old Crag Tooth," Andross said. "Their very first batch. It's worth a fortune. I opened it especially for you." His former savagery had evaporated, but Kip would never forget it. Andross waved Grinwoody away.

"My lord…" Grinwoody said. "I must protest. This one has shown reckless disregard before. I worry for your safety."

Kip was still blinking, trying to recover his breath and his wits.

Andross said, "Do you know, I paid more for this whiskey than I did for Grinwoody?"

Trying to repair his façade of calm detachment, Kip said, "The market price of slaves was a sadly overlooked part of my education."

" 'Education'?" Grinwoody asked coolly.

Andross laughed. "His owner noted his intelligence and was training him as a legalist before his ability to draft manifested, and was putting him into Blackguard training. He wasn't the only dual-use slave I bought, of course. The others were very interested in honor… prestige…making a difference. Grinwoody said only two things to me. Do you remember, Grinwoody?"

The old slave inclined his head but made no move to finish his master's story.

"He asked, 'Will you beat me if I don't deserve it?' I told him no, and I've kept my word. I've only beaten him twice. Both times for impertinence. Both times in the first year. After he understood the boundaries, we've gotten along quite well. And then when I asked if he would die for me if necessary, he said, let's see, how'd he put it? 'For you, yes. I'd prefer not to die for a lesser man.' A lesser man, you understand, Kip? This slave, this nothing, he dared to judge his betters, but not so far that he wouldn't do his duty. He didn't really want to be in the Blackguard, because Blackguards have to guard whoever happens to be Prism or on the Spectrum or sits in the White's High Seat or, horror of horrors, the Black's Low Seat if necessary. He could tell that some of them were great, whilst some were merely born to a lucky station. He fulfills his duties to the utmost, but he doesn't step beyond his station. You understand?"

"Oh, that's a very subtle lesson, High Lord Promachos," Kip said. "I won't forget who's who here. I guarantee it."

Andross lifted the bottom of the box out and revealed two decks. "Look through these while I tell you the stakes."

"I'm not going to like this, am I?" Kip asked, accidentally saying it aloud.

"That depends," Andross said. "How's your marriage?"

Kip's heart went cold. "What kind of question is that?"

"You disobeyed me when you went to Blood Forest," Andross said. "My direct order. Did you think I was going to let that slide?"

Kip shuddered, and he wasn't rightly sure if it was from disgust or rage or fear.

"If I went to Rath, Eirene Malargos would have put me in a cage," Kip said. "Metaphorically if not literally. She'd never have let me leave the palace."

"Much may be accomplished from a single building, if it's the right one," Andross said. "I should know."

Kip realized the old man had practically ruled the world from the Prism's Tower, so he couldn't exactly contradict that. "Only if one's already established the right contacts out in the world. I'm a young man, not an old one. I don't have the web you do. What I did was far more valuable to you anyway."

"At this point, the outcome is less the issue than your obedience is."

"You're upset because I showed you that you were wrong," Kip said. "You're so far removed from every human emotion, you have no idea what loyalty even looks like. I could be the king of Blood Forest right now if I hadn't decided to come here and save your ass, old man. You want me to leave? I'll go."

"You seem to think I'd give you that option."

"You seem to think I couldn't take it."

Andross sighed. Then he lifted the pistols from his lap. He cocked them. One stayed close to his body, a backup, out of reach. The other he extended over the table, the blade under the barrel reaching like an accusing finger. Kip didn't move back, and Andross tapped that dagger point against his forehead. "Kip, you didn't come here to save *me*, and those you came to save can't leave with you, so we both know you're not going anywhere. It isn't in you to run from a fight, not even one you think you'll lose. You leaving was always a bluff, and I've called it."

It was true.

"You're an asshole."

Andross chuckled as if it were a compliment. "A man who'll never risk being seen as an asshole is a man who doesn't believe in anything."

"You only believe in yourself," Kip shot back.

"No," Andross said. "Not for a long while now." He set the pistols down on the table between them. He spun one so it pointed toward him.

Kip realized he might mean a couple different things by it, but he didn't care to guess. "So what do you believe in?"

Andross took a sip of his whiskey. "I believe I'll finish the game."

Kip threw his hands up. "Always the game!"

Andross opened a drawer and pulled out two *zigarros*. He trimmed one with the dagger pistol's blade. He looked toward the window and sighed like a cat soaking up the sun, and then touched a sub-red-infused thumb to set the zigarro alight as he puffed at it. He offered the other to Kip, who accepted. He trimmed and lit his own, only then noticing that Andross was glancing at his luxin-reactive Turtle-Bear tattoo as he did so.

Orholam! Was everything Andross did about gathering intelligence?

"Look at us, Kip. While others scurry about like ants whose home has been stepped on, we smoke and drink and play cards and decide the fate of the world. What happens to our world for the next century turns on the next twenty minutes here in this room, and none of those below even know it. Doesn't it make you feel like a god?"

"I don't want to feel like a god," Kip said. But he wasn't sure that was true. He'd told Tisis he was going to die, and he believed it. But he didn't want to die.

He sipped the whiskey, and even he could tell that it was very smooth. It almost didn't taste like chewing on peat. He sucked on the zigarro, and couldn't tell much about it except that blowing smoke was itself actually kind of satisfying. "What are the stakes?" he asked, defeated.

"If you win," Andross said, "I'll make you Prism. And I'll protect you from Zymun, who's plotting to kill you. There are caveats, though. Not even I can do such a thing instantly. The Spectrum would find its spine and rebel if I forced such a thing through with no notice at all, and we can't afford that now. But Zymun will be dealt with, and you'd be Prism-elect for the next year. But you'll have the full force of my powers protecting you during that time. I swear that, should you win this next game, you'll be the next Prism."

Janus Borig had told Kip he wasn't going to be the next Prism. But she was a Mirror, not a Seer, right?

But Zymun being dealt with? Kip having the authority to be able to defend these islands, without interference?

Maybe Janus had meant Kip would die before he became Prism.

"That's a...tempting prize," Kip said. "I'm guessing you have some truly odious stakes you wish me to offer in return." His chest was tight. He knew this old spider.

"So suspicious, dear grandson." Andross puffed on his zigarro, the ash glowing red with each puff like the evil eye winking at him.

"And...?" Kip said. "What are your stakes?"

"King Ironfist will arrive very soon. He has a young cousin whom he's going to make the Nuqaba. Maybe already has. She's eighteen, maybe nineteen years old. Devout, though everyone knows her dear older cuz will be directing her every move."

"King *Who?*" Kip interrupted.

Andross looked genuinely shocked for a moment. Then a big, toothy-cat grin spread on his face. In the least convincing voice he could probably manage, he said, "Oh, Kip, I'm so sorry. Do you really not know? Have you not heard about it from every tongue in the city? Your old commander's turned traitor."

"Sure. Right. No, he hasn't. Now, what were you saying?"

"This actually depends on you accepting the reality of the situation," Andross said, growing serious.

"I don't see what you gain from that kind of lie," Kip said. "I can check on it in no time, and we've both got things to do."

Andross said, "Not a lie."

"Ironfist wouldn't betray the Chromeria. His brother *died* for me."

"Yes—because of me, as he sees it. And then his insane, treasonous, drug-addled sister the Nuqaba died under mysterious circumstances—which he also blames the Chromeria for."

Rightly, Kip guessed. And just like that, he believed it. He'd changed since he'd left the Chromeria, why wouldn't Ironfist? Andross had stripped him of his position, and then tried to murder him? Oh God. "So he's declared himself *king?*" Kip asked.

"There are places in this world where one is either at the top or dead. Perhaps he believed Paria was one of those. Regardless, we need to bring Paria back into the fold. For the war, and for all the other wars that will follow if we don't."

"You seriously lost Paria? Brilliant leadership, grandfather!"

"And you're going to help me get it back," Andross said, eyes flashing.

"What's this got to do with this girl, Ironfist's cousin or whatever."

"If I win, you marry her."

"Wha—I'm already married."

"Ah." Andross gestured with his zigarro as if Kip had a point, as if it were too bad.

Kip's brow furrowed. What in nine hells? "Not even a promachos can absolve centuries of Magisterial teachings against polygamy, and I can't imagine the Parians would countenance having their Nuqaba be the second wife of anyone."

"Of course not," Andross said blandly.

"You're not suggesting..."

"Ruthgar's fate is tied to ours now. They cannot leave us. Your marriage to Tisis has accomplished what the satrapies required. Now you'll put her aside. Your marriage will be annulled—you were a minor at the time of your oaths, and you both married against the consent of your families. It will simply be acknowledged not to have happened. Rather than lose face, Eirene Malargos will have to pretend it's mutual. Marriage dissolved, excused as the passions of youth, and so forth. No problem. Your failure to produce a child will actually be helpful. A child would have been a complication."

Orholam's agonies. It was exactly what Tisis had predicted, only much earlier than even she had guessed.

"Why would you do this to me?" Kip asked, breath short.

"The Parians have a fleet and the best mundane fighters in the world. We need both. In fact, with what you've told us about the White King's fleet, we now need them both far more than I thought we did just a week ago. And he and his fleet are almost here. If we are to have any hope of victory, Ironfist must be convinced to join us. A man who's declared himself king. A traitor, you understand, must be convinced to make common cause with us, or the empire will end.

"He will demand we recognize him as king. He will want guarantees—and we will be in no position not to give them to him. Naturally, losing Paria would be our fallback position. But better to lose Paria than the whole empire. What I hope to accomplish? Immediate rapprochement with Paria, albeit with special status granted to Ironfist himself for the rest of his life. He will be rewarded with very choice 'presents' at your wedding as 'small symbols of our long love for Paria and its leadership.' Ironfist will be made very wealthy; he will have enough power and the control of his Nuqaba to make sure he isn't betrayed or imprisoned in the future; and we will have saved the empire from this immediate crisis. And if I don't miss my guess, as a wedding gift Ironfist will grant you substantial lands in Paria that the Guiles haven't owned since my grandfather's and great-grandfather's time. You will spend your time between your lands and the major Parian cities, making sure no new rebellion is planned against the empire, and making as much of yourself as you will. When I die, you will take over family Guile, having been given all the advantages I never had.

"Naturally, that's only one way the negotiations may go, but I need to know what cards I have in hand so I can do the best for the Seven Satrapies that may be done, and after that the best I can do for the

Guile family, and after that the best for my grandson's oh-so tender feelings."

"This is disgusting," Kip said.

"This is *survival*, you preening microcephalic baboon! Exactly which part of survival do you object to? Morality's a warm blanket, but it's not worth dying for, and it's useless to the dead. *I* have been the one who's paid the price for our survival until now. *I* have been the one who killed so that others might live, who took the beating sun on my own shoulders so that others might play in my shadow, safe and ignorant and innocent and carefree. Now it's your turn. You want the power? You pay the price."

Kip tried to keep a level voice, tried to speak to Andross in a way he could understand. "You're asking me to go back on my oath."

"I'm asking you to save a million lives with your semen and your tears—and you'd prefer they die instead?"

"I swore Tisis a solemn oath. I—"

"When you swear to do what you don't have the power to do, that makes you a fool, not a liar."

"I swore a hundred times!"

"You swore a hundred times because you knew the keeping of that oath was out of your control. She asked you to because she knew it, too."

Kip's heart was aching already. He was willing to break Tisis with his death but not with his betrayal.

Not even if it saves tens of thousands of lives in this battle alone? Hundreds of thousands or a million eventually?

He said, "You loved Felia, you adored her, she was the heart of your heart. I know she was. Even those who hate you remark that she, *she* was the one thing in this world you loved. Would you have betrayed her? Would you have betrayed her for all the world?"

Andross's face grew still and his eyes, gleaming like iridescent-edged razors, turned inward. "For all the world, Kip, *I did*."

And Kip felt suddenly like a young dandy lecturing an old veteran on the costs of war.

This was war for the fate of the world. This was war as seen from the vantage of politics, with prices paid in grief and private wounds and terrible compromises and personal failures that could cost the deaths of entire families or entire empires. Andross was the high commander, sacrificing units to gain objectives, sending envoys to their deaths on mere slim chances, and making grand gambles that could cost everything. The currencies were different, but what warrior, having cut down an unarmed, fleeing enemy, could say that his way of fighting was cleaner?

If anyone should understand Andross Guile now, it was Kip.

Kip himself had thought Antonius Malargos a limited general for understanding tactics but never strategy. Andross must be looking at him the same way right now.

The old man spoke again, almost gently. "That bit where we'll excuse your first marriage as foolish young love isn't a convenient lie, son. I gave you this year to enjoy life as lesser men may. But this is our yoke. Lesser men give their sweat in labor, give their blood in battle, and give their tears, but their love is their own, if they're strong enough or lucky enough to claim it. Our duties are different from theirs. Our bodies are pampered, but we pay the price with our souls. We belong not to ourselves. All men are brothers in this, all are captives twisted on the rack until the executioner, Life, has wrung all our vital fluids from us: sweat, and blood, and tears from the commons; and blood, luxin, ink, semen, and tears from us.

"We need those ships and those men, grandson. Excellent mundane fighters, against the bane? Who else has a chance? Ironfist's fleet could stop the armada and the bane before they even arrive! And Ironfist likes you. If I tie his family back into ours, we can survive this.

"I'm getting ahead of myself, but naturally, should we survive, you'll have to produce an heir immediately, especially after not producing one with your first wife...but even should Ironfist make the marriage contingent upon children being born to our families, it still buys us a fleet for this week. So after the battle, stop drafting sub-red for a while. Impedes fertility."

Maybe I could go back to Tisis afterward.

No. Her sister Eirene would be too insulted to accept that. And not just Eirene. Tisis understood politics, but she wouldn't understand this. She would never forgive him if he didn't fight for her to the death. Rightly so.

But it wasn't his death he would be fighting to, if he refused this.

It was death for everyone.

Without the Parians, the Chromeria was doomed. Maybe they were doomed even with it. But without it, they didn't have a chance.

But...Tisis!

Kip thought he was going to throw up.

"A wet cloth for your face, my lord?" Grinwoody asked, polite as a handshake from a stable-mucker. Kip hadn't even noticed his return.

"But if I win this game," Kip said, "all those things will still be true. You'll still need the fleet. You'll still want everything else long-term, too."

"I have another grandson to marry off, worse luck for that poor girl. If you win, I'll just have to gamble that with time so pressing, Ironfist won't be able to look too deeply into Zymun's affairs or his character. I had hoped to spend him elsewhere. But I'll have you know: if you win—if you become Prism, things might actually be worse for you. Ironfist might already know about Zymun's character. Then you won't be able to blame me when you put Tisis aside."

"You make this sound like it's all cold intellect and unblinking rationale. It's not."

"Oh?" Andross asked.

"You're *punishing* me."

"Oh, absolutely."

"Why? I brought an army of drafters back here! I've done more for this family than anyone. And more for the Seven Satrapies, too!"

"Your disobedience destroyed my plans," Andross said.

"Your plans were shit! You underestimated me. You thought I was worthless, so you gave me a worthless post as a hostage in Ruthgar's court."

"I don't like to dwell on plans that went nowhere—"

"Because you can't admit that what I did was better. You, O Mighty Andross Guile, you were wrong!"

Andross shook his head slowly. He tamped the ash off his zigarro. Finished his last sip of whiskey, then stopped Grinwoody from pouring him more. "My tea now, I think," he said. Then he looked at Kip once more. "Finished?"

"Yes," Kip said.

He was only delaying the inevitable.

He was going to have to play, wasn't he?

"Then know this," Andross said. "If you'd obeyed me and gone to Eirene Malargos, the Nuqaba would have been obligated to stay another week or month while the preparations for your official wedding to Tisis were made. In that time, with your help—or without it, if you chose to be worthless—that insane bitch who put out Gavin's eye would have been assassinated. Things were arranged so the blame would've fallen on the White King. Regardless, the Parians would have spent the last year united and rallying troops for us. And without that Nuqaba at their doorstep, whom they'd considered untrustworthy and hated and been preparing their defenses against, the Aborneans would've built us another navy. The Parians then would've been deployed on those Abornean ships and circled the satrapies behind the White King—claiming Garriston first, then Ru. That navy would've attacked any supply lines the White King mustered near the coast. The White King would've had to try to deal with that threat. Depending on how many troops the White King sent back from his front lines to deal with that, Blood Forest might not have fallen. But you're right, I was willing to let it fall, to win the war.

"Instead, the Nuqaba lived. And her indecision about whether she was willing to commit treason outright and join the White King ending up freezing Ruthgar, Paria, and Abornea while the White King got stronger everywhere. All that, grandson, is on you. All that happened so you could go play boy soldier. Then Ironfist showed up and took power, and everyone was frozen again, because no one knew which way he would jump.

"So, Kip, you ask if I'm punishing you? The truth is your punishment. If you'd obeyed me, you may well have been stuck in Rath for a year, but there'd be no need now for you to annul your marriage to Tisis. Nor would I have let Eirene treat you like a hostage, much less a prisoner. Do you really think I'd let the world see a Guile disrespected?"

"If you'd told me, I wouldn't have..." Kip said, but he sounded pathetic.

"And you showed me you were trustworthy when?" Andross asked sharply.

In the last year, Kip had begun to feel that he was a somebody. That he had something to contribute. That he was smart, brilliant even. That he'd done good things.

And he had. But they'd been small things, with no understanding of the big picture.

So now he was the author of his own misery. The identities fell from his too-narrow shoulders, and their drawstrings caught about his neck as they fell, strangling him—Kip the Hero, General Kip, Satrap Kip, King Kip. Everything he'd done had made things worse than if he'd done nothing.

How does grandfather do this? How does this man make all my accomplishments look like shit before my own eyes?

And if he can still do this to me—even if it's not fair, and I fear that it is—then does that not, in itself, prove that he is better than I? Ten thousand men might follow me to likely death, but Andross can turn a hundred thousand by his will and word alone.

Who, then, is the greater? Who's smarter? Who's more worthy to lead?

Andross seemed loathsome because he wasn't Gavin Guile. But if this loathsome man could and would save a million lives, what made him loathsome? The dying might march into the grave smiling behind Kip's banners, yet they would still be marching into the grave.

How exactly did that make Kip better than his grandfather?

How we must seem like insects to this man. Kip was a smart

man. He knew that now. Without arrogance, without joking self-deprecation. It was a fact. But Andross Guile was as high above him as a man was over dogs.

By chain, or beatings, or simply by voice and with wagging tail and lolling tongue, in the end, Kip would obey him.

He might as well take the offered treat.

"I'll play," Kip said, and it was a betrayal, and it was inevitable, and it was freedom. "But there's a condition."

Chapter 82

~The Master~
Three years ago. (Age 63.)

"It's over, dear," she says. "We were wrong. Join me in the Freeing this year. Maybe we can find forgiveness for our sins together."

"We just need to hold out," I say, adjusting my dark spectacles even as the sun sinks low on the horizon. "The world needs us."

"So we believed," Felia says quietly.

"The time's fast approaching. We knew what we were in for. Forty years—that's only a few more!"

"So we believed," she says.

"The Lightbringer is to be the greatest man of his era. Who else could it be? Who is greater than I?"

"You are a great man, Andross Guile," she says calmly.

"You're patronizing me."

"Never," she said, and I believe her.

"You're mollifying me, then? Why? Are you *afraid* of me now?"

"It was never your greatness I questioned."

"That? Again? After all these years?! You think me a monster now?"

Her tone sharpens for the first time: "Do you think me a fool? You think you can hide your *eyes* from me? Your wife?"

I look away. "Something can surely be done. I'm not finished yet—"

"Take them off!" she snaps.

I remove the dark lenses, revealing my broken halos.

Her jaw tightens first, but then her mouth quivers.

"It's not—it's not like they say," I say. "It's not madness."

"Of course you would say that. They all do."

"BUT IT'S *ME*!" I roar.

It is exactly the wrong thing to shout when one is a red wight. But she doesn't shrink. Closes her eyes only for a moment. There is no fear or tension on her face when she regards me.

God. She thinks I might kill her. That I really am mad. And yet she shows no fear.

I cannot imagine such courage.

"It's me," I whisper. "I always was special. I always was different. I was meant to do—to, to be ... but somehow it's all gone wrong. This can't be happening. I couldn't—*we* couldn't have been wrong. We worked it out perfectly."

"There's only one man in the world who could have fooled you, my dearest," Felia says.

"If there is, I've not met him," I scoff.

"A man unmirrored indeed," she says quietly. "I meant *you*."

"You think I wanted this? That this was all self-delusion? The hundred prophecies, the, the things we've seen? You think I wanted to do what we've *done*?"

"I think reason is the devil's whore."

"I hate that line. Always have."

"You've always misunderstood it," Felia says. "It doesn't mean reason itself is corrupt. It means we use her to get what we want. *We* are the devil, and our reason is nothing more to us than the means by which we achieve our gratification. There's always a purpose behind the questions we ask, and there's always an answer we're really seeking, even if we keep our preferences secret even from ourselves."

"Now, that is a handy rhetorical bludgeon," I sneer. "I can be accused of being nefarious or deceptive or malign at will. I'm simply so sneaky that I don't even know it myself."

She takes a deep breath. "I don't think you wanted to hurt... anyone."

"I'm not so fragile. You can say his name," I snap. The red is rising in me.

She tries. But a wave of grief goes over her face. Maybe I can say his name, but she can't. She hasn't said Sevastian's name three times since he died.

'Since he died.' Curious that I put it that way. Even in my own mind. I've always put it that way, even when I only *think* about him, don't I?

"I love you, Andross," she says finally.

"I've never doubted that."

529

"You should've. Because I didn't, at first."

"What do you mean? You mean when we courted? Of course you did. I still have your letters. I still have that night at the pyre dances with Ninharissi emblazoned in my mind as with flames."

But the memory doesn't even elicit a smile, though it always has in the past. "No," she says. "I had an instinct about you. I was so young. But somehow, I felt the heart of you, more clearly and instantaneously than I have ever understood another soul in all my life. Perhaps Orholam Himself gave me a special *charism*. Or a burden. For I didn't choose you blindly. That's my curse. I chose this. When my father put you off for an entire week? We made up all that stuff about Ninharissi later, after it was taking me too long. We did it because we worried it would sabotage the start of our marriage, and make you think twice about me."

"What?!" I ask.

"Did you really think my father became the richest man in the empire by being an affable goof who laughed too much at his own jokes like a simpleton? Or that my mother was the boozy, brazen older lady susceptible to a bit of flattery? Andross, come on. We Dariushes are oranges all. Even my little brother fooled you."

"What? He was eight years old!"

"He said you seemed to think he ought to be quite impressed with some knickknack you drafted for him. A bat or something? He tried to be polite, but thought you were a bit daft."

"It was a dragon, and it breathed fire! And I swore that little shit to secrecy." I'm suddenly glad he's dead. Little fucker. I hope he was inside the palace when they torched it.

Of course, I can't say any of that aloud. I can't tell Felia anything she'll find wight-ish.

Gods fucking in a fire, what am I going to do if she threatens to report my current state? One look at my eyes and... The law's the law. That law applies even to men normally above it. It's the one law that can't be bought or bent. Voluntarily or not, wights must die. All the Chromeria's power rests on that plank.

She goes on. "I asked my father to put you off while I went to sit vigil, to ask what Orholam intended for me."

"I thought that was when I was still on my way."

"I try to wrap the little deceptions in as much truth as possible, so I don't have to worry so much about slipping later on. I haven't got your memory."

I say, "I figured that was simply a good way to go party with your
friends for a while."

"If by 'party' you mean 'pray,' and by 'friends' you mean Janus Borig."

Janus Borig, one of my least favorite people. "The Mirror. That lying bitch."

"Are you so surprised a Mirror should deceive?"

"Did she lie to *you*?" I ask. "Or was I special in that, too?"

"Never to me," Felia says. "She confirmed that I was right about you."

"Right about what?" I ask gruffly.

"That you were unstoppable. That you would become the most powerful man in the world one day. That if any impediment stopped you from proving yourself peerless, you would smash it. That you would not be a Prism, but you would be a promachos one day. And that if you couldn't rise within the structures of the Seven Satrapies, you would go outside them and rise regardless and take vengeance on all who stopped you. That you were a bad man, but one who had goodness in him. Goodness, we both hoped, that might grow."

"You did tell me you were afraid of me, that night," I say.

"'Afraid' was the most tepid and colorless word I could find for how I felt about you," she says.

"Thank you for that, dear. That is a story I could have gone down to the grave not knowing. Lovely that you share it now. Thank you."

"I fell for you soon after that," she says mournfully. "I did. Even though I could never claim real ignorance about what I was doing. I didn't know what awaited us, but I knew who I was getting into it with."

"You believed in me. And you loved me from the beginning. This is the raving of an old woman. You're losing your mind. I can't hold it against you. I don't. Age is a cruel matron. You're saying things that have never been true."

"You think me senile? Me?! *I'm* the mad one? Not you, the wight?"

"You wouldn't have approved of the things we did if you hadn't believed. You wouldn't have joined me in them."

"Andross, I didn't love you so much I wanted to take over the world with you. I loved the world so much that when you did, I wanted to be there to keep you from destroying it."

"You believed in what we're doing. I know you did."

"Maybe I did. For surely the Lightbringer must be a man unstoppable. And then I fell in love with you, and I justified everything. I made my reason a whore. If you were the greatest man ever, that made me the right hand of the greatest man ever. That made *me* special. That justified my sins, my suffering. Whatever was good for us was surely for the good of all. It is the same convenient deception the powerful so often believe. And for it, I know I'll answer. But it didn't matter what I believed. Not really. The Lightbringer might be greater than Lucidonius himself, so of course you would believe that person must be you. Lightbringer! Ha! You went to Lucidonius's statue and wept, because by the time he was your age, he'd conquered the world. You think you're the Lightbringer because you couldn't bear to stand in another man's shadow! You needed it. You need it still. The text of every prophecy was illuminated by that need in you. How many prophecies did we skip as incomprehensible or decide were clearly not authoritative or corrupted because they didn't fit you?"

She's trembling with rage that should be mine.

If there's proof that breaking the halo doesn't necessarily make one a wight, it is this: she raves; I listen.

"Look at you!" she shouts, despite those that might hear through these walls. "You've gone *wight*! You think that's bringing light? It's over! We deluded ourselves!"

"You think I don't know that?!" I shout, flinging a crystal decanter to shatter against the wall.

But she goes on, heedless, voice cracking. "We sacrificed our boys for our ambition. We *murdered* our sons! Our own sons!"

"Felia, stop it! Stop it!"

"My sons, Andross. My *sons*. Better I had put them in pagans' fires as babes. Sevastian! God curse me, all these years gone and I still see his sweet, trusting face every time I close my eyes!"

There is no answer.

"We sold our souls for this wretched dream. We sacrificed our sons with our own hands. Our beautiful boys. To our pride. Not just yours, Andross. Mine too. I thought I was part of something so important, but we're nothing but schemers. We're just like everyone else. You hold on to whatever you need to, but I'm finished. I deserve death, and I will have it. I will join the Freeing this year," she says. She's been bringing this up for five years. But this time is different.

"I forbid it."

"If you stop me, I'll reveal what you are. I want my own apartments, Andross. Immediately. I won't share a room with you anymore. Your face is as revolting to me as a bloody mirror."

Chapter 83

Andross had already been extending a pair of decks toward Kip, and his eyebrows dipped, lips tightened. "Yes?"

Kip's heart had leapt into his throat.

'You won't be the next Prism,' Janus Borig had told him. But was she telling him—or was she steering him? But Kip wasn't so worried about whether the prophecy was predicting the future or forming it; he was wondering how it could help him.

Like, if I play to become the next Prism, I'll definitely lose. But if I play for stakes *other than becoming the next Prism*, maybe I can win? But how could the outcome of the game be affected by the choice of the stakes? It was the same game, and Kip certainly wasn't going to play differently depending on what he won; he had too much to lose to give it anything less than his best regardless. It didn't make any sense.

And Andross was the cold, unblinking master of Nine Kings. He wouldn't play differently, either.

Unless... unless the stakes were high enough to rattle even Andross Guile.

"Please," Andross said languidly. He sipped his almond tea. He didn't offer Kip any. "Take your time. I've no other pressing matters to attend to while you sit there in uffish thought."

Janus Borig had said something else that night she died, hadn't she? Not just 'You won't be Prism.'

"If I win, I don't want to be named Prism; I want you to publicly acknowledge me as the Lightbringer."

The teacup hovered halfway to Andross's mouth. His lower eyelids tensed and his eyebrows moved almost imperceptibly—merely surprise, or was that fear?—then his lips narrowed and his eyes tightened, back into an expression Kip had seen before.

"Now, that was interesting," Kip the Lip said. "Why would you be afraid of that?"

The anger hardened. "Not 'afraid.' It's certainly audacious. I guess you learned something about overawing your opponents when you demanded to be made satrap in Dúnbheo. Well done. It won't work here."

"My God," Kip said, ignoring him. "You think *you're* the Lightbringer!"

The stricken look on Andross's face was priceless. And it was   533 confirmation. Kip was so surprised, he laughed aloud and clapped his hands.

Andross's face went black. He banged down his teacup and snatched up a pistol and bolted out of his seat, sending his chair crashing. He cocked the jaw and pointed the pistol at Kip's upturned face. His hand trembled.

Kip looked at him, serene.

Andross's finger lifted from the trigger. He lowered the cockjaw, clearing his throat. Then he put the pistol back down on the table and sat in the chair, which Grinwoody had put back in place.

Grinwoody mopped up a bit of spilled tea.

"Yes, I do," Andross said. "Forty years of preparations, and gathering prophecies, and sacrificing...everything. Everything, that I might save our empire, and our very world. Well done, Kip, you have found me out. I daresay not even Grinwoody had guessed it. Had you, Grinwoody?" he asked, turning to him.

"No, my lord. I stand in awe, sir, that one could possibly conceal something so profound about one's identity from the person at your very shoulder." The slave bowed deeply, respectfully.

"But...but you're not even a full-spectrum polychrome," Kip said. This he hadn't meant to say aloud.

"Am I not?" Andross asked.

"Holy shit," Kip breathed. "You kept yourself from drafting half your colors for forty years?!"

"It was the least of my sacrifices, I assure you. But—" He raised a finger suddenly, as if to forestall questions about what the other sacrifices were. "But I'll admit that it's not escaped my attention that there are certain ways of reading the prophecies that could indicate you are he, and certain qualifications that you currently lack might, after all, not emerge until you're older. I've thought about this no small amount. So...yes. Yes, should you win, I will begin paving the way immediately; I will protect you; and I will fully champion you the moment you're ready to announce your identity—in the unlikely event it's not immediately apparent to the whole world."

"Wait..." Kip said. "Just like that?" He'd imagined getting a little more pushback. "I'm asking you to tell everyone I'm the most important person in history, not you. And you're okay with playing a game for that? A single game. Where I could get lucky."

"I think luck shall have very little to do with it," Andross said.

"I'm asking you to wager everything you've spent forty years pursuing," Kip said, though he wasn't sure why he was arguing against his own case. "That's like twice as long as I've even been alive."

534

The irony of Kip taking his side evidently wasn't lost on him, as Andross suddenly smiled. "There is now nothing in the world that could keep me from this game, and this wager. For you see, I won't be playing against you, Kip. I'll be playing against Orholam Himself. For the answer to the question 'Who is the Lightbringer?' is not a name; it's not a man or a woman. The answer to that question answers how Orholam interacts with the world—if He does so at all.

"I'm asking you to wager the most important thing in your life," Andross said. "It's only fair that you demand the same of me. Grinwoody, the decks."

Kip sat stunned, silent. There were too many questions—what prophecies did Andross know that Kip didn't? If he were a full-spectrum polychrome, why had he had Kip View cards for him? What did this all mean?—but the cards were in front of him now, and those questions would have to wait. He had to win first.

Shaking himself, breathing deeply, Kip began studying the play decks Andross had constructed mostly from Janus Borig's new cards.

He looked up. "You didn't."

"Seemed appropriate," Andross said.

The old man had constructed decks to reflect the coming fight. There weren't enough legendary characters who'd earned their own cards to fill two entire decks, but he'd done as well as he could. Plenty of wights on the one side, the White King, drafters aplenty, lots of ships, and seven bane. "Six bane?" Kip suggested.

"Your people may have only seen six, but I believe superviolet will show up. That Danavis girl has a way of doing her own thing. In the last months, I've had reports from Aslal, Smussato, Cravos, Wiwurgh, Garriston, and Ru of a woman matching her description, traveling alone, with no obvious transportation. The ravishing fairy princess in white and gold with amethyst eyes. Not the color of amethyst, but with jewels crusted over her very eyes themselves. And at the joints of her fingers, in some later accounts. Always inspecting old ruins. And the prophecies suggest seven will come."

Kip felt sick. He believed it. No matter what she'd told Kip, he'd held on to some small hope that she was going to stay out of the battle, that she hadn't forgotten herself completely.

"We could've been a good team, you and I," Kip said, finishing up with the White King's deck.

"Pick a deck," Andross said impatiently. "Ah, one moment." He grabbed the Chromeria's deck before Kip could pick it up and snatched out a card, handing it to Grinwoody. "Won't be needing this."

"What was that?"

"Gavin's card. Since you established he's not coming back in time, if he ever does."

"I'd like to see that card," Kip said.

"Really, right now?" Andross said. "It's not an original. You can't View it."

"Oh. Right. I . . . later, then."

"If you win," Andross said.

"That weakens the deck," Kip said. Certainly his father's card would have to have been a powerful one.

"Then pick the other deck, moron. Hurry it up. I've got other things to do today."

"So, just to clarify, the stakes are my remarriage against your full support—"

"No, not your remarriage only. Your full obedience in all things until I die," Andross said. "Against my full support, until I die. All you want, against all you have," Andross said. "Isn't that the wager life always offers?"

"Agreed," Kip heard his voice say. "More liquor, calun."

As Grinwoody poured for him, Kip turned the next card of the Chromeria deck, and chuckled. "Now, that's a good one. After all you said about him, you gave the Chromeria Ironfist?"

"Without Gavin, the Chromeria needs Ironfist, or it loses every time." Andross rubbed his nose for a moment. "Think of Nine Kings as an aid to thinking, the way an abacus is an aid to arithmetic. At some point one should grow beyond the need for the physical prop, but the cards are actually best for those like you, who have difficulty looking at their friends and seeing them as a list of strengths and weaknesses—you, who would vacillate before spending two lives even if their deaths are necessary to forestall ten thousand more. This is why Nine Kings is more valuable for you, but I am better at it, and better at politics as well."

"What you miss," Kip said, "is that my friends will fight for me in ways they would never fight for you. When led by one they know loves them, they perform better than a number on a card could possibly capture. Everything that is most important about this game can't be captured by a game."

"Then you take the Chromeria deck," Andross said. "Perhaps the cards will fight *extra hard* for you."

Kip shouldn't have let him get away with that, shouldn't have let him get under his skin. The Chromeria was clearly the inferior deck, but his victory would be all the sweeter when he shoved Andross's nose in it like pressing a dog's nose to his shit.

536

It was a mistake, and Kip knew it, but he couldn't stop himself. "Fine, I'll take it."

Andross separated the decks and shuffled them under Kip's watchful eyes.

Kip reshuffled and let Andross cut both decks.

The old man smirked. "It takes years to become a proficient cardist."

"With your memory?" Kip asked.

"It's the dexterity that's challenging as one ages, and finding the time for the continual practice."

It was as close to an admission as Kip was likely to hear. "How many times have you cheated me that way?" Kip asked.

"You think I had to cheat, before?"

"Had to?" Kip said. "No. But you're the kind of man who likes to guarantee victory, aren't you?"

"I'm also a man who likes a challenge."

"No doubt the only reason I'm still alive," Kip said as they dealt out their cards.

"There are others."

"Oh, pray tell," Kip said lightly.

Andross waved it away, studying his cards instead.

"Huh, would you look at that," Kip said. "Never realized it before, but the Ironfist card actually has a perfect empty place for 'King' to be written in. The other cards don't have that spacing. It can't be an accident." Actually, Kip's hand had a nice collection of earlier attack soldiers and defenders, but it needed a noontime striker like Ironfist.

Andross gave him a disbelieving look. "You're trying to get into *my* head?"

"Me?" Kip said. "Just making conversation. I think you've radically underestimated the power of this deck."

Andross played a Pagan Priest, and Kip had to respond with a Lightguard—boy did that stick in his craw, using those bastards. "Odd that those cards don't come with a betrayal mechanic," Kip said. "Limitations of the game, I guess."

"I've found them quite loyal where they should be."

"Really? Is Aram still sucking at Zymun's teat?" Kip asked.

"Oh, yes," Andross said. "He much preferred to report to me secretly on what Zymun is doing than be executed for his little indiscretion."

'His little indiscretion'? Setting the Lightguard on Kip and murdering Goss, rather than letting them escape, was an *indiscretion*?

537

"If I punch you in the face, do I lose automatically?" Kip asked.

Andross merely considered him with his dead, shark's eyes.

"Aram's men murdered a friend of mine," Kip said. "One of the Lightguards demanded to see me, and Goss said he was me. They shot him. No other words spoken. So I know all this is a game to you, but you can go fuck yourself."

"You want justice for that? Fine. These are small matters for men such as us. Tell you what: as a gesture of goodwill, I'll execute the man who pulled the trigger, and Aram too. Done and done. The triggerman immediately. Aram's an officer too difficult to replace on the eve of a battle, but if he lives through the battle, he'll be hanged next week."

Orholam's balls, but Andross Guile was cold.

"I don't know what my problem is," Kip said. "I've spent a lot of time with you now. You've hit me, you've stolen things from me, you've cheated me, you've threatened to enslave my friend, your people have tried to murder me several times—"

"Only once on my orders," Andross said, "but do go on."

"And yet I still keep trying to engage you as if you had a soul. Why is that? I'm not usually a stupid man. When I spent a little time with Zymun, I knew instantly that he was all serpent. He's one of those people incapable of the higher human emotions. He's defective. Born crippled, if you will. Soulless. It's not really his fault, is it? He could never be much better than he is. He sees what he wants, and he can't help but try to take it. But you... you don't have that excuse. If you're a monster, you made yourself monstrous. You had a choice. More than one, I'd bet. And you chose darkness every time. I should hate you to the depths of my soul, and yet I don't. I actually like you, and I'm stuck here wondering, is that because you still have that preternatural Guile charm that I really wish I'd inherited, or is it because somehow you're my blind spot, or is it because intuitively, beyond all rationale, I see some spark of life deep in you? You should have been more than a great man; you should have been a good man."

"Your turn."

They played the next few turns in silence.

Andross was playing slowly. It wasn't like him. It was, however, a good strategy when your deck is significantly stronger—

There was a sharp rap on the wall. Grinwoody announcing someone.

And then Kip saw that Andross really was running the game as a simulation of the battle to come. The old man wouldn't attack until noon, when he could play a bane, just as the White King wasn't

538   attacking until Sun Day.

Andross really thought he was going to get some insight about the battle from this.

"High Lord, there's someone here to see you," Grinwoody said.

Andross's lip curled. "Grinwoody, I didn't think that you could possibly fail to understand what this game means. Or what 'I'm not to be disturbed' means."

"It's Satrap Corvan Danavis, my lord."

"What?! How did he get here so fast?"

"Upon your command that you not be disturbed, I turned away the messenger bringing news his ships had been spotted, and also the messenger who announced Danavis was coming directly here. You've been cloistered for quite some time."

"Grinwoody." There was a warning in Andross's tone.

"My apologies, my lord," Grinwoody said. "I'll show him in immediately."

Andross bundled his cards back together, squared the edges, and laid them facedown on the table. He put his teacup on them, and drew on his zigarro while Kip followed his lead, each watching the other closely to make sure neither took advantage of the disruption to cheat. Then they both rose and moved away from the table, each giving it a wide berth, and for the same reason.

"Kip!" Corvan cried out when he saw him.

Kip's heart warmed instantly. Kip knew a lot of people who'd changed monumentally in the last two or three years, but Corvan was almost exactly the same—except he'd grown out his mustache and hung little gold beads into it, as he'd worn it long years ago before he'd moved to Rekton. In a world of friends and foes as shifting as the mists, he was solid. Here was a man who was simply himself, whose idea of hiding his identity had been moving away and shaving off his famed mustache, without even changing his name. His eyes held the same old mix of sternness and contentment, with an undertone of abiding grief, but there were no regrets there. He looked strong.

They embraced, and Kip felt like a child again for half a moment. Except now he was taller than his old guardian.

"I hear those books you kept pilfering from my shelves have done you some good," Corvan said as he released Kip. "Though I've not heard a tactician's account of the Battle of Dúnbheo yet. Everything I hear is all giant bears and last-second traps and magic."

"I'll be happy to fill you in," Kip said, letting the man turn to the promachos.

"Satrap Danavis," Andross said respectfully. "Welcome to the Chromeria. We are so sorry to hear about your bereavement."

539

"I received your funerary gifts. They helped ease my burdens, Promachos. Thank you."

Andross gestured that it was nothing.

"Now I feel like an asshole for not sending anything," Kip said. "I'm sorry, sir. I only found out you'd even remarried at the same time I heard of your wife's passing—yesterday. I'm so sorry."

"They were the best days of my life," Corvan said. "And we knew they would be short. She told me all along, though she couldn't guess the details until recently. An assassin from the Order of the Broken Eye, we both believe."

"From the Order?!" Kip demanded, irate.

"A Seer is most dangerous to the most dangerous people," Corvan said.

"Grandfather, you didn't hire them for that, did you?" Kip asked.

The air suddenly tingled as if they were all waiting for a bolt to strike and its thunderhead to blow out all the windows.

"No," Andross said coolly.

"Oh, good," Kip said. "He had to be thinking it, and I thought it would be good for him to see your face when I asked. I thought he might be too polite to ask."

"On the matter of my wife, I wouldn't let etiquette—or anything—get in the way of my vengeance," Corvan said.

"I only ask," Kip said, "since you've had such a good working relationship with the Order in the past."

Again, the clouds boiled, but no thunderbolt struck.

"When one is in power, one must frequently deal with unsavory elements," Andross said, "worse than assassins, even. Which is why sometimes one must hold one's nose and deal even with traitors. But that doesn't make one a traitor oneself, does it, Corvan?"

Corvan Danavis was quivering with the effort to contain himself. "A traitor? You refer to King Ironfist, I suppose?"

"He brought you here, didn't he?"

"I've arrived here with an army, just in time, from what I hear. Without Ironfist's fleet, we'd not be arriving for another two months."

"Has your army disembarked, then?" Andross asked.

"No. I came on ahead. The White seemed eager that I should see the state of the defenses immediately—"

"And *King* Ironfist doubtless told you to go on ahead."

"Yes," Corvan said.

"Without your soldiers. Who are isolated on their own ships, perhaps? Ships disarmed, ostensibly so they have room for more soldiers?" Andross suggested.

Corvan froze as the implications dawned on him. "He... he wouldn't."

"You've not brought us an army, Satrap," Andross said. "You've brought Ironfist ten thousand hostages. You were right, Grinwoody. All his years serving at the highest level, and Ironfist has no loyalty at all."

"It grieves me to be right," Grinwoody said. "He is of my own tribe, my lord."

"Well, we'll deal with all that presently," Andross said. "First things first."

"He's disembarking himself to negotiate the surrender," Corvan said. "Or... at least that's what he told me."

"He meant it. Only, he didn't mean *his surrender*," Andross said icily.

Corvan cursed under his breath.

"But he's disembarking? When? Soon?" Kip asked. "Shit! We've got to finish this game quickly, grandfather. I've got to make sure my commander doesn't find out Ironfist's here."

"I don't imagine King Ironfist will have any trouble with one of your puppies," Andross said.

"This one he might," Kip said.

"You're in the middle of something?" Corvan asked. "I'm sorry I interrupted with such bad news. You're in the middle of... a game?" He didn't bother to conceal a note of disbelief.

"Hardly," Kip said, "but please stay. That is, if you don't mind watching."

"I'd be delighted to see the era's greatest mind at work."

"Thank you—" Kip and Andross said at the same time. They even sort of inclined their heads the same way. That was weird. Kip hadn't been around this man at all growing up.

The blood is strong.

Corvan said, "Your pardon, my lords, a slip of the tongue. 'Greatest *minds*.'"

"After I win," Kip said, "I'd like to go over some ideas on the Jaspers' defense with you."

They took their seats, Grinwoody having already scuttled about on his little roach legs to provide a chair for the satrap.

Kip brushed the art on the cards with his fingertips in frustration. He had to settle for playing a Lightguard, though the sun was high enough he could have played a more powerful card if he'd had it.

Andross played the Red Bane.

Kip flopped Cannon Island onto the table. "This deck isn't good enough. If Janus Borig had had time to complete—"

"No sniveling," Andross said. "You had first choice of decks."

"Here I could have been king of Blood Forest," Kip muttered.

"I think we've had quite enough of kings," Andross said. He dropped another bane, and attacked.

Kip didn't defend, soaking up the damage like he was the damned Turtle-Bear.

"Why isn't there a Turtle-Bear card?" Kip asked suddenly. Surely he had to be important enough to get a card, right?

"A what?" Andross asked, not that interested.

"Come on, you were looking at it earlier." Kip put down his cards, pushing his chair back. He showed off his tattoo. Swapping spectacles of various colors, he quickly worked through the superviolet, which gave the edges their nice borders, then as he drew in blue light, zig-zags of blue shot through his forearm, just above the wrist. A rounded rectangle. Kip drew green, and color suffused the outlines. Yellow, and the colors gained richness.

Corvan Danavis inhaled sharply. "What did you call that card?" he asked.

Kip ignored him until he finished, and the tattoo stood sharp and clear on his forearm. "Turtle-Bear. I'm the Turtle-Bear," Kip said.

"Where did you get that?" Andross asked easily.

"Fighting Abaddon," Kip said, as if it were a small thing. "Like I told you."

"The art style's Atashian, isn't it?" Corvan asked. "I recognize that creature, though I've never heard it called a turtle-bear."

"What *have* you heard it called?" Kip asked, though now, in look-ing at it, it seemed different than he remembered. The Turtle-Bear that had been seared into his arm had been a fat, round little thing, furry in all the wrong places, awkward as Kip himself. Now it seemed elongated, stronger, not nearly so ridiculous, like a juvenile...

"My maternal grandmother was Atashian," Corvan said. "She had this ancient brooch that looked like that. She told me Atashians believed men were born with two natures. One was usually symbol-ized by the monkey: the chattering dung-flingers of the forest—social, passionate, but all-reliant on the tribe, attacking those the group dis-liked without an independent thought in their heads, warm, caretak-ing, but always looking to the group for approval. The other nature was usually symbolized by the snake: cold, dispassionate, patient in ambush, not shaken from the truth by anyone or anything, but also uncaring, heartless, rejecting company heedlessly. They believed that only when one brought these natures together, not lukewarm but cold and hot in the appropriate times, fur and scale, could one be truly wise. Only by bringing the contrary animal natures together could one become fully human, whether monkey and snake, or dog and scorpion, or turtle and bear. And the greatest of these become dragons."

"A Dragon would be helpful now," Kip said lightly. He looked at Andross Guile, who was watching cold as an asp. "Don't suppose you've got a Dragon in the deck I missed?"

Andross's eyes glittered darkly.

"Luxin-reactive tattoo dyes. A nice parlor trick," Andross said. "An art lost long ago. We'll talk about who in Blood Forest holds this secret, if we live long enough. In the meantime, let's finish the game, shall we? Here, this will drain your excess luxin."

Andross handed Kip a little cylinder much like the testing sticks used in the Threshing. Kip pressed his finger firmly on the black point and watched his colors swirl down into the stick's bone-white body. Unlike the ivory of the testing sticks, though, here the colors dyed the stick fully their color and then faded in turn, swirling away like smoke.

They all waited until every color was gone, and then a few more seconds.

Without looking up, Andross said, "Grinwoody. The integrity of our game is intact?"

"Absolutely, my lord. I watched most carefully."

Andross picked up his own deck and motioned that Kip could do the same.

Kip picked up his cards.

He had two turns left before Andross won. No more stalling.

Andross played another bane. That he appeared to have an insurmountable lead wasn't slowing him down.

Kip supposed he could should feel flattered for that.

He did not feel flattered.

Andross pushed his eligible cards forward to attack Kip's sad selection of defenders. Cannon Island could take out the Blue Bane but would be destroyed. Kip's Lightguards and galleys couldn't stop the other bane, and any of the Lightning cards Kip might have could only take out a few of Andross's galleys, which was pointless.

The game was over. Kip was dead. He was going to lose everything.

Kip didn't lay down his cards, though. He played two Lightning cards, killing the attacking galleys.

"Petty," Andross said.

Still not touching any of the cards, Kip said, "I block the Blue Bane with Cannon Island. Oh, and I block the Red Bane and Dagnu with Ironfist."

There was no Ironfist on the table. Everyone stopped for a moment, then double-checked to see if there had been some mistake.

"I see he has an interesting Rage mechanic that kicks in when he defends against a superior attack."

Everyone in the room looked at Kip like he was mad.

Check it yourself, Kip wanted to say. But you don't tell your prey how good the meat in the trap will taste. You let the bloody scent in the air do the convincing.

"That card's a Lightguard," Andross said.

"Oh, but he's fighting *extra hard* for me," Kip said archly, and he thought, like Súil did.

If there was one thing Andross Guile couldn't stand, it was condescension.

The old Red angrily snatched up the card in his hand, and the trap snicked shut. His fingers broke the delicate layers of luxin across the face of the card, shattering the spiderweb-thin portrait of a Lightguard that Kip had copied with paryl and then laid atop Ironfist's portrait.

"This is—" The old man went wide-eyed as he saw Ironfist staring out of the card. He was uncomprehending for a long, long moment. "This is impossible," he breathed.

"I believe my Ironfist kills off both of your bane and your Dagnu," Kip said. "Good round for me. Shall we—"

Andross held up a finger. "Grinwoody?" he hissed without turning.

"My lord," Grinwoody's voice trembled. "He hasn't touched that card since he played it. I swear. He has no sleeves. The number of cards remaining in his deck is correct. I..."

But Andross's eyes tightened. He sniffed. Then he wafted the card toward his nose. The luxin scent, tiny as it was, must not have dissipated fully. "You cheated," he said. "You're disqualified. You lose."

"I did nothing disallowed by the rules."

"You substituted a card!" Andross said.

"No, I played it legally at noon. Nor did I announce it as anything other than it was," Kip said. "Some men simply don't look under the surface to see things as they truly are, grandfather."

"You little fuck!" Andross jumped to his feet.

"So help me, if you hit me—" Kip started.

"What? What will you do?" Andross demanded.

"The question isn't what I'll do," Kip said.

Andross's eyes twitched tight. Then he glanced at Corvan.

Corvan hadn't moved, but he sat with the languid grace of a killer.

"Whose play will he back, grandfather? Corvan practically raised me. How much loyalty have *you* inspired in him? Grinwoody was so intent on the game, did he search the satrap before he came in? Thoroughly?"

Corvan leaned to one side, and a large pocket on his cloak seemed to gape open a bit; it held something heavy.

A vein throbbed in Andross's neck as he mastered himself. "Then let's finish the game. I've got a chance yet." He dropped a musket on one of his wights. It left each player with a sliver of life.

Kip drew a Blackguard and dropped it onto the table. With a Blackguard backing him, Ironfist was able to attack twice.

"And that's game," Andross said, his voice tight, his eyes unfocused. "You win, and you may have doomed us all."

"Nice playing you, too. Let's never do it again," Kip said.

"Get out of my sight before I do something red," Andross said, not looking up.

Kip and Corvan left, with Kip expecting a musket ball between his shoulder blades at every step.

Outside the door, Cruxer was nowhere to be seen. Dammit.

The satrap looked at Kip appreciatively. "Slipping an Ironfist in under your opponent's guard." Corvan shook his head. "That was subtler work than Gavin would've even attempted."

"My father's a colossus. I'm a flea in his shadow," Kip said. He still couldn't believe what had happened.

"He has no greater supporter, but I recall Gavin Guile building the mammoth Brightwater Wall in five days yet still failing to change the fate of one small city. You, on the other hand, may have changed the whole world by drafting a portrait I could cover with my thumb. That is not the work of a flea, Kip. That's the work of a *dragon*."

Chapter 84

"Quiet," Ben-hadad said as they paced out the circle of Wrath/Mercy halfway up the Prism's Tower.

Walking ahead of Teia, Quentin froze in place. She ran into him, losing her grip of paryl and shimmering back into visibility.

She looked around quickly, but there was no one in the halls. "Sorry," she whispered.

"What is it?" Quentin whispered to Ben.

Ben looked at them both quizzically. "It's...quiet?" Ben-hadad said. "Oh, you both thought—no, I didn't mean for you to be quiet."

"Oh," Quentin said, straightening. "Yeah, I don't like to bother anyone, so I memorized when the various lectures and special events are in session so I can encounter the fewest people possible."

"For all the levels?" Teia asked. "Not just where your room is?"

"Well, I didn't know when I might need to drop in someplace else, and I already had the scheduling book..."

"Of course," Teia said. "Totally logical." When your brain is the size of a watermelon.

"I thought we'd like to avoid people as well," Quentin said. "Though with all the preparations for the defenses and for Sun Day itself tomorrow, there are more people about than usual."

"They aren't still having the parade, are they?" Teia asked.

"Of course they are," Quentin said. "There's tens of thousands of terrified pilgrims in the city. You want to take away the one thing that will give them hope? Plus, we don't know for sure if an attack will even come tomorrow. Honoring Orholam first might seem like the worst idea militarily, but there are a lot of us who think it's the best idea. Naturally, there have been some compromises on the parade route and the disposition of drafters. It will be the least, shall we say, lavish Sun Day celebration in many years."

"Worst Sun Day ever, you mean," Ben-hadad said, shooing them forward to walk once more, silently counting out his paces.

"On the contrary," Quentin said.

"How so?" Ben asked. "Fourteen more paces, I think."

"A pagan invasion, on Sun Day itself? Where we have scant hope of victory?" Quentin asked.

"Yeah," Teia said. "We're agreed on that much."

"It seems to me such a time is precisely when Orholam must show His power."

"Or else we're fucked," Ben-hadad said.

"Yes! So He *will* show His power."

Teia and Ben both looked at Quentin like he was out of his mind. Ben shook his head.

"Three more paces."

Quentin said, "I'm not saying I'm eager for the—"

Ben said, "I don't know where you found this guy, Teia, but—"

"What do you mean, where *I* found him?!" Teia said, and then stopped at an unfamiliar voice.

"Teia?" a girl repeated, looking straight at Teia. In front of them was a discipula, carrying a mop and bucket. She wore her hair in a bun with flyaways everywhere, was maybe fourteen years old, and looked even younger.

They had never met, Teia was sure of it.

"Teia Darksight?" the girl said.

"Huh?" Teia asked. A flash of fear shocked her like a flash grenade. She'd thought herself quite nondescript.

"You're Teia Darksight," the girl said, wide-eyed.

"Oh dear," Quentin said.

"O's itchy bung!" Ben-hadad said. He flowed forward just as the girl squeaked and brought her hands up to her cheeks, dropping her bucket.

Ben-hadad snatched the mop bucket out of midair and popped the handle of the mop back up into his hand with a dextrous flick of his cane. Teia had almost forgotten that for all of his technical genius, Ben-hadad had made it through Blackguard training, too.

"It *is* you!" the girl said, paying no attention to Ben-hadad or the impressive feat of dexterity he'd just performed.

Maybe not fourteen yet, then, part of Teia thought. Ben-hadad was annoyingly handsome.

But another part of her was already doing what was necessary. Paryl shot from Teia's fingertips and into the girl's chest. In a moment, Teia had the knot ready to slam home to sever the nerves that told the heart to beat.

She'd loused up. She'd let herself feel at home here, in the building that had once been her home. And now she had to kill this girl. This pale, wispy thing, all knees and elbows and big baby eyes and crooked teeth, mopping the halls as punishment for some mild transgression— this girl had to die. An hour ago she'd probably been jabbering complaints about this harsh magister or that reading that was way too hard.

That was just and right; it was as it should be.

Every painful stage of life is dictated by nature to make a woman. But nature's abortions are frequent and rude. Today, this girl would be one more civilian dead in a centuries-long war that only Teia could end. A necessary corpse. One innocent, who had to be killed because you couldn't trust an entire war's outcome to the discretion of a fourteen-year-old. An innocent, murdered because Teia had loused up. Teia had killed innocents before, but those had been innocents she'd been forced to kill. This was forced only by her own error. She'd let down her guard.

A woman like her could never, ever let her guard down.

This girl was innocent, but was her life worth so much more than a slave's life?

"Teia *Darksight*?" Ben-hadad asked. And Teia realized it had only been an instant that she'd stood paralyzed with the killing threads in her hands.

"Don't you know?" the girl asked. "She's the first paryl drafter in centuries!"

"No, she's not," Ben-hadad said, puzzled. "There've been a doz—"

"But everyone knows her! Mistress Teia, will you show me—"

Flaring her eyes to their fullest spooky black, Teia roared aloud at her. It was a cry of a damned soul. It was every old warrior's plaint, every penitent's wail.

But she did what had to be done.

The young girl squeaked and bolted.

"Subtle, T," Ben-hadad said. "I'm sure she won't tell any of her friends about meeting you now."

But Teia barely heard the jibe.

Ben-hadad didn't know.

He didn't know how bad this was. They hadn't had that long together. She hadn't gone into specifics. He didn't know the stakes. He thought they were just messing around in areas where maybe someone might realize they shouldn't be.

"Subtle...T," he continued. "I think you've got a new nickname! Subtle T!"

"Is this the door?" she asked. Subtle T was exactly the kind of name that could stick. It sounded laudatory to outsiders, but could either be praise or a quiet mock among comrades.

It made her miss the Mighty. These damn boys. It made her miss her old life.

Patch or no patch, she could never be part of the Mighty now. It was a fantasy to think she could ever pick up where she'd left off.

She'd never stopped to think what would happen after she took down the Order, had she? It had seemed such an impossibility, her mind had simply refused to go further.

There was no further.

But enough of that now. Teia had to be present, had to be sharp. Enough of thinking about that girl—that poor, innocent girl who would tire in a few minutes as her heart was slowly starved of blood, who would go lie down to nap and never rise.

"Yeah, this should be it," Ben-hadad said.

Silently, Quentin was staring at Teia. She hadn't told Quentin about everything she could do now, but Quentin knew.

Ben knocked on a door.

"What are you going to do if someone answers?" Teia asked.

"Hadn't thought that far ahead," he said. But he flicked down his blue lenses, and his hand filled with a blob of blue luxin.

The dread sat heavier and heavier in Teia's stomach.

Ben-hadad shrugged, deciding no one was coming, and jammed the blob of open blue luxin he'd drafted into the lock, solidified it, and turned. "I'm not really sure why the Chromeria even bothers to have locks," he said.

"Hold on," Teia said, feeling ill. "I've just made a terrible mistake."

She fled down the hall after the girl.

She was lucky. The girl had reached the slaves' stairs and realized she'd left her mop and bucket. She'd be in big trouble if she lost them. But the girl was still shocked when Teia approached on silent feet. She held her hands up in front of her face defensively, like Teia was going to hurt her.

"What's your name?" Teia asked quietly. She started working instantly to unravel what she'd done. Orholam have mercy, she'd gotten good at laying death traps, but not so good at removing them.

"Clara."

"What do they have you mopping for?" Teia asked.

Clara gulped. "Atarah called me a slatte—ahem, a name. So I tried to slap her, but I sort of missed? and I broke her nose instead. Two months I've been mopping after lectures every day."

"Ha," Teia said. "In the Blackguard, you'd not be mopping for that slap."

"I know! Why are the magisters so—"

"You'd be mopping for the miss," Teia said.

The girl's brow wrinkled and her mouth pursed.

"Look," Teia said. "I'm sorry for scaring you."

"I wasn't scared!"

"Truth is, Clara, you scared *me*."

Clara looked incredulous.

"I'm not supposed to be here," Teia said. "Well, I sort of am. It's complicated."

Orholam, I can't kill her. You're the god who spares the innocent. Can You keep this girl's mouth shut? Because I can't do this anymore. I can't kill the innocent anymore, not to justify a hundred other murders. Not to justify saving a thousand lives someday, maybe.

"I'm working for the White," Teia said very quietly. "It's a secret mission. I'm not supposed to be on the Jaspers at all. If you tell anyone you saw me, people will die. Me among them. Can you…can you not tell anyone you saw me for one week? I'll probably be dead by then anyway. It'll be a juicier story if I turn up dead, and *then* you can tell everyone. But if you tell anyone now—even your friends—Clara, I can't even tell you how bad it could go. A lot of people will die. Good people."

Clara shrugged, offended. "I can keep a secret!"

Right, and how many fourteen-year-olds will admit they can't? "One week," Teia said. "Two if you can. Unless I turn up dead, then tell whoever you want."

Her duty had become like that old little flask of olive oil that she'd gripped so hard in her fist that her fingers cramped. Holding on to it had meant everything, everything. Now she prised her fingers open one by one.

Orholam, this is Your war. If You want us to win, You're going to have to handle this little girl. I'm done killing innocents.

"You're serious," Clara said. "I thought you were just going to make love with that boy and were looking for an empty room."

"Ben?" Teia said. Oh hells. Now she'd said Ben's name.

"He's cute!" Clara said.

"Cute?" Teia asked. "No! I mean, sure, he's fine. But he's like my brother—look, I'm not talking about this!"

"Will you show me paryl tricks?" Clara said. "I think it's what I want to study. I'm a yellow myself, but I love research, and no one's done credible research on paryl since Aldib Muazon."

This was turning all sorts of directions Teia hadn't expected. But maybe this was salvation. "If…" Teia said. "If you show me you can keep one secret, I'll tell you more."

I am *screwing* the future me.

But I'm totally fine with screwing the future me. If I'm alive to be screwed, that's a win.

"It's a deal. Can I…can I get my mop?" Clara asked.

I almost killed this girl, Teia thought. "Of course."

In five minutes, the girl was gone, happily humming.

Teia didn't know if she'd just signed a hundred death warrants, but somehow the worry that she had sat side by side with a specter of faith that it was all going to work out.

She was afraid to examine that specter for fear it would fall apart at a touch, but it sat there, quietly, at the corner of her eye. And when she took a breath, it was a little less tight than her breaths had been for a

year.

The room, as it turned out, did have a secret door, hidden behind a hinged bureau. The magister who lived here was using it to store her extra clothing and books and a couple skins of good brandy.

Of course some of the secrets would have been found over the centuries by others.

The next hidden room they found had been converted to a private drug den, with narcotic plants growing everywhere next to an access to the tower's lightwell and pornographic texts on the shelves. The next, on another floor, hidden among the married couples' apartments, appeared to have been found but then lost again for decades, with a heavy coating of dust, a desiccated rat on the floor, and a single pair of wadded-up men's underclothes that looked brittle with age.

There was a story there that Teia wasn't sure she wanted to know.

As they found each, Ben-hadad seemed to home in more easily on the next, as if not just the architecture but the architecture of the builder's own mind was opening up to him. "Last one," he said, "it's on the way. Then I'll take you to the place I think it really is now."

The access room to that one was occupied, but Ben-hadad came up with some breezy lie and the old magister toddled her way off to lunch.

In the hidden room behind her apartments, they found a corpse, nearly skeletal, facedown, with the back of his head caved in.

"Dead many years, I'd guess," Ben-hadad said.

"But when he was fresh, how could they not smell him?" Teia asked. "These rooms aren't airtight."

"The infirmary occupies the entire floor below us. I'd imagine many unpleasant aromas escape. Or perhaps the occupant was herself the murderer, and had stayed long enough that the odors disappeared. A mystery."

"But not our mystery," Teia said.

"Agreed," Ben-hadad said. "If we make it through all this, we'll dig deeper and see if we can get him justice."

They left that room undisturbed, and with as little evidence of their passing as possible, in case the current occupant was the murderer herself, as unlikely as that seemed. Regardless, they wouldn't want to spook her.

But they didn't head back to the slaves' stairs.

"This last one..." Ben-hadad said. "This last one's special. We can't use the stairs. It's accessed from the lift."

"From the lift?" Teia asked. "But the lifts have got to be the most frequented areas in the towers."

"Not at the top levels they're not."

The idea that the Old Man of the Desert might have access to the top levels of the Chromeria shot a chill through Teia. But it wasn't like it was a new idea to her. She'd figured the Old Man had to be a high-level diplomat or noble or even Blackguard. Of course he'd be rich, and he'd have access to all sorts of disguises. But knowing that his lair was within spitting distance of the Blackguard barracks—an assassin lord, right under the noses of those whose main purpose was to stop assassins?—sickened her. It made it real. Ironfist wasn't just a one-off. They were everywhere.

"It would have to be quick to access," Teia said.

"It's between floors. You get to it from the back of the lift. A quick pause, set the brake, reset the weight to an empty lift, and the lift returns to the top floor automatically."

"So the Old Man has to be someone who gets on the lift alone often," Teia said. It narrowed her list a little. A Blackguard captain? "No, never mind. That isn't true," she said. "I was assuming the Old Man would have to visit his lair often. But he might only visit fortnightly, or even monthly. Anyone who takes these lifts regularly would have many chances to be alone briefly enough to get into such a room."

She wasn't going to find out who he was in time. She was going to fail again.

Teia went invisible, and they all got on the lift.

It was surprisingly easy to find, when they knew where to look. It was two and a half floors down from the top of the Prism's Tower. Just below where security started.

They pushed against the wall, and a narrow section simply sank in and swung open on hidden hinges, the seam invisible in all but bright light.

There was a small vestibule on the other side with a brake so that an empty lift could be halted on its passage up or down.

Teia carefully checked the vestibule for traps, then they released their brake on the lift and soon watched it go, summoned by someone far below.

After parting a curtain and stepping into the darkness beyond the vestibule, they found a stone letterpad with the entire Old Parian alphabet on it.

Her heart sank.

When Quentin moved forward to examine it more closely, she said, "Careful. It'll be trapped, somehow. The wrong code could wash the whole room with fire, for all we know. Maybe this one, maybe the one beyond."

Quentin stepped away gingerly.

With paryl, it was obvious that five of the letters had been smeared with finger oils more often than any of the others. Some of the letters looked like they hadn't been touched in years, and some had maybe been touched irregularly.

Teia relayed everything to Ben-hadad, who wrote down the letters in groups according to how much they appeared to have been touched.

"Well, there's good news," he said.

"You've taken up code breaking in the last year?" she asked.

"Not that good."

Of course not. She hadn't thought she'd be so lucky.

"It's long," he said, "and people are lazy, so it'll probably be a word, or a phrase. Unfortunately, that means there'll be repeats of letters, which makes breaking the code harder. And we don't know how long the phrase is. And I don't know Old Parian well enough to guess at letter frequencies. And it's possible that if we make any errors, something bad will happen."

"I'm still waiting for that good news," Teia said, as Ben watched the lift shaft to time an approaching lift.

Weights plunged past them, and a moment later, a group of discipulae chatting with each other zipped by, none of them noticing the three in the darkness.

"Ah," Ben-hadad said, "*that's* what this drawing is. Correct number of weights on the line to tell you the lift is empty. Nice engineering all around. Here's an empty one now."

Weights plunged past their faces; the desired number, apparently, because Ben applied the brake, and stopped the empty lift in front of them perfectly.

"You were saying?" Teia prompted.

"I was? Oh, oh, right. Well, if there's one great thing about being brilliant, it's that other brilliant people like talking to you. I know someone who might help."

"Might?"

"She didn't like me that much. Back in the day. That was a long time ago, though."

"Who are you talking about?"

"Magister Kadah."

"Kadah! You've got to be joking. The woman's a bitter little tyrant!" Teia had strong memories of her being the worst of their magisters.

"Yeah, but she's also the only magister I know with an interest in cryptology. Six hours."

"Six hours?" Teia asked. "To figure this out? How—"

"Actually, I have no idea," he said. "I was just picking a number. Quentin, you memorized which magisters are lecturing where, right? Of course you did. You can point me in the right direction. Now, let's get out of here before someone notices how long this lift has been stalled."

Chapter 85

The world had not stopped moving simply because Kip was spending hours gambling its fate with his grandfather. Andross had handed Kip a few things and then hustled out of his apartments to take care of a dozen tasks for the defense of the Jaspers. As soon as he himself stepped out of the old man's apartments with Corvan Danavis, he was met by no fewer than five messengers, not only updating him on the state of the defenses and the disposition of his forces but also asking that he request horses or oxen and wagons and various other things the Foresters needed permission for.

Kip directed those to report to the new high general, Corvan Danavis, who took it all in hand easily and promised to take care of it.

Winsen and Big Leo were there to guard Kip. Kip sent one of the messengers to find Ben-hadad—he was going to be figuring out mechanical things, so he needed the man's engineering brilliance. Then he sent Winsen to go find Cruxer to summon him urgently.

"You tell him *anything* you have to to get him to come to me, you understand?" Kip said.

"Your wife said not to leave you for any reason," Win said.

"And I'm telling you to move your ass to save Cruxer from doing something stupid. Come back with him."

Winsen, nonplussed about being pitted against Tisis, looked over at Big Leo for help, but the big man shrugged. "As soon as you get back, there'll be three of us with the boss."

"You say that like Breaker's the real boss," Winsen said, but he left.

Corvan was scanning documents that had been brought to him by the numerous messengers that were also waiting for him—he'd learned it was faster and more accurate, he said, than listening through an entire report.

Not much seemed to surprise him about what he heard and read, though at one point, he said, "The Chromeria's stockpiled that much black powder? The books never tell such things, but if we win, Karris will be the reason. Brilliant. Go on."

His messengers were soon given orders in a clipped shorthand that they scribbled on parchment as he spoke. He'd checked his own outgoing messages, approved them, and sent them out before Kip was finished hearing the second of his.

They spoke together as they made their way to the lift.

"You brought how many war hounds?!" Corvan asked. "Cwn y Wawr–trained?"

"I'd more say they *are* the Cwn y Wawr," Kip said, triggering the summon plate for a lift.

"Great, great, great. A hound's speed and slipperiness will make them perfect message carriers. It'll help with a real problem of communication. The battlefront is going to be the entire circle of the walls if we've got seven floating bane to deal with."

"Uh...maybe you can rotate them through messenger duty?" Kip said. "They'll serve where ordered, but you ever try to get a terrier to ignore a rat? Believe me, once you see them in their armor, you're going to want them fighting on the front lines. Or as a reserve."

Corvan nodded, and explained his strategies in broad strokes. He knew the Jaspers like the back of his hand, and had clearly been thinking about this for weeks, if not months. Bonus of being married to a Seer—who had also told him not to tell everyone at the Chromeria exactly what he was preparing for, for some reasons that she refused to explain—a drawback of being married to a Seer.

"I wish we had hours and hours," Kip said as they got on the lift. He decided to take it down with Corvan, though he needed to go up to the roof.

"There are hard things we need to talk about, son," Corvan said. "I've...got a lot of explaining to do to you. And forgiveness to ask."

"There's nothing to forgive," Kip said. "You cared for me more than anyone. And I, the son of your enemy. The man who cost you everything."

"That's...not...It's far more complicated than that. And not at all clean. I'm afraid I shall lose whatever respect you have for me."

"Never," Kip said. "Master Danavis...I mean, High General

Satrap Danavis, I've been in impossible positions now myself. Sometimes men do things in the heat of a moment, but I judge men by what they do day after day."

The cloud didn't move from Corvan's visage, though, only darkened.

"We need to talk about your daughter, too," Kip said. "But not here. Someplace absolutely secure."

Corvan shook his head as if it weren't necessary. "I met with her briefly some time ago. I know what's she's decided. I can guess where she'll be tomorrow." Corvan's jaw tightened, and his brow furrowed against his grief.

"I'm so sorry," Kip said.

"Me, too," Corvan said, his face not moving a whit.

The lift had taken forever, but finally a free one came and they got on.

"We'll talk more," Kip said. "But you...you think your soldiers are going to make it to join in the defense?"

"Yes," Corvan said.

"Which means you agree with me that Ironfist is going to relent. Your wife tell you that? I knew in my heart he couldn't be a traitor. Not really."

"Kip, she didn't tell me that. She said...she said someone's going to die before Ironfist's people join us. Someone who could avoid it, but almost certainly won't. Someone who doesn't deserve to die."

Kip blinked. "Could be a training accident, then. Someone disembarking from the ships, slipping or something."

"Could be," Corvan said, but his eyes were pained.

The lift stopped, but he didn't open the doors.

Corvan looked down at his feet. "In the Prisms' War, I found purpose and friendship and status, and at its end, I lost all those, and my best friend, and my wife, and I...I did things. I got lost for a long time, Kip. I wish I'd been better to you. A lot better. You deserved more."

"We've work to do," Kip said. "We'll talk later. Oh, one last thing!" He leaned close to Corvan and whispered in his ear, even then cupping his hand over his mouth so his lips couldn't be read, even though they were alone in the lift. "As satrap, you're entitled to Blackguard protection. Refuse it. You understand?"

The Blackguard had been infiltrated by the Order. If they were going to make a move, just before or during a battle was exactly when the Order would do it.

Corvan understood. He held on to Kip's forearms for a moment. "I don't know that He cares. I'm not sure that He even exists, but may Orholam guard you, son."

"And may He bring you light in your long night, sir," Kip said.

Then they parted ways, and Kip wondered if it was the last time he'd ever see the man.

Chapter 86

Commander Ironfist had been a legendary figure before he left the Jaspers. Striding victoriously into Karris's audience chamber, every eye upon him, King Ironfist was utterly terrifying.

In accord with Parian customs since the time of Lucidonius, the old Commander Ironfist had dressed modestly, wearing long-sleeved tunics and a carefully folded ghotra to cover his hair. That modesty was a centuries-old antidote to the more-ancient-still flamboyance of the pagan Parians who had come before them. In the Paria of old, the kings and queens had preferred to delight the eye and boggle the mind.

King Ironfist joined the ancient kings now, and he certainly over-awed all who saw him. His hair—uncovered—was twisted with gold dust and glue, into a great free crown of jumbled curls around his head. On one eyelid, cribbing from the Nuqaba, was painted the ancient Parian rune for Justice. On the other was Mercy. He wore an eye patch, flipped up now, which could be lowered to cover the one or the other.

On the patch was stitched a fiery orb, an orange eye aflame. His tunic was as tight as a Blackguard tunic, sleeveless, revealing biceps that looked like they could shake the pillars of heaven. But instead of modest black, this tunic was all bold checks of gold and white, brilliant as the sun itself, belted with white leather around a slim waist that emphasized the enormous breadth of his shoulders.

On his left wrist, he wore a manacle and a cruel heavy chain. According to the tale, it was the chain he'd literally torn from a rock wall trying to save his sister, the Nuqaba, from being assassinated. He wore a necessarily broad gold bicep band with a hook by his elbow, from which he suspended the end of the chain so that it was held tight along his forearm.

Ironfist was a king who'd broken chains. Now he used his chains to make war.

At his heels, sniffing the air like wolves first catching the scent of a sheep pen, were two enormous war hounds, a terrible midnight and a smaller albino.

But more frightening than the vestments or the hard tattoos or the new scars or the uncharacteristic showiness of his garb or even the damn-near horse-sized dogs was the look of dull rage in his eyes.

Karris had known angry men. Habitually angry men were always dangerous, but unfocused, undisciplined. You had to keep an eye on them the same way Karris would keep her eye on those hounds, but when such men attacked, it was usually with more ferocity than skill.

For her entire tenure in the Blackguard, Karris had also known dangerous men. Such men would use force when necessary, coolly, passionlessly, and with great skill.

But when a dangerous man got angry, you could be in for something else altogether.

Ironfist's quiet brother, Tremblefist, had gone into a battle rage once, and thereby earned himself a Name. It had taken the blood of five hundred to quench the Butcher of Aghbalu's rage. Ironfist was his brother's equal with a blade, and far more experienced than that young man had been.

Karris had never wanted to see Ironfist truly angry. She had prayed she never would.

Today, her prayer had been denied.

"High Lady!" Ironfist boomed, coming forward on quick steps. Two warriors flanked him, draped in bold colors, a man with a bocote-wood lion helm with lion's teeth and a woman with claw scars on her face and wearing a baboon helm. Each was as tall and lean as the hellstone-tipped spears they carried. Drafters, and if Ironfist had deemed them fit to accompany him before his old command, they were surely formidable warriors indeed.

Not one of the twelve Blackguards attending Karris wasn't sweating.

Ironfist motioned to his *Tafok Amagez* to stay back—right at the point where the Blackguard were about to challenge them to stop. He knew. He knew everything about the Blackguard's defenses, every seam, every weakness. If anyone could take apart the Blackguard, it was Ironfist.

He said, "How you've changed since you came under my tutelage when I was a new trainer, and you that scrawny noble girl hoping to find a purpose in the Blackguard."

She said nothing. Let him set the landscape of this discussion. She owed him that much.

Besides, if she didn't hear him out, she wouldn't know where to put pressure and where to yield so fast his weight carried him off his feet.

" 'The Iron White' they call you now," he said, sweeping a quick hand at the gathered nobles and courtiers and Colors and every maid and servant important enough to finagle their way into this meeting. He moved it so sharply, not a few of them flinched. "And that, not so long after you dropped Karris White Oak to become Karris Guile, then Karris the White. It seems you've gone through many names in a short time."

"And you, many masters," Karris said. The retort hit like a whip-crack.

He blinked as if slapped, but he didn't even slow his walk. Two steps silent, three, before he paused, just outside where the Black-guard would stop a man—but still too close for *this* man to get.

Then he said, "Yet now you've lost your name altogether, and I my masters."

"Have you?" she asked, but she said it gently, quietly. "Have you, my old friend?"

Something in his mien wavered like a blossom struggling to open on a day of jumbled sunshine and rain.

Then it closed tight again.

He put his hands down to his sides and patted the heads of the great war hounds. It was, of course, forbidden to bring war hounds into the audience chamber. A war hound was either a heresy or a target: either an animal that had already been will-cast, or an innocent beast that might be will-cast under your nose by malevolent forces.

Karris had allowed them in without complaint. What else could she do? She'd allowed Kip to keep his, albeit not in the audience chamber itself.

At Ironfist's tap, the smaller white hound with its pink eyes sat. Ironfist reached up and pulled down his eye patch over the Mercy tattoo, leaving only Justice.

Damn, damn, damn.

"Perhaps we could move to a more private setting?" she asked now. Ironfist was a reasonable man. Had been, anyway. Perhaps she could find that man again, if only she could get him away from all the eyes that demanded he act like a king instead.

But there was little or nothing of the old Ironfist here. This man looked indeed like the kings of old: harsh and terrible and primal. He said, "The Chromeria's secrecy and lies are what have brought us here. You need my fleet. You need Seers Island's army. The White King's armada will arrive tomorrow, and attack then or the next day. You have no time. "

"You need us as much as we need you," Andross Guile called out from the side entrance of the audience chamber. He walked in quickly, confidently, like a man twenty years younger. "We can win without you. On the other hand, you know that if the heathen destroys us, he'll come for you next. The King of Wights is not a man to be content with less than all the world. Joining us is your only hope of stopping him."

The crowd in the audience chamber was riveted. For some, this was confirmation of the rumors that the White King was coming. Others were hearing it for the first time. All of them knew Ironfist by name at least, and all of them knew he'd declared himself king. Hell, not a few of them probably liked him more than they liked Karris or Andross.

Karris had a sudden paranoid thought wondering if he'd arranged for a coup. What if he'd packed this chamber with his own loyalists?

But no, surely Commander Fisk would have guarded against such things. Right?

But still, her throat was tight. Who knew where else traitors lurked, if Ironfist himself could be one?

King Ironfist was looking at Andross Guile with open disdain on his face as the old man took his seat next to Karris. "Horseshit. You offer your help for hypothetical troubles while you yourself face extinction now. We're not equals here, so let's skip the oily preambles, snake. You need my armies. I'm here to tell you the price for them."

Astonishment rippled through the crowd. No one talked to Andross Guile like that. *No one.*

And then anyone who remembered that Andross had stripped Ironfist of his command of the Blackguard saw the depths of the antipathy between the men. This was not going to be pretty. This was why Karris hadn't wanted Andross here.

Andross didn't say anything immediately. Didn't bring his old commander to heel with a word.

And if he *didn't*, everyone saw, it had to be because he couldn't. Thus, Ironfist was telling the truth when he announced their weakness. The Jaspers really were that vulnerable.

And suddenly, the people were afraid.

Perhaps, working with paints mixed from vermilion rage and white-hot anger and black vexation, a painter as talented as Janus Borig might have been able to capture the spirit of Andross Guile now being publicly humiliated by a *slave.*

560

But he mastered himself and merely twitched a hand as one would to a servant: 'Go on.'

Karris knew she should intervene, soften the grind of stone on stone between these two men: Ironfist, fed up with the years of injustices, and Andross, unable to believe a slave would step so high out of his proper place.

But she had no words. Her heart was in her throat.

King Ironfist tilted his head, thoughtful, almost taunting.

It was coming now. Ironfist would propose the alliance, the kind that could only be sealed by her marriage. She would have to marry Ironfist tonight. With this attitude, he wasn't going to let his men off their ships until it was done. And 'done' meant signed, sealed, and consummated.

Though she was a grown woman, somehow she hadn't let herself think that last part through. She would see it through. She knew that. She wasn't going to faint this close to the finish line. But how could she bear to take this angry stranger's weight upon her? Once they were behind closed doors, would he become, somehow, her dear friend again?

But there would be no reprieve, no hoping he might delay the consummation, no blotting herself out with drink as she'd done with the real Gavin Guile—Ironfist might know that story, and he could give her no excuse to annul the marriage. She would take him to her bed, and she would do it sober, and she would meet his eyes while she did it.

Would she feign pleasure while she betrayed the only man she'd ever loved?

Orholam have mercy, what if she *felt* pleasure?

Would she hold back some position, some act, hoping to hold on to some piece of her own soul?

For some reason, until now, Karris had thought of dishonoring her office and dishonoring Ironfist and Gavin as somehow external: those would be acts others would judge unfairly, not understanding why she did them or how much good she was accomplishing. When she'd thought of her betrayals, she'd imagined only before she did what had to be done, and after.

Now she couldn't help but imagine the *during*.

But she would do it. To save her people, she was going to do it, even if for every moment of it she imagined Gavin somehow walking in on her, she was going to do it.

Finally, King Ironfist spoke, looking at Andross. "I gave you the best years of my life. My brother, Hanishu, did, too, and then he died

561

for you. And in return, you threw me out like garbage, and then you ordered the murder of my sister." Now the new king stared at them both, and Karris wasn't spared the heat of his gaze.

She suddenly felt things sliding off-kilter, like a wagon too heavily loaded careening down a thin mountain road suddenly jumping out of the safety of the ruts to where the cliffs waited.

"This is not a negotiation. This is an ultimatum," King Ironfist said. "You've taken my family from me. You want my help? I want a dead Guile. You, old man. Or you, Karris. Or Kip. You decide."

"Or Zymun?" Andross asked quickly, as if he were merely gathering information.

"Ha! How much of a fool do you think I am?" Ironfist barked. "No. I'm not here to solve Guile problems. I'm here to be one. You decide. I'll be back at midnight to see the deed done. If you don't, we join the White King."

Without another word, without a look back, Ironfist and his retinue strode from the hall, their footsteps echoing loudly in the utter silence of hundreds of noblemen and women who could only stare at one another in wide-eyed fear.

Andross had thought he was so smart. Andross had been so sure Ironfist would do the rational thing, the thing Andross would do. But Ironfist wasn't rational; he was grieving; he was furious, and he was hell-bent on revenge.

Ironfist was sounding a death knell that couldn't be unrung. The satrapies would die—if not tomorrow, then next year. After this, even if Paria and the Chromeria together defeated the White King, this blood Ironfist demanded *would* be answered with blood. But Karris couldn't blame him. Not in the least. Ironfist hated injustice; it was something she'd always admired about him. And she and Andross had murdered his people first.

And now it was going to bring them all to ruin.

Chapter 87

Kip looked around the open top of the Prism's Tower and tried to enjoy the sunshine, tried to breathe. It was a beautiful day, and the view was peerless, but he couldn't help but look to the horizon, as if the White King's armada would appear at any moment. He went to the edge, where the great cables he and the Mighty had once slid down to safety had been repaired and once again concealed.

It actually might be a good way to get messengers from the Chromeria out to every corner of the Jaspers as quickly as possible. They had signal mirrors for many messages, but he'd have to mention the option to Corvan.

Kip sighed. He was just trying to take his mind off the tightness in his chest.

Big Leo was standing watch, impassive, and it reminded Kip of the last time they'd been alone.

What had Big Leo said to him? That every time he tried to be someone else, he failed, and when he was only himself, he succeeded?

Kip looked down at his arm. I'm not Gavin Guile. I'm not Andross Guile. I'm the fucking Turtle-Bear.

He had to figure out the Mirrors himself.

That would have been a lot more comforting if he'd figured out anything at all, but even finding the mechanism on the roof by which Prisms balanced had taken him an embarrassingly long time. A multi-faceted crystal hung there, and one could address it standing, or actually strap into a raised frame.

Huh, that was strange.

Kip eventually figured out the leather belts and the locks and strapped himself in. He released the pins, and the huge crystal swung down hard toward his face. He jerked back against the belt with a squawk as it banged to a stop a thumb's breadth from his forehead.

"You all right there?" Big Leo asked sardonically.

Kip cleared his throat. "C'mon, that didn't make you nervous at all?"

Big Leo just stared at him.

"As you were," Kip said.

Tentatively, he rested his face against the crystal. He could see through the lowest clear layers as the rest pressed against his skin. He reached his will into it.

Nothing. No, not quite nothing. It felt like he'd put on a yoke that hadn't been hitched to a plow. The leads were there, just untethered.

"Get me out of here," he told Big Leo.

"That was quick," Big Leo said.

"Well, I am a genius of magic," Kip said.

Big Leo looked at him flatly. "But seriously."

"We need to go downstairs," Kip said. At least, that's where he hoped the answers were. "I'm blaming this all on you if it doesn't work."

563

"Mmm-hmm," Big Leo said.

Wiseass.

They made their way past checkpoints again. On the way up, they'd been staffed by Blackguards Kip and Big Leo hardly had known. But apparently they'd gone and gotten others.

Their welcome was warmer than Kip had expected. The Lightguards had had all the time in the world to paint Kip and the Mighty as murderous traitors. At the very least, the Mighty had left the Blackguard at a time when they'd really needed good people.

Instead, he saw Gill Greyling waiting for them.

"Gill!" Kip said. "They made you a trainer? Those poor nunks!"

The man flashed a huge smile. "I get along with the slow and clumsy." Kip laughed as they embraced.

"Where's Gav?" Kip asked.

He felt it instantly. Every face fell.

"No!" Kip said. But he saw the truth of it on Gill's face. "How?"

"We'd been out looking for your father. Gav had been pushing it for a while, drafting too much. We got ambushed by some wights. He saved two of his brothers in the fighting, but blew his halos."

"He make it back here?"

"Yeah. The White herself took care of him for the end."

Kip muttered a curse.

"You should go see her, Lord Guile," Gill said. He called him Lord Guile, not Breaker.

"Yeah, I know," Kip said. He supposed Gill thought Breaker was his Blackguard name, and though it was forgivable under the circumstances, Kip had still abandoned the Blackguard.

"Promise me."

Kip squirmed. It wasn't like Gill not to let things go. "Look, we didn't leave things so—"

"She's got one son she can't abide and one that she loves but drove away. Promise me."

"I'm not really her *son*. She made that very clear—"

"Gav spent his dying breaths making her see what kind of a cockroach Zymun is. She gets it now. But if you make my brother's sacrifice moot, you're turning your back on us. Or have you already done that?"

Kip swore under his breath. "Come on! Don't be—fine! I'll do it. I gotta go handle some trivial life-and-death stuff first. Let's do this again, though. It was fun."

He pushed through them, but stopped before the lift and turned. He cursed again. "Gill. Trainer. I'm sorry. About..."

564   "I know," Gill said.

Moments later, Kip and Big Leo stepped off the lift at the tall, wide-open level that housed all the tower's mirrors. Dozens of mirror slaves were hard at work prepping for Sun Day. It was the biggest day of the year for them. Not only were there all the festivities and parades to prepare for, many of which required special lenses and tight coordination, but they went on all day long, on the day of the year with the most intense sunlight.

Mistakes in coordinating the mirrors not only were deemed harbingers of bad luck, but they could also send errant burning hot rays into the crowds of pilgrims. Small smudges on the mirrors could turn them into a smoking ruin. Untrained or sick staff could fall to their deaths with the rigors of the long, long day. Thus, today was filled with everything from checking the health of the slaves here and on the Thousand Stars throughout the Jaspers, to checking and filling the cleaning solutions for the mirrors themselves, to drilling the star-keepers on hitting their sequences during the parades.

Kip had served with the mirror slaves before; it was a favorite punishment for nunks, and the slaves had laughed at the nunks' sweating and bumbling, saying that day was nothing compared to Sun Day.

There were no nunks here now. Kip figured they'd probably just get in the way. He started looking around for the slaves' overseer, but couldn't see one immediately. That was odd. Usually the overseers made a real effort to distinguish themselves above their fellows.

"I see how, I just don't understand why, Overseer Amadis," a boy said.

Kip homed in on the conversation and wove through the workers to the east side of the tower. The boy who'd spoken was watching as an older man swung a mirror from one position to another. But the mirror he was swinging was blackened, melted.

"Because we've got no backup mirrors. We use what we've got," the old man said.

"Why not take it out altogether?"

Overseer Amadis looked up at Kip. "My lord, will you give me one moment to deal with this?"

"Of course."

He turned back to the boy. "Because it's the counterweight to Valor's mirror. We've got two hundred twenty-seven position changes tomorrow, and without this mirror in place, that bolt in the frame may snap."

"But why do I have to clean it? It's *melted*!" the boy asked, but then his head dropped. "My pardons, Overseer."

A female slave nearby who was scrubbing the floor on hands and knees shook her head. "Little Alvaro doesn't want to work. Thinks he's too good for it. Surprise, surprise."

"Because if you keep it clean," the overseer said, "maybe it'll make it through the day without shattering. It's brittle as is. And because everyone else needs to clean theirs. Letting your mirror get dirty is the worst thing we keepers can possibly do, isn't it, Ysabel?" the overseer said, turning to the sneering woman scrubbing the floor.

She turned back to her labors, muttering.

Kip looked from her to the blackened mirror. Clearly there was some story there, but it didn't have anything to do with him.

"Alvaro," Amadis said, "son, you're only just coming out from under the cloud of suspicion she put on you. You serve well tomorrow, and you get moved to a rotation on the real mirrors. If you loaf because it doesn't seem to matter to you... You're a smart kid. You want them to look at you like you looked at Ysabel a year ago?"

The boy shook his head with a fair facsimile of humility, accepting his correction.

"Sorry about that," Amadis said. "These two should not be kept together, but we make do, like everyone. How may I help you, my lord?"

"I'm afraid I'm going to throw a wrench into your plans," Kip told Overseer Amadis. "But it's for something more important than Sun Day, I promise."

Unsurprisingly, the overseer was less than delighted at what Kip wanted. There were things a slave—even an exalted one—couldn't promise. Every warden would have to be summoned to sign over control of the mirror towers in their neighborhoods. Orders would have to be cleared with the appropriate authorities. The luxiats in charge of the Sun Day parades would have to confer.

Kip understood immediately, likely more than Amadis did.

This man didn't have the power to say yes. He wasn't an arrogant ass jealous of his small bubble of authority, but he served those who were. No one wanted to be held responsible for saying yes, so everything would go as slowly as possible. The luxiats in charge of the parades would confer, then decide they couldn't approve such a thing themselves, and summon a High Luxiat. He'd be briefed at length, then deliberate. Then he'd decide he couldn't decide himself, and so on until Sun Day of next year had passed.

"At long last," Kip said to Big Leo, "it turns out my time getting stonewalled in Dúnbheo was valuable for something after all."

Big Leo grunted and stretched against the massive chain he wore draped around his neck. It actually made a few slaves stop what they were doing. He didn't ask Kip to explain, though. Sometimes, he was at least as difficult in his own laconic way as Winsen.

Kip said, "Overseer Amadis, you have access to messengers, right? Good. Send urgent messages directly to the High Luxiats and High Lord Black and the luxiats in charge of the parades and the wardens that Lord Kip Guile requires—well, all the things I've asked for, you parse them out appropriately to the appropriate ones. Tell them I require those things immediately. Stop all your work with the mirrors, right now, until you've done that. In your messages, note that I've written down their names specifically, and that those who fail in providing what the Jaspers need for our common defense immediately will face the full wrath of the Guiles. Treason will be suspected of those who work against our common defense, punishment will be meted out swiftly if not overly carefully, and more loyal replacements found."

"Well, that oughta do it," Big Leo rumbled.

"I can promise you *our* full cooperation, my lord," Overseer Amadis said. "Starting immediately. These mirrors will be slaved to the gem before you can reach the roof." He swallowed.

"That feel good?" Big Leo asked as they headed to the exit.

"Nah," Kip said.

Big Leo said nothing.

"Maybe a little."

"—know why you think you're special, Elos?" a boy was saying at the same moment. "Because you're an arrogant little shit."

Kip stopped at the door. Had he heard 'Elos'? Like that green wight Gaspar Elos way back in Rekton? He could have sworn…

He looked back, but all the slaves were hard at work, double-time.

Nah, must have imagined it.

He headed back to work.

Chapter 88

It was no pleasure to cut through the layers of defense Kip had set up at his headquarters. If Teia could do it, so could other Shadows. The best of them anyway.

Fine, there was some pleasure in it: for the first time, she was able to experience the blend of using her magical and her physical dexterity without having to dread why she was doing it. Before now, an infiltration meant she was going to commit murder.

Today, she was simply going to . . . what exactly?

She wanted to talk to Kip before they died. Maybe she knew something that could help him. Maybe she could *do* something to help him. Hell, she was an assassin, wasn't she? She could probably make all sorts of his problems go away.

And for Kip she'd do it. No questions asked.

After all, what was one more soul in her ledger?

There was one paryl drafter in Kip's entourage. Slow girl, paryl leaking out of her like a sieve, inefficient, unfocused. Teia could have gotten past her without even being invisible.

Still, she had to be careful. Anyone who glimpsed a heel or the eyes of an otherwise-invisible intruder was going to shoot first and ask questions later, literally.

Teia was good now, but enervating a finger before it twitched on a trigger? She wasn't that good. And paryl certainly wasn't going to stop a musket ball.

It took only half an hour of being on the street until she slipped into Kip's suite, not completely certain that she'd managed to silence the hinges from outside the door, though she had wrapped them in layer after layer of paryl.

This was not Kip's suite, she realized as she got inside.

It was Kip *and Tisis's* suite. And Kip was gone. Tisis sat at a large table, quill in hand, scribbling. She looked tense.

Teia took a step forward. The plush rug under Teia's foot sank pleasantly, but then—

Click.

Oh shiiiiit.

"I would hold very still, were I you," Tisis said, laying down the quill and raising her gaze, studying the emptiness in the air as if she might see through Teia's invisibility. She took a deep breath as she realized she really couldn't. "Trouble with being a Shadow: your eyes have to be visible to gather light, so you like to only look up in little glimpses, huh? Keeps you from studying ceilings carefully."

Gathering the folds of the master cloak between her eyes and Tisis, Teia looked up to one side. Half a dozen muskets and crossbows pointed at various angles toward her and around her, in case she jumped away from the trap she'd just stepped into. All of them were behind a sheet of glass thick enough to defeat paryl from penetrating it, but thin enough that a bolt or musket ball would have no such difficulty. She assumed the other side had another half-dozen as well.

"I'm not here to hurt you," Teia said.

"Teia, I presume?" Tisis asked.

Teia shimmered into visibility and took down her hood. "Benhadad's work?" she asked, pointing a thumb to the death trap. *Thanks for telling me about this, Ben. Jackass.*

"His design. An underling did the work. That's why it's not armed yet."

"It's not armed?"

"I know how bureaucracies work. I figured that if someone ordered an assassination by a real Shadow, getting permission and then setting it up would take at least until this evening, whereas *you* might come immediately. But that was just a guess. I'm glad I was right. Nice to, um, see you."

"I'm, uh, real glad to see you again, too," Teia said. Because getting caught in a stupid trap like a moron is *exactly* how I wanted to reintroduce myself to Kip's gorgeous and competent wife. "So I can step off this?"

"Of course," Tisis said.

Bobbing her head to look down at her feet, Teia stepped off the pressure plate.

A *thwang* and the sound of breaking glass made her head snap up. Shards of glass fell from its frame in front of the weapons to the floor, shattering. One crossbow had discharged.

Teia'd heard too many tales of men being fatally wounded without realizing it to feel relief immediately. Had that been a breeze she'd felt on her neck?

She reached up to the back of her neck. It was dry, mercifully dry. But something tickled her neck. She pulled it into view: a clump of her hair, cut by the crossbow quarrel.

If Teia hadn't dipped her head to look at her feet...

Their gazes locked.

"I am so, so sorry!" Tisis said, horror writ on her features. "I swear to Orholam that wasn't me trying to..."

"Murder me and pretend it was an accident?" Teia asked.

"Orholam's hairies," Tisis said, "this is so not how I wanted this to go."

Teia heard running footsteps summoned by the sound of the breaking glass. She dove and rolled out of the way, shimmering out of visibility and throwing her hood up even as the door banged open.

Three people she didn't recognize dressed in cloaks of the Mighty burst into the room—along with one person who made her heart leap. Cruxer!

"A malfunction," Tisis said smoothly. "And a potentially *lethal* one. Commander? Do you have an answer for this?"

If Cruxer were chagrined, he gave no indication. The man had turned into a slender version of Ironfist in his time away. "I'll look into it at once, milady."

"Send someone to do it. I wish to speak with you privately."

Cruxer's back stiffened. He gave a hand signal to dismiss the other Mighty without even picking up the glass or the bolt embedded in the wall.

After they were gone, Tisis said, "Adrasteia?"

Teia stood and at some distance, and slowly—she knew Cruxer's reaction speed—she shimmered back into visibility.

His face blossomed open with such intensity of joy at seeing her that she almost started crying. He stepped across the room in two steps with those long legs of his and wrapped her in an embrace.

And then she did weep, with body-shaking, unstoppable sobs. She could only bury her face in his chest. For some reason, she'd thought Cruxer would disapprove of her, would judge her, would despise her for what she'd become.

It took her a while to pull her shit back together.

Orholam's balls. Crying in front of Kip's wife. Let me go hop on that pressure plate a few more times.

Finally, after what felt like hours but had probably been less than a minute, Teia cleared her throat and stepped back.

"So...I guess Kip's not around?" Teia asked. "Breaker, I mean." She was still trying to get used to the idea that she was accepted into the Mighty, so she had the right to use their Mighty names.

"He's at the Chromeria," Tisis said. "From the secrecy of your visit, I assume you're in danger?"

"Why are you in danger?" Cruxer asked.

"He doesn't know?" Teia asked Tisis, indicating Cruxer. About me infiltrating the Order? About Ironfist becoming King Ironfist?

"Kip said your mission was your secret and your burden—he only shared it with me because I needed to know to help him rule—but he wouldn't extend that circle further until we got here, where it might affect Cruxer's work. Commander, I would have told you a few hours ago, but things have been..."

He dismissed it with a wave of his hand. "I'm not entitled to all secrets, and I trust my Lord Guile completely." He frowned momentarily. "Which is not to say I don't want to know now, although I was just about to head to the Chromeria. I heard Commander Ironfist was seen heading there from the docks, with like a Parian honor guard or something?"

"Ironfist?" Teia asked, her voice strangled. "He's here?"

"Yeah, I know!" Cruxer said. "I'd heard he'd left the Jaspers, and there were crazy rumors he'd been fired—like how there always is," Cruxer said. "I wish it hadn't taken a war to get us all back together, but I can't tell you how many times as I've led the Mighty I've asked myself what Ironfist would do in a certain situation. I can't wait to thank him. And...well, even ask his opinion of a few things. I mean, I've missed him almost as much as I've missed you, Te—what's wrong, Teia?"

She couldn't seem to get her voice to work right. Her stomach was in full riot. "You...you really don't—you don't know?" She looked over to Tisis, who seemed just as clueless. Which meant Kip didn't know, either.

Tisis said, "I mean, we know he lost his position here. Kip meant to speak with his grandfather about that, and see if he could be reinstated. He's been furious about it."

"It is so much too late for that," Teia said. "You...didn't hear about Paria?"

"What about it?" Tisis asked.

"Who cares about Paria now?" Cruxer said. "He's here. He's all right, isn't he?"

"We were deep in Blood Forest," Tisis told Teia, "and the river was blockaded. We had no news, no messages at all for several months, and few before that."

Teia hadn't written anything to them about Ironfist being in the Order; she didn't dare trust any messenger, and they'd had no secret code together anyway. But she'd figured for sure Kip would have heard about Ironfist declaring himself a king! If he hadn't, or hadn't had a chance to pass it along, then Teia was about to become the bearer of worse news than she'd even imagined. The Chromeria was so connected to the events of the wider world that she'd forgotten how long it could take for the deeper parts of the satrapies to hear about events elsewhere. In war, picking out the reliable from the rumors made it twice as hard.

"What's wrong with Ironfist?!" Cruxer demanded.

"He's in the Order of the Broken Eye," Teia said.

Tisis went still with shock, but Cruxer laughed. "Ha, Teia, this isn't the time to make jokes. Orholam's balls, you scared me! But seriously that's not funny. What *is* wrong?"

Then he processed the horror on her face.

She said, "What *did* Kip tell you about why I stayed on the Jaspers?"

Cruxer glanced at Tisis, then back to Teia. "He said there was some threat to Karris that only you could help with. You can see threats with paryl no one else can. You thought Orholam was calling you to stay here."

Who would have thought that a man nicknamed 'the Lip' could keep his closed so well? But as much as Teia usually would have thanked Kip for that carefulness, now it just meant she had to march further out of the shadows to tell them the whole truth. "That's...all true. But it's not all the truth. Cruxer, I've been infiltrating the Order of the Broken Eye for Karris, trying to get the information to destroy them from the inside."

"You?" He grinned, but with a hint of desperation, as if he felt his disbelief crumbling. "Come on. Like some kind of spy?"

"And an assassin." It felt like a sinkhole had opened in her gut and it was swallowing all the world.

"A what?" He smirked, cocking his head. But his eyebrows were drawing down, and upturned corners of his mouth collapsed down around bared teeth.

"The White ordered me to do everything I had to in order to get in as deep as I could."

"And?"

"So when the Order sent me to kill the Nuqaba, I did. She was Ironfist's sister."

"Teia, what the hell?"

It all had to come out. Disastrous as she'd always known it would be.

Shame rolled over her at what she'd become, but she stabbed deep, lancing the boil. "Ironfist was there, Crux. As I killed her. That bitch had chained him to the wall. She was delusional, high, totally... murderous. She was gonna kill him. Her own brother. But—but he begged me to stop. Begged me not to kill her. Told me how he was in the Order himself, how this had to be a mistake."

"Well, well, surely—he was lying to save her, right? I mean, that's his sister, and he, he wouldn't want you to become an assassin, Teia. He's a good man. Honorable. He'd only lie to save you and her, you know that! That's the kind of man he is."

"He didn't know the assassin was me, Crux. Not at first. He couldn't see me, but he knew it was the Order coming for her. He was
calling out names of...of the other Shadows that he knew personally.

He knew way too much for it to be a lie. He said he'd joined them when he was a boy, asking them for vengeance on his mother's killer. He was appealing to an Order assassin like...like we were on the same side. I couldn't believe it, either. But it's true."

"No," Cruxer said, and his face contorted.

Teia could have stabbed Cruxer in the back herself and not seen such a look of profound betrayal.

"Cruxer," Tisis said softly. She moved toward him tentatively.

"He was with them all along?" Cruxer asked.

He saw all the confirmation he needed in Teia's face.

"I have to go see him," Cruxer said. "This is *horseshit.*"

"Cruxer, you can't," Teia said. "If you say *anything*, it'll get me killed. The Order will find out I'm a mole, and, and—Cruxer, you don't know what I've done to take these bastards down."

"Doesn't matter."

"No!" she shouted suddenly. "You don't tell *me* what doesn't matter! You listen to me. You shut up and listen."

His lips curled into a snarl. "Make me, assassin."

She buckled. "Cruxer, you can't."

"I won't give away your dirty secrets," Cruxer said. "What do you think I am?"

"Cruxer, you can't. He's...he's got the orange bane. Or seed crystal or whatever. At least, his sister did. I'm sure he took it when he became king. I don't know what it does to people."

He stared at her for a moment. "Goodbye, Teia. Tisis."

"Commander, I forbid you to go," Tisis said. Her voice was reluctant but firm.

He shook his head. "The Order tried to kill your husband once already. You really don't want me there with him?"

"Cruxer..." Tisis said, pleading.

The commander said, "Breaker will seek Ironfist out the moment he hears he's at the Chromeria. I have to go tell him."

"Someone else—"

"This is a matter of defense, and that's my domain. My apologies, Lady Guile." He bowed sharply and was out the door before either of them could gather any other arguments.

The expression on Tisis's face reflected the same dread Teia was feeling.

"Can you catch up with him?" Tisis asked.

Teia would have to sneak, while Cruxer could simply ride. "No," she said. "But I'll try." She drew her hood back on.

"One moment," Tisis said. She walked back toward her desk and 573 opened a drawer. "I know we may not get another chance—well, ever, so…For reasons that don't matter right now, Kip thought he couldn't give this to you himself. But he made it for you, and I want you to have it."

She pulled out a length of faintly luminous fine yellow chain with spearheads on either end. A rope-spear of woven yellow luxin?

Teia held it in her hands, baffled. "He *made* this?" The chain was so finely woven it was as supple as rope, but with yellow links. It would be virtually unbreakable.

"He was working on some magic to make it less visible or more visible—even glowing if you wanted it to—but I don't know how far he got with that. You'll have to ask him."

Teia wanted to study it, wanted to test the weight and the magic, but instead she wrapped the weapon expertly around her waist in a quick-releasing knot. "I…" What could she say to this woman, for whom she'd only had evil thoughts?

"Should go," Tisis said. "We'll speak again." There was a little drop-off in her voice though, as if she was consciously holding back 'I hope, if we live.'

Teia turned. She didn't know how to do this. And there was work summoning her that she *did* know how to do.

As Teia closed her hood around her face, and began to shimmer out of visibility, Tisis said, "One more thing. He gave it a name. He called it 'Sorry.'"

Teia paused. Then she went.

Chapter 89

In all her years as a young noblewoman, then as a Blackguard, and then as the White, Karris had never heard the audience chamber so quiet. The courtiers filed out in silence. The Blackguards cleared the room in silence.

Now she and Andross stood in silence.

She stood at the great windows, watching the sun go down. A summer squall, disappointingly small, was blowing in off the horizon.

When she'd been in this room before, there had always been a buzz of voices, chattering and tittering as this or that noble tried to prove himself a wit through his whispered observations. Even as a

Blackguard clearing the chamber of threats—or more often, simply collecting forgotten bags or scarves and the like—there had always been the small talk of work. Since she'd become White, moments of silence had become treasures.

But not moments shared with Andross.

The sun set. There was no green flash after the last sliver of sun disappeared, no divine promise that it would all work out.

Andross stood at a window, looking out on the futile drizzle of the late-spring rain, lightning illuminating his figure inconsistently, even the rumble of thunder seeming somehow impotent.

For the first time in a year or more, Karris was reminded that he was indeed an old man, ancient for a drafter.

"I didn't even think it worth mentioning that he might demand the price in blood," Andross said. Karris didn't know if it was even meant for her ears, he said it so low. "He shouldn't have been able to seize power at all. Satrapah Tilleli Azmith was there, ready to rule. Messages had been sent. She knew the danger Haruru was creating. She was going to return Paria to its loyal course. What are the odds she'd have a stroke the same night?"

"Zero," Karris said.

"Excuse me?" Andross asked. Then, sharper, "What did you say?"

"I had her killed. She was the Nuqaba's spymaster. I found out that you'd ordered the Nuqaba murdered, and I judged Azmith an even greater threat."

He looked at her with those tired eyes, and she couldn't tell if the brief flicker of life in them was surprise that she'd learned of his own contract, that she was capable of ordering a murder herself, or surprise that she would admit it.

Then Andross snorted. "Of course you did. And you used some goddam amateur to do the deed. My assassin does his job professionally—then yours comes along and bungles everything mine was accomplishing. Of course Azmith was the spymaster! That's how I knew she was practical enough to deal with."

Karris wasn't about to tell him that his assassin not only wasn't a man but was also the same assassin as hers.

But still, how could I have sent Teia into that?

I didn't, though. She was already being sent. I was just trying to take advantage of a bad situation and turn it into an opportunity. I was trying to be someone other than who I am, and I've reaped...this.

Andross had murdered the Nuqaba; it was his fault that Ironfist was furious. But Karris had murdered Azmith; it was her fault that Ironfist had become king.

"There was a moment there," Andross said, "when Ironfist demanded blood, and I swear I saw relief on your face."

"Relief?" Karris said. "You think I'd choose blood over marriage? Especially this marriage? Ironfist has been my dear friend for many years, and in case you hadn't noticed, is quite a handsome and powerful man. If I cannot have my Gavin, I could hardly hope for a better marriage."

Andross narrowed his eyes at her for a long moment, then said grudgingly, "I suppose so."

"It should be you," she said, "who dies."

He laughed. Waited. Then chuckled. "That's all you're going to say? You're not even going to make a case for it? Tell me how old I am, maybe? How I've 'lived my life already'? Surely you can dig deep and find some reason why the actual promachos is less important than a White."

"You know all the reasons I could bring up, but there's only one that matters."

"Oh?" Genuine curiosity filled his face. He stood up straighter, and something of Gavin Guile appeared in him.

Karris said, "You should volunteer to die because you love Kip. I know you do. I know there's something more than avarice and power in you."

At that very moment, there was a crack of thunder and lightning, the faint sizzle from the antennae above the tower as it was hit.

Andross laughed immediately. *Immediately* he laughed. "Love? Kip?" He laughed again.

That goddam lightning. A surge of hatred at this old man had coursed through her as fast as the lightning strike, but it had also been illuminated by that lightning striking at exactly the wrong moment: she doubted her words for a moment even as she said them—and he saw it.

"You didn't leave things so well with Kip, did you?" he asked.

She had no answer for him. But he caught the guilt in her eyes.

He said, "I'm the promachos. This is a matter of war. I could simply choose. I could make my life easier for once and choose that *you* die. But I won't do that. That'd make things too easy for you. When you were young, your choices ruined my family, and you've pretended ever since then that they weren't your choices at all. Now it's your family on the line, your boy, and your choice. I choose this much: Ironfist won't have my blood. So. You're the hard-ass; you're the *Iron* White. You choose who dies. This is your fault, so as I recall you telling me once with such great glee, 'You shit the bed, you clean it up.'"

Chapter 90

It was time. It was all for this.

Ironfist had demanded apartments in the Prism's Tower befitting his high status and bullied an underchatelaine until he was moved to the one with the secret exit he'd discovered years ago.

The execution was scheduled for midnight. He guessed that tonight's outing might take an hour. Maybe even two. But there was no way he was going to cut it too close, so he was giving himself four hours. A king didn't have to explain himself to anyone, so he'd simply retired to his rooms early.

His own guards outside his door had been joined by a pair of Blackguards that he didn't even recognize.

Things had changed a lot in his absence. After the loss of so many Blackguards at Brightwater Wall, he'd sped up the training of replacements himself, but he couldn't imagine that two nunks who'd been made full Blackguards in a year's time could possibly be up to the high standards he'd maintained for so many years.

It irked him to think of poorly trained men and women in his beloved 'guard, but that was outrage that belonged to another life. Besides, it had been under his leadership that a single cannon shell had taken out so much of the Blackguard.

One shell, one lucky shot, had obliterated several hundred years' worth of training and magical excellence and more than a million danars in recruitment and training and contract costs.

Ironfist hated guns. Hated how they could render moot so many thousands of hours of training. But tonight he checked his own carefully. He carried a fine Parian flintlock, as excellent as any Ilytian work, or so the smith had insisted. Ironfist double-checked the black powder and frizzen plate, and twisted the cockjaw screw a bit on the flint so it was held tighter. He put the pistol carefully in its holster bag and drew his ataghan. He checked the forward-curving blade and that its fit in the scabbard wasn't too sticky.

He'd already instructed his Tafok Amagez not to disturb him until it was time for the execution. They knew to obey. He was dressed in white and gold. He didn't bother with a disguise. If he were seen, he was too recognizable for any disguise to be of much use.

The passage was too tight to bring everything he wanted to bring. As a big man, he'd always been tempted to carry too much for missions simply because he could. The line between wanting to be prepared and actual paranoia was slippery. Especially when the rumor he'd heard involved actual, literal immortals.

Taking a deep breath, he tucked the bit of lambent white luxin he'd kept for so long into the pistol bag. The orange seed crystal he draped around his neck, and tucked under the tight cloth against his skin. He might hate the thing, but he couldn't deny it was useful sometimes.

Enough delaying.

He pulled on the bedpost, twisted a brazier, and pushed on the wall. It opened on not-quite-silent hinges. Perfect. That meant no one had been oiling them in the past year.

The secret passage was not so much a passage as a pit. There was a tiny ledge and then a ladder with many broken rungs rising and dropping into darkness. From the top, every prime-numbered rung had a trap built into it, either breaking off or triggering knives or something equally pleasant. The traps and the tightness could easily turn the whole shaft into a slaughterhouse, so Ironfist hadn't told Kip and his Mighty about this exit on that day they'd needed to escape, the day Hanishu had died.

One of Kip's friends had been killed and another crippled because of Ironfist's decision. But that's what commanders do.

And kings, he supposed.

Closing the panel behind him, he mounted the ladder in the secret passage.

The moist, cold wind licked at his face as he descended in utter darkness. Just beneath him, rung thirty-seven was already broken off. There had once been horizontal doors to shut out the humid breeze, but they'd been left open, and the hinges had rusted open in some time period when no one had known or taken care of this secret. That was what had exposed the secret to a young Watch Captain Ironfist: the sound of that damp wind, circulating air up and down the crooked shaft, and on some few nights *whistling*. It had driven Ironfist crazy until he found an entrance.

Someone else had known of the passage, and Ironfist had never found out whom. The whistling only happened rarely, and he'd later realized it had been when that other person exited one of the lower levels on a windy day.

Skip forty-one. Whoever had created the ladder had helpfully left Old Parian numbers inscribed in the ladder every twelfth rung, so one could enter at any entrance and not have to memorize which rung a particular one might be. The trouble with skipping rungs, however, was that you had to count with both your feet and your hands—and the numbers started at the top of Prism's Tower, though Ironfist had never found an exit or even eavesdropping holes up that high.

Maybe some previous Prism or White had filled those in, but it wasn't exactly the kind of thing Ironfist could have asked anyone about.

Ironfist hadn't done this climb often enough that he was comfortable doing it quickly. And before now, he'd always made his ascents and descents during the day, so that he could burn a lux torch without worrying that the light would shine through the cracks into all the rooms along the route and announce his presence.

Now the darkness whispered to him as he slithered through its fist. Small men probably think that being a big man only has advantages. The squeeze between rungs forty-three and forty-seven argued differently. Ironfist had to remove his sword belt and pistol bag and hold them above his head, and then he had to wedge one shoulder down into the vise. He got stuck.

He couldn't breathe, and he almost forgot everything. His lowest foot was touching forty-seven, the next trap rung. He had to skip that one.

He was wedged in tight, taking little shallow breaths.

I've done this.

But never in this hellstone darkness.

He closed his eyes. They weren't doing him any good anyway. He visualized what he knew to be true. Then he expelled all his breath and slid.

The forty-eighth rung was as jarring as ever. His shin pressed so hard against the forty-seventh rung that he was terrified it would trigger whatever trap lay there, as ever.

Funny how he never remembered that in time. Not ha-ha funny, rather ha-ha-I'm-glad-I-didn't-wet-myself funny.

But he'd made it. And from there, he worked down to the bottom of the ladder without incident. He found the hinges by touch, and applied oil to them, using a boar-bristle brush to push the oil into all the cracks as well as he could. A little noise above had been comforting. Here, it could be catastrophic.

Then he listened at the hidden door for several minutes.

This door opened to the passage between the back docks and the Chromeria's main hall. Large, serious gates covered both front and back. Ironfist had had one of his men surreptitiously check that his keys to the gates still worked. They did.

Thank Orholam for lazy or ignorant successors. Of course, usually a commander of the Blackguard trained his or her successor for a year or more. Ironfist had simply been deposed and banished. That still stung. He'd valued that office far more than he valued being a king.

After hearing only silence, he opened the door. The hinges were quiet, but not silent, and his heart thudded with tension.

Waiting was agony for any soldier, but Ironfist thought he hated it more than most. He was a frontal-assault man, not a skulker in shadows.

But then he was in the passage, and there was no one in sight. He closed the hidden door carefully, and headed toward the back docks.

It was a relief to see the gate, because there was light there—even the natural darkness of night was brighter than that terrible passage, and the moon was shedding considerable light.

In peacetime, only the front gate was guarded—after all, the gates guarded a tunnel with only one exit and one entrance, so why guard it front *and* back?

But this wasn't peacetime. There were two Blackguards stationed at the back gate.

Ironfist didn't know who these men or women were—men, judging by the silhouettes in the darkness—but he had to be willing to kill them. If necessary.

But it shouldn't be necessary. Having found an escape tunnel, Ironfist had figured no one would build an escape tunnel that would lead to a locked iron gate. It had taken him months, but he'd found it: a simple hidden room that had a crawl hole out the back.

It was open to the outside, and a skulk of foxes had taken up residence in this cozy cave. Which meant that even after Ironfist's first, horrific encounter, it still—years later—stank of musk and fur. He'd liked foxes, before.

Responsible commander that he'd been, he'd collapsed the tunnel so that there were no secret entrances into the heart of the Prism's Tower.

But he'd only collapsed the outermost few feet. He could dig through it if he must.

If the Blackguards stationed back here stayed exactly at their stations until they were relieved rather than walking back into the tunnel when they heard their replacements coming, it *would* be necessary.

He really, really didn't want to deal with the stench of a fox den and the pains of digging underground. It would add an hour to his night. It was only going to take a few minutes for him to find out.

In a quarter of an hour, the shift changed. At a call from deep inside the passage, the Blackguards outside opened the gate, came inside, closed and locked it behind them—and then walked into the tunnel to meet their replacements, chatting in worried tones about the impending execution and the looming fight.

Good luck, at last!

Ironfist slipped out soon after they passed his hidden room, then slipped out through the gate, locking it behind him.

Thank Orholam. He'd been starting to worry about time.

He walked at a low crouch until he was well out of sight on this cold, drizzly night. The Blackguards might chat with their reinforcements for several minutes, or they might come immediately. He wasn't going to risk anything. Not tonight.

Only steps away from the boathouse where his objective lay, a voice called out from a shadow, freezing him.

"I never thought you could do this. Not you."

Cruxer!

Cruxer couldn't have been more than eighteen years old now, but there was no trace of a boy in his voice or his eyes. His sword was already drawn, tunic dripping with rain. He'd been lying in wait.

"How did you—" Ironfist began. But it was the wrong question. If only he had the Guiles' golden tongues.

"I went to your rooms to speak with you. Some of your men are still loyal to the Chromeria," Cruxer said. "They told me you asked one of them to test your old keys on these gates. So I know something's back here. Perhaps you're to let in some invaders? Order assassins, maybe?"

"No," Ironfist said, but he felt a chill down his back at the mention of the Order.

"You're in the Order," Cruxer said.

"I...was." Ironfist didn't consider himself the most emotionally attuned man, but the orange seed crystal against his skin magnified his awareness of currents of feeling—and Cruxer felt as jagged as shattered hellstone, all dark glittery points ready to slice.

"All those years you were commander. They were all a lie."

"No."

"You infiltrated the Blackguard for the Order of the Broken Eye," Cruxer said.

"I thought I could hold them together," Ironfist said. "That they didn't need to be opposed. That the old wounds could be healed..."

"So you're a weasel as well as a traitor," Cruxer said.

And suddenly Ironfist saw that this young man was as hard and unforgiving and as foolish as he himself had been at that age. And as dangerous.

"Cruxer, stop. You're already in my zone."

The kill zone was the area inside of which an armed opponent

581

could complete a lethal assault before you could defend yourself. It could be a surprisingly large area, especially for a tall, quick man with a long reach and good training, like Cruxer.

Ironfist wasn't going to just let him stroll inside the zone, but making a move toward his own ataghan would start them down a path to misery. When blades sing, words fall silent.

"Son, I can tell you everything, but you need to give me time to explain."

"Time?" Cruxer asked. "How much time does it take for the orange bane to corrupt a man?"

Ironfist was stricken. *Shit.* He knew about the orange? The seed crystal was barely covered by his tunic's neckline. If Cruxer saw it, what would he do?

"This isn't you doing this, is it?" Cruxer said. "The orange bane has changed you, hasn't it?"

"It has affected me," Ironfist admitted. "But—"

"Did it give you the idea to make yourself king?"

"Well...maybe. I'm not sure, but—"

"And to demand blood for blood?"

"I—that's not what you think."

"Treason and murder aren't what I think?"

"I'm not going to go through with it! Son, you know me!"

"I know you? Which *you*? I looked up to you. You were everything to me. Everything I dreamed of becoming. You were the standard I fell short of. And it was all a lie. You're here opening the gates for the Order," Cruxer said.

"No, no! This is my *vengeance* on the Order. *They're* the ones who killed my sister."

"Your sister was *insane*. A loose cannon in storm-tossed seas. She was trying to kill you. You want me to believe—How about your brother's death? You don't blame that on the Guiles?"

Ironfist hesitated. "No. Not—"

"Liar."

"Fine! I'm furious! But for the greater good, I can let it go," Ironfist said.

"Like you let your integrity go?"

Ironfist's chest expanded as he drew in air sharply, his teeth baring.

"Were you serving the greater good when you joined the Order?" Cruxer asked, his voice raw.

"I thought so," Ironfist admitted. "Things were different then. The Order was just a tiny regional power halfway across the world from here. And they were the only ones who could save my sister. I thought

I could keep my vows to them and to the Blackguard—I was all the way over here!"

"Our Blackguard vows include renouncing all other vows. And reporting them."

"I was a kid! I made a mistake. You're telling me you're perfect, Cruxer? You've never made any mistakes? I seem to remember different."

"You're right," Cruxer said, his face haggard. "I loved Lucia, and I got her killed. But I decided not to compromise my integrity ever again, and that's the difference between us."

Cruxer wasn't taking his eyes off him. The young man was totally keyed up. And if Ironfist remembered his speed correctly, Cruxer was well within killing distance. Any wrong move Ironfist made was going to end badly. "Son, you have to believe me. I'm here to do the right thing."

"Through treason and murder?"

"I know it looks bad. It's a stratagem."

"That the orange revealed to you," Cruxer said.

Ironfist felt pierced through. He'd lied to Cruxer already, and the young man had seen through it. If he was caught in one more lie, this would be over. "Yes," he said softly. "It's for the greater—"

"Say 'the greater good' one more fucking time!"

"Easy, *easy*. Cruxer, please..."

"We're soldiers! We're guardians! That's who we are. We *obey*! The greater good isn't for men like you and me to decide!"

"Son, sometimes you still don't know your ass from your elbow. A man never gets to put his conscience in someone else's care. Every one of us has to decide what the greater good is."

Cruxer's face hardened, and Ironfist knew he'd made a mistake. Cruxer said, "You come upstairs with me now. You cancel the execution and I'll let them decide what to do with you."

"I can't do that. We have to play this my way."

"Oh, we do?" Cruxer said, stepping forward.

"Yes! Dammit, Cruxer, stay back!"

If Cruxer attacked, he'd lunge with that sword, but Ironfist wasn't exactly unarmed. People saw the heavy chain on his arm and thought of it as costuming, or a slow offensive weapon if he unslung it. But as it was, tight from wrist to elbow to shoulder, it could also make a bit of a shield.

Ironfist said, "I'm here for Gavin Guile. My contacts told me he's here. Locked up in a special cell beneath the Chromeria. There's a hidden entrance out here. I can save him. I'm the only man on earth who can save Gavin Guile."

"Really? He's been here all this time?" Cruxer said, scoffing. "Fine, then! Let's go upstairs, tell Karris."

"We *can't*. The Old Man's here. If he gets word—and he will!—if he even suspects what I'm planning, he'll kill Gavin before we can move."

"Oh, the Old Man of the Desert himself? Him, too? This gets more convoluted by the moment, doesn't it? But then, lies do that, don't they?"

"The Old Man'll be at the execution. I have from now until then to save Gavin Guile, and you are burning precious time here, son."

A flicker of doubt crossed Cruxer's eyes.

"We need Gavin Guile or we're doomed. He's the Lightbringer," Ironfist said.

"No, he's not," Cruxer said.

"He drafted white luxin at the siege of Garriston. I saw it. I have a piece of it. Here in my bag. I can show you!"

"Don't you pull anything from that bag! You think I'm an idiot?"

"Cruxer, you *know* me. Let me explain."

"Toss me the pistol bag."

"I'm not tossing you my bag. Just—I will move *so* slowly. You have every advantage—"

"*Slowly.* That's the key, isn't it? I know something about will-casting now, *Commander*. Takes a few minutes to will-cast a person if you don't want them to notice, doesn't it? You're doing it to me right now, aren't you? Bet you've got orange seed crystal in there, huh?"

"No, no!" Will-casting?

"Then why are you stalling?"

"Because you're right on the edge and I don't want either of us to die for no reason!" Only then did Ironfist realize he'd just lied, sort of. But he wasn't will-casting with the orange seed crystal. He didn't even know if he could do that.

He did have it on him, though, barely tucked out of sight in the neckline of his tunic, and if Cruxer saw it, he was going to think Ironfist was lying about everything else, too.

But as sweat trickled down between Ironfist's pectorals, he saw Cruxer's temperature drop, just a little.

"We can save him together," Ironfist said. "We wait until the very moment of the execution, and we bring him up there with us. He might be in rough shape, but you and I can keep him *safe*. Against the Order, you understand? We can't let anyone else get close. I didn't tell anyone, because we can't *trust* anyone."

"What are the names of the other Blackguards loyal to the Order?" Cruxer demanded.

"Goddam, son. You think they tell us?"

"*Yes*," Cruxer said. And the way he said it suggested a door closing, a last chance was passing. Of course he believed that, though. Ironfist had been the commander. He had to know.

"Grinwoody," Ironfist blurted out. "Grinwoody's the Old Man of the Desert. The head of the Broken Eye. Hiding in plain sight. As close to power as you can possibly get, but invisible. And if we give him even five minutes' warning, he'll spring some backup plan. He'll escape. He's smarter than you know. But if I can—"

Cruxer scoffed. "I ask for *Blackguards* and you offer up one old slave?"

There was no time to tell Cruxer the plan. He wouldn't believe it anyway. "Son. Everything I've done—declaring myself king, everything! It's all been for this. Only I can save Gavin Guile. Only I can stop the Order. Only I can pay for what I've done."

But while Ironfist kept his voice contrite, level, there was rage rising in him, too.

I can't let you stop me. This is bigger than you. It's bigger than me. This is redemption for all my betrayals and failures. This is the future of the Seven Satrapies.

Through the orange crystal, he could feel the war raging in his young protégé, scared, angry, guilty, wanting to believe, and not daring to.

Ironfist was turned the wrong way to see if the Blackguards had already appeared at the gate behind them, but every time Cruxer raised his voice, Ironfist thought, What if one of the reinforcements is Grinwoody's man?

Even if they weren't, any of the Blackguards would seize him and take him inside. And if they did that, he would lose everything.

Cruxer said, "You're listening behind you. You waiting for some of your traitor friends to join you?"

"Cruxer, let me show you. I'm gonna pull the white luxin from this bag."

But his hand was closed around the pistol's butt. His thumb pulled the cockjaw back almost to the place where it would click. But he couldn't cock it. If Cruxer heard that sound, he'd attack.

If he twisted his wrist, he could drop the cockjaw without drawing the pistol from the bag. It would have a very good chance of firing half-cocked. It would be faster even than Cruxer's sword thrust.

"Don't you do it!" Cruxer said.

And in the strain on Cruxer's face, Ironfist saw not the boy before him but Cruxer's father, Holdfast. Holdfast had been too much older than Ironfist for them to really be friends, but the older man had looked out for him. And when he'd died, there'd been that same expression on his face.

"I'm stopping," Ironfist said gently.

"You taught me everything," Cruxer said, his features contorting. Maybe he was beyond backing down now. "You taught me to protect my ward no matter what. You taught me it was better to yell a Nine Kill wrongly than to remain silent and let my ward die. I want to believe you. But you lied before. I can't give you another chance. I can't let you kill Kip. He's the Lightbringer. I'm sorry. I loved you. Now, draw. Please. I can't kill you in cold blood. Draw!"

But against every instinct screaming in him, Ironfist slowly uncurled his tight fingers from the grip of his pistol. He took a deep breath.

Cruxer's eyes flicked down, and Ironfist realized that something about his motion had popped the orange seed crystal out of his neckline and into view, where it burned with inner light.

He saw the look in the young man's eyes even as the orange sent him the feeling: Cruxer felt stricken, betrayed.

Cruxer said, "I believed you. You almost—" And then he lunged with perfect form and incredible speed.

He was even faster than Ironfist remembered.

In the tales, a duel between grandmasters is a wondrous thing. Each arrives in the prime of his powers. Neither is given some unfair disadvantage of injury or being weaponless. In the tales, a duel between grandmasters is a match of intellect and strategy as much as one of pure physique.

This lunge stabbed through Ironfist's left arm and side even as he twisted. The blade had passed through the center of a link in his great chain as he was bringing it up to block. Then, caught in that chain, the blade flexed hard—and snapped.

Cruxer tried to retreat, but he was off balance from the unexpected forces of the sword catching and then snapping. Ironfist's shoulder collided with the younger man's stomach. They went down together.

Ironfist drew a knife even as he was landing on the younger man's legs.

Slashing for Cruxer's hamstring, Ironfist cut into his calf instead. He rolled away.

There was no time to gauge wounds. Ironfist scrambled away

on hands and knees toward his bag, which had fallen to one side, while Cruxer lunged away to create distance. Blue luxin flashed from Cruxer and hit him, knocking Ironfist over and on top of his bag.

Ironfist rolled and saw Cruxer rising up to one knee to draw a pistol from some kind of holster at his hip.

Lying on the ground, Ironfist pulled his own pistol from his bag, but he was too slow.

The holster gave Cruxer the advantage. He finished his draw and pulled his trigger as Ironfist's gun was still coming on target.

And nothing happened. Wet from the rain in its open holster, the frizzen didn't spark. Cruxer was cocking the jaw again when Ironfist fired. Powder roared in a burning-white flash that blossomed into a black cloud between them.

But Cruxer didn't stop. Ironfist had missed. Cruxer cocked his pistol and aimed deliberately.

Ironfist threw himself down again as Cruxer fired.

The concussion deafened Ironfist, but Cruxer missed.

At least as far as Ironfist could tell. Battle was like that. Sometimes you could be dead ten seconds before you realized it.

Ironfist stood, blood gushing from his arm and side. He felt suddenly faint.

He collapsed at Cruxer's feet.

Tossing his pistol aside, he fumbled toward his bag. He wanted his protégé to know the white luxin was real. He wanted Cruxer to know it was all real. Maybe, maybe Cruxer could save Gavin. Maybe Ironfist's lies hadn't doomed them all.

But with one foot, Cruxer flipped Ironfist over onto his back. He must've thought Ironfist was going for another weapon.

Ironfist looked up into the judgment that stood over him.

Then Cruxer tottered. His face twisted with irritation.

Then he collapsed beside Ironfist.

The young warrior gasped bloody foam a few times, a bullet hole in his chest sucking air as his lungs filled with blood.

Ironfist hadn't missed.

Cruxer made no gestures. Said no final words. And Ironfist couldn't read the expression in his eyes.

"I tried... Oh God," Ironfist said. "I tried."

But there was no absolution here.

He pushed himself up to his knees, fumbling to show Cruxer the white luxin—to show his dying eyes that it was true, it was all true.

But Ironfist stumbled, couldn't stand. Suddenly weak, he fell face-down again.

There was a lot of blood. His blood.

It was all going dark. He wasn't going to make it.

I'm dying, he thought.

He was frightened.

Chapter 91

Karris lay on her face, her body surrendered to the ministrations of Rhoda's magical hands. It was good to be reminded that the body could be a temple of joy. That there was dancing, and hugging, and pleasing touches, and that life was not only war and death and unconscionable choices.

She wished she could lie abed with Gavin one last time, holding each other and speaking softly, or making love, either would be her choice of how she would spend this evening that would end in a night of blood, a failure that would echo into history. But the world is a broken place. As far as second bests went, a massage from Rhoda was better than most got.

A knock intruded on the pleasure of Rhoda scraping the warm oil from Karris's limbs with a strigil. "Lord Kip Guile, at your pleasure, High Lady," the Blackguard Stump said.

Rhoda packed hot towels all around Karris's limbs and torso. It was a natural break in the massage, as the heat worked in to Karris's body. Karris sighed, and dismissed Rhoda. "Send him in," she said.

Kip walked in. He'd obviously never been here, because he seemed surprised to see the massage table, and more surprised to see Karris on it, undressed—though she was covered.

Then there was a tiny expression of anger. If she hadn't been looking for it, Karris would have missed it. It said, 'You're getting a massage, now? What a bitch.'

Good. Karris wanted him angry. Time and distance and high office tends to put blocks up between you and other people. She didn't have time for horseshit. And she deserved his rage.

"I treated you terribly before you left," she said.

It was as if she'd written out the painful memory on a parchment, rolled it up, and swatted him across the nose with it like an unsuspecting dog. But he covered it quickly.

"Ah, you mean when my little joke failed so spectacularly?" Kip said. "My apologies again. I didn't understand the gravity of that subject, and dealt with my awkwardness . . . well, awkwardly."

She didn't cut him off. "Kip, when a person in his midteens acts immaturely, that's entirely forgivable and even appropriate. When a person in her fourth decade does, it's neither.

"Kip, a long time ago, I abandoned my son, and the guilt of that has never left me. So when you showed up and were so . . . you . . . I felt Orea Pullawr had manipulated me; that she thought the loss of one son could be made up by substituting another—as if I'd misplaced a pair of boots and she bought me a better pair. I was angry at myself and at others I'd trusted and at the world. I wasn't angry at you. Actually, it was the opposite. I was angry because Orea's plan was working so well, and I couldn't imagine how unnatural I must be to allow a child who was not my own to fill the ache I had for the one I gave up."

Kip said nothing, but she saw she had his total attention.

"I've realized a few things since then. First, that last part was horseshit. A parent's love isn't a barrel of water to be rationed among those dying of thirst, where more for one means less for another. A parent's love is a new channel cut through the self to the divine essence, a river that cannot be exhausted or even fathomed, only experienced. You know how Garriston used to have irrigation canals everywhere?"

"I saw where they used to be," Kip said. "All filled with sand and scrub now."

"That wasteland was what my life was when I first got to know you, Kip. Opening a new irrigation canal threatened what was working for me. Not working well, granted. But I knew the rules there. I'd adjusted to desert life. I treated you terribly because I was scared. If you'd been here since then, I could have apologized sooner, and . . . well, that's past now. The second revelation was . . . I don't like your brother."

"Half brother," Kip interjected.

She turned her head so she was facing away from him. She said, "And he doesn't even seem like that much. He has few of your talents and fewer still of your virtues. I don't even know if I can love him even in the abstract, and I've been trying." Her throat closed off. She swallowed, but she couldn't go on.

"And yet you summoned me, not him," Kip said flatly. "I heard about Ironfist's ultimatum. Everyone has. He wants a dead Guile. And here I am. I can't believe he's really doing this."

"He's not taking visitors. The Tafok Amagez wouldn't even knock on his door."

"Thanks for trying. I guess," Kip said.

"Ironfist said he wouldn't consider Zymun, Kip."

"He did?" Kip asked. "Oh. The rumor left that part out. Well. That's too bad."

Karris snorted. That was putting it mildly. "Andross's first choice, naturally, was to eliminate the threat at its source. Kill Ironfist, or detain him and forge orders—something. But before we could make plans, we were told that if Ironfist is harmed or doesn't give the order in person, his men will sail away immediately. His ships have orders to fire on anyone who tries to approach. Ironfist knows how convincing Andross can be, so he's simply not letting there be communication at all."

"And what about my people?" Kip asked.

"They're already here. Which, ordinarily, would mean their fate is tied to ours. But with your skimmers, we know they could leave. But they won't. You won't allow it."

"Even if I'm dead?" Kip demanded.

"Goodness sometimes makes one predictable."

"Thank you? I guess?" Kip said. "Funny how quickly things change, huh?"

"How so?"

"This morning, Andross wanted me to wager my marriage to save the Jaspers. I thought I was deciding everything with that game. I even thought I won. And now it's not my happiness you'll take, it's my life, and my game didn't matter at all. Even Andross Guile's best-laid plans go awry. In different circumstances, it'd be almost enough to make one hopeful, you know? That he didn't foresee everything. If a peon like Ironfist might disrupt his schemes, maybe I could, too. Not that this is the disruption I would have chosen."

She lay there, silent, facing away, hardly able to breathe. She didn't want him to see her weep.

"Hard to believe Ironfist turned into such an asshole. It just doesn't seem like him."

"We assassinated his sister," Karris said. The time for lies and hiding was finished. "Although I never heard a good word about her, he loved her. He always thought the stories that trickled out about her were planted by her enemies. She was his blind spot. After his brother died helping you escape, she was all he had left. We ruined him, Kip. I took away the last thing holding him up."

She couldn't see Kip's reaction, but this was the grandson of

Andross Guile, the son of Gavin. "Ah," Kip said, "I get it: our family took everything from him. Andross cost him his life's work as commander. I cost him Tremblefist. You cost him Haruru. I guess I can understand that rage. Everyone's got a limit."

They waited in silence. Karris's towels had gotten cold, and her stomach felt tight and uncomfortable. Rhoda would be poking her head in at any moment, if she hadn't already done so discreetly.

Kip cleared his throat.

"Fine," Kip said. "My people will fight under High General Danavis's command, as you asked. I would like time to write one last letter to my people expressing my wishes. And one to my wife. Naturally, I'm sure you'll read both before you pass them along. You'll likely..." He cleared his throat, having difficulty. Karis was still facing away. Tears poured down her face. She held her body tight so the sobs wouldn't betray her. "You'll likely need to imprison Tisis until all this is over, or she'll do something everyone regrets. I'll make two copies of the letter—she may burn the first." He laughed, but it was a short, forced sound closer to a cough. "Passionate woman. You would've liked her."

"High Lady?" Rhoda's voice came in as she did. The physicker began pulling away the towels, heedless of Kip's presence.

"When is the execution?" Kip asked.

"Within the hour," Karris said. She winced as Rhoda put icy-cold hands on each side of her neck. "We need to make sure that High General Danavis has time to integrate and deploy the forces. Even waiting this long is cutting it close."

"Not enough time to take care of everything," Kip grumbled under his breath.

"Who among us gets that?" Karris asked. Her stomach twisted.

She heard him take one step toward the door. Then he stopped.

"*Fuuuck*," Kip said suddenly under his breath. "You're not getting a massage. You're being anointed for burial. You didn't choose me. You chose *you*."

She didn't answer. Couldn't. She hadn't been able to muster the resolve to tell him yet, and even now her will failed her. She rolled over and sat up. Rhoda covered her, expertly using first her own bulk and then a robe to maintain her patient's dignity—such as it was.

"You?!" Kip demanded. "But you're *needed*!"

Needed?! What did he know about unmet needs? The very word pushed her enough that she could finally speak. "Kip. Do you want to know one of the deepest horrors of life? None of us is needed, not truly. It's just nicer for those who love us if we're there."

"I won't accept that. That's horseshit!" Kip said. "I won't let you die for—"

"For you?"

"For Andross! For Ironfist's stupid pride!"

"Kip, I'm not doing this for them. Or even for you. Not if I'm being honest with myself. I'm not that selfless. Really, what have I got left? My husband is gone and likely won't ever return. The friend I admired so much, who became like a father to me in the Blackguard, wants me dead—and I can't blame him for that. My son Zymun is a soulless manipulator, rapist, and murderer incapable of human feeling. I have only my work, my Blackguards' love, and my hopes for you and your life. All those things demand I do this.

"How could I live with myself if I asked you to die in my place? How monstrous would history think I was? Would they call me Karris Ironheart perhaps if—after you offered me a piece of motherhood—I not only spurned you and drove you away but then, when you finally came back to save us all, I rewarded you by demanding your death? No. No. This way history at least will be fooled. I'll become another heroic Karris sacrificing herself for the Chromeria. It's a lie, but one that might inspire others to do better than I have. I've known I was going to die in this battle for some time. This is—this is just like having my Freeing a bit early, is all."

"No," Kip said plaintively.

"You won your game. Go enjoy your victory and your life. Both are more fleeting than you know."

"You cannot—"

But another cramp hit Karris's stomach, this one insistent. "Now, if you'll pardon me," she said. "I decided that defecating as one dies isn't commensurate with the dignity expected of the White, so I took a laxative earlier. Shitting uncontrollably now seemed better than doing so later, but I'd rather you not watch."

Chapter 92

Get up, whinger. One more lap.

Ironfist woke. He was cold. Freezing cold. His cheek was in a pool of something sticky.

So, not dead. Not yet. He tried to move.

Everything hurt. Two places were utter fire, but his whole body hurt like he had a terrible fever. Everything ached. Lying still hurt marginally less.

I know I'm the fool who chose a team race, but you're the fool who agreed. Get up.

It was how he'd encouraged his little brother, when they were mere teens in that awful mountains-to-desert race that capped the novennial Philocteian Games. They'd always loved running, but they'd never expected to be among the best. But somehow, the better runners had fallen out through injury, and the young princes had suddenly become the bearers of their clan's pride.

Clamping his arm tight to his side, Ironfist sat up. He gasped. His injuries tore open afresh, both arm and chest.

Nearby, Cruxer lay dead in the midst of guns and a broken sword and a pool of blood. A lot of blood.

But the spiritual pain was blunted by the physical.

Ironfist blinked until the black spots retreated from his vision.

The Blackguards who should have come to the back gate had never come. Even with the musket shots, no one had come.

Up. Up!

Ironfist must surely be running out of time before the execution. He looked at the stars, but he'd never paid enough attention to know at what hour certain stars rose and set at this time of year. He couldn't tell how long he'd been unconscious. Besides, it didn't matter. All that mattered was saving Gavin Guile.

"One more lap," he said.

The great race ended with two laps in the hippodrome before cheering crowds. Hanishu and Harrdun had no idea that they'd nearly caught up with the Tiru-clan bastards they'd been following across the desert until they arrived in the hippodrome itself. The men were walking, beaten, exhausted. One was limping. They looked at Hanishu and Harrdun's entrance with frank terror.

Like young antelope, Hanishu and Harrdun had found sudden energy. They'd closed the gap. They'd passed the men, laughing as they headed into the final lap.

They were going to win. *Win!*

Forty thousand people were on their feet, shouting, cheering. And then the young men passed the Tiru section. Their tribal rivals had been aghast, in denial on the first lap.

This time, they were furious. They began pelting the boys with stones, crockery, coins, anything they could throw.

Ironfist had given Hanishu the inside, intending to make the last lap a friendly rivalry, to see if he could pass him in the final stretch.

But that put Hanishu closest to them, so he caught the brunt of the Tirus' fury. A cup hit him in the knee, midstride, and then a gruel bowl smashed over his ear.

Hanishu had gone down, nearly unconscious.

"Come on, brother," Ironfist said aloud now, his worlds blurring together. "Everything we've done up to now has been for this. No surrender, or it's all for nothing."

Using his good hand while keeping his other arm clamped tight to his side to try to slow the blood loss, Ironfist pushed off the ground. He swayed, faint, and reached out. He braced himself on the boathouse to keep from falling, a sudden wave of vertigo cresting over him.

After he steadied himself and the dizziness passed, he opened his eyes.

He was a good ten paces from the boathouse. There was nothing to steady himself on.

Hanishu had stood, staggered, and fell again as the Tiru runners came back into view around the corner behind them, catching up.

Harrdun pulled him to his feet and braced him with an arm, and tried to pull him to a jog.

But his younger brother's knee gave out after the first step. He fell again, pulling Harrdun down with him.

Hanishu had started weeping. 'I can't. I can't. I want to, but I can't.'

"Don't you make me carry you," Ironfist said aloud now.

Two more teams had just entered the stadium. There was a near riot in the stands where other fans were attacking the Tiru for their stone-throwing.

With trembling arms and trembling legs, he'd picked up his little brother. Hanishu clung to him fiercely, trying to distribute his weight, trying to help, even as he'd doomed them.

Ironfist had jogged a few steps, but he couldn't keep it up, not after all the leagues they'd run. He slowed to a walk, and then it was all he could do to stagger forward one slow step at a time.

And then the hippodrome erupted in cheers and also shouts of outrage as the Tiru team crossed the finish line to win, and the brothers were both weeping.

And then another team passed them. And another. And Hanishu broke down as his big brother carried him. 'I failed you. I failed you.'

God *damn* this whole world to fire. Those were the very words Hanishu said again last year as he'd lain dying in Ironfist's arms. As if the failure were his.

The last hundred paces were agony. Someone offered to help, but Ironfist hadn't even been able to see them. There was only the finish line, and his brokenness and his rage and a tenacious love for his brother that said, *I will not quit.*

"We don't quit, brother. We don't quit," he'd said then and said now.

The last forty paces were a blur of unvariegated pain. The acid in his muscles, the roar of the crowd—helpful or hostile, he couldn't tell—building to a crescendo, and the burning of the sun. He wept—ashamed as a boy is foolishly ashamed of tears—and none judged him. He wept, and those walking behind him, a throng swollen to hundreds, perhaps thousands, wept with him.

They finished fourth, collapsing across the line, and that placement only because the fifth- and sixth-place clan teams had seen what happened and slowed to a walk behind them, and refused to let anyone else pass them.

They fell—and were instantly lifted on shoulders and paraded through another lap, the actual victors forgotten.

Their defeat had garnered more acclaim and support for their clan than any victory would have. Their grit and courage in adversity had not only made them famous, but had guaranteed their Tlanu-clan ascendancy.

Mother had been assassinated soon thereafter. And once a rival to his big brother, bitter at his constant defeats, Hanishu had changed utterly. He'd suddenly worshipped Harrdun, taking his few victories over his big brother with quiet joy and his own defeats with equanimity.

The two had become best friends.

And it had all been for evil.

If Ironfist hadn't decided on a whim to join that race and forced his little brother to be his partner, if Ironfist hadn't carried his little brother that one lap, Hanishu wouldn't have come to the Chromeria to join his big brother. He'd still be alive.

Ironfist slogged now to the rear dock and the hidden door in the little boathouse that disappeared into the secret bowels of the Chromeria. It was right where his last Order contact had said.

Even the Old Man needed people to do the actual digging, and even the Old Man had recruitment problems—if you simply kill your workers every time they dig a tunnel for you, you run out of workers.

He ducked his head to enter yet another tight, loathsome place. He was fully in the darkness before he realized that this time, he didn't need to worry about anyone seeing a light. His thinking was coagulating like the blood matting his tunic.

Cracking open a mag torch, he was blinded by the glow—too stupid in his present state to look away.

The path forked and he took the higher way. Soon he caught sight of a blue arc off to one side of the path. Like a tangent line, this path had been cut through the rock to intersect with a blue sphere at only one point. The path was above the luminous sphere, looking diagonally down on its contents.

Ironfist braced himself on the rock and looked down. Gavin Guile wasn't inside.

But *something* was. A vaguely man-shaped mass of glittering blue motes swirled in the cell. The cell itself was broken, a hole gaping in one side, and shards of blue luxin littering the area beyond. But jagged hellstone glimmered in that tunnel, trapping the glimmering creature.

The pieces tumbled around Ironfist's besieged brain like the individual colored tiles of a mosaic refusing to coalesce into an image: Gavin, in the first year after the False Prism's War, once asking, 'Ironfist, your family were priests long ago, right? Do you know what happens when the djinn die?'

It had been an odd question, but Gavin had been an odd young man.

Gavin wasn't in there, and Ironfist was dying. He had to move on before his time ran out.

He pushed off the wall and kept walking, leaning heavily on the wall.

Ironfist had known nothing special to tell the Prism, no family secrets. But he'd delved into the subject for some months before finally abandoning it as nothing more than the Prism's whim.

That piece, and Gavin's fierce insistence that he hunt wights alone—though not always alone. Sometimes he'd fought the Blackguard most to fight alone when the wight was the most powerful, and let others come to help him when one seemed least dangerous.

Ironfist reached the portal to the green cell. Gavin wasn't there, either. Some skeletal tree-thing, like climbing ivy twisted around itself, dragged branch claws against its circular walls, fists knotting.

Not here either, go on.

The djinn were the old gods. To the pagans, they were immortal gods, spirits who sometimes partnered with favored humans—high priests or heroes—and might extend a human's life indefinitely. The Old Parians had believed the djinn were malignant, that they waited until the hour of death so they could take possession of a body, a host that was always a drafter, in whose body they might then walk the earth. Sometimes they waited for old age; other times they prompted young heroes and heroines to an early death through heroism or suicide. Thus, with their stolen bodies, these spirits might experience physical life—sex and food and time and human relationships, parenthood, even the feel of the wind across one's face—treasured novelties for the otherwise incorporeal.

The yellow god in the yellow cell was like a taste of sickly sunlight. It was liquid gold coruscating and crashing like ocean waves as it alternately threw itself against the walls and then meditated quietly, lights sloshing about its incorporeal figure, eyes like unquiet stars.

No Gavin.

Weakening further still, Ironfist moved on. Hallucinations. These must be the hallucinations of trauma and fear of impending death.

After all the study Ironfist had done, Gavin had never inquired about the djinn again. Ironfist had dismissed it as the young Prism's capricious, capacious intellect shining its light every which way, even into dead histories.

As for Gavin's question, everyone supposed that the djinn simply slipped back into a spirit form when their host finally died, for even their magic couldn't keep a human body alive forever.

And that was the final piece of the mosaic.

That was why Gavin had hunted alone on those times. He was hunting the contemporary equivalent of high priests, the men and women who might be hosting immortals. He hadn't been hunting men; he'd been hunting *gods*. With each successful hunt, Gavin had brought a host and djinn here. Somehow he'd figured out how to bind the spirit of the immortals within this prison. Maybe he'd even made the prison itself.

But now Gavin wasn't in the orange, and there was no obvious escape route from this one. The orange thing sat, quiet, just a little orange man, not scary, not fascinating, just pathetic. Just longing to be free.

An altogether understandable wish, and why shouldn't he be free? Ironfist wondered if there wasn't some way he could help the poor—

It's a hex. Many, many hexes together, Ironfist saw now, swimming under the surface of the thing's orange skin.

He blinked and looked away. He didn't dare look again.

But he buckled at the next step, and he wouldn't have been able to stand if he hadn't been helped.

He took up the mag torch again. "Tore open my wound pretty good," he said to—

To whom? He looked around him.

Who'd helped him up just now?

And what had kept him from falling outside, when he'd been ten paces from the boathouse?

Most mortals can't see them. You only can because you're so close to death, where the veil thins between your world and reality. This next part is going to be hard for you.

The voice seemed so familiar, but Ironfist couldn't place it.

Ironfist pushed along the corridor. Past the red immortal—Dagnu, he realized now—who was in the form of a man yet looked like a thousand tiny embers catching flame, descending as ash, and catching flame and climbing again. It turned and glared fire at him as he staggered past.

Gavin wasn't in there.

Gavin wasn't in the superviolet cell that hurt the eyes.

Gavin wasn't in the sub-red inferno, where a face of flame floated.

Gavin wasn't in the black cell, where Ironfist couldn't see any creature, but could feel a malignant presence watching him back.

"I can save you," a quiet, calm, reasonable voice from that cell said. "*He* cannot. I can heal you. What use are you in this condition? Do not believe what the liars have told you. You know they're liars, do you not? They weaken the strong, and you, you could be very, very strong indeed. With my help."

But Ironfist had been around men and women more persuasive than himself for his entire life. Simplicity was the cloak that fit him.

Every time he tried subtlety and lies, it turned to blood.

Like today.

Oh, Cruxer. Orholam forgive me.

He stepped away.

Touch this.

Under his fingers he found hellstone, and he pressed it hard, making sure he was drafting nothing, making sure the magic of the old gods didn't cling to him.

How did he know to do that?

But then, within sight of the exit, he suddenly grew faint as the realization finally crested over him like a tsunami wave. He was leaving. He'd searched all the prisons.

Gavin Guile *had* been here. He had—unbelievably, horribly, unthinkably—been imprisoned with these things.

But Gavin was here no longer. Which meant...

It meant Ironfist had murdered Cruxer for nothing.

He fell to the cold stones of the tunnel. His mag torch finally sputtered out, leaving him in darkness.

It was all for nothing. He'd come too late. He'd faltered on the last lap. If Gavin wasn't here, and no one had heard of him since he'd left, that meant he was dead.

Ironfist had failed. He had tried to compete in subtlety with the Orea Pullawrs and the Andross Guiles and the Amalu Anazâr Tlanus of the world, and he'd failed.

He sank down, down. He could go on no longer.

God, he cried out, damn me! Give me what I deserve! Let me die. I'm finished. No more. No more.

You're not dying today, brother. I won't let you. We're not going to quit. Not today.

What? Ironfist thought.

Something was glowing in the darkness.

"Don't you make me carry you," Tremblefist said.

It wasn't real. Couldn't be. Ironfist knew that. He was dying, and his mind was playing tricks. Torturing him or comforting him. It wasn't reliable, that was all that mattered.

He lay down.

"You are the most loyal man I know," Tremblefist said. "I *know* you, brother."

A hallucination. A bitter memory. Ironfist settled his head against the stones to die.

"You think they cheered only because you carried me?" this phantasm of Tremblefist said. "Do you not remember your own wounds?"

No. He hadn't been harmed, had he? Hanishu had taken all the brunt of the Tiru fans' rage.

And then he remembered the blood. He'd taken blows in the face, a broken nose, a sliced forehead. Two or three broken ribs. He'd forgotten those.

By the time he'd crossed the finish line, he and Hanishu had been a gory mess together.

"I begged you to quit. I knew my wounds were temporary, but I was afraid you would die. You said, 'I don't know *quit.*'"

"I've learned," Ironfist said bitterly.

Hanishu flashed an exasperated smile, exactly as he had done in life, except that Ironfist could see the wall through his form. "This doesn't happen, you know," Tremblefist said. "We peaceful departed, we don't return. And I am at peace, brother. But he told me that uncommon loyalty deserves uncommon rewards. You took a wrong turn, associating with the Order to avenge mother and protect Haruru. But you're no traitor, brother."

After Teia had killed Haruru, making himself king of Paria had been the only way Ironfist could get back to Little Jasper safely, and become too important to be killed or simply sent away by the Order's people or Andross Guile's. Becoming king had been the only way to muster an army and bring it here.

It had been the only way he could hope to get vengeance on his uncle.

The plan had been to relent at the last moment before the execution and say, 'I've changed my mind. Instead of a Guile, I'll let myself be contented with the blood of one of those most useful to them. That slave, Grinwoody. He's your right hand. I'll take *him*. Now.'

Andross Guile would take the deal in a moment, and the Old Man of the Desert would never see it coming. Even if he had Blackguards in his employ, even if they were in the room, they didn't know Grinwoody was the Old Man, so they wouldn't know to try to save him.

That was the trouble with keeping your identity secret from your own people.

It had been a good plan. Devious. Very orange. It might have even worked, if not for Cruxer.

But it was all too late now. All for nothing.

At least they wouldn't go ahead with the execution without him. Would they?

What if they did? Would there be more blood on his tally?

"I failed, brother," he said, and the tears were hot and bitter.

We all fail. It's why we don't walk alone.

And for the first time in a long time, Ironfist didn't feel alone.

He felt himself lifted in strong arms.

No one had lifted Ironfist since he was a young child.

He clung to his brother like the lost, and wept, and he wept as a man weeps: weak and unashamed.

At some point they had emerged into starlight and moonlight and night and the lapping waves. A figure approached. Voices spoke, Tremblefist's rumbling through his chest, as Ironfist drifted between consciousness and not.

And then he was handed off. His brother Hanishu took Harrdun's face in his big hands one last time, and kissed his forehead in blessing, and then was gone.

Ironfist must have been delirious, because he felt like the man now holding him was not nearly large enough to hold him, but the little round Parian managed not only Ironfist but also his own bags and jugs, and was also carrying him very quickly. They passed people, and everyone they passed seemed to be turning their backs or suddenly inattentive, yawning or rubbing their eyes.

And then the man set him down on his feet inside the lift that could take him to the level of the audience chamber, where there would be many Blackguards. Ironfist tottered, eyes bleary. His side had been bandaged; he couldn't remember when.

"Do I know you?" Ironfist asked. The man smelled of...kopi?

The man smiled, and his face shone. "Come now, she's almost here. "

"Who?"

"The one who's gonna save your life." The round little man squinted. "Probably." Then he seemed to flit out of and then back into the space he was standing, his jugs and cups clinking. Ironfist must have blinked or something. "Hmm. Well, if anyone *can* save you, she's the one."

Chapter 93

Don't hit him in the face, Kip. That is not how adults solve problems.

"We need to go ahead with this," Zymun said. "I mean, I don't want to any more than any of us. But I don't think we can afford to wait."

But if he *were* going to hit him in the face, Kip had a coin stick in his left pocket that fit in his burn-scarred left fist perfectly. No sense breaking your hand on the eve of battle.

The most important people in the Seven Satrapies had gathered in the audience chamber tonight: the High Magisterium, the Colors, nobles, the Prism-elect, the promachos, the White, Kip, at least twenty Blackguards, a veritable army of scribes who served them all, and one chubby little Parian ambassador, who looked like his heart was going to fail him.

Carver Black said, "We all agreed we need to give the signal by midnight or the soldiers won't have time to deploy before dawn."

"Midnight is the deadline the king has decreed," the ambassador said timorously, then swallowed and sank back into himself.

"We know what he said, traitor," Caelia Green snapped. "And believe me, we're going to interpret whatever amnesty comes along with this deal for Ironfist as narrowly as possible. It may not cover *you*, for instance."

"Midnight's in four minutes," Zymun said, as if he were just a clock, uncaring of the outcome, merely reminding everyone.

Uppercut, right in the jaw. Maybe I'd break some teeth that way. I could be spared the sound of his insufferable voice for a while.

"I'm ready," Karris said, coming back from the side, where she'd been talking one more time with the luxiats; praying, Kip guessed. She'd already said her goodbyes to all the Blackguards earlier. "I don't feel the need to scrounge about desperately for a few more minutes."

She was radiant, not just with her normal beauty and resolve, but there was an inner light, a deeper strength to her. There was nothing grim about her determination. She was, suddenly, a rock. All these events swirled around her, the stream diverting, but the rock unmoved.

Only Kip stole a glance away toward Zymun, to see if even this could affect him. But Zymun flashed a wink at Kip instead, and then while pretending to blow his nose, he poked himself in each eye.

The hell was that about?

"I'm ready, too," Zymun said. He moved forward, blinking, misty-eyed, his face lacquered with sorrow.

The little piece of shit.

"You can't possibly be serious," Kip said. "Ironfist isn't even here yet. You're not going to wait to see if he's changed his mind?!"

"He gave us the ultimatum," Zymun said. "Time is of the essence. If we wait, we endanger everyone. You heard the scouts! The White King's ships are within a league now, and not stopping for the night. By dawn they'll be setting up the siege. If we don't get those soldiers—"

"Enough!" Karris said. "I said I'm ready. I don't want to see hatred in my old friend's eyes again anyway. There is no yielding in him once he's set his course. Maybe it's better this way."

Zymun grinned at Kip, and Kip saw that a few others caught the expression and bristled at it. "Very well, then, *daughter*. To your place."

"One of her beloved Blackguard kin has agreed to be the one who—" Andross began.

"I'm the Prism," Zymun said firmly. "It has to be me. This is my duty and should rest on my soul. Mine is the protection of this empire, and mine is the shepherding of this flock. Even in this. Right, mother? You wouldn't deny us this last, holy moment together, would you?"

Kip's knuckles popped, he was clenching his fists so hard. He'd come here tonight ready to die. Because even if you think you know what's going to happen, when death is in the offing, and Andross Guile is in the room... well, he's Andross Guile.

"Of course not," Karris interjected. Her face twisted as she added, "son."

Zymun grinned in victory, changed his look to unconvincing sadness an instant later, and took the spear-point-bladed knife from Blackguard Commander Fisk.

There was a kneeling pillow at the front center of the podium. Zymun extended his hand to Karris. "Come, daughter," he said. As if he were Prism already.

Kip looked at Andross and found Andross staring back at him, but his eyes were inscrutable.

He was really going to let this happen.

They all were.

Though Kip had shown up ready to die, Zymun, of course, had never once thought that *he* might be the Guile to die. To him, this was all a game, a show for his entertainment.

To Kip, it was a nightmare he couldn't wake from. He could see why Andross didn't want to depose Zymun today: he was a figurehead without any real power, but for the people of the Jaspers, losing another Prism on the very eve of a battle for their survival would be a devastating blow to morale. He was handsome, and the son of the beloved Gavin Guile—that's all most of the people knew. Andross wanted Zymun to strut through whatever of the Sun Day events they could manage, maybe read a speech Andross had written for him, and then quietly go away right afterward. And Kip was needed for the islands' defense.

So it had to be Karris.

She made a sign of benediction to the crowd. "My faithful ones," she said, "I've run my race. I pass my light on to you, my friends. You fight like hell. Orholam be with you. And please, when we are victorious over the pagans—*when* we are, for I have no doubts of that—do not hold the shedding of my blood against Ironfist or the Parians. I am not without blame in this. Take no vengeance for me, but stitch Paria back into these Seven Satrapies with grace and mercy, as Orholam would will it."

There were quiet sobs in the room. The Blackguards were all stony-faced sorrow. Karris took a few moments to make eye contact with them one last time. Many in the crowd looked on with abject horror, while others simply seemed titillated.

This is not happening.

Karris looked at Kip, and her mouth pursed with regret. She nodded to him in farewell.

Then she knelt on the pillow.

"We're not doing anything yet," Andross said loudly.

Usually, that would have been the end of it, but Zymun didn't move. He'd put his hand on Karris's forehead, ostensibly in blessing, tilting her head back to expose her throat.

"Grandfather," Zymun said, his voice dripping contempt, "this is now a matter between the Prism and his faithful. This is sacrosanct. For the sake of the Seven Satrapies, I'm afraid I can't allow you to—"

Kip had been with the Blackguard long enough to recognize the small move with his right hand backward, drawing the knife back to get space to apply more force to ram it home.

All the tension in Kip's muscles exploded at once. Sweeping in from Zymun's left side, he caught the young man's right hand just as the knife swept forward. Kip pushed the knife wide as his own mass collided with Zymun, driving him away from Karris. Then Kip's right elbow flashed up, cracking across Zymun's head as Kip blocked his heel with his own foot.

Zymun went down, boneless.

The fight was finished before the gasps were.

Kip could tell suddenly that a lot of the people here hadn't seen the telltale twitch that foretold murder. To the untrained eye, his action must have looked like an unprovoked attack.

"He was moving to kill her," Commander Fisk announced sharply. "We train constantly to see tells of such a move, and Kip trained with us. He saw it, too. This was defense of life, not an attack. I know what I saw, and I swear this to be true."

Twenty Blackguards gave silent affirmation. Kip hadn't even thought of the Blackguard, but he realized why he was the first to react: they were trapped between their next Prism, a White who'd abdicated her protection by them, and a not-quite order from the promachos. Their loyalties and their oaths of obedience had tangled, slowing them.

"You dare? You dare lay your hands on me?" Zymun hissed at Kip from the floor, blinking his eyes.

"Grandfather," Kip said loudly but without turning from the snake. "May I remind you of your earlier promise?"

Irritated, Andross announced, "Blackguards, Kip is under my full protection. Act accordingly."

604   Zymun lunged at him, scrambling to draw a pistol, but the

Blackguard—happily absolved of contradicting loyalties—restrained him quickly and with more force than strictly necessary.

"Take Zymun to his apartments. Our Prism-*elect* has much to pray about this night," Andross said.

Zymun was dragged out, spitting and trying to bite the Blackguards, who had no trouble handling him.

"One minute to midnight," Carver Black said.

Karris hadn't moved from where she knelt on the pillow. "Commander Fisk?" she asked. "Will you do me the honor?"

"That is your will?" he asked.

"It is."

Quietly Fisk added, "I wish we could lose a different Guile."

"I know," she said. "You're a loyal friend, Commander. Thank you."

Commander Fisk looked at Andross, but the old man made no gesture one way or the other. So then Fisk looked at Kip and extended his hand for his knife.

Kip hadn't even realized he was still holding it. "Hell no," Kip said. "This is insane. You *know* Ironfist! He would never do this! This isn't his heart. We wait!"

"My lord has the luxury of disobeying orders," Commander Fisk said. "I wish I had the same." He took a knife from another Blackguard. "Karris, Archer, sister, High Lady Guile, forever our Iron White," he said, "it has been my honor to serve with you, and to serve you. May Orholam reunite us in gentler lands."

"And may He bless you with light and warmth, Commander. Now, stop delaying, old trainer of mine. It's taking everything in me not to try my hand at fighting you one last time, to see if I could win now, as I couldn't so very long ago."

Taking a deep breath as he came to stand over her where she knelt, she pulled the neckline of her blouse open, looking up toward heaven and pulling the skin tight so that the gaps between the ribs were visible.

Then there was a cry outside the audience chamber in the hall. Kip couldn't make out the words, but an instant later he saw Trainer Gill Greyling go sprinting past the open door—not into the audience chamber but past it toward the lifts—shouting, "Stop, stop, stop!" with the urgency of man who knew he was too late.

Chapter 94

Teia'd had terrible premonitions all the way here, but the last thing she was expecting when she finally made it invisibly to the Chromeria's lifts was to be greeted by the lift gate opening to reveal a bloody, badly wounded Commander Ironfist.

"Get in, quickly. Timing is everything," a dark, plain-dressed Parian man with him said to her. The lift was otherwise empty.

For a moment, Teia wondered if she was hallucinating the whole thing. First, she was invisible. Second, Ironfist was the utter opposite of invisible—and yet, no one else seemed to have seen him.

She stepped in, and the lift shot upward.

The Parian heaved a sigh of relief. "Haven't cut it that close since Cwellar—or is that next? Oh, no, that's next. Actually—that's right now!" He pulled the brake and turned to Teia. They were only a few floors up. "Give it a hundred and four count from right...now. Then go as fast as possible. Blackguard immediately on the left is an Order agent. Has orders not to let Harrdun make it alive to the audience chamber. Or he'll be on the right if you run late."

He turned to Ironfist, who was slumped against the wall. "You. You'll have to choose between vengeance and life."

"For whom?" Ironfist growled.

"No time."

"Wait," Teia said. "Who are you?"

"No time!"

The little man ducked out of the lift, cups and canteens clanking.

Teia threw her hands up. How was he—

She poked her head out into the hall, but he was gone. Not around the corner, the corners were too far away. He was just *gone*.

She stepped back into the lift. With Ironfist. Not Commander Ironfist, she remembered now. How had she forgotten? King Ironfist. Who'd last seen her when she was assassinating his sister, as he begged her to stop.

Shhhhiiitt.

"You're not gonna ask?" he said, his voice deep and cloudy with pain. He waved to the blood drenching his once-white-and-either-green-or-red garb—it was certainly red by now.

"The Order?" she asked hopefully.

"No."

"Orholam have mercy." Cruxer.

"Not much, He doesn't. But I...I can't blame this on Him."

Teia's heart froze. "Did he...?"

"He's dead."

No. She wasn't going to believe it. She wasn't going to think about it. "The Order," she said, suddenly finding some fire. "You know things about the Order."

"Enough to know they'll ask your soul and then stab you in the back." He looked at her with lidded eyes, exhausted from pain and blood loss and whatever ordeal he'd been through, but also hard and bitter. "But then, you know that."

"I'm infiltrating the Order for Karris. She's trying to stop them once and for all."

"You can't stop them." He tried to laugh. Coughed instead. "Look at me."

"What? What do you mean?"

"I'm convinced they've half the immortals of hell protecting them. How else does Cruxer find me just then?"

"Don't talk about him—don't! Don't! We're running out of time. I have to stop them, or it's all for nothing!"

"Ha. That's what I said, too. The execution. Can't be more than a few minutes from now. Hope they don't go ahead without me. Don't you see? It was all to get him." He blinked his eyes, swayed.

Huh? "No, you are not dying now. Who? Him *who*?"

"My uncle. He's the Old Man of the Desert. Kept himself secret all these years, but a secret's a weakness, see? Only way to get him was...this. He sent you to kill my sister. After everything I did for him. His own niece."

Ironfist sagged, and Teia braced him, feeling tiny against his big form. "No, no, no. You stay with me! I can't do this without you."

"You killed her. My sister. I begged you not to. I begged."

"Yes, and I'd do it again. She was gonna kill you. But I'm sorry. I'm sorry you lost someone you loved so much, but she needed to die. She was already gone by the time you were in that room with her. She was gonna get everyone killed."

Ironfist blew out a little breath, and his eyes softened. "I know," he whispered. "Oh God. Cruxer. Teia, I—"

"Don't. I can't talk about—Who is he? What's the Old Man's *name*?" Teia pressed.

Orholam's balls, how many seconds had passed? They had to go!

"I gave everything for this. Only I can do it. Can't trust anyone. That's not the plan."

Teia threw back her hood. "Trust *me*! Commander, please. Let *me* be the plan!"

He looked at her and she felt those eyes that she'd looked up to for so long weighing her, seeing her now, not only as an adult but as someone he approved of.

"Amalu Anazâr Tlanu," Ironfist said. "Amalu Anazâr is the Old Man of the Desert." He breathed a deep sigh as if stepping out from under a weight that had been crushing him for years.

"Wait, wait, there's no one named that who's got access to upper levels of the Prism's Tower. He's got some disguise, some other name?"

But Ironfist's eyes had drifted shut. He leaned more heavily on Teia.

"No! Don't you die on me!"

Eyes still closed, he said, "Easy, nunk. Just resting my eyes a bit before this last part. You lose the count already?"

"What?"

"Almost time," he said. He opened his eyes and there was something of the old Ironfist mettle in there. "I gotta get to that audience chamber and make sure nothing else goes to shit."

"Are you—"

"Grinwoody," he said.

It crashed around her ears like a pagan temple collapsing. Grinwoody? *Grinwoody*, Andross Guile's right hand. All the secrets of the world passed through that man's fingers. Another Order master assassin, this one dressed in the invisibility cloak of slavery.

Teia, a former slave herself, hadn't seen it. Hadn't thought to look there first.

She drew herself up. "I'll get you past the assassin or assassins at the door, but then I gotta hand you off. I've got work to do. What's that count at?" Teia asked.

"One hundred one."

"I knew you'd know," she said, making sure she was filled with paryl and clouds of it hissing from her fingers. She threw the brake, and they shot upward.

She glanced over at her old commander. "You look terrible."

"I've felt better, too," he said as the floors blurred past. With one hand, he took off a necklace and shoved it into a pocket. "Hood back on, kid."

Oh, shit! Teia scrambled to pull her hood back into place, a process made awkward by the long knives in her hands. "Who was that guy?" Teia asked as if she weren't flustered.

"Karris's kopi seller, maybe? She loves that damned stuff."

"Hey, watch it," Teia said. "A Blackguard guards his tongue."

They both chuckled at that, though Ironfist broke off immediately in pain.

"Six in the foyer at an event like this?" Teia asked. She was standing to his left to put herself between him and the threat.

He grunted. "I'd have more, but there's a war on. Could mean more." As if it took supreme effort, Ironfist levered himself off the wall to stand with his feet wide. "By the way," he said, unhooking the heavy chain that ran from the wrist manacle to a hook on his left bicep, "you're still just the backup plan."

Then the doors opened.

Through their training, the half-dozen Blackguards in the foyer were all glancing at the opening lift door, and they gawked at the sight of King Ironfist sodden with blood, even his face sticky with the stuff, his many-colored finery soaked with gore. Teia wasn't looking at the faces, though—she was staring at their hands.

They all moved forward. It was what they were trained to do, to move toward danger, to confront whatever shocked or threatened them in order to give aid or to defend the defenseless behind them. For Teia to find the threat with that much sudden motion all coming toward her, all of them armed to the teeth, was nearly impossible. Left side, left side—

Right side!

A young Blackguard she didn't know stepped forward, wide-eyed with fear, too fast for a paryl pinch to his nerves. Ironfist was moving to meet the threat himself, but he was way too slow. As the young man lunged, Teia dove beneath Ironfist's rising arm and slashed up with both knives.

Her first missed the blade she was trying to intercept, but passed cleanly through the young man's wrist. Hand and blade went spinning. Her other blade sank deep into the young man's groin.

Then Ironfist's open hand slapped into the young man's face, and stopped. The chain wrapped full around the would-be assassin's head. Then Ironfist tore back in the other direction, snapping the young man's neck and flinging his body away.

Behind the first ranks of Blackguards, Teia saw Gill Greyling coming running, shouting at his men to stop, stop!

But the problem of training people to react with instant lethality to threats is that *they do*. One of the veteran Blackguards was reaching for the sleeve of a young man next to her, but four Blackguards were already attacking.

A wall of paryl heat blasted out of Teia as it had once at Ruic Head. Everyone nearby fell back, feeling as if their skin were on fire.

"Naught Naught One! Naught Naught One!" Gill Greyling shouted, "Stop, stop, stop! I saw everything! Stop!" He arrived only a second later, interposing himself between the Blackguards and Ironfist.

Ironfist collapsed into Gill's arms. "Get me in there," he gasped.

But Teia was looking down the hall, past all the Blackguards who were rushing this way—even men and women who should have known better, who had been taught to stay at their stations. But she saw one person moving in the opposite direction.

Not a Blackguard.

Any civilian would rush toward the excitement to see what was happening. This one disappeared against the flow of the crowd.

A lookout, Teia guessed. To warn the Old Man.

But two dozen Blackguards and innumerable civilians who hadn't been allowed into the audience chamber were crowding into the foyer.

Teia pushed through them, ducking and dodging, not caring if anyone saw her. She saw Grinwoody, not twenty paces away, pop out of the door of the audience chamber and then run toward the lift on the opposite side of the tower.

It took her far too long to win her way clear of the crowd and go after him. The Blackguards who were stationed here had abandoned their posts. In the lifts, she felt the lines for vibration. Up. He'd gone up to the Prism's and White's level.

She didn't know of any escapes above her—was he gathering his papers?—no, wait, she didn't know of any escapes from higher in the tower *except from the roof*!

But two minutes later, she was on the roof. Alone. He hadn't triggered the escape lines. He had some other escape.

She'd missed him. The Old Man of the Desert was gone.

Chapter 95

Teia was shaking badly. It was irritating as hell.

But when the battle-juice rush disappears, the body reacts, and she'd never had quite as much of its rush as she had in saving Ironfist (she hoped she'd saved him, anyway) and nearly killing the Old Man of the Desert.

Grinwoody. That devious, slippery little bastard. That *toad*, sitting at Andross Guile's elbow for all those years.

In all her hunting, she'd looked past him a hundred times. She hated that everyone overlooked slaves, that everyone considered them beneath notice—and she'd done it herself. She'd *been* a slave. She *was* a slave. And she'd looked right past him.

She was so mad at herself, she wanted to kill something. Scratch that. Some*one*.

In fact, that was just the thing for it. But she had to find him first.

With the commotion she and Ironfist had made downstairs, there were only two Blackguards on the entire floor. But she'd been drafting paryl for hours, and she was tapped out.

Not to mention trembling.

Blackguards were going to be coming back to their stations soon, and she was in no state to fight or evade them with any dexterity. In fact, she was having trouble maintaining invisibility.

Shit.

She needed rest. For a moment, she thought of going to her little closet. But that was where she'd had that dream. Nightmare.

Abaddon.

He was looking for her.

She wasn't going to sleep there again.

Belatedly, too late maybe, she took up a position outside the Old Man's secret room in the lift shaft. He'd gone up when he fled, not down, so she knew that he hadn't come here first. Would he come this way at all?

If he were going to flee permanently, she assumed that he would come to his office first. She assumed this was his office. She assumed that he would have riches and supplies in a go-bag in here, and that he would at least stop for that.

It was a lot of assumptions, but she had to get lucky sometime, right?

Every time a lift went past her, she tensed, and tonight, the lifts were never still. Panicky people at first, then guards and Blackguards and Tafok Amagez, then messengers, then nobles, then more messengers all through the night.

After a few hours, she told herself she had to be patient, that the Old Man was being patient. He needed to get his stuff, but he couldn't afford to arouse suspicion with the lifts as busy as they were.

Teia assumed that at some point, Ben-hadad and Magister Kadah would finish their work on the code, so they would meet her here.

It had been much longer than six hours now, but surely the woman would eventually get it, right?

But the night passed. Teia dozed standing, jerking awake every time a lift passed. None ever paused, even for a moment, and the darkness was a warm embrace.

No one ever came. She'd gambled her hours and lost.

So sometime after dawn, she made her way to Magister Kadah's room. Maybe the woman had worked out how to open that door. If not, at least she could give Teia a place to sleep.

She knocked on the door with their agreed-upon series of taps.

Shit, Teia thought, she didn't think she could have missed them. Maybe they'd decided to sleep a few hours to tackle the code afresh.

Anyway, she *definitely* needed to tell someone else that the Old Man was Grinwoody. She didn't know if Ironfist had had the clarity to realize how important it was to get that out. To Karris only, if possible. Grinwoody would have other people who were in the audience chamber—they would tell him immediately if Ironfist had blurted out his name.

If that happened, Grinwoody might flee forever. Might have already, actually. Dammit.

But first, she had to tell Ben the Old Man's identity.

She tested the door. It wasn't locked.

That didn't seem wise.

"Hey, you two," Teia said, "please tell me you're not—"

The room was lit an eerie orange-red from testing lanterns the magisters used to teach discipulae.

But she barely noticed the wave of feeling that hit her with the light when her nostrils were assailed with a familiar smell. Blood.

Teia could see a woman's body crumpled behind a workbench to her left, and from behind a desk to her right, a pool of blood spread out.

Ben-hadad. No!

Teia jumped—backward. She threw her hood back up and snapped the cowl shut over her face, going fully invisible again. Pulling a long dagger under the cloak, she drew in as much paryl as she could hold and sucked in a breath, then froze.

Nothing.

Was that a moan from behind the heavy desk? Ben-hadad?

She shot a puff of paryl smoke around the corner of the door into the room. The paryl itself would be an attack—and visible to Sharp, if he were here, if he were looking. But there was no sudden violence. Her clouds of paryl didn't billow around any shape.

If he were in the room, her first move would be vital, and she couldn't stand at the open door forever. So Teia shot little darts of paryl into every corner of the room, even at the ceiling above the big desk, into the curtains at the window—anywhere large enough to conceal a man.

Nothing.

Only then did Teia turn to look at the woman lying on the ground. Magister Kadah. Teia's paryl had gone into her chest, where Teia could feel that the woman's heart was still.

Another moan from behind the desk. Ben!

The orange desire for connection and the red compassion overwhelmed her. Ben-hadad! No, please tell me I didn't get you killed! I can save you! Teia rushed over to her friend.

At her steps, a scintillant shimmering *something* concealed in the shadow of the desk itself uncurled. Something smashed across her face.

Her nose fountained blood as she staggered backward.

She saw Ben-hadad first. He lay on the ground, eyes wide, gagged, limbs bound but seemingly unharmed. Crouching over him was Murder Sharp, somehow out of control of his shimmercloak, contiguous patches of it invisible and then flaring colors intermittently.

She was already slashing blindly with her dagger before the first gush of her blood hit the floor. But she felt pinches in both her knees.

Nerveless, her legs buckled under her and she tumbled across the floor. Her elbow went numb.

Before she could think, she felt a hand grabbing her hair. She saw Murder Sharp raising a sap in his other hand. "Ah, Teia," he said. "I've missed you so much."

His voice was all warm honey, but in his eyes she saw something that made her blood run cold: paryl crystals like purply shrapnel had exploded through the whites of his eyes. Murder Sharp had broken the halo.

He hugged her briefly. "You're the only one who understands," he said. "But I should really kill you."

Then, as he sat back up to sit on her stomach, he slapped her face. Not softly, but it wasn't hard enough to wound her.

But it did scatter all the paryl she'd been drawing in.

"None of that," he said, and his voice was softly scolding, as if she were a naughty lover. Her stomach knotted in fear. He'd lost some of his faculties, it seemed, but none of the ones that mattered. He knew exactly how and when she might be dangerous. He was only losing his inhibitions.

That was not good news.

"Nice trap, huh?" he said, pointing to the orange-and-red training light. "Only forgot how susceptible I am to these myself. Seems like it's gotten worse recently." He pointed at Ben beside her on the floor, his eyes rolling with rage, tears of helplessness streaming from his eyes. "But you see how kind I'm being to you, Adrasteia? I let your friend live. I never do that."

He sighed. Stood, and turned out the lights to plunge the room into total darkness.

His voice took on a tone as black as the room. "I wish I could let you live, too."

His weird, uncontrolled shimmering pulsed in the darkness, and she saw him illuminated for an instant, raising the sap high his hand, and then he swung it sharply into her temple.

Chapter 96

It had been a long night, and Karris's initial elation at being alive to greet the dawn had long since faded to fear.

King Ironfist had stayed on his feet for only a few moments after he'd been brought into the audience chamber, clearly conscious through heroic effort of will alone. He'd ordered a stop to Karris's execution and ordered the deployment of all his troops under High General Danavis's leadership. Then he'd searched the crowd as if looking for some face, while begging Karris to come aside to hear something private. She went to him instantly, but he'd finally succumbed to his wounds.

He hadn't stirred since.

Naturally, the Chromeria's best physickers were with him, and his own Tafok Amagez, and Blackguards. There had been some chaos at the lift, apparently a *Blackguard* had attempted to assassinate him? The Tafok Amagez didn't trust the Blackguards (understandably enough, Karris thought, though of course the Blackguards were in full denial mode) or the physickers, and the Blackguards didn't trust the Tafok Amagez or the physickers, and the physickers wanted everyone to get the hell away from their patient.

Karris had no idea what the private thing Ironfist had hoped to tell her had to do with, and now there was no getting Ironfist away from the Tafok Amagez. After an attempt on their king's life, they weren't going to allow anyone near him until he was conscious and safe.

It was a fight she wished she had time for. She didn't.

Sun Day Eve dawned with thousands of Corvan Danavis's and King Ironfist's warriors disembarking and carrying supplies to their respective stations. High General Danavis was in his element, orchestrating a million details with ease and efficiency. There were a thousand logjams and bottlenecks that could happen with deploying so many troops and supplies, and with Danavis in charge, people simply were given orders and went, and when they arrived, they found the supplies they needed arriving at the same time, or already there, or arriving immediately after them.

It was a level of technical virtuosity that people didn't even see: *of course* black powder, wadding, flints or match cord, bullets, and ramrods will arrive in the same place as a thousand muskets, they thought. *Of course* that place would be centrally located to where the men who were trained in their use and needed them could get them in an orderly and timely fashion. But with what Karris and her luxiats had been doing in the last month to prepare the islands' defenses, she knew now how hard all of this was, and she simply stood back in awe.

But not in rest. She had her own details to oversee.

Not least of which was the fleet visible with the morning sun. At first everyone had assumed they were seeing the vanguard of the White King's fleet, coming in from the west.

But this fleet was alone, and small, not followed by an armada— and flying the flags of Ruthgar and the Malargos clan.

Karris took a skimmer out to them to divine their intentions: Eirene Malargos hadn't come herself (smart, in case we all die, Karris thought), but Karris learned that her luxiats had prevailed upon Eirene to send everyone they could spare.

And by 'her luxiats' they meant *Karris's* luxiats, Karris soon realized, for three of the young men who'd been so convincing to Eirene Malargos had been part of Karris's little group of faithful scholars.

'Everyone they could send' seemed an exaggeration, because Malargos had only sent five thousand men. But the five thousand were Ruthgar's best, and they were outfitted better than any of the other contingents. In addition, Eirene had sent desperately needed supplies. Not only black powder (most precious since Atash had fallen), but also good muskets and, most valuable of all, ten thousand sets of mirror armor.

Ten thousand!

Karris had thought all her entreaties to Eirene Malargos had fallen on deaf ears, but all the while the woman had been stockpiling and commissioning gear whose cost must have bankrupted even her. And Eirene had done it all silently, so that it might be kept secret from the White King.

The rest of Sun Day Eve passed in a blur of preparation: Kip was frantic with his Mirror preparations, too distracted to even talk to her; Andross was entirely absent except for when he popped in and demanded some of her smartest luxiats; Zymun had constant demands (not in person, as she refused to see him, but his messengers sought her out everywhere). The last couldn't be ignored entirely: there were forty drafters who needed to be Freed tonight, before dawn of Sun Day. Normally, she'd postpone the ceremony entirely, but these drafters were unable to fight and were fearful of what the arrival of the bane would do to them.

Truth to tell, she was, too. No one wanted them to go rogue at such a time.

That meant Zymun would get to kill them. The sick little piece of trash. She arranged to have him flanked by the most intimidating Blackguards she could in order to hem in his most disgusting tendencies, armed with strict orders on how to handle him if he got out of line with his somber duties. She also had to make sure he wasn't armed or accompanied by his Lightguard cronies.

If Karris hadn't had so much else to do, maybe she could have done better, but she—and the poor broken drafters who would be Freed—were simply going to have to make do.

In the afternoon, Koios's armada was spotted. It was, indeed, as large as Kip had claimed. The Parian fleet that Karris had hoped might save the Chromeria went out to fight them. By attacking with half of his skimmers, the Parian admiral attempted to goad the armada into raising the bane once more. Once those were raised, the armada would lose all mobility.

But Koios didn't take the bait, and the admiral wasn't willing to commit (and thereby lose) all of the skimmers in order to make the prize too tempting to ignore, so the battle devolved into a largely conventional one. Worse, not only did Koios have more ships, but the Parian admiral had emptied his fleet of drafters, lest they be immobilized by the bane as well. The Parians' superior cannons were matched and finally overmatched by the Blood Robes' superior magic.

The sea battle lasted the entire afternoon, but the White King's fleet was too large, his wights too numerous, and though his barges behind the front ranks were ungainly, the Parian fleet wasn't able to reach them.

The Parians broke off after taking heavy losses. They'd inflicted too few in return.

By evening, in a wide ring on the horizon, the White King's fleet had encircled the entirety of the Jaspers. They were besieged.

Orholam, she thought as she watched the sun descend, this is Your fight. Without You in this, we die.

As the sun disappeared beneath the horizon, she watched for the green flash.

But there was none.

Chapter 97

Teia woke to the sound of a man weeping in the darkness.

"That fucking *bitch*! Why'd she have to call me that? This is all her fault. This is some witchery. This is…goddam."

Sharp.

A weight of dread settled on Teia's chest. She was trapped in black-as-hell darkness with a paryl wight. Her arms were bound in front, hugging herself, elaborate knots under her fingers, and she was wearing…a dress?

She did not want to think about how she came to be wearing a dress.

"It's the darkness," she said aloud. She didn't know why she didn't spend minutes faking sleep while she checked the knots and tried to escape. Maybe because Sharp had always been so masterful with knots. Maybe she had some compassion for the sick, broken wretch.

Or maybe she was just giving up.

"Huh?" Sharp barked. "What are you on about?" He sounded angry, embarrassed.

Perfect.

"We're sensitive to darkness, just like we're sensitive to light. A black mood is literal for us." No one had told Teia about that part, though she should've figured it out long ago. Sharp hadn't told her, and just as obviously, the effect was exaggerated even further for a paryl drafter who went wight.

Something flared, shielded by Sharp's body, and then a flame took—in a special, single-spectrum lantern. The room was illuminated in a monochrome, either red or green.

If that was green, Teia was not going to do well. Sharp, turned wild when he was already feeling like this?

But no. She was certain it wasn't green. She could feel it now.

Finally, at the end of her life, finally she could tell the difference between green and red. She couldn't *see* the difference, but she could feel it: finally she could do consciously what she'd done in that terrible Order ceremony so long ago.

Not that it did her any good. It was red light. Big deal. She couldn't draft it, couldn't use it against Sharp in any way.

"No, no," he said at the light. "That's almost worse. Elijah ben-Zoheth. Damn that Seer." He strode toward Teia and snatched up a black bag from a table, but he didn't pull it over her head. "I shouldn't have brought you here. But ever since she called me that...The Separated One. The Cutoff." He scrubbed his fingers through his hair angrily. "I wanted you to be the one, Teia. You're the only one who could understand me, you know? You know, you'd be my disciple, and you'd look up to me, and you'd ask me things. You'd rely on me. And, and as you got more and more experienced, our relationship would change. We'd become partners, with a profound respect between us, and have a thousand adventures, and then one day you'd look at me, and you would still see all this"—he gestured awkwardly toward his face—his *teeth*, Teia realized—"but you wouldn't care. You wouldn't care that I'm older, and I'd say, 'No, no, no you have to find someone your own age,' but you'd set yourself to winning me over and..."

Red light. It was definitely, definitely red light.

Wait. What was he talking about?

"Ridiculous, huh?" He looked up at her face just as her first shock had worn away to be replaced with revulsion.

He saw her expression, and his own darkened instantly.

Ah, shit, Teia. A little pretending would've gone a long way right there.

"Yeah, I know," he said hoarsely. "Stupid. Instead we gotta do it this way."

"How'd you find me?" Teia said quickly.

"You really gonna try to stall me?"

"You did kidnap me a second time. If that wasn't to talk over our little contest, why would you do that?"

"No, it wasn't that. More the loneliness. So maybe sort of? But more for...another reason. A darker one." He scowled at the candle. Reds were not known for their deviousness. He threw the bag over her head, and then she heard the flare of a candle again. A normal one, apparently, because he sighed. "Oh, that's much better. Don't know why it's affecting me so bad these days."

"You know, I ran across you at the corner of Farbod and Low," she said. What time was it? How long had she been unconscious? Were they underground?

"Really? Why didn't you kill me there?" Sharp asked.

"Thought I had a chance at the Old Man. I followed him instead," she said.

"You always did have guts," he said. "But now, tell me, why didn't you come after your father? I sat on him for *weeks* waiting for you to make your move."

"You did?" she said. "I had no idea where he was." Still don't.

"What?! I left hints everywhere! I mean, I went to all your old haunts and left things that'd point you to him. Blackguard taverns. Parks you liked. That place where you bought fruit."

"Well, I was *avoiding* those places because I thought you'd be stalking me at them." He'd known where she bought fruit?

"Huh. Good thought," Murder said. "Great discipline. You always had great discipline. Just tended to try things that were a little much for your skills. It's too bad."

"So how did you find me?" Teia asked. She did not like him using the past tense about her.

"When your friends came. The Mighty. I knew you'd go to them right away. Trouble was, there's a bunch of them. But Kip and Ben-hadad split off from the others. Really thought you'd go for your old bed buddy first, see if he wanted a quick roll while his wife's head was turned. But then I camped out on Ben-hadad. Scared the hell out of me once I realized they were working on cracking open the Old Man's office! I was like, Do I go report this right away, or wait? So I split the difference and waited until they had the solution—or thought they did. Anyway, I knew you'd come. How could you help it? Patience is so key in our work, isn't it?" He sighed. "Forget about earlier. Don't know what got into me. Never been the sensitive type before."

Did he not know he'd gone wight? How could he not know?

Because he had no one to tell him. He'd been alone so long, he'd become a monster and he didn't even know it.

Could she use that?

Murder Sharp said, "You're not getting out of here, Teia. You're too resourceful for me to leave in this room until after the walls come down. You have to die. Just one more soul on my tally when you could have been so much more."

" 'After the walls come down'?" she asked.

"The Order's made a treaty with the White King. Our people mob the gates, a few Shadows take down the cannon crews, and they reward us beyond our wildest dreams."

"But that's—that's, you haven't even explained—"

"It doesn't matter," he said sadly. He seemed back in control now. Himself again.

"Well, sure it matters—" Teia said.

"It doesn't matter *for you*. Your part ends here. I'm sorry."

"Please," Teia said, fear gripping her throat. She'd been testing her bonds. There was nothing she could do. She couldn't even move her extremities.

She'd missed her chance. Drafting now was impossible.

She tried it anyway, her eyes flaring wide.

"Uh-uh-uh," Murder Sharp scolded. He tore the bag off her head, gripped her hair in a fist, and pulled her face up, almost gently. But she had no illusions he would stay gentle if she resisted.

He looked at her, eye to eye, and then he kissed her forehead gently, like a father. "I want to ask you a favor," he said.

"I want to ask you one back," Teia said quickly.

He laughed. "Not really in the position, are you?"

"I'll do anything you want if you hear me out."

"That's not how this works," Murder Sharp said.

"My father. They'll kill him if they learn I betrayed them," Teia said. "He doesn't know anything about this. You know that. He's just a merchant. Can you have them let him go?"

She was actually surprised at how level and calm her voice came out. Sharp seemed to be surprised, too.

"I've got no reason to help you," Sharp said.

"No...no, you don't. But maybe, maybe a little redemption is better than none. Maybe that's how you close a little bit of separation, Elijah ben-Zoheth."

He snorted. "You got balls," Sharp said with a little smile that showed his everyday dentures: plain, white, but not so perfect as to draw attention. "I wish we didn't have to do this."

"Me, too," Teia said lightly.

He laughed. Then he looked down at her body and shook his head. "I can't believe I put you in my mother's dress. What the hell was I thinking? Anyway...about my request."

He cleared his throat, suddenly awkward.

"Anything," Teia said.

He cleared his throat. "You've got a beautiful lower left dogtooth.

Immaculate. Gorgeously, flawlessly formed, from all I can tell. Its only defect, I think, is that it's a bit large for your mouth—but that makes it perfect for mine. I would like your permission to...um, add it to my best pair of diplomatic dentures. You know the ones. I find a beautiful smile cuts right through people's defenses. Melts them inside. It's magical, really. But I shouldn't like for my best smile to be tarnished by some shadow of guilt that I'd...violated you. You'd be part of something perfect, long after your death. It's immortality. Of a sort."

"Orholam have mercy," Teia whispered.

"Well, clearly *not*," Murder Sharp said, laughing suddenly. "But I will. I've had poor luck with teeth when I've killed the donor in advance—the rot sets into the tooth so, so fast it seems. That's why you're still alive, actually. I can't risk losing your perfection in such a way, so I intend to sedate you before relieving you of it. You'll feel very little. But you will be alive." He pulled forward two vials on the table. He cleared his throat again. "Two lovely tinctures here: first, I give you a heavy dose of poppy dissolved in brandy. Tastes wretched, but it'll give you a total euphoria, and some say visions akin to entering the afterlife, if there is such a thing. This second one is...a marvel. A wonder. Very odd. The Braxians were trying to find an opposite to nightshade—you know it?"

Teia did, of course. In drops applied to the eyes, nightshade or belladonna caused the pupils to flare wide, allowing drafters to soak in more light—or women to look more comely. It also made you blind if you used it too often, so the Chromeria frowned on its use, preferring drafters to learn the skill of widening or tightening their pupils at will.

"What would the opposite of belladonna do?" Teia asked. "Constrict pupils? Oh...to starve drafters of source light."

"Yes, yes, I'm always forgetting how sharp you are. Aha. Sharp. Anyway, the different narcotics they tried at first were too obvious when used at the doses necessary. I actually don't know if they ever found what they were looking for, but they stumbled across this: *lacrimae sanguinis*. Eaten or drunk, this poison takes a few hours to make its way to the eyes—I've not had enough occasion to practice to find out how long exactly. But in a few hours, it *sets* somehow. It crystallizes within the eyes. Then, upon the pupil contracting or dilating strongly, the poison's released into the body.

"One drop is supposed to be able to kill a dozen men. I'll give you two. Then I'll leave my drapes open. You'll have pleasant poppy dreams all night, and when light flashes over the horizon with the dawn of Sun Day, you'll die instantly." He cleared his throat again. "It is as kind as I can be while I do what I must."

"That...does sound very kind," Teia said.

There was nothing else to say. She'd failed. This was the end for her.

Her heart pushed through the thickets of panic and found, suddenly, the barren plains of resignation. Her breath slid from her mouth like a bit falling from her teeth.

She felt strangely better. Death wasn't the freedom she'd choose, but it was one kind of freedom.

Unless there was a hell.

She'd find out soon enough.

"Just the one tooth?" she asked, her voice level and scoured clean of fear.

With a slurping sound, he took out his dentures and set them aside. He began washing his hands in a basin, with soap. But even still, he never took his eyes off her for more than an instant. There would be no surprising him with paryl.

"Oh, I pride myself on my tidiness. I won't deface you unnecessarily." He dried his hands on a pretty, nicely folded cloth, unhurried. There was some element of ritual, of nearly erotic fixation, barely contained, in his voice. "I want you to know, Teia, I'll think of you always when I wear them."

"You'll help my father?" she asked.

He put a blindfold over her head, but didn't lower it over her eyes yet.

He stared at her in the half dark of the hidden chamber for a long moment. A last, guttering goodness flickered in his eyes. She hoped it was an assent.

"Open your mouth," he commanded, filling a tiny silver spoon full of dark liquid. Behind him on his table sat shining tools: a jaw stretcher, pliers, more awful things. She'd not be able to see or speak once he got to work on her.

"Murder?" she said.

"Yes, Adrasteia?"

"Fuck you."

He flashed a sudden grin, showing broken stubs of teeth beneath his gleaming, violet-shrapnel eyes. "They all say that."

She opened her mouth and accepted the bitter drops.

Chapter 98

One day wasn't nearly enough time to get ready, but through the triple miracles of preparation, competence, and the total focus of every human on the Jaspers, things were actually coming together. Kip had meetings with Tisis and the generals. Tisis would be managing Corvan Danavis's scouts and intel, and the generals simply needed to hear Kip say to their faces that he really did want them to follow every order Corvan Danavis gave them. It was worth the half hour Kip spent recounting all of Danavis's exploits and brilliance and showing Kip's own absolute faith in the man. These generals would be repeating the stories to their own men and women. Plus, they needed to see that what Kip was doing was intimately tied to their success.

He spent all of two minutes with his wife that weren't practical and tactical.

"Have you seen Ben-hadad?" Kip asked. "I could really, really use his big brain on this."

"No," Tisis said. "I haven't seen Cruxer, either."

Kip felt the cold hand of dread around his heart. They knew the Order was here. "What?" he said. "I assumed he was with you, making sure the new members of the Mighty were squared away."

"I know, and I thought he'd be here. But none of the others have seen them, either. Ben I could imagine disappearing to work on something he thought was important and forgetting to tell anyone. But Cruxer? Kip, he was really upset about Ironfist's betrayal... and then Ironfist shows up half dead..."

Ironfist hadn't woken. It wasn't certain that he would.

"Orholam have mercy," Kip said. He swallowed.

"I'll let you know the instant I hear anything," Tisis said. He saw the agony in her eyes, but there was also a steel practicality there. They both had things to do, at opposite ends of the Jaspers. No matter what. Even if Cruxer was dead.

And she was right.

"Likewise," Kip said.

They held each other then, forehead to forehead, all too aware that it might be the last time. Their parting kiss was both too much and too little by far. And then they went to their work again: he to the Chromeria, and she to set up scouts and signal-mirror communications lines.

Kip had to bust a few heads—one nearly literally, he'd bruised his knuckles—but he'd gotten control of all the Thousand Stars right around the time the White King's fleet had arrived on the horizon.

Probably not coincidental that the last stubborn jackasses were convinced by that.

Then he got the missive.

"Downstairs. Now. Not a suggestion.—Promachos G."

"Downstairs?" Kip asked the messenger. At least Andross hadn't sent the message through that smug jackass, Grinwoody.

Ferkudi and Winsen accompanied him as he followed Andross Guile's servant down the lifts, then through the small door that headed to the back docks. Hard-faced Blackguards stood at either side of the door, lips tight. They wouldn't meet Kip's eyes.

Oh no.

Kip's neck went tight. He couldn't draw a full breath.

His feet seemed to move independently of his will. He was being carried along by pure momentum and social expectation.

If he didn't find out, maybe it wouldn't have happened.

But he couldn't stop himself. The world was closing in, vision narrowing even as the tunnel widened out.

More Blackguards. More stony faces. No, no, no.

He walked down the path toward the docks toward Andross, who stood impassive over...something.

A body, of course, Kip knew. Covered.

He saw Gill Greyling there, opposite Andross, on the other side of the body. Gill stood ramrod straight, face still, but his eyes streamed tears, and he swallowed as Kip came close. He backed away to make room for Kip.

The body had been covered by Blackguard cloaks. It was a sign of the tremendous respect they wouldn't have given to one who wasn't one of their own.

"Aside from laying their cloaks on him," Andross said, "nothing's been touched, in case you wanted to examine things for yourself. When you're ready, I'll tell you what we know."

It had to be Andross here, didn't it?

Kip squatted down beside the body and pulled back the cloak. He felt the same shock he'd felt before at seeing the dead, somehow never quite dulled, and this time sharper than ever: this face looked like a poor facsimile of Cruxer's face. Cruxer was so much more handsome. Vibrant. Funny. Kind. His spirit had always suffused his flesh, made it continually more beautiful than...this cold visage.

And yet the cold visage was all that was left. He was lying on his side, and that side of his face had purpled from pooled blood.

"Sometime before midnight, I'd guess, from the bodies I've seen after battles," a voice intruded. Winsen.

Kip nodded.

"I went after him," Winsen said. "Like you told me to. Ran all over these damn islands. He didn't take the news of Ironfist betraying the Chromeria well. He thought Ironfist was going to kill you."

"Your young commander's broken sword is here," Andross said. "The blade matches Ironfist's wound and there are grooves cut into Ironfist's chain that match it, too. Both of their pistols had been fired."

But Kip didn't need the explanation. He'd known what was going to happen long before it did.

"Why a sword rather than his spear?" Kip asked. Cruxer was better with a spear.

"Easier to hide?" Winsen guessed. "Blackguards on duty last night never saw either of them. At least that's what they say. You want to talk to them?"

"If they lied to you..." Kip began. They'll lie to me, too, he meant to say, but the words were too much effort. It was the most he could do to shake his head.

Would a spear have made the difference?

Oh, Cruxer.

"This?" Winsen said. He didn't sound moved at all. "Dying like this? For your lord? It's what we do. It's what we signed up for. And Cruxer loved it. He fought the best warrior in the world to a standstill. Stopped him. Saved your life. This isn't a bad death."

"Every death's a bad death," Andross said.

Kip didn't know what to do with it, but he loved his grandfather a little bit for that. Sure, sure, dying to save someone is noble—but you're still fucking *dead*. But this wasn't Winsen's fault, not really. He'd been born with very little feeling himself. When things were fraught, he jumped the wrong way sometimes. This was actually Winsen trying to comfort Kip.

Well, aren't we all a bunch of fuck-ups?

"Have you told the rest of the Mighty?"

"I sent them messengers at the same time I sent yours," Andross said.

Funny, Kip thought, Andross hadn't used this opportunity to be an asshole. Maybe he was just biding his time, though.

But he couldn't keep his attention away from the thing that had been his friend. He took a tremulous breath. He squatted down beside the man who'd put his life and honor on Kip more than once. He brushed some dirt off Cruxer's cheek.

The softness of the gesture was a mistake. The corralled horses of his passions burst through the fences, he fell from his squat to his knees, and a single sob racked him before he could silence himself.

He flashed to anger. I need you now! You can't abandon me here! You have not been relieved of duty, goddammit!

Then he breathed, just thought about his breath. In. Hold. Out slow. Hold.

"Breaker. Lord Guile. *Lord Guile*," Winsen said. "There are messengers. It's urgent, they say. Everything's urgent today."

Kip caught sight of his forearm. The Turtle-Bear. What could it do? What could Kip do? Suffer. Keep going. That was all that made him special.

You and me, buddy, Kip thought, looking at the tattoo. This is what we're here to do: fight and die.

I just hoped that I'd be the first of us to go.

He stood. Cleared the tears from his eyes with calm fingers. Brushed off the wet knees of his trousers from his kneeling.

"Who do I make commander of the Mighty?" he asked Winsen, his voice level, professional.

Winsen's mouth twisted. "They all love Ferk, but he's too big of a goof. A commander's gotta work with people all the time, and Ferk gets people wrong near as often as I do. Guess that cuts me out, too. Ben-hadad's too smart, too distracted, too arrogant. Tisis could do it, but it's an all-the-time kind of a job, and she's got too much else to do. Can't be any of the scrubs. That leaves Big Leo, I guess."

"You make a good case," Kip said. "Tell him you chose him."

Winsen frowned. It was going to make it impossible for him to carp and complain about Big Leo's orders all the time when the Mighty knew *he* was the one who'd picked him. Which was why Kip had done it. Winsen's insubordination would be the biggest threat to a new commander...well, other than the encircling, overwhelming army.

So maybe it was all moot anyway.

Kip straightened his back. He looked over at Gill Greyling. "Thank you, for this. And convey my thanks to your people. Please take care of him?"

Gill nodded. He understood.

"I got shit to do," Kip said, and he walked over toward the messengers.

Chapter 99

Teia was high as a ... Teia was high as an eagle? Teia was high—as high! Teia was...

Shit. Teia was giggling.

"Mmm, yith hehl funneh," she said around the jaw cage holding her face immobile, mouth open for Sharp to work. She laughed at her garbled words. "Harf?" Sharp. "Remimd meh to hell you humfing."

'Hell you,' not 'tell you.' That was hilarious. She laughed again.

And then the pliers were in her mouth, and she couldn't talk at all.

And then, as the blood gushed in her mouth, she didn't want to. She twisted her jaw just as the tooth released and wailed into the rag he hurriedly stuffed over her face. Even laudanum couldn't make someone tearing out your tooth enjoyable.

He loosed the bolts securing the cage to her jaws. She turned her head and spat blood.

"Sharp," she said.

Some blood dribbled a wet line down her cheek, down her neck.

"Yes?" he asked, turning away from studying her bloody, perfect tooth. "I find last words really do only tend to be worth as much as any other words, but if it'll really make you feel better..."

Her head lolled. Opium really was a tell of a thing. "I just, mm, wanted to let you know, I'm going to have to kill you for that. But! Good news! You won't have to save my dad. I'll do that myself. But thanks. For offering. Quite decent of you. Really feel like...mm... like we could have been friends..."

"Me too," Murder Sharp said. He popped her tooth in his mouth and sucked at it to get the blood off.

"If you weren't a sick fuck, I mean."

"Now, that's no way to speak to—" His face scrunched. "Why's your tooth taste like almonds?" He spat the tooth into his hand, suddenly horrified.

There was a nice, well-defined crack in the tooth, as if it had been engineered to break that way. Teia's one little twist as it pulled away from her jaw. A last bit of white gel leaked out into his palm from that crack. He'd sucked down the rest.

"You were always looking at that tooth like a horny teen boy stealing glances of cleavage." Teia laughed. Not that *she* had cleavage.

"You—what did you do?"

"I'm actually glad you finally took it. It's been killing me for six months," Teia said. There was something really important she was supposed to remember. What was it again? "Six months, worrying that damn poison tooth was going to crack and leak death into my mouth."

Murder Sharp staggered and sagged against the door. "I can't... You didn't."

"Oh! That was it!" Teia said. "How long's that other poison last? The light one, lacrimae sanguinis? Does it wear off?"

"You ungrateful bitch. I would've..." Murder Sharp slid down the door. His stomach cramped, but he didn't vomit. Not yet. Cyanide was the only poison potent enough for such a job that Karris had had access to, and it gave an ugly death.

"When's it wear off?" she asked.

"You *shamed* me," he said. "I shared with you. I trusted you. And this? This is...oohhh." He fell over and puked noisily.

"How long's it last?" Teia asked. "Please."

"Stupid, stupid bitch." He puked again.

"I'm stupid?" Teia asked. "Who's the one who had his enemy tied up and didn't finish the job? Who kidnapped me *twice*?"

A silly smile painted his puke-strewn face. "Stupid because... I never dosed you with the lacrimae sanguinis. Just the poppy. I couldn't kill you, Teia. I couldn't—"

And then the convulsions began. His feet drummed against the stone floor.

It took forever, and he was incapable of speech from then on. His eyes raging at her, then rolling back in his head. His dentures had flown from his mouth and lay in a pool of vomit. He gnawed at the floor with his broken teeth, dug his fingers into it.

It was awful, and it was long, too long in her drugged stupor, before she realized she could draft paryl if she wanted to.

Unless he was lying about that. Tricking her.

He was a cunning one.

Well, she had shit to do in the next day, and she'd need paryl to do it. Might as well find out now.

She took one breath, let her fears gather in the wind in her lungs, and then blew it all out into the world. Then she flared her eyes before she took the next breath.

And didn't die.

That was nice.

She looked at the tiniest cutting tool on Sharp's tray and with ridiculous amounts of paryl was just barely able to lift the little thing and float it to her hand. She cut herself free of her bonds.

Then she walked over to Sharp's desk and took out his favorite dip-lomatic dentures, the blindingly bright white ones.

Taking a glass of water, she gently rinsed out his mouth. He coughed weakly as some went down the wrong way. But then, in between convulsions, she put his dentures in his mouth, giving him some dignity back. As much dignity as a man dying spasming in pools of vomit can get, anyway.

"I'm sorry," she said. "For speaking cruelly. Good night, Elijah ben-Zoheth."

He couldn't speak now. The light was already dimming from his eyes. She didn't know if he heard her at all. With paryl, she squeezed his spine to stop the pain and then stopped his heart, too.

It was a mercy too long delayed.

She stood and looked down on him. There was nothing peaceful in the tension-locked corpse.

She found her split tooth and tucked it into his clenched fist.

"I feel bulletproof," she told the dead man. "And I don't think that's such a good thing right now."

For a while, she looked around the secret office, and realized that she kept forgetting what she was looking for.

"Oh!" she said suddenly, holding it up triumphantly. "The master cloak. Sharp, silly, you never even asked me about it!"

She put it on, and felt a little more herself. Then realized she was still wearing the dress Sharp had put her in. His *mother's* dress? Yuck. And he'd undressed her to put it on her? Double yuck.

Eventually, she found her own clothes, feeling a little better when she realized that she was still wearing her own underthings. Sharp had been a sick man, but at least he wasn't *that* kind of sick. It took her a while to get dressed. She might have dozed off for a few minutes. Or hours. She'd never used opiates before, so she wasn't sure how long it was going to take for them to wear off.

But there was no time to wait until she was at her full strength.

She gathered up her things, and everything of Murder Sharp's that seemed like it might be useful. Before she went, she closed his dead eyes. There was nothing tentative or overly gentle in her motions. He was just meat now.

Giving him this last kindness wasn't for him, it was for her. He'd become a monster, but she had the seeds of the same mon-ster in her. And there had been something in him that hadn't been all monster; his goodness was always poking through at the oddest moments.

But she'd killed better.

Next stop, the Order of the Broken Eye's holiday, the Feast of the Night's Coming Triumph. Or whatever the hell it was called.

Maybe she'd be sober by then.

Chapter 100

"Thank you for coming," Andross said. "I know it's been a terrible day."

His note had politely mentioned he would withdraw all support from Kip's martial positions tomorrow if they *didn't* come, so here, late at night, the Mighty had gathered in Andross's stateroom. Their moods ranged from sullen to stoic to jagged. The demands of duty could only block out so much grief.

Suspecting a trap, Tisis hadn't come.

"Koios will attack at dawn, if he's able," Andross said.

"Most of the tacticians think he'll wait. He's only just setting up his siege," Kip said.

"The tacticians have the tactics right, but the strategy wrong," Andross said.

"It'd be a terrible move," Kip said.

"No, not terrible. Simply not his strongest. If the White King can shut down our drafters—which he believes he can—then he is already vastly more powerful than we are. He doesn't need to play it safe, surround us, lay siege, and summon his troops to exactly the right area to focus an attack. He can just attack."

"He's been patient elsewhere," Kip said. "Why on this, the most important battle, would he rush headlong?" And why are you having this conversation with us, rather than with High General Danavis?

"Because he has to attack on Sun Day," Andross said. "His sea battle with you slowed him. I'm sure he would have preferred to get here earlier and set up at his leisure. Now he has to rush in. There's no other choice."

"Wouldn't he want to *not* attack on Sun Day?" Kip asked. "He's a pagan."

"Maybe usually. Not this time. Thumbing his nose at Orholam is worth a few thousand more dead to him," Andross said.

"Ah," Kip said. That made sense. Not only could Koios satisfy his personal animosity against Orholam—probably the most important reason—but he would also show the Seven Satrapies that Orholam was powerless on His holiest day, in the very center of His power.

All remaining resistance would fold after that. The old gods would have shown they were more powerful than Orholam at His greatest. Although it would make this battle more difficult, it would make reigning afterward much easier.

Koios was still playing the long game.

"So let's win, shall we?" Andross said. "To that end, I have gifts for you."

Kip and the others looked at one another. Gifts? Andross Guile?

"Commander Leonidas," Andross said. A slave brought forward a huge rosewood box that he seemed to have difficulty carrying.

"Leonidas?" Kip asked. "Big Leo?"

"I know, I know, it sounds like a girl's name," Big Leo said sheepishly.

He opened the box.

"Oh, you shouldn't have." On the top was a thick black leather coat with a high collar. Across the chest was the Mighty's sigil in white leather. He picked it up; it was obviously very heavy, with chain and plate woven in beneath the leather.

"Oh, you *really* shouldn't have," he said, looking into the rosewood box. Lifting the coat had revealed, on velvet, a hammered, heavy copper chain with links the size of fists. There were two gloves inside as well. Big Leo looked at Andross, who nodded.

Leo put on the gloves and lifted the heavy chain. Each link had a black stripe around its burnished circumference. Then he looked at the tips of the thumbs of his gloves. "Oh, hell, yes!" he said, and flicked his thumb against the chain.

Nothing happened.

"Chain's copper so you don't throw a spark accidentally when it's wrapped around your own body," Andross said. "Forefinger and thumb."

Kip didn't know what he was talking about. But Big Leo looked down at his gloves. He held the chain out and flicked his thumb against his forefinger, throwing a spark.

The entire chain caught fire as the atasifusta wood in each link whooshed into flame.

"Holy shit," Ferkudi said.

Big Leo whipped the fiery chain in frippering circles, passing it over his arms, around his back, striking one end out like a spear, whipping it down like a hammer, and then winding it around an arm.

Then he sort of spoiled the terrifying effect when he giggled like a little kid.

That actually made it more terrifying.

"I know I just said this, but *holy shit*," Ferkudi said.

However, the chain on his arm continued to burn. Atasifusta, the ever-burning.

Ah, thus the leather. Still...

Andross said, "When you're done, do this." He laid a hand on Big Leo's arm. Red luxin poured from his hand, coating the burning chain. First it flared up into fire, red luxin being flammable, but then the luxin crusted over, blackened in every place, extinguishing itself and the chain.

When Big Leo moved his arm again, the red luxin broke to dust with the smell of tea leaves and tobacco, his arm and the chain unharmed. He was also given a helm: naturally, it was a lion with a mane like fire.

Andross motioned for the young man to step back. "Don't say thanks. Express your thanks by keeping Kip alive."

"Yes, my lord," Big Leo said.

"Ferkudi del'Angelos," Andross said. Ferkudi stepped forward. "I hear you're a grappler." His armor was the same, albeit without the covering of leather, and thus much lighter. But his, too, was black and adorned with the Mighty's sigil: the man with head bowed, arms out, radiating power. His weapons were twin double-bladed hand axes, each with one blade of steel and the other blade of a single wavering obsidian edge. Each obsidian stone itself could have purchased a castle. Nothing could cut through luxin like those. He, too, was given gloves, with hellstone points at the knuckles.

Andross said, "Wights will either flee in terror or seek you out especially. I order you to kill at least one of their petty gods, understood?"

"With pleasure, High Lord," Ferkudi said.

The hand axes were completed with sword-breaking hafts and an ingenious back sheath. Ferkudi took a bear helm.

For Winsen, there was the lightest armor, befitting the archer's small size. His helm was a snake. And there was a short bow inside. It was beautifully wrought with horses in some ancient art style, but at first Winsen sneered at it. He did admire the arrows, two quivers full, half of them tipped with obsidian. He looked at them in the light. "Flawless, best fletching I've seen, too. But as for the bow, it's beautiful, but...a short bow? And it's got a sight? I think I'll keep my—"

"It'll pierce armor at three hundred paces. Test it if you don't believe me. My man will instruct you on its care."

Winsen couldn't help himself. He lifted the bow and drew the string, his broad back knotting with the effort. It was clearly harder than he'd been expecting. Then he walked away with it, muttering obscenities in appreciation.

"Ben-hadad," Andross said.

Ben was, surprisingly, little the worse for wear. A servant had found him around noon, tied up, and since then he'd been more fixated on Cruxer's death than on his own narrow escape from it. He'd quietly told Kip of Teia's kidnapping and the work he'd been doing but that his door code was wrong, and when they'd cut through a wall to get in, it was to the wrong room. Sharp would be holding Teia somewhere else. Maybe nearby, which meant Ben-hadad had to revisit his earlier work searching for hidden rooms: he'd missed something.

But that work would take him hours if not days. Teia would be dead by then, if she wasn't already. Ben had told Kip he instead needed to concentrate his efforts on checking the siege defenses and all the various machinae that were going to be used in the Jaspers' defense.

With anguish, Kip had agreed. The battle hadn't even begun, and two of his Mighty were already dead.

He wanted to make the Order pay dearly for that, but he knew he wasn't going to. He was going to die before he could do anything about them.

Andross gave Ben-hadad a coat that was similar to Ferkudi's.

Ben felt it and said, "What's layered underneath this?"

"Mirrored steel scale, like all of them," Andross said. "It's not as strong as plate, but not nearly as heavy, either. Try not to test its effectiveness too much."

Beneath the coat there wasn't a weapon. Instead, there was a pair knee braces.

"I, uh, am actually almost finished with my backup brace," Ben-hadad said, gesturing to his current, solid brace. Kip had broken the other when he'd raised the Great Mirror. "Parallel discovery, I guess? But thank you? Definitely will save me some hours tonight."

"These are Commander Finer's own knee braces," Andross said. "Before he went wight and tried to kill his Prism, he developed these. Instead of using open luxin, he reinforced the joints with sea-demon bone. I think you'll also find that wearing two of them, you can do much, much more than you did with one."

"Two? And sea-demon...?" Ben-hadad's eyes widened. "Of course! Why didn't I think of that? This is—thank you! Thank you very, very much!"

633

"While you're at it, you may also take the *sharana ru* I'd intended for Cruxer," Andross said.

"No, I can't," Ben said, though the curiosity in his eyes was plain. A tygre striper?

"It's not going to do him any good," Andross said.

An uneasy silence descended on them.

"I can't," Ben-hadad said finally.

"Don't be a damned fool. Cruxer died because he couldn't adjust to realities shifting under his feet. Don't follow his example in this." Andross drew a tygre striper shaped like a white spear from Cruxer's box and veritably threw it at Ben-hadad. "Kill a god for me."

Looking to the rest of the Mighty, who nodded their approval, Ben-hadad kept the thing. The spear was long and thin, with a steel spike at the foot and a graceful steel blade at the top, below which were embedded jagged obsidian teeth in the haft.

Turning to Kip, Andross said, "We'll have the appropriate funerals, if we live so long. Now, where is your stubborn bride?"

Kip said, "I guess she's not that eager to see you again. Strangely enough."

"Strangely enough, I'm tempted not to give her her gift, then. But whatever. Take it."

Kip stepped forward and opened Tisis's chest. Inside was a red dress, high-necked and long-sleeved and heavy and adorned with the Mighty's sigil as well. "Armored?" Kip asked.

"As much as possible without being obvious. I figured that her duties wouldn't be martial, but that she may well not stay away from harm, either. The Guile women seem to hold in common a lack of an aversion to danger."

"This is Felia's dress, isn't it?" Kip asked. Andross had merely had a tailor add the Mighty's sigil to it.

Andross pursed his lips. "I hate how you do that."

"So, do I get anything?" Kip said flippantly.

"Oh yes," Andross said, his eyes twinkling. "I spent a long time pondering if I should give you armor so fine you couldn't turn it down but that would make you look like a raging asshole."

"Nice," Kip said. Though I kind of do that on my own.

"But I figured you already do that on your own."

I hate how he does that.

Andross gestured and a slave brought out another box. In it was armor to match the Mighty, albeit with the colors reversed, the armor entirely white, with the figure of the man in black, head bowed, silhouette suspiciously like Kip's own these days. "White, huh? That's a little raging-assholey," Kip said.

"I couldn't give up the idea altogether."

"By which I mean, thank you, grandfather."

"Stop. I'm getting weepy."

"Is there a weapon for me?"

"I thought you'd enjoy going into battle armed with your wit," Andross said.

"But you'd not want me to go into battle defenseless."

Andross didn't smile. He simply held out his hand. In it was a single Nine Kings card.

In a flash, Kip remembered the other cards, but the memories were fragmentary: Andross the Red, and The Master. Now this, a *third* card for Andross Guile, called simply The Guile. In Janus Borig's exquisite style, it showed an old man seated in darkness, eyes glowing red-gold. The faintest glow outlined his head against the darkness. His fingers were colored claws, in each color.

One of each color, because Andross was a full-spectrum poly-chrome. Well, that would have been nice to remember before now. Or maybe Kip would have guessed it was merely symbolic of having the other Colors on the Spectrum under his fingers.

"Cute," Kip said.

"Not quite turtle-bear cute, but I like it."

"You're a motherfucker."

"In more ways than one."

"That's all you've got for me? Scorn and a card?" Kip asked. "You give them weapons; you give me knowledge. Ordinarily, I'd see deep meaning in that. Today it's just a distraction. It's always games and bullshit with you, isn't it?"

Viewing the cards only took an instant, but it might louse Kip up for hours or days. Another Andross Guile card? How bad might it be to View that? Forget it. Kip would either want to murder the man standing here in front of him, or worse, he might understand him. Either way, Kip might be shaken for hours. Hours he didn't have.

Andross said, "Also, I'm ready to tell you your family history. Your mother's history. Your father's. Your uncle's. Mine. It'll be deeply unpleasant for both of us, but perhaps it's time."

"Forget it. This is my family," Kip said, gesturing to the Mighty.

"Your choice," Andross said, with that air that implied, as ever, that Kip was a fool.

Kip tucked the card away carelessly, like it was trash. "Funny thing is, grandfather, after all the time I've spent with you, I've come to a belated but very important realization: you just aren't worth getting to know better. Thanks for the armor. Goodbye."

He picked up his helm from the slave on the way out. It was a dragon's head. With *fur* on it. Sonuvabitch.

Chapter 101

Teia was only half-unlucky. All things considered, that felt pretty good.

Between her capture and falling asleep for 'just a moment,' she'd lost much of the day, though she finally wasn't high anymore. She'd first gone to see if Ben-hadad was still tied up, but he was gone. Rescued, she assumed. Or at least she hoped so.

She wanted to find her friends, to tell them everything. But there was no time to hunt them down. She had other hunting to do.

Atevia Zelorn wasn't at any of his warehouses; he wasn't at any of his favorite taverns or brothels on Teia's way—but he was at his own home. Her favorite wine merchant/serial cheater/Braxian high priest hadn't left yet.

She crouched invisibly outside one window until he made his excuses to his beautiful wife and headed out for his 'long-planned business meeting.' She said, "Please don't get drunk tonight? I promised the children we'd attend the predawn pyrotechnics. They're still having a few, I hear... despite everything."

If Teia had her way, those would be the last words the woman ever said to her husband. Atevia made his promises and headed out, climbing up into a wagon that his slaves had brought around.

Teia timed her own climbing up into the back of the wagon with Atevia climbing up into the front seat so that no one noticed the weight displacement, and then she carefully tucked herself in with the great wine barrels, spreading the master cloak out over herself.

They stopped half an hour later, and men unloaded the barrels and brought them into a dingy little workshop. Teia had gotten very good at taking little glimpses and moving when the timing was right. She dropped off the far side of the wagon so that when the cloak flared from the fall, no one would have a chance to see her momentarily visible legs.

Atevia Zelorn put on a new cowl before he climbed down. This one was lined with fine mail.

The man or woman who received the shipment had one very similar. He or she didn't speak, and moved carefully, so it wasn't until Teia risked a blast of paryl through the new person's clothing that she was able to tell the other figure was a woman.

The woman held up a gloved hand to Atevia, fingers extending, twice.

"Ten minutes. Fine, fine," Atevia said, putting a growl into his voice. It wasn't the greatest disguise, but there were more men than women in the Order, so perhaps he figured it was good enough. Or maybe he just didn't care.

He stepped outside, and the servants opened the barrels. The woman dismissed them and then moved from barrel to barrel. She held a small vial in one hand. It stank. Teia recognized it as a common emetic.

The hell?

But then she understood. The woman sniffed and then tasted each wine in turn, stirring them first with a big ladle.

Satisfied they weren't poisoned, she put aside the emetic. Then she went to her workbench and pulled out bundles of wrapped vegetation. She worked with the speed and efficiency of a physicker or an apothecary, inspecting the leaves of several plants Teia didn't know and numerous poppy bulbs. Then she began counting out the leaves into piles, rejecting those too old or dry, and cracking the poppy bulbs and collecting the brown seeds into cups. Leaves of three different kinds of plant went directly into the wine, each counted out, and then the poppy was ground with a mortar and pestle, added to the barrels, and stirred.

The woman tasted a tiny amount of the resulting drug cocktail. She cocked her head as if it tasted wretched but that that couldn't be helped. She rinsed her mouth with water and then spat it out.

She looked like she was finished.

Now.

Teia ghosted across the floor and poured Murder Sharp's lacrimae sanguinis into each of the barrels. She used it all.

She didn't make a sound. She didn't stumble. She didn't scuff the floor. She didn't pour that liquid death from enough of a height to make a splash. She didn't even breathe.

But the apothecary paused. Sniffed.

Suddenly, Teia smelled it, too. A tangy-sour stench that would have been buried under the taste of the poppy or even the wine, but now, floating at the top, not stirred in, and with the container still in Teia's hand, uncorked, it wafted through the room subtly.

Subtly, except to a trained apothecary.

The woman stepped close, sniffing again. "What is—by the old gods, is that lacrimae—"

Teia grabbed her spine in a paryl fist, then grabbed the woman's head before she could tumble to the ground. Teia cracked the apothecary's neck with a sharp twist.

She felt the breath sigh out of her.

Sometimes you can't wait to see if your paryl knots hold.

"Ready?" a voice outside asked.

No time!

With strength she didn't know she had, Teia heaved the woman up over her shoulder and dumped her into the half-empty barrel of water from which she'd drunk earlier.

Teia tore off the woman's chainmail-lined cowl and pulled it on herself. She willed the master cloak to ape the woman's white cloak, went visible, and heard the scuff behind her at the door. Without turning, Teia held up one finger. One minute, please.

She used her body to block the man's view of the water barrel. Orholam have mercy, it had no lid!

Calmly, hoping the man had turned away or gone away—Teia couldn't hear if he'd left over the sudden pounding of her own heart—she peeled the gloves off the woman's hands, tucked her hands down, and put the gloves on. Checking that the cowl was firmly in place, she finally peeked over her shoulder.

The servants were standing there now, and Atevia Zelorn was coming.

Calmly, Teia grabbed the cloths that had been wrapped around the leaves and draped them over the water barrel, and the woman's protruding shoe.

Then she bent and picked up the vial of poison she'd dropped earlier. She corked it and put it among the other vials and weights and alchemical accoutrements on the workbench.

Teia had never been so glad to be wearing a full-face covering. She was sweating. She didn't sweat easily, but she was drenched now. She walked to the wine barrels, gave them each a few deep stirs, and then stepped back. She waved the men forward, hoping they knew what to do.

The woman she'd just murdered had seemed the quiet type, right?

The men affixed the lids, pounded them down with mallets, and then rolled them to another cart.

Atevia Zelorn climbed up into his seat. Teia gave a halfhearted little wave goodbye, nodding her head to him, and turning away.

"What the hell?" he asked. "Come on. You know how this goes, Muriel. You're the cupbearer."

Cupbearer. He meant poison tester, the one who had to drink the wine publicly first to certify it was safe.

"Makes no damn sense," Teia muttered, but her stomach was knotting with fear. "Why would I taint the wine?"

Zelorn said, "What makes no sense is that the Old Man demanded I use my best Ambrosia Valley Barbera for the bloodwine. After you put all that shit in it, I might as well have used Bilgewater Red."

"If I were going to poison the wine, wouldn't I just prepare an antidote for myself beforehand?" Teia said. An antidote. Yeah, that *would've* been a good idea, wouldn't it?

"It's tradition. It doesn't have to make sense. Now, get up here."

Teia grumbled her assent and climbed up. Her heart was thudding.

How many poisons did Murder Sharp have in his lair? Why'd I have to pick the one with no antidote?

Chapter 102

There had to be a way out.

Their little cart clattered over cobbles as darkness fell on Big Jasper. Teia'd always had quick hands. Maybe she could... What? How do you taste test poison and not die?

Every dodge she thought of was stupider than the last: Maybe she could swap glasses? Yeah, except you didn't poison *some* of the wine, T; you poisoned it *all*. Are you really going to pin your hopes on someone showing up with another random glass of wine that you can swap at the last moment?

Maybe she could try to keep her veil on and pour the wine down her neck? But her robes were white; the wine was red. Maybe it could work, though! Her robes were actually the master cloak. Maybe she could keep willing it to stay white. Maybe it would!

But she didn't have any way to test it.

And if they noticed anything suspicious, they'd kill her. Worse, they would throw out the obviously poisoned wine. Everything she'd done to get here would be for nothing.

No matter how she turned it, there seemed to be only three possible outcomes here: she successfully faked drinking the poisoned wine, she got caught faking drinking it, or she actually did drink it.

Two of those ended with her very dead.

She'd not come this far to end up dead.

They reached the Crossroads, and it was packed with people. There were merchants moving trade goods at the last minute for tomorrow's festivities—if those went ahead—or doing business before the battle. Some people. Orholam's chafed nutsack.

There were Lightguards trying to set up a checkpoint—on one of seven intersecting roads, but not the others. Morons. There were people already partying, and all the food and wine vendors to cater to them. Some yellow pyroturges were doing tricks in the evening air, elaborate creations bursting apart with sparks and flashes.

Three carts met them, and three horsemen, nondescript, faces hidden as if cold. One pointed to a barrel, and without a word, Atevia levered off the lid. He handed a ladle to Teia, and she clambered into the back of the wagon.

Suddenly, all eyes were on her. Three barrels of wine, three carts. The poisoned wine wasn't going to one of the Braxian congregations. Each was getting a barrel. If Teia did this, she would wipe out the entire Order with one stroke.

There were no other ladles. No big ceremony with her confronting two glasses and trying to figure out how to drink from the right one. It was just a dozen eyes on her. One ladle, and the choice of life or death.

Teia dipped the ladle deep into the barrel, drew it forth, and then held it out toward each of the men, so they could see that it was brimming full.

Here's to you, my dead slave brothers. I accept your judgment. I accept my punishment.

She lifted her veil and drank it all. She presented the empty ladle to them, and whispered, "Good enough?" to show she didn't still have the wine in her mouth.

"Thank you, Mariel," one of them said, his voice obviously modulated with one of those collars. But she knew.

The Old Man himself. Grinwoody.

Teia stiffened. Atevia had called her Muriel. Teia threw her hands out, like 'What the hell?'

"So it is you," the man said. "Just checking. Never seen you drink so deeply before. Guess it's not a normal night, is it? Men, load the barrels." He turned to one. "Oh, and search her."

The man did, roughly but quickly. Inexpertly, too, in Teia's opinion.

She could only wish that actually mattered. A vial of an antidote hidden in a body cavity sounded like a really great idea right about now.

"She's clean," the man said.

The Old Man pulled out a coin purse.

Teia waited. She had no idea if Muriel usually declined payment, so she didn't push the act.

But she widened her eyes briefly, only to see paryl leaking from a shell around the nondescript man who'd just searched her. A Shadow.

A lousy one, obviously, from the spectral bleed she could see, and by the fact he hadn't noticed she was a paryl drafter herself—though if she'd been holding paryl when he touched her, that would have gone very differently. This moron Shadow had just been yanking her around while he 'searched' her by shooting paryl through her clothing. He was too inexpert at keeping his spectrum tight enough to search her from any distance.

Well, lucky me, Teia thought. Watching carefully, she caught the flash of super-fine mail around the Old Man's legs and wrists.

Some subtle paryl attack was not likely to get through that in time. She'd have to go straight through Grinwoody's eyes for a clot in the brain.

But she'd already poisoned the wine. If she killed him now and thus revealed herself, who in the Order would dare to drink wine an assassin had mixed for them?

If she tried to kill Grinwoody now, she wouldn't be killing anyone else. Patience, T.

The coin he pulled out was unlike any she had ever seen. Large, silver tarnished, dark except for the relief of a broken eye. The obverse showed nine crowns.

"Barricade your shop tonight, Muriel. The fun begins half an hour after dawn. If anyone attacks you or yours, you show them this." Half an hour after dawn? That would be once the Sun Day parade was in full swing.

Which was insane. A battle was probably going to happen, and they were going ahead with the parade? She'd heard a dozen speculations for why on the streets—some with a more cynical take than Quentin's—that it was to keep the pilgrims from panicking, and that by honoring Orholam, they hoped to twist His arm into helping them.   641

Others guessed that this way the Chromeria's defenders knew exactly which streets would be free and which blocked by the crowds, or said that even though it was going to be much smaller than usual, the new Prism had demanded it.

Some kind of Order attack during *that*? Perfect. Just perfect.

But Teia nodded. She was already feeling fuzzy. Her stomach was several degrees past the warmth of a swig of brandy. That would be the alcohol and various drugs, she guessed, probably not the lacrimae sanguinis. Not yet.

Watching the wagons rattle away in various directions down the streets, leaving her in a crowd simultaneously tense and joyous, scared and jubilant, facing a holy day and an army intent on their annihilation, Teia couldn't help but feel empty. In their hopes and fears, they were tonight connected with one another, with the whole city and the whole religion. They were about to face the greatest fight of their lives, but they were doing it together.

Teia's fight was over. She was abandoned, alone, and not for the first time in the last year, unspeakably lonely.

Just as she'd vowed, she was going to finish her big mission. She was going to make a difference, forever. She was going to succeed; it was just that she'd be dead by the time it happened.

So you win after all, Murder Sharp. Or let's call it a tie. But points to you for doing it the way the Order always does its best work. They couldn't corrupt me until I helped them do the job. And you? You couldn't kill me... until I helped.

Chapter 103

"Breaker! Sir! You need to wake up!"

Kip couldn't have been asleep more than an hour. He sat up and started at the looming form of Big Leo standing over the bed. Tisis yelped. Kip might have yelped, too, but she was louder.

Thank you, honey.

"What's going on?" Kip asked.

"My lord," Big Leo said. "It's *Teia*."

"What?!"

"But she's ... not herself."

"Get her in—" Kip started to say.

"I'm already here!" Teia said. She held her hands up in the air as if presenting herself for applause. Her face was flushed; her skin was glowing. Her lips were dry and her eyes were dilated.

"I couldn't leave her out there," Ferkudi said, poking his head in, apologetic. "She was hollering."

"Wow," Teia said as Kip got out of bed. Tottering on her feet, she stared at him appreciatively—even brazenly, considering his wife was right there—shoulders to abs to underclothes and back up. "You are looking *good*." She rubbed her forehead. "Orholam's balls, I am so high right now. This was not how I wanted to do this."

He hurriedly pulled on his tunic and trousers.

"Teia, it's so good to see you again," Tisis said, coming around to Kip's side of the bed. "How can we help you?"

"I am *really* sorry for glancing at your husband's bulge," Teia said. She winced. "I can't believe I just said that. You have been so kind to me, and..."

For his part, Kip was looking at Tisis, who seemed utterly unperturbed.

"Can we get you some breakfast?" Tisis asked, as if Teia were an expected visitor in the morning. Tisis was wearing Kip's favorite green silk negligee, the one whose straps had been torn off and mended several times. She calmly pulled a wrap around herself, and Kip felt a jolt of admiration for his bride's cool calm. "Do you need medical attention?"

He knew how Tisis had felt about Teia in months past, but now she was choosing to see Teia as a young woman who was not in a good way, but also maybe not quite responsible for it. She saw Teia's suffering, not her behavior.

It made him love her even more.

Teia covered her face with her hands, contorting with such shame and self-loathing it made Kip ache for her. She gestured toward Tisis. "Guess I don't need to ask what you see in her, huh? All this and kind, too? Her *hair* even looks good. She's been *sleeping* and her hair looks good. How does she do that? I bet she's not even a murderer!"

"Teia?" Kip asked. This was not like her. He'd expected that she would change in the time they'd been apart, but even given that, this wasn't her.

"The poppy's wearing off," Teia said. "I wanted it to, but..." Teia repeated curses under her breath for a few moments, then she looked up plaintively. "I just really wanted to see you, Kip. I'm sorry to be like this. I can't even remember all I wanted to say to you, but I just really wanted to see you one last time."

One last time? "Teia? What's going on?"

She looked up at him, and her eyes filled with regret. "Kip, I'm dying."

Chapter 104

Quentin had only two types of clothing now: the disgustingly rich and the obscenely wealthy. Either one would have nauseated the old him. Over the last year, he'd warred with himself every day as he'd slowly grown accustomed to the weight and wear of this garb.

As part of his punishment—being the example of a luxiat led astray by the world's riches—he was forbidden to wear anything less expensive than his second-best set in public. In his rooms, he'd worn literal sackcloth for several months. Then, realizing that he was taking pride in mortifying his own flesh—O Pride, thou insidious beast!—he'd taken to wearing a fine but simple robe in private.

But today, long before the sun rose, after Kip had awakened him and told him what was required, Quentin put on his finest robes with something akin to a healthy pride: today these robes would help him do what needed to be done. He actually had to ask a servant to help him dress: there were layers to these things! Pearls in their hundreds, real gold twisted in the brocade, a mink collar dyed murex purple. Fawn-skin boots, silk laces, and jeweled rings for every finger.

He looked like everything he had always hated, but today it would all be for Orholam's glory. That which had been a scourge unto his back was now the armor for his battle. A great and glorious gamble. He would be tested to his limits.

He might not survive it.

From his apartments in the blue tower, he made his way across the Lily's Stem, greeting a few luxiats on their way to matins prayers. One offered him a coin, and he took it humbly. If the Order came to suspect what Quentin was doing, he'd not get a chance to put it into the hands of the poor who needed it, but this, too, was his personal spiritual discipline: trusting that Orholam would cover his flaws and failures and still get His work done on this world, even if Quentin weren't here to do it, even if Quentin misused some moiety of the bounty with which Orholam had trusted him.

He arrived at the west docks an hour before sunrise. The docks were crowded with the faithful, still hoping for a parade. But not only the faithful thronged here. Last-minute reinforcements to the fortifications above the docks and to the surrounding walls were being shored up by dozens of workmen. Nearby buildings had been cannibalized for lumber and bricks, beams torn from centuries-old homes while their owners wept.

On the opposite side of that wall, crouched in the bay like a panther outside the door, the Wight King's navy waited.

Quentin hated being the center of attention, and as he looked at the stairs up to the wall, he felt faint. Several soldiers were looking askance at him. The bored crowd, some huddled with their sleeping children, others simply looking for some entertainment to fill the next hour until sunrise—all stared at him and openly speculated as to why he was here rather than in richer quarters.

Men and women will die today in droves. Orholam hasn't asked me to pick up a sword for that battle.

He asks not what we are unable to do.

He has asked me to fulfill *this* duty.

Ergo, this duty is a duty that I am able to fulfill.

Of course, Orholam never promised we shan't soil ourselves in the fulfillment of said duties.

For some reason, that lightened Quentin's heart.

'Just pretend to be Gavin Guile, but…you know, holy,' Kip had told him.

It wasn't quite a ringing endorsement of Kip's father, but it was good advice.

This'll be my first sermon, Quentin thought. Most likely my last, too, the not-so-encouraging part of him added.

As far as prophetic sermons go, this really is cheating, isn't it?

But then, if the prophecy doesn't come true, I'm going to look like a fool immediately. And fatally.

Oooh boy. His heart hadn't felt like this since he'd walked out before the crowd to face Orholam's Glare.

Gavin Guile. Just put on your Gavin Guile.

Taking a deep breath, Quentin walked toward the soldiers stationed at the bottom of the steps.

Chapter 105

In the first light of what would be his final Sun Day, Gavin was circling to where his sword and his death lay, when he beheld an impossibility.

Directly opposite where the stair had spilled Gavin out onto the tower's crown, the sun was rising, but now, the sun in all its brilliance, bearable only in small glances, seemed to *widen*. Blinking, he shaded his own eye against Orholam's with a hand. His pace slowed.

What the hell is going on? But Gavin wet his lips and kept moving.

The sun in the sky split into twin orbs, as if they were Orholam's own orisons glaring judgment across the horizon. As if, most times, He gave the world only half His attention, and now Gavin had all of it.

Both of God's eyes, open, burning white.

Just as Gavin had given up on finding Him, He was *here*—and He was angry.

Fear threw shackles at Gavin's heavy limbs, but he staggered forward. He would not be a man who cowered—not even before God Himself.

And those few extra steps back toward his sword were all it took. The second eye moved out and out, and then was halved, eclipsed by nothing Gavin could see. Then it disappeared entirely.

Gavin stopped, shaken from his fear by curiosity. He stepped back, and the second celestial eye reappeared. Then he stepped back farther, to where the second eye had split from the first, and in a few steps, they merged once more.

He knew he should get the blade before he investigated any mysteries, but he took a few more steps back to the stairs where he'd entered.

Now there was nothing visible at the crown of the hill.

But it *had* to be there.

The sword, you moron. Arm yourself, *then* investigate mysteries.

Gavin circled the promontory once more, quickly now, keeping his distance.

Orholam's single eye split again, and again both eyes glowered down at Gavin in judgment.

Gavin gritted his teeth and took a step—up the hill. And then another, climbing the hill at an angle with the sun.

There was something *off* about those burning eyes.

Then all the pressure on his heart released at once, and he blew out a huge breath.

There weren't two eyes up there at all. It was a mirror!

God *damn*.

A mirror, set atop this hill at just the right angle so that pilgrims coming here at dawn on Sun Day and following the path Gavin had would see exactly what Gavin had seen. It was just a bloody mirror! Up on the hilltop, casting that illusion with every sunrise, the angle worked out precisely: the path, it seemed, even had markings that had to be a calendar, so that the priests could have pilgrims stand at exactly the right spot each day.

It was all religious flimflam, a swindle, chicanery. A con for the desperate and credulous.

But still…an impossibly thin, huge, perfectly clean mirror? Clean, after centuries and doubtless thousands of storms? That in itself was well-nigh miraculous.

Granted, it was still a lot more credible than that God Himself was staring at him.

Gavin approached the mirror, the time and angle of the hill making the 'eyes' hold steady. He squinted against the brightness to study the fraud.

But as soon as he did, they moved. Not the way they should have, given his own motion.

His steps faltered.

No, surely not. They must've only *seemed* to move wrongly.

But Gavin was frozen, his muscles going taut as a bowstring fully drawn.

Heart thudding, mind screaming that he should have grabbed the sword first, Gavin circled farther.

The eyes seemed to move, but now fully independent of Gavin's steps.

No. No! He'd just puzzled it all out. This was all a Sun Day deception like those Gavin had taken part in so many times himself.

But now as he took another step, it was undeniable. The reflected eye should eclipse from the other side as Gavin circled, leaving the sun alone in the sky.

Instead, the sun tore away to hang in the sky alone in its rightful place.

But twin orbs glided down within the mirror, side by side, like eyes.

Gavin stepped back on his heel toward the sword down the hill behind him, but he couldn't tear his gaze away.

The orbs settled at the top of the promontory at the height of a man's face, at his eyes.

The very air distorted at the crown of the hill, and something there—perhaps even a mirror, as Gavin had suspected—seemed to bubble outward, as if something was pushing its way out from the mirror and into the world.

What was happening there was hard to make out, looking up the hill against the monotone brightness of the sky, except for where every downward angle from the figure's pushing in made the mirror reflect black ground instead of the bright sky.

The face itself was unbearably bright. Gavin held up a hand to block the searing light. Through his spread fingers, Gavin saw a silvery foot slide forth. Then a gleaming arm with muscles etched of marble, then a perfect body with mirror-skin.

The godling took three steps out before he seemed to recall that here he needed to breathe. Gavin could hear the breath, this far away. If this was all an illusion, it was more sophisticated than any Gavin had ever heard of.

The mirror-skin of the being resolved, melting into or morphing into humanlike skin. Humanlike except for its utter perfection. As if in deliberate mockery of Gavin, it, too, wore only a loincloth. Its eyes, now not quite so brilliantly hot as the sun itself, were still unbearably bright, blotting out the man's features. Gavin couldn't scan that alien face for whatever deception or malice might lie there.

Gavin's disbelief managed one more gasp. This was all a magical deceit—sure, maybe an ancient and fiendishly complicated one—but Gavin was no simpleton desperate to buy clever drafting.

The eyes. The eyes were the key!

He looked down to see if his own shadow moved as that bright being moved; no hex-casting, no illusion could cast such light that it actually threw shadows. The lack of shadows would reveal that this was mere will-casting.

The phantasm started circling down the hill, as if giving Gavin room, as if Gavin were a skittish wild beast. But Gavin welcomed each step the thing took away from the mirror—if this were will-casting or hex, the magic would be placed where everyone must look, the mirror itself.

But then he saw that his shadow was splitting, trembling, synchronized with those lantern eyes as they bobbed with the creature's every step.

Fear shot down Gavin's spine. It was real.

Worse—what if the godling were circling, not to alleviate Gavin's fear but...it was heading toward the Blinding Knife!

Gavin shot away like an arrow loosed. Up the hill, the godling shot forward, too, rushing in at an angle toward the same prize as if he and

Gavin were twinned eyes in a mirror, the light of heaven and the light of earth being called together here at the center of all things.

But the god was better positioned. Gavin didn't dare look toward him for fear of it slowing him even half a step. He could feel the deity closing.

Then It cut in, not going for the prize but leaping at Gavin instead, as if he himself were the prize.

They went down hard, slamming to the beautiful and utterly unforgiving black stone of the tower's roof.

And that resolved his last doubt with a thuddingly physical crash: you can't get tackled by an illusion.

Coughing, gasping, Gavin lashed out immediately. If he'd learned nothing else from his life, it was that he who strikes first often strikes last. But with their legs entangled, his kick glanced off solid muscle.

Gavin lashed out with knees and elbows, kicking to create some distance.

Whatever else this being was, Its flesh wasn't marble or luxin or pure will; it felt like that of a man.

And It fought like a man, too, grabbing Gavin's ankle as he tried to pull away to run the last steps to the sword. The godling twisted Gavin's ankle so hard that he had to flip sideways, or risk his leg being broken.

Gavin rolled, tearing his ankle free, but losing all forward momentum. He tried to stand, losing where his opponent was as he tried to claim a position between the being and the blade.

The godling crashed into Gavin again, blasting him off his feet and landing on top of him, two steps from the blade.

This time Gavin was on the receiving end of the knees and elbow strikes. He blocked, blocked, thrashed ineffectually. He'd never been a great grappler. The Blackguards he'd trained with never much wanted to slam their elbows into the Prism's head, and in Gavin's real-world fights, he'd only rarely come within range of a sword, much less fists. Drafting and shooting had always been enough. If anyone had come within grappling range, Gavin had been able to count on a Blackguard dealing with the threat instantly.

It had become one part of his training Gavin let rust into disuse; not even Blackguards could excel at every martial art, and Gavin had needed to be so much more than only a warrior.

The man went for a chokehold, and Gavin barely had the presence of mind to shoot an arm up through the grip before his opponent could choke him from consciousness.

Even as he strove to break free toward that damned blade—it was a hand's breadth from his straining fingertips!—a chill cut through the heat of flight and fear and the raw vibrancy of battle juice: Gavin couldn't fight this Opponent with some easy and obvious short-term goal animating his every move.

Trying only and immediately to grab the sword would make him too predictable. Back when he'd had his powers, fighting a monochrome drafter while standing between the man and his spectacles had always been easy. Drafters in those positions always thought they only had options *after* they had their spectacles and thus their power, so they always moved to grab their spectacles first, even if it put them in the jaws of an obvious trap.

Gavin would need to use every resource instead; this fight wouldn't end in seconds; it might stretch minutes. How long it took didn't matter. Whether he grabbed the Blinding Knife didn't matter. Victory was all that mattered.

Gavin stopped trying to roll toward the sword and pushed hard into the godling's pull.

The reversal threw them both over, away from the Blinding Knife. Gavin scissored his legs around the man, straining to lock his feet together.

"I know you," Gavin said.

"You don't even know yourself."

"You're—"

The Opponent twisted, grunting, throwing repeated knee strikes, mostly deflected. They had to take as much out of him to dish out as they took Gavin to absorb. The fire in his eyes was smaller now, but just as intense if not more. Gavin couldn't stare at him for long lest he be blinded.

"I...had seven goals," Gavin said. He had to talk in short little gaspy fragments. He'd probably been fighting for only two minutes, and it already felt like years.

"For every seven years. You think I don't know?" the godling said. He didn't seem nearly as out of breath as Gavin was.

"Took—" Gavin shifted as he took another shot in the ribs. He lost the thought. "Was careful not to even, uh, think about it out in the sun. In case." In case the Order was right and Orholam really did see and maybe even hear everything done in the light.

"Thought darkness could hide your blasphemy?" the godling asked.

"Blasphemy? Ha! One can only blaspheme against a god!"

Gavin lost his grip on a sweat-slick arm, then he lunged for a better hold and missed.

They broke apart from each other, both rolling, both standing, chests heaving, throwing glances at the sword but neither of them making a move for it that might leave him vulnerable.

"But then," Gavin said, "that's what you wanted everyone to think, isn't it? That you're God."

"Deception is your forte, not mine." There was something familiar in his voice. A bad copy of Gavin's own. Another mockery.

"No, no," Gavin said. "You dazzle and distract rather than hide, but it's still deceit. I'm a liar and I know a liar when I see one. So I've suspected your game all along." They circled each other, each keeping their weight low, hands up.

"You came to lay your suspicions to rest?"

"I already have. I was right. I've suspected it ever since I became Prism," Gavin said. "Assassin. Traitor. Genius. Warlord. Liar. We have a lot in common. But only *you* founded a religion that conveniently made exceptions for your worst behavior. The man who lives alone is either a god or a monster, and I know which you are, and I'll admit you're more than a man now, but you're not Orholam, the creator God, the Almighty Lord of Lights. You? You steal our lives and our magic to fuel your own. You're nothing more than a leech. You're not the creator God, Orholam. I—"

"No—"

"I know who you are, and I'm not here to beg a boon of you, Emperor Lucidonius," Gavin said. "You ascended to godhood, and I will, too. I'm not here to praise you. I'm here to replace you."

Chapter 106

"Listen, O ye beloved of Orholam!" A voice rose above the crowds thick in the streets, mere minutes before dawn. In a normal year, the call would have been inaudible over the sharp snaps and explosions from the pyroturges and the *oohs* of the crowd and the din of food sellers and the chatter of conversation. This year, there was an air of quiet dread.

People had come great distances to join the Sun Day festivities on Big Jasper. When they'd heard of the invasion, a few had left, but most hadn't believed it would really happen, or perhaps their homes had been lost already to the Wight King's armies and they had nowhere else to run, or perhaps they believed Orholam would surely protect them here.

Kip had taken a position at the seawall by East Bay with the majority of his raiders. He was halfway glad to be here: he was happiest being with his people in this fight, but he thought that he really ought to be atop the Prism's Tower with the mirrors. Andross had let him practice on them to his heart's content yesterday, but had claimed that today there were prophecies to be fulfilled. One, he claimed, said that the Lightbringer 'will ascend the heights only at the last, where others have tried and failed.'

It was one thing to follow a prophecy because it had good advice anyway; it was another to follow one that seemed to be forthrightly *bad* advice.

But it actually didn't matter whether Kip trusted him or if Andross was deliberately sabotaging Kip's chance to be the Lightbringer. Andross was the promachos. His word was law. Within the Chromeria itself, Kip had to obey him. And Andross had said Kip wasn't to come back to the Chromeria until the bane rose.

Kip wasn't sure why that hadn't happened yet. Perhaps the Blood Robes planned to wait until the Chromeria committed its drafters to the fight. Perhaps, with the bane spread around the islands rather than grouped as they had been when Kip had encountered them at sea, there were simply technical difficulties. Deploying as quickly as the White King's army was doing was certain to cause all sorts of problems. After all, an amphibious assault was an incredibly difficult undertaking, and it wasn't something the Blood Robes had ever practiced; nor had they ever deployed on this scale or at this speed.

Please let them be running into unforeseen problems.

Please let us be able to take advantage of those.

Once the bane did rise, Kip would have to leave the front lines quickly. In theory, it would take a while, so he should have plenty of time to get back to the Chromeria.

Regardless, he needed to be here for a while, at least. At least until they found out if Teia had been right.

They believed this was the area most likely to be attacked first. West Bay was covered by the batteries of Cannon Island. Little Jasper itself was so rocky and tall, with sheer walls above the sheer rocks, that it was well-nigh unassailable. One or two ships might land at the back docks, but the only passage into the island from there could be guarded by half a dozen men and held for days. Naturally, they'd put an entire platoon there.

The only important thing to be done still was to get every drafter to bleed themselves a bit with some hellstone. The orders had already been given, and stressed, and repeated, but telling a war drafter not to draft before going into battle was like telling a swimmer not to hold his breath before diving.

"I come to you with a word from Orholam Himself!" Quentin shouted. He'd bribed his way to getting atop the gatehouse, and everyone could see him.

Kip's men had quietly accompanied Quentin everywhere he'd asked this morning. He'd made four or five stops. This was to be the last before dawn.

Teia, please tell me you weren't merely drunk last night. If nothing happens here, you—and I—will have ruined Quentin.

From where Kip and his men stood, Quentin's voice wasn't loud. There was still time left now, in the last few minutes before dawn, where Kip should be making his own big speech.

In Kip's experience, men usually fought because they didn't want to let the man next to them down, then because their commanders would kill them if they didn't, and finally because they might get loot or revenge.

What was he supposed to tell his people that wasn't already obvious? *We're on an island. We're surrounded. There's nowhere we can go, nowhere to run away to. We win or we die.*

"My friends!" Quentin said, and he was resplendent in his luxiatlord's attire. "Be strong and take courage. You have trembled through the long night, but dawn is coming. We, the Magisterium, have long used our words to sway your hearts. Today Orholam shall reveal whose heart inclines to the light and who wishes to hide in darkness. Let me speak to you one last time, for three minutes only. I take as my text a commentary on the end of mercy by Doni'el Machos."

Quentin read the words without drama, without inflection, merely a loud and clear statement of fact: " 'The wrath of Orholam burns against them. Their damnation doesn't slumber, the pit is prepared, the fire is made ready, the furnace is now hot, ready to receive them, the flames do now rage and glow. The glittering sword is whet, and held over them, and the pit hath opened her mouth under them.' "

He closed the scroll, although Kip was certain that the action was mostly to signify that he was finished quoting. Quentin had quoted longer selections from memory many times. The young luxiat continued, with no passion in his voice other than pity. "My dear wayward sheep, today is the day of judgment. Orholam's luxiats have become corrupt. His magisters clad themselves in golden rags, as if rags might 653 save." He held up the front of his own fine tunic as if it were loathsome to him. "Orholam's own drafters have grown proud in their strength, so this day, Orholam will deny our drafters His luxin that we may learn to lean upon His strength instead.

"Among us, men and women of all stations have worshipped other gods, have conspired with Orholam's enemies, and have betrayed Him and us both. Traitors stand among us, but Orholam knows what is done in darkness, and Orholam will drag their shame into the light. These are words you've heard before, words you've discounted as mere metaphor. But I tell you that when the dawn comes—*literally: this* dawn, *this* day, today, minutes from now—when Orholam's Eye rises over these walls, some of those standing with us will die. They will be unable to bear the full light of Orholam's gaze. And they will perish."

Oh, shit. Quentin had gone way past what Kip had told him to say. Quentin had been supposed to go out and say, 'Hey, don't be afraid if some people get ill. Orholam's in charge. Those loyal to Him are going to be fine.' But no, Quentin had thrown it all in, like a first-time gambler with no sense of responsibility.

If Kip and Teia had led him astray, Quentin wasn't merely going to be ruined; he was going to get lynched.

"But when it does happen," Quentin said, "be not afraid. Orholam sees. Orholam hears. Orholam cares. Orholam saves. He will slay these traitors who are intent on betraying us to the King of Wights. Orholam will slay them, not to cause your hearts to fear but to save your very lives and your souls.

"This day is not a battle of brother on brother. Nor even between men and those wights who once were men themselves. Today, Orholam Himself fights beside us against the legions of the damned. When you grow faint, His immortals shall uphold you. When you grow weary, they shall bear you up. Though ye fall, O beloved of Orholam, ye shall rise again. And if any part of this doesn't happen, slay me as a false prophet!"

Quentin paused. The crowd had fallen utterly silent. They seemed caught between hope and despair, with disbelief overall. When did any luxiat speak so plainly?

Some knew him or knew of him, and those who did whispered about Quentin to their neighbors, and the sound of the whispers ebbed and flowed.

The sun, still below the horizon for those here at the waterline, was casting its light on the tallest towers of the Chromeria now, its light descending slowly and surely.

The people turned and looked. Some looked ill. Was that the lacrimae sanguinis affecting them, or just people scared to death?

Quentin said, "I close now with a few final words from Doni'el Machos:

" 'Orholam stands ready to pity you; this is a day not only of judgment but also of mercy; you may cry now with some encouragement of obtaining mercy: but once the time of mercy is past, your most dolorous cries and shrieks will be in vain; weep now in repentance, or weep in the very throes of your damnation.' "

Atop the gate, limned in the rising light, Quentin fell to his knees and lifted his arms in supplication, or perhaps greeting.

Kip felt sudden, intense anxiety for his friend.

What if the poison took too long to take effect?

The sunlight filled the square, its hand touching all the people who'd been listening so intently to Quentin—and, as far as Kip could tell, word of Quentin's sermon must have spread like wildfire, because it seemed like the whole island held its breath.

And now we find out if Karris's luxiat corps is any good.

Kip nodded to a standard-bearer, who waved a signal flag.

In obedience to Karris's luxiats, mirror slaves and the star-tower slaves around the Jaspers reacted instantly, spinning the towers' mirrors, sending great beams of sunlight across the crowd. Not only here but also working light over every wall, every gate, every sector of the city: if the lacrimae sanguinis was released by a sharp constriction of the pupils, Kip wanted to make certain that no one had a chance for their eyes to gradually get accustomed to the light of the day.

But what if even that didn't make things go fast enough?

People were blinking against the sudden rays that had just bathed them, wondering if that was Quentin's miracle. Then many seemed angry.

What was this? Flashing light over the crowd? Was that supposed to impress them?

"Lieutenant Commander," Kip said. The man was General Antonius's right-hand man, and he stood at Kip's elbow, ready to take orders, hand nervously on his dagger, no doubt because of the restive crowds. "I think we have about two minutes to rescue Quentin before this crowd turns. Lead your men quietly into place right now, then grab him before they do."

"I'll stay with you, my lord. I'll send a detachment."

Kip turned, irritated. The crowd was starting to buzz. Someone cried out angrily. "False prophet! Kill him!"

Kip snarled, "Lieutenant, was there something unclear about my orders?"

The lieutenant commander had drawn his dagger, but Kip barely noticed it. He'd fought alongside this man many times. All Kip could see now was that the whites of the lieutenant commander's eyes were suddenly flooded with bright crimson, as if the irises had cracked on every side and a dam had broken.

This man wasn't a red drafter. That red filling the whites of his eyes wasn't luxin; it was blood.

Kip and he seemed to have the realization at same moment. The commander had been poisoned. That meant—

"Light cannot be chained!" the commander screamed, lunging.

A heavy chain spun out of nowhere and slapped the attacker down to the ground as easily as a man smacks a mosquito on his arm. One instant the man was leaping at Kip with lethal intent, and the next all his momentum had been redirected into the ground at Kip's feet.

Kip cursed as the man convulsed once, fingers and limbs stiffening as if in instant rigor mortis. He looked up at Big Leo. "It somehow actually slipped my mind that the Order might try to assassinate *me* again."

Big Leo wrapped the heavy chain back around his chest. "Didn't slip ours."

In the few seconds Kip had been distracted by the assassin, pandemonium had broken out. In his own ranks, a dozen men and women had dropped dead, and thousands were reacting to the assassination attempt on Kip and to the dead nearby.

Things were far worse in the square. Nearly a hundred people were dying or lay dead already, hidden weapons spilling from hands that had been tucked away under coats and cloaks, men and women with blood hemorrhaging from their eyes, lurching into the innocent, convulsing to die with limbs crooked tight like spiders'.

Most of the traitors were congregated directly around the gate—and, as if this death were contagious, the people around them were surging back away from them.

Kip heard screams reverberate throughout the island as others were dying in droves in the far corners of Big Jasper, just as suddenly.

Quentin jumped to his feet as the people roared. "Be not afraid!" he shouted. "Orholam fights with us. Orholam fights with us!"

Only Kip knew the truth. My God, he thought, and he wasn't sure if it was a curse or a holy invocation of the divine mystery: Teia's just wiped out the Order of the Broken Eye.

656   All of it.

Today a great warrior like Big Leo might kill twenty of the enemy. Maybe, *maybe* forty. He would be accounted a hero for such valor.

If her estimates were right, in one day, of the empire's most dedicated, most cunning, most dangerous, and most implacable enemies, Teia had just killed *four hundred.*

And no one would ever know. Despite all Quentin's talk of Orholam's mercy, like a mighty man levering apart the pillars of a pagan temple, Teia had killed the enemies in their hundreds only at the cost of killing herself.

Kip climbed up on the wall.

The masses of people were cheering now with new hope, but Kip's eyes were drawn to the horizon, because among the cacophony of alarms and screams of horror and disgust and shouts of praise and relief, he'd heard the whistle of the lookouts, and he saw the horizon darken with the long shadows of the White King's approaching armada.

It seemed much, much bigger than Kip remembered.

Then his eyes were drawn to the waves—and, illuminated in the angled rays of dawn—what was swimming in undulating ranks beneath them.

Chapter 107

Gasping between his words, Gavin said, "You're...really...fucking strong."

"Annoying, huh?" Lucidonius said, hands on his knees.

They were standing within two steps of each other, not even pretending to be on guard against a sudden move from the other.

Gavin had tried sudden moves when they'd rested briefly before. His moves were no longer at all sudden.

Truthfully, they were hardly even moves now.

And it was getting worse. He'd noticed it immediately, how the ascended man's eyes mirrored the sun, slowly shrinking in apparent size as the sun rose, but growing in intensity.

Lucidonius obviously wasn't as tired as Gavin was, nor as bloodied. He had only a split lip while Gavin's nose had bled and clotted, bled and clotted. His cheek swollen from a collision with the marble, elbows throbbing, knees abraded.

Gavin had noticed that Lucidonius's body, too, seemed to grow stronger as the sun did. Somehow the godling's magic was tied to the rising of the light. On realizing that, Gavin had made desperate attempts to end the fight quickly.

Those times had been the times he'd come within a hair's breadth of losing. Now there was only endurance, not the thought of victory.

They'd reached the sword not once, but several times. It now lay not far from the Great Mirror itself. Gavin counted that as his only victory. If Lucidonius were smarter, he would attempt to throw the Blinding Knife off the tower. As long as it was so close to the Great Mirror, Gavin had a chance.

"Shouldn't you be...you know, on your way elsewhere?" Gavin asked.

"Where's that?"

"It's Sun Day. Don't you go visit the poor assholes giving their lives for you over at the Chromeria?"

"I wish I could go help them in their hour of need. I'm needed here."

"Hour of need?" Gavin asked. He wouldn't call the Freeing that.

"The Jaspers are under siege. The White King has floated seven bane and tens of thousands of soldiers and drafters for the attack. And there are traitors within the walls."

"And yet you're *here*. While they worship you."

"They don't worship me."

"You know what I mean. Whatever you want to call yourself, Lucidonius, it doesn't change that they're dying because they believe your words."

Lucidonius stood and dusted himself off. "You seem to have recovered your strength, if not your sense of irony. Ready?"

"How'd you do it?" Gavin said, not least because he most certainly was *not* ready.

"Are you hoping I'll get distracted now, or that I'll give you instructions?" Lucidonius asked.

"You give me too much credit. I'm just buying time to rest. But seriously, you ascended to *godhood*. How?" Not that Gavin wouldn't take any opening if the creature offered it, but he didn't expect that. Lucidonius was too sharp for simpler ploys to work.

"Oh, you're hoping I'll wear myself out a little bit, just by me using my breath to talk while you rest?"

Gavin didn't deny that had been his thought, but he pressed in. "You're not nearly as tired as I am. What's the harm? I'm the only one in the world who could possibly understand you. Even if only partially."

"And people think Andross got all the cleverness in the Guile family."

"People think wrong. My mother was more clever by half," Gavin shot back. He was defensive of Felia now, and he wasn't sure why. Maybe because he'd only recognized her particular genius after she was already gone. Maybe because she'd always championed him, even against his father.

"Brilliant people, Andross and Felia, each in their own way. Complementary in their gifts, but twins in their arrogance."

"Fuck you," Gavin said.

"People think Andross got all the temper, too," Lucidonius said wryly.

Gavin leapt for him, swinging a fist for the godling's throat. Most men will duck their head at an incoming blow, so a low shot could catch the chin or the nose, and no one fights well either unconscious or blinded by involuntary tears.

But he missed. Of course.

He was too slow, and so they began slugging it out again, absorbing blows but too exhausted to do much damage.

From the first moment Gavin had noticed Lucidonius's strength was tied to the sun, he'd thought of a terrible strategy. It was still a terrible strategy, but it was slowly becoming the only one left to him.

If Lucidonius got stronger as the sun rose, then would he not also weaken as it sank?

Gavin would have to last through the entire day to find out.

It was still two hours until noon. Of Sun Day. Gavin had chosen to fight a creature whose strength was tied to the intensity of the sunlight... on the longest fucking day of the year.

Chapter 108

The Blood Robes came down like wolves on the fold,
their forerunners bedecked in the white and the gold.
For the sons of Orholam they bore the scourge and the flail,
and to hell they would ride before they would fail.
—Gorgias Gordi

It had a certain beauty to a battlefield commander, seeing an attack so exquisitely timed, a surprise played at the perfect moment. Sea chariots pulled at great speed by sharks or dolphins, impossible to see at this distance, came roaring forward by the score. With battle standards whipping in the wind, showing the golden broken chains of the pagans and the colors of the new nine kingdoms, and scoops in the hulls designed purely to throw water into the sky to make great rooster tails as they pulled, everything about the sea chariots was designed to be a scintillating spectacle. Wights piloted each craft, and rank by rank they roared into cannonball range.

The boom of the cannons began immediately, but the craft were tiny, fast, and well spaced. The cannons would only catch a few of them.

But the forerunners made far too small a strike force to have any hope of success, which is why they had to be a distraction.

Kip looked beneath the waves, and there he saw them, already penetrating the bay, rounding in behind the seawall, simply swimming under the great chains meant to keep ships out. He'd heard the rumors of them in Blood Forest: even as Gavin had turned his gifts to making a craft that could move faster over water than any others ever had, some of Koios's wights had turned their own gifts to remaking their bodies so that they could move swiftly and silently under the water.

"Wights!" Kip shouted. "Beneath the waves! Coming in fast!"

They called themselves the Daughters of Caoránach, who would snatch off his boat anyone who dared go out on a moonlit night too close to the waters, and they wailed whenever they took blood. Their cries echoed in the dark over foggy lakes and rivers, chilling men and women to the bone. Others called them river demons or lake demons.

They would still just be men, wights encumbered on land by bodies designed for water.

"*Caoránaigh!*" someone shouted. "It's the caoránaigh!"

Kip cursed. "No! They're only men! River wights! Arms, to arms!" The last thing his people needed was the psychic shock of seeing their childhood nightmares come alive.

He hated this part of a battle, when you suddenly see the whole of the enemy's strategy and you need everyone to hear you at once. There were too many orders to give, too many people shouting for everyone to hear them.

"Protect the gates and cannons! Look to the bases of the towers and walls," someone shouted beside him. "Get me my signal banners, now! Aleph Company, in reserve! After we repulse the first attack, you're going to reinforce the secondary attack on the seawall!"

Corvan Danavis had just arrived, with his booming voice stomping through everyone else's shouts.

Kip looked down into the courtyard and saw a massive influx of the high general's soldiers, come to reinforce the gates.

"You!" Corvan shouted at Kip. "I'm here now. That means you can't be."

They'd discussed this. Corvan wouldn't allow for the possibility of one lucky shell taking out so much of the Chromeria's command and control. (Incidentally, it also put him in charge without having anyone else around to second-guess him—'slow him down,' as he put it.)

"I got this," Kip said. "Until the bane rise, I can—"

"This could be a—" The boom of cannon took out Corvan's last word, but he didn't even flinch. He repeated, "Trap. You get to Tower Twelve—"

"I know it's a trap. The river wights—"

"No, I mean all of it! They could be using the *entire attack* to raise the bane. You draft chi, so you can throw your will out farther than anyone. Get to Tower Twelve, and send me a signal if they're raising the bane. We have to know when to tell our drafters to stop drafting."

Shit. Corvan was right. And Kip was doing exactly what he shouldn't do—arguing with the man he'd put in control. "Yessir!" Kip said. "My apologies. Right away."

"Marksmen to the fore!" Corvan shouted back at his men. Signal flags were hoisted, orders were repeated in shouts to warriors back in the lines. "Aim especially for any of these river dogs who look like they're trying to throw up a flare or any sort of signal."

He was in his element, juggling the big picture and the small with ease.

The caoránaigh had burst from the waters and were scaling the towers. Others were attacking the gates directly, throwing great streams of fire and missiles in every hue, leaping over spiked fortifications with baffling ease. They were not at all encumbered by their amphibious form.

The rattle of musket fire deafened Kip. He wanted nothing more than to watch the battle unfold, to see the spectacle of gouts of water leaping into the sky as the cannons' explosive shells hit ships or waves, throwing death into the chariots' ranks. He wanted to marvel at the sinuous forms of these river demons, that made even his heart twist with fear.

He wanted to fight.

But he had orders.

"I know the fastest way to get us to that tower," Big Leo said, his copper chain held in his big hands over his shoulders. He wanted to fight, too.

"Son," Corvan said.

Kip glanced into the courtyard. Corvan's men had somehow already moved all the Order of the Broken Eye's dead aside to make room for their own ranks.

If those Order traitors had been alive to mount even a halfway-decent assault on even this one gate from within, the caoránaigh would have made it to the walls unnoticed, and breached the gates if they'd not been opened from within. Then they'd have gone for the cannons, but even if they hadn't gotten that far, the White King would have rushed in and immediately had a foothold on the island itself.

If the White King took the wall at any point, that would be the beginning of the end for the Chromeria.

And he would have had that already this morning, if not for Teia.

If not for Teia's sacrifice.

Kip wondered if she was still alive, cocooned as she was in a pitch-black room, her eyes bandaged, everyone hoping that maybe, maybe her eyes could be kept from dilating or contracting and that that might save her. That maybe her body would process the poison slowly, and she might live.

But she was out of the battle. She would help no one. Just like that, before Kip had even fired a musket, Teia's battle was done.

Beside Kip, Winsen's bowstring thrummed, but Winsen didn't even watch his arrow arc through the morning air. He was gazing enrapt at his bow the way another man might gaze at his lover disrobing for the first time.

Kip watched the arrow fly—which would usually be impossible, but here he could actually watch it fly, because this arrow streamed yellow-and-blue magic, burning and sizzling in the air. Two hundred fifty paces away, a caoránach jumped up to clear a spiked palisade, and was met—*in the air!*—with the glittering arrow. Its limbs jerked every direction as the arrow hit its chest with a small flash. It dropped flat on its back to the ground.

"Not bad," Winsen admitted.

He didn't mean the shot. He meant the Andross-gifted bow and arrows.

"Remind me never to piss you off," Ben-hadad said.

"Hey, Ben," Winsen said.

"Not right now, asshole," Ben said. He was rubbing his knees as if uncomfortable with the new fit and with wearing a brace on both legs.

Kip cursed. He'd gotten frozen with the spectacle and the anticipation and the battle juice pumping in his veins.

"Son!" Corvan said again, louder.

Kip looked.

Corvan said, "This battle's gonna have surprises for all of us—but that means them, too. You're doing fine. We're going to win here. Your friend probably bought us a few hours and a whole lot of confidence." He gave a wolfish smile. "Now, get the hell out of here. I have a feeling the bane attack is coming soon."

Chapter 109

The superviolet bane was not much to Aliviana's liking. It had been largely finished before she arrived at Azuria Bay, of course. The unskilled drafter she'd replaced as the Ferrilux had no imagination, nor sense of aesthetics, nor even the realization that the bane could be shaped as it grew.

So it had grown as it would, many-faceted crystals growing up many-faceted crystals. A floating island of large crystals, growing in spirals upon spirals, the greater echoing the smaller.

A cannon shell exploded fifty-two paces from her bane. Some small amount of shrapnel tore through her left port bow.

Aliviana Ferrilux fixed it, found a drafter who'd been injured, and dumped her out into the water.

Changing the bane, she'd decided, would be too massive an expenditure of her time and effort, so she was stuck with it. Her hatred of it was illogical. She could have made the bane invisible. Even with the vast amount of water the structure displaced, she could have crafted illusions such that the water here looked like the water elsewhere. Instead, this mess of crystals with every possible polarity made the floating island actually somewhat visible, even if one missed the giant bowl of missing water in the waves.

She hated a lot about things that she couldn't quite figure out these days.

For the two hours before dawn, she'd been picking the superviolet crystals off her face and hands, elbows, knees, neck, groin. You'd think this would be a simple thing: superviolet luxin was so fragile that a vigorous shake ought to do it.

But she'd learned in the last year that what the Chromeria's drafters did with superviolet exploited only a fraction of its potential. With what Aliviana now did? The body had to learn how to deal with so much magic, and it simply didn't handle all of it well. Her mortal body failed her immortal will. She would figure out fixes later. Work-arounds. Eternity would be a long time.

For now these crystals grew on her skin like barnacles on the hull of a boat, slowing her down. If she tore them off, they too often tore her delicate human skin—which seemed to be thinning all the time. This was especially bad on her face. The tears left her with scars to which the crystals accreted even more quickly. It was slowly immobilizing her face from showing even the few emotions she now betrayed. But she didn't want to lose function, not in anything, not because of magic she didn't control. That reeked of failure.

Another cannon shell exploded, closer. She fixed the damage with an irritated thought. Soon it would be time to rise.

All this power, yet I'm losing control over my own body.

Perhaps this was what it was like for humans to grow old? She would have to think on that.

Beliol had offered to help her with this, of course, groveling as he did, the little spirit. She rejected him this time, as she usually did. And as usual when rejected, Beliol quickly went on his way. He treated his time on this world as if it were precious. Any chance he might have of worming his way further into Liv's thoughts, he took, but when rejected, he acted as if he had other places to be.

He grew more powerful the more Aliviana depended on him. She'd figured that out almost immediately, though she hadn't let on, she hoped. Theirs would be a game played over centuries, she thought. He was, likely, malevolent. But he had limitations, too. She would be careful not to put herself under his power. The groveling might stop at the most inconvenient time.

She saw the signal from her partner, her god of gods, Koios. She couldn't help but roll her eyes as she thought of him and his overly intricate battle plans.

Battles. It was so hard to concentrate on them.

Just tell me who wins and who's left alive at the end, please. I have things I need to do once we get to that point.

When everyone lets down their guard in victory, that's when things get really interesting. Aliviana was looking forward to that.

Oh, right. The signal.

The Chromeria was funny like this: for all that their powers came from sunlight, for all that they worshipped a god they believed to exist literally above them, the cretins so rarely looked *up*.

Aliviana gathered her powers and lifted the bane up, out of the waves and into the sky.

Chapter 110

"Put on the wraparound blue spectacles," Kip told the messenger. "Ride as fast as you can. Tell High General Danavis the orange bane rises. Go now!"

Blue was the best color to use to sharpen the mind against orange. He didn't know how well it would work, though. The Chromeria's damnable fear of teaching hex-casting left them ignorant of how best to defend against it. After all, 'Don't look at the hex' isn't very useful advice during a battle, when the hex might be painted on your enemies' very shields and helms. How are you supposed to fight without looking at your enemy?

For more than an hour now, Kip had been carefully scanning the horizon with chi, as instructed. He'd toyed with melting open the silvery globe of gallium he wore on his neck to access the chi bane, but he had no idea what he'd *do* with it. He'd drafted chi only a handful of times in his entire life, and none of them had been pleasant. He hadn't jumped on any opportunity since then to practice with it.

It was just another mistake he'd made. He should've practiced to find out what he could do with chi instead of vaguely thinking that it could be used for signaling, and that it was better in his own hands than in someone else's. No, he should have brought the Keeper with him. *She* should be doing this.

But bringing the Keeper with him would have been a death sentence for her and her sect, and maybe for Kip, too. Consorting with heretics? Bringing a bane to the Jaspers, at the very time the White King was? With her masks and gaudy armor and tumors, the Keeper wasn't exactly concealable, either.

"Breaker, sir? Should we go?" Big Leo asked.

"Not yet," Kip said. "I've got my orders." He wasn't supposed to come back until he saw a signal, Andross had said.

What signal?

'You'll know it when you see it,' Andross had said.

Which drove Kip crazy.

Quit that. Too much thinking. And the wrong kind.

Kip had thought he understood the old soldier's maxim that the waiting is the worst part of war. He'd waited before. He'd waited to spring traps. He'd waited to order men to fire. He'd waited for the rush of the battle's beginning.

But once it began, he'd always been *right there*, in the thick of it. Now the battle was about to begin—but not for him.

He was going to watch. Once the bane rose, he'd make his way up to the top of the Prism's Tower to do what he could from up there. Which might not be much of anything at all.

He might be stuck watching all day, depending on what the Wight King did. Watching, while others died.

With the bane still submerged, and with the great number of the Blood Robes' ships and sea chariots, all of them in constant motion, the bane were initially hard to find, but Kip had finally discerned their locations with chi and had sent word to Corvan. The high general had rearranged his defenses appropriately—and without any help asked or needed from Kip on where to put them.

At regular intervals, Kip had shielded his eyes and gazed in chi toward each arc encircling the island, then in paryl, then he put on each of the colored spectacles he carried at his hip in turn, hoping to see something. He kept it up now so that he didn't get caught unawares by the others rising. It was easy to get war-blind and focus all your attention on only the one threat in front of you.

But he'd spent his time debating with himself about what he should do: Use the chi bane? Don't use it? View Andross's card? Don't View it?

That was what he wanted: a magical salvation, a solution from out of nowhere to solve all his problems for him, because he was so goddam special.

A lifetime ago—and only three years ago—Gaspar Elos had asked him, just before Koios White Oak (and Zymun, that asshole) had burned down Rekton, 'Do you know why you think you're special?' And had laughed as Kip's young heart had welled with hope that he was the prophesied one, the one chosen to do great things—'Because you're an arrogant little shit.'

Kip shook his head. Wrong thoughts. Not the time.

Corvan's books had taught him years ago that a commander should use his quiet hours to obsess over two questions only: what does the enemy know, and what are the enemy's problems? If you knew those two things, you might guess what he would do. If you knew the enemy himself, you would know.

He felt it more than saw it. A trembling under the waves. Movement.

Kip squinted against the reflection of the rising sun in its many-colored glory.

"Why has the orange waited so long?" Tisis asked. "Worse leadership? Fewer drafters?" Her spies had said that the orange 'god' was considered distinctly inferior to the others, and the orange corps of drafters and wights smaller and poorly trained compared to the others. This last, at least, was one benefit of the Chromeria's tight strictures on orange—it had made orange drafters less useful. Thus, fewer lords and satraps went to the expense of sponsoring orange drafters, which meant fewer were around to defect to the Wight King.

"This is the first time they've done this," Kip said. "With the bane all separated from each other, not able to share drafters and crews, it's a lot harder than when they were on the open sea."

Kip thought about their problems. The sheer complexity of separating your navy—not even just your army!—with many of them out of sight behind the mass of Big Jasper, trying to coordinate any attack, with no way to fix the little problems, meant that little problems could get big. Fearful subordinates waiting to make decisions, commanders unreachable who would have been easily found if they'd been on land—an amphibious mundane and magical assault by an inexperienced navy?

But Koios's main problem was that he wanted to attack *today*, and he was so certain that the bane would make all the difference that he didn't care about the losses he would incur.

"With as heavy as orange is, it may be harder to raise," Kip said. "And if they want orange to join them in their first assault, they have to wait until it's ready. And, you know, stuff goes wrong. I think we can take a glimmer of hope at seeing that though the Blood Robes are monstrous, they aren't diabolically perfect. If they were..."

"If they were...?" Tisis asked.

If they were, they'd have hit us right after dawn with a first attack on the bay as the Order attacked. They'd have hit us with a fear hex.

It was still a good plan, but now the main problem for the Blood Robes was all the Chromeria's gun emplacements, especially on the towers, which due to their height could lob shells and cannonballs farther than any of the Blood Robes' ships could return them.

He cursed. "Orange isn't going to join the attack; it's going to lead it. A fear hex. Something like that. They're gonna try to sneak it up on us somehow." He squinted against the blinding orange light of the sun rising in the east.

"The rising sun," he said. "They're using…"

And then it was nearly upon them.

Thin, mysterious fingerling clouds had been streaking along the tops of the waves, hidden by the dazzling sun and to-and-fro of the sea chariots throwing water high into the air, burning torches that hissed smoke out in a dozen colors to confuse the eye.

A great flock of birds rose suddenly from the Blood Robes' every ship, black against the rising sun. Another distraction, mostly.

"Blue spectacles, now!" Kip shouted. "Those'll be razor wings." He threw a signal flare into the sky to tell the gun crews on every tower to ready the nets they'd prepared to string up on poles above them to catch the deadly bombardment coming.

But Kip's eyes were again down: those misty fingers hit East Bay's seawall, and sidled over it, slipping past the ships sheltering in the bay.

Kip turned his back to address his people. He didn't want to see whatever hex was coming. "Remember," he called out to them, "you cannot trust what you feel; trust what you know to be real. The bane will lie to you, so hold to what you know is true. Your brothers and sisters will fight and they'll die for you. Be not afraid. Be not afraid! Though hell itself march against us, be not afraid in what you do!"

What the hell? Speaking in rhyme?

Shit! Liv. Somewhere, the superviolet bane was out there, too!

Kip turned and roared, all turtle-bear.

The wave hit the city's walls at every tower hard enough to make them shake, gushing water, dropping all the moisture it had picked up from the sea in a sudden rain. But the physical force of the attack was purely ancillary—the attack itself was the wave of fear blasted over Kip with the force of a tsunami, leaving him breathless and panicked, frozen.

His heart was lodged in his throat. They were doomed. This was like nothing they'd prepared for.

They were all going to die. It was all his fault. He didn't know the first thing about anything. He was just a child, a child in the face of gods. Literal gods.

Everything he'd mocked, everything he'd sneered at was suddenly here and more real than he could have imagined.

"Hey," a distant voice said.

668

Kip could hear the war dogs whining.

He was going to get them all killed. Everyone. It was too late already. They were already dead. Kip's heart was seizing in his chest with grief and dread as he was enveloped in the soft orangey cloud.

He was losing everyone he loved, and there was nothing he could do about it.

He heard the clatter of a sword falling from someone's hand.

"Hey! The hell is wrong is with you all?" Winsen said.

Suddenly a hand was rubbing Kip's face, scrubbing it as if to brush away water—or luxin. Winsen's face appeared in Kip's sight.

Winsen, the broken man who'd never really understood danger or avoiding it. Winsen, the literally fearless, was standing in front of Kip looking puzzled. He had a hand drawn back, preparing to slap Kip.

"I'm good," Kip said, coming back to himself. "Get the rest of us. Cwn y Wawr!"

He turned to them, some on the tower, more below. The handlers were almost as bad off as everyone else on the towers and walls, catatonic. Some had wet themselves. Their war dog partners were whining, alarmed, not understanding. Some of the dogs licked their humans, and a few of those had been roused by the fearless love of their canine friends.

"Eyes!" Kip shouted to them. "Their eyes!"

The dogs, preternaturally intelligent, understood immediately. Through growling or tugging or even bracing on their partners' shoulders and licking their faces, the dogs dragged their masters' attention to themselves and cleared away the hex. Most people snapped out of the hex immediately, but some seemed broken by the terrors they'd just suffered.

"Here they come. Everyone!" Kip shouted. "You know what to do!"

The White King's armada was rapidly resolving from a black mass of ships into individual ranks as the sun rose and as they sailed closer.

But all the Chromeria's ships sheltered by the seawall sat as if dead, crews paralyzed.

The gun emplacements were the target, not anyone inland. The first attack was going to come not from the bane but from the armada. The armada was going to try to land, and if the Chromeria's cannons didn't do something soon, they would land unopposed.

That couldn't happen.

Kip shouted, "Winsen, you get to High General Danavis! Wake him if he needs it, tell him how we are! Cruxer, go—shit!" Cruxer was dead. "Big Leo, you run out to the ships with the Cwn y Wawr. Wake them up, get them fighting. We need those cannons now. Meet me above East Bay. Messengers, you wake all the rest of the gun towers—no one goes alone, though. Terrified people might get violent. You, you, and you, take your regiments and rally the rest of the island. Let them know we just got hit with magic, and it's already dissipating. It's not real. We can stand! Gun crews, start firing rounds—I know they're out of range, just do it! It might wake some people. We got this! Go!"

Chapter 111

When Karris burst into the Spectrum's council chamber, none of the damned Colors was there except Klytos Blue, slumped in a chair at the great windows, watching the battle beginning to unfold.

"You stupid sack of shit!" she said. "What have you done!"

In a low voice, nearly catatonic, he said, "We were all gathered already, dividing last-minute responsibilities for the day and the battle, trying to decide what to do to calm the pilgrims. Where to have them take shelter—"

"We agreed not twelve hours ago to cancel this parade—and now I hear Zymun pulled drafters off the wall and soldiers from their posts in order to have it anyway. And with the Spectrum's blessing! What the hell were you thinking?"

Klytos wouldn't meet her eyes, still watching the dawn and the approaching armada and the eerily silent cannons below. Woodenly, he said, "He came to us directly from the Freeing. He hadn't washed. He—he was covered in their blood. There was a manic gleam in his eyes. He called it his due. He's not wrong."

"You know he was never to be declared Prism. Andross is going to be furious—"

"It was his second Sun Day as Prism-elect! And—and if Kip is right and the tower array can be used as a weapon, only a Prism can keep using it for any length of time! How long can anyone else live drafting that much power?" Klytos asked. The little weasel.

Karris grabbed his shoulder and hauled him around, forcing him to face her. "But the Spectrum doesn't make a Prism just by saying a few words!"

A little smile suddenly played over Klytos Blue's lips, though the mad, hopeless gleam never left his eyes. "Oh, I know that," he said. "Andross managed to root out most of the Spectrum who know how Prisms are made, but some of us figured it out. We can't *make* a Prism anymore, which means we're all going to die in this battle. But you Guiles always survive the calamities they bring on the rest of us. Not this time."

"Why declare him Prism?" Karris demanded.

His smile dripped poison. "Without being made a Prism by the Blinding Knife, anyone who gets up on that array is gonna die. Kip already promised to, so there's one dead Guile. But why take only one when we can get two?"

Karris slapped him.

He crumpled against the wall and cowered.

She rubbed her temples, thinking what to do next.

Wild-eyed, Klytos was looking around at the Blackguards. "You all saw that! I'm the Blue. She's *assaulted* me! Take her into custody immediately!"

From where he stood at Karris's left hand, Gill Greyling drawled, "Apologies, High Lord, I must've been distracted. I saw nothing." He looked around at the seven other Blackguards in the room. "Anyone?"

Around the room, lips pursed in chagrin. Heads shook.

"I heard something," one of the new kids volunteered. "Sounded like a shit plopping on the floor."

Twenty-year-olds, Karris thought.

Klytos snarled from where he was on the floor, but he was too much of a coward to physically attack a Blackguard. "You should be thanking me! You know what Zymun is!"

Karris shook her head. She knew what she had to do now. She was gonna have to go find Zymun and try to make him do what had to be done. There was no way it was going to end well. She had no authority over him now, and nothing to bribe him with. "Klytos, you fool, you've given Zymun almost unlimited power. What's he ever done to make you believe he'll use it for good?"

Chapter 112

The sounds of cannons roaring to life from various towers around the great walls announced the progress of the Cwn y Wawr to Kip's ears. Those gun crews began their bombardment immediately, their elevation giving them significantly greater range than the armada.

The first shots splashed harmlessly wide or short, but soon the gun crews fell back into their training. They'd zeroed their shots on buoys at set distances, and now, even though the Blood Robes had sunk those, the gun crews' captains had them memorized.

Odd, Kip thought, how when you were far enough away, the sights of distant timbers exploding and fires billowing from a ship were satisfying. But when up close, one felt only awe at the destructive power of humanity, and horror at the bloody carnage and shrieks of the limbless dying that attended every successful shell, the innocent crews being dragged to their watery rest.

The men pulling those oars were surely prisoners of war. Allies. Friends. Men whose names had once been posted on Big Jasper's lists as lost.

Yet Kip couldn't hate the gun crews when they shouted with joy after a successful shot. War is the wily orator who gets us cheering horrors.

It looked like the Chromeria's forces were being roused from their torpor, but before Kip could descend to the lines to make sure of it, Einin said, "My lord, that's far enough. Commander Leonidas ordered me to keep you back from the lines."

Kip glared at her. "Big Leo?" he asked instead of complaining. He should have known the new commander wouldn't let him put himself in danger.

"Yessir. Uh, he hasn't made it clear to us nunks what we're allowed to call him."

Regardless of what Andross had commanded, Kip should probably go up to the mirrors now, but what if the army messed up again? What if they needed him?

The razor wings reached the towers. Netting hung above every gun crew, and archers and musketeers armed with blunderbusses were posted with them.

Some of the will-cast birds were shot out of the sky. Others made it to the nets, tangling in them before exploding or bursting into flame.

A musketeer drawing a bead skyward on an incoming razor wing stepped backward into a cannon's line of fire just as the gun crew, looking out to their own distant target, touched the linstock to the breech. Kip cried out, but they were too far away, there was too much noise.

The woman simply disappeared in the black-powder cloud that bellowed from the cannon's muzzle. Kip caught a glimpse of her legs flying, launched off the wall.

The razor wing splashed fiery death amid the gun crew a moment later.

"I would love it if we went back to the Prism's Tower now, my lord," Einin said nervously.

He shot out chi at all the bane again. He couldn't see all of them from here. That was a problem, though he thought he'd have felt if any of the others were rising from the depths. Where was Liv?

Out beyond the bay, some of the larger ships of the armada had turned broadside and stopped, apparently within their range now. He extended a hand and someone gave him a long-lens.

The ships were dropping anchors. Huh. Ah, to give themselves more stable firing platforms. The gun crews on the open decks, many of them bare-chested, were all very dark-skinned.

Ilytians. Dammit. Best gunners in the world, with the best guns. That meant the pirate kings were indeed working for the Wight King. Karris said she'd tried to bribe them away, but apparently after Gavin and Kip had sunk Pash Vecchio's great ship, the *Gargantua*, he'd been beyond the reach of promises—and she hadn't been willing to send him boatloads of coin merely in the hope that a pirate would act in good faith.

Kip watched the Ilytians fire their first rounds, the flash of light and the puff of rolling black smoke visible long before the sound could be heard.

He wanted to give an order to someone to focus on those ships, but it was unnecessary.

As those ships set up their bombardment, the rest of the fleet charged the East Bay.

Kip wondered where Corvan was.

Maybe he was content to lead from some safer, clearer vantage. Maybe there was an emergency somewhere else Kip didn't even know about.

The Ilytian gun crews had a lucky early hit. Or Kip hoped it was luck, as a tower top exploded a hundred paces away.

The Chromeria's army—here mostly Kip's people, selected because they were battle-hardened—immediately jumped to the labor of trying to salvage guns from the emplacement that had been blown to pieces, working in the gore and slime of a crew exploded by shell. The teams were all arranged for this, ready to determine what large guns could be salvaged, ready to wheel in and set up smaller cannons or use teams of oxen to lift cannons that had merely fallen when shell demolished tower foundations and the like.

Backup gun crews waited a safe distance from the front lines, jittery, wanting a chance to fight, but knowing that when their chance came, it would be because that spot they were to step into was a target whose range and position had already been found.

This was to be a marathon with no end until victory or nightfall or death.

Falling behind meant that the armada would make landfall, and the Blood Robes making landfall would be the beginning of the end.

But now, despite all the defenders' work, it looked like it was about to begin anyway.

The withering fire had grown sporadic as supply lines were stretched, powder stores exhausted. Ships that should have been easy pickings instead sailed all the way to the mouth of the bay.

The enormous chains barring the armada's entry to East Bay were attacked first. As the armada approached, caoránaigh swarmed out of the water where they'd been swimming unseen, cast luxin ladders up the great links, and climbed up like monkeys.

Kip had thought they'd be clumsy out of the water. *Great.*

A few of Kip's best marksmen—joined in this by many of the Blackguards' Archers—picked off dozens, but there were always more of them, and with their swimming abilities, even the charges dropping off into the sea was little more than a setback. Eventually, the wights packed charges against the links of the chain, swinging and swaying dangerously, and set fuses.

A few wights jumped back into the water too late and were killed by the explosions, but the great chain fell, having slowed the Blood Robes for only minutes.

Now there were only big guns to demolish the ships.

Kip sent a message that they should deploy sharpshooters and Archers on the other side of Big Jasper in case the wights did the same there, and then he gathered his army.

The orders and reports didn't stop simply because the battle had been joined in earnest.

Through the fires and flames, the armada limped into the bay, the first ships smoking, half their oars broken, decks awash with blood. But they landed, and the galleons and coccas behind them pushed hard forward, even as wights and drafters disembarked to throw luxin planks down on the water itself, connecting ship to ship in one large floating mass so men could swarm from one to the other without slowing to use boarding nets.

A messenger said, "Sir, that problem with the sect of luxiats calling for drafters not to touch hellstone to drain their internal luxin has been put down."

"Oh?" Kip asked, not really paying attention.

Kip could only watch the battle plan unfold below him. The people, military and civilian volunteers both, had been briefed on exactly what to do. No orders from the rear were even going to make it to them now.

Like all battle plans, it didn't go as planned.

"Turns out High Luxiat Amazzal went down there himself, with a cane. He was beating men left and right as he reprimanded them. Quite impressive, I'm told."

"Good, good," Kip said.

Brave fools up and down the length of the seawall stayed at their gun emplacements rather than retreating, as if to erase their early paralysis by staying and firing until the bitter end.

There was no way to save them. Once the armada touched the seawall itself, wights and drafters tore through the stakes and spikes and fire traps and other passive defenses and mounted the top of the wall with frightening speed.

They poured down the length of the seawall like oil wicking up a lantern, dyeing it with their own colors and the red of blood as they massacred the gun crews one after another. One crew set off an explosion with the last of the black powder.

The smoke lasted longer than the obstacles did. The drafters lay great planks of luxin down on the flames and debris, and their men charged right over it.

Kip saw combined forces of drafters and nondrafting soldiers used in ways that he swore the White King must have learned from him.

But even as the Blood Robes were wicking toward the killing field waiting for them at that end of the docks, the rest of the armada had pushed deep into the bay itself. Some of the sailors made the same kind of last stand, but mostly their cannons had been arrayed in such a way that they didn't have the angle to shoot in toward the city, and the men retreated as they were supposed to, if not quite in the good order one might hope. Some were trampled by their panicked fellows, or torn off the plentiful ladders at the walls so that some vicious ally could reach the top a heartbeat earlier.

They weren't Kip's men, and he hadn't been here long enough

to even start instilling discipline in these civilians, but it was still a helluva thing, watching men be killed by their friends.

And there was nothing to be done about it.

The big guns on the walls kept pounding the armada, which was all rafted together now. Ships that should have sunk were instead buoyed up by their fellows. It was probably a waste of powder, although it did help bait the trap.

As more of the armada pressed against land and the docks and the tethered ships that had been the Chromeria's artillery, more and more men charged out, making a beachhead.

What struck Kip was that it was almost all men. Not drafters. Not wights.

The pagans had achieved an almost perfect inversion of the Chromeria's values: in battle the Chromeria would save its people by spending those who had gone wight and the drafters closest to breaking the halo first, because those were closest to death or insanity. The Blood Robes were saving their wights and drafters by spending their people, because their people were farthest from magic and godhood.

All the White King's promises of freedom and of a new order, a utopia where all would be made right, were belied.

For the Chromeria, the privileges of power were paired with prices. Drafters were expected to stand in the *first* line of defense, as the promachos did. Human nature being what it is, they didn't always do so, but that was the deal, the expectation. By contrast, the nine kings would happily rule a wasteland, if they could rule.

Orholam damn them.

How many of these invaders about to die just wanted a better life, or hadn't dared to stand against the White King when his armies had marched through their lands and had pressed them into his armies? They weren't quite innocent, but they were men, not monsters. They deserved a second chance, and Kip couldn't afford to offer them one. Not right now.

"Still not time to go?" Ben-hadad asked. He'd come back, as had others of the Mighty.

Kip looked around again, though he still didn't know what he was looking *for*. "No."

They'd pushed in far enough. Thousands of men were clambering over the moored ships and onto the docks, between the boathouses and warehouses.

"Raise the red," Kip commanded.

The men had been waiting for it. They raised a red flag, and immediately, the cannons atop the walls began firing incendiary shot at the

Chromeria's abandoned ships and docks still moored within the bay. Pyrejelly had been drafted into barrels and hidden away yesterday. The last order for all the sailors abandoning their ships was to open those barrels and splatter it about.

The Blood Robes had surely suspected fire, but they expected nothing as ferocious as the holocaust that swept in upon them.

The men and women of Big Jasper stood agape, watching a spectacle such as they would never see again if they lived a hundred years. The intensity of the flames was matched only by the intensity of the screams as every dock, every ship, and the whole length of the seawall went up in sudden flames. In a few places, the incendiary luxin hadn't been set or had failed, but it didn't matter. The flames jumped gaps and burned everything.

"Fire crews ready?" Kip asked.

"Yes, sir. Watching the wind carefully and spread out appropriately. Looks like it's in our favor."

One of the worst things about commanding was that sometimes you see what's going to happen some minutes hence, and you know how to stop it, and there's time to stop it, but your people won't listen to you.

Such was the commander of the armada's plight.

Kip could see him waving his arms and screaming. The drafters had made his situation much worse by connecting the ships. With no incendiaries aboard, the floating-island armada caught fire far more slowly than the docks had, but they were lashed together. They couldn't push apart from one another to make gaps too large for the fire to pass. The ones at the back were having great difficulty breaking free to retreat.

After a few minutes, though, he rallied enough drafters and officers, and cut deep, setting a fire line where he gave up fully a quarter of his fleet. At this line, they would break away from the island and abandon all those on the side nearer to Big Jasper.

It was what Kip had been waiting for.

"Catapults, go," Kip said. The crews knew where to aim.

Catapults. Who used catapults in the age of gunpowder? It was one of Corvan's discoveries when he did a personal inventory of the Jaspers' defenses. They'd been kept for decades beyond their obsolescence by Carver Black, who couldn't bear to sell them off for a pittance for lumber, yet hadn't been able to replace them all on the meager budget he had to buy cannon.

The catapults now hurled barrels of red luxin and sub-red charges skyward and onto the armada—behind the lines where all the drafters and officers were working. They exploded in the air, or even in the water, flinging pyrejelly everywhere on the ships and even floating on the waves.

Suddenly, those people, the only ones on the armada under control and not panicking, had fire before them and fire behind. They were cut off.

Kip and Corvan had expected to get a quarter to a third of all the attackers—though only half of the armada had attacked this side of Big Jasper. They'd expected a retreat, and then after the fires died down, a second attack later in the day. They'd arranged killing grounds and lines of retreat, choke points and ambushes.

They weren't going to be using any of those. Not on this side of the island. With the fires still roaring and men still screaming their despair and pain, Kip sent half his army to the other side of the island, and a messenger to High General Danavis asking for orders.

Most of the observers didn't realize it yet, but there would be no fighting on this side of Big Jasper for at least a few hours. They'd already won the first round here. This part of the armada was dead. The poor bastards just had to decide if they went by fire or water.

The rest of the armada wasn't going to attack here again, not until the fires had gone out, not until they could reorganize.

It was a great victory.

But Kip's heart was as light as a millstone.

"What's he *doing*?" Ben-hadad asked. He meant Koios.

Ben understood the heart of the problem. Karris had told them that Koios wanted to burn the whole world down and start over, that he didn't care how big his losses were, but Kip hadn't known if he should believe that—calling your enemy's every failure somehow part of a brilliant larger plan was more likely to be paranoia than anything; after all, Koios's first attack could well have succeeded.

But maybe paranoia was the right response. Why hadn't Koios raised all the bane?

"If he wins with his first assault, he seems invincible in the field," Kip said. "But if he loses, and then ultimately wins when he attacks with the bane, he shows his future subjects that nothing can stand against his magic."

Ben-hadad wrinkled his nose. "Or he just loused up the incredibly difficult task of a combined amphibious and magical assault because he met a strong defense."

Kip shrugged, admitting that was possible, too. All he knew was that his fight wasn't over; his fight had barely begun. Everything all the Chromeria's people had accomplished here could be wiped out in a moment if Kip failed.

Behind Kip, someone cleared his throat.

"High Lord, I come from Promachos Andross Guile," a young man reported. "He requires your presence at the Chromeria. You are to join him at the back dock. He said it has to do with the Lightbringer."

"Now?" Kip said. "The plan was that I go to the mirrors next."

"There have also been...developments with the Prism-elect."

Kip swore under his breath. Was Andross actually trying to make good on his bet? Or was it a trap?

It was surely past time for Kip to take over the mirrors. But the promachos was the ultimate authority in a war. If Kip was going to start disobeying him now, he'd have to do it for some better reason than simple gut instinct.

"Sir, my apologies," a young woman interrupted, coming in. "A message from High General Danavis. He says to send half your men to West Bay."

"Already done," Kip said.

"Also, he says under absolutely no circumstances should you go to the Chromeria. There have been developments with the Prism-elect."

"What the hell?" Kip asked.

"Danavis said no more, sir," the woman said, but her face was pained.

"But you know more than that. Tell me," Kip demanded.

"The Prism-elect had himself declared Prism, and we've heard there was some kind of scuffle or, um, skirmish? between Lightguards loyal to Zymun and Blackguards loyal to the White."

Kip surveyed his Mighty: goofy Ferkudi, now grim; Winsen, languorous; Ben-hadad, intense; Big Leo, sinisterly smirking. They would follow him to hell and back. Only Kip couldn't promise the 'back' part, not today.

"Well, obviously, High General Danavis has the right of it," Kip said. "It's madness to go to the Chromeria and charge into some situation we know so little about."

He looked around at his men.

"So we're going?" Big Leo asked.

Ferkudi said, "The horses are already saddled."

Chapter 113

"I see what you're doing," Gavin growled.

They held each other, arms locked, heads against each other's necks, bodies crouching low—though in their exhaustion, not so low as proper wrestling form dictated. Lucidonius grunted, tried to butt his head against Gavin's cheekbone, but with their closeness, he couldn't get any force into it.

"You think I don't know?" Gavin demanded.

Lucidonius only drove him in a circle with little steps.

The sun had swollen fat with the day's many injuries. It limped now along the last of its lonely path home, hemorrhaging gouts of light, spattering streaky cirrus clouds with arterial glory, seeking some safety, but its horizon-home held only its warm, waiting deathbed.

Lucidonius said nothing. His eyes were dimming with the dimming of the sun, and though they still burned, Gavin's gamble was paying off: Lucidonius was weakening.

He fought with merely a man's strength now, while Gavin swelled stronger. From beneath the smooth skin of his practiced social proprieties, the day's battle had made his long-sunken veins of rage jut forth, declaiming his righteous fury at the god who lied.

"The mirror!" Gavin snarled. They were within a few steps of it. Lucidonius had ever angled them back toward it, over the course of the year's longest day. "I know what it is."

He was a black drafter. Born that way. Born special. To have that ability wasn't a curse. Nor a blessing, either, for to call it a blessing assumed there is one who gives the blessing. This simply *was*, an accident of birth or propitious parentage or both. It was simply another way Gavin was different, better than others, yes, he'd not be afraid to say it now. *Better*, but also isolated from them thereby. He was also unhappier than those blind, those deceived.

His way was harder. He could see what others couldn't—that wasn't fair. But now, through the black gem—which was nothing less than a physical manifestation of all that made Gavin *Gavin*—he saw that the mirror itself was an elaborate trap for him. The godling had come from the mirror. It was a portal to his home. It was where he had power.

Gavin said, "It's not just mockery, is it? It's much—"

Lucidonius must have thought Gavin would push into his home.

Gavin would invade, to try to find what had given Lucidonius the power of a god and take it. But the god would have all his defenses in there.

The mirror would be where Gavin could be trapped, slain.

Gavin took some breaths as Lucidonius shifted his grip on a sweaty shoulder, trying to get some advantage. "It's even more insidious than that, isn't it?"

"You see punishment where there is mercy," Lucidonius said, as if Gavin were a tremendous disappointment.

"Mercy? You've arranged this! It's all perfectly designed for me. Even you. Your appearance itself! I'm the *Prism*! You think I don't know what an elaborate deception looks like?!"

"On the contrary." Lucidonius breathed raggedly into his ear. "You are the very son of deception. And it's time for that to end."

And then he collapsed.

Gavin staggered into him, and then over him, tripping and tumbling over the man. But Lucidonius grabbed his leg as Gavin fell, and wrenched on it, twisting to slam him into the ground.

There was a strain and shooting pain as Gavin's hip almost popped out of its socket, but Lucidonius's hands slipped. Gavin's back hit the ground, and Lucidonius was pulled off balance. His grip had now slid down to Gavin's foot. But he didn't let go. He was pulled down, losing his balance, aiming a knee—

Gavin caught him with both feet.

Then he launched the man off him toward the mirror, kicking both legs as hard as he could.

Lucidonius slammed into the Great Mirror, and the entire surface wobbled and deformed. His whole body seemed to sink into it a little.

Instead of leaping for the sword, Gavin leapt forward, trying to press his advantage. He punched Lucidonius in the stomach, but the muscles there were taut, tensed for the impact. Gavin's left-handed uppercut missed its huge swing at Lucidonius's chin, and he stumbled forward.

To avoid even touching the mirror, Gavin slammed his forearm into Lucidonius's chest in order to regain his balance. But as the mirror rippled once from the force of Lucidonius's back smacking into it again, rather than trying to break free, the man hugged Gavin's forearm to his chest.

He rolled sideways, trying to throw Gavin into the mirror.

Gavin threw up his right hand to stop himself—

Once, on a bitterly cold morning in the mountains of Paria when he was first Prism, Gavin had followed the blue wight he was hunting out onto a frozen pond. Ever since a blue had murdered his brother

Sevastian, he'd always held a special hatred for them. It had made him foolish that day. The pond was a trap. The wight's magic had strengthened the ice—for himself. Gavin would never forget the feeling of the ice holding his hesitant first steps easily, but then flexing under his weight, and suddenly buckling.

His magic had saved him that day.

He had none now. Slapping his hand against the mirror felt exactly the same as the ice had felt that day. Where for Lucidonius the mirror seemed gelatinous, forgiving, for Gavin it was frozen, momentarily stable. His hand stopped, held his weight from an icy plunge as his palm tingled, bits of lightning shooting up his forearm, enervating it.

The mirror cracked under his hand like the sound of a musket shot. Gavin snatched his hand away. The mirror was a death trap. Lucidonius wanted to obliterate him.

The moment itched a memory in him, of a dream where he'd stood on the top of a tower, as a giant approached—but there was no time!

I need more time! he'd shouted in his dream.

He turned now and saw Lucidonius, picking up the sword.

Gavin's heart dropped. He'd been distracted mere seconds, but it had been seconds too long.

But then he saw something worse than seeing his foe armed: Lucidonius turned. His eyes were coals now, still-hot mirrors of the descending sun, but no longer so blindingly bright that they obscured what his face looked like.

"Fuck you!" Gavin roared at the sight of that face. "You want me to think I'm losing my mind!"

"Again," the man said quietly.

"Yes, again! You drove me to madness once, Orholam. Your lies. You cost me everything! And now, *now* you come back?!" Somehow, Gavin slipped from addressing the godling as Lucidonius to Orholam once more.

It wasn't a perfect facsimile, but the god wore a face that could have been Gavin's own.

"I'm not your shadow, Dazen," the god said. "You're mine. You are a dim reflection of what you could have been."

"Lies. From you, *Orholam*. I took such joy in you when I was a child. When I was a boy, I thought I was going to be a luxiat, do you know that? The incense. The ceremony. The hymns. I loved it all. Do you remember? Or did you even notice me then? And then, after I became Prism, when I celebrated the highest and holiest days, they were bitter gall to me. Because I *knew*! And now you stand, wearing that face like mine, stepping from a *mirror*? As if I fight myself here?

As if I'm mad already? But I see clearly now. I am the Black Prism. I am the dark center of creation. And now the world's light and life will feed me as it has fed you for four hundred years, Lucidonius. I will be immortal as you are."

"I'm not Lucidonius."

"It doesn't matter who you say you are. You have to die. You have to die or Karris dies."

"You have it exactly backward...brother."

The final word struck Gavin in the stomach, driving the breath from him, and if the figure had moved then, he could've slain Gavin easily.

No, this was a nightmare, the way the giant fist coming down to crush him had been from that earlier dream. Gavin must be feverish. He must be mad.

No! No. He was *here*. This was *real*.

So this was all calculated. It was a trap.

"You're not Orholam," Gavin said. "And you're *nothing* like my brother. Don't make me laugh."

"Usually, we mortals don't get to serve as messengers," the man said as if Gavin hadn't spoken. "But He was making an exception for one brother. And we Guiles *can* be very persuasive."

"What'd you do, Lucidonius? Try to mold the illusion to look like me as much as you could, and hope the brightness of your eyes would blind me to all its shortcomings?"

"Flaws? Please, brother," the godling said. "*I'm* the handsome one." His eyes twinkled with good humor, and he held the blade casually, but kept enough distance between them that Gavin wasn't going to be able to take him by surprise.

"Well, that's a little bit like him, I confess. But it's still not good enough."

"Brother. You've tried to hold out until nightfall. What do you hope comes with the darkness?"

"Your power is faded already," Gavin said.

"Indeed. Mine is. Orholam's is not."

Gavin sighed. "Orholam. Lucidonius. Me. Now you're someone else again? It's so tiresome. Just pick one, huh?"

The god laughed. "Oh, is this Gavin complaining, or Dazen, or He Who Would Be Orholam himself?"

"I...I—fair enough."

Gavin wondered if Karris were already dead. Gavin would have one small opportunity here. Grinwoody had proven himself patient above all things, so he wouldn't be impatient with all his plans on the 683 line. He wouldn't kill Karris *before* sunset. He wouldn't even kill her at the very moment of it, surely, as if he were a timepiece. Surely he would wait, if only a few long moments, to see if all his plans might still work out. To see if Gavin might yet come through.

Or so Gavin had to hope.

There would be a few moments soon, just after sunset, where Lucidonius would be at his very weakest. Gavin would wrest the blade away then, and kill him, whether or not he'd told Gavin how to ascend to godhood.

Karris was worth Gavin delaying godhood.

She was worth Gavin losing it.

"You have the sword. I'm at your mercy," Gavin said. "Surely now you can tell me how you ascended."

"Are you waiting only for sunset, or do you hope to delay me until full dark?" the god asked. He seemed amused at Gavin's attempts. "That is quite a long time from now, on the longest day of the year. What's your plan?"

Not stupid, Lucidonius.

"I don't think I need full dark," Gavin said. "A little more and I'm going to take that blade from you and ram it through your heart."

"It wouldn't be the first time," the god said, looking mournfully at the blade.

"Nice try," Gavin scoffed. "I mean, as guesses go. I suppose all that black luxin at Sundered Rock messed up even your vision, huh? I didn't use the Knife to kill Gavin."

Lucidonius shook his head. "It must be exhausting, seeing lies and schemes everywhere. But I suppose I shouldn't be surprised. You've been so steeped in your shame that you never saw how deeply father was lost in his. Of course, he's very good at hiding it. From you most of all. For many years now, he's been killing everyone who knows, exiling those who might even suspect. As if the Lightbringer, of all people, would bring darkness." He expelled a long breath.

Gavin waved that all away. "Lightbringer?" Gavin said. "Father? You think he believes in that? Father's not remotely superstitious."

"Where you turned your shame in, he has turned it out on the world. But you, brother, do you think that when Orholam's Eye sets, that He can no longer see? His light burns unceasing, though all the earth turns its back and sees darkness. In the darkness, He gives us celestial lights that we may be reminded of Him, and the world turns once more. And to you, it is given to be a mirror set on high, to shine light even to the depths and bring others hope of the swiftly coming dawn."

"What are you, insane?"

"I never said *you* killed me."

It was such a non sequitur that Gavin couldn't even respond for a moment. "Ah, I see. Now you're simply throwing as many words at me as possible. My confusion *is* the point. But I know how this works. I remember what you just said. I'm a Guile. It's what we do. I might have lost a few things because I drafted black, but I certainly fucking remember killing Gavin."

"And with all the memories you lost, I'm so sorry you kept that one."

"Oh, I'm sure you are, as it gives the lie to your little—"

"Brother. Peace. I never said I was Gavin."

"You just—" Gavin suddenly couldn't breathe as the implication of Lucidonius's words slipped through his defenses like a knife between a child's ribs.

The godling said, "This is how I would've looked now, had I lived. You needed to exhaust your rage, fighting all through the day, so I begged for the duty. I didn't expect to get it. But then I worried that the young face of him you loved so well might push you to madness."

"No." Gavin wouldn't allow this. "Not *him*. Don't you...don't you defile *him*," he whispered.

"Dazen, there is no gentle way to lance a boil. Nor an easy way to bring a betrayal to light."

"Says the man who poses as a god?! Take off that face! And you stop talking *right fucking now*," Gavin said.

"There's work yet to do, big brother. And only just time enough for it. The sun sinks, and your son is dying."

"Don't you—see?! This is exactly what I was talking about! You throw more and more at me, hoping to confound me. Hoping to get me tangled up, hoping to distract me from—"

"It's not your fault. I don't blame you."

"You fuck!" Gavin nearly leapt to attack him, sword be damned. "I said don't you dare—"

The creature who pretended to be Sevastian did the last thing Gavin expected: Sevastian tossed the sword to him—or *at* him, somewhat, for though hilt-first, it was no gentle toss.

Gavin cut his fingers as he bobbled the blade. He retreated, stunned back into recognition of their fight and the blade and the peril he was in.

But 'Sevastian' made no move to attack, nor even to close the gap between them.

Gavin came down with the blade in his right hand, without his adversary so much as attacking. He was so stunned that his adversary had given up every advantage that they'd fought for throughout the entire, long day that he nearly forgot his rage, Guile though he was.

"Before any of us were born, father came to believe he was the Lightbringer," Sevastian said.

"Stop it now," Gavin said. "I have the monopoly on the madness here."

"He thought only he could save the world. That he was the most important person in history."

"Well, that much does sound like father," Gavin admitted.

"He thought that if he didn't save the world, no one would. He laid out a path, and as he always did, he pushed through every obstacle. But one time, he got outmaneuvered, outplayed at the great game. High Lord Ulbear Rathcore saw the size of father's ambition. Before father was even on the Spectrum, Rathcore pushed an obscure rule change about the Prism sacrifice through the Spectrum that he thought would stop father's ambitions."

Ulbear Rathcore? Gavin had barely known the older man, only that he resigned from the Spectrum and left the Chromeria around the time when his wife, Orea Pullawr, had become the White. That was decades ago. Orea had only spoken of him with fondness, which had seemed odd, given that they'd lived apart for as long as Gavin could remember. Rathcore had never even visited the Chromeria again, and as the White, Orea couldn't leave it.

"Wait. What? What? The Prism *what*?"

"Centuries ago now, Vician was the last true Prism. Born, not made. But when it came time to step down and surrender his powers, he murdered his successor instead. And then he murdered all those he could find with the gift, renewing his own powers—for a time—with theirs. He cowed and bought off the Magisterium and the Spectrum, and they helped him, rather than fighting him. But true Prisms stopped being born, even after Vician was gone. Some say those with the gift were still being born, but that a faithful luxiat had used black luxin to destroy the knowledge of how to find them. Others said it was Orholam's own punishment for the Magisterium's faithlessness.

"But by repeating Vician's murders, the Magisterium found they could *make* a Prism, and instead of an outsider upending their power every generation, they could choose one of their own to be the new Prism, which they liked very much indeed. Unfortunately, unlike a true Prism's powers, this made-Prism's powers would fade over the course of at most seven years. They knew what they made was a fraud, but some thought if Orholam wouldn't save the world from the luxin storms and warring gods, they would do it themselves. So they renamed their murders *sacrifices*. They found when they sacrificed adults, it might take dozens to fill a single jewel of the Blinding Knife with a color. It was as if days of life and power were being transferred. Then one had the diabolical idea to sacrifice a child, one whose gift for drafting had just awakened. And to the world's sorrow, it worked. Perhaps it was yet another test for the High Magisters: would they stoop so low?

"Of course they did. With a child, they'd get a full color from one murder, sometimes two. And it was so much easier to hide the death of one child, separated from her parents for tutelage at the Chromeria. A sudden illness, the High Luxiats would claim. With all the influx of pilgrims around Sun Day—often bringing the ill, hoping to be cured—who would notice the deaths of seven or ten children every seven years? The High Magisters never chose their victims from important families. Like predators, they hunted the weak and outcast children, the friendless ones. As if Orholam, who commands the exalted to bring succor to the lowly, would have them bring death instead."

The pieces were snapping together for Gavin. He remembered some of his mother's last words now. She had told him, with a peculiar intensity, 'You are a *true* Prism.' He'd thought she meant he was a good Prism, that he served well, despite the fraud of replacing his brother.

She would've known he thought that; she would've intended it. She'd given him a piece, knowing he would remember it, believing that he would put it in place when the time came.

And it fit. Perfectly.

His chest felt banded with iron. He couldn't get enough air.

He remembered bafflement among the older High Luxiats and the High Magisters as his seven-year anniversary of being Prism had approached. He could tell they expected something from him, and fearing to give them the wrong response, he'd given them none. Was he supposed to have been buying their allegiance, so that he could renew his reign? Was he supposed to react with dread?

Gavin's ignorance must have seemed feigned to them.

Meanwhile, Andross Guile had been removing or buying the silence of everyone who knew. And if the High Magisters and High Luxiats figured it out, what were they to do? Move against the first True Prism in centuries? Orholam's own blessed? His coming saved them from another round of murders—and to open the secret would be to reveal their own guilt.

And doubtless Felia had been working her own magic, too, to

protect her last living son. She'd had men killed for him, she'd confessed to him. Felia, who was never fierce, except for when she was defending Gavin.

Their power was built on the murder of children, every seven years? No wonder so many Prisms had only lasted through one term, or been driven by shame into drunkenness and self-destruction.

It had been a cancer in the very heart of the Chromeria.

Children?

"But the Freeing," Gavin said. "Surely a sip of power a hundred times over would equal the full gulp? Surely they could have used all those..."

"Sometimes. For certain colors, as long as they had the Blinding Knife. But those drafters who come to be Freed have almost nothing left of their power. They have none to give. The children selected for the sacrifice—one lightsplitter, and one or two for each color—were always confined in a special ward in the infirmary just before Sun Day. They were drugged so that they would feel ill. When a particular child's color wasn't required, she would simply recover from her 'illness,' and never know how close she had come to death."

So that was why father needed the Blinding Knife. It was what transferred the power. And this was why they'd always tried to select Prisms who were already polychromes—fewer colors needing transfer meant fewer murdered children. But the Chromeria cared about installing men or women from the right families more. They'd told themselves they killed the innocent to save the innocent of all the Seven Satrapies...but they'd killed the innocent to serve their ambitions, too.

"Who knew all this?" Gavin asked.

"Those at the very top. The circle was kept very tight. Any luxiat who didn't show enough moral flexibility to ignore matters of doctrine for matters of political necessity was derailed long before he could rise high enough to endanger them all. And the Spectrum has always been made up of political creatures. Most of them didn't even see it as an existential hypocrisy: to keep themselves and everyone else safe, they were happy to trade the lives of a few poor slaves, or commoners' children; whom they saw as hardly better. Most of them kept the secret simply because they thought its discovery would at worst make them look a bit heartless."

Gavin had thought himself the worst man in leadership at the Chromeria, an unparalleled deceiver. But they were all liars, black hearts in colored robes.

Perhaps that revelation should have been a relief. It was quite the opposite.

"You said...you said father got outflanked. What was the rule? What was the change?"

Behind the creature that called itself Sevastian, the spiderweb of cracks from Gavin's fist had spread up the mirror like sin. Cracks now reached nearly to the top of the Great Mirror and to every edge.

"The new rule was that no one could serve on the Spectrum while an immediate family member also served, in any capacity, whether as Color or Prism or promachos or the White or the Black. Everyone liked that, because Orea's name had been put forth several times to become the White, and people feared what she and Ulbear might do together. By tradition, such rule changes are required to have contingencies, in case an unforeseen emergency requires it, so Ulbear proposed a contingency that simply seemed outrageous. If two family members wished to sit in such high offices simultaneously—which at the time only applied to Ulbear and Orea—they had to supply one of their own children for the Prism sacrifice."

And then Gavin saw it coming, like the windup to a gut punch, when his arms were bound and there was no defending himself.

The man went on. "Father didn't even learn who'd pushed that rule through for years. No one thought it would apply to anyone but Ulbear Rathcore ever again. He resigned to let Orea join the Spectrum, thereby cementing the precedent, binding it into law and tradition both.

"But for father's plans, Gavin had to be made Prism, and father could only protect him if he himself were on the Spectrum, too. Father believed that the prophecies indicated he could only become the Lightbringer if he were the promachos first. So the price for father's ambition—and, he thought, the price to save the whole world—was that he sacrifice his sons. One to die after his term as Prism, and one..."

And then Gavin remembered it again, vividly. That wound on his little brother's chest. A single thrust, at an angle that had always seemed wrong. It wasn't the perpendicular angle of an intruder stabbing a child lying flat in his bed. It was an angle downward, through the ribs to the heart. As if the child had knelt before an adult, submissive to the blade.

"Father could only fully save one of his sons," Sevastian said, gently, as the dying sun finally touched the horizon. "He chose you."

Chapter 114

Karris watched the pagan armada approaching her beloved isles from her balcony. Her young luxiats, many of them now trained in rudimentary battlefield medicine, were awaiting her orders for where to deploy. She would be joining them as soon as the battle began in earnest with a large contingent of Blackguards. They would be medics and helpers to any civilians caught up in the fighting, doing the unseen work of making war slightly less hellish.

Then, if they saw a place where they were needed, she and the Blackguards could at least give one hammer blow of reinforcement.

She had a slim hope that that wouldn't be necessary today.

"High Lady," one of Karris's room slaves said, a young woman, round and shy. "The new Prism has taken the roof and installed himself on the balancing array. He's, he's using the mirrors to kill people."

That answered the question of where the hell Zymun was, though it wasn't the answer she wanted. "Well, that's a relief."

The girl looked ill. "Yes?...But...he seems not very careful in who he's burning? He's laughing, Mistress. He cut through our lines, must have killed a dozen men. Just said oops, and laughed and laughed. He's talking to someone who isn't there. He's bragging that even the immortals serve him now."

"Have the Blackguards seen this?" Karris asked. Though no current Blackguard had ever done it, they *were* sworn to kill Prisms if they became a danger. Not that any Blackguard would expect to have to do it on a Prism's *first day*.

"No, Mistress. They're all stationed farther out, as if he doesn't trust them. Only the Lightguards are near him."

So they might not know.

Karris cursed under her breath, but it was loud enough to further scare the young girl, who had some idea of the gravity of the situation she'd found herself in.

As she tucked pistols into her waistband behind her back, Karris said, "Why don't you go to your quarters for a while? Go see your friends or family. It may not be safe for you here."

The Blackguards were sworn to the Prism first of all. Technically, they had an equal duty to the White, but if Karris initiated violence and they didn't believe Zymun was mad...they would put down the threat. Many of the old hands hated Zymun and would want to side with Karris, but what would they think their duty was? And what would the new kids do?

Karris rolled her neck and checked her ataghan and the old scorpion held tight against her forearm. She was resplendent in her white-and-gold silk directly over her mirror-armor breastplate. It was the only practical part of her armor. She had no helm at all; instead her hair had been dyed in many colors and woven together in braids to show the unity of the Chromeria, and the white-enameled mail was so light that it probably wouldn't survive more than a single blow—nor would she.

She was meant to be seen as ready to fight today, not to *actually* fight.

One last glance toward the shores. Despite the constant cannon fire, the bane were getting close.

Karris had intended to go to the roof and take the White's escape lines down to get to the battle lines wherever she was most needed, as quickly as possible.

She wasn't going to be getting that far.

Zymun was murdering friendly soldiers, for fun. If that was the case, who would definitely be foremost in his sights?

Kip. And Karris. And Andross. And anyone who vexed him in the least, but these first of all, because only they had the power to stop him.

So. There it was. She had been so certain that she would die in this fight. Perhaps she'd been right. Perhaps she'd only been wrong about the day.

She was a warrior. That was why Orholam had selected her. Because she was ready to die.

Maybe, in order to do what she must, she'd even had to be ready to die in dishonor—because what was worse than a mother who killed her own child?

Zymun, son of my shame.

Maybe all that was preparation for this.

She had no more feeling than that. She'd grieved already. She had no wish to die, but she wished even less that others would die because she did nothing.

Five paces at most, she thought. Three would be better. Two pistols, just in case.

And with that, it was simply a thing she needed to do, and it jumped to the front of her list:

☐ *Get close enough to get a clean shot.*

How many of the Blackguards remembered how fast she was? Definitely Commander Fisk. He wouldn't have forgotten. She'd have to hope he wasn't up there with Zymun.

She double-checked her powder and shot, checked that the flints and the frizzen were clean and dry, then practiced her draw of the two pistols from her belt. She pulled a crease out of her tunic at the back, cocked the pistols, and tucked them back into her belt.

Gavin, you would've done this smiling. You would've come out of it successful and with everyone cheering you. What is this last bit of fear in me?

Maybe it's that you won't understand. But if I hesitate, Zymun may move against me first.

My love, I only hope that when you hear of this, you're proud of me. I hope you understand. I hope it matters.

She took one last deep breath, and put on a neutrally pleasant face. She was going to need it to get close to Zymun.

She opened the door.

Commander Fisk stood there, his hand raised to knock. His expression was pained. "High Lady," he said.

There were twenty Blackguards with him. At least. Oh, no.

He cleared his throat. "High Lady, we've come to arrest you. For treason."

There were Lightguards beyond the Blackguards, too.

"Treason?" she asked.

"Please don't make this any worse than it has to be," he said.

Chapter 115

"There was a storm that night," Dazen said, his own voice sounding far away. "Mother was away. Father and Gavin were off on one of their trainings, leaving me behind. Again. You know I loved you, but I . . . I felt so left out. Like I got put at the kids' table at dinner. But I was supposed to take care of you."

"We had a great day," Sevastian said, "scouting out the ruins of the old Varigari manor, where father was building the new house, remember? We forgot lunch, and somehow you convinced that tavern owner to give us the full spread? She thought you were so cute."

"I forgot about that," Dazen said. Those events had been overshadowed by the night's.

"A great day together," Sevastian said with a smile. "But all day is a long time to be stuck caring for a brother so much younger than you. You'd had no breaks."

"You're trying to let me off easy."

"You were mature for your age, but you were still young," Sevastian said. "Would you judge any ten-year-old so harshly if it weren't you?"

But Dazen couldn't even hear him. "The storm was shaking the entire house. You were scared. You wanted to sleep in my bed with me. I was scared, too, but I thought Gavin would mock me if he found us. I called you a baby. You wouldn't go. You held on to me, and I said you couldn't stay because you'd pee the bed. You hadn't peed the bed in two years, but I knew saying it would shame you. You didn't get angry." A hot tear coursed from Dazen's good eye; the black eye was incapable of tears. "You hunched your shoulders, defeated... your little shoulders shaking, and you went without a word. Like you respected me. Like my word was law, and I'd just used my power to crush you. That's who I am, Sevastian: I'm the one who finds himself in power by accident and then uses it to crush what's good."

The sun was almost all the way down now, and Sevastian's eyes were merely warm embers, filled with such compassion that Dazen couldn't bear to look at them.

"I knew I should go to you," Dazen said. "But I hardened my heart, and I slept. I *slept*, peaceful as a man without a conscience."

"Exhausted, yes. Petty, yes. Even cruel at times, as a child," Sevastian said. "But a lack of conscience was never your problem, big brother."

"If I hadn't turned you away... If I hadn't pushed you out..." Dazen said.

"I'd be alive." Sevastian shrugged.

Dazen flared hot. "What? Like, 'Oh well'? 'Shit happens'? Like, 'Water under the bridge'?!" He could feel the blackness growing inside him, like the black seed crystal in his eye was growing like a twining ivy, climbing down his throat, interlocking with the darkness that had so long lived in his heart.

He wanted to strike down his brother now with the sword. How dare he trivialize all Gavin had endured? This wasn't Sevastian. This was madness indeed. He—

"If..." Sevastian said.

"What?"

"I'd be alive, if... C'mon, brother. I already gave you this. Show that mental flexibility that's made you the wonder of the Seven Satrapies."

But he hesitated only a moment, and Gavin couldn't regain his bearings so quickly. He could barely disentangle his thoughts from his rage.

Sevastian said, "I'd be alive... *if* I'd been killed by a blue wight with some grudge against our family. If I were killed by a blue wight, as you've thought all these years, then your rejection that night cost me my life. Or maybe it would have come and killed both of us. A blue wight would've been able to handle two children, don't you think?"

Gavin frowned, off balance.

"Father didn't take any chances," Sevastian said. "He could have framed a groom or a governess for my killing, easily. Instead, he emptied the house of nearly everyone through a dozen different errands and excuses. Why else would two young scions of the Guile house be alone? We were *never* alone. Brother, please. We didn't fall through the cracks of a busy household. He arranged it to look like we had. But he didn't want to murder any more innocents than he had to, not even a groom or a governess. But do you really think that if he found me sleeping in your room instead of my own, he would have given up the whole endeavor? All his plans undone so easily? Does that sound like our father? Or would he have had a backup plan? Do you think a *servant* left that wineskin we found after dinner?"

Dazen was reeling. He knew dimly that father had changed after those days, at the same time that his elder brother had, but Dazen had thought father's hardening attitudes had been because he'd preferred his eldest son, Gavin—and that father blamed Dazen for not protecting Sevastian... from a wight.

But all that aside, Dazen didn't know what Andross had really been like before he'd become the bitter, conniving spider of the second half of his life.

"I wasn't even killed in our home, brother," Sevastian said.

Dazen said, "That can't be true. I came to your room. I tried to tell myself for years that I was coming to apologize, but I know that wasn't true. I was wakened by a cry. I remember it."

"Father carried me home. He was arranging the evidence in my room: the blue luxin shards, the torn window latch, the note. He'd donned the blue mask and cloak. But he faltered when it came time to arrange my body the way he'd planned. It broke him. I think he lost all faith that night, and yet his path was set. It was his cry you heard, not mine. And then you burst in and caught him... like that. His favorite son, catching him in his moment of greatest shame."

Dazen couldn't breathe for the longest moment.

"But...but, how could he?" Dazen said.

"The murder? The act itself? He didn't. He made Gavin do it."

Just when Dazen thought it couldn't get any worse. It was an upper-cut to the chin after a gut punch makes you drop your guard.

Sevastian said, "They didn't and don't understand exactly how the Blinding Knife works. What's necessary. What's not. They didn't dare let me die for nothing. Prisms or Prisms-elect were always the ones who'd wielded the blade before. Father told Gavin that this was why we Guiles held high office, that this was what made Guiles worthy of all the power and prestige and riches that flow to us: sacrifice. He told Gavin that if he wanted to be great, he mustn't shrink from his duty. He told him that they were literally saving not only the Seven Satrapies but the whole world, that all of this rested on Gavin doing what he must."

And there it was at last. Not only why the real Gavin had changed so, so much after that night.

Here also was why Gavin must have felt betrayed—betrayed by Orholam Himself!—when Dazen had shared with him that his own powers were expanding and expanding. Dazen was a polychrome now, and adding new colors every day! Dazen said what if he could split light, too? Wouldn't that be amazing? He was just like his big brother, wasn't it exciting, Gavin?!

How could Gavin feel anything but threatened to his very core by the news? Gavin had murdered Sevastian to get those powers, Sevastian, whom he loved.

Dazen was telling Gavin that he'd been *born* with them?

Gavin had murdered their beloved little brother for nothing—and, without even knowing what he was implying to his guilty older brother, Dazen was telling Gavin that *he* was the one who should really be Prism.

...Or how had that happened? Dazen thought that he'd remembered... Hadn't he himself killed the White Oaks to take their power? Hadn't he stolen power with black luxin?

Why was he confused about that? Had he remembered it being that way, or was that something he'd been told? What was wrong with his memory?

His left eye throbbed. He rubbed it.

The pain helped Gavin refocus. It felt oddly good. None of that mattered now, anyway.

The last edge of the sun disappeared from the horizon.

"It really is you, isn't it?" Gavin said. But he was worried all this was a hallucination. "Karris is going to die if I don't...try, anyway, to kill this—" He waved toward the mirror. "And you, I guess. I don't know." He looked at the Blinding Knife in his hand. Could he really use it to kill his own brother a second time, this blade that had stolen both brothers from him, and his father, too? And his mother.

Was he going to use this blade to serve *Grinwoody*? For some slim hope that that monster back at the Chromeria might spare Karris?

Really?

"Time's running out. What am I supposed to do?"

"Be Dazen," Sevastian said.

"I don't know who that is anymore," Dazen said.

There was an echo of the little boy Sevastian had been as the man before Dazen turned his palms up helplessly, but then he tossed his head to the side as if very-unsubtly subtly trying to direct Dazen's attention.

Dazen turned and saw his brother was trying to get him to look at the Great Mirror. He snorted and then shook his head. "Goddammit, Sevastian."

"Rather the opposite, I hope," Sevastian said, suddenly serious.

Dazen looked at the Great Mirror. In all the long day of fighting, he'd never had a moment to spare to question the thing. The monument stood impossibly thin and tall, without supports, the wind bothering it not at all: an immense mirror, flawless except for that great crack, with only his experience having touched it and some old Tyrean Empire filigree as evidence that it was a physical thing at all, resting as if weightless on the ground as it did.

He'd only seen glimpses of his own image reflected there. Hadn't wanted to look longer, maybe.

Now Gavin sneered at his second self. The figure seemed to flicker, seemed to split his head, as if his eyes were sending him opposing visions. He rubbed his right eye, wondering what was wrong with him.

Through his dead eye, through the black seed crystal embedded there, he could see himself truly. Only his memory could be so perfect. Or maybe this was how madness felt—normal. He examined himself.

Here behold Gavin Guile, in all his glory. Ha!

As he barked a laugh, aloud, he saw the empty tooth socket where his dogtooth had been. He'd broken it out of his own head in his bid to escape prison beneath the Chromeria. It had been a longed-for freedom that was as much a lie as all his years of service. His dogtooth was gone.

Nor was that the last of his deformities. He held up his left hand, as if waving to that loathsome figure: Hey! Looking good! The hand had only two fingers and a thumb.

It—he—was gaunt, one-eyed, hardly more than one-handed, gap-toothed. He, who had been beauty itself. He was revealed, finally, as the wretch he had always been. A cripple outside where he'd been a cripple for years within.

He'd told himself he was a victim of circumstance, who'd only chosen to survive.

His heart plummeted.

That was all lies, wasn't it? He'd *chosen* to pursue his young love Karris after he'd barely met her, knowing his father would be outraged, knowing his elder brother would be furious. He'd *chosen* to strike the White Oaks when he was afraid. He'd *chosen* to keep that gate locked when he thought Karris's lady-in-waiting had betrayed him. He'd not intended for anyone else to die, maybe, but he'd left her to the fire, to die a horrible death.

Gavin hadn't merely chosen to live; he'd chosen *to kill* so that he could live.

'You know this is wrong! I see it in your eyes!' a drafter had said to him on the night of a Freeing, furious, eyes straining his halos.

How many times had Gavin heard some variation of those words? At every single Freeing. And often in between.

Gavin staggered. Shying away from looking at his brother, he braced himself on the Great Mirror.

Like spring ice, the cracked mirror gave way. His hand plunged through it.

A chill shot through his entire body as if his blood were icing over, and when he ripped his arm back from the mirror's cold grip, his hand was *gone*.

He backed away from the mirror in horror, stumbled—fell.

Cracks spidered from the hole in the mirror toward every edge.

Pushing off the ground, Gavin leapt to his feet, certain some monstrous threat was about to pounce through it at him.

Then he realized he had pushed off the ground with both hands. He couldn't help but glance at his hand. It hadn't been lopped off; he hadn't lost it...but his flesh and bones had turned invisible; only weird, thick, dark veins remained, still opaque. As he turned his wrist, to his color-blind sight his veins were like black thorns waving in the wind, pulsing with a gentle darkness.

He flexed the fingers of his glassine right hand. His hand was still there, whatever this illusion was, merely invisible except for the thorns within it.

Up the mirror's pure gleaming surface, the cracks shot toward heaven. As they finally touched the top of the mirror and every edge simultaneously, a boom like thunder shook him and the tower, then modulated with the *wom-wom-wom* of a great temple bell.

It was so low it shook his belly and palpated the air in his lungs. The Great Mirror trembled.

High above, over the top of the Great Mirror, blood began pulsing. Not spilling down the mirror's surface as if poured out from a glass, but pumping, as if each of the myriad hearts Gavin had stilled was waking from death to condemn him. Rivulets streamed and stuck and raced together toward the ground, widened. The blood doubled and redoubled until not even a finger's width of shining glass remained clean. Like a curtain dropping, the blood draped the mirror entire.

It draped it *red*.

All the world was black and white...and now red, as if Orholam, who gives and takes away, had now given him the cursed gift of seeing his own crimson guilt in vibrant color. In his world of gray and the leeched nothingness of white and the triumph of gathering midnight-black, the vermilion hues sank into his skull like daggers into his eye sockets.

Red, everywhere red.

And in the blood mirror, Gavin saw himself again.

As every Freeing came around, Gavin had braced himself, and he'd felt bad...and he'd done the murdering expected of him. And he'd wept and he'd repented privately and he'd gotten drunk and he'd tried to forget. And the next year, he did it again. Over and over.

What would the Spectrum have done if instead he'd stood up on Sun Day and used his platform to declare, 'This ends now! I will not kill in your name. This is evil. It is finished!'

What if he'd spent his life trying to find some other way? Things had been different before Vician's Sin; they all knew that. What if Dazen, who routinely did the impossible, had turned himself to the impossible task of fixing the Chromeria and the Seven Satrapies?

Instead, Gavin had spent all his charisma on himself. He'd hidden when he could have fought.

The blood reached the bottom of the mirror. It poured out onto the obsidian of the tower's top, rushed past his feet, sticky.

He could smell it.

He'd been made for more than this. With his natural gifts, Dazen could have been more. Should have been more.

He'd secretly dared to be a god? He'd not even been a *man*! Alone, isolated by his own secrets and shame, he'd become a monster.

I have nothing to give you, Dulcina Dulceana had said at the Freeing, *but my time. Take my five minutes, and rest.* She'd been so quiet, so still yet welcoming, her presence had been an enveloping peace, like the warmth of hot springs on a chill night.

He'd taken her five minutes. Her action: her offer, her sacrifice, and her love, had been beautiful, pure. Where time was the measure of wealth, he, the rich man with many flocks, had taken a poor woman's last beloved lamb—and devoured it before her eyes.

And then he'd slaughtered her. He'd cast from this world that young woman whose very presence was healing. He'd cost the whole world all she could have done.

He regarded the broken thing in the Great Mirror. Here was 'Gavin' Guile. Any accusation he could level against his father, any sin of which he could accuse the Spectrum, any cupidity and vice he hated in others, all that he despised, lay living and breathing and strong in him.

The climb up the tower was supposed to purge his sins? It had only revealed them. He'd held on to a core of himself, an ambition, a pride. He'd held on to the sword, thinking: Judge me, O God? You dare? I am broken, but I will rise in bitter triumph. I submit to the truth of Your every accusation, but soon...I will *be* God!

He looked at the mighty blade in his maimed left hand and transferred it to his thorny, strong right. He felt a gathering darkness in the blade that echoed the gathering darkness of the night and within him. Gavin was not a holy man; he was a man wholly dark. The black sheathing the blade was the same black that had become his left eye, that had burrowed deep. Perhaps it wasn't hiding, as he had thought. Perhaps it was incubating.

Woe to the world when it hatched.

It had spread from his heart throughout his body, reaching even to his hands, to the black blade.

Or perhaps, seed crystal that it was, the black eye had simply titrated all the darkness that was already within him, latent. It wasn't foreign, alien, other. The black was his true self.

What if it is yourself that you fear? Your power?

His vision shivered once more, and in the blood mirror through his truth-seeing black eye Gavin saw great wings sprouting from his back, unfurling with a crack. He saw his form swelling with power, growing invincible. He would take, and punish, and live. Live forever. What could he not do, given time? He would make all things right. Fix all he'd broken. Even himself.

But visible from his mortal eye, the self remained, aghast, ashamed at him.

Take the blade, and strike—or they will take everything from you! Strike! Be the god you really are! You've suffered enough. You deserve this! All can be healed! Rise from ashes, glorious!

Closing his left eye, he looked once more upon the man in the mirror. Lips cracked, skin burnt, hair lank, eye patch leering, his whole aspect a shadow of a shadow of the glory of his former self. There were only skeletal remains of Dazen Guile. He'd killed him. He'd killed everything good. And why? In order to extend an existence he hated?

Why would you kill an innocent to give another day to a person you despise? He had failed in every good thing he'd tried to do. He was loathsome. Everyone he loved would be better off if he were dead.

Let this be the end.

He braced the hilt of the gun-sword on the ground and set the point of the cruel sword between his fifth and sixth rib. Then he shifted his weight, adjusting to get it right.

Of all the things not to fuck up, falling on your sword had to rate pretty high.

"Dazen!" Sevastian said. "*Elrahee. Elishama. Eliada. Eliphalet.* He sees. He hears. He cares. He saves."

Gavin snorted. "And yet here I am, on His front porch. Knocked on the door. Hell, I even punched a hole in it! He isn't here, brother. Never was. This tower's a monument to nothing. And you're nothing but my madness."

"Dazen, if Orholam came to speak to you in the flesh, you still wouldn't listen. Didn't, for your whole climb and for your whole life. But you listened to *me*. So who's the right messenger to send to you?"

"You're not a messenger. You're a hallucination." But tears were flowing. He was so ashamed and he could hide none of it now.

"A hallucination who tells you things you don't know and kicks your ass?"

"Hey, you didn't kick my ass!"

"You just don't want to admit you lost a fight to an eight-year-old boy."

From its brief levity, Gavin's heart dropped again.

"It was supposed to be you, wasn't it?" Gavin said. "You were the best of us. You were supposed to be the Lightbringer."

Sevastian took a deep breath and pursed his lips.

"So we're lost. Father *killed* the Lightbringer."

"Sometimes the wicked win a battle. Sometimes those who hear the call say no to it. Men have power. Our actions matter, even unto eternity. But the ultimate victory is still assured."

"We killed the fucking Lightbringer, Sevastian."

"A Lightbringer," Sevastian said. "Perhaps. Or perhaps I, too, would have been turned aside, corrupted, or killed. Who's to say? What I know is this. If God needed perfect mirrors to bring His light to the world, it would be a world forever dark. Imperfect mirrors also—"

Gavin scoffed, pointing at himself. "Imperfect?! What, you see *this* as mildly flawed? Look at me! You know what I was! What I am."

"I see. I see and I'm not turning away."

"How can you not?"

Sevastian pierced him with a gaze that combined the best of Felia and Andross Guile and yet was somehow fully his own. "Because I love you, brother. I see the you that's *you*, under all this. Yes, it's ugly, it's disgusting, but you can be more. I know what you can become, even still. There's still work for you to do."

Gavin sneered. "Not for me. I'm finished. It's sunset. I've failed my mission. Karris is dead by now. I've betrayed half the people in my life, and failed all the rest. My time's up."

He remembered then his dream. In the dream, his hand had looked like this—this thorny, skeletal abomination. He'd been on a tower like this, and a giant had come striding up to smash him in judgment. Orholam Himself. And Gavin had known he deserved his fate, but still begged for more time.

It had been more than a dream. It had been prophecy.

And had done him just as much good as prophecy usually does.

He braced the hilt of the sword on the stones once more. The blood would make it slick.

He was so very tired of his lies, and his false bravery, and his false fronts, and his falsity on every human axis of virtue. His lies had gutted every word of praise uttered for him, denuded every moment of triumph, hamstrung every victory. Now it was time to let every lie die, no matter how precious.

"You know, for all the awful shit you did," Sevastian said, "you had some good things about you. Even as Gavin, you were amazingly brave. You would risk your life to do amazing things at the drop of a hat. Not sure why you'd give that up, right at the end, when you could do the most amazing thing of all. If you had the guts, that is."

"What?"

"If you're gonna kill yourself, why don't you go out like a man?"

"Huh?"

"Like you said, the front door's right there." He motioned to the Great Mirror, still streaming blood. "The Mirror of Waking is open. Why don't you go inside?"

"It's a trap," Gavin said.

"So what do you care if it is? You climbed all this way to confront 701

God Himself, and at His doorstep you're just going to kill yourself? Really? You're just going to lie down in the bog and wait for the muck to close over your face? No fighting, huh?" He faked a yawn. "Out of all the things you've been called, brother, I never thought at the end you'd opt for 'boring.'"

Gavin narrowed his eyes. "Why are you egging me on?"

"I'm a little brother. It's what we do." Sevastian grinned, and if his version of the Guile grin was more innocent than Gavin's knowing grin, it was equally mischievous, and more winning. Gavin's grin had always said, 'Look at me, aren't I wonderful?' Sevastian's said, 'Look at us, aren't we wonderful?'

Even here, even now, Gavin couldn't hold on to all of his anger.

"You're kind of a dick," Gavin murmured.

"I'm a Guile."

"That's what I said."

"That's what I meant."

Ah. Acknowledging the truth, but drawing the parallel so as to shoot the insult back to include Dazen, who was a Guile as well.

Sevastian was joyfully quick.

It made the ache of losing him deepen. Had he lived, Sevastian would have been a peerless friend. A man keen and sharp and strong. The best of the Guiles, surely. If he'd lived, might not his goodness have moored Dazen to some integrity?

They all would've been so different: Gavin, father, mother, and Dazen, too.

But Gavin was staring at the mirror now with something like purpose. Sevastian was right: he had climbed all this way. He had to know.

And if it cost his life to find out, so much the better. Right?

But first... "I'll lose you if I do this, won't I?" he asked.

"For a time," Sevastian said, his voice low.

"A long time?"

"I hope not, for my sake. I miss you. And I hope so for your sake and the world's."

Gavin looked at him, as if one last look would tell him if this were all real or madness, but his vision still bifurcated with his two eyes. "All right, then. Delusion...Brother. Whichever. Thank you." He took a deep breath, but there wasn't air enough in all the world for him to be ready for what he was going to do next, so he simply said, "Now, enough fuckin' around."

Without another word, he charged the cage that held the monster he'd been fleeing for his whole life: he ran at the Great Mirror. His reflected self—bloody, crimson, deformed, raw, haggard, and hard—ran at him. They screamed their defiance of each other and their acceptance of death, and crashed into each other.

Chapter 116

"Would you look at that?" Kip said as the Mighty crested the last hill before heading over the bridge to the Chromeria. All around the Jaspers, the bane were now visible, just under the surface, slowly rising, and coming in closer toward the shore every moment, propelled by magic and the will of their dark gods.

By now all the drafters on the Jaspers had pressed their fingers on hellstone to empty themselves of all the luxin in their bodies, and Kip should have been up on the mirror array, even though the bane weren't *doing* anything yet.

"You still with me?" Kip asked. "Even if...?" He didn't make eye contact with the Mighty. He hadn't told them about the game, about the Lightbringer stakes. There were lots of reasons for that. He didn't want to tell them what he'd wagered against it, for one. Tisis wasn't going to take that well, once he told her—and he would, just not hours before a battle. Andross could well refuse to honor his debt, might find some loophole.

Truth was, he didn't *feel* like the most important person in history.

Winsen said, "We've placed our bets. We're yours, asshole."

That it was Winsen who said it warmed Kip's heart unexpectedly. He nodded to the enigmatic man, his friend.

"Just wish we coulda done right by Crux before the end," Big Leo said.

"Bollocks," Ben-hadad said. "Fighting for what's good and right? Fighting for what we believe in and for each other? We *are* doing right by Cruxer and by every other friend we've buried in this war. Enough. Let's—"

They all stopped talking as above them a sudden beam of light shot from the Great Mirrors atop the Prism's Tower.

"What the—" Big Leo said.

"Zymun," Kip said. "*Bastard*. That's my signal. The one I can't miss."

They rode across the Lily's Stem and saw several Lightguards go running, doubtless to tell their master. Kip and his Mighty and fifty of the best of the Cwn y Wawr and numerous units fortified by Daragh the Coward's men made their way to the grand atrium. Forty Lightguards stood in ranks before the lifts, and another twenty before the slaves' stair entrance.

The Lightguards were sweating and pale. Not the best of that august company. Kip's men couldn't help but sneer at them, but one of Andross Guile's secretaries at the mouth of the passage that led out to the back docks spoke up, "My lord! High Lord Guile! The promachos awaits you out back!"

Kip couldn't attack those Lightguards, even though he'd heard they'd had some kind of skirmish with the Blackguards. The Lightguards were at least nominally Andross Guile's men. Attacking them would start a civil war.

Now was not the time.

So Kip simply walked past them. He reached the Blackguards at the gate to the passage to the back docks. "The old man back there?" Kip asked.

They nodded jerkily.

Kip left the majority of his men there—he didn't want to get stuck on the wrong side of a choke point. Then he walked through, only Ferkudi and Big Leo and a dozen of his best following him.

There were Blackguards at the back gate, of course. New people Kip didn't know. Another two stood on the dock, scanning the water for sea wights who might be swimming below. But Andross Guile wasn't with them. With four more Blackguards watching over him carefully, he was off to one side, on the small beach, staring out over the Cerulean Sea.

Kip approached him alone, coming to stand where the very beach was wet with little lapping waves.

"Do you want to know what's bathetic?" Andross Guile said, standing at the waterline.

"What?" Kip said.

"I'm standing here because of a translation my wife was unsure of, in a dead language, on a partial scroll, which may have been dictated to a poor student by a prophet who himself was rejected by the Chromeria's leading scholars—a prophet of a god I don't believe particularly cares about us." He shook his head. "And yet here I stand. It's a stubborn thing, the faith of one's youth."

"Oh," Kip said. "I was actually wondering what the word 'bathetic'
means."

"Haven't Viewed my card yet, have you?" Andross asked.

"There's a war on," Kip said. "Did you not notice?"

"We have so many things in common, you and I," Andross said.

"Some," Kip admitted. Not many.

"Both outsiders, both drawn inexorably to the center of all things, both overlooked, both with a tenacity to outlast stones and shatter cities. We approach life with hearts broken but heads unbowed. We both are surrounded by the mighty. We were both great from our youth: I recognized as a young man with a destiny, you...well, that other meaning of 'great.' Depending on how you parse such things, one might say one or the other of us has brought down gods. Only you have killed a king, but if today goes well, I'll add kings to my list, too."

"Both wasting our time on a beach?" Kip offered.

"Odd. Flippancy is a trait of the fearful, not of those who inspire fear."

"Do I look fearful to you?"

After a moment, Andross said, "No."

"Then can we move this along? I saw the sign you told me to look for. I have places to be."

"No, you have one place to be. This place."

"Sir?" a young Blackguard interrupted. "Pardon me, High Lord Promachos. It's the Prism, sir. Er, Prism-elect?"

"Yes?" Andross said, irritated.

"Commander Fisk wanted me to tell you...He's, um, the Prism-elect that is—He's sort of gone crazy, sir? Not like battle exhausted or catatonic, sir. He's using the mirrors to burn people, apparently on purpose. He's laughing. Our people, sir. The bane are almost to the shore, but he's mostly ignoring them. Said it's like ants under a glass."

Andross sighed heavily. "Well, that's inconvenient, if not a total surprise. Kip, remind me the next time you louse something up that you aren't half as bad as your brother."

"He's only my half brother, so there you have it," Kip said. "What were you hoping he'd do?"

"Oh, exactly what he's doing, but half competently. He was supposed to get angry you'd been favored and get on the mirror array to defend the islands until he burned himself out, broke the halo, and needed to be put down by the Blackguard."

"What?" Kip asked.

"He was supposed to 'ascend to the heights and fail'—thus clearing the path for you to...be what we said. Young man," Andross said to the Blackguard, "tell Commander Fisk this falls under the Fourth Oath. You'll find him stationed with our young Prism."

"The Fourth Oath, sir, yes, my lord." But the young man had a panicked look on his face, like he was failing a sudden quiz.

Andross sighed again. "In the last extremity, your duty to protect the Prism is replaced by your duty to protect the Seven Satrapies *from* the Prism. This, you damned fool, *is* the last extremity."

"Oh! Yessir!" the Blackguard said.

Then he ran.

Kip turned to follow him.

"Hold," Andross said. "The bane will come ashore in mere minutes. I've lookouts posted to let me know the moment it happens." He pointed up to the orange tower where a man with a hand mirror stood waiting on a side balcony of a tower above them, ready to relay the signal.

"I don't understand," Kip said. "What does it matter?"

"For one reason—that you can look at two different ways. There was a lost prophecy hidden in a forbidden scroll at the Great Library in Azûlay. I recovered it at...great cost to our family, not least yourself. It said the Seven Satrapies would be plunged into a thousand years of night if the Lightbringer didn't stand on the shores of the Jaspers when the bane made landfall—as in literally where the water touches land. So one way of looking at that is this: if you're not standing on the shore when the bane land, you can't be the Lightbringer. The other way is that if you *are* the Lightbringer, you'd damned well better be standing on the shore, or it'll mean a thousand years of night for all of us.

"Either way, Kip...when history calls your name, you raise your damn hand."

"Are you telling me *that's* why you've been standing down here holding your dick while you could have been stopping Zymun?" Kip demanded. "Because of some idiotic prophecy?"

"He'll be stopped soon, regardless," Andross said. "A bet thirty-eight years in the making is about to be decided. The last card flipped. I'm not about to walk away from the table now. Zymun's nothing. He's got no money, no connections, certainly no friends. And very little time left. "

Kip said, "No money? It doesn't matter who has the *money*; it only matters who has the *guns*!"

"You're missing the forest for the trees."

"One of those trees is on fire!"

"Kip. This is your last chance. Two minutes. Maybe five. If you're the Lightbringer, you've got to be *here*. If you leave, I *will* take the mantle of that office from you. Someone must save this empire, and if you won't, I will."

"By standing here?" Kip said, "All this time. Everything you've seen and heard of me, and you still don't know me at all, do you? I don't care about being the Lightbringer. I—"

"Yes, you do. There's a time to lie about the scope of one's ambitions. I should know. I've done it for all my life. But that time is past."

Zymun was killing people. The bane were landing, and Kip wasn't helping the defense. But Kip felt that old surge of longing, to matter, to matter so much that no one could ever deny it, no one could underestimate or minimize or ignore him ever again. To have the respect he'd won from a few people be in *everyone's* eyes.

At the cost of a few extra dead defenders, people who would never know that Kip could have saved them but didn't. Here's all you could ever want, and the price for it will be paid by someone else.

"I do want it. But I want to save my friends more. To hell with your prophecies. The Lightbringer can't be the one who stands around waiting for the light. He's the one who brings it."

"Kip! Grandson," Andross said to his back, and his voiced seemed almost kind. "If you want to survive up there on the array, don't draft. You're no Prism. The power will break your halos in moments. It'll burn you out. You break our enemies with your *will*. Earn your name, Breaker."

Kip glanced back at him over his shoulder, eyebrows drawn down. "As much as you don't know me, grandfather...maybe I don't know you, either. Farewell, sir."

* * *

Andross watched as Kip ran back inside.

Very little of the fat boy he'd once been clung to the man Kip had become, except his compassion, his loyalty. Andross liked that about him.

Too bad. His leaving early surely meant that he, too, would ascend the heights and fail.

Light flashed across Andross's face and he looked up to the signalman with the hand mirror high on the side of the orange towers: *The bane have made landfall.* That signalman was merely passing along a message from another spotter. It would have taken several moments at each station to confirm the message and then pass it along. Kip *might* have still been standing on the shoreline at the moment the bane landed.

Inconclusive. How annoying.

But, after all, Kip was still only the backup plan. Andross sent a man on ahead to order his supper sent to his stateroom. It was going to be a long day, and he'd need his strength. He'd take a bite to eat and await Kip's failure before heading up to the mirrors himself.

"I thought You'd beat me," Andross said aloud, slowly turning a bitter gaze to the heavens. "But perhaps I may yet snatch the victory from Your greedy hands."

Chapter 117

A thunderous waterfall blasted Dazen off his feet. He tumbled and rolled across bright marble, coming to rest with his head in his arms, bruised and battered and dazed, eyes stinging from the force of the blast.

But he wasn't *wet*.

And as far as he could tell, he wasn't *dead*, either.

He moved to push himself up off the ground and saw his arms. Both had gone fully invisible, except for those black thorns within them. He sat up to his knees and saw his dream made flesh: the black thorns were everywhere twined through his transparent flesh, everywhere weakening him, wrapped around his heart, infiltrating it in such fine threads it turned the sadly palpitating, pitiful pink organ gray.

He didn't dare look at the mirror. His whole body was a playground of jagged dark thorns, and he didn't want to see it, didn't know if he could handle loathing himself more.

Okay, he thought. Maybe I'm dead after all. This *could* be hell. A very tricky introduction to it, what with the bloodfall and the bright colors, but—

The *colors*. They struck him all at once. God *damn*.

Dazen stood and took in the world. The stone at his feet was white marble, here. So too was everything changed, better. This was like a bright reflection of the real world.

No, that was exactly backward, he thought; *this* was the real world, and he'd lived in the dim reflection of it for his entire life.

The mirror stood just as tall here as it did atop the tower in his world, but the cataract here poured pure water. It flowed clear and bright and everywhere it brought life. Instead of howling, the wind soughed sweetly.

The tower itself was shaped somewhat differently, but Dazen lost all track of his thoughts as he saw the sunset.

His heart swelled within its black-barbed cage as he beheld the polychromatic miracle of a sunset once again. Here, with the sun just down, every hue wielded the weight of glory.

A long moment passed before he remembered to breathe.

For the first time he could remember since he was a boy, his mind went quiet. He turned from wonder to wonder, to see the winking stars brighten in their realms, to see the million gradations of color from the blackness of the night yielding to ruddy vitality on the horizon. The cosmos stretched luxuriant above him, around him, embracing him.

He could stay here forever, watching wonders unfold like the petals of a flower opening and opening anew. But then he felt his skin tingling. Reluctantly, he looked at himself again. Frowned.

A droplet of the bright water standing suspended on his invisible arm suddenly soaked into the skin, like rain into thirsty soil—and his skin blossomed from invisibility into visibility. Everywhere he'd been immersed—so, everywhere—Dazen saw his skin not so much reappear as seem to grow anew at the touch of the water. He held up his left hand, which was tingling sharply, and saw his pinky and ring fingers grow afresh from the hacked-off stubs the Nuqaba had left him with. He tapped the whole, perfect digits with his thumb, bewildered. There was *feeling* in them.

He dropped his hand to his side, though, and felt a flash of rage.

This wasn't real. This could only be some new kind of torture. It was a trap, right?

And now he looked around intently, as he should have from the very first moment, for his Enemy.

But he could see no one else. He circled the tower peak slowly, to see if anyone hid behind the mirror.

The tower itself looked slightly odd, so once Dazen had assured himself that he was alone, he went to one edge. The tower itself wasn't *black* as it was on his side of the mirror. Here it was lambent white, all the way up.

On a whim, Gavin went to the side where he'd left the old prophet below him.

Of course he wasn't there.

"Orholam isn't here, either," Gavin said.

He suddenly barked a sad laugh. Orholam isn't here.

There's nothing here.

It's beautiful . . . and there's nothing for me here.

I came all this way, and now I've lost everything, and there's nothing here.

Every effort had been wasted. Deluded.

Then he felt something tingling deep within him. He knew instantly what it was. It was as if a flame had touched an old black wick. He looked up to where the sky was still blue—and drafted blue luxin into his palm. Then he did the same with red. And with every color in turn.

His gift had been restored.

But only to torture him.

He sighed out all his hope. He released the colors from limp hands and groaned.

Maybe he should climb down the tower. Maybe he should try to live here, in this better world, where he was whole. Maybe there were versions here of all the people he had known . . . though that didn't make sense. Sevastian and the old prophet were gone.

No. There was nothing for him here. It was perfect, and he was not. No matter that his skin had regrown, he could still feel those black thorns inside his body, sapping his strength, rending his flesh anew with every movement, no matter that here he healed immediately.

He'd made it here. Alive. He'd invaded Orholam's own realm. But he didn't belong here.

He looked at the great waterfall. He knew that when he went through it again, back to his world, he'd lose his fingers and his powers and even his color vision. Again.

He'd thought he might die, invading this realm, and instead he'd found life. Now, going back, he would find his drab life, adorned only with all the encroachments of death.

The black eye throbbed. It felt like it had been loosened in his skull by the cascading water, and now it ached. Gavin rubbed around it, carefully. He couldn't bear to touch the damned thing here.

He took one last look around, locking the colors in the vault of his memory, and then before he could lose his courage, he took one last deep breath of air, so pure it made his lungs ache with goodness, and ducked quickly back through the waterfall—

—emerging soaked in blood.

He was disgusted, angry, full of contempt for the meanness, the stench, the sticky grotesquerie of all this world. It could be all he had just seen, and was relentlessly not.

Beauty is possible, but we choose ugliness.

He scraped the streaming, steaming, sticky blood from his face, and eyes, using his hand as a strigil to scrape away all the accusatory gore. His two fingers were gone again, as he knew they would be. Dogtooth gone. His sight once again black, white, and red.

Of course the red remained.

His gift was gone. Of course it was.

And his brother was gone. Sevastian, the one last good thing in this world was gone.

And yet Gavin lived, still. As ever.

Then he saw a familiar figure. The old prophet was sitting over at the edge of the tower, watching the sunset, heedless of the slow cascade of blood, sitting in it, apparently unperturbed by the mess. Apparently, the bloodfall from above had alarmed the old man and spurred him to make the last bit of the climb to find out what the hell was going on.

Gavin wondered how big the gap had been when Orholam had jumped it. Probably small. Old bastard.

Gavin walked over toward him. The sword was on the way. He picked it up, bloody as it was from the endless stream pouring past it. Gavin was exhausted. What was he gonna do? Hack apart the mirror, hoping it accomplished something?

He'd carried this damn blade halfway across the world. What had it done for him? It was as useless as he was.

He was sick of it. Sick of his own shit.

Without thinking too much—hell, he'd thought too much for his whole life—he simply threw the blade.

The throw was as pathetic and weak as he was, in body and in will; he couldn't even commit to throwing it hard. He threw it sort of to Orholam, sort of at him, and sort of toward the edge, that it might fall into oblivion.

He didn't even choose, merely tossed it away. But then, it was trash, like his plans; he didn't care about it anymore.

The blade clattered and slid and stopped short of the edge and Orholam both.

The old prophet turned and looked at it, then at Gavin, then turned back to looking at the horizon without taking any more interest.

Gavin strode over to the old man.

The old man didn't respond, so Gavin sat. He dangled his feet off the edge of the bloody tower.

Orholam didn't say a word. Gavin was reminded of their days rowing together. After a long hard day of rowing, sometimes, a rest would come, and they would simply sit. In such times, there would be no chatter. Bone-weary, there was nothing to say, but there was a silent communion in the rest from their mutual labor.

As they had then, now in the cool of the evening, they sat together.

What did anything matter now? There was no rush. It was too late. Someone else was steering the ship. Someone else calling the cadence. A broken-down slave wasn't going to change history.

Gavin was about to be cut free from his oar and tossed overboard; he was human jetsam.

In his dream of this tower top, Gavin had begged the approaching giant for more time; he'd wanted to fix things. Fix himself, he supposed, as he'd held his black-marbled heart in his hands, as if he could disentangle the living and the dead flesh knotted together using instruments as blunt and clumsy as his fingers.

The truth was, he was hopelessly broken, and time wasn't going to fix him. Now he was out of time. But maybe he'd been out of time for years. If he'd had another century, he would still be himself.

But a stillness descended on him as he sat there with the old man. He beheld the horizon, and though he saw only in a bichromatic palette made painful by his recent vision of the sunset in full color on the other side of the glass, he was filled to overflowing with wonder. What was absent to his blinded eyes was yet *there.*

He could remember beauty, could remember how this gray-scale tone would correspond to a lemon yellow blushing to sweet tangerine. Velvet violet was stitched with subtle seams into the soft samite blanket of night, embroidered with silver points of light.

It was there, and he knew it was there, knew it was more real than what his eyes could presently see.

"What do you miss most?" Orholam asked quietly, not turning.

They'd failed together, Gavin supposed. Orholam had climbed up here, after he'd been 'told' not to come, and perhaps he believed now he was being punished for his disobedience by finding nothing here. His world had to be shit right now, too.

What came to mind wasn't what Gavin expected, though.

"When I called down that...holocaust at Sundered Rock, I didn't know what it was going to do. Not exactly. I mean, I knew it was going be bad, but...I came to, standing there, naked. The black just devoured *everything.* And that hot day turned cold. Bitter cold. Frigid. Even my brother's body was cold. I couldn't tell how long it had been—if I'd been unconscious on my feet for hours, or if the hellstone magic sucked in even heat and it had only been moments.

"You know, I was the one person on that battlefield who should have understood what had happened, and I was...baffled. My skin was hairless in spots, but unharmed otherwise, but my clothes had disintegrated? I felt I had broken the world, like I'd cracked open an egg and something terrible had been released. But in that moment, there, among the dead...even the dying didn't seem to moan. Or maybe I was deaf. I don't know, but it was so still, as if a ripple of what I'd done was traveling out to infinity. Amid all that, I experienced this moment out of time, as if passing realms had locked here and the pressure had built until the earth heaved and everything fractured. Suddenly the landscape was changed, and you could only pray that the tensions had been relieved and that the aftershocks wouldn't destroy you.

"Something had happened that was bigger than I could even understand...but it had passed, and these stupid, normal, boring-ass concerns came rushing back. Like: I was naked. And I couldn't find my friends. And first it, it, it wasn't even that I was afraid they were all dead or that I'd killed them. I couldn't even think that far ahead. I only knew I was *lonely*. After all that? After this conflagration of magic the likes of which no one had ever seen or even heard of? No one cared if some guy on the battlefield was naked and his hair didn't look right or some shit. But I was *cold*, and I saw Gavin had clothes and there—at the end of the fucking world!—it made me remember this one time when we were kids.

"We'd stopped on one of the little islands my father owned on our way between Rath and Big Jasper and we snuck out late one night and hiked up the mountain to look for this old ruin—which we'd been forbidden to do, of course. And we'd been going for hours and there was a sudden storm, and I'd left my cloak back at my room, and I thought Gavin was going to tell me what an idiot I was. He'd even reminded me to bring it. But instead of mocking me or hitting me—" Gavin's voice cracked suddenly. He had to clear his throat hard. "Instead Gavin...Gavin hugged me under one arm and gave me his cloak. He said he was too hot. The damn liar. Asked me if I'd wear it home for him."

Gavin cleared his throat, irritated. "He didn't deserve—I mean, at Sundered Rock I was naked and stupidly embarrassed about it and he had clothes and was dead, and I, I just took them. It seemed really practical, you know? He didn't need 'em, right? But I looked back at it, and I stripped the dead like a looter. I stripped my brother's corpse like a grave robber. It was like I'd planned, you know, with Corvan. I mean, it was one possible outcome of like six: set a bunch of smoky red luxin on fire, come out as Gavin, take charge of his armies and pretend to be him...I've never had a plan go so flawlessly and so poorly.

"After that I used black luxin again, on purpose. To wipe out some memories. And I...what I was left with was my hero worship for my big brother. Like remembering that night in the storm. I thought he was the perfect Prism, that I could never measure up to him. I tried to be what I thought he'd been. And in the last couple years...I've seen and started to remember all the terrible shit my brother did. His cruelty. His meanness and fear. Some of it excusable because he was a child and scared and...and some of it not, not at all, regardless. And you know, learning about who he really was—seeing the truth about him? It's been like losing him all over again. My family was shit, and I was shit, but I had a hero, and then I lost him for a second time. He wasn't ever who I'd thought he was. He did some awful, awful shit I can never forgive him for. But at the same time...he wasn't all bad. He was still the big brother who gave me his cloak."

Gavin had to swallow again.

"So I guess, you know, I guess I miss my big brother. And I miss Sevastian. And I miss my mother, who never let me in all the way, even though she loved me. I trusted her and she had my back, but she didn't trust me. Not with the truth. She was ashamed, I guess. And I miss my father, or the man he was before all this...I miss the man he should've become. The grandfather he should've been to Kip. I miss Kip, and the father I should've become for him. I miss all the things I cost me. I miss Karris, and the great years I should've had with her. I miss Corvan, who was my best friend, and who I abandoned. I...shit. I miss things that never were and mourn things that ought to have been. Ridiculous, huh? It doesn't matter now. It's too late."

Gavin tried to shake it off, finally turning to look at the old prophet with a lopsided half grin. "So, should I complain some more about my unhappy decades as the richest, most powerful and admired man in the world? It's all pretty much the same, though: 'Ugh, all this rich food doesn't taste good while I'm feeling so guilty.' 'Poor me! All these women want me, but I'm in love with one who I've given good reason to hate me.' The story's a real tearjerker! But what about you? What were you doing then, Orholam? Oh, you were enslaved and chained to the oar all those years? Beaten daily, nearly drowned a dozen times? Yeah...that does sound *almost* as bad as I had it. So, you know, maybe I can be done." He turned up the corners of his mouth and gestured over to the old man. "But really. I've gone on enough. What was your family like before the whole call-to-prophecy-and-running-away thing happened? What do *you* miss?"

Orholam cocked his head, lips curling in a smile. "Can I tell you a story?"

"It *is* your turn," Gavin said.

"Not my story."

"Meh, it's still your turn. Maybe a cryptic parable will do me good." Gavin doubted it, but he owed the old man this much, and he was embarrassed at how he'd gone on.

Orholam said, "After Dazen Guile killed his brother at Sundered Rock, he built a prison. Not one cell or two, but an eightfold prison."

"Uh. Look, I know this story. How 'bout that cryptic parable instead? A prophecy? You can even make it rhyme. I can't even tell you how ready I am for some awkward rhyming couplets that don't quite fit a meter."

Orholam said nothing, and Gavin felt like an asshole. "I just said I'd listen, and I interrupted first thing, didn't I?"

Orholam said nothing.

Gavin sighed. "I built it because I went mad. I wasted—"

"No."

"What do you mean, no?"

"In your climb through the seven circles to reach this, the roof of the world, you've seen that you were worse than you knew. It's time for you to see that you were also better."

"Better?"

"Dazen built those prisons because he knew what men had wrought. In seeking immortality and power, man had released the infernals into this world. The gods of old, the immortals, could walk here. The Chromeria had obscured the knowledge as well as it could, but such could not be hidden forever. And so Dazen dedicated himself, alone, to fighting those whom the Chromeria denies even exist. He discovered that to wield the greatest power, the infernals have to partner with a human host, a drafter who will share her or his body with them. And so to expiate his sins, Dazen became a hunter. Not a hunter of wights, but rather of the powers who prey upon those dying drafters called wights, all over the world."

"This...isn't..."

"He couldn't kill these gods. That took something beyond him, something he didn't have, the Blinding Knife, which his brother and father had lost. But he, who so often did what others called impossible, did the impossible once more. With the greatest secrecy and cunning, one at a time, he imprisoned eight of the immortals. One for each of the seven Chromeria-recognized colors, and one of the greater elohim in the black prison. Chi and paryl were too rare or too careful for him to find, and white, he was certain, was a myth."

"What are you—" But Gavin's throat was tight. It was hard to breathe. Why was it hard to breathe?

Orholam said, "So it was that after he had imprisoned these immortals, he came to believe that the only person who might undo his labors was he himself, for he knew himself corruptible and corrupted already. So rather than seek more power, this remarkable hero sought to throw his power away: he brought death and oblivion into his own heart. This true Prism sacrificed what was more precious to him than even his own life—he sacrificed his Guile memory and his own reputation, even in his own mind."

"No," Gavin said. He could barely form words over the encroaching tears, could barely breathe. It was impossible. It was lies. "No. That's all very flattering, but you don't know. You don't know me."

But then he remembered the voices from his prisons. They hadn't known him. They hadn't spoken quite right. If he'd cast bits of *himself* into those walls, they'd have spoken to him differently. The infernals cast into those walls hadn't known what lies the others had told him, so each had tried its own tack against him, bluffing.

The last one had cursed him, called him ℧ᘄᒋᲤᘄᒋ. That was a tongue Gavin had never known, nor Dazen, either. It was a word not made for human throats. It was the slip that should have given the whole game away.

Gavin had hunted wights, so he remembered. He'd wanted to eliminate all the blue wights in the world. That much made sense, after Sevastian, but he'd not hunted only blues; he'd hunted *every* color. Why?

Had it been simple equanimity? A feeling of duty to all of the Seven Satrapies? But after a while, he'd stopped going so often after certain colors, hadn't he? He'd let local drafters or the Blackguards handle such things, sometimes, unless it was on his way somewhere else. But then he'd still insisted on going alone to others. Totally alone. Sometimes.

They'd always been furious. Orea Pullawr had been furious. Why would he endanger himself like that? Why go alone? Why go alone sometimes but not other times?

Because he had to be alone when he tried to trap an infernal. Because he could protect himself from their malign will, but he couldn't protect anyone who went with him. Anyone who went with him, he might have to kill himself.

It was true.

"No," he said. "I killed for power. I'm the bad guy. I've *always* been the bad guy."

"You've lost a lot of yourself. It's what evil does: it promises an easy way out of one problem at the cost of causing worse ones. But I saw you at the hippodrome."

"The hippodrome? When they put out my eye? You were there?"

"You didn't draft black. And you wanted to. You knew you could."

"Good thing, right? Lucky. It would have killed Karris. And Ironfist. I mean, fuck all the rest of the tens of thousands of people there. Me, I only care about my friends." He bared his teeth, but couldn't make it a smile.

"You did the right thing. And it cost you your eye, but you believed it was going to cost you both your eyes and your life. It did save Karris and Ironfist—but you didn't know it was going to do that. That wasn't why you held back. The world may never know or understand, but that was your greatest moment. Dazen, you laid down your life for people jeering at you and enjoying your torture."

"I was broken. I just couldn't do it again."

"And you didn't use it to kill your father."

"A mistake."

"You despised the pilgrimage, and yet you tried to take it honestly."

"Turns out I'm none too bright," Gavin said.

"Did you find your answer?"

Gavin spluttered a half laugh. "Ha. That would be no. And it would also be plural. Answers. Not just one. A million questions, and no one even here to listen to me whinging."

"No. There's only the one question."

"Really? And that would be...?" Gavin asked.

"Can I show you something?"

"Uh...is that the question? Because I'm pretty sure that wasn't my question. Nope. Not just 'pretty sure.' Sure. Sure, sure."

"Can I show you something?" Orholam repeated, insistent.

"Only if it looks good in black and white," Gavin said. "Maybe with some red thrown in for flavor?"

The old man reached out a gnarled hand, still nearly as callused as it had been when they'd pulled an oar together.

Gavin hesitated for a moment, then took it. How was the old guy going to—

Chapter 118

~How the Simple Confound~
(One year ago.)

"You think you're special, don't you?" Overseer Ysabel says.

"No, Mistress."

"Do you know why you think you're special, Alvaro?"

I've only heard you ask this of half the mirror slaves in the tower. "I don't think I'm special, Mistress. I only wanted to watch the execution. I'll stay out of the way, I promise."

Of any of us, the overseer is the only one who thinks she's special. She claims she was taken into slavery illegally, and maybe it's true. You have to be smart, dextrous, and lucky to get assigned to the big mirrors in the Chromeria's towers. Ysabel isn't smart or dextrous, so we've all decided she must be very, very lucky. Some say she was really pretty when she first arrived. I can't see it. Maybe she's just a good bluffer: Ysabel pretends to be from the lower nobility. She claims her name's Ysabel Elos, and her big brother Gaspar is going to come save her from this life. Any day now.

Any day. Right.

She's been saying that since before my parents sold me into this life after their brewery burned down and they lost everything. It was arson, but good luck convincing a magistrate of that on Big Jasper. Tyreans don't win lawsuits against their Ruthgari competitors. Not here. So my parents signed the forged documents saying I'd been taken in war, and took the meager sum. They figured slavery for one of us was better than starvation for all of us.

I was the smartest and quickest of my siblings, already able to read and good with an abacus. They could get twice as much for me as for any of the others, and I'm the big brother. It's my job to protect the others. I volunteered.

We're all slaves here. Everyone's got a tale of woe. But even slaves look down on liars like Ysabel 'Elos.' She's a petty tyrant. Our work is good and necessary. We bring light into darkness. But Ysabel is a bloody stain on her office, besmirching what should be pure.

She sees it on my face: how I despise her.

She picks up her small cat-o'-nine-tails.

All the other overseers use only unbraided, uncured leather in their cats. It has been decreed by the master of the Chromeria's lands and properties High Lord Carver Black himself, that we not be whipped like common slaves. We're slaves, but we're precious ones. Privileged. We work alongside our manumitted older brothers and sisters who've bought their papers, and came back to work, now paid triple. We've all been educated in optics and angles and even enough magic to understand our drafters' needs and operations. We're highly trained so as to keep all the mechanisms in perfect repair, from clearing lightwells to greasing the gears, and ordering new ones fit to exacting specifications, inspecting, and then replacing them. Most of all, we're the keepers of the precious Great Mirrors themselves, which we polish with vinegar and water and special heavy silk cloths up to eight times every day.

Other lesser slaves are given certain holy days off. They pity us because we take none. They don't understand. Our duty is holy, and it is most important at the holiest times. With the heat and light these mirrors endure, a dirty mirror could shatter on any day, but the risk is doubled on hot, sunny days, and doubled again during executions, such as today, where all the minor mirrors add their full intensity to the sun's own.

Lowly as we are, we direct Orholam's Eye.

Slaves we are, but we're star-keepers. We're not to be beaten like common field hands.

A smack with nine loose, soft cords is allowed to rouse anyone whose attention is wandering. But Carver Black gets furious when anyone damages valuable property, and we are surely some of the Chromeria's most valuable property of all.

But Overseer Ysabel doesn't care. She's boiled her cat-o'-nine-tails hard, and to one of those tails, she's tied an old piece of broken mirror. You might get hit half a dozen times and never get caught with that shard. Or it might get you every time, slashing or even sticking into your flesh before being torn free.

"Execution's starting, Mistress," one of the older men says quickly. Amadis pretends not to even be aware of me, but I know it's an attempted rescue.

The overseer steps toward the edge of the tower, and I'm tempted to charge her back and push her out of the tower. Amadis glances at me and shakes his head.

He's right. I'm no Guile, to get away with such things. They'd put me up on Orholam's Glare myself if I murdered an overseer.

In fact, I might not be the only one to die. Slave rebellions always meet brutal ends.

The overseer comes back. "They're jabbering, like they do. We'll have to be quick. Tunic."

The others go silent. Overseer Ysabel whips a slave's buttocks when she intends to draw blood and doesn't want Carver Black to see it on our bodies afterward. The humiliation is merely a bonus for her.

I do her one better, though. I hitch up my tunic and pull down not just my trousers but also my underclothes. I stick my rear end out at her to let her know my opinion of her.

Gasps go up.

I'm a damned fool.

I know she's going to beat me terribly. Some brighter part of me is shrieking about the stupidity of presenting one's naked underside to a savage woman intent on humiliating me. I will my stones to pull up into my body. Orholam have mercy on the stupid and insane.

"No disrespect, Overseer," I say. It's much too late, though. "You said we were in a hurry. Just wanted to make it easier for you to give me the beating I deserve quickly. And I want to keep my underthings from getting shredded. They're my only pair, and I'm a clumsy hand with stitchery."

Even as I lie, I know it's not very convincing. I can't put my heart into it.

My attitude'll get me killed someday. They've all told me that.

Please not today.

I don't dare turn around to see her face, but my heart is straining with hope that she'll run out of time and that the execution will call her to deal with me later—Maybe I can run away!—when the cat-o'-nine-tails falls.

It's never good . . . but this is not bad. And just the once.

"Do you know why you think you're special?" she asks quietly, and I know we're not even close to finished.

I should stall, but the words escape before I think of it. "Why, Mistress?"

"Because you're an arrogant little shit," she says. She laughs like hell's own gatekeeper.

She whips me harder than I've ever been whipped in my life. My breath leaps from my throat, tears to my eyes. Then again. Forehand and backhand she strikes, as hard as she can.

The mirror slaves are dead silent. Under the fires, I feel my skin slice open. Feel hot liquid pouring down my legs.

"Ow, fuck!" she says. The lashes stop.

I fall to my knees.

When I dare to turn, I see her holding her forearm. She's been hitting me so hard, she hurt herself.

I can't even find thoughts, though. Not even to mock her.

"Mistress, please," Amadis says. "It's enough. There's so much blood. He won't be able to hide it from High Lord Black if you do any more. He'll miss shifts as it is!"

"No, he won't!" Overseer Ysabel shouts. She slaps my face and I crash to the ground.

I hear her cursing when I regain my senses. She's still holding her forearm.

The stupid cow just hit me with the same arm she's injured.

I stay down, weeping. There's no pride left in me to hold back tears.

"Get up! Now! Or it'll be forty more," she barks at me. "Amadis, you take the 'cat'! You get to give the rest of the lashes for your attitude."

He moves slowly, but she knows that game. Every slave knows that game. She kicks him.

I stand as quickly as I can. I hate her. I hate living this life. I've only made it all worse for myself. She'll beat me to death and push me down one of the lightwells. It's happened before.

"Ten more, now, as hard as you can, or I'll double it and you'll get them, too," the overseer says.

Amadis hits me. Hard. I almost fall down. Though he's hit me with the side with no glass so he won't maim me, he's much stronger than the overseer.

I shouldn't hate him for it, but I do.

It's his fault. He stopped me with his warning look. I should've pushed her out of the tower when I had a chance. Better to die than to hold out hope.

He hits me again and I fall.

"Mistress!" one of the older women says. "There's the signal!"

She curses aloud. "Places, everyone, places. On six! And you, Alvaro, get out of here!" she yells at me.

"Five!"

Everyone scatters back to their mirrors, pulling heavy dark spectacles over their eyes. There hasn't been an execution on Orholam's Glare in years. Everyone expects perfection, exact synchrony from the mirrors with steady and precise movements. Anything sloppy not only reflects poorly on all the star-keepers, but could actually end up with innocents down below being killed by the intensity and heat of the sunbeams we focus.

"Four."

I stand, blearily. My underclothes and trousers are still at my ankles. I pull them up. It's agony. I can't help but put a hand on my buttocks. My hand comes away bloody.

"Three!" Then she shouts at me, "Out of the way! Get out of my tower or I'll throw you off!" I'm not really in the way, but I'm near her and her own mirror, which is in pride of place at the east side, and I know I need to get out fast. There's murder in her voice.

"To Position One," she shouts. "On my mark!" She reaches up to grab the big frame at the same time everyone else does.

Then she yelps and lets go, the strain hurting her injured arm. She turns her back, cradling her arm, cursing. Everyone stops, wondering if they should continue without the count.

For an instant, I'm between her and her Great Mirror. The great disk is beautiful. Flawlessly gleaming. It's our holy duty to care for the mirrors. It's our whole reason for being.

"Back to your posts!" she shouts, furious, and at the whipcrack of her voice, scared to draw her ire themselves, everyone turns away.

And for one moment, every back is turned toward me.

I swipe my hand quickly, leaving a trail of blood across her mirror. Then I duck my head and go to the stairs, not daring to turn until I get to the door.

She's back at her place behind her mirror, with an apprentice helping her now.

They didn't see it. They don't know.

"On a two count!" she barks, as if it's their fault that they're starting late.

I hold my breath, certain someone's going to see, someone's going to shout out what I've done.

"Position One," she says. "On my mark!"

The smaller mirrors start turning to gather their beams to send to the Great Mirrors.

"Go!" she says.

My heart swelling with terror, but with triumph, too, I go.

Chapter 119

They slapped manacles on Karris's wrists and hustled her to the lifts. "We don't want to give anyone a chance to do something stupid," Commander Fisk explained to the Lightguard captain. "Karris commands a lot of loyalty around here."

Not everyone could fit on the lift, though, so there was an argument. Fisk was livid. "We're only going down three damn floors. Are you kidding? Every moment we stay here arguing—fine! Just do it!"

Five of the twenty Blackguards got off the lift, muttering, and six Lightguards pushed their way on.

"It was crazy," Fisk said as they finally set the weights. "I was watching his eyes. He went from nothing to pressing the halos in every color. He doesn't have much time left."

"That's nice," Karris said as the lift came to stop on a residential level. "Except that it doesn't seem I do, either."

There were a dozen Lightguards waiting here. Obviously killers. "We need to get on," one of them said. "Prism's orders. You all get off."

Karris wasn't being taken to a cell.

Fisk pushed against the Lightguards in front of him. "Sure. Fine, but can you get the hell out of the way so we can get off?"

As the last to have entered the lift, the Lightguards on the lift had to exit first. Several stepped off before others hesitated.

Fisk clicked his tongue twice, and suddenly Lightguards were flying out of the lift into their murderous compatriots, kicked or thrown out by the Blackguards. Someone threw the counterweights, and the lift dropped like a stone.

Only one of the Lightguards held on to the Blackguard who'd pushed him. He tottered at the edge of the rapidly growing height above the descending lift.

But someone grabbed his arm, and he didn't fall on them.

They slowed the lift, and Karris looked at Fisk.

"You didn't think I was going to side with that little shit, did you?" he asked, unlocking her manacles.

"I…"

"We're with you, Iron White. Blood and bone."

"I know you all loved Gavin, but you don't have to transfer any oath of—"

"We loved Promachos," Fisk said, using Gavin's Blackguard Name. "Still do. But this has got nothing to do with him. We're yours, blood and bone."

"Blood and bone," the others swore.

She compressed her lips tightly and nodded, looking quickly at each, eye to eye. "Thank you. Thank you. All right. We've gotta get off Little Jasper completely," Karris said. "We're not safe as long as—" She cut off as they reached the ground-level grand atrium, and the lift stopped, revealing a semicircle of at least forty Lightguards, all of whom were pointing muskets at the lift.

One of the Blackguards muttered, "That's unfortunate."

Say this about Blackguards: facing death, they still guarded their tongues.

Several hundred people who were sheltering in the grand atrium or who had business with the Chromeria on this fraught day stood watching, confused and then aghast that people they'd thought were on the same side were pointing muskets at one another.

Gill Greyling murmured, "We can take 'em."

Say this about Blackguards, too: facing death, they still never said die.

It made them excellent people not to listen to in certain situations.

A young Lightguard with a brace holding his leg straight and a crutch with a blade along the front edge announced loudly enough for the whole crowd to hear him, "Commander Fisk! I have to say I warned our High Lord Zymun that you would betray him. He wanted to give you a chance. So hard to find loyal commanders for the Blackguard these days. But we do have an admirable replacement. Gentlemen, it's my honor to introduce you to your new Blackguard commander: me. You may call me Commander Aram. Brothers, sisters, all of you, surrender your muskets. Now."

No one moved. The crowd murmured.

"That's an order," Aram growled.

Fisk was tense as a drawn bowstring, but he growled, "Do it." He drew his own pistols, careful not to point them toward the jittery Lightguards. But instead of sliding the pistols to the any of the Lightguards, he slid them hard down one of the gaps between their lines.

You never arm your enemy.

The rest of the Blackguards followed in quick succession, doing the same.

"High Lady," Aram went on, annoyed, "I'm afraid to say that I'm under orders from our new emperor, the High Lord Prism Zymun Guile, to take you into custody on charges of treason."

"Treason?" Commander Fisk said loudly. He wasn't addressing Aram, though. He was speaking to the other Lightguards, and the whole room. "High Lady Karris Guile, treason? Our Iron White is heading out to do battle for us all. She goes to join the Lightbringer himself. Are you telling me you're gonna *murder* her? For that spoiled boy up there? What is he offering you Lightguards? Money? She goes to fulfill prophecy. She goes to save our island, our empire, and our very lives. If she doesn't go, we all die! Hard to spend your bribe money when you're dead. And after you discharge those muskets, consider this: what happens to you?"

"What do you mean what happens to—? Look," Aram said, "we have our orders, and we obey them, unlike—"

"Here's the thing," Commander Fisk said. "We Blackguards are better trained than you are. But the *damnable* thing about muskets is that they wipe out most of the advantage of training. At least for the first volley, especially close up. That works against us today. But it works against you, too."

"Huh?" Aram asked.

A young man in the crowd beyond the Lightguards had picked up one of the Blackguards' discarded pistols. Now, swallowing, he pointed it at Aram.

"I think you should let the Iron White go," he said, his eyes wide, his voice squeaky. He looked like he could hardly believe he'd found such courage in himself. He blinked, then, embarrassed, he cocked the pistol.

In an instant, others were picking up the muskets and pistols near them, as well, and pointing them at the Lightguards.

And then dozens of other people around the atrium produced muskets—with the threat of an invading army, everyone who owned a weapon was carrying it today.

In moments, the semicircle of Lightguards found themselves goggling as they were encircled by civilians and diplomats, bristling with dozens and dozens of muskets.

Chapter 120

Gavin gasped, jerking his hand away from the old man. "What was that? A vision? You're a *will-caster*?" he demanded. "You might have told me! That could've come in handy a few times in the last few years, you know. And what the hell was that? Some slave kid? Mirrors? Why show me—"

The old prophet said nothing.

"Wait, that will-casting *has* come in handy, hasn't it? You've been twisting me to your will for this whole climb, haven't you? Was this all a deception, then? Have I actually seen any of this?"

Orholam sighed. "We know ourselves by how we see ourselves mirrored in others' eyes. So when a man lies habitually, he distorts the mirror he holds up to the world. In fooling others, he loses himself. Those who praise him? Those who love him? He knows they must simply be fools. He hates himself because there's a gap between what he is and what he believes himself to be. If the gap grows too large, it becomes a tear, a schism. A man torn asunder lives in madness. So, my friend, do you know who you are?"

"I'm a guy trapped on a tower in the middle of nowhere with a lunatic."

"You've tried to be the Trickster. It doesn't fit you. So you failed at trickery, and it made you fail at what you *are* made to do, too. Some try to blot themselves out with drug or drink, but you needed stronger stuff. You sought to unmake that which God Himself hath wrought. You used black luxin. You were afraid to be who you are. Ever in front of thousands, you thought you could stand alone, all while you secretly tried to buy redemption on the cheap. It's why you took the pilgrimage seriously, but utterly wrongly."

"Is this about the *blade*?" Gavin asked.

"There are many reasons to make a pilgrimage, but the most common is believing a pilgrimage is a shortcut to redemption. It's also the worst reason to make one. As if one might carry a rock for a while and be finished with pride. Carrying a burden so heavy it hobbles you is a good metaphor for sin, but it's only a metaphor. Confusing the image of a thing with the thing itself is the root of all sorts of trouble."

"Let me guess: life itself is the pilgrimage?" Gavin asked.

But the old prophet hardly slowed. "You Guiles are eagles watching a sunset in a still mountain lake. You dive into it instead of soaring as you were made to do, and flap your wings in the water and curse the world because you can't fly and you find it hard to breathe—and with your splashing you destroy the image of the sky, too."

"Thanks," Gavin said. Asshole. "So if I'm not who I think I am, then who am I?" He was trying to be flippant, but he was too exhausted. The day's long fight had taken it out of him.

"You like to figure things out. Figure it out. Besides, I've already told you."

No, you didn't. "What does this have to do with that slave Alvaro?"

"Who's asking?"

Ugh! God! Gavin *hated* prophets!

Dazen. Dazen hated prophets. Dammit! He still thought of himself as Gavin. Half the time. It was excruciating, holding himself together. "I'm Dazen Guile," he said. His voice came out firmly. A strong, steady statement of fact. Mostly.

"No, you're not."

"Well, shit. A one-in-two chance, and I still blow it. What, then? I'm Gavin indeed?"

"You're asking me?" the old man said. "And you're going to listen?"

"Yes!" Gavin said, exasperated. This was surreal, infuriating. He'd stepped into a circus world, a hall of mirrors. Up was down, left was right, and though he could finally remember everything he'd lost to black luxin, he couldn't even firmly pin down his own name?

Orholam said quietly, "You're not a trickster. You're a protector. You're the one who goes out before his people into battle. Is that enough, or do you need more hints?"

"Promachos?" Gavin asked, but something in him cracked. "That's what Ironfist called me. I come all the way up here just to get my Blackguard name a second time?"

But he was being defensive, holding the prophet off mentally. Stalling. It had felt good when Ironfist called him that. It had felt real, and strong, and true. And that had been a treasure. He'd held off the name then, too, even as he'd craved it. 'I'm not the man you think I am,' he'd told Ironfist. Ironfist had replied, 'Are you not the man I've served these past ten years?' 'I am.' 'Then perhaps, my lord, you're not the man you think you are.'

Orholam went on. "Harrdun saw what you did, for decades, and at Garriston you gave him undeniable evidence, no matter his other feelings about you."

Dazen cocked his head. "At Garriston? What, making Brightwater Wall?"

"No!" Orholam laughed. "That part *infuriated* him, how seemingly effortlessly you could create such a wonder, and how you so easily turned people's hearts to you. I mean at the gate."

"I got his people killed at the gate," Gavin said. "I should've finished it faster."

"You laid down your life for your friends at that gate, and in so doing, you drafted white luxin. He found a piece of it. He wears it still."

"White luxin? Me? That's not—"

"Dazen or Gavin, you have been what you thought you needed to be in order to be Promachos. It's who you are. And you are at your most powerful when you stand for those who have no one to stand for them."

The words smote him like a giant's fist crashing down around him.

But instead of crushing him, he felt his dead heart stir once more, pounding for at least one moment again within its dark and thorny cage—life in him pulsing against the death garrisoned in his body. It was truth, smashing him as painfully as a man pounds a drowned swimmer's chest, breaking ribs to save his life, making him gasp in pain in order to help him breathe at all.

But he knew this was nothing more than one last skirmish in an old, losing war. It was too late. He'd not drowned in water that might be spat out, leaving his lungs clear. He'd drowned in blood. Rivers and seas of it.

And yet...

Tears coursed from his eyes. *Promachos.*

His mind cast back to a thousand times he'd thrown himself into danger to save those who couldn't save themselves. The best times of his life had been when he'd saved others, whether by going after wights, sinking pirates and slavers, killing bandits, stopping the Blood Wars. And the worst times of his life had been the times he'd failed to protect those he'd loved: He'd failed to protect Sevastian. Failed to protect Marissia. Failed to protect Kip. Failed to protect Karris— because he couldn't do it alone. And he'd always been alone.

"I stand for them," Gavin said. "Well...stood."

And then his voice lowered to a low, piteous tone utterly unbefitting the Prism he'd once been. It was the voice of that helpless boy, in an empty, beautiful mansion in a storm, holding the lifeless body of his little brother. With a voice shot through with tears and weakness, he said, "I stood for them. Who stands for me?"

Gavin looked away. He didn't dare see what might be in the old man's eyes now. He couldn't handle pity, and one I-told-you-so and Gavin was going to throw himself off this goddam tower.

He didn't need an answer. When had he given anyone the chance to stand for him? Or even beside him? When had he asked? No, Gavin had wanted to be the big hero, partly from vanity so he'd be *seen* as a hero, and partly from pride that only he could do whatever was required, but also partly from fear at losing whomever he might have asked.

Gavin said, "I failed everyone I love, and I've not loved those who deserve it and needed it. What do I...what do I *do* with that?"

When Orholam didn't answer, Gavin began to lift his gaze to the old prophet, when he saw a tear splash in the blood between them, a momentary pinprick bleaching the red stream. "Love as you are, Dazen. Sometimes a broken mirror serves best."

"Ha! Oh yeah? When?! When bits of it are tied into a cat-o'-nine so it can tear flesh, like with that little shit Alvaro?" Gavin turned away. He couldn't look at Orholam's face. "Besides, I wasn't looking for an answer."

It was a lie, though. Of course he was.

"Your dark night was lived every day in the sun. And was darkest on the brightest day of the year. In the full view of unseeing thousands, you felt alone."

Gavin grunted an assent.

"If only there were someone you could have talked to."

"I had no one."

"I was suggesting you might have talked to Me."

Ha. "I feared if I looked too closely, the whole thing would fall apart."

"It would've," Orholam said.

Gavin blinked. "What do you mean, like maybe afterward I could have put it back together better or something?"

"No. Not alone. But there would've been many willing hands, ready to help."

"If they had a leader maybe. Sevastian."

"No. You. There was always a key role for you to play."

"Right. Whatever."

"I sent others, over the centuries. Some denied the call. Others were killed. Others were seduced, corrupted before they could fulfill their purpose. The sea demons, for example."

"The—wait, what?"

"Lucidonius was to be the Lightbringer. He turned aside. Chose conquest. Sought godhood. And then, in terror of my judgment, he sought immortality. He soul-cast himself into the gentle creature that had been his servant and friend. Lucidonius became the first sea demon. He swims still. All the later ones took their inspiration from him."

He swims still? Gavin's jaw went slack. He'd fought Lucidonius himself: the greatest of the sea demons had smashed the *Golden Mean* onto the reef.

"Wait, wait, wait, how come no one at the Chromeria told me this?" he asked. "I was the Prism. The emperor! I was even promachos for a while!"

"Would *you* tell Gavin Guile how to find immortality, knowing what it would cost everyone else?" the old prophet asked.

My God. That was the real reason Karris Atiriel had created the Blackguard: they guarded the black secret. What had seemed the contradictory goals of guarding his life and ensuring his death weren't opposed at all: they guarded the Prism and his honor—by forcibly marching him to an honorable death, if necessary. As brothers in arms would kill a compatriot drafter out of mercy if she broke the halo, so the Blackguard would kill the Prism before they'd let him become a monster forever. "You're telling me the sea demons are all former Prisms?"

A gentle head shake. "Most were, and all those who remain are, but the magic is *possible* for others."

It was all suddenly too much.

Too much explanation. A prophet might know many hidden things, sure, but *all* of this? So clearly? Plain answers and not a god-damned rhyme in the whole thing?

Gavin took a step back. His throat suddenly felt like a fist had clamped around it.

As if retreating from a snarling dog, pretending his heart wasn't laboring, he staggered to his feet, and stepped back and back.

The old prophet watched him, amused. He didn't pursue him.

That didn't make Gavin feel any better.

There was something sinister in that amusement, wasn't there? Gavin's heart clenched with the old feeling like he was going to die.

He reached the spot he wanted at the edge and craned his neck to look over to the level below him.

Gavin was standing directly above that gap he'd had to leap across before he could climb the final stairs to the tower's top—the gap where he'd left Orholam.

An old man was still down there, directly below Dazen, on his knees, scowling at all the blood. He looked up suddenly. "Gavin?! You're still alive! Hey, is there someone up there with you? I thought I saw someone's back a few—hey, Gavin!"

But Dazen had whipped his head around, startled back from the edge. The doppelgänger was still up here, now standing mere feet away from him, though Dazen hadn't heard him move. It was holding the gun-sword.

A chill shot down Dazen's spine. His breath caught. He took a step backward and felt his heel shift on the empty air beyond the tower's edge.

The doppelgänger poked the gun-sword into the bloody ground and folded his hands atop it as if it were a walking stick and he simply a kindly old man.

Looking between the two copies of the same man, one before him and one below him, Dazen addressed the deceiver on the tower's top with him. "You tricked me! You're not Orholam!"

The old man leaned on the gun-sword. He smiled. "Oh, but I Am."

Chapter 121

"Where the hell'd they go?" Kip said.

He and his men had been bracing for battle with the forty or fifty Lightguards that had been guarding the lift. He'd even come up with a plan to get the jump on them, but it hadn't been a good one. He'd expected to spill blood.

But the thugs were simply gone.

"We, uh, detained them," a soft-looking young nobleman said. He appeared to be the last person who could have done such a thing.

Kip and his men looked at each other. Someone triggered the lift to summon it. They weren't going to slow too much to investigate a mystery right now; they needed to get to the roof.

"The Iron White came. She showed us how," a woman volunteered.

"And Commander Fisk," the first man said. "The stones on that guy! I'm surprised he doesn't have to travel with a wheelbarrow."

Kip lifted an eyebrow and the man fell silent. "They left? Just now?"

He got nods all around.

"They were going to kill her! They were taking her to execute her!" someone said.

"We've got those bastards disarmed and locked in a storage room. Do you want to—"

Kip shook his head as the lift arrived. He didn't want to look a gift horse in the mouth: not having to have a battle with the Lightguards here was a huge boon, but Andross had assumed Commander Fisk would stay at his post upstairs with Zymun. Fisk was supposed to be using those giant stones of his to lead the Blackguard in killing Zymun after he went wight.

I can't exactly be mad that Fisk is saving Karris instead . . . but as a general, I'm furious.

Of course, Andross surely hadn't told Fisk his plan. Andross never told anyone his plans for fear they'd screw them up. So it was Andross's fault. In a battle, there were too many moving parts to manage every detail, too many players acting in extreme ways for even an Andross Guile to predict everything.

There was no one for whom Fisk would leave his post—except for Karris, and only if her life were in danger.

The lift took them up to the penultimate level, where they had to switch lifts to get to the highest level.

Kip's chest felt tight. "You feel it?" he asked as they set the weights.

Nods all around. The dull thrum of the bane could be felt in all of their bones, but that was the next fight. This one was enough for now.

The Mighty were checking their weapons, never mind they'd checked them minutes before.

The lift opened to the Prism's and White's level of the tower. The Mighty and the best of their compatriots presented a hedgehog of muskets, drawn arrows, spears, and crossbow bolts—to an empty foyer.

No one stood at the checkpoint here, or farther down the hallway. It made things infinitely easier for Kip and his people—this hall could be held at the checkpoints by a dozen men with muskets for hours.

Good luck? Kip was so unfamiliar with the creature he didn't dare trust it.

"Superviolets, sub-reds, out!" Big Leo said, suddenly every bit the commander.

Kip, with nothing to do until others finished their work, thought idly, 'Commander Big Leo'?

Huh. That did sound a bit awkward. 'Commander Leonidas'?

Hmm. Maybe so.

If we live.

The superviolets and sub-reds streamed out of the lift, checking for traps. Kip thought again of Teia. Orholam, but it would have been nice to have Teia here. She was so fast, so sharp.

And so absent. Curled up in her darkened room, shivering against the lacrimae sanguinis in her very eyes, hoping it might wear off before it killed her.

They all wanted to be with her, to give her all the comfort and companionship she deserved. Kip had a million things to say, a thousand apologies—but war silenced all.

They motioned an all clear, and Big Leo motioned everyone forward. Kip wasn't allowed to lead, not into what could be an ambush.

They made it all the way to the doors to the roof. What was wrong with the Lightguards? Not even a lookout out here? It was odd to be reminded that the enemy could be poorly led, too. Even at the top, it wasn't always geniuses and masterminds. Sometimes it was just thugs willing to work with the worst kinds of masters. Sometimes it was the amoral, selected primarily for their skills at bootlicking.

Still, no soldiers here didn't mean Kip wasn't going to barge into the middle of a hundred on the other side of these doors.

So the Mighty stacked up at the doors to the roof, forty men. Ferkudi—with no sign of the silly, dopey, spacey Ferkudi he so often lapsed into—was giving rapid hand signals to the warriors in the stack.

For the space of a few heartbeats, Kip saw the young man blurred with the boy he had been. Big, soft, dopey Ferkudi, the butt of all the jokes, the oblivious knucklehead who could oddly do long calculations in his head had turned into this lethal warrior, this leader of men.

And yet he was Ferkudi still. He wasn't one or the other; he was one or the other as the situation demanded.

Kip loved them both.

And he was terrified that he was going to get his friend killed.

But not terrified to inaction.

Kip checked his pistols' load and action and flint and frizzen. No luxin, not now.

Big Leo looked to him. Kip nodded.

The commander gave the tempo with one hand. Took a breath.

Three. Two. Boom!

They charged up the stairs onto the roof, fanning out.

In mere seconds, the forty were on the roof, guns pointed every direction.

There were a mere dozen people on the roof: six Lightguards, who raised their muskets to the sky instantly; two trembling courtiers; two messengers; and two scantily clad young slave women.

No Zymun.

"Where is he?" Kip bellowed into the face of one of the courtiers.

"Sir, I—"

"Where?!"

"He had to...he had to answer the call of nature, sir."

"He broke the halo," one of the women said with a hollow tone. She had the look of one who'd been traumatized by Zymun and was courageously fighting to reclaim herself. "His eyes bled. Sub-red. They took him downstairs."

The courtier looked at her with rage. Advancing on her and lifting a hand, he said, "We were ordered not to—"

Big Leo pummeled the man across the jaw.

The courtier skidded across the ground, unconscious, maybe dead.

Kip turned to Ben-hadad. "Take twenty men. Arrest him or kill him."

"And if they look to fight back? It'll threaten civil war," Ben said.

"That war would end as soon as he's dead," Kip said.

"Got it," Ben said. And left.

Kip realized that his friend was not even going to try to arrest Zymun.

But it just wasn't a priority now.

"Quickly, my lord," someone said.

Kip turned to the enormous crystal that hung suspended between great iron arms, half of its circumference enshrouded in mirrors. Kip grabbed the straps and golden hand grips and beautifully carven sigils of Prisms past and levered himself into place. Others strapped him in.

Just in time.

For roaring over the horizon, already nearing the Jaspers, the first of the lux storms was coming.

Chapter 122

Dazen couldn't claim that he dropped to his knees out of piety, but he certainly dropped to his knees.

There was no denial. The pieces snapped together all too tightly. There was even a certain whimsy to it: Dazen had deceived the world to hide his identity; Orholam had deceived Dazen by hiding His own—and He'd hidden behind His own *real* name.

"I brought you a tribute," Dazen said, motioning to the gun-sword he'd discarded. "I see you found it already. Good handiwork. Shoot an apple clean out of a fool's mouth at forty paces. Farther if you're not on a heaving ship. Or if you're God, I suppose."

He didn't know why he was doing this. Maybe no form of address seemed right, coming from him. Certainly not all the high-priestly benedictions he'd parroted, those rote noises from a liar, who'd believed they were lies every time he'd said them before in his life.

"You call this a tribute?" Orholam asked, patting the blade.

"A certain prophet told me bringing an offering was customary."

"Oh, you're following what's customary now?" Orholam asked.

"Worth a shot...?" Gavin asked. He wanted to stand, but he hadn't the strength for it. Blood swirled around his knees and over the edge. "No pun intended. Gun-sword. Shot. You—" He stopped at Orholam's look. "Right, you probably know what I intend, huh?"

Orholam didn't look amused. "You wouldn't give your garbage to a beggar and expect his gratitude. You threw this away. Should I be grateful for you giving Me your garbage?"

He had him there. "Uh. I dunno. Thought maybe you could use it?"

"You think that to accomplish My will I need an old sword that's lost its edge?"

Dazen said, "Probably not? Wait, are you calling *me* an old sword?"

"Haven't lost your edge, after all."

"Or at least not all my edge," Dazen said.

"Lot of edge up here, if you lose it."

Dazen couldn't help but crack a smile.

Yep. This was it.

Certain proof.

He'd gone mad.

This wasn't how this would go, if it were real. If it were real, there would be 'thee's and 'thou's. There would be ponderous grammar straight out of Doni'el Machos.

Orholam merely studied him in the fading light.

"You know," Gavin said, "I hadn't thought of you having...well, *personality*. No offense. You know what I mean, right? I kinda like you. Despite myself. You oughta come down every once in a while. Mix with the locals."

"That's a great idea. I'll have to consider it." There was a certain flatness to the tone. A little jab at Gavin's honestly giving *suggestions*. To God. As if *God* had never thought of them.

Gavin scowled. "You...you already do? Walk around incognito and all?"

Orholam merely lifted his eyebrows.

"Damn! Er, sorry. Well then, you really should come visit the Chromeria. Sit in on a Spectrum meeting. You'd straighten a few things out real quick, I think."

"Quick? In a committee meeting?"

Dazen laughed aloud. "No, you're right. I can just imagine you floating in, all glowy, trumpets blaring, ready to orate, and Klytos Blue suddenly interjecting, 'Point of order! Has the gentleman in the clouds of glory been granted the floor?'"

They laughed together.

Madness was more fun than it had any right to be.

Then Gavin said, "Comedy must really suck for you, huh? I mean, you've gotta always see the punchline coming, right?"

"It's all in the delivery," Orholam said. He gave a sly grin. "Speaking of which..."

Dazen swallowed. "I'm not gonna like what you say next, am I?"

"No." The joviality was abruptly gone. "You're supposed to deliver a tribute."

"So you were really serious about the garbage thing? Like, the gun-sword doesn't count?" Gavin said. "I mean..."

"Oh, I'm not above using others' garbage. I'll use a stone the builders reject as a cornerstone, but *you* can't give Me as tribute what's garbage *to you*. That's no sacrifice. I'm a healer to healers and a servant to servants, but to kings I'm a king—not a slave."

The last layer of denial fell away as Dazen saw finally the sense of it. He wasn't mad.

Orholam wasn't one simplistic personality. He was vast. One person could only behold so much of Him. Encountering Him was like trying to see a gem the size of the earth itself, made of every color inside and outside the visible spectrum: the human eye and a mortal's mind's eye could only behold so much and so truly. Gavin himself was a wit, funny and kind, but at the end of the day, he was definitely the emperor, and he wouldn't allow anyone to forget it. So Orholam appeared to him thus, a divine mirror, so that Gavin might have some hope of understanding a part of the truth, a corporeal synecdoche: a part standing in for the whole.

"I've got nothing that's a fitting tribute for You," Dazen said. "I'm broken-down trash myself."

"I accept."

"What?"

"You! I accept! With delight! An excellent tribute. None finer."

"Me?! You don't need me. You just said—"

"Does a king need friends?" Orholam asked.

"What? What?" Dazen knew how Gavin would've answered, but he also knew it would be wrong.

"Does a father need his children?" Orholam asked. "Does a mother need the babe in her arms?"

"Of course not. But...yes? Not *need* need, but that's totally different. What are You saying?"

Dazen thought of his own father and what it had done to Andross to think he didn't *need* his children. He thought of his mother, who'd been so broken by her own loss. And he thought of Kip, and what he himself must have done to Kip, thinking the boy didn't *need* need Dazen to stand in as his father.

Dazen said, "I see what You're saying, though it's not exactly an apt meta—"

736 "Perfectly apt. Will you come be My son?"

What?! Dazen couldn't wrap his head around that. It didn't make sense.

But what was perfectly clear was the ruin he'd left everywhere in his wake. He could see in color sharper and more jagged than all his memories. He could remember sliding the dagger home into ribs, over and over, until he was numbed to the deed.

And he'd done it thousands of times. Thousands.

He'd known the Freeing was wrong, and he'd done it anyway.

Gavin knew what he was. Orholam had to know it, too, or he wasn't Orholam.

A wave of self-loathing crested over him, a tide of blood guilt as unending as the blood river coursing past his knees. Gavin didn't deserve acceptance, forgiveness, or anything soft and good, certainly not love, certainly not from Orholam Himself.

He sucked in a breath, and it was heavy with the stench of fresh blood. It was time to end this. "You gave me a chance, before. Not one—hundreds. Every voice that cried out and told me what my conscience had already shouted at me was another. You even put me in chains, but I saw myself as an emperor in chains, but never a slave. I could never see myself as a wretch, wretched as I was. 'I wouldn't give trash even to a beggar,' You said. And You're right. You want me? Fine. I'm yours. But not as a son. I don't deserve that. That's not a punishment. Let me pay for all those deaths with all my remaining life. Let me be Your slave."

"No," Orholam said. "If I wished to rob humans of their will, would the world be so full of trouble? No. Slavery is what happens when men act on their desire to be gods, and slavery shows what kind of gods you'd be. How about a son who strives to be the best son he can be?"

"Then I swear to honor and obey You with all my strength."

"Really?"

"I'm Yours. To spend as You will."

Dazen looked up and saw eyes harder than a hurricane sky. And he was reminded that all the temporal power of even the greatest emperor was but an intimation and premonition of the power and passion he beheld here.

"Accomplish something with me, would You?" Dazen asked.

"Conditions? Already?" Orholam asked, and His voice was soft as stone.

"None except Your nature." Dazen could only pray it was true, that he wasn't as wrong about that as he had been about so much else. With a trembling hand, he touched Orholam's foot.

737

"First, then," Orholam said, "you've brought something detestable into My presence. You cast away nine boon stones to make the leap here, but you kept one."

"What?!"

"Give Me the black boon stone."

Gavin gulped. "Whatever do You mean?"

But he knew what He meant.

Orholam pointed a very pointy finger at Gavin.

No. Not at Gavin. At his *eye*.

Mother Dark herself. The black seed crystal that had become his eye. Orholam wanted *that* for tribute?

"I'm...uh, You don't want that," Gavin said. He swallowed.

"I want you to give it to Me."

"Give me some time and I'll...I'll devise a more fitting gift." He was a coward.

"No, you won't."

"Do You think I'm lying, or that I won't be able to make a fitting gift? On second thought, don't answer that," Gavin said with a weak grin.

But Orholam didn't smile this time. "Is this what your obedience looks like?"

"I'll *die*. Don't You know what You're asking?! I have nothing left— and You'd demand..." But Gavin had fought enough. He was tired.

His hands slumped down into the blood.

Maybe he'd see Sevastian now. Maybe he'd see Karris.

He'd sent Orholam rivers of blood—unasked for, he knew now, as his heart had always known. It was only right that Orholam should demand his own blood in return.

He sighed, and with his breath went out all defensiveness, all hope that he could deceive his way out of this one.

The old Gavin finally, finally breathed his last, and died.

Dazen sank into the stones and bent back his head to stare into eyes that blazed with judgment hotter than the noonday sun.

Orholam was nothing if not fast. He braced Dazen's forehead with a hand, knotting his hair between His fingers to keep his head in place. Dazen could feel the evil eye twist and buck in his skull of its own accord, as if it were a living thing and it knew what was coming—

Then Orholam's hand stabbed into his face, and it felt like his hand went into Dazen's flesh whole, through and into his head.

It clamped down on the eye and wrenched.

Dazen gagged at the pain. Agony shot from eye to brain, down his neck and down his spine, everywhere through his chest and radiating through every limb. As Orholam twisted His clenched fist, as if drawing out a parasitic worm, Dazen's body bucked of its own accord. Every muscle clenched. He gagged, and his hands flew up to fight off his persecutor—

But he willed them be still. He flung his hands out and willed them stay spread as wide as if he were nailed in place.

Something gave within him, tore.

Orholam's fist turned over and over, like He was coiling rope around His hand. At the same time, like a wet cloth to a fevered man, Orholam's other hand was cool on Dazen's forehead. It was the only comfort in a world of suffering.

And then Orholam ripped the thing out of Dazen's left eye socket and threw it on the ground.

Dazen gagged and gasped and coughed, breathing fresh air for the first time in eternity. He sank to his haunches, almost fell—but then his one good eye caught sight of the black Thing.

It twisted on the ground like a legged serpent made entirely of thorns. Every surface was a shard of obsidian, curled in hooks and barbs. And it lived.

Shocked from being torn free and flung down to the ground, it twisted its form together now, at once like a lion crouching to pounce and a snake coiling to strike. Baleful eyes, unblinking, blacker than the gathering night, stared primordial nyxian hatred at Dazen. It had been created to kill him if he removed it, and from his knees, gasping still, breathless, frozen with horror, there was no way Dazen could defend himself before it attacked.

The Thing lunged at his face—

And things happened so fast Dazen could scarcely comprehend them. Orholam flashed suddenly colossal. He was the giant from Dazen's dream, immense beyond belief. And Dazen saw the fury in His sun-bright eyes, and a fist the size of the tower itself came crashing down in judgment.

On his knees, Dazen barely fit between the fingers of the clenched fist as it smote the entire top of the tower.

The tower shook from the concussion. Thunder crashed, but it was thunder beyond mere sound. Every hair stood on end. The air itself shouted with a triumphant yell. Lights fired in every color Dazen remembered and a myriad he didn't know—for one instant, even his color-blinded eye could see. And a shock wave spread out, as great waves rippling in the ocean give an angle to see momentarily into the ocean's depths, for an instant, Dazen could see into the Thousand Worlds as if here his realm and the heavenly realms overlapped. He could see figures, bloodied warriors joining a victory shout.

And then...all was normal once more. That shock wave disappeared into the distance in every direction, ripples in the pond of time, but Dazen still knelt here. Orholam, masked as the old prophet once more, stood again before him, now looking oddly and entirely mundane.

The black Thing, broken now in a hundred places, writhed yet.

And it twisted, relentlessly, toward Dazen.

Orholam stepped forward and crushed its head under His foot.

It squirmed and snapped in its death throes, snapping at His heel, and died.

But Orholam nonchalantly tore away the dead Thing and tossed it off the tower.

He turned and quirked a grin at Dazen, and though every crease remained on old Orholam's face, and His teeth were just as crooked and stained as before—though nothing was changed—every seam of the old man's visage leaked out glory.

Dazen dropped to his face.

The midnight, hungry stone beneath him seemed now merely bright black. The air tasted fresh. The ache in his finger stubs felt somehow clean, a body doing what a body was made to do when it had been injured. His vision, still black and white, somehow seemed crisp.

He was changed, as if he'd been made anew.

"Get up," Orholam said with a voice that seemed to resound with hidden undertones of power. "We've business to finish."

Dazen glanced up, but it was still old man Orholam. "The giant? Was that...?" he asked. As if that were the most pressing question to ask Orholam Himself.

"The same one from your dream? Of course. You've had such a terrible attitude about prophets, so I made you one." He lifted his eyebrows, and Dazen, remembering he'd been told to get up, stood quickly.

"Obedience," Dazen said. "Yeah, not my strong suit."

Orholam looked at him levelly. Right, Orholam knew that.

"What would You have me do, sir?" Dazen asked.

"There's one matter we must attend to first."

"Huh?"

"Traditionally, pilgrims who deliver a boon stone may ask Me a boon."

I get to ask a...what? After all that? After what I just saw?

But his mouth was already running away, unmoored from sense. "Seems like a stupid tradition, though, doesn't it? I mean, 'Here's my pride rock, now gimme stuff'?"

Orholam laughed aloud, and Dazen was struck by the sound. He was actually enjoying Himself, as if talking with Dazen was something that could bring Orholam joy. Absurd! And yet, here it was. "Traditions," Orholam said, "like people, tend to fall short. I work with what I'm given."

He was serious, and suddenly Dazen was baffled.

What could he ask for? How could he *dare* ask more? He'd seen his brother again. He'd been condemned to death and been given back life.

It wasn't that there was nothing he wanted. He thought of them all now: His fingers back. His eye to see again. His powers. His position. More than any of those, he wanted his wife and his son.

He thought of asking for them to survive. He thought of framing some request so broad and precisely legalistic that he might get back everything good and nothing bad from his old life.

He would have done that, too. Old Gavin would have, that man of guile, the master of land ways and sea ways, breaking the rules to win the game.

But here, after what he'd seen, it not only seemed witless to try to gull God Himself, but it seemed breathtakingly ungrateful.

Dazen still wanted it all. He wanted everything good for those he loved even more. His mouth opened to ask for Karris and Kip to live, to thrive, to have all that was good in the world.

But then he stopped as he gazed out toward the great seas and the reef that circled this island. "They suffer?"

He didn't have to clarify. Orholam knew how his mind skipped around and how it focused intently on things others ignored. The One who knew the punchline to every joke knew Dazen spoke of the sea demons, the monsters he could so easily have become, his predecessors in power and in pride and in loss and in striving for what they could not have and what they could not be.

"They've chosen to be separated from Me forever," Orholam said. "That's one of the better descriptions of hell."

Gavin had been a son of separation himself, where delicacies turned to ash in your mouth. It was the land of madness and murder and a life drained of color. It was a life that was worse than death. "Then for my boon, I ask that You cut their punishment short. Or their penance. Or whatever it is. I ask that You release them from this suffering," Dazen said, and he knew that his words were a foolishness beyond understanding. What was wrong with him?

"You think they didn't have a fair chance? That they didn't know what it meant when they made their choices?"

Dazen knew he was being audacious, presumptuous, but this, too, was how he'd been made. "I know that people make choices about eternity before they understand what eternity means. I know I threw away a thousand second chances before I took the last one. I know they probably won't take it, but...what if they do? So for my boon, my lord, I beg that You offer these undeserving one more chance."

Orholam studied him. "You stand broken and powerless, stripped of all you loved, with all your world in the balance, your son and your wife fighting for their very lives, and for your boon you ask clemency for strangers?"

"My wife and son are Yours. If You don't care for them even more than I do, You're not who You say You are. If You're not who You say You are, what use is a boon? But I think You are. My wife and son are loved, by me and by You and by thousands of others. The sea demons..." He thought of them: feeding on light itself but living in darkness, alone, outliving everyone who'd ever loved them, twisted into something hideous by their own choices.

Dazen's heart emptied all at once, like a dam bursting and all his hopes rushing out, like he was doing something disastrous—but right. "The sea demons aren't strangers. They're me."

"O Dazen," Orholam said, and his voice was soft and his eyes were proud. "Here at your end, you are indeed a man after my own heart. So let it be. Come. Your penance awaits."

Chapter 123

Kip flexed his burn-scarred left hand, working the stiffness out of it before taking the intricately engraved golden bar in his grip. It fit like they'd been made for each other.

"Breaker, I don't mean to minimize the challenge you're taking on there," Ferkudi said from the edge of the roof where he was looking out over the Jaspers, "but whatever you're going to do, could you... maybe...you know, start?"

With his free right hand, Kip pulled the mirror array's crystal to rest against his forehead, exactly where the pagans said the third eye resides.

"The bane have all made landfall," Big Leo said from beside

Ferkudi. "Thousands of drafters and wights are swarming from every one of them. We're surrounded."

"Not all the bane. Superviolet's gone," Kip said.

Liv had found her old loyalties were stronger than she'd expected after all. She'd withdrawn from the fight. Thank you, Liv.

He drafted superviolet and put his right hand on the other grip—and suddenly felt his awareness cast out of his body as if he'd been catapulted from himself, far out into the ocean.

"Whoa, whoa! What was that?!" He yanked his hands away from the grips. It had not done that before. It was as if the presence of the bane had somehow charged it up.

Everyone was staring at him, unnerved.

"Not that I'm surprised or anything," he said with a weak smile.

"Boss?" Ferkudi asked.

"No worries," Kip said. "I got this." He checked himself. This wasn't what had happened yesterday, but yesterday he'd practiced using only the barest amount of superviolet and no other colors—knowing that the bane would deny him the use of them. He'd already had so much to learn. The superviolet let him focus the mirrors. Today—dammit, when had he drafted a little bit of blue? Probably just spectral bleed from the superviolet, and this bluer-than-blue beautiful day.

He emptied himself of blue on the nub of hellstone he kept at his belt, then tried again with only superviolet. Now he was simply directing the mirrors as he had yesterday.

Andross had told Kip not to draft on the array, told him drafting with so much power at hand would burn him out in seconds or minutes. He was—irritatingly—surely right. But if Kip drafted not through the array but before he touched it, and then it still worked without frying him, then maybe that was worth exploring.

So he lifted his hand, drafted a bit of blue—and now he could cast his vision wherever he wanted.

He blew out an exasperated breath. Why did he always have to figure things out the hard way? Could no one leave a short instruction book chained to these magical devices?

There was no time to waste, though.

He launched himself back to where Zymun had last focused the array, far out in the sea, but saw nothing there.

Why that bit of the sea? No reason?

Zymun must have kicked the mirror array when they'd hauled him off it after he'd blown his halos.

Kip drew his attention back to Big Jasper.

743

The array snapped into focus instantly, the entire thing lifting him bodily on an articulated arm to point him wherever he willed. This damn thing was one of the wonders of the world. Of course it was: it had been made for the Prisms themselves. Probably it had been made so they could look out for bane.

If he were a Prism, if he could split light and draft as much as he wanted, this battle would be finished in ten minutes.

Did Koios know that? Had the White King attacked *now* because he knew the Chromeria had no Prism to defend the Jaspers, or was he just that lucky?

It didn't matter.

Kip's vision had passed over the armada as he'd brought his will back to the Jaspers, but now he went back. They were bombarding Big Jasper's cannon towers. A gunner stood on deck, linstock in his hand.

A spotlight the size of the gunner's whole body suddenly lit him up as hundreds of mirrors turned toward him. He turned, shocked at the heat, throwing his arm up in front his eyes at the glare.

Kip sharpened the focus convulsively.

A beam of light no thicker than a thumb shot through the man's upraised arm and then out the back of his head.

He dropped, and every part of his head that passed through the beam as he fell was burnt through. His open skull smoked on the deck, and a hissing furrow was carved deep into the sea beyond him.

Kip's self was pulled with it, as tightly focused as the beam itself, plunging into deep waters sizzling and hissing to steam. He pulled back.

Someone was yelling at him, but he realized he'd done the wrong thing.

He didn't have time to kill men one by one. He widened his focus.

In a broad spotlight that encompassed the entire ship, where men were standing agog, a hundred hands put up in front of eyes in the same way the gunner had, Kip found an open barrel of black powder on the deck behind the cannons.

He tightened the beam once more.

The powder keg exploded in his face.

He threw himself back as the explosion overwhelmed him.

His hands came away from the grips and he found himself in his own body once more.

"The storm, Breaker! The lightstorm! Kip!" Ben-hadad was yelling. "Come on, brother!"

"You're back?" Kip asked, blinking. "When did you get back? Did you get Zymun?"

"No," Ben-hadad said. He seemed relieved Kip had finally heard him. "They're regrouping. We think they're going to attack us up here—it doesn't matter. Kip, you gotta do something about the lightstorm."

"Lightstorm? Oh, right!"

Superviolet was so alien, so orderly, and so damned curious that Kip had been working his way from the small-scale applications to the larger ones without even fully realizing it. He'd momentarily lost regular human concern—like for the crackling, seething sapphire tornado streaming upward from the seas around the blue bane.

He turned away from the exploded, burning, sinking ship and moved his will to the skies.

Within the brewing blue lightstorm were tens of thousands of razor-edged crystals of blue luxin. Some smaller, some heavier, different shapes from square caltrops to edged planes to spikes.

It all spoke of a mind that was experimenting. Curious. And new to what it was doing, just as Kip was—but also as sharp as the razor rain itself would be, because this storm was almost ready now. It was ready long before any of the other incipient storms brewing over the other bane.

Kip hadn't willjacked anyone in a long time. It was counted too dangerous to be taught to nunks like he'd been when he'd left the Jaspers. But it had also been one of the first things he'd ever done.

Will-Breaker, they'd joked about him, long ago. And Andross had repeated it, not joking at all.

We'll see about that.

Kip charged at the blue lightstorm with all the bristling fur and snarls and momentum of a turtle-bear. He caught the Mot completely unawares, and blasted her off her feet, scattering her powers completely. He knew her then as Samila Sayeh, the instant his will collided into her and snatched away the reins.

She'd been lifting the entire storm to bring it down on the defenders at the walls. Kip snatched it away and brought it down on the sub-red bane floating next to the blue and on the armada's ships nearby.

Fist-sized blades fell from the sky, cutting the air with a frightful sound, thousands of edged weapons falling unexpectedly from the sky. Bodies were slashed; timbers chipped and exploded under the relentless rain.

The sub-red bane blossomed with fire at each strike. Every sub-red crystal in its surface had to be sealed from the air lest it burn openly. The razor rain cut them open.

Men and drafters and even wights howled at the intensity of the sudden flames. It was too much heat and fire for most of them to redirect away from themselves, so fireworkers though they were, they burned to death.

Their leader, the Anat, lost his concentration. The lightstorm he'd been gathering spun away from his hands; the sealed sub-red crystals he'd been gently wafting upward lest he break them simply escaped.

Kip quickly dropped one hand from the mirror array to suck in a bit of sub-red.

Only then, disengaged from the array, did he hear the clash of arms nearby, the grunts of men fighting, the thud of fists on flesh.

The frame whipped him around in an instant, and he saw that the Lightguards were trying to reclaim the roof. They must have made an unexpected push, because a dozen of them had made it onto the roof.

A Lightguard dove off to one side, where his musket had fallen. All of Kip's men were already engaged, either fighting or trying to block the door once again. The Lightguard scrambled to his feet, right at the edge of the tower, and lifted the musket toward Kip.

Big Leo's chain crashed upward, knocking the musket toward the sky as it discharged, and then wrapping up around the Lightguard's body and head, smashing his arms against his chest.

"Ignore us!" Big Leo shouted as he hauled the man effortlessly into his own waiting elbow with the sound of cracking bones. "Help them!"

And so Kip did.

As fast as his attention shifted, so, too, did Kip's position. The frame snapped around and pointed him back to the sub-red lightstorm.

It hadn't gotten away yet.

Kip snatched it up and flung the mass of delicate crystals down toward the sea and the armada, not daring to throw it toward the red bane, lest the god there redirect it as easily as Kip had.

Then he caught sight of the Anat himself, hands skyward, confused. Kip hadn't even crossed wills with him, merely picked up the storm after he'd let it go from his nerveless fingers.

But now, seeing Anat so exposed, Kip brought the mirrors to bear.

Concentrated light stabbed through the god, and he burst into flames.

He staggered about in the flames in agony and his mouth opened.

He must surely be shrieking, but Kip heard no sound through the array.

One down. Five to go, and then the Wight King himself.

The next ones were going to be harder. They were going to be aware of him coming now, and of what he could do. The Wight King himself was currently too far away, out on his dragon-ship, for the tower to make a burning beam, or Kip would have gone after him right away. But Kip exulted nonetheless.

For the first time, he dared to think he might make it through this, after all.

He could do this. He was *made* for this.

Next!

Chapter 124

"This can't be happening!" Ben-hadad cried from beside the musket-ball-riddled door. "I lost my knee on this stupid roof last time. I am not—"

He spun in and leveled his crossbow directly at the face of a roaring Lightguard charging the door. He was back to the doorframe's shelter before Big Leo even heard the twang or the *thunk* of crossbow bolt hitting face.

The door shook from the force of the Lightguard's falling body.

At the beginning, they'd tried not to use lethal force. They didn't want war—not even with the Lightguards. Not today.

But protecting Breaker was more important. After several of the Lightguards had spilled onto the roof and one attempted to shoot Breaker, all bets were off.

They were doing this damn thing again. But this time, they knew how to flee. They just couldn't.

Musket balls rattled into the door once more. Twelve muskets, right now. Either eleven or twelve had fired, and with their reload speed—

He shouted through the door, "You poor bastards. Fighting us? You're just gonna die! I mean, look at this! Even without us having luxin we outclass you by leagues. You cretins are even terrible shots! My grandmother can shoot better than this." Ben poked his head in front of the hole he'd just shot through to stare at them spitefully. "You don't shoot for the *door*, you morons; you shoot for the *holes* in the door. You know, so you could maybe hit someone?"

He jerked his head away half a heartbeat before the hole splintered once, twice, and again. Other shots thudded into the door.

Ferkudi looked askance at him from the other side of the door-frame. "I think you win it again, Ben."

"What's that?" Ben-hadad asked, drawing his sea-demon-bone crossbow easily. With will, he tightened the string until one dial for each string showed the appropriate tension. He fitted bolts into each channel. Toward the door, he yelled, "That's better! At this rate, you'll be through this door by Sun Day next year. Nicely done!" He poked his head briefly in front of the hole again.

It splintered instantly.

"Someone's onto me," Ben-hadad said appreciatively. He rubbed at a streak of blood a flying splinter had left on his forehead. "Wait, what were you saying, Ferk? What do I win?"

"Stupidest Smart Guy in the Mighty. Are you joking with this? What are you trying to prove, Ben?"

"C'mon, Ferk. It's all part of my cunning plan."

"Cunning plan? To get your head shot off?"

"Nah. The hole wasn't big enough. Didn't want to risk my life to widen it myself. Besides, if they keep shooting at the door, we're not going to have anything to defend here."

"Hole? What?"

"Cover on three?"

Ferkudi nodded, lifting up his blunderbuss. "Two," he said.

Ben-hadad pulled a fist-sized grenado from a pouch, all swirling with red and yellow luxin. He pulled the string to allow the two ingredients to mix.

On one, Ferkudi poked the bell-shaped muzzle of the blunderbuss against one of the holes he'd shot through before. Everyone on the other side took cover as his shot rang out, spraying hot metal into the hallway and their faces.

A moment later, Ben-hadad's large grenado sailed through. He instantly dropped to the ground, not because he was injured but to look through a hole that had been shot low in the door.

There was a shattering as of glass, then a whoosh of fire, then screams. The discharge of a musket.

"Damn, I'm good," Ben-hadad said. He stood up—easily, due to Finer's braces, which he wore on each knee now, though not without pain—and poked his crossbow up the hole. Each string twanged in turn. He rested his back against the doorframe once more and looked over at Ferkudi with a waggle of his eyebrows. "Mmm?" Ben-hadad prompted.

"Let me guess. Two headshots?" Ferkudi said.

"Ooh! Can I play?" Winsen shouted from behind them.

"No!" Commander Big Leo boomed from his position by Breaker.

"How many is that now?" Ben-hadad asked as they both reloaded their weapons.

"I dunno," Ferkudi said.

"What do you mean you don't know? I've been calling them—" Ben-hadad asked.

"No reputable witnesses," Ferkudi said.

"Are you—"

But then they both cut off at a sudden distortion in the air. It passed through both of them as if an enormous wave had passed, bending all reality. For a moment, it was as if they'd been color-blind for all their lives and were suddenly seeing—seeing not just the world but into realms beyond the world.

And then the shock wave passed like a ripple in the pond of time, heading rapidly west.

"Anyone know what that was?" Ferkudi asked.

"No!" Big Leo barked. "Hold the door!"

Chapter 125

The red bane was in disarray. The Dagnu had been intending to attack with Anat, Red with its brother color Sub-red, but with Anat dead, Dagnu now was scattered and stupid with rage. It would take him several more minutes before he could attack.

In the meantime, the orange was launching a storm of pure horror at the island. Shapes congealed and morphed in the very clouds, dropping from the sky toward Big Jasper like the shot from a trebuchet.

Kip drafted a bit of orange to get ready for the combat, forgetting to take his hand from the mirror array first.

In an instant, a burning like brandy gives your throat and gut flashed through his entire body. He'd tried for just a taste of orange; he'd just quaffed a full tankard.

He'd surely burned through a third of his halo.

It left him gasping, nearly gagging.

His hands dropped from the array as he grunted and struggled to breathe. There was musket fire here, the sound of the Mighty, talking, tense but not panicked. He could understand no more than that, so dazed was he from the amount of luxin he'd just burnt himself with. He gasped, huffing. Then, shaking himself like a turtle-bear who'd just taken a blow to the snout and was shocked that anyone would dare such a thing, Kip grabbed the array again and launched himself at the orange bane.

Where are you, Molokh?

It wasn't hard to find. Though shielded from a mirror strike behind the bulk of a castle-like superstructure, Kip could follow the djinn's hold on its lux storm.

Kip hit the Molokh with such righteous fury he could feel the man bowled off his feet. The last thing a slippery orange ever wanted was a direct confrontation—and Kip brought it, screaming all his psychic fury at what the Blood Robes were attempting. His will hit the Molokh with such force, he felt the man's will simply snap. The petty god collapsed, unconscious, broken.

And again, Kip seized a lux storm and threw it down.

Kip split the cloud of nightmare, with the first half of it hitting the reds—who were defenseless against it, especially scattered and emotional as they were. The other half he threw at the yellows.

They liked to believe themselves perfectly balanced between emotion and reason. Now they found out how many of them were only deluding themselves.

This is why the old gods of the nine kingdoms kept to their own lands, Kip thought. They were always the greatest threat to one another. With the orange coursing through him, he could feel the connections between the bane and all their magic, not just the logical ones but the emotional ones as well. He could also hear through the array now.

Oh, you've got to be kidding.

Of course. His time with the cards had prepared him for this: Blue gave sight in the array, just as it did with tapping the cards. Supraviolet gave the structure and logic of the array and of the world itself. Orange had given him smell and a sense of the others in the world. So green would give touch, the sense of embodiment. Yellow would let him hear. Red would be taste; and sub-red pure emotion.

Kip sought Corvan Danavis's command structure at the Great Fountain, and found it immediately. He looked for the figure of the general himself and found his awareness covered three-quarters of the distance between them, and then all of it. He could see Corvan barking directions rapid-fire to one man and then another. He could see the lines on the man's face. But he couldn't hear him.

Opening his awareness the smallest quantum to yellow—which translated to two of the smaller mirrors automatically dropping a yellow lens into their light streams—Kip could suddenly hear Danavis shouting, "—two hours until dark. You have to hold the walls until then. No drafting!"

Touching a bit of every other color brought all his senses together, just as the cards had taught him. He could cast some semblance of his self to any part of the Jaspers almost instantaneously.

Oh, he was going to kick ass now!

Even as he gathered his next attack, he could see that the Wight King must have sent urgent messages out. The bane were changing tack. The great, devastating lightstorms were being dissipated or hurled back out into the seas by the very gods who'd generated them.

They'd finally figured out that Kip would use their greatest weapon against themselves.

He cursed. Maybe he could get one last bane before the lux storms got away.

But as his will jumped through the array once more, he noticed something unexpected. Samila Sayeh was back in the blue bane. She was so damned resilient, she'd returned to the battle immediately, and this time she wouldn't be taken unawares.

Worse, the Sub-red was moving again. What?! The Anat was dead!

Kip had definitely killed the man. His will jumped across the gap, and he could still see the body, but hidden from his line of sight—deliberately, no doubt—there was another will here, taking control. Another Anat. A woman had simply stepped forward into the old one's place, taking up the mantle as easily as one would pick up a crown and settle it on one's head.

There was no telling which of its powers she could use, but at least she could make it move. It seemed that as long as there was a sub-red wight with the will for it, there would be no end to the Anats. Kip would have to kill every last wight here.

No!

What had seemed so easy moments ago suddenly felt impossible. There was no way Kip could kill every single wight attacking Big Jasper. Even Gavin couldn't have done that!

Kip stopped altogether, watching with growing tightness in his throat.

Each bane was an island unto itself, an eighth the size of Big Jasper. They had surrounded Big Jasper and they covered much of its shoreline, the blue bane pressing from Cannon Island to the seawall, sealing West Bay. It glittered like cut sapphires in the sun and crept forward on a million crystalline teeth, each sprouting off its leading edge, being smashed forward by the weight of the bane behind it, and digging in, devouring territory like a hungry mouth. Around a great central tower, great faceted stalagmites sprouted everywhere. At the island's edge, those shards shattered ships and docks, soon to roll over homes and bodies.

The green bane lay in a tentacled mass of vegetation and horror south of the blue, across the wall from the neighborhood of Weasel Rock. The yellow, blinding as it flashed from liquid to solid to light, and the orange bane, dull as an oil slick but just as iridescent and oddly fascinating under the weight of its hexes, were on the south and southeast sides of the island. Red and sub-red together sealed East Bay, making a conflagration that smoked and steamed as it hit the water, bubbling ever forward like lava meeting the sea.

If killing the chief wight of each color didn't stop the bane, what could?

The seed crystals. They had to shatter the seed crystals. They were what empowered the wights to become nearly gods. They were what spawned and controlled the entire magical islands that were the bane.

Kip threw his will toward the green bane now clambering up the very walls with great wet roots like tentacles, shattering rock and burying defenders. He'd barely made it to the surface of the bane when something there knocked him off his feet with incredible force. It seemed to grab at him, sucking him toward it.

Someone—some *thing*—was trying to willjack him.

Kip hit back instantly, but it was like punching a brick wall. He slammed against it again and again, but he felt it clinging to him, clinging to green, pulling him in, in. His mind felt bloodied from his strikes, dazed, and the green's grip on him only strengthened.

He felt probing against his mind, as if yellow were reaching out for him, too, with glee.

Launching himself backward, cutting off green and yellow, Kip snapped back to his own body. He dropped his hands from the array's grips as if they were hot coals.

"What was that?!" Big Leo asked.

"Did you feel it, too?" Kip asked. "Same thing as at Ru, wasn't it?"

"Breaker, there's blood coming from your ears."

Kip touched his ears and looked at the wetness on his fingers. "Just blood," he said. "Not spinal fluid."

Not that bleeding from your ears is good.

"Zymun's here with his drafters!" Ben-hadad called from where he stood beside the door to the roof. The door itself was mere splinters now, held together with every color of luxin, put into some honey-combed pattern Ben-hadad must have made up.

"Stop all your drafting now," Kip commanded. "Something's changed. Their influence is spreading over the islands even now. And move."

In moments, he was going to lose the ability to draft any color at all. So he threw everything he had into doubling and tripling the strength of the barricade Ben-hadad and the others had drafted in front of the door.

Then he turned his will back to Big Jasper. Samila Sayeh was charging up her own tower, halfway to the top, and somehow seemed at war with some unseen figure for control of her own bane-island. She had the blue seed crystal in her hand.

Knowing it might be the last chance he had to draft at all, Kip used the mirror to hurl a spear of sub-red and red interlaced into solid flame at her and the blue bane's central tower.

It felt like he'd walked past a catapult's release lever and nudged it; instead of throwing a stone, it threw every bit of red and sub-red luxin Kip might have been able to draft in forty years, all at once.

But he felt like he'd been kicked just as he released the burning spear.

He was spinning in the array.

For a long moment, Kip held still, gasping. His eyes throbbed. He could tell he'd gone from the occasional drafter of fire to suddenly now straining his halos in both sub-red and red.

"Who grabbed the array!" Kip yelled. "Who spun me?! Who the hell spun me?!"

As his eyes cleared, he looked at the Mighty. They appeared as baffled as he was.

If he hadn't physically been spun, and he hadn't willed himself to spin, then only superviolet hijacking the controls could have done that.

At that moment, something like a shock wave passed over them. Like an immense ocean swell, bending vision, Kip suddenly could see realities overlaid as they'd overlaid the world when he'd been at death's door before.

Without spectacles, he could see superviolet tentacles reaching down from above, withdrawing by the moment, as if caught out. He spun within the array and saw her there: in the air, high above him, floating on an invisible bane, was the woman who'd once been Aliviana Danavis.

Liv.

But she wasn't alone. With her was a creature of immense proportions, masquerading as a small, unctuous thing. It held the superviolet seed crystal.

And now, everywhere Kip looked, he saw them, with every bane. Immortals. This was why the colors were locking down. Koios's most important wights knew some of the bane's powers, but the old gods— the immortals behind the old gods—they knew *all* of their powers.

Now those immortals had come to join the fight.

Kip saw at least one for each color, all of them exposed, momentarily, by the great wave passing over Big Jasper, all of them with alarm etched over their once-beautiful faces, looking east to the source of that wave.

If the superviolet could take control of the mirrors as it had just tried to do, this battle was finished.

Kip brought his will and all the light collected by several thousand mirrors upon the superviolet thing reaching down for him.

The superviolet bane was as subtle and fragile as a shameful secret. It blasted apart under the sledge of Kip's attack like fine porcelain.

But Kip didn't withdraw after one attack. His attention focused hard on that entire floating island of beautiful, breakable crystals. It was like letting the Turtle-Bear off its leash in a crockery shop.

His will burrowed through the superviolet island, leaving trenches of shattered luxin all the way down to the waves, shearing off huge sections that dropped toward the waters. The immortal was recovering from its shock, but seemed leashed to stay within some certain distance of Liv. So it leapt this way and that like a mad dog on a chain.

Until Kip found it, seized it, and with his will like one big paw, he seized the sharp, spiny seed crystal and squeezed it as it twisted snake-like in his grasp.

All the mirrors of the island focused to that one point the size of Turtle-Bear's fist, and the seed crystal blew apart.

The reaction was instantaneous. The entire superviolet island fell to dust.

Liv fell from the sky, and Kip lost her.

That's the goal. That's how we win.

We can do that.

With a mere thought, Kip triggered the escape chains out to Big Jasper and Cannon Island, then he dropped the handles of the array.

"Listen to me," he said to the Mighty as the chains spooled out flawlessly. Karris's repairs were perfect.

They all looked at him. With the door to the roof seemingly impregnable, there was for the moment nothing at all for them to do.

" 'Avoid battle, seek victory,' remember?" Kip asked. He knew they did. "I was doing this all backward. I'm not my father. I'm no Gavin Guile, the Promachos who goes ahead of everyone else and fights alone. I'm Kip Guile, and the only way we can win is if we fight together. I've been raised here for one reason. I don't know if I'm the Lightbringer, but I know I can bring you light." Kip looked every one of them in the eye in turn. "You're going to hate my next orders, but if you don't follow them, everyone on this island is going to die."

Chapter 126

"We don't defend," Karris said, taking weapons from Commander Fisk. "We attack."

No one looked at her like she was insane. Orholam have mercy, but they trusted her.

She thought again about the Lightguards they'd left behind, tied up in a storeroom, guarded by nervous civilians who probably would lose their courage as soon as they lost their Iron White's presence. Part of her had wanted to execute them on the spot, especially their greasy commander, Aram.

The Iron White, murdering a crippled captive?

Forget it, it was done.

As she led her people to the Lily's Stem, she unsealed the adhesive to the eye caps she hadn't worn in a long time and applied them around her eyes. She dispatched messengers to Corvan Danavis, which forced her to go with her gut. She couldn't wait for messages to go back and forth; she had to make a choice now, and let Corvan know what she was going to do.

Her luxiats had dug up everything they could find about the seed crystals and the bane. It hadn't been much, but some ancient writer had taken care to preserve a line revealing that shattering the seed crystals could break the bane when they were small. He or she had guessed that it would work even when they were large.

Karris herself was a red/green bichrome, and she didn't know how much those bane might mess with her if she attacked them—but the blue bane was right here, floating jammed in the strait between Cannon Island and Big Jasper, grinding slowly through as if it had will. It looked like it was trying to move directly onto Little Jasper.

She didn't have anything else to go on.

"Blue! Let's go!" she said.

"High Lady! Wait one moment!" a voice called out behind her.

She spied a man carrying a large satchel, running from the Chromeria toward her. Andross's slave Grinwoody?

"High Lady, please, let me accompany you. Please. I made a promise that I wouldn't leave your side today."

"What? No," Karris said. "What's the promachos doing?"

"He's in the infirmary, High Lady. Deathly ill. I'm afraid he's been poisoned. Before he lost consciousness, he was angry with me for not stopping it. Ordered me to get out of his sight. Demanded I go serve you and get myself killed if I could. I dare not disobey him. I dare not be there when he wakes...if he wakes, Mistress."

Grinwoody looked utterly miserable.

The Order! Karris swore. They were everywhere. Dammit!

Andross wasn't easy to work with, but today was a day when the Chromeria needed all hands to work defending it.

"I trained with the Blackguard," Grinwoody said. "And yes, it was long ago, but I'm not useless in a fight." He opened a satchel and handed out a fortune's worth of lux torches in every color to the Blackguards, and the finest Ilytian pistols. "Please. I owe Gavin a debt. He did me a, a great favor once. Let me fight beside you."

Well, Karris *had* just been thinking how she needed every hand possible to defend the Chromeria. She nodded sharply, not turning from studying the blue bane where it lay in the water. She looked hard at the topography of the thing, its bristling porcupine shards sticking into the air and confusing the eye about the underlying structure, but she could see that it rippled and folded as the structure slowly crawled up and down the hills and valleys of the seabed beneath it.

Blue drafters were already attacking the walls, being answered with small arms and small cannon fire, and being mostly repulsed, though the enemy drafters were less concentrating on the attack and more simply building a series of interlocking ramps for those behind them to follow. When the main attack came, there would be no scaling ladders—the soldiers, drafters, and wights would attack at speed.

The defenders were trying to blow apart that blue luxin as fast as it was drafted, and all the drafters they could hit, too.

And she suddenly had a plan. She was no blue drafter, but she'd always had an affinity for the blue virtues. She knew how blues thought: rational, logical, straight lines.

So she'd be circuitous.

They ran together through Big Jasper at the speed Blackguards run, but she decided to make a stop before they reached the wall. It took two stops instead, and two baffled shopkeepers who initially thought they were looters. Grinwoody, who'd fallen behind on the run, caught back up in the second shop. And though winded, he wasn't exhausted, nor did he complain. Pretty good for an old man.

Then they made it to the walls, to the side of where the main attack was coming. The nearest commander looked delighted at getting Blackguards to reinforce his line, then baffled.

"High Lady?" he asked, stunned to see her here herself.

"I'm not here to help. Not directly," she said. She was already sliding a knife down her tunic, splitting the silk, then tearing it off to expose the mirror armor beneath. The Blackguards had it easier, merely shucking off their tunics and trousers, exposing their own mirror armor beneath.

"Maybe now's a good time to tell us the plan?" Commander Fisk asked.

"We've got Blackguards posted on Cannon Island. We go save them."

"What are the blue cloaks and dresses for?" he asked.

"The blue bane will be our bridge to charge over to Cannon Island."

"They'll see us coming as soon as we cross over the wall," Fisk said.

"Yep."

"They'll know exactly what we're doing."

"Almost," Karris said. "Cannon Island's citadel and guns are a huge prize for whoever holds her. But here's the key: that hill right there makes a valley right behind it where they'll lose sight of us before we climb back up to Cannon Island. When we get into that valley, six of us don the blue clothes as camouflage, and we skirt around the back of the blue bane out of sight. The rest of you go on and save Cannon Island. We go in the opposite direction and stab them in the back."

They immediately froze up. There was one impossibility to her plan. It involved them leaving the White. They were Blackguards.

"No, she's right," Gill Greyling said, speaking up for the first time. "Sometimes the best way to protect your ward is to leave her."

Commander Fisk rapidly picked out six Blackguards—all fast, and rather than picking massive, wide-bodied men, he picked only those with more slender body types, who'd be harder to spot among the forest of blue crystal trees. He made himself the seventh choice.

"Seven?" she asked.

"Lucky number," he said.

As for that, she herself and Grinwoody would actually make it a pagan nine, which might well be the wights' lucky number—but now wasn't the time to quibble.

"Our goal is the seed crystal," Karris told her people in case she died before the job was finished. "Killing the Mot is secondary. When we kill the seed crystal, the entire bane-island will turn to dust. So when you feel that blue crystal go, get ready to swim."

'When,' she'd said, not 'if.'

Chapter 127

"We don't defend," Kip said. "We attack." He was already back in the mirror array. "I'll slave a light to each of you with superviolet. They might not check until too late. You'll maybe get one chance to draft—just one. You reach up with your will, and you'll get lit up with your color, as much as you can use, and all the wights around you will be drowned in the worst colors for them. The bane will react. They'll shut you down within seconds, so only use this as a last resort, and then empty yourself with black or you will die, got it?"

They didn't ask stupid questions.

Kip looked around at them quickly. Dammit, but Kip could really use Teia's skills now. He really could use Cruxer's, too—but there was no time to think about that. You use what you've got.

"Ferkudi," Kip said. Ferkudi was a blue/green bichrome and thus susceptible to control from either of those colors. "Go kill the red bane. The Dagnu wears the seed crystal on a necklace. You kill the god, smash the crystal. The bane will fall apart and everyone'll be able to draft red again."

Big Leo was a sub-red and red. "Big Leo, you go to the blue. There's a squad there that's about to need help badly. Smash the blue seed crystal.

"Winsen, green is yours. Try stealth. The seed crystal's hidden at the top of the highest tree-thing. The Atirat's important, but it's a distant second."

Ben-hadad was a blue/green/yellow polychrome. "Ben, I killed the Molokh, but a new one's stepping up. Destroy the orange seed crystal. Wait—on second thought, orange and sub-red both have new masters. It'll take a few minutes for us to figure out how adept they are with their new powers. You make your own call once you get down to Big Jasper."

"Got it," Ben-hadad said. Of all the Mighty, Kip knew he could trust Ben to figure out the best strategy while weighing his own and the others' capabilities.

Einin was an orange/red/sub-red polychrome, which meant Kip couldn't send his newest Mighty against either of the softer targets. "Einin, you're on yellow. That one might be the most likely to be a one-way trip. You up for that?"

"With all due respect, milord, fuck off. I pull my weight," she said. She didn't raise her voice; she was just done with being the new kid.

Kip said, "Glad to hear it. I'm signaling High General Danavis to give all of you a distraction as soon as possible. May help, may not. I've already signaled for backup from the Cwn y Wawr. They may come, may not. Things are hot down there."

He slaved mirrors to each of them, and a red one to Danavis, too, for good measure.

"This is what we need to do? You're sure?" Big Leo asked. He wanted to fight Kip, wanted to say he should stay by his side, but he also trusted him to lead.

Cruxer would've never left, no matter what. But Cruxer was a pain in the ass.

"It is," Kip said. "Mighty...This is it. We aren't all coming back from this one." They all looked back, unflinching. "I love you bastards. Now, go make Cruxer proud."

They didn't linger. They were warriors. They were veterans. They'd already said everything they'd been able to say to each other, and understood all those things they couldn't say. So now they nodded to one another one last time. Saluted Big Leo. Saluted Kip.

Ferkudi gave hugs, because—well, Ferkudi.

Then they loaded up in turn, and whooshed off the tower toward their targets. Winsen went alone, but the rest of them were followed by whichever of the probationary Mighty were of the appropriate colors and were physically able to go. That left Kip only the nunks and some soldiers who were too wounded to go join the fight.

Kip sent his messages, several times, and then tried to dazzle the 759 enemy wherever he could. He was confined now to using the mirrors for a fraction of their power, but he could still burn wights one at a time, still signal, and still bathe whole groups of wights coming over the walls in their opposite colors to make things difficult for them.

It didn't always stop them even from drafting, but it did confuse them, and it gave Danavis's defenders a small edge, one neighborhood at a time.

Twenty green wights were climbing the wall over at Weasel Rock, climbing, dropping down to the ground, and bouncing up ever higher until they reached the very edge. Kip turned fifty mirrors to send bursts of white light straight into their faces as they pulled over the wall. Blinded, they gave the defenders atop the wall a chance to cut them down.

At East Bay, dozens of red wights with burning hands were hurling fireball after fireball. Kip turned mirrors to flood them with blue.

Fists went up and defenders turned toward the sources—blue drafters. Danavis had stationed blue drafters opposite the red bane, superviolets across from sub-red, red across from the blue, and so forth to minimize the proximity and hopefully the impact of the bane on the drafters.

As those blue drafters started drafting—why were they drafting?! They'd been ordered not to touch blue! But maybe they were just that desperate. Maybe there was something in that neighborhood worth their lives to save.

Kip felt more than saw something emanate from the blue bane toward them—a thousand tendrils of paryl. Those were the strings through which the blue drafters could be paralyzed.

How did the bane do that? What was the mechanism? If Kip could see *how* the bane reached out to control the drafters of their color. He could stop it.

Orholam's balls. Paryl, the master color. Of course. The immortals could use paryl, at least when in conjunction with the bane. He didn't know how it worked, but he didn't have to exactly.

Maybe there was still hope here.

Kip slapped that wave back, ripped it apart with paryl himself.

Then he blinked, blinded from having opened his pupils so wide.

If paryl was half of the answer...

With chi, he could see written in the very bodies of the drafters what colors they used and how much they were holding. He could see through walls.

He sank into the fight.

The situation was desperate—wights and Blood Robe drafters

were pouring over the walls in half a dozen areas, but now Kip had a tool. The blue drafters in East Bay could, for the first time in the battle, actually draft. And they did.

The control began sliding back out of Kip's grasp immediately, and he shot messages in brief flashes of light to the blue drafters—but he knew now that he could do this, at least once, with each of the colors in turn.

It might be enough to make it until sundown.

It might be enough to give the Mighty a chance to kill those things.

Corvan had made no distractions thus far, but Kip himself could be one. Kip would make himself such an inviting target that even the gods would get war-blind.

His senses were burning. His skin was burning. Once before, when he'd sunk the great ship the *Gargantua*, he had been this alive, this focused on everything all at once.

That polychrome over there needed green and yellow, but was about to need blue when he reached that corner. Kip slaved mirrors in those colors to him.

Those red wights were low on their source. Kip flooded them with yet more blue.

Kip put whole neighborhoods under diffuse green.

He fried a Blood Robe marksman's hands as he tried to take a shot at Corvan Danavis from a nearby rooftop.

Kip's eyes felt like he'd not blinked in many minutes. His bones felt hot from chi. This was ruining him, he knew. Already colors felt dangerous, his halos straining. He checked the position of the sun. It was getting close to sunset.

He could make it, probably.

But they had to win this battle today. Because Kip was going to be finished by the time they reached sunset. If the battle stretched into a second day, they'd lose, because Kip wouldn't be there to fight regardless.

There was no time for reflection or regret. Nothing was static on the battlefields of Big Jasper. Already the wights were reacting, and the gods themselves were, too. One tried to willjack Kip in paryl, and he barely slipped away.

Below, Corvan Danavis was moving forces and slipping men through neighborhoods that were disconnected from the battle zones. It was either a mistake based on bad intelligence or a stratagem too subtle for Kip to understand immediately. There were still two major breaches of the walls over—

Suddenly everything went blank.

Weird. An aftereffect of widening his eyes to paryl? He hadn't broken the halo, had he?

No, no, he was sure he hadn't. He wasn't drafting any colors at all now.

They could do this! By Orholam's beard, the wights were drawing back in half a dozen places.

They were going to win this! Or were they being drawn back because the immortals had figured out that the Mighty were attacking them? Kip needed to make sure—

Everything went blank again, and Kip reeled.

Another punch knocked his hands off the controls and he was suddenly back to his own body. Strapped in and taking blows.

He was spun around and walloped in the stomach.

Kip retched, but he didn't look at his attacker; instead, drawn by a familiar voice's yell, he saw a dozen men lock shields and plow into the remaining Mighty nunks on the top of the tower. The injured men tried to push back. They dropped their weapons and pushed, pushed, feet scrambling desperately, but the strength of the Lightguards was too much for them.

The injured men were bulled off the edge of the tower.

The next punch hit Kip hard in the jaw and he crumpled. Men released his limbs from the array and he fell to the ground.

He had trouble focusing his eyes, and his limbs were trembling from the exertions he'd been through, but he looked up and saw the cruel idiot grin on Zymun's face.

There were bodies everywhere. While Kip had been sunken into the array, Zymun's men had taken the tower.

"Looks like you did some good work here," Zymun said, looking out over the islands. "Looks like we're winning!"

"Winning?" Kip asked. "Maybe for the moment, but I have to consolidate our—"

"Everyone," Zymun said to the men around him, "when you're asked, *I* did all this. I'm the savior of the Jaspers. You'll be rewarded for your little white lie. Or you can be skinned alive. Your choice."

"What are you even talking about?" Kip asked. "The Jaspers aren't even close to being saved yet. I need—"

Zymun kicked him in the stomach. "As for this trash," Zymun said. "He attacked me, the Prism."

"Zymun, this is not the time for this! Are you insane?! You're doing this now?"

"That makes him a traitor. We've got enough sun left. Hot day.

But we'll have to move fast. Don't want anyone to get ideas about saving him."

"You have to listen to me," Kip said. "Zymun, you can't do this."

"I can't? Brother, I already am. I'm gonna burn you, Kip, as I've been trying to burn you since I lit the fires at Rekton."

Kip almost went blank with fury, but he came back to himself. "I don't mean *killing me*. I mean you can't handle the mirrors how I can. You can kill me an hour from now, for Orholam's sake. Just wait that long! Let me save the city!"

"I know you're afraid to die. Beg me. Beg me, little Guile."

"Of course I'm afraid, you sheep-swiving shit-for-brains! If you take me off these mirrors, you'll doom us all! How long would it take you to blow your halos? Oh, no. You already have! Zymun, mine are intact, and I'm still working. I'm better at this than you are. I'm the only one who can do this."

The Lightguards were shifting uneasily. But they'd already killed men for Zymun, injured men. They were in too deep to risk disobeying him now.

"If you can do it, I can do it better," Zymun said. "And look, we're already winning. They'll withdraw for sunset."

"Sir," one of the Lightguards said nervously, "maybe we should..."

"Maybe we what?!" Zymun roared, grabbing the man by his lapels. The man was too shocked to do anything, too scared to attack his commander until he realized Zymun was running him toward the edge of the tower. Too late.

Zymun flung the man off the edge and turned immediately, not even watching him fall.

Pointing at Kip, he said, "We do not leave an enemy like *this* holding the biggest weapon in the goddam world. Do you morons understand?"

They understood.

"I, the Prism, will save us personally," Zymun said. "Aram, can you handle a small task for me, or are you going to louse it up like you did the last one?"

"Anything, High Lord Prism. To the death."

"Good. Send our people to seize the towers' Mirror Rooms. Send the rest with us. I want no rescue. And find his wife while you're at it. I'm going to put my brother up on Orholam's Glare. We're gonna watch him burn."

"Yes, my Lord Prism," Aram said, and Kip could feel all the cripple's bitterness seething and bubbling with joy. "Gladly, sir."

Chapter 128

"Why are they being so slow?" Gill Greyling asked. "They can't have missed us, can they?"

Still in the first phase of their plan, they'd crashed into the rear of the blue pagan drafters assaulting Cannon Island—and they were demolishing them. A few of these blue drafters had begun to transition their bodies, making themselves wights by degrees as they incorporated luxin into their skin, over their eyes as lenses to give themselves plentiful blue source, and along their arms or elbows to make spears or scythes or whatever other weapons they could dream up. But none of them seemed like they'd fought against any force tougher than terrified civilians before.

Slow, predictable, and amateurish, they didn't even realize how much danger they were in until Karris's Blackguards had cut through half of them.

Karris wasn't sure if her small force in mirror armor had been assumed to be mere soldiers (not drafters, and thus inconsequentially weak, to the Blood Robes' way of thinking) or if the blues were simply so inflexible. But what she did know was that the fact that the Blood Robes weren't quick to turn around to fight them meant that the Blackguards holding Cannon Island were still alive and holding it.

"Feels like there was some kind of war within blue itself, sir," Tamerah said. She was a blue drafter herself. "But...it's over now. I think we can expect an attack from the center of the island any moment."

"We got this," Commander Fisk said to Karris, though they were still outnumbered by more than two to one—even without the reinforcements coming. "What are you going to do if the seed crystal is at the top of that?" He nodded toward the vast spire in the center of the blue bane reaching toward the sky, higher by the moment.

"Signal us when you take the guns," Karris said. "We might need you to knock it down for us."

"I'll make sure we save enough powder," Commander Fisk said. "Orholam go with you."

It killed them to let her go without them, and it killed her to abandon them just as they were about to be attacked, but Karris and her strike force peeled away, heading into the deepest part of the valley and out of sight. Then they donned blue robes or cloaks or dresses, or whatever they'd taken from the stores to camouflage themselves, securing these around their bodies with whatever was available so that the clothes wouldn't interfere with their fighting. Karris produced the jar of boot black she'd grabbed from the store, and they each dulled their mirror armor in the places where it might flash and give them away through the gaps in their clothing, at their shins, and elsewhere.

Then, after everyone reloaded their discharged muskets, they were off again.

They circled the back of the bane without even seeing anyone, and then charged the center, flitting from great crystalline outcroppings and sapphire forests to empty, gleaming villages of static topaz laid out with straight boulevards of arithmetic precision. It was as if the wights both reviled the natural world and longed for it at the same time, mimicking it in these weird facsimiles.

"Here we go!" Gill said.

Karris hadn't even seen anyone up ahead, but moments later, missiles of blue glass streaked for her head. They shattered and sheared apart on Gill's mirror shield, though she'd ducked, maybe even enough to evade them.

More missiles streaked in, and all life became dodging and deflecting and slicing with her own shield edge and, once, stabbing the shield far off to one side to catch a missile that Gill had turned his back to as he threw a wight to the ground for the kill.

The shock of the missile was greater than she'd expected, and she left her guard open for too long. A blue drafter appeared from nowhere with an ash lance, coming up for her guts.

His head flew half apart as Grinwoody's blunderbuss discharged, but the dead man still completed his step blindly thrusting. But Grinwoody's old training of never assuming a dead man knew he was dead had him already moving in toward the threat. He smashed the butt of the blunderbuss against the lance, sending it safely away, and the dead man took no second step.

There was no thanks. No time for it. Tamerah had been mortally wounded in the clash, blood shooting from her neck, then slowing, slowing, even as her breath did, and the nearest Blackguard took her in his arms, that her last sight would be of one who loved her.

They pressed on. A thousand paces left, and no chance to look to see how many wights and drafters were between them and that great tower.

In the next clash, she raked her scorpion across a blue drafter's belly, opening it with all four claws. She dove under a musket blast.

The man who'd shot at her was dead before she regained her feet. Gill's spinning spear flung blood in a wide circle.

Glancing back, she saw Grinwoody parry too slowly and take a blue spear in his guts—though a formidable warrior, the old man was no longer in his prime. But the luxin spear tip shattered on Grinwoody's mirror armor and merely jabbed the old man with its wood shaft. It was still a blow that drove the wind from the old man's lungs.

Karris lunged with her ataghan, but the wight attacking Grinwoody was a hair too far away. The point of her ataghan barely poked the back of its head, knocking it off-step, but not piercing its skull.

It was enough. Grinwoody stepped into its arms and drove a blade up under its ribs, wrenching the blade around before twisting it away.

Behind him, Rivvyn Shmuel dodged into the path of a monstrously huge blue wight and ran him through with a slender spear, but the wight threw great arms around him, and lifted, then threw layer upon layer of luxin around his waist and legs. Shmuel drew twin daggers and stabbed in a frenzy, over and over, trying to kill it before it could immobilize his arms. Then, as the huge wight fell to its knees, Shmuel calmed and buried one dagger in the base of its skull.

The dying wight went boneless, but Shmuel was bound to it with blue luxin and was dragged to the ground. He disappeared under a half-dozen wights.

Gill and Karris killed the wights atop the Blackguard as he fought them from beneath, but by the time they got them all, Shmuel's throat had already been ripped open. With one hand, he was holding his life's blood in while the other held a dagger drenched in his enemies' blood. But now his grip relaxed, and blood poured out. His eyes dimmed.

Forward again—ever forward—though now with only five Blackguards.

Three hundred paces out now, not far! They sprinted up a rise, not daring to slow to reload muskets, and suddenly found themselves facing a double line of Blood Robe musketeers. More than twenty of them. The front row kneeling, the back row standing, all muskets leveled.

But their officer, facing the Chromeria, gave no order to fire. His eyes were on the tower.

An instant later, Karris and everyone else saw why.

With the speed and dazzling, eye-burning intensity of a falling star, something streaked in a fiery crimson-and-sapphire line from the top of the Prism's Tower to the great blue tower at the center of the bane.

It lasted only one blinding moment, and seemed like it had been jerked away from its low, intended target up and to the side.

Karris found herself tackled, thrown to the side out of the way of the firing line, but the blue officer still gave no orders. The other

Blackguards were cutting into the musketeers' ranks with astonishing speed and efficiency.

Blues were slashed, spun, muskets seized, muskets discharged into others, kneeling men knocked down, stabbed on the ground even as the Blackguard attacked the next and the next.

Twenty-four men, killed by six, in *seconds*.

But Karris was looking back up toward the Prism's Tower, where that incredible magic had come from. Her heart swelled.

Someone was looking out for them. Someone saw, someone cared, someone was trying to save them.

They ran on.

She saw that two great lines now stretched from the top of the Prism's Tower, one to Ebon's Hill and the other to Cannon Island. Small figures were zipping down each one.

So her repairs had worked. Good.

But still, those guys must have balls of steel. Zipping down the escape chains into *this*?

With a spear, Grinwoody moved down the line of falling pagans, stabbing and twisting, stabbing and twisting. He said, "Sure didn't think I'd go out like this."

The others had been taking advantage of the lull to reload.

"What?" Karris asked. Having mounted this rise, they finally had a good view of what was around them in every direction. Behind them, the Blood Robes had caught on to their incursion, and several hundred were chasing to catch up with them. The sides were open, but led nowhere, and would be closed off in minutes.

Between Karris and her goal of the great blue plinth were hundreds and hundreds of blues—*thousands*—with more coming by the moment, called back from the front lines to stop her attack. Against Karris and her six.

Her heart cratered.

The blues were already between her little force and the bane. And the bane itself was sheer-sided, with no helpful steps for her to charge up like the bane at Ru had had.

But...the tower's perfection was marred, not far from the base.

A single line left by that falling-star strike from the Prism's Tower cut across it as if it were a bamboo shoot cut with a sword.

Except dropping blue luxin the width of the sword-cut meant dropping an entire tower's mass onto the crystalline blue luxin beneath it. Luxin that was marvelously strong on one plane but otherwise fragile on others.

A sharp report echoed across the plain of this weird blue island,

and Karris saw cracks race up the tower's face, and slower ones run down from the cut as well.

They shattered into vast crystals the size of whole buildings and fell in many directions, not least toward Karris.

"Oh, shit," Gill said.

She found herself thrown into a crack and buried under a pile of protective bodies just as chunks of razor-sharp blue luxin rained from the sky. Gill threw the shield above them, only to have it ripped away by some blow or from the vast chalky wind of gritty blue dust blasting over them.

A minute later, they stood, binding cloths over their faces so they wouldn't breathe the sharp blue dust. Miraculously, none of them had died, though everyone other than Karris had at least small cuts from flying frostglass. The same could not be said for many hundreds of the enemy. A great portion of the tower had fallen into the bulk of the pagan army. Others had been sliced to ribbons by the sideways-flying shrapnel.

Hundreds more, farther out, couldn't have actually been injured, but they were stunned to immobility, their wills shaken by the cataclysm that had befallen what they'd thought impervious to attack.

Others were slowly recovering, moaning under the blue dust and the rubble.

Karris gave hand signals to advance. The blues might be broken altogether—or they might recover at any moment.

Soon, Gill pointed sharply in one direction and took the lead.

That was right, Gill was almost a blue drafter; he'd barely failed his testing in it, and hadn't tried again, afraid he would be named a polychrome and become too valuable for Blackguard service. He must be feeling something.

They climbed over the rubble of blue luxin shards, sharp enough to cut through a careless boot and the foot inside it. Not a few times, Karris felt more yielding ground beneath her foot, only to find a body, bleeding an all-too-human red into the dust.

But many, many of the wights and drafters were recovering. Far more of them than she would have imagined still seemed to be alive, even here.

Then, suddenly, they were upon *her*.

The Mot was still alive. Crippled and broken, she'd tried to draft luxin wings to glide from the top of her collapsing tower, but she'd been too slow.

Under the ice-blue skin, shimmering in a million facets so that it could move, Karris recognized the woman: Samila Sayeh, one of the legends from the Prisms' War. She'd fought for Gavin at Garriston.

She and her longtime lover Usef Tep, the Purple Bear, Karris thought. Or had they fought on opposite sides?

That was right. Opposite sides during the war, then lovers afterward.

But Samila had fought *for* Gavin.

"Samila?" Karris asked. "You're with them?"

The woman wore a black luxin collar. She tapped it. "Slave," she said with difficulty. And Karris understood. Somehow, Samila had been given the choice to serve Koios or die.

"Red light and blue," Samila said, wincing. Something was wrong with the woman's spine, for sure. But Karris wasn't sure what Samila was talking about. The red and blue stroke from the Prism's Tower that had doomed her?

"He died, you know. My Purple Bear," Samila said. "Usef, left me alone. Not his fault. Irrational to blame him. Irrational to be so angry. But Usef helped me feel passion. Made it acceptable for a lady of my stature and intellect."

She grinned, and suddenly there was something young and mischievous and fierce in her old, cold eyes.

"He loved a big show. Going out with a bang. Iron White, listen!" She suddenly clamped her eyes tightly shut. Then she hissed, "The djinn are real. When they find a powerful drafter who pleases them, like me, like the nine kings of old, they may possess her, trading power for power. Then at the moment of death they *take*—but she doesn't want this broken body. She wants to flee! But she's vulnerable now. You can bar them from this realm forever, maybe from all the Thousand Realms together. But only if you can strike fast, before she escapes my will. Do you have the Blinding Knife? Quickly now, before—"

Her face contorted as if something had just caused her tremendous pain.

"Quickly!" Samila grunted. She gritted her teeth. "The Knife!"

But Karris didn't have it.

And then Samila Sayeh died. And Karris had the terrible feeling that somehow she'd focused all her energies the wrong direction.

Just then a huge young man with a flaming chain in his hands and black armor with the sigil of Kip's Mighty on it came running up. Karris's Blackguards nearly panicked until they recognized him; it was their old compatriot, Big Leo. One of Kip's men now. Behind him came thirty more of Kip's elite drafters.

Big Leo's gear was bloodied, with some of the black lacquer rubbed off his armor from luxin bolts, showing the mirroring beneath it. 769

"Wait," he said. He looked down at Samila Sayeh. His war chain went out, and drooped. "You're all done? You did it without me?"

"Gimme that," Gill Greyling said off to one side. "C'mon!" He snatched a glowing blue stone that Grinwoody was trying to tuck away.

Big Leo looked bereft. "But—but do you know what we had to do to get all the way out here?...And—and I came all this way to..."

"Thanks," Gill said, throwing the blue seed crystal on the ground. He drew a musket and shot it. The glowing crystal blasted apart as if it were just a globe of glass.

"I don't know if you should have done that just—" Grinwoody started to say.

But Karris cut him off, her eyes locked on the horizon between Big and Little Jasper. "What the hell is *that*?"

They all looked. Two fans of flame like wings were jetting into the air at the northern tip of Big Jasper.

"Forget it!" Karris barked. "This island's coming apart! Run! Unless you wanna swim, run!"

Chapter 129

This can't be happening.

There was a veil of surreality over the entire walk. Kip thought he was too smart to get sucked into thinking the same things over and over, swirling 'round and 'round like a ship spinning down Charybdis' maelstrom until it was devoured whole, helpless. Yet here he spun.

He can't get away with this.

This can't be happening.

Someone's gonna step in to stop this any moment now. They've got to.

How can he think he'll get away with this? This isn't happening. This can't be happening.

Part of Kip knew that Zymun *wouldn't* get away with this. His congenital lack of fear was also a lack of sense; it *would* get him killed. Maybe tonight. Maybe tomorrow. With the friends Kip had, and the other desperate actors in this city, Zymun certainly wasn't long for this world.

But he didn't need to be alive tomorrow in order to kill Kip today.

Zymun had the most willing men with guns in the immediate vicinity. Even as one suicidal fanatic with a musket could prevail against the entire Blackguard itself, Zymun was rendering moot all the long-term, careful plans of those more skilled and better trained than he was.

The Chromeria's drafters were locked down now by the bane. Cowed by the shock of being separated from the power that defined them. None of them were going to step forward against the thugs of the Lightguard, not now.

And thus Kip passed through the gates from the Chromeria.

Footstep followed footstep, dozens of Lightguards walking beside him, before him, behind him. One of them had even had the wit to throw a red cloak around Kip's shoulders to hide his bound hands behind his back. Many of those they passed now wouldn't even know Kip was a prisoner.

Everywhere around the walls of the city, the battle continued, even as the sun sank low in the sky. The attention of everyone sane in this city was turned to the walls and to the horrors that lay outside them. Every friend Kip had was off fighting, doing vital work to save the islands.

Zymun, overconfident in victory, wasn't even manning the mirror array.

Orholam's Glare came into view, perched as it was at the base of the Lily's Stem, just on the Big Jasper side of the bridge. There would be no rescue. Kip knew how far away all the people who would come to his aid were now: too far.

I knew this would happen, he thought. I knew I was going to die on this island.

He'd had the temerity to think it would be a heroic death, that he might accomplish something as he died. Hell, he could've died on the mirror array ten minutes ago and counted it a good death. A noble death.

This? A traitor's death on the Glare?

How could anyone find meaning in that?

When the Chromeria used the Glare, they did it at noon. It was a horrible death, burning—but it was done in half a minute. How long would it take Kip to die, with the sun low in the horizon? How much torture would he endure?

And then they arrived. The simple walk was finished without any theatrics, without any attempts at rescue, without anyone even crying out for them to stop—a brisk walk across the Lily's Stem like Kip had made hundreds of times before.

No one even knew.

The Lightguards had found Tisis somewhere, though she was supposed to be on the far side of the city. Maybe she'd come when she saw him on the array. Kip didn't think her presence was a mercy.

He felt pulled away from himself, watching himself walk, watching himself look at his wife.

He didn't know what to say to her. She was going to see him die, like this. She was going to watch him burn to death, rave, shriek. It was not the last view anyone should have of someone they loved.

"You can look away," he said. "When it gets awful."

"You did *not* just say that to me," she said, her voice jagged as hellstone.

"I wanted to see that fire in you. You know, since you're going to see fire in me soon."

She didn't even smile, her face falling. "Goddammit, Kip."

"I always prided myself on being able to do hard things," he said, forcing a little smile. "But you know, I'm not coming to this fresh..."

She was right on the verge of tears, and he was afraid he was, too. He looked away. He'd seen men die by fire. There was no stoicism equal to it. Such a death was never less than ugliness itself.

He said, "Please don't judge me for... for how I go."

"Judge you?" she asked, her voice cracking, and he dared a single glimpse, seeing her tears of loss and rage and impotence streaming down her face. "Never!"

His hands were bound behind his back, so he said, "There's a, uh, card in my pocket. Can you take that out for me?"

The Lightguards let her. Indeed, a couple of the young men—kids really—among them looked sickened by what they were about to do. If there had only been five or six Lightguards, Kip might've been able to turn that to his advantage. But not with forty.

"Can you press it against my forearm?" he asked. "I owe a favor to someone."

She looked at the card. "This asshole? You owe Andross Guile nothing!"

"I owe him our marriage," Kip said simply. He didn't look at her, still. He thought maybe he had enough residual luxin in his body to trigger the card.

She pressed the card to his skin. It slapped down as of its own volition, tap, tap, tap.

He grunted at the flood of Andross's memories. A lifetime passed in a few moments, and then Kip was back. "Hmm. Damn. I was kind of hoping the old man maybe helped construct Orholam's Glare or something and knew a secret way for me to...well, not die. No such luck. No magic way out."

It was really the wrong time to try to comprehend what he'd just seen. But he had duties.

"You tell Andross I Viewed his card. Tell him...tell him my respect for and loathing of him have both grown immensely. He should laugh...I love you," he said. He could see the steps to the platform up ahead. They didn't have any more time. "You have given me one perfect thing. In a life suddenly overfull with blessings, you were the brightest and best gift of all."

He took a quick breath and blinked back the tears.

"Now, go, quickly. I have to maintain this tough-guy façade for a few more minutes."

"Kip," she said quietly, "you will always be a dragon to me."

"Oh, that is adorable," a voice broke in. Zymun. "My little dragon-poo. And what is she? Your little bunny-kins?" He pushed past her. His halos were shattered, and red raged through the whites of his eyes, but either no one noticed or no one dared say anything. "I know I should be up on the array, but I...I just couldn't miss this," Zymun said. "Plus, you do have so many friends. I couldn't bear to have you so far out of my grasp. Good, let's do this! Places, everyone!"

Kip was marched straight up the platform. They started strapping him to the frame.

Facing out, he saw a small crowd gathering. The execution hadn't been announced, and most of the civilians of Big Jasper had taken to cowering in their homes, anyway, but this sudden gathering of people at one of the most important intersections in the city garnered attention.

Kip saw a messenger from Corvan Danavis at the Great Fountain heading toward the Chromeria. She pulled up her horse.

She saw Kip and recognized him, and immediately turned her horse around. She galloped away.

Too late. Even if she cut past all the other messengers coming and going around the high general at the Great Fountain, even if Corvan Danavis himself heard her immediately, even if he had horses waiting and issued the orders immediately—even if he disregarded the fact that attacking the Prism would be treason—Corvan still wouldn't arrive in time.

Kip appreciated that they were trying, though.

The Lightguards cinched the straps tight on his arms and legs.

"Hurry up," Zymun said. "The sun's not far from the horizon. Is it going to be hot enough to kill him?"

"Easily, sir. I mean, it's not gonna turn him to ash, but he'll burn," one of the men strapping Kip in said. "He'll die faster if we remove the colored lenses first, but burn or pop, he'll go all right! Your choice."

Kip felt a sudden reverberation in blue, and Zymun tensed, too. It seemed he and Zymun were the only blue drafters in sight.

Blue suddenly felt free once more.

Big Leo had done it! Damn, and he'd done it fast, too! Holy shit, Big Leo.

Maybe Big Leo could...but no. He was several thousand paces away, and if the bane evaporated in the next minute or three, he was going to be several thousand paces away and *swimming*. And he didn't know Kip was here.

Big Leo wouldn't be coming in time.

Funny thing. Zymun had said, 'You do have so many friends.'

It was true. Kip had no doubt that his friends would drop everything and run for him when they heard about his need.

When had that happened?

Growing up, he'd always been the outsider, the kid scared of being rejected again. And look at this! This life he was leaving? How could the son of a drug-addled prostitute hope for even a day of *this* life? Kip had tasted honey that few in the history of the world had tasted: he'd had meaningful work, and friendship with titans; a great marriage to a strong, good, beautiful woman; and a father who'd been willing to die for him. Kip had had a couple years of a life that old chubby Kip of Rekton would have happily died to have for a single day.

How could he face his death with anything but gratitude?

Yet he was still afraid.

He'd seen immortals coming with the bane when that strange wave had passed. Maybe... "Rea?" he whispered. "Are you here?"

"Of course I'm here!" the immortal, all invisible, said in his ear.

She was weeping.

That meant she couldn't stop this.

"Will you..."—his voice choked—"will you help me be brave? I don't feel very brave right now."

The frame lifted him suddenly into the air.

The mirrors grated on their gears as they began to turn into place.

"Look, and *see*," Rea said.

Kip blinked. It wasn't like looking in paryl or superviolet, but rather more akin to looking through that immense wave that had passed over the Jaspers. It felt like his eyes were only slowly bending into focus, his mortal lenses unaccustomed to seeing this spectrum:

what he was seeing was more real than reality.

First, his eyes fell on the normal people of the crowd gathering around the great intersection. They were weirdly, undeniably themselves but different, as if now he could see the whole self. The outward things, such as their beauty or plainness, their clothing, the shape of this nose or that pallid tone of skin all remained, but faded by comparison: This boy shone with goodness. That nursemaid streamed prayers like incense but more real than drafted luxin as she carried her ward toward his home. Others walked in darkness. A butcher hungered for the spectacle of an execution to fill the dark, empty gnashing of his pain. A fisherman radiated casual cruelty, his hands twisted by violence.

But then, in the gaps between the mortal gawkers, he saw *others*, unencumbered by mortal trappings.

Glassine figures glowed as if lit from above, then slowly resolved into people. People he knew. He saw Luisa Sendina of Rekton, who'd not only fed the addict's boy: serving up compassion in food, but also speaking to him, listening to him despite the chaos of her own five children. He saw sweet Isabel—Orholam have mercy, she'd been a child!

What was going on?

Then he saw Gaspar Elos, the man who'd gone green wight whom Kip had met that night before the burning of Rekton. He was wight no longer. He stood with folded arms and a little smirk on his lips. He moved a finger to his head, as if tipping a hat that he wasn't wearing.

Janus Borig appeared decades younger, but still chewing on a long-stemmed pipe, studying him with a portraitist's intensity. At his gaze meeting hers, she brightened and winked at him. The radiant woman next to her—the Third Eye?—curtsied perfectly in a swirl of golden cloth.

The hulking mass of a shaggy red-bearded man could only be Rónán Arthur, Conn Ruadhán's twin. He put his hand to his heart in salute.

Felia Guile stood at the back, his grandmother, her back ramrod straight, an apologetic half smile on her lips and her eyes bright.

Goss stood next to Gavin Greyling, each in their blacks. They nodded to him: *You got this. You can do it, brother.* And then they snapped to attention, saluting him.

Tremblefist appeared—no, not Tremblefist any longer, *Hanishu*, not in his blacks but in his Old Parian garb, with the frailties and brokenness of life fallen away from his soul. He nodded with fierce approval.

Next was the young commander beside them: Cruxer. Kip felt a flaring of anger at the same time he felt a surge of love and longing and emptiness. Dammit, Cruxer, *dammit.*

But the anger melted. Here was Cruxer purified, his earthly rigidity gone. Lucia—who'd died for Kip, if accidentally—dear Lucia, whom Cruxer had so loved, stood next to him, and they were at peace.

It had taken Kip until now to understand. These were all the people who'd loved him, who'd already gone on before. They'd gathered, a great cloud of witnesses, to stand for him in his final hour. They'd come so that he wouldn't die alone.

And then his eyes fell on one thin woman standing off to one side. Mother.

Once, long ago—though he carried the words as if it were yesterday—she'd said to him, 'You're nothing. You're not special. And if anyone really knew you, they'd hate you as much as I do.'

Mother, how much were you hurting when you said those words? How much did you hate yourself afterward for saying them?

For he knew she had.

For he remembered her, on a different night, sober two days and shaking in her vomit-stained blankets, not for the first time. But this time she'd come to his side when she thought him asleep; she was weeping. She'd touched his cheek with a trembling hand. 'I'm so sorry. I am gonna beat this, and I'll be the mother you deserve. I love you, Kip.'

She'd failed that time, though, as she had before.

But they'd all failed, hadn't they?

Kip could stare at most of them and name a fault, even a crime, but instead he saw them with love, and that changed everything.

"Thank you," he whispered to Rea, to all of them. It was enough.

He could do this, because even if he failed to die well, it didn't matter. Who, out of all the people that mattered, would think less of him?

The moment passed and the vision passed as Kip was ratcheted into place, but the peace clung to him like the smell of smoke after a bonfire.

Zymun didn't order Kip turned upward to face the sky, as they did with traitors and wights to keep them from lashing out at the audience. No, Zymun didn't want to miss the agony on Kip's face, and he obviously wasn't worried that Kip would kill innocents.

The mirrors were all coming into alignment, covered with their cloths, heating up.

"Oh, Kip. Just in case you get any ideas: you make any move to attack me or my men, I kill Tisis. Even if you stop me, my men'll do it. You stop the man with a gun, another's got a knife. Probably went without saying, right? But—"

Suddenly, a fruit seller stepped forward. Kip had never seen the man before in his life. "Lord Guile!" he shouted, interrupting Zymun, who stopped, thinking the man was speaking to him. "No, not you," the man said. "Kip, I have a word for you. A word from the Lord of Lights Himself! I've no idea what it means, but I never do. Orholam says, 'Remember blubber.' "

"What the—? Who is that?" Zymun demanded. "Seize him!"

But the fruit seller ran off, and the Lightguards didn't try very hard to catch him.

Kip started cry-laughing. An *inappropriate* word from Orholam? Only the inappropriate *could* be appropriate for Kip. Andross Guile, the smartest man Kip had ever met, had been unable to conceive of a god who could be both big enough to create all the Thousand Worlds and small enough to care about each living thing on them.

But Andross was wrong. One terrified fruit seller who hadn't dared to be a prophet had proven the smartest man in the world wrong. Orholam saw. Elrahee. Orholam heard. Elishama. Orholam cared. Eliada.

It was as if He were saying, 'Kip, I waste nothing. You fear that you'll scream for mercy? I made you for this yoke. I've already made you so that you won't.'

Blubber can take punishment. Fat kids are tougher than anyone knows, especially themselves.

"Start it now!" Zymun ordered. "Just the colored mirrors. I don't want to wait anymore. Let's see him pop!"

Kip had avoided looking at Tisis. Hadn't thought he could take the sight of softness and care. He should have known better.

Zymun had forced her to her knees, and there was a bright-red handprint across her cheek—he must have slapped her—but though her eyes streamed tears, she stared defiantly, proudly at Kip.

I can't protect her, Orholam. They're gonna kill me, and that leaves her alone with that animal. And with an army coming over the walls. Orholam, I can't do anything for her.

That was the real reason he hadn't dared look at her. He was leaving so much work undone. He was leaving people who counted on him.

Orholam, You are Eliphalet. Save her, please.

For Kip could not. There was only one thing he could do for her now.

He could die well.

He could do that. He could suffer. That was his one great talent, after all.

He met her gaze, and hoped his eyes said all that his lips wished to.

During normal executions on the Glare, the mirrors were covered with black cloth until all the mirrors were in place, but Zymun afforded Kip no such decency and didn't wait until the mirrors got killing-hot.

They seared him instantly.

Kip was already exhausted from his ordeal directing the mirrors. But fat kids know how to take punishment.

Zymun didn't keep Kip covered until all the mirrors were brought into line. He didn't care how executions on the Glare were usually done, or about minimizing the condemned's suffering. He wanted the opposite. As soon as the city's mirrors could be turned, Kip was pummeled with hot light in every color.

Green hit Kip first, tearing his eyes open like a too-large swallow of water—except that the swallowing just wouldn't end. He felt a crack as deep as his bones, taking his breath, stabbing his eyes, and sending shivers down every limb as his halos blew out.

Slivers of luxin exploded out of the white of his eyes, blinding him momentarily. Blood trickled down his face.

Then sub-red burrowed into him like hot coals pressed sizzling through his eyeballs.

It was pain unlike anything he'd ever experienced. When he'd fallen in the fire and burned his left hand, he'd squeezed it convulsively into a fist—but here the fist was his mind itself, crackling, cooking, splitting in the heat like an overcooked sausage.

Breaking the halo shattered the boundaries of his self. He was suddenly connected to all the green around him. The green drafters on the Jaspers felt like beacons; the bane felt like a star come to earth. It was dazzling, it was beautiful, it was insanity itself, and it called to him.

And then he was connected to the sub-reds, and to the red bane.

And then orange hit him.

Yellow.

Superviolet. Each like the blows of a spiked mace cracking his skull, again, again, again. Crushing him.

It was like someone was gagging him, forcing impossibly too much light into his eyes at the same time that someone else brought a sledge down on his fingers, on his wrists, on his knees, his ankles, his groin.

For a drafter, there was only one choice on Orholam's Glare: to not draft and explode from the buildup of luxin, or to draft and be forced to draft more than any human possibly could. Every conversion generated heat.

Converting so much meant burning up.

'Did you cast sub-red, or fire?' Janus Borig had asked him once, oddly intense.

Writhing against his steel bonds, Kip vented fire now in the only safe direction he could, waves of it bursting from the outer edges of his arms and forearms like wings reaching out wide and up into the sky.

But he couldn't vent it all. He was only prolonging things.

"Why is this taking so long?" he heard a distant voice demand.

As he felt his heart convulse in an irregular, belabored beat, too late he figured it out. Puzzles and prophecies. *Remember blubber.* What is it about blubber?

Blubber bounces back.

He was the Turtle-Bear. He was a dragon. He was sitting passive before all these mirrors, acting as if they had no will, acting as if he didn't either, when instead the mirrors were pressing one message in upon him with great force from every direction—one word, one command: die.

He didn't have to be passive. He could fight.

He didn't have the mirror array, but Kip had seen how it worked, and he could draft all the colors it could. He could surely not equal its power, but with the superviolet bane broken, he could mimic its function.

He left alone the mirrors nearest him—the Great Mirrors focused on him—so that Zymun wouldn't think he was attacking, and then Kip shot his will up through the mirrors reflecting killing light into him, and found the mirror array on the Prism's Tower roof, still connected to all the mirrors through superviolet. Manipulating it was like trying to use a spoon to eat, if the spoon's handle were a pace long, but—clumsily—he began to press his will on it, and he began to turn distant mirrors.

The blue bane and the superviolet were defeated, and Kip knew the drafters of each were on Big Jasper—he could feel them.

Kip couldn't attack Zymun without risking the man simply shooting him. But he could help the islands' defenders.

So Kip, flawed mirror that he was, burned for his friends, shooting blue and superviolet light to every corner of Big Jasper, spotlighting friendly drafters so they'd have a source, helping them repel the attacks at the walls. He slaved mirror towers nearest to superviolets to them, arming them for their fight.

And then he had an idea about paryl, the bane the Wight King didn't have.

If he were fast enough, before he died, he could use the master color on the very—

He felt the mirror array snatched away from him, and his will locked with one who stood at the top of the Prism's Tower, and they communicated at the speed of thought, mind to mind.

'You attacked me,' Aliviana Danavis said. But she wasn't Liv now. She was the Ferrilux.

'You attacked me first,' Kip told her.

'I did not! And I am Ferrilux; I cannot lie.'

'Your immortal attacked me through you,' Kip told her.

She hesitated. But it would change nothing, he could see. He'd insulted the goddess of Pride in the worst way possible: he'd handled her. Humiliated her.

'You failed,' she said. 'I left a door open for you to win here, but you missed it. You lose. I won't join you in a loss. Can't. Goodbye, Kip.'

And then she tore away the control of all the mirrors from him, easily.

He threw his will against her, but hers was the will of a goddess now. Superviolet controlled the mirrors, and the superviolet goddess would not let anyone be her master. A Ferrilux does not yield.

Maybe he could have beaten her had he been fresh. Maybe if he'd thought of it instantly. On a good day, his will might be second to no one's. But today wasn't a good day.

He knew Aliviana's will now, felt the sheer scale of it. He couldn't beat her. She had faded far from the young woman who'd half hoped Kip might rise; she'd changed even since she'd made a plan involving the Great Mirrors and repaired and activated them for him. She'd lost interest in that plan now.

He saw then the outlines of it, barely. Superviolet is orderly, and concerned with divining order where others couldn't see it. She had hunted down, visited, and repaired the ancient Great Mirrors in every arc of the Seven Satrapies.

They were the answer to a question Kip hadn't known enough to ask. What were the Great Mirrors for? Communication. Defense. Artillery. Source. But they were also lightwells. Not figuratively, the way the term had come to be used now, meaning 'where the buildings were kept wide apart so the sun could still reach the ground,' but literally: vast repositories of light against the night.

'Give them to me,' Kip pleaded. 'It's not too late.'

'No,' she said. Stern. Simple. Like an experienced mother to a child pleading to stay up far too late. Her mind was made up. Kip simply needed to die so she could get on with other things she needed to do.

The less he fought, the better it would be for everyone.

His strength was fading fast, and hers was implacable. It was like trying to scale a sheer wall that got taller by the moment.

Kip had promised himself he wouldn't scream. A turtle-bear might scream plaintively, wheezing in pain like some pathetic, persecuted fatty.

Dragons don't scream. Dragons don't beg or grovel. Dragons roar.

"MORE LIGHT!" he shouted. He shouted as if all his soul were carried in the sound.

He could feel their shock, their wonder. All but the soulless one.

"How's he still alive? Why aren't these other mirrors on him?" Zymun demanded from somewhere far away, his voice tinny with distance, insignificance.

"High Lord, there was a problem with their filters. You asked for colors only. So we—"

"He's not burning! You promised he'd *burn*! Do it! All of them! Now!"

And though she could have stopped them easily, Kip's onetime friend Liv let them turn the mirrors on him—all of the Jaspers' mirrors. She did more than let them. She helped them.

White light poured over him, into him. Light he couldn't split. He was no Prism.

As he roared, Kip gathered his remaining will and threw light back into the mirrors with all his fading strength.

But with the mirrors locked into place by the goddess herself, each reflecting light from Orholam's Eye straight to Kip, he was only throwing light harmlessly back toward the sun.

It was a ruthlessly closed system, a thousand mirrors each focusing their light to the greatest mirrors, and those focusing those concentrated beams on Kip.

He was burning to death, flames venting out to the sides uncontrollably in great wings. Tears sizzled on his cheeks. He felt the gallium necklace soften and melt on his chest, the chi bane burning another hot point into his skin.

And then something cracked.

Under the heat of Kip's returned onslaught, a single flawed mirror high in the Prism's Tower—its surface blackened and half melted from a past execution—suddenly shattered.

A weak beam of light shot through the broken mirror's empty frame, throwing light out to the east.

It wasn't enough.

Kip couldn't wrest control of the mirrors from the goddess. She was too strong. He'd broken his halo in every color; his will had failed.

He'd failed.

I'm so sorry, friends. He looked at them one last time through the blazing glory of the light, and found, oddly, that he could actually see them. The chi bane touching his chest helped his gaze cut through everything. He gathered up the vision of his wife, his friends, the Chromeria he'd loved, and held them in his eyes.

He wouldn't finish this job.

Unless—

Chi! He could use chi to reach the seven Great Mirrors around the satrapies, and—

But no. It was too late. Ferrilux held the array now.

Besides, he was too weak to throw chi to the ends of the earth.

His strength was at an end, his body shutting off, his talent burnt out, red burning out to black, yellow numbing to cold gray, green winking out, blue dying, and with each turning off, the heat in his body ratcheted ever skyward, his thoughts collapsing, focus dulling, his light dimming.

He thought, too late—far, far too late—that he couldn't split white light—but maybe he could draft it.

And so he could.

It filled him, then, with one last gasp of power, a glorious final breath of life and light and happiness, all flooding too late through his broken limbs and broken talent and broken mind.

His last thought was of that sole, single shattered mirror in the tower—one mirror out of a thousand mirrors, melted and broken and as failed as Kip himself—but pointed, as Kip finally was, in the right direction.

Releasing all else as even his pain grew wan and distant, Kip threw a last gasp toward that broken mirror, throwing white luxin woven through with sustaining chi back into the array. It was a cry into the darkness beyond the horizon, whose answer, if answer there ever was, he would never hear.

And as a single beam escaped, all the thousand mirrors minus one remained in their executioners' stations, functioning perfectly, concentrating the fading light of the setting sun on the condemned, burning him to death.

He sank against his bonds into the burning white of Orholam's Glare, a mighty man with arms outstretched, and his head slumped at last, as his burden overcame him.

Chapter 130

Ferkudi had barely hopped off the little platform that had sped him down the escape chains when a groom shouted to him from the open yard of a nearby smithy. "My lord, do you need a horse?"

After a quick glance around, Ferkudi realized *he* was the 'my lord.' "Yes!" he said belatedly, looking back up the escape chain, where the other blues out of the prospective Mighty were coming. "Five of them! But who said to—why?"

"High General Danavis said, 'Anyone comes down those chains, they'll probably need a good, fast horse.'"

Ferkudi clambered up into the saddle. He loved horses. He and horses understood each other. Two of his five men had already reached ground.

They readied their horses while Ferkudi sat in the saddle, suddenly awkward that he wasn't helping; he was just sitting on his horse like he thought he really was a 'my lord.' He looked up at the next man descending, and noticed the arrows flying up in the air at him. There were reports from muskets, too, but those had been a constant from everywhere. "They shoot at you?" he asked. He hadn't really noticed if they'd shot at him. He'd been watching the whole battle unfold, all the ships and the bane, and the descending sun.

It looked like it was going to be a real pretty sunset tonight.

"Yessir. Used a glove on the line to brake now and then to make myself a tougher target."

They waited together on their horses. The groom held the last two and looked up at Ferkudi.

He blanked, then dug in a pocket for a coin. He offered it to the man.

"Milord!" the man said, scolding. "It's a war. I don't need a gratuity."

"Oh, right, right." Ferkudi tucked the coin away and busied himself with checking his weapons, as if that took his full attention. The twin hand axes were right where they'd been a minute ago, on his back, double-bladed, their hafts slotted to be sword-breakers—which also meant they caught on pretty much everything. The leather gloves with their hellstone studs at the knuckles were also unchanged. He tightened the chin strap of his bear helm...then loosened it. As he'd done before.

He really needed to make a new hole in that strap, halfway between one and the other.

The next new Mighty, Arius, jumped off his platform early, hit the ground, rolled, and hopped up into his saddle instantly. Show-off.

Still. Pretty deft.

Ferkudi heard a curse, and watched with the others as the last of his Mighty slid down the remainder of the escape chain, swaying crazily, barely holding on. Ferkudi was out of his saddle instantly. Caught him.

The man had been hit with several arrows. One under his ribs. One was stuck under his helmet's chin strap and made the skin of his opposite cheek bulge.

There was no way the man should still be alive, but he'd held on. Ferkudi took him in his arms and lay him on the ground.

He whispered praises and a blessing in the man's ear, and when he raised his head, the man's eyes were glassy, unseeing. They left him there, only taking the time to array his limbs somewhat and beg the groom to take care of him.

Then they saddled up and rode, hard.

He had no compunctions about taking four horses out of he didn't know how many. His was the farthest assignment away from the escape-chain disembarkation point. They avoided blockades the defenders had set up, asking questions and cutting through strange narrow alleys, with the sounds of muskets and fighting everywhere growing more intense.

When they reached the wall near Overhill, it became plain how desperate things had gotten here.

"Where the hell's the rest of the Seventh?" Ferkudi asked a poor woman struggling to beat out the sparks that had landed in her family's thatch roof.

The woman slapped a sopping-wet dress against the spreading flames. "Half those bastards took some nobles' coin to defend the walls near their own houses up south. Commander here done nothing to stop 'em when they left."

Without a word, Ferkudi spurred his horse onward.

At the wall, he leapt out of the saddle and slapped the stallion's flank. "Good boy!"

No need for him to die, too.

As he mounted the wall without so much as being challenged once, he saw the wan terror on the defenders' faces. He knew this music here. This was what people look like right before they break.

He reached the top of the wall with his Mighty hard behind him.

A hellscape greeted him.

The red bane was a charred landscape that broke open in red seams everywhere it folded over, some of them afire, the rest ever threatening to take fire. The whole seemed to have the rigidity of a beached jellyfish that somehow yet moved, oozing up the shoreline toward the wall.

One of the Mighty said, "How do we invade *that*?"

Thousands of drafters and wights were surging from its surface toward the walls.

From the Prism's Tower, Ferkudi had seen how Kip had set this whole bane afire by throwing the sub-red lux storm against it. From the charred bodies, it was clear that hundreds and hundreds of the enemy had died in that attack—but there were still so many more, and while the mundane soldiers had died in droves, the drafters and the wights had survived.

Now, whatever the reds' original plan had been, they attacked without any discernible plan at all—and they attacked with rage to spare. They had no siege engines, no siege ladders, instead merely throwing themselves against the walls and using red luxin to clamber and stick and boost themselves as well as they could. It was stupidly inefficient, even insane, as the Chromeria always said.

But the numbers were on their side, and as fast as the few defenders atop the wall could pick them off with arrows and musket balls, still the rest climbed faster, heedless of their own dead, heedless of all but rage.

"We wait for our chance," Ferkudi said. "Corvan Danavis is gonna give us a distraction. Maybe that'll be it."

"And until then?"

Some of the attackers had torn up still-burning trees and had flung them against the walls as makeshift ladders. The defenders couldn't dislodge them.

"Until then we keep these poor bastards alive. We defend the wall," Ferkudi said, hopping up and sprinting. His men ran hot on his heels along the top of the wall. They were spotted instantly, and soon missiles spitting flames were crackling past their heads.

They rammed into a tree and hurled it back from the wall, astonishing the scrawny defenders—surely the worst of the city's worst—who'd been unable to move it at all.

But it wasn't enough. Somewhere a hundred paces down some reds burst into view on top of the wall and lit into terrified defenders.

Ferkudi and his men cut through those fleeing.

His axes sent limbs spinning. As each of his axes got stuck—one in a Blood Robe's shoulder joint and the other pinched between a screaming wight's ribs—a wight popped into view over the top of the wall, and Ferkudi butted his bear helm into the thing's face, sending it flying off the wall.

The next minutes passed in that odd blur of fighting—every moment lasting an eternity and every minute gone in a blink.

The reds reached the top of the wall in new places every minute, and Ferkudi spread his Mighty out. Most of the other defenders had disappeared, which at first Ferkudi thought was good—no one in his way as he ran back and forth.

Then he realized how bad it was.

One of his Mighty, Arius, went down with a leg wound. The nearest man, Amastan, flashed hand signals: Arius would live, but he'd fight no more today.

And then, inattentive for a moment while he tied a tourniquet around Arius's bloody leg, Amastan took a spear through his armpit. Dying, Amastan clawed a pistol from the bag at his hip and handed it to the wounded Arius, even as he used his other hand to hold the spear piercing him in place. From his back, Arius shot the pagan drafter in the face, and they all collapsed on him.

Suddenly, the wall felt very, very empty.

Screaming defiance, Ferkudi reached up with his will and triggered the mirrors. He was flooded with blue light from a half-dozen directions in the waning light of the day. He jumped up on the battlements and bellowed his challenge at the Blood Robes below.

It drove them mad. Drafters who'd been unstoppably far to one side for Ferkudi to possibly fight abandoned attacking where they were and came to join the horde directly in front of him. They climbed over one another, crushing each other, making a ramp of their very bodies, heedless of everything except trying to kill him.

He hurled blue-luxin javelins into them. He broke reaching arms. He smashed faces with his knees and with his hellstone-knuckled fists. He carved great crimson wounds into their crimson bodies. Split heads with his glittering hand axes. Smashed once-men into each other. Extinguished flaming wights with blunderbuss gusts of blue luxin. Picked up wights and hurled them bodily from the walls.

But what he completely forgot was to let go of blue.

It should have helped him remember, blue should have, rational as it was.

But even blue can't overcome the full grip of battle fury.

He didn't remember the danger until he felt something twisting around his very will. It froze him, and locked up all the luxin in his body.

He couldn't move. He stood with a Blood Robe's chin in one hand, a fistful of his hair in the other, broken-necked. The dying man dropped from Ferkudi's grip, almost taking him down with him. Better that he had. Now Ferkudi was exposed at the top of the wall, defenseless, hands extending, muscles straining against the empty air, his inchoate yell the only thing that could escape.

A red wight hopped up to the top of the wall a few paces away. His hair was slicked back to his head with white, fire-retardant gel and, uncommonly for a red wight, this man had no fresh burns or burn-scars whatsoever on his half-naked body, over which red danced and flickered. A *careful* red wight.

He balled fire in his hand, even as others mounted the wall and coiled to unleash it in Ferkudi's face, when something dark and soft hit him from below. A wet cloth?

Ferkudi couldn't even move to see where it came from. The wight threw down the wet dress—and was pierced through the ribs by a spear.

An instant later, he realized that the roaring of blood in his ears had been joined by another roar, and he heard impacts around him, saw bricks flung from inside the city pelting the Blood Robes taking the wall, and then hundreds of men streamed into view. The woman he'd seen beating at her flaming thatched roof with that wet dress pulled the spear from the wounded wight's ribs and stabbed him with it again and again.

Then she stood, looking for Ferkudi's approval. She looked scared and exhilarated, and her grip on the spear was all wrong.

Ferkudi noticed others claiming the top of the wall now, too: men in tradesman's caftans, women in burnouses. They'd picked up the weapons dropped by the fleeing soldiers, and now suddenly even the soldiers were returning.

And Ferkudi was at the heart of it all. He was the frozen heart of it all.

They rallied around him, saving him, and saving themselves and their own homes.

But Ferkudi felt the blue twisting deeper into him, vengeful, seeking to still his very heart, his lungs. Breathing became slower, slower, and panic rose in him.

And then it snapped.

Mot's hold on blue was dropped, and Ferkudi fell.

"What was that?!" Arius asked. The people had carried the wounded Mighty to be together so that they could be protected together.

Ferkudi lay gasping, and slowly felt sensation and control returning to his limbs.

And then Mot seemed to wink out of existence altogether, and the blue was truly free.

"The blue bane is broken," Arius said, and a big crooked-toothed smile lit his dark face.

"Good, good," Ferkudi said, pushing himself to his feet, his legs trembling. "Now we can attack."

"What?" Arius asked.

Ferkudi took a step. His leg folded and he caught himself on the edge of the wall. He picked up one of his hand axes from a Blood Robe's split skull. Had he *thrown* this ax? That never worked! And then he found his other one, stuck where it had split another drafter's mouth. Yuck. The guy wasn't dead, either.

Ferkudi slashed the man's throat and gave him a moment to die before retrieving that one. "Where's Itri? Where's Yuften?" he asked. "We gotta go. We got orders!"

"Itri got burned. Bad. They gave him poppy wine. He's out, but... we're gonna have to give him the black mercy. Yuften's got a broken arm."

"It's my off hand! I can fight!" Yuften said, limping into sight. Apparently the broken arm wasn't his only wound. "I'm with you, sir! To the end!"

"Are *you* hurt?" Arius asked.

Ferkudi checked himself. There was a lot of blood on him, but none of it seemed to be his. He'd had some hair singed off—that's right, now he remembered extinguishing the flames with blue. He was sore in a dozen places and knew that by tomorrow that would expand to a hundred. But he didn't seem to be injured, just exhausted with the bone-deep weariness and the shakes that come every time after the terror and thrill and total muscular exertion of a battle. And Ferkudi had never fought so hard or so long in his life.

He sucked down some watered wine from a skin someone put in his hand, and watched the red drafters and wights falling back.

"Shit," he said at a sudden thought. It could be mere exhaustion and lightsickness. But maybe it was more. "How are my halos?"

Arius looked at him. "Strained to the absolute limits, sir."

"But not broken?"

Yuften said, "Wouldn't lie to you, sir."

So merely exhausted, lightsick, and half-dead. It didn't make Ferkudi feel better. Nor did the adoring looks in all the people's eyes—even the woman who'd saved his life.

"We have our orders," he said plaintively. He looked at the people and the few soldiers standing atop the wall, all jubilant at their victory. They were already talking of what they'd done, sharing stories and asking each other if they'd seen some dragon's wings or fire wings or something down north on the island, and something about a beam of white light like Orholam's finger stretching across the sky. (Ferkudi did remember a white light, briefly, there at the end.) They were all thrilled with themselves—but they weren't proper soldiers. These were people defending their homes. They wouldn't leave this wall to go charging across that hellscape out there, not even if led by Ferkudi.

And if they did? They'd be massacred in the first counterattack.

The people had rallied. Ferkudi had saved the wall at its weakest spot...but he'd saved nothing else. He'd spent the last, best portion of his life's strength on this fight, and he'd changed nothing. The red bane remained. Dagnu still ruled it, and the seed crystal was intact.

They'd be back tomorrow at first light, and Ferkudi wouldn't be able to stop them.

'Avoid battle, seek victory,' Breaker always said. Ferkudi had gotten caught up in a battle instead, and he'd won it. But he'd guaranteed the Blood Robes would win the next battle, tomorrow.

He sank down, and sat on a ledge. He didn't even have the strength to stand now.

He'd had his orders, and he'd failed.

Chapter 131

"You're a tenacious little bastard," Karris said. She'd regained her breath from the run, and had been in the only group that made it off the blue bane before it dissolved and dropped everything and everyone on it into the waves.

"I accept the compliment," Grinwoody said, hands on his knees, dripping water, chest heaving.

She hadn't been waiting for him—not specifically—but she had needed to re-form her forces here, just outside the city walls. Half of her people had been dropped into the water, and not a few of those in water deep enough to drown men wearing armor. She'd sent her good swimmers to save those they could while she did the necessary work of cataloging the wounded, gathering weapons and armor, and coordinating the attack on the yellow bane.

Destroying them *all* was the only route to victory. Even if she didn't have much hope of it.

The wall's defenders had lowered ladders for them, and now she climbed up to start sending the necessary messages, but first, she grabbed an officer's long-lens to see what she could of the Jaspers situation.

Her Mighty were cleaning up the stunned blue wights and drafters on Cannon Island. Good, as far as it went, but with the blue bane dissolved, her people were marooned out there, useless to her for at least another hour.

She turned the lens toward the green bane, her next target. The officer's long-lens wasn't very good, but she thought she saw—yes, another. A green wight fell, seemingly at random. The drafters under his control stared at one another, baffled. Karris couldn't see why, either; then, when the Blood Robes were looking the other way, she saw a small form pop up out of the vegetation covering the forestlike surface of the green bane.

The archer sprinted forward a few steps, bow in hand, then dove down out of view again. He was running toward the great central tree-thing that dominated the middle of the green bane.

He popped up again, and she saw him loose an arrow, but couldn't see any target anywhere in bow range of him. Then she saw an enraged giant grizzly burst from a cage the greens had been keeping it in, surely more than three hundred paces away from the figure. It stood on its hind legs and roared as greens scattered. The giant grizzly went berserk, but Karris was already looking for the little archer: Winsen, she saw now. She was sure of it.

Winsen was attacking the green bane—by himself.

Madness. But she was too far away to do anything for him.

She slewed the long-lens to the yellow bane, overshot and saw the Great Fountain.

No, no, no! It was being attacked.

She put the lens down, and turned to shout to her people to move immediately, when a messenger from Corvan came galloping in. Several other messengers were already waiting for Karris, but he practically rode over the top of them.

790   "High Lady White!" he shouted. "Urgent message from High

General Danavis: Good work stopping blue! Forces have breached the walls in three places we know and are assailing the command post at the Great Fountain now. We can hold. Don't reinforce us. At least one platoon of the White King's best has been tasked with finding and killing you personally. Don't go to green next. Go to Orholam's Glare. Now!"

"What's at Orholam's Glare?" Karris asked, hardly able to absorb all the bad news. Then she noticed the Thousand Stars. All of the city's mirrors were pointed exactly where they would be for an execution.

What?!

"Have you not seen the great wings of fire?" one of the other messengers asked, turning to point.

But just then, an incredible beam of incandescent white light leapt from somewhere on Big Jasper's north shore up to the Great Mirrors (Orholam's Glare?) and out to the east. The beam was the width of a man's spread arms, with a mass, a weight, to it. It was whiter than white, like mother-of-pearl and ivory lit from within.

Karris had seen something like this, just once, at Garriston—and that, drafted by Gavin himself, was but a candle to this inferno. She had no question now what it was: white luxin.

But no one could draft that much.

No one could draft that much—and live.

And then it stopped.

Who could possibly draft so...?

Oh, God.

*　　*　　*

"So it's too late," Dazen said as the sun set and the darkness gathered. Orholam had just told him of the battle being waged and lost beyond the horizon. Of Kip strapped in, being executed. Of Karris being hunted by her own merciless brother.

Here, in Orholam's own presence, it was perhaps impossible to feel fully hopeless, but Dazen felt an emptiness vast as the space between him and those he wished he could rush in to save. It's what he would have done, before.

Now he was a shell of that man. Clean, perhaps now. But broken. Useless. The consequences of his choices lying before his eyes.

"Too late?" Orholam asked. "What do I look like? A broken-down old oar-puller?"

"Please don't try to cheer me up."

"You'll need this later," Orholam said. He stepped away from the gun-sword He'd been leaning on. Somehow, its tip had sunk deep into the marble of the black roof they stood on.

" 'Later'?! Is that a joke? There *is* no later! The sun's down!" Kip was dying. Karris was dead, or would be any moment—and there was nothing he could do to save them. Dazen swept his hand out in the direction of the Chromeria as the last light died. "It's all darkness now! Look!"

Just as Dazen's hand waved to the dark hopelessness of the dead horizon, a wide beam of white light shot out squarely at him from exactly where the Chromeria must be.

Its brilliance nearly blinded him. It was so intense there was a physical weight to it. It almost knocked him off his feet. Merely standing in its path felt like sucking in a great gasping breath after being submerged in a lake for far too long. It was pure, unsealed white luxin, a torrent, like someone had pumped the crank of a well and hope and courage and life shot forth, one time—then stopped.

And it was gone.

"What was that!?" Dazen breathed.

"That was Kip. Fighting. Dying." A tear rolled down each of Orholam's cheeks, but He seemed proud of Kip, even in His sorrow. "That was your answer."

"To what?"

"The only question."

"Why?" Dazen asked, weeping.

"Yes. Why all your suffering? Why Alvaro's? Why Kip's?" Orholam said.

Dazen wept harder. "It was his cry for help, wasn't it? I should have been there to save—"

"Stop. You're not getting it. Kip outgrew his overt self-pity before his father could outgrow his subtler kind. He wanted your help, yes, but not to save his own life. He wanted your help to save those you both love."

Dazen raised his hands, supplicating, disbelieving. "How can I possibly...?"

Orholam was studying the descending night sky. The moon hadn't yet risen. "Awfully dark out here," He said. "Dark enough a drafter of black could find source in the sky, don't you think? That's one color you can still draft, isn't it?"

The consequences of doing that settled around Dazen's neck like a mantle of iron. Softly he said, "It'll obliterate me."

"It will, if you let go of Me," Orholam agreed.

Dazen looked angrily at him. "I don't understand what You think I can do from here."

"I don't require your understanding."

"Just my obedience," Dazen said bitterly. "Got it."

"And your strength," Orholam said.

Dazen stood, laboriously, and in the process got his hands thoroughly bloody. He didn't feel strong. He hadn't felt strong this morning, before everything this awful day had thrown at him. He followed Orholam to where He'd left the sword as if in a trance.

He didn't want to die, but now, finally, he was ready. If it was all for this, then so be it.

Orholam extended a hand to him, and Dazen took Orholam's clean hand in his own bloody, three-fingered one.

"You remember the coordinates?" Orholam asked.

"I never forget anything. You know that. But...uh...coordinates?"

"Kip gave you the position of the Chromeria. But there's only one drafter in the world strong enough to throw magic that far."

Dazen shrugged. "Kip was strong enough."

"He was."

Was. That little word was a punch in the guts.

It pissed Dazen off, and not at Orholam this time.

It sank into the cool ashes of his heart and blew the embers to flame. They'd killed Kip. They'd murdered his son.

He was going to make them pay for that.

He had a sudden thought. "The bane are there?"

Orholam nodded. "Kip and Karris got two. There's five left."

"Five on one. That's hardly fair," Dazen said.

"Five on one?" Orholam asked, amused. "Not five on two?"

Dazen looked at Him, opened his mouth, shut it. "Yeah, that's what I meant." *I'll just do the magic part, and the fighting part. You...do Your thing. Whatever that is.*

But the time for sniping was finished. Impossible magic, against impossible odds?

That's what I do.

He breathed out, widening his pupils and gazing toward the darkest part of the sky.

Before, he'd wrestled black luxin to obliterate, to destroy others, and to destroy himself, to rip himself asunder and blot out parts he hated. It had been the sum of all wild beasts, bucking against him like a mustang, whipping its tusks toward his belly like a giant javelina, charging him like an iron bull—and in all the fights, he'd been a brute with a whip, determined to break the beast. Like a cornered, injured animal, the black luxin had been all violence and madness, both against his enemies and against himself.

Now, entering the great beast's demesne, he extended an open will with his open right hand, offering partnership, not mastery.

And the black came roaring from the night upon him—charging over the horizon and into Dazen's undefended, wide-open eye. Dazen lay supine, exposing his belly to the snarling maw of the great wolf Death.

Here am I, Death. Let us walk together one last time, and fight each other no more.

The beast paused, snuffling at his bloody open hand, even as the magic filled Dazen's eyes and made his bones hot within him.

A shiver passed through him, from the crown of his head, down his spine and hands, which burned hot with blood, and to the heated soles of his feet, rooted in the blood that connected skin to tower.

Without the scent of fear inflaming its predator's nose, but accepted, respected, the great black beast calmed. Then its power entered him.

Even at Sundered Rock, he hadn't drafted so much. He drew and drew, taking all the dark night into his soul. He drew, lancing those darkened memories for all his own old poison, all the hatred and envy inside him, all the cruelty of taunting victory he'd unleashed before. He connected the darkness above with the old darkness within, though each was punctuated by its celestial lights. He was beyond fear now. How could he be daunted? He could give no more than everything in him, and that was exactly what he planned to do.

He threaded his fingers tight through the beast's mantle and then with a yell of defiance, Dazen slapped its flank: Take all this, and go! Go!

The black luxin leapt toward the horizon like a war hound on a lead seeing a cat and leaping to the hunt. It nearly tore Dazen's arm off. He could only nudge it this way and that, directing his fraying will toward the Chromeria.

It took all the excellence of Dazen's superchromacy to maintain the exact tone. The slightest flaw would mean madness or agonizing death or the obliteration of memory and self or even time.

Even the descending starlight eroded the black as they flew across so many leagues, and Dazen had to cushion every quantum that infected his streaming black, had to split it away from the stream and push more power into it, like a sprinter shrugging off battering rain, forging through buffeting winds—and he lost precious luxin continuously as he did it, a hundred times a second. Dazen could feel the black unraveling in his grasp, like the southern lights dancing across the sky, defying his control.

And as the magic unraveled, it unraveled him. He braided the open cords together again and again, weaving them tight with fingers that felt a million paces away. He himself was dissipating, losing awareness altogether into the cold dark, but he pulled himself back to consciousness again and again.

This was for Karris. This was for Kip. This was for Marissia. This was for mother. This was for Gavin. This was for Sevastian...

He couldn't fail them. He couldn't fail them *again*.

But then he was there. He couldn't see the islands, he couldn't see anything, but he could *feel* the entirety of Big Jasper and Little Jasper both, those shapes he knew and loved so well. He could feel the physical and magical shapes of the bane, each one extending overlapping bubbles of control far beyond themselves. No red drafter could draft red within the red bane's bubble, nor green in green's, nor yellow in yellow's, and so on.

Dazen didn't have enough time or will or magic or life left to obliterate the bane. They were too far away, too dense, too numerous, too different from one another.

The control he would need to find the seed crystals themselves was far too fine for his skills. Father had always told him he needed to develop his fine-drafting skills, but Dazen had always ignored him, believing more was better: always the hammer, never the tweezers.

There they lay: all the bane, everywhere around the islands, like leeches clinging to the Chromeria's face. He could pierce those bubbles of drafting control easily with the black, but to find five single figures—these so-called gods?—in the few seconds he had left? To find the bane's hidden seed crystals?

It would be like trying to pick a lock with a feather duster.

His will, thus overextended, began to fray apart now in hopelessness. The black he'd flung so far dissipated into the amorphous clouds as the magic finally pulled itself away from his fingers.

And then he felt her.

He wouldn't have thought he could know anyone from this distance, but he couldn't have missed her, not if she'd been twice so far away. Her will burned in the evaporating cloud he'd thrown, like a lighthouse burning white in the black of a lost captain's night.

Karris!

*　　　*　　　*

Karris's Blackguards and all the other soldiers they'd recruited on the spot had made it halfway to Orholam's Glare when they'd been jumped by the White King's platoon of assassins. Forty men didn't seem like they'd be a problem against her hundred and fifty, especially when fifty of them were her Blackguards—who'd appeared from all over the island, escaping from the Chromeria and abandoning Zymun, or the promachos, or the Colors to find and join their Iron White.

Forty *men* wouldn't have been a problem. Forty *wights* was a huge problem. They were clad head to toe in white, gloved and hooded to hide what colors they drafted. In moments, she was in a fight for her life.

And no fair fight. Every one of the Blackguards except the monochrome blues were feeling it. The bane had tightened their grip. Anyone who had the least luxin left in their bodies had to fight against luxin locking up inside them—and every drafter except the youngest had some luxin permanently in their bodies.

Even those who'd carefully drained their power with hellstone were slowed. The best off fought as if in a high wind. Those worse off fought as if in water, sluggish, their old strength turned against them.

But then she felt *something*. The air turned colder, somehow murky, as if a dry fog had rolled in. The city darkened perceptibly. Night had arrived on sprinting feet instead of its usual gentle wings. But, in the fighting, everyone around her missed it.

She stepped back from the fight, back into the mass of Blackguards here to protect her.

There was something familiar—

She gasped.

Gavin!

She opened her will to him, and she knew. He was dying.

She felt his strength faltering, fraying. Her heart froze.

Live, damn you, live! *You come back to me!*

*   *   *

But it was too late. He was dying. He was failing her, *again*.

He could feel her weighed down by the bane's oppressive power. Her light dimmed, her limbs heavy from the very luxin that lived in her, shackled, unable to defend herself from the death he knew was stalking her. He could feel the lock and knew how he might release her from it, but from this distance, it was like feeling the teeth of a key with a fingertip.

No.

No, not while he had breath.

He released all else and clung to her, his lighthouse, the white in the foggy seas of his black.

*　　*　　*

Karris was frozen, even amid the clash of arms around her. Gill Greyling, blood splashed across his face, was shouting something at her. '*Retreat. We've failed. We can't…*'

Mere words.

It was like they didn't even notice.

Don't do it, my love. Please, no. Gavin, what are you doing?

There was something fatal and final she could feel in Gavin's will.

Please, no. Forgive me, my love, but I gave up on you once—don't you dare do it, too. Don't you dare!

And then he was gone.

*　　*　　*

"More darkness," Dazen gasped as he dropped the luxin. He pulled his hand angrily out of Orholam's. "I need more black! More black!"

The sky above was dotted now with thousands of stars, shining, brilliant. The descending darkness should have given him more source, but it only made those points of defiant light shine all the brighter.

Orholam said, "Even eagles must sometimes dive into a lake to hunt, no matter that it momentarily destroys the lake's reflection of the sky."

"What are You even talking about? Reflection of the—"

Dazen looked at the sword stuck into the black crust covering the tower.

When he'd stepped through to the other side of the mirror, the tower in that other world had been white. It had been as it ought to be, maybe as it had been on this side of the mirror before Vician's Sin, before the relentless tide of the Chromeria's murders.

Surely now every bit of the black tower was covered in a great cascade of blood flowing from the Mirror of Waking.

There was an entire tower's worth of unadulterated black luxin at Dazen's feet. Pure, concentrated darkness, and the blood of martyrs connected him with all of it.

Dazen plunged his hands again into the flowing blood, smeared it up the blade until it made an unbroken line to his hand.

He gazed at the bloody thing that would be the instrument of his own execution. He had lived by the blade, wrongly sacrificing the innocent. It was only right he himself should be its final sacrifice.

This is for you, Vell Parsham, my first murder. You tried to warn me.

She'd said, 'End me now, Lord Prism, but someday, may you end it all or *be ended*. Know that Orholam is just, and tremble.'

This is for you, Edna, who thought your sins so black you couldn't speak them. I understand you now as I couldn't then.

This is for you, Titrit, whom I despised. I came to despise myself more.

This is for Dulcina Dulceana...He couldn't think of her, but he remembered her words and his own disbelief at her quiet, her peace. She'd said, 'You've been doing Orholam's work all day, and will do so all night and through the morrow. Let me give you a gift. The only gift I have. The gift of my five minutes. You may speak or we can be silent. You can Free me first if you prefer solitude, or at the end if you prefer company. As you will.' She'd believed in him so much—she'd been so generous of spirit that she'd given him her last five minutes: a poor woman giving her last mite to a man whose treasury overflowed.

Her grace had broken him.

Going in to his first Freeing, Gavin had believed in two gods, and with her had died his faith in the wrong one.

This is for you Aheyyad Brightwater, that flower I plucked too soon.

This is for...this is for all of you.

Standing beside him, Orholam extended His hand again. Even though He'd just been holding Dazen's bloody hand moments ago, His own hand was clean. "You want to do this with Me, or alone?"

Dazen slapped his hand into the old man's. He didn't know what, if anything, Orholam was going to do, but he'd been a fool trying to do everything on his own for long enough. If a bit of help would help him help those he loved, he wasn't gonna turn it down.

He braced his feet wide, and taking a deep breath, he put his right hand on the blade before him. His source was a perfect black, unpolluted, deeper than the darkest night, but even with such a source, drafting from a color's luxin was never efficient; it always generated heat and discomfort, even if you only drafted a little.

Dazen didn't plan to draft a little.

Dazen never did anything *little*.

He threw his will down into the whole tower. Everywhere the blood touched, his will connected with the old black luxin.

It shot up into him like an erupting geyser, and filled him, impossibly fast. Beside him, he saw omnichromatic fire erupting from Orholam's other hand, as if He were scraping the dross from all the black and venting it, allowing Dazen to be filled with purest black alone.

Dazen became the lens focusing a vast well of black light onto a point hundreds of leagues distant.

Then Dazen was filled beyond bursting, and with one last, mighty shout, he threw all his will into one final burst toward that dimly flickering light on the horizon, his beloved White...

*　　*　　*

With a foot kicking hard against the wight's chest, Gill Greyling cleared his spear from the still-standing body of his foe, and in the same motion, lengthened his body out as if he were a striking serpent, smashing the spear's butt directly into the throat of a red wight swinging a war hammer wreathed in flames at Karris's back. Before the wight even hit the ground, Gill's spear had spun an arc to slash through his crushed throat.

Ending threats forcefully and with finality, Karris thought dimly. It was what they were trained to do.

But she was a ghost. Already dead inside, she walked the battlefield with the other spirits of the dead lingering only shortly on this side of the veil. The air had shifted. The black-luxin fingers that had reached from beyond the horizon were gone.

Gavin's will had let go. He was gone. Finally gone.

She had given up on him. She'd failed him. She had thought she wouldn't know when he died, that such thoughts were the nonsense of young fools in love. But she knew now.

She knew.

And then the air shifted again. Something to do with the black luxin. As if its withdrawal hadn't been the withdrawal of an attack abandoned but the temporary withdrawal of ocean after an earthquake.

Even the wights seemed suddenly discomfited. Men and wights both paused in their fighting, backing away from their enemies.

"What is it?" Gill asked. "What's happening?"

Karris was looking out to sea toward her lost love, so she saw it first.

Far out beyond East Bay, the lights of a ship winked out. Then another's, far to one side. A burning ship's fires simply disappeared. Then she noticed that the stars on the horizon were gone.

Her breath caught in her throat as she saw it for what it was. Like a sandstorm thundering across the desert, towering into the night, an immense black wave broke over the horizon, wider than the Jaspers themselves, and as high as the clouds.

In the distance, she heard screams at its onslaught.

As if the sea were swelling and devouring all before it in a massive wave, every light on every ship was extinguished in turn, into the bay, and then over the towers, over the walls, and then—in the time it takes to suck in a startled breath—over the Jaspers entire.

All went utterly, utterly black. Blacker than mere night. This was the black of blindness, after a life spent working light. It penetrated everything, soaking everything as water does—then scouring it away with all the strength of an earthquake's wave.

Eerily, it was silent.

And it was, unmistakably, unquestionably, Gavin.

Then, just as the wails of alarm and despair were rising up from women and men struck blind and dismayed at their sudden loss—the wave was gone.

As light returned to their eyes, Karris could feel the wave dissipating. It had been held together this far, but it wouldn't last even another league. Gavin had...

"*promachos*," Gill whispered, awed. "That was *him*. That was Gavin, wasn't it? I could *feel*— How could he draft so much? What did he do?"

A snap and hiss popped next to them, illuminating the merely natural dark of the night with glorious green light. Samite grinned in that wild light.

"The bane," she said. "Their power's broken. We can draft!"

Numerous bane-islands were still out there, so at first no one believed her, but then there were slowly the snaps and hisses of glorious colors coming alive from burning mag torches. First a few, then dozens of them drenched the Blackguards and their allies in heady, potent light.

The twenty remaining wights turned and fled.

It was still night. Their position was still precarious. They had only whatever magic they could draft off of their mag torches. But now— now they had a chance!

Gavin had reached from beyond the grave to give them one chance.

He had died to bring them light.

"To the Glare!" Karris shouted.

She would mourn her husband. Later. She was a warrior.

Warriors know how to honor a hero's sacrifice: first you finish the fucking fight.

Chapter 132

If there was one thing Corvan Danavis excelled at, it was being able to ignore a little personal danger (say, a battle raging around him) in order to focus on more important things. It was part of what made him an excellent commander, and in truth, he'd never understood how other people couldn't do it.

Which was why right now he was cursing in the face of a shaking messenger, spit flying as he bellowed, "How old is this message?! And don't tell me you don't fucking know!"

"Maybe, maybe half an hour, sir? Less?" the messenger said. "I came straight here, but the others—"

"An hour?" Corvan demanded.

"Uh, maybe? Maybe, sir. Yes. There was so much fighting, and I wanted to make sure I got through safely so I didn't—"

"Get out of my face!"

Two of Corvan's bodyguards, one from either side, suddenly threw their shields up in front of him as a fireball the size of a woman's head arced toward him. It bounced off their shields and rolled into the crowd behind him.

Nope. Not a fireball the size of a woman's head. A literal flaming woman's head. Odd.

The messenger blanched. A coward. It was the last trait a messenger could afford—but one didn't find out which messengers could handle the job until they'd been through a battle or two.

A distraction, Kip said. Kip needed a distraction.

The city was in a bad way. Corvan had just had news that the wall bordering the poor neighborhood of Overhill nearest the red bane was nearly abandoned, most of its defenders lured to the walls elsewhere in the nobles' neighborhoods, or even worse, lured to guard their houses against the looters they feared during the battle.

If the city survived until tomorrow, Corvan was going to find those damned nobles and put them on the walls as rank infantrymen themselves.

But first came survival.

Corvan had found any plan with too many working parts tended to fall apart in direct relation to how many parts depended on other parts doing what they should, so his battle plan was simple: defend and delay. As islands, the most obvious weakness of the Jaspers was that they were easy to lay under siege.

But anyone laying them under siege was, in effect, under siege themselves. Karris had directed the isles' fishermen to deliberately overfish the nearby waters, not only to stockpile dried fish but to deprive invaders. Fresh water was an even bigger problem for a besieging armada, so where there were springs that drained into the sea, Corvan had massed defenders in greater numbers than any other general would have. If the fight lasted long enough, the availability of potable water might actually be the key to the victory.

Everywhere, he'd prepared the defenders with how long to hold their walls, and what to do when they lost them, and how to signal everyone else that such loss was imminent.

The defenders would stagger their losses, hopefully containing those to nonessential areas. A few natural ambush choke points could be used if the local commanders dared.

Corvan liked to push certain decisions down the chain of command as much as possible. Men paralyzed waiting for orders that might never come through the chaos of battle were dead men, not defenders.

Today the hope had been to hold the Blood Robes off the walls.

Unsurprisingly, that hadn't worked out.

The next plan had been to make them pay in rivers of blood for every street they took, delaying them until dark, when the Jaspers' defenders would no longer be at a disadvantage.

But there were places the Chromeria couldn't afford to lose, full stop: some of the gun emplacements that could be turned against the city and the Chromeria itself, certain neighborhoods, the Lily's Stem—and the Great Fountain. Corvan had set up his headquarters here to stress to his people how it was the linchpin to their defense. Not only was it the most abundant source of fresh water in the city with its artesian well, but it sat at one of the five great intersections of the city. That made it hard to defend, but also easy to dispatch reinforcements to anyplace in the city that needed it.

The battle had come here, in surprising force.

The razor wings and bomb wings and the crawling vermin will-cast to burrow into the street barricades before bursting into flame had waited until the assaults by tens of thousands of Blood Robe soldiers. Kip had warned Corvan of this: the use of munds as cannon fodder and auxiliaries.

It had meant a catastrophic loss of life for the attackers, especially as the bane had been so confused, so late in locking down all the Chromeria's defenders.

The defenders had lost neighborhood after neighborhood, including some sections of wall with their most powerful guns—all spiked before they were abandoned, luckily.

But the Blood Robes hadn't broken off the attack here, even as full dark was gathering.

Why weren't they withdrawing?

After all, at night the Blood Robes were deprived of their greatest advantage—their drafters and wights. Why wouldn't they wait until tomorrow to attack again? Were they hoping to take the city before full dark, and were giving their attack a few more minutes to succeed? Did they think Corvan's forces so close to breaking?

He thought them wrong, though not by much.

That was when Kip sprang his own gambit: attacking the bane themselves with small squads. Suicidally small squads.

Kip, repulsing unbelievably strong magical attacks, was trying to wrest victory directly from the enemy while their forces were at Corvan's throat.

It was just the kind of move Corvan would have attempted as a young man, though not, he thought, with such small forces.

His people had fought the Blood Robes to a standstill. Indeed, some of the invading soldiers had even withdrawn to their bane.

Corvan swore aloud again, suddenly putting the pieces together.

Those Blood Robes had withdrawn to protect their bane from Kip's Mighty. Kip's men had been striking at the heart of the White King's power and had needed the distraction Kip requested so they wouldn't be overwhelmed.

But the messenger was a coward.

Corvan's damned messenger might have gotten not just the Mighty but *everyone* killed.

Was it too late now?

Kip's men might have saved Corvan's forces here, but could he save them now?

What could serve as a suitable distraction?

Was that it? His wife, Polyhymnia, the Third Eye, had called him her Titan of the Great Fountain. He'd set up his defense here partly because of that.

But *that* plan couldn't work because of the bane's influence locking down red.

Magic rocked the isles again and again. Not only the loss of blue—there were reports of white?! Some even claimed to have felt black.

But even as detached as Corvan liked to think he was in the midst of issuing orders and hearing reports and dodging razor wings, he realized he couldn't even comprehend everything that was happening elsewhere. There were at least two battles happening here simultaneously, probably three, all overlapping one another.

And he might be screwing up all of them.

Now, why weren't these damned Blood Robes retreating with the coming night? Why?!

Then, suddenly, the black luxin returned in an enormous wave.

Dazen!

The wave scoured the islands, breaking the bane's control of all the drafters, freeing them to do what they could.

The defenders and attackers were equally astonished, breaking from fighting for a few moments and then rejoining the fray. But even that didn't make the Blood Robes flee.

And then the black wave was gone.

Corvan immediately deployed his drafters, but the sun was already so far down that they had little source. Some had mag torches, but those were rare and expensive—Corvan left it to the drafters themselves to decide if they needed to use them.

It allowed some pushback at key places, but there weren't enough mag torches to fuel the defense.

Why the hell had Kip stopped sending light from the mirror array?! He hadn't been answering the messages they'd flashed to him for a while now. And *now* was when they needed him on the mirror array most. These few minutes could make a real difference!

"Send messages to Kip again. Tell him if he's got any more tricks, now would be a good time—"

"Sir, the superviolets say that the Ferrilux has seized the mirror array," an attaché said.

"What?!" he demanded.

Ferrilux's bane had been killed, but *she* had not. And she'd taken the array, which likely meant Kip was dead.

Dammit, Aliviana.

But he couldn't think of her as his daughter. Not right now. And maybe it wasn't her anymore. Maybe she wasn't in control anymore. Maybe she was a victim, too.

So why would Ferrilux seize the mirrors as night came? Why put herself in such peril that she would try to take the mirrors even without her bane or her wights?

He looked out at the other bane once more. Each had some kind of central spire, a high point. He'd thought them mere lookouts, good areas from which the Blood Robes could see what was happening even behind Big Jasper's walls.

804

And then he got it. The bane had brought lightwells, like great mag torches.

That was why Ferrilux wanted the mirror array.

The Blood Robes were bringing sources to the fight. With colors from each of the towers and the mirrors, the wights would be able to attack with magic, all night long, anywhere in the city.

Aside from the purely strategic disadvantage of fighting all those wights with no magic themselves, Corvan realized that in mere minutes his people were going to be fighting street to street against literal monsters in the dark.

The terror would be overwhelming.

"Sir! We've got more wights massing to attack. Hundreds at least!" an attaché shouted over the din.

"What colors? What colors, Lieutenant? And don't you dare say all of 'em!"

"Sir..." Her face strained. "All of them."

Chapter 133

Andross Guile crawled across the stateroom floor, drool and vomit dripping down his chin.

White luxin. Goddam. Kip had drafted white luxin before the end. The little barnacle on Andross's ass had had the audacity to try to control the mirror array from Orholam's Glare itself. And that fire! It had confirmed one thing, anyway, Lord Dariush had been right: the Atashians' Dragon and the other satrapies' Lightbringer weren't the same person.

Or maybe they were, and Kip had failed, and they were all doomed.

Andross threw up again, retching on an empty belly.

The slaves were gone. Not a one of his household had stood by him. He had treated them so well, and this is what he got?

When the spasms passed, he pulled himself to his feet. He was past the worst of it now. Two bites into his garlic-and-almond chicken before he'd stopped. Two distracted bites before he'd recognized the tastes weren't *exactly* garlic and almond, and stopped, and forced himself to vomit. Not garlic and almond, but two poisons whose odors most resemble those: arsenic and cyanide.

He braced himself against the doorframe, and slowly, slowly checked his Ilytian pistol. There was a chance that an assassin might come and make sure the job was finished. Then, reassured, he opened the door.

No one was outside. All the Blackguards had abandoned their posts, either traitors or men and women who put their loyalty to Karris above their loyalty to anyone else on the Spectrum. Certainly Zymun had had no Blackguards attending him when he'd murdered Kip. Zymun was stupid, but he wasn't that stupid.

Andross tottered across the hallway to Felia's old chambers. Opened the door slowly, in case its occupant had been given a musket.

"Who's there?!" a young woman called out.

"It is I."

"Who the hell are you?" Teia demanded from the couch. Good, good. He would have been furious if they'd put the little runt in Felia's bed.

"Andross Guile. Your promachos."

"Is Grinwoody with you?"

"I'm alone," he said, coming into the room.

Teia relaxed visibly, taking her finger off the trigger, but still resting it along the musket's guard and still keeping the musket pointed in his general direction. Her head was wrapped in numerous layers of thick cloths, and he could see she was listening closely for any quick movement. "Where is he?" she asked. As if she had the right to ask questions of him—but he was too sick to fight right now.

"Gone."

"How'd you know they brought me here?" she asked.

"They couldn't keep you in the infirmary; it would be the first place the Order would look. And they didn't know of any of the hidden rooms except those the Order obviously knew about already. That left them without many good options."

"You just...know all of this?" Teia demanded. "You really do have people everywhere, don't you?"

"In truth," Andross admitted, "I heard them arguing about it outside my door." He hoped to elicit a smile, but Teia was past charm.

"Grinwoody is the Old Man of the Desert," she said.

"Really? Is he now?" The red in him flared up. "Now, that information would have been very valuable *before he poisoned my supper*."

"He poisoned your— Oh shit! So that's why you look like that."

So she could see through her head wrappings?

All right, then. Actually, good.

"You're a miserable failure, Adrasteia, but I'm going to give you another chance."

"What are you talking about?"

"You were supposed to kill the Order, right? Grinwoody got away. And you've missed all the fighting today. Good people have died. Friends."

He could see her swallow. She wanted to ask, but didn't.

"I can't do anything," she said. "I'm not here because I want to be. I drank lacrimae sanguinis. Had to, to get them all to drink it. I don't even know if it wears off, but I'm weak as a puppy and—"

"It does."

"What?"

"Wear off."

"How would you know that?"

"I studied poisons quite a bit when I first got into politics—seemed a prudent defensive measure. Luckily, that was before I took on Grinwoody, else he'd have known about the mithridatism."

"The what?"

"The reason I'm still alive. But never mind. If you make it two days, you'll live. But your vision's fucked. Permanently. You have only two options. Open your eyes to widest paryl or tighten them to superviolet, then keep them in whichever position you choose, if you can. That lacrimae sanguinis does something to the muscles regardless. If you tighten your eyes, which is what the scholar I read recommended, your pupils will stay as pinpricks permanently. Your vision will always be dim, and incredibly nearsighted, and you'll never draft paryl again. But if you widen your eyes to paryl, you'll only ever see in paryl. You'll lose all the other colors, and you'll have to wear the darkest lenses at all times and even wrap your eyes with cloth or you'll risk even normal light blinding you forever—even in the paryl spectrum."

"I already went to paryl," Teia breathed.

"Huh. That's that, then. At least you can draft."

"At least I can draft?!" she said, rage bubbling in her voice.

"You'll most likely die before the night's out, so it's no matter."

"You're a real bastard," she said. "And I can't even *move*, so go to hell."

"I'm the promachos. And I've got orders for you. Enough chitchat."

"You're not hearing me," Teia said. "I can barely even breathe. I can't go do anything for you!"

"Sure you can. You just need the right motivation. A goddess has just seized the mirror array. I can't get to her unseen, which means *I* can't stop her. But *you* can. I'm not sure what she's planning up there. It'll be ruin for us if she still controls the array tomorrow morning, but I don't know what she can accomplish with it at night. What I do know is that if the enemy wants something—"

"You deny it," Teia interrupted. "I know. Kip is my friend, remember?"

"Was," Andross said bluntly. "Kip's dead. I watched him die from my window. In between bouts of vomiting, that is."

The wind went out of Teia's aching lungs. "You can't be..."

"Someone put him up on Orholam's Glare. He was trying to take control of the Prism's mirror array from there. I would've said such a thing was impossible, but he almost did it. Until the Ferrilux stopped him. She killed him. So you need motivation? How 'bout vengeance?"

* * *

It took them a few minutes to make it to the Prism's and White's level of the tower. There were no Blackguards anywhere.

They made quite the pair, walking arm in arm, supporting each other as they staggered down the eerily empty halls: Teia, with Kip's chainspear, Sorry, around her waist and one of Felia Guile's long silk scarves wound several times around her head and tied tight over the dark spectacles she was wearing, layer on layer meant to protect her eyes; and the trembling Promachos Andross Guile, who'd stripped off his pukeencrusted tunic but hadn't realized he still had stray vomitus in his beard.

She wasn't gonna tell him, either.

Several minutes ago, after assuring her she'd be able to draft a small amount without any problems despite the lacrimae sanguinis, he'd seemed pleasantly surprised when she'd done just that—and hadn't keeled over dead.

He hadn't known. Not for sure.

As they climbed the stairs to the door leading out to the rooftop, Andross said, "If she becomes aware of your presence, you're dead, you understand? I can silence the hinges of this door if you can't, but she may well have set up some additional safeguards, if not traps—"

Then everything went black.

Not just dark. Everything went the black of the grave. Teia wondered for a moment if some light source had triggered the lacrimae sanguinis and this was death, this was her brain blowing out and darkness closing over her forever.

And then light returned. Albeit only the light of paryl cast from Teia's own hand. She heard her own gasping breaths echoed by Andross's. He'd been as scared shitless as she was. "What was that?" she asked.

He didn't answer for a moment. Then he said, "That was black luxin. An incredible amount—it means she'll be weak. Quick! Go!"

Teia staggered up the stairs at a half jog. There was no door. It lay in fragments.

The report of a musket made her drop to the ground, though if it had been on target, it would have been way too late.

Teia tried to roll, but merely flopped, her body too weak to do what her mind commanded. She struggled to rise.

The mirror array was empty, but the harness still swung on its hinges. She heard the clang of a dropped musket as she finally stood.

A moment later, so belatedly she couldn't believe she was still alive, she finally remembered and went invisible. She must be in worse shape than she thought.

But it didn't matter. Aliviana Danavis was staggering around the tower, face and arms encrusted with superviolet, some of it bleeding where it connected with her skin.

"Gavin Guile!" the woman cried. "He makes the very immortals tremble! What has he done? How could he—? So much...so much black. I've never...Ahh!"

She flung a hundred daggers of superviolet toward the open door, as if the feat were an afterthought. They rattled into the stones behind where Teia had been standing moments before like an iron rain.

Teia ran toward her.

She had no weapons. She had no weapons! She hadn't drawn the chain-spear off her waist. What was she thinking?

But the Ferrilux seemed to be collecting her wits already. "Yes, yes, you're right. Of course you're right. I— What? Who's coming? No, you mayn't take control! I know your—"

And then Teia crashed into her—and shoved hard, launching her off the rooftop.

Teia stepped to the edge, and as she passed out of sight, Aliviana still seemed to be falling fast—but using only paryl as she was, Teia couldn't see all the way to the ground.

Moments later, she heard the crunch of a footstep behind her.

"Well, color me less than impressed."

"Is she dead?" Teia asked. "I can't see that far."

"I can't see her body from this angle," Andross said. "And if you think I'm going to lean out really far for you..."

"I'm not gonna *murder* you!" Teia said.

"And I'm not gonna bet on you. Made that mistake once."

"Yeah, fuck you. That was me *as* the bet, not you betting on me."

"Fair point. I'll let the disrespect pass unpunished for that and   809 your…reasonably good service here. The job's done, or done enough. One hopes, anyway. I never believe an enemy dead when I can't see the body myself. But you may go. Crawl back in your hole and die, or try to live. You seem like you could be useful. If you live, I'll have work for you in the days to come."

She turned, her heart falling. If she lived, now she was to be Andross Guile's assassin?

Was there really no way out?

"Oh," Andross interrupted. "Before you go. Help me get strapped in, would you? I have to see if I can figure out what the Ferrilux was trying to do."

Chapter 134

"Is the black powder ready?" Corvan asked. The battle was raging at the barricades all around the Great Fountain. Corvan's drafters had all burned through their mag torches. The Cwn y Wawr war hounds had each fought like a dozen men, but now every one of them bore wounds and was exhausted, panting, those intelligent eyes seeming to bear full knowledge of their coming deaths. The men Kip had recruited from Daragh the Coward's forces had fought as if every last one of them wanted to win medals, and every last one of them would've earned one, too.

But the end was coming, and they knew it, and those hard men seemed to have no regrets that this was how they would face it.

"Yes, sir, powder's ready," his lieutenant, Lorenço, answered. Corvan's usual attaché, Miriam, had leapt into a razor-wing attack, saving him. Her throat had been cut. She'd been alive when they'd carried her away, but hadn't looked good. "But…sir, can you tell me what you're planning?"

Something had happened with the mirror array atop the Prism's Tower—perhaps the Ferrilux had been killed—because the mirrors were doing nothing. Maybe that was the only reason the Great Fountain—and the city—still stood, but it wasn't enough.

Corvan had been right that the bane had meant to be sources for the Blood Robe wights and drafters all through the night, and losing the mirror array was a setback for them—but not the total catastrophe Corvan would've hoped.

The bane themselves, with single mirrors each, couldn't reach many parts of Big Jasper, and they could only focus their light on one area at a time.

Some were more adept at this than others, clearly, already shining light to one area for ten seconds, then another for ten, then another, then repeating the pattern so that its drafters could go to any of those spots to refill their powers when they needed to.

Corvan had already sent orders to his drafters to attempt taking those new source depots—but his orders weren't getting through now.

If the Ferrilux had kept the mirror array, the defenders would have been facing limitless magic that could be applied pretty much anywhere, pretty much instantly. As it was, the defenders were merely facing superior numbers of drafters and wights with lots of magic, while they themselves had none.

The dam was straining, and Corvan guessed his forces had only minutes here before they were overwhelmed. Hell, even if they held here, it was surely only minutes until key points elsewhere in the city broke.

If they hadn't already.

He wondered if any of Kip's Mighty were still alive.

He wondered if a distraction *now*—so very long after they'd requested it—could still do them any good.

"You ever try to read your wife's mind, son?" Corvan asked. The young Ilytian was a newlywed.

"Yessir," Lorenço said. "Doesn't usually go well for me."

"Me, neither," Corvan said. 'Titan of the Great Fountain,' dear? Could you have been slightly less opaque for once? Loudly, he said, "Listen up! If I'm incapable of command, Lorenço will act as high general. He has my full faith. I took command of armies when I was younger than he is now. Got it?!" There was a small chorus of agreement, but many were too tired or too hurt to reply.

"You take these next moments to shore up the barricades. Messengers, get on your marks. No gawking! That's for the enemy to do."

He cracked open two red mag torches and began filling himself with power.

Dazen, I wish you could see this. You would've loved it.

He sketched out the arcs in his mind. It was actually going to work a lot better in the dark. Half pyroturgy, half luxin imbued with will—and a shit ton of black powder.

Looking one last time at his people, he said, "Pleasure. Honor. All the shit. Keep fighting. And get back farther. This is most likely just gonna blow me up."

He crouched to jump and then sheathed his entire body in red luxin. He looked over at Lorenço, who was standing by the black powder launch pad with the linstock in his hand.

'Titan of the Great Fountain' my ass.

"Lieutenant," he said. *"Now."*

With a loud report, the first of the powder barrels was flung sky-high.

Chapter 135

"I'm...not dead?" Dazen said, opening his eyes. "I'm not dead!"

"Yet," Orholam said.

Dazen glowered at Him. "Well, that's not a very nice joke after what I just went through."

"It's funnier in other realms."

That didn't make him feel any better. "When You say 'yet' what kind of time frame are You operating on?"

Orholam shook His head.

"I mean, I feel like I've been dead for three days," Dazen said.

Orholam lifted an eyebrow.

"I suppose I have You to thank for this? Being alive, I mean? In the more immediate sense, I mean, not in the sense of 'I made all this shit and that means you, too, especially the shit part.' "

"I want you to remember this, a little later," Orholam said.

"Which 'this'? This, the You saving me, or *this* this, my impertinence?" Dazen asked. "I'm doing it again, aren't I?"

As the last fog of the black departed from him, Dazen noticed that the tower he was kneeling on was now awash with water, not blood. And the tower's entire shell of black luxin that the blood had covered over was gone. Dazen now knelt on radiant white luxin like what he'd seen on the other side of the Great Mirror of Waking—an entire massive edifice of the luxin he'd so long believed mythical.

"Are you ready to continue?" Orholam asked.

"Continue?" Dazen turned his hands palms up. "I thought that was my penance. What, that didn't count?"

"It counted for quite a lot."

Dazen expelled a breath. "Thank You, by the by," he said, standing with great effort. He was exhausted.

"You're welcome."

"What's next?" he asked. The waning wick of his life was already smoldering on its last wax. "I can only draft two colors—if you call black and white 'colors'— Wow, am I scattered after that."

He looked at Orholam. Then at the tower. Then at Orholam.

"This one is going to be death, isn't it?"

"No, no. This will be—"

"Oh, good!"

"—a good penance," Orholam said, nodding. "And life for many."

Dazen wrinkled his brow. "You say that as if we're somehow in agreement."

"Promachos, hurling black luxin across half the breadth of the satrapies was a well-nigh lethal and well-nigh impossible magical test—"

"Yes! It was! Thank You!"

"—that allowed you to do exactly what you wanted."

Dazen had no answer for that.

"Doing impossible magic to overcome ludicrous odds and smash my enemies?" he said. "That's what I do!" So maybe he did have an answer.

"Did," Orholam said quietly. It was the gentlest whipcrack Dazen had ever heard. It had a sound of finality to it.

Dazen had the sudden and too-slow-arriving insight that Orholam was accustomed to having the last word.

Orholam continued, "There was never a question of your will or your ability, Dazen, so such a test is hardly a test at all, much less a penance."

"So You're saying *this* is the one that's going to be hard for me," Dazen said.

"Yes."

"As if the first one was so easy," Dazen groused.

"The first counted as an answer to your greatest question: 'Could you ever be the man you were before?'"

In a tone inappropriate from a son to his father, Dazen snarled, "And what's this gonna answer?"

"My question is, 'Is that the man you want to be?'"

Dazen's stomach turned, and fear hit him like cold water chilling his throat, icing his belly, and filling every limb with doubt. What could such a test possibly be? "Just when I was starting to like You," he said. His bravado was thin, but on a cold night a thin cloak is better than none, and this night was starting to feel cold indeed, in the gale of Orholam's gaze. "What do You want me to do?"

"Touch the mirror."

I already did that, Dazen thought. But he was smart enough not to say it, barely. He moved over toward the great shining thing, torrents of clear water gushing over its surface and onto his feet, threatening to wash him away as he came close. But he reached through the water and touched the metal.

The waters ceased.

And he saw himself.

Behind him, Orholam said gently, "Behold Dazen Guile, who thought himself the least of his brothers."

He saw himself, the image crisp and clear in the starlight. He stood slouching, with two fingers cut off, his dogtooth smashed out, cheeks hollow from privation, back striped through injustice and bowed through travail—and yet still here. He'd been a great beauty before the last few years: muscular, strong-jawed, broad and tall, agile and self-possessed with a winning smile and prismatic eyes. No wonder they'd loved him. They'd seen the flawless bark of the great sequoy, not the rot within, the roots withered, waiting for the next great wind to topple him. He studied himself—with only one eye now, but that one eye was bright and clear.

He'd been hiding all his life. Now he hid no more.

Diminished though Dazen was, he was not devoid of all virtues, not even in his body. He was still tall, still broad, and strength was rallying in his every limb.

He studied what he'd long avoided, and there was now no detail obscured, no truth denied. Here he stood in the cold light of eternity, and by some magic greater than chromaturgy, all that was wretched and self-deprecatory and judgmental and hating fell away like a serpent's scale from his eye.

He had seen through Orholam's mask of being an old prophet, and beheld something ineffably beguiling beneath the old prophet's age spots and deep wrinkles and snaggle teeth.

And now he saw something of that same beauty in himself, an image of the divine.

Here was Dazen Guile through the eyes of charity.

And as unwilling tears flooded his eyes, he realized that—wonder of wonders!—he was *glorious*.

Beneath all he'd despised, there had been someone worthy of love here all along. His eyes had simply been too clouded to be able to see it.

He looked at Orholam and was able to see more of Him than he had before. "You...You really went to a lot of trouble for me."

"More than you know," Orholam said briskly. "Now, throw your will into the mirror, and take up the work your son has left behind."

" 'Work'? You mean some magic? I just threw a *volcano* of black luxin at the Jaspers. I wiped out everything magical there. Surely I spoiled anything Kip was trying to do."

Calmly, Orholam said, "White luxin is not overwhelmed by black."

Dazen thought of a thousand reasons why that wasn't necessarily the case, and then realized who he was talking to. "It is really frustrating to argue with you," Dazen said.

"I get that a lot," Orholam said. "Ditto. Oh, by the by, hurry."

Chapter 136

Quentin had arrived too late. He'd spent all day serving: first carrying food and water, later attending to the wounded in the poorest parts of the city, comforting the dying when he could. In the first hour, he'd been tempted to shed his ridiculous golden robes, but there was something about seeing a rich luxiat lower himself to service that had not only inspired other luxiats but also scared townsfolk to join him in his labors wherever he went.

As a lone servant, he would have been invisible, but lifted up, he'd been able to bring light to neighborhoods in need of hope. So he'd served in his uncomfortable clothes in the soot and smoke and blood—neither danger nor magic moving him—until he saw he saw that white beam shooting out to the east.

He'd run immediately, praying, praying he not be too late.

He was too late.

The traitor had already been lowered from Orholam's Glare, and a blonde-haired noblewoman held his body, weeping.

The crowd in the square was large, angry, confused, scared. They'd been witness to magic such as they'd never seen—such as no one had ever seen. But the man who'd done it was dead, and the city was still under attack. It seemed like everything should have changed with so much magic, but nothing had.

Blackness had rushed over the city entire, as if even the light mourned the dead man, and abandoned them with his passing. But then that, too, was gone, and nothing had changed, unless it had changed for the worse: everyone had expected the Blood Robes to withdraw with the coming of night, and they'd redoubled their efforts instead.

"Are you quite done?" Zymun asked.

Then Quentin saw the woman as her face lifted in tear-streaked rage, and every bad premonition he'd had was confirmed. She was Tisis Guile. Which meant the body she held was Kip's.

Quentin pushed through the crowd, aided by his narrow-shouldered frame and his garb, which made some people step aside for him.

He lost the next thing Zymun said, but from his intermittent glimpses of the Prism's gleeful face, he could tell it was cruel. Nor did he stop even as Quentin moved closer and closer, taunting her so much that even some of the Lightguards looked uncomfortable.

"—dear. You know we've a tradition in the Guile family of passing around our whores. My own mother rushed from my uncle's bed to my father's as soon as she figured out which one was a winner. Some people might call that slatternly or opportunistic. Terrible things to say about a woman in such a vulnerable position, though. She was just making the best of it, wasn't she? And look! Now she's the White, and no one even talks about her tawdry early days. Me? I don't call a woman like her a disloyal whore, I call her *practical*. Besides, who wants to share a loser's bed? You ought to consider trying her approach: find out what it's like to be fucked by a winner, for once. Tonight, maybe? I can promise you won't remember Kip's name by dawn. Hell, you might not even remember your own."

He looked up at his men, and the Lightguards laughed belatedly like the sycophants they were. Some of them chuckled awkwardly instead, like men who suddenly felt like they'd gotten into something much worse than they'd bargained for.

Tisis launched herself at him, screaming incoherently.

He slapped her hard, as if he'd been waiting for it.

Then he leaned over, just as Quentin finally made his way to the front.

"Careful, sweetheart. I'm going to interpret that pathetic attack as spirit, fire, whatever you want to call it. But do it again, and I call it treason. And you've seen what I do to traitors." He turned. "Now, then, what's happening up on top of my tower?"

Tisis's nose was streaming blood, but she rose to her hands and knees.

Just in front of her, one of the Lightguard shifted his weight and put a hand on his hip, flaring his cloak out around where his pistol was tucked, cocking it with the back of his hand as he did so, as if by accident. He cleared his throat to cover the sound, looking away.

Zymun's back was turned, and the Lightguards were turning with him to head back to the Chromeria.

Tisis leapt to her feet, grabbing the pistol from the Lightguard's belt. She leveled it at the back of Zymun's head, not a pace away.

But a spear butt flashed up between them and threw the pistol into the sky. And in a blink the spear's holder—the Lightguard commander, Aram—was holding Tisis, his spear under her neck, choking her.

"Treason!" Aram shouted.

Several other Lightguards took up the shout. It all had the feeling of something poorly choreographed. The people in the square looked merely horrified.

"My lord!" Aram said loudly. "What should we do with this traitor?"

Zymun put his hand to his heart as if sorely wounded. "No, no, no. Tisis, why?!" He lowered his voice. "Thank you for giving me the excuse, my dear. Oh, and just so you know—that pistol wasn't even loaded. You stupid, stupid girl."

He turned back to the crowd. "The Glare is too cruel for this poor woman. And I shouldn't want her to have to wait for justice. Who knows what might happen before tomorrow? Put a rope up on the Glare, and hang her. Immediately."

"No!" someone cried out in the crowd.

Zymun went purple. "What? You saw what she just tried to do! She tried to kill me!"

"Mercy, my lord, mercy!" someone shouted.

Others began to take up the chant.

"Enough!" Zymun screamed. "Who *the fuck* do all you people think you are, anyway? I am the High Lord Prism Zymun Guile. I am untouchable. Invincible. To dare to raise your hand against me is to die! And anyone who says different will share this traitor's fate. The next to shout for mercy will hang beside her. This I swear!"

The crowd fell silent, aghast. A young man stepped forward as if to shout—but his family grabbed him and clamped a hand over his mouth.

"What's the holdup?" Zymun demanded. "Hang her!"

The Lightguards shuffled their feet. "Sir, there's... We don't have any rope. All the supplies like that have been taken for the barricades. We—"

Zymun cursed them. "No one has *rope*? Surely someone here has rope! And someone, give me a musket. No, no, a blunderbuss. We Guiles are hard to kill, and I need to make sure about my brother."

Quentin could tell no one was going to offer rope, not even if they had it.

Suddenly, he found himself stepping forward. "My lord! High Lord Prism, I don't have a rope, but... but I do have this good strong belt."

"Off with it, then. I have things to do."

Quentin began unwinding his silk belt. He said, "I have a confession to make, High Lord Prism. As you are now the head of our faith, it is forbidden for me to keep secrets from you. Too long the High Magisterium has violated this dictum. With Gavin Guile, we—"

"Oh, hurry it up," Zymun said. To a Lightguard, he said, "There, that blunderbuss. It is loaded, yes?"

"Lord Prism," Quentin said loudly, "by the command of the promachos and the White, I was invested as a luxor."

"A luxor?" Zymun asked.

"Yes, my lord. My sacred and, until now, *secret* duty is to root out filth in the Chromeria."

"Good, good," Zymun said, checking the flint. "I can certainly put you to work—"

With a tone of certainty and authority that Quentin had never before heard in his own voice, he declared, "In the eyes of God and the Magisterium, you, sir, are filth."

"What?" Zymun asked, looking up, more surprised than outraged.

None of the Lightguards had thought to train a musket on the effete little rich-robed young man who was helping them. His two hands came up, and the two hammers of the most expensive pistols money could buy came down.

They fired simultaneously, blowing off half of Zymun's head.

Both pistols had fired. Ilytian handiwork. One had to admire that. The Ilytians made fine pistols.

Chapter 137

This time, the magic came easily. It hit Dazen like liquid joy, spreading throughout his body as if he were a starving man eating a ripe peach, licking the juice from his fingertips, exulting in the sweetness.

As black had marched him like a prisoner to the brink of death, so white freed him and filled him with vigor. Within moments of beginning to drink from the fountain at his feet, he felt as if he had slept a long, full night in a feather bed and awakened to a gentle dawn, his bride warm beside him and the smells of a fine repast filling his nostrils.

White luxin was Orholam's warm regard for the world.

How did we lose this? How could we let this go?

Like that sleeper waking, stretching his arms, Dazen stretched out his magic luxuriously toward the Chromeria, and the pains stretching thus brought him were pains leaving his body. White blazed out from him to the horizon and beyond, toward his beloved islands, his beloved wife, and all those many others he loved there. It was a great gift—a privilege!—to bring such light.

Dazen's will burned white through the darkness, over the face of waters as if tracing the white-luxin line Kip had thrown toward him back to its source.

As he raced back, he felt a whisper of will in the fading white luxin Kip had cast. Was it a prayer? Desperation, but no message was discernible at this distance as the luxin was disappearing. Dazen's heart leapt. It was Kip's will, Kip's voice!

Kip was alive?!

But then he realized, like a distant cannon's flash outruns the sound of its firing, that what he was sensing now, becoming clearer and clearer with every league his will came closer, was only the last echo of his dead son's voice. And yet he grabbed after it, desperately, that this one remaining piece of Kip might not be lost to him.

The message became clear only as Dazen closed on the Jaspers themselves.

"Please! God! Please, someone finish what I've..."

And that was it. Weakly, the voice and the will that had sustained it had trailed off.

Dazen had just heard his son's final words.

And now the final filaments of the magic decayed so that even that message was lost. Bereaved afresh, Dazen's will burst back through the still-smoking broken mirror that the slave boy Alvaro had sabotaged, and thence into the mirror network itself.

Kip was gone—dead and removed now from the execution scaffold and the mirrors' grasp. No trace of living will remained, but the luxin he'd been weaving had not yet decayed completely, though it was unraveling by the moment.

What were you doing, son?

It had something to do with the mirror array, but Kip hadn't averted the larger mirrors from himself—as any sane man being baked to death on Orholam's Glare would've been trying to do. Why not?

But there were seven fading streaks, like dim arrows of chi and white luxin. And then those, too, were gone.

And now nothing of Kip remained.

Finish what I've begun? What have you—

Seven arrows. Seven different directions: if Dazen extended the lines, one pointed to each of the seven satrapies.

The closest one was Blood Forest. In a blink, Dazen followed it like an arrow pointing him the right way, and there found his answer. There was a Great Mirror here, standing afresh in a place where no Great Mirror had been known to be mere months ago.

Dazen's will jumped to follow the next line, and the next.

Every line of Kip's magic pointed to a Great Mirror, some buried, most forgotten, and only the ones at Ru and Apple Grove fully operational.

But why?

And regardless, what use were mirrors at night?

And then, as Dazen explored the mirrors, he found the answer for that as well. Each mirror tower held an odd reservoir, like liquid luxin of its own color within or beneath it. Tyrea's Great Mirror outside Rekton brimmed with sub-red, a shrine outside Idoss stored red, Ru's Great Mirror stored orange, Blood Forest's held yellow, Melos— capital of the ancient united kingdom comprising most of Ruthgar and Blood Forest—held green, Paria held blue, and Ilyta superviolet.

But why would Kip look for more light as he was dying from too much?

Because he wasn't looking for it for himself.

Kip had given his life trying to bring light for his friends, who would need it to fight in the darkness. As night fell, the Chromeria's drafters had no source—but here was a network of mirrors and light-wells throughout the world, with every color the defenders needed.

One source of color in each of the Seven Satrapies, and Dazen himself stood atop an immeasurable source of white like a wheel's axle around which all of them turned.

Kip had pointed the way. Kip had discovered the design, so long forgotten, but only Dazen could cast his will so far that he might finish the tapestry Kip had begun.

To raise even one tower holding a Great Mirror from its great hiding place underground would have daunted any drafter in the world. Only Dazen—maybe—had the strength to raise them all.

So he did it.

He cast his will to the easiest first, the mirror in Ru at the pinnacle of the mighty pyramid there, and he lashed its Great Mirror to his will. He felt the mirror turn and then shiver as it came into place, as if it were made for this, as if the mirror was settling into an old groove—and felt it lock, not on him but on the Great Mirror right behind him.

Of course.

Connected once again to its ancient network, under its cascading gardens and beautiful waterfalls, the surface of the Great Pyramid of Ru suddenly flowered with orange runes and ancient designs. Dazen heard cries of fear turn to shouts of delight as the people of Ru came forth to see this wonder. But he had no time to enjoy it with them. He'd already moved on.

The Great Mirror in Blood Forest at Apple Grove had already been raised by Kip—but there were children playing at the base, in the way of the gears. They might be crushed if Dazen moved it without warning.

He shook the Great Mirror, beginning the process. It threw several off their feet.

Then he moved on. He'd come back.

Outside the ruins of Kip's home village of Rekton, within sight of Sundered Rock, he found a fallen statue, perhaps of the old Tyrean Empire warrior-priest Darjan. It once guarded and marked the mirror's location. Dazen realized then that at least some of the Great Mirrors were older than Lucidonius, older than the nine kingdoms he'd conquered. They were at least as old as the Tyrean Empire, fifteen hundred to three thousand years old.

Now the crumpled statue seemed to guard nothing more than an orange grove, but still a slow mist of paryl rose from the very soil. It shivered at Dazen's touch, and a puff of superviolet joined it, allowing his will to thread down and down through seemingly solid earth.

He gathered color after thickening strands of color into his grasp like the fibers of a rope. And taking it full in hand, heaved heavenward.

821

The earth split, tree roots tore, and in a fountain of dirt, a spire shot into the sky.

Dazen laughed as the magic poured through him.

He glanced in wonder and awe at Orholam beside him and found Him smiling His own delight and encouragement: 'Go on!'

Dazen sank into it once more. This was his old strength, doubled and redoubled. He felt virile, potent, alive in a way he'd not felt in years. The joy of drafting came back to him. It was like, after being buried alive and breathing as shallowly as possible, he'd suddenly broken free of the prison earth and was taking the deepest breath of his life. He was strong.

No, 'strong' didn't cover it. He had the might of a Titan.

A vast disk shot into the air, and then, with a pulse of magic that had lain dormant waiting for this moment, it vibrated, and all the dirt and detritus of long ages jumped off its surface and it gleamed as sharply clear as the day it had been made. On protected gears and belts undecaying, on luxin and old infusions of will, the mirror swiveled to answer Dazen's call.

And his will shot away again. To an abandoned temple atop the first soaring butte of the Red Cliffs outside Idoss.

Then to a high valley between green round-shouldered mountains in Ilyta, where the superviolet mirror had been buried beneath the banks of a river. Bandits had set up a camp on this forbidden ground, a camp that had become a village. If he raised this mirror without warning, houses would be destroyed, and perhaps innocents kidnapped for ransom or slavery or even children crushed.

Dazen shook the earth hard, laid a hex foreboding doom, and moved on.

In Paria, near two vast and trunkless legs of stone, the blue mirror lay hidden under the lone and level sands. A brickwork floor opened smoothly on centuries-old hinges, swallowing half a dune effortlessly, and the mirror rose.

In Ruthgar, the green mirror rose from the heart of a butte over the verdant grasslands outside the once-great city of Melos, setting a nearby herd of iron bulls stampeding.

Back to Blood Forest, where for the first time he realized that though the well of white luxin might be limitless, his own endurance was not. He blinked, and wondered how long it had been since he'd blinked last.

The children had scattered. Some still watched from a distance, clinging to a wary young man near Kip's age as if he were a father to them all. A safe enough distance.

Dazen knew what he was doing now, and he pulled the Great Mirror to its groove. This one was a different design, though, from some other people, some other time, claimed and retrofitted by later conquerors but not made new.

This mirror was connected, communal somehow. It spoke to... trees? He felt root speak to root, and his will was drawn from this mirror to others, deeper into the forest, all the way to Dúnbheo and Green Haven and other, smaller mirrors. It wasn't a luxin-based web, though, so Dazen couldn't raise all of them directly.

Instead, he turned the first mirror toward them—and they answered! The Great Mirrors of Dúnbheo and Green Haven didn't even need to be raised; they'd never been hidden in the first place. Some of the smaller mirrors were broken, nodes that lived only in memory, but others had rested shielded within the trunks of great trees. Now coiled roots pushed out, and others, stretched, pulled taut. Working like ligaments and muscles, with no gears anywhere, the tree roots worked together to heave several dozen mirrors across the satrapy into position.

Had this been the work of some empire Dazen had never heard of? Was this the magic of the pygmy peoples?

But there was no time to study the marvel, or even to wonder at it. Dazen felt his body gasping, his own strength stretching him too far.

Back to Ilyta, where some people had scattered, but others had come bearing their muskets and long knives. Bandits, Dazen hoped. But maybe just the sons of bandits, only trying to defend their homes from something that filled others with dread.

Brave men, regardless.

Dazen shook the earth once more. One last wordless warning to people who could die in a war they didn't even know about.

Some fled, but others stood their ground, shaking their spears as if some monster stomped between their homes. You've built your home on the monstrous, you fools. As did we. The cowards who ran would live, while the brave died.

Dazen could wait no longer.

Houses shattered and tore apart, the earth rent, a spire shot into the sky, and then the superviolet mirror slashed through the village. The brave fell and the rubble of their own homes crushed and buried them.

He flashed back to his own body, staggering.

No, not yet. He'd taken seven colors, but there were nine. He sank deep into the mirror to feel for those last two, but found only a single trace: a bane atop Hellmount, far, far to the west, pulsing like the sun, its slopes littered with the burnt bones of the dead who'd tried to approach, to claim it for themselves. But there was no mirror nor lightwell for that great chi bane, nor anywhere else. Nor for paryl. Even the ingenuity of the drafters of old had never subdued those colors.

No wonder the Chromeria had always feared those colors. Light cannot be chained indeed. Not all of it anyway. The mystery always escapes us.

Finished, he came back to his body again.

He felt disconcertingly wonderful, but he knew it was a false strength now. He'd lifted weights with the strength of a thousand men, but his muscles were going to give out on him without warning at any moment.

The whole thing must have taken only a few minutes, because even as he gasped on the sweet night air, he could feel the distant Great Mirrors still finishing turning, still settling their beams onto the Great Mirror behind him.

And then, as more strength came into his hands than perhaps had ever been held by one person, he realized that he was deeply and truly *fucked*.

The Mirror of Waking began to spin. Suspended on nothing at all that he could see, it began to turn into a blur, on several invisible axes. The air filled with its sound, and wind whipped over him.

Dazen felt the lightwells under each of the seven Great Mirrors in their far-spread satrapies slowly uncorking themselves like shaken bottles of bubbly wine. They would blast perfect, pure light in their respective spectra, pulsing in time with each rotation of the Great Mirror behind Dazen. Thus, basically simultaneously, Dazen could direct light from every arc of the Seven Satrapies to any point and to as many points as he wished.

He had under his will as much power to distribute as he could hope.

But no matter how good it felt, he was damn near dead. Drafting white was like sprinting downhill—deceptively effortless, so long as he kept his feet under him. Giving him this much power was like giving that downhill sprinter a hard shove in the back.

He'd done what no other drafter could have done. No other drafter in the world could've handled that much magic. No other drafter could've reached so far. Other than Kip, no one could've lifted so much as a single one of those towers alone.

He'd raised five.

But now? Even if he could handle the light, somehow *feeling* the colors needed despite his color-blindness, even if he could survive more than another few seconds of so much power, the Chromeria was far beyond the horizon. The mirrors themselves could settle into their old grooves to find one another, but it would be impossibly fine work to strike at a single foe on the island or to take the mirror array and use it himself.

Dazen couldn't strike down wights from here. He'd broken the bane's control of magic, but he couldn't fight those floating islands from here, couldn't unwind their magic and drown the wights in their thousands. Not from here.

He couldn't save the Chromeria.

He was a runner collapsing on the last lap, begging that someone carry him to the finish line.

Without warning, the colors bubbled forth from their long imprisonment. Dazen didn't know what else to do but throw them toward the Chromeria. First, they effervesced across the sky, but then he wrestled them back to a tight beam. One last act of white will.

In the now tightening spray of colors, he felt a vortex reaching out, giving him a point to aim for. It was an answering Will, some desperate or brilliant drafter who intuited that now, in the middle of the night, after the wash of black luxin had freed the skies, she or he should mount the Prism's mirror array.

Maybe there was some hope after all—

Dazen felt the colors sucked in, suddenly. One two threefourfi—all of them!

A full-spectrum polychrome.

A man—yes, it felt like a man—of chthonic strength and titanic will.

Across the immensity of the space between them, their wills meshed like the gears that had raised the Great Mirrors, and without words they knew each other.

Father.

Dazen?

Dazen felt a shock of revulsion ripple through his entire body. The gears ground to a halt.

His father—and since when was Andross a full-spectrum polychrome?—his father wanted him to hand over control of the mirror array.

On the one hand, it was the obvious solution. Andross was there. No one else was. Who else could handle the magic? Who else had the will and concentration and pure fortitude?

But at the same time, it was a horror beyond countenancing.

If he gave his father this power, Andross Guile would be seen rescuing everyone. *He* would be hailed the Lightbringer. If Dazen gave him this, everything Andross had ever done would be excused. Forgiven. No, not even forgiven, *lauded.*

'Murdering children? That must have been so hard for him!'

'Yes, yes, but he was wiser than the rest of us. He knew what was necessary to save the world. He did that for us. He was a man of vision. A *great* man, willing to do what was necessary for all the rest of us. A hero.'

Everything in Dazen shouted *No!*

Anyone but him!

Tears of rage poured. Dazen felt a cooling reassurance from the old monster, and a repeated demand that Dazen give him control of the array. *Now.* Like that was more important than anything.

You murderer! You killed Sevastian! You killed all that was good. We had everything and you killed it all. Don't you dare say it was for the world. It was for you, your pride! You always had to be the best. You always had to be right. You always had to prove yourself smarter than anyone else! Always, always!

But the distance was vast, and they couldn't hear each other's words.

Orholam, please, no! Not this. Not this.

Dazen held all the weight of the empire's salvation in his hands. He knew to hold on to the magic any longer would kill him, but to give it to that beast was impossible. His fists knotted white.

He felt a presence, and he opened his eyes.

Orholam stood in front of him.

He knew.

As they locked gazes, Orholam's left eye deepened and morphed, and Dazen saw standing there a throng, silent in their penitents' garb, but adorned in their Sun Day finest cosmetics and jewels. More than two thousand women and men, each with Dazen's knife wound over their hearts. His victims from all the Freeings. His peaceful accusers.

Around them stood a vast multitude: the fathers who'd never dreamed their sons would die before them; the husbands so devastated at losing their wives they couldn't even care for their children; those children, who'd lost their mothers; the orphans who'd had only one parent to begin with; the bereaved spouses hastily and unhappily remarried; the families who held together but always kept an empty seat at every dinner, every feast, and tried to tell themselves that it was all for the best, that this was Orholam's will, though they could never fully believe it. Because it wasn't.

They were his victims all. Dazen's murders had rippled out into the world in a swamping wave greater than he'd even imagined. Not one corner was untouched.

He wept.

He couldn't look anymore, didn't dare to keep on seeing the truth of what he'd done—but in tearing his gaze away, he was arrested by another image, this one in Orholam's right eye. Andross cradling a dying Sevastian, the long blade yet in his hand, blood still leaking from Sevastian's chest. 'Did I do well, father? Did I make you proud?' Sevastian asked.

He died before the weeping Andross could find the will to speak.

Then, a mercy: Orholam's eyes were merely eyes once more. But there was only truth reflected in both His eyes, and none of it was soft.

Orholam said, "I've forgiven your many, many murders. Will you forgive him one?"

Chapter 138

Though Gill was one of perhaps half a dozen people who understood what he was seeing, he felt no less awestruck than everyone else he saw turning to the north, their eyes widening, jaws slack.

In the distance, rising into view from the Great Market, though the market itself was hidden by Ebon's Hill, was a creature from legend. Outlined in fire, a titan emerged as from the earth itself, stretching skyward. It seemed to pluck a barrel from the ether, took it in its fist, and then hurled the thing, flaming, into the ground somewhere in the Blood Robes' ranks. The flash of light was followed a moment later by the sound of the explosion.

When Corvan Danavis had told them what he planned, he'd said, 'Should be a last stand to remember.'

And no one watching seemed to notice that the flash also showed the red titan had no body. The outline of fire was all it had—all it was—an outline of burning red luxin stretching high into the darkness of the night, grabbing barrels shot or lofted into the air. The titan moved with astonishing fluidity, and it really did throw the barrels of black powder, but with the benefit of forewarning and distance, Gill could see it for what it was—amazing drafting.

To everyone else, it was as if a great djinn had risen from the earth to intervene in the battle.

But then, just as they emerged into the great avenue running from the Chromeria to the Great Market, getting their clearest view yet, Gill heard the sound of a pistol shot.

His and Big Leo's were two of the only faces that turned toward the sound. Near the base of Orholam's Glare, a body fell dead, practically headless.

High Lady Karris's luxiat slave, Quentin, held two smoking pistols over the body, a surprising, powerful gravitas in the usually tremulous young man's face.

The Lightguards nearby were flinching back from the pistol shot, some cowering, others lifting their weapons instinctively, as if to block.

They were holding Tisis Guile as if she were their prisoner.

Now the Lightguards, shaken, were recovering. Some were pulling their own muskets toward Quentin, who'd dropped the pistols and had thrown his hands up in surrender.

Someone was going to shoot him.

"Stop!" Karris shouted beside Gill, and she ran toward the Lightguards. Gill ran beside her with Big Leo only one step behind, and the people crowding the square melted back for her and Gill and the rest of the Blackguards cutting through.

Deprived of their leader, caught out in the open with everything going wrong for them, the Lightguards panicked. They dropped Lady Tisis. Some dropped their muskets. Half a dozen, including—Gill saw through the gaps in the crowds—that crippled bastard Aram, ran back toward the Chromeria, moving with surprising speed despite his crutch.

And then they were there. Gill had expected to find some poor bastard dead, but instead he found two.

The man Quentin had shot was bleeding still, blood somehow still pouring from his shattered braincase onto the paving stones, but slowing, slowing, even as they arrived. Lady Tisis had been punched several times at least, and looked in terrible condition emotionally—but not seriously wounded. Gill didn't concern himself with her further for now.

No one else appeared armed.

Though many looked afraid of the Blackguards, of Karris, of glowering Big Leo with his great chain, no one in the crowd appeared threatening, or guilty, or shifty.

A flash from behind him made Gill whip his head around. A last flash of red light from the Great Market, the following sound of a distant explosion, and now the titan was gone.

828   High General Danavis had said he had a better than even chance

of dying if he tried whatever he was planning—and almost no chance of not breaking the halo, which was really the same thing. Gill could only hope that he'd accomplished what he hoped, that he'd made those pagan bastards pay.

Part of Gill wanted to urge Karris to take them all to the general, to help them in whatever desperate straits they were in. But that wasn't his role. He was a trainer of the Blackguard, not a general.

As he turned back to things nearer at hand, Gill realized that the young man whose wreck of a head was still pumping blood on the ground could only be Zymun Guile.

He sought his ward's reaction, but the White's face was a cipher. She was already looking to Tisis, who was moving, pushing people out of her way.

"Zymun was about to hang Tisis," Quentin told Karris. "I was too late for . . . High Lady, I'm so sorry."

Tisis reached where she was going, kneeling, pulling a body into her lap, and the crowd melted back to let Karris see.

To let Karris see *Kip*.

Dead.

Beside Gill, Big Leo dropped to his knees, dropped his big chain with a clatter to the stones.

But Gill didn't even look at him. Big Leo wasn't his ward; Karris was. And if he lived a hundred years, Gill would never forget the expression on her face now.

It wasn't denial, for in her face there wasn't rejection, but instead the note of confirmation of something suspected. He saw in her face her last hope for happiness die. It was as if she'd thought, At least I'll have one good thing, and though it was less than I wanted, I shall make myself be content with this.

And now she'd had that last good thing snatched away and smashed before her eyes.

Gill turned away, telling himself his job was to scan for threats, telling himself that he should give her the dignity of mourning in private, telling himself he was the wrong person to comfort her in this. She should be comforted by a mother, a father, a husband—but she had none of these: they'd all been stolen from her.

Well, then, surely she needed a friend her own age, not him, not a man who worshipped her, who was ten years younger. It would seem presumptuous to even step forward to try to be a comforter. He wasn't the one who could be that for her—

Suddenly, she keened, and her scream was so incoherent that everyone who heard it understood perfectly.

Eyes turned away, faces filled with shame around the square.

"*NO!*"

She seemed to almost attack Tisis as she pulled Kip's body into her own arms. She froze, trembling, muttering her denials under her breath as she stabbed fingers into his neck to feel for the pounding of life there.

Finding none, she stood, Kip's body sliding limp, gracelessly, out of her lap. She staggered as one drunk.

Her eyes searched the crowd unseeing, wild.

Gill felt a surge of shame. He should guard her in this, too. Protect her somehow from this shame. But he didn't know what to do. When Gav had died, they'd known what to do for him, how to honor him; Karris had stood with him, somehow. But he had nothing.

She keened again.

He felt sick.

She was the Iron White. They shouldn't see her like this.

"High Lady..." he said quietly.

She shook with her weeping or with rage, the red rising in her against this evil day.

Tisis looked up at her, haunted. "He didn't try to save himself. Even to the end, he was trying to bring light to us. He was fighting for us. To the very end."

"No!" Karris shouted, decorum abandoned, spit flying. "This isn't right! This isn't happening!"

"High Lady, please..."

"You don't understand! He's not dead! He's not dead. Oh, *God...*"

Gill reached a hand out to steady her, but she slapped it away angrily.

"Karris, please, the people—"

"No!" she shouted at him. "Don't you tell me about—YOU! I know you!"

Suddenly her ire turned on a man in the crowd. An artisan by his dress. He looked familiar, but it took Gill a moment to place him. That was it: the kopi seller from her favorite little stand. Parian by his look, but Ilytian by his accent. Gill couldn't remember his name or any other connection, though.

Karris quieted as the little man came forward uncertainly. Speaking to the rest of them, she said, "Send everyone to go aid High General Danavis, if he yet lives. If he doesn't, he'll have left someone competent in charge."

"High Lady..."

"That's an order!" she bellowed. "I have work to do."

Gill waved to the others to go.

Big Leo and his Mighty didn't move, and Gill didn't insist.

"You, Jalal. You saved me," Karris said quietly to the weathered old artisan. "That day those men beat me. Andross's men. When they beat me to teach me a lesson. I thought . . . but it was *you*. You carried me back to the Chromeria, didn't you?"

The old man said, "Who are you, child?"

"Who am I? Who am *I*?!"

Even to Gill, it seemed a strange question. Was the old man blind?

But Karris. Oh, his beloved High Lady Karris White. His Iron White was edging into hysteria.

Tears spilled down his cheeks and he dashed them away. This was unseemly.

"I'll tell you who I am," Karris said, cheeks wet, but with hidden heat like a coal burnt to white ash suddenly breathed upon to glow a sullen red. "I'm the fatherless daughter, the bereaved sister, I'm the widow, I'm the impure White, I'm the leader who failed—but there's one thing I won't be. I'm the slip of a girl who'll run through brick walls, and I won't be the mother without a son. Because who *I* am doesn't matter."

"Oh, but you're wrong."

But she barreled ahead. "*You* carried me through all this. You were there when I was broken down, beaten up. And you will *not* leave me now! You promised me that you'd repay me for the years the locusts have eaten. You promised! And I believe. Orea told me, and the Third Eye confirmed it. So you swore it! HE IS MY SON! And you will *not* let him be dead. You can't!" she screamed the last. "You *can't*, because if he's dead, then you're a liar. You can bring him back. I know you can! If you will it, you can give him back to me. And you have to, or your word is good for *nothing*!"

She was barely keeping her feet.

Gill's heart lurched. War had broken strong men and indomitable women before, but Karris?

Not his Iron White, please no.

Did she even know how she sounded?

"I don't care!" Karris shouted at everyone around her as they looked away, embarrassed for her, brokenhearted. "I don't care how you look at me. You think I'm crazy? I don't matter! *He* does." She pointed ferociously at the kopi seller. "You all think they could kill my Kip? You morons! You think they could kill Kip on Orholam's Glare? Orholam's *Glare*? How could Orholam look on my son with anything but favor? And mercy. And mercy. *Please* . . ."

"High Lady, he's dead. Let him go," Gill said.

Tears streamed down her face. "I failed, don't you see? Don't you understand?! I reached the end of myself, and I failed—but Orholam cannot. He *cannot*. It's what I do now that matters, right? And I believe. I believe."

She sank to her knees and took the hand Tisis offered. And together they wept.

"Please," Karris begged the old man. "Please, tell them. Tell them who you are."

"Who do you say I am?"

She looked up and through her tears she said, "I say you're the one who holds the wind in his fists. I say you're the one who wraps up the oceans in his cloak. I say you're the one whose every word proves true. I say you're the Lord of Lights. I say you're stronger than death, and…" She sank farther, lying prostrate, her face on the very cobblestones, stretching her hands toward the old man as if he were unimaginably far away. "I say I'll praise you, though you slay me."

Only then did the old man move. He came forward, and he knelt beside her. "I'm afraid," he said, "that you have been very much misled."

She expelled a breath, so hopelessly that she clearly wished it were her last.

"Shh, shh," he said, brushing back her hair behind her ear as if soothing a child. "Very much misled about the extent of your failures, and even more so about your own worth, Karris *Agapêtê*. Be still, child. Be still. For about this at least you are right: your son isn't dead, only sleeping."

Karris took a sharp breath, and Gill's hand convulsed on his spear. What new insult was this? Was the old man mocking her?

But Karris lifted her head, and the hope in her voice as she spoke to the old man hurt Gill most of all. "Then you'll wake him?" she asked.

"Of course," he said, slinging his pack around and pulling out his little cups, and filling them with his dark, steaming brew. "What do you think kopi is for?"

His eyes twinkled as with many lights. And as he gently poured the drink into Kip's mouth, suddenly the night lit with incandescence above them all.

Every eye turned to the Prism's Tower as a great white light from the east hit it, unimaginably pure and bright.

The whole tower lit with color, and then, too, did all the other towers of the Chromeria in turn as every one of the Thousand Stars flared to life throughout Big Jasper—radiating first with white light, then with every color under the sun.

Then, under the control of some masterful hand on the mirror array, the night filled with light. Directed by some great intelligence that could hold a hundred details at once, the Thousand Stars blossomed and turned—here shooting red source, here focused tight and hot enough to burn some unseen enemy, here giving blue or green, here flooding the enemy with light they couldn't use, and in fifty other places seeking out friendly drafters to give them exactly what light they needed.

Faces turned heavenward, seeing hope brought to their despair and light brought into their darkness. Cheers broke out throughout the square and throughout Big and Little Jasper.

But Gill, after checking for any immediate threat from the outpouring of magic and seeing none, saw little more of it. He saw only his mistress's face, and she saw only Kip—and her son suddenly took a deep breath, and sat up, eyes opening.

Only as Kip breathed out, smiling as if waking from a pleasant dream, did Gill realize that the old kopi seller had disappeared.

Chapter 139

"This here is the point where you make a decision," Orholam said.

"You've got to be joking," Dazen said. "I thought that's what I just did." He was an old cloak drenched in the rain and now wrung out, and there was nothing he wanted so much as to hang up in the air to dry a bit. He'd just given father everything the old cancer had wanted for more than forty years. Worst, he'd given father vindication. It made Dazen's heart hurt. Could he not just curl up in a corner for the next decade or two?

Orholam said, "You came all this way for one reason. Did you forget it already?"

To kill You? Oh, not that. "To save Karris?" Dazen asked.

"You still want to?"

"What are you talking about? She's on the other side of the world. Me drafting anything is impossible at this point. Like, I *thought* it was impossible before, but now? It's really, really not happening."

"A man is more than his magic, Promachos."

Wow, that sounded like a deep lesson, but c'mon… "What can I do? You got another ship and crew tucked away inside the reef somewhere I didn't notice? What's the rush now? It'll take me weeks or even months to get back. Everything will be over by then. There's no way I can get back in time to help."

"Time. Psh," Orholam said.

"Easy for You to say."

"What about your glider? What'd you call it, 'the condor'?"

"That would be handy. You know, if I hadn't destroyed it in Tyrea, hundreds of leagues from here. You gonna make me a new one?"

"Right now I prefer making things new to making new things."

"You are *really* hard to understand sometimes," Dazen said. "It's lost. Broken. I destroyed it so no one could learn its secrets. And I couldn't fix it anyway, now."

"Like I said, fixing is *My* specialty," Orholam said. "You want to fly with Me?"

Dazen said nothing for a moment. "You're serious."

"I seem to recall you rather enjoy it."

"Flying? What?!" Dazen's exasperation was as unbounded as the night sky.

"That vexation you're feeling?" Orholam said. "Been feeling that for you. For years."

This did not make Dazen feel less vexed.

"But, you know," Orholam went on, "it'd be hazardous. It *is* pretty dark out, and some people say Orholam can't see at night."

Dazen glowered.

It turned out that the reckless, winsome Guile grin had nothing on God's.

"So what is this?" Dazen demanded. "You've actually got a condor up Your sleeve? No, You'd have to do me one better, wouldn't you? An eagle or something?"

"A machina, up My sleeve? That'd be cheating. Now, hurry. It's a long fall if you miss the timing."

"Timing? What timing?"

"For the jump! You do remember where the gap is on the level below this, right? Go through that gap—or it'll be a short fall."

Dazen said, "You want me to *jump*? Off this tower? In the dark?"

"Admit it, your last leap of faith was terrible," Orholam said.

"Huh?"

"I'm giving you a do-over. A second chance," Orholam said. He bent his knees, readying himself to run. "It's what I do. Any moment now. Three...Two...Oh, don't forget the blade!"

"Right!" Dazen turned back. The gun-sword was still sticking out of the now-white tower.

He yanked it free. Behind his back, he heard Orholam yell, "Now!"

He turned.

Orholam was gone.

Oh no. No, no, no!

Fear grabbed at his legs to hold him in place. It was probably already too late. If the timing was so tight, then he'd surely already—

Dazen kicked Fear in the face.

As he sprinted toward the edge, he shouted, "I can't believe You're making me do this!"

And he leapt.

Chapter 140

"Can you fight?" Karris asked. Baffled, the crowd was torn between gasping at the dazzling spectacle of lights above them or at the young man silently healing at their feet. Healthy skin was surfacing from beneath his burns, and where he'd been burned bald, hair was growing in speedily—but as if it were natural, as if this were something that happened every day.

But none of them mattered.

"Yes," Kip said tentatively, then, gaining strength, "Yes! Let's go kick some ass!"

Big Leo hauled Kip to his feet as easily as Karris might lift a quill.

Kip immediately collapsed again.

"Well, that's awkward," Kip said, looking at his limbs like they were purposely embarrassing him.

"Son—can I call you son?—I'm so glad you're alive," Karris said, "but other people are dying. My people. Right now. If we live, we'll—"

"We'll do all sorts of things," Kip said. "Got it. But you need to go. So go."

"You showed me how to win," Karris said, and she felt like the Iron

White again as she said it. "We have to kill the White King. And that's on me. It doesn't matter that it looks impossible. And our best chance is tonight, right now. Who knows how long this will last," she said, pointing to the spectacle of many lights dancing above them. "Right now is the only time we're going to have the advantage. We win now or we lose. Kip, I love you. Can I take Big Leo and the Mighty?"

She knew she sounded scattered, but there were too many things to do all at once.

"Yes," Kip said at the same time Big Leo said, "Uh-uh. I'm not leaving you again."

"*Leonidas,*" Kip said.

"Don't call me that."

"Big Leo, you can't think I'm in danger now," Kip said. "Orholam Himself saved me. I'm gonna be fine. You think He did all that to let me get killed two minutes later?"

"I'll stay," Tisis said.

"Me, too," one of the nunks of the Mighty said.

"See?" Karris said.

"Besides, you didn't help at all with the blue bane," Karris said. "Think of this as a second chance."

"Leo didn't help with the blue?" Kip asked. "I thought— Holy shit, man, the rest of 'em are never gonna let you live that down."

"Fine. I see how it is," Big Leo said. He looked at the nunk volunteer. "But not you. Anyone who volunteers might be Order. I'm not sure they're all dead." He pointed to two of the other nunks at random. "You and you, but keep ten paces out."

"Yes, Commander," they said. The original volunteer looked offended, but kept his mouth shut.

Big Leo loosed his big copper chain. "Wight King's flotilla's that way, right?"

"Straight down the main street," Gill said. "But we'll have to make it through the Great Market and maybe even past the orange—"

But Big Leo wasn't paying attention. He swung his great thick chain over his head, and suddenly, it took fire, whooshing with each great circle. "Let's go kill some pagans! For the Iron White. For the Lightbringer!"

And then as they roared in return, he ran, as if he didn't care if he had to do it all himself, as if he'd simply take all the glory for himself, and if they missed out, so much the worse for them.

In a moment, everyone followed—not only the Mighty, not only Karris's remaining Blackguards, but practically every able-bodied civilian in the square, too.

Karris looked at Kip, shrugged, and then hopped off the platform. Gill was holding a horse for her.

"Go on," Kip said. "That's your battle cry. That's your advantage. You shout it every chance you get: 'The Lightbringer is come.'"

But she glanced back, and as he said it, he wasn't looking at her. He wasn't looking at the battle. He was looking up at Andross Guile, limned in light at the top of the Prism's Tower.

Chapter 141

Gavin had once said, 'The only thing more dangerous than winning a battle is losing one.'

Now Karris knew what he meant.

Not once, but *twice* as she and her people fought across Big Jasper, Karris saw jubilant Chromeria forces rush around corners and blunder into each other—and go blasting away at one another with muskets and magic before they realized they were killing their allies.

She'd only been saved from the same by the great beam of white light that followed her everywhere she went—Andross tagging her somehow, which had not only saved her from friendly fire but also drew enemies.

Not that she should really complain.

Nor was there was any way to do so, if she'd wanted to.

But it did make what she'd hoped would be a simple jog across Big Jasper into a running battle that took the entire night.

Her forces had torn into the weakened northern flank of the White King's drafters encircling the Great Fountain, and demolished them. A young general named Lorenço was commanding in Corvan Danavis's stead. He was relieved to see them, and delighted to give over command.

But Karris didn't want to command, and it took valuable time to get the strike force she wanted out of him. She also reclaimed her own Blackguards that she'd sent on before her to help High General Danavis. Lorenço believed the grievously injured high general was dying, and had put him in the care of physickers nearby. Karris would have liked to thank the man or at least say goodbye, but there was no time.

Once she had her force, she didn't go out of her way to save others or even to attack shaken Blood Robes—not much, anyway. And yet, for every company they encountered that simply melted at the sight of them, others fought tooth and nail. Clearly, many had no idea of what had happened out of their own sight, and most of the Blood Robes thought they were still winning and that the Jaspers would soon be theirs.

Nor was fighting in the middle of beams of light an unqualified advantage—for some of the Blood Robes were canny enough to use the darkness to spring traps, especially with will-cast animals: Karris's people were attacked by wolves, a tiger, a giant javelina, and even a bear once.

But everywhere they went, they shouted, "The Lightbringer has come!" and with their ever-burning coruscation of every color and the heavens alight with untimely scintillance, the Blood Robes believed them and were sore afraid.

The idea spread through their battlefields like a slow, stubborn fire.

Karris's people forced the Blood Robes in their sector all the way back to the wall they'd climbed on their way in and smashed them against it, men and women suddenly panicking that they would be left inside the city they had worked so hard to enter.

As she crossed the wall itself, from that higher perch, she could see her brother's own dragon-ship out beyond the orange bane—but first her eye was drawn to the yellow bane, which cracked open like an egg and blazed brightwater skyward in great fountains shooting up into the night.

A lone figure was running along the shattering shell, dodging enemies and splinters and shards of yellow glass. He ran to one yawning edge of a sudden abyss, much too far, and *bounced*, ludicrously high and far to the other side.

Landing, he split a yellow wight nearly in half with a spearlike thing—a tygre striper?—who in the world knew to how fight with one of those these days?

But it could be nothing else. It bent and straightened—now plastic, now rigid—as the warrior cut through half a dozen yellows in turn, all fleeing him or fleeing to get off the crumbling yellow bane. The young man sprinted with great long strides, impossibly long and fast, and Karris realized his very legs must be fitted with the same kind of sea demon bone that made the tygre striper directly susceptible to the Will.

"Shit, I don't see Einin," Big Leo muttered. Then he shouted, "Benhadad! Ben!"

And then Big Leo was gone, taking the Mighty with him to rescue his comrade, who, truth be told, didn't look like he needed rescuing.

In minutes, though, they all re-formed on the orange bane.

It was the last place Karris wanted to be. You couldn't trust your very eyes here. The orange bane was virtually paved with uncured lumber and flat stones—anything the Blood Robes had been able to find to make themselves pathways on the oleaginous surface. To step off the paths and streets was to risk sinking to the waist in orange goo.

Karris immediately feared traps, but nothing happened as they charged across the surface. There were few oranges, and they'd not been expecting a counterattack, so perhaps for once, Karris and the Chromeria's defenders would get lucky.

And then the surface of the bane shifted as if in an earthquake, and behind them an orange hill rose and rose.

They ran, faster, and faster. Ben-hadad blitzed on ahead of them all, with his great inhuman loping strides, looking for traps or ambushes or even safe havens.

But then they were plunged into darkness as the hill rose so high that the mirrored light from the Thousand Stars could no longer reach them.

And then the bane settled behind them—and split open ahead, yielding to the wood decks of the White King's own dragon-ship flotilla of a dozen galleys lashed together.

Its eerie white wooden skin bristled with ivory, metal, and luxin spikes, and its mouth gushed fire from spouts out its draconic mouth.

Karris and her people were out of range of that fire, but she saw hundreds of his warriors leaping out onto the orange bane.

She recognized their standards: these were Koios's personal guard, maddened, screaming, carrying their own colors forward into the night.

Karris had fewer than three hundred elite warriors with her, many of them better drafters than fighters, now trapped in the darkness with no mag torches left. Dawn was achingly close, but too far off to make a difference—and suddenly, alone, her three hundred were facing thousands of the White King's best and freshest troops.

For the moment, the Chromeria was winning this battle. Hell, they might win the battle outright, regardless of what happened in the next few minutes to Karris.

But that didn't make a whole lot of difference right here, did it?

As Gavin had said, 'Dead winners and dead losers have only one thing in common. Unfortunately, it's the most important thing.'

Chapter 142

The great, winged machina must have flown directly at the tower, nosed up hard to vertical at the last moment to avoid a collision, and stalled just in time to catch Orholam gently.

In jumping late, Dazen was going to get nothing *gentle*. He plunged after the falling condor, seeing Orholam nonchalantly pulling Himself into a finely carved wooden seat and tying a rope around His waist, even as the machina fell sideways, slowly spinning.

Dazen fell only slightly faster, head angled down like a boy diving into the water, sword flopping about hazardously in the air.

He realized that the principles of flight, which he'd only been starting to master when he'd made the first condor, also applied to his body. There was probably something smart and dextrous he should be doing right now.

Orholam have mercy, it was as if they were two horses racing each other, and he'd taken the outside track to doom. He started to pass the condor, too far away to grab on to the tail or the seats, coming equal to its nose before the condor, now headed straight down, began falling as fast as Dazen was.

But then the condor swooped, raising its nose and swerving into him. He bounced off its nose, the machina smacking his head and knocking the wind from his lungs, and the sword almost out of his grasp. He slid down its back. Or, more appropriately, *up* its back, as it was inverted, still falling. As Dazen slid, he grabbed for Orholam's chair, or his legs—anything. But his three-fingered left-hand grip failed him again. He slid up to the tail, and there clung with his hands and knees gripping the winged machine like a bad rider clamped helplessly to the back of a spooked horse, feet braced against some small protrusions of the tail that hadn't been there in his version of the machina.

The wind tore at him as if he were as welcome as a tick, but he held on. He wasn't going to die. Not yet.

"Hey!" a baritone voice shouted at him. "Can you move your feet, please?"

"I'm not back here for fun!" he shouted back.

"Get your feet off the elevator flaps or we're gonna hit the trees."

Dazen looked up, not at the speaker, but at the horizon. The condor was leveling out slowly, but it needed to climb *rapidly*, or it was going to smash into the hills ringing the plain around the mountain
840 tower's base.

He scooted forward and pulled his feet off the nubs where he'd braced them and instantly felt gears shift and the tail flex. He tucked his head tight against the condor's back as it shot up into the air.

He didn't move again until it leveled out. Then he scooted slowly, slowly forward, until he reached the windbreak on the condor's back. He took the only other chair. Chairs? That was a nice innovation.

No one had even offered to help him.

"Thanks for the help!" he said. "No, I kept the sword, too. No problem."

Orholam and the captain of the air machine glanced at him as if he'd only just boarded.

"Oh, did you hit your head?" the captain asked. "Sorry about that."

He didn't sound sorry at all. "Not your fault," Dazen said, though Orholam could have given him warning.

"I know," the captain said. "I meant I'm sorry you hurt yourself. I was being polite."

Real polite.

Dazen returned the favor by staring at the man. The man had apparently also hit his head recently, as there was an ugly lump and abrasions across his forehead. But that wasn't the main thing that made Dazen stare. This man was ethnically unlike anyone Dazen had ever seen: fine, straight black hair, broad cheekbones, and skin folded across his upper eyelids.

No, scratch that. This man was unlike any Dazen had ever seen in real life, but not in art. There'd been a statue of a man like this at the beginning of the pilgrimage. Or...no. Not a man like this. *This* man.

Not this *man*, this *immortal*.

"Oh, hey, I've seen you before," Dazen said. "It's an enormous pleasure to get to meet you in person! I saw your statue. You must be really special!" Being overly friendly was sometimes the best way to irritate the surly.

The immortal grunted.

"This your island?" Dazen asked, relentlessly chipper.

The immortal grunted again. Maybe a no.

"Dazen Guile. Nice ta meetcha!"

The immortal glowered at him. "I know who you are."

"You're an immortal, huh? How's that work? What do you do?"

The immortal looked over to Orholam. "My lord? Permission to abandon ship?"

"Denied," Orholam said happily.

"This is about my failure with V, isn't it?"

Vee? Dazen felt like a child among adults talking over his head.

"Not a failure, not yet," Orholam said. "And this is no punishment."

"Please don't say it's a reward"—the immortal cleared his throat and added quickly—"my most gracious lord. I beg you."

Orholam said nothing.

"So it is a reward," the immortal grumped. "And since you said 'Not yet,' you're sending me back to her."

"If it's possible," Orholam said.

"What would keep me from going back to—oh." The immortal got quiet, then squared his shoulders. "So we're heading into one of *those* kinds of fights," he said.

Great. We're going into a battle that gives the immortals pause?

"There's victuals and a wineskin in the pack, and blankets," the immortal told Dazen, nudging it with his foot, but not moving from the wheel. "Eat. Sleep."

After devouring the best food of his life, Dazen did.

He woke to a hand on his shoulder.

"You'll want to see this," Orholam said.

The sun was beginning to lighten the sky. Dazen felt a hundred times better.

Orholam pointed over the edge of the condor.

They had to be hundreds of paces in the air. Dazen felt a brief moment of vertigo, then saw them—streaks in the water. "Are those...sea demons?" he asked. "What are they doing here? I thought there were only eight left."

"Seven of the eight accepted Orholam's mercy last week," the truculent immortal said, though Dazen hadn't been asking *him*.

"Last week?" Dazen asked. "But I only asked the boon for them yesterday. That *was* yesterday, right?"

"It was," Orholam said with a twinkle in his eye. "But I knew you'd ask."

"But what if I hadn't?" Dazen asked.

"That's Karris Atiriel at their head. Unable to reverse Lucidonius's soul-casting and bring him back home, after her years as Prism, in order to join her husband, she became a sea demon herself."

"I thought she *established* the Blackguard," Dazen said. "Wasn't half their purpose—"

"Her intention was that no one would ever again do what Lucidonius had done, even as she planned how to copy him herself. Instead, her success proved to others that drafters less gifted than Lucidonius might also succeed. Now, after all these centuries, she's ready. She's finally chosen to abandon her husband to the self-destruction that he loves more than he loves her or anything."

Dazen absorbed that for a few moments, then asked, "But what are they doing *here*? This doesn't look like *release*. They're still sea demons."

"They serve, Dazen. Broken as they are. In gratitude to you, they asked that before they die, they might use what they've become for the good of the people they loved, and for you."

Dazen was about to find that very touching, when he saw something atop the sea demon. A platform? "What's that on her *head*?" He squinted against the distance, but he lost it.

Orholam was grinning. "That? You're gonna love it. Do you want to know the last part of your penance, Promachos?"

There's *more*? No, I do not want to know about any more penance! "Yes, please?" he said.

"There *is* no last part of your penance, but you will have opportunities to show that you've changed."

"That sounds a lot like penance."

"I know. Just like this next part could look a lot like a leap of faith, but it really isn't."

"What are you talking about? A leap? We are going to land together, right? I can suggest some really—"

"Not together, and we're not landing. This is your part. I'm not getting out of the machina," Orholam said. "Now, remember, the sea giants despise the bane, but they're susceptible to their influence. In particular, Karris Atiriel is highly sensitive to the orange bane, even still. Do your best to destroy it before she arrives, would you?"

"Sure, but I still don't—"

"Good. Kip will really appreciate it. Put this on. Oh, and one last thing," Orholam said. He handed Dazen a canopy-pack and the gunsword.

"What?" Wrestling the pack on, strapping it tight with Orholam's help, Dazen saw a fleet of ships and the bane like floating islands dotting the waves in the first gray light of the morning. The condor was closing fast. He felt disoriented. Why had all this waited until now?

Orholam embraced him, and at first, Dazen was too stunned to even return it. For all that Orholam looked like a reedy old man, His hug redoled of an unstinting strength that was unmistakably maternal: a mother gathering her hurt child into her arms, fierce in defense, gentle in encouragement.

"Never forget," Orholam said softly. "I see you. I hold you in My eyes."

Then He threw Dazen off the side of the condor.

Chapter 143

"Brother! I don't want to kill you. But I will," Karris shouted.

Her people were doing better against vastly superior numbers than they had any right to be doing. It helped that everyone on both sides had exhausted both luxin and gunpowder, which left her with her Blackguards—not to mention the Mighty, who'd now been joined by all two dozen prospective members, and Ferkudi, and Winsen (who'd apparently destroyed the green bane *by himself*).

Somehow they'd followed Karris, despite everything.

Or not Karris, she knew. Ferkudi and Winsen had come to fight for Big Leo and Ben-hadad. They fought for one another, like brothers do.

But not her brother.

Koios had lost patience and joined the fray himself.

He cut a swath through all of them, his own men first, heedless, murderous, then the Blackguards as well, battering them with jets of luxin, impaling men with great spikes, even blasting Gill Greyling far off to one side.

Coming finally in front of her, he threw one hand up, and a cage of blue luxin shot up around her from the ground at her feet. Then he threw his other hand up, and the ground beneath them shot into the sky, making a craggy blue-luxin tower only wide enough for the two of them. She would have expected orange, here on the orange bane, but Koios had always been most adept with blue.

Karris snapped off one of the bars imprisoning her, and then another. But there was a lethal drop on every side. There was nowhere to go.

"Give up now," he said. He pulsed with every color, rivulets of light cascading from his head and down his body, his luxin armor now more like a carapace than a suit. "Your people die. But you don't have to join them."

"You're losing," she said.

"Am I?" he said, and she hated that she could still hear echoes of his old voice in this monstrosity. He shook his head. "I have a dozen seed crystals in reserve. I can grow new bane in a day, and the Ilytian pirate kings' reinforcements will arrive tomorrow. I overextended today in my eagerness. But nothing you've done has accomplished anything. Not a thing. You've delayed me by one day. Tell me, do you think your people can fight again tomorrow as they did today?"

"You're lying," she said, heart sinking. "It's all lies."

"Let's see about that," he said. He pulled out a brilliant green jewel, holding it with a thumb and forefinger.

He waved his other hand, and the blue bars of Karris's cage disappeared.

Karris darted forward, but she felt the green luxin inside her body suddenly stiffen.

She skidded on her knees. Against her will, her hand opened, and the scorpion tumbled out of it.

"Worship me," he said. "The very immortals weary of your Chromeria's tyranny. They fight for *me*! I am a god of gods!"

"You're a slave and you don't even see it," Karris said.

He sighed. "They've brainwashed you. It's so very sad. I loved you, sister. I loved you so much. I love you still, but not like this, sister. Not like this." As he rolled the green jewel between his fingers in the first of dawn's light, its color flashed like a green wink. Her hands came up, palms spread as in supplication. He smiled at her, but it was an ugly smile, and in his other hand, a blade sprouted, longer and longer.

"Say the word, sister, and live. Or...I'll just to have to remember you as you were, before they corrupted you."

*   *   *

Dazen was drifting downward beneath his canopy, trying to slow the thudding of his heart and choke down the tightness in his throat. Without drafting, he didn't have the margin of error he used to have in everything.

But Orholam Himself threw me. It's gotta be a perfect throw, right?

However, it quickly became apparent that he wasn't going to land on Big Jasper at all. He was headed for the darkness of the ocean.

Surely there's going to be a crosswind coming soon?

Any time now.

There was no crosswind.

But what he did see as he fell was a bane—orange? maybe red—and a flotilla of ships all lashed together, and then a battle of some sort. A circle of Blackguards and some others were holding off many, many more enemies.

All right, all right, maybe this is the right place after all. Good throw, old man.

He pulled out the Blinding Sword and pulled open the breech. There was no powder. Dazen started checking his pack to see if he had a powder horn somewhere.

Surely he had a powder horn somewhere.

The Blackguards were all in a circle around a narrow tower of some sort—and they all had their backs to it, making a last stand—and there she was atop the tower, his Karris, confronting a polychromatic wight.

And she was on her knees.

But Dazen was coming right down behind that big rainbow bastard. Dazen found the powder horn and tugged it clear of the canopy-straps.

Cutting this close, Orholam old boy.

He uncapped the powder horn with his teeth—

And then something invisible caromed off him, sending him spinning up and sideways, tangling the cords of his canopy and throwing him wildly off course. The powder horn went flying, and he nearly lost the sword, too.

He saw a flash of light that illuminated two winged figures fighting, tumbling through the air away from him, locked in combat.

Spinning and swinging wildly off course, Dazen gripped the sword with white knuckles, trying to get his bearings. He was fast approaching the luxin tower—but not the part where he wanted to land.

He was too far away. Now he was going to land behind Karris, at the very, very edge of the tower. He might not be able to stay on it at all.

He had only moments to make a decision.

Without black powder, he couldn't shoot the gun-sword, but he *could* throw it like a spear. That worked, once in a while, throwing your sword. Once in a long while.

Almost never.

And throwing a sword like a spear while spinning and swinging...?

But Dazen was the Promachos. That was who he was! He was the hero who arrived on the wings of the dawn and saved everyone at the last second. He could make the throw! He had to!

Or...he could give up all that.

* * *

"Hey! Hey!" someone shouted in the air above them. The voice was familiar.

Locked in place by the green seed crystal's influence over the green luxin in her body, Karris couldn't move, but she saw Koios look up quickly, alarmed, blinking against the glare of Orholam's rising eye.

A black blade landed across her open hands. It cut her palm as it slid through her grip, and the black luxin sucked greedily at the green luxin in her blood.

And suddenly, as the green luxin immobilizing her was devoured, she was freed.

But then Koios saw her moving, and saw the blade in her hands.

He lunged at her, blade extending.

Karris was nothing if not fast—it was the reason she'd made it into the Blackguard—so she lunged faster, batting Koios's blade aside with a forearm and ramming the black sword home, all the way home into the Wight King's chest.

For a moment, it was as if nothing had happened. No blood poured from around the blade. Then, abruptly, it was as if he were collapsing in on himself. She realized what was happening: the blade was sucking every bit of luxin out of him in turn: sub-red, then red, orange, yellow, green, blue, and superviolet—

—until Koios was, quite suddenly, merely a burned man with rage and disbelief in his wide eyes, wearing a necklace with colored and black jewels on it. She ripped the necklace off him and threw it off the tower.

Then she ripped the sword out of his chest. There was no blood, still, which stunned both of them.

He threw a hand at her to lash out with magic, and she moved the sword desperately to parry the attack—but no luxin missile flew from him.

Koios looked down in horror at his mortal flesh.

His head shook, no, no. He threw his hand forward again, again, as if trying other colors in turn and finding none of them.

His eyes filled with fear. He backed away, desperate. "Ye immortals! My servants! Come to me now! I command it!" Koios cried. "Save me now!"

Extending his arms, he leapt off the tower as if he fully expected to be caught.

His body crunched on the deck of the ship far below, crushed.

"Um. Hate to be a bother," a voice called out behind her.

Gavin? "Gavin!" she cried.

Her husband stood with his toes on the very edge of the tower, his hands cartwheeling as he tried to keep his balance.

"Uh…" he said. "Hi, honey. Help?"

Then, before she could move, he plunged out of sight.

She was at the edge the next instant, as if she hadn't had to cover the intervening space.

She looked down, afraid of seeing his broken body beside her brother's far below, but instead she saw Gill Greyling. He'd almost climbed the entire tower, coming after her—and now he'd snagged Gavin out of the very air.

Twisting as he held Gavin's wrist in his hand, the Blackguard said, "I lost one Gavin, sir. I'm not losing another."

And then she was helping hoist her husband up the tower. The battle immediately below them was finished—the Blood Robes had broken at the sight of their master leaping to his death.

And then her husband was up, and safe, and in her arms.

The dawn was glorious, but there were a million things to do. But none of them mattered right now. The feelings were too big to hold in for one more moment.

She had never cried so hard in her life.

Chapter 144

"Will you...uh, will you look at my eyes?" Kip asked Tisis. He'd thought that it was simply the night, bleeding the colors from the land as it does, but the rising light of the incipient dawn was making it clear. There was something wrong with the colors; they were wan and weak. He said, "I blew my halos. On the Glare. It's been really nice holding and being held by you, but now...I have to know."

Tisis took a deep breath. She'd hadn't looked in his eyes since the beginning. But as she looked at him now, she seemed relieved. "They were stark white, right after. All the way through. Now they're blue. Just your natural blue."

"No halos at all?" he asked.

"No, none."

"Well..." he said. "That's, um, great. I guess." He wasn't going to have to be Freed in the next few days, so that was something.

"What's wrong?" she asked.

"I can't draft," he said quietly. Grief speared through his stomach. That was why the colors felt weak, emotionless. His vision now felt as impoverished and textureless as a drafter's vision is compared to the immortals'. He was seeing the way munds do.

"What?" she asked. "No. Maybe you're just tired? Lightsick?"

He shook his head, forcing a smile. "My life was spared, but not my powers. I've tried every color. They're gone. They're all gone."

"Oh, honey," she said, putting her hand to her mouth.

He could've been the Lightbringer; now he couldn't even draft. He was a mund. Many drafters would have preferred death to that. He would have, a year ago. He looked away. "Do you think—do you think you can love a man with broken eyes?"

She didn't get mad at him, which he would have deserved. She only squeezed him tight.

"I'm so sorry," she said again.

"Me, too," he said, wiping his eyes clear. He took a deep breath. "And now let's be done with that." He was almost surprised that the words rang true. "I think . . . I think I'm kind of finished with self-pity. It probably should've taken less than *dying* to figure out how good I've got it, but I do. I'm here. With you. So I'm a mund. So what?"

"A mund?" she objected, a smile turning her lips at last. "Kip Guile, the last thing you are is *mundane*."

Did you think I would forget you, little Guile?

"Huh?" Kip asked Tisis. She and Commander Fisk were helping him stand.

"I didn't say anything," she said.

He was wobbly, but maybe he'd recover quickly if he walked around a bit. "I think I've figured something out about myself: I really hate watching a battle."

The view from the elevated platform was excellent. Though Ebon's Hill hid everything in Weasel Rock and Overhill, Kip could see West Bay and East Bay and the still-burning fires at the Great Fountain. The predawn light was just beginning to tell the tale of how much damage the Blood Robes had done to the city. Smoky plumes rose from numerous areas, but Karris had stockpiled water and firefighting supplies, and organized neighborhood teams, and it seemed those fires weren't spreading. The rattle of muskets was still constant, sometimes in volleys, but more often in crackles around the entire island. Few of the cannons were firing at this hour. Most had either been silenced or were waiting for the dawn to better reveal their targets.

The superviolet, the blue, the yellow, and the green bane had been destroyed. As far as he could see, the rest were still afloat. He didn't want to think what that probably meant for Ferkudi and Ben-hadad. He wanted to rejoin the fight, but he knew Commander Fisk and Tisis weren't going to let him do that. Probably they wouldn't have let him fight even if he started turning cartwheels. But they were right, he was in no shape for any of that. He was useless.

It was not a good feeling.

Now, what was that voice he'd imagined?

"What was *that*?" Tisis asked.

"What?"

"In the water!"

But whatever it had been, Kip missed it—and turned his aching head and burning eyes as far as possible while doing so. He immediately regretted the action. All right, definitely not in any state to fight. He might as well volunteer to go fall on an enemy's spear.

"It went right past the Lily's Stem," Tisis said. "Here I was about to suggest we get back to the Chromeria to be safer, but... if that thing hadn't turned it could've taken out the bridge without even noticing."

"A sea demon?" Kip asked.

Then he heard a throaty boom of some huge cannon and turned. Few other cannons were firing now, and none sounded like *that*.

"What was that?" Tisis said. "I think I know that gun. Orholam's beard, is that The Compelling Argument?"

"The what?"

"My sister tried to buy it off a merchant Phineas something maybe? He wouldn't sell, and said he'd never make its like again. Swore it was destined for someone else, but demonstrated it for her to try to drum up other business."

Kip could only see a wisp of smoke in the air in the direction he'd heard the blast. Sometimes cannoneers wrapped burning sackcloth around a shell to be able to watch its trajectory. In a few more moments, he was rewarded with another shot, arcing identically to the first, to thud into the sub-red bane.

Commander Fisk had a long-lens to his eye. He handed it to Kip with an odd look. "Please tell me I'm not crazy."

In the half-light, though, it was hard to find anything.

"Find the old Tyrean embassy. Couple points right of it, halfway out in the bay," Fisk said.

"Where's his ship?" Kip asked. For in the water, there appeared to be a ship's square forecastle, moving at speed, undulating, floating without the advantage of a ship. A man danced to an inaudible beat, with hot points of light burning in his beard as he loaded a huge cannon all by himself.

"*Gunner?*" Kip said. What was that forecastle resting on?

Gunner fired again, then jumped up on the barrel of his big cannon and danced from one foot to the other, eyes straining as if waiting for something. He pumped his arm as if successful, though at what, Kip had no idea.

A moment later, the entire sub-red bane *exploded*. Light flashed over the islands and a cloud mushroomed in the early morning, smoke rolling in on itself.

"Did he just—?" Tisis asked.

"He sure seems to think so. And—is Gunner on top of *a sea demon*?!"

"Not sure," Fisk said.

But whatever it was, Kip wasn't going to see it, because Gunner and his floating forecastle disappeared behind the Tyrean embassy.

"Enough. This one is under my protection!" someone shouted.

Kip looked around. It was a familiar voice this time. But there was nothing to be seen. A feeling of foreboding came over him. "Rea?" he said. "Rea Siluz?"

Tisis looked at him. "Who?"

"Nothing," Kip said. "Were you going to go wrap that wrist and get some poppy?"

When Aram had deflected her pistol during her attempt to shoot Zymun, he'd sprained her wrist. It was very swollen now, but she hadn't wanted to leave Kip, hadn't left all through long hours of the morning.

"Yeah." But she looked at him oddly.

"Commander Fisk?" Kip said. "I'll stay right here, promise."

As they went, Kip walked to the very edge of the platform and craned his neck. A rain of burning embers was still drifting down from the sub-red bane—luckily for the city, most of it was landing in the water. Kip could just barely see Gunner's forecastle—now resting on the seawall of East Bay. The pirate was gesticulating furiously, but he didn't appear hurt, and the forecastle deck was leaning at an angle as if it had been dumped off the sea demon's back.

Kip stepped back, and something brushed his shoulder.

There was no one on the platform with him, but that touch made his whole body tingle. He looked at his shoulder. The sleeve was cut open—and *smoking*. The barest line of blood welled up as he gripped his arm.

The premonition he'd felt suddenly resounded again in his gut with all the urgency of a sick man who'd ignored the first belly twinge and now was about to vomit.

Abaddon.

He tilted his head back and saw—and he saw in glorious, weighty, more-real-than-real color, because as he was drawn inexplicably, inexorably into that overlapping realm by the great immortal's presence, he was seeing not only with his physical eyes, but he was seeing as *they* saw.

As Kip's eyes focused on this other world, he saw Abaddon, king of locusts, spinning a tight loop in the air, something like a black blade seething in his hand.

Rea Siluz staggered near Kip, her arm drooping, and he could only guess that she had just deflected a blow from him.

And not for the first time.

But she didn't pause. She leapt instantly, faster than human thought, bringing up a blazing sword—

The concussion of their collision blew away Abaddon's illusory body and face. The black, smoking fragments dazzled Kip's eyes but not Rea's. Abaddon beat her back, and with hammer blows of sword on sword and sword on shield, the immortal battered Rea out of the air like a man swatting a moth to the ground.

She fell to the street below the platform, elegant armor scraping on the cobblestones, baffled, afraid.

Ten paces out, the two Mighty nunks looked around as if they'd heard something. But they hadn't been drawn into the bubble; they couldn't see them.

The locust thing that was Abaddon drew Comfort, his mother-of-pearl-handled multichambered pistol, and shot rapidly at Rea's prone form.

Rea blocked the shots with shield and then sword, getting knocked back and back, finally falling to the cobblestones. She looked more shocked at his power than in fear for her life, though.

Smoke curling lovingly from his pistols around his body, he paused in firing, not to reload: that pistol never needed reloading. "Concede this world to me, Aurea." He gestured to his pistol. "This is no Sundering Blade, but if I kill you with it here, you can still never return to this realm. Go. Tell yourself that you'll be back someday. I've won today."

Why was he telling her that? There must be some shred of a chance Rea could still win, or he wouldn't be giving her a chance, right? Or was there some old affection between them that Kip couldn't even guess at? *Aurea?*

Rea looked at Kip, and he could swear he saw an apology in her eyes.

Then, taking advantage of her distraction, Abaddon fired at Rea, but she'd already winked out of the space where she'd been lying a moment before, fleeing.

She'd abandoned this world.

But then it made sense, didn't it? If there really were a thousand worlds, that left nine hundred and ninety-nine more for her to fight for, didn't it? One battlefield lost didn't mean much, on that scale.

The nunks who were supposed to be protecting Kip seemed to have heard the final shots or the ricocheting of the musket balls off the street, because they charged toward the platform now.

And died, instantly; their heads obliterated with a single shot each.

Abaddon holstered his pistol and landed on the platform in front of Kip. He didn't bother to re-form the illusory mask of a human face, instead staring at Kip out of the same insectoid monstrosity that Kip had last confronted in the Great Library.

Some part of Kip had really, really hoped that was a hallucination brought on by the cards.

"You hoped I'd forget you?" Abaddon asked, a rusty voice from a throat not made for human phonemes. "You thought you might triumph here?"

"Yes?" Kip said.

Abaddon's face clacked and chittered. Kip had no idea what emotion that was intended to convey. Then the creature said, "Where is my cloak?"

"It's right over there. Can't you see it?" he asked, pointing to the far side of the platform.

Abaddon's fist lashed out and cracked Kip's ribs. He fell and almost tumbled off the platform. He groaned, holding on to the corner post, staring out to East Bay in the half-light.

Rea, please tell me I'm not really alone here. Please.

"The master cloak. Where is it?"

"You've made a big mistake," Kip said, facedown, woozy. "Huge. Gigantic."

Gunner was out there, so far away Kip could barely see him, standing as if he was holding a long-lens up to his eye. With the hand out of Abaddon's sight, Kip tried to gesture to Gunner: 'Shoot here, yes, here!'

"Me?" Abaddon said. "No, no, no. You have no idea, do you? This battle was never about Koios and this little empire. It was about the fate of this entire world. Even now your Wight King calls out for our aid—and will get none. The djinn have been freed from his control. The bane will grow again—in a single day, with my help. We'll inspire such bloodlust that these barbarians will scour these Jasper Islands. Massacre everyone. Even now, look! Are your worthless mortal eyes keen enough to see the black sails of Pash Vecchio's fleet on the horizon? The pirate king comes with our reinforcements, and what do you

853

have? No one comes for you. You've been abandoned. What's your last hope? Some sea demons? Do you know how weak those really are against the right magics? It's been a defense worthy of song. But none will sing of what you did here. None will be left to do so."

"It's funny you mention my eyes," Kip said. "Because you're right. I am blind to other realms. I don't know them, nor understand them when I see them, and when they affect my life, I'm left breathless and dazed. But I'm not the only one blind."

"I know. All your ilk are the same, save some few Seers, who catch glimpses and believe they see all and know yet more."

"I mean *you*," Kip said. "How many humans have you known, over how many ages? How many worlds? And yet you don't understand us at all. I'm blind to the other worlds, but you're blind to the workings of love, of self-sacrifice. You look at the space they occupy, but it looks empty to you. You can't even imagine how they work. You can't imagine caring about anything other than yourself. It makes you stupid, Abaddon. It makes you predictable. It makes you weak. Do you know what humans can do? We can *suffer*. If you just give us one solid thing to brace our will against, we will move the world. We will hold on. Past reason. Past belief. Do you know what we know that you don't?"

"I should take you to join my menagerie. Perhaps a thousand years of torment will teach you some respect. What are you hoping for, little Guile? Orholam's hosts have abandoned this realm. I feel not the touch of a single one of them now. Soon we shall free our brothers and…" He trailed off, his head twisting to the side. "I see something about a *gunner*?"

"Thanks," Kip said. "Sometimes it takes a while for a compelling argument to come together."

"What?"

Kip reached out and touched Abaddon's foot. Abaddon could move way too fast for Kip to mock him out loud, but he thought, You're in my bubble of causality now, bitch.

The immortal looked at him, his head tilting. "We seem to have such trouble communicating, you and I."

Kip couldn't help it; he glanced toward the seawall protecting East Bay, where he could just barely see the lonely foredeck of a ship that had been run aground, and the black cloud of smoke that had been belched from its mighty throat. Kip shouldn't have looked, but perhaps Abaddon was so crafty he would think Kip's glance itself was a distraction, a misdirection.

854   Between the raised platform at Orholam's Glare and Gunner's

mighty Compelling Argument soared the old Tyrean embassy. There was a space no wider than a man's forearm is long through which a cannonball might clear the embassy and still hit the platform.

Indeed, though Kip was visible, the embassy probably blocked Gunner's view of Abaddon.

Kip didn't care. He hoped Gunner put the exploding shell straight in his own lap. His life for Abaddon's? Yes. Absolutely yes. This is for my nunks, you bastard.

But even as the first diced heartbeat passed, Kip saw that the shot was simply too far, even for Gunner.

The cannonball—a smoking, flaming streak—was heading wide. Either Gunner had miscalculated to try to miss the embassy or the cannon itself simply wasn't accurate enough. The shell was going to miss.

Then he and the immortal saw the same impossible thing: the flaming missile was *curving*—curving *in midair*—

Curving toward them.

Kip scrunched up into a fetal position, turtle-bear once more, one last time, hunching around Abaddon's ankle—they had to be touching for the immortal to be stuck in Kip's world and time.

Over him, Abaddon threw his arms up in defense.

The concussion rocked the world. Kip's sight went black with a slap.

And then he became aware of shrapnel raining down on him. And—ow! shit!—it was really hot!

Kip scrambled to his knees, flicking burning pieces of metal and wood from his clothes and skin, little burn holes dotting his tunic and trousers. But he was too weak to stand.

Abaddon stood before him, above him still, knocked back five paces by the cannon shell still raining down around them. His coat and cloak had been ripped away in the blast.

His burned and blackened wings unfurled in a crack of rage, but whatever wounds had torn his wings, they weren't new; they'd happened long ago, in millennia beyond counting. Abaddon was unhurt.

Kip's deception and Gunner's excellence and a curving, exploding cannonball had done *nothing* to this immortal except knock his clothes awry.

"ᗝᘺᒋᕤᘺᒋ!" Abaddon bellowed in that voice that reverberated in tones above and below human ken. "You think any mortal weapon could kill me?"

He leaned over, pained by his long-ago-broken ankles, and picked up his sword, which he'd lost in the blast—now disguised as a cane once more.

855

"I don't need to kill you," Kip said, though his heart dropped.

"What? Are you hoping your father will arrive with the sword?" Abaddon asked, derisive. "He's a league away, killing that idiot Koios. Do you think with the master cloak abroad that I'd actually *lose track* of the one blade that can hurt me in this world? No. He'll not come in time for you. Now, *where is my cloak?*"

He lifted a foot and casually stomped on Kip's head.

It felt like Kip had been kicked by a horse. But blubber bounces back. "Get out of here," Kip said. "You bug me. Ha. Get it? You're an insect?"

"You can die easy now or you can die over the course of ten thousand agonizing years. Last chance." Stomping on Kip's head with each word for emphasis, he said, "Where. Is. My. Cloak?"

That was the magic of the master cloak. Even the immortals couldn't see it. No wonder Abaddon was a bit put out that Kip had taken it.

"I have a better question," Kip said, nose streaming blood. "Keep firing as fast as you can. It reloads itself."

"Enough of this," Abaddon said. "As fast as—what?"

"A better question than 'Where is my cloak?'" Kip said quickly, "would be 'Where is my . . . pistol?'"

Abaddon reached for his holster to draw his revolving-chambered pistol, Comfort. It wasn't there to be found.

Teia was fast. She'd always been fast.

A hole appeared through the middle of Abaddon's left eye as a gush of gases and smoke jumped out of the empty air to Kip's left. Only the pistol's barrel protruded from the invisible master cloak. One report followed on another. Five shots. Ten shots. Fifteen. Twenty, as fast as she could fire them, perforating the immortal relentlessly.

Teia said nothing. She wasn't the kind of assassin to give a lecture to announce her presence.

She also wasn't usually the kind to miss with half of her shots, but then Kip saw why as she dislodged the master cloak and her head became visible: she was firing blind. She wore a scarf around her eyes and had also ducked her head into the crook of her elbow to shield her light-sensitive eyes from the muzzle flash of the pistol every time she pulled the trigger, only taking a quick, unsteady peek every few shots until Abaddon collapsed, hemorrhaging blood everywhere.

With a word to her, Kip took the pistol from her hand, then stood over the immortal, whose chest and arms were drenched with several shades of impossibly vivid green and black and red blood, the colors already fading in Kip's sight as the immortal's life faded and their realms separated once more.

"I know I can't kill you without the Blinding Knife," Kip said. "But I can banish you, can't I?"

He shot Abaddon in his nasty insectoid head. Twelve times. Then his chest a few more. Then the joints of his flailing limbs. Then his stomach—who knew where this immortal kept his heart? No point taking any chances. "Get...out...of my world!"

Kip kept firing until the color faded and the immortal's blood boiled, turned to smoke, and blew away with an ungodly stench. The rest of its flesh followed. In moments, nothing was left but Abaddon's clothing.

"Dammit, Teia. Took your time, didn't you?" he said.

"Is that a thank-you?" she asked. She was sitting with her head against her knees. "When'd you see me coming?"

"I didn't. But I knew you wouldn't sit out a whole battle," he said. "We'd never let you live that down."

She gestured to the chain-spear still wrapped around her waist. "Faced an immortal, and I forgot to use your gift. Sorry." She flashed a wan smile. "I guess it's aptly..." She trailed off. "I'm not feeling so good, Kip." She twitched. Her skin blanched deathly pale.

He barely caught her before she collapsed.

"It's gonna be all right. We'll take care of you, Teia," he said, his chest tightening.

"I know," she said. "I know."

Chapter 145

"Form up," Big Leo ordered. "One last time."

They were all standing looking out toward the pirate ships anyway.

"Might as well make an easy target for 'em, huh?" Winsen said.

"Running's still an option," Ben-hadad said. "They might not get us all."

"Says the man with bouncy legs," Winsen said, but he took his place in the formation.

"I tried so hard to bribe them," Karris said, resigned. "They shaved my messengers bald and had them beaten. Never even listened to the offers. Offers that would have put us in debt for a hundred years, by the way."

Dazen said, "This is personal. I sank Pash Vecchio's great ship, his pride and joy." In the time it had taken them to safely get back down from the White King's high platform, the pirate king's fleet had pulled within range, with a great ship the twin of the *Gargantua* coming to point-blank. "I guess when you make enough enemies, it's gotta catch up with you sooner or later."

Karris sighed, then straightened her back to stand tall. She looked around at all of them as if to lock them in her mind's eye now. "Where's Grinwoody?" she asked.

"Grinwoody?" Dazen asked.

"Yeah, he fought with us all night," Karris said. "Saved me a time or two."

"Good fighter for an old guy," Big Leo said.

"He what?" Dazen asked.

"Haven't seen him," Big Leo said. "Not since we came out here. Maybe he fell behind?"

No one else had seen him, either, and no one had as much interest as Dazen did in pursuing the inquiry, as they were staring out at hundreds and hundreds of pirates bearing down on them.

"Pirate king's a mercenary, right?" Ben-hadad said. "So...surely he's gonna want to switch sides again now that the White King's dead? Right?"

"Ben, Ben, Ben," Winsen said as if he were a child. "The leadership of one side is dead, and he's got the leaders of the other side staring down the barrels of a thousand guns. You really think—"

"Not a thousand," Ferkudi interrupted. "Don't exaggerate! Twelve port pieces, twenty hail shots, two top pieces, thirty breech-loading swivel guns, six slings, six fowlers, and we don't have to worry about the culverins and demiculverins and sakers—they're probably not gonna waste long-range guns when we're this close, right? And less than half the total could be pointed our direction at once since they can't broadside us with both sides simultaneously—though with the muskets and pistols all those pirates are pointing...And then there's the other ships— huh. Yeah, maybe a thousand guns, after all. Never mind."

Winsen went on as if Ferkudi hadn't spoken. "Pash Vecchio's a vulture. What do you think he's gonna do?"

"Hold us for ransom?" Ben-hadad said hopefully.

"A vulture with a grudge," Dazen said as the other ships of Vecchio's fleet continued to fan out. He was reminded how slow naval combat could be before its sudden sharp end. "It's a big mistake to think people will always act according to their best interests rather than according to your worst. How's the light for you all?"

"Not enough to do anything against that many guns," Big Leo said.

"Why haven't they fired yet?" Karris asked.

"We'll get mockery first, I think," Dazen said. "Pash will want to make sure I know who's killing me."

"Maybe he'll only kill *you*," Winsen said, switching places in line to be farther away from Dazen.

A big man stepped out into view on the deck, a big man in ruffles and brocade and more jewels than a beach has sand. He wore a waistcoat under his coat, but no tunic, showing dark-olive skin under many gold chains. He looked something like a huge, obscenely rich version of Gunner.

"And there he is," Dazen said. "Sometimes I hate being right."

"Huh, where'd you pick up that keen understanding of what a super-arrogant guy will do?" Winsen asked.

"Win, shut it," Big Leo said.

"Yes, sir. Sorry, sir. Dying makes me grumpy, sir."

"Gavin Guile!" the pirate boomed between ranks and ranks of men with muskets all pointed at Dazen. Vecchio was broad and happy and intense and spoke in the tone of a man who wouldn't be ignored. The man was also holding two exquisite flintlock pistols, entirely plated in gold.

"Pash Vecchio? Your Majesty," Dazen said.

"I see my reputation precedes me!" Vecchio said. "Or did you recognize the ship?"

Even as he smiled, Dazen swore under his breath.

"Do you know? Someone sank its twin!" Pash Vecchio said. He spun his gold pistols around his fingers, not precisely pointing them at Dazen and not precisely not. "All hands on deck, too. Terrible loss."

"Terrible loss," Dazen agreed, pained. Please, let this not be out of the frying pan, into another frying pan closer to the fire.

"There's a battle on, Guile. And is that High Lady Guile with you there? Who would *believe* my luck? You're even more lovely than I'd heard. And, given the soot and blood you're covered with, as formidable too."

"Thank you?" Karris said.

"Why don't you both hop aboard my newest little treasure?"

'Treasure.' That didn't bode well. Not that there was any option to disobey. The ship had hundreds of well-armed pirates on it, in addition to the sailors. Imprisonment was better than death, but Dazen had had quite enough of imprisonment.

He gritted his teeth and refrained from doing anything stupid, climbing up the extra-long gangplank to get onto the ship.

The Blackguards and the Mighty lined up on the deck with Dazen. No one had moved to disarm them without the Pash's order, but no one had stopped aiming their muskets at them, either.

"Here's the thing, Lord Guile," Pash Vecchio continued, "O sinker of a ship I adored, a ship that cost me a hundred million danars—"

"That much?" Dazen said. "You should really talk to the shipwright about that. The powder magazine would be considerably more secure if—"

"Silence!" Pash Vecchio said. He licked his lips. "We talked. It was rather...more direct than peregrinational."

Pirates. Did they all try to impress with their verbal gymnastics, or was that an Ilytian trait?

But Pash continued, "What I was trying to say—and there's a battle waiting here, so let's not drag this out—is that you, Gavin Guile—"

"—Dazen Guile—"

"—you sank a ship I loved. I was very, very...very, very, *very* perturbed about that. Disturbed even. Mad even. Mad. *But* it turns out there's one thing I love more than my flagship. And you managed to find it."

Oh, nine hells. Seriously? What did I do now?

"My daughter. Behold, the pirate queen!"

A girl jumped out of the door to the captain's cabin. Dazen recognized her. Orholam's balls. It was his mother's room slave.

"High Lord Guile," Fiammetta said. She bowed instead of curtsying, as she was wearing short trousers, a vest, and somewhat fewer gold chains than her father. She had a beatific smile, and had grown out her bright hair in curls. She was either adopted, or took quite a lot after her mother.

This was the slave girl he'd sent home, practically on a whim, guarded by the Cloven Shield mercenary band. She hadn't said she was even *from* Ilyta; she'd said she was from Wiwurgh, in Paria.

But of course she had.

Because what do you do if you're the intelligent daughter of an incredibly wealthy pirate king? You pretend that you're just a lowly slave unless things get really terrible, because you know he's going to save you and you'd like him to be able to ransom you cheaply, and you don't want to stir up his enemies who might kill or buy you to get back at him.

"Dazen?" Karris asked.

"My mother's former room slave, whom she'd ordered freed…but my father hadn't quite gotten around to freeing yet," Dazen said.

"Nor had any plans to," Fiammetta said.

"You never mentioned that," Karris said.

"Turns out," Fiammetta said, "Gavin Guile did those kinds of things quite frequently. Swooped in, saved people, left. Protecting his people, risking his life as if that was just what he did. There must be a hundred villages that have stories of the Prism himself coming and saving them from a rampaging wight, or bandits, or a rapacious local governor. He never cared what it would cost to make things right. And only Gavin Guile could track down an illegal slave ship, board it alone rather than sink it from afar, and free everyone aboard with no loss of life. He ended the Blood Wars. He saved an entire swath of Atash when the Blue-Eyed Demons decided they wanted their own kingdom to despoil and he put them down."

"Wait," Karris said, "that was you? We thought they'd turned on each other."

Dazen shrugged apologetically.

"You went *alone*?" she asked, and he wasn't sure if her outrage was that of a wife or of a Blackguard.

"The way I hear it," Fiammetta said, "he couldn't help himself. Traveled the empire and fixed problems wherever he went. Ships saved from storms. Cures brought from afar. The ruthless brought to justice. Practically invisible, yet bringing light wherever he went. People love a man like that. People follow a man like that."

"They *did*," Dazen said. Once. He tried to say it without bitterness. For good and ill, a Guile might never forget what he'd done, but other people certainly did.

"They do still," a woman's voice said from the recesses of the captain's cabin. "I traveled all over the Seven Satrapies, and everywhere I went, they told me tales of their Gavin Guile, who came and stood for them, who fought for them."

Dazen's knees almost went out from under him, and he heard Karris gasp as she recognized the voice.

"Everywhere," Marissia said, "they love him, and when I asked them if they'd fight for Gavin Guile in his hour of need, they *ran* to answer the call."

Dazen couldn't speak. He couldn't believe it, couldn't believe his eyes as Marissia strode out of the gloom.

Dazen crushed her in a hug, and Karris—gracious Karris!—joined him immediately.

He choked out, "I thought you were dead. I thought that was on me, too."

Fiammetta, who had apparently become a great friend of Marissia's, couldn't help herself. She crashed into the hug, too.

"But how? How?" Gavin asked.

Marissia said, "Your father's an asshole, but he doesn't always murder people when he can avoid it. He exiled me to one of those little islands he owns. I escaped."

"But how did you—?"

"Escape? Gavin Guile," Marissia said in a reproving tone, "I am not a woman without resources."

"I—"

"Enough!" Marissia said. She was radiant, smiling fiercely despite the tears streaming down her cheeks. "Come see!"

She pulled him out onto the forecastle, where she raised one of his arms, and the pirate queen Fiammetta came to his other side and raised the other. Thousands of voices roared at seeing him, not just those sailors on the great ship but the sailors on all the others around them.

Pash Vecchio's fleet had to make up more than a third of the White King's entire armada. And it was shifting into a formation that didn't make much sense if they were preparing to invade the Jaspers.

Marissia said, "Every one of these thousands you see here: every gunner, soldier, and sailor has told me some variation of the same thing: 'When I needed help most, Gavin Guile stood for me. How could I not stand for him now?'"

Dazen was speechless. Proud as he was, he'd never understood what people meant when they said they were humbled by a gift.

He understood now.

"This isn't Pash Vecchio's fleet, Gavin Guile," Marissia said. "It's yours."

Pash Vecchio cleared his throat awkwardly. "I was against all this, but... but you should really have a daughter. Then you'll understand." He glowered. "Come on, Orholam with the squirts, people, this is the part where we betray the pagans and destroy their armada. Isn't anyone going to give the order?"

"What order?" Dazen started to ask. Was this why the whole pirate fleet was coming to bear not on Big Jasper but on the White King's battered armada, into which they'd already driven a wedge?

O my sweet Orho—

"Fia?" Pash Vecchio said, unlimbering a massive curving sword. He flicked it spinning into the air.

Fiammetta jumped up to a gunwale and snatched it out of the air. She shouted, "Who stands with Gavin Guile?"

Pash Vecchio launched a signal flare even as she brought the blade down with an impressive flourish.

The people roared, and the thunder of many cannons rose like a chorus of a thousand voices, shouting:

"I stand, I stand, I stand with Gavin Guile."

Chapter 146

The goddess once known as Aliviana Danavis watched the battle play out from atop the Prism's Tower as the sun rose. She'd tended to her wounds throughout the night, pausing when her flesh required it and simply watching as Andross Guile directed astonishing quantities of light with deft control. She was glad, then, that he'd chosen to become an old man rather than a god.

The fall had not only nearly killed her, it had shaken her. More importantly, it had shaken Ferrilux's hold on her. The immortal was more cunning than she'd given him credit for, and if not for being hurried by this battle, he might have taken her over by degrees.

It was going to be a very long war between them.

She limped to the edge of the tower. Not everyone realized it yet, but the battle had already been decided. The pirate fleet was fresh and had better position, and the Blood Robes' leadership was in utter disarray, some ships counterattacking and colliding with other ships fleeing, contradictory orders, confusion—it had all the elements of an impending slaughter.

Nor was the fleet the only surprise: that, the hosts and their immortals might have destroyed. The dawn had brought sea demons, and they were devouring the bane from beneath. The fresh seed crystals with which the Blood Robes had planned to renew any bane they lost simply winked out of Liv's perception, ingested into those great cruciform mouths and digested by their great cetacean gullets.

Interesting. The sea demons were a conundrum she hadn't studied yet. She would have to, in the coming centuries.

She heard the clank of the mirror-array frame's metal on metal as it came to a rest. Then Andross Guile began unstrapping himself. He looked weary, and angry.

"What are You playing at?" he demanded. He wasn't looking at Liv. He was looking skyward. "Orholam! That can't be it. This was to be my last and greatest game. This was to be everything!"

She studied him, curious. He had summoned magic from the far corners of the empire. He'd empowered thousands of drafters through the entire night, and killed countless of his enemies by his own will. He'd saved the empire. Turned the war.

And it wasn't enough for him.

Suddenly, to Liv's left, the old spectral form appeared. "Kill him!" Ferrilux hissed. "We'll give you all power. Power such as Koios could only dream of. But kill Andross Guile now!"

With stony eyes, Liv met Ferrilux's gaze for a moment and then turned her back. Ferrilux hated being ignored more than anything. She smiled.

"How dare you take it from me," Andross Guile said to the heavens. "This was to be my greatest trial and my greatest achievement. But you had *them* do all the parts I didn't know if I could do."

He climbed out of the mechanism. He looked toward the door into the Prism's Tower, but no one came out.

Andross Guile, the Lightbringer, was utterly alone.

Gathering the superviolet to her to float her down, Liv stepped to the edge of the tower.

The battle was over now. There would be hours of murderous cleanup, but now it was only a matter of bloody time. Now it was just meat slaughtering meat.

The old man had dropped to his knees. "I don't understand," he said. "My whole life. My whole life..."

People, Liv thought. So strange.

She floated down from the tower and crossed the bridge. There was nothing for her here now.

It was a mistake. She had barely left the Lily's Stem when she saw him, being carried in a litter.

Her father.

He shouldn't have been able to see her, but there was something odd about people's vision when they were close to death. It was another thing she would have to investigate someday, she thought.

For the moment, she pulled her hood down, hoping this more mundane cloaking would save her the bother of speaking with him. But even surrounded by his soldiers and being hurried to the Chromeria, he saw her. "Stop! Stop!" he commanded them, and they did. He pushed a man out of his way, and stared at her, transfixed. "Aliviana?"

For some reason, she froze. He was dying, she saw. Internally bleeding in half a dozen places, as from a great fall.

His men piled up behind him, unready for the sudden stop.

He sat up, though it was a bad idea in his state, ignoring everything in the world for her. He was like that. A good man, Corvan Danavis.

"Oh, my Aliviana," he said. "You're here! You're alive!"

She looked at him, and she saw instantly what he couldn't bear to see, and thus, like a human, he did not see: the gulf between them was unbridgeable now.

He seemed to see it in her eyes, though, and then, finally his own eyes took in the superviolet crystal clumps at her joints and hands and by her eyes, and the placid stillness of her face.

He started weeping weakly, horrified. "Oh, my Aliviana, what have they done to you?"

That sparked something in her. Some old defiance. Some old, human outrage. It almost felt good.

" 'Done to me'?" she asked. "They did nothing *to* me. I chose this."

"Liv. No. My daughter. My darling one. Please. Come back."

Come back? To what? To being human and frail? To being subservient? No. There was a hierarchy, she saw now. But it was organized by power, not by affection. It had to be.

Nothing else made sense.

Though she couldn't have said why, with a dismissive flick of her hands, she healed the wounds that would otherwise kill him.

Then she departed, and she thought of Corvan Danavis no more.

Chapter 147

The lock on the door to Andross Guile's sitting room clicked, and Grinwoody stepped into the darkened room as he had so many thousands of times. He hesitated when he saw Andross sitting in his wing-backed chair.

"Please, sit," Andross said, lighting a lamp with one finger, gesturing for Grinwoody to sit in the other chair. There was a cocked flintlock pistol on the arm of his own chair. A measure of whiskey was waiting on the table for each of them. Andross had never said 'please' to Grinwoody, not in all their years together.

Grinwoody dropped his head, his mouth twitching at a hundred thoughts. Then he took off his servants' white gloves and tucked them away in a pocket. He sat opposite Andross.

They sat, sipping their whiskey, as if they were two gentlemen enjoying a pleasant summer day rather than mortal enemies whose paths had crossed as a battle wound down.

"Smoke, Lord Anazâr?" Andross asked.

"Please."

They smoked as a fleet and a city burned, as sea demons tore through the remaining bane and devoured the wights thrown into the water and the Wight King's fleet dissolved into chaos.

"It was an excellent gambit," Andross said. He didn't have to say that he meant Grinwoody's long betrayal, not his failed poisoning attempt. "Not only well conceived but also flawlessly executed. Breathtaking daring wedded to such patience? Few would be capable of it. To sublimate one's ego for so long? To become a *slave*? Astounding."

"Thank you. I learned from the best."

Andross inclined his head.

"So many temptations, you know?" Grinwoody said. "To step free of this garb, this face, these servile manners. Just once, not in front of a few subordinates, but to actually take my rightful place among equals."

"To be fully yourself," Andross said.

"Yes! There's something so grating about the world thinking less of you than you know yourself to be."

"Your Braxians put on masks once every few months, but for you, those holy days were the only time you got to take your mask off."

"Perhaps just a different mask," Grinwoody said, pensive.

"Lonely," Andross said, looking not at him perhaps but at his own reflection in the window.

After a pause, Grinwoody smirked. "Me, too."

"The Old Man of the Desert," Andross mused. "I've always liked that."

Grinwoody shook his head. "Your nightly bitter-almond tea was for mithridatism? That was...unexpected."

"Oh, I know. You might've chosen any of the dozens of poisons it won't work for. What can I say? The idea appealed to me when I was young and still romantic."

"Why did you keep it up?"

"Honestly? It was a convenient way to test new help. I'd tell them not to touch my special liquor. If they got deathly ill shortly later, I'd sell them immediately."

"I don't know whether I should be angry at you that you're so lucky or at my own error, or if I should be impressed that you kept the ingredients secret even from me for all these years. So why is it instead that I'm hurt that you didn't trust me enough to tell me?"

"It's a hell of a thing," Andross said.

"What? All your secrets? My infiltration? Trying not to make a single mistake, knowing it will get you killed, against an enemy who can make a hundred and never lose?"

"Betrayal," Andross said quietly.

"You goddam Guiles. It's not even fair, opposing you."

"You chose to be in opposition. You might have done otherwise."

"No, I think not," Grinwoody said.

"How'd you do it?"

"Which part?" Grinwoody asked.

"The hardest part. Getting me to buy you of my own accord."

"You actually weren't the target, oddly enough. You were my second failed attempt. I was trying to get purchased by Ulbear Rathcore. He seemed more likely to go far than you did."

"In a kinder world," Andross said. He sipped. "But...a *slave*?"

"Impossible to keep many secrets from your slaves."

"And if I were terribly abusive, what? You had a magistrate standing by? Witnesses who would swear you'd been enslaved illegally? That sort of thing?"

"Naturally," Grinwoody said. "I almost called on him a dozen times that first year. I did not like taking orders. Caused me quite some panic when he died a decade later. Then I realized I had assassins at my command. Getting a magistrate to authenticate papers wasn't going to be any problem. Now, your turn. Who was your assassin? Everyone drank the bloodwine. I nearly drank it myself. I usually do. You almost got *me*—but I had too much to do in the morning, so for the first time in many years I abstained. But no one else did. I have spotters to watch for such things. The only thing I can figure is that your poisoner must have drunk the lacrimae sanguinis, too. Who was it?"

Andross shrugged.

"There are only five people it could be," Grinwoody insisted. "And they're all dead. It was one of my high priests, wasn't it? Atevia Zelorn?"

"It actually wasn't my doing," Andross said.

Grinwoody almost dropped his zigarro. "You can't be serious. 867

All this time playing against you, and I'm undone...by some side player? Who?"

"Karris, I think," Andross said.

"Little *Karris*? *Karris* killed four hundred and thirty people?" Grinwoody sat back. "And here I thought that Iron White business was a pretention to impress the small folk."

"Then she became what she pretended," Andross said.

"Perhaps so." Grinwoody looked at his empty glass. He set down his zigarro, and glanced at the pistol. "But I did not."

"I thought you were my friend," Andross said suddenly. There was a ragged edge in his voice. In another man, it might have seemed close to tears.

"A mistake I never made of you," Grinwoody said.

"So I see," Andross said, all iron control once more. "Your papers are on the table. Take them as you go."

"My papers? You're letting me live?" Grinwoody asked. But he stood immediately. He was no fool.

"Good play should be rewarded, and you won. Far be it from me to snatch the fruits of twenty-three years of service from your lips. Far be it from me to deny your victory."

Grinwoody picked up the papers, slowly. "Do I look *victorious* to you?"

"No, but the game that you lost was some other game, against someone else. Nothing to do with me. Me you outwitted, *me* you convinced to expose my back. I have no excuses. Spying is a well-known stratagem in the great game, and betrayal a time-honored tradition. How can I begrudge you those?"

"You surprise me," Grinwoody said. "I hadn't expected to find you equanimous in defeat."

"You've never seen me lose."

"Except your temper."

"At setbacks. At delays in my game. But our game is finished. Now is the time for me to examine my loss, and to learn from it."

Grinwoody pursed his lips. "After all these years, you still are able to surprise me, my lord." His lips quirked to a frown. The 'my lord' had been reflexive, a mistake.

" 'Andross,' please."

"Yes. Of course."

Andross said, "There's an island off Tabes on the Ruthgari coast. Good little harbor, tricky approaches to dissuade raiders, and looks crude from without but is luxurious within. Comfortable for a household of fifteen or twenty. I meant to keep it secret even from you. Do you know of it?"

"Yes. Followed the money, of course."

Andross inclined his head. "It's yours. The deed's among those papers. Sell it if you wish. Fair wages, I think, for twenty-three years of your labors."

"But you purchased me."

"Yes. Yes, I did. And the man who sold you to me now owes me a great debt."

He said this without emotion, but the malice was clear. Grinwoody was a victor, but any others who had betrayed Andross were simply enemies. And his memory was long and long.

"Naturally," Andross said, "should I see you again, or hear of your interference…"

"Naturally," Grinwoody said.

He took his papers and walked to the door as if he expected Andross to shoot him in the back at every step. But he stopped when he got the door open. He looked back. He looked as if to experience this magnanimity from Andross Guile was itself a deep draught of bitter-almond tea.

"I want you to know something, *Andross*. In all my years of working with spies and murderers and traitors and scum," Grinwoody said, "I've never met a man who deserved betrayal more."

Chapter 148

"Sit down," Andross said. "We have to figure a few things out before we go out there."

"Do we really?" Kip asked. He came and took a seat, though.

The curtains were wide open in his grandfather's sitting room, windows open to the sun. Outside, the work of repairing the city—and the empire—was well underway. The funerals were over: by necessity, done quickly, efficiently even for the defenders, and expeditiously at best for the attackers.

The people of the Jaspers would mourn even as they rebuilt, but Andross was keen to give everyone reasons to cheer as soon as possible, to focus on victory and unity, not on the costs of what they'd been through.

"Yes, we must," Andross said. "You won our game. And though I told you that I would claim the mantle of Lightbringer if you left the beach, you never conceded that. I received the signal the bane had landed moments later, so you may have still been on the shore."

"Are we really doing this?" Kip asked. "I can't even draft."

"Nothing in the prophecies about drafting after becoming the Lightbringer. I managed to do pretty well at ruling for many years while only drafting on the rarest occasions."

Kip expelled an exasperated breath, looking away.

"The people need a Lightbringer," Andross said. "One man who will make the changes the empire needs."

"The *people* do, huh?"

"Have you Viewed my card yet?"

"Yes," Kip said. "But honestly, I'd like to address my current obligations before I delve any more into the past." Later today, he was going to visit Cruxer's mother, Inana, to tell her how her son had died, and how he'd lived.

Andross said, "I'll tell you Lina's story when you're ready. All that I know. But it's complicated, and no one in the tale comes out looking good. Not me, not her, not Corvan."

"You added that last part just to make me curious, didn't you?" Kip asked.

Andross stopped himself before he denied it. "I'd like to get it off my plate. And my conscience."

For a moment, Kip thought about forgiveness, and time. "I'm not ready. It might be a while until I am."

Andross paused, then nodded. "I forget," he said. "Felia would do this to me, too. Great leaps of intuition and then long, slow cud-chewing on facts that seemed simple to me. But she would chew and chew, and then suddenly understand a whole person or a whole family, it seemed. I could never guess where it would strike with her, nor, it seems, with you. How I miss her. I wish you could've met."

"We could've, actually. She came to Garriston for her Freeing. She never tried to talk with me. I've thought of that a few times. Seemed weird to me that she wouldn't want to meet her only grandson, bastard though I was," Kip said. "She was afraid I was *your* bastard, wasn't she?"

"Yes. Wrongly," Andross said. "Do you want to have that conversation, after all?"

"No. No. I should have liked to meet her quite a lot, though. It seems to me this family has kept far too many secrets for far too long, to our own injury."

Andross said, "We keep secret what we fear makes us weak, not realizing in our fear that it is the keeping of secrets itself that weakens us." He lifted his eyebrows then, as if surprised at hearing the sentiment from his own lips. "Let's let it lie for now, then, not a secret, but simply a difficult discussion that can wait a while. I do have another that can't."

"I figured, coming in to see you, that the meeting wouldn't be all rainbows and daisies."

"This will be known henceforth as Ascension Day. In the future, this will be a holy week—from Sun Day to Ascension Day, commemorating the great victory of Orholam's light over the forces of darkness, and celebrating the coming of His chosen one: me."

Kip nodded.

"You don't seem angry," Andross said.

"Are you worried about threats to your throne already?" Kip asked. "Look, if you need me to join Corvan in the Reconquest or want to exile me to Blood Forest or whatever, I'll go. I'll have requests, but I'll go, and I won't cause you problems."

"I know," Andross said. "And I don't like it."

"Huh?"

"I've been very carefully vague in my wording with all my commands, in everything I've done as promachos to prepare the islands for Ascension Day."

"Okay..."

"I'm saying, when we go out there to the blast of the ramshorns and the dancers and the pyroturges, we have to declare someone the Lightbringer. But it doesn't have to be me."

Kip felt like a turtle-bear charging into a granite rock face. "Huh?"

"You could've done everything I did."

"Not true," Kip said.

"You did more than I did."

"Arguable."

"You laid the groundwork for everything I did. You figured out the puzzle. I didn't!"

"That I can concede," Kip said.

"You paid more than I did, and if it weren't for *my* blunders with Zymun, *you* would've been on those mirrors all night. *You* would be being declared the Lightbringer in a few minutes. I should be, at best, an adviser to you, if not on the run for my life for everything I've done."

"I would've loved to have had you as an adviser."

"I know the truth. You and your father did the magic; I turned some mirrors."

"You brought source to thousands of different drafters simultaneously and battered and confused and burned wights and immortals until dawn. No one else could've done that. I couldn't have."

"Don't you *want it*?" Andross insisted. "Don't you *want* to be the most important person in history? It's this close! Reach out and take it! Play one more game with this as the wager. I'll do it! I'll do anything!"

"Anything, anything to prove it should belong to you?" Kip asked.

"You have no reason to believe I'll rule well."

"I believe you'll find reasons to rule well."

Andross's face reddened.

"No, no, I know I seem like I'm being flippant. And, fine, I sort of was, because I know how you love that, but mostly I'm not." Kip took a breath. "There are things in this life that I need. Things that I can hardly function without: My wife, a few close friends, hard work, the camaraderie of shared purpose, things to figure out. Some leadership, because I'm pretty good at it and I chafe under incompetence. But I don't need power. I don't need every eye to be on me every time I walk into a room. I don't need strangers to know who I am or be in awe of me. I wouldn't give up those first things in order to be the most important man in history. Because that man will also be the most isolated man in history. I've been isolated, and it's not for me. Not at all. If I were declared Lightbringer, could I make it work? I mean, you sort of get to define the job as you go, right? Yeah, maybe I could, with a lot of help. I might even be a good Lightbringer. But I don't need it. You? You do."

"I'm the best one for the job!"

"So what's your problem?" Kip asked.

"I didn't earn it! I didn't beat the overwhelming odds. I didn't show the magical genius. I didn't die twice. You did! *We* fulfilled all the prophecies—not me. I've spent my life preparing for this, and now I've proved myself to everyone except the people who matter—the son and grandson I'll defraud in taking it. How can I accept a crown I didn't earn?"

Kip gave him a sidelong look. "Maybe...rule as if it's a gift, and not something you're owed?"

Andross's temper flared for a moment, then cooled. "I wouldn't trust anyone with the power you're giving me."

"I know," Kip said. "And hell, in a month? I'll probably be kicking myself for this. You played a long game, and Orholam folded on His last card and gave you the victory. Now play the longest game. You're the Lightbringer. Now be the greatest Lightbringer anyone could imagine. Don't just win. Live victoriously."

Andross grew thoughtful, then scowled. "You know," he said, "I can't tell if you're wise beyond your years or just a dumb kid full of slogans."

"Me, either," Kip said.

Andross cracked a smile even as he shook his head. "Definitely gonna have to exile you somewhere."

"Somewhere nice?" Kip asked.

"No, just far away," Andross said.

"I could use a good wedding trip with my bride."

"Oh, Orholam have mercy."

"Also I need a job. I don't think I have any money."

"So it begins," Andross said darkly.

"Actually, I might've also put the family on the hook for a few expenses in Blood Forest. And everywhere else."

"What?" Andross asked. "And when were you planning to tell me this?"

"Why bring up a few little debts when we were all going to die?"

"How 'little' are we talking?"

"The Malargos family will have to help. And maybe some bankers. Definitely some bankers. Maybe all the bankers."

Andross said, heading for the door, "Hellmount's good for a honeymoon, I hear."

"Oh, grandfather," Kip said, stopping him before he went out. "I heard from the messengers that you also brought light to my people at the siege of Green Haven and saved the city. And definitely saved my friends. Thank you."

Andross stared at him for a few moments, then nodded and left.

Alone, Kip wondered if he'd done something very, very good or very, very bad. He turned to head out the other door and saw his father watching him. "How long have you been there?" Kip asked.

"You know," Dazen said, fiddling with the black eye patch he wore now, "when I was kid, when Sevastian died, I felt like I'd suddenly lost not just my brother but also my father. Growing up, I longed for someone who would mentor me, tell me how to do things—instead of just judging me when I failed. My father's work was always everything to him. The scraps went to Gavin, and I got nothing. I missed out with you—"

"Not exactly your fault," Kip said. "You didn't know I existed for most of my life."

"I'm not talking about those years. I mean since I found you."

"C'mon, you've been a bit busy saving the world."

"That was my father's excuse for all the terrible shit he did, too," Dazen said, "but..." Dazen cleared his throat. Adjusted his eye patch. "I mean, I see you do what you just did with your grandfather, and, Kip, I'm so damn in awe of you..." His eye misted up, but he kept going. "And...I'm so damn sorry. You needed a father. And now I'm too late." And suddenly tears were streaming down his cheek and his breath was strained. "I missed my chance. You're a man already now. And a fine one," he said, getting control of himself. "A better man than I ever was. And I want to be proud of you—but you did it all without me. How can I take pride in what you've done without my help? You didn't need me. To do all *this*, you didn't need me."

Kip squirmed. He *had* needed his father, not just in the early years but since then. He'd not meant this to go to casting guilt, but he didn't want to rush in and say anything untrue to try to brush it away, either. The wound was real. He didn't blame Dazen, but it still ached.

In many ways, he barely knew his father, and that very thought was edged with razor desolation.

Dazen was quiet for a long while, and Kip—as he never could have before—filled the silence not with words but with listening.

Finally, Dazen took a deep breath and said, "Kip, when I didn't deserve it, Orholam gave me a second chance—maybe a thousand-and-second chance. I don't deserve it with you, either, but...Kip, if it's not too late, can we start over? Can I try again at being your dad?"

Chapter 149

When a protocol officer had questioned where Gavin should be seated in the overflowing great hall (the whole Dazen thing would be dealt with later, Andross had decided), Andross Guile had given one of the most Andross Guile responses Dazen had ever heard: "The sun is not dimmed by the presence of other stars in the sky, nor even by the moon."

All in white with gold brocade, Dazen was seated on the platform. He was quite the subject of fascination, of course, and the marveling that he was still alive had already started to turn to what his new position might be. Clearly, he couldn't be Prism again. He couldn't draft. But no one expected him to do *nothing*. Certainly Andross didn't; he'd already started to float ideas about how to use his son's reputation and charisma to stitch the satrapies back together.

But every one of their meetings thus far had been public. They hadn't had to speak about the long night, or Sevastian.

For the moment, Dazen was quite content to be simply the White's husband, and he was happy to sit at her right hand rather than her at his. She was resplendent in her whites, but she'd dyed her hair from its harsh platinum white, now, back to her natural auburn. He loved it.

Andross had contrived some last-minute duty that kept Kip busy while everyone else was being announced and seated. Rather than being ushered in a side door at the front, though, in the hush of the hall, the young man came in from the back with Tisis. He walked with his head ducked, trying to be inconspicuous on the long walk up the center aisle, chagrined at being late.

Kip had learned a lot in the last few years, but he could still be charmingly naïve.

He had no nobles under his own authority, and all his own soldiers were outside the great hall, so perhaps he really hadn't expected anything.

The Blood Foresters stood for him first. Then the Tyreans, who counted him one of their own. His Mighty, seated in the front row as if family, stood, too.

Then, in singles around the hall, drafters stood. They knew what he'd done.

With help, King Ironfist (still 'king' technically, until some formalities were worked out) stood. He gave Kip the old Blackguard salute.

All the Blackguards followed suit.

And then everyone stood, from the High Luxiats down.

Dazen and Karris stood late in order to let Kip know that no one was standing because they were following their lead.

The youngest Guile looked humbled, honored, as his eyes went from face to face and he recognized friends young and old. Kip and Tisis embraced Dazen and Karris and took their places beside them.

One of Kip's Mighty, Winsen, coughed loudly. Suddenly there were gasps throughout the room, and then laughter spread fast on its heels. Those on the platform had to turn around to see it: at the front of the room, next to the staid official banners of Houses Guile and White Oak and Malargos, and Andross's banners and the Lightbringer's banner, and the banners for the various satrapies, a very ad hoc, homemade-looking banner unfurled. It appeared to be a child's drawing of a turtle with a shock of hair on its head and a goofy grin on its face, with big bear claws and wings of fire.

Seeing it, Kip immediately blushed and buried his face in his hands.

The audience roared with laughter and then cheered.

While a steward rushed to take the Turtle-Bear banner down, Kip turned to the Mighty and drew his hand across his throat.

They all made very unconvincing shrugs: 'Who? Us?'

Dazen couldn't stop smiling. In some ways, they were still just a bunch of damn kids.

But they loved one another, and that was priceless.

Naturally, Andross Guile waited until the furor had died down, and then waited some more. But once he'd begun, with all the usual pomp and spectacle Dazen expected from such a ceremony—the magic, the music, the processionals, a surprisingly brief prayer by High Luxiat Amazzal—the ascension ceremony was short and to the point.

The Colors and representatives for each of the Seven Satrapies and the six remaining High Luxiats (one had belonged to the Order and was dead) each knelt before Andross and swore their fealty to him as Prism, emperor, and Lightbringer. Everyone else in the hall was allowed to take the oath from their own seats.

Andross had moved fast in these first few days. Indeed, not just fast; he'd moved like a man who'd been making a list for decades of all that would need to be done.

It wasn't impatience, either. Amid all the work of cleanup and reconstruction and burial and immolation of enemy corpses, there was still the euphoria of their improbable victory. Only the war was on people's tongues. Lesser stories—such as vast banking families being given ultimatums, and certain troublemakers being thrown in prison, new laws curtailing slavery and the capture of fugitives, restructuring in the Magisterium—these didn't even need to be hidden: they simply weren't that interesting in comparison to all else that had happened.

Andross had gathered the Spectrum and High Magisterium and suggested a sentence of death or bereavement (a term he claimed he'd dug up somewhere, but he may have simply invented it) by the Blinding Knife for the Blood Robe drafters and wights who'd been captured. The suggestion was unanimously approved.

Bereavement was, he claimed, what had happened to Gavin when he'd been stabbed with the Blinding Knife and had lost his magical powers but not his life. Andross planned to use the opportunity to figure out the exact mechanics of the blade: Did it matter who held it? Did what the wielder wished to have happen to the condemned change what the blade did?

Karris's young luxiats—whose ranks were suddenly swelling by the day—were reclaiming lost knowledge, including some from books older scholars swore previously had left entire pages blank. Dazen didn't know if this was a reclamation against the old workings of black luxin, or if Andross was instructing his forgers among the scholars to insert his own preferred teachings.

But the crux of it was that the luxiats claimed that before Vician's Sin, retiring drafters at the Freeing simply *retired*. They were Freed, not of their lives but of their bonds of service—and also their magical gifts, as Dazen had been.

Except that some also *died*, judged by Orholam Himself, it was said. So drafters, never certain what they would receive at their judgment day, would still approach it with fear and trembling. Sun Day would remain a somber and holy occasion, but also one filled with joy for the righteous.

So they claimed. The world would find out soon enough.

Dazen had only begged his father to wait a little while. He had an intuition he wanted to explore.

Andross had granted it, saying the scholars could use the extra time anyway.

In the meantime, the Blood Robe drafters were held in mirrored cells or darkness or in rooms carefully draped with colors they couldn't draft. Andross hadn't even suggested utilizing the dungeons Dazen had crafted and been held in, and Dazen certainly didn't want to think of them ever again.

Surprisingly enough, Dazen rather enjoyed all the pageantry, though most of his enjoyment came from the fact that he wasn't the person on whom the entire ceremony depended for once.

Then Andross stood and spoke. "We have endured much, and we have many labors before us. Changes are coming. I shall not restore to us some mythical golden age from the past. The only golden age open to us lies before us. If these satrapies are to endure, they must rest upon a foundation of justice. This will be hard, for many of us have suffered such grievous injustices that we've allowed ourselves to inflict injustices on others, as if we each were impartial judges who happen to rule in our own favor, always. This coming age will bear great fruit, but we will have to till the rocky soil of our own hearts to plant that fruit so that our ch—so that our children and our children's children may enjoy it."

He pursed his lips, and then, in a less practiced voice that suggested he was diverging from the speech he'd memorized, he said, "Some of us have done things in this war...even done things to win this war for which we must repent. I foremost among us."

Dazen had more than a merely healthy cynicism for his father's every act and word, but this hit like a right cross. Confession? Contrition? From Andross Guile? Was this another put-on? Another trap?

But from where Dazen was seated behind the old man, he hadn't been able to see his face, couldn't tell if this was just another game, another manipulation, and already Andross was back to his scripted remarks.

"This is the project we begin. As we fought together, we will work together, all of us: luxiat and noble and drafter and farmer and fisherman and smith. We will mourn together, and we will celebrate our victories and Orholam's. We will bind up the wounds of these Seven Satrapies, and we will make them stronger, and more just and more honorable than they were before. By the grace of Orholam, despite our many losses, the list of our allies and friends has grown in these dark hours, and those who sacrificed to serve in our darkest hours shall not go unrecognized in the light."

Andross was a plain speaker, given to sentences too long for many people to follow, and it wasn't the kind of speech designed to draw forth applause, but it did anyway. These people needed it.

"Oh. There is one other matter," Andross said with obvious relish and a smile. "The much-delayed official wedding of my son to Karris White Oak. This will begin tomorrow. The party will continue for a week. And as a special additional pleasure, my grandson, Kip, will soon celebrate his own long-delayed official wedding to Tisis Malargos as soon as her family arrives. As we'll be celebrating already, I'd like to join my ascension celebration to their parties. Naturally," Andross Guile said, "you are all invited."

He smiled, and the years sloughed off him as the people roared their applause. He actually looked more than surprised; he looked delighted, as if the acclamation was soaking long-dry soil in his heart.

Dazen, obedient token and good son, stood and waved, to even louder applause. Kip copied him from across the aisle and got his own applause—just as loud.

Then Karris stood, and then Tisis, and the applause grew louder still.

Dazen grinned at Kip, and saw his son had the same fool grin he did.

Must run in the family.

"Not a bad speech, old man," Dazen said after all those on the platform had recessed off to one of the side rooms.

"Felia wrote it," Andross said. "Thirty-eight years ago. Not all of it, of course. But she told me to give them some reason to cheer at the end." He pursed his lips. "She should be here."

"She did all she could to make it so the rest of us are," Dazen said.

Andross expelled a slow breath at that. He seemed different. They walked together out a rear exit of the hall. They were about to go separate ways, but now they paused.

The new Lightbringer said, "Kip was right, you know: I'm the right person for this time. I know the personalities, the old feuds, the true stories behind family myths, the economies and the familial ties. With help from more handsome and tactful faces, I can bind up these satrapies as no one else could hope to. I know what can be broken and what can only be bent slowly. I can make these lands better—safer, stronger, richer, fairer, more just, more open, more free. I have perhaps ten years left to my mortal span, twenty if I'm disciplined and fortunate, and I will make this land endure—not fall apart under a weaker personality or less capable hands."

"Why are you telling me all this?" Dazen asked.

"Son, you know how I view vows."

"Yes."

"This office? I vow to do my best to be worthy of it."

Dazen nodded his thanks and turned to go.

"Oh, and one last thing. Not that it will mean anything to you," Andross said to his back. His voice lowered. "Not that it should. It shouldn't. But I'm grateful for both of you. Proud of you."

Fists tightening, Dazen barely suppressed the urge to spin and punch his old man in the face.

You *dare*?!

He wanted to scream Sevastian's name in the old murderer's face for an hour. And then Gavin's name for just as long.

He wanted to shout, 'I gave you my empire; I gave you my victory; you don't get to have my family, too!'

But... it was a step. A tenuous step, beginning a long climb toward wholeness for this broken, quarrelsome, ravaged family. Dazen could sabotage it now—and god*dam* but Andross deserved to be pushed into the abyss—or he could help. They weren't going to complete it today or this year. Maybe they never would. Maybe they were too broken. Maybe forgiveness was too hard.

But he could take one tiny step. Couldn't he?

"Well, then—" Andross said, turning away.

"Thank you," Dazen said. He couldn't look back, couldn't risk meeting the old man's eyes. That was too much, for today. "Thank you... father."

Chapter 150

After the ceremony, Kip went to the infirmary and spent some time with his old Nightbringers who were wounded, bringing comfort and cheer where he could. Not all the living were well, but they were all being tended to admirably.

With that realization, he made to where two more wounded awaited him: Teia and Ironfist.

At the lifts on the way there, Kip was surprised to find Ferkudi, Ben-hadad, Winsen, and Big Leo. They'd been waiting for him.

"Where's Tisis?" Big Leo asked.

"Taking care of the real work so I can goof off with you layabouts," Kip said. He smiled. "It's good to have all of us together again. Most of us, I should say. Dammit. Sorry."

"No, you're right. Cruxer should be here," Ben-hadad said. He swallowed.

"And Goss," Ferkudi said. "And Daelos."

"And others," Big Leo said. "Lots of others."

In the battle, they'd all proven themselves heroes. But Kip hadn't needed a battle to show him that.

They made it to the private room Teia and Ironfist were sharing. It was guarded by an honor guard of Tafok Amagez *and* the new Mighty *and* the Blackguards. After knocking, Kip stepped inside the door, then slipped through the black curtains, careful not to let in any light that might kill Teia.

"You in here?" Kip asked, not really serious.

"Sadly," Teia said. "Some old guy keeps telling me stories about the glory days or something."

"If I could move, I would so kick your ass for that," Ironfist's voice said.

Kip shifted his vision to the sub-red to be able to see in the utter darkness. At least he still had that.

"It's so dark in here," Ferkudi said. "Why doesn't someone—"

"Ferk, no!" Kip said, but he was too late.

Ferkudi threw open the curtains. The day was blinding bright. Ironfist flinched, and Teia shrank back, throwing her hands over her eyes.

But then nothing happened.

"Well, I guess that answers how long that lacrimae sanguinis stays active," Kip said.

Then Teia collapsed.

"Oh, no!" Ferkudi said. "What happened?!"

"You idiot!" Ben-hadad shouted. "What have you done?!"

Then Teia suddenly grinned, and Kip noticed that she was wearing black eye caps over her eyes. She reached over to her bedside table, though, and placed two slightly-less-unsettling leather eye patches over them.

"Orholam's hairy butt crack, Teia," Ferkudi said. "You nearly stopped my heart."

They all looked at him, incredulous.

Winsen said, "You *do* realize that's the opposite of what just happened, right? The literal *opposite*."

Ferkudi looked back at them for a moment, then, chagrined. "Oh. Oh, I mean... sorry, Teia. I wasn't thinking."

"I really missed you, Ferk." She sat up and hugged him. "But that hurt like hell, and if I ever get out of here, I'm definitely gonna kick you in the stones for it."

He looked uncertain. "Am I supposed to let you do that?"

"No, you're supposed to try to stop me. I'm just telling you because I know you can't."

She grinned then, and Kip could see that she was trying things out, trying to see if she could fit back in with her friends' old banter. 'Do I have a place here?'

Ferkudi looked confused. Did this go in the Box? It was obvious that Teia wasn't going to be out sparring with them anytime soon—if ever—so where was she going to have a chance to make good on her threat?

C'mon, Ferkudi, please...

"Challenge accepted!" Ferkudi said, and Teia's smile exploded light everywhere.

"So, Winsen," Ironfist said gruffly. "What's this I heard about? You killed a bane?"

"Eh. Wasn't so hard," Winsen said. "Sort of embarrassing, actually. Breaker told me I had to shoot the crystal. I missed it ten times. Target this big. Only two hundred paces away. Ten misses. Ten."

Of course, he was discounting how he'd sneaked and fought his way across the bane—alone, evading hundreds of wights and drafters and soldiers, and killing so many he'd had to start retrieving his arrows and theirs, not to mention saving lives on *other* bane from his perch.

"Better than I did!" Big Leo said. "I didn't even make it to my bane before Karris and Gill killed it." Of course, he didn't mention that he'd been instrumental in leading the final assault on the White King, and saving Karris's life a half-dozen times.

881

"Better than I did!" Ferkudi said. "I never even made it past the wall." Of course, he'd *held* the wall. For a long, perilous time, he'd held the wall nearly alone against Dagnu until the astonished locals had rallied to him.

"Better than I did!" Kip said. "I barely even made it out the front door!"

They laughed.

"Better than I did!" Teia said. "I barely made it out of my room."

And again.

Then they looked to Ben-hadad, who painted a disconcerted look on his face. He'd saved Einin's life (she would recover, but was in the infirmary now) and then killed Belphegor and destroyed the yellow bane. "Wow," he said, "sounds like you all did terrible. *I* kicked ass."

They laughed and jeered.

Winsen said, "Yeah, sure. You know I saved your bouncy butt three different times, don't you, Froggie?"

" 'Froggie'? *Froggie?!* Don't you dare!" Ben-hadad said.

"It's the Spring of Doom!"

"The Leaping Lancer!"

"It's the Hopping Death!"

"Someone save me from the Sprinting Cripple!"

Ben-hadad shook his head stoically, muttering as he realized he simply needed to take his punishment and hope that they didn't stumble upon a new Name for him.

Finally, Ironfist said somberly, "You all were...superlative." He didn't say 'unlike me,' but they all heard it.

Their joviality died.

"Don't do that," Kip said. "You were trying to save the Chromeria and destroy the Order before they killed us all. Cruxer fucked up. We know you tried."

"Maybe if I'd slowed down, he could've heard me. I was trying to be like...like Andross Guile, and I should've just been me." Ironfist winced at his pain.

"You brought an army, a navy, and the best general in the world," Kip said. "Without *any* one of those, we'd all be dead. Truth is, we all failed. Anyone here *not* able to think of something you could have done differently that wouldn't have saved lives? Anyone?"

They shook their heads, one at a time, and some looked away.

"There's no shame in it," Kip said. "Cruxer shouldn't have gone after Ironfist. He should've been guarding me. Maybe he would've saved me from Zymun and Aram. He failed us, but without him I wouldn't be standing here. Most of you wouldn't, either. He was our heart. Sometimes you do your best, and it's not good enough. That's why we have each other."

"I know I butted heads with him a lot," Ben-hadad said, "but I really loved that asshole."

"I love all you assholes," Winsen said. "Well...like, most of you. Mmm...maybe more like 'tolerate.'"

"Gah!" Big Leo said, and he reached his enormous arms around as many of them as he could and swept them into a huge hug.

"Careful, careful!" Ironfist said from his bed as they tipped over.

Kip leaned into the entire mass, and they all tripped and went slipping over Ironfist's bed.

In a moment, they transformed back into the children they had recently been: laughing, tickling, shoving, flicking one another in the stones, and trying to crawl out from under the pile.

"I should've never have resigned!" Ironfist shouted. "I'd give you all a hundred laps for this!"

"You didn't resign!" Ben-hadad said. "You got fired!"

"Stop reminding me! Ow! Not the chest, off the chest!"

They soon headed out—the blast of light from the window had Teia sicker than she'd wanted to admit.

As they went, Kip realized that in the coming days there was going to be a lot of swinging between laughing and crying, teasing and mourning, telling stories and sitting silent, hugging and fighting. It was all right.

No, it was better than all right; it was *good*.

It's what families do.

Chapter 151

With the normal difficulty of a woman getting married the next morning, Karris tried to set her to-do lists aside and enjoy the massage.

☐ *Enjoy massage, dammit.*

"Seems really fast to try to organize a wedding, much less one on this scale," Rhoda said, working Karris's wrist high over her head with her magical hands. "How are all the details going?"

Karris sighed, and Rhoda pulled hard on her wrist, extending all the muscles in her arm and shoulder and into her rib cage. "Aha!" Rhoda said.

"You tricked me into that," Karris complained. She grunted. "Not. Ow. That I'm complaining."

"Extensions today. You really beat the hell out of yourself, didn't you?"

"It was a battle, so mostly it was other people beating the hell out of me."

Rhoda *tsk*ed. Her hands quickly cataloged the weird places Karris was sore, then tapped her tight sartorius. "So, this got this tight from *riding*? A horse, I mean?"

"Rhoda!"

The loud masseuse laughed. "No, no, good for you two. It is so good to see you happy, High Lady. I'll be securing your wrists so you can relax your upper body while we do these extensions." She got to it, covering Karris with warm towels as she rolled onto her back. "There's a bit of a trick to doing this so it won't leave any hard-to-explain bruises the next day. If you want me to show you or your husband how it's done..."

Karris closed her eyes and shook her head, smiling.

"I'm sorry, High Lady, I didn't mean to overstep." Of course, Rhoda didn't sound at all sorry. "Try to relax into these."

She told herself that she was the reason they were doing a big wedding in the first place. She'd demanded one, way back when. It had seemed like a good idea at the time.

Having a few months to plan it probably would have been a good idea, too. It did make sense, from a political perspective. Andross was showing the big happy family, and using all the love and adoration the people had built up for Gavin and Karris, and Kip and Tisis, to add a halo effect of love and adoration to his own rule and legitimate himself. Hard to rebel this week when last week everyone saw you smiling with your father.

"Oh, that's a little tight," Karris said.

"We just have to hold that until I finish this leg," Rhoda said. But she didn't work ten or fifteen times down Karris's left leg as she had on the right. Instead she wrapped it up with the scarf and secured it to the table, as she had done with both wrists and her other leg.

Eyes still closed, Karris said, "I guess I can see why people who really like the feeling of vulnerability might—"

"Aha, see this tension in your neck?" Rhoda said, her fingers massaging Karris's jaw. "Open."

Karris opened her mouth. "Rhoda, I think I'm done with this. I'd like—"

Something was stuffed into her mouth, and when Karris tried to spit it out, her eyes flying open, there was no red for her to draft, no green, and then thick strong fingers jabbed deep into the pressure points behind Karris's ears.

Before she could scream, a gag so thick it held her jaw open and tongue down was secured across her face.

Rhoda scrubbed her hands through her wild hair. Her face was tracked with tears.

Karris bucked against the bonds, but they only tightened. She tried to scream, but almost no sound emerged, certainly nothing that would alarm the Blackguards outside the door, who were used to being banished from the room and chided for investigating any little moan of pain.

Visibly summoning her courage, Rhoda put one hand behind Karris's head and one under her chin, preparing to snap her neck. Then she stopped. "He told me not to talk to you. But you have to know. I don't *want* to do this. Everyone spies on the Jaspers. I thought he was just another noble, except he paid more than anyone. And when he saw I could keep my mouth shut, he paid more still. And then I got invited to the parties for the people he trusted...I thought it was all wild parties and free thinkers and free spirits, you know? The Order? I thought they were just people who wouldn't be held down by stupid rules. It was all way before you became the White. I never meant you any harm. I mean, I never thought they'd really turn any of that stuff into action. They were all talk. I want you to know, I love you, Karris. I didn't go to their party, and I told him no. Told him I was out. I promised him my silence, and I told him I wouldn't do it. That I was done."

No. Please, Orholam, no!

Rhoda's face contorted with grief. "He killed my mother for that! And now he's holding my brother. The only family I've got left. He'll kill him if I don't do this. I'm sorry. I'll die for this. But it's what I have to do."

Rhoda took a deep breath and stepped forward, putting her hand on Karris's chin. Then there was a sound like someone's back being slapped, and hot light flashed from within Rhoda's chest, bright enough it shone through her clothes. It burned in flashes up and down her spine, making her neck glow.

Flash-boiled from the inside, her eyes went cloudy gray an instant before she collapsed out of sight as if boneless.

A godawful sound of cooking gases hissing out of the entry wound filled Karris's ears. Then the smell of horribly burnt meat and viscera filled the room.

"Too bad," Andross Guile said, his face appearing over Karris. He settled the towel primly back in place over her nakedness where it had fallen away in her struggles. "I'd really hoped she would talk more."

He loosed her feet, then her hands, and then, as she took out the gag for herself, he opened a robe for her, turning his gaze aside.

It gave her a moment to collect herself. At first she wanted to hit him or throw something, maybe not at him maybe right at his damn head, what did he think he was doing here, did he think she gave two shits about getting dressed when she'd just— Okay, fine, she did care a little about getting dressed, what did she even ask first? What the hell he'd done to her friend? Could he not have stepped in a little tiny bit earlier? She'd almost had her damn fool neck snapped!

"How long were you there?" Karris asked, despite herself.

"I had a suspicion she was the last of them, and you were the most likely target for Grinwoody's wrath."

"What?! Why would *I* be his target?"

"Because I told him you were responsible for destroying the Order."

Her jaw dropped. "You set me *as bait*?"

He didn't bother to answer. "I was hoping she'd say if there were any others left, but you heard her; she's the kind who kept her mouth shut."

The door exploded open so suddenly Karris almost flipped, and Blackguards were suddenly all over the room. They'd smelled the burning and heard a man's voice.

The next minutes were filled with the predictable—scouring for other assassins, moving Karris and Andross to a secure room, (eventually) getting Karris fully dressed again (thank you!), and surely taking care of the body. Andross seemed irritated by the whole rigmarole, but he played along.

Sometime later, they continued. "Are you going to send someone to save Rhoda's brother?" Karris asked.

"Of course not. I'll not do her a good turn in return for her treachery. But I will send my best men to find her brother, so we can kill the Order people holding him. If our people save him as an ancillary cost…" Andross shrugged. "Sometimes one must do good in order to obtain what one desires."

Karris shook her head. "Wow. You know, once in a while, I think there's some things you can't admit about yourself, High Lord. You like secrets, so I'm gonna tell you this one."

"It won't be a secret if you tell me," Andross said as if utterly disinterested, but she didn't believe it; if he really didn't want to hear what she was about to say, he'd have interrupted her to talk about something else.

"Oh, I trust you to keep it quiet," she said. "It's this: I think there's a sliver of kindness growing in you. You better watch out for that."

He looked at her critically, nonplussed. "Look at you. Full of hope. Naïve despite all evidence and experience to the contrary. Making people feel better about themselves wherever you go. Leaving them eager to be with you, and follow you. You do make an excellent White."

Karris held her breath, and when he moved to speak, she interrupted. "And I'm going to choose to believe, right now, that the next words out of your mouth are *not* going to be a clever put-down that undercuts everything you just said."

He grinned wolfishly, eyes glittering. "Of course not," he said after a moment.

She wondered if he'd changed his mind about what he was going to say next, but she couldn't read anything except amusement in his deep eyes.

"You saved me," she said.

"Mmm."

"You didn't have to. I'm one of the few who can stand in your way now, and I've showed I will if I think it necessary. You could've waited at the door and listened from there. You could've had people seize Rhoda and interrogate her after she killed me. Then you could've installed your own White. It would make your life a lot easier. The assassination of a White? It would have prompted the Spectrum to give you every remaining power that you don't already have. And don't tell me it didn't occur to you."

Andross sniffed. He motioned to his new body man, whom Karris didn't recognize. The slave set down what looked like a ledger book on a side table. "Your wedding present."

He hadn't answered her question at all. What? Now? A book?

With a polite tone and wearing her most pleasant diplomatic expression, she said, "You're too kind. A book. Is it hollowed out for the asp hidden inside?" She scrunched up her face. "Shit! Sorry."

But he seemed to inflate with immense pleasure. "Aha. The triumph of experience over hope. So it happens even for our peerless White," Andross said.

Karris tried again. "What is it?"

"The genealogy of the family Guile."

"A...genealogy?" she asked, arching her eyebrows. Gee, I'll have to crack that open while I eat my sawdust sweetmeats.

"You're young. I know you've no interest in it now. But someday you might. And the answer is the same," he said.

"The answer?" she asked, baffled.

"To both questions."

"Sorry...both?"

" 'Why would I give you this boring old book?' and 'Why did I save you at such cost to myself?' "

She opened her mouth, closed it. "Yes. Those would've been my two questions...when they occurred to me about an hour from now. So...why?"

He studied her, and his eyes seemed to soften. "Because you're family."

Then he left.

Chapter 152

"Darling," Karris said with a note in her voice like he'd just come back from the bathroom and he'd forgotten to tuck something away.

"Yes?" Dazen asked, double-checking his clothes. They'd decided to process forward together. Different satrapies had different traditions on such things, and he'd been nervous that he (being so recently thought dead) might actually get more applause and cheering than she did. Probably a silly fear. And Karris wouldn't have cared if he had. But hell, they *were* already married, and they were a team, so they were walking together.

"Your *hand*?" she said.

He lifted his right hand.

"The other one. Did you think I wouldn't notice? What is *that*?"

He looked down at his left hand and wiggled his fingers. "Just think of it as a bit of, uh, cosmetics. Surely today of all days, you're not going to object to a little harmless hex-casting, are you?" he asked.

" 'Harmless'?" she whispered loudly. "You can't go out there with a hex-crafted fake *hand*."

"Honey..." he said. And he gave her the most innocently charming Dazen Guile smile she'd ever seen. Or at least he hoped it was. "I just didn't want anything about *me* to distract anyone from *you*."

She actually blushed, and straightened her dress. It was a gorgeous something with lots of details that he couldn't really notice except for the fact that they united together beautifully to heighten his eagerness to take it off her.

Then she looked back at him sharply. "Wait…the tooth, too? You did not!"

He gave a lopsided grin to bare his dogtooth. "Go on, try to guess. Denture or hex?"

"*Honey*! I am *the White*," she whispered, looking around at the various attendants who were trying to give them a few private moments before they went out together. "You can't—"

"Relax," he said. "C'mon, it's what I said last night, and that worked out, didn't it?"

She shook her head, blushing again. "I am gonna make you pay for that. And this."

"I look forward to it," he said. He looked at the shut great doors, with the Blackguards ready to open them at their signal. "Shall we?"

"No, wait," she said. "I have something for you."

"Hmm?"

"A wedding gift."

"A wedding gift? Well, now I feel like the louse," Dazen said.

"Don't worry. At first I planned to give you something truly awful, like make you Nuqaba," she said.

"Endless rituals and bumping into the people who burned out my eye in the first place? I'm not sure how happy I could've pretended to be about that."

"Yeah, I thought it might be too awkward. Too many Guiles at the top as it is," she said.

"High Lord, High Lady," a steward said. "Whenever you're ready. Or…the musicians can loop this song another fifteen times, as you will."

"Oooh, I love the sassy ones," Dazen said.

"But…now I'm lousing this up because I'm pressured," Karris said. "Anyway, it did make me think of your eye patch. And your eye. All you've given for these satrapies. I couldn't stop thinking of that Parian metaphor about the evil eye and justice and mercy. And I can't stop thinking how you had that harsh kind of retributive justice burned out of you. You gave up the evil eye. You have no condemnation to give. And I thought there's something beautiful in that.

"And I don't want people to look away from your eye patch because you've been wounded. I want them to see it and be reminded of what you sacrificed for them." She took out a white silk eye patch with subtle embroidery, white on white. "I'm having others made. Jeweled ones nearly as prismatic as your eyes used to be. Different expressions. I figured I can play dress-up with you every day." She looked up at him, nervous. "I'm kidding. I mean, I am having some made, but you don't have to wear it if you don't like it. You don't have to wear any of them if you don't like."

"I love it." He took off his black eye patch and closed his eye, ducking his head while she put the white eye patch in place.

"Ready?" she asked.

The great doors opened. They processed forward together, but the cheers and the music and the voices were all hushed to Dazen's ears. These first days with her had been full of such wonder he could hardly believe it. He felt like he was continually being reminded of things he adored about her that he'd somehow forgotten in the time they'd been apart. He felt so united, so whole.

They'd wanted to stay up late last night, just talking—so they did. Talking, connected, they wanted to make love—so they did. Resting safe in each other's arms, they wanted to tell each other everything, so they did.

In these first days, conflicts seemed but trifles easily overcome, and all the demands on their time were somehow met, and only heightened their joy of reunion at the end of the day.

They weren't children; they knew this was a special time and a fleeting one, but there was nothing cynical in that recognition, nor at all resigned to eventual stagnation: they were, simply, in the first great thaw of spring, and they were enjoying the warmth of the sun, without demanding that it never rain or snow again.

The ceremony went on, with more speakers and more prayers than Dazen would have liked (one of the trifling conflicts), and he kept stealing glances at her as if to memorize every detail of her irrepressible smile.

Then they faced each other, held each other's hands, and renewed their vows.

As they finished, he said, "Do you mind if I maybe show off a little?"

"Dazen Guile," she said. "If I was bothered by you showing off, I wouldn't have married you. Twice."

"So I had this dream last night," he said.

"You're telling me about this now? We're supposed to process out."

"They'll wait," Dazen said. As if twenty thousand people weren't watching. "So this dream... Orholam was talking to me and He said, He said that because I asked a boon for others and not for myself, that He wanted me to carry a new message for Him in a special way for all those wounded and left bereft by this war. He said with Him, sometimes the healing is fast and sometimes it's slow, and oftentimes it's not finished while we still live. But with Him, it's never, ever partial."

"That's a good message, honey." She smiled and squeezed his hand. His maimed hand.

First her expression flashed apologetic, then she looked down, confused. That was the hand whose fingers were illusions.

But the illusions had held.

"So yeah," he said. "I kind of lied? I didn't really forget my wedding gift to you. Orholam's really?"

"*What!?*"

He locked his gaze with hers, and as if they were all alone, not in front of thousands, he pulled off his eye patch.

He'd thought this moment was going to be a gift for her, but instead he was awestruck anew by the unmerited favor he'd been shown. For he didn't simply see his bride through the new eye as well as he would have seen her through the old eye he'd lost. He saw his bride through eyes made new. He saw her truly, lit by an unstinting compassionate light, and he knew her every strength and every fight and every wound as he had never known them before, and his heart swelled as if to cover every hurt and rejoice in every joy.

His feelings for her had smoldered for most of his life, banked patiently as if against his will, a stubborn affliction almost, a strong but by now unsurprising love—but now it surprised him, after all, as his love leapt up at seeing this divine creation before him, a jewel with more facets and color and depth than he'd ever imagined, and his love was suddenly burning white-hot, as when they were young, but with an abiding strength beneath it like old oak, tested and true.

Her eyes went wide with wonder and alight with such joy as he would have never dared hope for her.

Finally, he rejoined the stream of time, and took a breath, and realized it was his first breath in some time. And he squeezed her hand with the hand Orholam had made whole.

"Now, for the fun part," he said, grinning reckless foolishness. His body felt so full of hope and light he couldn't contain it. "I'm not sure how this is gonna go. Or *if*, honestly. You ready?" he asked.

She didn't know what he was talking about, but her grip was as strong as iron and her face was radiant.

"Whatever it is...Hell yeah!" she said.

The high drapes opened and bathed them in Orholam's light.

Dazen raised his hands and it was as if all the goodness that had been pouring into him through these days came bubbling out to bless everyone he loved here—and his love had grown a dozen times over— and with skill and brilliance and no small amount of audacity, never stopping to consider whether he could really do what he was about to attempt, without giving it a little test first just in case, but simply believing, as if he were Prism once more, about to dazzle the thousands with spectacle and wonder, he called the colors to him.

He called. And they came.

Epilogue 1

An hour before his second wedding, Kip looked in the full-length mirror on the wall of the small parlor and marveled: part of him supposed that most anyone could look presentable if they were worked on by the most tenacious hairdressers and personal stylists, and he certainly had been thrown upon the untender mercies of those predators as they dug for any shaking sliver of attractiveness to drag out of its den and into the light to be devoured—but instead his wonder was directed at how he himself saw that schlub.

Seeing himself now, somehow he felt like he saw better than he ever had.

The cosmetics, the clothes, the hair, the shaved and lotioned skin, the anointing oils, the posture, the dazzling bright colors and pleasing patterns: these were all the lampshades we settle over our light hoping to cast a hue and color others will find acceptable. We hope we'll find it acceptable, too.

But others don't even see that color, for they view us through their own lenses, filtering our already-filtered light in ways we can only guess. Nor do we see ourselves true, for we wear our own lenses, and sometimes the eye itself is dark, and how great the darkness!

Kip had been so certain for so long that there was nothing he could do to make himself acceptable that he'd hidden his light altogether. The mirror had been an enemy who, overwhelming in his might, had simply needed to be avoided. But the mirror is ever a liar: when you yourself cut out half the light by which you see, how can the mirror be anything but?

'Let me see my skin, but with no pink tones.' . . . 'Oh, how awfully pale and ugly I am.'

We see others not as they are but as we see. We see ourselves not as we are but as we see—and as we are seen, for we each cast our light on each other, too. Surrounded by those who cast only brutal light, we see some truth, and sometimes necessary truth, but a lie if we think it all the truth.

Kip had been shedding filters and lampshades for the last few years now. Being stripped of drafting was different, though. It not only changed his sight, but it changed the very light he cast in the world. It certainly was changing how people saw him.

He'd gone to the Threshing Chamber immediately, hoping his loss might be temporary. But the testing stick had shown nothing. He'd kept it like a bad-luck charm: he was a mund.

Others had paid more in this war. Others had worse injuries. This burden wasn't going to be easy, and yet…he felt hopeful. As one must wear clothing, one must wear shades—clothing itself is one of them!—one must present oneself to the world, and yet he felt that now he could bring more of his light to the world than ever before. He looked now into the mirror and felt, well, *approval*.

"Looking pretty good there, soldier," he said. He straightened his back—not that these clothes let him slouch much—and then he flexed a bit.

Someone whistled behind him, and he felt the blood rush to his face. He spun.

It was Rea Siluz, in a shimmering burnous, a strand of pearls at her neck, and a bright galabaya down on her strong brown shoulders. She was literally radiant. Skin bright and luminous, eyes brighter still and mischievous. A smile like a current in a river where you thought, 'That's a nice smile,' and then suddenly you were three leagues downstream wondering what had happened. Every part of her was beautiful and strong and potently feminine, and the sum was more than its parts.

"Wow! You're just—wow!" Kip said. He suddenly understood why people had worshipped the immortals.

"I didn't want to underdress for your big day. Still…" She seemed to dim a bit. A couple of smile lines appeared, and her teeth suddenly seemed less than perfectly straight, and her proportions shifted slightly. "Better?"

"Perfect for starting a riot," Kip said.

She sniffed. "Here you said you loved a spectacle." But she shifted still further, until she looked like the prettiest mother in the city rather than in the history of the world.

"You came," he said, smiling broadly. His heart welled with appreciation. "I wasn't exactly sure how to send you an invitation. The luxiats looked at me funny when I asked."

"It's a big day. Days of profound healing capture our attention as much as days of war."

"It's so good to see you again. But I have to admit, I'm still not really sure why I'm doing this. I'm—well, look," Kip said. He picked up the Threshing testing stick and showed its lack of colors to her. "I'm not even a drafter now. Not a satrap—oops, missed that bet, I guess. Not a king. Not, not anything. And don't get me wrong, I'm pretty much delighted just to be alive, but I don't really understand doing the whole big-spectacle-wedding thing."

"It's not really for you," Rea Siluz said.

"And if you're going to get married a second time, don't you usually go more casual rather than more formal?" Kip asked. The entire island was celebrating the party of a century. "Seven days! Do you know I have to give *four* speeches, and that was with me *winning* the argument about how many I had to do!"

"Kip. It's not for you."

Kip knew it wasn't only for Gavin and Karris, and certainly not for the much-lesser-known Kip and Tisis. It was a celebration of victory, and of life. It was as necessary as midwinter festivals amid the chill and death of every year. The people had mourned, and now was time to celebrate.

"So I had this question," Kip said.

"About me running away when you faced Abaddon," Rea said.

"Well, I wouldn't put it that way," Kip said. He paused, then admitted, "Out loud."

She laughed. She'd apparently forgotten to tone down the beauty of that sound.

"You said once that you were less than he had been but more than he currently is. I kind of took that to mean you're more powerful than Abaddon."

"Kip, our power isn't measured by numbers in a ledger."

"But...I didn't really misunderstand, did I?"

"No," she admitted.

"And you don't lie, do you?"

"Oh, my little Guile bulldog. Next you're going to ask—"

"Why did he kick your ass?" Kip said.

"Why indeed?" she asked as if baffled.

Or as if teasing him.

Kip cocked his head as the possibility dawned on him. "You...you didn't."

She nodded.

"You *let* him win?" Kip asked, outraged.

"I prefer to put it that I wagered on you, Kip. Yes, I had the power to push him out of your world for a time, but only you could bring him fully into it and thereby make him vulnerable to being banished from this world forever."

"Well...dung," Kip said. "I mean, well done."

"Good job, little one. Controlling that tongue will be harder for you than killing 'gods' ever was."

"Hold on. You're not going to leave now, are you? This feels like goodbye. Before this torture of a wedding, too. You got dressed up and everything!"

"There are...oddities to how mortal and immortal time overlap. Every moment I am with you is a moment I cannot be elsewhere in the other realms. My liege has few warriors as gifted as I."

"Is that an answer, or a dodge?" Kip asked.

"A dodge," Rea admitted happily. "But don't worry, my tenacious Turtle-Bear, it is granted to me that I may come to you in your moments of deepest need. You see, Kip, you are the mirror in blood of my own deepest temptation."

"Huh? That doesn't sound good."

"When the Thousand Worlds were young, many of my dear brothers and sisters fell. Much is given to us, as the first created of the Am. But we have no bodies, though we can filter our light such that we put on bodies for a time. But we don't experience a body as an organizing principle of our selfhood, as you do. We are not given in marriage. We have no children. Thus, even as your kind wish to taste our powers, never realizing the costs therein, so our kind thirst for what you humans have that's denied to us. The rebels among us promised us that we *could* have it all, that we could transcend the bounds laid out for us. And in some things, they did not lie, though they knew not all the truth, and spoke less. My great temptation was to be a mother, as you mortals experience such things. Motherhood is a true and good and beautiful thing. How could one impugn such a desire?! I thought. A true and good and beautiful thing—reserved for others? What an outrage! This I longed for: to be a demi-creator, to be all the source of sustenance and love to one utterly dependent on me. To experience the unquestioning love of a babe looking up from the breast, though unknowing, utterly dependent, utterly sated, utterly adoring? It is a true love, a mother's. It is godly and good—but it is a love and gift and burden meant for mortals, not my kind. I was tempted to covetousness, because here was a love *denied* me. Who could deny me *love*? If He denied me this love, He must not love *me*. Was that not the work of a tyrant? Surely the Name above Names was holding out on me.

"Rather than apprehending my pain according to the Love I knew, I apprehended His love according to my pain. Thus misapprehending, my pain threatened to turn His no to anger and thence to rage and thence to rebellion.

"Each of the elohim were tempted thus, according to our station and our weakness. Some weren't even close to rebelling. I was close, but ultimately did not. I made the right choice, though it has meant sacrifices. I volunteered for you, Kip, but you are so fit for me that I might as well have been assigned. You are...so much of what I love about mortals. And my Lord has allowed me to taste as much of human motherhood with you as I can bear. I will be here for parts of today, and I will be there at future moments of great joy for you, and I will be at your end, if it is at all possible."

"What do you mean, as much as you can bear?" Kip asked. He was tearing up, and he wasn't sure why.

She stopped as if gut-punched, and her glory dimmed palpably. But when she spoke, it was with a steady, quiet voice. "As human parents do, I got to taste what it means to fail my child."

"What?" he whispered.

"In that closet..." she said, and a grief as potent as all her earlier glory flowed from her, palpably darkening the room.

She didn't have to say another word. There could be nothing else she was referring to except that lightless, godforsaken closet where Lina had locked him and gone on her binge, blotting out her cares and worries and mind and recollection of her son. The closet where his mother had forgotten him. Abandoned him without food or water to the rats for three days while no one noticed. While no one cared to look for him.

And suddenly, Rea was weeping, too, and he knew that she could see that closet right now. He knew, instantly, that she could see it in the present moment, with an immediacy before her eyes that even he could no longer feel. She was seeing Kip screaming as the rats began biting him, as the blood poured down his back and as he threw himself against the walls, scratching and clawing for an escape that didn't come. She could see his fear turn to terror, turn to despair, turn to madness. She was watching the pain that would shape and scar his entire life, even now as she spoke.

"I was supposed to be there, Kip." She could barely breathe the words over her sobs. "I was supposed to save you."

"What?" he asked as bitter tears spilled down.

"I was elsewhere, fighting, doing good. I knew I could get to you in time. But when I entered your time, Gader'el and Suriel were waiting for me in ambush. For three days I contended with them while you suffered. I want you to know—and I am allowed to say this much—*I* wasn't with you. But *He* was. When I arrived to save you, He was already there."

"But He did nothing," Kip said as he wept, the wound opening afresh.

"He spoke to you."

"No. I was alone." But Kip could remember it now. A few words only, in the many hours. A few calm words, but they'd kept his sanity.

"Kip. What if, in your darkest moment, He was there, all along, weeping with you?"

"If He saw me, if He cared, He could have saved me. He could have saved me with a word."

"Indeed. And that's the problem, isn't it?"

"What? 'Indeed'?" Kip asked. "What does that even mean? I don't understand Orholam at all."

"If even *we* could, I don't think my friends would have rebelled. What I know is this: A tapestry made of only white threads is perfect, but blank. When He starts letting us add our own colors, things get more interesting."

Kip scoffed. "Color metaphors are a little bitter for me at the moment," Kip said, holding up the blank color stick again. Then he shrugged as if he didn't care. "I prayed that He would help me escape that place."

"And you did."

"I didn't pray that He'd get me out after three fuckin' days."

"You asked Him to get you out immediately and He said no. I don't know why, Kip. But I know that sometimes when He says no to our desires, His no is mercy. I envied mothers, Kip, and now, having loved like one, I see how profoundly I'm not built for that blessing and that burden. For we immortals never forget. You Guiles have a miraculous memory—a gift of a redeemed sin from one of my kind deep in your ancestry—but we immortals carry all our memories before us at all times. I experience it as the present moment, always. My failure and your suffering will never *not* be before my eyes."

Her compassion was so genuine and so costly that Kip didn't shoot back in anger, but he couldn't keep the bitterness from his tone. "So there's some greater good that makes it all fine?"

"I didn't say that," she said. "I can't answer every tragedy, but I know my Lord's character and I know His power. I choose to trust Him, and though I've doubted that choice at times, I've never regretted it."

"I suppose I'm the last person who should shake his fist at Orholam," Kip said. "Sure, I've been through some shit, but look at what I have. I should just shut up forever." On the one hand, he'd saved his friends, his wife, and more thousands than he could know. He had been given his life back, when he should be dead. But on the other hand, he'd lost his best friend and many others, and he'd lost his powers and his claim to being the most important person in history.

Why, in the darkness, in the quiet, did he keep looking at the wrong hand?

Her tone was gentle. "He doesn't want you to shut up, Kip. I know you're not thinking just about the closet. You're scared that you lost your identity when you lost your magic, and even though you chose this, it still hurts. You're still scared, despite everything."

Kip scowled. So much for nonchalance. "Stop...understanding me and stuff."

"Kip. It's okay to be angry."

"I feel ungrateful," Kip said. "Greedy. I'm alive! Cruxer's not. I've got it amazingly great, and I did the right thing, and people love me—but sometimes all I can think about is what I'm never going to be." He must've pressed his fingers against that testing stick a hundred times, praying stupidly, blindly.

"I think if your prayer in that closet might have a lesson, it was this: sometimes, Kip, the answer isn't 'No.' It's 'Not yet.'" She smiled at him and stood. "Now, please excuse me, but you've got a wedding to attend, and there's a young woman in another realm who has a gift for getting in trouble that may rival your own. Not sure if my assignment to her is a reward or a punishment for how I've done with you."

"Bit of both?" Kip said.

She looked up for a moment, and he got the impression again that she was seeking permission for something.

"Don't blink," she said, grinning suddenly at him.

Rea Siluz's figure shimmered, and burst into something *other*. She didn't get any bigger, but suddenly the room seemed to strain to contain her essence. To look at her carried a sensation for the eyes like when the ear hears a perfect harmony reverberate with overtones and undertones as the waveforms dance in joy. She was brighter than color, more alive than the sun on green grass. She wore black dragon's-scale armor etched with designs in fire, and a helm of gleaming gold, and her eyes shone with lavender mischief. Her presence had a physical weight to it, like walking from a cool basement into the anvil of the desert sun. Kip dropped to the floor.

"I told you I love a spectacle," Rea said, and she smiled fiercely, and that smile was terrifying and sexy and breath-suckingly, knee-weakeningly, eye-blindingly bright; it was a flame that beckoned on a cold night and a fire that burned like a forge.

Kip's tongue failed him. He averted his eyes. He had to. The very room seemed more alive in the light of her presence. He nodded at the floor.

I remember.

I didn't take it seriously.

Holy shit.

She flared golden wings out broader than the room; they went right through the walls. There was a hum of gathering energy. Then she beat those enormous wings once and shot out of the world.

Slowly, he stood up and dusted himself off.

Always fooling around with people—people?—he shouldn't. One of these days that was really going to bite him in the ass. He saw the testing stick on the floor. He'd knocked it down as he fell. He reached over and picked it up.

For an instant, the testing stick's edge seemed to flash green like a quick wink at sunset. Kip scowled.

He looked at it more closely, but there was no color in the ivory. None.

He pressed his finger on the stick again.

Nothing.

Must have imagined it.

Epilogue 2

The dawn prayers atop the red tower had concluded. The young women and men, discipulae and luxiats both, departed quietly, as was required, allowing those who remained to continue meditating and praying. But the moment their feet touched the stairs, they immediately broke into happy conversation, eager to dive into days full of instruction and labors mental, spiritual, and—as the Jaspers needed workers for repairs and healing—quite physical.

A few worshippers and contemplatives remained, huddled in warm layers against the early morning's cool wind, hoping to hoard a treasure of quiet calm in their hearts against the chaos of the coming day.

Teia was here on her physicker's orders, sitting with her father. Every day she was supposed to try to last one minute closer to dawn before shielding her eyes once more behind layers of leather and her pitch-black spectacles. She couldn't even make it halfway to dawn yet, but it was good to sit beside her father.

Her physicker's hope was that her contracting pupils would break down the crystals of the lacrimae sanguinis slowly so that the poison might be worked out over months without killing her. In the meantime, contracting against the hard crystal matrices would help her keep her eyes from atrophying so that she wouldn't be blind when the poison did dissipate. He said 'when,' but she'd heard the 'if' he was hiding.

What it actually meant was that she felt incredible pain and nausea every day, to the point where sometimes she hoped to die.

Really, they had no idea whether it would work and she'd be rehabilitated, or if they were simply daily tearing open again a wound that would otherwise heal.

Even if it worked, she had a long, long road ahead of her. She most likely would never work for the Blackguard again.

So now she was on the disability dole, like a Blackguard who'd had a limb blown off. Her injuries weren't visible, weren't debilitating in the same way, but she was just as useless to the Blackguard. A sudden flash of light—such as, oh, every single time someone drafted, or lit a lantern, even the flash of sunlight on steel—might kill her. Even if it didn't, it could blind her permanently, and it would definitely incapacitate her as she seized up, vomiting.

So she was forced to wear impossibly dark spectacles and the eye patches over both eyes.

"Baba," Teia asked, "what are you supposed to do with a bird with broken wings?"

He put his hands on her shoulders, and when he finally spoke, there was a hitch in his voice. "I don't know what you're *supposed* to do. But I would hold her. Just hold her."

And so he did, embracing her silently, not trying to fix anything. He was not, perhaps, a great man who shook the pillars of the earth, but he was her father, and for today at least, for this hour, his embrace blunted the jagged black edges of her hellstone thoughts.

He held her as she cried, and in some deeply aching, wordless place inside her, just a little, something thawed.

Finally, she cleared her throat and said, "Come on, Baba. We've gotta go get ready soon so we can be there when Kip and Tisis get married. Again. Nobles are weird."

Her father grunted. "So...do I have to thank Kip for sending those bandits to find me and save me from the Order *before* I can punch him in the nose for breaking my little girl's heart? Or can that wait until afterward?"

900

"Baba! Don't you dare! And he didn't break my heart. I'm fine. And those men aren't bandits...anymore. Daragh's men were the only ones disreputable-looking enough to get into that neighborhood without raising any eyebrows."

But they'd barely started heading inside when someone barked from the stairs, "Hey! Shithead!"

"Excuse me?" Teia's father asked.

"Not *you*. That stunted little crotch fruit of yours," Winsen said. "Hey, layabout! Sluggard! The hell you doin' up here still?"

"What are you talking about?" Teia asked. "This is what I've—"

"*Training?*" he said as if she were as dumb as a bag of rocks. "I know you've got a nice gig here, getting fat and fartin' around with daddy. No disrespect, buddy—though I'm not sure why I oughta respect you. You clearly have none for yourself or you'd not have spawned our navel lint of doom here."

"Wh-what?" Teia's father said.

"Teia," Winsen barked, "vacation's over!"

"You flea-bitten, pox-eaten son of a whore!" Teia said. "You shit-licking, vomit-slurping, fart—er, sorry, Baba. Winsen, you *know*—"

"Oh," Winsen interrupted. "Shit. Right." Something hit her chest. She snatched it out of the air before it hit the ground. At least she still had her reflexes.

"What's this?"

"Here, come inside."

Inside, where it was much darker, Teia examined them in paryl.

They were glasses—no, more like small goggles, barely more than eye caps connected at the bridge of the nose. She shed her dark spectacles and eye patches, keeping her eyes shut tight, and put them on. She frowned. These new eyepieces had wide, curving lenses to preserve her peripheral vision, but otherwise fit tightly to the angles of her face perfectly, with leather cushions blacking out light from the sides or below. But the lenses were *clear*.

Not helpful.

"What're these?" Teia asked.

"This is the fun part," Win said, and he smacked the frames at her temples.

She cried out as tiny spikes stabbed into her skin and the lenses suddenly darkened.

"What are you doing?!" Teia's father demanded.

"*I* told 'em we should cut you loose like so much deadwood," Winsen said, "but Ben-hadad and Breaker been working on this all week. Ferkudi stole materials. Quentin translated some maybe-heretical books. Big Leo covered for everyone. Not that they all don't have more important stuff to do, in my own humble and disregarded opinion, thank you very much! They copied some ideas from Breaker's old spectacles, which were supposedly made by Lucidonius himself or whatever. Then they added some new tricks. These'll darken or lighten almost as fast as your own eyes can dilate or constrict—and you won't even have to think about it. There's, ehh, *maybe* some slightly or totally forbidden will-casting in there, though you won't hear me telling the tale. They'll allow you to isolate whatever spectrum you want—including superviolet, which you couldn't see before, so I guess that's a bonus? Breaker had to beg Súil to help. She claimed the paryl nearly fried her brain." Winsen shrugged. "Guess that explains what happened to make you the way you are, using paryl all the time. Anyway, now you can see. Without dying."

Teia couldn't breathe. She hadn't drafted paryl since that night, when she'd used the barest sliver necessary to make the master cloak work—and only for the few moments necessary to attack Liv and later Abaddon. The latter had left her shivering and puking, certain she was going to die. But this... Maybe Teia wouldn't be able to draft the paryl cloud that made her invisible to even sub-red drafters, but she could suddenly—maybe? maybe!—do everything else.

She felt like a champion sprinter going from losing a leg to merely having a limp.

She tried to change the spectrum she was seeing. The goggles worked flawlessly, instantly, dimming and focusing the light so she could see once more.

Dumbstruck, she glanced at her father—and looked away fast.

He was *blubbering*. Oh hell, she was gonna lose it, too.

"I dunno," Winsen said, resigned. "I voted against taking you back. But the others said, 'It isn't a vote, Winsen. Once you're one of the Mighty, you're one of us forever, Winsen.' Bah!"

Oh, nine hells.

Her boys. Her *brothers* hadn't forgotten her. As she'd been blind, they'd seen her. As she'd been in the dark, they'd found her. They'd known. They'd understood. As she'd pulled away, they'd pursued her. They'd all been working to restore her. They'd saved her, body and soul. Her brothers—abrasive, idiotic, absentminded, cranky, wonderful, beautiful, brilliant, steadfast, and self-sacrificing as they were—her brothers had worked tirelessly to make her whole.

—And then they'd sent *Winsen* to give her the news. He was the worst!

A sharp little laugh burst from her lips. Winsen! Of course it had to be Winsen. Because they couldn't treat it like it was a big deal.

"Win?" Teia said.

"Yeah?"

"You know, for the longest time I used to think you were an asshole."

"Oh yeah?" he said, waggling his eyebrows. "And now?"

"Oh, I still do. I just used to, too."

Epilogue 3

Dazen waved his empty hands around the corner before he entered the hidden room. "Please don't shoot," he said. "It'd feel ridiculous to die now in some silly accident." He poked his head around the corner.

Ironfist lowered the flintlock unsteadily, grumbling, "What makes you think it'd be an accident?" He looked like what he was: a man who'd recently lain on the brink of death. They'd hidden Ironfist away in Murder Sharp's old lair.

"Aren't you supposed to be somewhere?" Ironfist asked. Maybe he'd just woken.

"No. It's all fireworks and celebrating now. Kip and Tisis are good and hitched. Re-hitched? Anyway, I'd just be a distraction right now. Don't want to steal the spotlight."

"Still got the old magic, don't you?" Ironfist said. Then his brow furrowed. "Poor choice of words."

Dazen waved it away. He came in, ignoring Ironfist's frown at the big, wrapped-up sword he was carrying. "So, are you enjoying your time...uh, resting, or do you have one more adventure in ya?"

"Weddings and hobbling around watching sycophants rush to kiss the royal...ahem, *ring* isn't exactly an adventure."

"You seem to be forgetting what happened the first time I tried to marry Karris. You know, when our eloping somehow turned into the Prisms' War?"

"I actually did mean to come to Kip's ceremony," Ironfist confessed. "How long have I been here?"

"Long enough for Gill to get bored watching you sleep."

"That's not really an answer," Ironfist said.

"Well, you didn't answer me, either."

The two men stared at each other. Then Dazen waggled his eyebrows. They both knew Ironfist was a man of action. He had to be bored out of his mind. He wasn't in any shape for a battle of wills. "What's the *adventure*?" Ironfist asked grudgingly.

"Epic derring-do. Legendary opponents. And total secrecy. Even afterward. I expect you to be too weak and say no, but I thought you'd be furious with me for going to face so much danger without asking you. 'I would have come,' you'll say later. 'If you'd waited for me, you'd still have your legs,' you'll say. *Pfft*."

"Have I ever told you that you're a real piece of . . . work?" Ironfist asked.

"Look, they told me you were cranky, and I knew you were going to be too weak to come. But I just knew *someone* would be mad if I didn't at least ask my old friend along."

"Friend?" Ironfist asked. He swallowed, but then growled, "I don't even like you."

"A sadly common malady among my friends," Dazen said.

Ironfist laughed despite himself, then winced at his wounds. "Orholam's beard, mercy."

"You know what I came for?" Dazen said.

"Figured there'd be an ulterior motive. It's yours anyway. Always planned to give it to you." Ironfist pulled open a drawer on his bedside table and tossed a white stone tied on a leather thong to him.

Dazen caught the white luxin and looked at the lambent stone, then lifted his white eye patch and stared at it more. "I really drafted this at Garriston, huh?"

"Why're you still wearing the eye patch?" Ironfist asked.

"It's a bit intense to see everything without it. Maybe I'll be able to build up some tolerance to it eventually, but for the time being it looks like I'm going to have to labor under the burden of having a slight aura of mystery about me."

"You can make anything look good, can't you? It's annoying. Not to mention the getting-healed-instantly thing. Everything works out for you, doesn't it? No wonder you don't have friends."

"It's true, there's just not many people with the ego strength for it. That's why I've had to go for pirates and prophets and beautiful women and Blackguards and traitors and kings. Sometimes traitorous kings even—king, really. Singular. Don't want to exaggerate. The other king wasn't as friendly as you are."

Ironfist only shook his head.

"I figured it out," Dazen said.

" 'It'?"

"History."

"A suitably humble claim."

"Not all of it. Just the relevant bits," Dazen said. He took out the sword from where he'd propped it carelessly on the ground and unwrapped the cloths around it.

Ironfist goggled at it. The Blinding Sword didn't look at all the same as he remembered. A dark, molten and shimmering iridescence swept down the entire blade. There was a depth to it, like staring into the night sky, with all the colors of creation seen twinkling in the muted seven stars on the blade. Entire sections of it dulled though as it turned, as if it were covered in a polarizing lens.

Dazen started tapping the white luxin on the blade, then on the pommel. He rubbed it down its length like a whetstone.

"What are you doing?"

"Well, she told me not to draft or I'd draw the wrong kind of attention. Not that I'm eager to draft just now. You ever run a long race and it wipes you out, and then a few days later you think you've recovered and you run again and then you realize, no, you really, really haven't recovered? That's how I feel about drafting right now. Like I don't know if I tore some muscles or if they're really tired, but either way, I hurt like hell."

"What are you talking about?" Ironfist said. "Who told you not to draft? What 'attention'?"

"I'm trying to awaken the white luxin in the sword. I know it's there." He stared up at the ceiling. "C'mon, you *told* me white luxin isn't overcome by black."

He tossed the chunk of white luxin to Ironfist, then passed him the sword. "Here, you try."

"Try what?" Ironfist demanded, but before the words were out of his mouth a scintillating shine flashed down the length of the blade in every color. The muted seven stars surfaced through the darkness and now shone as hot in the blade as Orholam's Eye at noon. In the light of the blade, every color in the room suddenly glowed brighter, sharper, and more real.

"Great! That'll do," Dazen said. He took the sword from Ironfist's limp hand and quickly wrapped it back up in the cloths, as if worried someone would see it, though there was no one else in the room, and no windows, and no one who even knew where it was hidden.

"Huh," Dazen said, now that it was fully covered once more. "Guess that's what I get for thinking I'm so special. Good job. You can probably put away the white-luxin chunk now. It might draw attention, too. They weren't terribly specific."

"Who?" Ironfist looked at him, but he looked more troubled than in awe. "What have we just done?"

"Not 'we.' You. You just fixed the sword. It's what I figured out. Before Vician's Sin, drafters used to retire. The Knife passed through a drafter's heart, purging her of the buildup of toxic luxin but also taking away her drafting. You ever hear about this?"

"Some."

"Between the drafter's conscience and the Prism's judgment and Orholam Himself, other things might happen: a blue drafter who'd misused his Color would find himself blind to blue, where one who'd used his Color well might find himself granted more drafting ability even than before—even more years, or an additional color. A faithful artist might find herself made a superchromat, or a traumatized woman might find her memories eased or even erased. And lastly, some few would be judged worthy of death for what they'd done with their gifts. And the sword would then blind them to all color forever—or to all light forever, with death. It prefigured the final judgment of the afterlife, not only for drafters but also for those who watched, and they called it the Freeing, because once judgment is rendered, we're freed from fear, and because so often mercy prevailed. You know about Vician's Sin now?"

"The others told me, yeah."

"After Vician's Sin, the white luxin went dormant in the blades—all of them. The Knives would still kill and steal, but unbalanced by white, the Knife almost always killed, and it never gave gifts. Orholam sent prophets to call the Chromeria to repent, but they beat and killed the prophets, and when Vician finally died, the Chromeria began murdering innocents in order to make their own Prisms and to cover up their sins. The stories kept leaking out, so they commissioned their most fanatical as luxors to suppress the truth, even wielding black luxin to erase lines from books and from memories. Handling the black luxin repeatedly corrupted the luxors more than they already were, whereupon the purgers themselves were purged and the crime deemed complete.

"The Chromeria henceforth was a house of hypocrisy, its jealousy for power held side by side—sometimes within the same heart—with all its acts of mercy and tending to the indigent and sick."

"And you think we just fixed it?" Ironfist asked.

"We? *You.*"

"Why me? I didn't do anything!"

"Despite all your doubts, you held on to the white luxin, didn't you?"

"Doesn't seem like enough, does it?" Ironfist rubbed his lower lip. "You really believe Orholam intervenes personally?"

Dazen snorted. "How's your prayer go? 'God hears. God sees. God cares. God saves'? I more than believe it now. I know it."

Ironfist looked away. "Do you know this word 'ebenezer'?"

"What's that, Old Abornean... some kind of stone?"

"The word's Old Abornean, but the practice is ours. Means 'rock of remembrance.' When a great event happened in our communal life, we would set up a stone there so we'd be reminded every time we saw it. A great event in our own lives might even necessitate replacing our name. My birth name, Harrdun, means 'gazelle.'"

"Let me guess, 'rhinoceros' was already taken?" Dazen asked.

"If you're going be so you, I'm gonna need more poppy."

"Fresh out," Dazen said. It wasn't true, but he needed Ironfist sharp for what they were going to do next. "Please, go on."

"After... a race I did, they called me Izdârasen Winaruz."

"They gave you a double name *for a race*? Must have been some race. What's it mean?"

Ironfist seemed reluctant, but said, "'He Carries His Hope with the Strength of a Lion.' But, you know, that's way too long to ask the trainers to shout at a Blackguard scrub—"

"And it was a Parian double name, so everyone would have known you were a big deal. For winning a race."

"We didn't win," Ironfist said. "Anyway, it was a burden, so I welcomed it when they named me Ironfist. Not too flashy, not too original, but solid. I wanted to be hard enough to protect those I loved, because I didn't believe that Orholam cared about me. I'd accepted early on that I wasn't important enough to attract the attention of the maker of all things. So I remade myself into one who would be strong, and one who would be important. I took it as Orholam revealing to me who I was. I was become a hand raised in violence, my flesh turned to iron. To save my sister's life, I'd already sworn myself to the Order, and now to save my brother from our family's enemies for his murders at Aghbalu, I had proven our worth to the Chromeria. I had to become the best. So I did. But to save them, I lost them. And myself.

"Then that day at Ruic Head, *He* spoke to me. Orholam Himself. He helped me. Helped me in war. I had turned myself into someone utterly worthy of rejection, but He accepted me. He saw. He reached out his hand to save me, and I took it, and I...then didn't acknowledge it in the days after that battle. I didn't come clean. Didn't change my name or my life. I was too embarrassed. I had too much to lose—like the Magisterium in your story, after Vician was dead.

"I knew, at the very least, that confessing would mean I would lose my position as commander. Even self-confessed, an Order traitor as the commander of the Blackguard? Unthinkable. Would Andross Guile be content with less than my head? And then, how would I blunt the Chromeria's rage with my sister? What about the Order's? I...I had to think it through.

"But I didn't. Not really. I simply fell back into my old ways, telling myself I'd come clean soon—and then I lost it all anyway. And when my uncle was there, right in front of me, and all he asked for was the black bane...Though he is what he is, he was the last family I had left. I obeyed him from sheer habit. And then I left, ashamed. And then my brother died, and I learned he'd been trying to save me for all those years, to stitch back to wholeness a man split down the middle—while himself so wounded and guilt-stricken from Aghbalu. He served, for me. I damned myself by seeking vengeance and to save my sister's life. I saved her life, but I lost her soul and mine. My brother served humbly instead, and somehow I missed him for all those years. Right beside me, standing faithfully in a blind spot so large I missed the best thing around me. I had my chances to turn around. And with every one I didn't take, I brought a little more hell to earth. I even killed my best student, a young man like my own son. It's too late for me, Guile."

"Maybe Orholam has something to say about that?" Dazen said, gesturing to the sword Ironfist had just fixed.

"I can't explain that! But look, I can't make up for what I've done. The misery I caused in my arrogance."

"You'll never balance the scales," Dazen agreed. "So what?"

"I...I don't follow."

"Becoming a good man's easy. Act like one, even if it's an act. Some say, 'Who you are is what you do.' They're wrong, but not all wrong. What you do forms who you are. Then who you are forms what you do. It's a vicious cycle, or a virtuous one, depending. One act doesn't undo all of who you are, but a thousand acts make you who you are. So it's simple, though not easy: stop creating the wrong you. Stop trying to prove to yourself that you really are the bad man you believe you are despite what others say, and simply start doing good. Even if deep down you're a bad man, if what you do every day for the rest of your life is good, you'll be a bad man indistinguishable from a good one."

"Why go on at all?"

"Because there's a whole lot you can do, you moron. Not for yourself. For everyone else. If you had a scrub who loused up a hundred times but finally figured out what to do, and then he decided to volunteer for the Freeing because he believed those hundred mistakes made him a fuckup forever, would you send him off to the luxiats to die?"

"This is different."

"You thinking you're so different is what got you here."

"You just don't get it," Ironfist said.

"Fine. You know who did?"

"You mean who did get it?"

"Yeah. Your brother," Dazen said.

"I'm not sure I want you talking about him."

"He couldn't balance the scales. He was the Butcher of Aghbalu! By your logic, because he couldn't take away all the misery he caused, everything he did in the years between that massacre and his dying—including his dying for Kip and those boys—*all of it* was worthless. Because he couldn't balance the scales."

"I never said that."

"You're measuring yourself by a standard that'd make you furious if anyone used it on your own brother."

"It's not the same thing."

"My point exactly. It should be. You want to be a man of integrity? Start by having one set of weights and measures for others and yourself."

"You don't understand."

"You're seriously going to tell me how higher moral standards should apply to *you* than to your brother, who was a better man than you by far? *You* are getting up on your moral high horse? Ironfist, you're a liar and a traitor and an apostate and a pagan, a man who ordered murders and a coward. So that's a little rich, isn't it?"

Angry clouds gathered in Ironfist's brow, but they sat there and then receded some as Ironfist nodded.

Dazen said, "Arrogance is a ladder, and your ladder got you to the top of the mountain. The top of the Blackguard. You know what you find on mountaintops? An amazing view—and no life. No food, no water, no shelter, no companionship. Maybe it's time you come down. Life isn't a climb; it's a marathon. If you want to make it across the desert sections, you should run carrying water, not a ladder. Your arrogance got you here. Maybe it's time you left it behind. Maybe it's time you pick up some water and join the race. Your arms are strong from climbing; now they can carry extra water for others. You'll find stragglers along the way who need it, I think. But get your ass *moving*, because you've got a lot of catching up to do."

Ironfist sat with that for a few moments, and Dazen couldn't tell how much was sticking. Then Ironfist said, "Hearing this from you is a bit much."

"Who better to teach a lesson than one who had to learn it?" Dazen asked. "I'm not saying I'm ahead of you in this particular race. I'm saying you won't be running alone."

"You're some real motivational motherfucker, aren't you?"

"Watch it. A Blackguard guards his tongue."

"I'm not a Blackguard anymore."

"Yeah, about that..." Dazen said.

"What about it?" Ironfist asked suspiciously.

"We've got space in the newest cohort. Could use a good nunk."

Ironfist laughed. "You're an asshole."

"I know. It's why you always liked me."

"No, no, I never did."

"At the end you did."

Ironfist grunted. It might have been an admission.

Dazen decided to take it for one anyway.

"Actually, a space did open up," Dazen said. "Commander Fisk had some things go real sideways in the battle. He's asked to retire. Said he'll give us one more year as a trainer, though, more maybe, if we can get the right replacement as commander. And we *really* need him as trainer with the state the 'guard is in."

"You're asking me to be the commander of the Blackguard again?" Disbelief.

"Seems like."

Ironfist's jaw tightened with suppressed emotion. "There are others who can do the job."

"Oh, I know, you're not that special," Dazen said. "But I already offered it to all of them. Every last one said they'd love the job, but they'd rather serve *under you* instead. Threatened to resign en masse if you didn't get it, actually. So if you don't take the post, the Blackguard is *finished*. It'll be a hundred years before it recovers. If ever."

Ironfist's lips compressed, and his forehead tightened. He whispered, "They didn't really..."

"They did. But honestly, I don't think they like you *that* much. I think they just really want a chance to hit you with one of those

Blackguard Names. You know, one of those sort-of-respectful, more-kind-of-mocking things?"

"They want to change my Name?"

"Yeah, I dunno, maybe Ironfist's too flashy and original for 'em. I don't know if they conspired on this or what—they're so insubordinate sometimes—but you'd have to accept the new Name if you came back."

"Do you know what it is?"

"Yeah."

"Well?"

"I think they're gonna call you 'Rex.'"

Ironfist laughed, then winced. "'Commander *Rex*'? Those little shits!"

But the man seemed to glow. He was suddenly soaking all of this up, a great treasure of joy that he would examine later. His Blackguards meant so much to him, and that they loved him still was favor he didn't believe he merited. It was precious to him beyond all words.

Then he pressed his lips together, and his eyes hollowed. "I miss 'em," he said. "All of 'em we lost the day you made this." He gestured to the white luxin. "And since. My sister. And my brother most of all."

"Me, too," Dazen said quietly.

"So is that it?"

"There is a condition," Dazen said, taking Ironfist's acceptance for granted.

"Yeah, I figured," Ironfist said. "Several, I guessed. You are still a Guile."

The truth was, if Dazen hadn't been at least a little bit of an asshole as he delivered his offer, he knew that Ironfist would get stuck in his own head, and might actually have turned it down. Being an asshole about it directed Ironfist's gaze outward, to the job, to the people who needed him, to the personalities he saw himself needing to rein in.

But that was fine. Dazen could pretend to be an asshole when required.

Pretend.

He said, "There's just the one condition—well, for me. A few other people have to sign off on this, and they might really need convincing, but you know what? I *am* really convincing."

"Hadn't noticed that about you," Ironfist said.

"So here's the thing," Dazen said as if it pained him. "I need you to get up, like, right now, while everyone's distracted with the big wedding spectacle, and come do that thing with me."

" 'That thing'?" Ironfist asked, sitting up more in bed. He was trying to look irritated, but Dazen could tell he was on the hook already. A man like Ironfist needed to be needed, needed to be active, or he'd just die. "You mean that adventure? I thought you were joking."

"Nope. Has to be you. Has to be now, while everyone's distracted."

Ironfist hesitated. "What are you going to do with the Blinding Knife while everyone's distracted?"

"We, you mean. As in 'What are *we* going to do?' "

"No, I meant *you*. I'm not touching that thing."

"Right, agreed. That's fine. And *I* meant you're going to help me get there to do what I have to do. So you can parse that as us doing it or as me doing it while you help me, I mean, whatever floats your—"

"Gavin!"

"Dazen."

"Whatever!"

"Well, here's the thing. You've been there, too, like I have. And there's no one else I can trust to not succumb to them. And we've only got one chance to do this. Any other time, and I'm afraid they'd have allies show up. I know you don't feel well right now. And regardless of how good I look, I'm not at my full strength, either, so I guess we'll just be wounded warlords together."

" 'Wounded *warriors*,' you mean?"

"Eh, you and me? Come on. We're a bit more than just 'warriors,' don't you think?"

"Just shut up and tell me."

Dazen finally got serious. "It's now or never. I've always been proud, Harrdun. I've always wanted my greatness to be known, to be acknowledged. This? This will be the greatest thing I ever do, and no one will ever know it. That's my penance. Or at least my way of showing I've changed. Maybe you'll find some penance in it, too."

"Gavin," Ironfist said, low and dangerous. He was halfway out of his bed now. "What are we gonna do with the Blinding Knife?"

"The wedding's a huge spectacle, not just on the mortal side but this... *librarian*? I dunno. One of them who likes Kip has arranged some spectacle on the immortal side, too. The truth is, both the mortal and the immortal spectacles are merely a distraction for two old warlords—one of whom is the last person you'd expect to go all hooded-man-sneaky— to go quietly to do something only they could possibly do, right under the noses of hundreds of watching immortals, while hoping that the right half of them are watching the wrong thing. We'll have no allies with us, none. No help whatsoever. It'll just be you and me, against the eight of them. We'll take them one at a time, though, at least if we're lucky."

"Wait. Uh-uh. Gavin, you are *not* going back down to those cells to face those—"

"Oh, yes I am. And unless you want to explain to my widow afterward why you made me go alone, *Commander*, you are, too." Dazen gave him the big smile that he knew Ironfist hated. "Ironfist, buddy! C'mon! We're gonna kill us some gods." He spun the scintillating sword on its point. "You in or what?"

Acknowledgments

Wait a second, are you one o' them curious readers who reads acknowledgments? Even though you *know* your name isn't going to be here? You shouldn't be here! Book's over! Scram!

Fine. One more paragraph. I know you're a fast reader, and it's hard to not read a little bit more than you meant to, but after this one, stop.

There are few authors who have nearly a million and a half words' worth of riveting story to tell. The jury's out on whether I'm one of them, and that jury includes *you*. So my first thanks goes to you—even though you don't listen so well. Many of you first discovered me with my Night Angel trilogy and might've frowned at seeing that my next trilogy wasn't even set in the same world. Worse, the trilogy then became a tetralogy, then a pentalogy. (The man can't even count to three?!) But you gave Lightbringer, and me, a chance.

I've given my all to repay those acts of faith with these books. I will never take such trust for granted. I hope and strive to bring you joy and more.

Thank you for your graciousness as this final book took an extra year. For me it was worth the ink, sweat, and tears to present you with something I can be proud of.

Thank you to my editor, Brit Hvide, who took on a series after it was already a million words long—and an author who had difficulties understanding the term 'deadline.' Thank you for working to give this project the time and space and the pacing and polish it needed. Few authors understand the complexities of your job, but thank you for all you do.

Thanks to Bryn A. McDonald for taking on the mammoth task of producing a book of this size and complexity, and to my heroic copy editors. (Hi! Yep, I'm totally stetting that!) Thanks to Lauren Panepinto and your team for consistently brilliant covers and so much more besides. No one finds out what's in a book if they never pick it up, so pretty much all my success is because of you. (Bring this up the next time you ask for a raise.) Thank you to Laura, Ellen, Alex, Paola, Nivia, and to the rest of the team at Orbit US, UK, and AUS.

Thank you to my translators. I can't even tell how ingenious you are, because I are American and thus more polygluttonous than polyglotinous, yet I know from my brief, bruising encounters with little Latin and less Greek how much effort goes into your work. I *do* think of you when I write plays on words—and usually just laugh. Writing is pain. Should translation not be? (But seriously, sorry for the Gunner chapters.)

Thank you to my beta readers: John, Tim, Elisa, Heather, and John again for also being my gamma reader, and Keith for being my alpha to omega reader.

Thank you to my agent, Donald Maass. You have been a tireless advocate and a straight shot of sanity. Thanks to Katie for all the follow-up e-mails to foreign publishers and for the continual education on a complex business.

Thank you to Simon Vance, my audiobook narrator. With your skills, you bring all the benefits of adding talents together and none of the drawbacks. I am so glad you were brought to this project under false pretenses.

Thanks to Joseph Mondragon. I came across your synopses of Lightbringer online and realized to my great chagrin and greater delight that they were *better* than mine. (Turns out that writing a huge book and describing briefly what happens in it are different skills. Who'da thunk?) So I did what people do on the Internet and stole your work. I hope you never read this. Please don't sue me. (I'm kidding. I got his permission.) Joseph's (somewhat edited) work appears here. Any errors are mine—but would be seriously ironic.

Thank you to my assistant, the Dread Pirate CAPSLOCK. Though your predecessor should have most likely killed you in the morning, I'm flabbergasted by your unending brilliance and towering intellect. You're a paragon of strength, resilience, humility, and hilarity. Thank you for being the person who makes those last-second edits and additions to the manuscript that sometimes even I don't see before they show up in print.

Going a bit further afield now—no, no, go ahead, you can quit reading anytime! Thank you to Dante Alighieri, for literally writing a character named 'Dante' meeting the greatest poets of all human history in the afterlife and having them welcome him to join them at their fire as an equal. Whenever I worry my pride may be getting the better of me, I think of your—

Dante: Hey! It's not arrogance if it's accurate!

Brent: I'm not so sure about that, bucko. And putting your enemies in literal hell?

Dante: Bucko? Psh. Call me Dan. Now, come on, why don't you join us at the fire? I'll introduce you to everyone you don't know. Oh, don't worry. They all know *you*! We were just having a great discussion about how amazing Lightbringer is.

Brent: Yessir, whatever you say, Master Alighieri, sir…uh, Dan.

But seriously, I've always had a keen understanding of which fire I don't belong at, and—more's the pity—that's one of 'em. But my sincere thanks to you and Homie and Bill and Eddie for showing me how high the bar can be. Even if you are laughing at me as I Fosbury Flop right under it.

Tim Mackie, thank you for the glimpses into the Ur. My thanks to the Monday Night Irregulars, and my thanks to those who have stood in the gap for me when it seemed my help was caught up over Babylon.

My deepest gratitude to the one who ended that storm at the exact right moment and brought me diamonds in moonlight. I've been a lot of trouble.

My thanks to Dr. Jacob Klein for decades of dumbing down ancient Greek and Latin and philosophy for me. Some of it is going to stick any day now. Call it purgatory for that impressive jumping spinning sidekick on the racquetball court that was supposed to miss my face.

Thanks to my brother, Kevin. Kristi says whenever I speak Andross Guile's lines, I imitate your voice. (Weird!) Without the dirt-clod incident, the pitch-black locked closet with the spiders crawling under the door with their glowing red eyes, and the plastic zippered under-the-bed laundry bags, I'd probably have a lot more brain cells, but I wouldn't be able to write claustrophobic terror nearly so well. Huh, this makes you sound mean. Sorry. Please don't hurt me.

Sorry to that one guy who wrote me the angriest e-mail I've ever gotten—for writing a world in which color differentiation is so important that color-blind drafters are discriminated against. I appreciate your yearning for a kinder world. A world where all people knew what was true and beautiful and acted on it would have only one drawback: writing fiction there would be impossible—and probably unnecessary. In my worlds, characters believe many ugly things that I don't. Indeed, some even believe beautiful things I don't. Some authors confront the truth that people suck by imagining a world in which people don't suck in some particular way; I choose to say, "People suck. What do we do about that?"

Thanks to my *akhuya* Ishak Micheil for the Arabic translations. Any errors are either Teia's, because she was doing her best to translate phonetically what she heard, or your practical joke on me. But you wouldn't do that, right?

Thank you to Thomas McCarthy, for the Irish pronunciations, translations, and the patience with our Internet-translated (i.e., wrong) declensions.

Thank you to the late Mitch Hedberg. Sorry for stealing the 'I used to...I still do' joke form that one time. I put you in the acknowledgments to make up for it...?

To my dearest Kristi, without whom no one would be reading these words. When we were thirteen years old, I thought, 'That girl is going to make an amazing wife someday.' I love being right.

When we were planning our wedding (twelve years later, readers!) and you said you thought you should work the day job so that I could write full-time, I wanted to say YES! so badly that I was almost afraid to. An artist on a mission can be a terribly inhumane creature, as willing to make others suffer for his art as he is willing to suffer for it himself. I've tried not to be that careless creature—and too often failed. Thank you for suffering with me, for learning with me, and for laughing with me. Thank you for helping me understand my story-children as much as our real ones. Your singing makes the stars shine brighter.

Oh, and for you stubborn, quirky readers who read to the very last line of the book: Thanks for supporting me in doing what I love. You deserve to be rewarded. Flip the page for a special, secret little thank-you gift for you.

BUT JUST THIS ONCE! Don't you expect me to do it again!

Postlude

In the burned-out ruins of Master Atevia's house, Teia stepped into the cool, dark room and hung the master cloak on a mechanical peg, much like another one she remembered. She had only time to make out two figures in the room, one seated wearing spectacles and the other standing at his right hand.

As she closed the door behind her as if her heart weren't in her throat, an altered voice said out of the darkness, "You'll pardon my caution, I hope."

It had been three months since the Battle of Sun Day, and this morning, she'd found the note in her pocket, inscribed with the Broken Eye, telling her how to get to the Old Man of the Desert's secret new offices on Big Jasper. That she'd received a note instead of a knife in the back meant the Old Man didn't know (at least for sure) that she was the one who'd poisoned the entire Order. That the note had been planted in her very pocket suggested that he had at least one last Shadow.

Andross had given Grinwoody the chance to run, but he just couldn't do it.

That was why she was here, foolish as it was. She had too many friends upon whom the Old Man still wanted vengeance.

"What the hell happened to all of us on Sun Day?" she asked. "I've been trying to find out, but everyone's just claiming it was an act of Orholam. No one's telling me anything."

"Not even your friend the White?"

"You know how that infiltration went, don't you?" Teia said. "I've been demoted for being absent without leave. I've been lucky to keep my place in the Blackguard."

"You were at the Feast of the Dying Light," the Old Man said. "I wasn't aware you were invited. You were supposed to be watching Gavin Guile."

"I'd just got back. Master Sharp took me to the Feast, just for a bit, he said. Said I shouldn't miss out on the holiest day of the year and my first chance to drink the bloodwine and see the community I was giving so much to serve. Then, afterward, he saved me. He guessed what the poison was and told me our only hope to live through it. But he drank too much of it. I watched him die."

"As I watched many more," the Old Man said.

"What happened?" she asked.

"One of the high priests betrayed us, a man named Atevia Zelorn. He poisoned the wine. He gave his life to betray us. This was his home. He was acting, I think, on Karris Guile's orders. We will have our vengeance soon."

Teia cursed as if she hated the White.

You just couldn't run away, could you, Old Man?

"So what's the plan?" she asked.

"We build anew," the Old Man said. "I still have riches. I still know who's weak, who can be bribed, who can be blackmailed, who's fearful, who can be conned or seduced. Best of all, I still have several shimmercloaks. You and Aram will be the foundation on which we rebuild the Order."

"Aram?!" she couldn't help but say.

The man beside Grinwoody in the dark didn't speak, but he gave a satisfied, arrogant little grunt.

Grinwoody spoke for him. "Aram is sharp and bitter and unquestioningly obedient—and a better fighter than most people would guess, considering. And in a sign that our gods have power beyond the Chromeria's knowing, I've discovered that Aram is a lightsplitter. You, Adrasteia Sharp, my strong right hand, you will train him. You two will be our first team of the new era."

So there it was: the admission Teia had been hoping for. There were no others. This was the last root of the Order, the last tiny smoldering ember.

"No," Teia said. "That's *not* how it's gonna be."

"Excuse me?" Grinwoody said. "Young lady, if I have to teach you lessons in obedience as I did your master, I—"

"It was me," Teia said. "I never left the Jaspers. I told Guile you planned to betray him. I killed Halfcock and Aglaia Crassos and Ravi Satish. I followed Atevia Zelorn, and I poisoned the bloodwine. All of it was me."

Full-spectrum light suffused the entire room as Grinwoody hit some hidden switch as Aram snapped into a ready position with his spear. The look of black rage suffusing the Old Man's face was fearsome to behold.

"Well, now you've made a very big mistake. Why would you tell me such lies? Do you think this is a game?" The Old Man slapped a hand down, triggering something that slapped a bar down over the cloaks hanging on the pegs, clicking as it locked them into place. He threw back his hood, released the voice-changing collar. "Aram, kill her if she moves. Child, do you *want* to die?"

"Oh yes, but not today, I think."

His eyes narrowed. He didn't believe her. He didn't think she was capable of all she'd done.

She said, "You know, Sharp liked to think of the Order as piranhas. But he told me once that there's a fish that hunts piranhas. Vampire fish, they call it. Fangs longer than my fingers. Said he never could get those fangs to work in his dentures. Too long to fit in his mouth without stabbing himself, he said. He thought that was appropriate, because though he always entertained a fantasy of killing you, he was never willing to bleed to do it."

"So you killed Elijah, too?" Grinwoody had his hand under the desk, clearly holding a pistol.

"I found this mask in his workshop. With some help from my friends, I finished it. And now I'm going to finish what Elijah started, and what you started, too." She pulled out the alien, skeletal half mask. With leather loops over the ears to hold it up, it covered only from the forehead to the upper lip. Vampire-fish fangs hooked down from the upper jaw. A black cloth draped below that to conceal the lower half of the face and the neck. The cloth was imbued with orange luxin to make an illusion of a skeletal, monstrous neck and a toothy lower jaw snapping up to meet the hungry upper fangs.

Teia said, "You wanted to make me dangerous. I've become ever so much more than that. Do you want to know the biggest secret about my shimmercloak?"

Grinwoody stood, a pistol in each hand, trembling with rage, but he didn't fire yet. He needed to know. He always had. His eyes shot a glance to her shimmercloak, locked to its peg.

"The secret is..." She lowered her voice to a whisper. "I don't need it anymore."

Before she settled the mask into place with its illusory teeth, before the Mist Walker disappeared, before the report of the muskets, before the thuds of flesh and the final hopeless begging, before the blood leapt onto the walls, before the last gurgling breaths of evil men drowning in their own blood, she flashed a smile at them, and her eyes were an open grave, and her teeth were very sharp.

Character List

Abaddon: Also known as the god of locusts, the Day Star, the Lord of the Flies. One of the chief immortals of the Two Hundred. Often depicted with crippled ankles, giant insect wings, and pallid features.

Adrasteia (Teia): One of the smaller Blackguards, a skilled paryl drafter, and a luxor for the Iron White. She is a double agent in the Order of the Broken Eye.

Agnelli, Lucia: A Blackguard scrub, she had a forbidden romantic relationship with Cruxer. Murdered by Quentin Naheed during a training exercise.

Aleph, Derwyn: Commander general of the Cwn y Wawr.

Aliyah: Married to Halfcock in secret. She has a teenage son from her first marriage, Eliazar.

Alvaro: A young, rebellious mirror slave.

Amadis: An older man, overseer of mirror slaves on the Jaspers.

Amazzal: One of the six High Luxiats, most notable for his commanding presence and rich voice.

Amzîn: Awkward young Blackguard, charged with protecting the White.

Appleton, Aodán: A nobleman and member of the Council of the Divines for the Blood Forest city of Dúnbheo.

Aram: A failed Blackguard scrub with a grudge against Kip Guile and Cruxer. Elevated to commander of Zymun Guile's Lightguard.

Arius: One of the newest members of the Mighty.

Arthur, Rónán: Deceased twin brother of Conn Ruadhán Arthur. Full-spectrum polychrome and member of the Shady Grove willcasters.

Arthur, Ruadhán: Conn of the Shady Grove will-casters.

Arun: Manager of an inn on the Jaspers.

Asafa ar Veyda de Lauria del Luccia verd'Avonte: Keeper of the Word, Chief Librarian of the Great Library in Azûlay, Katalina Delauria's father.

Aspasia: Karris Guile's room slave.

Azmith, Akensis: A scion of the Azmith family. Killed by Karris White Oak during the choosing of the White.

Azmith, Caul: A Parian general, the Parian satrapah's younger brother. Briefly served as commander of the Chromeria's allied armies. He led his troops to devastating losses against the White King at Ox Ford, almost shattering the alliance, after which he was demoted. His family seeks to return him to power.

Azmith, Tilleli: Parian satrapah, older sister of Caul Azmith and spymaster for Paria's Nuqaba. Andross Guile had intended for her to take power after his assassin killed the Nuqaba, but on Karris's orders, Teia killed Tilleli as well.

Beliol: Incorporeal (imaginary? immortal?) assistant to the Ferrilux.

Ben-hadad: A former Blackguard, Ruthgari, and a member of the Mighty. A blue/green/yellow polychrome and a brilliant engineer.

Blue-Eyed Demons, the: A mercenary band that fought for Dazen Guile's army during the False Prism's War. They later attempted to set up their own kingdom. Stomped out by Prism Gavin Guile.

Blunt: A Blackguard watch captain.

Bonbiolo, Benetto-Bastien: One of the four Ilytian pirate kings, rumored to trade under the pseudonym Marco Vellera.

Borig, Janus: A Mirror who painted true Nine Kings cards. Was assassinated by the Order of the Broken Eye.

Brightwater, Aheyyad: Orange drafter, grandson of Tala. Defended Garriston by designing the murals on Garriston's Brightwater Wall; given the second name 'Brightwater' by Prism Gavin Guile.

Brook, Justinia: Served as White two hundred and twelve years ago.

Buskin: A venerable Blackguard and excellent archer.

Caelia Green: A talented drafter, a dwarf, and formerly a servant of the Third Eye. Named Green on the Chromeria Spectrum after Gavin Guile decreed Seers Island a satrapy, New Tyrea.

Carver Black: A non-drafter, as is traditional for the Black. He is the chief administrator of the Seven Satrapies. Though he has a voice on the Spectrum, he has no vote.

Clara: A young and diminutive discipula.

Cumán, Cu: A nobleman and member of the Council of the Divines in Dúnbheo.

Council of the Divines in Dúnbheo: A group of elderly noblemen in Blood Forest. They are Aodán Appleton, Ghiolla Dhé Rathcore (nephew of Orea Pullawr), Breck White Oak (third cousin of Karris White Oak), Cúan Spreading Oak (grandson of Prism Gracchos Spreading Oak), Culin Willow Bough, and Lord Golden Briar (newest member).

Crassos, Aglaia: The youngest daughter of a wealthy noble family, she lives at the Chromeria as a Blackguard sponsor. A sadist who enjoys the pain she inflicts on her slaves. Has a powerful hatred of the Guile family, and Teia—whom she once owned.

Cruxer: He was perhaps the most talented, dedicated Blackguard of his era, now one of the Mighty.

Daelos: A Blackguard, very small but intelligent and talented with blue. Left behind at the Chromeria when he was gravely injured fighting as one of the Mighty.

Danavis, Aliviana (Liv): A yellow/superviolet bichrome drafter from Tyrea. Formerly a discipula at the Chromeria whose contract was owned by the Crassos family. Grew up in Rekton with Kip Guile. Daughter of Corvan Danavis. She served the White King for a time; now the superviolet pagan god, Ferrilux.

Danavis, Corvan: A red drafter. A scion of one of the great Ruthgari families, he was also the most brilliant general of the age and the primary reason for Dazen Guile's success in battle during the Prisms' War. Now the satrap of Seers Island, he is married to the Third Eye.

Daragh the Coward: The bandit king of Blood Forest. Known for his many scars.

Dariush, Lord: Felia Dariush Guile's father. A wealthy Atashian noble and art collector. His full name is Roshe Roshan Dârayavahush.

Darjan: A warrior-priest of the Ancient Tyrean Empire. A statue of him once stood near the orange groves in Rekton, known as the Broken Man.

Daughters of Caoránach (pl. caoránaigh): Wights who have adapted their bodies for living in water. Also known as 'river wights,' they took their name from the mother of demons in Blood Forest folklore.

del'Angelos, Ferkudi: A member of the Mighty. A goofy and awkward blue/green bichrome who excels at grappling. Gifted mathematician/statistician but misunderstands social cues.

Delarias, the: A small farming family in Rekton.

Delauria, Katalina (Lina): Kip Guile's mother, died in King Garadul's siege of Rekton. She was a librarian in Paria before fleeing in disgrace, eventually settling in the Tyrean town of Rekton.

Einin: A new member of the Mighty from Blood Forest. Orange/red/sub-red polychrome, mother of ten.

Elos, Gaspar: A green wight, he saved Kip Delauria's life before the destruction of Rekton.

Elos, Ysabel: Particularly cruel overseer of mirror slaves; sister of Gaspar.

Essel: A Blackguard Archer. Her young mother, Delilah Tae, was a sub-red drafter and one of the first drafters Freed by Prism Guile.

Estratega, Gaspar: One of the most famous and brilliant military strategists in history.

Fiammetta: Felia Guile's trusted room slave, manumitted by Lady Guile in her will, though Andross didn't enact this provision of his wife's wishes. Gavin eventually did, sending her home with protection.

Finer: A legendary Blackguard commander who developed knee braces with sea-demon bone before going wight and attempting to assassinate his Prism.

Fisk: He barely beat Karris White Oak during their testing as scrubs to enter the Blackguard. He rose through the ranks to become a Blackguard trainer, then served as commander after Ironfist was fired.

Galden, Jens: A magister at the Chromeria, a red drafter with a grudge against Kip Guile.

Garadul, Rask: A satrap who declared himself king of Tyrea; his father was Perses Garadul.

Gates, Anjali: A senior diplomat in the Chromeria who came out of retirement to serve the Iron White.

Golden Briar, Cathán: Cousin to both Arys Greenveil and Ela Jorvis. Eva Golden Briar's elder brother. He replaces Arys Greenveil as the Sub-red on the Spectrum after she dies.

Goss: A Parian Blackguard inductee, one of the best fighters, and a member of the Mighty before he was killed by the Lightguard.

Greenveil, Arys: Served as Sub-red on the Spectrum. A redheaded Blood Forester, cousin of Jia Tolver, sister to Ana Jorvis's mother, Ela. She has thirteen children by thirteen different men and died giving birth to her last son.

Greyling, Gavin (Gav): A legacy Blackguard. Younger brother to Gill Greyling, named after Gavin Guile. He is Freed by Karris White after he breaks the halo on a reconnaissance mission to find her husband.

Greyling, Gill: A legacy Blackguard. He is the elder brother of Gavin Greyling, and the more intelligent of the two.

Greyling, Ithiel: Late Blackguard. Father of Gill and Gavin Greyling.

Grinwoody (né Amalu Anazâr Tlanu): Andross Guile's head slave, secretary, and right hand. Worked as a Parian legalist before entering Blackguard training; his contract was bought by Andross just before his swearing in as a Blackguard. He is secretly the Old Man of the Desert, the head of the Order of the Broken Eye.

Guile, Abel: Andross Guile's elder brother and the heir to the Guile 'fortune' before he signed it over to his brother.

Guile, Andross: Father of Gavin, Dazen, and Sevastian Guile, husband to Felia Guile. He drafts yellow through sub-red, although he is primarily known for drafting red, as that was his position on the Spectrum. Now the promachos, and the longest-serving member of the Spectrum.

Guile, Darien: Andross Guile's great-grandfather. He married Zee Oakenshield's daughter as a resolution to their war.

Guile, Dazen: Younger brother of Gavin. He fell in love with Karris White Oak and triggered the False Prism's War when 'he' burned down her family compound, killing everyone within.

Guile, Draccos: Andross Guile's father. Notorious for gambling an entire hyparchy for the hand of a woman, the young Orea Pullawr, on a horse race. He lost the race, the woman, and his family's entire fortune. It was revealed decades later that his opponent, Juldaw Rathcore, had cheated. The Spectrum refused to expel the Rathcores at that time, leaving the Guiles as wool traders. Implicated in the murder of his brother, but as the only witnesses were slaves whose testimony was thereby inadmissible, the case wasn't prosecuted by local magistrates or the satraps. (Orea ended up later marrying Juldaw's brother.)

Guile, Felia: Born Firuzeh Eszter Laleh Dariush, a brilliant linguist and orange drafter from Atash. Wife of Andross Guile, mother to Gavin, Dazen, and Sevastian. Cousin of the Atashian royal family. Freed at Garriston just after the first battle with the Color Prince. Her mother was courted by Ulbear Rathcore before he met Orea Pullawr.

Guile, Gavin: The Prism. Two years older than Dazen, he was appointed Prism at age thirteen.

Guile, Kip: The illegitimate Tyrean son of Gavin Guile and Katalina Delauria. He is a superchromat and a full-spectrum polychrome. Leader of the Mighty, married to Tisis Malargos.

Guile, Sevastian: The youngest Guile brother. He was murdered by a blue wight when Gavin was thirteen and Dazen was not yet eleven.

Guile, Zymun: A young drafter and former member of the White King's army. Also known as Zymun White Oak, he claims to be the son of Karris and Gavin Guile and has been declared Prism-elect.

Gunner: né Uluch Assan, legendary Ilytian pirate famous for having killed a sea demon. His first underdeck command was as cannoneer on the *Aved Barayah*. Worked for Dazen Guile during the False Prism's War. He later became captain of the *Bitter Cob*.

Halfcock: One of the oldest Blackguards at forty years old. Sub-red/red bichrome. Refuses to retire.

Hill, Ruarc: A nobleman and leader of Dúnbheo.

Holdfast: A Blackguard. His son is Cruxer and his widow is Inana, another Blackguard.

Holvar, Jin: A woman who entered the Blackguard the same year as Karris White Oak, though she is a few years younger.

Hanishu: Tremblefist. A Blackguard. He was Ironfist's younger brother and was once the dey of Aghbalu. His Nine Kings card is the Butcher of Aghbalu.

Harrdun: Ironfist. Former commander of the Blackguard, a blue drafter. Parian. Brother to Haruru (the Nuqaba) and Hanishu (Tremblefist). Member of the Order of the Broken Eye. Takes the title of king of Paria after his sister is assassinated.

Haruru: The last Nuqaba in Paria, she was assassinated by Teia for the Order of the Broken Eye.

Inana: Cruxer's mother, and once a Blackguard. Widow of Holdfast, also a Blackguard. She retired from the Blackguard in order to marry him.

Izemrasen: A ghotra-wearing Parian, forty years old, green drafter. He lost his legs after breaking his back during his training to enter the Blackguard. Now a scout-drafter for Kip Guile's Nightbringers.

Jalal: A friendly storekeeper. Karris's favorite kopi seller on Big Jasper.

Kadah: Formerly a magister at the Chromeria who taught drafting basics. Now a researcher for the Chromeria.

Kallikrates: Teia's father. He ran the silk route as a trader before losing everything due to his wife's reckless behavior.

Keeper of the Flame, the: A chi drafter. Member of a secret religious order in Dúnbheo.

Kerea: A Blackguard and an Archer.

Klytos Blue: The Blue on the Spectrum. He represents Ilyta, though he is Ruthgari. A coward and Andross Guile's tool.

Leonidas: *Aka* Leo. A member of the Mighty, hugely muscular, drafts red and sub-red. Better known as Big Leo.

Lorenço: One of High General Corvan Danavis's lieutenants.

Lucidonius: The legendary founder of the Seven Satrapies and the Chromeria, the first Prism. He was married to Karris Shadowblinder.

Malargos, Antonius: Cousin of Eirene and Tisis Malargos. A handsome young red drafter. Later a military leader of some skill for Kip Guile's Nightbringers. A devout follower of Orholam.

Malargos, Eirene (Prism): The Prism before Alexander Spreading Oak (who preceded Gavin Guile). She lasted fourteen years.

Malargos, Eirene (the Younger): The older sister of Tisis Malargos. She took over the family's affairs when her father and uncle didn't return from the False Prism's War.

Malargos, Tisis: A beautiful Ruthgari green drafter. Her father and uncle fought for Dazen Guile. Her older sister is Eirene Malargos, from whom she will likely inherit the wealth of a great trading empire, as Eirene has refused to bear children. Now married to Kip Guile.

Marissia: See 'Rathcore, Marissia.'

Miriam: High General Corvan Danavis's attaché and lieutenant commander.

Muazon, Aldib: The last academic to credibly study paryl.

Muriel: The apothecary for the Order of the Broken Eye.

Nabiros: One of the Two Hundred. Legendary spiritual being. Also known as Cerberos.

Naheed, Quentin: A young luxiat, genius polymath, erstwhile assassin, now humble servant of Orholam and slave to the Iron White, Karris Guile. He wears rich clothing as a warning to other luxiats of what sins their vanity may lead them to.

Nuqaba, the: The keeper of the oral histories of Parians, a figure of unique and tremendous power due to her ancient office as both religious leader to the Parians and guardian of the Great Library of Azûlay. Within her satrapy, she rivals both the satrap of Paria and the Prism in her influence.

Nuri (Nuriel): An immortal, one of the elohim.

Orholam: From the Old Abornean Or'holam, literally 'Lord of Light/ Lights.' Referred to by His/Its titles rather than by a name as a sign of total respect. The deity of the monotheistic Seven Satrapies, also known as the Father of All. His worship was spread throughout the Seven Satrapies by Lucidonius four hundred years before the reign of Prism Gavin Guile.

Orholam: A nickname for a pious slave rower on the *Bitter Cob* who claimed to have been a reluctant prophet of Orholam. Due to Captain Gunner's superstitions, he was assigned to the seventh seat in the galley's ranks.

Pansy: Gunner's first mate on the *Golden Mean*.

Parsham, Vell: Freed by Gavin after the False Prism's War.

Pen, Ulgwar: Leader of the Eighth Stoa, scholar who wrote about shimmercloaks and invisibility.

Pheronike: A spy handler for the White King and a sub-red drafter. It was discovered while he was being executed on Orholam's Glare that he was hosting the immortal Nabiros.

Polyphrastes: Religious scholar who wrote *Dictions*.

Presser: A battle-scarred Blackguard.

Proud Hart, Lady: A beloved artist and historian in Dúnbheo.

Ptolos, Euterpe: Satrapah of Ruthgar.

Pullawr, Orea: The White who preceded Karris Guile. A blue/green bichrome who refrained from drafting for decades in order to prolong her life. She served as the White for nearly thirty years before she was assassinated. She was married to Ulbear Rathcore before his death twenty years prior to her own.

Ramir (Ram): A Rekton villager and a bully who was murdered when Rask Garadul destroyed the village.

Rathcore, Marissia: Gavin Guile's room slave, Orea Pullawr's granddaughter. A red-haired Blood Forester who was captured by the Ruthgari during the Blood Wars, she served Gavin for more than ten years (since she was eighteen) as his room slave—secretly spying for her grandmother.

Rathcore, Ulbear: The late husband of the White, he has been dead for twenty years. An adroit player of Nine Kings.

Red Leaf, Bram: The rotund, rosy-cheeked ambassador to Satrap Willow Bough of Blood Forest; nobleman who holds land on the Blood Forest coast.

Rhoda: Masseuse for the Blackguard and the White.

Sadah Superviolet: The Parian representative, a superviolet drafter, often the swing vote on the Spectrum.

Samite: One of Karris White Oak's best friends. Now one-handed after a war wound, she has become a trainer for the Blackguard.

Satish, Ravi: An unscrupulous banker and slaver involved with Aglaia Crassos, and a low-ranking member of the Order of the Broken Eye. From one of the families dispossessed and bankrupted during the False Prism's War.

Sayeh, Samila: A blue drafter for Gavin Guile's army. She fought for him in the defense of Garriston.

Seaborn, Phyros: A member of the Omnichrome's army. He was seven feet tall and fought with two axes. Liv Danavis's protector and guardian. His family was destroyed by the Guiles after his brother crossed Gavin Guile. Killed by Liv Danavis when he tried to enslave her for the White King.

Shadowblinder, Karris (née Karris Atiriel): A desert princess. She became Karris Shadowblinder before she married Lucidonius, and succeeded him as the second Prism of the Seven Satrapies. She founded the Blackguard.

Sharp, Murder (né Elijah ben-Kaleb): An assassin of the Order of the Broken Eye who has at times worked for Andross Guile when the Order endorsed the assignment.

Shmuel, Rivvyn: A light-skinned Abornean Blackguard. A red drafter who fought particularly bravely in the Wight King's War.

Siluz, Aurea (Rea): Fourth undersecretary of the Chromeria library. She helps Kip once or twice.

Siofra, Sibéal: A pygmy drafter of Shady Grove.

Spreading Oak, Alexander: The Prism before Gavin Guile. Became a poppy addict shortly after becoming Prism. He spent most of his time hiding in his apartments. Son of Lord Bran Spreading Oak.

Súil: A weak paryl drafter living in Dúnbheo recruited by the Mighty.

Talim, Sayid: A former Prism. He nearly got himself named promachos to face the nonexistent armada he claimed waited beyond the Everdark Gates.

Tallach: A giant grizzly partnered with Conn Ruadhán Arthur. His littermate, Lorcan, was paired with Ruadhán's twin brother, Rónán.

Tamerah: A Blackguard, a blue monochrome.

Tana: A legacy Blackguard.

Tawleb, High Luxiat: An important luxiat who was mentoring Quentin Naheed and directed him to assassinate Kip Guile. Once discovered, he was executed on Orholam's Glare by the Iron White.

Tep, Usef: A drafter who fought in the False Prism's War and later against the Omnichrome's armies at Garriston. He was also known as the Purple Bear because he was a disjunctive bichrome in red and blue. After the war, he and Samila Sayeh became lovers, despite having fought on opposite sides.

Third Eye (née Polyhymnia): A gifted and powerful Seer, the leader of the original Seers Island inhabitants, and wife of Corvan Danavis before her assassination by Murder Sharp for the Order of the Broken Eye.

Tlatig: One of the Blackguard's most skilled Archers.

Tzeddig: Blackguard trainer who mentored Samite and Karris's cohort.

Valor: A mirror slave and former Blackguard trainee.

Vanzer: A Blackguard and a green drafter.

Vecchini, Phineas: A cannon-caster, and retired cannoneer.

Vecchio, Pash: The richest and most powerful of the pirate kings. His flagship was the *Gargantua*, the best-armed ship in history. Gavin and Kip Guile sank it. He is reputed to be less than happy about this.

Vician: The last True Prism known to history.

Web, Daimhin: A legendary hunter from deep in Blood Forest, famed for taking his prey with only a knife. Known in his native tongue as *Sealgaire na Scian.*

White Oak, Karris (later Karris Guile): The newly appointed White of the Spectrum, also known as the Iron White. Former Blackguard and a red/green bichrome. Married to Gavin Guile.

White Oak, Koios: One of the seven White Oak brothers, brother of Karris White Oak. He disappeared after the disastrous fire that killed nearly all of his family and destroyed their estate; years later he emerged as the Color Prince in Tyrea. Now known as the White King, or the Wight King in the Chromeria's propaganda.

White Oak, Kolos: One of the seven White Oak brothers, brother of Karris Guile.

White Oak, Rissum: A luxlord, the father of Karris White Oak and her seven brothers; reputed to be hot tempered but a coward.

White Oak, Rodin: One of the seven White Oak brothers, brother of Karris Guile.

White Oak, Tavos: One of the seven White Oak brothers, brother of Karris Guile.

Wight King, the: Aka the White King, the Color Prince, Lord Omnichrome, Crystal Prophet, Polychrome Master, and pejoratively, Lord Rainbow. Leader of a rebellion against the rule of the Chromeria. He has re-formed almost his entire body with luxin. Reputed to be a full-spectrum polychrome, he posits a faith in freedom and power, rather than in Lucidonius and Orholam. He was formerly Koios White Oak, one of Karris White Oak's brothers. He was horribly burned in the fire that triggered the False Prism's War.

Willow Bough, Briun: The satrap of Blood Forest.

Winsen: A mountain Parian, and one of the Mighty. An unparalleled archer.

Zelorn, Atevia: A respected wine merchant and secretly a priest of the Order of the Broken Eye.

Glossary

Aghbalu: A Parian dey, this inland region is mountainous, its inhabitants known for their height and blue drafting, as well as a fierce independence from the coastal Parian deys.

Anat: Pagan goddess of wrath, associated with sub-red. See Appendix, 'On the Old Gods.'

Angar: A country beyond the Seven Satrapies and the Everdark Gates. The Angari are matrilineal, remarkable for their blond hair and fair skin, sailing skills, emphasis on hygiene, and brewing of an alcohol from honey.

Ao River: A river on the border of Blood Forest and Atash.

Apple Grove: A small town in the interior of Blood Forest, a part of the White Oak patrimony for generations.

arrachtaigh: An ancient Blood Forest term meaning 'monster.'

Aslal: The capital city of Paria. The Eternal Flame, at the heart of the city, was lit by Lucidonius at his inauguration as Prism.

ataghan: A narrow, slightly forward-curving sword with a single edge for most of its length.

atasifusta: The widest tree in the world, believed extinct after the False Prism's War. Its sap has properties similar to high-density red luxin, which, when allowed to drain slowly, can keep a flame lit for hundreds of years if the tree is large enough. The wood itself is ivory white, and when the trees are immature, a small amount of its wood, burning, can keep a home warm for months. Its usefulness led to aggressive harvesting, and this, coupled with slow growth, caused its extinction.

Atirat: Pagan god of lust, associated with green. See Appendix, 'On the Old Gods.'

auditarae: Scholars dedicated to the preservation of contemporary and ancient history. They memorize speeches and lectures using auditory cues and vocalizations of the speaker, writing annotated copy akin to a musical text, noting accents, rising or falling volume, pitch, speed, obvious sarcasm, physical movements, and other verbal flourishes or delivery idiosyncrasies.

Azûlay: A beautiful coastal Parian city, where most of the satrapy's trade happens. The satrapah and Nuqaba live there, making it the locus of religious and political power in Paria.

Azuria Bay: A small coastal town on the Blood Forest coast, near the Ruthgar/Blood Forest border.

balancing: The primary work of the Prism. When the Prism drafts at the top of the Chromeria, they can sense imbalances in magic and can draft enough of its complementary color to stop the imbalance from spiraling out of control.

bane: Aka lightbane. An old Ptarsu term, which most likely referred to a temple or a holy place, though Lucidonius's Parians believed they were abominations. The word is now used to refer to enormous concentrations of single colors of luxin, grown from a single luxin seed crystal, that extend control of that color far beyond its own boundaries. As temples to false gods, they are also called *loci damnata.*

Bay, East, and Bay, West: The two bays on Little Jasper. Each is protected by a man-made seawall that keeps its waters calm.

beakhead: The protruding part of the foremost section of a ship.

Belphegor: Pagan god of sloth, associated with yellow. See Appendix, 'On the Old Gods.'

bich'hwa: A 'scorpion,' a weapon with a loop hilt and a narrow, undulating recurved blade. Sometimes made with a claw.

Big Jasper (Island): The island on which the city of Big Jasper rests just opposite the Chromeria (which is on Little Jasper Island). Big Jasper is where the embassies of all the satrapies reside. Inhabited by the Ptarsu and enslaved pygmies before the Lucidonian expansion.

Blackguard, the: An elite guard at the top echelon of the Chromeria. The Blackguard was instituted after Lucidonius with a unique dual purpose: to guard the Prism and to guard the Prism from him- or herself. They are commonly seen as bodyguards for the Prism (and other members of the Spectrum).

Blinding Knife: Aka Knife of Surrender, Bonding Knife, Blinder's Knife, Hellfang. Magical, mythical weapon used by Prisms and in the ceremony installing new Prisms.

Blood Wars, the: A series of conflicts that began after Vician's Sin tore apart the formerly close allies/sometimes united kingdoms of Blood

Forest and Ruthgar. The war started and stopped repeatedly over nearly four hundred years, until Prism Guile put a decisive end to it following the False Prism's War.

Blue-Eyed Demons, The: A famed company of bandits whose leader attempted to set up a kingdom after the False Prism's War. Put down single-handedly by Prism Gavin Guile.

blunderbuss: A musket with a bell-shaped muzzle that can be loaded with nails, musket balls, chain, or even gravel. Devastating at short distances.

Braxos: A legendary, now dead city thousands of years old, cut off from the Seven Satrapies by the Cracked Lands, which were reputed to have been formed with magic during the Ptarsu expansion centuries before Lucidonius.

brightwater: Liquid yellow luxin. It is unstable and quickly releases its energy as light. Often used in lanterns.

Brightwater Wall: Its building was a feat to match the legends. This wall was designed by Aheyyad Brightwater and built by Prism Gavin Guile at Garriston in mere days before and while the rebel King Garadul's army approached.

burnous: A long cloak with a hood, common in Paria and elsewhere.

caleen (masc. calun): A diminutive term of address for a female (or male) slave, used regardless of the slave's age.

Cannon Island: A small island with a minimal garrison between Big Jasper and Little Jasper. It houses formidable artillery.

Cerulean Sea, the: The great body of water circled by the Seven Satrapies.

chirurgeon: One who stitches up the wounded and studies anatomy.

chromaturgy: Literally 'color working,' it usually refers to drafting, but has been expanded to cover the study of luxins and will. See also Appendix, 'On Luxin.'

Chromeria, the: The ruling body of the Seven Satrapies; also a term for the academic institution where drafters are trained.

Chromeria trained: Those who have or are studying at the Chromeria school for drafting on Little Jasper Island in the Cerulean Sea. The Chromeria's training system does not limit students based on age, but rather progresses them through each degree of training based on their ability and knowledge.

cocca: A type of merchant ship, usually small.

Colors, the: The seven members of the Spectrum. Originally each represented a single color of the seven sacred colors; each could draft that color, and each satrapy had one representative. Since the founding of the Spectrum, that practice has deteriorated as

935

satrapies have maneuvered for power. Thus a satrapy's Color could be appointed to a color she doesn't actually draft. Likewise, some of the satrapies might lose their representative, and others could have two or even three representatives on the Spectrum at a time, depending on the politics of the day. A Color's term is for life. Impeachment is nearly impossible.

Compelling Argument, The: The greatest masterpiece of famed cannon-caster Phineas Vecchini.

conn (fem. *banconn*)*:* A title for a mayor or leader of a village sometimes used in far-northern Atash, but more common in Blood Forest.

Corbine Street: A street in Big Jasper that leads to the Great Fountain of Karris Shadowblinder.

Cracked Lands, the: A region of broken land in the extreme west of Atash. Its treacherous terrain is crossed by only the most hardy and experienced traders.

Crag Tooth: A fine whiskey with a sublime nose hinting at rose and cinnamon, made in distilleries at the edge of Blood Forest in the highlands above Green Haven. It evinces orange and raisin flavors under powerful chocolate.

Crater Lake: A large lake in southern Tyrea where the former capital of Tyrea, Kelfing, sits. The area is famous for its forests and the production of yew.

Crossroads, the: A kopi house, restaurant, and tavern, the highest-priced inn on the Jaspers, and downstairs a similarly priced brothel. Located near the Lily's Stem, the Crossroads is housed in the former Tyrean embassy building, centrally located in the Embassies District for all the ambassadors, spies, and merchants trying to deal with various governments.

culverin: A type of cannon, useful for firing long distances because of its heavily weighted cannonballs and long-bore tube.

Cwn y Wawr: The 'Dogs of Dawn,' a Blood Forest martial company of archers, mastiff handlers, tree climbers, green drafters, and masters of camouflage. A semisecret society found in the deep parts of Blood Forest.

dagger-pistols: Pistols with a blade attached, allowing the user to fire at distance and then use the blade at close range or if the weapon misfires.

Dagnu: Pagan god of gluttony, associated with red. See Appendix, 'On the Old Gods.'

danar: The primary unit of currency in the Seven Satrapies. An average worker makes about a danar a day, while an unskilled laborer can expect to earn a half danar a day. The coins have a square hole in the middle and are often carried on square-cut sticks. They can be cut in half and still hold their value.

    tin danar: Worth eight regular danar coins. A stick of tin danars usually carries twenty-five coins—that is, two hundred danars.

Deimachia, the: The War of/on the Gods. A theological term for Lucidonius's battle for supremacy against the pagan gods of the old world.

Demiurgos: Another term for a Mirror such as Janus Borig; literally 'half creator.'

dey (fem. *deya*): A Parian title. A near-absolute ruler over a city and its surrounding territory. (Equivalent to the Atashian/Tyrean 'corregidor.')

Diakoptês: An ambiguous term. Literally 'He who rends asunder,' but a looser translation could be 'Breaker.' In Braxian belief, both the name and title of Lucidonius and the name or title of a similar figure, possibly a reincarnation of Lucidonius, who will come again to break or heal the Cracked Lands.

discipulus (masc. pl. *discipuli*, fem. *discipula*, fem. and mixed gender pl. *discipulae*): Those who study both religious and magical arts, usually at the Chromeria.

djinn (fem. *jinni-yah*): Immortals also known as the fallen, or elohim, or gods, or the Two Hundred. Alternate spelling *jinn*. A fuzzy, much-debated religious and historical term, as the reality of such beings, much less their nature(s), is unknown.

drafter: One who can shape or harness light into physical form (luxin). See also Appendix, 'On Luxin.'

Dúnbheo: Also known as the Floating City. Sits in the middle of Loch Lána, the great lake in Blood Forest.

elohim: Immortals or gods (see entry for 'djinn'), spiritual beings of some sort.

'elrahee, elishama, eliada, eliphalet': A Parian prayer meaning '[Orholam] sees, He hears, He cares, He saves.'

Embassies District: The Big Jasper neighborhood that is closest to the Lily's Stem and thus is closest to the Chromeria itself. It also houses markets and kopi houses, taverns, and brothels.

Everdark Gates, the: The strait connecting the Cerulean Sea to the oceans beyond. It was supposedly closed by Lucidonius, but Angari ships have been known to make it through from time to time.

evernight: Often a curse word, it refers to death and/or hell. A metaphysical or teleological reality, rather than a physical one, it represents that which will forever embrace and be embraced by void, full darkness, night in its purest and most evil form.

eye caps: A specialized kind of spectacles. These colored lenses fit directly over the eye sockets, glued to the skin. Like other spectacles, they enable a drafter to draft her color more easily.

False Prism's War, the: A common term for the brief but violent war between Gavin and Dazen Guile. The 'False Prism' is a reference to Dazen, who claimed to be a Prism even after his older brother had already been chosen and installed.

Ferrilux: Pagan god of pride, associated with superviolet. See Appendix, 'On the Old Gods.'

flashbomb: A weapon crafted by yellow drafters. It doesn't harm so much as dazzle and distract its victims with the blinding light of suddenly evaporating yellow luxin.

flying pulpit: Skimmers used for scouting, designed by Ben-hadad. These boats dispense with the weight of a deck entirely. They are held from the waves by only a narrow horizontal foil giving lift and the drafter's vertical reeds, which also provide propulsion. Though they require great muscular and magical strength and endurance, they are the lightest and fastest skimmers in existence.

Four Festivals, the: Seasonal celebrations in the Seven Satrapies.

   Sun Day: Summer solstice, the longest day of the year; aka the Braxian Feast of Dying Light.

   Feast of Light & Darkness, or Waning Light: Autumnal equinox.

   Feast of the Longest Night: Winter solstice, the shortest day of the year; the Luxlord's Ball is also on this night.

   Feast of Waxing Light: Spring equinox.

Free, the (see disambiguation with 'Freed, the' below): Those drafters who reject the Pact of the Chromeria to join the White King's army, choosing to intentionally break the halo to become wights. Also called the Unchained. (Similarities between 'Free' and 'the Freed' are deliberate; the White King's pagans use it to appropriate the Chromeria term.)

Freed, the (see disambiguation with 'Free, the' above): Those drafters who accept the Pact of the Chromeria and chose to be ritually killed in the Freeing (see entry below).

Freeing: The ritual death of a drafter immediately before or after they break their halos. Performed by the Prism every year as the culmination of the Sun Day rituals. A sensitive and holy time, it is accompanied by both mourning and celebration. Each drafter meets personally with the Prism for their Freeing. Many refer to it as the holiest day of their lives; pagans take a different view.

frizzen: On a flintlock, the L-shaped piece of metal against which the flint scrapes. The metal is on a hinge that opens upon firing to allow the sparks to reach the black powder in the chamber.

galabaya: A robe-like dress, common in Paria.

galleass: Originally a large merchant ship powered by both oar and sail. Later, the term referred to ships with modifications for military purposes, which include castles at bow and stern and cannons that fire in all directions.

Gargantua, *the:* A veritable floating castle, it was Ilytian pirate king Pash Vecchio's flagship, with one hundred and forty-one light guns and forty-three heavy cannons. Sunk by Kip and Gavin Guile.

Garriston: The former commercial capital of Tyrea, at the mouth of the Umber River on the Cerulean Sea. Prism Gavin Guile built Brightwater Wall in an attempt to defend the city from Koios White Oak, and very nearly completed it before the pagans took Garriston.

gciorcal: A traditional dance of the Blood Forest pygmies involving paired, spinning dancers.

ghotra: A Parian head scarf, used by many Parian men to demonstrate their reverence for Orholam. In Old Parian tradition, a man's hair is a sign of his virility and dominance and thereby his glory. Most wear it only while the sun is up, but some sects wear it even at nighttime.

Golden Mean, *the:* The finest ship to ever sail the Cerulean Sea. An Ilytian galleass, white teak with a brightwater sheen to its hull; it has forty guns on tracks and a masterpiece culverin on the forecastle named The Compelling Argument.

Great Chain (of Being), the: A theological term for the order of creation. The first link is Orholam Himself, and all the other links below (creation) derive from Him.

great hall, the: Located under the Prism's Tower, a revered space in the Chromeria that is converted once a week into a place of worship, at which time mirrors from the other towers are turned to shine light in. It includes pillars of white marble and the largest display of stained glass in the world. Most of the satrapies have a great hall in their respective capitols, but none parallel the hall beneath the Prism's Tower.

Great Library of Azûlay: An ancient library in Paria, the building itself is more than eight hundred years old and is built on the foundations of another library at least two hundred years older.

Great Mirror(s): A set of enormous mirrors, spread out among the entire Seven Satrapies.

Great River, the: The river between Ruthgar and Blood Forest, the scene of many pitched battles between the two countries.

great yard, the: The training yard at the base of the towers of the Chromeria, used primarily by the Blackguard.

green flash: A rare flash of color seen at the setting of the sun; its meaning is debated. Some believe it has theological significance, citing Karris Atiriel's sighting of it the evening before the battle in Hass Valley. The previous White, Orea Pullawr, called it Orholam's wink.

Green Forest: A collective term for Blood Forest and Ruthgar during the years of peace and unity between the two territories—in contrast to when the same territory was called the Blood Plains, after Vician's Sin incited the Blood Wars.

Green Haven: The capital of Blood Forest, on the far side of Lach Lána.

Greenwall: The massive, living, defensive wall surrounding Dúnbheo, still known to outsiders as the Floating City, though it long ago adjoined the shores of Lach Lána.

grenado: An explosive clay flagon full of black powder with a piece of wood shoved into the top, with a rag and bit of black powder as a fuse. Can also be made with luxin and can be hurled at an enemy along an arc of luxin or in a cannon. Often filled with shot/shrapnel, depending on the type used.

Guile palace: Family palace on Big Jasper, distinct from their residence on Jaks Hill in Rath. The Guile palace was one of the few buildings allowed to be constructed without regard to the working of the Thousand Stars, its height cutting off some of the light paths.

Harbinger: Corvan Danavis's sword, inherited when his elder brothers died.

haze: A narcotic. Often smoked with a pipe, it produces a sickly-sweet odor.

hellhounds: Dogs infused with red luxin and enough will to make them run at enemies while lit on fire.

Hellmount: A snow-capped peak far to the southwest, near the Atashian border.

hellstone: A superstitious term for obsidian, which is rarer than diamonds or rubies, as few know where the extant obsidian in the world is created or mined. Obsidian is the only stone that can draw luxin out of a drafter if it touches her blood directly.

hippodrome: A large oval stadium, dedicated primarily to races among horses, chariots, or athletes. Often serves as a public gathering place for executions and other important state functions. They are most common in Ruthgar and Paria.

hullwrecker: A luxin disk filled with shrapnel, designed by Blackguard Nerra. It has a sticky side so that it will adhere to a ship's hull and a fuse to allow the attackers to flee before it explodes, punching a hole in the ship's hull and spraying shrapnel in toward the crew.

Idoss: An Atashian city, now under the control of the White King's armies.

incarnitive luxin: A term for luxin when it is incorporated directly into one's body. See also Appendix, 'On Luxin.'

Jaks Hill: A large hill in the city of Rath overlooking the Great River, notable for its wealthy estates. Castle Guile dominates the area.

Jaspers, the: Two small islands in the northwestern corner of the Cerulean Sea. The Chromeria is on Little Jasper. Legend has it that the Jaspers were chosen for the Chromeria by Karris Shadowblinder after the death of Lucidonius because they were part of no satrapy, and therefore could be for all satrapies.

javelinas: Nocturnal animals in the pig family, often hunted. Giant javelinas are rare but can reach the size of a cow. Extremely dangerous and destructive, giant javelinas have been hunted to extinction in all satrapies except Tyrea.

ka: A sequence of movements to train balance and flexibility and control in the martial arts. A form of focusing exercise or meditation.

Keffel's Variant: A set of rules for Nine Kings to make the game especially quick.

Kelfing: The former capital of Tyrea, on the shores of Crater Lake in the southern end of the satrapy.

khat: An addictive stimulant, a leaf that stains the teeth when it is chewed, used especially in Paria.

kopi: A mild, addictive stimulant, a popular beverage. Bitter, dark, and served hot.

lacrimae sanguinis: A mysterious and singularly deadly Braxian poison.

Ladies, the: Four statues that compose the gates into the city of Garriston. They are built into the wall, made of rare Parian marble and sealed in nearly invisible yellow luxin. They are thought to depict aspects of the goddess Anat, and were spared by Lucidonius, who believed them to depict something true. They are the Hag, the Lover, the Mother, and the Guardian.

Laurion: A region in eastern Atash known for its silver ore and massive slave mines. Life expectancy for the enslaved miners is short and conditions brutal. The threat of being sent to the mines is used throughout the satrapies to keep slaves obedient and docile.

league: A unit of measurement, six thousand and seventy-six paces.

Lightbringer, the: A controversial figure in prophecy and mythology. Attributes that most agree on are that he is (will be? was?) male, will slay or has slain gods and kings, is of mysterious birth, is a genius of magic, a warrior who will sweep, or has swept, all before him, a champion of the poor and downtrodden, great from his youth, He Who Shatters. That most of the prophecies were in Old Parian and the meanings have changed in ways that are difficult to trace hasn't helped. There are three basic camps: those who believe that the Lightbringer has yet to come; those who believe that the Lightbringer has already come and was Lucidonius (a view the Chromeria now holds, though it didn't always); and, among some academics, those who believe that the Lightbringer is a metaphor for what is best in all of us.

Lightguard, the: Andross Guile's personal army, nominally established to defend the Jaspers, answering only to him. Mercenaries, ruffians, veterans, and any others willing to fight for the Red. Primarily washed-up Blackguards and the sons of poor nobles. Their clothing is in contrast to the Blackguards', white jackets with garish brass buttons and medals.

lightsickness: The aftereffects of too much drafting. Only the Prism never gets lightsick.

lightwells: Holes positioned to allow light, with the use of mirrors, to reach the interiors of towers or sections of streets.

Lily's Stem, the: The luxin bridge between Big and Little Jasper. It is composed of blue and yellow luxin so that it appears green. Set on the high-water mark, it is remarkable for its endurance against the waves and storms that wash over it. Ahhana the Dextrous was responsible for designing it and engineering its creation.

linstock: A staff for holding a slow match. Used in lighting cannons, it allows the cannoneer to stand out of the range of the cannon's recoil.

Little Jasper (Island): The island on which the Chromeria resides.

longbow: A weapon that allows for the efficient (in speed, distance, and force) firing of arrows. Its construction and its user must both be extremely strong. The yew forests of Crater Lake provide the best wood available for longbows.

Lord Prism: A respectful term of address for a male Prism.

Lords of the Air: A term used by the White King for his most trusted blue-drafting officers.

Luíseach: A Blood Forest term for the Lightbringer.

luxiat: A priest of Orholam. A luxiat wears black as an acknowledgment that they need Orholam's light most of all; thus they are sometimes called a blackrobe.

luxin: A material created by drafting from light. See Appendix, 'On Luxin.'

luxlord: A term for a member of the ruling Spectrum.

luxors: Magisterial officials empowered by the Chromeria at various points in its history to bring the Light of Orholam by almost any means necessary. They have at various times hunted paryl drafters and lightsplitter heretics, among others. Their theological rigidity and their prerogative to kill and torture have been hotly debated by followers of Orholam and dissidents alike.

magister: The term for a teacher of drafting, history, and religion at the Chromeria. It always retains its masculine ending: *magister*, regardless of the instructor's gender. This is a relic from when all teachers were male, female drafters being considered too valuable for teaching.

mag torch: Used by drafters to allow them access to light at night, it burns with a full spectrum of colors. Colored mag torches are also made at great expense, and give a drafter her spectrum of useful light, allowing her to eschew spectacles and draft instantly.

Malleus Haereticorum: 'Hammer of Heretics.' The title for a luxor commissioned to destroy heresy.

match-holder: The piece on a matchlock musket to which a slow match is affixed.

matchlock musket: A firearm that works by snapping a burning slow match into the flashpan, which ignites the gunpowder in the breech of the firearm, whose explosion propels a rock or lead ball out of the barrel at high speed. Matchlocks are accurate to fifty or a hundred paces, depending on the smith who made them and the ammunition used.

millennial cypress: A tree known for its immense age and ability to grow in damp conditions.

mirror slaves: Also known as star-keepers, they are highly trained and educated slaves who manage and maintain the Thousand Stars on the Jaspers. The star-keepers are usually petite children who work the ropes that control the Thousand Stars. Though well treated (for slaves), they spend their days working in two-person teams from dawn till after dusk, frequently without reprieve except for switching with their partners.

Molokh: Pagan god of greed, associated with orange. See Appendix, 'On the Old Gods.'

Mot: Pagan god of envy, associated with blue. See Appendix, 'On the Old Gods.'

mund: Mild pejorative for a person who cannot draft.

murder hole: A hole in the ceiling of a passageway that allows soldiers to fire, drop, or throw weapons, projectiles, luxin, or fuel. Common in castles and city walls.

Narrows, the: A strait of the Cerulean Sea between Abornea and the Ruthgari mainland. Aborneans charge high tolls on merchants sailing the silk route, or simply between Paria and Ruthgar.

Nekril, the: Will-casting coven that laid siege to Aghbalu before being destroyed by Gwafa, a legendary Blackguard.

norm: Another term for a non-drafter, a person who cannot create luxin. Pejorative.

nunk: A half-derogatory term for a Blackguard inductee. Most nunks will eventually become full Blackguards. (Cf. 'scrubs,' those who are trying out to become inductees. Most scrubs will not become nunks but will 'scrub out.')

Odess: A city in Abornea that sits at the head of the Narrows.

old world: The world before Lucidonius united the Seven Satrapies and abolished worship of the pagan gods.

ora'lem Or'holam: Old Parian phrase loosely translated to 'hidden light of God' or 'the hidden Lord of Light(s).'

Order of the Broken Eye, the: A secret guild of assassins and conspirators, originally from the old city/kingdom of Braxos now beyond the Cracked Lands in western Atash. They specialize in killing drafters and have been rooted out and destroyed at least three times. The pride of the Order is the Shimmercloaks, or Shadows, pairs of purportedly invisible, unstoppable assassins.

Orholam's Glare: A giant mirror on Big Jasper, set on a platform before the gate to the Lily's Stem. Used to execute drafters convicted of the most serious crimes.

Overhill: A neighborhood in Big Jasper.

Ox Ford: A town at a crossing of the Ao River on the Atash/Blood Forest border. Recently the site of a disastrous battle in the Wight King's War.

Pact, the: Since Lucidonius, the Pact has governed all those trained by the Chromeria in the Seven Satrapies. Its essence is that drafters agree to serve their satrapy and receive all the benefits of status and sometimes wealth—in exchange for their service and eventual death before they break the halo.

Palace of the Divines: The ancient residence and meeting place of Dúnbheo's Council of the Divines, in Blood Forest.

Pericol: A city on the coast of Ilyta.

petasos: A broad-brimmed Ruthgari hat, usually made of straw, meant to keep the sun off the face, head, and neck.

Philoctean Games: Novennial celebration of athleticism in the Great Hippodrome of Aslal in Paria.

physicker: A medical professional who attends to common ailments and injuries.

polychrome: A drafter who can draft three or more colors.

portmaster: A city official in charge of collecting tariffs and managing the organized exit and entrance of ships in his harbor.

Prism: There is only one Prism each generation. They sense the balance of the world's magic and balance it when necessary, and can split light within themselves to draft any of the seven colors at will. Technically the emperor of the Seven Satrapies, other than balancing, their role is largely ceremonial and religious, with the Colors, the satraps, and the Magisterium working hard to make sure that Prisms rarely wield true political power.

Prism's Tower, the: The central tower in the Chromeria. It houses the Prism, the White, and superviolets (as they are not numerous enough to require their own tower). The great hall lies below the tower, and the top holds a great crystal for the Prism's use while he balances the colors of the world.

promachos: Literally 'one who fights before us,' it is a title that may be given for a brief duration during a war or other great crisis. A promachos may be named only by order of a supermajority of the Colors. Among other powers, the promachos has the right to command armies, seize property, and elevate commoners to the nobility.

psantria: A stringed musical instrument.

pygmies: A rare, fierce people of the Blood Forest interior, they claim common ancestry with the people of Braxos. Nearly extinct. They can interbreed with humans, though with great danger if the mother is the pygmy, death in childbirth being the norm. Some Blood Forest chiefs and kings in the past saw fit to kill pygmies, declaring it a morally neutral or even laudable act. The Chromeria declared pygmies human, and such killing to be murder; pygmy numbers have never recovered from past massacres and disease.

pyroturges: Red and/or sub-red drafters who create wonders of flame, known particularly for their wonders in Azûlay.

raka: An archaic but serious insult, with an implication of both moral and intellectual idiocy.

Rath: The capital of Ruthgar, set on the confluence of the Great River and its delta into the Cerulean Sea.

Rathcore Hill: A hill opposite (and somewhat smaller than) Jaks Hill in the city of Rath. The hippodrome is carved into its side.

ratweed: An addictive, toxic plant whose leaves can be smoked for their strong stimulant and hallucinogenic properties.

reedsmen: Drafters used to propel skimmers.

Rekton: A small Tyrean town on the Umber River, near the site of the Battle of Sundered Rock. An important trading post before the False Prism's War. Now uninhabited after a massacre by King Rask Garadul.

Ru: The capital of Atash, once famous for its castle and ziggurats, still famous for its Great Pyramid. The castle was destroyed by fire during General Gad Delmarta's purge of the royal family in the Prisms' War.

Ruic Head: A peninsula dominated by towering cliffs that overlooks the Atashian city of Ru and its bay. A fort atop the peninsula's cliffs guards against invaders and pirates.

satrap **(fem. *satrapah*):** A political ruler of one of the seven satrapies. Always paired with a Color. The satraps/satrapahs always reside in their respective satrapies, while the Colors reside on the Jaspers, representing their interests, both political and magical. Power used to largely reside with the satraps or satrapahs, with the Colors being more like their ambassadors. Now power largely resides with the Colors, with the satraps being reduced to provincial governors.

seven: A unit of measurement for weight, equal to the weight of a cubit of water. A *sev* is equal to one-seventh of a seven.

Seven Lives of Maeve Hart, The: A Blood Forest epic.

Shadow: Another term for an assassin in the Order of the Broken Eye. Shadows are lightsplitters, and any lightsplitter can use a shimmercloak to make her- or himself invisible in the visible spectra. (Only paryl-drafting lightsplitters can make themselves invisible to subred and superviolet, and that with difficulty.)

Shady Grove: A region within Blood Forest where pygmies reside. Decimated by the diseases brought by invaders, their numbers have never recovered, and they remain insular and often hostile to outsiders.

shimmercloak: A cloak that makes the wearer mostly invisible, except in sub-red and superviolet.

Skill, Will, Source, and Still/Movement: The four essential elements for drafting.

Skill: The most underrated of all the elements of drafting, acquired through practice and study. Includes knowing the properties and strengths of the luxin being drafted, being able to see and match precise wavelengths, et cetera.

Will: By imposing will, a drafter can draft and even cover flawed drafting if her will is powerful enough.

Source: Depending on what colors a drafter can use, she needs either that color of light or items that reflect that color of light in order to draft. Only a Prism can simply split white light within herself to draft any color.

Still: An ironic usage, made up for the mnemonic (Skill, Will, Source, and Still is easier to remember than Skill, Will, Source, and Movement). Drafting requires movement, though more skilled drafters can use less.

slow fuse/slow match: A length of cord, often soaked in saltpeter, that can be lit to ignite the gunpowder of a weapon in the firing mechanism.

soul-cast: An extremely dangerous, difficult, and forbidden type of magic. To soul-cast is to blot out and replace the soul of an animal with the soul of a drafter. The animal's body may live for days afterward, but its vital spark is extinguished. It damages the caster in more insidious ways. It has been done to humans both living and dead and is considered a black magic. Even if not lethal to the drafter attempting it, soul-casting is grounds for execution on Orholam's Glare. It is believed that only full-spectrum polychromes might successfully soul-cast themselves.

spectrum: A term for a range of light; see also Appendix, 'On Luxin.'

Spectrum, the: The high council of the Chromeria that is one branch of the government of the Seven Satrapies. Each member of the Spectrum is paired with a satrap/satrapah of one satrapy. The Color is supposed to represent the magical interests of their paired color. In practice, it is rarely so simple.

subchromats: Drafters who are color-blind, usually male. See also Appendix, 'Subchromacy and Superchromacy.'

Sun Day: A holy day, the longest day of the year. For the Seven Satrapies, Sun Day is the day when the Prism Frees those drafters who are about to break the halo and go mad. The ceremonies usually take place on the Jaspers, when all of the Thousand Stars are trained onto the Prism, who can absorb and split the light.

Sun Day Eve: An evening of festivities, both for celebration and for mourning, before the longest day of the year and the Freeing the next day.

Sundered Rock: Twin stone monoliths in Tyrea, sitting opposite each other and so alike that they look as if they were once a single stone mountain that was split down the middle.

Sundered Rock, Battle of: The final battle in the False Prism's War between Gavin and Dazen Guile, near Rekton.

superchromats: Extremely color-sensitive people. Luxin they seal will rarely fail. Overwhelmingly female. See also Appendix, 'Subchromacy and Superchromacy.'

Sword of Heaven: The luxin-imbued lighthouse of Azûlay.

Tafok Amagez: The elite guard for the ruler in Paria, composed entirely of highly trained drafters. Comparable to the Blackguard—though both forces will strongly deny it.

thobe: An ankle-length garment, usually with long sleeves.

Thousand Stars, the: The mirrors on Big Jasper that enable the light to reach into almost any part of the city for as long as possible during the day.

Threshing, the: The initiation test for candidates to the Chromeria. Through subjecting the initiates to things that most commonly instigate fear and providing appropriate spectra of light, it usually reveals the initiates' ranges of drafting ability (with some uncertainty around the edges).

Threshing Chamber, the: The room where candidates for the Chromeria are summoned to be tested for their abilities to draft.

Tiru, the: An ancient Parian tribe.

tromoturgy: A form of hex-casting, 'fear-working' or 'fear-casting' banned by the Chromeria, as are other forms of direct manipulation of emotions; man being created in the likeness of Orholam, any assault on the dignity of man's body (violence, murder) or his mind (emotion-casting, torture, slave-taking) is considered sinful—except as allowed by just-war theory and the rights of rule.

Túsaíonn Domhan: 'A World Begins.' The name of a luxin-infused mural-ceiling created by a legendary Blood Forest woodwright.

Two Hundred, the: Apocryphal. Two hundred of Orholam's progeny who rebelled and came to the world to rule over men and magic. See also 'djinn.'

tygre striper: Also known as the *sharana ru*, said to be carved seademon bone. Sources contest that the even rarer whalebone makes superior weapons. It is the only known mundane material that reacts to will, becoming hard or flexible depending on the user's.

tygre wolves: Fierce creatures of deep Blood Forest, untamable, but able to be directed by will magic.

Umber River, the: The lifeblood of Tyrea. Its water allows the growth of every kind of plant in the hot climate; its locks fed trade throughout the country before the False Prism's War. Often controlled by bandits.

Unchained, the: A term for the followers of the Color Prince, those drafters who choose to break the Pact and continue living even after breaking the halo.

vechevoral: A sickle-shaped sword with a long handle like an ax's and a crescent-moon-shaped blade at the end, with the inward bowl-shaped side being the cutting edge.

Verdant Plains, the: The dominant geographical feature of Ruthgar, enabling the farming and grazing that give Ruthgar its immense wealth. The Verdant Plains have been favored by green drafters since before Lucidonius.

Vician's Sin: The event that marked the end of the close alliance between Ruthgar and Blood Forest, and purportedly led to Orholam's raising White Mist Reef and the mist itself at the center of the Cerulean Sea. Exactly what it was or what happened has been concealed as much as possible by the Magisterium.

warrior-drafters: Drafters whose primary work is fighting for various satrapies or the Chromeria. Usually far inferior in drafting to the Blackguard, who are the foremost warrior-drafters in the world.

Weasel Rock: A neighborhood in Big Jasper, dominated by narrow alleys.

White, the: The head of the Chromeria and the Spectrum. She (or he) is in charge of all magical and historical education at the Chromeria (as opposed to purely religious instruction, which is the demesne of the High Luxiats). She is in charge of all discipulae and matters political and social regarding the Chromeria (where the Black is in charge of matters mundane, practical, and martial, and is subordinate to her). She presides over the Chromeria, though her power is limited to casting tiebreaking votes—a rarity, as the Spectrum gives one vote to each of its seven Colors (the Black having no vote ever, though he is allowed to speak and attends meetings).

White Mist Reef: The reputed site of White Mist Tower. Sailors who have gone in the waters near it report the sounds of a reef from the crashing waves and claim to have seen many sea demons nearby. (Though, given that the mist is a mist and thus impedes all sight, these are likely fabrications.)

White Mist Tower: A meteorological phenomenon. A tower of cloud spinning from the sea into the sky, with its purported base on White Mist Reef. Sometimes seen from afar, especially after storms clear the clouds that usually rest throughout the middle of the

Cerulean Sea, though possibly it is simply a trick of the light similar to mirages in the desert.

wight: A drafter who has broken the halo. They often remake their bodies with pure luxin, rejecting the Pact between drafter and society that is a foundation of all training at the Chromeria.

will-blunting/will-breaking: A form of drafting used to directly attack another's will by connecting emotionally and intellectually with them, and thereby forbidden by the Chromeria as an assault on man's mind and dignity.

will-cast: To infuse another living creature with one's will. An extremely dangerous practice among drafters, it is forbidden by the Chromeria but still practiced among pygmies in Blood Forest.

will-craft: Aka oath-binding. Binding an oath, sworn between two or more drafters, to a physical object. The object is referred to as an 'oath stone.'

will-jacking: Aka forced translucification. Once a drafter has contact with unsealed luxin that she is able to draft, she can use her will to break another drafter's control over the luxin and take it for herself.

Wiwurgh: A Parian town that hosts many Blood Forest refugees from the Blood War.

zigarro: A roll of tobacco, a form useful for smoking. Ratweed is sometimes used as a wrapping to hold the loose tobacco to allow use of both substances at once.

zoon politikon: 'Political animal.' From the Philosopher's treatise, *The Politics.* His theory was that man can only reach his *telos,* his end or highest good, when in a community, specifically a city large enough to meet all his needs: physical, social, moral, and spiritual.

Appendix

ON LUXIN

The basis of chromaturgy is light. Those who use this magic are called 'drafters'; a drafter is able to transform a color of light into a physical substance within their body. Each color luxin has its own properties, but the uses of those building blocks are as boundless as a drafter's imagination and skill.

The magic in the Seven Satrapies functions roughly the opposite of a candle burning. When a candle burns, a physical substance (usually wax) is transformed into light. With chromaturgy, light is transformed into a physical substance, luxin. If drafted correctly (within a narrow allowance), the resulting luxin will be stable, lasting for days or even years, depending on its color.

Most drafters (magic users) are monochromes; they can draft only one color. A drafter must be exposed to the light of her color to be able to draft it—that is, a green drafter can look at grass and be able to draft, but if she's in a white-walled room, she can't. Many drafters carry delicate and expensive colored spectacles developed by Lucidonius himself, and later improved upon by the Technologist, so that if her color isn't available where she stands, she can still use magic.

Monochromes, Bichromes, and Polychromes

Most drafters are monochromes: they are able to draft only one color. Drafters who can draft two colors well enough to create stable luxin in both colors are called 'bichromes.' Anyone who can draft solid luxin in three or more colors is called a 'polychrome.' The more colors a polychrome can draft, the more powerful she is and the more sought after are her services. A full-spectrum polychrome is one who can draft all seven colors in the visible spectrum. A Prism is always a full-spectrum polychrome.

Merely being able to draft a color, though, isn't the sole determining criterion in how valuable or skilled a drafter is. Some drafters are faster at drafting, some are more efficient, some have more will than others, some are better at crafting luxin that will be durable, and some are smarter or more creative at how and when to apply luxin.

Disjunctive (Discontiguous) Bichromes/Polychromes

The spectrum of visible light exists in a consistent order: paryl, sub-red, red, orange, yellow, green, blue, superviolet, chi. Most bichromes and polychromes simply draft a larger spectrum on the continuum than monochromes. That is, a bichrome is most likely to draft two colors that are adjacent to each other (blue and superviolet, red and sub-red, yellow and green, etc.). However, some few drafters are disjunctive (or discontiguous) bichromes. As could be surmised from the name, these are drafters whose colors do not border each other. Usef Tep was a famous example: he drafted red and blue. The Iron White is another, drafting green and red. It is unknown how or why disjunctive bichromes come to exist. It is only known that they are rare.

Subchromacy and Superchromacy

Subchromat: One who has trouble differentiating between at least two colors, colloquially referred to as being color-blind. Subchromacy need not doom a drafter. For instance, a blue drafter who cannot distinguish between red and green will not be significantly handicapped in his work.

Superchromat: One who has greater-than-usual ability to distinguish between fine variations of color. Superchromacy in any color will result in more stable drafting, but it is most helpful in drafting yellow. Only superchromat yellow drafters can hope to draft solid yellow luxin.

Outer-Spectrum Colors

For more than four hundred years—from the time of Prism Vician until the beginning of the Age of the Lightbringer—knowledge of outer-spectrum colors (i.e., paryl and chi) was suppressed by the Chromeria. Paryl exists far below sub-red on the spectrum; chi is equally far above superviolet. During this age of suppressed knowledge, very few people understood the unique properties of these types of luxin, much less their usefulness. The idea that there are more than seven draftable colors was theologically problematic for some; paryl and chi were considered not only blasphemous but quite deadly.

But if colors are to be so broadly defined as to include colors only one drafter in a million can draft, then shouldn't yellow be split into liquid yellow and solid yellow? Where do black and white luxins fit? How could such colors even fit on the spectrum? As ancient knowledge of the four suppressed colors—white, black, chi, and paryl—is carefully rediscovered by luxiats, our understanding of their properties and distinctions will propel us beyond our horizons, into uncharted academic waters. The prospect is thrilling to many of us.

PHYSICS

Luxin has mass. If a drafter creates a luxin haycart directly over her head, the first thing it will do is fall to the ground and crush her. Luxin density, from heaviest to lightest, is as follows: red, orange, yellow, green, blue, sub-red,* paryl, superviolet, chi. For reference, liquid yellow luxin is only slightly lighter than the same volume of water.

(*Sub-red mass is difficult to determine accurately because it rapidly disintegrates into fire when exposed to air. The ordering above was achieved by putting sub-red luxin in an airtight container and then weighing the result, minus the weight of the container. In real-world uses, sub-red crystals are often seen floating upward in the air before igniting.)

Tactility

Each type of luxin has a unique feel, as follows:

Sub-red: Again the hardest to describe due to its flammability, but often described as feeling like a hot wind.

Red: Gooey, sticky, clingy, depending on drafting; can be tarry and thick or more gel-like.

Orange: Lubricative, slippery, soapy, oily.

Yellow: In its liquid, more common state, like effervescent water, cool to the touch, possibly a little thicker than seawater. In its solid state, it is perfectly slick, unyielding, smooth, and incredibly hard.

Green: Rough; depending on the skill and purposes of the drafter, ranges from merely having a grain like leather to feeling like tree bark. It is flexible, springy, often drawing comparisons to the green limbs of living trees.

Blue: Smooth, though poorly drafted blue will have a texture and can shed fragments easily, like chalk, but in crystals.

Superviolet: Like spidersilk, thin and light to the point of imperceptibility.

Scent

The foundational scent of all luxin is lightly resinous. The smells below are approximate, because each color of luxin smells like itself. Imagine trying to describe the smell of an orange. You'd say citrusy sweet and sharp, but that isn't it exactly. An orange smells like an orange. The below approximations are close.

Sub-red: Charcoal, smoke, burned.
Red: Tea leaves, tobacco, dry.
Orange: Amandine, rich.
Yellow: Eucalyptus, mint.
Green: Fresh cedar, resin.
Blue: Light mineral or coca.
Superviolet: Faintly like cloves.
Paryl: Saffron.
Chi: Metallic, like the air during a lightning storm.
*****Black:** No smell, or smell of decaying flesh.
*****White:** Honey, lilac.
(*Mythical; these are the smells as reported in histories and legends.)

METAPHYSICS

Any drafting feels good to the drafter. Sensations of euphoria and invincibility are particularly strong among young drafters and those drafting for the first time.

Generally, these pass with time, though drafters abstaining from magic for a time will often feel them again. For most drafters, the effect is similar to drinking a cup of kopi. There are vigorous ongoing debates about whether the effects on personality should be described as metaphysical or physical.

Regardless of their correct categorization and whether they are the proper realm of study for the magister or the luxiat, the effects themselves are unquestioned.

Effects on Personality

The benighted before Lucidonius believed that passionate men became reds and that calculating women became yellows or blues. In truth, the causation flows the other way.

Every drafter, like every woman, has her own innate personality. The color she drafts then influences her toward the behaviors below. A person who is impulsive who drafts red for years is more likely to be pushed further into 'red' characteristics than a naturally cold and orderly person who drafts red for the same length of time.

The color a drafter uses will affect her personality over time. This, however, doesn't make her a prisoner of her color, or irresponsible for her actions under the influence of it. A green who continually cheats on his spouse is still a lothario. A sub-red who murders an enemy in a fit of rage is still a murderer. Of course, a naturally angry woman who is also a red drafter will be even more susceptible to that color's effects, but there are many tales of calculating reds and fiery, intemperate blues.

A color isn't a substitute for a person. Be careful in your application of generalities. That said, generalities can be useful: a group of green drafters is more likely to be wild and rowdy than a group of blues.

Given these generalities, there is also a virtue and a vice commonly associated with each color. (Virtue being understood by the early lux-iats not as being free of temptation to do evil in a particular way, but as conquering one's own predilection toward that kind of evil. Thus, gluttony is paired with temperance, greed with charity, etc.)

Sub-red: Passionate in all ways, the most purely emotional of all drafters, the quickest to rage or to cry. Sub-reds love music, are often impulsive, fear the dark less than any other color, and are often insomniacs. Emotional, distractible, unpredictable, inconsistent, loving, bighearted. Sub-red men are often sterile.
Associated vice: Wrath
Associated virtue: Patience
Red: Quick-tempered, lusty, and love destruction. They are also warm, inspiring, brash, larger than life, expansive, jovial, and powerful.
Associated vice: Gluttony
Associated virtue: Temperance
Orange: Often artists, brilliant in understanding other people's emotions and motivations. Some use this to defy or exceed expectations. Sensitive, manipulative, idiosyncratic, slippery, charismatic, empathetic.
Associated vice: Greed
Associated virtue: Charity
Yellow: Yellows tend to be clear thinkers, with intellect and emotion in perfect balance. Cheerful, wise, bright, balanced, watchful, impassive, observant, brutally honest at times, excellent liars. Thinkers, not doers.
Associated vice: Sloth
Associated virtue: Diligence
Green: Wild, free, flexible, adaptable, nurturing, friendly. They don't so much disrespect authority as not even recognize it.

Associated vice: Lust

Associated virtue: Self-control

Blue: Orderly, inquisitive, rational, calm, cold, impartial, intelligent, musical. Structure, rules, and hierarchy are important to them. Blues are often mathematicians and composers. Ideas and ideology and correctness often matter more than people to blues.

Associated vice: Envy

Associated virtue: Kindness (Gratitude)

Superviolet: Tend to have a detached outlook; dispassionate, they appreciate irony and sarcasm and word games and are often cold, viewing people as puzzles to be solved or ciphers to be cracked. Irrationality outrages superviolets.

Associated vice: Pride

Associated virtue: Humility

Paryl: Also called spidersilk, it is invisible to all but paryl drafters. It resides as far down the spectrum from sub-red as most sub-red does from the visible spectrum. Believed mythical because (apart from a paryl drafter's) the lens of the human eye cannot contort to a shape that would allow seeing such a color. Paryl is the color of dark drafters and night weavers and assassins because this spectrum is usually available at night. Renders the drafter much more susceptible to empathy, able to absorb emotions in a way other drafters cannot.

Chi (KAI): The upper-spectrum counterpart to paryl. (Often referred to in tales as 'as far above superviolet as paryl is below sub-red.') Also called the revealer. Its main claimed use is nearly identical to paryl—seeing through things, though those who believe in chi say its powers far surpass paryl's in this regard, cutting through flesh and bone and possibly even metal. The only thing the tales seem to agree on is that chi drafters have the shortest life expectancy of any drafters: five to fifteen years, almost without exception. If chi indeed exists, it would mostly be evidence that Orholam created light for the universe or for His own purposes, and not solely for the use of man, and would move theologians from their current anthropocentrism.

Legendary Colors

Black: Destruction, void, emptiness, that which is not and cannot be filled. Obsidian is said to be the bones of black luxin after it dies.

White: The raw word of Orholam. The stuff of creation, from which all luxin and all life was formed. Descriptions of an earthly form of the stuff (as diminished from the original as obsidian supposedly is from black luxin) describe it as radiant ivory, or pure white opal, emitting light in the whole spectrum.

LUXIN AND LIFESPAN

General Effects. At this point, it has been established beyond question that drafting shortens the lives of those who do it, and almost all scholars accept that this is not because those who draft are intrinsically more fragile, but because of the act of drafting itself. The reasons for this are unknown, but the more luxin drafted, the shorter the drafter's life. It is believed that the body will heal some amount of the damage drafting does. Thus, a drafter who drafts minimally daily will be able to draft far more cumulatively than one who attempts to draft a great deal in a short period of time. The Chromeria encourages drafters to honor Orholam's gift of our lives by drafting in moderation, except in emergencies.

Various Colors and Lifespan. It's been noted that, even as drafters of the various colors tend to evince particular personality traits, so too do those who draft certain colors seem to live longer. Only one color has been proven to the Chromeria's satisfaction to never be safe to use: chi always kills its practitioners, almost always within five to ten years. As Life is one of Orholam's Seven Great Gifts and being party to the wanton destruction thereof cannot be within Orholam's will, the Magisterium successfully enjoined the Chromeria to cease teaching chi-drafting three hundred forty-two years ago.

As for the rest, debate rages on the exact causal connections, but it has been noted that superviolet drafters tend to break the halo earlier, while at the opposite end of the spectrum, paryl drafters may live to a full natural span. Lightsplitting paryl drafters may, indeed, live much longer than most munds. However, this last is uncertain, given their overall small numbers and the fact that many of those recorded as such belonged to the Order of the Broken Eye, where names were often handed down to give the illusion of immortality to enhance the Order's reputation and intimidate opponents.

ON THE OLD GODS

Sub-red: Anat, goddess of wrath. Those who worshipped her are said to have had rituals that involved infant sacrifice. Also known as the Lady of the Desert, the Fiery Mistress. Her centers of worship were Tyrea, southernmost Paria, and southern Ilyta.

Red: Dagnu, god of gluttony. He was worshipped in eastern Atash.

Orange: Molokh, god of greed. Once worshipped in western Atash.

Yellow: Belphegor, god of sloth. Primarily worshipped in northern Atash and southern Blood Forest before Lucidonius's coming.

Green: Atirat, goddess of lust. Her center of worship was primarily in western Ruthgar and most of Blood Forest.

Blue: Mot, god of envy. His center of worship was in eastern Ruthgar, northeastern Paria, and Abornea.

Superviolet: Ferrilux, god of pride. His center of worship was in southern Paria and northern Ilyta.

ON TECHNOLOGY AND WEAPONS

The Seven Satrapies are currently experiencing an age of great leaps in understanding. The peace since the Prisms' War and the following suppression of piracy has allowed the flow of goods and ideas freely through the satrapies. Affordable, high-quality iron and steel are available everywhere, leading to high-quality weapons, durable wagon wheels, and everything in between. Though traditional forms of weapons like Atashian bich'hwa or Parian parry-sticks continue, now they are rarely made of horn or hardened wood. Luxin is often used for improvised weapons, but most luxins tend to break down after long exposure to light, and the scarcity of yellow drafters who can make solid yellows (which don't break down in light) means that metal weapons predominate among mundane armies.

The greatest leaps are occurring in the improvement of firearms. In most cases, each musket is the product of a different smith. This means each man must be able to fix his own firearm and that pieces must be crafted individually. A faulty hammer or flashpan can't be swapped out for a new one, but must be detached and reworked into appropriate shape. Some large-scale productions with hundreds of apprentice smiths have tried to tackle this problem in Rath by making parts as nearly identical as possible, but the resulting matchlocks tend to be low quality, trading accuracy and durability for consistency and simple repair. Elsewhere, the smiths of Ilyta have gone the other direction, making the highest-quality custom muskets in the world. Recently, they've pioneered a form they call the flintlock. Instead of affixing a burning slow match to ignite powder in the flashpan and thence into the breech of the rifle, they've affixed a flint that scrapes a frizzen to throw sparks directly into the breech. This approach means a musket or a pistol is always ready to fire, without a soldier having to first light a slow match. Keeping it from widespread adoption is the high rate of misfires—if the flint doesn't scrape the frizzen correctly or throw sparks perfectly, the firearm doesn't fire.

Thus far, the combination of luxin with firearms has been largely unsuccessful. The casting of perfectly round yellow luxin musket balls is possible, but the small number of superchromatic yellow drafters able to make solid yellow luxin creates a bottleneck in production. Blue luxin musket balls often shatter from the force of the black powder explosion. An exploding shell made by filling a yellow luxin ball with red luxin (which would ignite explosively from the shattering yellow when the ball hit a target) was once demonstrated to the Nuqaba, but the exact balance of making the yellow thick enough to not explode inside the musket but thin enough to shatter when it hit its target is so difficult that several smiths have died trying to replicate it, probably barring this technique from wide adoption.

Other experiments are doubtless being carried out all over the Seven Satrapies, and once high-quality, consistent, and somewhat accurate firearms are introduced, the ways of war will change forever. As it stands currently, a trained archer can shoot farther, far more quickly, and more accurately.

ON CHROMERIA PROHIBITIONS

Tattoos. From a time when factionalism ran high, before all the noble houses had intermarried so much, before single families existed with a kaleidoscope of skin tones within single generations.

At the time, for a number of reasons, the Parians had been more isolated and were more uniformly dark-skinned, which gave numerous drafting advantages that some of them interpreted as being expressions of Orholam's favor on them as the people who had united under Lucidonius first.

Colored lenses could be lost or unavailable when needed, and were initially prohibitively expensive, so lighter-skinned drafters had taken to tattooing blocks of their own colors on their skin so they'd always have a source available. But color tattoos didn't work nearly as well for darker-skinned drafters, which included most of the Parians, who were the politically dominant force at the time.

Rather than lose their advantages, several of the most powerful families united to argue that wights were hiding incarnitive magic behind tattoos. They successfully rammed through a prohibition on tattoos, conveniently ignoring that naturally very dark skin could hide incarnitive magic and luxin-packing just as well.

Incarnitive luxin. A term for luxin when it is incorporated directly into one's body. This is forbidden by the Chromeria as debasing or defiling Orholam's work (the human body itself) with man's work and is seen as a slippery slope to trying to fully remake the body and become immortal. In certain cases, the luxiats have turned a blind eye to more minor or prosthetic uses.

Pets

<u>Dogs</u>: Being highly susceptible to will-casting, dogs are not allowed on the Jaspers. Ships carrying dogs that so much as dock without permission face a small fine, while disembarking with a dog may result in seizure of the ship and striping for shipowner and the dog's owner and death for the dog.

<u>Cats</u>: As they are necessary to control the populations of mice and rats, cats are allowed on the Jaspers. That they're highly resistant to will-casting also plays a part. The Beneficent Hiram D., the renowned will-caster of Blood Forest, testified on the matter before the Magisterial High Court, saying, 'Cats shrug off all attempts at either being mastered or cajoled to do what they don't wish to do, either amused or profoundly insulted that a human would even make the attempt. Before investigating this matter on your lords' instigation, I wasn't afraid of cats. Now I am.'

<u>Other</u>: Other animals are allowed, prohibited, or subject to taxation in accordance with how domitable they are. Horses, for example, must display a registered brand, pass yearly inspection, and pay a duty, making them a luxury item beyond even the already heavy expenses of keeping them fed and stabled on an island.

One more small, silly scene just for those
of you who can't stop until the very last page:
www.brentweeks.com/shawarma-scene
—Brent

THE END